ELA, THE OUTCAST;

OR,

THE GIPSY OF ROSEMARY DELL.

A ROMANCE OF THRILLING INTEREST.

BY THE AUTHOR OF "ANGELINA; OR, THE MYSTERY OF ST. MARK'S ABBEY;"
"GALLANT TOM; OR, THE PERILS OF A SAILOR ASHORE AND AFLOAT;"
"THE BRIGAND; OR, THE MOUNTAIN CHIEF;" "THE MANIAC FATHER;"
ETC. ETC.

"What should be the traitor's meed,
 Who leaves that fair one thus to weep?
Like her's, his flinty heart should bleed,
 The tares he sow'd to reap.
Where'er the traitor strayed, should rise
Looks of scorn from lovely eyes :
Condemned to hopeless woe ;—his fate—
All mankind's scorn, and woman's hate
Without appeal, through life to bear,
 On earth reproach, in Heaven despair!"

A N.

LONDON:
PRINTED AND PUBLISHED BY E. LLOYD, SALISBURY-SQUARE, FLEET-STREET,
AND SOLD BY ALL BOOKSELLERS.

PREFACE.

I CANNOT close the present edition of the Romance of "ELA, THE OUTCAST," without expressing my most unqualified gratitude to the Public for the extraordinary success with which they have again been pleased to crown it—a success, I will not presume to say it has not merited, for that would be an insult to the judgment of its numerous readers. In proof of the deep interest as a work of fiction it has excited, I need only state that its weekly sale has been *thirty thousand copies*, and the present is *the nineteenth edition!* Independently of this, the tale was very cleverly dramatized by Mrs. Denvil, and performed at the Royal Pavilion Theatre for nearly one hundred successive nights! Encouraged by the patronage bestowed upon "ELA, THE OUTCAST," "ANGELINA," "GALLANT TOM," "THE BRIGAND," and many others of my humble productions, I take the opportunity of informing my kind friends that I have another tale in the press for revision, entitled "EVELINA; OR, THE PAUPER'S CHILD," and which, I trust, will be found equally worthy of favour as my other efforts ; and in the meantime I beg to subscribe myself

THE PUBLIC'S MOST GRATEFUL SERVANT,

THE AUTHOR.

January, 1850.

ELA, THE OUTCAST;

OR,

THE GIPSY OF ROSEMARY DELL.

London:

PUBLISHED IN PENNY WEEKLY NUMBERS BY E. LLOYD, SALISBURY SQUARE, FLEET STREET,
AND SOLD BY ALL BOOKSELLERS.

No. 1

ELA, THE OUTCAST;

OR,

THE GIPSY OF ROSEMARY DELL.

A TALE OF THRILLING INTEREST.

CHAPTER I.

If pity reigns within thy breast,
Oh, let the houseless wand'erer in.
ANON.

A VIOLENT storm had succeeded a beautiful day, in the spring of the year 1791, and the honourable Mrs. Wallingford was seated in the parlour of Wallingford Hall (a noble edifice, situated in the north of England), endeavouring to abstract her attention from the horrors of the tempest in the innocent sports of her two lovely children, who were gambolling together at her feet. A cheerful fire blazed briskly in the grate ; and the comfort and elegance of all within presented a striking contrast to the misery which reigned without. But nothing could tend to alleviate the heavy depression of spirits, under which that amiable and lovely lady suffered, occasioned not only by the sympathy she felt for those poor, houseless wretches who were exposed to " the pitiless pelting of the storm," but she was deprived of the society of her husband, the honourable Edward Wallingford, whom business of importance had called from home for several days past.

The rain descended in overwhelming torrents, the thunder rolled in heavy peals, that seemed to shake the mansion to its foundation, and was succeeded by vivid flashes of forked lightning, which shot fantastically across the fine lawn fronting the house, and glared awfully in at the parlour windows that descended to the ground.

"What a dreadful night," soliloquized the amiable lady, casting her eyes fearfully upon the dreary prospect; "alas! what must be the lot of those poor creatures who are exposed to its horrors ; hungry, hopeless, shelterless ! Heaven protect them !"

Overcome with her terrors, she was proceeding to summon her waiting mind, the simple but faithful Dorothy, when between the pauses of the thunder, a shriek, long and piercing, vibrated in her ears, which seemed to proceed from the direction of the lawn. She started, and hastened to the casement ; for it was not yet so dark but she could plainly distinguish objects at a considerable distance ; but she had no sooner reached it, than a flash of lightning blazed across her eyes, and alarmed, she sank in a chair, completely unable to move. A second shriek, more loud and piercing than the first, again aroused her, and she started up with the intention of ringing the bell for the attendance of her servant. Before she could do so, a loud kicking or knocking against the outer door, arrested her purpose, and immediately afterwards the crying of a child was clearly audible.

Ever sensibly alive to the distresses of her fellow-creatures, Mrs. Wallingford immediately repressed her own terrors, and rang the bell violently. In a few minutes Dorothy appeared with astonishment and excitement depicted in her countenance.

"Oh, madam," exclaimed the maid, raising her hands and eyes, " do pray hasten to the hall ; there is such an occurrence."

"What has happened to excite curiosity, Dorothy ?" inquired her mistress; "explain to me the meaning of the violent knocking, and those cries of distress that I so lately heard."

"Pray pardon me, madam," replied the simple attendant, " but I really am in such a flusteration that I cannot explain anything. Ah! I knew there was something going to happen by the dream I had last night. Do you know, madam, I dreamt——"

At this juncture the loquacious Dorothy was cut short in her speech, by the cries of a child again being heard.

"Oh, do come, my lady," importuned Dorothy, " I'am sure you will pity it ; poor little thing, it is so pretty too, and has such lovely black eyes ; but it is so ragged, and so wet, and its tale is so pitiful. Now do come, my dear lady."

The humane Mrs. Wallingford needed no solicitation on the part of her domestic, to urge her to the performance of an act of charity ; it was enough for her to know that a fellow being was in distress, to arouse all the energies of her benevolent heart, to render them assistance ; she therefore put no more questions to Dorothy, but accompanied her to the hall.

The object which struck her attention was a little girl, apparently about six years old. Its tattered, ragged, wet, and miserable. Its tattered frock, of many colours, only just descended below its knees, and its legs and feet were entirely naked. An old straw hat barely covered the back of its head, from beneath which and over its sunburnt shoulders, descended in wild but picturesque disorder, a rich profusion of natural black silken ringlets. Its complexion was dark, but its features were peculiarly noble and expressive, and its fine black eyes, although suffused with tears, darted forth a lustre which could not be looked upon without admiration.

Upon hearing Mrs. Wallingford approach, the little stranger raised her eyes, and gazed with the most impressive looks of supplication towards her.

"Poor child,!" said the lady, "why did you not take her to the fire, Dorothy? How wet, —how cold she is—Tell me, who are you, my dear?"

"I am called little Fanny, ma'am, sobbed forth the child,—" but mamma will die, my poor mamma will die, and then what will become of me?"

"Where is your mother, child?" eagerly inquired the lady.

"Oh, ma'am," answered the child, weeping violently, and wringing her hnnds, "mamma's so ill; we have both walked such a long way, and we have had very little to eat; but at last poor mamma could not walk any farther, so she laid down all in the rain, just above here in the dell; and I know she will die, ma'am, if you will not help her; oh, pray do, and I will bless your name when ever I say my prayers; do not let my poor mamma die."

With these words the child threw herself on her knees, and looked up in the face of Mrs. Wallingford most piteously. That lady was deeply affected.

"Do not weep my poor child," she ejaculated, rising her gently from her knees, and gazing upon her compassionately, "I will render your unfortunate mother all the assistance in my power. Dorothy desire Ralph, and two or three of the male servants to attend me directly."

Dorothy curtseyed and hastened to obey her lady with much alacrity, and Mrs. Wallingford taking the little stranger kindly by the hand, (whose intelligent eyes sparkled with gratitude), led her into the parlour, and placed her before the fire.

Ralph having made his appearance, was ordered with his fellows to provide themselves with torches immediately, and other things necessary, and hasten in the direction which the child had pointed out, in quest of the distressed stranger, while a messenger was despatched to request the speedy attendance of the medical gentleman who was employed by the family.

Ralph and his companions evidently did not admire the task allotted to them, for the storm still raged with unabated violence, and it was some distance to Rosemary Dell; but ever ready to obey the orders of their mistress, to whom they were all much attached, they stifled their objections, and having procured lighted torches, and what was requisite, they proceeded to hasten on their mission.

No sooner did the child behold the preparations for rescuing her unfortunate parent from the perilous situation she had described her to be in, than she wiped the tears from her cheeks, and hastening from the fire prepared to follow them.

"What would you do, child?" asked Mrs. Wallingford, gently seizing her arm, and arresting her design.

"Oh, ma'am," cried the poor girl, struggling to escape, "I must go to my poor mamma; if she should be better, she would die with fright when she missed me from her side. Oh pray do let me go to her, there's a dear good lady. Besides, the men may not be able to find the way, and I can conduct them to the very spot without any trouble."

At this Ralph looked ominously at his companions, shook his head, and whispered to them that it was his opinion, that this child was the offspring of one of the numerous gipseys, who sometimes infested that neighbourhood; and that this was nothing but a scheme to entrap them, and to be revenged upon them for certain tricks they had played them the last time they encamped in Rosemary Dell: besides this was about the time that the tribe usually visited that spot, and he had seen several suspicious looking characters lurking about for several days past. In this sage opinion his companions who boasted of rather less courage than himself, perfectly coincided, and their teeth began to chatter, and they evinced other symptoms of fear, which did not escape the eye of their mistress; but before she could remonstrate with them on their cowardice, her attention was withdrawn to the child, who seeing the parlour window open, bounded suddenly from the hold of Mrs. Wallingford on to the lawn, and beckoning Ralph and the others to follow, flew along totally regardless of the storm, with a speed that made the clowns puff and blow most immoderately to keep up with.

The tempest seemed rather to have increased than abated; and the frightful glare of the torches carried in the trembling hands of the servants, only served to add to the horrors of the scene. The heavy torrents of rain that had fallen had completely flooded the place, so that they were frequently above their knees in water; and it seemed to be a matter of impossibility for any human being to survive many minutes in the awful situation which the child had described her mother to be placed in. Mrs. Wallingford, in whose bosom the adventure had excited a deep interest, watched Ralph and his companions with anxious eyes, until entering upon the Dell, they were hid from her view; she then hastened to give her orders for the reception of the unfortunate wanderer.

In the course of twenty minutes, the noise of Ralph and his companions convinced her that they were approaching the hall, and hastening to the parlour, her conjecture proved to be correct, for the men were rapidly advancing towards the house, bearing something which appeared to be a human form, while the child hastened before them, every now and then turning round with affectionate solicitude, and gazing upon the burden they carried.

Ralph and his companions now entered the room, supporting the senseless form of a woman, who was completely saturated with the rain to which she had been so long exposed. She appeared to be about thirty years of age; her features were regular and handsome. Her complexion was a bright olive, on which the cankerworm of care had set its destructive mark. The contour of her forehead and eyebrows was fine in the extreme. Her hair was black as the plumes of the raven, and flowed in long tresses over her shoulders. Her figure was tall and powerful, and although somewhat attenuated, yet bore the remains of grace and elegance. Altogether she seemed to have moved in a far better sphere of life than her present appearance bespoke.

Her dress evidently marked her for one of the gipsey tribe, and yet her handsome features bore that nobleness of expression which rendered her connection with them unaccountable.

She was attired in a dark stuff gown, covered with patches of various colours, which seemed to be placed there by design rather than necessity. Her shoulders were covered with a short scarlet cloak, and a coarse straw hat surmounted her head.

Soon after the wretched wanderer had been brought to the hall, Dr. Hartley arrived, and after eyeing the form of the invalid with no small degree of astonishment, proceeded to apply such antidotes as his knowledge dictated. During the proceedings, the affectionate child clung round its unfortunate mother's knees, and looked up in her pallid countenance with the utmost solicitude and anxiety; and when she beheld her again breathe more freely, although still insensible, she evinced her extacy in the most affecting manner.

In the course of some inquiries which Dr. Hartley put to the child, for although in other respects, a worthy man, he was prone to inquisitiveness and suspicion, he elicited a confirmation of the woman being one of a gang of gipsies, who had frequently taken up their abode in Rosemary Dell, much to the annoyance of the persons who lived around, that she had been on a secret mission to a distant part of the country, and was to join the rest of the gang at Rosemary Dell; but illness had overtaken her on the road, and, to add to her difficulty, upon reaching the Dell, she found that the tribe had not yet arrived: overcome with fatigue, illness, and disappointment, she had at length become insensible, as the child had before described, who, with a courage and

presence of mind, remarkable at her age, hastened in quest of the nearest habitation in which she might obtain assistance.

The unfortunate woman evinced symptoms of slowly recovering, but she still remained unconscious of all that was going on around; and Dr. Hartley, after prescribing what was necessary, having to visit another patient, was compelled to depart.

When the Doctor was gone, Mrs. Wallingford, who felt an unaccountable interest in the fate of the stranger, paid her the most affectionate attention, and watched the progress of recovery with the greatest anxiety. She had just mentioned to Dorothy the propriety of placing their patient in a warm bed, when she breathed a deep sigh, and opening her full black eyes, fixed them with wild scrutiny upon the features of Mrs. Wallingford, and then round the apartment.

"Where am I?" she exclaimed in a tone of voice that penetrated to the very soul of her auditors, and fixed them in mute attention and astonishment. "What vision of mystery is this? surely I dream, Ah! my child! my darling, the only hope besides that of revenge which makes me cling to the wretched existence it is now my lot to bear!—If it were not for thee, my loved one, oh, that this happy insensibility had lasted for ever."

"Mother, dear, dear mother," sobbed forth the poor child, climbing on its parent's knee, and looking into her care worn face with indescribable love.

"My girl! my own fond cherub! Oh, amid thy wretched parent's miseries, there is a joy unspeakable in knowing that thou really lovest me, that thou art yet unacquainted with that base hyprocrisy which has made the mother the despised, the degraded, abandoned being that she is." And she hugged her child with frantic fondness to her bosom, and kissed her forehead, cheeks, and lips vehemently.

"But how came I here?" she continued after a pause; "what right now has the outcast Ela beneath the roof of luxury and splendour?—Is this done to mock me?—The barren wild, the rugged mountain, the shade of the oak for her canopy, the rude shelter of the gipsey tent, and the sterile earth for her couch, are now all that Ela the outcast may expect. Tell me, women, why am I brought hither?"

As the mysterious woman thus spoke, in an authoritive tone, she arose from her chair, and fixed her piercing eyes sternly upon the countenances of Mrs. Wallingford and her maid. The lady was much alarmed by her behaviour, but fearful of the consequences of revealing her feelings, she endeavoured to suppress her terrors, and in a voice of mild persuasiveness she replied:—

"Fear not, my good woman, I beseech you,

believe me that here you are in the society of friends."

"Friends!" almost shrieked Ela in a tone of irony and contempt, which made Mrs. Wallingford tremble, while an expression passed over her strongly marked features, which was almost terrific;—"Friends!" she repeated, laughing hysterically; "Ha! ha! ha! Base, infamous, accursed title;—the scorpion that bears a thousand stings; the basilisk that tempts innocence to ruin!—The honeyed poison conveyed by the tongue of treachery, which I have sucked deep into my veins, which rankles at my heart, and scorches up my brain: which has made me what I am!—Lady, look on this emaciated form, this careworn visage, this tattered garb;—this form, this face, were once as fair as thine, and as costly garbs bedecked this person as those thou now wearest? what think ye then, has wrought this change? I'll tell thee, 'tis that delusive phantom called a friend! a shameless hypocrite, who —— fool? why should I thus waste words upon a subject that boots thee not, and for which thou mayest perhaps only mock, revile at me after, and call me madwoman?—Farewell, lady; this is no place for Ela?"

Mrs. Wallingford was so overcome by the empatic manner in which the mysterious woman pronounced this wild speech, that she was unable to utter a word, Ela hastily grasping her child by the hand, was about to quit the apartment, when a sudden thought seemed to strike her, and turning back, she said in a more subdued tone:—

"Lady, I perhaps have been too hasty; thou hast sought to do me a kindness and I thank thee? I would know the name of her to whom I am indebted."

"My good woman," said Mrs. Wallingford, mildly, "I have done no more than a simple duty towards a fellow creature; but if you should at any time need assistance, rest assured that Mrs. Wallingford——"

"Wallingford!" reiterated the woman, in a voice almost superhuman, and her eyes dilated, her bosom heaved, and her whole frame became convulsed with strange emotion; — 'Wallingford;—and—and—thy—husband's name, —tell me, speak!"

"'Tis Edward Wallingford;" faltered forth the affrighted lady;—"for Heaven'sake, why do you grasp my arm so fiercely?"

The eyes of Ela appeared to flash fire, and she clutched the arm of Mrs. Wallingford with a vehemence that made her scream, while she looked into her countenance with an expression approaching to ferocity. "And have I then," she cried in a voice hoarse with rage, "have I then once more wandered beneath the accursed roof of the villain Wallingford;—Have I lived to receive a kindness from her for whom I was abandoned, left to misery, degradation, shame?

Oh, revenge, revenge, thou art now within my grasp, and——"

"Oh, mother, dear mother!" lisped forth the child, imploringly, embracing her parent's knees, and looking up to her with supplicating innocence; "do not say such wicked words; do not hurt this poor lady, who has been so kind to us."

"Mysterious, awful woman," ejaculated Mrs. Wallingford, while Dorothy was completely petrified with horror, and unable to move or speak; "what do you want with me? For mercy's sake leave go your hold!"

"Ah woman," exclaimed the gipsey, with an aspect of alarming ferocity,—" well mayest thou shrink from me : I have cause to curse and hate thee and thine; thine head reposes in the bosom which has sheltered mine, and should do now; thine offspring enjoy that wealth and luxury, that by right belong to this poor child; yes, this, the child of my weakness, the child of thy husband,—thy Edward Wallingford!—Say that I am mad,—I am an outcast, a wandering vagrant, a despised wretch;—who is it that has made me so? Thine! thine! thy Edward Wallingford!—But think not I covet him of thee; no; I detest, abhor him, curse him!—when thou seest him again,— when thou pressest him to thine heart, whisper in his ear that thou hast seen Ela; her whom he vowed to love, to protect;—her whom he basely deceived—betrayed!—Tell him that her poor broken hearted father lived to pardon his wretched daughter, and that his latest breath was employed to heap a bitter curse upon the betrayed of his child!—Tell him that Ela still lives for revenge; that as he has been her curse, so she has sworn to be his bane till death! This tell the villain, Edward Wallingford!"

As the distracted woman uttered these words, she snatched her child up in her arms, and bounded through the open window on to the lawn, and at that moment a vivid flash of lightning darted across her form, and gave her rather the appearance of a spirit of evil than a human being.

Overcome with the power of her emotions, the unhappy Mrs. Wallingford screamed and became insensible, while the cries of Dorothy quickly brought the other domestics to the room, who conveyed their mistress to bed, and instantly sent for Dr. Hartley.

CHAPTER II.

IT was a dreary evening when the Honourable Mr. Wallingford mounted his horse, and accompanied only by one faithful attendant, prepared to leave the mansion of his friend, Sir Walton de Bourville, where he had been on a visit for the last week, on business. He had not intended to have departed so soon, but a few hours before, he had received a letter from Dr. Hartley, apprising him of the indisposition of his beloved wife, and requesting him to return to Wallingford Hall with all possible despatch.

Mr. Wallingford was naturally very much alarmed at this information, which was not a little increased by a strange presentiment of some calamity that was about to befal him; and which, although he was not much given to superstition, he had found it impossible to vanquish. He therefore lost no time in complying with the urgent request made in the letter from the worthy Doctor.

Although he was a considerable distance from Wallingford Hall, he had determined at all hazards to perform the journey that night; he therefore spurred his horse into a brisk gallop, and gave free indulgence to the moody thoughts that oppressed his mind.

The moon was only at intervals partly visible, and shed a murky ray upon surrounding objects, which scarcely penetrated through the darkness. The wind blew bleak and cold, and whistled in fitful gusts among the surrounding foliage, like the hollow moaning of some poor wretch in his last extremity. But Mr. Wallingford took no notice of the weather, for his mind was fully occupied with other subjects.

The way they had to travel was dismal and disagreeable, and the road was also bad and dangerous; but Mr. Wallingford continued his speed unabated, although his horse several times stumbled, and put him in danger of being thrown.

"This is a dreary road, sir," remarked Andrew, who was not very well pleased at being taken from the hospitality of De Bourville castle so abruptly; "and the night is none of the pleasantest; a cheerful hearth and a glass of grog would be no bad exchange for this, methinks."

Mr. Wallingford, who was naturally proud and haughty, and never encouraged any familiarity with domestics, returned no answer to these observations; so the garrulity of Andrew was "nipped in the bud," which was a most vexatious thing for a person who was fond of giving free indulgence to his loquacious propensities.

In this gloomy manner, they proceeded for about three hours, when they reached an inn; and, as both their horses were somewhat jaded, Mr. Wallingford was compelled, much against his will, to put up for a short time.

Our traveller was all upon the thorns of impatience during the time he was there, and Andrew was just in the midst of the felicity of discussing a glass of hot brandy and water, when he was aroused by a summons from his master, who commanded him to prepare to resume the journey.

"Why," said the landlord of the inn who, at that moment entered the room, "you will surely never think of continuing your journey at such a late hour as this, sir; besides, the wind blows a perfect hurricane, and there is no knowing the dangers you will have to encounter in crossing the forest. There are a great number of those fellows the gipseys about, and they would no more mind murdering a person on the highway, than they would about stealing a goose from a farm-yard. If I might be so bold, sir, I would advise you to remain here till the morning, I'll warrant me you will not find—"

"My good man," impatiently interrupted Mr. Wallingford, "I thank you for your advice, but cannot avail myself of it; go I must, and were there ten thousand more dangers than those you have enumerated, they would not have the power of thwarting me in my design. Well, Andrew, are the horses ready?"

Andrew answered in the affirmative, and accompanied his master to the door, where they once more mounted their steeds, and pushed on their gloomy journey with redoubled speed; while the landlord hastened to wait upon a goodly host of customers in the parlour, muttering to himself as he went along:—

"Well, that is one of the most foolish, obstinate, headstrong gentlemen I ever saw: to prefer riding through the forest such a night as this, to the comforts and hospitality of 'The Royal Sovereign;' well, well, I pity his taste."

In the meantime, Mr. Wallingford and his domestic pursued their journey with unabated speed, and soon entered upon the forest which the landlord of the inn had spoken of. It certainly was a dreary place, almost rendered impervious by the thick clustering foliage; and the moon's rays scarcely or ever penetrated it. The wind howled most tempestuously, and swept in dismal gusts among the branches of the trees, threatening at times to tear them up by their roots.

At length they broke from the thickest part of the forest, and entered upon an open narrow space, and here the horse of Mr. Wallingford had not proceeded far, when it shyed and suddenly made a full stop, and in spite of the spur would not stir an inch. Mr. Wallingford was very much astonished at this, and was unable to account for it. The moon for a few seconds had been hid behind a cloud, but presently it reappeared, and shedding a flood of light upon the traveller's path, quickly revealed to him the occasion of his horse's terror.

The object upon which the eyes of Mr. Wallingford and the terrified Andrew rested, was the tall and bony figure of an old woman, leaning upon the ruined trunk of a tree, and her large, black, and bloodshot eyes, fixed with an intense and mysterious expression upon the countenance of Mr. Wallingford. Her cheek bones were high, her hair black and matted; her skin brown and shrivelled, and upon her chin grew a grizzly beard. She wore a dirty dark dress, on which was inscribed a number of mystic characters, and her legs and feet were entirely naked. A disgusting malicious grin overspread her pointed features, which had an expression truly unearthly. In fact, her whole appearance had more the character of the hideous creation of a disordered imagination, than a thing of life and reality.

Standing in the lurid reflection of the moon's rays, this mysterious form looked particularly awful; but Wallingford whose mind was a stranger to fear, eyed it with the utmost coolness and unconcern, and then in a voice of command, he said—

"Frightful old crone, what mean ye by crossing my path? Begone, or I will trample you beneath my horse's hoofs!"

"Ha! ha! ha!" laughed the hag, at the same time pointing her bony fingers towards our hero; "Ha! ha! ha!—How bravely ye threaten, Mr. Wallingford! But ho! that proud and haughty blood of thine will be cooled anon; 'tis working now!—Aye is it! The moon shines sadly upon this dreary scene; so are the fortunes of the *noble* house of Wallingford!"

"Avaunt witch!" exclaimed Mr. Wallingford, who was surprised at hearing her mention his name; "let me pass, or by my soul I swear I will do thee harm!"

"Harm me!" screeched the frightful being, while a sardonic grin overspread her loathsome features, that was revolting to gaze upon; "Ha! ha! ha!—how the braggart likes to snort and foam; oh, forsooth 'tis noble and brave to trample on virgin innocence, to leave the mother and the offspring of illicit passion to misery and disgrace. Indeed 'tis brave and honourable doings!—Ha! ha! ha! 'tis rich food for me to feast on, but listen, Wallingford of the Dell:—

A curse shall attend the deceiver's race,
His reward shall be misery and disgrace,
On his home the e shall fall a deadly blight,
That shall turn his days into dreary night.
The heart that his treachery sought to break,
Shall live a fell revenge to seek;
Sorrow and pain shall triumphant lord
O'er the proud house of Wallingford!"

"Foul hag! let me pass!" exclaimed Mr. Wallingford, worked up to a perfect pitch of frenzy by the mysterious import of her words. A wild and supernatural laugh that resounded through the forest, was the only reply he received, and the awful being never changed her

position in the least, but stood gazing upon him him with a look of the most demoniacal exultation. In a transport of ungovernable rage, Mr. Wallingford spurred on his horse, and the next moment he was precipitated to the earth, while another peal of laughter shook the forest.

On recovering himself from the effects of his fall, he rose upon his feet and looked around him, but the hag was gone.

It was several moments after this strange adventure ere Mr. Wallingford could regain his usual equanimity, but when he did so, he aroused his domestic, who on the first appearance of the hag, had thrown himself upon his face on the ground; and ordering him sternly to remount, he did the same, and digging his spurs deep into the sides of his horse, he started through the wood with the speed of lightning, and was soon far beyond its gloomy confines.

Midnight had long flown, before Mr. Wallingford arrived at his mansion; where he found everything in a state of alarm and confusion. The fright Mrs. Wallingford had experienced in her interview with Ela, had had the most dangerous effect upon her constitution, which was the more alarming, owing to the delicate situation she was in. Fit had succeeded fit, and Dr. Hartley had been unable to quit her bedside for an instant.

Mr. Wallingford was in a state of distraction, and was rushing into the presence of his unfortunate lady, when Dr. Hartley, who had heard of his arrival, came in and prevented him, assuring him that such a procedure might be attended with the most serious consequences, Mr. Wallingford was therefore compelled unwillingly to submit; but he questioned the worthy doctor narrowly, being confident that something particular had occurred during his absence from the Hall, to occasion this sudden and unexpected change. Dr. Hartley having elicited all the particulars of what occurred at the meeting of Ela and Mrs. Wallingford, from Dorothy, thought it would be imprudent to conceal the facts from Mr. Wallingford: he therefore detailed everything as minutely as he could, and forbore to make any remarks that might seem impertinent or ill-timed. He, however, added that the morning after these occurrences, the gipsey's encampment was discovered in Rosemary Dell.

During this strange recital, Mr. Wallingford evinced the utmost agitation, and when the doctor had concluded, he arose from his chair, folded his arms, and paced the apartment for several minutes, muttering incoherent sentences to himself. At length he turned to the doctor and said,—

"Mr. Hartley, these wandering wretches must not be suffered to do such things as these with impunity. As a magistrate and lord of the manor. I have the power not only to drive them off my estate, but to punish them as vagrants, and I am determined to do so without any loss of time."

"This may be all very proper, sir," answered Dr. Hartley, "but it is a task of more difficulty, in my humble opinion, than you seem to think; at any rate I would suggest that you forbear all proceedings for a day or two, until the result of your lady's illness is known."

Mr. Wallingford made no reply to this, but he breathed an involuntary sigh, and hastened to his study, where he remained for several hours.

The following morning, Mrs. Wallingford was delivered of a dead infant; and for the first time for many months, an universal gloom reigned over the mansion.

————

CHAPTER III.

O, listen to a tale, whose weakest point
Shall excite your deepest interest.
ALFRED THE WANDERER.

IT was about eight years prior to the events recorded in the preceding chapters, that an unusual scene of bustle and activity was observable in and around the gothic castle of De Montford, which was romantically situated on the margin of one of the most delightful lakes of Cumberland. The cause of this was the return of the earl's son from the continent, on which occasion that hospitable nobleman had resolved to give a grand entertainment to all the nobility, gentry, and his tenants for several miles around, and which was to be got up in a style of feudal grandeur.

The day upon which this festivity took place, was the first of May, and no sooner had Aurora unfolded the curtains of the east, than the bells of the different churches commenced a merry peal, and universal delight reigned around.

Small parties of peasants, attired in their best apparel, were seen jogging cheerfully across the green sward, while here and there a tall may-pole reared its gaily decorated head, and round it danced to rustic music, small groups of happy and contented youths, with maidens, whose modest beauty and simplicity would have done honour to the poet's lay or the pencil of the artist. All business appeared to be suspended in the neighbourhood on that day, and everybody seemed to do his best to augment the pleasures of that jocund scene.

The great centre of attraction was De Montford Castle, to which crowds of persons were hurrying in all directions. The ancient building was fitted up with much taste, elegance, and magnificence, for the reception of the noble guests who had been invited to do honour to the banquet, and to welcome the young lord to his native land. The grand banquetting hall was laid out with admirable taste, and decorated with the armorial bearings of the house of De Montford; while from the lofty battlements of the building, the splendid banners of the family waved proudly in the wind, and seemed to flutter in gladsome union with the cheerful hearts that bounded below.

Not the least gratifying sight was to view the ample preparations that had been made for the enjoyment of the poor. Long tables laid out beneath the umbrageous foliage of the oak, the poplar, and the chesnut trees in the grounds attached to the castle, were loaded with good old English fare, at which the rustic guests were allowed to enjoy themselves in the manner most congenial to their feelings and their habits, and to make themselves as happy as the good cheer and the occasion might prompt them to be.

It was a complete rustic holyday, and as the hour at which the young nobleman was expected to arrive approached, and the illustrious guests, with their gorgeous equipages, drove along the principal avenue in rapid succession, the delight of the numerous assemblage increased, and their joyful shouts rent the air.

Beneath the wide spreading branches of a venerable oak, sat a group of persons who attracted particular attention. It consisted of an aged man of noble and expressive countenance and portly demeanour, although only attired in the simple dress of a farmer; a lady-like woman, and a young girl about twenty, tall, graceful, and elegant, with a countenance surpassingly lovely; and dark eyes whose brilliancy penetrated to the very soul of the beholder.

This was Gilbert Sherwin, (the name he was known by, although it was rumoured that he was an Italian by birth, and had formerly moved in affluent circumstances), his wife and only daughter, the beauteous and accomplished Ela.

The great attention which was paid them by Mr. Charlton, (the steward of the Earl De Montford), was beheld with extreme jealousy by a cluster of women, who were notorious for their love of tattle, and their propensity for backbiting their neighbours. Totally regardless, however, of the envious and malicious looks with which his behaviour was watched by these scandal mongers, Mr. Charlton conducted them to the seat before mentioned, and spread before them the choicest viands, treating Ela in particular, with the most marked respect.

There was also in the same happy party, a clean and homely looking dame known in the neighbourhood as blind Alice, accompanied by her son, a tall handsome young man named Edwin, who was paying his addresses to the farmer's lovely daughter.

"Only observe that impudent minx," observed Miss Deborah Griggs, who formed one of the amiable coterie before mentioned, and who was no less remarkable for her ugliness than her excessive vanity; "it is really quite disgusting to behold the boldness of the hussey; setting her cap at all the men that approach her. I am sure since she has resided amongst us, she seems to have quite bewildered the heads of all the fellows, but for my part, I can't see what there is to admire in her."

"Nor, I either," coincided another *young* lady, who had lingered through thirty-six dreary years, without making so much as a single conquest; "but I dont know what's come to all the men now-a-days, when they can tolerate such ignorance and forwardness as is daily displayed by this poor beggar's girl. Beauty indeed!—I am sure they must be gifted with very different eye sight to that which *some people* possess, if they can recognise any thing pretty in such an ugly brunette as her."

"That's very true, Matilda," said another of of this worthy party, tossing up her head to the convulsive agitation of her pink cap ribbons, and her artificial flowers; "and *I* think, if Mr. Charlton must have a wife, after keeping a bachelor for so many years, he might have more prudence than to fix his choice upon a bold forward slut, whom nobody knows, and who, to say the least of her, is a proud upstart minx."

"But do you really think, Miss Snarl," inquired the first speaker, "do you really think it is a fact that Mr. Charlton is making love to the girl?"

"Think," returned Miss Snarl, "why a person must be blind if they couldn't see it. What does he want to visit Gilbert Sherwin's so often for, I should like know? and what makes him always show the jade such marked attention in company?"

"Poor Edward Hartfield, what will he do?" said Matilda.

"Oh!" rejoined Miss Snarl, "what indeed? See how disconsolate the poor lad seems now, and she looks upon him with as much contempt as if she were a princess, and he only a beggar. Well, if I were him, I should choose some other pretty and respectable girl in the neighbourhood, and he need not look far for that matter, for I'm sure he is much too good for such a conceited slut as that Sherwin's daughter, as fine as she may think herself; and——"

How far the last speaker might have suffered her scurrilous propensities to lead her, we cannot say, but at that moment she was interrupted by the joyful shouts of the numerous persons assembled; and it was soon ascertained that young Lord Edgar De Montford had arrived. The humble guests arose with one accord, and cheered him vociferously as he passed along the grand avenue.

Lord Edgar De Montford was a handsome youth of noble bearing; but he was accompanied by one, whose manly beauty and elegant figure excited general admiration. This was the honourable Mr. Edward Wallingford, who had been the companion of Lord Edgar on his travels, and was sworn to him by the strongest ties of friendship.

Edward Wallingford was at that period just of age, and was accounted one of the most handsome and accomplished young men of the day. And indeed report did not belie him, for a more interesting object could scarcely be imagined. At times, he betrayed a certain degree of hauteur, that somewhat deteriorated from his other merits; but there was a certain fascination in his general demeanour which more than counterbalanced every other failing.

The two nobleman received the congratulations of the company with becoming courtesy, and walked through the gardens, and seemed to greatly admire the scene of festivity that was got up for their reception. When they arrived at the place were the family and friends of Farmer Sherwin were seated, they made a full stop, and the eyes of Edward Wallingford immediately rested on the lovely countenance of Ela; her fine black eyes met his earnest gaze, and it was evident from her blushes, and the confusion she betrayed, that their admiration was mutual.

Gilbert Sherwin and the rest arose and paid their respects to him, and it was not till he was reminded by his friend, that Edward could withdraw his gaze from the fascinating object that had attracted it; he then appeared to leave the spot with regret.

Never, perhaps, had Ela appeared more beautiful than she did on that occasion. She was attired in a petticoat of white, which was just short enough to reveal to the gaze a foot that would have fitted Cinderella's famed glass slipper, and an ancle gracefully and beautifully turned. A dark velvet bodice, made to fit close, shewed to great advantage her delicate waist, and a neck and bosom formed in perfection's mould. The soft tinge which faintly suffused her cheeks, gave additional beauty to her complexion, which was dark, while her hair, which was black as jet, sported in natural tresses over her shoulders. Upon her head she wore a simple rustic straw hat, adorned with flowers, and a rose, (the emblem of herself), breathed its perfume in her bosom.

As the maiden timidly raised her sparkling eyes, and beheld the astonishment and rapture with which she was being contemplated by Edward, her confusion may be better conceived than described. The deep blushes that overspread her cheeks, made her appear more lovely than ever, and as it was not possible for the gentleman's behaviour to pass unobserved by every person present, had Ela heard the rude remarks and splenetic observations that were lavished upon her, she would have retired immediately from the gardens, confused and abashed.

There was one who had remarked the attention paid by Edward Wallingford, towards Ela, and the manner in which she had received it, with the most intense and painful anxiety; that person was Edwin Hartfield. Entertaining as he did the most fervent affection for Ela, the slightest incident was calculated to excite his jealousy. Besides, although Ela had always treated him with the utmost respect, there was not that ardour in her manner, which emboldened him to think that she felt for him a warmer passion than friendship. Mr. Sherwin 'tis true, raised no objection to his paying his addresses to her, but he was confident that so doatingly fond of his daughter was he, that were she to object to accept him as a husband, he would never attempt for a moment to bias her inclinations.

Ela it is true entertained that respect for Edwin, which she had never felt towards any of the young men who had sought her hand, yet her heart could not acknowledge him in the character of her husband, although she had resolved to be guided entirely by the wishes and advice of her parents, upon whom she doated, and sooner than cause them the slightest pang, she was ready at their command to sacrifice her hand, notwithstanding she felt that her heart could not wholly accompany it.

" Did you observe that beauteous creature, Edgar ?" remarked Edward Wallingford to his friend, as they turned away from the place where Ela was seated.

" I did," replied the young lord, " she is certainly very pretty for a rustic."

" Pretty !" exclaimed Wallingford rapturously, " by heaven ! she is more lovely than Venus. Know you who she is ?"

" I do not," replied Edgar, smiling, " but by Jove, Wallingford, you appear to be quite in love at first sight. If you are particularly anxious upon the subject, here is Charlton, who I dare say can inform you."

" She is the daughter of Gilbert Sherwin, a farmer whom you see with her, sir," answered the steward to the interrogatory put to him ; " but report says that Sherwin is only an assumed name, and that he is an Italian nobleman by birth, whom misfortunes have reduced to his present situation. He has resided in the farm he now occupies about four years, and a more honest and well behaved family does not exist."

" I feel an interest in this family, and must endeavour to learn more about them;" said Wallingford, turning round and taking a farewell look at the damsel who had so enslaved his senses. He then walked with his friend into the castle.

The revelry in the grand hall of the castle was kept up with great spirit. The inebriating contents of the wine cup were freely quaffed, and sentiments delivered in honour of the Earl De Montford and his son. Never were the hospitality, the luxury, and the magnificence of the English noble more ostentatiously displayed. Whichever way the eye turned, some fresh rarity it encountered to call forth praise and admiration. The hall presented a dazzling mass of beauty and splendour. In the evening there was a grand ball in the state apartments, that were adorned with couches for those who became exhausted from over exertion. Here reclined the young and lovely, listening to the fulsome strains of adulation. But amid all the gaiety of the festive scene, surrounded as he was by some of the most beauteous females in the country, and basking in their admiring smiles, Edward Wallingford felt restless and unhappy. The beauty of Ela had forcibly struck him the moment he gazed upon her, and he was unable to erase her image from his mind,

With passions naturally impetuous, and accustomed from childhood by his foolish fond parents, to give free indulgence to them, the Honourable Edward Wallingford, at the age of eighteen, was one of the most reckless libertines in Naples. Purity shrunk from his approach, and parents guarded their daughters from his presence with watchful eyes; for few could resist the wily tongue and handsome person of the gay young Englishman.

Unused to restraint it cannot be supposed that Wallingford could easily forget an object which had so deeply interested him; he at length, therefore, seized an opportunity to escape from the Hall, and strolled forth into the gardens with a determination of seeking out and addressing the beauteous girl who had so entranced his senses. He sought anxiously amongst the various groups of revellers, but although he beheld her father and the others, he looked in vain for the object of his search.

Disappointed and vexed, he was about to return to the castle, when a loud shriek assailed his ears, which seemed to issue from a small alcove at the further end of the garden. He hurried with all possible speed to the spot, and tearing aside the foliage, beheld the beauteous Ela struggling in the rude embraces of one of the drunken revellers of the castle.

" Villain !" exclaimed Edward, as he rushed

into the alcove, wrenched the senseless damsel from his grasp, and with a violent blow of his clenched fist, felled him to the earth.

If Wallingford had thought of Ela after they first met in the gardens, no less had his image occupied her mind; sensations entirely new to her had filled her bosom, and for which she could not account, but above all the handsome stranger reigned predominant in her thoughts. The festive scene around her lost all its charms, and the conversation of Edwin became irksome to her. With an unwilling heart she consented at the request of Edwin and her parents to join the other lads and lasses in a dance, but at the first opportunity she left them without informing them of her intention (a most unusual thing for her to do), and retired to the alcove before mentioned to indulge in her secret thoughts. She had not been there many minutes, and before her parents had missed her, when she was alarmed by the abrupt entrance of one of the gentlemen from the castle, and his behaviour quickly convinced her that he was flushed with wine. What followed has already been related, and thus was the very object who had occupied her thoughts, providentially made the instrument of her delivery.

While Edward Wallingford still held his lovely and unconscious burthen in his arms, with emotions of delight indescribable, Edwin Hartfield, followed by Ela's parents entered the alcove.

The countenance of Edwin betrayed at once the jealousy of his disposition when he beheld the insensible form of Ela supported in the arms of the handsome young nobleman; but Wallingford noticed not the envious gaze with which the youth eyed him; the felicity he at that moment experienced in pressing to his bosom the lovely object which had so much attracted his admiration, completely superseded every other consideration, and much as he felt enraged at the insult to which she had been exposed, and the alarm in which it had placed her, there was a feeling of inexpressible delight mingled with the thought, as he had been the fortunate means of her preservation. So great was his rapture in enfolding the insensible damsel to his breast, that he became quite unconscious that any other person observed his conduct, and in a delirium of transport, he pressed his lips to hers. This action aroused the jealous rustic, and advancing rather rudely towards the young gentleman, he attempted to take Ela from his embrace at the same time exclaiming;—

"Hold, sir, her friends be present now, and with your permission, will take the trouble off your hands."

Edward Wallingford's naturally proud spirit rose at this impertinent speech from a peasant, and looking sternly upon Edwin, he was about to return him an answer in accordance with his feelings, when Mr. Sherwin interposed, and with an air of nobility, yet respectful gratitude, taking the form of his lovely daughter from his arms, and casting a reproving glance towards the hasty lover, he said;

"To you, Sir, I owe a debt of gratitude for the generous and manly way in which you have stood forward in the defence of insulted innocence; I need say no more, Sir, for I am confident your self-approving conscience will be a far greater reward than any compliment I could possibly pay you."

"I am indeed happy, Sir," observed Wallingford, "to think I have been the means of saving your lovely daughter from insult. But pray allow me to assist her into the castle, where proper aid may be immediately procured towards her restoration."

"You are very good, Sir," replied Mr. Sherwin, "but there is no necessity for anything of the kind; she has merely fainted from fright, and a few minutes will restore her; besides, I am but a short distance from my farm, and thither I think we had better convey her."

"At any rate," said Wallingford eagerly, "allow me to assist you to your residence, and——"

"Nay Sir, excuse me," interrupted Edwin as the young nobleman offered his arm towards the support of Ela, "that office I am fully capable of rendering, and could not think of allowing you to leave your noble friends."

"Insolent peasant," thought and half muttered the indignant Wallingford, as he was compelled to resign his lovely burthen to her father and Edwin, "but," he observed aloud, "will you permit me, Sir, to call and enquire to morrow after the state of your daughter's health?"

Mr. Sherwin nodded assent, respectfully, and with the aid of Edwin, supported his daughter from the castle to his farm, which was in the immediate vicinity, while our hero followed them with his eyes, and folding his arms, stood for a few moments in silent meditation upon the felicity he had so briefly enjoyed.

Young and sanguine, it was no wonder that Wallingford received an impression stronger than he had ever before experienced, from the superlative charms of the farmer's daughter, but it was a feeling that was quite new to him; a passion absent from all sensual ideas, a passion that, had not his pride interposed, would have urged him on to consider there could be no greater happiness in existence than in wooing the lovely Ela, and making himself master of her affections and her hand. Wrapt in these thoughts, he returned to the grand banqueting hall of the castle, where the revelry was still kept up with unbated spirit; but the occurrence of the last half hour had deprived his mind of its usual elasticity, and although he was compelled to mingle in the festivities that were going forward, he did so with a heavy heart, and a demeanour that could not be wholly hidden from his companions. The wine-cup passed merrily round, and daylight had peeped through the gothic windows of the castle, ere the company thought of separating. It was a great relief to our hero, when the guests departed, and he was permitted to retire to his chamber, where, throwing himself upon his couch, his thoughts reverted to the adventures of the evening, and in vain he courted the balmy influence of sleep. Before he arose, however, he determined to avail himself of the permission which had been granted him by the fascinating object of his admiration, and to pay them in form a visit on the following day.

We must now return to Ela, who, before they had reached the farm, recovered her senses, and with them the recollection that it was to Wallingford (who had so deeply interested her) she was indebted for her preservation from the insolence of the inebriated gentleman who had so much alarmed her. She looked around her, and her heart felt a strange disappointment, when she found that her rescuer was not present. At that moment she felt that—could she have gazed upon the handsome stranger, and thanked him for the generous aid he had afforded her—it would have been one of the most felicitous periods of her existence. Edwin, ever fond and attentive, made the most solicitous enquiries after her health, but she received the same with a coldness and indifference which she had never before shewn towards him.—Alas! her heart from that moment (so quick is love in the execution of its duty,) was entirely estranged from that being who would have laid down his life to have made her happy.

She was glad of the excuse she had of retiring almost immediately to her chamber, where, throwing herself upon the couch, she gave herself up entirely to the thoughts that occupied her mind; among which the form of Edward Wallingford reigned above everything else. She compared his noble bearing, his handsome countenance, his gentlemanly deportment, with that of Edwin; and her heart, susceptible to the tenderest emotions, could not help acknowledging the superiority: and when she considered the difference of his rank, and her own humble circumstances, the utter hopelessness of her soaring to his affections recurred to her with redoubled force, and inflicted in her bosom a pang she felt it impossible to allay, or to eradicate. She was convinced of the impropriety of indulging even a thought of an object placed so far above her, but alas! when she tried to forget him, his image returned to her thoughts in more vivid colours, and she felt truly miserable.

"Oh, that I had never seen him," she soliloquized, " then what anguish, what misery might have been spared me. Poor Edwin, generous, affectionate, what an injustice are these thoughts to your merits."

After a restless and miserable night, she arose unrefreshed at an early hour in the morning, and hastened to join her parents in the breakfast room. Mr. and Mrs. Sherwin were very much concerned to see her looking so ill, and would have sent for immediate advice, but she prevented them, and assured them that she should soon be better, and would take a walk in the meadows adjoining the farm immediately after breakfast.

As soon as the repast was over, Ela walked forth, and had scarcely left the farm five minutes, when Wallingford, in accordance with the permission he had received from Mr. Sherwin, made his appearance, and made the most tender inquiries after her health. The farmer and his wife were concerned to see his arm in a sling, and anxiously asked him the cause. He endeavoured to evade the question, but after some pressing, was compelled to reply that the gentleman who had insulted their daughter on the previous night, enraged at his interference and the blow he had struck him, had sought satisfaction of him that morning, and in the encounter he had received a wound in the wrist; but he assured them it was very slight, and that it was not attended with the least danger.

Mr. Sherwin expressed his regret that he should have been exposed to such an unpleasant and dangerous adventure, owing to his generous interference in the behalf of his daughter; to which Wallingford returned a suitable reply, assuring him that he felt extremely happy to think that he had been made the means of rescuing so lovely an object from insult.

Wallingford felt greatly disappointed that Ela was not present, and after waiting a considerable time in hopes of her return, expressed a wish that he might be permitted the honour, during his stay at De Montford Castle, of paying the farm occasional visits. To this Mr. Sherwin, who was a reserved and mysterious man in his habits, returned a very unsatisfactory answer, and Mr. Wallingford departed.

In the meantime, Ela, deeply occupied with the thoughts entirely new to her mind, continued to wander through the delightful scenery that entirely surrounded Sherwin Farm. Completely absorbed by her own reflections she was totally unconscious of the distance or the lapse of time, until a neighbouring church-bell aroused her to recollection, when she turned back and proceeded to retrace her way home. She had not proceeded many yards when a strange voice repeating her name caused her to look up; and to her surprise and confusion she beheld standing in her path, the noble and interesting form of Edward Wallingford. Ela suddenly paused, and blushing deeply, hid her face, when the young gentleman approached, and, taking her hand respectfully, expressed the extreme pleasure he felt at seeing her about, and hoped that she had not suffered materially from the alarm she had experienced the night before. It was some moments before Ela could make any reply to this, but at length, with the modest and blushing artlessness of maiden timidity, she thanked him for his kind inquiries, and made a suitable acknowledgment for the service he had rendered her. With every sentence the crimson blushes suffused her cheeks more deeply, and the enraptured Edward thought he had never before beheld so lovely an object. He requested permission to conduct her home, and Ela felt it impossible to refuse. On the way thither, the conversation gradually became more interesting to both. Their ideas upon every subject seemed to assimilate. Edward was surprised and delighted at the accomplishments of one so humble, which convinced him of the truth of the rumour that they had not always been in their present circumstances; and Ela felt a pleasure in Wallingford's society, which at the time was indefinable—a pleasure she had never experienced before. Wallingford saw her no farther than the entrance to the farm, where he bade her an affectionate adieu, to which her heart did, although her lips refused, respond to. From that hour the feelings of Ela underwent a change; from that hour Edward Wallingford was never for a moment absent from her thoughts; and to herself she was compelled to acknowledge that she loved him with all the strength and constancy of woman's fondest passion. The different circumstances in which fortune had placed them, had no power to stifle her feelings: she knew the imprudence, the hopelessness of her love; but every effort to erase it from her heart, only made it the more indelible.

CHAPTER IV.

" Oh, God! assist me in this trying moment,
Preserve my wife, my child, or let
The same moment seal our fates!"

THE real name of Gilbert Sherwin was Angelo Beranzio, an Italian nobleman, whom certain misfortunes, which it is not at this period of our narrative prudent or necessary for us to explain, had compelled to abandon his native country, and with a very limited sum of money to seek refuge in England about ten years before. For a few years, hoping an arrangement of his affairs, he had lived in the most frugal manner upon the residue of his property; out at length, despairing of a settlement of

his rights, and his money becoming rapidly exhausted, he was compelled to seek for some means of providing himself and family against the heavy vicissitudes that attended him. This to a man who had moved in the most affluent circumstances, and who had been totally unused to follow any pursuit for a living, was a very severe trial; but possessing more than ordinary strength of mind, Beranzio was enabled to surmount all difficulties, and assuming to himself the name in which we have introduced him to our readers, he removed with his wife and daughter to the farm; to which he attended with the most assiduous care, and which in the course of a few years, by his industry, had become no inconsiderable property.

Great as was the change in his circumstances, Signor Beranzio, (or as we shall henceforward call him,) Gilbert Sherwin, possessed a mind which was enabled to surmount all difficulties, and blessed in the society of an amiable wife, and lovely daughter, he began to think himself happy. To Ela he devoted the most affectionate attention, and beneath his care and instruction, she became as accomplished as she was beautiful.

Possessing such extraordinary charms, it is not to be wondered that Ela should soon excite attention and admiration in the other sex, and it was not long ere her father received many very respectable offers for her hand, to all of which, resolved alone to consult the happiness of his daughter, he gave a respectful but positive denial. Circumstances of a peculiar description brought the family of blind Alice more intimately acquainted with that of the farmer, and Mr. Sherwin could not but entertain the warmest esteem for Edwin, who possessed many inestimable qualities, far more valuable than wealth, and who entirely supported his afflicted mother and sister Rosa, by his industry. The young man immediately formed the most ardent attachment for Ela, who also imbibed the strongest esteem for him, which Mr. Sherwin perceiving, when the former acknowledged to him his passion, raised no objection to his paying his addresses to his lovely daughter. Thus were affairs situated, when the events related in the preceding chapter took place.

The following day, and for a week after the occurrences at De Montford Castle, Edward Wallingford daily visited the farm, and every time he went there, the confusion and blushes of Ela too plainly evinced the pleasure she felt at seeing him. Wallingford was indeed a most engaging young man, and his conversation deeply interested Mr. Sherwin, but yet, at the same time, he had not failed to remark the particular attention he paid to Ela, and the satisfaction with which she received it, and he was too well acquainted with the world not to know that prudence compelled him to put some restraint upon it. He therefore determined, on his next visit to tell him candidly his mind, and to request him to discontinue coming to the farm. He forbore to say any thing for the present to his daughter upon the subject, although he was convinced that the handsome person and elegant manners of Wallingford had made a deep impression upon her, for her behaviour to Edwin Hartfield had for the last few days been cold and indifferent, and that kind-hearted youth evidently suffered severely by the change. He was, however, saved the trouble of this resolve, by Mr. Charlton, the steward of the Earl de Montford, who frequently visited him, informing him that Mr. Wallingford had received an unexpected summons from his father, and had made his departure from the castle the evening before.

Mr. Sherwin was very well pleased with this information, but Ela plainly shewed as she heard it, how deeply she lamented the circumstance. She became dull and spiritless, and avoided society as much as possible; wandering from home in the romantic shades that surrounded De Montford Castle, and recalling to her mind the image of him, who was, fatally for her peace, too deeply impressed upon her mind for her easily to forget.

Thus passed away a month, and Edward Wallingford having settled the business for which his father had required him, returned to Montford Castle. During his absence, his thoughts had continually dwelt upon the beauteous Ela, and it was therefore with no small pleasure he hailed the opportunity he should have of once more beholding her. It was a beautiful day, when he returned to De Montford Castle, and filled with the anticipation of once more seeing that lovely girl, who had so deeply interested him, he was in unusual spirits. In the evening he excused himself from the society of the earl and his son, and took a stroll among the delightful scenery with which the castle was encompassed. The moon had just arisen in radiant glory, and shed a broad flood of light upon the surface of the expansive lake, on the margin of which the castle stood. A lovely calm reigned over everything, which wrapt the soul in soft enthusiasm, and the flowers that closed their leaves for the night, had left behind them a delightful fragrance, which perfumed the air, and came sweet and refreshing to the senses. Wallingford was a great admirer of the beauties of nature, and he contemplated the tranquil scene with the most pleasurable feelings. He continued to wander on, unconscious of the distance or the lapse of time, so wholly was his mind engrossed by the beauty of everything around him. Unthinkingly he strolled to the

summit of a lofty hill which overhung the valley where the farm of Gilbert Sherwin was situated, and the moon's rays streamed full upon the white walls of the neat but humble building.

As his eye rested upon the farm, Edward Wallingford's heart bounded with indescribable emotion; he paused, and folding his arms, from the summit of the hill contemplated that rustic habitation which sheltered her for whom his heart felt so deep an interest.

"Curses light upon adverse fate," soliloquized the youth, "which has placed an inseparable barrier to our ever being united together!—Oh, had Fortune, fickle jade, still continued to smile upon her, how proud should I have been to have offered to her my heart and hand—how gladly would my father have received so fair, so virtuous a daughter! But it cannot be: and therefore it is madness to think upon her ' But to forget her, alas! that I feel is impossible!"

As these thoughts crossed Wallingford's mind, he paced the hill to and fro, in a state of agitation, and sighed deeply. He half resolved to hasten to the farm, but the lateness of the hour, and the suspicion which might be attached to his motives by the parents of Ela, restrained him. He, however, felt it impossible to withdraw himself from the spot, and remained with his eyes fixed upon the farm, in silent meditation.

Suddenly he was startled by the appearance of an unusual light in one of the casements, which in a short time increased, and shed a lurid glare upon the scenery below.

"Good God! what can this mean?" exclaimed Wallingford, starting down the hill. He had not proceeded many paces, when a loud crackling noise assailed his ears; the next moment the light became stronger, and at length a torrent of flames poured out of the broken casement, and convinced him too surely that the farm-house was on fire.

"Kind heaven assist me to preserve the unfortunate Ela!" cried Edward in a tone of the utmost distraction, as he rushed with breathless speed towards the farm. Ere he reached it, the flames burst forth from every part of the house, and illuminated the atmosphere with an ensanguined hue for miles around. With the speed of lightning, Wallingford burst open the door, and he had no sooner done so, than Gilbert Sherwin with the air of a madman, in a terrible state of alarm, rushed out!

"My wife! my child!" exclaimed the wretched man; "oh, God! they will perish!"

"Where are they? Speak, quick! or all will be lost!" cried Edward, hurriedly.

As well as his agitation would permit, Mr. Sherwin pointed to the room in which he supposed they were, which was the one where the devouring element was raging most terrifically; and without waiting to hear another word, the brave young man darted into the passage, in spite of the flames by which he was on every side surrounded, and the dense clouds of smoke that nearly suffocated him. Thrice did the dreadful impetuosity of the fire, which crackled and roared hideously, force him back, and in vain he tried to discover the staircase; but nothing could daunt the intrepid youth, and at that moment when hope seemed entirely lost, and the flames had apparently cut off all chance of rescue, a female shriek guided him to the right direction, and stimulated him to fresh exertions. Through fire and smoke, he darted up the half consumed stairs, and at length he reached the apartment, which he supposed to be the one whither he had been directed by Mr Sherwin.

"Ela! dear Ela!" he cried in a half suffocated voice, "where are you?"

At that juncture a loud shriek vibrated in his ears, and a female threw herself senseless into his arms. Imagining it was Ela, and in the confusion of the moment forgetting that her mother was placed in the same situation, Edward wildly threw the inanimate form over his shoulder, and hastened down the burning stairs, which now tottered beneath his weight. It was with the utmost difficulty he gained the door, and deposited his senseless burthen in the arms of the distracted Mr. Sherwin, but what was his horror, when he discovered that instead of the form of Ela, it was that of her mother!

"Horror! horror!" ejaculated the farmer; "My Ela! she is lost!"

At this agonizing moment, a piercing shriek attracted their attention to the casement where the flames were raging most furiously, at which appeared the unfortunate Ela, wringing her hands, and screaming aloud for help.

"But a moment!" vociferated Edward; "one instant only, and I will save you, or perish in the attempt!"

Quick as thought, Wallingford sprang up, and catching hold of the branch of a tree which grew by the side of the door, clambered into its top-most branches, from whence he was with difficulty enabled to reach the casement. With a desperate effort of strength, which only the danger of the moment could have supplied, he clung to the bough with one hand, and clutching the form of Ela with the other, dragged her in safety to the tree, and no sooner had they descended, than the roof of the building fell in with a loud crash, burying everything beneath it, and filling the air with a dense column of black smoke, and myriads of sparks.

"Father of mercy!" cried Mr. Sherwin, as the intrepid Wallingford, completely exhausted

with his unusual exertions, resigned his precious burthen to his care; "Father of mercy, I thank thee for the preservation of all for which I cling to life, my wife!—my child!"

CHAPTER V.

"In vain we yearn, we pine on earth to win
The being of the heart, our boyhood's dream."
Sir E. L. Bulwer.

It would be a fruitless task to seek to describe the transport of Gilbert Sherwin, even when he beheld the whole of his little property consumed, and himself left houseless and a beggar, as he pressed his wife and darling child in safety in his arms; overcome by the strength of his emotions, the old man wept like an infant, and raising his hands towards heaven, invoked a blessing upon the head of their preserver.

The feelings of Wallingford were too powerful for utterance, but his first and immediate care was to see to the safety of those for whom he had ventured so much. A great crowd of persons had now gathered to the spot, among whom was Edwin Hartfield, whose ecstacy upon finding that Ela and her parents were rescued, may be better conceived than described. In a transport of joy, he forgot all those feelings of jealousy that had before distracted his bosom, and poured forth his gratitude to their deliverer in the most unbounded terms. He would have had them immediately taken to his parent's cottage, but Edward suggested that de Montford Castle would be the most convenient asylum for the unfortunate family for the present, and to which, of course, Edwin could raise no reasonable objection; so thither they were conveyed immediately, followed by the commiseration of the numerous persons assembled.

The hospitable earl received the houseless family with much compassion, and Ela and her mother were immediately conveyed to bed, and medical attendance called in to their aid.

Notwithstanding Wallingford had received several hurts in his perilous adventure, he would not submit to any assistance, until he was assured that Ela was perfectly safe, when he suffered his wounds to be dressed, and having received the praise and congratulations of every one for his intrepid conduct, retired to his chamber. His mind was, however, too busily occupied in thinking of the awful adventure of the night, and upon the situation of Ela and her parents, to suffer him to sleep, and with the first dawn of day, he hastened from his apartment, and anxiously enquired after the condition of Ela and her mother. He was delighted to hear that they had not suffered any accident, only excessive alarm, and that they were now rapidly recovering. In a short time afterwards, Mr. Sherwin requested to see him, and he then once more expressed in eloquent terms his gratitude for the inestimable service he had rendered him. Wallingford pressed the old man's hand fervently, and assured him that the happiness he felt in having been made the instrument in the hands of Providence of saving two of his fellow beings from an awful death, more than repaid him for any danger he might have incurred in so doing.

But in the course of the day, Edward Wallingford experienced a pleasure which he would have encountered any hazard to enjoy, which was in hearing from the lips of Ela herself, the warm expression of her gratitude. Never did she before appear half so lovely in his eyes as with artless simplicity, and deepening blushes, she spoke those words of sincerity her feelings dictated; while the soft tremour that agitated her frame, told that she felt even more than she dare give utterance to. Edward could have listened for ever to the music of her voice, and he left her with regret and a stronger impression of affection than ever.

The prospects of Gilbert Sherwin were now gloomy and cheerless in the extreme; the conflagration had destroyed all the little property he had been for years so industriously cultivating, and he saw himself, his wife, and daughter, left without a home, or the means of getting a bare subsistence. He had indeed drank deep of the poisoned chalice of misfortune, and fate seemed resolved that he should drain it to the bottom. The awful calamity had excited the sympathy even of those who had formerly viewed him with envious eyes; for his industry, honesty, and integrity, were ever known to be most exemplary. Wallingford deeply commiserated the misfortunes of the worthy family, and in vain tried to think of some means by which he could render them assistance; but he knew the proud spirit of Mr. Sherwin, which spurned at the idea of lying under an obligation, and he knew not how to act. He determined to consult the earl upon the subject, and immediately sought an interview with him.

The Earl de Montford had already settled the business, and with a humanity which redounded highly to his credit, had, the day following the fire, requested the attendance of the farmer in his study, where commenting in the most flattering terms upon the honourable manner in which Mr. Sherwin had ever conducted himmself, and expressing his sorrow at the unforeseen misfortunes that had fallen upon him, presented him with the title deeds of a vacant farm on his estate, in the immediate neighbourhood, and would not listen to any objection which Mr. Sherwin offered, to accept of his munificence. Two days afterwards saw them in their new

habitation, which was a much more commodious and valuable one than that which had been destroyed, and peace and content soon again cheered the hearth of Gilbert Sherwin and his family.

From this period Wallingford became a daily visitor at the farm of Gilbert Sherwin, and in those hours experienced all the felicity that an ardent passion can create. He had frequent opportunities of conversing with Ela, and once or twice he had met her alone when out. These were dangerous meetings for the peace of Ela; the wily tongue, and handsome person of Wallingford were too powerful for her; besides had he not generously risked his own life to preserve her and her mother's? She felt confident that the difference in their circumstances would never permit him to make her his wife; she knew that it was wrong to indulge a hope so futile, but in spite of every effort to resist it, her heart too soon acknowledged that she loved him fondly, ardently; and ere many weeks had elapsed, Edward Wallingford elicited the fatal confession from her lips.

Gilbert Sherwin was too experienced in the ways of the world, not to notice the particular attention which Wallingford bestowed upon his daughter, and also the evident pleasure with which Ela received his advances; he had observed it, and he knew the impropriety of allowing it to continue; but he still knew not well how to break the connection. What could he say to the preserver of his wife and daughter? What reasonable motive could he advance for refusing his visits to the farm? He was placed in a situation of the utmost difficulty, from which he was fortunately relieved by an accident.

Mr. Sherwin had occasion to be absent from home for a few days, and the time of his return was not known to Ela. This was a blissful chance for Edward, and Ela hailed it with no less pleasure—for they could then indulge without fear of interruption in their rural walks, and in giving free expression to their sentiments. It happened, however, in one of these rambles, that seeking a retired spot not far from the farm, they were giving free scope to their sentiments, and Edward was vowing eternal love to Ela, when Mr. Sherwin returned from his journey, and having occasion to pass the place, overheard all that they said, and presented himself before them. Their confusion was manifest, and the farmer stood for a few seconds and contemplated them in silence, during which time his heart underwent many painful emotions to think that prudence compelled him to cast a blight upon the hopes of those whose feelings seemed so closely to assimilate.

"Mr. Wallingford," he said, "I have

long suspected what this has now confirmed; think me not harsh or ungrateful, considering the difference that fortune has made in our circumstances—and the utter hopelessness of my daughter ever becoming your wife, if I request that henceforward, you forbear to visit my residence, or to seek an interview with Ela !'

"Mr. Sherwin, Sir," exclaimed Edward, in a state of the utmost agitation, "hear me, I entreat——"

"I cannot, Sir," interrupted Mr. Shewin, "I owe you an eternal debt of gratitude, but fate has placed an insuperable barrier between you and my child; therefore, I trust that you will see the policy of restraining your feelings, and adhere to my request. Ela, follow me."

Ela arose; she knew the justice of her father's words, and much as it pained her to yield to his decree, she could not disobey. She left the spot, and accompanied her father to his home, and as she left the place, the expression of deep emotion in her countenance convinced Wallingford of the sincerity of her passion. Mr. Sherwin saw how deeply his daughter's heart was engaged to Edward, and he pitied her from his soul; he therefore forbore to upbraid her for what had happened, but pointed out to her, the utter hopelessness of ever becoming his wife, and endeavoured to reconcile her to the painful alternative. That night was one of the most wretched that Ela had ever passed; she knew the justice of her father's resolution, but to forget Wallingford, alas ! he was too completely interwoven with her every hope to do so, and she therefore could contemplate nothing but misery before her.

Mr. Sherwin being now convinced of the situation of his daughter's mind, was determined to urge her marriage with Edwin Hartfield, he therefore summoned her into his presence the following morning, and after pointing out to her the fallacy of ever becoming the wife of Edward Wallingford, and the trouble which might attend her by entertaining a hopeless passion, begged of her to endeavour to make up her mind to receive Edwin Hartfield as her husband.

For several days past Ela had not seen Edwin; so great had become her passion for the too fascinating young nobleman, that much as she esteemed his amiable qualities, she could not endure his society, and know that she might probably be compelled to give him her hand, when another would undoubtedly possess her heart. She, therefore, candidly acknowledged to her father her love for Edward Wallingford, but assured him, though it might break her heart in the struggle, she would never give him cause to complain of her disobedience to his wishes. She would have added, that she would endeavour to forget Edward ; but,

alas ! her heart choked the expression of such a promise, and thus the interview closed.

Ela now felt a sadness at her heart which she in vain tried to shake off. Edwin Hartfield was a youth who possessed so many excellent qualities, that without decidedly inspiring her bosom with love, he had imperceptibly almost stolen upon her best esteem, and she felt he was every way worthy of her hand, which, had she never beheld Wallingford, she would not have hesitated in bestowing upon him, and the bare thought of being the cause of rendering a being she so much esteemed unhappy, made her truly miserable.

Ela partook but slightly of the morning's repast, and then strolled from the farm into the adjoining fields. It was a beautiful morning, and the early zephyr breathed fresh and reviving upon her, impregnated with the odour of the opening flowers. The feathered songsters from every leafy branch warbled forth their sweetest carols, and all around betokened a delightful calm, enough to soothe the bosom to peace and tranquillity. But unable to dismiss the gloomy thoughts that obtruded themselves upon her mind, Ela wandered on, and unconsciously took the path which led directly to the cottage of blind Alice, which was situated on the brow of a hill, and was remarkable for its extreme neatness and cleanliness, being kept in order by the dame and her only daughter, the pretty and industrious little Rosa.

As Ela proceeded, her thoughts reverted to the painful events of the last few hours, and her mind became quite abstracted from the beautiful scenery that on every side surrounded her. She had nearly arrived at the foot of the hill, on which the cottage of Alice Hartfield was situated, when a simple ballad, sung with exquisite taste by one of the sweetest voices she had ever listened to, vibrated on her ear. Ela well knew the tones, and looking up, she became conscious where she was, poor blind Alice being seated on a rustic bench beneath the honey-suckled casement, knitting, while by her side sat little Rosa, warbling in tones that might have delighted the most insensible heart her mother's favourite song.

Rosa was not more than twelve years old, and was extremely beautiful. Her eyes, that beamed with innocence and content, were a cerulean blue, and her complexion altogether was extremely fair and transparent. Her bright flaxen hair hung in natural tresses around her neck, and sported playfully with every breath of wind ; and her figure, which was very tall for her age, already exhibited that grace and elegance which a few years would ripen into perfection.

Ela stood a few moments and listened to the song which Rosa was singing, but hesitated whether it would be prudent, in her present state of mind, and after the injunctions of her father, as regarded Edward Wallingford, to visit the cottage. But recollecting that Edwin would be at his employment, (whom she feared to meet), she walked on, and had only just began to ascend the hill, when she was observed by Rosa, who, apprizing her mother of the recognition, joyfully ran down the hill to meet her.

"Oh, Miss Ela," said Rosa, taking our heroine cheerfully by the hand, "I am so glad you have come to see us; my poor mother has been talking about you all the morning, and my brother left home so ill and melancholy, that we did not expect he would be able to remain at work."

"I am sorry to hear that," said Ela, with a sigh—"pray what is the matter with your brother, Rosa?"

"Why, I'm sure I can't say," replied Rosa, "though I have heard my mother say it was love; and I am certain, from what I have before heard, that she is correct; and no wonder indeed, where there are such pretty and amiable young women as Miss Ela Sherwin in the neighbourhood."

Ela blushed deeply at the artless girl's observations, which pained her severely, but could not make any reply.

"For several days, you know, Miss," continued the talkative little Rosa, "you have not visited our cottage, which was very unkind, and last night brother Edwin came home in such a melancholy state that it was enough to break anybody's heart to see him; and from all that I could learn, you were mentioned as the cause of it; but I couldn't believe that, for I know you are too kind and too good to make any other person unhappy."

She pressed the hand of the interesting child in silence, and Rosa continued:—

"But, dear me, Miss, you are looking very pale and ill; I hope there is nothing the matter with you. Ah! Miss, although I am only a little girl, I think I can guess what is the cause of the grief of you and my poor brother. But why don't you marry him; then you would be my sister, and I should be one of the happiest girls in the world. Oh! I should feel such a pleasure in doing all I could to deserve the love of such a sister as Miss Ela!"

It was a fortunate thing for our heroine that they had now walked up the hill, and arrived at the cottage; for the conversation of the simple and affectionate Rosa pained her extremely, and she regretted that she had unconsciously strayed towards the dwelling of blind Alice.

"Here is Miss Ela, mother, come to see us," said Rosa, putting the hand of our heroine in that of Alice, who left off knitting the moment her name was mentioned, and evinced the utmost pleasure at her presence.

"Ah! Miss Sherwin," ejaculated the poor old woman, with a sigh, "I thought you had quite deserted us; and your conduct for the last few days has thrown a blight upon the hopes of my unfortunate boy, which I fear will make him wretched for many a day to come. Oh, Ela had you but seen him last night, I'm sure your heart would have pitied him! Poor lad, it is his first love, and alas——"

"Pr'ythee, my good Alice," interrupted Ela "spare my feelings, as I pity those of your son."

"Pity him," reiterated the blind woman, with a half satirical laugh, "there was a time not far distant when you did not deny you loved him; the change is very sudden, young lady, very sudden, and very—no, 'tis not unaccountable: perhaps the young gentleman at De Montford Castle, the ——"

"Alice!" interposed our heroine, seriously, "recollect, that to the young gentleman you so ironically speak of, I owe the life of my mother, and that of myself;—can you then wonder that I feel unbounded gratitude towards him?—Nay, more, I will not deny it, for I know not why I should, although mine he never can be, I love him, and—"

"In wooing him," hastily rejoined Alice, "doom my poor son to perpetual misery!"

"Say not so, Alice," observed Ela, "indeed you wrong me; there is an insurmountable obstacle to our ever coming together; indeed my father has commanded me to forget him, and to look upon Edwin as my future husband;—but alas! my heart tells me that such a decision would only make me miserable, and be doing an injustice to your son, whom I am certain possesses virtues deserving a better fate, and that must ever possess my esteem. I would therefore have him forget me in any other character than that of a dear friend, feeling confident that I could never love him as my husband, and I would not bestow that hand upon anybody wilfully, which could not be accompanied by my heart. Therefore would I entreat of Edwin to show the proper fortitude of his sex, and endeavour to vanquish his unfortunate passion, and ere long he may meet with one who may be equally as deserving of him as Ela!"

"Oh, no, no, no, Ela!" cried Alice; "Edwin's love is too ardent, too sincere, to be so soon extinguished. His whole soul is wrapt up in you my child; no other maiden, be she ever so lovely or amiable, will have the power to wean his young affections from that object on which they have first been placed: melancholy despair will prey upon his constitution; he will sink to an untimely grave, and poor old Alice will be left alone, as well as in darkness in the world!"

"Oh, no dearest mother, do not say so," said the gentle Rosa, weeping bitterly, "you will still have your little Rosa near you, who will watch over you, toil for you, and think no trouble great if she can only win a smile of approbation from her poor blind parent, or do the least thing to lighten the darkness of her declining days. Come, mother, pray cheer up, you afflict Miss Ela to see you sad; I will try that pretty song you used to say you liked to hear me sing so much; anything I will do, but you will break my heart, if you talk in that dismal manner!"

With these words the affectionate child threw her white arms around her mother's neck, and kissed away the tears that were streaming from her sightless eyes.

Ela, who was much overcome by the scene, lent her aid to that of the affectionate Rosa, and endeavoured to soothe the mind of poor old Alice, in which they were at last successful; the topic of conversation was changed, and our heroine remained there until evening, talking upon a variety of subjects, and not noticing the flight of time, until an observation from the old woman, which bore some reference to Edwin, reminded her that it was near the hour of his return from his daily employment, and feeling inadequate to the task of meeting him for the present, after what had transpired, she arose, and making an excuse to Alice, departed from the cottage.

The vermeil tints of the setting sun were gradually sinking behind the western hills, as Ela directed her way towards home. The air was mild and serene. No sounds were heard, save the lowly bleat of the sheep, the bark of the shepherd's dog, or the whistle of the rustic, as he plodded his way, with a contented mind after the toils of the day, to his humble home. Our heroine, whose mind felt depressed at the idea of the pain she was the unfortunate cause of bringing upon a worthy family, walked slowly on, buried in deep reverie, when she was aroused by hearing her name repeated in a man's voice, and turning round, she saw Edwin, whom she had passed, running towards her. She was sorry that he had seen her, but perceiving that his face was pale, and his whole demeanour agitated, she stopped till he came up to her.

"Ela," said the youth, in a tremulous voice, while his eyes beamed forth an expression of gentle reproach, "this is unkind, very unkind, thus to avoid me! What have I done; in what way have I offended you, that you pass me by as though I were a stranger?"

"I did not see you, Edwin," said Ela, blushing and trembling, as he took her hand, and pressed it with more than his usual fervour—"I had been to your mother's, and——"

"Was hastening home" rejoined Edwin, "without waiting to exchange one word with me. Ah! Ela, how great a change has a few short days wrought in everything around me,

in you, whom of all others I had fondly hoped would never change,—at least," and he corrected himself, "never so change, as to shrink from speaking to him, who if he could injure you by word or deed, or even by a single thought, would curse himself as a wretch unfit to live!"

"You wrong me, Edwin," answered Ela, much affected, "you greatly wrong me by supposing I could ever treat with coldness and disrespect one whose merits have ever induced me to esteem him as a friend."

"A friend!" repeated Edwin bitterly,—"oh, how I hate that name; so dull, so insipid! so cold, in all that my ardent hopes have connected with you. A friend; it is the word which has thrown a blight upon my young, and perhaps too sanguine hopes, and——"

"Do not talk so, pray do not, Edwin," interrupted Ela, "you know not how you afflict me, you do not—But you are ill; I see you are!"

"Ill!" exclaimed Edwin, the expression of his eyes beaming wild, as they rested upon the countenance of our heroine: "yes, yes, I am ill, I am indeed ill, but 'tis here, Ela; there has something fallen here, which neither doctors nor medicine can cure; Oh, Ela but a few days since, this heart was light and buoyant; hope had fixed its bright temple there, and pointed to you as the beacon of my future happiness. But all is darkness now; your coolness has told me that I am no longer loved, and——"

Ela tried to answer, but her agitation choked her utterance, and she remained silent.

"It is so," hastily continued Edwin, "it is so; your silence proclaims it. Oh, Ela, this is more than I anticipated. Even in my boyish days, when people talked of love, and my young imagination began to imbibe a notion of that tender passion, my vivid fancy pictured to me, in glowing colours, one bright, one beauteous, one gentle form, such an one as I then thought I could only love; and, strange as it may appear, that ideal form haunted my fancy for ever afterwards. It was the subject of my thoughts by day, the vision of my slumbers by night. With all the fervour of youthful passion glowing within my bosom, I looked around me for one being that might realize the object my ardent imagination had created. I saw bright eyes and gentle forms, and listened to tender words, uttered by silvery voices; but all fell far, far short of the lovely portrait my fancy had drawn, until Ela met my sight. Oh, how my heart palpitated the moment I beheld her. The shadow that haunted me by night and day, stood before me; only arrayed with more than tenfold beauty than that which my thoughts and hopes had pictured. Need I say I loved? I adored!—And when that lovely creature, for whom I seemed by fate predestined, smiled upon me, nay, even blessed me by the assurance that she was not insensible to my passion, oh, what bliss was mine! What ideal scenes of future transport did my delighted eyes conjure up. Alas, little did I think that my prospects were to be so sadly crushed, and so dark a night of despair was to succeed the golden sunshine of my hopes."

While Edwin thus energetically spoke, his fine eyes sparkled with uncommon lustre, and the tenderness of the subject upon which he was speaking, imparted an eloquence and enthusiasm to his manner, which Ela had never before witnessed. He had drawn her arm within his, and they were slowly walking towards the farm. The moon had arisen clear and bright, and was shedding her lucid beams across the green pastures they were traversing. There was a gentle melancholy in all around, which was in unison with their feelings. Ela sighed, but was too much overpowered by the fervour of Edwin's words to make any immediate reply.

"You are silent," said Edwin, "am I then so hateful to you that you will not even deign me an answer to my words! Alas, alas! then have I truly cause to be wretched."

"Edwin," observed Ela, mustering up all her fortitude and resolution; "why will you afflict me by forcing me at the present time to make an acknowledgment, which candour compels me to disclose? I know the strength of the love with which you have honoured me and fully appreciate your merits, but, would you, oh, would you have me bestow on you my hand, when my heart is another's?"

Edwin Hartfield clasped his forehead with intense agony on this declaration, and walking a few paces from her, he remained silent, though the heavy sighs that escaped his bosom, showed the mental anguish he was suffering. At length he returned to her, and looking despairingly in her face, he ejaculated,

"It is so then, my worst surmises are realized, and my fate is sealed. "But oh, forgive me, Ela; love has made me a selfish being; but Heaven forbid that I should bring sorrow upon that heart which can never be mine. No, from this night, to my own breast, shall my misery be confined, and though my heart break, my tongue shall never more utter a word that may wound you!"

"Enough, Edwin," replied our heroine, "your promise the more convinces me how worthy you are of my esteem! Strive then to smile upon the frowns of fate, and forget that I——"

"Forget you, Ela!" interrupted Edwin, with a melancholy smile, "yes, when the shadow of death shall fall upon these eyelids; when the green turf in the old churchyard wraps this form, but till then, never."

They had now arrived near the farm, where they paused, and Ela timidly ventured to suggest that they should part. Edwin looked at her a moment with the most intense emotion; he tried to speak, but could not; then suddenly raising her hand to his lips, he kissed it fervently, and heaving a deep sigh, rushed hurriedly from the spot, and was out of sight in a moment.

———

CHAPTER VI

Stay wretches! whither would ye bear me?
My cries shall make the air resound! Oh,
help!—ANON.

FILLED with the most melancholy thoughts, Ela stood for a few seconds to endeavour to recover her usual spirits before she hastened to the farm. Suddenly she was alarmed by hearing a shrill whistle from an adjacent copse, and the next moment she found herself rudely seized by two ruffians, disguised in masks and large cloaks.

Ela screamed with terror, and endeavoured in vain to release herself from the grasp of the men.

"Unhand me, villains!" she cried, " oh, help, help!"

"You call for help in vain," exclaimed one of the villains, " but fear not, we do not intend to harm you; you must come with us, resistance is vain."

With these words the ruffians endeavoured to force her from the spot, towards a carriage which was standing at a short distance, upon which the unfortunate girl renewed her cries for help more loudly than before; at that critical juncture, when the men had nearly forced her to the vehicle, a rustling was heard in the bushes, and presently the form of a man jumped before them.

"Hold scoundrels!" uttered the voice of Edwin, whom the cries of Ela had attracted to the place, and immediately rushing upon them, he felled one of them to the earth, and endeavoured to rescue Ela from the grasp of the other.

"Stand back, fool!" vociferated the ruffian, drawing a pistol from underneath his mantle, and presenting it at the head of Edwin, " I would not harm you, but if you are obstinate, you must take the consequence."

"Villain! release that trembling maiden," cried Edwin, rushing upon the man, and grasping him by the throat. The next moment the report of the pistol was heard, and Edwin with a deep groan sunk to the earth, weltering in his blood; Ela uttered a terrific shriek, and immediately became insensible.

How long she had remained in that situation, she had no means of judging, but when she recovered her senses, she found herself in a vehicle which was proceeding at a rapid rate, the blinds of which were drawn closely down, and on each side of her were the two ruffians that had seized her.

She clasped her forehead, and in a moment recalled to her recollection the horrible event which had lately taken place. The unfortunate Edwin, wounded and bloody, returned to her imagination, and with a frantic groan she exclaimed,—

"Good God! Where am I? Whither are you conveying me?"

To this the man made no reply, but forcing a gag into her mouth, prevented her uttering another sentence. The vehicle proceeded with increased speed, and it was evident from its jolting that they were travelling over a hilly part of the country. We will not attempt to describe the thoughts of our heroine in this dreadful situation; in whose power could she be? What was the meaning of the outrage; but above all, the awful fate of the unfortunate Edwin, and the dreadful state of agitation her parents would be in, agonized her mind to distraction.

It was a tempestuous night, and the thunder rolling in heavy peals, and the rain pattering terrifically upon the top of the carriage, increased the horrors that racked the mind of Ela.

"It was an unfortunate job," said one of the men to his companions, breaking from the deep silence they had hitherto maintained, "and I am afraid we shall get into a pretty mess by it."

"How could I help it?" replied the other surlily; "the headstrong fool wouldn't take my warning, and he has therefore paid for his temerity. We must make the best we can of it, that's all!"

The fellows now relapsed into silence, and Ela was left to the indulgence of her distracting thoughts. In this manner the carriage proceeded at a rapid rate, for about two hours, when it suddenly stopped, and the men opening the door, threw a mantle over Ela's head, and assisted her to alight.

"What, ho! mother!" cried one of the ruffians, hammering on a door with his fist; "come, move yourself, are you going to keep us waiting here all night?"

"Hey day," replied a harsh female voice, opening a door which creaked heavily upon its hinges, "why what a bustle you are in. You are still as impertinent and as surly as ever, I find."

The men made no remark upon this answer, but laid hold of the arm of Ela, and forced her along what appeared to be a narrow passage, and up a winding flight of stairs; they then took the mantle from her head, and she found herself in a gloomy apartment, rudely furnished,

and which only received light from a narrow casement, placed very high in the wall.

"If you will promise not to create any alarm," observed the ruffian who had shot Edwin, "we will now remove the gag from your mouth, and you may partake of some refreshment. But I warn you that you are where your cries will be unavailing, and will only compel us to use that severity which we do not wish, for no harm is intended you."

He now removed the gag from Ela's mouth, and the two fellows immediately left the room, and locked the door after them. In a few minutes the door was again unlocked, and an old woman of forbidding aspect, entered with some provisions, which she placed on a table, and was about to retire, when Ela, wound up to frenzy, grasped her arm and implored her to inform her where she was, and for what purpose she was torn from her home in such a clandestine manner. The woman released herself from her hold, and shaking her head, pointed to the victuals, and left the room, without making her any answer.

In the utmost despair at the horrors of her situation, and the mystery that was attached to it, Ela wrung her hands, and gave way to a violent flood of tears. Who could be the authors of this shameful outrage, and what could be the motives that induced them to it? She was lost in a chaos of fruitless conjecture. Poor Edwin, too, what was his fate? Had not his generous interference in her behalf brought him to an untimely and dreadful fate, and that too, so speedily after she had blighted the fond hopes he had formed of making her his bride? Her parents, too, what must be their distraction at her mysterious disappearance; and last, Wallingford, her dear Wallingford, oh, what anguish would her abduction cause him! The refreshments which the old beldame had brought to her remained untasted on the table, and she was giving way to the agonizing thoughts that racked her brain, when she heard the heavy door of the dreary apartment she was in again unlocked, and the old woman entered. There was something so peculiarly revolting in the aspect of this harridan that it chilled the heart of Ela to look upon her, and stifled the appeal she would have made to her compassion. She advanced to the table with a sardonic grin upon her features, and observing the untouched viands, tossed her head and exclaimed:—

"So I suppose this homely fare is not good enough for you. Hey-day, the world has come to something when poor people bring up their brats to ape the fantastical airs of your fine folks. It will be well for you, young woman, if you can always get such food as this. But no matter, perhaps you may find your appetite by the morning, you will need it to prepare you for the long journey you will have to take. You will stay here to night."

"By what right am I brought hither; why am I torn from my friends?" demanded Ela, more firmly; for the harsh and disgusting conduct of the old woman had aroused her utmost indignation.

"I dare say you will know that by-and-bye," replied the old woman; at all events, I don't think proper to satisfy you, so you may save yourself the trouble of asking me. Come, I can't wait here all night, follow me to the chamber allotted to you."

Ela knew it was useless to remonstrate with such a heartless old beldame, she therefore sighed deeply, and followed her as well as her trembling limbs would permit her to do, up a narrow flight of stairs, and into a room which although small, had rather an air of comfort about it, compared with the apartment she had just left.

In one corner there was a small stump bedstead, and the only furniture the place contained besides, was a table, a chair, and a small swing glass.

"There," said the old woman, placing the lamp on the table, "you will sleep comfortable enough; better than thousands of poor creatures who I dare say deserve it as well as yourself. The bed is aired, and I reposed in it myself only last night, so you need not be afraid of catching cold. You will be ready to rise early in the morning."

Ela needed not the latter injunction, for her mind was too much distracted to render any idea of repose at all probable. The casement was barred like that of the other room, but it was not placed so high in the wall, and by standing on the chair, Ela was enabled to reach it. The storm had now entirely subsided, and a beautiful moonlight had succeeded. From the confined limits of the iron bars, Ela was enabled to gaze upon the scenery beyond. It was a wild, mountainous track of country, but in what part it was situated, she, of course, had not an opportunity of forming the slightest conjecture.

At length, tired of gazing upon the monotonous scene, she descended from the chair and paced the apartment in an agony of mind we need not attempt to describe. The parties below had evidently not yet retired to rest, for their voices frequently met her ear, and they seemed from their boisterous mirth to be enjoying themselves vastly. How Ela shuddered to be in the power of such wretches, whose designs she could form no idea of. She could not think of venturing to bed, but paced the chamber to and fro', and mentally implored Providence to protect her. The noise of the persons below at last subsided, and all became as still as death in the house; and Ela, completely exhausted with the fatigue of travelling, and the agitation of her mind, threw herself upon the couch and closed her eyes, but sleep was denied her, and she pressed a restless pillow till the first streak of day darted through the narrow casement, and the next moment she heard a person ascending the stairs. The door was thrown back on its hinges, and the old woman entered.

"Well, come," she said, seeing Ela up and drest, "this is well; I like to see young people mind what is said to them. Follow me below, where there is a repast prepared before you resume your journey."

"Tell me, I implore you," ejaculated our heroine, encouraged by the softened tone in which the old woman addressed her, "in whose power am I, and whither are they taking me?"

"I have before told you, young woman,' answered the beldame, relapsing into her former surliness, "I have told you that is a business I will not explain. This, however, I can assure you, that you will come to no harm, and indeed there is many a poor girl like you, who would bless her lucky stars all the days of her life, if she should only meet with such a chance. Come, come, your conductors will be getting impatient."

Ela said no more, for she found it was no use, and therefore followed the woman into the parlour, where her two unprepossessing conductors were seated at a table, and making a hearty breakfast of milk, eggs, and home made bread. The old woman pressed Ela to join them in the repast, and at length she yielded to her repeated solicitations, and partook slightly of the refreshments on the table. While this was going forward the driver brought the coach round to the door, and having finished their meal, the men arose, and prepared to depart.

"Young lady, observed one of them, as he proceeded to wrap the mantle around Ela, "I suppose you perceive by this time that it is quite useless to seek to oppose our will. We have before told you that we do not intend to harm you, and are only obeying the orders of a superior, who will sufficiently explain every thing to you when you see him, and no doubt to your satisfaction. We would indulge you as far as we have the power, and therefore, if you will promise us that you will make no outcry, or attempt to alarm the passengers, we will not place the gag again in your mouth."

Ela shuddered with horror as she looked in the countenance of the man, from whose hand the unfortunate Edwin had received the fatal bullet; but as she was well aware that it would have been complete madness to have offered any resistance to such wretches, she promised to comply with his request, and having entered the vehicle, it was driven off at a rapid rate.

It would be tedious were we to attempt to describe minutely the lonely journey; suffice it to say that they continued to travel the whole of that day, only stopping for refreshment, and to change horses at the most obscure inns, where the men appeared to be well known, and Ela, therefore, knew that an appeal for aid would be disregarded. Towards night they seemed to emerge from the country, and by the noise and bustle that prevailed on all sides, and the numerous lights, Ela imagined that they were passing through some large town. The idea of this almost tempted her to break her promise to her companions, for surely among the numerous persons she saw passing and repassing, there would be some who would pity and assist her; but her companions, who appeared to read her thoughts, frowned, and reminded her of her promise, telling her at the same time, that she would severely repent the last infringement of it; she accordingly repressed her feelings as well as she could, and remained silent.

The number and beauty of the shops surprised her, and she was lost in a multitude of thoughts that crowded rapidly on her imagination. Surely this must be London, that she had heard so much about, but in which she had never before been, and as this idea occurred to her, the thought of the distance she was from home, and from any assistance from her friends racked her brain to frenzy. After driving for more than an hour through many conspicuous streets, the scene again became changed, and they entered upon what appeared to be a country road. Having proceeded along this for some time, the vehicle at length stopped before a large, respectable looking house, and here her companions informed her that their journey was at an end, and once more enjoined her to caution and silence.

The driver having descended from his box, knocked at the street door, which was almost immediately opened by a young woman who looked like a servant. The two men alighted first, and then assisted Ela out of the vehicle, and conducted her into the hall, exchanging at the same time a significant glance with the girl, who gave one of them a light, and immediately disappeared, though not before Ela imagined that she eyed her with something like pity. The men beckoned our heroine to follow them, and then ascended a handsome flight of stairs, that were carpeted, and ushered her into an apartment which was elegantly furnished, and brilliantly lighted up. They then bowed, and left the room without saying a word, and locked the door after them.

Ela looked around her with the most indescribable amazement, and could scarcely believe the evidence of her senses, the change was so great and so sudden. She had scarcely time, however for reflection, when the door of an ante-room was thrown open, and looking up, Ela uttered an ejaculation of astonishment, when Edward Wallingford stood before her!

CHAPTER VII.

"Oh, that deceit should wear so fair a form,
And with a gentle visor hide deep vice!"
                                        SHAKSPERE.

PETREFIED to the spot, the astonished damsel had neither power to move or speak, but Wallingford rushed towards her with apparent transport, and throwing himself on his knees at her feet, pressed her trembling hands to his lips, and kissed them passionately, at the same time looking up in her face with an expression of love and supplication.

"Ela!" he cried, "beauteous girl, will you not speak to me? Will you not say you pardon me?"

"Wallingford!" answered the maiden in a trembling voice, "for Heaven's sake explain this—Why am I dragged from my home, my friends? Why am I brought hither, and you here!"

"Oh, Ela," exclaimed Wallingford, "forgive me; I am the author of it all!"

"You, sir," said Ela, turning more ghastly pale, and shrinking from him.

"Yes, beauteous girl," ejaculated Edward, again seizing her hand; "this is all my doings; but oh, forgive me for that which the impetuosity of my love, and the fear I entertained of seeing you wedded to another had led me to perform!"

"Mr. Wallingford," said Ela, coldly, "rise, sir, this posture ill becomes you! If you have one spark of honour or humanity left, restore me to my friends, and never let me again behold one who could act so cruel, so heartless, so treacherous!"

"Ela," replied Wallingford, rising and endeavouring to lead her to a seat, "if you would not see me expire in your presence, if you ever loved me, do not reproach me for that which the strength of my affection has urged me to do! By Heaven, I swear that I intend you no harm! 'tis true my behaviour may appear cruel, unpardonable, but my intentions towards you are only those of the strictest honour, and sooner than act the villain I would perish!"

"Talk not of honour, sir," said Ela, scornfully, "was it honour that prompted you to tear clandestinely a defenceless female from her home, subject her to insult, and leave her parents to break their hearts! Wallingford, if you would have me not curse you, if you would not bring down the maledictions of my parents upon your head, you will take immediate steps to restore me to that home you have made wretched; and seek to make that reparation to the poor blind woman of whose only protector you have been the means of depriving her. Alas! unfortunate Edwin!"

And overcome with the intensity of her

anguish, occasioned by the melancholy fate of the kind hearted rustic, Ela sunk into a chair, and covering her face with her hands burst into a convulsive flood of tears.

Wallingford offered not to interrupt her grief, but paced the apartment for a few seconds in evident agitation. At length, throwing himself by her side in a chair, he once more took her hand, and looking up into her countenance with a mingled expression of adoration and supplication exclaimed in a faltering voice:—

"Hear me, dearest and loveliest of women; no one can regret the accident to which you allude, more than I do, but it is not so bad as you fear; it is true Edwin Hartfield was wounded, but very slightly, and is now likely to do well. Oh, Ela, did you but love with half the ardour that I do, you would not treat my conduct with such severity. I knew that your father, knowing the disparity of our circumstances, would never consent to my paying my addresses to you: in fact he had told me so, and desired me to discontinue my visits to the farm, I could not exist out of your sight; and my torture was augmented by knowing that your father had promised Edwin your hand, and that in a few days you would probably be torn from me for ever. It was this idea that prompted me to take the step I have taken; it was then I formed this stratagem, and lost no time in putting it into execution, for I flattered myself that you loved me, and when convinced of the honour of my intenions would not hesitate to forgive me. It was by my orders that you were seized and conveyed to this place, which belongs to a lady of the utmost respectability, and who will treat you with every kindness and indulgence. Here then, did I intend you to remain until I could make arrangements for our union, when I might once again restore you to your friends, and solicit their forgiveness."

Wallingford paused, and seemed to await Ela's answer with the most painful anxiety. She made no reply for a few moments, during which interval she sobbed convulsively, and her whole frame evinced the utmost emotion. At length she looked up at Edward with a mingled expression of unsubdued love, reproach, and doubt, and in tremulous voice said:—

"And think you, Mr. Wallingford, that I can calmly yield to your proposal, and know the misery my parents must endure at my mysterious disappearance, and the horrible uncertainty of my fate? Oh, no, no, If indeed you love! If you really intend to act as becomes a man of honour and a gentleman, lose no time in making what reparation you can for the indiscretion you have been guilty of, and restore me to them; and then I swear to grant you my hand, in spite of every obstacle that may present itself!"

"Alas! Ela"! returned Wallingford, "that is impossible! It is madness to think of it! your father would never consent, and I should be driven to despair. In a week I promise to marry you, and then as the wife of Edward Wallingford your parents will be happy to receive you with open arms, and to pardon all that has happened. Here, under the protection of my friend, Mrs. Fitzosborne, you may remain quite safe until I have arranged all the preliminaries, and I will not even visit you, if you desire it, until I come to make you my bride!"

It would be a painful task to detail minutely all the specious arguments Wallingford made use of to obtain his guilty wishes; rather let us pass over the event as speedily as possible, and suffice it to say that Ela loved too passionately, he succeeded too well, and that fatal night saw her ruined, degraded, and hateful to herself.

It was not till the next morning that the unfortunate Ela was aroused to a full sense of her misery, and the fatal imprudence of which she had been guilty! Her remorse, and her anguish were so violent that Edward began to be alarmed for her reason, and endeavoured to soothe her by every means in his power; vowed eternal constancy and honour, and sought to compose her distracted mind. This was, however, a more difficult task than he had at first calculated upon. Ela was inconsolable, and raved of her parents, invoking their curses upon her own head and that of her seducer. Wallingford was afraid to leave her the whole of that day, and called in the aid of Mrs. Fitzosborne, whose prepossessing manners and apparent sincerity, at last had some effect, and Ela became more calm.

Mrs. Fitzosborne had evidently been brought up in a superior manner. According to the account which Wallingford gave of her, she had been married to an officer in the army, who dying about two years before, left her a handsome independence, upon which she took the house she at present occupied near the village of Hampstead, and resolved for the future to retire from the bustle and gaiety of life. Upon a closer intimacy with her, however, there was a certain vivacity approaching to levity in her manners, which seemed greatly at variance with this decision; but of her real character there will be enough in the course of this narrative.

That night Wallingford also remained with his victim, and in the morning, after breakfast, he left her to see immediately, as he said, about the arrangements for their nuptials. He strictly enjoined Mrs. Fitzosborne not to suffer her to leave the house on any account for a minute. But he had no occasion to use this precaution; the deed was done, and Ela confiding in his promises, felt not inclined to escape. For whither could she fly? What could she do, without money, without friends, and in a strange place? She dared not encounter the reproaches of her unfortunate parents, whom she had so cruelly degraded, and she endeavoured to soothe her mind with the thought, that but a few days would elapse, when she would become the wife of him for whom she had sacrificed her honour; for Edward Wallingford could never, never be the villain to deceive her!

But what were Wallingford's thoughts, what his intentions? Had he ever, or did he now intend to make Ela his wife? No! 'tis true he had loved her; but could he ever select a bride from the hut of the peasant—the child of poverty? Never! the noble house of Wallingford had ever been pre-eminent in the wealth and rank of its members, and should he now bring disgrace upon it! No! his pride revolted at the bare idea! Such were his thoughts as he left the house of Mrs. Fitzosborne on the morning we have mentioned, and added to which was his bitter compunction for the crime he had committed, and the consequences that might follow! He cursed himself for a villain in having so basely betrayed and ruined one so fair, one so good, so fond as Ela! for he was not yet so callous to shame, as to exult in his triumph! One moment he was half resolved to return to the house of Mrs. Fitzosborne, and acknowledging the impossibility of fulfilling his promises seek Ela's forgiveness, and offer to make any reparation in his power! Then again he vowed to marry her, but soon his pride arose more powerful than before, and he was left in a state of doubt, irresolution, and distraction, almost insupportable. To drown his thoughts he flew to the wine cup, and that night, flushed with the inebriating beverage, he obtained a temporary respite from reflection, only to feel its poignancy more severely in the morning.

In the course of a few days, Ela became more composed, the apparent sincerity of Edward having re-assured her. The uncertainty of the situation of her beloved parents, it is true, tormented her mind, but with the idea that in a few short days she should be a wife, and her crime might never be known to them, she endeavoured to console herself. Wallingford was with her every day, and his affection seemed rather to increase than abate. She frequently pressed him upon the subject of their marriage, and at length he informed her that he was enabled to fix upon the time when it should take place, which was on the third day from that time; but he added, that as it would be prudent and consonant with both their sentiments, that it should take place as privately as possible, he had made arrangements for it to be solemnized by a friend of his at the house of Mrs. Fitzosborne, in the presence

only of her, and a gentleman of his acquaintance in whose confidence he could rely.

This proposition seemed so reasonable to Ela, that she could not raise the least objection, and her mind felt relieved of one half the burden which had previously oppressed it.

The evening appointed for the celebration of their secret nuptials at last arrived, and about eight o'clock, Mrs. Fitzosborne entered the apartment of her fair prisoner, and told her all was ready. Ela gave her her hand, but was forced ultimately to lean on her hand for support, for her frame trembled violently, and her heart palpitated as though there was something dreadful going to happen to her. They entered the drawing-room, where Ela beheld the clergyman, Wallingford, and another gentleman, waiting. Her face was covered with a long veil, so that her features could not be seen by any one. Edward advanced towards her; he pressed her hand vehemently in his own, and spoke to her words of comfort; but his voice trembled, and he seemed impatient for the ceremony to be over. In another moment the clergyman had commenced reading the service, and soon afterwards, Ela, the confiding Ela, supposed herself to be the wife of Edward Wallingford.

No sooner was the ceremony over, than the clergyman and the other gentleman left the house, and Edward embraced Ela, and called her his wife, and by every other endearing title. Oh, how happy did our heroine then feel! Words are inadequate to express the weight of grief which had been taken from her mind. Alas! she little suspected what cause she had for care. Little did she imagine that him she now thought all perfection, all honour, had basely, villanously deceived her!

And let it not be supposed that the seducer was yet so far steeped in crime, as to triumph in his treachery; to exult over his unsuspecting victim. No; in secret he cursed, he abhorred himself for what he had done; yet the strength of his love, and the fear of losing the object of it for ever, prevented him from throwing himself at her feet, acknowledging the baseness he had perpetrated, and offering to make her what reparation remained in his power. Unable, however, to endure the smiles of her whom he had ruined, deceived, after a day or two he excused himself from Ela, telling her he thought it better that he should seek an interview with her parents, and ask their forgiveness for the clandestine manner in which they had acted, and the anguish they must have caused them. To this proposition Ela acceded with delight, and parted with him with the fondest affection, uttering a thousand prayers for the success of his mission.

And how had Edward acted towards the too-confiding girl, who had yielded up her every hope of happiness to the indulgence of his illicit passions? Need the reader be told that he had deceived her—basely, cruelly deceived her? Need we inform him that he had acted, in the latter part of the drama especially, with the most heartless treachery? That the supposed marriage was all forgery, a shameless subterfuge? Nor did the guilty party escape without the severest punishment which can be inflicted upon a sensitive mind, namely, that of a self-rebuking conscience; but yet, so strong was the frenzy of his love for the unfortunate Ela, that virtue was made subservient to it. It was after the celebration of the supposed marriage that the pangs of a self-accusing conscience more poignantly attacked him, and unable longer to endure the presence of her his treachery had seduced—her that his pride would not suffer him to make a just reparation to, became doubly guilty; and to escape her sight, although at the same time he only existed in it, he formed the stratagem we have detailed in the previous pages.

Of course it was never his design to seek an interview with the parents of Ela; no, he dare not face those poor individuals upon whom he had heaped such misery. He felt that he deserved their curses, and yet he had not the strength of mind to make them that reparation he had a right to do.

In the meantime, Ela, fully confiding in the specious promises of Wallingford, and thoroughly believing herself to be his wife, after a lapse of two or three days, began to feel herself comparatively happy; for she was convinced that her parents were too doatingly fond of her, to suppose for a moment, (after Edward acknowledging to them that she was an unwilling party to the abduction which had taken place,) to attach the smallest blame to her; and her affection for Edward increased, when she thought of the pecuniary sacrifice he had made in making her his wife.

To Mrs. Fitzosborne, who displayed the greatest urbanity of manners, she became much attached, and the hopes that she held out to her of a speedy reconcilliation with her parents, and the consequent happiness that would attend upon her in an union with him to whom her whole heart was devoted, made her feel confident and content.

A week elapsed before Edward re-appeared at the house of Mrs. Fitzosborne, and our readers may readily judge the anxiety with which Ela flew to meet him. He embraced her with the utmost transport, and to her eager inquiries about the success of his mission, he replied that they might hope everything; that her parents, although at first they reproached him for the stratagem of which he had been guilty, and which had caused them such hours and days of suffering, gradually yielded to his arguments, when he informed them of Ela's innocence, and that she was an unwilling party in the whole affair; but when he assured them of their marriage, and showed them the proof of the same, they became satisfied. They, however, insisted that he should make no delay in seeking an interview with his father, and asking his forgiveness for the step he had taken, and that obtained, they would be ready with open arms to receive him as their son-in-law.

"And then, dearest Edward," exclaimed the delighted Ela, while tears of joy chased each other down her cheeks, "then shall we indeed be happy—then shall I once more behold my beloved parents, and receive a blessing from their lips. Dear, dear, old souls, oh, my heart throbs to meet once more their fond embrace!"

The conscience-stricken Wallingford turned away at this; he could not bear to hear Ela give utterance to such bright anticipations of happiness, and know how utterly impossible it was that they should ever be realized.

"But what of Edwin?" added Ela after a pause, "oh, tell me, is he better? Alas! how will he bear the news of my marriage?"

"Ela," said Wallingford, with an air of jealousy and displeasure,' 'you must remember that you are now the wife of Edward Wallingford, and that every regret expressed, especially towards a mere rustic, is a —— but no matter, I will not rebuke you, Ela; I know you meant no harm: pardon me—but such is the vehemence of my love, that the least thing excites my jealousy. Edwin Hartfield, you will no doubt be glad to hear, has quite recovered from his wound; and from all that I could learn, evinces little concern at your loss."

Of course every tittle that the now-guilty Wallingford had uttered, was totally untrue. Still he had heard, by the means of one of his domestics, of the true state of affairs; and the account given filled his heart with the most bitter anguish and remorse. He was informed that Mrs. Sherwin had been confined to her bed ever since the disappearance of Ela, and that all hopes of her recovery were at an end; that the farmer himself had been in a state bordering upon distraction, and had instituted the most diligent inquiries as to the author of the base plot, and the retreat of his daughter, to no purpose. As for Edwin, his wound was of a more serious description than it had been represented; and its most alarming effect was delirium, the medical man being afraid that if ever he recovered from the wound, it was a matter of doubt whether he would regain his senses.

"And have I been the accursed cause of this misery and ruin?" soliloquised Edward, when the above account reached him; "oh, Wallingford, how have you degraded yourself in the eyes of the world; how lowered yourself in your own estimation!"

As these thoughts crossed his mind, Wallingford paced his apartment with hasty steps, and continued to upbraid himself for what he had done. At one time he was half resolved immediately to seek the presence of the unfortunate Ela, and throwing himself at her feet, acknowledge his perfidy, and solicit her forgiveness. But this thought was abandoned as soon as formed—for of what use would such a step prove, he ruminated;—would it not be cruel to arouse his victim from her delusive dream of happiness; and what return could he expect but her bitterest curses? No! he shrunk afraid from such a step. So well had Wallingford arranged his plot, that he was never for a moment suspected by the friends of Ela, of being the cause of it. But we are digressing.

"But," suddenly ejaculated Ela, after she had given free indulgence for a few seconds to her joy, "did they not send me a line, not a word to assure me that they still love me —still believe me good and innocent; and that they long once more to behold me to——"

"Ela," interrupted Wallingford, somewhat staggered by this question, "you must allow for the agitated state of your parent's feelings, which totally incapacitated them from writing; but they desire me to say all that you could wish:—they told me to inform you—but enough—be assured that they do feel all that you desire, therefore be happy."

"Oh, yes, dear Edward," cried the poor unsuspecting girl, unutterable delight sparkling in her tearful eyes, "upon that assurance and the certainty of your love, how can I be otherwise than happy?"

At this juncture, luckily for Wallingford, whose feelings would presently have betrayed the duplicity of which he had been guilty, Mrs. Fitzosborne entered the room, and thus broke the chain of a conversation that was becoming insupportably painful to our hero.

CHAPTER VIII.

"Oh, she was formed the heart to win,
And he, alas! but to betray."
                              ANON.

So happy had the information of Wallingford made Ela, that the fortnight which he told her must intervene before he could seek the presence of his father, passed away on rapid wings, and every moment which brought the time nearer for them to seperate, filled the bosom of our heroine, with the mingled feelings of regret and hope. The affection of Edward seemed to increase every day, and in fact her wishes

were ever studied by him with avidity, and he appeared only to exist in her presence. Mrs. Fitzosborne, too, had succeeded in prepossessing herself in her favour, her manners were so kind and lady-like. She was indeed a most accomplished woman, and seemed to make it her sole study to render Ela comfortable and contented with her condition. The elegance of everything around her also afforded Ela no small delight: the furniture was so handsome, and the garden and scenery that surrounded the house so beautiful. Then Mrs. Fitzosborne was a finished musician, of which Ela was an enthusiastic admirer, and could herself play the piano with much skill and judgment. In fact, could she but have heard from the lips of her parents a ratification of the information she had received from Mrs. Wallingford, Ela would have been truly happy.

The day before that fixed for the departure of Edward, he appeared unusually low spirited; and from the abstracted state of his mind, it was plain enough to be seen that he was deeply agitated. Ela, whose quick discerning eye was ever ready to notice the most trivial change in him to whom her whole soul was devoted, remarked his melancholy with the utmost alarm, and inquired of him the cause. Wallingford endeavoured to evade the question, and denied that he was depressed in spirits; but Ela was convinced, and pressed the interrogatory.

"Indeed, my dearest Ela, you are mistaken," he observed—"I am well, very well, and too happy in your love to feel the smallest portion of uneasiness. If, indeed, my bosom feels the slightest regret, it is that occasioned by the necessity of our separation—but it will not be for long—and when I again return to you, I trust it will be to assure you of the anxiety of my father to behold you, and to restore you to your parents.

With these words he kissed her passionately, and Ela was satisfied. We will pass over their separation on the following day, which was one of the most affectionate description. Ela, after Edward had left her, felt a void in her heart, which even all the endeavours of Mrs. Fitzosborne failed to supply. Occasionally strange doubts and fears crossed her mind, for which she was entirely at a loss to account; and she felt a foreboding and uncertainty when she thought of her parents, which often fell upon her heart like a blight.

Mrs. Fitzosborne tried by every means in her power to amuse her; sometimes she read to her her favourite authors; at others they sought to stifle melancholy by music; but more frequently did they seek that enjoyment which nature must always afford to the sensitive mind by rambling among the pleasant scenery of Hampstead.

Edward had faithfully promised that his

absence should not exceed a fortnight, but when that time passed away, and he did not return. Ela began to feel very unhappy, and apprehensive of something having happened to him. In the same manner, another week elapsed, and still Wallingford returned not. Ela became truly wretched. Mrs. Fitzosborne endeavoured to compose her agitation, and to convince her that his being unable to see his father had been the sole cause of his lengthened stay; but when another week passed over, and still brought no intelligence of him, Ela became completely inconsolable, and turned a deaf ear to all the arguments and expostulations of her supposed friend.

"His conduct is cruel, 'tis unpardonable," she exclaimed, "surely he might have written to me. But not a line—not one sentence in explanation; what am I to think?"

Mrs. Fitzosborne could not very well answer this question, but she still tried every effort to convince Ela of the inviolable constancy of Wallingford, and that something particular had occurred, which he would no doubt satisfactorily explain, to procrastinate his return. These remarks had the effect of partially appeasing the violence of her anxiety, but her mind was still far from being at ease. Edward was now doubly endeared to her, for she felt that ere many months would elapse, she might present him with a pledge of their mutual affection; and who is there that has experienced the feelings of a mother, especially towards her firstborn, but will duly appreciate her thoughts, her anxiety, her emotions?

On the same evening after this conversation had taken place, Ela excused herself early from the society of Mrs. Fitzosborne, and retired to her chamber, but not to rest. Her mind recalled in the most vivid colours all the occurrences of the last month or two, and as she reflected, the uncertainty of her fate came to her thoughts so forcibly, that she shuddered at the apprehensions her own disordered imaginations conjured up. Should Edward have deceived her! Should she not after all be his wife! Should he now abandon her! These thoughts passed rapidly in her mind, and she was surprised they had never occurred to her before; they were so horribly reasonable. Then again she reflected! What might be the actual situation of her parents; might that not have been misrepresented to her; and instead of their imagining her to be the wife of Wallingford, might they not have heaped their maledictions upon her head, believing her to have brought disgrace and infamy upon their aged heads?—No! No!—these thoughts were too terrible to be encouraged! Wallingford, the noble-minded, affectionate Wallingford, could never be so base, so treacherous, so heartless!

It was a lovely evening, and Ela sat by the window of her chamber, which overlooked a vast space of fields and pastures, that were now illumined by the chaste light of Cynthia. Suddenly Ela thought she heard the sound of horses' hoofs approaching the house, and her heart bounded with hope, as she listened to every tread, as they became more and more audible, and were evidently advancing towards the mansion. A loud knock at the street door, more than ever convinced the delighted Ela, and she flew rather than ran down stairs to meet him whom she supposed it to be; nor was she mistaken, it was indeed Wallingford, and the next moment she was pressed fervently to his bosom.

"Ela, my beloved Ela," cried Edward, "pardon the anguish I must have caused you by this painful delay!—but indeed it was unavoidable."

"Oh, name it not, dearest Edward," answered Ela, whose features glistened with transport, "the pleasure of your return more than repays me for the anxiety your prolonged absence caused me. But you look pale and agitated; oh tell me, Edward, surely you have been ill."

"No, my love, no, you are mistaken," hastily returned Edward, who did indeed look pale and careworn, "I have been quite well; but let us hasten to your chamber, I have much to tell you, to which I must request your most serious attention."

Ela felt a melancholy foreboding as Edward made use of the latter words: but she merely looked earnestly in his face, and suffered him to conduct her into the apartment.

"Ela," said Wallingford after a pause, during which he appeared to be endeavouring to collect himself for some unpleasant task, taking her hand affectionately; "it is now necessary that I should inform you of certain particulars connected with myself, which it may afflict you to hear, but to which I request your cool and patient attention. In early life my father became bound by the strictest and most imperative ties of friendship with a gentleman about his own age, who had been brought up with him from childhood. So strengthened was this intimacy by years, and a reciprocity of sentiments, that they revered each other with a brotherly affection. They both married about the same period, and in due course of time I was born, and in a few weeks afterwards the lady of my father's friend presented him with a daughter. Looking upon this as a dispensation from Providence to unite their families more closely, in the enthusiasm of their friendship they made a vow that if we lived we should be united, and in order to further their wishes, the young Amelia and myself were brought up almost entirely beneath one roof, and every opportunity afforded us to imbibe that attachment towards each other in our early days, which would ratify the future marriage they had so foolishly and rashly decided upon. When we had both attained the age of eight years, Mr. Herbert was compelled by family affairs to take up his future residence on the continent, where he resolved his daughter should be educated and remain until the proper period might arrive for the celebration of our nuptials. In consequence of this, I have never since beheld Amelia, and indeed so little regard did I pay to a vow made in a moment of enthusiasm, and to the probability of the question ever again being urged, that I ceased to think upon Amelia in any other light than as the playfellow and companion of my boyish days. Time, however, has shewn me the fallacy of this opinion, and the imprudence of which my father and Mr. Herbert were guilty. The father of Amelia has lately died, and in his last moments, after consigning his daughter to the protection of her uncle, he expressed an earnest wish that the compact made between my father and himself might be carried into effect. Amelia's uncle promised faithfully to obey the request of his dying brother, and immediately communicated the particulars to my father, who hourly expects them to arrive in England, and has commanded me to prepare to meet the lady as my future wife."

During this recital Ela had undergone the most agonizing emotion, her bosom throbbed, she turned ghastly pale, her whole frame trembled violently, and at the conclusion, she would have sunk upon the floor had not Wallingford caught her in his arms. Utterance was entirely denied her, and she gazed at Edward with a look of stupified horror !

"Ela! dearest, beloved Ela !" cried Edward, in a tone of distraction, "for Heaven's sake do not look upon me thus ; already am I driven to madness ; oh, have some sympathy for my anguish, and rather than heap reproach upon my head, advise me how to act ! The command of my father paralyzed me, and of course I dare not enter into any explanation of the purpose for which I had visited him !"

"And is this then," exclaimed Ela, fixing upon Wallingford a look that penetrated to his very soul, "is this then the reward for my love, my constancy, my too confiding faith in him I thought could rather die than deceive me ? Is it for this I have been torn from the roof of my parents, whose hearts I have probably broken ? Whose curses have perhaps been invoked upon my head ! Oh, Edward, this is cruel ; surely you might have confided to me this dreadful story before ; and thus have saved me the misery, that I fear is now too certain to be my doom !"

"I know I merit your reproaches, Ela," answered Wallingford ; "I should have told

you this before ; but I repeat that I never anticipated for a moment that I should be called upon to fulfil the accursed vow !"

"Edward Wallingford !" exclaimed Ela, in a tone that startled him, and fixing her brilliant eyes seriously upon him—"Edward Wallingford, am I not your wife! Your lawful wife !"

"Dearest Ela," replied Edward, with strong emotion depicted on every feature, "you are ! you are !—and here I swear that none other can, or shall possess that heart, which is indissolubly yours !"

"In that then you have not deceived me !" continued Ela, solemnly.

"Spare me, dear Ela," ejaculated Edward almost stifled by the violence of his feelings, clasping his forehead, and pacing the room wildly ; "think you, I could ever—"

"Deceive you" he was about to add, but conscience, that severe monitor smote him, and choked the words in his throat !"

"If then," resumed Ela, earnestly, "if then you have not deceived me, if I am really your wife ; if you are sincere in your vows, and I alone share your heart, why deceive your parent by suffering him to entertain hopes that cannot be realised ; why not confess to him your marriage, and acknowledge me your bride ?"

"I confess the reason of your questions,' replied Wallingford, " and intend to do so ; but it cannot be done so precipitately ; my father is a very obstinate man, and the intelligence must be broken to him cautiously. He has given to me a fortnight to prepare myself to meet miss Herbert, and in that time, I solemnly vow to make the necessary disclosure ; and shewing him the absolute impossibility of my complying with his commands, abide by the consequences. Till that period arrives, my beloved Ela, rest content, and be assured that whatever may be the result, your Edward will be too well rewarded in knowing himself the master of your fondest affections, to deem any trouble he may have to encounter, worthy a single pang !"

"Dear Edward! I cannot doubt you !—"exclaimed Ela, convinced by the earnestness of his manner, bursting into a passionate flood of tears, and throwing herself into his arms! "Let what may occur, the certainty of your constancy will uphold me, and I will endeavour to be happy !"

Wallingford kissed her in silence, and afterwards informed her that it was his intention to write to her parents the next day, informing them of all that had happened, and inclosing any letter that she might feel anxious to send to them. This promise quite re-assured Ela, and she became composed. Soon afterwards they were summoned to supper, and the remainder of the evening was passed in perfect happiness.

Alas! little did Ela imgaine the perfidious part Wallingford was acting towards her; little could she suspect, that deceit and treachery the most foul lurked within the bosom of that man she deemed one of the most noble and honorable of his sex.

The story he had told her of his engagement to Miss Herbert was only in part true, and in fact, circumstances had occurred, that had almost entirely broken off the correspondence of the two families, and the father of Wallingford thinking that Mr. Herbert had repented of a promise made in youth, thought no more about the matter, and never above once mentioned it to his son. Wallingford had been summoned to attend his father on family affairs, which it was imperatively necessary should be arranged without delay, as his father had been for some time in a bad state of health. It was during his brief stay there, that Edward began to think more seriously of his unfortunate connection with Ela, and the effervescence of his passion having abated, he could more coolly deliberate upon it. He now saw and cursed the folly of which he had been guilty, and was apprehensive of it reaching his father's ears, which would entirely ruin him. Even if he he had no will to consult but his own, could he ever make Ela his wife? A girl who was a beggar in rank and fortune, and who had beauty and accomplishments alone to recommend her? No! his pride revolted at the idea! Then ought he not to endeavour to extricate himself from the dilemma in which his imprudence had involved him as soon as possible? Had he not better at once make known to his unfortunate victim, the fatal truth that she must sooner or later hear? He almost resolved not to return to her again, but at once make the disclosure to her by letter. But no, he could not, callous as he was daily becoming, make up his mind to abandon that girl he had brought to ruin, without another interview; he therefore resolved, after a prolonged absence to return to London. His interview with Ela, however, which we have just described completely overturned all his former resolutions; he trembled at the thoughts of the bitter and deserved reproaches she would heap upon him, and he had not the courage to make the confession. He felt convinced that his first determination was the only one he could ever put in practice, and he was resolved in a few days, therefore, to return to the country. But he sought to appease the upbraidings of his conscience, by mentally vowing to provide amply for Ela and the offspring of their unlawful passions! But what could ever reward a soul like Ela's for the disgrace and treachery he had brought upon her and her parents?

The fortnight Wallingford had promised Ela to remain in London soon elapsed, and during that time she had been far from happy. Edward had become less ardent in his asseverations, and did not court her society so much as before, and frequently absented himself for whole days together.

Mrs. Fitzosborne too, she thought, seemed less kind and attentive to her than formerly, and when she found her frequently weeping at the thoughts of this unaccountable change, she rebuked her in terms that seemed harsh and uncalled for.

On the morning of Edward's departure, however, he seemed to treat her with more than his former impassioned fondness, and they parted in the most affectionate manner.

"Heaven bless and preserve you, dearest, best of women!" were his words, "in a month we shall meet again, till then farewell."

"You will write to me in the meantime, my love!" said the weeping Ela, hanging around his neck.

"Without fail," replied Edward in a half-stifled voice, and covering his face with his hands to conceal his emotion, he tore himself from her arms, and rushing out of the house, mounted his horse, and was out of sight in a moment. Ela immediately retired to her room, where throwing herself upon a couch, she gave free vent to her feelings in a copious flood of tears. Her mind was tormented with the most dismal forebodings, which she found impossible to conquer.

Day after day flew away, and Ela looked anxiously for a letter from Wallingford, but every day she was doomed to be disappointed. It was strange, she thought; surely something particular must have occurred to prevent Edward fulfilling a promise so solemnly made. What could it be?—She was lost in a chaos of the most agonizing conjectures. To add to her perplexity, the behaviour of Mrs. Fitzosborne became every day more cold and repulsive, and she treated her anxiety with utter indifference, if not absolutely with derision. She was frequently from home all day, and did not return till very late at night, and at such times her conduct was actually insulting. Poor Ela felt truly wretched when the third week elapsed, and still no letter; she was quite distracted. In the same way the fourth week passed away, and had expired three days, when a letter arrived to Ela directed in the handwriting of Wallingford; with a trembling hand she broke the seal, and proceeded to read the contents, but she had scarcely perused half a dozen lines, when she uttered a piercing shriek and fell insensible in the arms of Mrs. Fitzosborne.

CHAPTER IX.

Deserted, left a prey to grief,
And the corroding anguish of deep shame.
CLAREMONT.

The contents of the fatal letter which had taken such an effect upon the hapless Ela, was couched in the following language :—

" DEAR ELA —For such you must ever be to be, though untoward fate ordains that we may meet no more!—Ela, I feel, and none can more poignantly feel the anguish and shame that I have brought upon you ; none can more bitterly repent than I do the deceit of which I have been guilty. Would to God that I might have been suffered to have repaired my errors by making you my wife. But that can never be, my father's word must be obeyed, though it break my heart, and he threatens me with his eternal displeasure should I not marry her to whom he has devoted me. Beloved girl, could you but read my heart, you will find how fondly, how firmly it is still attached to you and the dear innocent you will shortly bring into the word, the fruit of our imprudent passion. May heaven shower down its choicest gifts on you both. I cannot dwell longer upon a subject which strikes a thousand daggers to my heart; farewell then for ever, most lovely and beloved of women, pity and forgive your penitent, heart-broken,

EDWARD."

P. S.—Inclosed is a checque for £300, which sum will be remitted to you yearly to any address you may forward to my agent."

In vain was every endeavour resorted to to restore Ela to sensibility; a medical man was of course immediately called in, who applied the proper remedies without effect. Ela remained completely delirious for three or four days, and on regaining her senses she was surprised to behold several strange faces around her.

"Where am I ?" she cried frantically, "why am I brought hither ; and Mrs. Fitzsosborne, where is she?"

"Why, madam," said an elderly woman with a disagreeable countenance, "in the first place you are in the same house as you were before you was taken ill; in the second place Mrs. Fitzosborne has left here these two days—"

"Left, left," interrupted Ela, trying to recall her scattered senses; "where has she gone, and Mr. Wallingford—what has become of him ?"

"Poor thing," said a young woman who had acted in the capacity of maid to Mrs. Fitzosborne, " poor thing, her mind still wanders ; we had better leave her, and let her strive to compose herself to sleep."

"Sleep !" cried Ela, " no, no, no, I cannot sleep ; do not leave me, I tremble to be left alone. What is the occasion of all th confusion."

" Why, ma'am said the young girl, " the whole of it is, that two days after you was taken in, Mrs. Fitzosborne, as she called herself, left this house, having disposed of the lease and all the furniture to the mistress of this good woman, who is expected to arrive from the country to take possession of it every day."

" Yes," added the old woman, "and a pretty kettle of fish it would be to let her find her best bed-room occupied by a sick person, it would be as much as my situation is worth, and I'm sure I'm not a going for to do that here; good places is not quite so numerous as parish churches now-a-days."

" What has happened ?" repeated Ela, taking no notice of the harangue of the ill-tempered old woman, "tell me. I beseech you !"

" Why, ma'am answered the girl, " if you must know, though I don't think I am doing right to inform you, in your present situation; after you received that letter——"

" That letter !" screamed Ela, "ah, I recollect it all now. It was no dream then, no wild illusion. Give me the epistle, let me again peruse the confirmation of my misery and his perfidy."

" No, pray don't read it now," implored the girl, " be advised ; I'm sure you are not in a fit state to do any such thing at present."

" Give it me, I entreat, I command !" cried Ela frantically, and making an effort to get out of bed ; and the young woman thinking that the consequences might be less fatal if she complied with the request, than if she refused it, gave her the letter which she had treasured in a box against her recovery. With eager hands she snatched the letter from the servant's hand, and cast her eyes over the well known characters ; every sentence she read seemed to scorch her brain, and when she arrived at the conclusion, she burst into an hysterical fit of laughter, and throwing herself back in the bed, again became insensible.

" Well a very pretty pickle we're in truly," remarked the cross old domestic, "I wouldn't have had such a thing happen for five guineas ; however, ill or well, out she must bundle before my mistress comes here ; a nice name we should all get, if we were known to harbour the likes of her indeed !"

When Ela was again restored to sensibility the delirium of her anguish was abated, and she was enabled to look with wonderful calmness upon the misery of her situation ; it was the calmness of utter despair and hopelessness. She now viewed herself as a lost, degraded, wretched creature, who would be despised by her own sex, and insulted by the other ; the destroyer of her parent's happiness, and an alien from society ! But what were her

thoughts connected with the name of her seducer? The revolution in her feelings was as rapid as it was powerful: she now thought of him with hatred, disgust, and contempt, and doubly detested herself that she should have been the easy dupe of such a villain! The Italian blood which flowed in her veins, was excited to boiling, and in her heart she cursed him as the fell destroyer of her innocence, the devastator of her home, and the deliberate assassin of those who had given her being; for she could not imagine that they could live against the loss and supposed and apparent culpability of her in whom their very existence was centered. Oh, how dreadful were her sufferings as the latter reflections crossed her mind with fevered rapidity! We will not seek to pourtray them, for who is there that cannot imagine them?

It must not be supposed that Wallingford

had acted in the base manner we have described without a severe struggle with his feelings, and bitter and agonizing were his thoughts after he formed the resolution. Had it not been for his inordinate pride, and the fear he entertained of offending his parent, it was very doubtful whether he would not ultimately have married the much-injured Ela.

In two days more the housekeeper of the new tenant, again urged her unfeeling request for Ela to leave. It was then that she felt the full horrors of her situation, destitute of a home, and in a strange place, with resources very limited. The cheque sent by Wallingford had been purloined by the worthy Mrs. Fitzosborne, before she left the house, and had it not been, Ela would have shuddered at the idea of taking that money, which might be said to be the wages of her infamy. She had a few pounds of her own by her, and some articles of jewellery, which would be sufficient to support her for some time; but whither could she go; on whom depend for protection, especially in her present delicate situation? To remain beneath that roof where her ruin had been effected, was abhorrent to her feelings, and she was as anxious to leave the house as the old woman was to get rid of her. She reflected for some time without being able to come to any conclusion how it would be most prudent to act. At length she bethought her of asking the advice of Ellen, the young girl who had shown that good naturedness of heart that had somewhat preposessed her in her favour.

Ellen reflected for a few moments, and then said—

"Why, ma'am, I'm sure I pity you from the very bottom of my heart, and I would do anything to serve you. It is a shocking thing for a young lady like you to be placed in such a situation. I have got an aunt who lives in Howland Street, Tottenham Court Road, that has two daughters only; she is a poor woman, but I think if you could put up with such accommodation as she could afford you, till you have made some arrangements with your friends, which I hope and trust you will soon be able to do, she will upon my recommendation let you lodge with her. She is a very clean body, and a feeling woman too, and would do all as laid in her power to make you comfortable."

Ela sighed deeply at the word comfortable, her comfort she knew would never again be restored in this world; but she thanked the kind hearted Ellen warmly, and gladly availed herself of her offer. That evening Ellen hastened to her aunt Mrs. Bentley, and on her return informed our heroine that that good woman had willingly agreed to receive her on the following day. Ela heard this with all the pleasure that may be imagined, and the next morning removed to the house of the hospitable Mrs. Bentley. There we must for the present leave her, as her adventures will be recorded on a future occasion.

We return now to Wallingford, and it must not be supposed that he was exempt from punishment for the villanous treatment he had inflicted upon the unfortunate Ela. He had rendered her an outcast from her friends, a stranger to her parents, whose gray hairs he would probably be the cause of bringing with sorrow to the grave. He recalled to his recollection the beauteous state of innocence and content in which he had first beheld Ela; how soon he had suffered his sinful passions to throw an everlasting blight upon that happiness, and as he did so he breathed an involuntary curse upon his own head. In vain he flew to the wine cup to try to drown those harrassing thoughts; the remembrance would rise up in spite of all his efforts, and every time in more vivid characters than before. This anguish was augmented by the uncertainty of Ela's fate, he having made every inquiry after her, without gaining the slightest clue.

In the midst of this misery his father died, and thus did he receive additional cause for anguish. True, he was now his own master, and had no one to question his actions, should he think proper to make Ela his wife; but he feared he had proceeded too far to render such a step practicable, and still his pride revolted at the idea of uniting himself to one who was so far beneath him in rank and station, and at whom the finger of scorn and opprobrium might at some future period point.

While he was thus placed in a state of doubt, perplexity and anguish, he received a letter from Mr. Herbert, the uncle of Amelia, informing him that they should be in England in the course of a month, and expressing a wish that he would be willing to fulfil the vow which his late brother and his (Edward's) father had made. To this letter Wallingford returned no answer, and before the expected arrival of Mr. Herbert and Amelia he had formed a determination to return to London, not only with an idea of endeavouring to regain his spirits by change of scene, but with a determination of seeking out the retreat of Ela and her child, a twelvemonth having then elapsed since he had abandoned her. On the way to London he formed a number of resolutions, how he would act if he succeeded in discovering Ela,—how he would sue for her forgiveness, and provide for her and her child. They should be brought up in affluence and comfort, everything but making Ela his wife he would not hesitate to do. The nearer he approached to London the greater his anxiety increased. "Good God," he reflected, "what may now be the situation of Ela and her child! my child?—Perhaps wandering the streets, houseless, ragged and hungry—the ridicule of the vulgar, and the scorn of the great!—Oh, what a villain must I have been to consign them to so cruel a fate!"

No sooner did he alight from the coach than he hurried to Hampstead, where he learnt from the housekeeeper of the new proprietress that Ela had quitted the house two or three days after she received his letter, accompanied by Ellen; that she had managed to ascertain that it was Ela's intention to take up her residence with the former's aunt, whose name she was unacquainted with, and whose place of abode she did not know, any more than that it was somewhere in Howland Street, Tottenham Court Road, and that she was a poor woman, with two daughters who took in needlework.

To Howland Street Wallingford drove without delay, and after a most tedious inquiry, discovered the name and residence of Mrs. Bentley, of whom he immediately sought an interview. Upon making his business known, that good woman wept, and raising her hands ejaculated,

"Ah! poor dear young creature, her's is indeed a sad fate, and that of her helpless babe of whom she was so fond, and used to kiss it, and weep over it till she almost broke my heart to look at her! Lackaday! what a shocking thing for a pretty, good-tempered, and accomplished young woman like her, to be brought to such misery!"

"My good woman," said Wallingford, to whose heart every word of Mrs. Bentley's penetrated, "do not keep me in suspense;—does the lady live with you now?"

"Ah! no sir," replied Mrs. Bentley, "and sorry enough I am for it; for I'm sure I was as fond of her as if she were one of my own daughters!"

"And whither has she gone," eagerly demanded Wallingford, trembling with anxiety.

"Alas! sir," said Mrs. Bentley, "I wish I knew; but I am much afraid that some bad fate has been her portion. It is now more than two months since she left me. She had exhausted all her little stock of money, and although I am sure she was heartily welcome to share with me while I had half a loaf in the world, she could not brook to eat the bread of obligation. One morning when we arose at our usual hour, we were surprised that Ela did not make her appearance to breakfast; so thinking she might be ill, I went up into her bedroom, where I was paralyzed to find that she was not, neither had she apparently entered the bed at all on the previous night, for it was not tumbled in the least. On the table was a note, however, which explained everything!"

"Quick!—the contents of the note!—Tell me!" ejaculated Wallingford.

"In it," replied Mrs. Bentley, "she

affectionately thanked me for what I had done for her, though God knows that was little enough, but as much as my limited means would allow me; and informed me that she could no longer rest until she had sought out her poor parents, and begged their forgiveness. Thither she said she had departed the night before; and from that time to this, I have never seen or heard anything of her!"

Here then Wallingford was in as great a state of uncertainty as before, and knew not which way to act; for he dared not make inquiries in the neighbourhood where her parents resided. He therefore entreated Mrs. Bentley to make every inquiry in her power, and promising to call upon her again in a day or two, he departed to his hotel in a state of mind bordering on frenzy.

CHAPTER X.

"Canst thou minister to a mind diseased,
Pluck out a rooted sorrow from the brain?"
SHAKSPERE.

SEVERAL weeks rolled on, and still Wallingford was unable to gain the least clue to the retreat of Ela. He had, however, sent a person to the part where Gilbert Sherwin and his wife had dwelt; who was unable to learn more than that Ela had been seen there in a most wretched condition, but had soon left the village, and no one knew whither she had gone. Her father and mother were both dead, and Edwin Hartfield had enlisted for a soldier, and left the country.

This melancholy intelligence drove Edward almost to madness, and a thousand times he cursed himself for a heartless scoundrel. With avidity he flew to the society of his gay and thoughtless companions, with the hope of drowning reflection in the vortex of dissipation.

Among these votaries of folly he happened to meet with an old schoolfellow of the name of Rackett, who was one of the wildest men of fashion of the day. Pleasure and improvidence were the only deities he worshipped, and virtue was an article he laughed at. Among the ladies of the fashionable circles, he was a great favourite; for as well as being a smart, handsome-looking fellow, he possessed an ample stock at command of those sweet nothings so pleasing to the women, commonly placed under the denomination of small talk; and plenty of the best taking witticisms and flattering *morceaux* at his tongue's end.

Of this gentleman Wallingford became the almost constant companion, and attended with him with avidity every public assembly or scene of extravagant folly. He had made Rackett the confident of his *liason* with the unfortunate

Ela; and when the latter saw him at times thoughtful and melancholy, he would rally him severely upon his still thinking upon a rustic beauty after so many months separation, and when she had probably become acquainted with some other "*protector*," and thought no more about him, or only with feelings of contempt.

"Wallingford," said Rackett one afternoon to his friend, observing him to be sinking fast into a moody silence, "are you engaged tonight?"

"No," replied Wallingford; "but I do not feel disposed for company, and I think I shall retire to rest early."

"'Shaw! you shall do no such thing," said the other. "I confess, Wallingford, I begin to grow out of all patience with you, you so give way to those confounded dull fits, that I am fearful I shall catch the mania, and in the course of time be the counterpart of yourself.'

"If you are apprehensive of so great a calamity as that befalling you," rejoined Edward, faintly smiling, "I advise you by all means to give up my company, and seek the friendship of those whose feelings are more consonant with your own."

"I shall do nothing of the sort, I assure you," answered his gay friend; "but of this I am determined, that I will either cure you of your gloomy moods, or never own my name to be Rackett again. You must accompany me to the Opera to-night; it is for the benefit of Signora Lemarre, the lively *cantatrice*, and all the *elite* of the fashionable circles are sure to be present."

"I would much rather decline going," observed Wallingford—"I do not feel at all disposed for pleasure."

"And that is the very reason that I insist upon you accompanying me," returned Rackett; "so no more idle excuses—the thing's settled, and go you must."

Wallingford found it would be useless to hold out, so he gave an unwilling assent; and Rackett set about ordering the requisite preparations."

On entering the theatre, they found it crowded in every part with a brilliant audience, and Rackett's eyes wandered with astonishing rapidity from box to box, till they finally settled upon one, which immediately absorbed his whole attention.

"By Jupiter!" he exclaimed, seizing the arm of Wallingford, and directing his gaze towards the box, "this is very lucky—there is the little angel who is at present the magnet of attraction in the fashionable world. Look, Wallingford, do you see that lady in the white satin dress; you must acknowledge that she is lovely in the extreme, or else you are a worse judge of female beauty than you would wish me to believe."

Wallingford instinctively cast his eyes towards the lady to whom Rackett directed his attention, and was immdiately struck with her uncommon loveliness. She was not more than two and twenty, with a complexion fair as the opening lily, and a cast of features that would have graced a Madonna. Her eyes were a beautiful cerulean blue, and her hair, which was a bright flaxen, hung in natural tresses upon her shoulders. A soft tinge of retiring modesty upon her cheeks, added an exquisite charm to her countenance, which was perfect. Her figure was elegantly formed; and altogether she was one of the most interesting objects the eyes of Wallingford had ever encountered.

"Well, I see by your looks," remarked his jocose friend, laughing, "that you are not yet past redemption, so come along, I must introduce you." And without waiting for any reply from Edward, he took him by the arm, and hurried him into the box where the lady and her friends were seated.

"Permit me the honour, Miss Herbert," said Rackett, forcing Wallingford up to the lady, "to introduce to you my friend, Mr. Wallingford.—Mr. Wallingford, Miss Herbert!'

At this singular meeting with the lady to whom he had been introduced, Wallingford was so thunderstruck that he could not speak.

If Wallingford was astonished and confused, the beauteous Miss Herbert scarcely betrayed less perturbation; upon hearing the name of her former playfellow mentioned, her frame trembled, she looked timidly up, turned ashy pale; but speedily recovering herself, she smiled courteously upon Rackett, and curtseying distantly to our hero, turned from him with a look of indifference, and immediately entered into conversation with her own friends.

The rest of the evening was past most miserably by Wallingford; the beauty of Amelia had perfectly captivated him, while the coldness with which she treated him was a punishment, although severe, that the manner in which he had insulted her, rendered him fully deserving of.

"What a lovely being," he soliloquized, as he gazed in rapture upon her, "what bewitching modesty, what grace, what elegance; cursed fool that I was to sacrifice so much felicity; but it is too late now—Amelia could never pardon me; besides, is it at all likely that perfection such as her's should be without numerous admirers—one of whom may also have engaged her heart?"

This thought was distraction; and it was with the utmost difficulty that he could find patience to endure it. For the first time for many, many days, Ela was entirely banished from his thoughts; and when she was again recalled to his recollection, it was only to draw a comparison between her and the lovely Amelia, which deteriorated greatly from the pretensions of that betrayed and new unfortunate female.

It was a great relief for Wallingford when the performance was over, and he and his friend left the theatre, for he could not bear to contemplate such surpassing loveliness without deeply reproaching himself for the folly of whch he had been guilty,

Having seen Amelia and her friends to their carriages, Rackett seized the arm of Wallingford, and hurried him on towards the hotel at which they were staying.

"Well, and what think you of my friend, Miss Herbert," he demanded as they walked along—"is she not a sweet creature?"

"She is an angel!" exclaimed Wallingford, in a tone of rhapsody; "I never beheld so beauteous a countenance, so enchanting a figure, and such lovely eyes, in my life before."

"What!" cried Rackett, "and do you confess that the lady is handsomer than that certain little dark-eyed beauty for whom you have been sighing and moping, and fretting yourself into a consumption for so many months past?—Egad, Wallingford, Miss Herbert, if she was aware of your sentiments, ought to feel highly flattered."

"Indeed, Rackett, replied Wallingford, "the lady ought, and no doubt, would feel quite the contrary; but enough of that,—tell me—that is—of course the lady must have many admirers?"

"There's a question to ask," rejoined Racket—"why, do you think the men are all blind or stupid, which they must be, did they not admire when they behold perfection?"

"I confess you are right," answered our hero; "Miss Herbert is as near perfection as anything mortal can possibly be. But I mean, do you think that there is one that she beholds with an eye of favour?"

"Now that is quite another question," replied Rackett; "but what in the name of wonder, makes you so inquisitive all at once, Wallingford?"

"I may have stronger motives for my curiosity than you probably imagine, Rackett," said Edward, "but let that rest for the present, and oblige me by answering my question."

"Well, your conduct this night is perfectly inexplicable to me," observed Rackett, "but as you seem so deeply interested in the matter, I will endeavour to satisfy you. In my opinion then, although Miss Herbert is actually surrounded by lovers, she views not one of them with any more tender feeling than that of friendship."

"Impossible!" ejaculated Wallingford warmly, "a mind formed in such an exquisite mould as Miss Herbert's can never be insensible to love."

"And that may be all very possible, and very true," answered his cheerful friend, "and pray my dear fellow, is it equally impossible think you, that Amelia's heart should be pre-engaged?"

"True!" cried Wallingford with vivacity, as a latent gleam of hope shot across his heart, "but do you know whether such is really the case?"

"Why, she rejected my suit," answered Rackett, "and I think that's almost proof positive."

"Nonsense!" exclaimed Wallingford, pettishly, "and is that your only reason?"

"No," said Rackett, "I have stronger reasons for believing so, nay, more, I am pretty certain, that Miss Herbert's heart has been devoted to one being for many years, a man who by his indifference, has rendered himself totally unworthy of such a treasure, and I am likewise confident, that in spite of his treatment, her heart still retains all its former affection for him."

"Oh! do you really think so?" eagerly cried the delighted Wallingford but suddenly checking himself, he added; "but what an idiot must that man be, who could so readily dash the cup of happiness that was offered to his lips."

"He must be a maniac; an ass, a—a" added Rackett, warmly.

"And do you really think so?" demanded Edward, smiling,

"That do I, most sincerely," said his gay companion, "and if he were present, I would not hesitate to tell him so."

"Then you have the opportunity of doing so," returned Wallingford, "for I am that maniac, that ass, that——"

"Can I believe my ears!" cried the astonished Rackett.

"Indeed you may," answered our hero. "Ah, Rackett, you may well call me a fool; but listen,"

Mr. Wallingford then proceeded to explain everything to his friend, and when he had concluded, the latter having paused for a second or two, slapped him on the shoulder, and cried,—

"Do not despair, my boy, after all, your case is not decidedly hopeless; true, you have no doubt offended the lady's pride, which is the worst thing any of our sex can be guilty of, but I am fully persuaded that Amelia still loves you, and as I am on particular good terms with her, I will take upon myself the task of negotiating the business; but what is to become of the black-eyed beauty, Wallingford? I presume she is forgotten already?"

An inexpressible pang shot through the heart of Wallingford at this question, which completely saddened all the sanguine hopes he had but the second before indulged in; and ere he had time to reply, a female voice screaming for help, attracted their attention toward Westminster Bridge, at the foot of which they then were, and by the light of a lamp near, they were horror struck at beholding, mounted on the balustrades, apparently about to spring off, the figure of a female, while a woman beneath, had hold of a portion of her gown, and was making every effort to arrest her rash determination. Wallingford and his friend hurried towards the spot, but ere they reached it, she had broke from the woman's hold and immediately precipitated herself into the water, with a heavy plunge. Wallingford waited for no more, but rushing with the speed of lightning down the steps of the bridge, threw off his coat, and dashed into the water, to the unfortunate woman's rescue.

The night was very dark, the only rays being thrown upon the liquid tide by the glimmering lights upon the bridge, so that Wallingford had no easy task to perform. The woman had twice sank, ere he could discern her, and was about to sink the third time, when Wallingford put forth his whole strength, and at length succeeded in grappling a portion of her dress, by which he dragged her to the bank.

By this time the woman who had attempted to prevent her committing the dreadful act, came to the spot, and proved to be one of those unfortunate beings, who having strayed from the paths of virtue are compelled to get a revolting and precarious living in the public streets. She expressed apparent sympathy for the wretched creature, who was quite insensible.

" Do you know her, my good woman?" asked Wallingford.

"Yes, sir," answered the young woman, with a low curtesy, " she lodges in the same house with me, in Orchard-street, Westminster; and I really think that it is misery and starvation that have driven her to this awful act. She used to get a scanty subsistence by taking in needle-work; but lately she has had scarcely anything to do, and I do believe that neither her nor her infant have scarcely tasted a morsel of food for the last two or three days, and none of us could assist her, for we were all nearly as bad off as herself. This evening she said she could endure it no longer, and that she was resolved to get victuals for her poor little innocent, or perish."

A strange trembling came over Wallingford while the woman was giving this account, and without waiting to hear another word, he bore the senseless form of her he had just rescued up the steps, and took her beneath the light of the lamp; while he hastily parted the long and dishevelled tresses of raven hair from her countenance, but uttered an involuntary groan of agony, when in the pale features of her he had just dragged from the jaws of death, he recognised those of Ela—the betrayed, the deserted Ela.

" Good God! can it be?" he cried, and throwing the senseless woman over his shoulder, he flew rather than ran towards a doctor's shop on the other side of the bridge, followed closely by the astonished Rackett, who was perfectly at a loss to unravel the mysterious affair.

"Stop! stop!" he vociferated, "for goodness sake, Wallingford, are you mad?"

But Edward heard not what he said, so completely was his mind absorbed in what had happened. Having arrived at the shop, he intreated the man to use his utmost skill with the least possible delay, with which request he complied, and while he was endeavouring to restore her to sensibility, Wallingford was pacing the shop in the utmost state of distraction, and perfectly deaf to the anxious inquiries of his friend Rackett, who began to think that he had taken leave of his senses.

The doctor having tried his utmost skill ineffectually, recommended that the wretched suicide should be conveyed home to a warm bed as speedily as possible.

"You say you know where this la— poor woman lodges?" said the agitated, Edward addressing the before mentioned female, who had been a silent and astonished spectator of all that had passed.

" Yes, sir," she answered, " I repeat, that I live in the same house."

"Will you accompany me with her?" hastily demanded Wallingford.

"Certainly sir," answered the woman, "but it is such a wretched place, and not at all fit for such a gentlemen as you to——"

"For God's sake, call a coach directly," interrupted our hero, "every moment of delay is fraught with tenfold danger; I will myself attend her to her lodgings."

" Why surely your senses have forsaken you, my dear fellow;" said Rackett, " your clothes are now wringing wet, and such a rash step might be the death of you. Come with me to the hotel immediately, and change yourself; this good woman no doubt will see to the safety of her companion."

" As your friend justly observes," interposed the doctor, "such a step in your present condition would be highly imprudent and dangerous; I therefore beg of you to follow his advice, and I will myself accompany this poor woman, and see to her safety before I leave her."

It was with the utmost difficulty that the doctor and Rackett prevailed upon the distracted Wallingford to accede to this request, and having seen Ela into the coach, followed by the doctor and the female, into whose hand Edward slipped some gold, with strict and earnest injunctions for her to see to the safety f her unfortunate companion, he suffered him-self to be led away by Rackett, in a state of mind, more easily conceived than de-scribed.

CHAPTER XI.

" Oh, bitter was that female's lot,
By ev'ry misery surrounded."
THE FORSAKEN.

How shall we attempt to describe the bitter remorse, the soul harrowing anguish that Wallingford experienced that night? In vain did Rackett seek to compose him: he could not be persuaded to retire to rest, but paced his chamber the whole of the night, calling upon the name of Ela, and accusing himself of being her murderer. What a villain did he now consider himself, when he found that his black treachery had been the cause of bringing the unfortunate Ela to the lowest depths of misery, to that awful state of destitution and despair which could have urged her on to self-destruction. Her child, his child too, oh the thought was madness! What a heart-rending tale had the few words of the woman who had sought to save her from an untimely fate, spoken to his guilty conscience.

"And should she die!" he cried in a tone of intense agony, clasping his forehead; "Oh, God! the bare supposition drives me to frenzy! Alas! What a scene of misery has my accursed perfidy, pride, and treachery effected! Ela, can I ever know peace again, when I reflect upon what I have brought thee to? Oh, no, no, no; and should she recover, how dare I meet her reproachful eye;—how live and hear her curses?"

Again he paced his chamber with disordered steps, and groaned aloud with mental agony. With the first dawn of day, he hastily dressed himself, resolved to hasten to the place where his hapless victim lodged, and learn the worst. Rackett would have persuaded him from this, but finding that he was determined, he insisted upon accompanying him.

Bitter as was the anguish of Wallingford at the misery in which he had beheld Ela, and the awful circumstances in which they met, that anguish was increased tenfold when he and Rackett entered the dirty, confined, and filthy neighbourhood in which she had been compelled to seek a shelter for herself and infant. It was situated up a narrow alley in Orchard Street, which seemed scarcely capable of rendering shelter to the living, the very air of which was pestiferous, and whose aspect was revolting in the extreme. The houses, or rather hovels, for they deserved no better title, were fast crumbling to ruins, and everything denoted the squalid misery and abject poverty of these poor creatures who were compelled to inhabit them. Filth of every description be-strewed the muddy ground, and the threshold of every house was bestrewn with rubbish and dirt.

"My God!" exclaimed our hero, "and is it in such a place as this, my villany has driven what was once one of Nature's fairest works, to seek a retreat? Oh, monster, monster!"

Rackett sought to compose his friend, and then knocked at the door of the house to which they had been directed, which was shortly opened by the female whom we have before mentioned. Edward breathlessly inquired after the unfortunate.

"Oh," replied the woman, "she passed a very bad night, but is now remarkably better, and has insisted upon arising. She has often anxiously inquired the name of her preserver, but as I did not know it, of course I could give her no information upon that point. Shall I take your name up to her now, Sir?"

"Oh, no, no," hastily replied Wallingford, "conduct me immediately to her room."

The woman curtseyed very obsequiously and obeyed, preceding our hero and Rackett up a dark, narrow, and dismal staircase, until they stopped at a door on the third floor, to which she pointed, and whispered "that is the room." She then hastened away to another part of the house.

Wallingford now paused and trembled, his heart throbbed violently, and if it had not been for Rackett he would have fallen. A low moaning sound from within the chamber, and the faint cries of a child aroused him to recollection, and with a faltering hand he ventured to open the door, but so gently, that the person within could not hear him.

Wallingford paused once more at the thresh-hold, and his whole frame shook with emotion as his eyes rested upon the misery of the scene beyond. It was a large dreary room; the plastered walls of which were dropping to pieces. In an obscure corner was a skeleton grate, in which a fire seemed to have been re-cently kindled, and to which it had probably for many months before been a stranger. The only articles in the room were a common deal table, a broken chair, and a crazy bedstead hung round with tattered bed-furniture, whose original colour was not discernable, so thickly was it encrusted with dirt. This bedstead stood in a nook by the side of the door, so that Ela, who was seated at the foot of the bed nursing her infant, could not perceive any person who entered till they were in the middle of the apartment. Edward still faltered, and his heart smote him bitterly. He tried to collect himself, and advanced a few paces into the room. Aroused by the noise of his footsteps, Ela left off rocking her infant, and said in a faint voice, "Is that you, Charlotte?"

"Ela, poor, deeply injured Ela!" ejaculated Wallingford, and unable longer to contain himself, he started forward and stood before her!

A ghastly hue overspread the before pallid features of Ela, when she beheld the destroyer of her peace in her presence; her large black eyes darted forth an expression of bitter hatred and disgust, her bosom throbbed convulsively, she uttered no sound, but laying her infant on the bed, stood and gazed upon Wallingford, with a glance which smote him to the soul.

"Ela! dear Ela!" cried Edward, "speak to me; do you not know me?"

A smile of irony passed over the countenance of Ela, which dissolved itself into an expression of scorn and abhorrence, as she replied:—

"Do I not know ye! Yes, for a villain, a monster, a wretch unworthy of the name of man. The seducer of female innocence, the betrayer of the unwary; the murderer of my parents, the destroyer of my peace; my curse, my bane!—Do I not know ye!—Base traitor, can you stand in my presence—in the presence of her who, but for your accursed arts might now have been good, and virtuous, and happy—can you gaze upon the misery you have occasioned, and ask me that question? Begone, hypocrite. Villain, no longer scare my eyeballs with your hated image."

"Ela, for mercy's sake, drive me not mad," ejaculated Wallingford, advancing nearer towards her, and looking into her face with the most earnest supplication.

"Drive you mad," shrieked Ela, "ha, ha, ha! And came you here to endeavour to persuade me that you have a heart; that you have the sense of feeling. Hark ye, Edward Wallingford, if you be sincere, now will I make you feel still more. In this wretched habitation for days has your Ela, as you once called her, and her child—your child—felt all the horrors of hunger, until at last driven to frenzy, what did I? Shall I tell you? Have you courage to listen to it? Yes, your callous heart can endure that and more. Know then that last night, driven to despair, and goaded on by the cries of my poor helpless babe, your babe, Wallingford, I left it on its hard pallet, and started forth, resolved to sacrifice everything, yes, even my eternal salvation, to procure it food. In vain I sought, I had sunk so low, so wretched, that even the revellers in female guilt looked at me with an eye of scorn, and mocked and reviled me. For hours I walked about, until my weary limbs would support me no longer. The full horror of my situation then started vividly before me, and scorched my brain; I heard in imagination, the anguished cries of my poor little innocent for food, and I had none to give it. Could I return to my miserable shelter, and witness its

agonies, without having the power to relieve it? No. I could not; in that moment I felt myself a thing of hate, of scorn, an outcast, degraded, despised, hopeless. What was life to me, but a curse, a mockery? Why not then end it? The water rolled beneath me; I looked down upon it, it was dark and gloomy as my doom, and seemed to invite me to my fate; I breathed one prayer for my infant, and plunged as I imagined into eternity; but some cursed spell was upon me, some officious hand saved me. Now, Edward Wallingford, art thou not disappointed, that thy crimes have not made me a self murderess, as well as the abandoned wretch I already am?"

"For the love of Heaven, Ela," ejaculated Wallingford, "do not rack me."

"Heaven!" repeated Ela, with scorn, "what have you to do with Heaven?" Dare such a villain as you appeal to the judgment seat of the Almighty? You, who have broken my poor parents' hearts, who brought their grey hairs with sorrow to the grave. Listen, I have not told you all yet. I have not told you how I endured the scorn and contumely of the world when I became a mother; how, I was compelled to be beholden to strangers for the common necessaries of life, for me and my offspring. Shall I tell you how I at last resolved to re-visit my home, the home that had at least once been mine—that home you had rendered desolate—and seek the pardon of my parents. Oh, yes, it is a goodly story, and you may like to hear it. Know then I left the place in which I had too long eaten the bread of honest charity, at night, and with the child in my arms, commenced my weary journey. I travelled on for many a weary mile, until exhausted nature could endure no more, and I laid me down with my infant nestled to my milkless breast, and sought repose. Repose for me! The word was mockery. But I stretched my weary limbs upon the sterile earth till morning's dawn, when I resumed my toilsome journey. Shall I tell you how I contrived to support me and my child—your child, Wallingford, during that wretched pilgrimage? Why, from the charity of those I met on the road; nay, start not—they though strangers, were kinder far than those who pretend to all that's noble, good, and virtuous. At length I reached the village from which your treachery tore me. It was a lovely day, the sun shone forth in golden panoply, and the birds carolled their sweetest lays, as if in mockery of my misery. It was one of those bright days that I had passed so happily when surrounded with all the joys of home. My way lay through the old church yard; I stopped at a new made grave; instinctively I knelt before it, and breathed a prayer for the souls of those who rested beneath it; a rest I yearned to meet. My eyes rested

upon a small stone at the head; I read the characters upon it; hear me, Edward Wallingford, on that simple stone was inscribed the name of her who bore me."

"Oh, God! oh God!" cried Wallingford with intense agony, while drops of cold perspiration bedewed his quivering temples. "Spare me, Ela—in mercy, Ela—in mercy spare me."

"Hear me out, Wallingford," replied Ela, with awful calmness; "think not that I wept; no, my eyes were dry, my heart was deadly calm and I felt a secret delight—aye, delight, at that moment,

for I thought the poor old woman had better rest there, than be alive to see the misery of her once innocent child. I gazed but amoment upon that lowly grave, pressed my infant closer to my heart, and walked from the churchyard. With firm steps I tred the path that led to the peaceful habitation o my parents. I paused upon the threshold of the door; and then, indeed, I trembled. I listened—the voice of pain smote my ears, I threw open the door, and the next moment I was on my knees, at the bedside of my dying father."

The last words were spoken in a tone that

thrilled to the very soul of the distracted Wallingford, he threw himself in a seat, covered his face with his hands, and groaned aloud. Ela paused, and seemed to watch his emotions with something like revengeful satisfaction.

In the same fixed and stern attitude Ela stood for two or three seconds, and watched the agitation of Wallingford in silence. Rackett had been a silent spectator of the singular scene, in fact the impressive behaviour and extraordinary beauty of Ela, amid all her misery, had astonished him, and rendered him mute.

"Edward Wallingford," at length resumed Ela, with a calmness that was even more awful than her frenzy, "Edward Wallingford, I repeat I knelt beside the bed of my dying father, for his soul was quickly hastening to eternity; the poor old man whose heart you cruelty had broken, was about being summoned into the presence of the Almighty power, at whose judgment seat he was prepared to stand with a conscience clear and unblemished. Oh, Edward Wallingford, methinks if you could but have been a spectator of that scene, it would have wrung your—yes, even your flinty heart. The poor deserted outcast humbled to the dust, wept like a child, but could not give utterance to a prayer for forgiveness. The good old man extended to me his hand, already damp and clammy with the dew of death; he bade me rise, blessed my name, kissed my cheek vehemently, and as his lips gave utterance to a malediction upon the head of the seducer of his daughter—that daughter, Wallingford, received him in her arms a corpse."

"Oh, God!" cried Edward, distractedly, "this torment is insupportable; Ela, if you ever loved me——"

"Loved you!" interrupted Ela, "villain!—Look at me now; look at what I have suffered; at the confidence I placed in your specious promises, and asseverations; gaze upon the features of this little infant, and then repeat if Ela had ever loved—but you must hear the termination of my story. It is a goodly sequel. Rather than accept the charity of strangers, I disposed of every little article that was left of my parents' humble property, and buried him in the old churchyard, in the same grave which bore the ashes of my mother; I hallowed the sacred spot with my tears, even till night had spread its grey mantle over the face of nature, when pressing my babe to my bosom, I turned from the spot, and bade farewell to the scene for ever. With the scanty remains of the money I had made by the sale of my late father's effects, returned to London, and took a humble attic in an obscure part of the town, where I endeavoured to support myself and my infant by such jobs of needlework as I could get to do, though that was little indeed,

for the poverty of my appearance, and the miserable place in which I lived, rendered people suspicious, and I oftener received an insult rather than employment. But I cared not for myself, no. I felt that all I could suffer would be only a just punishment for my accursed credulity; but could I calmly contemplate the sufferings of my unfortunate infant? Oh, no, no, no—every cry it uttered when it sought in vain the nourishment of my breast, was worse to me than as though I had had a dagger sheathed in my heart. Three dreary months of winter I endured this state of wretchedness, and many a day have I passed without so much as a morsel of food entering my lips; but miserable as were my circumstances then, I was ordained to endure worse; unable to pay the rent of the lodging, the landlady insisted upon my leaving it, and I came hither, the abode of poverty and crime. I cannot recount all the horrors I have endured since I have been here, until at length driven to desperation, I last night left my infant, sleeping, unconscious of its mother's anguish, and resolved to make any sacrifice to procure it food. The spell that was upon me followed me there, and mad, distracted, I sought to terminate an existence that had long been a curse to me. Now Edward Wallingford you have heard my tale, say, are you not satisfied with the work of your base, your guilty soul?"

As Ela thus finished her melancholy narrative, she fixed her eyes upon Wallingford with a look that thrilled his soul with agony, then sinking into a passionate burst of anguish, she pressed her infant vehemently to her bosom, and bathed its innocent face with a flood of tears.

"Merciful powers!" cried Wallingford, in a voice almost choked with anguish, "and has this indeed been all my work! Oh, how bitterly do I now feel it. Ela, I acknowledge I have been a villain, a cruel, guilty wretch! —but if repentance, if remorse, can but restore——"

"Restore!" reiterated Ela, relapsing into her former wildness of demeanour which had given to her looks and actions the semblance of insanity; "can repentance, Wallingford, restore me to that peace, that innocence, that happiness I formerly enjoyed? Can it bring back my poor parents from that grave to which your baseness so prematurely sent them? Can it——"

"Oh, Ela, in mercy spare me," implored our hero, "I have indeed been guilty, but yet not so guilty as you would believe! For months I have been brought to a sense of the enormity of my conduct, and my life as been miserable, a curse to me! Amid every scene of pleasure your image has ever been present to me, and I have prayed again and again to meet you, that I might throw myself at your feet, implore your forgiveness and offer you all the reparation in my power! Heaven knows the days of misery, the nights of distraction I have passed! How anxiously I have searched for you, how bitter has been my torment at the fruitlessness of my efforts! Last night Providence made me the instrument of saving you from an untimely fate; surely that was an augury of our future happiness; pardon me, dearest, best of women, and I swear that henceforth my whole study shall be to dissipate from your mind those horrors that now embitter it! Ela, on my knees, I implore you. Forgive me!—in mercy forgive me!"

Ela gazed a moment solemnly upon Wallingford who with impressive earnestness had thrown himself on his knees, and was looking up into her pale countenance with an expression of agonizing supplication. Her bosom heaved convulsively, her form trembled. At that moment her infant awoke, and gazing upon Edward, smiled innocently in his face, The feelings of Ela could endure no more: she laughed hysterically, and with a passionate flood of tears, sunk upon Wallingford's bosom, and became insensible. We must pass over this effecting scene, for no language of ours will do justice to it! Wallingford hastily summoned the woman we have often mentioned before, to the assistance of Ela, and then requested that Rackett would leave him, as he was resolved not to quit the house until he had seen Ela restored to tranquillity. Rackett assented, for the scene agreed not with his taste, and they were left alone.

That night Wallingford never for a moment quitted the wretched abode of Ela, and when daylight broke in upon its gloomy confines, it discovered Ela and him seated calmly side by side, the former with her infant enfolded in her arms, and gazing with melancholy fondness alternately upon its lovely features, and the countenance of him to whom her heart was still enthusiastically devoted. Yes, Ela was calm; nay, comparatively happy, for hope and confidence had once more spread their bright delusive visions before her imagination, Edward had repeated again and again, his assurances of endeavouring to repair the injuries he had done her; and bestowed upon their infant all the exuberant fondness that a parent could lavish upon his offspring; and had vowed that nothing should persuade him to quit her presence, till she was delivered from her present wretchedness, to a comfortable situation. All this had Edward promised, nay swore, and at the time he did so, he was sincere; his compunction for the wrongs he had done her were so great, that he thought he could not do enough to make reparation. "I will never more forsake her," he mentally soliloquised,

"she shall never again know the bitter stings of misery; my whole study shall be the happiness of her and her child, my infant; I will be its protector from the snares that have ruined its mother. This, this will I do at every hazard, at every worldly and selfish sacrifice!"

Wallingford really felt as he then thought, for Ela appeared to him again, in all the purity of loveliness, by which she had at first fascinated his breast, that state of innocence and happiness, from which he had been the means of hurling her, and he wondered that he could ever have been the villain to cause her so much misery.

Edward's liberality to the people of the wretched abode in which Ela had long sought a refuge, had been the means of procuring her attention and comparative comfort; refreshments had been obtained, and Ela having been persuaded to partake of them, felt her long exhausted spirits partially revived. Wallingford had expressed his resolution to see her placed in a comfortable lodging, without any delay; he therefore the same day left Ela to put his plans into execution, after repeating his before mentioned vows.

Were we to give an analysis of the real sentiments of Edward Wallingford, we fear the result would be anything but satisfactory to the reader. Pride, love and principle were struggling for supremacy in his mind, but it was evident which had the ascendancy. The effervescence of the delight with which he had effected a reconciliation with Ela, had partially subsided, and the imprudence and absolute impossibility of his ever making her his wife recurred to him with redoubled force. But surely, he reflected, Ela could not be so thoughtless as to entertain such an idea? He had not led her to hope such a thing, and she must be aware that circumstances had placed an insurmountable barrier in the way of such a plan. No, no, all that he could do to render her happy, except that he was ready and determined to do; he would be to her a friend —a brother—but a husband, he never could! To his child too, he would perform all the duties of a father, so far as prudence would allow him; he would see to her education, and watch her conduct with a vigilant eye. These thoughts naturally recalled to him, the image of the gentle Amelia Herbert, her whom he had so insultingly slighted, and with whom he might have been so supremely happy. A pang shot through his frame at the reflection, and he could not help contrasting the mild and placid features of Amelia, and the wild glances, and savage demeanour of Ela, when they had encountered each other in the miserable den she now occupied, and the contrast was certainly all in favour of the former. But yet was Ela still lovely; and when Edward thought upon what she was when he first beheld her, pity, remorse, and admiration, combined to render him wretched. Time alone can efface from our hearts, those we have once loved with all the strength of youthful passion.

"Cursed misfortune!" he exclaimed as he walked on towards his hotel, where he had promised to rejoin Rackett, would to Heaven Amelia had but met my sight ere I knew Ela, then would this painful conflict have been spared me!"

Having thus soliloquised, Wallingford resolved once more to see Amelia Herbert, and by some means explain to her the reason of his former neglectful conduct towards her. But of his unfortunate connection with Ela, he would not mention a sentence; no, he would not wound her amiable heart by the recital, neither could he make up his mind to mention a circumstance that must render him contemptible in the eyes of every person of principle and honour.

Wallingford strove to convince himself of the propriety and integrity of these designs, but his mind was far from being satisfied, and in that mood he arrived at the hotel, where he found Rackett dressed and prepared to accompany him in quest of aparments for Ela. As they walked along, Rackett aroused his companion from a deep reverie into which he had fallen, by observing :—

"By Jove, Wallingford, I acknowledge that I am quite fascinated with your taste; this Ela is one of the loveliest creatures the poet's imagination, or the pencil of the artist ever drew. Such a woman would be a magnet of attraction in the higher circles; by heaven, it is next to sacrilege to see her buried in obscurity!"

Wallingford sighed; "you are a perfect enthusiast in these matters, Racket," he replied.

"I plead guilty to the charge," returned Racket, "but such a woman as that would make even a stone an enthusiast."

"Oh," added Wallingford, "had you seen Ela formerly you would indeed say she was lovely."

"Was lovely," repeated Racket, "by Jupiter, she is still the most beautiful woman I ever beheld. The brilliancy of those black eyes is sufficient to penetrate a heart of adamant; her long silken lashes, her exquisite arched eyebrows, her lips, her teeth, and then her commanding figure—by my soul, Wallingford, she is as near perfection as anything can approach. There are few indeed that can equal her, even now that the mark of care is upon her cheeks; for instance, Amelia Herbert would not bear the least comparison with her.'

"Hold, Racket," said Wallingford, ardently, "I must not listen to such observations ; Amelia Herbert is worthy every encomium, she is both,

chaste as purity can make her, and beautiful as one of heaven's fairest inhabitants."

"Ha! ha! ha!" laughed Racket, "well upon my word, I have made the discovery that I wished, with difficulty ; you are a sad dog, a devil of a fellow!"

"Let me beg of you, Racket," observed Edward seriously, "to reserve your levity for some more fitting occasion."

"Nay, nay, be not offended, my dear fellow," said Racket, "I am delighted to think you entertain the sentiments you do towards Miss Herbert, she is worthy of them. Besides, Ela must herself be convinced of the utter impossibility of————"

"Enough, my friend," interrupted Wallingford,—"you appear to understand my sentiments, and for the present let us drop the subject. I must request you to maintain the most inviolable secrecy upon this unhappy affair; Ela's name must not become the subject of ridicule and scorn among the wild and thoughtless."

"You may depend upon me, Wallingford," replied Racket; "not a sentence upon the subject shall ever pass my lips, in the presence of any one but ourselves!"

CHAPTER XII.

"When lovely woman stoops to folly,
   And finds too late that men betray
What charm can soothe her melancholy,
   Oh! what can wash her guilt away?'
                                    GOLDSMITH.

WAALLINFRD and his companion were not long in obtaining respectable apartments in the vicinity of Islington, and having represented Ela to be a young widow, and Edward her only brother and protector, the landlady appeared perfectly satisfied. They therefore hurried back to Westminster, to remove Ela from her miserable residence as speedily as possible.

Before Wallingford left the house in the morning, the woman had suggested to him the propriety of Ela and the child being provided with such wearing apparel as would prevent suspicion, and set the busy tongue of scandal at rest ; Edward, therefore, had left the means of carrying such a plan into execution, and when he and Racket returned to the disgusting abode, they found Ela and the infant attired respectably, and the former looking happier than she had done for months before. A coach having been procured, Edward and Racket proceeded to lead Ela from that abode in which she had experienced so much sorrow, and Wallinford having liberally rewarded the woman of the house, they were driven off with all possible speed to the neighbourhood of Islington.

The mistress of the house was an elderly woman, of urbane and matronly appearance, and she received Ela without the least apparent suspicion. By the orders of Wallingford when he had taken the apartments, she had a pleasant repast prepared for them, but Ela and Edward's minds were too much occupied with other thoughts, to suffer them to enjoy it, and Rackett was left to the almost exclusive discussion of it. The apartments were extremely comfortable, and handsomely furnished, and everything around had an air of peace and respectability, but, in spite of all, Ela felt wretched, for what comfort, she reflected, could be her's when she was beholden to Wallingford for all, and was compelled to live under an assumed character, which, if ever discovered, would degrade her in the eyes of every respectable woman? Wallingford was scarcely less sad and wretched than Ela, and unable to endure with patience the crowd of conflicting ideas that tormented him, and he was glad when the time arrived for him to retire from her presence.

Wallingford hurried early to his chamber that night, and so refreshed was he by sleep, that when he visited Ela in the morning, he was perfectly composed and apparently happy. But it was easy to perceive that Ela felt very, very different; for though she attempted to smile and greet him with an ardent welcome, it was evident the canker-worm of care was upon her cheeks, and that the poison of mental anguish and self-reproach was rankling at her heart. Her eyes, which were inflamed, were sufficient evidence that she had been weeping, and her countenance was pale and dejected. But very different was the effect this change wrought upon the mind of Wallingford; instead of exciting his sympathy, it lessened and cooled the ardour of the passion he had entertained for the unfortunate victim of his treachery, and as he compared the melancholy, emaciated looks of Ela with the serenity and chaste beauty of Amelia Herbert, the contrast appeared so powerfully to the disadvantage of the former, that he began to feel astonished how he could ever have considered her the perfect being his former admiration had depicted her to be.

As Wallingford's admiration for the unhappy Ela diminished, so did Rackett's appear to increase; he made no secret of his thoughts from Edward; he was an experienced rake, and used to setting feelings or principles at nought; his vanity was the principal passion that prompted him in his illicit career, and he considered that Ela would be a "splendid creature," as the phraseology of the libertine has it, to sport with him in his cab, or in a box at the opera. He would be the envy of all his gay and dissipated friends. Such were Rackett's thoughts, which received encouragement as he daily remarked the indifference with which Wallingford began to view Ela; the restraint he seemed to feel in her society; and he often ventured to rally him upon the subject, and to throw out such hints as could not be mistaken by one object to whom they were directed. And Wallingford, too, listened to him, patiently listened to remarks that should have aroused his utmost indignation. Rackett perceiving his advantage, did not fail to follow it up by every artifice he knew so well how to use. He seized every opportunity of placing Amelia in the most alluring point of view—of eulogising her charms—her modest pretensions to his heart; and it was a theme so consonant with the sentiments of Wallingford, that he listened with avidity and admiration.

A fortnight passed away, and Wallingford daily became more cool and distant towards the unfortunate Ela. He would sit for hours in her presence, and scarcely exchange one kind word with her. Ela could not but remark this, and many a bitter pang, many a sleepless night did it cost her, but still she was ready to attribute it to any other cause than the right one; he must be ill, or family affairs, into which she had no right to inquire, afflicted him. Surely after all his vows, after all the expressions of remorse he had uttered for his past misconduct, he could not again be the villain to deceive her. She dared not question him upon the subject; no, she would not evince such a doubt of his sincerity. Alas! she was fated too soon to be deceived.

"Wallingford," exclaimed Rackett, one morning when he entered the apartment of his friend; "throw off those looks of sadness with which you have been wont of late to clad your countenance, and look

'Like patience sitting on a monument,
    Smiling at grief.'

I have good news for you!"

Wallingford looked at his jocose companion with doubt and anxiety.

"Ah, I see," continued Rackett, "that you are in a state of suspense, and as I am one of the most merciful fellows in Christendom, I will hasten to relieve you. You know I promised you that I would exert my influence to bring about an understanding between you and Miss Herbert."

"Ah!" ejaculated Wallingford, eagerly, "and are there, then, any hopes for me? Do not deceive me, Rackett; this is not a fit subject for you to sport upon."

"Oh! the deceit, the hypocrisy of mankind!" cried Rackett, laughing, "but a few days since, Edward, you were all rapture, all transport at the thought of being restored to the forgiveness and love of Ela; you were vowing eternal constancy to her, and forming plans for her future happiness; but, weugh! in a moment, the name of Amelia is mentioned, and—"

"Do not torture me, Rackett," interrupted

our hero; "you know my situation—the dilemma I am placed in—the impossibility of my ever being more than a brother, a protector to Ela: and my own feelings—her feelings, will never suffer me to think of her in the degrading character of my mistress; but Miss Herbert—"

"Well, well, Wallingford," added Rackett, starting, for the candid and plain way of putting the question was more than he was prepared for; he had not yet ventured to come to such a conclusion himself, although his conscience too plainly told him it was a just one; but he found it was impossible for him to refute it, and hanging his head abashed at the consciousness of his own villany, he suffered his companion to proceed:—

"The fact is, my dear fellow, I see nothing so very heinous in the business, after all; as you just now observed, you were evidently designed by nature for a domestic man; Amelia is worthy of you, and I see no obstacle in the way of your attaining your wishes; at least, I am determined to serve you all that is in my power, and I am generally pretty successful in such matters. By way of a preliminary I have procured for you a private interview with Miss Herbert, and no doubt you will soon be able to effect a reconciliation with her; in the next place I not only acknowledge that Ela has won my admiration, but that I am quite willing to release you from the burthen."

This heartless proposal fell like a dead weight upon the heart of Wallingford, and aroused him for a moment to a sense of his own enormity, to make a bargain for the person of Ela with another man! The idea was horrible! It was revolting; it was with difficulty he stifled his indignation, but the thoughts of Amelia recurred to him, and will it be believed that Wallingford at length brought himself not only to listen quietly to the proposal, but actually to accede to the base, the cruel stratagem. That very day, Edward was admitted to the interview with Miss Herbert, and he succeeded even beyond his most sanguine expectations.

Week after week now passed away, and every succeeding one brought more cause of sorrow to the hapless Ela. Wallingford hourly treated her with more distance and reserve, and often absented himself from her society for two or three days together; at length she was too fatally aroused to a full consciousness of his infidelity, and her own deplorable situation. But yet she dared not express her too-well founded suspicions to Wallingford himself; she felt an unaccountable dread of the consequences, and much as she felt the dependant and humiliating situation in which she was placed, she resolved to endure it all till the storm cloud burst over her devoted head, for the sake of her infant. To Rackett, however, who had lately shown her the most respectful attention,

and who she believed acted solely from motives of pure and disinterested friendship and sympathy, she hesitated not to confide her thoughts; and the interest he seemed to feel in her situation, and the pains he took to console and reassure her, won for him her warmest esteem.

Wallingford had more than once surprised them in these moments of confidence together, and the glances he had fixed upon her, stung Ela to the heart, and filled her bosom with apprehension. But yet, surely, Wallingford could never be so ungenerous, as to suspect a man who evinced such devoted friendship towards him, or to suppose her capable of encouraging any but the purest motives. Poignant was the anguish these reflections caused her, and many a sleepless night she passed in consequence.

A whole week now elapsed, and Edward did not visit her. Rackett pretended to endeavour to quiet her uneasiness by informing her that he had been suddenly called away into the country on business;—"But then," thought Ela, "not to leave me a line, or send me a word in explanation; surely this is cruel, cold, neglectful!"

The crisis of Ela's destiny was now rapidly approaching: the following morning, while she was expressing her apprehensions to Rackett, who never missed a day visiting her, the landlady put into her hand a letter which had just been delivered by the postman. She broke the seal, and what was her wild despair, when she read in the well-known characters of her seducer the following lines:—

"Your behaviour of late has convinced me of my folly in supposing that I possessed your undivided affections. But I will not upbraid you, I have perhaps no right to question your actions, but since I am convinced of this, of course, you cannot expect me to be more to you in future than
Your friend and the protector to your infant,
          EDWARD WALLINGFORD.

"The villain!—the base, heartless monster!" screamed Ela, worked up to a pitch of frantic wildness, and tearing the letter into a thousand pieces; "then he has at length thrown off the mask, and stands confessed in all his natural enormity! Weak fool that I have been, to trust a second time to one who before so cruelly deceived me! Oh God! preserve my senses, for you, my poor child, in this trying moment!"

Completely overcome with the torrent of emotions that crowded upon her brain, Ela sunk in a chair, and covering her face with her hands, she sobbed aloud! Dreadful was her agony in that moment; she felt as though a hundred serpents were gnawing at her heart, as though a furnace was scorching up her vitals! Rackett ventured to approach her, and endeavoured to take her hand:—

"Beauteous Ela," he exclaimed in a tone of the greatest compassion, "for Heaven's sake calm those frantic feelings, compose yourself!"

Ela raised her head and gazed intently upon Rackett; the lightning of her eyes darted through her tears, and her voice assumed a tone approaching to supernatural, as she exclaimed:—

"Compose myself!—mockery! cruel mockery! Has he not abandoned me? Has he not cast me from him as a wretch unworthy of notice; Am I not again to be plunged into that horrible abyss, from which he lately rescued me, only to make my future torments more acute? Am I not again to become a wandering outcast—the despised, the loathed of mankind, to have contumely, reproach, scorns heaped upon my defenceless head; to see this little innocent whom he calls, "MY child!' exposed to want and cold! to—"

Choked with the violence of her anguish, she could proceed no farther, but wept hysterically. Rackett exerted all his powers of rhetoric to calm her feelings, and after some time he succeeded, and pressing her infant with delirious affection to her bosom, she listened to Rackett as he thus proceeded :—

"For mercy's sake do appease your anguish, dear Ela : he has still promised to be a protector to you and your child! He cannot be the villain to break that promise! but even should he, still has Ela nothing to fear from the frowns of fortune, in me she and her child shall ever find a guardian, a friend—"

"In you!" cried Ela, starting, and fixing upon the libertine a look that seemed to search his inmost thoughts.

"Yes, Ela, dearest Ela, in me," repeated Rackett; "nay, do not eye me with that look of scorn and suspicion; I repeat my words, the time has arrived for revealing the truth, and if by so doing I am driven from your sight, that promise will I solemnly keep. Ela, now that Wallingford has forfeited all claim upon your affections, hear me, dearest girl, on my knees I acknowledge to you the ardent love I have so long in secret felt for you—"

"Mr. Rackett," interrupted Ela, with strong resentment depicted in her features; "this insult, and at the present moment is cruel, is ungenerous. Begone, sir, I will no longer listen to you—,'

"But you must, you shall, dear Ela," he replied with vehemence, "I would not deceive you, neither can I bear to see you deceived; read this paragraph, and you will then perceive that Edward Wallingford is lost to you for ever."

A mist seemed to obscure the vision of Ela, as she took the newspaper from the hand of Rackett, and endeavoured to peruse the paragraph to which he directed her attention. She passed her hand across her burning forehead, and casting her eyes upon the paper, read the following words :

"It is now confidentially known that the Edward Wallingford Esq. will in a few days lead to the Hymeneal altar, the wealthy and beautiful Miss Amelia Herbet, the——"

The wretched Ela could read no more, but with a wild shriek, she sunk in the arms of Rackett in strong convulsions !"

Rackett immediately rang the bell violently, and summoned the landlady, and the female domestic, who conveyed her to the chamber and sent for a doctor, while Racket awaited in the apartment until he heard of her recovery. This did not take place for several hours, and she was then so ill that the doctor would not suffer her to be spoken to; Rackett, therefore strictly enjoined the lady of the house to pay the most careful attention to her, and promising to call again in the morning, he took his departure.

CHAPTER XIII.

"Alas how short the step
From bliss to misery, from misery to crime !"

WE will pass over the many struggles that the hapless Ela had with her conscience before she could bring her mind to accede to the wishes of the unprincipled Rackett; the bare idea of becoming the mistress of any man was so horribly repugnant to her feelings, that she shrunk from it with disgust and shame ; but the mistress of Rackett, honourable, disinterested, and attached as he seemed to be was doubly revolting. In spite of all his specious conduct Ela's quick discernment soon penetrated through his hypocrisy, and she despised him accordingly ; but how doubly did she despise, nay, loathe Wallingford, who could tamely bring his mind, after all his earnest vows and asseverations, his tears, his pretended remorse, his oft repeated protestations, Wallingford the betrayer of her innocence, the father of her child, to abandon her, nay, absolutely sell her to another ; the bare idea aroused all the hot blood which flowed in her veins, and had Edward at that moment been present, she felt that he could have become a murderess !

From these maddening reflections, she turned to a gloomy retrospect of her former sufferings, her horrible deprivations, the wretched abode in which she had sought a refuge, and the depraved beings with whom she had been obliged to herd—her starving child ! its piteous cries ; and—these thoughts decided her ; she would dare anything for the sake of her poor babe. Rackett had promised to protect it; and many as were the bitter pangs it cost her, she at length yielded to his proposals.

It was necessary that they immediately removed from their present residence, for the landlady could no longer be deceived, Ela having betrayed everything while in a state of unconciousness, and she shuddered at the thoughts of the scorn and disgust with which she would look upon her. Accordingly, Rackett, having attained his object, took a handsome house to which he speedily removed Ela and her child, and a short time afterwards beheld her as his avowed mistress, and mingling with him in all those scenes of fashionable folly and dissipation in which his degraded taste led him; the magnet of a giddy throng, the envied of all the wild and unprincipled libertines of the day. But think not it was with a willing heart that Ela thus acceded to the dictates of her "protector;" oh, no; many a bitter pang, many a scalding tear did it cost her; and it was plain to be seen although she was compelled to assume the smiles of gaiety, and to listen to the senseless nothings that were uttered to her by the unprincipled companions of Rackett, that heart was the abode of a deep, corroding care, and that she loathed herself and all around her, but her darling Fanny, in whom her soul was wrapt!—And Wallingford had heard of all this; nay, more than once, although after his marriage he had studiously avoided the society of his former companions, he had come in contact with her, and seen her dressed in all the elegance and luxuriance of fashion, the object of universal admiration among those from whom admiration was degredation! He had seen her, and Ela too, had beheld him, and when their eyes met, the look of ineffable scorn and hatred which she had cast upon him, stung him to the heart. Fortunately he had never been accompanied by his wife on these occasions. But could Wallingford be happy? Could he gaze upon Ela, formed as she was to have mingled in scenes of happiness and virtue, and not reproach himself for a villain? He could not!—And unable to contemplate the ruin he had caused, he hastily arranged the business which had called him temperllay to the metropolis, and returned home, to endeavour to find solace in the virtuous endearments of his wife.

A twelvemonth elapsed, and Edward remained almost entirely secluded at Wallingford Hall, but he had a friend in London, to whom he had entrusted all his secrets, and who constantly forwarded him intelligence of Ela and her paramour. Every letter that he received, came fraught with more painful intelligence. The reckless career of extravagance Rackett was pursuing, it was evident could not last long, for his fortune had been greatly impaired years before, and when he became acquainted

with Ela it was very limited indeed. What would then become of Ela and her child? The thought was madness! Must they become degraded, despised outcasts upon the face of the earth? Must the child be brought up in crime and made familiar with vice? He would have given his whole fortune to have rescued that child from a fate so dreadful, and the thoughts of the impracticability of such a design, (for Ela, he was convinced would never part from her offspsing,)drove him to distraction.

Too soon Wallingford's worst fears were realized, he was made acquainted with the utter ruin of Rackett, who after being released from a prison had left Lendon, and no one knew what had become of him; Ela, who would not abandon him in his misfortunes, had become the companion of his flight, and all clue to the place of their destination was entirely lost. This account so embittered the mind of Wallingford, that he became in spite of the affection of his wife, a perfect misanthrope, and secluded himself as much as possible from society.

His health became gradually impaired, and the faculty declared that unless he had a change of scene, the most serious consequences might be apprehended. Mrs. Wallingford heard this opinion with the utmost alarm, and urged upon her husband the necessity of complying with the advice of the medical gentlemen without the least possible delay. The only thing that grieved her more than all, was that her delicate situation would preclude her from accompanying him, but she endeavoured to stifle these feelings in her anxiety for Wallingford.

As *ennui* seemed to be the principal malady under which Wallingford was suffering, the doctors thought a journey to London, and mihgling as much as possible in its scenes of gaiety, might have the desired effect, and when our hero heard this proposition, he yielded to it without much difficulty; for a hope sprang up in his bosom that he might be enabled to hear something of Ela and her child. The necessary preparations were therefore made without any further delay, and after an affectionate separation from his wife, Wallingford started on his journey.

Our hero being anxious to get to his journey's end, gave the horses and the postilions very little rest; they travelled the whole of the first afternoon, and at night found themselves in the intricacies of a wood, and the postilion was just about to stop to inform his impatient master, that he was entirely unacquainted with the way when an accident occurred to the vehicle, and it broke down, but without injuring either the driver or Mr. Wallingford.

They were now placed in an awkward dilemma, for it was impossible to proceed till

ELA, THE GIPSY OF ROSEMARY DELL.

the carriage was repaired, and they neither of them knew where they where, and whether there was any habitation near in which they might obtain a shelter for the night. It was a very dark night, and there was scarcely any light penetrated through the thick canopy of foliage above their heads. Wallingford looked around him in despair, but it was no use to hesitate, so he despatched one of his servants to see if he could find any habitation, while he and the others remained with the horses and the carriage.

The man was gone a long while, and Wallingford at last fancied he had lost his way, and therefore sent the other domestic in quest of him;

and wrapping his cloak around him seated himself on the steps of the vehicle to await their return.

In this situation he had not been long, when he thought he heard a rustling among the branches, the next moment the light of a small lantern streamed full upon him, and he beheld standing before him the figure of a man. Wallingford started upon his feet, for the idea of robbers immediately occurred to him, and he remembered with regret that he had not taken the precaution to bring any weapon of defence with him.

"Who are you, and what do you want?" demanded Wallingford in a stern voice.

"A man whom misfortunes have made desperate," was the reply, in a cool and determined voice.

"What do you seek?" asked Wallingford.

"Money," returned the fellow, "which I must have, or your life."

"Villain!" exclaimed our hero, preparing to defend himself.

"Nay, you may spare your abuse," answered the ruffian, in the same cool and deliberate manner, but the tones of whose voice sounded familiar to Wallingford's ears, "you may spare your abuse, I have known my title long enough. Come, your money;—I would not harm you, but money at all hazards I must hav! I'm armed——"

"Rascal!" cried Wallingford, rushing upon the man, whom he perceived held a pistol in his hand; he fortunately grasped his arm, and in the struggle the pistol was discharged in the air. The conflict now became fierce and desperate, for the robber was a powerful man, and resisted to the utmost. Twice they fell to the earth, and struggled fiercely; but the second time Edward succeeded in getting his antagonist under him, and pressing his fingers upon his throat, compelled him in a hoarse and half-stifled voice to implore for mercy. At this critical juncture, a light glimmered between the branches of the trees, and the footfalls of persons approaching, became audible. The next minute the two domestics of Wallingford approached, bearing with them a lantern.

"What ho, William, Richard," shouted their master, "Hold the lantern here."

The men obeyed, the light shone full upon the countenance of the prostrate robber, and Wallingford started to his feet with a cry of astonishment, when he recognised the features of his former companion, Rackett!

Yes, it was that unhappy man, but what a change in his appearance. The once gay and fashionably dressed young man, was now pale, care-worn, emaciated; covered with rags, and bearing all the semblance of the most abject and revolting misery!

Rackett had recognized Wallingford at the same moment, and although almost overpowered with the fierceness of the combat, he staggered to his feet, and gazed completely paralyzed upon our hero,

"Rackett!" at length exclaimed Mr. Wallingford. "Good God! is it possible?"

"Aye, you may well ask the question!" answered Rackett; "we meet under rather different circumstances to those in which we parted. Fortune is a fickle jade, a jilt, and so I have found her to my cost at last! Well, it can't be helped; Mr. Wallingford, I am your prisoner. Do as you like with me, I am quite indifferent now."

"For Heaven's sake, wretched man," said Wallingford, "what has driven you to this desperate and guilty course?"

"Shall I tell you, Ed—Mr. Wallingford, I mean?" answered Rackett, in a bitter, sarcastic tone, "it was her who——"

"Hush! hush!" interrupted the alarmed Edward, "I know what you would say, but do not speak it here. Accompany me where we may confer in private."

"We have succeeded in finding an inn, not far from here, sir," observed one of the men, "and the landlord is prepared to accommodate us, but we must be compelled to leave the carriage in the wood till the morning."

"That will do," said Wallingford hastily, and then turning again to Rackett, he said, "pray attend me to the inn; we have much to say to each other before we again separate."

"What, in this miserable dress; with these suspicious looks?" remarked Rackett, with a bitter smile, "oh, no, no; it won't do, my dear fel——Mr. Wallingford, I mean. There was a time you know that I didn't even care a shot for a bailiff, but now——"

"No matter," interrupted Wallingford, quite shocked at the awful change in one who had once been the idolized of fashion's giddy throng. "Will you promise to meet me, in the morning?"

"Where?"

"I care not, so that it be any where where we can converse alone, and without fear of interruption," answered our hero.

"Then we cannot choose a better place than the present," observed Rackett; "there is not much fear of our being interrupted here."

"Well then let it be here," said Wallingford, "on this spot if you like."

"Good," returned Rackett, "what time?"

"Six o'clock," answered Wallingford.

"I'll be here; that is if I——" said Rackett.

Wallingford guessed what he was about to say, and he interrupted him, and pressing his purse into the unfortunate man's hand, he bade him good night, and proceeded to follow his domestics to the inn, while Rackett bounded into the thickest part of the wood, and was immediately lost to view.

We need not attempt to describe the thoughts of Wallingford after this singular and unexpected interview, but his principal idea was of Ela and her child; were they still with him, the companions of his crime? The thought was too horrible to dwell upon. When he had retired to his chamber, he threw himself upon the bed in his clothes, and gave himself up to reflection. The morning found him awake, and the bell of a neighbouring church warned him of the time. He prepared to hasten to the wood in which he had appointed to meet Rackett. He got there some minutes before the time, and Rackett had not arrived, but exactly as the clock struck six he emerged from an opening among the trees, and bowed to Wallingford. His personal appearance was the same as the night before, but his countenance, though pale, was cheerful, and there was the same reckless smile in his eye which had gladdened it in the days of his prosperity.

"By Jupiter, Wallingford," he exclaimed laughing, "it was a fortunate thing you did not throttle me last night, or you would not have been able to have gratified your curiosity this morning;—I did not bargain for such a trial of skill, I assure you——"

"Rackett," interrupted Wallingford, shocked at the callous levity of his manner, "I am deeply, sincerely sorry to meet you under such degrading, such infamous circumstances as we met last night!"

"Oh, I suppose you have come here to preach a sermon," said the other; "if so our interview is at an end for the present. What's the use of repining? that won't make circumstances any better."

"But what can have driven you to this desperate, this guilty course of life?" asked Wallingford.

"What," replied Rackett, coolly, "why, that which drives most people to it, I believe—a want of money."

"You must indeed have been improvilent in so short a time to be reduced to such a state of misery," said Wallingford.

"Why, I must confess," returned Rackett, "that I had the happy knack of making the money fly; but I'll tell you, Wallingford, if I had never beheld that devil's imp, Ela—"

"Rackett!" interrupted Wallingford fiercely, "dare you apply such epithets to her—"

"Who has been my curse, my ruin," rejoined Rackett; "her confounded temper first drove me to madness, and then her accursed extravagance beggared me, and made me the inmate of a debtor's prison. True she remained with me there as long as I could put up with

her temper, when we cut the compact and separated!"

"And could you make up your mind to abandon her, after she had made such a sacrifice for you?" demanded Wallingford, with agonizing emotion at the thought.

Wallingford shuddered at this idea, and he felt a kind of relief in the thought that at any rate, Ela and his child were not the companions of the abandoned wretch who stood before him.

"And what has become of her?" eagerly inquired the distracted Wallingford.

"I neither know nor care," replied Rackett, with the same heartless coldness and indifference; "but I doubt very much whether she has picked up with another victim to—"

"Rackett!" interrupted Wallingford, almost choked with indignation, "if you have forgotten all respect for yourself, or her whose protector you once styled yourself; recollect that she—she is the mother of my child!"

"Ah! to be sure," said Rackett. "I forgot myself; I beg your pardon, Mr. Wallingford, I have no doubt you are eager to be made acquainted with their fate; and I am sorry I cannot satisfy you. The fact is, I have not heard or made any inquiries after her since I left London, at which time she was living in a lodging house, in a place called Charles-street, Drury-lane.

"And the number!" hastily asked Edward.

"Don't know," laconically answered Rackett; "but I dare say some of the girls who lodge in the same street knew her very well, and you will, therefore, not find much trouble in tracing her out, if she still lodges there, and you are going to London"

Wallingford finding this was all the information the unfortunate man could give him, was anxious to get away from him, for he felt a sensation of shame, abhorrence, and disgust in his presence, that was almost unendurable. He was, however, constrained to stay until Rackett had related to him in his usual style all that had occurred to him from affluence to poverty, from poverty to crime.

"But Wallingford," ejaculated Rackett, as they were about to part, "what would the amiable Mrs. Wallingford think, if she were to be made acquainted with your connection with Ela?"

A sudden thought rushed upon the mind of our hero, which filled him with apprehension, and looking earnestly in the face of Rackett he exclaimed,—

"Surely I need not fear such a disclosure from your lips!"

Rackett seemed to understand him, and to exult that he had taken his observations as he meant them. He paused, and seemed rather at a loss how to reply.

"Why, no, of course not," he at length said, "how could you think of such a thing? Besides, it is not at all improbable that before have such an opportunity, if I were so I may be safely cooped in some gaol or other."

"That, at any rate, I will endeavour to avert," said Wallingford; "surely you are not yet so abandoned, as to discard the means that may restore you to a place in society?"

"Why no, to be sure," answered Rackett, "if I had money, I might then think of reforming, but reformation upon an empty stomach and an empty purse are very unpalatable!"

"What do you purpose doing, if I provide you with the means?" asked Wallingford.

"Why, I think of trying my fortune in Paris," replied Rackett; "it is a famous place, and I have not the least doubt but that there I should soon find the means of raising me in the stirrups again.

Wallingford heard this with pleasure, for he thought he should then be rid of a man, whom he had now cause to fear, as he could plainly perceive he would make his knowledge of Wallingford's unfortunate *liaison* with Ela, the means of extortion; and there was nothing he dreaded so much as the tale reaching the ears of his wife. Commending, therefore, his design, Wallingford thrust into his hand a considerable sum of money, and wishing him success, he tore himself away, and hastened back to the inn.

The anguish of Wallingford now as to the fate of Ela and the child, was redoubled, for the story of Rackett had given him every reason to surmise the worst; he resolved, however, to use every possible endeavour to ascertain their retreat, and was anxious to prosecute his journey to the metropolis with the least possible delay. The vehicle was soon mended, and Mr. Wallingford was enabled to resume his journey, which he completed without any further accident the next day, and he had no sooner alighted in London, and before he would scarcely allow himself time to take any refreshment, than he started by himself on foot towards Drury-lane.

Charles Street, Drury Lane, was at that period, namely, about thirty years ago, as it is at the present day, one of the most filthy and blackguard places in London. Crime, misery, and indolence made it their common haunt. The very aspect of the ill-shapen houses seemed to speak of the vice and squalic misery contained within. The footpath, for pavement it could not be called, as well as the middle of the road, was always redolent of filth, and the threshold of every door was continually blocked

by clusters of low ruffians and dirty vulgar women, whose countenances spoke volumes of vice and infamy.

By the presentation of some silver to a girl who appeared more decent than the rest, Wallingford found no difficulty in discovering the house at which Ela had lodged, and saw the woman who rented the truly wretched den. She possessed a most forbidding countenance, and when he made the necessary inquiries, she answered him in a tone particularly disagreeable. She said "that she knew nothing of her, and she didn't suppose as how she would ever call upon her to leave her card of address, as she had valked hoff an' forgot to pay a fortnight's rent, an' it comed very hard upon her, who vos a 'onest, hindustros ard workin' woman, with a large fam'ly, an' a sick 'usband."

Wallingford, who perceived that if he wished to unlock her garrulity upon the question so important to him, it could only be done by a golden key, put half a guinea into her hand, which had the desired effect, and the woman became as communicative upon the subject as her knowledge would allow her; which, however, could throw no light upon where she at present was. From her story, he managed to elicit a dismal recital of Ela's sufferings. It appeared, from her statements, that she had been used in the most brutal manner by Rackett, who had, after they were reduced to poverty, long been supported by Ela, who pledged every article she possessed for that purpose. Notwithstanding this, he was continually applying the basest epithets to her, and upbraiding her with being the cause of the trouble which had been brought upon him entirely by his own imprudence and dissipation. This had not been confined to words alone, but was often followed by blows, and this was all because she could not procure sufficient means to support the villain in drunkenness and debauchery. At length he was taken to prison for debt; but, in spite of his brutal treatment, she did not abandon him until her heart was completely broken, and she declared that nothing should induce her ever again to have anything to do with Rackett. To add to the horror of this tale, the old woman informed our hero that Ela had eloped with a man and his wife, who had lodged in her house, and had robbed her, and not only her, but other people, for, a few days after they were gone, the officers of justice had come to search their apartments.

Wallingford had heard enough. He left the house heartsick; the poignancy of his emotions was augmented instead of abated. Ela was, then, the companion of the most depraved, and her child was fated to be nursed in the lap of guilt! Ignominy could alone attend them, and was he not the sole cause of all? But still he resolved not to abandon his design of endeavouring to find Ela out; but day after day elapsed, and he was equally unsuccessful. At length he received a letter from Wallingford Hall, which informed him that his lady was seriously indisposed, and he was, of course, compelled to return home with all the speed he was able. The birth of a son drew his attention from all other subjects, and filled his mind with the brightest anticipations, and time had almost succeeded in effacing from his memory all recollection of the unfortunate Ela and her child, which was only re-called in the melancholy manner related at the commencement of this history, to which period we will now return.

CHAPTER XIV.

"Come, stain your cheeks with nut or berry,
You'll find the gipsy's life is merry!"

MRS. WALLINGFORD remained in a very precarious state for several days, during which time the agony of her husband was almost insupportable. At times she was quite delirious, and then she mentioned the name of Ela, and left the distracted Wallingford too much reason to fear that the secret he had guarded for so many years, was now known to her. The bare thought of this was enough to turn his brain; how could he ever again face that amiable lady after his base conduct was known to her; and would not the disclosure break her heart? She could never survive the knowledge of the guilt of that man to whom her soul was devoted, whom she had thought without a fault, without a single error, or rather would she not despise, abhor him for his contemptible villany towards a poor confiding girl?

The re-appearance of Ela, and that among the gipsies, was a source of the most unqualified astonishment to him and filled his mind with consternation. He knew the hot blood that flowed in her veins—the hot blood of Italy, which had long been fermented by cruelty and injustice, and he knew not to what length she might carry her revenge. Were he now to seek an interview with her, and endeavour to reclaim her, and induce her to let him become the guardian of the child; but no, he felt the utter uselessness of such a thought, and he trembled at the very idea of encountering her whom he had reduced to such misery and shame.

After racking his brain for some time to no purpose, he determined to consult Dr. Hartley how to act; and, accordingly, he immediately solicited an interview with that gentleman upon the subject. This was a disagreable task, for it would naturally lead to the exposure of many things he was anxious to hide, and must degrade and lower him in the estimation of the doctor, who was a man of the utmost integrity and soundness of principle. He had, however, no other alternative but to disclose the facts to this, the only person he knew in whom he could thoroughly confide such an important secret. He entered upon the narrative timidly, and frequently paused in the course of it to watch the effect it might have upon Dr. Hartley's countenance, the result of which was anything but encouraging. He endeavoured to gloss over the blacker parts of the story, and to make his conduct appear less culpable than what it really was; but the doctor was a man not to be deceived, his frequent shake of the head convinced Wallingford that he was not upon this occasion. He was vexed, lowered, and impatient.

When Wallingford had concluded, he asked the doctor's advice upon the subject. That gentleman made no immediate verbal reply, but he shook his head frequently, and then gave utterance to a reproachful "Ah!" and looked at Mr. Wallingford until he repeated his question with more vehemence than before.

"Mr. Wallingford," at length said the worthy doctor, solemnly, "I am sincerely grieved at the recital, nor can I help candidly expressing my opinion upon the subject. You have been very much to blame, very much to blame, sir, and ——;"

"You must, sir, if you please," interrupted Mr. Wallingford, impatiently, "make some allowances, I presume, for the folly and impetuosity of youth. But I asked not for reproaches; I know that I have acted wrong, very wrong, that wrong I wish to repair, and I request your advice for the most certain and efficacious means of effecting my wishes."

Dr. Hartley once more shook his head, placed his gold-headed cane to his lip in a thoughtful mood, and made no immediate reply.

"Mr. Wallingford," resumed Dr. Hartley, "if this little unfortunate is your offspring;"—

"Upon that point I may say I am certain," impatiently interrupted our hero.

"Then, sir," returned the doctor, "justice demands that you should become its protector; that you should take it from the power of its wretched parent, with whom, if it remains, it must certainly be nursed in the lap of infamy and crime."

Mr. Wallingford liked not the plain manner in which the doctor spoke, and the evident reproaches his looks cast upon his conduct, and he hesitated a few moments before he made any reply.

"I would gladly do as you suggest, Mr. Hartley," he observed at last, "but I am afraid that the task is more difficult than you seem to imagine; the mother would not be easily prevailed upon to part from her child, and to me, above all, I am fearful would not deign to listen—"

"Indeed!" interrupted Mr. Hartley, with a suspicious look, "and yet by your story I had been led to imagine that this woman possessed far less gentle feelings than this would show, especially in her present state of misery and distress."

"I—I—see you do not understand me, sir," replied Wallingford, with much confusion.

"Indeed I do, sir," returned the worthy doctor, "but we will waive that subject for the present. It is an unfortunate affair, but if I can in any way assist you, of course you may command me. No time must be lost: perhaps money might prevail upon her."

Wallingford shook his head, doubtfully. "You appear to think money would have no effect, sir," observed Mr. Hartley, "however, we must see what can be done in the business. This evening I will seek an interview with the woman; but, although I do not wish you to see her if you would rather not, I think it would be better for you to be close at hand, in order that you may ratify any agreement I may make with her."

"It will be decided entirely by your judgment, my dear sir," answered Wallingford, "do as you think proper, and glad shall I be to accede to any proposal which may be the means of bringing about so desirable an object. Indeed, for a long time, have I reflected with bitter remorse upon my folly and imprudence, which, although pardonable in one so young, has——"

"Pshaw! my dear sir," interrupted the plain spoken doctor, impatiently, "you are to accompany me this evening, then?"

Mr. Wallingford replied in the affirmative, and was about to add some further observations, when he was startled by hearing his name repeated in a man's voice, and turning towards the spot whence it proceeded, he was surprised at beholding the figure of a man, squalid and ragged in appearance, standing before the parlour window. In one hand he bore a thick oaken staff, and with the other he beckoned our hero towards him.

"Mr. Wallingford!" repeated the man in a tone of command; "do you not know me?"

"Rackett!" muttered Edward to himself, as he recognised too well in the pale countenance of the man, the features of the once gay and fashionable exquisite whom he had never expected to behold again.

"Shall I walk in, or will you condescend to walk to me?" said Rackett, placing one foot upon the window-sill;—"it's not very civil of you to keep an old friend standing here."

"One moment, pray," exclaimed Edward, in vain endeavouring to stifle his emotion;—"my dear sir," he continued, turning abashed towards the doctor, who was eyeing the man, and Wallingford alternately, with looks of suspicion and reproach, "will you excuse me?" The doctor bowed coldly, and left the room, and as he quitted it, Rackett stepped in at the window, and advancing to the side of Wallingford, unceremoniously took a chair, and gazed firmly at him with a mingled expression of exultation and sarcasm.

"Well, Mr. Wallingford," he said, "I suppose you never expected to see me again. No doubt you thought that I should either have dropped off the hooks before this, or quite have forgotten my old friend and companion."

"Rackett," said Wallingford, proudly, "your present appearance and conduct convince me that I ought only to recollect our former friendship with shame. I desire you to quit my house immediately, and never more attempt to insult me by your presence!"

"Ha! ha! ha!" laughed the abandoned wretch, scornfully; "very fine, upon my soul! Why, what a devilish proud fellow you are, Wallingford! But you know it is no use to me: I am not to be so easily shyed, especially when I have come some hundreds of leagues for the express purpose of seeing you. Come, come, ain't you going to introduce me to Mrs. Wall——"

A passionate exclamation from our hero prevented the conclusion of this speech. The cool impudence and sarcastic irony of Rackett perfectly astounded him, and it was with great difficulty that he could refrain from using forcible means to eject him from the house; but when he thought of their former connection, and how much he was in the villain's power, he feared him, and stifling his rage and offended pride, he thought it would be best to endeavour to attain his object by persuasion.

"What is your object in seeking me out?" he inquired, "what is it you want?"

"Why, in the first place," replied Rackett, placing the remains of a hat in a very dilapidated state on a table, "I want something to eat, for I am devilish hungry; a glass or two of wine would be very acceptable, for I have not tasted a drop for many a day, and last, though not least, I must have money!"

"Villain!" exclaimed Wallingford, completely aroused by the insolent tone in which this demand was made; "if you do not immediately leave the house, I will have you taken into custody."

"Well, as you like, I am quite used to prison so I don't mind it at all," answered Rackett, laughing; "I should have a very interesting story to tell the worthy magistrates, no doubt; such a one as would amuse all the old women in the parish for the next twenty years to come."

"You appear, then, in the character of an extortioner," said Wallingford scornfully.

"Well, may be I do," returned the other, "it matters not to me what you call me: I want money, and money I must have; you are the only person I can, at present, apply to, and if you refuse me, why I must adopt another plan, which, for your sake, I would fain avoid. You understand me?"

Wallingford made no reply to this; he bit his lips, and paced the apartment with disordered steps. The unexpected appearance of Rackett, at this time especially, filled his bosom with apprehension; he knew he had it in his power to increase his misery, and that, to keep him quiet, he should be compelled to yield to his insolent demands whenever he thought proper to make them. To be obliged to endure the menaces of such a wretch, was doubly annoying and degrading to Wallingford's proud spirit, and bitterly had he reason to curse the hour when he first became acquainted with him.

"Rackett," observed our hero, appeasing his chagrin as much as possible, "abandoned as you ever were, can you have sunken so despicably low as this? can you be so entirely lost to shame, to principle?—"

"Tut, tut, tut," interrupted he, "what the deuce is the use of preaching of shame or principle to a man with an empty stomach, and without a penny in his pocket?"

"And if I were to accede to your demands," returned Wallingford, "of what use would it be? Did I not, on our last meeting, supply you with ample means to replace you in a creditable position in the world, and did you not promise—"

"Promise, ay, so I did," returned Rackett, "but you see my cursed good nature and love of life prevented my keeping my word. I went over to Paris; of course I could not help making some appearance in that gay city while I had the means. I met with some of my old companions; I was lured to the gambling table, where a cursed run of ill-luck soon left me without a single sou. I became once more a desperate man, and—enough; I served at the galleys until an opportunity presented itself of making my escape, when I could not resist the temptation of once more seeking you out, to inquire after your welfare, and make a further claim upon your exchequer. I thought too, perhaps, as you were so anxious to discover the retreat of Ela, you would be obliged to me for any intelligence I might bring you concerning her and your child; I therefore came to tell you that they are in your neighbourhood, and I—"

"Hold!" ejaculated the enraged Wallingford hastily, "by Heaven I will not tamely suffer you to talk to me upon a subject which has caused me all the misery I have ever known. I am acquainted with all that you can tell me about that wretched woman!"

"Perhaps not!" returned Rackett, with a bitter smile. "Would you like to be convinced, Mr. Wallingford; if so, I am ready to gratify your curiosity to impart to you a secret which it is necessary you should know for the sake of your own honour, the peace of her you *call* your wife."

"Call my wife!" cried Wallingford, his eyes sparkling with indignation, "base slanderer, dare you pollute my ears with such a base insinuation? I repeat, that if you do not instantly depart, and forbear to come into my presence again, I will give you up to that punishment your guilt fully merits."

"Well, I can go," said Rackett coolly, and rising from his chair as he spoke, "but mark me, Mr. Wallingford, before a week is over, unless you purchase my silence, Mrs. Wallingford shall receive a full and substantial account of all your *liaisons*; nay, more, I will impart to her ear, and that of Ela also, the secret I would fain confide to you alone. Good day to you, Edward Wallingford!"

"Stay, Rackett, wretched man," cried Wallingford, as the former made a motion towards the window, alarmed at the dark hints thrown out by his words; "you would deceive me?"

"I would undeceive you," returned Rackett with a mysterious expression of countenance that made Wallingford involuntarily tremble.

"What mean you," said the latter, "what is the secret you have to impart to me; or is it merely a stratagem to excite my alarm, and to induce me to yield to your illegal demands?"

"It is neither," said Rackett, "and I am prepared with sufficient proof to substantiate what I assert. "Do you wish me to proceed?"

"I do, I do," replied Wallingford in great agitation, and thrusting into his hand a well-filled purse, which Rackett weighed with a look of satisfaction; "but be quick, for should you be seen here by any of my servants, I do not know what might be the consequences."

"Well, then," said Rackett, again seating himself by the side of Wallingford, "I need not remind you that the false marriage by which you purposed quieting the apprehensions of Ela was concocted by me!"

"No, no, proceed," hastily replied Edward, "the supposed clergyman," continued Rackett, "was also a friend of mine, whom you had never before seen."

"Yes, yes, what of that?"

"Now, Wallingford, prepare yourself to hear what I am about to impart," said Rackett more seriously and narrowly watching the effect his disclosure was taking upon our hero; "that marriage, which you supposed was a mere deception, was——"

At this critical moment there was a knock at the parlour door; and Wallingford trembling with excited curiosity, and apprehensive of Rackett being seen, motioned to him to depart, and as he left the room he whispered in his ear—"For Heaven's sake, if there is any truth in what you were going to reveal, write to me as soon as possible, but do not again venture here!" Rackett smiled exultingly, and nodding his head assentively, stepped from the window and hurried across the lawn, leaving Wallingford in a state of the utmost suspense and agony. Being summoned to the chamber of his wife, Wallingford hastened to obey. But it was with a heavy heart that he entered the presence of the invalid, not only from the suspense and doubt created in his mind by his recent interview with the abandoned Rackett; but how could he meet that amiable being when he knew that the secret of his guilty interview with Ela was probably known to her, how bitter would be her upbraidings, how just but poignant her reproaches!

"But surely," he mentally ejaculated, "she will pardon me for an indiscretion youth alone caused? She will not reproach him whose whole study has been to make her happy; the father of her children! Oh, no, no, no, I know my Amelia's gentle nature too well to believe her capable of that!"

Thus endeavouring to assure himself, he entered the room of his wife, and approaching her couch, kissed her pale cheek affectionately. Mrs. Wallingford started at the touch, and looked wildly up in his face. Although she did not utter a word which he could construe into reproach, it was evident from her looks how severely she felt the knowledge of his culpability.

"My dearest Amelia," he said, looking fondly in her face, and pressing her hand to his lips "I trust, in spite of our unfortunate bereavement, we shall again be happy, and—"

"Happy!" ejaculated Mrs. Wallingford, wildly, "oh, no, no, we shall never again know happiness; the fatal die is cast; did she not breathe a malediction upon our heads? Did she not wish her child, your girl, to curse us? Yes, even now her awful looks, her vengeful eyes are present to my imagination; her imprecations ring in my ears! Oh, Wallingford, the curses of the injured, the betrayed, are surely not always breathed in vain! But your child, oh! Wallingford, Heaven's just voice commands you to save that poor child from destruction, if you cannot reclaim its unhappy parent;—I will not reproach the little innocent;—no, Wallingford, I will protect it, love—bestow the same care upon it as my own children. Say, then, will you not snatch it from ruin and poverty?"

"I will, I will, dearest Amelia," replied Wallingford, with intense agony; "I will yield to your every wish, and ——" Before he could finish the sentence, Dr. Hartley abruptly entered the chamber, and he peremptorily insisted that not another word should be said upon so painful a subject, and which could only serve to render the situation of Mrs. Wallingford more dangerous. He requested our hero to withdraw, which he reluctantly obeyed, completely absorbed in the anguish of his conflicting thoughts. About half an hour after, the doctor rejoined Wallingford in his study, and inquired if he was ready to depart to the dell. Wallingford replied in the affirmative, and they immediately left the hall together. Wallingford felt a great relief that the doctor did not question him about Rackett, and they walked on in silence for some distance. The sun was just beginning to descend behind the western hills, as they walked on in the direction of the dell, and his departing rays tinted the horizon with a sanguine hue. No sound was heard, save the lowly bleating of the sheep, or the barking of the shepherd's dog, and Wallingford began to fear that the gipsies had left the dell. When, however, they arrived upon its brink, they beheld the encampment, and the light of the fires in the tents. They also perceived several of the gipsy children playing before the tents; but the elder persons seemed all absent. While they thus stood, uncertain how to act, one of the children, who had observed them, bounded up the side of the acclivity on which they stood with the lightness of a young fawn, and Dr. Hartley had only just time to desire our hero to conceal himself behind a clump of trees that grew just by, when the same little black-eyed girl who had sought the sympathy of Mrs. Wallingford in behalf of her mother, stood looking up in his face with a smile of innocent curiosity.

"Would you please to see any of our people, sir?" said the child with an intelligence of expression that surprised Mr. Hartley, who gazed upon her beautiful features with pity and admiration.

"I think your name is Fanny, my little lass?" said the doctor kindly.

"Yes, sir," replied the child, "and my mother——"

"Yes," added Mr. Hartley, "do they not call her——"

"Ela, sir, is her right name," added the child, "but she is called by our people the—"

"Never mind that, my dear," interrupted Mr. Hartley; "is your mother in the tents?"

"No, sir," replied Fanny, "there is nobody in the tents but old Zelta, who is so surly, that I am almost frightened to be where she is. Mother and the rest of the tribe have gone to the fair, but I expect they will soon be here, and hark! they are coming now. I hear their voices on the breeze, singing the gipsies' favourite song. Do you not hear them, sir?"

"I do," answered the doctor, as the voices of the tribe burst gradually upon his ears; "now, my little maid, will you hasten to your tent, and when your mother returns desire her

MORNA'S MALEDICTION UPON ELA.

to come to me, as I wish to speak with her? But mind, do not let any of your people hear what you say, and request her to come unaccompanied;—do you understand?"

"Oh, yes, sir, I will do as you desire," said Fanny, and in a moment she flew towards the encampment, and was out of sight directly.

"Mr. Wallingford," said Dr. Hartley, when he rejoined his companion, "never did I behold so lovely or intelligent a child as that; any one might be proud to claim her; it would be dreadful indeed if she were left to the contamination, the inevitable destruction with which she is now surrounded."

"Alas, sir," said Wallingford, "believe me, I feel all you say." And he spoke sincerely; with what astonishment — with what admiration had he gazed from the place of his concealment upon the little beauty; and as he looked, how bitterly did he reproach himself for the treachery which had been the means of placing her in such a dangerous situation! He was interrupted in his reflections by the voices of the gipsies, which sounded nearer, and at length they were able to distinguish the following words, sung with boisterous glee, but possessing a sort of harmony which riveted the attention, and could not be heard without considerable pleasure :—

"The gipsies lead a life of glee,
         Fal de ral lal lal lal la ;
There's none more blithe or gay can be,
         Fal de ral lal lal lal la.
In our coarse built tent, when the fire burns
         bright,
We gather around its cheerful light ;
And our cup we quaff devoid of strife,
Then, oh, how merry is the gipsies' life !

We sigh not for the halls of state,
         Fal de ral lal lal lal la,
In our own free tent there are none so great,
         Fal de ral lal lal lal la.
No care on the gipsy's brow is seen,
And he sleeps on his grassy couch so green,
With a heart more light than was ever known
To beat in the breast of the heir to a throne !"

As the last verse vibrated on the ears of Wallingford and Dr. Hartley, the tribe gradually wound round the brow of a neighbouring hill, and descended into the dell. Wallingford's eyes eagerly watched every one, and at length they rested upon a form, which, although attired in the wild garb of the gang to which she belonged, was impressed too strongly upon his memory ever to be effaced. He clutched the arm of the doctor breathlessly, and pointed towards her. Mr. Hartley signified by a nod that he understood him ; but he motioned him to withdraw, and Wallingford retired to the place of his concealment.

Dr. Hartley watched the gipsies as they entered their tents, and when Ela approached the entrance of hers, he perceived Fanny, who had been waiting for her, draw her aside and whisper to her. Ela seemed to hesitate at first, but at length, having seen all her companions enter, she turned towards the hill upon which the doctor was waiting for her, and slowly approached.

"You desired to speak with me," said Ela, when she stood before the doctor; "what would you ?"

Doctor Hartley gazed upon the fine figure and still handsome features of Ela, with the most unqualified admiration, as he replied :

"I would be your friend, my good woman, if—"

"Friend," interrupted Ela, with a look of the utmost contempt ; "I want not your friendship, there is none in man; you came from one whose assistance I would scorn to accept ; no, sooner would I perish of hunger, sooner would I see this dear child dying for want than I would—"

"Hear me patiently, my good woman," interposed the doctor, kindly ; "I would not persuade you to accept assistance from—him of whom I am the messenger ; but—"

"Then what can he now render me ?" demanded Ela, haughtily, "can he recall the past? —can he make me once more the innocent, happy girl I was ere I beheld his hated form ? Is it in his power to restore to me those parents from the premature grave into which his cruelty plunged them ?—Can he render justice to my child, his child ?"

"But he can aid you in abandoning this state of crime and imfamy;" observed the doctor, quickly.

"I would despise his offer," replied Ela, "were it even possible for it to be made available. No, I would not leave the gipsy tent, the emerald turf, and the restless life of the wandering tribe, for all the ostentatious panoply of wealth! But know you not that no one can desert the gipsy gang without being sure of being consigned to death? Stranger, if it is all you sought Ela for, our meeting is at an end."

As she thus spoke, she turned to depart, but the doctor gently arrested her purpose.

"Stay, stay, my good woman, I beseech you," said he, "I will be brief;—if you will not yourself desert this wretched life, surely you will not refuse to let your child be taken care of, and brought up—"

"Ah! I see it all now!—you would rob me of my treasure, my own sweet child," ejaculated Ela, as she raised the little Fanny in her arms, and pressed her convulsively to her bosom; "you would bereave the wretched wandering outcast of her only joy—teach her to scorn and curse her broken-hearted mother ! —But it shall not be ; no power but that of the Almighty, shall tear her from me !—The child of shame—so would he call it—can find no friend so good as her mother, though she be despised and—"

"Oh, Ela, wretched Ela," cried Wallingford, who, unable longer to bear the violence of his agony, had broken from his concealment ;— "in mercy listen to my supplications—you know not what I feel for you—for that child— do not then turn a deaf ear to my entreaties— but—"

"Fool! wretch! deceiver !" exclaimed Ela, as she fixed her full black eyes fiercely and contemptuously upon the countenance of Wallingford, "think ye again to deceive me? —Do you suppose that I will again lend a willing ear to your base falsehoods, your treacherous asseverations ?—No! I would rather, dearly as I love my child, place my fingers on its throat and rob it of life, than it should receive a favour at your hands !"

"Oh, Ela, drive me not to madness," ejaculated Wallingford, clasping his hands with intense emotion ;—" I would in some measure repay the injuries I have done to you in my care and attention to this poor child! Let me then have her, I earnestly supplicate you !—"

" Ha! ha! ha!" laughed Ela wildly, as her eyes beamed forth an expression of savage exultation, " oh, this is glorious revenge ! This is more than I expected ! Now at last then, do I know how to wring your flinty heart !—Yes, I repeat, I will keep this child, and the knowledge that my resolution will afflict you, will fall upon my seared heart, like drops of balm. May your thoughts and cares ever be connected with her ;—may the recollection of her render your nights sleepless, your days wretched, and may a curse light upon your children—"

" Hold ! hold ! fierce ungovernable woman !" exclaimed Doctor Hartley, " I shudder to hear your dreadful words ; do you not tremble to—"

" What !" interrupted Ela, with increasing violence, " tremble to heap curses upon the head of that villain who has accursed me ?— He who thrice deceived, and finally sold me to the polluted vices of the villain whom he acknowledged as his friend. Yes, there stands the wretch, and he dare not deny it—Edward Wallingford, I defy you to contradict me,— ah! you tremble with conscious guilt !—Edward Wallingford," continued Ela, while her eyes darted forth an expression which penetrated to his heart, and made him feel abashed and confused, "are you so lost to truth as well as honour, to attempt to deny that you basely, cruelly, heartlessly, bargained with that vile wretch Rackett, to take me off your hands !— Did you not, without a blush, without a pang, deliver over to the hateful embraces of that villain, her you had seduced from virtue and happiness ; her you had solemnly vowed to love and to protect with your life ?—Did you not make me a dependant upon his charity ; his tool, his scorn ; and all to remove every obstruction to your union with Amelia Herbert, the child of wealth, for whom I was despised ? Deny that you did this, and great as have been the injuries you have heaped upon me, I will freely pardon you !"

" Ela !" cried the distracted Wallingford, covering his face with his hand, " oh, spare me, spare me !"

" Ah, you cannot deny it !" ejaculated Ela, while a saturnine expression enveloped her countenance ; " wretch ! and can you after this shameless acknowledgement of your black infamy, dare to appeal to me for mercy ?— Oh, it is but a tithe of the anguish you will

yet endure. A curse, a heavy curse light upon you and yours ; may a blight fall upon your fortunes ; may your property decay ; sickness and death attend your wife and children ; may every fresh misfortune be but as a prelude to greater sufferings !—May your bride fly your bosom, and seek shelter in the arms of dishonour and crime ; may you live to see all you love perish, and die alone, and in a foreign clime, with no one near to soothe the agony of death, or drop the tear of pity at your fate !"

Petrified to the spot as Ela uttered these bitter maledictions, Edward Wallingford was unable to move or speak, but he felt each word she spoke as forcibly as if a poniard had entered his heart. He knew how well he merited her bitterest reproaches, and he felt degraded and humiliated in the eyes of Dr. Hartley, in a manner that wounded him more than all. Ela, as she uttered the last sentence, fixed upon him a look of the most ineffable scorn and hatred, and, snatching her child to her bosom, bounded down the hill and vanished into one of the tents with the speed of lightning.

Dr. Hartley had listened to every word she had spoken with the most profound attention, and his looks betrayed the thoughts he entertained upon the subject, and the abhorrence with which he viewed the conduct of Wallingford. He sunk beneath the doctor's keen glance, and being unable to utter a single word in extenuation, he moved towards the Hall in silence, followed by Mr. Hartley.

CHAPTER XV.

" My conscience has a thousand several tongues."　　　SHAKSPERE.

NOTWITHSTANDING his disappointment in the interview just described, and the vexatious circumstances attending it, Wallingford was resolved to make another effort to rescue Ela from her wretched course of life, and to get the little Fanny under his protection. That child was ever present to his mind's eye, and the more he pictured her image in his fancy, the more interested he became. He had observed with wonder the extraordinary likeness the girl bore to his little Christabelle, and that circumstance alone, independent of the other claims she had upon him, drew his heart insensibly towards her.

Mrs. Wallingford began to get better, and, when her husband returned, she questioned him upon the subject of his interview with Ela, for she had guessed it was for that purpose the doctor and him had been absent from the Hall. Wallingford would have fain evaded her interrogations, but she was resolute, and he therefore related as briefly as possible the non-success of his mission. Mrs. Wallingford made no remark upon this subject, but she sighed deeply, and it was evident how poignant was the anguish she mentally endured.

"But I do not yet despair, my love," Edward continued; "at any rate I am determined to make one more effort to snatch the child from misery and shame. To-morrow I will visit Rosemary Dell alone, and I have no doubt——"

"Alone!" interrupted Mrs. Wallingford, with a shudder, as she recollected the revengeful looks and expressions of Ela, "oh, surely you would not entrust yourself among these lawless, reckless, wretches!"

"Fear not, my dear," replied Edward, "they will not harm me; they would not dare to do so; besides, what motive could induce them to such a course? If I can but see that unfortunate alone, I might prevail upon her to accede to my wishes."

Mrs. Wallingford appeared satisfied, and her husband fixed upon the following day to put his plan into execution. The interview he had had with Rackett had caused him the most serious uneasiness, and he in vain sought to fathom the mystery he had to reveal to him. He felt, however, that, whatever it was, it would be productive of fresh misery to him; and he a thousand times regretted the circumstances that had brought him and the villain Rackett together again. He knew he was a dangerous enemy, and to conciliate his friendship was fraught with every degradation and shame. He waited with the most painful anxiety the arrival of a letter from him, explanatory of the subject which so deeply engrossed his thoughts, and formed a thousand speculations upon the nature of the information he had to impart to him. The following day he was just preparing to depart for the Dell, when a servant informed him that a gentleman was waiting in the parlour, who requested to speak to him. Wallingford hastily descended to the room below, and upon opening the door, was surprised and vexed to see Rackett, coolly seated by the casement, and whistling a part of an Italian air, with as much unconcern as possible. He had exchanged his miserable apparel for a gay and fashionable suit, and with the exception of the haggard appearance of his features, he looked as well and as cheerful as when he had been in the days of his prosperity.

"Rackett!" exclaimed Wallingford, "is it possible? How foolish to venture here again! I thought I told you——"

"No matter what you told me, my dear fellow," added Rackett, with his accustomed familiarity, "the fact is, here I am, so that settles the business. Besides, why should you be so devilish fearful of my coming here?—I am a little better in appearance than I was

yesterday; nobody knows me here except Amelia, and as you do not seem inclined to let me see her, why,—"

"Well, well, enough," hastily interrupted Wallingford;—"what is it you have to impart to me?"

"Something which I dare say you will not thank me for," replied Rackett; "it is a secret on which your very happiness hangs! Are you sure there are no listeners?"

Wallingford went to the door, and looked into the hall, and then returned to Rackett, and said—"It is all right; pray be as brief as possible; speak low!"

"Well, then, Mr. Wallingford," resumed Rackett, watching the countenance of our hero narrowly while he spoke; "you must know that your marriage with Ela was no cheat; it was a real clergyman who performed the ceremony; and Ela is justly Mrs. Wallingford, and—"

"Lying miscreant!" exclaimed our hero, worked up to a pitch of frenzy; "and have you the effrontery to attempt to impose upon me by such a vile fabrication as that? Despicable scoundrel, leave me this instant, or by Heaven I swear that——"

"You will send me to gaol, I presume," rejoined Rackett; "but I will dare you even to that, and I will there repeat my assertions, of the truth of which I can bring forward sufficient proof! I told you you would not thank me for the information."

Wallingford paced the room in great mental anguish—should the villain have indeed spoken the truth; "but no," he uttered aloud, "I will not believe it, it is impossible, it is a villanous plot to extort money from me, but it shall not succeed."

"There you and I differ in opinion," said Rackett, with the most consummate *sang froid;* "I do not deny that I expect to draw upon your purse occasionally to keep the secret, but if you act handsomely the affair has no occasion to cause you much anxiety. Ela has no idea of the fact, and I can secure means to keep my witness silent. The whole of it is, Wallingford, I am tired of leading the life of privation I have so long endured; I must enter into the world again; you can enable me to do so without materially injuring yourself; act liberally by me, and you need not fear the consequences."

It would be impossible to describe the state of Wallingford's mind at this moment; doubt, fear, shame, and rage struggled in his bosom, and he paced the apartment in a state of perturbation that rendered him entirely incapable of uttering a word. Rackett watched the effect his story had upon him with evident exultation, and did not attempt to interrupt him, but coolly resumed his whistling, as though he was perfectly at his ease.

"Rackett," at length said our hero, "if you

have spoken an untruth, you must be a more heartless, debased wretch, than I would fain believe you to be. But it is impossible. I will not believe your words, where are your proofs?"

"Oh, if you wish them," said the other, "I will satisfy you by to-morrow night; meet me at any place you may think proper to appoint, and they shall be forthcoming. If you are then convinced, you have but to give me a sum of money, which I shall demand, and my silence, nay, my absence from the country will be secure."

"I will meet you!" said Wallingford, clasping his forehead.

"To-morrow night?" exclaimed Rackett.

"Yes, yes," replied our hero.

"Where, and at what hour?" demanded Rackett.

"In the copse near Rosemary Dell, at the hour of eight," returned Wallingford.

"Very well," said Rackett, "then I suppose you do not care how soon this interview is terminated."

Wallingford made no reply, but hastily shook his head, and walked towards the door. "Good day, Mr. Wallingford," ejaculated Rackett, with a satisfied smile, as he left the room, "I will not fail to be punctual."

When Rackett had quitted the mansion, Edward remained for a few moments in a state of stupefaction, so much was he bewildered with the information he had received from him. "Good God!" he at length ejaculated, "should this dreadful tale be true, how doubly guilty am I!—What disgrace, what anguish, what ruin have I not brought upon an amiable woman! But no! no! no! I will not believe it; it is too horrible to be true—it is all the invention of that base wretch to rob and intimidate me." And so improbable did it appear, that Wallingford became more composed, and endeavoured to dismiss the subject from his thoughts altogether.

The evening was now far advanced, and Wallingford, having had a severe conflict with his thoughts, somewhat regained his composure, determined to start on his adventure in the Dell. He did not wish to be observed leaving the house by any of the domestics, he, therefore, disguised himself as well as he could in a large cloak, and left the Hall quietly, taking the direct road to the Dell, towards which he walked with hasty steps.

Darkness had completely enshrouded the earth by the time Wallingford had arrived upon the summit of the hill which overlooked the Dell, and where the doctor and him had had the interview with Ela before. All was darkness and silence beneath him, and he began to fear that the gipsies had departed from the Dell, when suddenly a thick column of smoke ascended from the closely clustered trees, and immediately afterwards the cheerful blaze of

the camp fires convinced him that his apprehensions had been unfounded. The light enabled him to see pretty clearly all that was passing in the tents, and he perceived that the gipsies were seated on the ground partaking of their evening meal. The tribe consisted of about thirty rough savage-looking men and lads, with seven or eight females, with several children, who rolled upon the earth in a state of semi-nakedness. The whole party surrounded a large iron pot, which was suspended over the fire, and a coarse, fierce-looking woman was distributing the viands among her companions. Wallingford looked anxiously into the tent, and among the group for Ela, but he was unable to recognize her. At length the woman who had been serving out the eatables, addressed herself in a harsh and disagreeable voice to a child, in whom Wallingford immediately recognized Fanny, who instantly darted out of the tent, and speedily returned from the adjoining one, leading in her mother. It was easily to be observed Ela was the object of some displeasure among the gang, for part of them eyed her with looks of the greatest ferocity, while others apparently took her part. The old woman before mentioned particularly evinced the most savage feeling towards her, spoke to her in tones evidently harsh and passionate, and by her gestures seemed to appeal to her companions, most of whom appeared to coincide with her. Wallingford watched the proceedings with the utmost trepidation and anxiety; the critical situation of Ela kept him in a state of the most inconceivable suspense, and bitterly did he reproach himself for being indirectly the cause of her present degradation and danger. Ela did not seem to entertain the slightest apprehension, but, on the contrary, she eyed the repulsive looking woman with glances of ineffable scorn and defiance. She stood for a few minutes and listened to the coarse abuse of Morna, (for so was the woman called), with silent contempt, but at last she addressed some words to her in reply, which Wallingford could not hear, and then seated herself with her child between her knees, with the greatest composure, and commenced eating the rude meal of which her companions had already partaken. With what powerful emotion did Wallingford watch all these proceedings, and was uncertain how to act. He, however, thought it best to remain quiet, till the gipsies had finished their meal, when he thought they would retire to rest, and he might be enabled to gain the desired interview with Ela. The meal was despatched, but not one of the gipsies offered to stir, and it was evident, from their replenishing the fire, that they meant to remain up some time longer. Some beverage was now brought in a keg, horns were filled, and they proceeded to enjoy themselves in a very extravagant manner. The mirth was boisterous the men chaunting occasionally a verse or two of a rude song, in which most of the females joined in chorus. But nothing could apparently change the malevolent thoughts of Morna towards Ela, and every now and then she poured upon her a torrent of vulgar abuse, whilst Ela bore it all with the most firm indifference, although Wallingford could perceive, by the expression of her countenance, the tumult that was raging in her breast. As the cups passed freely round so did Ela partake of their contents, and with every fresh draught Wallingford beheld with fear, that her long stifled rage was gradually arousing itself into a blaze, which might be attended with the most dangerous consequences. As the effects of these libations became more apparent, the ferocity of Morna increased, and the cool sarcasms with which Ela replied to her vituperations, exasperated her to such a degree, that, had she not have been withheld by her companions, she would have rushed upon the object of her wrath. Wallingford trembling with apprehension, and anxious to learn the cause of the quarrel, ventured to descend nearer to the tents, and, throwing himself on the grass, was able to gratify his curiosity. He soon learned that the occasion of the tumult was, the discovery which had been made of Ela having conversed with our hero and Dr. Hartley, and a supposition, on the part of Morna, that she had received a sum of money which she refused to give up to the tribe, and, moreover, that she intended, the first opportunity which offered, to abandon them. Morna had ever, it seems, viewed Ela with the most bitter jealousy and hatred, and she was therefore ready to seize upon every trivial opportunity of annoying her, and setting her at enmity with the rest of her companions. The liquor every one had drank had taken such an effect, that those who had before been inclined to take the part of Ela, now listened to the accusations of Morna with something like credit, and the altercation became stronger, and assumed a more alarming aspect. What incited them still more to take the part of Morna was, that they were very short of cash, and they were willing to suppose that two such fine gentlemen as Wallingford and the doctor would not have made Ela anything but a very handsome present.

" A murrain light upon you, hell cat!'' exclaimed Morna, her eyes flashing fire ; " the curse of the tribe should descend upon your head. Are we to be robbed by a—''

" To be sure we will not," cried a ferocious looking wretch, " give us the money, treacherous hag!" As he spoke he grasped the arm of Ela fiercely, and tried to drag her from her friends. The rage, the agony of Wallingford was intense, —he could hardly endure the painful sight, but

how could he assist her ? To rush amidst such a gang of ruffians would be throwing himself into the jaws of death, and without rendering any service to the object of his commiseration. The struggle now became fierce, all the men joining in it, and Wallingford trembled for the safety of Ela, when suddenly he beheld her wrest her arm from the grasp of the ruffian, and make a plunge at him with a knife which she held in her hand. The blade entered his arm, and the fellow staggered back with an imprecation of rage.

" By hell, the cat has stabbed me !" cried the villain.

" Yes, and lay but a finger upon me again, and I will plunge it in your heart!" cried Ela, with a look of fierce determination ;—" nay, I will sheath it in the body of any one who dares to insult me! You know I will not fail to keep my word, Wolna !"

" Well spoken, Ela," exclaimed a tall, sturdy looking man, starting on his feet in the midst of the belligerents; "by the infernal host I admire thy hot Italian blood ! Why do you annoy the girl ?—I would stake my neck that Ela has spoken the truth; that she has never received the money."

" I swear," said Ela, vehemently " that not the smallest coin did I receive from those men you suspect; had I taken it from the wretch whom Morna imagines gave it to me, I should expect a heavy curse to fall upon me. I would rather my knife should open a passage to his heart than I would receive one kind word from him. It is he, the wretch, on whom my bitterest hate is fixed ; on him my soul thirsts to be revenged ; and if he had been unaccompanied yesterday he should never have returned to his house alive."

" Beware, Ela," cried one of the partisans of Morna, " these passions may not only place your neck in the halter, but bring destruction upon our tribe."

Ela made no reply to this warning, but she looked disdainfully upon the speaker, and the others, evidently awed by her manner, did not offer to interrupt her again. The quarrel subsided, although Morna still eyed Ela with fury, which the latter returned with glances of the most supreme contempt. She took her child on her lap, and hugged it fondly to her bosom. The cups were again replenished, and the revelry became more boisterous. Tired and disgusted with the debasing scene he had just witnessed, and horror-stricken at the threats Ela had made use of, Wallingford hurried from the spot, and made his way towards his mansion.

He was walking hastily along, and buried in a deep reverie upon what he had seen and heard, when suddenly a loud discordant laugh vibrated on his ears, and made him start back with astonishment and alarm. Raising his head, he was surprised to behold standing across his path the hateful figure of the same frightful hag who had obstructed him a few weeks before in the forest. The moon, which had arisen, shed a broad flush of light across her person, which rendered her appearance particularly awful and ghastly, and her large supernatural-looking eyes gleamed upon the countenance of Wallingford with a sardonic expression of exultation:

"What ho! Edward Wallingford," she cried, in her usual disagreeable tones. "Well met! Ha! ha!"

"Croaking hag, why do you again obstruct me?" ejaculated Wallingford, who was really terrified at the appearance of the frightful being.

"Great things are brooding in the web of fate, Edward Wallingford," returned the hag, "a cloud hangs over the house of the betrayer; but it will burst anon! Hey, will it?—Oh, 'twill be glorious sport when it happens. Ha! ha! ha!—

A curse shall attend the deceiver's race,
His reward shall be misery and disgrace,
On his house shall fall a deadly blight,
That shall turn his days into dreary night.
The heart that his treachery sought to break
Shall live, a fell revenge to seek;
Sorrow and shame shall triumphant lord,
O'er the proud house of Wallingford!"

"Foul fiend! I'll hear no more," cried Wallingford, rushing desperately on; but the hag had vanished, and he heard her wild laugh repeated by a hundred echoes. Unable longer to bear the tumult of thoughts that crowded on his distracted brain, Wallingford made with all possible speed to his mansion, and rushing into his chamber, threw himself into a chair, and gave way to the innumerable thoughts the events of the last few hours had given rise to. He had not been in this situation more than an hour, when he was startled by hearing a strange tumult in the hall below, and at intervals the groans of a person apparently in great agony. He hastened down stairs, and eagerly inquired of a domestic the cause of the disturbance.

"Oh, sir," said the man, "such a shocking event; you know that gentleman who called upon you this morning?"

"Ah! well—what of him?" asked his master, eagerly.

"Me and Robert, sir," replied the servant, "had occasion, not long since, to pass near the Dell, when we found him lying on the ground, stabbed in several places. So, as we didn't know where else to take him, and thinking he was a friend of yours, we brought him here."

"Has he been able to speak yet?" demanded Wallingford, who was horror-struck at such an unexpected occurrence.

"Oh, no, sir," answered the domestic, "although he has tried several times. Poor gentleman! I do not think he will ever speak again. Depend upon it this job has been perpetrated by some of them rascally gipsies."

Wallingford stayed to hear no more, but hurried into the apartment where Rackett, bleeding profusely from two or three wounds in the side, was being supported in the arms of the servants. When he saw Wallingford, he became very much excited, and made a desperate effort to speak; but it was all in vain; the cold dew of death was upon his temples, and in the midst of the struggle he fell back in the arms of the attendants, and expired with a groan.

Dreadfully shocked at this unforeseen catastrophe, Wallingford stood over the corpse of the late wild and reckless votary of dissipation, and gazed upon his countenance, ghastly and livid, with the convulsive agonies of the death struggle, with emotions too powerful for delineation. His eyelids were unclosed, and the glassy expression of those eyes that had been wont to sparkle with such vivacity, seemed fixed upon the countenance of his former friend in a manner which thrilled his soul with horror.

"Poor gentleman," observed one of the domestics, "what a shocking fate has his been! Depend upon it those cursed gipsies are at the bottom of this dreadful deed; surely, sir, you will immediately issue orders for the apprehension of the whole gang!"

This suggestion startled Wallingford; it was probable, too painfully probable, that the unfortunate Rackett had been murdered by some of the tribe. Ela, too! Surely her revengeful spirit could not have led her to the perpetration of such a horrible crime? The thought was madness! Yet circumstances but too strongly inculpated the gang, and it would be his duty to apprehend them, in order that a thorough investigation might take place. Ela amongst the rest!—Oh, God! what a horrible exposure would this lead to, what disgrace, shame, and degradation would it bring upon him; the public would become acquainted with the misdeeds of his past life, through the means of Ela, who, he was convinced, would feel a malicious exultation in revealing the whole painful history!—What suffering, what anguish would it cost his amiable partner; he knew that she could never survive the shock, and he could only then look upon himself as a murderer. His heart sickened at the thought; his brain whirled round, and sinking into a chair, he buried his face in his hands, and groaned aloud. Astonished at his extraordinary emotion, the servants stood looking significantly at one another, and shook their heads. At length, Andrew ventured to suggest, that the corpse had better be removed, and immediate steps taken to apprehend the murderers. This aroused Wallingford to action.

"Right, right, Andrew," he observed, "bear the corpse of the unfortunate man to the north wing of the Hall, and then return here, for my further orders; but mark me, at the peril of my displeasure, act with caution and prudence in this affair, for should a sentence of it reach the ears of your lady, in her present situation, it might be attended with the most fatal consequences." The servants bowed, and the corpse of the ill-fated Rackett was borne out of the apartment. When left to himself, Wallingford gave unrestrained indulgence to his feelings, and traversed the room with hasty strides; which ever way he looked, nothing but misery presented itself. Should Ela, indeed, have committed the rash act, he must ever upbraid himself as being the cause of leading her to it; and should she be convicted, brought to an ignominious death! Ela, the once lovely, the once guiltless, the mother of his child, the interesting little Fanny! Could he ever hold up his head in society again; could he ever again know peace?—would not his guilt, his heartless treachery, be made known to every one?—would he not become the common talk of the land, the scorn of the rich, and the contempt of every well-formed mind? Fanny, too; what would be her fate?—Would she not be upbraided as the offspring of a murderess?

"Oh God!" he cried, "give me strength, for this is more than I can endure!"

He was interrupted by the entrance of Dr. Hartley, who arrived very opportunely to consult upon, and advise him how to act. He had been apprised of all that had happened, and had seen the body of the unfortunate man.

"I much fear," said the doctor, after a pause, "that the surmises of the servants are too true as the perpetrators of this awful crime, he was found near the Dell, and—"

"Yes, yes," hastily interrupted Wallingford, "but Ela—"

"It is a sad piece of business," replied the doctor with a sigh, "but of course she is as deeply inculpated as the rest, and must be apprehended with them. Justice demands that there should be no delay in the matter, and whatever may be the result, and however painful it may be to your feelings, your duty as a magistrate commands you to apprehend the tribe immediately. If the crime was committed by them, it is evident their object was not plunder, for, upon searching the person o the murdered man, a considerable sum of money was found upon him!—"

"Ah! that still more horribly confirms my worst suspicions," groaned Wallingford; "should Ela have seen him, to what desperate lengths might not her revengeful mind have urged her!"

"And why should she feel a spirit of revenge towards this unfortunate man?" quickly returned the doctor, fixing an inquiring look upon Wallingford, who shrank from it abashed; —"did she know him?"

Our hero hesitated, but he had no alternative but to explain everything to the doctor as briefly and explicitly as he possibly could. The doctor listened to him with much anxiety. when he had concluded, he shook his head.

"It looks very black, very black," he said, "but there is only one course—suspicion rests upon the gang, and they must not be suffered to escape before they have proved away the foul stigma from them. Let your domestics arm themselves, and accompanied by Ralph, the constable, who is already in attendance, proceed at once to the Dell.

"I will myself attend them," said Wallingford; "I would not see her and her child left to the rough treatment of these ignorant persons. I will go with them."

"In your present state of agitation," remarked Dr. Hartley, "that would be madness, and might be the very means of divulging that which you are anxious to keep secret from your wife, namely, the whole of the horrible event. You remain at home, and I will attend the men. It is late, and doubtless the capture will be easily effected, as the gipsies have, in all probability, retired to rest."

Of course Wallingford could not object to the propriety of this proposal, and the domestics having armed themselves with such rude weapons as they could lay their hands on, the doctor buttoned up his coat, clenched his stout cane firmly, and issued from the Hall, followed by the posse of men, many of whom were far from fancying the job, but, according to the boasting of Ralph, he was more than a match for the whole tribe, single-handed, and the edge of his courage had furthermore been sharpened by sundry potations of ale, which he had been drinking with some friends at the "Blue Hog," when he was summoned to attend the Hall.

The night was very dark, and the road by no means a good one to travel, but as they were all acquainted with every inch of the ground, it did not so much matter. On the way to the Dell, the doctor strictly enjoined them to do nothing but by his directions, and he had already formed his plan of attack. They soon reached the hill which over-looked the Dell, and descended cautiously, reaching the bottom with much difficulty. All was darkness around, so that Dr. Hartley concluded that his imagination had not deceived him, and that the gipsies had really retired for the night. Still, as they advanced towards the spot where the encampment had been, he was surprised that they did not hear the barking of their watch-dogs, but his astonishment was indescribable when, on reaching the place, he found it vacated, the tents gone, and the ashes

(THE GIPSIES' ENCAMPMENT AT ROSEMARY DELL.)

of the fires the gipsies had kindled, were the only signs that they had been there at all. Anxious as the doctor was to bring the perpetrators of the murder to light, he could not help feeling gratified that he was saved the painful task of apprehending the unfortunate Ela and her companions, while on the other hand, the sudden flight of the tribe was a still stronger evidence of their guilt. He was determined, however, not to give up the pursuit here, and therefore ordered the men to follow him. After traversing the most likely road for the gang to take, for about five miles, without being able to trace the slightest clue to them, the doctor thought it would be useless to prosecute the search further for that night; they therefore prepared to return to the hall.

During their absence, Wallingford had suffered the most dreadful anguish; he pictured to his mind Ela arraigned at the bar as a murderess, revealing the whole of his guilt, and uttering the most horrid denunciations against him. Then the words of Rackett recurred to him; his declaration of the validity of their nuptials; and the eagerness he shewed to give utterance to some important secret, in the agonies of death; and he could scarcely retain his reason within bounds. Should he have spoken the truth! But no, the story was too improbable—he would dismiss it from his mind as too absurd to be entertained; and he endeavoured to think that Rackett in his dying moments was anxious to confess to him how he had attempted to deceive him. In the midst of these reflections, in the pauses of the wind, he would listen attentively, expecting, yet dreading every moment to hear the voices of his domestics and their prisoners, and then would the form of Ela and her child recur to him in stronger and more impressive colours than ever. At length he was aroused from a deep lethargy into which he had sullenly fallen, by a knock at the hall door, and soon after the doctor presented himself, and acquainted him with the result of their journey.

"Thank Heaven!" exclaimed Wallingford, involuntarily, "I am spared the horror of—"

"Nay, sir," interrupted Doctor Hartley, "it may not be so; of course every means must be adopted, and they may yet be apprehended. Their abrupt departure looks doubly suspicious, and we are bound to use the utmost vigilance to detect them. You said, I think sir, that you saw them yourself in the dell, but a short time ere the murdered man was found?"

Wallingford hastily replied in the affirmative. "And they then appeared not likely to be preparing to depart?" interrogated the doctor. Wallingford shook his head, and groaned, for the remembrance of the scene he had witnessed in the gipsy tents came forcibly upon him.

"It is strange—very strange," remarked Dr. Hartley. "However, nothing more can be done in the business to-night; I will be with you early in the morning, and advise with you, what will be best to be done; in the meantime endeavour to calm your agitation as much as possible, for should Mrs. Wallingford become acquainted with the circumstances, I would not answer for the consequences."

With these words the doctor left the hall, and Wallingford sought his chamber, and endeavoured to gain a short respite from his cares in the arms of sleep.

CHAPTER XVI.

There is a spell upon my fate;
My days, my nights are doomed to woe,
And a curse lights on all who dwell around me.

By the break of day, the news of the assassination having spread like wildfire, and the sudden disappearance of the gipsies being observed, suspicion universally lighted upon them, and by the order of the proper authorities persons were sent to scour the country in all directions in search of them, and a large reward was offered for their apprehension; but all trace of them was entirely lost. Doctor Hartley and Mr. Wallingford, notwithstanding the delicacy of the situation in which they felt themselves placed, were indefatigable; but every effort was vain, and the dark deed remained enshrouded in the same mystery as it was on the night the murder was committed. A coroner's inquest had sat upon the body, after which it had been decently interred at the expense of our hero. The affair soon ceased to be talked about, and, by degrees, Wallingford became more at ease; but there were times when the uncertainty of the guilt of Ela, and the damning suspicions against her, came with such force upon his mind, that he was hardly able to endure the poignant anguish it engendered. The uncertainty, too, of her fate, and the little Fanny, was ever uppermost in his thoughts; he remembered but too painfully the scene he witnessed in the gipsy encampment, and among such a set of wretches what could he expect but murder? He shuddered and endeavoured to erase it from his thoughts.

It was a fortunate job, notwithstanding the noise, the catastrophe had made in the neighbourhood. Mrs. Wallingford had not heard a sentence about it and in her presence Wallingford had succeeded so well in stifling his emotions, that he gave her not the slightest cause to imagine that anything out of the ordinary way had happened. To the delight of her anxious husband a favourable change had taken place, and she was rapidly recovering, and as she regained her health, her spirits likewise gradually returned, and she seemed to have entirely erased the events which had caused her so much pain from her memory; or if she had not entirely forgotten them, she seemed determined not to recur to the subject again. Once only did she mention the name of Ela, and inquired after the child, when Wallingford briefly informed her that he had been unsuccessful in his efforts to persuade Ela to relinquish her offspring, and expressed his deep regret, with which sentiment Mrs. Wallingford coincided, and there the matter dropped.

Their whole care and attention was now devoted to their children, the little Walter and Christabel, whose growing beauties were sufficient to excite the greatest admiration, and whose wonderful intelligence, for their tender years, was a theme of astonishment to all who saw them. Christabel was a lovely, arch, playful little girl, with brilliant eyes, and cheeks of roseate hue. Her form already exhibited grace and elegance, while her every action was expressive of dignity and rank. But there were times when Wallingford gazed upon the features of this sweet child, that a pang of bitter sorrow darted to his heart, for it was impossible for him to help noticing her extreme likeness to the little Fanny, which daily became more apparent; and at such times as these he dreaded to meet the eye of his wife, lest she should read his thoughts, and awaken the sorrow she had formerly felt. But in Walter, his son, the twin brother of Christabel, his very soul was centered; and with the feelings of exquisite pride, he beheld that boy who was to inherit his fortunes and his honours, daily becoming more noble and prepossessing. Walter was indeed a fine boy, quiet, quick, generous, and affectionate. His features were the index of his mind, and on them was imprinted every benevolent feeling. To his sister he was devotedly attached, and he was never more gratified than when he could present her with some toy, or get up some healthful game to please her.

Thus rolled away two years, without anything worthy of note occurring, and the sorrows of Wallingford being softened by time, he began to hope that nothing would again occur to disturb his present tranqillity; but alas! an event was about to take place which showed him how futile were these hopes.

On the anniversary of their children's birthday, Mr. Wallingford determined to get up a festival, and accordingly everything that mirth and hospitality could dictate was provided to celebrate the joyous occasion. The gentry around were, most of them, invited; a dinner was prepared for the tenantry, and the poor people of the neighbourhood were also provided with a plentiful repast on the lawn. The scene was of the most animated description, and nothing could exceed the festivity that prevailed. Wallingford, as he accompanied his amiable wife, and their two lovely children, round the tables at which the numerous guests were seated, and received their shouts of esteem and gratitude, felt supremely happy, and Mrs. Wallingford plainly evinced how warmly she reciprocated his sentiments. It was a sultry day, although in October, and Mrs. Wallingford feeling rather faint from the weather, and the excitement of the occasion, requested to be permitted to retire to her chamber for a few minutes. Wallingford saw her to the door of her apartment, and leaving her in care of her waiting woman, he returned to the lawn, to

watch the joyous sports of the humble guests he had invited to share his hospitality. As he was about to descend the second flight of stairs he caught a glimpse of a strange female figure, rudely habited, which seemed to emerge hastily from an apartment beneath, and immediately descend the stairs with silent steps, as though she was afraid that some one would overhear her. Surprised at this circumstance, and suspecting the woman was after no good, Wallingford called upon her to stop, but at that moment she had gained the hall door, which was open, and turning round, she looked up at him, utterred a laugh of scorn, and immediately disappeared. The woman's countenance was nearly hidden by a close bonnet which she wore; but there was something in her eyes as they glanced upon him, reminded him of one whom he had never thought to behold again, for it was now two years since the gipsies had visited Rosemary Dell. But still he dared not believe that his surmises were right. Increasing his speed, he rushed out of the hall, and looked around him, but he saw nothing of the object of his curiosity. He inquired of several persons whether they had seen a female answering the description of the woman, but they all replied in the negative. He then returned to the apartment, from which he thought that he had seen the woman emerge, to ascertain whether her object had been plunder, but he found everything there as it had always been, and after in vain racking his brain to endeavour to imagine who the woman could be, and what the object of her visit, he sought to persuade himself that it was only one of his rustic guests, who had done it for a frolic. He kept the circumstance carefully from Mrs. Wallingford, fearful of alarming her, and once more returned to the lawn. Still he could not erase the impression from his mind which had entered it, and folding his arms, he stood moodily ruminating on what had occurred, and quite unconscious of the gladsome scenes that were passing around him. He was suddenly aroused from this lethargy by hearing his name pronounced in a harsh voice close to his ear. He started, and his surprise and alarm were not at all diminished, when on turning round, he beheld the frightful visage of the old hag, who had twice before obstructed his path, grinning wildly upon him. Wallingford was no coward, but the appearance of this strange being at that time, and the recollection that she was always the harbinger of evil, made him tremble, and he was totally unable to utter a word. The hag watched his agitation with evident delight, and at length interrupted him with her usual loud and demoniacal laugh.

"Ho, ho, Mr. Wallingford," she croaked forth, "brave Edward Wallingford, why is thy cheek pale, thy lips livid, and thy limbs trembling?—Does my presence alarm ye?—Ha! ha! ha!—'tis good. I like to make the *would-be* brave shake and quiver;—'Tis good, 'tis good!"

"Mysterious being," exclaimed Wallingford, "why do you cross my path?—What would you with me now?"

"Hark ye, Edward Wallingford," replied the hag, pointing her long, bony fingers towards him, "I came to warn you;—a calm has long rested upon your home, the betrayer has been at peace, while the victim wanders in wretchedness and misery with the offspring of thy treachery;—but the storm is rising, aye it is; —I see it coming;—behold there is a black cloud now hanging over thy noble house;—it will burst, it will burst, and woe betide the inhabitants:—

"'Tis coming, 'tis coming, the hour is nigh,
When the tear of anguish shall fill thine eye,
When thy fair-haired bride of her darling 'reft,
To weep and wail with thee shall be left!"

As the strange being uttered these prognostications, she suddenly bounded from the spot, with more than human speed, and was almost instantaneously out of sight. Horror-struck by what he had heard, Wallingford stood for a few moments, unable to move from the spot;—opposed as he was to superstition, there was something so peculiarly awful and impressive in the words and appearance of this mysterious being, that he could not divest himself of terror in her presence. Besides, she had never appeared to him but some calamity always befell him, and coupled with the form he had seen in the hall, it was enough to make his mind ill at ease. But anxious to conceal what had happened from his wife, he endeavoured to compose himself and to regain his usual equanimity. He at first succeeded better than might be expected in this effort, when Dr. Hartley approached him, and requested to speak a few words with him. Mr. Wallingford complied, and laying hold of the doctor's arm they walked forward.

"I would ask you, Mr. Wallingford," said the doctor, seriously, "whether you have walked near Rosemary Dell this morning?"

"I have not," answered our hero, with trepidation, for he dreaded something of which his mind had a presentiment, and which the solemn expression of the doctor's countenance led him to imagine he was about to impart.

"The gipsies are again encamped there," added the doctor. Wallingford turned pale.

"Is it possible?" he gasped; "after so long an absence, and the circumstances of suspicion that attended their departure, I never imagined they would venture into this neighbourhood again."

"And their returning does not look much like guilt, at any rate," rejoined the worthy doctor; "however, there they are, for I myself saw their tents this morning, and I am only surprised that the alarm of the villagers

should not have communicated the circumstance immediately to your ears."

"And have you seen or made any inquiry of their people?" eagerly asked Wallingford, "anything relative to—to—Ela, I mean?"

"Ela is not with them, neither is her daughter," the doctor gravely answered.

"Thank Heaven!" ejaculated Wallingford; Dr. Hartley frowned, but said nothing, and Wallingford after a pause continued;—"But are you certain, my dear doctor?—How know you?"

"From a woman of the tribe, who had met with an accident on the road, and to whom I afforded assistance," answered Dr. Hartley; "but I cannot learn where she is, no more than that she still belongs to the gang—indeed she could not leave it and live. No doubt she is on some secret mission in another part of the country. But her child——"

"Ah! what of her?" demanded Wallingford, with violent emotion;—"do not keep me in suspense—what has——"

The good doctor shook his head mournfully, and looked reproachfully at Wallingford, as he said;—"I have been unable to ascertain anything satisfactory of that poor child; by some she is stated to be dead, by others not; but it is evident she is separated from her mother, who has latterly even become more wild and reckless than she was before, and my informant stated that she was looked upon with terror by the whole of the tribe. She is an unfortunate woman indeed; it is horrible to see the wreck of that which might have been the ornament and admiration of society."

Wallingford shuddered, for he keenly felt the reproach conveyed in the doctor's words, and conscience told him that he was the cause of the wreck spoken of.

"And yet," continued Doctor Hartley, who had watched narrowly the expression of our hero's countenance, "in one respect I hope that the report of the death of the poor child may be well founded, for brought up to the life of misery and degradation, she would have been without any hope of rescuing her from it, is it not better that she should die before she has become acquainted with guilt, and—"

A deep groan from Wallingford interrupted Doctor Hartley, who seeing how keenly he felt the observations he could not help making, although he condemned his conduct, in mercy forbore to proceed further. Changing, therefore, the tenor of his conversation, he said:—

"That those parties are not present, is a circumstance which you cannot regret, sir, as it is your duty to apprehend the tribe on suspicion of the dreadful crime laid to their charge; of course, you will use immediate steps to satisfy the minds of the public on that point"

"The rascally gang shall not escape, depend

upon it," ejaculated Wallingford with avidity, "too long have their presence caused trouble to me and my neighbours; they have been suffered to do so with impunity, and they have grown insolent upon it, but by to-morrow's dawn, they shall all be in safe custody, and if nothing transpires to implicate them in the crime of which they are suspected, I will take good care that it shall be their last visit to Rosemary Dell."

A deep sigh near him caused Wallingford to turn round, and to his vexation he beheld his wife, who had come from the Hall to look for him, and had overheard the principal part of the conversation between him and Doctor Hartley. Wallingford had been anxious to keep from her the knowledge of the gipsies having encamped in the Dell, but he saw too plainly, from the melancholy expressed in her countenance, that she had become acquainted with the secret, and that it had awakened all those sorrows he had been so anxious to see buried in oblivion. Wallingford took her arm affectionately. "My love," he said, "pray let not this circumstance alarm you; let it not recall events, the recollection of which can only renew our sorrows;—come, come, let me conduct you to the Hall, our guests are waiting our presence."

Mrs. Wallingford made no reply, for she saw the emotion of her husband and she stifled her own feelings. Wallingford had related to her such parts of his unfortunate connection with Ela, as might serve partially to exonerate him from that culpability in which Doctor Hartley was disposed to view it; and fondly attached to her husband, she had readily lessened her sympathy for Ela, and felt inclined to view it as youthful indiscretion on both sides; but when Wallingford, with that consummate hypocrisy which guilt and shame assumes to mask itself, represented to her that she had, after he had provided her with every comfort, willingly become the mistress of Rackett, and by her extravagance brought him to ruin, it worked upon her the effect he desired it should have, and although she did not cease to pity Ela, she considered that the misfortunes she had met with were no extenuations for the violence of temper she had subsequently displayed, and the bitterness of the revenge she entertained against Wallingford. But well as her gentle mind could reconcile itself to this, her sentiments were still the same towards the hapless little Fanny,—child as it was, enshrouded in all is native innocence, who should blame it for the faults of its mother? and when she drew the comparison between that poor child's situation, and that of her own offspring, nursed in the lap of luxury and independence, the night when, barefooted and wet, she came an innocent pleader for assistance for her mother, arose to her recollection, and filled her bosom with anguish.

"Dear Amelia," observed Wallingford, as he linked his arm within that of his amiable wife, and led her towards the Hall, followed by Doctor Hartley, as a sudden idea crossed his mind, "I have long been thinking that a change of air and scene might be of the utmost benefit to us both, and this circumstance has the more strengthened my desire;—say, are you willing to accompany me to Cheltenham, or any other place that you think may be conducive to the establishment of your health?"

"But our darlings," said the affectionate mother, looking inquiringly in the face of her husband.

"Of course my love," replied Wallingford, "they shall accompany us; I would not be separated from them for the world."

"Then I am willing, dearest Edward," said Mrs. Wallingford affectionately, "and Heaven ordain that when we again revisit these scenes, it may be to experience no more interruptions to our happiness."

Wallingford kissed the cheek of his lovely wife, and led her into the Hall, where, in the mirth that prevailed, he endeavoured to dissipate the recollection of the unpleasant events of the day; but in spite of his exertions they would rise up, and prevented him from enjoying a scene that at any other time would have afforded him such infinite pleasure. The company separated at an earlier hour than had been anticipated, and Wallingford gladly sought his couch, but his mind was too busily occupied to allow him to rest, and he lay revolving in his brain the occurrences of the day. He was glad that Ela was not among the tribe, and he determined in the morning to put his former design into execution of apprehending the gang, hoping thereby to prevent their ever returning to the Dell, and thus securing to himself that peace and safety which he could not hope for while they were in the neighbourhood.

CHAPTER XVII.

"Danger and calamity so fast succeed each other,
That my burning brain can scarce endure the shock."
OLD PLAY.

No sooner had Aurora unfolded the curtains of the east, than Mr. Wallingford arose, firmly resolved to put the design he had formed the previous night into execution. Descending to the Hall, he found the domestics already assembled according to his instructions, and armed with such weapons and implements as were available. In addition to these was Farmer Fallowfield with several of his men, the former being stimulated to assist in the capture, from having imbibed sundry prejudices against the ribe, owing to his suspecting that they had at different times committed depredations upon his property. Besides the parish constable there was another great man in his own estimation, who had come to take part in the proceedings, yclept Abel Crankey, parish clerk, sexton, undertaker, and grave-digger. Altogether, they made a pretty formidable host, and far outnumbered the gipsies, of whom there was supposed to be no more than six men, with about the same number of women, children, &c. Wallingford having kept his intention a profound secret from his wife, they left the mansion as silently as possible, and without waiting for Dr. Hartley, who had promised to be one of the party, but had not yet arrived, they proceeded at a pretty brisk pace towards Rosemary Dell. On the way, Mr. Wallingford continued to be guided alone by his directions, as any precipitate act might not only thwart their designs, but also be attended with the most fatal consequences, as the desperate character of the ruffians they had to deal with must be pretty well known to them all.

"You zay right, zur," observed the honest farmer, "a more howdacious set o' varmint does not exist, and it is quoite time as they wur brought to justice. I remember very well th' last toime they wur in the Dell, I wur continually bein' robbed; I lost three lambs in one week, and as for my hen roosts, they wur pratty well emptied afore they went away."

"Oh, shocking, shocking," added the sexton; "besides, only look at the stuff they put into the young women's heads, about sweethearts, children, and all such loike."

"Young women's heads," remarked a third, 'yes, and old 'uns too; why, the last time they were in the Dell, my dame wur foolish enough to go to 'em, to have her fortin told, as they calls it, when they informed her that she was to marry a second husband, a rich squire, and ride about in her carriage, and have a *revenue* o' sarvants to wait upon her; and I do believe it has turned her brain, for ever since then she has led me a worse life than a dog, snubbing and snarling at me, just for all the world as if she wur trying to worry me into my grave, so that she might have a chance of realising the predictions of the confounded gipsies."

"And do they not always bring sorrow and sickness with them whenever they come?" said another. "Look at his honour's respected lady, for instance, did there not seem to be a spell laid upon her whenever they comed? Was she not always attacked with illness whenever they made their appearance?—and did not I lose two as fine children as ever drew the breath of life by a fever, when they took up their abode here?"

"Well, well, their time may be reckoned nearly up, I think," added the farmer, "for if some of them do not swing for the murder of that poor gentleman, who was slain by them and nobody else, say my name's not Farmer Fallowfield."

"Saving your honour's presence," said the constable, addressing himself to Mr. Wallingford, "your late noble father, God rest his soul, was too indulgent to the fellows; he never offered to disturb them, and, in fact, used to send many little presents to them into the bargain."

Mr. Wallingford silently assented to this, and by that time, having arrived on the summit of the hill which overhung the Dell, they prepared for action. They saw them collected around their fire, having apparently just finished their morning meal, and they did not observe the approach of their assailants. As Wallingford cast his eyes into the Dell, and recollected the scene he had there witnessed two years before, his heart palpitated, and a cold tremor agitated his limbs; but quickly recovering himself, he proceeded to descend into the Dell, the men following closely behind him. In his eagerness for the combat, however, the honest farmer forgot the injunctions of Mr. Wallingford, and giving a loud hurrah, the moment they reached the Dell, immediately alarmed the whole tribe, who jumped to their feet, the men looking at them with a look of scornful defiance, while the women and children set up a simultaneous yell. Wallingford told his men to be firm, and boldly approached the ruffians, who did not offer to move, but seemed determined to abide by the consequences, and not to be taken so easily as some of their assailants had calculated upon. When Wallingford had got within a few paces of them he stopped, and exclaimed in a tone of authority:—

"I arrest you all in the name of the king."

Upon this the women set up a loud yell, more wild than the other, which was re-echoed by the children, and the men's countenances became more sullen and ferocious. At length one of them, who seemed to possess some little authority over the others, advanced a step or two towards Mr. Wallingford, and fixing his scowling eyes steadfastly upon him, said:—

"And would you drive us, Squire Wallingford, from that spot, where our people for centuries have sought and found a shelter; where your fathers ever allowed us to remain undisturbed, and even deigned to visit our tents? What harm do we? We rob no one—we purloin alone from the hedges, and—"

"Oh, you lying scoundrel," interrupted the farmer, the whole of his wrongs rising to his mind at once, "do you not rob the honest farmer of all you can lay your rascally hands upon? I know it, have I not suffered?—But

I shall live to see you all hanged, and that will be some consolation."

"I come not here," proudly remarked Wallingford, in answer to the words of the gipsy, "I come not here to waste time in argument with you or your fellows. I advise you to yield quietly, as we are prepared to enforce obedience if you are obstinate."

"Ha! ha! ha!" scornfully laughed the man, while his companions joined in the demonstration of contempt; "we scorn all that your force can do; the Gipsy yields himself not tamely into the talons of the vulture; mark me, Squire Wallingford, you will find us no cowardly foe; death is our motto, rather than lose our liberty!" As the fellow thus spoke, he brandished a stout cudgel, and every one of the men exhibited a similar weapon of defence. The eldest of the women, whom Wallingford recognized as old Morna, drew a knife from her bosom, with fierce and threatening gestures; immediately there was a cry among the rest of the women: "To your knives!—To your knives! Blood for blood!" and rushing into the tents, they quickly returned, each armed with a long knife, and placing themselves by the side of the men, seemed determined to use them the moment any attempt to apprehend them was made.

"Squire Wallingford," said the man who had first spoken, "we give you fair warning; we caution you to reflect before you proceed to a violence that may cost you and your companions bloodshed, if not your lives. Why are we driven like dogs from the spot in which our forefathers made their occasional home? What harm have we done? Of what do you accuse us?"

"Of murder!" answered Wallingford, "of the murder of an unfortunate man the last time you took up your habitation in the Dell, about two years since!"

"By the infernal host, it is false!" exclaimed the gipsy vehemently, which assertion was reiterated by his companions, and they clutched their cudgels more firmly, and showed by their ferocious and determined looks that they were prepared for the worst.

"That you must endeavour to prove in another place," replied Wallingford; "are you prepared to yield quietly?"

"With our lives only," cried the gipsies in a breath.

"Then take the consequences;" exclaimed Wallingford, firmly, making sure of vanquishing them, and giving a brief order to his adherents, they rushed on in a body, and endeavoured to seize upon the ruffians; but no sooner had they advanced within reach of their cudgels, than half of them were laid prostrate by the well-directed blows of the gipsies, who evidently knew well, from long experience, how to use their cudgels. The women seemed anxious also to rush on with their knives, but the men restrained them, so they kept aloof, eyeing the battle with malignant triumph, and by their piercing cries adding redoubled terror to the scene. The conflict did not last long, the gipsies fighting with determined courage and consummate skill, while the partizans of Wallingford, on the contrary, having been discomfited at their first onset, relaxed in their bravery; in spite of the entreaties of Wallingford, they gave ground fast, and at length, finding the case completely hopeless, they were compelled to make a precipitate retreat, followed by the whole of the gipsies to the entrance of the Dell, heaping upon their heads the most bitter denunciations, and the children shrieking terrifically.

The shameful defeat vexed Wallingford more than the blows he had received in the contest, which were not a few; while, on the contrary, Farmer Fallowfield, Abel Crankey, and the rest, notwithstanding their vaunted courage, felt no inclination whatever to renew the contest. Wallingford was determined, however, that the gipsies should not escape, and therefore resolved to dispatch a messenger immediately to the nearest town, which was ten miles off, to request assistance to apprehend the scoundrels. On his arrival at the Hall he met Doctor Hartley, to whom he related the circumstances of their defeat, but who expressed no astonishment at it.

"These men are desperate characters," he observed, "and are sworn to defend their liberty at the peril of their lives. But if you wait for assistance from Waterfield, it will give them time to effect their escape, which you may depend upon it they have already set about putting into execution. Surely you can find among your tenants, and the farmers' labourers, a sufficient force to overpower the rascals."

"It has been very unfortunate," replied Wallingford, "that this is the day of Hollyoak fair, and the men are all at it; therefore I have no other alternative but to wait until my messenger arrives from Waterfield."

It was late in the evening before the servant returned from Waterfield, accompanied by the expected force. It was very dark, and threatened to be stormy, notwithstanding which, however, Wallingford, accompanied this time by the worthy Doctor, lost not a moment in departing for the Dell. They numbered now a sufficient force, and all well armed to easily overcome the gipsies, and they therefore made sure of success. They were, nevertheless, doomed to be disappointed, for on reaching the Dell, they found that the tents were removed and the gipsies had departed. The farmer who had attended them, seemed much chagrined that they had lost the opportunity of revenge; but our hero was really not sorry that they had departed, as their apprehension would have been the means of making some unpleasant disclosures, and probably would have renewed all the anguish of his wife. Doctor Hartley evidently read his thoughts, but whether he approved of them or not, was uncertain, as he did not make any observation or allusion to the subject. They now prepared to retrace their steps towards home, while the men who had been sent for from Waterfield, hastened on towards Hollyoak fair, thinking it was not at all improbable that they might meet with the gipsies there.

Wallingford, Doctor Hartley, Farmer Fallowfield, and the others, had scarcely left the Dell, when the storm which had so long threatened, commenced with great fury; fierce flashes of lightning darted along the skies, succeeded by heavy peals of thunder; and presently the rain descended in torrents. They hastened their speed, and were proceeding with the greatest rapidity, when between the flashes of lightning the farmer suddenly stopped, and drawing the attention of his companions, exclaimed—

"Surely that is the reflection of a fire; some building has been struck by the lightning!"

They all looked in the direction to which the farmer pointed, and were convinced that he was not mistaken, but that there was a dreadful fire raging somewhere in the neighbourhood.

"Good God!" cried Wallingford in a voice of consternation, "the reflection is in the direction of the Hall! Surely it cannot be!" The eyes of the others all followed those of Mr. Wallingford, on this horrid suggestion, and they were not much longer left to doubt, for presently the flames ascended to a fearful height, notwithstanding the heavy fall of rain, and throwing a broad blood-red light upon their path showed them the towers of the ancient hall, with the left wing, appropriated to the nursery, rapidly falling a prey to the devouring element!

"Horror! horror!" groaned the frantic Wallingford, "my wife, my children! Oh save them! Save them!"

"Lose not a moment, for Heaven's sake!" cried Doctor Hartley, whose agitation was scarcely less violent than that of Wallingford, although he retained more self-possession; "they may yet be saved, if they are not rescued already!"

Wallingford rushed forward like a madman, and soon heard the shrieks and cries of the domestics, and the noise of the persons engaged in extinguishing the devouring element. Followed closely by Doctor Hartley, he rushed into the burning pile, calling frenziedly on the names of his wife and children; he was driven back nearly suffocated by the smoke, and returned to the lawn, shrieking wildly with the intensity of his feelings; and had scarcely gained the entrance, when standing erect across his path, the red glare of the ravaging element gleaming fearfully upon her, stood the revolting form of the sybil he had twice before seen; who uttering a loud laugh, and pointing to the fast falling ruins, disappeared in the smoke that quickly enveloped her form. Overcome with his emotions, Wallingford uttered a deep groan, and sank senseless to the earth.

CHAPTER XVIII.

"She's gone! the cherub whose sweet prattle,
And whose angel looks, filled each beholder
With delight, and thoughts of Heaven."
                    "Ethelred," a poem.

THE fire was confined to that wing of the building in which it had broken out, which was entirely destroyed. But dreadful was the news Wallingford was fated to hear when he recovered his senses;—his wife and son were rescued from the flames, but his darling Christabel had perished. The account given by Agatha, the nurse, who had been in the service of the family from a child, and her father and mother also, was to the effect, that having put the little Christabel to rest, at the usual hour, she retired into her own sitting-room, to employ the time before retiring to bed in needlework. The storm coming on with such violence, alarmed her, and in order to see the more to the safety of her little charge, she put down her work, and hastened up the stairs, when to her horror she was met by the flames, which burst forth from the very apartment in which the ill-fated child was. She screamed and raised an alarm, but all attempts to enter the room were useless, the flames raged so terrifically. Horrible indeed was the anguish of Wallingford at this dreadful tale, and the unhappy mother, who had, in the confusion that prevailed, become acquainted with the awful fate of her darling child, had become delirious, and Dr. Hartley entertained very little hopes of her recovery. Wallingford's feelings were too harrowing to be described; but his anxiety as regarded his wife, made him struggle hard to sustain his fortitude, and he succeeded with wonderful effect.

The occasion of the conflagration could only be accounted for by the lightning, as Agatha had protested that she had left no light burning in the apartment, when she quitted her tender charge; but to add to the calamity, although the ruins underwent the strictest search for days, not the slightest signs of the child's remains could be discovered.

This, added to other circumstances, at times induced Wallingford to believe that his child had by some miraculous means not perished at

RACKETT AND THE LEADER OF THE GIPSIES.

all, and to add to this strange opinion, the appearance of the Sybil at the very moment of the scene of destruction recurred to his recollection, and her previous prognostication:

"'Tis coming, 'tis coming, the hour is nigh,
When the tear of anguish shall fill thine eye,
When thy fair-haired bride of her darling 'reft,
To weep and wail with thee shall be left."

These words, too, uttered only the night previous to the dreadful occurrence, all carried suspicion with it, that the woman, from some motive of revenge, had contrived to gain access to the house, and taken the child for some sinister object; and to aid to the mystery, had set fire to the apartment. But then what cause could this mysterious being have for such a crime? He had never seen her before he encountered her in the forest, and knew not of any cause for offence that he could have given, more than the expressions he had made use of towards her on that occasion. He had instituted strict inquiries about her, but no one knew her, and he had never seen her among the gipsies!—Ah! here a dreadful thought crossed his brain; this woman might be connected with the tribe, although not seen among them; and should she have been employed by them to effect their revenge;—should Ela have employed her as an agent! The idea came with horrible conviction to his mind; he remembered the threats Ela had made use of on the night he had watched the gipsies in the Dell, and the bitter malice with which she nursed her hatred and vengeance against him and his.

"Good God!" he cried, clasping his forehead, with dreadful agony, "can her cruelty have led her to such a fiendish crime as this? —If it has, awful indeed is the retribution she has sought!"

Then he recollected the woman he had seen in the Hall on the day of the festival, corresponding in figure and looks with Ela, and the certainty of his conjectures came more vividly on his imagination.—Filled with these distracting thoughts, he rang the bell violently for Agatha, determined to question her more minutely on the subject. The poor girl entered her master's presence trembling violently, and her agitation was not by any means diminished when she beheld the wildness and frenzy of his looks.

With trembling haste Wallingford again questioned her minutely as to the origin of the fire; but she declared that she was unable to account for it in any other way than the lightning having struck that part of the building in which the child was sleeping, as she was positive she had not left a light burning in the room when she left it.

"And, dear sir," she continued, sobbing, "what other way could the shocking accident have happened, unless some person had a spite against your honour, and contrived means to get into the building; for I now recollect that when I came down stairs, I found the front door ajar, but I thought perhaps some of the servants had entered with their private key, and forgot to close it after them. But then, you know, sir, that they have all been strictly examined, and they declare that none of them had occasion to leave or enter that part of the building at that time."

"Agatha," asked the agonized Wallingford, looking solemnly in the face of the trembling domestic, "once more I enjoin, I implore you, to recollect yourself; did you observe any strange people lurking about the Hall in the course of the day?"

"Oh, dear no, sir," answered the girl, after pondering for a moment or two.

"You knew the gipsies were again in the Dell," added Wallingford, with fearful haste; "are you sure that you saw none of them near the house in the course of the day, or before the dreadful calamity occurred?"

Agatha gave a convulsive start at this question, and turning ghastly pale, clasped her hands, and fell upon her knees before her master, looking up in his face with terror and supplication

"Speak—tell me all," cried Wallingford, with fearful agitation, when he remarked the strange effect his question had upon the poor girl.

"Oh, yes, I will, sir," sobbed forth Agatha, "I will tell all, if you will but say you'll pardon me;—oh, I shall never forgive myself; but I'm sure I thought no harm of it."

"Girl, keep me not in suspense," demanded her master, "it is worse than death. If you have done wrong through error, I will forgive you; but do not attempt to conceal a single iota from me."

The agitated Agatha then proceeded, as well as her fears and her sorrow would permit her, to inform her master, that on the morning before the fire took place, she had met, while she was walking with the unfortunate little Christabel, near the Hall, an old gipsy woman, who had persuaded her to have her fortune told, and who, before she went away, had put several questions to her conceing the family, of which she had taken no notice at the time. That when she returned from her walk, she had observed the same woman lurking near the spot, and that she continued to watch her until she entered the house.

"But," continued the poor girl, "how could I ever imagine for a moment that her and her tribe could entertain such a shocking feeling of revenge against my dear master and mistsers, as to commit such a dreadful crime as this?"

"My fatal conjectures are confirmed!" exclaimed Wallingford, pacing the room with a wild air; "it is the diabolical work of that fearful woman;—amply has she fulfilled her cruel threats. Oh God! sooner would I that my poor child should have perished in the flames than have fallen into the hands of such atrocious wretches!"

Overcome with his emotion, he threw himself into a chair, covered his face with his hands, and groaned aloud. The wretched Agatha, who fancied herself now the sole, although the innocent, cause of this misery, again threw herself on her knees, and once more implored him to pardon her. Wallingford, however, heard her not, although he motioned her to retire, which she obeyed, trembling and heart-broken. Wallingford remained for a few moments after she had retired, completely absorbed in the agonizing thoughts that his interview with Agatha had given rise to, then suddenly starting upon his feet, and looking wildly around him, he exclaimed :—

"Why do I remain here? why thus apathetically give way to despair, when my child, my Christabel, calls upon me to rescue her from the clutches of the fiendish wretches that have torn her from her parents' arms? By all my hopes of mercy, I will not rest until I have discovered their retreat, torn my child from their power, and brought the miscreants to punishment! That woman—her whom I once thought purity itself—oh! curses light upon her head! But I will find her, if the earth is contaminated with her hated form. I will tear the dreadful secret from her polluted heart! My child—my poor unfortunate Christabel!"

Scarcely knowing what he did, the wretched parent clasped his forehead, and rushed out of the room. He darted out of the house, and was hurrying precipitately forward, when he suddenly encountered Dr. Hartley, who was about to visit his unfortunate patient, Mrs. Wallingford.

"For Heaven's sake, my dear sir," said the good doctor, arresting his progress, "where are you going, and what is the meaning of all this agitation? Surely no new calamity has happened, to increase the troubles of this sorely-afflicted family?"

"She lives! she lives! I know it all now!" cried Wallingford, with a half-frantic laugh.

"What? who?" hastily demanded the doctor, who began to fear that the recent occurrence had turned his brain; "of whom do you speak?"

"My child, my Christabel!" answered Wallingford—"she is not burnt—I am convinced she is not! But oh! I am certain ever. that fate would not be half so fearful as the horrible one I fear she is now doomed to suffer."

"Pray explain yourself, my dear sir," said the astonished doctor, leading him back into the house.

Wallingford paused a few moments to collect his scattered thoughts, and partially to regain his composure, and then proceeded minutely to detail to Dr. Hartley all that had transpired on his recent interview with Agatha, and the reasons he had to suspect that the fire was the work of Ela, for the purpose of abducting the little Christabel, and thus gratifying her cruel revenge by bringing her up to all the degradation and misery to which her own child was doomed. The doctor listened to him with the most inconceivable interest and astonishment, and there appeared to be so much reason and probability in his suspicions, that he was almost inclined to adopt them.

"But then," he observed, after a moment's reflection, "we have had sufficient proof that Ela was not in the tribe."

"Oh, that was merely a stratagem," exclaimed Wallingford, "the better to carry her atrocious design into execution. But I am so convinced that my conjectures are well founded, that I am determined to sacrifice fortune, happiness, nay, life itself, to find this infamous woman out, and wrest the victim from her power, if the murderer's knife has not already made that impossible!" Wallingford groaned as this awful thought suggested itself to his mind. "Besides, if she had indeed perished in the ruins, is it not utterly improbable that not the slightest portion of her remains should be found, when several articles of her bed were found, and scarcely at all damaged by the fire?"

The doctor again weighed every circumstance connected with the mysterious and awful catastrophe, in his mind, and the more he reflected, the more he became convinced of the truth of Wallingford's conjectures. He, however, endeavoured to appease the agitation of Wallingford, and suggested to him the propriety of using the utmost caution in furthering their inquiries, so that they might lead to a perfect unravelment of this mysterious affair, and bring the abominable perpetrators of the outrage to that punishment they so severely merited. Wallingford was convinced of the prudence of these suggestions, and promised to adhere to them; but he immediately set his designs into motion, by offering a large reward for the apprehension of the gipsies, or to any one who could inform him of the retreat of Ela. These preliminaries once set on foot, his mind became somewhat more composed, but as he watched the perilous and melancholy condition of his beloved wife, he suffered the most poignant misery. The wildness of her delirum had subsided into a calm but painful aberration of intellect, and it was a truly piteous sight to hear her at intervals, in a voice of the most heartrending pathos, exclaim—

"Poor little cherub, and would no one put forth a helping hand to save her from that dreadful fate? Oh, 'twas cruel to see her innocent career thus terminated.—Hark! how the flames hiss and crackle!—Look, look, she flies to the window, and supplicates for help! —Good God! why do you all stand by and heed not her piteous shrieks?—Hark!—again —mother, she cries, mother!—Oh! horror! I cannot get near her; the flames obstruct my way!—The black smoke suffocates me!—I choke—oh!"

She would then sink into a state of torpidity, and would not speak for several hours: at intervals, however, bursting into paroxysms of tears, and clasping her aching temples. In this state the unhappy lady continued for several weeks, and Doctor Hartley gave very little hopes of her recovery; but at length the violence of her disorder abated, and the doctor with delight pronounced her out of danger. But he told her affectionate husband the urgent necessity of removing her without delay from the scene of her sufferings, and also to endeavour to recruit her health by a journey to some watering-place. As all the inquiries instituted by Wallingford for the discovery of the retreat of Ela or the gipsies had been ineffectual, he readily complied with the doctor's request, and leaving Wallingford Hall in the care of Agatha and her parents, they departed on their journey.

CHAPTER XIX.

" There is some awful myst'ry in this
We cannot unravel. What form is that?"
ETHELRED.

IT was on a cold inclement night, although in October, when the frost was upon the earth, the snow descended in large flakes, and "ice-bounded were the brooks," about six years after the events lately recorded had taken place, that around a blazing fire in one of the rooms of Wallingford Hall, were seated a group of three.   The two was composed of Agatha, old Anthony, her father, and Jenny his wife. The old woman had just been recounting one of her marvellous legends, until she had nearly frightened her simple daughter into fits, and a pause had ensued, during which they listened to the rage of the storm without, and watched the bright embers in the grate, with feelings of honest gratitude to the Providence that had provided them with so comfortable a home in that boisterous season of the year.

" Mercy on us," suddenly broke forth the old man, " what a terrible night it is ; the snow descends like a funeral shroud, and the wind rattles the casements of this old building as if it would blow them away."

" Ah !" ejaculated the old woman with a long drawn sigh, " and it is now just six years ago that the dreadful event took place, which I shall never cease to remember to my dying day. Poor dear little thing, I wonder if she is really alive !"

" I do not doubt it, Jenny," said her husband, " and what makes me think it the more likely is, that ever since that dreadful night, which is six years ago, those cursed vagabonds, the gipsies, have never ventured to show themselves near the spot ! Ah, poor little innocent, well do I recollect the morning when I met her with Agatha, the morning before the fatal night——"

" Oh, pray do not, my dear father," said the weeping Agatha, " spare me, spare me ; I never cease to think of it, and to pray to Heaven for forgiveness for my imprudence."

" And so you ought, girl," returned her father solemnly ; " it was a terrible job, and I should never forgive myself if I were in your situation, that I shouldn't.   But I will not upbraid you, my girl. I know you did not do it wilfully, for you was too fond of the poor dear child, as who could help being who witnessed her innocent gambols, and heard her coaxing prattle ?   But let us change the subject, it is such a melancholy one, it makes the tears start in my eyes whenever I think of it.   Is it not almost time that your husband called, Agatha, to see you home ?   But it is such a rough night I don't know how he can get here, so you had better sleep where you are."

" Oh, Giles does not mind the weather," replied Agatha, " and I know he will come ; but hark !—I thought I heard a voice at the hall door ; and there is the bell ; it is Giles, no doubt."

The bell was a second time rung more violently than before.   " Well, bless my soul," added Agatha, " what a hurry he is in, to be sure ; he won't give one time to get to the door."

" You'll recollect that it is a night not fit for a dog to be out in," said old Anthony, " and no wonder that the poor lad is impatient ; for my own part, I think he was very foolish to venture out, when he knew you was safely housed."

Before the conclusion of this speech, Agatha had hastened to the door, and admitted her husband, who seemed in a state of confusion, and had evidently been running, for he was almost breathless.

" Why, Giles, lad," said his father-in-law, drawing him a chair by the fire-side, " what in the name of goodness made you venture out such a boisterous night as this ?   There are very few husbands would have done the like, when they knew that their wife was safe with her parents ; come, sit you down and warm yourself, for you must be half perished."

" Let me get my breath first," said Giles, shaking the snow from off himself ; " I have been running ready to break my neck."

" Running !" reiterated his wife, " why what the deuce is in the wind now ?—What makes you so flurried ?"

" Such a piece of news," returned Giles, " I never was more astonished in my life, and it it had not happened I should not have come here to-night, for I knew you would make Agatha stay with you ; but I could not rest until I had come here to tell you all about it."

" Well, what has happened ?" exclaimed they all in a breath ; " do, pray, explain yourself, and do not keep us in such a state of suspense."

" Ah, you may well say what has happened," returned Giles, " I never was so astonished in my life. What do you think, would you believe it; why, those infernal gipsies are in the neighbourhood again!"

"The gipsies! impossible! at this time of the year, too," cried the old man.

"You forget that it was at this time of the year they were in the neighbourhood last," rejoined Giles.

"Right, right," replied Anthony; "but then the weather was as mild and serene as the middle of summer, and we do not often see winter set in so severely in the month of October; but you must surely be mistaken, they cannot have taken up their abode in the Dell, or they would all perish."

"True they have not fixed their habitation in the Dell," returned Giles, "but they have not far from it; but you must let me tell the story my own way, and do not interrupt me."

"Very well, very well," said his anxious listeners, "but go on."

"Well," began Giles, "you must know, after I left work, I was hurrying home to get out of the cold and snow, which I never remember to have seen so severe before at this time of the year, when, just as I came to the old Manor House, near the Dell, which you know has been left to decay for many years, I was suddenly startled by seeing lights blazing in the windows. Unable to account for such a singular circumstance, seeing that no one for years has been bold enough to enter it, on account of its being reported to be haunted, I could not help having the curiosity to stop and watch, for which you will say I am entitled to a claim of more courage than most people. Well, I planted myself behind a clump of old trees, where I could see all that past without being observed myself, and I had not been there many seconds, when I saw the lights moving about, and presently afterwards, two men and a woman came from under the archway, whom I knew by their appearance to be gipsies."

"Nonsense," said old Anthony, incredulously, "you must have been mistaken! robbers they might have been —"

"Well, for the matter of that, Master Anthony," rejoined Giles, "there's very little odds, for they were robbers, no doubt, as well as gipsies, or else they do not very well support the character of the rest of their tribe; but that they were gipsies I am certain, for I had the courage to speak to them, and inquired if they intended to take up their residence in the old Manor House for any time, and they replied in the affirmative, for they said that they could not travel about as the weather had set in so bad; and they might walk a long way before they could find such a shelter as their present one."

"If I am not much mistaken," exclaimed Anthony, suddenly starting from his chair, with more alacrity than could have been expected at his age, "I am much mistaken if they do not find themselves in another habitation, though; the county gaol shall hold the rascals before the morning."

"Why, where in the name of goodness are you going to, father, such a night as this?" asked Agatha, seeing the old man put on his hat in great haste, and seize his walking stick.

"To Doctor Hartley's immediately," replied Anthony, "to tell him of the whole affair, and consult with him on the subject; these wretches must not be suffered to escape, when they have so much to answer for. Giles, I must get you to attend me."

"I do not see of what use that will be,', observed Giles, "for the men I spoke to say they do not belong to the tribe that were in the habit of visiting Rosemary Dell, and, indeed, I never saw their faces before."

"We will, at any rate, not take their assertions for it," said Anthony; "six years is a long time, and you may have forgotten the faces of the rascals. However, the subject is too important to let it pass over slightly, so off to Dr. Hartley's I go at all hazards, and hear what he thinks of the matter. Will you attend me, Giles?"

Seeing the old man was resolute, Giles could not refuse, so he accompanied Anthony from the house, much to the chagrin of Agatha and her mother, who did not at all relish the idea of being left to themselves in the mansion at that time of night, and especially when they knew themselves to be in the vicinage of such reckless customers.

"It was very foolish and headstrong of my father," said Agatha, when her husband and old Anthony had left the Hall, "to venture out on such a wild-goose chase as this on such a night; for my own part, I don't see why the morning would not have done as well, especially as Giles says that the gipsies, who have made their retreat in the old Manor House, are not in any way connected with those who used to come to the Dell."

Her mother coincided with this opinion, "and," she added, "to leave us two poor lonely women in this large dreary mansion by ourselves; your father has forgot all the gallantry for which he was so noted in his youthful days. Goodness me! with such characters in the neighbourhood, we might be murdered and the house robbed before they came back."

"Oh, mother," cried the simple Agatha, trembling, and looking round her, "you'll frighten me to death, if you say such things as that!—Oh, dear! what's that? Did you not hear a noise?"

"Nonsense!" replied Jenny, "it was nothing but the wind. You get more timid every day, Agatha."

"No, no, I'm not, mother," returned Agatha, still trembling, and looking fearfully around her; "but I'm sure, after such dreadful doings as have taken place on this spot of late years, it is enough to make any one feel qualmish like. You remember that poor gentleman who was murdered near the Dell, and brought here; I saw him after he was dead, and his face looked so pale and ghastly, that I'm sure I have never been able to get him out of my mind ever since. I could almost fancy I see his glassy eyes fixed upon me now."

"Oh, Agatha, for God's sake don't," exclaimed the old woman, who was in truth almost as terrified as her daughter; "I wish the plague had all the gipsies, for they are the cause of nothing but misery wherever they go. But, dear me, I forgot; the parlour shutters are not closed, and if any one should be so inclined, they might easily enter the Hall. You must accompany me, Agatha, to secure them."

"Oh, goodness!" ejaculated Agatha, turning very pale at the bare idea, "I would not go for the world; let us bolt the door, and we shall then be safe enough till father and Giles return."

"Nonsense; of what use would that be, when the entrance is not secured?" interposed Jenny; "come, come, it can soon be done, and if you will not attend me, I must e'en venture and do it by myself."

Agatha could not reasonably allow her mother to do this; so much against her will, and trembling all over like an aspen leaf, she suffered her mother to take up the lamp, and laying hold of the skirt of her gown, she followed the old woman up the stairs. They paused at the parlour door and listened, being both afraid to enter without taking this precaution, but all being still they cautiously entered the apartment. Jenny, having satisfied herself that no one was lurking in the room, proceeded towards the window to fasten the shutter, while Agatha stood trembling aside; but before her mother had reached the window, she uttered a terrified cry and pulled her back.

"Oh, mercy!" she cried, "come back, for God's sake, come back;—there, did you not see!—"

"See what?" answered her mother.

"Why, that form," returned Agatha, "that figure which hurried among the cluster of trees yonder? Oh, I'm sure I was not mistaken. I saw it as plainly as I see you. You would be so foolish as to venture here—we shall be murdered, I am sure we shall! Oh, dear! oh, dear! oh, dear! How cruel it was of father and Giles to leave us in this manner!"

"What nonsense you talk, child," said the old woman, who began to regain fresh courage as her daughter's decreased; "it was only your own shadow you saw as I put back one of the shutters—and—ah! gracious me!—I did see something then myself; it was the form of a

woman. There is something wrong. I'll close the shutters, at all events; and then we can go up stairs in the drawing-room, and watch with safety the proceedings of the party, if we only conceal the light."

With these words, the old woman closed and bolted the shutters, with much more courage than could have been expected at her years, and turning to her daughter, endeavoured to reassure her, preparing to leave the room and go up stairs. In this effort she partially succeeded, and they ascended the stairs on tip-toe, as though they were fearful that somebody would overhear them. Having taken a hasty survey of the apartment, and ascertained that there was no danger, they left the lamp in the lobby, and walked in. They approached the window, which commanded a view of the whole of the lawn and a considerable distance of scenery beyond.

The snow had ceased to fall, and a bright moonlight had succeeded, which, as it beamed upon the deeply-covered earth, had a beautiful and fairy-like appearance. The trees, covered with the pure fleece, formed a variety of picturesque and fantastic shapes in the light of Luna. Objects were distinctly visible for some distance, and it was one of those lovely nights which frequently succeed a snow storm, and raise the soul in admiration at the wondrous works of Nature.

The timid Agatha, from the slight glance which her terrors would allow her to take at the object which alarmed her, had not been able to form the least conjecture of what it could be, whether a male or a female form; but Jenny was certain that it was a woman, and she was inclined to think, from what she could distinguish of her apparel, that she was a gipsy. However, let it be who it might, Jenny felt convinced, though she did not mention her opinion to her daughter, that their design could not be a good one, to be stealing in the grounds around the mansion at that time of the night. Jenny continued to look earnestly from the window, while her daughter stood at a respectable distance, and trembled from head to foot.

"There it is again!" said the old woman, suddenly drawing Agatha to the window, and pointing to the figure which was now clearly distinguishable, not many yards from the house. It was the form of a woman, miserably attired, but her step was noble and majestic, and would have led a person to suppose, had it not been for her dress, that she moved in the higher circles of life. She approached boldly, till she stood exactly opposite the window where the old woman and her daughter had placed themselves, and glanced stedfastly up at the building. Jenny was convinced that she was a gipsy, and whispered to Agatha that she was a good mind to speak to her, and ask her her business; but the foolish girl endeavoured to dissuade her from it.

"Oh, no, mother, for goodness sake, do not do so," she urged; "suppose any of her companions should be near at hand, who knows what might be the consequences?"

"Nonsense," replied the old woman, "your foolish fears overcome your reason; what if she should be accompanied by any of her tribe? when they know that they are observed, it is not likely that they would attempt anything wrong, however evil their designs might have been. I will address this woman, at any rate, and know the worst."

With this resolution, the dame opened the casement, and leaning forward, she said in a voice of such firmness and command as it was possible for her to assume,—

"Why are you wandering in the grounds of this mansion at such a suspicious hour of the night, woman?"

"Where guilt lurks not there is no suspicion," returned the woman in a firm voice, after starting when she was watched; "I would speak to Mrs. Wallingford," she added.

"There is no Mrs. Wallingford here now, my good woman," returned old Jenny, with remarkable self-possession.

"Ah! can it be?" eagerly inquired the stranger, in a tone of something like exultation. "Is she then no more?"

"Your questions are mysterious," observed Jenny; at any rate, you cannot be very well acquainted with the person of whom you speak, or you would be aware that it is six years since she resided here."

"So long? Six years! No, it is impossible," remarked the woman, and she placed her hand to her forehead, as though she was endeavouring to recall her recollection; "yes, it is so—the time now rises more vividly to my recollection; it was the very period when —" The stranger here paused; and after a second or two passed in silence, in which interval she seemed to be indulging in some painful reminiscences, she raised her head, and in a voice of great emotion and eagerness, interrogated, "Tell me, then, that man she called her husband—whither has he gone?"

"Well, I'm sure," observed Agatha, who now found courage to speak, "I never heard such impertinence in my life: that *man, he,*—"

"'tis well he is not here to hear you, woman, or woe betide you. But if you have any particular wish to know where Mr. Wallingford is, he is where he should be, to be sure—with my lady, his amiable wife."

"Accursed disappointment!" cried the mysterious woman, in a voice in which despair and chagrin were mingled.

"Well, as I live," said Agatha, as she caught a full view of the woman's countenance in the moonlight, and drawing her mother aside, "as

I live, this must be the very gipsy who was sheltered by my mistress so many years ago, when the little girl came and implored assistance for her; what can she want here?"

"If it is as you say, Agatha," returned her mother, "she may probably have some intelligence to communicate about the poor dear lost Christabelle; I will go down and open the door to her, for I do not fear that she means us any wrong."

"Oh, no, for goodness sake do not venture to do so, mother," said Agatha; "who knows but some of her gang may be lurking near the spot, who may rush in, murder us, and plunder the house; if she had any good intentions, would she have chosen such an unseasonable hour as this to put them into execution?"

"At all hazards, I am resolved to do as I say," replied Jenny, peremptorily. "I do not see any reason for your apprehensions."

Before, however, Jenny could put her design into execution, the woman had turned away from the spot on which she had before stood, and slowly retreated towards the cluster of trees, from which they had at first seen her emerge, and was hidden from the view; but Agatha would have it that she saw a form still moving about among the cluster of trees, and shortly afterwards was positive that she beheld her joined by a second person. Jenny, however, whose sight, of course, was not so good as her daughter's, could not perceive anything of the kind, and as she felt persuaded that the woman had retired, she suggested that it would be useless for them to remain longer in that room, and proposed that they should return to the kitchen. To this, Agatha was not inclined to raise any objection, and they hastened once more to the cheerful fireside below, to talk over the mysterious adventure of the night.

A considerable time had now elapsed since Giles and Anthony had left the Hall, and Jenny and her daughter began to feel very anxious for their return. They listened attentively for the bell, but another hour passed away, and they did not return. Agatha began to feel tired, and the old woman was just beginning to doze in her arm chair, when they were both aroused by a violent pulling of the bell, the barking of the house-dog, which they had not heard before, and several voices apparently engaged in angry discussion, among which they distinguished those of Giles and Anthony; and, as they imagined, the supplicating tones of a female at intervals.

"Goodness me, what can be the meaning of all this rumpus?" said Jenny, taking the lamp and rising from her chair; "follow me, Agatha, directly, and let us open the Hall door."

This was done, and the old woman and Agatha were absolutely astonished at the scene they then beheld. The tall and elegant figure of a female, apparently about fourteen years of age, was struggling in the grasp of Anthony and Giles, and, in piteous accents, imploring their forbearance. A short distance from them was the woman whom they had before beheld, who was rushing impetuously forward, and in a voice, hoarse with indignation, commanding them to desist, and to release her child from their ruffian grasp. To add to the terror of the scene, the dog barked more furiously than before, and threatened every moment to seize upon the fragile form of the shrieking girl.

"For Heaven's sake, what is the meaning of this, Anthony?" demanded the good old dame, advancing, and endeavouring to interpose in behalf of the struggling and terrified girl; "what can you want to do with the poor child, that you handle her so violently? Off, off, Carlo;—do not alarm yourself, my poor girl, the dog shall not bite you; off, off, Carlo, I say!"

But the dog did not mind the orders of his mistress on this occasion, continuing to bark furiously, and threatening every minute to make a spring at the object of his rage; while Anthony, not heeding the remonstrances of his kind-hearted wife, continued to drag the girl towards the house, and Giles, although he did not continue to take any part in the proceedings, stood by, and seemed to approve of what was going forward.

"Oh, Giles," cried Agatha, whom the piteous supplications of the poor girl had deeply affected, "why do you stand by staring in that stupid manner? surely the poor thing cannot have done anything to deserve such treatment as this. Father, do call the dog off, and relinquish your hold of the girl."

"Spare me, spare me, good sir," implored the girl; "indeed we came here with no bad intent; we have done no harm, indeed we have not."

"Very likely," replied Anthony, "but no thanks to you for that, I'll warrant; no doubt if we had not interrupted you, your devilish minds would have contrived to do us some harm. All is fish that comes to your infernal nets, anything that will save you the trouble of getting your living by honest industry. You care not what troubles you bring upon the hard-working poor; but you shall not escape so easily as you think for this time;—you must explain what caused you to be lurking about the Hall at this strange hour, and likewise satisfy me upon another business about which I shall question you."

The girl again protested her innocence of anything wrong, and implored the old man to let her go to her mother, whom the dog was now pursuing, and who, as she retreated with her face turned towards them, called loudly and fiercely upon them to release her child from their clutches. At length, Giles, moved by the entreaties of his wife, and the supplications

and tears of the poor gipsy girl, seized the dog, and dragging him into his kennel, secured him; which Ela (for it was her) no sooner beheld, than she advanced towards the group, and placing herself between Jenny and her husband, exclaimed in a voice that shook the place, while her large and still brilliant black eyes darted fire,—

"Menial, dastard, release your hold of that trembling maid, my child! Miscreant! dare you to drag her like a criminal to the house of which she should be the mistress?—Hold off! hoary-headed ruffian, or tremble for the consequences. Fanny, kneel to the slave of your father, and the curse of her who bore you be upon your head!"

As the infuriated woman thus spoke, she grasped the arm of the old woman with fearful violence, and her whole frame shook with indignation.

The last words of Ela made old Anthony start with strange emotion, as a sudden thought crossed his mind.—"Mysterious!" he cried, "surely my ears deceived me; *father* did she say?—Oh, no, no, it is all a base plot to deceive me; this cannot be the child of my master—the pretty, smiling, innocent Christabelle. Base, lying, hell-cat, this falsehood shall not avail you; at any rate, if the tigress escape, I will secure her cub!"

Without uttering another word, Anthony threw the form of the girl over his shoulder, and was proceeding to enter the Hall, when his progress was arrested by a loud shriek from Jenny, and turning round, what was his consternation to behold her forced upon her knees, while Ela stood over her brandishing a knife, which she seemed ready in a moment to plunge in her bosom.

"Wretch!" shrieked the gipsy, "if you would not see me bury this knife in the heart of your wife, release my girl from your rude grasp; nay, think not I will flinch from my promise; one minute more, and you refuse, her you have vowed to love and cherish shall be stretched a breathless corpse at your feet!"

The astonished Anthony beheld the look of determination with which she eyed him, and the pitiful cries for mercy uttered by his wife at once decided him. He relinquished the form of the gipsy girl, who flew with the speed of lightning to her mother, while Anthony hastened to the protection of his affrighted wife.

"Stand where you are," ejaculated Ela, savagely, "advance but another step towards me, and I will bury my knife in your throat!"

"Mighty fine indeed," said Anthony, attempting to laugh at the gipsy's threat; "but come, release my wife, and hasten after your devil's imp, who—"

"Presumptuous serf!" interrupted Ela, advancing a step or two towards him, and

[Dr. Hartley prevented questioning the beautiful Gipsy-girl.]

brandishing the knife, "venture to utter such a word again, and I will tear your heart from your vile carcass. Beggar, wretch, grovelling hind, the lickspittle of a villanous master, and yet dare to apply such an epithet to the eldest child of that master! To the child of Edward Wallingford."

More astonished and bewildered than ever, Anthony started back aghast.

"Woman, whatever may be your motives I know not," he said, "but for pity's sake do not attempt to sport upon that subject; this, the child of Edward Wallingford; for pity's sake then, explain—"

"Ha! ha! ha!" laughed Ela, scornfully, "explain, what to the dastard slave of Edward Wallingford!—Old man, get thee gone, and think yourself lucky that Ela's knife has not let out your heart's blood for your insolence and daring—"

At this moment a shrill whistle was heard, and directly afterwards several men jumped through a thicket and advanced towards Ela and her child;—alarmed at their appearance, and doubtful of their actual intentions, but feeling rather inclined to believe that their design was to rob the Hall, Anthony and the others hastily retreated into the house and secured all the doors, fearing an immediate attack. They waited for several moments, but nothing occurring to verify their apprehensions, Anthony and Giles ventured up stairs, and looked out of the window, and were agreeably astonished to find the coast entirely clear; Ela, her daughter, and the men had all departed.

CHAPTER XX.

"Deep in her heart the spirit of revenge
Is buried; no power in life can root it out."
THE MANIAC.

VARIOUS were the speculations which this mysterious adventure gave rise to in the breasts of the humble inmates of the Hall, but after considerable deliberation they all came to the conclusion that the gipsies could not have wanted to do them any harm, or else they would have attacked the house when their numbers were so superior. The assertions of Ela that the girl was the child of Mr. Wallingford, was a source of great doubt and perplexity to them, but at length tired of ruminating upon a subject which they could not satisfy their minds upon, they gave it up, and retired to their separate chambers.

Before partaking of breakfast the next morning, Anthony could not rest until he had hastened over to Doctor Hartley's to acquaint him with the particulars of the last night's occurrences, in addition to the facts he had before disclosed to him. During the night he had been able to sleep but very little, but had reflected more seriously upon the events that had taken place, and the statement of Ela; and the more he ruminated upon it, the more inclined he felt to believe the truth of her words, to pity her hapless fate, and to regret the rough manner in which he had behaved to her daughter. The conduct of his master, Anthony, who was rather a sensible man, he could not help censuring most severely. He looked upon him as the ruiner of the hopes, fames, prospects, and happiness of a woman who might have been borne to ornament society, and he began to view the troubles that had of late years attended the house of Wallingford as the retribution of an offended God for the sins of his master. It was in this vein

that the old man reached the house of Dr. Hartley, and immediately communicated to him all the particulars of the strange affair.

Although the time that had elapsed had served to weaken the interest which the worthy Dr. Hartley had taken in the melancholy events connected with the unfortunate Ela and her child, yet when Anthony, the night before, had informed him of the unexpected appearance of the gipsies at the old Manor-house, all the circumstances came full upon his mind, with all their former strength and impression, and anxious to elicit all the particulars he could relative to the catastrophe which had caused the disappearance of the little Christabelle, (for he, himself, strongly surmised that she had not perished in the flames which had consumed the nursery) he had, prior to Anthony's second appearance, come to the determination of applying to a magistrate for the apprehension of the gang, in order that the dark suspicion that rested upon their heads, might be thoroughly investigated. With this design the good doctor was about to leave the house, just as old Anthony entered, and recounted all the circumstances that have been detailed in the preceeding chapter. The doctor was greatly astonished at what Anthony related, and paused for a few moments to reflect upon it.

"Unfortunate woman," said he, "death then has not yet mercifully terminated her misery, although the gipsies told me she was no more. Poor creature, it would have indeed been a blessing to her, had the cold grave long since closed over her sufferings; and her poor girl, too, you say, Anthony, that she accompanied her mother?"

"Yes, sir," returned the old man, "and a fine tall girl she is, too, now; a handsome girl, yes, and the very picture of my master. Ah! it is a sad job, and I'm sure I could never have believed it of him, for goodness knows a more amiable young gentleman apparently there could not be. Ah! sir! sure enough we do indeed live in a deceitful world when,——but there, it is not my place to say anything about the matter. But certainly, sir, it is a duty incumbent upon all good men to see that something is done to save the wretched mother and her unoffending offspring from the shame and infamy with which they are now surrounded. Surely my master can never wish it to be said that a child of his was left to wander about in such a state of dire misery and disgrace, when he is so amply provided with the means to rescue her from it. And good God, sir! should the poor little Christabelle be still alive, and be in the power of the gipsies, may she not be instructed in the same guilty course? Alas! that ever I should live to see such troubles come upon the noble house of Wallingford."

"Your surmises, Anthony," said the worthy doctor, "bear too horrible a probability to be quietly rejected;—Ela's disposition is naturally revengeful, and should she have formed the stratagem to get the poor child into her power, so that she might train her up to a life of shame, and to be a curse to her parents,— still we have no certain proof that Ela was with the tribe at the time of the fire. But we are only delaying that time in idle surmises which might be employed in gaining more certain information ; we will, at all events, venture to visit the Manor-house, and see if we cannot obtain an interview with her. If, as you say, she wished last night to obtain an interview with Mrs. Wallingford, it is not at all improbable that if she had any hand in the supposed abduction of the little Christabelle she may be aroused to feelings of compunction, and wish to make a disclosure of all she knows."

"Ah, to be sure, sir," coincided Anthony, "do not let us delay a moment."

Notwithstanding, Anthony expressed such an anxious wish to hasten their departure to the resort of the gipsies, it must be acknowledged, that when he recollected the manner in which he had offended Ela the night before, and the ferocious disposition she then evinced, he did not feel altogether comfortable as to the likely result, but relying on the presence of the doctor to secure him from any personal violence, he mustered up all the resolution in his power, and attended Mr. Hartley, without any visible signs of apprehension.

From the doctor's house it was a direct line to the old Manor-house, which, standing on an eminence, might be seen at a considerable distance. It was yet early, and as the last grey tints of morn rested upon the ancient fabric, it had a peculiar, venerable, and solemn aspect. It had been formerly a very spacious and elegant structure, but the hand of neglect and time had committed sad ravages upon it, and there was only a very small portion of it that was not dilapidated and dangerous. It had for many years been left untenanted ; for what reason no one precisely knew, although it was attributed to various causes, all alike improbable, but the most common report among the lower orders was, that some dreadful crime had been committed within its walls, and that the ruins were haunted by the troubled spirit of the murdered person, and no one among the rustics would, in consequence, venture near it after night fall, and scarcely in the day time. This superstitious terror made it a secure retreat for the gipsies, and they could not have chosen a better spot. The approach to the building was by no means easy, for the ruins lay scattered thickly about, and many of them were hidden from the view by the brushwood and underwood which grew thickly around. The gipsies were all collected in the open space which had formerly been the court yard, and were seated upon the straggling lumps of moss covered stones that had tumbled from the walls, while others were gambolling about with their sun-burnt visaged children, or the dogs, of which they had a number, and between them, appeared to divide their affection equally. No sooner had Doctor Hartley and Anthony approached any way near the building, than the dogs set up a simultaneous bark and gathered themselves together around their companions, who, however, seemed to take very little heed of the approach of strangers, from which it appeared they did not apprehend any danger, or else were well prepared to resist it.

Doctor Hartley could not help gazing upon the scene with feelings of admiration and interest, for it was one that would have realized the most picturesque described in a romance ; the straggling groups of coarsely attired, but hardy looking men, women, and children, arranged in various tableaux, before the old grey towers of the ancient ruins, all an effect peculiarly expressive.

The men now eyed him and Anthony more keenly, but not one of them offered to move towards them. Dr. Hartley looked eagerly among them, but in vain, the objects upon which his thoughts rested, did not meet his gaze, and after the lapse of a moment or two, he turned to his companion, and gave it as his opinion that Ela was either not among them, or had kept out of the way designedly. To this opinion, Anthony was compelled to assent, and added, "that what astonished him more than all, was, that the men should treat their presence with such indifference, and that the females should not, ere this, have attacked them with their importunities."

"It is indeed strange," replied Mr. Hartley, "and I cannot account for it; at any rate I will endeavour to ascertain the reason of their conduct ; it would be complete folly for us to return home without some satisfactory result."

With this opinion Anthony agreed, so Doctor Hartley noticing that one of the females was watching them more narrowly than her companions, — motioned her towards them. After exchanging a word or two with a tall, stout-looking man, who was leaning on a formidable cudgel, who nodded his head, she stepped cautiously over the ruins that were scattered about, and soon afterwards stood before the doctor with an air of self-possession and determination.

"What would you with me, stranger," she demanded, "would you read the "Book of Fate," and know your future fortune, it is only to cross my palm with—"

"Psha!" interrupted the doctor, peevishly "I sent for you upon no such foolish errand;

but I think this is not the first time we have met."

"Very likely not," said the woman, and her full dark eye rested scrutinizingly upon the doctor's benevolent features; "I have been a wanderer in many lands, and gazed on many faces—where has your honour before beheld me?"

"In the Dell, Rosemary Dell, I mean," returned Mr. Hartley, "when you was attended by Ela—does she not still belong to your tribe?"

"She does not, your honour," answered the woman, "at least I know not of one who bears that name. There are our women, your honour, see you the one you mean among them? But you must be mistaken, or you would not have said you had seen me with the female, before, in Rosemary Dell, for I never remember to have been at least thirty miles within this place till the night before last!"

"You tell an untruth, woman," said Doctor Hartley, sternly; "can you have the effrontery to deny that six years since I saw you with the woman of whom I speak in the Dell?— It is useless; every feature of your face is as familiar to me as if it were but yesterday. You may save yourself the trouble of denying it, for—"

"And think you then," said the gipsy with a look of scorn, "think you that I would fear to own it, were it so?—Ha! ha! ha!—I am not used to qualms, ha! ha!"

"Do not tire my patience, my good woman," said the doctor, "you see plain enough that you are not unknown to me. Perhaps this may make you a little more communicative," he continued, slipping some money into her hand, "come, inform me how I may see Ela, I have something of the greatest importance to communicate to her."

The woman paused, and placed her finger to her lips, as though she was deeply ruminating. then suddenly turning to the doctor, she said, while a sarcastic smile played about her mouth, "I am sorry, since you have behaved so liberal, that I cannot afford you any information upon the subject, no more than to tell you that there is no female called Ela among our tribe; but if it will afford you any greater satisfaction, I will ask them if they ever heard of such a woman as you describe."

"Woman, do not tantalize me," exclaimed the doctor angrily; "you perfectly understand me, but seek to baffle me with your evasive answers. You may call the person I mean by a different name, but I am certain she was with your gang no longer since than last night."

"And you saw her, I suppose you mean to add?" inquired the woman, looking at him earnestly.

"She was seen, but not by me," returned the doctor; "my companion here, not only saw her, but spoke with her."

"And did he know her before?" interrogated the gipsy."

"I did not," answered Anthony, "but I am certain she was the woman."

"She did not tell you so, though," returned the woman, "nor that she belonged to the tribe who have sought a temporary shelter in the old Mannor-house?"

"Why do you ask these questions, woman?" demanded the doctor, sternly, his patience being completely exhausted by the woman's evasive and bantering conduct; "do not think that I intend to let you play with me, with impunity. The woman I seek is known to you well, your name being, I remember, Morna, I therefore caution you how to behave, or you may find that forcible means may not be the pleasantest mode of making you speak the truth. See Ela I must and am determined; and here will I remain till I do."

"Then a pleasant time to you, I say," laughed the woman, "you will need no little stock of patience, I assure you, to fulfil your determination."

As the woman thus spoke, she turned quickly upon her heel, and retraced her steps to her companions, leaving the doctor and old Anthony vexed and bewildered. Having rejoined her female companions, the men quickly gathered round her, and it was evident from their gestures that the account she was giving them; had anything but a peaceable effect upon them; they talked very loud, and looked rather fiercely towards the intruders, as though they were undecided how they should act. Anthony began to apprehend that their conduct boded them no good; and he half repented of his eagerness to attend the doctor, (who was immoveable) on such a hazardous expedition. From Mr. Hartley, however, he concealed his fears as well as he was able, though he had some difficulty in doing so, more especially when he beheld one of the tallest and stoutest of the men, armed with a thick oak cudgel, quit his companions and walk towards the spot where they stood. Doctor Hartley, however, entertained no such fears, and he watched the approach of the man unmoved. When he had reached within a few paces of the doctor and Anthony, he paused, and leaning carelessly on his staff, said :—

"What is your honour's business that you tarry here so long?"

"I presume you know it from the woman to whom I have just now spoken," replied the doctor; "perhaps you may also be inclined, if I reward you accordingly, to answer me more explicitly, and satisfactorily than she thought proper to do."

"Tell me what you would inquire," returned

the man, putting forth his hand eagerly, as he saw the doctor pull out his purse.

"I would ask you," said Mr. Hartley, where the woman is, one of your tribe, I know, whom you called, or now call, Ela?"

The Gipsy paused, and appeared to endeavour to recollect himself, and at length turning to the doctor, said:—"Ela, I have certainly heard the name before, and now, if I recollect right, black Mark's wife used to be so called; if so, your honour's errand is a hopeless one, for last night she quited us abruptly, and no one can form the least conjecture whither she has gone."

"Is this true?" demanded Mr. Hartley, with a penetrating look.

"I can have no object in deceiving you," replied the man; "if that is her you mean, it is quite unlikely when you may behold her again, though her husband is gone in search of her."

"Her husband!" ejaculated Mr. Hartley, "is it then possible that she has united herself to——"

"A wretch, a vagabond, an outcast; so you would term one of the gipsy tribe;" added the man, "but it is nevertheless true; and a bargain bad enough she is for any one. The tigress is not to be dreaded more than is her you call Ela in her moments of wrath!" Last night her husband, who is himself not one of the best tempers in the world, had some angry words with her, and not without cause either,—for she absented herself from us and could not be found until late, when Mark and one or two more of our men went in quest of her, but I do not know where they found her; but they not only came to words, but blows upon the subject; and, in consequence, she eloped last night, and her husband went in search of her. We have heard nothing of them since, and know not whether they may think proper to return. They had better, though, for woe betide those who abandon those companions they have sworn to stick to with their lives; they never live long to run the risk of betraying their secrets."

The tale told by the gipsy was of such an extraordinary description that he was lost in amazement while he reflected upon it; but the fact of Ela being absent from the tribe at the time mentioned, and the circumstance of her being followed by the man who called her husband, corresponded so exactly with the events which had taken place in the Hall, that he could not help placing reliance on its accuracy. But the thought of Ela being so lost to all her former feelings as to unite her fate with that of a wandering ruffian, without a name or home, the scorn of humble industry, and the heir of the gallows, was more than he had been prepared to hear, and he had not yet succeeded in reconciling it with his thoughts when

he was aroused from his reverie by the sound of a light footstep on the grass, and immediately afterwards the following words were sung in a voice of the most plaintive sweetness:—

Oh! scorn not the poor Gipsy girl, though rude she be
Rude in her speech and her garb, as you see;
On your hearts let kind Charity only alight,
And the future she'll quickly unveil to your sight!
Then pity the Gipsy girl, gentlefolks, do!—
The wanderer now makes her appeal to you.

As the voice ceased, Doctor Hartley beheld emerge from behind a portion of the ruins near which he was standing, the tall and elegant figure of a young girl, apparently not more than fourteen years of age. Struck with her interesting appearance, Mr. Hartley turned to the man and inquired who that girl belonged to.

"She belongs to me," replied the man, "it is Esther, my daughter."

"Impossible!" exclaimed the doctor, "it cannot be!"

"And why not?" demanded the man, with a contemptuous look; "think you it is only the offspring of the wealthy that can be comely to look upon; there is no better blood flows in the veins of your kings and princes than that which animates the wandering Gipsy. Think you I tell a falsehood, as you do? perhaps her mother may be more successful in convincing you. I will call her if you wish it, for yonder she is." As the man said this, he pointed towards a coarse, fierce-looking woman, who was seated at the entrance of the ruins, employed in making cabbage-nets for sale.

"No, I will not require you to do that," said the doctor, "I can put some question to the girl herself which will probably be most satisfactory."

"Hold!" cried the man fiercely, and intercepting the doctor's progress, at the same time brandishing his cudgel in a threatening manner; "the shepherd's staff is always ready to protect the lamb from the wolf; beware, you deal with one who knows not fear, and who is ready to take offence, and seek immediate retribution."

"The man is mad!" said the doctor, calmly, "you mistake my intentions, but that the girl is positively not your daughter, your violence convinces me."

"Indeed," sneered the Gipsy; "your sagacity may deceive you, old man, at any rate it cannot benefit you to know whether she is my child or not."

"Perhaps it does, more than you may at present imagine, but which you may know by and bye to your cost," returned Mr. Hartley, firmly: "Anthony," he continued, "look earnestly at that girl, and tell me whether you do not recognize in her the same that you last night beheld?"

No sooner had the doctor said this, than the man seemed to gripe his cudgel more firmly, and he scowled upon old Anthony in the most threatening manner. The latter was so afraid, that although he knew the girl was the same he had seen with Ela, he dared not venture to acknowledge it, and for a second or two knew not how to answer.

"They all resemble one another so much," he at length replied, "that I really could not speak with any degree of certainty as to the girl's identity."

"Psha!" ejaculated the doctor angrily, "then all I have got to say in the matter is, that you must have been blind at the time. But I am determined not to give up my inquiries so easily—I will immediately seek the aid of a magistrate, and in less than a couple of hours the whole tribe shall be lodged in the cage; we will see what effect that will have in making them speak the truth."

"Perhaps your honour will think better of the matter," said the man more mildly, as the doctor turned away from the spot, followed by the trembling old Anthony, "surely there is no offence in a man swearing to his own child;—but perhaps you will be better satisfied when she answers for herself; I will bring her to you."

When he had thus spoken, the Gipsy hurried away towards the spot where the girl was standing, and Mr. Hartley paused for him to come up with him.

"It is the very girl, sir," whispered old Anthony, "I knew her in a moment, but the looks of the ruffian made me afraid to acknowledge it. We had better leave here directly, for depend upon it, they mean us some harm, and what could we do against such a host of villains?"

"I shall do no such thing, let the consequences be whatever they may," said the doctor sharply,—"I am surprised, Anthony, that a man of your years, should suffer your groundless and cowardly terrors to make you tell an untruth,"

Before Anthony had time to make any reply to this rebuke, which he probably might have done rather warmly, the Gipsy had came up to them, leading the girl by the hand, who seemed to restrain her real feelings under a mask of indifference.

"Now, your honour," said the man, addressing himself to Doctor Hartley,—"perhaps you will be pleased to question the girl yourself."

The doctor looked earnestly in the girl's interesting countenance, as he said:—"Tell me, my good girl, what is your name, and who are your parents?"

"Esther Darwin is my name," answered the girl, "and I am the daughter of——"

"Psha! girl!" cried the worthy doctor, testily, "enough of that nonsense; you know

that you are speaking falsely; it is painful to see depravity in one so young, but no doubt you have been ably instructed by the persons whom you are connected with. However, could you not be induced to forget what you have imbibed, and reveal the facts? Here is money," continued he, exhibiting several pieces of silver, "all of which shall be yours if you will tell what was your original name, the one prior to your being called Esther Darwin, come now, that's a good girl."

The Gipsy girl looked eagerly at the money, and was about to stretch forth her hand to receive it, when the man fixed upon her a significant look, and frowned awfully. It was enough—the girl well understood his meaning, and shrinking back abashed, apparently at the idea of what she had been about to do, and then in a faltering tone, and in evident confusion she said :—

"I want not your money; I have told you the truth, and am not to be tempted to swerve from it for paltry lucre." The man, upon this, turned a look expressive of his satisfaction and then addressing himself to Mr. Hartley with a smile of malice and scorn, he said :—

"So you would tempt the offspring of the Gipsy outcast to deny those to whom she is indebted for existence ?—But you are deceived, the Gipsy girl is beyond temptation!"

"You are an incorrigible rascal!" muttered the doctor to himself, as he turned away, much to the satisfaction of Anthony, who had been momentarily expecting to see the Gipsey's wrath arise to violence. He could not but reprehend what his own timid fears made him construe into Mr. Hartley's obstinacy and head-strong folly, in thus braving and provoking the anger of a tribe of wretches whom he considered would no more mind cutting both their throats than they would in purloining the fowls from the hen-roosts of the farmers. He hurried on rapidly after the doctor's heels, every now and then looking back fearfully, to see whether any of the gipsies were following them. When they had got into the main road, which led towards the village, he paused to take breath, and the doctor also stopped.

"Well," said Anthony, "we are out of that scrape, and thank Providence for it, I say.

"And pray," said the doctor, "why should you feel so particularly grateful?"

"Why?" repeated Anthony, "that we have escaped with whole skins, or our lives, to be sure. You seemed to think there was no danger to be apprehended, sir, but I narrowly watched the gestures of the rascal, and am confident that he was within the turning of a straw of inducing his companions to fall upon us, and, no doubt, they would not have done so by halves."

"Why, certainly, Anthony," replied Mr

Hartley, "these wretches are capable of anything, and could they have gained any advantage by so doing, no doubt they would have verified your suspicions. But I confess such an idea did not strike me when I was speaking to the fellow. I felt confident that all he was saying was infamously untrue, and I could scarcely keep my impatience within bounds when they so obstinately persisted in their assertions. The race of Wallingford is predominant in every lineament of that girl's features; about her age, Mr. Wallingford's only sister expired, and the likeness is so striking, that I could scarcely believe but what it was Emmeline Wallingford who stood before me."

"Well, sir," said Anthony, "that may be your idea, but you will excuse me if I differ from your opinion; for my own part, the poor girl is much more like her mother, Ela, as she is called. She has just her eyes, and her cast of features; notwithstanding, I still strongly suspect that it is my master's daughter, for even when uttering such a palpable untruth, she looked too noble and dignified to be the offspring of a low-born hind. Ah! poor girl, after all, she is much to be pitied, I really do not think she spoke from her heart, but from intimidation, and being fearful of punishment, if she did not utter what the ruffian wished her. I watched his looks while she was speaking, and feel confident that my surmises are right."

"On that point, Anthony," observed Doctor Hartley, "I must perfectly agree with you. I am resolved not to be easily thwarted in my designs, which are to get her away from the gang, and probably we may then be able to elicit something about Christabelle; I will immediately seek the aid of Squire Dormington, who is the nearest magistrate; at any rate, I will walk over to him, and advise with him the best way to act."

With these words, Doctor Hartley and Anthony separated, the latter making his way to the Hall, where he related to Jenny all that had taken place, with many embellishments and notes.

"It is very singular, Jenny," continued the old man, "and I scarcely know what to make of Doctor Hartley. I thought he would be all anxiety to inquire about the poor little Christabelle, about whom we are all in such a quandary; but instead of that he scarcely ever mentions her name; all his care seems to be devoted to this girl, this gipsy woman's daughter, who, although I dare say she is our master's child, and ought to be taken care of, has got too old in sin, and has become too abandoned to be reclaimed."

"Hush, Anthony," said the dame, "I am surprised to hear you talk so. You would paint the poor girl blacker than I really believe her to be, and I am ashamed of you. Poor thing, the fault of her sins, if she be indeed sinful, rests not on her head, but upon those of the wretches who have brought her up and sought to corrupt her mind. I am sure I was quite struck with her beauty last night, when with the tears streaming from her large black eyes, she supplicated your forbearance, as you endeavoured to force her into the house. Real guilt can never inhabit her bosom, and no one shall persuade me to it."

"Nonsense, dame," said the old man, angrily, "you are blind half your time, that's certain, or else you would never say that. However, I question much whether you would not have altered your opinion of this girl, had you been present at the interview me and the doctor had with the Gipsies, and heard her insolently declare that her name was Esther Darwin, and that her and me had never before met. I am certain the marks of my fingers must be still imprinted upon her skin by the manner in which I was obliged to hold her last night, and had her arms been bared there would have been sufficient proof of the bold falsehood she was uttering."

"It is very extraordinary that the gipsies should compel her to utter such an untruth; what could be their motive for it?—And then her mother; I wonder where she can have gone! Oh, Anthony, how terribly frightened I was as she stood over me, and threatened to bury the glittering knife in my heart, she did look awful then, and I shall never forget it; there was something so wild and unearthly in her appearance, with her sunburnt features distorted with rage, and her brilliant black eyes starting from their sockets with fury. But, after all, I will not think that she would have been inhuman enough to put her threat into execution. Where do you imagine she has gone to, Anthony?"

"No farther than the place where all the rest of the gang are living, dame," replied the old man; "depend upon it, the story of her elopement is as false as the one her daughter told to us, and was invented only to screen her from the punishment which she thought probably she had incurred by her behaviour last night."

"Dear me," ejaculated Jenny, "I do not think as you do; for I now just recollect that Farmer Fallowfield told our neighbour Goodson, this morning, that he happened to be passing near the direction which the gipsies would take on their way to their retreat from here last night, when he heard the most piteous shrieks in a female voice, also the curses of men, and the howling and barking of a dog or two, but that being unattended he was afraid to interfere, and made his best speed towards home."

"Good God!" exclaimed Anthony, "this does indeed look suspicious, but surely the ruffians cannot have taken away the wretched woman's life!"

"Oh! good gracious!" cried the kind hearted dame, with the utmost horror depicted on her features; "if that dreadful surmise should be true; oh, poor unfortunate woman; I hope it is not so;—no, no, the girl, let her be what she may, can never be so deeply steeped in iniquity as to remain with the murderers of her mother, and keep their guilt hidden from the eye of retributive justice."

Anthony shook his head, by which he meant the dame to understand that he entirely differed with her upon that point:—"I know not what to think," he observed, "I should be very sorry to suspect the girl of such brutal, such unnatural behaviour without a cause; but when I weigh every circumstance in my mind of the effrontery with which she denied her real name and protested that she had never before seen me, I find it very hard to divest my mind of the suspicion which haunts it. Still, now I think on it, once or twice when she caught my eye and the doctor's unwatched by the ruffian who was with her, she appeared to hesitate, and I could perceive that she had a difficulty in restraining her tears: and I do think we might have had a different tale from her lips, if we had been lucky enough to have got hold of her by herself."

"Well, well," said the old woman. "Heaven grant that the mystery may soon be unravelled, and that those who are guilty may be brought to justice."

"There's no doubt that will be," replied Anthony "for Doctor Hartley has now gone over to Squire Dorrington, and he will not return from there, you may depend upon it, without coming to some satisfactory conclusion; Mr. Hartley's the man to sift such an affair to the bottom, and especially where it involves the happiness of so many human beings, he is sure not to rest until the affair be fully elucidated."

Thus ended the conversation between Anthony and his wife, and the former hastened over to his son-in-law's to make him acquainted with all that had occurred. As for the good old dame, her curiosity and suspense was so much excited that she could not rest until she had gone round to all her neighbours, and mentioned the particulars to them, and various were the surmises that were formed upon the mysterious subject, each individual, of course, failing to come to anything like a satisfactory conclusion. They all agreed, however, in thinking that the unfortunate Ela had been murdered, and the old women raised their hands, and shrugged up their shoulders, and prognosticated evils too numerous to mention, if the gipsy tribe were suffered to remain there any longer.

CHAPTER XXI.

"What dismal thoughts these secret haunts create,
Here crime and misery perchance reside.'—ANON.

DOCTOR HARTLEY lost no time in pursuing his way to Squire Dorrington's, and immediately on his reaching home, and apprising his family of his safety after his interview with the gipsies, from which there was always danger apprehended, he proceeded on his way to the house of the magistrate. Unfortunately, upon his arrival at that gentleman's house, he learned that he had gone to London for a few days, and disappointed and vexed, Mr. Hartley returned again towards home. It may be necessary to inform the reader, that the doctor's way led immediately across the Dell, and at the foot of the eminence upon which stood the old Manor House the retreat of the gipsies. The ruins overhung the hill we have so often mentioned, and at the foot in the Dell was an old out-house, which had been for some years unused, and which was supposed to have a secret communication with the Manor House above, although, from a fear of its being the haunt of robbers or hobgoblins, no one had yet had the temerity or curiosity to ascertain the truth or falsehood of such a report.

Just before the doctor reached this place, the heavy clouds which had long overhung the horizon broke, and a violent storm commenced. Mr. Hartley looked around him for a second or so to see if there were any building near where he might stand up until the storm abated, and his eye rested on the old out-house, to which he hastened with all possible speed. The door was closed, but a slight push served to force it open, and the doctor entered. He now remembered the report of the connection it had with the ruins above, and his curiosity was of course immediately excited. He looked around the place which was very dark and damp, but feeling round the walls, and knocking on them with his fist, he noticed one part of the wall, or rather wainscot, sounded more hollow than the rest, and following up his researches, his hand touched upon a piece of brass, which he pressed, and immediately a door flew open, and revealed to him a flight of stone steps, which descended into a cavern beneath, but which was involved in such impenetrable darkness, that he could not discern its construction or dimensions minutely. He was about to descend the steps, but he recollected that he had not the means of prosecuting his inquiries without a light, and there was no knowing the danger he might run into if he were too precipitate. The doctor was, however, very well pleased at this discovery, but wondered that the gipsies had not made themselves acquainted with it, and secured it against intrusion. It occurred to him that Ela

[The Doctor elicits from the Hag a fearful Narrative.]

had not quitted the ruins, as the man had stated, but that they had particular reasons for not wishing to see him; should this place actually communicate with the old Manor House, he thought he might safely gain access to the place without fear of discovery, and probably become acquainted with all their secrets. He determined at all hazards to put his design into execution that evening, and perceiving that the storm had now abated, he left the place, and after closing the outer door as well as he could, to prevent any person from suspecting that it had been interrupted, hastened to his own home.

Sanguine with the hope of the success of his designs, and totally regardless of the risk he would run (for, should he be discovered by the Gipsies, they, no doubt, would wreak a summary vengeance on his head), he partook of a hasty meal, and arming himself with a pistol, and taking with him a lamp, and the utensils for kindling a light, he once more left his house, and proceeded towards the Dell. When he arrived there he looked up, and could perceive the Gipsies fires burning briskly in the ruins, and presently afterwards he could hear the voices of the men, in boisterous mirth, and at intervals the barking of the dogs. Satisfied that they were secure, Doctor Hartley advanced boldly to the building, pushed open the door, and closed it as well as he could after him, piling some old rubbish against the inside so as to make it seem secure. He then kindled a light, and proceeded to open the secret door he had discovered in the afternoon. The doctor held the lamp over his head previous to his descending the steps, and was enabled as well as the rays of the light could penetrate through the deep gloom below, to observe that it was a cavern hewn out of the hill with much care, several feet below the surface of the earth. He also perceived an archway branch off to the left. Closing the secret door after him, the doctor descended the steps, and soon stood in the cavern. It struck very cold and damp, and the atmosphere was noxious and oppressive.

After looking cautiously around him for some seconds, to make sure that he was not observed, and all being buried in profound stillness around, the doctor became more confident, and moved towards the other entrance, which he had observed on the steps, and he found that it led to an inner cavern larger, but similarly contrived to the one he had first entered. No sooner had he emerged into this, than the thick and noisome vapours curled around his light and almost immediately extinguished it. While he was occupied in rekindling the fire in the lamp, the doctor thought he heard a noise, like the closing of a ponderous door, which, at first, somewhat startled him; all, however, afterwards was as still as death, and he concluded that it was the door of the outhouse which had been shook by the wind, Doctor Hartley proceeded across the cavern to another archway which conducted him into a long and gloomy passage, the full extent of which the rays of his lamp could not penetrate and which seemed to be rather the work of Nature than of art. Along this the doctor proceeded, pausing every now and then to listen and look around him, and as he advanced it became lower, until at length he was compelled to stoop to prevent his head from coming in contact with the roof. Having arrived at the end of this place, the doctor was surprised to find a stout door with massive hinges and bolts, the key of which was in the lock. Here he paused and hesitated how to

act; it was now evident the place had been more but recently entered so that, it was than probable that it was known to the present lawless occupiers of the old Manorhouse, and should he be surprised in that situation, his death, no doubt, would be the inevitable consequence.

A few moments reflection served to do away with this impression as erroneous: it was evident that had the gipsies been aware of the secret communication to their retreat, they would have used proper precaution to secure it against intrusion; he therefore unlocked the door, and found himself in a small stone apartment, in which was a pitcher, and a straw mattrass. The doctor shuddered, for it was evident that this wretched cell had been used for some vile purpose, and he began to entertain strong suspicions that the reports raised about the former possessor of the old Manor-house were not altogether without foundation.

There was a door on the opposite side of the dungeon (for such it undoubtedly was), which was standing open, and the doctor perceived beyond it, a narrow flight of ruinous steps that appeared to lead to a kind of corridor above. These, Mr. Hartley ascended with some difficulty. At the top of this staircase another door of oak presented itself, and which opened with a spring, which was very ingeniously concealed on the other side, and might have passed for a long time undiscovered, without a person was well acquainted with the secret. It opened upon an apartment completely delapidated, and to the walls of which the cobwebs hung in all directions. The casement was broken all to pieces, and was placed very high in the wall, but the doctor getting upon a heap of rubbish was enabled to peep out, and perceiving himself upon the summit of the hill, he knew that he had entered the ruins of the old Manor house. The discovery afforded him much satisfaction, for he reflected that in the apprehension of the gipsies, who were all desperate villains, there would sure to have been some blood spilt, but now they might be surprised and secured, before they had the power to offer any resistance. He was advancing towards a door which he perceived in the right hand corner, when a confused murmuring of voices arrested his steps, and he put down his lamp behind the door, for fear that its rays might betray him. He then advanced cautiously to the door and listened, but although he could hear a confused sound of many voices, he could not distinguish any particular tones, or make out a sentence that was uttered. The persons speaking, he had no doubt, were the gipsies, but as it would be complete madness for him to proceed further, which would be the means of immediately betraying himself into their power, and having succeeded in finding the way to secure the tribe without any danger, he retraced his steps to the out-house again.

He had scarcely gained the door of the out-house when the storm again commenced, and he was about to re-enter, when by the light-ning's flash he perceived a shadow on the ground, and looking up, to his surprise, he beheld the tall figure of a man standing exactly opposite the door-way, and gazing with an eye of suspicion upon him.

"Who are you, and what do you here?" demanded the fellow, in a gruff and authoritive tone, which was by no means prepossessing.

"I cannot conceive what business that is of yours, my man," answered the doctor, firmly; "by what right do you put the ques-tion?"

"It's enough for you to answer my in-quiry," said the man, "what right I have to put it rests in my own pleasure; you'd better hasten from hence as soon as possible."

"You are an insolent fellow," replied the doctor.

"You had better be more choice of your words, I can tell you, master," said the ruffian, who brandished a thick ash cudgel, "I am one who will not be trifled with; so you had better depart while you are safe; I give you timely warning, and I would not have you be long in deciding."

"Think not to intimidate me by your threats, fellow," returned the doctor, firmly, for he possessed a mind not easily to be daunted by menaces; "I have sought a shelter here from the fury of the storm, and until it has abated it is my determination not to quit it."

"You had better change your mind, I again warn you," observed the man; "my patience is nearly exhausted."

"That matters very little to me," replied the doctor, drily, "perhaps a dusted jacket would be quite as well as a wet one, so I'll e'en—but eh!" he continued, as a flash of lightning darted vividly across the man's face, and shewed him more distinctly his features; "if I mistake not, your name is Mark, and you are the husband of Ela——"

"Ah!" ejaculated the man, starting, and immediately thrusting the doctor violently forth, he rushed into the building and closed the door after him.

"Rascal!" exclaimed the infuriated doctor taking the pistol he had brought with him from his pocket, "you shall pay dear for this out-rage." But recollecting the danger he stood in if the gang should be alarmed, he turned away and hurried across the Dell towards the turn-pike-road.

As Doctor Hartley pursued his way towards home, he revolved in his mind various schemes of revenge against the man who had so grossly insulted him, all of which he rejected as soon as he had formed them; nor were Ela and her offspring absent from his thoughts; he could not help the more and more deeply regretting the life of degradation to which they were exposed, and he was still more anxious to rescue them from it, and place them among a respectable order of the community. Before, however, he could devote his attention to this, he must endeavour to find out whether there were absolutely any just reasons to suppose that the little Christabelle instead of being destroyed in the conflagration of the nursery, had been abducted by the tribe for some sinister purposes or the other. This was daily becoming a mere currant report, and although the good doctor had his doubts of there being any just ground for such a sup-position, he resolved to use every means, and to exert all his energies to arrive at the truth; for that purpose, and the better to promote the success of his plans, he decided upon not interfering further at present with the Gipsies at the Manor-house, although the outrage committed by Mark had at first tempted him to seek an immediate and ample re-venge.

Thus ruminating, Dr. Hartley took no notice of the battle of the elements, for the storm again raged with all its former fury, but walked on towards his house. He had not, however, proceeded any great distance on his way, when he was aroused by hearing a num-ber of persons speaking together, and looking up, he perceived that it proceeded from a mob of persons assembled at the door of "The Old Oak," tavern, who were evidently discussing something of importance. Hastening up to them, he saw that the party was composed of several of the village rustics, who, as soon as they beheld him, seemed to express much satis-faction at his presence.

"What is the meaning of this, Humphrey," inquired the doctor addressing one of the men, as he hastened into the parlour, where there was a raising fire, and which seemed to invite him to dry his clothes, which were exceedingly wet from the pelting of the storm.

"Why, sir," replied the man, "you see Giles has been over here, and informed us that he had seen a man and woman whom he was certain was the one who had caused so much disturbance in this place some years back, and who your honor is so anxious to secure, enter the old out-house underneath the hill, and so, as we knew that you would be very well pleased to see her apprehended, Giles and Far-mer Fallowfield, with a lot of his labourers have not long since started by the back road to see if they cannot surprise them, and bring them here."

"That was very imprudent," said the doc-tor without first consulting me on the subject;

for the utmost caution is necessary, the Gipsies being very powerful and desperate, or the very object we have in view may be thwarted. Should they fail in their attempt, the tribe will, doubtless, not afford us another opportunity in a hurry, as they will, of course, leave the spot immediately."

"They will act with the greatest precaution, I have no doubt, sir," returned Humphrey; "for that reason they have gone the back road, and should they succeed in surprising this woman and the man alone, they may bear them away before the rest of the gang are aware of the circumstance."

"It must take its chance," said the doctor, "though I have very little hopes of the success of the stratagem. I wish I had been with them; at any rate I will wait here till their return and know the result of it."

The worthy doctor now ensconced himself in the chimney corner, and impatiently awaited the return of the party; but he was convinced from what he had seen himself that they would be unsuccessful, and he was fearful that should the gipsies be alarmed, it might be attended with the most serious consequences, as they would not fail to wreak their vengeance on the heads of all those who had made themselves parties to the plot.

Half an 'hour had elapsed in this manner, and Mr. Hartley, whose patience was entirely exhausted, had just come to the determination of going with the remainder of the persons assembled at the tavern to the Dell, and see if the others were in any danger, when one of the men returned to the house and apprised him that his friends were approaching, and that they had the woman in their power,

"I hope you have treated her gently," said the doctor, delighted at the unexpected result which had attended the expedition.

"As for that that, sir," answered the man, "we have behaved to her as well as we could under the circumstances; but she is such an arrant jade that we had no easy task with her, I can assure you, for she resisted like a man. We met them a short distance before we came to the out-house, which was lucky for us, for before the gang could be alarmed, we were far enough away."

"And what became of the man, who you say you met with her?" inquired Mr. Hartley.

"Oh, he adopted the wisest plan," said the other, "seeing the odds he had to contend with, he no sooner beheld us approach than away he scampered as fast as his legs could carry him, and so we e'en suffered him to escape, for we thought as we had got the woman that was the principal part of the business. We had no very easy matter with her, for she is a regular tartar, and can use her tongue, too, I can tell you; I have seldom heard a fouler one. But here they come."

The noise of the men was heard in the passage, and directly afterwards they entered the room in which the doctor was awaiting them, but he started back with vexation and disappointment, when he beheld instead of Ela, the disgusting visage of a woman, whose dark features were distorted with rage, and whose eyes flashed with malevolence and revenge.

"Unhand me, dogs, you know not the lioness you would hold in you lair!' shrieked the old sybil, "off, off, ye dastard hinds, and know that my curses bitter and sure shall light upon thee and thine for this,"

"The devil!" exclaimed the doctor, "why do you bring this old hag hither? I did not want her."

"You hear that, fools," cried the gipsy, as she laughed contemptuously on her captors, "you see you have laboured hard to no purpose; but release me, and let me go about my business."

"Giles," observed Mr. Hartley, "you have acted very stupidly in this affair, and should not have taken upon yourself to do so, without in the first place consulting me; you know very well that this shrivelled old wretch was not the woman I wished to secure."

"It is true, sir," said the abashed rustic, "I know'd this wur not un, but then yer see, I acted all for th' best, and I thought you would be very well pleased wi' me for it; besides, I thought this old woman might be able to throw some light upon the business, which I know you are anxious to learn."

"Well, well," returned Mr. Hartley, "I commend your zeal, and that of your companions, although it has not this time been used in a manner that I exactly wished. But is this the woman you observed enter the old out-house this morning with the man?"

"No, I am sure it wur that she devil and no other that alarmed us so at the Hall, the other night;" replied Giles, "and it wur that which tempted me to undertake this job. So I hastened first to my father-in-law's, who wur not at home, an' then I went to your house, sir, with the intention of asking your advice upon the matter, but you wur also out; so as I knew how eager you wur to get th' woman in your power, I consulted wi' Farmer Fallowfield, th' consequence o' which was, we resolved upon doing what we have done, thinking we should agreeably surprise you when you came to hear of it."

"And a pretty business you have made of it you clown," said the old woman, scowling upon him; "but, I suppose, now you have satisfied yourselves by half shaking my bones out of my skin, I may be permitted to depart."

"Hold!" cried the doctor, arresting her as she was skulking off, "I do not mean to part with you quite so easily, woman. I have some questions to put to you, which you will do well to answer explicity. The fellow who was with you, his name was Mark, was it not?"

"I believe they call him so," replied the woman, her countenance expressive of the utmost spite and malice.

"Do not seek to evade my question," said the doctor; "you do know his name?"

"And what boots his name to thee?" demanded the old hag, with a bitter scowl. "Our people are not used to babble if those of your class are."

"This language will do you no good," said Mr. Hartley, for I am resolved to know the particulars before you are suffered to go about your business again. This man has been lurking about the out-house all the morning, and more than three hours since he assaulted me, and refused me shelter in it. What were his motives for such conduct?"

"Why put the question to me?" said the old hag, scornfully. "How should I know his motives, and if I did, it is not among the gipsy tribe that you must seek for tattlers."

"Odds dickens!" remarked one of the rustics, "but you give us a pretty good speciment o' your tattling on the road. You did not forget to use your tongue then, and I never heard such a one before in all my born days, though I have had to do wi' a good many vixens in my time."

"And ye merited all ye got from me, dolts and savages as ye are," said the woman. "Call yourselves men, and use a poor old woman, who has seen seventy-five years over her head, in the cruel manner ye did! A murrain light upon you all, say I, and the maledictions of her who now speaks to ye, never yet failed to fall upon the heads of those who had incurred her wrath."

"I thought you told me that the woman was treated with proper forbearance," said the doctor angrily, addressing the man who had preceded his companions to the tavern to inform the landlord and the others of their approach: "even abandoned as she is, her age and sex ought to have secured her from such treatment. Giles, what was the reason of this?"

"Why, sir," returned Giles, "th' fact is we did try to treat her as gently as we could, but it was all no use. She was a perfect devil, and was not contented wi' abusing us in the most *shockingest* language as ever I heard, but she fought just like a man, and was stronger than a good many men too."

"The tigress lays not tamely down and suffers the huntsman to take her," answered the woman, looking with increased malice upon the surrounding group.

"Have you seen this woman before?" asked the doctor, of the village constable, who, of course had been one of the party in the capture.

"Why, haply I mought, sir," answered the official, scratching a very sandy head of hair, and looking more closely into the woman's face; "Ye'es I am almost sartin sure as I have; let me see, whoy danged if I doant think as how she be th' vary old 'ooman as fought so hard, when his honor Squire Wallingford and us had th' tustle wi' th' gang. Ye'es now I'm sartin sure it be her, and I recollect they called her Zelta. There's an old wretch for you; why burning too be good for her by half."

"Has the constable spoken the truth, woman?" demanded Dr. Hartley, sternly. "Is Zilta your name?"

"It is not," answered the gipsy; "that fellow has spoken false. My name is Naormy. I am willing to answer your honour's questions, when they are reasonable, but I will not bandy words with these senseless curs."

"This is not the first time you have been in this neighbourhood," observed the doctor, fixing his eyes with stern scrutiny upon her. "If my recollection fail me not, some few years since I have seen you with the rest of your tribe that used to visit Rosemary Dell."

"It is even as you say, master," said the gipsy, "but many years have passed away since that time. It is more than twelve summers since."

"I will not believe you, woman," cried the doctor; "you are seeking to deceive me, and I warn you to beware. You must answer me explicitly, and tell me precisely where you were, and what you were doing at the time me and the constable have spoken."

"And does your honour think it a reasonable question to ask a poor old woman, whose memory is wrecked, and whose home is the wide world, where or what she was doing at so distant a period as *six years* since?" inquired the hag, hurridly, and before she had time to recollect herself.

"Ah! mark that all of you," ejaculated the doctor, eagerly; "you heard what she said not a minute since, that it was twelve years since she had been before in the neighbourhood, and now she says it is *six years*, the very period to which me and the constable alluded. This is sufficient; you have said enough to convince me that you was not only present on that fatal occasion, but that you participated in the savage transaction which threw two hapless parents into such a state of misery, that nothing can again rescue them; now, mark me, and be assured that I am determined—unless you instantly and fully disclose every particular, and how the child was disposed of—yes! it is plain enough, your looks betray you"—added the doctor with much agitation, for the old woman started convulsively, and turned as pale as death when he mentioned the child; "you know all about it, and little did you or your infamous associates imagine that those whom you had so cruelly injured, had elicited the manner in which you gratified your demoniacal vengeance; but woman, remember,

'God is just,
And when the measure of man's crimes is full,
Will bare His red right arm,
And launch His lightnings!'

But your safety depends entirely upon your speaking all you know, and in being the means of discovering where the child is to be found!"

"Ha! ha! ha!" scornfully laughed the old beldame, "I thought you had discovered all, with the aid of that God you mention; but yet it seems, after all, the work is but half performed. But I do not know what you would have me say; you hint 'tis true that a child has been lost, and of course the poor wandering Gipsy tribe are always blamed for such misdeeds as that: But what want we with the brats of your people? Think you that the Gipsy tent is not as likely a place for children to be borne in, as the costly chambers of your women? The poor old wanderer before you has seen her children's children thrive into goodly trees, and——"

"Psha!" interrupted the doctor, "enough of this nonsense; it is not to the purpose, and you seek by every means to evade the questions I put to you; but your design will fail, and can only have the effect of drawing upon you a punishment, which, by candour and truth, you have the means of avoiding. Answer me, woman, will you tell me where is the child of Mr. Wallingford, and where it is now concealed?"

"I know nothing about it," said the woman fiercely, "and cannot therefore answer your interrogatories. Why, then, do you persist in asking me what you will not believe, unless I speak falsely. I will swear—but am I mad? Who will believe the Gipsy's oath?"

"Dare you swear, woman," said the doctor passionately, "dare you, have you the effrontery to swear that your real name is not Zelta, and that you were not in this neighbourhood on that fatal night when the nursery of Wallingford Hall was lighted by the brand of an incendiary, and its owner's infant daughter taken away? Ah! I see you hesitate; but if you pause to answer me that question, perhaps you will more readily reply to another which I shall put to you."

"Name it," said the woman eagerly; "I am ready to satisfy your honour, as far as I have the power, but——"

"No matter," interrupted Doctor Hartley, "answer this question fairly, and I will instantly cause you to be set at liberty; at least as soon as all doubts are removed from my mind, and moreover than that, you shall be handsomely rewarded for your trouble, and the inconvenience you have been put to in being brought hither. Inform me, is not Ela with the tribe at the Old Manor House, and is not the story that they told me of her having eloped, all a falsehood? Be the means of bringing her to me, and you shall be immediately set at liberty."

The old beldame laughed demonically, and shaking her head, said—"You speak in riddles, that even my art cannot solve; in truth I know not what you mean."

"Infamous old wretch," passionately exclaimed Mr. Hartley, "this is insupportable, and I will no longer endure it. I will see what effect prison, and the power of a magistrate will have upon your stubbornness, who upon the evidence that can be brought forward against you, must commit you for trial. I am better acquainted with the place where your diabolical companions have taken up their residence than you may perhaps imagine, and before daylight to-morrow morning I trust I shall have them all in prison with you. Knobbs, secure this woman in the cage to-night, and in the morning I will be with you to attend upon Squire Dorrington."

Knobbs, who was particularly zealous in his profession, and moreover had a very strong aversion to the Gipsies, from whom he had received many a cracked crown and bruised shoulders wanted not to be told twice to execute this order, and prepared to lay violent hands upon the woman for the purpose of taking her into custody.

"Use her gently, Knobbs," ordered Mr. Hartley, seeing that the constable was proceeding to handle her more roughly than was consistent with his, the doctor's, notions of humanity; "I would not see her ill-treated depraved and guilty as she doubtless is."

"Oh, very well, your honour," observed Knobbs, in a tone of evident dissatisfaction "of course I shall do as you desire, though for my own part I must say that I think it is no much matter how you sarve such an old wretch as this, and if I had my will I should care no more about hanging her up to the sign-post outside, than I should of eating my supper."

The old woman scowled upon him with a look of the most ineffable contempt, although she was evidently much impressed by the firmness and solemnity with which the doctor had addressed her.

"Ah! you may look as black as you like my lady," resumed the constable, "I don't care a rush what you think me; I don't mind your curses and your spells, and all the rest of them things that belong to your gang. The cage will cool your courage I'll be bound, and if any of these lads don't mind keeping my company I will watch you myself all the night. Who'll agree to what I say?"

"Take care of her, Knobbs," said Mr. Hartley, as he rose to return home; "but do not use her more harshly than is absolutely necessary."

"Very well, sir," replied the constable, and the doctor left the tavern.

They had not to go far before they came to the cage, it was next door to the tavern, and Knobbs having had a fire kindled in it for his own comfort and that of one of the men who had, upon the promise of a good supply of ale, agreed to keep him company, they walked into it, giving the old woman a seat in one corner, where she became very dejected, and did not offer to reply to any of the observations made by the officious Mr. Knobbs. The idea of going to gaol had completely taken her courage away, and folding her arms sullenly, she seemed to be lost in rumination.

CHAPTER XXI

"I will admit my guilt;
I am a wretch unfit to live,
But oh, how unfit to die !"—ANON.

DOCTOR HARTLEY having changed his clothes, upon reflecting more maturely upon what had occurred, could not refrain from paying the old Gipsy woman a second visit before he retired to rest, trusting that he might by persuasion elicit from her such information of the mysterious affair as he was most particularly anxious to learn.

During his absence she had never once changed her position, nor had she uttered a word, and when he entered her temporary place of confinement, he found the two men, in whose custody she was, smoking their pipes, and quaffing ale out of a quart pot, as jovially as if they were attending a merry-making.

The entrance of Dr. Hartley aroused her, and she looked at him steadfastly for a moment, but she almost immediately removed her glance, dropped her head upon her chest, and relapsed into her former sullen position and demeanour.

"Knobbs," said the doctor, as he was apparently again preparing to leave the room, "let your prisoner have a good supper, and such other moderate refreshment as she may require."

"Very well, sir," replied Knobbs, if it is your pleasure it shall be so."

"Never mind, it is my pleasure, and that is enough," interrupted the doctor reprovingly. He was then about to retire, when the Gipsy woman again fixed her eyes upon him and said,—

"A moment, your honour, I would ask you a question."

Doctor Hartley turned eagerly back, and encouraged the old woman by a look to proceed.

"Did I understand you right," she said slowly, "that the child's father of whom you speak was abroad ? "

"You did," answered the doctor, "I am informed that he is now at Brussels; but if you speak the truth, I know that he will freely not only forgive you for the share you have had in the villanous transaction, but will give you something that will enable you to live in peace for the rest of your existence."

"I understand not your definition of the word peace," answered the woman scornfully; "but I have too long known the happiness of freedom, to brook confinement in my old days."

"Do as I require," returned the doctor, "and I will not detain you another moment."

The old woman paused a minute or two, and seemed to ruminate, then, as if soliloquising with herself, she muttered, "Why should I hesitate to act the traitress to her, who did so by me ? It was not my fault that any harm came to the poor child; and if she steeped her hands in its blood, that blood be upon her own head !"

"Horror !" exclaimed the terrified doctor, "what awful deed do your words imply ? Keep me not in suspense; I—"

"In the presence of those busy clowns ?" said the old woman, pointing contemptuously at the constable and his companion; "no, no; what I reveal, must be only to you."

"We will go to a private tavern next door," said the worthy doctor; "and you, Knobbs, and your friend can accompany me to the house, to be ready if I should need your further assistance."

The indefatigable Mr. Knobbs did not much approve of the conduct of the doctor, and he doubted much whether he should not be guilty of a dereliction of duty, or, at any rate, imprudence, by suffering a person who had once been given into his custody, out of his sight, but a little *palmacetti* ointment, administered by the doctor, served very suddenly to cure him of his scruples of conscience; and taking his place by the side of the old woman, to be sure that she did not escape, he proceeded to obey Mr. Hartley, who being shown into a private room with the Gipsy, the others retired and left them to themselves.

"Be quick, woman," said the doctor, when they were alone, "and keep me not in a state of anxiety that your recent insinuations have rendered horribly insupportable. What have you to tell me ? "

"A tale that will doubtless interest you deeply," answered the woman; "you suspect that I was implicated in the occurrence of which you have spoken; in those conjectures you were perfectly right. 'Tis true that the infant was placed in my care, but of the manner in which the incendiarism was performed,

I cannot say anything, no more than that our men were the designers and perpetrators of it. I repeat, to me the child was entrusted, and having had many a goodly child of my own, it was secure from harm at my hands. It was, in truth, a lovely youngster, and might have won the affection of the hardest heart. There are hearts that can feel, your honour, in a Gipsy camp, much as your people despise the poor outcasts."

"Well, well, go on, my good woman," said the doctor impatiently.

"But the poor child," continued the woman; "was not so fortunate as to gain the attachment of all our people; no; one, a woman too, amongst us, and with a brat of her own, looked on it with hatred when she was informed who it was, for she was not with us at the time the event took place, though for what reason I know not; but she was absent on some secret mission, accompanied only by her own girl."

"Tell me," interrupted Doctor Hartley, hastily, "the woman to whom you allude was called Ela,—am I not right?"

"You are," replied the Gipsy, "Ela was her name, and I judge by that, that she was known to you, and perhaps you was acquainted———"

"No matter, no matter," said the doctor, "pray proceed."

"Be it so," resumed the old woman; "for two months I alone had the care of that child—I hid it for days, in the deepest of the forest glens—and only did I venture from my secret haunts, when darkness veiled the earth—no mother could have behaved to her with more attention than I did to that unconscious babe—to elude the vigilance of those who were scouring the country in all directions in pursuit of us, I travelled many and many a weary mile, with her concealed under my cloak at my back, and at night, when tired with walking, I sought repose in some lonely cavern or copse, with the child nestled in my bosom.—Many a narrow escape have we had of being discovered, and the spies of the wretched parents have been within a few paces only of our retreat—yet did the thoughts of injuring her, never once enter my mind.—At length your friends began to despair, and the chase abated. I then returned to the tribe, and found that Ela had rejoined them.—Methinks I even now behold her fiendish look when she beheld that child, and learnt its history;—she snatched it from me furiously, and looking upon it as though she could at that moment have twisted her fingers in its little throat, she exclaimed,—

"Curses light upon those who did not leave the brat to perish in the burning pile!"

"Good God!" cried the horrified doctor, "can such an execrable fiend exist?"

"Hear me out," continued the Gipsy; "I

upbraided her for her monstrous cruelty, and she affected to regret what she had said, and even pretended to weep; but the detestible monster was nurturing poison at her heart all the time. When we had been together for about a fortnight, fortune frowning upon us, we agreed that we would divide ourselves into small parties, and travel in different directions, in hopes that we might meet with better luck in that way. One of my boys and two women accompanied me. My son and one of the women pretended to be the parents of the child, and she was instructed to call me " granny" which the poor babe did, unconscious that she was not.—Two weary day's walk we had, and tired enough we were. On the evening of the second day, completely exhausted, and in truth rather overcome with the strength of the different potations I had taken, I was forced to lay myself down, with my little charge locked in my arms, for she began to know well then, and used to cry when any one offered to take her from me. I would fain cease here for it is a sad story and,———"

"No, no, for pity's sake go on," said the doctor with breathless impatience.

"About the hour of midnight," proceeded the woman, " the screams of the poor child awoke me, but the fumes of the liquor I had drunk had not yet evaporated, and I was stupified and confused; but yet, I have a horrible recollection of some one tearing the poor babe forcibly from my grasp, and when I came to my senses, I looked around me, but I was alone, the child was gone, and by my side was a pool of blood, which convinced me too fatally of the sanguinary crime which had been perpetrated."

"Good God!" exclaimed the distracted Mr. Hartley, " to what a dreadful tale have I been listening. But tell me, woman, why should your suspicions of the guilt of the foul crime rest upon Ela, when you say that she was not one of your party?"

"I'll tell you," replied the gipsy, " whom could I so well suspect as her who had evinced such hatred towards the poor child; and besides, I heard on rejoining our people at the place we had appointed to meet together again, that at a short time subsequent to the departure of my party from the tent, Ela had absconded no one knew whither, and when I returned to our people I found her among them, she having reached there only a short time before me, and accounted for her sudden flight from them by saying that she wished to put an end to the continual quarrels that were taking place between my sons Mark and Rupert, who were struck with her charms, and between whom we often thought murder would ensue."

"The wretches!" ejaculated the horror-struck doctor, " but continue your dreadful recital."

"After the lapse of several weeks, a fair

in another part of the country called us away, and thither Ela also accompanied us. In secret she and I had several quarrels, for I was afraid of falling out with her openly, dreading the fury of Mark and Rupert, who I felt certain would not have cared about murdering me, had they seen me offend the object of their fancy. More than once, too,

I ventured to hint to her my suspicions that she had not assigned the real motives for her so abruptly leaving the camp."

"And what was her reply?" hastily enquired Doctor Hartley, "surely she did not own to the bloody crime."

The old woman hesitated upon the question, and seemed to ruminate within herself the propriety of frankly or evasively answering it, but at length she said :—" She sneered when I hinted my dark suspicions, and breathed a heavy malediction upon the head of the murderer. 'Fool!' she cried, 'you know not what you say; those who did that deed deserve blessings instead of curses, in having rescued that child from a life of care and suffering. Oh, had I but have let out the heart's blood of my own off-spring when an infant, from what shame, crime, and trouble should I have released her; and oh, what bitter suffering should I have saved my-self!"

"Miserable being," ejaculated Mr. Hartley, while his mind was imbued with the most harrowing feelings of pity and disgust : "and this poor wretch is now married to your son, Mark? Come, come, do not seek to impose on me, for in the event of that, as I hope to be saved, I will immediately deliver you up to the hands of justice, where the truth will be wrung from you, and you may meet with severe pu-nishment."

" I am not attempting to deceive you," said the old Gipsy, earnestly; "I have no motive in doing so, since my liberty depends upon my speaking the truth. My son Mark, then, I assure you, is not the husband of Ela, on the contrary, he detests her as much as he before worshipped her. I have before told you that him and his brother Rupert often quarrelled about her, and once or twice bloodshed was the consequence. Ela, too, looked on at this unnatural strife, and she appeared to exult in it; yes, that woman has the spirit of a demon, and glories in witnessing the miseries of her fellow-creatures ; she, however, looked with an eye of scorn upon their battle, and only mocked their vows of passion; the boys, therefore, grew tired of seeking her favours, especially as she is not one of our blood, although she bears our name. So Rupert quitted our tribe and joined another party at Worcester, where he took unto him a wife; but this failed, as Mark had expected to make her look upon him with any greater favour, and her scorn went as far as insolence, and the most bitter and degrading revilings; the hot blood of my boy could not brook this treat-ment, and——"

" And where is Ela, where can she at the present time be found? That is what I particularly wish to know," demanded Doctor Hartley.

"I know not," replied Zelta, "if I did I would not hesitate to disclose her retreat, why should I? I owe her no favour."

"Nay, nay, no prevarication," observed the doctor, "remember my promises, which I am not bound to fulfil unless you adhere to the truth."

"I have adhered to the truth, as I hope to live!" returned the old woman. "At this moment, I know not where she is to be found."

"That is merely a subterfuge," said her interrogator, "you are well aware that but the night before last she was with your people; and, you also know, that she was seen but this morning to enter the old out-house with your son Mark, who afterwards assaulted me in a most ruffianly manner, at the entrance of the same place."

"You did not see her?" said the old Gipsy, looking earnestly at him.

"True," said the doctor; "but I am almost certain I heard her but to-day."

"Where?"

"In the room adjoining the one where your people usually assemble, in the old manor-house," replied Dr. Hartley.

"Ah!" exclaimed the old woman, with an inquiring look, "how gained you access there? You did not pass through——"

"No matter," returned the doctor; "this is rambling from the point. By your words, I can perceive that you are aware that she is at present with the gang ; at least, that she is secreted somewhere in the neighbourhood, and you would deceive me."

"By the planet which presided at my birth!" ejaculated the old woman, with energy, "since yesterday my eyes have not beheld her. Is it likely I should seek to conceal the woman I have so much reason to abhor? And I will tell your honour, that she belongs not to our people, although disgrace and infamy have led her to seek the protection and shelter of our camp. In the blood of old Zelta is all the spirit and fire of the real Egyptian, but she is a wretch beneath contempt, and sorry has been our lot ever since we admitted her amongst us."

"And at what place, and in which way was she introduced to your tents?" inquired Mr. Hartley, who could not help feeling a deep curiosity to hear the particulars of the Gipsy's narrative, and thought that by such questions as these he might gradually wean her to speak the truth.

"It is some years ago," said the woman, "and my recollection fails me now. I cannot say where it was that she first came amongst us; but it was in the evening, when the autumn moon was shining brightly upon our tents, and we were all gaily carousing, for Fortune had smiled upon us for weeks before, and we always enjoy her while we can be blest with her friendship. In the midst of our revelry, and when our jovial supper was smoking cheerfully before us, we were surprised at the sudden appearance of a man, whose looks were careworn, haggard, and fatigued, and who im-plored our aid for his wife, and only sister and her child, who were lying completely exhausted not far from our encampment, famishing for want, and dying with exhaustion."

"And did you heed his tale?" asked the doctor.

"Did we heed it!" repeated Zelta; "the Gipsy turns not a deaf ear upon the tale of misery and distress. Scorned as we are by your people, more gentle hearts throb beneath our dark skins than beat in half the bosoms of your fairest dames. The wretched appearance of the man immediately excited our warmest sympathy, and orders were given to some of our men to go and conduct the females to our tents. In the meantime, we compelled the man to sit down, and eat heartily of our meal. The poor wretch needed no second invitation, for he seemed almost starving, and eat so ravenously, that we thought he would have choked himself. But if our pity and compassion had been excited by the appearance of the man, how much more were our feelings aroused when the women and the child were carried into the tent? They had all the ghastly and unearthly appearance of the inmates of a charnel-house, instead of human beings; and their eyes glared with the intensity of their hunger, when they beheld the viands spread before them."

"We put no questions to them as to their early history, and what had been the cause of their being brought to such a state of destitution and misery; for our tribe need no reasons for what they offer in charity. Two days afterwards, when they had recovered their strength, and were about to leave our tent, our chief, who pitied their condition, asked them if they should like to join us; to which they immediately assented with avidity, and the proper oaths having been administered to them, they were received amongst us; fatal was the hour, for sorrow and trouble followed in their train."

"Indeed, how so?" inquired Doctor Hartley, who felt a great interest in the old Gipsy woman's story, and, moreover, remarked the serious tone in which she last spoke.

"Ah! bitter, bitter was the woe they brought upon us," replied the old Gipsy, with an expression of deep emotion, which struck the doctor most forcibly; "Zelta's curse be upon them, and great cause has she to heap her malisons upon their heads. You see, your honour, Milford, the man (which was the name we knew him by only), was a wretch whose thirst was blood, and who would willingly steep his hands in it, for the purpose of plunder. A few months before we admitted him and the women among our tribe, he had committed murder. The victim of his brutality was a kind-hearted farmer, whom he had met on his travels, and who was returning from London, where he had been to receive an account. This he thoughtlessly disclo-

sed to the villain Milford, whom he had treated on the road, and behaved with all the kindness of a brother towards him. How did the monster reward him? In the middle of the night he arose, and plunged his knife in his heart, and robbed him of all his money. He made his escape, but was hunted about from one place to the other, and sought refuge in all kinds of places, to escape falling into the hands of the officers that were sent in every direction in pursuit of him. Shortly after this, and when every penny of his ill-got money was gone, we admitted him into our tribe. The blood-thirsty villain could not rest even when he had no occasion to wet his knife in the blood of his fellow men; once more he sought to become an assassin, but he was thwarted, and was apprehended. When it was discovered that he was one of our people, although many miles at that time separated us, we had a narrow escape of all dying the death of a dog: he was condemned for the first murder, and died on the gibbet, and one of my boys, my youngest born, was sentenced to a life of perpetual slavery, because he happened to be near the spot at the time, but had nothing whatever to do with the crime."

"Can it be possible that this wretch, this Milford, was the brother of Ela?" said Mr. Hartley.

"The women said he was," answered Zelta, "but I believe them not; I know he was not; but they all merited the same, for, by my natal star, I feel confident that they all equally anticipated in the bloody crime."

"Oh, no, no," said the doctor, shuddering with horror at the dreadful suspicion, "it is impossible they could have been such fiends, and wear the female form. But were they suspected?"

"Ay they were," answered Zelta, "and arraigned at the bar too, for the crime; but Ela's silvery tongue, and her deceptive looks, served them; the jury were deceived, and they quitted the presence of the earthly judge unscathed."

"Merciful father!" ejaculated the horror-struck doctor, clasping his hands. "Ela, with the beauty of an angel, and a mind so accomplished, for the sake of paltry lucre steep her hands in the blood of a man who had never offended her; oh, I cannot believe it!"

"And why impossible?" demanded the Gipsy; "does an angel's heart always inhabit an angel's form? Are they all saints who wear the garb of sanctity? Is hypocrisy always unmasked, and open as the broad light of day? Do mankind so glory in depravity, that they endeavour to make their fellow men think them villains? You talk of paltry lucre, and yet you worship the gold you affect to despise. What think you of those who have it not? Do you not scorn and trample to the earth the poor wretch who has not the bright coin you now pretend to disparage? Wherefore then should you marvel that the despised victim of poverty should strive by every scheme to obtain that which may place him at once on a level, in the estimation of the world, with those who have oppressed and scorned him? It is the paltry lucre you speak of which makes the worldly gentlemen. What am I, a miserable old outcast, whom you would deem it but an act of justice to punish, as though I were some poisonous reptile, and to whom you would refuse the shelter of your humblest shed, for fear I should contaminate it; but let me be rich, let me possess the 'paltry lucre,' and my age and ugliness would be changed into youth and beauty; my smiles and favours would be sought after, and all who came before me would be clothed in the flattering garb of smiles and adulation;—doctors would fly to my relief upon the slightest appearance of indisposition; and if death ensued, tears in abundance would be shed, monuments erected to my memory, o'er which my virtues would be lauded, and your parsons would pray for my soul; all this would be the result of my having the paltry lucre, you have pretended to despise, to distribute for their use."

Doctor Harley was astonished at the strength of the woman's reasoning, and scarcely knew how to answer her.

"Your argument," he said at length, "I admit, is correct in some points of view, but surely you would not condemn all of our people, as you call them?"

"Oh, no," said Zelta, fervently, "not all, not all! I beg your pardon, sir, for the boldness of my speech, but I do not indeed condemn all of your people; there are sunny spots at times amidst the greatest gloom. To your honour I owe a debt of gratitude, for you have been kind to one in whose veins the blood of the poor old Gipsy woman flows, and I shall— I will ever remember it."

Dr. Hartley was surprised at the latter part of the old woman's speech, an he was anxious to know her meaning, but her looks and manner prevented him. It was no easy matter for an individual who had passed nearly the whole of his days in acts of philanthropy and benevolence, not excepting any particular class of unfortunates, to recall to his memory one particular case; but the energetic manner in which the Gipsy expressed her thanks, inspired him with a greater feeling of sympathy than he had at first felt towards her.

"But you have strayed from the subject, my poor woman," he said, in a softened tone, "upon which I wish to question you. The retreat of Ela, will you still deny that you know where it is?"

"Have I not sworn?" replied Zelta.

"And will you also swear as solemnly," hastily rejoined the doctor, "that if you are set at liberty, you will try all that is in your power to find her out, and make me acquainted with it?"

"Never!" exclaimed the old woman, relapsing in a moment into all her former fierceness, and seeming to acquire fresh energy from the question. "Think you that Zelta the Gipsy, who has been among the tribe ever since she came from her mother's womb, will now become a traitoress to one of her own people, and ensnare her into the hands of her enemies? No! I would rather mount the scaffold, old as I am, to-morrow, or dangle on the first tree we come to, than I would take the oath you ask me. Even were I so inclined, I could not do it and live; for we swear to be true to each other, and the gipsy's knife would be the reward of my treachery. I have already done more than I ought, in revealing what I have to you of Ela. I depended upon your secrecy, if you despise that, my fate is certain."

It is not easy to describe the chagrin and agitation of the good doctor when he found that every hope of attaining the object of his inquiry was thus thwarted. He bit his lips, folded his arms, and traversed the room for a few moments with great emotion. His hopes had been raised when the old woman had voluntarily disclosed the manner in which the little Christabelle had been abstracted from Wallingford Hall, on the night of the conflagration; and they were now as suddenly and universally destroyed. What to do with Zelta was the next thing that tormented him. He felt bound in honour to release her from her present confinement, and yet, if he did so, without some prior agreement with her, he felt convinced that she would take good care to keep out of his way afterwards. He, however, at last, thought that probably money might have a better effect upon the old woman's feelings than compulsory measures; he, therefore, placed in her hands a couple of guineas, telling her it was some amends for the inconvenience to which she had been subjected, and informing her at the same time, that her reward should have been much greater if it had been in her power to reveal what he was so anxious to know.

Zelta's aged countenance was lighted up with delight as she viewed the precious coin, and she could not restrain the expression of her feelings.

"Heaven preserve your honour, for this act of charity to the poor old Gipsy!" she ejaculated, with much sincerity in her tone and demeanour. "You have made the last days of poor Zelta happy, for now she will know that her bones will rest in the churchyard, and that a coffin will encase her cold remains, which would otherwise have been buried uncovered in some wild spot, or else disposed of to the surgeons for dissection. God bless your honour! and may you live many years to reflect on the good you have done, and anticipate a bright reward hereafter. Long, long, have I been scraping, and hoarding, and saving, and gone many a time athirst and hungry, to get together the means of interring my poor old bones, when my days shall be over. Halfpenny by halfpenny, and penny by penny have I saved, till I had got the value of a silver coin, and that I treasured as carefully as if it had been a drop of my heart's blood, and when I had got sufficient silver I changed it for a guinea, which I have here—I have here. God bless your honour! You have smoothed the path of the poor old woman to eternity, and may your last hours be those of peace, and your memory be revered while time shall last, for this your charity to her who so much required it."

While the old woman thus gave expression to the doctor of her gratitude, she drew from an ample pocket in her cloak, a small bundle of rags, which she proceeded to unroll carefully one by one until she came to an old leathern purse, from which she took the bright guinea in her grizzled hand, and after exhibiting it triumphantly to her benefactor, she deposited it with the two others she at first received, in the purse, rolled it in the rags again with the greatest care, and having consigned the precious parcel to her pocket, and repeating her thanks to Mr. Hartley, left the room, from which she had scarcely emerged, when she was pounced upon by Knobbs, who grasping her tightly by the arm, inquired with evident disappointment, if it was the doctor's intention to let her depart so easily; to which the latter replied in the affirmative, adding, that having discovered he was mistaken in the woman, it would not be of any use to keep her in custody.

"Take your hands off, you gaping idiot," cried the old Gipsy, as the parish constable released her from his hold, while her features assumed all their former fury and malevolence, "you hear your commands, dog! and thank your lucky stars that Zelta has not now the strength she once possessed, or by my natal star, I would——"

"Nay, nay, good woman, no more of this," interrupted the doctor, "but go about your business, I pray."

"I go, your honour," replied Zelta, nodding her head in compliance with her benefactor's wishes, and the next moment she disappeared from the house, from whence Knobbs would have followed her and committed summary punishment upon her for the abuse she had given him, had he not been withheld by Doctor Hartley, who gave him some additional *douceur*

by way of a soother, after the disappointment he had experienced at the Gipsy woman being allowed to escape.

CHAPTER XXIII.

"Although we wander once again
  Amid the scene of joy,
What bitter cares, what hopes and fears,
  Arise our bliss to cloy!"—THE PILGRIM

DOCTOR HARTLEY returned home after his interview with Zelta, but his mind was in a state of the utmost horror and confusion. Could the tale he had heard be true? He could scarcely believe that Ela, whom Wallingford had once described as all gentleness and love, could be the heartless wretch that the old Gipsy represented her to him;—a murderess! The murderess, too, of the child of that man in whose bosom she once reposed! The bare idea was sufficient to strike the most insensible mind with terror and disgust, and to a heart so sensibly alive, so painfully acute to the feelings of humanity as Doctor Hartley's, the reflections it caused were more than doubly painful. For more than an hour he paced his study, revolving in his thoughts every sentence he had heard, and the more he meditated upon it the more forcibly did the conviction of the truth come upon his mind. Good God! What would be the anguish of Wallingford when he was made acquainted with the dreadful fate of his child, and by whose hand she was suspected to have fallen? And what indeed would be the terror of Mrs. Wallingford, if, by any chance, it should come to her knowledge that her darling had perished by the assassin's knife, and that knife wielded by the hand of her whom her husband had plunged from the paths of rectitude into degradation and crime?

The worthy doctor could not bear to dwell upon that soul-harrowing subject, and after another hour spent in bitter reflection, he sat down to write a circumstancial account of all that had occurred. Having done this as carefully as possible, he retired, completely exhausted, to his chamber, and endeavoured to court repose; but his busy and restless thoughts kept him awake till the morning, when he arose and descended to his breakfast-room, intending to despatch his domestic immediately to post the letter he had written to Mr. Wallingford, when he found on his table a letter addressed to him, in a hand-writing which he very well knew. He hastily broke the seal, and skimmed over the contents. It was from Mr. Wallingford, informing the doctor that he, with his family, were on their route to the hall. In a tone of the greatest melancholy, which told how little absence from the scene of his troubles had tended to alleviate his sufferings, he informed his friend that the health of his lady still remained as bad as ever, that change of climate had failed to eradicate a disorder which, he feared, had no earthly cure, and which had its origin in a dreadful calamity which was impressed upon her memory in characters too indelible ever to be effaced, and that he had, however reluctantly, been at last compelled to yield to her own constantly expressed wishes to return to Wallingford Hall, especially as the medical gentleman had given it as his opinion, that the same should be complied with without the least possible delay. Mr. Wallingford went on to state in his letter, that he dreaded the period of their return, as he knew how poignantly all the occurrences of the past would be recalled to his beloved Amelia's recollection, and the probability there was of its accelerating her death.

Doctor Hartley was, on the contrary, gratified at the thoughts of the return of his friend, though he sincerely sympathized with him in the feelings he had so appropriately expressed in his letter; but how much more dreadful would be his anguish when he received the awful intelligence he had to impart to him? He almost trembled at the painful task which had devolved upon him.

Having partaken of a hasty breakfast he left his house to proceed to the hall, to inform Anthony of the intended return of the family, so that they might have everything in readiness for their reception. The old people were quite delighted at the intelligence, and sent for Giles and other labourers immediately to begin the work of preparation in Wallingford Hall.

Doctor Hartley waited till the arrival of Giles, who informed him, that him and two or three others, in passing near the old Manor House that morning, and not noticing the gipsies about as usual, had the courage and curiosity to approach nearer the ruins, but perceiving that there was nothing to create their apprehension, they had the further temerity, after hearing the awful reports that had gone about of their being haunted, to enter the ruins and search all over them, when they found that their surmises had been right, the tribe had abruptly left the place, no doubt fearful after the adventure of old Zelta, that they would all be apprehended.

The doctor was not at all displeased to hear this, as Mr. Wallingford and his family were about to return to the Hall, and after some necessary instructions, which he was authorized to make to Anthony, he returned home.

The news of the return of the Wallingford family to the seat of their ancestors, soon spread around the neighbourhood, and universal joy was the consequence amongst the labouring classes, and dependents of the gentlemen especially; for to them Mr. Wallingford had ever been a most liberal benefactor. Every person was disposed to give them a hearty welcome to their so long vacated halls; and while they deeply sympathized in the troubles that had fallen upon their house while they were last there, they sincerely hoped that there would not be a recurrence of them, and they breathed a simultaneous prayer that the amiable lady of Mr. Wallingford might be restored to perfect convalescence.

Of course Doctor Hartley had not divulged a sentence to any person of what had taken place in the interview he had had with the old Gipsy-woman Zelta, so that he was under no apprehension of the dreadful story of Christabelle's assassination reaching the ears of Mrs. Wallingford, unless her husband thought proper to reveal it; which, under her present precarious circumstances, was not at all probable.

The preparations at the hall for the reception of its master and his family were soon completed, for, of course, as Anthony and his wife constantly resided in it, it had been kept during the absence of their master and mistress in proper order.

When the morning arrived, which was the third one after Doctor Hartley had received the communication, it was ushered in by the ringing of the church bells, and most of the persons took a holiday, it being determined to get up a deputation to wait upon Mr. Wallingford and his lady, to congratulate them on their once more taking up their residence amongst them, headed by the village pedagogue, who had written a very eloquent address for that auspicious occasion. All, in fact, was festivity in the neighbourhood, with which they imagined not how badly the spirits of those they wished to do honour to would harmonize, notwithstanding Doctor Hartley had taken the trouble to go round to them, and endeavour to persuade them not to put themselves to an unnecessary inconvenience or expense, as he was fearful Mr. Wallingford would not be enabled to receive their demonstrations with becoming spirit and cordiality.

"Poor dear lady," observed old Jenny, the night before the expected arrival, as she and her husband sat chatting together in the kitchen, "how glad I shall be to see her amiable features once more, and hear her voice, which always spoke in such sweet tones to every one; but how grieved am I to hear that travelling has not had the desired effect upon her constitution! Ah! poor lady, if she was to die we should never have such another mistress, and the poor people would miss one of the kindest of benefactresses."

"You say right, dame," remarked Anthony, "it would indeed be a loss were it to please God to call our lady to his arms, but let us hope that she may live for many years yet, to shed around her those blessings she ever bestowed with so liberal a hand. Then there's Master Walter, too, oh, I dare say he has grown a fine lad by this time. Ah, poor child, had but his sister lived!"

"Oh, father spare me," said Agatha, who was present on that occasion, "it breaks my heart when you mention that shocking event. I'm sure I shall never be able to look my poor dear lady in the face again, to see her pale and suffering, and to know that I have partly been the cause of her affliction, though, Heaven knows, I did not do it wilfully, and I would sooner have laid down my life a thousand times than I would intentionally have caused one moment's uneasiness to a mistress to whom I was so fondly attached."

"Well, well, never mind, child," said the old man, "I know that you was not to blame, although one cannot help at times recalling the shocking event to our recollection with the most bitter regret. We will drop the subject."

And the subject was dropped accordingly, and nothing was talked of the rest of the evening but the preparations that were making for the welcoming of their master and mistress, of which they all most cordially approved.

But while affairs were thus going on at home, what were the sufferings of our hero and his wife? Six years had elapsed since the occurrence of the dreadful events we have so fully recorded in the former part of this history, and they had sought in foreign climes and varied scenes to forget what had happened, and Wallingford had, to no purpose, watched for an improvement in the health of his beloved partner; but no change of scene, no endeavour whatever could relieve their minds from the corroding care which perpetually oppressed them, nor could bury in oblivion those events which had stepped in between them and their future happiness. Mrs. Wallingford had never been able to erase from her recollection the scene which had passed between her and the wretched Ela; not a sentence she had uttered but what was stamped upon her brain in burning characters; and often when in the midst of her domestic pleasures, and while caressing her only darling, the form of that unfortunate woman would rise to her mind's eye, and imbue her thoughts with horror. Again would the awful maledictions of the Gipsy vibrate in her ears, and make her tremble for fear they should come true. In such moments, too, when Wallingford sought to lead her thoughts from those melancholy events to which they invariably leaned, and in tones of the warmest affection recalled to her recollection the days of their youthful courtship, the one maddening idea would burst upon her brain, and with it a train of others of the most insupportable description.

"Ah," she would reflect, "who shall believe those smiles of kindness; how know I but the heart of the hypocrite is hid beneath them? Even so, perhaps it was he was wont to look upon that wretched victim, who is now deserted and left to guilt and misery, and the offspring of his illicit passion is brought up to a course of infamy: it is dreadful to look upon. Oh, what anguish is there in that idea, and yet how true, how just. Then if he has once so cruelly deceived her that was pure and lovely, why should I think that were there no tie to compel him, I too in my turn might not be deserted. Oh, Wallingford, your guilt has proved the bane of our future bliss!"

Thus when alone would she give way to her emotions, and pass her time in tears and bewailings. But what even were all those pangs to the horrors she felt as she thought of the terrible fate her poor Christabelle had met with? In those moments she was completely delirious, and would rave in a frightful manner. The form of the child seemed to rise to her view, screaming for that help which no one could afford her; she heard the hissing and crackling of the burning ruins; she beheld the broad red glare upon the horizon, and the huge columns of smoke ascending amid the ensanguine reflection; she heard the shouts of the surrounding multitude, then one dreadful crash, and all was over; wound up to a pitch of frenzy beyond endurance at these agonizing thoughts, she would shriek, and become insensible.

Oh, how intense was the anguish of Wallingford in such moments as these, when he had none to accuse but himself as the cause of all the misery that had come upon his house. We will not, we cannot attempt to pourtray it: it is enough to say that his mind was a perpetual hell to him, and bitter indeed was the punishment he endured for his crimes. What rendered his misery still more severe, was the restraint he was obliged to put upon his feelings in the presence of his wife, and the smiles with which he was often obliged to clothe his cheek, while the cankerworm of despair was preying upon his vitals. The uncertainty, too, of the fate of Christabelle was perpetually tormenting him, and haunting him in his dreams at night. Could he but know that she had escaped that horrible death, and had afterwards sunk to an early grave, he could, he thought, be comparatively happy; nay, even if he could be sure that she had perished in the flames, he would have been more content than to know that she lived and was in the power of those wretches the Gipsies.

In order to prevent, as much as possible, the events of their past life being recalled to the memory of his wife, he had taken the precaution to take none but strange servants with them on their travels, and to go as little as possible into English society; but all this had not the effect he desired;—Mrs. Wallingford got no better; years passed away and still it was the same. There were indeed moments when she gazed upon the ripening beauties, quick growth, and promising qualifications of her son Walter, that hope would spring up in her bosom; but short indeed was the duration of that hope; should he also be fated to fall under the fatal malison which had been so dreadfully realized; this was the fearful idea that obtruded itself, and dashed the honied chalice in a moment from her lips.

In travelling through Italy, Mr. and Mrs. Wallingford took the opportunity of calling upon her only brother, who for some years with his wife had resided there; but what a melancholy moment did they arrive at. The remains of his wife were then lying in a coffin, and Mr. Herbert had but just before the entrance of his sister been given over by his physician. The only daughter of her brother was standing over his couch, and bathing his temples with her tears of anguish. Poor girl, she had lost one of the best of mothers, and death was fast closing the eyes of an affectionate father, when she would, as she thought, be left friendless and portionless in the world: but Providence watched over the poor orphan in the hour of her tribulation.

The meeting between Mrs. Wallingford and her brother, as may be expected, was of the most affectionate description, but he did not long survive her arrival. Before his death he most earnestly committed his beloved daughter to the protection of his sister, a trust which she promised to perform with the utmost care.

Maria Herbert was a beautiful girl, then nine years of age, just two years younger than Walter. Her features were exquisitely delicate; her mild blue eyes beamed with gentleness and sweetness of disposition, her skin was of the purest white, and her hair, which was a lovely chestnut, fell over her neck and shoulders in a rich profusion of natural curls. Her manners were so affectionate, and whole demeanour so interesting that it was impossible to behold her without loving her; and Mrs. Wallingford began once more to indulge a hope that she would prove a solace to her sorrows, and serve to banish the poignancy of that anguish which had so long afflicted her.

Mr. Wallingford too looked upon the poor orphan girl with feelings of the deepest interest, and beheld with gratitude, the pains she took at all times to lighten the sorrows of her aunt, and the alacrity with which she flew to fetch her any little necessary which she might require in her illness; indeed the heart must have been utterly callous which could be insensible to the winning sweetness of the gentle and beauteous Maria. Walter and her became the most inseparable companions when they could get together; they shared in each other's studies, for sweet indeed was that task to Walter, which Maria would learn also.

Thus did affairs stand, when Mrs. Wallingford, tired of travelling, expressed a wish to her husband that they might return home. The novelty of foreign climes had ceased to exist, and she urged their return home with an earnestness which her husband scarcely knew how to oppose, although he felt bound so to do, fearful that a return to those scenes, in which the fatal results that had caused them so much suffering, took place, might be attended with the most fatal results. But in vain he tried every argument in his power to endeavour to persuade her to relinquish the idea of returning to England until her health was far better; she had fixed her mind upon it, and the doctor having given it as his opinion, that her native air was more calculated to restore her to convalescence, since every other had failed, of course her husband had nothing more to offer in opposition to it, and immediately prepared for their departure, writing off to Doctor Hartley, as we have previously described.

Mr. and Mrs. Wallingford received the congratulations of the poor people on their return to the Hall, as they really felt; but the deep impress of care and suffering was upon their face, and it excited the heartfelt sympathy of all who beheld them. The beauty of Maria Herbert, and the fast ripening perfections of Walter, created universal admiration, and poor old Anthony and Jenny "were in a complete extacy of delight, as they paid their respects to their poor dear young master." Jenny, however, when she and her husband were alone, shook her head and said:—

"That is certainly a beautiful girl, Mrs. Wallingford's niece, and I am certain she is as good as she is lovely; I was prepared to love her the very moment I first saw her, for she is very much like our lady, and —— ah! Anthony, just such another sweet girl as this would poor little Christabelle have been, had she——"

"Don't mention it, Jenny," interrupted the old man, "I cannot bear to think on it; it has made sad havoc on the frames of our poor master and mistress; a sorry day has it been for them, when those rascally Gipsies were suffered to take up their abode in Rosemary Dell. I don't know how it is, dame, but my heart is full of melancholy forebodings of some other calamity, which I cannot account for, but have not the power to shake off. This day, which should be one of rejoicing too, is more like a funeral party than anything else. Ah, Jenny, I am afraid the troubles of the house of Wallingford are not over yet."

MR. BARNELL IS ATTENTIVE TO MARIA.

"Alack! I fear they are not," responded Jenny: "dear me, now I come to think of it, last night, too, I had such dreams——"

A summons from Mrs. Wallingford put a stop to this conversation, and Jenny hastened to the apartment of her mistress.

In the meantime Mr. Wallingford sought an early opportunity of being alone with Doctor Hartley, of whom he eagerly inquired whether anything particular had occurred lately. In as few words as possible, but yet hiding from him none of the facts, Mr. Hartley related to him the dreadful tale he had elicited from the Gipsy, Zelta. Good God, what a story for a parent to hear; his child, his little Christabelle, had, then, escaped from the flames, but to perish by the knife of a murderess, and that murderess Ela;—his once loved Ela;—her who had reposed in his bosom;—who had been all love and enthusiastic affection;—Ela, the mother of Fanny, his child—could it be true?—Ela an assassin!—the murderer of a child, too, whose innocence should have been its protection from such a monstrous deed. But no, no, no, it was impossible: it could not be;—the old Gipsy Zelta might have been deceived, or perhaps she told a wilful falsehood, to gratify the spirit of hatred which she seemed to bear towards Ela. He thought over all the gentleness and fondness of Ela;—her attachment to her parents; her warmth of feeling;—her urbanity and universal kindness, and he again thought to himself;—" By Heaven, this awful story must be unfounded in truth."

"Oh, that I could see this woman," said he, after a pause, "that I might question her narrowly, and see whether I could not detect her in a falsehood, to endeavour to prove that it was all a fabrication."

For a while this appeared so probable, that he began to try to efface the shocking story from his memory, and to believe that Christabelle still really lived, and that this tale had been invented by Zelta, partly to gratify her revenge against Ela, for some injury she seemed to think she had done her, and to render the concealment of the girl the more secure; but the idea vanished when he recalled to his memory the scene he had witnessed in the Dell some years before, between Ela and Morna;—her ferocious conduct on that occasion;—her threats;—and the readiness with which she joined in the riot, debauchery, and ribaldry that predominated afterwards;—the horrible certainty of the truth of Zelta's opinions darted upon him with irresistible force, and he could not help thinking that his poor child, his innocent little Christabelle's blood had been shed by Ela; Ela, the mother of his child, the object of his once ardent attachment. The latter thoughts inflicted a pang, if possible, more severe than the others, for was not—ought not Fanny, the daughter of the murderess, to be as dear to him as Christabelle? The glowing description which Mr. Hartley gave of the beauty of Fanny, wrung him to the heart; but nothing now could save her from the life of shame and infamy to which she had been brought up: for how was she to be reclaimed?—and was it at all probable, after the lapse of years, that the Gipsies would again make their appearance in Rosemary Dell? what would be the agony of his wife, should she ever become acquainted with the real fate of their little darling? He dared not entrust his mind with such a thought.

Mrs. Wallingford being fatigued with travelling, retired early to rest; but the mind of Wallingford was too much occupied by what he had been told, to permit him to follow her example; he therefore flew to his study, and there alone, and in silence, gave way to the bitter thoughts that racked his brain.

Wrapt in deep rumination, with his head reclining on his hand, and his elbow resting on the table, Mr. Wallingford took no notice of the flight of time, and the hour of midnight was past, and still he thought not of retiring to his couch. Suddenly, however, he was startled by hearing a stifled unnatural laugh in the room, and which seemed to proceed from behind him. He started up in a moment, and turning round, what was his astonishment to behold standing near the door of the apartment, the same hideous old hag who had several times before annoyed him, and whose appearance had ever been the harbinger of evil. She was gazing with an expression of malice and exultation upon Wallingford, who almost doubting the evidence of his senses, was paralysed to the spot, and continued to stare at the revolting looking being, unable to utter a word.

The hag advanced into the centre of the room, and pointing her long bony fingers towards Wallingford, said in her usual harsh, disgusting tones :—

"What ho! my Lord of Wallingford!—Well met—well met; I have news for thee; hey have I; 'tis goodly news, too, though you mayhap may not think so! Ha! ha! ha! welcome back to the Halls of thy fathers, Edward Wallingford; the scene of thy pleasures! Ha! ha! ha!"

"Mysterious being, what are you, and why do you appear to me?" demanded Wallingford, who felt awed at her manner, and although by no means predisposed to superstition, shuddered while in her presence, and shrunk beneath the unearthly glance of her eye;—"I never harmed you to my knowledge, why then should you perpetually seek to annoy me, and what is now the purport of your visit?"

"Ho! ho! Edward Wallingford," replied the hag, "then you do dread me? Ah!—you do not despise the threats of her you once called hell-cat, hag, wretch! Ha! ha! ha! The hell-cat, the hag, the wretch, will continue to annoy you; and whenever she comes to you, so sure shall some heavy calamity follow;—do you doubt my promise? Oh, no; I have always kept to my word. Hark ye, Edward Wallingford;—

"Though thy brain has been rack'd, thine heart been wrung,
Thou wilt suffer much more, thou in grief art young;
There's a curse on thy head, the deceiver's lot,
Try, seek all thou may'st, thou'lt escape it not.
Prepare for trouble, prepare for woe,
For that is thy fate on this earth below;
Fly where you may, go where you will,
The curse, the spell, shall attend thee still."

As these words rang in unearthly tones in the ears of the distracted Wallingford, a blue vapour appeared to encircle the form of the hag, which having gradually evaporated, he looked up and found he was alone.

"What dreadful mystery is this?" cried Wallingford, as he walked around the room; "Can I be awake, or have my senses left me? Mysterious being, where have you vanished; or am I the dupe of some infamous impostor?"

The latter words had scarcely escaped his lips when a hollow laugh, which seemed close to him, vibrated in his ears. He glanced hastily around him, but there was no one near him, and overcome with the strength of his conflicting feelings he covered his face with his hands, and became for a while unconscious. The morning found him feverish and unwell, but yet he had somewhat regained his composure after the strange events of the night. He made some enquiries of the domestics whether they had noticed any strange person the night before lurking about the house, or whether they had given admittance to, or seen any one leave, answering the description of the hag; but, of course, the reply was in the negative, and not wishing to make his domestics acquainted with his affairs, he dropped the subject, and pretended to be satisfied; but his mind was ill at ease, for he had never yet seen the hag but her visit was sure to be followed with some evil or the other.

The constant companions of each other, and associated by a reciprocity of tastes, sentiments, and dispositions, Walter and his fair cousin daily became less happy if they were separated from each other; and the Dell often re-echoed with their sounds of mirth as they bounded across it in all the sportive vivacity of youth. Time flew apace, and Walter was now eighteen years of age, and Maria two years younger, when Wallingford, for the first time, began to look upon the attentions they paid each other with an eye of suspicion. He had hitherto failed to perceive the consequences that might ensue through the connection which had been formed between the two young persons; in fact, he had looked upon them both as his children, and considered their affection only as that of a brother and sister; but he was very soon undeceived, and he then found out, too late, the imprudence of which he had been guilty in associating his son with a female so attractive as Maria. But why imprudent?—Surely there could be no sin, no discredit in this attachment? Was not Maria all that could be wished in charms intrinsic and extrinsic?—Was she not a match fit for an emperor? Then why should Wallingford accuse himself of having acted imprudently in having brought them so intimately together? But such did he think, and was at once determined that he would thwart their young passions in the bud. He

first sought the presence of his wife, to whom he revealed his suspicions, and mentioned his desires and designs upon the same.

It was on the day that Walter had attained his eighteenth year that his father had an opportunity of putting his plans into operation, and making his wishes more explicitly known.

"My dear," said Wallingford, addressing himself to his wife, as he entered the room, " of course our Walter has not forgotten you on this auspicious mornnig, pray what little token of affection has he given you? I dare say, something he has presented you with of a very handsome description, for he has been keeping his purchases such a profound secret."

"He has not, indeed, forgotten me, Edward," replied Mrs. Wallingford. "See here, he has bought me these handsome vases, and filled them with the choicest flowers, in which he always displays such excellent taste."

"Very true, my love," returned Mr. Wallingford. "I am not disposed to quarrel with Walter's taste generally speaking; and I must say that he has not been at all backward in displaying it at this period, although, in one instance, so far from acting judiciously, he has not only behaved imprudently, but in a manner which creates my astonishment."

"Oh! how can he so have erred?" asked Mrs. Wallingford eagerly, and yet half doubting whether her husband was jesting or not. I am certain, if Walter has given offence, it has not been intentionally done, and——"

"There, my love," interrupted Wallingford, you speak my sentiments; I trust that I shall have no occasion to rebuke Walter, when he knows my will, which must not be questioned. What I allude to is the present made by our son to his cousin, namely, a brooch in the form of a heart, a ring with a true-lover's-knot in the centre, and other things, such only as should come from a lover to his lady-love; but when they are sent by Walter Wallingford to Maria Herbert, I repeat, it is imprudent and quite out of character. I tell you, Amelia, gently but firmly, that I shall expect you will warn your niece that she has now arrived at years beyond childhood, and must act with more discretion in the company of Walter; not to allow him to treat her with any greater freedom than is consistent with maiden bashfulness and the manner in which they are related."

The countenance of Mrs. Wallingford betrayed the unqualified astonishment she experienced at this speech. "My dear Edward," she exclaimed, "what has occasioned you to speak in this manner? Why do you speak in terms of Maria, as if she had acted otherwise than as maiden modesty and virtue should dictate? I must confess I am at a loss to understand you."

"But, my love, I understand all quite well," observed Wallingford, quickly, "and only blame myself for not checking before the attachment which Walter and your niece have evidently formed for one another. But it must be put an end to forthwith, and I trust you will use your endeavours to instil into the mind of Maria the necessity there is for checking the passion immediately. Let her not be kept in ignorance of my opinion upon the matter, and that it is my wish, nay, my command, that she does not wear the trinkets which Walter has purchased for her. It would be highly improper, and I repeat, it must not be. I am satisfied that in this I am only acting with propriety, for I have watched them closely of late, and have too much reason to believe that they have encouraged a passion which can only be productive of unhappiness to all parties; and unless Maria acts as I wish, my opinion of her, and my behaviour to her will be greatly altered indeed. But I do not doubt that she will see the folly of acting contrary to my desires, when you have pointed them out to her, my dear Amelia, for she is a sensible and virtuous girl, and—but enough, you will, I hope, lose no time in speaking to her upon the subject."

Thus speaking, Mr. Wallingford quitted the room, and left his wife in a state of wonder, grief, and offended pride. She had taken particular notice of the emphasis with which he pronounced the words, "your niece," by which he seemed so eager to impress upon her recollection that for the behaviour of Maria she was accountable, and that he entertained an ample opinion of his own charity in having become the protector of her poor brother's portionless daughter. The idea pierced her to the heart, and with it her indignation arose; for it was evident that Wallingford looked upon her niece with haughty pride, and thought her unworthy of being made the bride of Walter Wallingford. Her wounded pride for a moment or two almost overcame her, but at length she sunk into tears, tears of the most bitter anguish, for she saw in an instant the misery that was in store for her, and the sorrow she must bring upon those two beings who seemed but created for each other, and whom she was convinced loved each other with a passion that it would be difficult to eradicate.

The watchful mother had for some time noticed that the passion of Walter for Maria was more deeply centered in the heart than that inspired by mere consanguinal ties, and he had contrived to rob her of her heart while she was unconscious of the loss, and before she had even ventured a thought upon the subject. In more than one of their interviews Mrs. Wallingford had, unknown to them, been a spectator, and upon one occasion all her doubts were set at rest by hearing Walter acknowledge to Maria, how deeply, how fondly he loved her, and in return to his repeated importunities, draw forth from the blushing maiden a similar

confession, and never dreaming that Mr. and Mrs. Wallingford would ever raise any objection, but on the contrary, fondly hoping that they would delight in such a union, they were supremely happy. True, poor Maria had sometimes her doubts; she remembered that she was an orphan, without a farthing of her own, and entirely dependent upon Mr. Wallingford and her aunt for support, and should that induce them to reject her as a daughter; but no, no, she could not believe them capable of such mercenary motives. Alas! Maria, although an intelligent girl, was a novice in the ways of the world, and to the selfish ideas that too often guide the actions of mankind: but it was not long her fate to remain in such ignorance.

CHAPTER XXIV.

" Alas! for all that I could ever read
Or learn in history,
The course of true love never did run smooth.'
                                    SHAKSPEARE.

WE must not forget to mention that on the day to which we have alluded, namely, the anniversary of Walter's birth, as the health of Mrs. Wallingford had greatly improved of late, her husband made up his mind that the event should be celebrated with a hospitality becoming his rank, and the heir of Wallingford, and for several weeks before, preparations had been making at the hall, and numerous invitations sent round to all the neighbouring gentry.

It was on this auspicious morning that the conversation we have described in the previous chapter took place between Mr. Wallingford and his lady, and when the latter had somewhat regained her composure after the shock, and saw the necessity and propriety of complying with his wishes, she had no great difficulty in persuading her husband to let that day of festivity pass over without their being made acquainted with the grief and disappointment that were destined for them. Mr. Wallingford yielded, for the request was so natural; and Mrs. Wallingford solicited him so earnestly, while the tears stood in her eyes, that he found himself utterly unable to refuse his assent to her request. But his brow became gloomy, and it was evident that he regretted having yielded, when, on the guests arriving, it was found that neither Walter nor his cousin were present, and, on inquiry, it appeared that they had been seen to leave the hall about an hour before. He bit his lips, and turned a look of reproof upon his wife as though he considered she was to blame in having induced him to grant such a concession. She felt abased, and could not but blame the imprudence of Walter and Maria, especially on such a day as that. She was more and more vexed, when on the arrival of the company, and inquiring after

Walter, some officious and thoughtless person intimated that him and his cousin were rambling the fields together, to hear that it gave rise to numberless jokes and remarks, which served to increase the gathering cloud on her husband's brow.

In the meantime, the two young people, not thinking for a moment that they were doing any harm, and forgetting the want of etiquette in not being present on the arrival of the persons invited, had taken an early ramble towards Rosemary Dell, which, since the Gipsies had left off visiting the place, as we have before mentioned, had become their favourite haunt. Walter had formed a little summer-house in the pleasantest part of the Dell, whither him and Maria often retired to talk over their little secrets and breathe their vows of affection. On the morning of which we are speaking, the sun shone forth with full meridian glory, and everything around was glittering in its radiant beams. Nature seemed to spring into tenfold beauty beneath his genial influence, and the birds carolled sweetly among the foliage, as if partaking of the general pleasure. The ardent youth locked the arm of Maria in his, and they left the hall. The day was inviting, and forgetting how strange their absence from the hall upon such an occasion as that would seem, they wandered on in the direction of their retreat.

They had taken their usual seat in the shrubbery that adjoined the summer-house, and Walter looking with the most fervent devotion in her countenance, which seemed more beautiful than ever, poured forth with the eloquence of youth and sincerity, his soul's adulation; when they were all at once startled by hearing a low sigh near them, and raising their eyes to the part from whence it seemed to proceed, they were astonished to behold standing in the path, and gazing fixedly upon them, the figure of a girl, who, from her air and apparel, they guessed to be a Gipsy.

She was a beautiful tall girl, with eyes brilliant as planets, and a mouth teeming with intelligence and vivacity. Her cheeks were roseate, and her complexion seemed not so dark as many of those erratic class of people, although it had received, perhaps, a deeper tint than nature had bestowed upon it, by art.

The girl paused a few moments when she found that she was observed, and then dropped two or three curtseys, and advanced timidly towards them.

"She is one of the Gipsy tribe," said Maria in a whisper to Walter, "and really she is very handsome; do you not think so?"

"She is pretty," returned Walter, "certainly she is pretty, but after all, how far short does she fall of the exquisite beauty of Maria?"

The maiden blushed deeply at this compliment, and made no answer. In the meantime the Gipsy girl had approached close to them, and fixing upon them a look of importunity, said,—

"Fair lady, if you will let me study the lines in your hand, I can tell your fortune. I can read to you the book of fate, and tell you the past, the present, and the future. Shall I tell you, lady?"

Maria smiled, but shrunk back timidly as the Gipsy girl spoke, but Walter, smiling, gently laid hold of her hand and extended it towards the Gipsy.

"Well, in truth, we must try the Gipsy's skill," said the youth; "no doubt she can tell us marvellous things, and among the rest, how long it will be before your wedding day arrives, Maria."

"I can tell you yet more marvellous things than that, sir," remarked the Gipsy girl; "there is nothing can escape my art."

"I dare say not," replied Walter, laughingly; "however, we will try your skill before we attempt to judge. Come, then, here is something to begin with, for I know that your art would fail unless the palm be crossed with silver or gold; now let us know who are to be our lovers, whether we are to have wealth, and if we—but come, come, whose fortune will you tell first, my fair *sister's*, or mine?"

"Hold, young man," cried the Gipsy girl solemnly. "Your sister!—It is not so;—and the name of sister should not be used lightly by your tongue. Your sister never was, and never could be so closely allied to your heart as is this young lady. Nay, I want not your money, I will not have it; the page of her destiny is easily read."

"And what is to befal me?" asked Maria, half trembling at the seriousness of the Gipsy's manner.

The girl shook her head, and looking earnestly in Maria's countenance, said, "Lady, you are born to grief, to baffled hopes, and crushed expectations. Even now the tempest is gathering over thy head, and ere many hours shall have passed away, it shall burst. The present source of your greatest happiness will then become your bitterest sorrow."

Maria turned very pale as the Gipsy girl uttered these words. and they seemed to tell upon her heart with all the force of truth.

"Enough!" ejaculated Walter, with a look of vexation, when he perceived that the Gipsy had alarmed Maria; "I like not the melancholy style of your prognostications, my good girl. Can't you try something in the lively strain instead? People seldom feel grateful to those who bring them bad tidings. Nay I will reward you well for your trouble; here is silver, and if you can but restore composure to this pretty face, I will not grudge you a piece of gold."

"I want neither your silver nor your gold,"

replied the girl, turning his hand away scornfully; "I will tell you the truth, and you will be afterwards ready enough to acknowledge that I am no deceiver. You say true, she is lovely, but beauty and sorrow are too oft allied; there are many as good hearts as her's that have been wrung, nay, broken; and deeply is she doomed to grieve. Disappointment shall overcloud her happiness, care shall make the rose give place to the lily on that fair cheek, and the tear of anguish shall flow from those eyes that now beam with such lustre; yes, and before to-morrow's sun shall rise, shall they be dimmed with tears; then shall she——"

"Psha!" exclaimed Walter impatiently, "I am sick of these melancholy prognostications; and then you utter them with so gloomy an aspect that it is enough to chill any one to hear you. Come, you have said enough of this lady, and now see what you can tell me. Here are lines a plenty for you to exercise your wondrous skill upon; can'st explain them to me? But perhaps you can tell me of something that *has* occurred to convince me that your art is not mere moonshine."

"You ask me a difficult question, sir," said the girl, "but I will try to satisfy you. The frowns of fortune have never yet scowled upon you: your life has hitherto been one of uninterrupted serenity. While an infant, the tempest raged, but it harmed you not, though one was doomed to perish in the blast, who would have shared in that affection, which you now enjoy undivided."

As the Gipsy girl gave utterance to the last words, Walter started and looked at her with astonishment, for her voice was full of pathos, and glittering tears rolled slowly from her bright eyes, her bosom heaved, and she was remarkably agitated altogether.

"Ha!" cried the youth, "what means this strange emotion?—Why do you weep?—Mysterious girl, are you really what you seem to be?—How know you this;—and——"

"How do I know it?" returned the Gipsy girl, "shall I tell you?—but," she added, checking herself; "no, no, it must not be; but mark me well, I know you, heir of Wallingford!"

"Why, in truth," replied Walter, smiling, "now there is not much sagacity in discovering that; I am, indeed, heir of Wallingford."

"You are considered so," said the Gipsy girl, significantly; "but should not the firstborn take the precedence?"

"True," answered Walter, carelessly, "but what is the solution of your problem, or has it really any meaning at all?"

"I could explain the problem, as you are pleased to call it, gentle sir," returned the Gipsy girl, "and—but no," and she appeared to check herself, "it must not be;—the time is not yet come;—I have made a vow and

nothing shall induce me to swerve from my oath."

A deeper melancholy overspread the Gipsy's countenance as she uttered these words.

"You know your business well, girl," said Walter, who, having regained his usual composure, was vexed to think he had suffered himself to have any of the semblance of being deceived by the girl's words. Still, in spite of all, he could not help feeling a deep and unaccountable interest in the mysterious girl. She seemed to mark his emotion with much pleasure, and fixing upon him a glance of expression, signified by sign that she was bound by an oath to silence.

"Yes," observed Maria, who had been for the last few moments a silent spectator of all that passed, "but surely there is no vow you can have made to prevent you from telling my cousin what fortune is to attend him?"

"Lady," answered the Gipsy solemnly, "have I not told you your fortune;—have I not said that sorrow was to be your portion, and the dark clouds of adversity that hang over your head, when they break, will not suffer him to escape their violence. If he—" At that moment the eyes of the Gipsy girl wandered hastily towards a cluster of trees, among which there was a rustling sound, and she uttered a half-suppressed shriek, and darted away like lightning.

"What a mysterious being," cried the astonished Walter, turning to Maria, as the form of the Gipsy disappeared among the trees; "who can she be, and what could make her take to flight so suddenly?"

Maria was thunderstruck with the singular behaviour of the girl, and could not, for a few seconds, return any answer to her cousin, but looked eagerly in the direction that she had taken, almost fancying that she could discover more than one form moving among the trees. As the girl started away, Maria's eyes had quickly followed her, and she was positive she beheld a figure, but it vanished so suddenly, that she could not tell whether it was the form of a man or a woman.

"I am astonished," said Maria, after a pause; "this adventure has assumed a character which I never expected it would. I cannot conceive who and what she is?"

"I think, my dear Maria," replied Walter, "it requires very little sagacity to solve that question. She is, depend upon it, nothing more than one of the Gipsy tribe, who has become more proficient in her trade than many of her companions; and, doubtless, by assuming such airs of mystery and cunning, finds it answer her purposes very profitably. She perceived that the old cant about wealth, happiness, prosperity, and such like, were not likely to have much effect upon us, and was, therefore, induced to try the other scheme."

"Your opinion is contradicted, by her refusing to take any remuneration," returned Maria; "and has she not now gone without seeking any recompense for her trouble?"

"It is a mere scheme," said her cousin; she will not fail to cross our path again at the earliest opportunity, and then she will make sure of getting a larger reward than she would have done otherwise. The cunning of these people is so great, that no wonder they contrive to make so many dupes as they do."

"That may be true, Walter," said his cousin, "and I believe it is; but although I have not seen much of these singular people, there is a certain air about that girl that I cannot help feeling a more than common interest in her."

"She certainly is an adept at her trade," observed Walter, "but depend upon it, after all, she is an impostor; we will however wait here awhile, and see if she returns."

Maria shook her hand incredulously, she had never heard much as regarded the Gipsy tribe, although she was aware that some events of a most extraordinary nature had occurred to her uncle and aunt through them, which had thrown a shadow over their path, and it was the fear of causing her benefactress any pain, and also from a repugnance to appear at all curious, that prevented her from ever questioning her aunt upon the subject. Consequently, not at all aware of the circumstances we have related in the early part of this history, as she was convinced Walter also was, she was quite unable to understand the hints that the Gipsy girl had thrown out, and the more she reflected upon her words, the more she became involved in wonder and perplexity. She had also marked with no little wonder the ardent looks of affection she had fixed upon Walter, but then she reflected who could gaze upon a youth so interesting, and good as her cousin, especially a young female, without emotion?

Much as Walter had endeavoured to appear indifferent upon the subject, Maria was not to be deceived, and she was confident from the expression of his eyes, that he felt an interest not less than her own.

"She will not come again," said Maria, when more than a quarter of an hour had elapsed; "I was certain she would not: ha! Walter, it is no use your attempting to deny that she has made a stronger impression upon your imagination, than you are willing to confess."

"Well, well," replied Walter, with evident confusion, "since you will have it so, I must acknowledge that I cannot get her so easily from my thoughts as I expected; but it was not the charms of her face, or form that struck me most forcibly, only I had really expected that she would have come back, to have sought for

some remuneration, and it therefore renders her real character the more unaccountable to me : for they are generally a selfish set of of beings, these same Gipsies."

"But do you think that she was not assuming the character she appeared in, or think you that she really was one of that tribe of outcasts, who have by depredation, and pretending to unriddle the secrets of futurity, become so notorious?"

"Most assuredly the latter, my dearest Maria," answered her cousin, "what reason have we to think that she was anything else?"

"Oh, surely one whose form and features were so exquisitely beautiful," remarked Maria, still incredulously, "one whose eyes were so softly expressive, whose manners were so gentle, could not belong to such a class of wandering degraded beings."

"How strange, Maria, it is," said Walter, "that you should appear to take so great an interest in this girl."

"I can scarcely account for it myself, Walter," answered the maid, "but yet I cannot advance any particular reason for imagining that she was not what she represented herself to be, with the exception that her manners and her appearance were so different, so superior, to what I have hitherto conceived those people to possess."

"Well, for my own part," observed Walter, "I did not think her by any means handsome, although she certainly had good eyes, with a wicked look; as for her figure, in the dress she wore, it would be, in my opinion, an absolute impossibility to judge what it was; but I had forgotten the time we have been here; what will my father and his friends think at our absenting ourselves from the Hall on such an occasion as this?"

"True," said Maria, "and I declare I had forgotten that it is necessary I should make an alteration in the appearance of my dress. How very thoughtless this is of us, Walter."

Walter smiled, and linking her arm within his, they walked forth from the Dell. As they proceeded on their way home, Walter was very grave and thoughtful, and it was very evident that the Gipsy girl occupied his imagination more than he wished it to appear she did. When they reached the hall, they found every thing in a state of confusion; and several strange sentences reached their ears of the occasion which had called them forth on that particular morning. Maria looked timidly first at Mr. Wallingford, and then at her aunt; and she perceived, with much pain and astonishment, that the former's countenance was enveloped in a forbidding frown; while the latter, who, upon all previous occasions, had ever greeted her with a benevolent smile, looked sorrowful and uneasy.

Poor Maria was wounded to the heart at

this very unusual behaviour, and, in vain tried to imagine what she had done to merit it; but how much more was she surprised and hurt, when Mr. Wallingford turning towards her with a look of bitter sarcasm, said:—

" I presume Miss Herbert admires the words of the poet, who says that—

" Beauty unadorned's adorned the most;" and, therefore, means to favour us by appearing at dinner *en deshabille*."

This pointed observation affected the gentle nature of Maria almost to tears, and hastily curtseying to the company, she retired to her dressing-room, where, unable longer to restrain her feelings, she gave vent to them in a copious flood of tears. The words of the Gipsy girl now came more forcibly to her recollection than ever, and the truth of part of the prediction made such an impression upon her that she felt she would have no easy task in eradicating. For the first time in her life since the death of her parents she felt truly wretched, and she dreaded having to appear before the company again; however, she struggled violently with her emotions, and, at length, succeeded in composing her thoughts much better than might be expected.

Among the guests who had been specially invited to the Hall on that day, was Lord and Lady Harlington and their daughter, the Honourable Euphemia Bamford, who, being filled with aristocratic pride and ignorance, seemed to think themselves the principal luminaries of the company, round which the other planets of the guests revolved, and twinkled so faintly as scarcely to be perceptible at all.

The Honourable Euphemia Bamford was rather pretty, but excessively bold, superlatively vain, and insupportably ignorant. She looked with the most supreme contempt upon all the other guests, and with the most spiteful feelings of jealousy and hatred upon every other lady in the room who happened to be better-looking than herself. She had been nursed in the lap of ignorance; educated by her aunt, a detestable old maid, who had the most inveterate hatred for the whole of the male gender, inasmuch as she had never been able to make a single conquest in the whole course of her life. It was expected that Miss Bamford, on the demise of the old lady, would have come into the possession of a handsome fortune, but she was doomed to be disappointed; she died very poor, and Euphemia was, therefore, sent home again to her parents, whose fortune had been considerably impaired by a very heavy family, and their own improvident style of living.

Of course, her parents were not very anxious to retain this bargain any longer than possible upon their hands, they therefore seized every opportunity of introducing Euphemia into the best of company, in the hope of making a wealthy conquest.

Among other persons to whom Maria had been introduced as forming the company, was a Mr. Barnell, who made himself insufferably officious and monstrously disagreeable. He paid Maria particular attention from the moment he was introduced to her, and she found herself, to her inconceivable vexation, compelled to take a chair by the side of him, for all the other guests were occupied as they thought proper, and to her astonishment and confusion, upon looking round for Walter, she found him paying his attentions to the Honourable Euphemia Bamford, and not appearing to notice any other person.

Mr. Barnell was an importation from Cockneyshire, and truly a bright specimen he was. He was a coarse, vulgar, mean looking man, with a very large nose, much carbuncled, small, piggish grey eyes, very high cheek bones, a broad face, short neck, high shoulders, sandy hair, short cropped whiskers, a wide mouth and very black teeth. His person was thick and clumsy, his clothes of the newest cut, but could not hide the excessive vulgarity for which he was so remarkable. He was reported to be very rich, which he had got, not by his own talents or industry, but by the good nature of a distant relation who had lately died and bequeathed him the whole of his wealth.

The mawkish attentions of this man to Maria were most disgusting to her gentle and sensitive nature, and she never felt so truly miserable before in her life. He put a number of the most absurd questions to her, which she scarcely knew how to answer, and there was a boldness and vulgarity in his general conduct, that was truly sickening. How did Maria long that the night was over, and to render her still more miserable was the situation of Walter, who seemed studiously attentive and polite to Miss Bamford.

She was very much surprised, however, at the sudden alteration in the behaviour of Mr. Wallingford, who was seated opposite to her, and appeared to watch her with looks of encouragement and kindness. All aspect of former wrath, if such he had really felt, had vanished, and he addressed her when occasion offered, in the most affectionate manner. This was singular;—it was completely inexplicable, and Maria was bewildered and surprised. To add to the vexation of Maria, it appeared likely that Mr. Barnell would be a frequent guest at the Hall, for he had but just taken possession of a new estate, called Woodbine House, which was situated but a short distance from Wallingford, and intended to reside there until he had succeeded in making a conquest of some rustic beauty, who had not received the contamination of a London course of tuition.

Maria sat in a state of misery that may easily be conceived; but her anguish was the mor-

(MARIA AND THE OLD HAG.)

augmented by observing her cousin so occupied with the bold and conceited Euphemia. But little she knew the state of Walter's thoughts, or she would have pitied him. Constrained to listen to her fulsome and ignorant observations, and narrowly watched by his father, who frowned ominously upon him if he observed him not superciliously attentive to the lady, his situa-tion, it may well be imagined, was anything but enviable. He was at a loss to conceive what could be his father's motives for placing him in such a wretched situation. Anon his eyes would wander to that part of the room where Maria was seated, and when he beheld her subjected to the loathsome attentions of Mr. Barnell, his blood mantled to his cheeks, and he could scarcely restrain his feelings within the bounds of decorum.

"Gracious, Mr. Walter!" suddenly exclaimed Euphemia, "I declare your cousin and Mr. Barnell seem to be quite smitten with each other!"

Walter felt his indignation rising, and he made no reply.

"Well, to be sure," continued Euphemia, "she might make many a worse bargain than that;—wealthy suitors are not to be caught every day, especially by those who are portionless, and not possessed of any great personal attractions."

Walter smiled contemptuously, and suffered his envious companion to proceed.

"Mr. Barnell is very rich, no less than fifteen thousand pounds a year, besides large landed property;—a very eligible match indeed for some young lady."

"As you seem to think so well of it, miss," replied Walter, sarcastically, "I wonder you do not endeavour to make a conquest of the gentleman."

"Oh, me, indeed!" said Euphemia, sharply, and tossing her head, as though she thought it would be a very great honour for any man to be blest with her smiles; "but perhaps," she added, and she looked significantly at Walter, who knows but my heart may have imbibed a prior attachment."

"Of course, Miss Bamford," said Walter, indifferently, "that is not at all unlikely; but with the feelings of your heart I cannot have anything to do."

Euphemia bit her lips at this reply, and looked as spitefully as she could; she then muttered something about some people's unpolished manners, and other people's consummate vanity, and looking disdainfully round upon the company, remained silent for a few moments, much to the relief of Walter, who was thoroughly disgusted.

"There are, certainly, some very beautiful women present here to-day," observed old Lord Harlington, in his usual snuffling tone, and breaking silence for the first time after dinner.

"Beautiful women!" ejaculated his daughter; "good Heavens! papa, what have you done with your taste? I'm sure, if a gentleman wants to see handsome women, he must not come to the neighbourhood of Wallingford Hall for them."

As Miss Bamford said this, she tossed her head, and glanced towards Maria, with a look of malice that did not pass unobserved by Walter, but he treated it with the contempt that it merited.

"The ignorant, vain girl," muttered Walter to himself; "my father must have some design in placing me in such a situation as this;— Maria too, is she not selected to entertain that low-bred, vulgar, insipid monkey, Mr. Barnell, with his fifteen thousand a year! Bah! I must soon, however, undeceive him with regard to any presumptuous notions he may have formed. Maria wedded to such a senseless brute— Psha! the very idea is preposterous! Let the dolt aspire to the hand of the conceited, frivolous Miss Bamford, and there, no doubt, he would succeed, for she is every way worthy of him, and I dare say she would, or at least her covetous and needy parents would feel very glad for her to have him in preference to me, who cannot boast of any such a fortune at present, at any rate."

It was a great relief to poor Maria, when after dinner, the gentlemen sitting themselves down to enjoy their glass convivially, the ladies were, of course, permitted to retire to the drawing room, to amuse themselves in the manner most congenial to their tastes. But Walter was forced to remain behind, and his vexation was not the least diminished by the events that followed. The toasts had been freely circulated, and Mr. Barnell had responded to each with the coarse conviviality of a tap-room ale bibber, when after coughing two or three times, looking inconceivably stupid, and grinning with an ignorant self-satisfied air upon everybody present, he got upon his feet, and proposed the health of their hospitable host's niece, Miss Maria Herbert! Walter started from his chair; his eye flashed with indignation, and his heart seemed to rise into his throat—in vain he attempted to get the glass to his lips; but his surprise and wrath were not a little augmented, when his father with a benevolent smile, in reply to the toast Mr. Barnell had proposed, begged leave in the most unqualified terms to return his thanks to that gentleman for the compliment he had so kindly paid to Miss Herbert!

"Good Heavens!" reflected Walter, "can I believe my ears? Or is this some strange delusion? Can my father have become so lost to his former sense of pride, as to take anything as 'a compliment,' and 'so kindly' paid, from such a vulgar numskull as Barnell, especially when addressed to Maria?"

He looked scornfully and indignantly upon Mr. Barnell, when his father had done speaking, at the same time took in his dimensions at a glance. His behaviour was not unnoticed by the company, and there was a low titter, and significant winks passed among them, which shewed that they enjoyed Walter's discomfiture amazingly. Walter marked these demonstrations with the most sovereign contempt, but the marked behaviour of his father did not escape his notice, and made him less at ease than he would otherwise have been. The conduct of Walter had excited that gentleman's utmost anger, and he found great difficulty in refraining from an open expression of his feelings. He motioned his son aside, and in a determined tone said—

"Walter, your conduct has excited my warmest displeasure, and I trust you will not repeat it; I particularly wish, nay, I am anxious to be on the best terms with Mr. Barnell, and I must request, that on pain of my displeasure, you will not, by any ill-timed and ridiculous display of your feelings, cast a cloud over my feelings!"

With these words Mr. Wallingford returned to the festive board, giving Walter a look which plainly evinced that he would not be disobeyed.

Need we attempt to describe the strange conflict of thoughts which raged in the mind of Walter, after this caution on the part of his father. His bosom swelled with offended pride, not for himself only, but for Mr. Wallingford, who had sunk so low in his own estimation as to consider himself honoured by the friendship of such a fellow as Barnell, who looked as if he had but escaped from behind a counter, or from a blacksmith's vice, instead of having the least pretensions to the character of a gentleman; or more especially to aspire to the affections of a young and lovely female; and yet this was the man whom his father wished 'particularly to be on the best of terms with,' and whose friendship presented prospects to his mind's eye, which he was fearful that his son's behaviour might o'er cloud. His father must evidently, he reflected, be suffering under some strange infatuation. But Walter had made up his mind, in spite of his father's warning, and whatever the consequences might be to himself, to thwart the impudent schemes of the hateful and illiterate cockney.

Tired of the company of the gentlemen, and anxious to seek out Maria, and to seize an opportunity to explain to her his feeling, he formed an excuse to retire, and led by the sounds of music to the drawing-room, there found most of the female guests amusing themselves in that manner. He eagerly looked around the room, but was very much disappointed when he found that Maria was not present, and hastening to where his mother was seated, hastily asked what was the cause of Maria's absence.

"Your cousin was taken rather ill," said Mrs. Wallingford, "and has retired to her chamber for awhile until she shall have recovered herself; but I caution you, Walter, and mind my words, lest you bring trouble upon us all, not to display so much attention to Maria, since it only tends to make your father angry."

"Impossible," exclaimed the astonished Walter, scarcely believing what he heard, "how can any attention I may pay to Maria, or any solicitude I may express in her welfare, excite the anger of my father? How has my fair

cousin deserved this? What can she have been guilty of to arouse the displeasure of Mr. Wallingford?"

Mrs. Wallingford put her finger on her lips and enjoined him to silence, in the presence of so many; she then motioned him to follow her, which he did into her closet, where she pointed to a chair, and begged of him to be seated, and earnestly solicited him to tranquillise his feelings. Walter was surprised at the extreme sorrow and agitation visible on her features, and obeyed her in silence.

"Walter," she began in a melancholy tone, "I had hoped that this day might have been allowed to pass over without my being compelled to mention a circumstance which will doubtless cause you pain, but which, nevertheless, I feel it is my duty to tell you, and to enjoin you to a strict compliance with the will of your father."

"Why what has either me or Maria done,' cried the impatient youth, "to cause this sudden change in the conduct of my father? Surely——"

"I implore you, my dear boy," interrupted his mother; "implore you by your love for me, to moderate your feelings, and listen patiently to what I must unfold."

"Mother," replied Walter, firmly, "you know that in everything consistent with my duty to you and my father, I have felt a pleasure in studying to please you, and Heaven forbid that I should cause you a moment's uneasiness; but in this you must pardon me; I never could play the hypocrite, and think you I can tamely submit to play the gallant to that hateful girl, Miss Euphemia Bamford, while at the same time my Maria is subjected to the annoyance of that ignorant man, Mr. Barnell? No, by my——"

"No foolish vows, my son," said Mrs. Wallingford, "alas! they will be useless, your father's mind is made up, and I see no reason why I should not—but, no matter, Walter, I will not speak of it on this day of mirth, tomorrow——"

"No, no," hastily rejoined Walter, "let it not be delayed a moment, you cannot make me more miserable than what I have witnessed this day already caused me to be; tell me, what of my Maria——"

"Your Maria, my poor boy!"—ejaculated his mother, with a deep sigh.

"Aye, my Maria," repeated Walter, with deep emotion, "is she not so; dearer to me than life itself?"

"Hold, Walter! This must not be;" observed his mother; "it would be the height of cruelty to encourage hopes that cannot be realised."

"And why not realised, my dear mother?"

"Because it is the will of your father;

answered his mother, with more firmness than might have been expected.

"What, the will of my father that I should not love Maria?" cried the youth, his lips quivering with emotion.

"As your cousin, still continue to love her, my son," answered his mother, "but——" and she paused, and looked affectionately upon him; "Walter, let it satisfy you that your father has been an observer of the attentions you have paid Maria, and he has commanded that they shall cease; he has desired me to caution Maria not to encourage them; therefore, my dear boy, do not seek by any obstinate vehemence to do that which can only end in misery to us all, much more to her for whom you express so much solicitude. Remember that your cousin is a poor friendless girl, at least with no other friends than——"

At this moment the door of the apartment flew open, and before Walter could make any reply, or his mother could even finish her speech, Maria entered. She looked pale, and was evidently agitated, though she made a powerful effort to suppress her emotions in the presence of her aunt and cousin; the latter of whom, in spite of all his mother had been saying to him, immediately hurried to Maria, and in a voice of the utmost tenderness, inquired after her health, and why the tears still trembled in her eyes and notwithstanding his mother cast upon him a look of reproach, he took her arm, and led her once more into the drawing-room, where, much to the chagrin of Miss Euphemia Bamford, who seemed to be actually thunderstruck, he led her to a seat at the opposite end of the room, and placing himself by her side, took no notice of the disdainful looks of Euphemia, or the insolent inuendos and jokes that were so freely bandied from one to the other. But in Maria's mind a number of conflicting thoughts, hopes, doubts and fears ran riot; the decided conduct of Walter filled her with pleasure, and removed from her thoughts an agonising fear, that amid the blaze of wealth and beauty with which he had been surrounded, he might forget her, or that he had really forgotten her in the society of Miss Bamford. As this idea crossed her imagination, she felt a sort of triumph, which lightened her bosom of half its care; but she was sadly perplexed and grieved, when she remarked the sorrowful look with which Mrs. Wallingford was observing her and Walter.

The pride of Miss Bamford and her parents, Lord and Lady Harlington, had evidently received a severe wound by the behaviour of Walter; and their chagrin could not but be apparent to everybody, except Mrs. Wallingford, to whom it caused the greatest embarrassment.

CHAPTER XXV.

"Oh, let me not the secret hear,
Thy words speak sorrow and despair
'Twere better far than cause this pain,
That I in 'gnorance remain."

THE MAID OF CASTILE.

MATTERS remained in this position for several minutes, and Mrs. Wallingford was obliged to act with the greatest precaution, to prevent an open rupture with Lord and Lady Harlington and their daughter, while at the same time, she might excite the jealousy and offend the other portion of her guests. From this dilemma, however, she was at length released by Euphemia herself, who watching her opportunity, walked over to Maria, and drawing her aside, with that apparent kindness of which she so well knew how to assume the mask, she observed that for months past she had been longing for such an opportunity as that, having heard of her in letters she had received from her friends, and from the flattering accounts they had given of her, being anxious to form an intimacy with her. Then she launched forth into a tirade of unmeaning rubbish, in which she pretended to pay her a great many compliments, but it was easy for Maria to perceive that she entertained a firm opinion that she was immeasurably superior to her, both in personal and intrinsic charms.

"Really, my dear Miss Herbert," continued the lady, you are a regular slayer of hearts and I question if there is scarcely a single gentleman that will leave this assembly without feeling the power of your beauty."

Maria blushed deeply at such levity, and made no reply.

"Ah! there you are again," said the flippant Miss Bamford, "it is that modest, downcast look and that pretty face, when suffused with blushes, that commits all the havoc. But, alas! I pity the poor unfortunate swain who is smitten with you, after Mr. Walter, for I am no diviner of these interesting promblems, and I do not think you can candidly deny, that of all those who are dying in love for you, none possesses so great a share of your affections as your handsome coz."

"All those dying in love with me, Miss?" repeated Maria, with undisguised astonishment and mortification;—"really I——"

"Nonsense, my dear child," interrupted Euphemia, "now you must confess that I am not far out in the conjectures I have formed? Of course, I do not blame you for not confessing to me, as I am no priest; besides, when you seem unconscious, you throw out more arrows than you are aware of; but you cannot but know the deep impression you have made on both my brother's hearts, and as for your cousin Walter —oh, he's absolutely gone past redemption.

There now, that will do, your very eyes tell me that I am right—and what necessity is there for denying it?—But apropos of lovers—what is your opinion of Mr. Barnell, your new conquest, the gentleman who paid you so much attention to-day, upon every opportunity? Do you not think that *he* is a remarkably nice gentleman?"

"I have not yet had an opportunity of forming an estimate of the gentleman's character, Miss," replied Maria, "and it is very improbable that I ever shall. I have heard my uncle, Mr. Wallingford, however, speak of him before to-day, as his having become the possessor of Woodbine House. I hope he may only be as good and charitable as its former occupant, Mr, Goodwin, in whom the poor people have lost a most liberal benefactor."

"Nonsense, my dear," said Euphemia, hastily, "what's the use of lamenting the death of some stupid old fogy? That is no answer to my question; what do you think of Mr. Barnell, with his great wealth?"

"Well then," answered Maria, "since you ask my opinion so earnestly, from the little I have seen of him, I must say that I think him remarkably annoying, and insufferably ignorant."

"What! a gentleman with fifteen thousand per annumn, annoying?" said Euphemia, "you perfectly astonish me."

"Indeed, Miss?" said Maria, "I did not think that I had said anything very remarkable."

"Oh, nothing at all remarkable," returned Euphemia, sarcastically, "but dear me, Miss Herbert, what a very pretty broach that is you wear in your bosom—and as I live it is a heart—oh, oh,—here's a secret discovered!—Don't blush! that's a dear; there's nothing at all unnatural in wearing a heart you know, in one's bosom;—now do tell me all about this, will you, dear? I am all upon thorns till I hear it. And I declare, too," she continued as Maria, deeply blushing, put up her hands to prevent her inspecting the gew-gaw, "a ring too—and the device—how appropriate, a true lover's knot:—why, I am more impatient than ever to be made acquainted with the generous donor; I dare say he was some elegant unsophisticated rustic youth; and no doubt he did not give his heart without having yours in exchange."

"Indeed, miss," returned Maria with the utmost confusion, when she beheld that Mrs. Wallingford had been listening to all that had passed between them, and was looking on with extreme vexation depicted in her countenance; "there is no necessity for your raillery; you are wrong in your surmises too, for these trinkets were given to me by a relation, a near relation!"

"Upon my word, then, I must apologise for my boldness," observed Euphemia, withdrawing her hand from the brooch; "really, I am very sorry, and perhaps Mrs. Wallingford will pardon me, for I presume that she presented you with them, and although I must confess, it is rather *outre* from a lady—still——"

"If there has been any lack of taste displayed in this business," said Mrs. Wallingford, "it is most assuredly on the side of my niece: who ought never to have accepted it, especially from the relative who gave it her. If she would save herself from remarks that she may consider unpleasant, she will immediately resign them to me, and I will give her in exchange these that I wear, which are by far more appropriate. Do, my love, relinquish those foolish baubles, and here is something that will make up for their loss."

With these words, much to the astonishment and agitation of Maria, her aunt took a beautiful diamond ring from her own finger, and removing the one which Walter presented to her, placed it in her bosom; she also presented her her neice with a valuable brooch of exquisite workmanship, in exchange for the one which had attracted Miss Euphemia Bamford's attention and occasioned her rude observations. Maria trembled, but she could not venture to offer a word in expostulation, somewhat to the astonishment of Miss Bamford, who was yet in considerable perplexity and mystery as to the exact cause of all that had taken place. She, however, began a long rigmarole dissertation upon the merits of the trinkets, which gave Maria an opportunity to escape from her, and she seated herself in another part of the room, and reflected sadly upon what had taken place, What could be the meaning of the ambiguous conduct of Mrs. Wallingford? She could in no way account for it; but yet, when she remembered the behaviour of her uncle to her in the morning, she could not help thinking that they had discovered the attachment which subsisted between her and Walter, and disapproved of the same. But why object to it? Had she done anything to render her unworthy of their son, or was it that she was a portionless orphan? Oh, no, no, she dismissed the latter idea almost as soon as it was formed, for she never believed her uncle and aunt would be so mercenary as to make the idea of money guide their actions, where the happiness of herself and Walter was concerned. But when she recollected the manner in which Mr. Wallingford had imposed the task of entertaining Miss Bamford, upon her cousin, she once more began to doubt. Nor had she been able to drive the recollection of the Gipsy girl and her singular prognostications from her mind, and the more deeply she reflected upon them, the more did she seem to feel their truth; yet did she never for an instant imagine that the girl used any supernatural agency; but she thoroughly believed that she was not one of the Gipsy tribe; but that she was some being interested in the fate of her and Walter, who had, by some means or other, become acquainted with what was passing, both privately and publicly in the families of Lord Harlington and Mr. Wallingford, and had adopted the disguise of a Gipsy girl for the purpose of warning her and her cousin.

Tormented with the tumult of thoughts that these ideas ideas gave rise to, Maria feeling a head-ache, took the opportunity of slipping out of the room, and thinking that the evening air might revive her, she walked forth on to the lawn, which she crossed in the direction of the dell. She had not proceeded many paces, however, when she felt her arm arrested by somebody behind, and starting round, what was her consternation to behold the countenance of a frightful old hag fixed upon her, while there was something so unearthly about the expression of the sunken eyes, that Maria was chilled with horror. She was attired in tattered clothes of a variety of colours, and bore in her left hand the long leafless branch of a tree.

Maria tried to scream, but her tongue clave to the roof of her mouth, and she became transfixed with terror.

The hag advanced towards her, and the sardonic grin which overspread her unearthly features, seemed to express a fiendish exultation at the terror evinced by the poor girl. Not a soul but themselves was near the spot, and the hall was so far distant that her shrieks could not have been heard. The mysterious being again grasped the arm of the horror-struck damsel, and fixing her eyes steadfastly upon her countenance, she said in a voice of supernatural solemnity :—

" Girl, thou tremblest ; ay, and well may'st thou ; I come to thee the harbinger of evil ! Ho! ho! ho! 'tis good, 'tis cheery work to wring the hearts of the worldly insects ! Listen to me, dependent on the bounty of the seducer, the libertine, the deceiver :—

"O'er thy head there hangs a fatal spell,
In sorrow and pain art thou doomed to dwell ;
The sigh thou'lt heave, the tear shall start,
And bitter's the woe that shall wring thine heart ;
In vain thou'lt seek, in vain thou'lt try,
From Fate's decrees thou can'st not fly ;
And ere many days their course shall whirl,
Weep and wail will the orphan girl !"

Maria heard no more ; overcome with her terrors as the frightful hag uttered the last fatal sentences, and relaxed her hold of her arm, she sunk on the earth insensible.

When she recovered her senses, she found herself in bed, and Mrs. Wallingford hanging affectionately over her ; a burning fever seemed to scorch her brain, and she had only a faint recollection of the past ; but what she did remember was impressed upon her mind in characters so vivid, that she felt convinced she could never obliterate them. Mrs. Wallingford

wisely forbore to question her upon the cause of her illness, and after some necessary attentions, she left the room for a short time, in hope that she would get some repose, leaving her in the care of Agatha.

The continued absence of Maria from the party at the time the incident took place which we have just narrated, had, of course, excited the astonishment and alarm of Mrs. Wallingford and Walter, more especially the latter, who evinced the most painful emotions, and requested that his mother would hasten to her chamber to enquire after her health. He had no sooner made the request than, looking up, he beheld his father scowling upon him in the most repulsive manner, and evidently, from his manner, greatly displeased at his behaviour. Mrs. Wallingford, however, who felt uneasy at the illness of Maria, in spite of the looks of her husband, which she well understood, hastened to her apartment ; and was surprised not to find her there. She returned to the room where she had left the party, and informed them of the circumstance.

" What can be the meaning of this?" cried Walter, starting hastily from his seat, and retiring from Euphemia. " Where can she be? Something wrong has happened ;—I will go immediately in search of her."

"Stay, sir," exclaimed Mr. Wallingford, frowning, " methinks your anxiety after your cousin has caused you to forget your gallantry. I dare say Miss Herbert will return when she is tired of her walk ; at any rate, I desire that you will remain here."

But Walter heard not the latter part of this mandate, having abruptly quitted the side of Euphemia and rushed out of the Hall, hastily desiring a servant to follow him. Wallingford bit his lips with vexation, for he quickly noticed the bitter smile of sarcasm and envy which overspead the features of Euphemia, and the significant glances that passed between her and her parents, Lord and Lady Harlington.

In the meantime, Walter hastened from the house, and searched every part of the grounds, without being able to trace anything of Maria, when, crossing the lawn in the direction she had taken, he beheld her stretched lifeless on the ground, as we have described, after her adventure with the frightful old hag.

We need not attempt to describe his anguish when he discovered her ; he lifted her in his arms, pressed his lips to her pale cheek, and endeavoured to recall her to animation ; while thus occupied, Mr. Wallingford and several of the guests and domestics made their appearance, and the former sternly approaching his son, snatched the form of Maria from his arms and consigning her to the care of the servants, commanded him to return to the Hall. Walter looked up in the countenance of his father in a supplicating manner, but the latter frowned upon him, and muttering,—" Foolish boy !" motioned him before him, in a way that told him he would not be disobeyed.

When Maria was restored to sensibility, the company had broke up and separated ; but although Walter had retired to his chamber, he found it impossible to hope for sleep, in the state of anxiety his mind was in with regard to his fair cousin. He kept continually sending to inquire how she was, and when he heard that she had recovered her senses, he was in such a state of agitation, that it was with the utmost difficulty he could refrain from rushing into her chamber and throwing himself at her feet. What could have been the cause of her alarm, what had occasioned her insensibility ?—Surely no one had dared to insult her ;—at the very idea, the blood mantled in the young man's cheeks, and he clenched his fists. Then the name of Mr. Barnell suggested itself to his memory, and his emotions and wrath increased,—

" The egregious blockhead !" cried the impetuous youth, starting to his feet, " if I thought he had presumed to—"

But then he remembered that the individual he was so ready to suspect, had been in the apartment all the time that Maria was absent from it ; and the folly of his suspicions at once presented itself to him.

He passed a wretched night, for he revolved in his mind the whole of the occurrences of the day, which had been one of the most miserable he had ever endured. The conduct of his father was no longer inexplicable to him ; for his marked expressions and looks as regarded Euphemia, and the manner in which he had forced the company of Mr. Barnell upon Maria, quickly unravelled the mystery. As he thought of this, Walter's bosom swelled with indignation, and he was at a loss to conceive what could have, in so short a time, changed the disposition of his father, who had ever been conspicuous for his pride and independence, as to make him act in a manner approaching to adulation towards the poltroon Barnell. As soon as he left his couch, he sent a female domestic to enquire after Maria's health, who returned and informed him that she was considerably better, and that his mother, early as it was, had been with her for some time. At breakfast, Mrs. Wallingford made her appearance, and she related the facts of the cause of Maria's illness, as they had been related to her by her niece. Mr Wallingford affected to treat the tale with indifference, and pretended to say that Maria had been labouring under some singular delusion,—but, in fact, he felt startled by the circumstance, for he had not the slightest doubt from the description, that the mysterious being who had appeared to his niece was the same who had so often annoyed him, and whose coming had always been the prelude to some painful calamity. He, however, sought to erase the idea from his mind, and in a careless tone said,—

" Maria is a strange girl, and is possessed of many romantic and foolish notions, which she will do well to divest herself of as soon as possible ; I must say that her giving way to this weakness on such an occasion as the party yesterday was in very bad taste."

" Well, for my part," observed Walter, " so little gratified was I with what took place yesterday, that I hope it will be a long time before we have any more parties."

" Ridiculous !" said Mr. Wallingford, angrily, " that observation is remarkable for nothing but its excessive absurdity ; however, it assures me that I was right in a conclusion that I came to yesterday, namely, that you have been too long nursed in the lap of your mother, Walter, and that I ought not so long to have suffered you to judge of the world by the notions of indulgent women, and foolish girls."

" Father," replied Walter, colouring with astonishment and indignation, " you have taught me hitherto how to view the world, and I have never sought another tutor ; if I may have derived but an indifferent taste for that world from such instruction, surely the fault is not mine."

Mr. Wallingford frowned, but evidently abashed, could make no answer ; but the tears stood in the eyes of his wife, and she turned her head away, and covered her face with her hands. Mr. Wallingford seemed to be too much confused for a few minutes to speak ; he bit his lips, and then arising from his chair, traversed the room two or three times, and returning to the table, addressing himself to Walter, said,—

" This morning, Walter, you must attend me to Lord Harlington's ; nay, sir, no objections, I command obedience."

" Sir'" replied his son, " of course, I must comply with your wishes, but—"

" No more, sir," impatiently interrupted Mr. Wallingford, " you know my will."

Walter bowed, and the repast being over, his father beckoned him to attend him, and they left the room together. When they had gone, Mrs. Wallingford, who had with much difficulty restrained her feelings, gave vent to them in a copious flood of tears. She saw at once the misery that was in store for Walter and Maria, and her heart was wrung with the most poignant anguish. After having in some degree vanquished her feelings, she went to the apartment of Maria, whom she found more composed, and who felt herself so much better, that she had but a few moments before rung the bell, with the idea of arising.

Mrs. Wallingford inquired affectionate after her health, and would have persuaded h to remain in bed for the present; but Maria declaring that she felt quite well, and that she had only been suffering from the effects of error, she arose, and attended Mrs. Wallingford to the parlour.

"But are you positive, my dear," observed Mrs. Wallingford, after they had been for a few minutes engaged in conversation on the subject of the mysterious visitant, "are you quite certain that you was not mistaken, and that you was labouring under some delusion excited by the pain in your head of which you had previously been complaining?"

"Oh, my dear aunt, how is it possible that I could have been so deceived, when I remember every sentence of the lines she uttered to me?" returned Maria: "I shall never forget the frightful expression of that strange being's countenance, the fiendish pleasure with which she seemed to mark my terror; and then, too, her words; alas! I know not how it is, but I have a sad presentiment that they will be realised; what took place yesterday, the more convinces me."

Maria sighed deeply as she recalled to her mind the behaviour of her uncle; the conduct of Euphemia, and the situation in which Walter was placed with that frivolous and vain woman, and the no less awkward position in which she had been forced with that disgusting ignoramus, Mr. Barnell.

"And what took place yesterday, my dear child," said Mrs. Wallingford, hastily, "that could give you any just cause to come to such a conclusion?"

Maria sighed again more deeply than before; and evincing the utmost confusion at the question, was unable to make any reply. This was an opportunity which Mrs. Wallingford had been waiting for, and she determined to break the ice at once

"Maria, my love," said her aunt, in her usual tones of affection, "it would be folly in me attempting to deny that I can answer the question I have put to you as well as you can yourself. Indeed, I am too well aware of your thoughts, and however painful it may be to me to request you, and you to obey, as you value my happiness and your own, you will cease to encourage ideas that can never be realised. You must no longer dwell upon the words, the sentiments, which the youthful folly and romantic notions of Walter has, I know, instilled into your mind. Now, tell me, my dear girl, and be not afraid to own it, that rash foolish boy, has he not confessed he loves you, and you have made a reciprocal acknowledgment. Is it not so?"

Maria blushed, and turned pale, alternately at this interrogation, but she in vain endeavoured to answer. Mrs. Wallingford looked upon her with an expression of pity, and it

was a second or two before she was able to proceed:—

"Yes, yes, my dear Maria," at length continued she, "I see it is as I suspected; your looks convince me of the truth of my surmises. Foolish boy, thus to give occasion for grief to wring that gentle bosom, which, but for that, might never have known what sorrow was. But you must dismiss the idea from your thought; it can never be gratified; Heaven knows, had my will been consulted, nothing could have afforded me greater felicity than to have seen my son wedded to his fair and gentle cousin; but, unhappily, my views and Mr. Wallingford's upon that subject do not happen to coincide; and, therefore, I beg of you no longer to allow Walter to anticipate what cannot take place. Mr. Wallingford, I am convinced, will never grant his assent to your nuptials;—he has formed other notions for Walter, and when you reflect, Maria, that I, your only real friend, whose affection for you, you can never have had the slightest cause to doubt, am placed in a most unpleasant situation by this circumstance, I know you will not hesitate a moment to comply with my request, and not suffer any future behaviour in Walter that may encourage him to act contrary to the wishes of his father." Mrs. Wallingford's voice faltered when she came to this passage, and taking the hand of her niece, she pressed it fervently, and looking tenderly in her face concluded:—"but never will the pride of Maria, I know, suffer her to indulge in a passion which has not the sanction of the father of the object of her unfortunate love."

Poor Maria looked up hastily through her tears, and endeavouring to smile, said:—

"Yes, my dearest aunt, you have, indeed, formed a right opinion of poor Maria; she will never do anything wilfully that might cause you a moment's pain; and Walter, he shall never, if I can help it, again be in my company except in the presence of my——Mr. Wallingford and yourself."

Mrs. Wallingford was struck with the manner in which her niece gave utterance to this speech, and she beheld with pain from the tenour of it, that she felt keenly the observations she had felt it her duty to make use of. Poignantly had Maria felt the expressions of Mrs. Wallingford, "your only real friend." "Alas!" she reflected, as she hastened from the presence of Mrs. Wallingford, "with what contempt, what disdain am I viewed by my uncle; I am considered only as a poor dependent on his bounty, but one degree above his lowest domestic. Oh, how has my young and unsuspicious mind misled me hitherto;— upon him I have ever looked as an affectionate guardian; but alas, now too keenly do I feel that I am only an object of charity;—a burthen from which he is anxious to be released."— Unable to restrain her feelings, the poor girl

MARIA AT THE OLD NURSE'S COTTAGE.

flew to the summer-house we have before mentioned, as the favourite retreat of her and
Walter, and throwing herself in a seat, she
buried her face in her handkerchief, and gave
free vent to the emotions that racked her
bursting heart.

_____

CHAPTER XXVI.

"Ah, was it well to sever
Two fond hearts for ever?
I can forget thee never, &c."
T. H. BAYLEY.

LONG, long did Maria sit and weep; and
revolved in her mind the injunctions of her

aunt; everything around her reminded her of Walter, whose image she had been commanded to erase from her recollection, and at the same time the interview with the mysterious Gipsy girl recurred to her recollection; an interview which had been the prelude to that sorrow and anguish she now so keenly felt. As these thoughts crossed her mind, she looked up, and glanced timidly around the place, almost expecting once more to behold that singular being, or the more awful one that had crossed her path the evening before. But all was still around, and no object met her eyes, save the gentle waving of the tall poplars which grew immediately before the entrance. Again she reflected on the misery of her fate, while the tears of bitter anguish glistened on her cheeks, and her temples throbbed and ached with the intensity of the thoughts that crowded upon her brain.

"Good God!" she exclaimed, "from what a dream of happy unconsciousness am I suddenly awakened;—what a painful certainty has the words of my aunt aroused me to;—I, that thought myself so blest, so fortunate;—what am I? My aunt talked of pride, but alas! what have I to be proud of? Am I not an absolute beggar;—without means of my own to support me? And could I ever have been so presumptuous as to aspire to the hand of Walter Wallingford, the son of my benefactor, the son of him from whom I have been receiving the bread of charity; the heir of the noble, the proud house of Wallingford. Oh, foolish, vain girl that I was; but I am well punished for my presumption. Ere this, too, doubtless Walter has heard his father's wishes and commands, and may be brought to a conviction of the imprudence he has been guilty of, in for a moment encouraging the hope of such a thing, in the bosom of one who was destitute of rank and fortune. But no matter;—I will struggle with my feelings, and though my heart break, I will let them see that the poor humble intruder upon their charity has sufficient pride to scorn to be the cause of any uneasiness to Mr. Wallingford. Yes, I feel my heart getting firmer; —I will think no more of Walter, and he shall be at full liberty to cease to recollect that I was ever anything more to him than his cousin. Let him become the acknowledged suitor of Miss Bamford ; it is a match his father, of course, can never object to ; for has she not all the pride of rank and fortune to recommend her? I will never reproach him for it, by look or word:—no, never shall he be able to judge from my countenance that the mercenary motives which guide the actions of him and his father excite my contempt and disdain. My heart may break, but never shall they know my real feelings. Let them be united, I——"

Completely overcome at the idea, she dropped her head upon the rustic table and sobbed aloud. She was suddenly startled by hearing some person repeat her name, and then attempt to take her hand, and raising her head, he astonishment and confusion may be easily conjectured when she beheld the form of the hated Mr. Barnell standing before her.

Maria was too much surprised and bewildered to speak, but Mr. Barnell, with the most impudent effrontery, advanced towards her, and attempted to take her hand as he said—

"Dear, dear, Miss Herbert, how it greives me to see you so afflicted ; indeed it does, Miss. What in the name of wonder can be the cause of it? Now do not think me rude, dear Miss Herbert, but who can behold those lovely cheeks suffused with tears, and feel unmoved? Indeed, I cannot, open your thoughts to me sweet girl, and——"

"Sir," said Maria, rising and recovering, while her bosom swelled with resentment as the vulgar being tried to take her hand, and glanced at her with a wretched attempt at love and admiration; "sir, I request you will forbear; allow me to pass, and I will acquaint my aunt that you have arrived."

"Nay, my dear Miss Herbert," answered Mr. Barnell, forcibly detaining her, "you must excuse me, but not so fast ; I cannot part with you till I have unfolded to you my mind, I will then accompany you to Mrs. Wallingford. Now pray do not be flurried, be seated, and listen to me patiently. Upon my word, Miss Herbert, I would not wound your delicacy for the world, for no one is a greater admirer of it than myself, and it is that which has so deeply interested me, more than anything else, ever since the first moment I beheld you; I assure you your beauty has quite captivated me, and——"

"In pity to my feelings, sir, do not detain me," interrupted Maria, whose cheeks were dyed with crimson blushes, and whose bosom swelled with offended pride and indignation; "pray suffer me to retire; for indeed your words——"

"Pardon me, Miss Herbert," replied Barnell, still detaining her, " but I cannot, indeed I cannot comply with your request. But, upon my word, my sweet creature, you need not be afraid of anything I may utter; I am always very particular in the language I make us of, especially to a charming, modest young lady like yourself. Believe me, I entertain not a single dishonourable thought towards you—I could not do so for the wealth of the Indies; you have quite charmed me, quite won my heart, and you are the only female whom I should feel proud to make the lady of Woodbine House. You probably have heard, miss, of my rank and station in life, and what great prospects I have of the future ?" Here the little great man pursed himself up, and seemed to think himself of very great consequence indeed. "My circumstances are such, Miss Herbert," he continued, "that I can follow entirely the bent of my own inclinations in my selection of a lady for my wife. I have no incumbrances whatever, I am entirely my own master, and you will be your own mistress, without any spiteful relations to annoy you, by reminding you that you came into their family without a fortune, as officious relations are sometimes apt to do; no, my charming girl, in my estimation you are in yourself more than the largest fortune could be, and no greater happiness can I feel than in being united to you. So I am sure we should be very comfortable together, for I am of a very amiable temper, as you have doubtless already discovered. Ah! why do you turn away from me? do not be so shy; but give your consent to my making proposals to your uncle, Mr. Wallingford."

"Not for the universe, sir," ejaculated Maria with great emotion; "indeed I cannot listen to any such arrangement; I feel honoured by your good opinion, but I am yet too young to think of changing my condition—I cannot think of a union that——but my aunt, sir, no doubt has already answered you upon that subject, and——"

"You say right, Miss Herbert," interrupted Mr. Barnell, with a look of offended dignity, occasioned by her unequivocal rejection of his suit. "Mrs. Wallingford has indeed answered me upon the subject, and I have her permission to pay my addresses to you." And as he made this avowal he raised himself to his fullest height;—pulled up his shirt collar, and demonstrated in every possible way his own opinion of his own importance, and the contempt he entertained of her approval or disapproval, when he had the sanction of her guardians. "And miss," continued the ignorant booby, "not only have my addresses been sanctioned by your aunt, but by the unqualified consent and approbation of Mr. Wallingford, who is sanguine as to my success as he says, when all the circumstances are considered, under which I press my suit."

"Enough," said the poor girl, weeping bitterly, "Mr. Wallingford has done his utmost, and bitterly do I feel my dependence on his bounty. But he shall find, poor and humble as I am, I will never consent to——But excuse me, sir:—you are not to blame, and I thank you for having been pleased to condescend to make me an offer which no circumstances whatever will tempt me to accept."

"But, my dear Miss Herbert, listen to me—for a moment only," ejaculated Mr. Barnell, as she tore herself suddenly from him, and bounded out of the summer-house with the speed of lightning; but she paid no attention to his voice, and ran with all the speed she could to the Hall, where she hastened to her own apartment, avoiding the sight of everybody, more especially Mrs. Wallingford, whom, after what she had heard, she dreaded to behold. She threw herself in a chair, and after weeping bitterly for several moments, thus gave expression to the violence of her feelings—

"'Tis true, then; my every hope is at an end, happiness and me are henceforth strangers. Oh, this is the cruellest blow of all; to think that I occupy so mean a station in the estimation of those I thought my dearest friends, as for them to suppose that such a detestable being as Mr. Barnell could tempt me to become his wife for the sake of his lucre!—Oh, wretched, wretched Maria, you will never again know peace! But," she continued after a brief pause, as a feeling of offended pride swelled her bosom, "am I a slave, that, because I have eaten the bread of charity they have provided, they should consider that they have a right to dispose of me to the highest bidder, without consulting my will or the dictates of my own heart? It cannot be; and yet haven't I but just listened to words that confirm it, and that from the lips of that man whom of all others I despise and abhor; nay more, was I not subjected to his loathsome adulation, forced to listen to his *generous* offer, which he made with so much parade, to make me the mistress of his hand and fortune, and that by the permission of my aunt and uncle!—By Heaven, I would hail death directly with pleasure, in preference to such a fate!—But Walter—oh, there have I still greater cause for sorrow and anguish; shall I not be mentioned to him after this, as the bride elect of the hateful Mr. Barnell?—nay, may *he* not also hear it with expressions of approbation, and thank the good fortune which has attended his portionless cousin in becoming the wife of the master of Woodbine House!—But hold, Maria, your grief leads you into error, and makes you ungenerous; —no, I will not, cannot think that Walter could act so; he could never wish to see his poor Maria so truly wretched."

As these thoughts occurred to her, she wept more violently than ever. But yet amidst this vehement grief her mind was firm and determined to maintain her dignity, and act according to the impulse of her heart and the dictates of her conscience, in spite of any severe trial which she might be put to. She felt that she was the victim of injustice and cruelty, and with that knowledge, her mind underwent a singular change, and she was resolved to let those who persecuted her see, that the gentle, quiet girl, as she had hitherto been, had still a will and resolution of her own, when they were called forth by a sense of undue oppression.

Long did Maria reflect upon the event of the morning and the words of Mr. Barnell, and endeavour to come to some satisfactory determination as to the plan it would be most prudent to adopt in her future behaviour to her uncle and aunt. What course could she pursue, if they insisted upon her receiving the attentions of Mr. Barnell, poor and friendless as she was, and yet she reflected, she was not entirely destitute, for after the death of her poor father she recalled to her mind, at the sale of his effects, there was a sum of about four hundred pounds left, which she certainly had a right to, unless Mr. Wallingford should be mean enough to claim that paltry sum for the expense he had been at in her board and learning. But no, she would not do him the injustice to believe that he would so far degrade himself, as to take advantage of that claim to deprive her of that trifling sum, and leave her without any resources. To be sure he might think by that means she would be compelled to yield to his wishes.

"But even in that idea he should be disappointed," exclaimed Maria, proudly;—"I will endure any hardship, suffer any privation, rather than become the wife of that hateful being. His wife!—Good God!—what fate could there be half so dreadful, so disgraceful as that? Have I not youth—have I not health—and strength—and why cannot I work for my living as well as many of my poor fellow creatures, to whom I am in nothing superior but education? Yes, I have, and resolution to combat with the change. Any fate is happiness, compared with that of becoming the wife of Mr. Barnell."

Just as she came to this conclusion, she was aroused by the sound of horses' feet on the gravel walk which led up to the hall, and listening with a throbbing heart, she heard the voice of Walter as he spoke in his usual tones of kindness to his groom. Her bosom heaved, and her brain throbbed with emotion at the well known and much loved accents, and she forgot in a moment the gloomy thoughts that had before occupied her mind. Could she but see him, and judge by his countenance what had been his adventure at Harlington Abbey, she thought she could be happy. She arose from her chair and approached the casement, but just as she had placed herself at it, she heard the hall door open, and just caught a glimpse of Walter's form as he entered the house. She returned disappointed to her seat, and became lost in a vortex of distressing conjectures.

She was startled from these by hearing the voices of Mr. Wallingford and his son, apparently in tones of anger. What could be the meaning of this? Maria was all agitation;—surely she could not be the object of this altercation, and yet her mind foreboded that she was. The apartment in which they were was immediately underneath her chamber, and she could hear everything they said by opening her door. She could not resist the temptation,

prompted by her curiosity, to endeavour ascertain what they were quarrelling abou She gently opened the door, and walked on the lobby, and there she could hear every wo that passed, for they spoke very loud, and we evidently both warm. Maria trembled as sh listened to what they said, for she could lea immediately that she was the subject of the quarrel. She soon understood the cause, Walt on his return had inquired for her, and on bein informed by Mrs. Wallingford that the last tin she had been seen was by Mr. Barnell in tl summer-house, burst through all the bounds decorum, and had not his father forced him o of the room, there is no doubt but that he wou have had a serious quarrel with Mr. Barnell.

"Nay, sir," said Walter in continuatio "I owe you every love and duty as a son. ar I trust that in all things you have ever foun me dutiful and attentive;—but I am dete mined that in this case I will not be pacifi until I have sought the presence of my cousi and from her own lips have an explanation Mr. Barnell's conduct."

"Walter," returned his father," I cautic you not to endeavour to anger me more tha you have done already. Remember, I a your father, and will be obeyed."

"And in all that is reasonable and just, sir said Walter, "I will not offer to disobey you but I must persist in seeking out Maria."

"Rash, ungrateful boy," exclaimed M Wallingford, "and it is thus I am rewarded f yielding to your request this morning? R member your promise, that if I did urge you request to Euphemia, you would obey my wishe in not seeking the society of Miss Herbert?"

"I did promise that I would not seek an clandestine interview with *my cousin*, sir, an *your niece*, as you once felt honoured to cal her," returned his son indignantly.

"And I should have felt it no disgrace stil to have called her my niece," observed M Wallingford," had she not abused my indul gence, and sought to crush my happiness b weaning you, sir, from your duty."

Maria gasped for breath, and leant agains the bannisters, as she listened to this crue speech. Unkindly as Mr. Wallingford had be fore behaved to her, she could scarcely credit th evidence of her senses, or believe that he coul utter such an ungenerous, such an unfounde accusation.

"By heaven! you wrong my Maria," replie Walter; "never by word or deed did she abus the kindness you *once* treated her with; he gentle nature, her integrity, and———"

"Bah!" interrupted Mr. Wallingford im patiently, "Why persist in offending my ear with a repetition of this fulsome tirade of non sense and inflated trash? I am sickened an disgusted with it. You are a novice to the way of the world, or you would not speak of Maria' immaculate charms with such enthusiasm. Experience will show you that a passable face and person, and a mawkish, amiable disposition, which, in fact, has never yet been tried, are not the only things to ensure comfort and happiness in matrimony."

"Never, sir!" cried Walter firmly, never can time, change, or circumstances effect any change in my sentiment of affection for my dear cousin. 'Tis true, I promised you that I would no more speak of my attachment until I had purchased that worldly experience of which you have so often spoken to me; but when you exacted from me such a concession, you did not inform me, sir, that you were going to sanction the hateful and sickening attentions of that detestable—"

"Hold, boy!" interrupted Mr. Wallingford vehemently, "this resistance is intolerable;—I command you, sir, on pain of my displeasure, to treat my friends with the respect they merit."

"And call you, father, this illiterate, low-bred man," returned Walter, "who but the other day was a beggar, and who has no virtues or good qualities to recommend him, your friend?" Oh, father, pardon the warmth which my surprise calls forth, but, indeed, my impatience overcomes my reason, when I reflect that you would throw her away whom you once loved, upon such a worthless dolt——"

"Psha! the boy is mad," remarked his father; "is not Mr. Barnell rich, possessing an income of fifteen thousand a year, and yet you would wish to make it appear that I am seeking to make a sacrifice of this girl who has not a penny in the world. Let me hear no more of this foolery, Walter; I think Mr. Barnell confers a very great honour on your portionless cousin by the offer he has made her, wealthy as he is, and with every prospect of shortly obtaining a title."

"No titles or honours, however great," observed Walter, "can ever make him more than a plebeian in birth, and an idiot in manners."

"Tut, tut, don't tire my patience," returned Wallingford, angrily, "I command you, sir, to return with me immediately to the sitting-room, and behave yourself with proper respect towards Mr. Barnell."

"Pray excuse me, sir," said Walter humbly, "I would rather remain here until Mr. Barnell has left the Hall; I wish not to hurt your feelings, which I must do in the presence of that man, to whom, I am confident, I could not act with civility."

A pause followed this reply, and Maria could hear Mr. Wallingford pacing the chamber to and fro with disordered step. She trembled for the consequence of this altercation to Walter, and the bitter things her uncle had said of her, had so affected her that it was with difficulty she could sustain herself.

"Then, sir," at length ejaculated Mr. Wallingford, "you treat my authority as a father with contempt?"

"Oh, no, no, my dear father, replied Walter, "you do me an injustice by such a thought, indeed you do. I should hate myself could I forget my duty to you; any thing else that you command me to do I will obey, but do not pain me by forcing me into the presence of that man whom I abhor;—how can I do otherwise than hate and despise him, while my Maria——"

"Enough," interrupted his father, obstinate as you are, I will submit to your will. Remain here, sir, but remember I have your promise that you will not seek an interview with Miss Herbert, or prejudice her against my friend."

"You shall be obeyed, sir," replied Walter, and the same moment Mr. Wallingford quitted the apartment. Overcome with the intensity of her wounded feelings, the hapless Maria staggered into her chamber, and throwing herself on her couch, sobbed aloud.

"Good God!" she reflected, "can I have been awake; no, no, surely it must all have been some frightful dream. Oh, Maria, thou art indeed truly wretched."

Her tears again flowed fast; but in the midst of her dreadful anguish, her heart beat with delight when she remembered the words she had heard Walter utter, which so plainly proved beyond a doubt, the sincerity and ardour of his affection for her; but, alas! how hopeless was this unfortunate passion, for although he had so firmly opposed the will of his father as far as regarded Euphemia; contrary as it must be to his wishes and repugnant to his feelings, yet did she feel certain, and indeed her wishes were for the same, that Walter's sense of duty would not suffer him to disobey the desire of his parents. It was distracting to imagine the misery, the grief, and disappointment that were, she knew, in store for her and Walter, more particularly while they were together, and then to know to what mortifications it would expose her aunt, who was evidently anything but a willing actor in the plot, filled her bosom with tenfold sorrow and regret. The contemptuous manner, too, in which Mr. Wallingford had spoken of her to Walter, had sunk deep into her heart.

"And shall I remain no longer to receive the bounty and protection of one who regards me with disdain, if not hate?" she cried wringing her hands with the intensity of her feelings; "no, no, however I may suffer, whatever misery may attend me, I will no longer remain beneath this roof; no more will I eat the bread of charity from one who looks upon me as a burthen. My poor dear aunt, and Walter, too, when I am away, will probably soon cease to remember me, and then——"

She could not finish the sentence; her sobs stifled the words in her throat, and she remained for some time with her face covered with her hands, in a state of stupor.

At length, however, she aroused herself, and became calm and composed; her innate pride made her feel eager to become the independent being she had determined to be, and to show Mr. Wallingford that she had a proper spirit, and was not the weak, timid, humble girl, he probably imagined her. She dried up her tears, and descended to the dining-room, with but little appearance of the grief she had so recently experienced, and the anguish with which her bosom was now distracted. The repast was a miserable one to all parties, apparently. Walter looked sad, and frequently, when his father was not watching him, his eye wandered to Maria, and in it was such an expression of love, and such poignant regret, that it wrung her heart. Mrs. Wallingford looked pale and ill, and Wallingford seemed to be far from being happy, although he endeavoured to appear so. and sought to engage his son in conversation upon different topics, but more especially upon what they had seen at Harlington Abbey, and talked of the beauty of the paintings: the taste they displayed in the gardens; the excellent arrangement of the parterres, and many other things, which seemed far from being interesting to Walter, who, when a question was put to him in reference to these things, invariably protested his entire ignorance of anything he had been talking about.

"Well, you certainly must have been blind this morning, Walter," observed his father, evidently chagrined, although he endeavoured all in his power to conceal it, and affected to smile, or you must have seen all that I have been mentioning."

"Indeed you are mistaken, sir," replied Walter, " I was not blind, as you have been pleased to imagine, and indeed had I been so on that occasion, I should have had very little to regret."

"Upon my word," said Mr. Wallingford, colouring, "you do not pay much of a compliment to Lord Harlington and his family, Walter. For my own part, I could not help noticing the improvements that have lately taken place at the abbey, which is now really a most magnificent specimen of gothic architecture; then Lady Harlington has such a refined taste, look at her grottos and hermitages, and the fountain in the centre of the garden, all designed by her, with the aid of her accomplished daughter. Really, Walter, I cannot imagine what you could be thinking about, not to notice and admire all these things."

Walter shook his head.

"I confess it may seem strange that I did not do so, sir," he observed, "but when I looked round and saw the cottages of the poor crumbling to ruins through neglect, and their comfort evidently unattended to, I might be wrong, but it really gave me quite a distaste for the empty show and parade which characterise everything at the abbey."

Mr. Wallingford looked displeased, but being unable to controvert the opinions of his son, the conversation soon dropped, and a painful silence ensued—painful to Maria, for her mind was occupied with the designs she had in contemplation, and she could not help noticing the perturbation of Walter and her aunt, the latter of whom looked uncommonly pale, and at intervals sighed deeply. It was several minutes before Maria could sufficiently combat her feelings to put into execution what she wished. At length, when she arose to retire from the table, she mustered all her energy, and turning to Mr. Wallingford, addressed him, in a firmer tone than might have been expected :—

"I have a favour to ask of you, sir," she said, "if you will permit me."

"A favour, Maria?" said Mr. Wallingford, with much surprise, "certainly, name it, and depend upon it, if it is in my power, I will readily grant it."

"I merely wish to have a few minutes' private conversation with you, sir," answered Maria, " if you will permit me, any time to-day when it is convenient to yourself."

"I will attend you in the library in a few minutes," said the astonished Wallingford, pressing her hand with every appearance of kindness. Maria curtseyed, and without daring to look towards Walter, whose eyes she was certain were fixed upon her in surprise at the request she had made, she took the proffered arm of her aunt, and walked from the room.

Mrs. Wallingford seemed to be very much agitated, but made no remark to Maria upon the request she had made to her uncle: when she arrived at the door of her sitting-room, she kissed Maria affectionately, while tears filled her eyes, and the latter walked into the library, and threw herself into a chair to await the arrival of Mr. Wallingford.

Maria tried to appear calm, but it was a moment of great suspense and anxiety, and she almost regretted having sought the interview; however, hearing Mr. Wallingford ascending the stairs, she made a desperate effort and recovered herself.

Mr. Wallingford approached her with curiosity and eagerness expressed in his countenance, and having fixed upon her a keen, penetrating glance, he awaited in silence for her to open the business she had desired to see him upon. Maria's heart palpitated, and a slight trembling came over her, for she had hoped that Mr. Wallingford would have brought her to the subject by putting to her some question or the other, and she was at a loss to know exactly how to broach it. Mr. Wallingford noticed her embarrassment, and took her hand, encouraging her by a look of kindness.

"Sir," said Maria, at length. mustering all her strength for the task she had imposed upon herself—"Pardon me for intruding upon your time, but I will not occupy it many minutes, for I need not many words to express all I have to say. The business which made me request a private interview is briefly this;—circumstances have made me wish to leave Wallingford Hall, for the present, and I beg you to inform me if, out of the small sum of money that was left me from the sale of my poor father's effects, anything remains, so that I may be able to put into operation a plan which has suggested itself to me?"

Maria paused, and held her head down in confusion; she dared not encounter the gaze of Mr. Wallingford, who, she knew, was contemplating her with the most searching glances.

"And may I presume to inquire, Miss Herbert," returned Wallingford, in a tone of irony that stung his fair companion to the quick. "May I presume to inquire, I repeat, what mighty project has suggested itself to your mind, and why you so suddenly wish to retire from Wallingford Hall?"

Maria, gentle as she was, felt her heart throb with resentment, at the bitter sarcasm with which Mr. Wallingford thought proper to address her, but she quickly recovered herself from her embarrassment, and with a look which reproached her uncle for his unkindness, replied:—

"This mighty project, as you have been pleased to designate it, has suggested itself to my mind because I wish not to make others miserable by remaining at Wallingford Hall; and since I felt that I was dependent on those —or on one, who—but I beg pardon, sir, I had better not proceed any further. I will, however, if it please you, explain the design I have in contemplation."

"By all means, Miss Herbert," said Wallingford, in the same accents of irony; "do let us have the plan by all means, for no doubt, it will be an excellent example for all other young women to follow."

"I trust, sir," observed Maria, indignantly, "that however ill-devised my plan may be, it has its origin in a proper sense of pride, and is such a one as no virtuous female need be ashamed to acknowledge. It is my wish, if I am provided with pecuniary resources, to go to the metropolis, where I think it is not at all improbable that I could get a situation as governess, or companion to a lady——"

"Aye, to be sure," interrupted Mr. Wallingford, laughing, "suppose we say as lady's maid. Don't you think that that would be about the thing for a young ambitious lady like yourself?"

"Anything, sir," returned the offended maiden, warmly, "anything, sir, however menial, would be preferable to the state of degradation, contempt, and dependence, I now feel myself placed in."

"Maria," remarked her uncle, "I have had enough of this ridiculous stuff, and will not listen to any more of it. But you are young and thoughtless, and inexperienced, therefore do I pardon you for a certain warmth of expression and style, which might otherwise sound to me very ungrateful. You romantic young ladies certainly entertain some truly preposterous ideas, which, if they were permitted to run riot, could only be attended with the most painful and ruinous consequences. You can have read very little of London, or you would at once see the absurdity, the downright madness of a girl like you thinking of going to that large and giddy place, in which you are a complete stranger, and totally unacquainted with any one."

"You are mistaken, sir," replied Maria, "I have got one friend there, and I know her to be a sincere one. It is to her I purpose going. She was my nurse, and was with my poor mother during the whole of her illness, and until she breathed her last. She is also the sister of Jenny."

"Jenny—Jenny," said Mr. Wallingford, "and who in the name of wonder is this same Jenny? it is not a very fashionable name, but you talk to me of her, as if I was intimately acquainted with her; is she one of your friends?"

"She should be one of yours, sir," observed Maria, vehemently, "seeing that she has been a faithful attendant in your family for so many years; I mean Jenny, Andrew's wife. Surely, there cannot be anything discreditable in their friendship."

"Probably not," returned Mr. Wallingford; "and they may be all very well in their way, but Maria Herbert should think higher of herself than to confide her thoughts and designs, and secrets, to such——"

"You wrong me, sir, by such a supposition," eagerly interrupted Maria; "I should indeed hate myself could I do as you say; but of this feel certain, their friendship and affection for me would stand the strongest test. Mrs. Arnold, Jenny's sister, is not in indigent circumstances; indeed, she is rather comfortably off, and has a small house in the vicinity of the metropolis, whither I intend to go, and stay with her until I can put my plan into operation. I therefore request you, sir, if anything remains of the trifle I have mentioned, to let me have it, so that I may not be thwarted in my wishes to extricate myself from a state of idleness and dependence which is so abhorrent to my own feelings, and probably so disagreeable to others."

"Not one shilling," exclaimed Mr. Wallingford; "do you think I am mad, Maria? Do you imagine that I would thus make myself a party to your ruin and disgrace? Never! and what else could follow, think you? Come, come, Maria, do not be so silly, that's a good girl, but for goodness sake do inform me how this pretty little plan of 'looking after a place,' has occurred to your mind?"

We cannot do justice to Maria's feelings of vexation and resentment at the tone her uncle had assumed; however, she stifled her feelings as much as possible, and with becoming firmness and spirit answered:—

"My reasons for coming to this determination, sir, are soon told. I find I cannot longer with anything like prudence remain near my cousin without causing uneasiness to you. Again I would not make you and my aunt uncomfortable; which, my remaining here, I feel convinced will be the occasion of. And then to endure the——"

"Pray proceed, Miss Herbert," said her uncle, "do not leave the sentence unfinished."

Maria, confused, mortified and embarrassed, faultered, and could not give utterance to a single word.

"You remain silent;" resumed Wallingford, "well then, with your permission, I will endeavour to do what you have only half accomplished. To endure the odious overtures of a gentleman, who possesses the trifling annuity of fifteen thousand a year, and who would have it in his power to raise you to that rank you were born to adorn. Who with a generosity deserving of all possible praise, has given his word that he will make as liberal a settlement upon you, as if you had brought him a splendid fortune. Yes, Maria, it is owing to these painful offers that you design to abandon the protection of your best friends, and to seek that of the lowliest of the lowly in a strange place, where you would be exposed to every temptation and vice, and where for a young and unprotected female to escape contamination, if not ruin, is next to an impossibility. Is this a sample of that nice sense of gratitude and feeling which I thought Maria Herbert possessed? But I will not reproach you, for I do not doubt that you already perceive the folly you have been guilty of. Nay, nay, do not weep, my dear girl, I will not reproach you: you must, however, promise me not to think any more of the metropolis, for the present, and do not go there till you go there as Lady Barnell of Woodbine House."

"By heaven, I would sooner breathe my last this moment," ejaculated Maria, in a tone of passionate emotion. Her uncle, however, took no notice of her observation, and so far from replying to it, did not seem to have heard it, for he was calm and indifferent, and walked to the other side of the apartment for a minute or two without speaking. At length, however, he returned to her, and taking her hand with a persuasive conciliatory smile, he said—

"Now, Maria, we have really had quite enough of this, and I must request you to compose yourself and accompany me to your aunt's sitting-room, and put her out of suspense, for I am certain the singular circumstance of your requesting to speak to me in private, strangely disconcerted her, and she is, in an alarming state of uneasiness and anxiety."

In spite of her anguish and indignation, poor Maria could not but comply with this request, and suffered, vexed as she was, Mr. Wallingford to take her arm, and lead her into the room in which were seated Mrs. Wallingford and Walter. Mr. Wallingford well acted his part, and cladding his face with smiles, and seeming to be on perfect good terms with his niece, his wife looked up with gratification, and her bosom seemed relieved from a heavy weight that had before been pressing upon it. Maria, who struggled with her feelings rather than disturb those of her aunt, also affected to smile, so that the former began to imagine that every obstacle was settled satisfactorily between them.

But did Walter labour under the same delusive idea? Oh, no; he was not to be deceived; the moment Maria had entered the room, he fixed his eyes upon her countenance, and that which was always an index of her mind, convinced him that the interview had been one of the most painful description to her, and that she was suffering the most intolerable anguish. Neither was Walter blind to the fact that his father's gaiety was merely an assumption, and that, in fact, his mind was but ill at ease. Walter was lost in wonder and suspense: what could have transpired at their late interview, and for what purpose could Maria have sought it? Conjecture was perfectly useless, and Walter abandoned it in despair.

CHAPTER XXVII.

"Mystery upon mystery, what fatal spell
  Directs my fate? Am I e'er to be
The child of sorrow and of pain?"
                              THE ORPHAN.

IN spite of the endeavours of Mr. Wallingford to appear unconcerned, and his efforts to engage all present in conversation, the evening seemed likely to be passed away in gloomy silence. Walter pretended to be perusing a book, but it was merely an excuse, so that he might have an opportunity of watching his beautiful cousin, while Mrs. Wallingford looked melancholy and distressed, only exchanging an observation occasionally with her husband. At length, Mrs. Wallingford, who seemed determined to arouse them from this state of misery, requested Maria to oblige them with one of her pretty songs, which

WALTER COMES TO THE ASSISTANCE OF MARIA IN THE SHRUBBERY.

recalled Walter from a state of gloomy rumination, and he smiled his willingness to hear
her, although he feared that she was too much
distressed to comply.   As for Maria, she was in
a state of mind that we scarcely know how to
describe, but which, from the occurrences of the
day, may be well imagined; she would have
made an apology, and excused herself, but her

aunt also urged the request, and unable to
refuse that beloved relative anything, especially
at a time like that, when she was temporally
happy in her unconsciousness, she seated herself
at the piano, and turning over the music-book,
almost unconscious of what she was doing,
sung a ballad of the greatest pathos, and the
words of which were appropriate to the state

of her mind, but ere she had got through the second stanza, her voice became inaudible, the violence of her emotions almost choked her, and unable longer to suppress her feelings, her hands dropped from the piano, and she burst into a violent flood of tears. Could Walter endure this sight? No; forgetting in a moment the promise he had made his father,—forgetting everything in his distraction at the grief of her who was dearer to his heart than life itself, he sprang from his seat, rushed to her side, and seizing her hand, exclaimed:—

"My Maria, my own, my darling Maria, what means this? Oh! in pity to me, explain the cause of this violent emotion?"

"Rash, foolish boy!" cried Wallingford, colouring with vexation, and tearing his son away from the weeping object of his solicitude; —"am I to be always annoyed and braved by this nonsense? Shame on you, Walter, you are as drivelling and effeminate as Miss Herbert herself. Nay, sir, do not attempt to answer me. I will no longer tamely submit to this foolery, performed by a disobedient boy and a weak, ridiculous girl. Follow me, directly, sir, to my study, and there I will listen to what you may have to say in apology for this froward conduct."

"Hear me, father, I implore," cried Walter, his chest swelling with the mingled feelings of anger and grief.

"Not here;" exclaimed Mr. Wallingford, passionately, "nay, sir, I insist upon your obeying me!"

Walter offered not another word, but casting a look of ardent affection and sympathy upon Maria, who had thrown herself into the arms of her aunt, he retired from the room, attended by his enraged parent.

"My love, my Maria," said the distracted Mrs. Wallingford, when they were left alone, "oh, speak to me, and tell me, what has been the cause of this?"

"Dearest aunt," sobbed forth Maria, raising her head from her bosom, and looking with melancholy fondness in her pale face;—"oh, let me retire;—in pity do not detain me;—it is done.—I am determined that if there are disturbances in your family, I will no longer be the cause of them. Pray let me retire, and do not ask to see me again until I——"

"Until you have done what, my poor girl?" asked Mrs. Wallingford, in a tremulous voice.

"Ask not to see me again," replied Maria sobbing, "until Mr. Wallingford may be convinced that I am not the weak and frivolous girl he takes me to be."

"Oh, my poor child!" exclaimed her aunt in a tone of compassion, "what will be the end of this misery?"

"I will end it," answered Maria hastily,— no, my account these disturbances shall never

occur again. But I grieve for you, my dear aunt, you have ever been so very, very kind to your poor Maria. Oh, pardon me, do pray pardon me!" In a paroxysm of passionate grief Maria threw her white arms round the neck of Mrs. Wallingford, and gave free vent to her feelings on her bosom.

"My dear child," said her aunt, "do not, I beseech you, give way to this;—pardon you, oh, what have you ever done to need my forgiveness?"

"Hear me, my dear aunt,'" continued Maria, and her eyes sparkled wildly through her tears;—"promise me, that in spite of whatever may occur, you will never entertain a harsh opinion of me—nay, understand me rightly,—I will never be guilty of anything to forfeit your good opinion, nothing that you may blush to hear of your niece;—let Walter do as his father wishes him, and when I can no longer be considered as an obstacle in the way of the views he has formed for his son,—when Walter shall be united to Lady Euphemia, then, and not till then, will happiness and content once more be ours."

"And why wait till then, my love, to be happy?" observed Mrs. Wallingford, embracing her fondly!—"No, no, we will be happy now; who knows that such an event as the one you mention may ever occur, and why therefore should we delay our pleasure?—I am sure, Maria, you will feel convinced that were it in my power, how willingly, how gladly would I give my assent to anything that might promote the peace and the pleasure of you and Walter; but alas, you know how little have I the power to interfere. The anxiety of your uncle to see his son established in a sphere of life where his abilities may have the chance to expand, renders him more apparently impatient and harsh than his heart really prompts him to be. Mr. Wallingford wishes his son to take an active part in public life, and from a union with the family of Lord Hartington, he has been led to imagine that all his fond hopes and ambitions will be realized, he has undertaken to introduce Walter with success; which has flattered your uncle's anxiety, he being himself long since by the private life he has led, and sojourning on the continent, estranged from all his former friends, and consequently, not in a condition to do so. And thus, my love, you will see the cause of his objection to the affection of yourself and Walter. And, indeed, cruel as he may seem to be in urging you to become the wife of Mr. Barnell, I must do him the justice to say, that I believe he really thinks he is doing that which will be the cause of your future success and happiness in life."

Upon the latter theme Mrs. Wallingford did not venture to proceed further, for she could see from the expression of Maria's countenance how painful it was to her. She knew that her husband had made up his mind to this match, and she dared not flatter the hopes of her niece that he would easily abandon it.

"Surely, my dear, something of a very unpleasant nature must have occurred between you and Mr. Wallingford, at the interview in the library," continued Mrs. Wallingford, after a pause; "and yet when I saw you enter the room with him, from both your countenances I was led to hope that everything had been satisfactorily arranged."

Upon the mention of that conference the blood deeply mantled the cheeks of Maria, for she recalled to her memory the insulting sarcasms Mr. Wallingford had made use of to her, and the manner in which he had seemed to take a delight to taunt her; but she suppressed her feelings as much as possible in the presence of her aunt, and after a minute or two's silence, during which she had been endeavouring to collect all her fortitude and composure, she said firmly:—

"My dear aunt, I am afraid that my weakness has caused much disquiet to you and Mr. Wallingford;—I am a silly girl, but I will end it; this is the last time that I will ever be the cause of these painful contentions."

Without staying to utter another word, Maria threw her arms round her aunt's neck, and having kissed her affectionately two or three times, she flew from the apartment.

We forgot to mention to the reader, that fearful the presence of Andrew and Jenny, and their daughter, might recall to Mrs. Wallingford's memory the dreadful events of former times, Mr. Wallingford had, several months before the time of which we are now speaking, discharged them from his service with a handsome annuity, and had given them a neat cottage on his estate. Maria, who was very fond of the old people, seldom missed a day without calling to see them, and taking them some little present or another.

When Maria retired from her aunt, she hastily repaired to her own apartments, and having in a moment made up her mind what she would do, she put on her hat and her scarf, and hastening lightly out of the hall, without encountering any one, she took the direction to Jenny's cottage. It was a beautiful evening, and the sun had not yet gone down, but Maria's mind was too much occupied with other subjects for her to take notice of the beauties of nature, which in her tranquil moments she so delighted to revel among. Having crossed the neat little garden, which old Andrew took such pains to cultivate, she tapped gently at the casement, and Jenny hastened and opened the door in a minute, and welcomed "her dear child" with her usual warmth of honest attachment.

"Ah, my dear young lady," said the old woman, joyfully, and rising from her seat, "I am very glad to see you, but what made you come so late? Hey day, why the poor child cannot be well; how pale she looks, do tell me what——"

Maria was unable to restrain the tears her mortified and agonised feelings called forth, and Jenny, alarmed at her emotion, was unable to finish her speech. However, she wiped the dust carefully off the chair, upon which Maria having seated herself, the old woman waited with much curiosity and anxiety to hear what was the occasion of her grief.

"Jenny," observed Maria, after a pause, during which she had somewhat recovered herself, "I am rather nervous and indisposed, that's all; but the reason I came here this evening was to ask you for the address of my nurse, Mrs. Arnold."

"I'll get you her letter directly, Miss Maria," replied Jenny, and although her curiosity was great to know for what purpose Maria wanted it, she suppressed it as well as she could, and took the letter from her chest of drawers, in which it had been carefully secured, among other esteemed relics. Maria eagerly unfolded the letter, and perused the contents, which breathed the utmost affection for her, and, in fact, it contained little else besides inquiries after her (Maria's) health, and how she looked; whether she wasn't a very fine young lady, and a very handsome one too, and expressing a fear that she should never behold her dear child again.

"Good, kind creature, how delighted would she be to see me!" observed Maria, as she folded up the letter and returned it to Jenny.

"Indeed she would," returned the old woman, "I verily believe my poor sister would go mad for joy."

"That pleasure will soon be her's," said Maria, with forced composure; "do you know, Jenny, that I have partly made up my mind to go to London, and there, of course, the first person I shall go to will be——"

Jenny started from her seat as if she had seen a ghost, and clasping her hands, stared at Maria with stupified amazement.

"Do I hear aright?" she ejaculated; "I cannot believe my senses; what you, my dear child, think of travelling to London by yourself?—goodness gracious!"

"I was prepared to hear you evince surprise at my design, Jenny," returned Maria, "but nevertheless my resolution is taken. I want to inquire of Andrew about the coach fare, for I must be economical, and wish to know, therefore, the cheapest coach."

"But surely, my dear Miss Maria," said the old woman, "you cannot be serious?"

"Indeed but I am, Jenny," answered Maria, "but why do you express so much astonishment at my intention? Is there anything particularly wonderful in my wishing to see that busy metropolis about which I have heard so much? —As to my talking about travelling cheap, it would be highly imprudent for me to act any other way, for you are aware how limited are my pecuniary resources."

"Ah! poor dear child!" said Jenny, "I am afraid that no good will come of this; but it grieves me to the heart to hear you talk in this strain, that it does. I cannot bear to think of it. And how came you to have such an idea? Something particular must have taken place to suggest such a thing to your mind. And if my mistress or your uncle were to hear you talk in that manner—what in the name of fortune would they think."

"Jenny," answered Maria. "I have not concealed my design from Mr. Wallingford; I told him of it to-day, and I intend also to make my aunt acquainted with my intention very soon."

Maria only said this to appease the apprehensions of Jenny, but it was far from having the effect desired.

"Heavens! my dear Miss Herbert," exclaimed the old woman, "surely you must be mistaken; can they who have always appeared to love so fondly, so easily agree to separate from you, to suffer you to go alone to that wicked place, London, and actually to suffer you to travel by the means of conveyance?"

"It is a matter of very little importance," returned Maria, "at least of not so much importance as you would give to it, Jenny; at any rate, I do not wish to enter farther into that subject at present. Will you be so good as to request Andrew to walk in for a minute or two from his garden, in which I saw he was engaged when I came here; or, if he cannot conveniently come, I will wait upon him?"

"My poor dear child," replied the old woman. "Andrew shall be here in a minute; but I do hope that you will not be tempted to do anything rashly; I hope you will see the necessity of changing your mind. Heigho!" And the old woman tottered out into the little garden, which Andrew cultivated with such care, and in as few words as possible made him acquainted with all that had taken place between her and "her poor dear child."

"Well," remarked her husband, when she had concluded her story, "it is no more than I expected. Ah! poor girl, I am afraid she is fated to experience a great deal of trouble. No one knows the disposition of Mr. Wallingford better than I do. Conquer his obstinacy when he has got a determination in his head, and you have only got another to beat, and, in that respect, Walter takes so much after him, that the two tempers clash together, and so I imagined that the finish of it would be that poor Miss Maria would be compelled to leave Wallingford Hall. Well, miss," continued

the old man, addressing himself immediately to Maria, "I do think, that to make the best of a bad job, your wisest plan certainly would be to leave the Hall for awhile. Mrs. Arnold, will, I am convinced, be delighted to see you, for you know how fond she always was of you, and there is nothing that she will grudge doing to render you comfortable, although to be sure you must expect to find everything humble. I cannot, however, think of your undertaking such a journey by yourself. I would not for the world allow it, when I know the danger to which you might be exposed. I am old, to be sure, but I shall be better than nobody with you, for I am very well acquainted with all the tricks of the London folk. So the whole of it is, I will, with your permission, be your companion, and Agatha, who has long been promised a trip, shall accompany us."

"Oh, yes," exclaimed Maria, joyfully, "that will be just the thing, I——no," she continued, as a thought suddenly struck her, "no that will not do either, for would not Mr. Wallingford and my aunt be vexed at the interest you would thus take in my cause? Oh, no, advantageous and desirable as I must acknowledge this design appears to be, I cannot make up my mind to involve you, my dear friends, in any trouble or vexation that may attend me."

"That is nothing at all to the purpose, Miss Maria," returned Andrew, "did you not say that you had made Mr. Wallingford acquainted with your intention, and that you were resolved to apprise your aunt of the same, and that Mr. ——"

"Do not misunderstand me, good Andrew," interrupted Maria, "although I own I informed you that I told Mr. Wallingford what I purposed doing, I never said that he expressed his approbation of the plan; on the contrary—"

"But," interposed Andrew, "have you not finally resolved to put your plan into operation, my dear miss?"

"'Tis true," answered Maria.

"For that very reason then, miss," replied the old man, "is it the more absolutely necessary that I should accompany you; and your uncle would certainly have greater cause to be displeased if I were to permit you to travel by yourself. But no matter, I cannot help it whether he is displeased or not;—what I intend doing is with the best of motives, and I feel confident that Mrs. Wallingford will, when she reflects maturely upon it, approve of my conduct."

To these arguments Jenny and her daughter, who were eager for the jaunt, joined theirs; the consequence of which was, that Maria was urged to assent to their wishes, and promised to be guided entirely by Andrew.

The next question was, when should they commence their journey? This was more strongly urged by Agatha, who would willingly have set forth directly, so anxious was she to see the wonders with which she had heard London abounded.

"Were it this moment," observed Maria, "nothing could afford me greater satisfaction;—but it is useless to think of acting so precipitately as that."

After a long consultation, and a great many demurrers on the part of old Jenny, who, to tell the truth, dreaded the loss of her daughter's society, it was finally settled that the following evening they would make their departure. Old Anthony had informed her the place where a cheap coach started from, and it was settled that he should borrow a cart to convey their luggage to the coach; but the latter subject troubled Maria very little, as she had made up her mind to take no more with her than she could herself carry, and she did not doubt but that Mrs. Wallingford would send them to her, as soon as she was made acquainted with the residence of Mrs. Arnold.

Everything being thus arranged to the satisfaction of all parties, Maria bade her humble, but honest friends good night, and made her way towards Wallingford Hall. As she proceeded she reflected upon the step she was about to take, and weighed it maturely, but under all circumstances, she could not but consider that she had resolved to act perfectly right, and that to remain any longer at the Hall would neither be prudent, or consistent with the spirit of independence she prided herself upon possessing. Yet when she thought of the pain her departure would cause to her affectionate aunt, she felt the most poignant regret that she should be obliged to adopt such a plan.

"Not many hours," she soliloquized with a sigh, "not many hours, and I shall be far, far from hence. But shall I regret the necessity that compels me to such a step?—No, since Mr. Wallingford's behaviour has made me look upon this no longer as my home, I should indeed be a mean and despicable being, could I continue to intrude upon his hospitality."

She had entered the gate which led into the shrubbery, and was proceeding towards the house, when she perceived that there were lights moving in the sitting room, and wishing to avoid all company in her present state of mind, and with the designs she had in contemplation, she was hastening towards her favourite haunt, the summer-house, when by the dim light of the moon she fancied she recognized a couple of objects proceeding before her. She paused and gazed more steadfastly, and was then convinced that she was not mistaken, and that the figures she had observed were those of two females. Her curiosity was aroused to the utmost pitch, and she watched them narrowly, yet fearing to advance too rapidly for fear they should observe her. At length, turning into a more open part of the grounds, the full light of the moon was thrown upon their figures, and Maria to her astonishment, saw that they were both of the Gipsy tribe, and in one she quickly recognised the graceful and prepossessing form of the girl who had so excited the curiosity of herself and Walter but a day or two before.

Maria's anxiety was now raised to the utmost pitch, and she lost all recollection of her own cares, in her curiosity to discover what was the occasion of the girl's visit to the gardens, and how they had gained admission. She followed them slowly, and saw them pass the summer-house, and turn round towards the back of it. "What can be the meaning of this?" reflected Maria, "why did they not enter the summer-house, I wonder, and what can be their object in coming here at all?"

With cautious and light footsteps she hurried forward, and entered her favourite retreat; and no sooner had she done so, than the sound of two voices in earnest discourse met her ear, which she doubted not proceeded from the females she had seen. She drew in her breath, and listened with the utmost eagerness, but little did she expect at that moment that she should be brought into their discourse.

"Ah, Fanny," ejaculated a merry voice, "you cannot blame me for loving him, after the eloquent description you gave me of him; did you not continually speak to me in terms of adulation concerning his handsome countenance, the beautiful expression of his eyes;—the gracefulness of his form, the melody of his voice, and—"

"Nonsense," replied the other, whose tones were quite familiar to the ear of Maria, although she could not recall to her mind where, and in what way she had heard them; "nonsense, you know I did not say any such thing; to be sure I reiterated the opinion of many others, that he was a good-looking and well-informed young man, and, as my mother has said, the very image of his father; but had I imagined that my description of him would have made such an impression on you, I would not have mentioned a word, because his heart is evidently in the keeping of his cousin, the fair Maria Herbert."

"Fal de ra, fal de la, fal, lal, lal, de ra!" sung the girl who had first spoken, and a more melodious voice never had smote the ears of Maria. "His *fair* cousin, mark my words, Fanny, will stand but little chance against me. What could her mild blue eyes, as you have described them, effect against my bright, black, sparkling orbs, which every one is enraptured with?—Oh, no, no, my girl, I would stake my existence, that, if I could only be in his company for about an hour, she would stand no chance with me. I would soon make him cease to remember his *fair* cousin, without even being compelled to have recourse to my spells."

"What a vain little creature you are, Esther," observed the companion of the first speaker ; "and how wildly you talk ; but come, since nothing will do but you must endeavour to see this young man, do not let us delay making the attempt, for we are running a great risk by loitering here, and should we be discovered, the cage undoubtedly would be our portion, and we should very likely be suspected of having a burglary in contemplation."

"Very true, Fanny," replied the other, "people are not very particular in what they accuse any of our tribe of ; give a dog a bad name and hang him ; so it is with us ;—however, I cannot think of attending you until I have adjusted my apparel, and made myself a little smart, because if we should have the misfortune to be apprehended on suspicion of committing some misdemeanour or the other, I should not like to falsify the opinion that I have generally heard expressed of myself, namely, that I am a most beautiful and fascinating girl. Heigho !—There now, who could injure me now ?—No one, could they ? no, not even your—"

A gust of wind, which at that moment burst through the shrubbery, stifled the conclusion of this speech, and it was two or three seconds before either of the girls spoke again. Maria was all in a tremor of anxiety and impatience, and scarcely ventured to breathe for fear she should lose a sentence of what they were saying.

"Beware, Esther," were the first words she could catch, which were spoken in the voice of the girl Maria had before seen, and who appeared to be older than her companion ; "beware, Esther, and keep all you know a profound secret, or you know not what may be the consequences ;—should you divulge,—my mother might——"

The wind again whistling among the bushes, once more buried the sound of the speaker's voice, and Maria was unable to catch the finish of the sentence of this, the most interesting part of the speech. She stretched forward her head as far as she could, and drew in her breath more powerfully, so that she might not miss a syllable of what they were conversing about, which had excited her deepest interest and curiosity, and at length she was enabled to catch the following words, which were spoken in the voice of the female Maria had heard called Esther :—

"Depend upon me, Fanny ;—I will never act so imprudently as you seem to fear I shall ; you know me well, Fanny, and ought, therefore to do me the justice to acknowledge that I am incapable of doing anything to injure you ; but remember if we encounter this young man, I shall expect that you will not act otherwise than fairly."

The reply to this speech did not clearly reach the ear of Maria, and at that moment she heard them starting, and looking out from her retreat, she observed that they were going in the direction of the Hall. She was enabled to take a minute survey of their persons, for the moon now shone brightly, and all the surrounding objects were brought as clear to her as the light of day.

They wore the apparel of the wandering tribe, and there was very little difference in their costume, with the exception that they had a couple of straw hats, and the younger one, or Esther, wore her's in a jaunty style, and her cloak was thrown tastefully over her left shoulder ; in fact, her appearance altogether was that of a buoyant, thoughtless girl, who seemed anxious to make a display, and who looked only upon the sunny side of the world. As Maria looked after them, the only conclusion she could come to was, that they were sisters, though Esther was apparently two or three years younger than the other, and was much shorter.

A tumult of conflicting thoughts raged in the mind of Maria, as she followed the footsteps of the gipsies at a distance, as to what their purposes could be in coming to the Hall, and being so anxious to behold Walter ; for that it was him and herself to whom they alluded in the words she had overheard them utter, she could not entertain the slightest doubt. But were they really what they seemed ;—were they actually gipsies, or was the disguise only assumed for some particular and secret purpose ?—Yes, she was certain that they could not belong to that degraded and wandering class of beings, for their language and the sentiments they had expressed showed that they were different, and as for Esther, she was the most vivacious and interesting girl she had ever beheld. But these thoughts completely racked the mind of Maria, for she was unable to form the least conjecture as to their real characters, and what could be the reason of their adopting such a disguise ? Such was her anxiety to endeavour to ascertain who they were, that she persevered in following their footsteps, though at any other time she would have been afraid to have been near them, and would have studiously avoided crossing their path. She continued to pursue them though at a proper distance, and watched them along the principal path until they had nearly reached the Hall, and here they both suddenly paused, and seemed to be alarmed or surprised at something, for they screamed, and turning round flew back again along the path in which Maria stood, and she was unable to avoid them. There was a start of simultaneous astonishment and confusion among the three, and they were fixed to the spot, eyeing each other with bewildered looks. At length Esther, the youngest girl, regained her equanimity, and grasping Maria's arm firm, in a peremptory tone said—

"You cannot advance further;—you must go with us, but do not fear, no harm shall come to you."

"I do not fear," answered Maria, in as calm and collected a tone as she could assume, "I am not apt to tremble at trifles;—but for what reason do you——"

"We cannot answer your questions here," interrupted Esther, "but if you hasten with us, we will satisfy you upon every point; come, come," she continued, as she urged Maria forward with gentle violence, "why do you hesitate?—you need not doubt us."

Maria made no reply, and wondering what would be the result of this singular adventure, she suffered the gipsies to lead her towards the summer-house, which she had just before left.

When they had gained the summer-house, they thrust our heroine in, and stood themselves at the door, as if to prevent her from leaving it. Maria began to feel alarmed, but knowing that there would be more danger in letting the gipsies observe her fears, she vanquished her emotions as much as possible, and awaited the result of the adventure with impatience. They paused a few moments at the door, and seemed to listen; then Esther addressing herself to her sister, for such Maria imagined the girl called Fanny to be, said:—

"It is a fortunate job, Fanny, they have not discovered us. Or, if they did observe us, they in all probability thought we were some domestics of the Hall; we are placed in a very awkward predicament; how shall we escape from it?"

"Well, I hardly know, Esther!" answered Fanny, "I have been much to blame in this affair, I am ready to admit, but it cannot be helped now, and we must therefore endeavour to make the best we can of it. But how foolish we are; while we stand here talking, the dreadful event we apprehend may have taken place."

"Oh, Heaven forbid!" ejaculated Esther, with much emotion, "but perhaps, after all, you was mistaken, Fanny, and it might not have been——"

"Nonsense!" interrupted the other impatiently, "I could not have been mistaken; too well do I know the expression of his ferocious countenance;—I saw him lurking among the bushes watching the opportunity to put his hellish designs into execution; not far from him, too, I observed the old man, and no doubt there might have been——Good God! perhaps the whole of our gang;—oh! Esther, should they discover us, our lives will be the sure forfeit of our curiosity;—jealous as they are of the most trifling circumstance, they would be sure to attribute our presence here to a design to betray them into the hands of justice."

Esther returned a quick answer to this speech but it was in a language that Maria did not understand, though she could not perceive by their gestures that it was something important. They continued to converse together in this strange language for several minutes, during which time Maria's agitation was very great, although she managed better than could have been anticipated to conceal it. She was now convinced that the two girls were Gipsies, and that they belonged to some gang or the other that had taken up their temporary residence in the vicinity, and had in contemplation some nefarious design. These thoughts made her feel very uneasy, and the behaviour of the two girls towards her was completely inexplicable. But after all, she could not help acquitting them of having any participation in the evil intentions of the rest of the gang, whatever they were, and this idea re-assured her, and made her feel a great reliance on her own safety. The moon was shining brightly, and the most distant objects were discernible, as plain as if it had been at noonday. But Maria's eyes could not wander from the countenances and forms of her companions, who stood immediately before her, and rendered her egress, without their permission, quite impossible. Nothing could, in her opinion, excel the beauty of the two sisters, as she believed them to be; they approached as near perfection as possible, but more especially the youngest. Her countenance was a lovely sample of nature's workmanship, and her figure put those of the three graces far into the shade.

Their discourse was brief, but apparently to the purpose, and when they had concluded, they turned towards Maria, and looking earnestly and searchingly in her face, the eldest one said—

"Is there no way of avoiding the path we have lately quitted?"

"Oh, yes," replied Maria, "there are two or three other ways; but the safest one, and that where you are less likely to be observed, is to take the one by which I entered the grounds, and so go round the gardens, to that part of the hall inhabited by the domestics."

"Did I not say so, Fanny?" demanded Esther; "so you see there will be no danger of her being seen if she goes that way."

"Right, Esther," returned the other, "she might do so certainly, but the question is, should we act prudently by suffering her to do so? Young lady," she continued, looking more inquiringly in Maria's face, "are you ready to swear, if we permit you to retire, that you will not divulge the particulars of this meeting to any human being, and that you will never betray the slightest thing at all connected with it, but to abide by our commands?"

Maria paused, for she knew not how to act She was placed in an awkward dilemma; but, then, surely two such young girls could never be so callous to all feeling as to attempt to injure her; so she mustered up resolution, and was resolved that she would not let them perceive that she was afraid of them.

"I cannot consent to what you ask," she replied firmly, "I will not swear to that which may be repugnant to my feelings, and opposed to virtue. Neither can I properly reply to you until I am made acquainted with the nature of your demands."

"As you refuse," returned Fanny, "there is no other alternative but that you must attend us; without you agree to take the oath we require of you, what guarantee have we that you will not betray us? Had it not been for the suggestion of Esther, I would not even have depended upon your oath, which would have been at the best but a hazardous proceeding, but since you decline our offer, I shall have an opportunity of indulging my inclination, so you must prepare to follow it."

"I would not hesitate to take the oath you ask of me," observed Maria, had I not determined to do precisely as you require; but to move from this spot, in your company, I tell you plainly it is not my determination. If I have already quietly permitted you to bring me back hither, my only motive for doing so was one of humanity, as I apprehended that you were in danger, though from what cause, I cannot, of course, conceive. If you think to intimidate me by threats, you are most egregiously deceived, and without I know the purport of what you would have me do, I will not promise that I will comply with any request you may think proper to make."

"You talk largely, young lady," remarked the elder sister, with a contemptuous sneer, but I would first have you ascertain the power of those whom you pretend to despise. But an instant, and we could summon to our assistance a number of daring persons, who would probably soon make you regret that you did not pay attention to our timely warning, and accept the terms to secure your safety."

"All this may be true enough," replied Maria, with great difficulty repressing her terrors, "but know you not that I am in the grounds of my relative, and that only by calling, I could soon bring him and the servants to my protection?"

"Ah! say you so, girl?" exclaimed Fanny, vehemently grasping Maria's arm, and looking fiercely in her face, "utter not a sentence, or your life shall certainly be the forfeit of your daring."

The girl continued to clutch the arm of Maria with great strength, and put Maria into such pain that she could scarcely help screaming. The menace, too, she had uttered with such an expression of savage determination, that Maria could scarcely help betraying the fears which beset her. She was, in fact, so overcome that she had not the power to make any answer, and Fanny and Esther again resumed their conversation in the language, which, to our heroine, was completely unintelligible. She trembled during this interval, and watched their countenances narrowly, and being convinced from their gestures that they did not intend to harm her, she became more composed, and made another strong effort to conceal her real terrors.

"I would ask you a question," said Esther, then turning towards Maria, "suppose we were to take your word, and suffer you to depart without exacting the oath we at first required of you, in what manner would you act?"

"Why, keep this interview an inviolable secret, certainly," answered Maria. "I do not deny that I would caution my friends to be on their guard, as some danger threatened them."

"But should they be curious to know how you obtained your knowledge?" said Esther.

"On that point I can easily satisfy them," replied Maria, "for cannot I inform them that persons lurking in the shrubbery have met my sight, and that to escape them I was compelled to turn back? In fact I need not conceal anything from them that will not implicate you."

"That will do," observed the elder sister, "but will you swear to do so, by all your hopes here and hereafter?"

"Readily," answered Maria, repeating the oath.

"Then we will rely upon you," said Fanny; "but mark me, young lady, much as you may affect to despise our power, and that of our people, if you even divulge one word of what has this evening here transpired, more than you are permitted to do, the revenge that will be taken against you will be certain and terrible."

As the Gipsy girl uttered the last words in an emphatic tone, she released her hold of Maria's arm, who, completely overcome with her terrors, darted off with the speed of lightning, in the direction she had described to the Gipsies. She had not proceeded far, however, in the path, when she was startled by observing the long shadow of a human form on the ground, and looking up, she beheld Walter running towards her.

"Dearest Maria," exclaimed the delighted youth, who seemed to be in a state of much agitation, "I have been searching everywhere for you, but in vain; oh, where have you been, my dear girl? my mother is dreadfully alarmed at your being so long away from the Hall, and my father has also expressed the greatest uneasiness. I do not know how to account for it, but their minds seem to be beset with some terrible foreboding, and yet it may be attributed partly to their having made the discovery this day, that a gang of Gipsies have taken up their residence in the wood close at hand, and that they had been there for more than a week. And yet, upon mature consideration, why should this circumstance so much alarm them? for the most they can run the risk of losing will be a little poultry; but my father has expressed his determination to go down to-morrow with a good posse of peasants and domestics, to scout them; therefore—but bless me! Maria

ELA'S UNEXPECTED APPEARANCE AT WALLINGFORD HALL.

you are not well! how pale, how agitated you look! what, for Heaven's sake, has terrified you that you thus shrink back?"

"Do not attempt to pass through the shrubbery," ejaculated Maria, faintly, and gently pressing her hand upon his arm in a persuasive manner.

"What mean you?" demanded the astonished Walter, "not pass through the shrubbery? for what reason? You really can never think of going home by such a roundabout and dreary way as this road?"

"Oh, yes, yes," hastily answered Maria, "I care not what road we take, or however lonely it is, so long as we can avoid the shrubbery." And then she looked fearfully around her, and almost imagined she saw several forms moving about in the dark shadow of the scenery beyond, and that she could see the dark eyes of the gipsies peering from among the bushes.

More than ever amazed at her conduct, and completely at a loss to account for it, Walter made no reply, seeing that his cousin's alarm seemed rather to increase than abate; and without offering any further opposition to her wishes, he took her arm, and walked with her into the road she wished to go; but he had not proceeded many paces, when a sudden idea appeared to dart across his brain, and stopping immediately, he looked searchingly into Maria's face as he said—

"By Heaven, there is some mystery in this, Maria, which I cannot fathom. Tell me, dear Maria, and do not keep me any longer in suspense, what does all this mean?—Whither were you hastening when I encountered you? from where did you come? I am convinced that you had not come from the Hall, for, for more than three hours, we have searched every apartment there for you, without success. As for the grounds, you were not there, for them I also minutely examined, and searched for you, without success, in our favourite summer-house."

"Three hours since, indeed, you could not find me there," returned Maria, "for I was then at the cottage of Anthony and Jenny."

"But you did not remain there till now, my dear girl," said Walter; "and where have you been since you left old Anthony's cottage?"

"I have been at our much loved spot, Walter," replied Maria; "but spare me, Walter; do not interrogate me further here; when we reach home I will satisfy your curiosity and anxiety in every particular."

"By Heaven, there is something more in this than you would wish me to imagine, Maria," exclaimed her cousin, "and I will not easily give up my inquiries You have seen some person who has insulted you, and they are now in the shrubbery!"

"You are mistaken, dear Walter," returned Maria, eagerly. "Indeed, you are; no one has insulted me, although I own that I have been alarmed; but in pity to me, Walter, do not longer linger here, and I again promise you that when we reach the Hall, I will explain to you everything, at least, as far as I know."

Walter paused, and his countenance was flushed with rage. "You only say this to prevent me from demanding satisfaction from the villain who has thus dared to insult you!" he ejaculated; "but for what reason should you evince towards him so much mercy and forbearance? why do you hesitate to pass the shrubbery under my protection? You know that the wretch has not the courage to——"

"Walter," interrupted his fair cousin, "your ideas deceive you; I have not seen the person to whom you allude, indeed I have not; but you will not run into the danger, I will—— but oh, Walter, do not treat my injunction lightly; indeed you would too soon have cause to repent not having followed them; for should you impetuously brave the vengeance of the tribe——"

"Tribe!" reiterated Walter, "what no you mean?—By Heavens! I cannot fathom the mystery at all. Every person seems to be panic-striken with the idea of the gipsies and you, among others, are now talking of danger being to be apprehended from the vengeance of the tribe. I have heard the mention of the word gang, I should say at least a hundred times this evening, but for the life of me I cannot conceive what we have to fear. do, my love, inform me, if you can."

Maria had, while he was thus talking, managed to persuade Walter to proceed to some distance on the road, so that her fears were now quieted as to his persisting in going the other way, and so come in contact with the two gipsy girls, so that she did no longer hesitate to inform him of all she had determined to divulge.

"Listen to me, Walter," she observed, "while I tell you something which will, no doubt excite your astonishment as well as it has done mine, and likewise show you the almost absolute necessity of being prepared to combat any danger that may threaten. Lurking in the path you wished to pursue, I not long since observed persons of suspicious appearance although I cannot tell you what their number were, but I am certain there was more than one. Now, I am at a loss to conceive what their object can be. but certain it is that it is not a good one, consequently it would be very imprudent not to provide against it. I fortunately evaded them, and, to escape them altogether, took the road we are now traversing and in which you met me. The other part of the journey I was accompanied by Anthony. Thus I have given you every particular with which I am acquainted, and as no doubt you are satisfied, do not, I beseech you, let us delay any longer hastening to the Hall, that Mr. Wallingford may be made acquainted with what I have just now informed you of. In all probability the object of the gipsy gang is robbery; at least, what else can it be? but if he is aware of their designs in time, he may easily provide himself with the means of thwarting them."

The astonishment of Walter equalled that of his fair cousin, whose statement he could not for a moment doubt the veracity of, for she had particularized everything so minutely, which had, indeed, cost her but little trouble, as the conversation of the supposed sisters had given her every idea of the intentions of their colleagues.

"And yet," observed Walter, after he had been for several moments absorbed in rumination, "and yet there is still a mystery hanging to this affair, which I in vain seek to solve. Why should my father and mother take such a particular interest in the appearance of these lawless wanderers, and why should Doctor Hartley actually put himself to the trouble of riding over to Wallingford Hall, for no other purpose than to apprise them that a gang of gipsies had taken up their residence in the wood ?—Is there anything so very extraordinary in such a circumstance ?—One would really imagine the that appearance of a few gipsies was a circumstance that had never been known in this part of the country before. To be sure I have heard that some years since this neighbourhood was much annoyed by gipsies, but what have they to do with the present gang? —And then, both Doctor Hartley and my father so strictly enjoined me not to say a word about it in the presence of my mother; and they both seemed to be in such a state of confusion and agitation ;—but their injunctions might have been spared, for my mother, it appears, had heard of the gipsy encampment through the loquacious tongue of her domestic, and while we were yet conversing upon the subject, she entered the room, evincing the greatest agitation and terror, and informed us of what she had heard, and added that some of the men had been asking alms at our stables. Why, I ask, should the locality of these vagrants be the subject of a moment's thought to her ?—Really, I am at a loss to imagine. True, as pilferers the gipsies have at all times been considered, but the importance that is put upon the appearance of these people in Ashdown Wood, would lead any one to suppose that they were a regular organized banditti, who would not hesitate at perpetrating any acts of infamy and violence."

"And is not such a supposition reasonable, Walter ?" asked Maria; "think you that the fellows whom I have before described as lurking in the shrubbery, are there upon any good intent ?"

"It does, indeed, look suspicious," replied Walter; "and is it possible that you were so close to the objects of alarm, as to be able to distinguish them so clearly ?—It is a providential thing that they did not observe you, or God knows what they might have been induced to—Merciful father ! What means that cry ?"

Walter suddenly stopped and listened, for the distant sound of a shriek had vibrated in his ears, and Maria had also heard it, and turned ghastly pale. But a moment only, and again a shriek more distant than before, in the voice of a female, arose on the air from the direction of the shrubbery, and Maria, trembling with terror, threw herself into the arms of Walter, and ejaculated—

"Oh, God ! they are murdering the poor creatures !—For the love of Heaven hasten to their rescue !"

"Fly to the rescue of who, dear Maria ?" demanded the bewildered Walter, " to whom do you allude ! what persons are likely to be in the shrubbery from whence the sound seems to proceed ?"

Ere, however, Walter could finish his interrogatories, Maria had become insensible, and, in a state of the most violent agitation, he raised her in his arms, and bore her towards the Hall, from which they were yet some distance.

The surprise and alarm of everybody in the house, when he made his appearance with his senseless burthen in his arms, may be very easily imagined : the servants were running about in all directions, in the greatest state of confusion, and informed Walter, when they hastened to his assistance, that they had all heard the screams, but that they had imagined they were uttered by Miss Herbert, to whose aid, as they thought, Mr. Wallingford and most of the male vassals had hastened, leaving their mistress in a state of the most violent alarm in the sitting-room.

"Immediately hasten," said Walter, to one of the women, "immediately hasten to my mother, and appease her terror, by informing her of the safety of my cousin; she will soon be better, it is only fright, and see, already she begins to revive; look to her carefully, while I——"

Resigning Mara to the care of the attendants, Walter did not stay to finish his speech, but immediately hurried out of the Hall, and rushed into the grounds to seek for Mr. Wallingford. He had not proceeded far in the direction of the shrubbery, to which spot, of course, he expected they had directed their steps, when he met his father running to the Hall, he not having been able to ascertain the cause of the shrieks that had so alarmed them; but it was quite evident that they had originated in some cruel outrage, as the door of Walter and Maria's favourite retreat had been broken completely off the hinges, the flowers trodden and trampled under foot to some extent, as if something had been forcibly dragged along, or that the persons had forced a path that way, for the purpose of more readily effecting their escape.

Although Mr. Wallingford had himself given up the pursuit, he had ordered his servants to persevere in it, and he determined on making his way back again o the Hall, to ascertain whether anything had transpired there which might serve to unravel the mystery.

On their way back to the Hall, Walter, in as few words as possible, related to his father all that Maria had told him about having observed strangers lurking about the grounds, and expressed his pleasure at her having been so providentially enabled to avoid falling into their clutches; but to his infinite astonishment, Mr. Wallingford did not seem by any means to coincide with his feelings upon the subject, but on the contrary, as soon as Maria recovered, which she had by the time they had arrived at the Hall, he asked her in a harsh, authoritative tone, what she did in that part of the grounds at such a late hour of the evening?

"What mean you, too, sir," he added, looking sternly at his son, "by thus setting my authority, and the promise you made me, at defiance, and seeking clandestine——"

"You wrong me, father, indeed you do," interrupted Walter, vehemently. "I did not go there to——"

"Psha!" exclaimed Mr. Wallingford impatiently, "you cannot deceive me, sir, so do not insult me by any of your forged excuses. Your behaviour is quite enough to convince me of the truth of my surmises, and I have no doubt Maria is equally innocent with yourself, and, of course, she was perfectly unconscious when she walked to the shrubbery, that she would be likely to meet you there!"

The indignant Walter was prevented from making any reply to this ungenerous speech, by the abrupt entrance of part of the male servants who had been in pursuit of the intruders, who informed their master that their endeavours had been entirely unsuccessful; and Mr. Wallingford, as soon as he heard this, retired from the room, beckoning Walter to attend him, which the latter did not attempt to disobey, though his bosom was swelling with wrath at the insinuation his father had so unjustly thrown out. As they left the room, Mrs. Wallingford entered to see after her niece, whom she was delighted to see recovered, and having heard the story of the gipsies Maria was said to have thought she had seen, she expressed the pleasure she felt at her having so fortunately escaped without being observed in return by them, as the consequences might in that case have been most alarming.

"It is very strange," remarked Mrs. Wallingford to Maria, after a while; "did you not behold any woman among them?"

This question Maria had never anticipated, and she was completely bewildred, and knew not how to answer. The confusion into which the interrogatory had thrown her niece did not escape the penetrating eye of Mrs. Wallingford, who in a moment ejaculated—

"Yes, it is as I suspected; my ideas upon the subject are confirmed; she has crossed your path; she has spoken to you, and it is only in pity to my feelings that you withhold what she has imparted. Oh, my dear Maria, never, never can this bosom know peace, after the pain that wretched woman has inflicted; never can I banish from my recollection the interview I have had with her; never can I obliterate from my mind, the words, the maledictions she uttered; oh, even now they seem to rise to my mind's eye with all the freshness of resuscitated horror."

"Dearest aunt," exclaimed the astonished Maria, "I do not understand you, indeed I do not; to whom, pray do you allude?"

"Ah!" answered Mrs. Wallingford, as a ray of pleasure passed over her features, "then I was mistaken, and so you have not beheld that unfortunate being. But why the look of alarm and confusion with which your features were clad not a minute since, when I alluded to your not having seen a female among the party who you say were lurking about the grounds? But enough for the present; your uncle is coming this way again, and I would not let him see the anguish that racks my mind; for well do I know the mental torment he at present himself endures."

As Mrs. Wallingford thus spoke, her husband returned to the room, and Maria made a hasty excuse to retire to her chamber; at the same time that she did so, she understood Mr. Wallingford to say that he should leave it till the morning before he resumed his inquiry into the cause of the event which had created so much alarm, the reasonableness of which Maria could not deny, as the most probable conclusion any person could come to was, that having been guilty of some violent outrage, they would not return there again for the present. They had, notwithstanding, determined to keep watch that night, in case of any attack, and therefore Mrs. Wallingford was prevailed upon to retire to rest, after having commended her husband to the care of Providence.

CHAPTER XVIII.

"I am a wretch now loathsome to the sight,
My face is wan, my eyes are hollow,
And every feature shows the ghastliness of
    care.
But once the bloom of beauty clad my cheek,
My form was redolent of every grace,
And sorrow passed me by unheeded!
Alas! how great the change!"   ANON.

THE apprehensions of the inhabitants of Wallingford Hall were not realised and the night passed away without any further disturbance, Walter, his father, and the male domestics sitting up and keeping watch. But a sad night it was to Maria and her aunt; they were, both of them, so painfully tormented by conflicting thoughts, that they courted sleep in vain. How bitterly did the circumstance of the re-appearance of the gipsies in the neighbourhood recall to the mind of the latter all the painful circumstances of the past—Ela and her unfortunate little Christabelle—every imprecation uttered by that unhappy woman was as fresh in her memory as if they had been spoken but yesterday, and too well, too, did she remember how awfully true the threats and prognostications appeared to be, in the loss of her darling child, and how narrowly she had escaped coming to a dreadful and untimely end at the hands of her companions, the gipsies; and what but misfortune, which had ever marked their coming, could she now anticipate, since they had, after so many years' absence, once more taken up their residence in the vicinity of Wallingford Hall? Yes, too cogent, alas! were the reasons she felt she had to apprehend calamity, when, even at the very period of their re-appearance, her son and Maria, whom she loved so fervently, were rendered miserable, and her husband, from whom she had ever experienced before such unbounded kindness and indulgence, had now, only within the last two or three days, become stern, mercenary, and inflexible in his ambitious views. What conclusion could she come to, but that the maledictions of Ela, the betrayed, the outcast, had once more fallen upon their house, and that it was her fate to behold those made miserable, to secure whose peace and happiness, she would willingly have sacrificed her own life? Overcome with the intensity of these thoughts, the hapless lady wept scalding tears of poignant anguish.

We despair of doing adequate justice to the thoughts that tormented the brain of Maria at the same time. They were even more poignant and bewildering than those that were passing in the mind of her aunt. Whichever way she turned, nothing but care and regret met her mental vision; the events of the preceding night were vividly impressed upon her memory, and a presentiment of her own fate was brought to her thoughts in characters she found it utterly impossible to erase. Then the likelihood that she was about to be separated from all those so dear to her affections, never, perhaps, to behold them again, weighed like a mountain on her heart. Oh, how deeply would her kind and affectionate aunt feel the deprivation of her society; and then the mysterious allusions she had made, and the painful story they seemed to refer to, racked her imagination in vain to elucidate. But amidst all these conflicting thoughts, she could not forget how necessary it was that she should see immediately to the arrangements of those preparations, indispensable to the design she had in contemplation; so at length her thoughts became entirely abstracted from everything else, and with many tears she set about selecting what was indispensable for her to take with her on her hazardous journey. Her heart was almost broken as she set about performing this melancholy task, and the articles she found it necessary to select and arrange, were associated with ideas that served to increase her anguish. It was with the most mournful regret that she threw by such articles as she considered would be unfitted to the different station of life she was about to enter upon, and required all her energy and fortitude to accomplish it. To take with her anything that could recall to her recollection the image of Walter, she felt would be very imprudent, but yet how great the struggle with her feelings to reject them. But propriety told her that she must henceforth endeavour to forget that such a being as Walter ever existed, and she therefore put among the parcel that she intended to leave for Mrs. Wallingford, every little present he had made her, and every article that could in any way interfere with and counteract the design she had formed. But oh, how swiftly did her tears flow, and how quickly her heart throbbed as she took up a small miniature of her cousin, and gazed upon it for the last time. It had been given to her by him three years before, and every lineament of his manly and handsome countenance was faithfully preserved. Maria had treasured this dear gift with the most sedulous care, and when alone had passed hours in gazing upon it, and pressing it to her lips. And must she resign this beloved relic? Might she not preserve that which had been her solace in many hours of melancholy? Yes, prudence dictated that it must go; and bitter as was the pang it cost her, she resolved to comply with the ordeal. But for a long while did she sit gazing upon it, and wondering whether she should ever, after she had quitted the Hall, behold the dear original again; and that if it was her fate to do so, what a change might have taken place, not only in his face, but his heart.

In this manner she occupied herself until daylight peeped through the casement; and she was aroused from the lethargy into which her thoughts had thrown her, by hearing Mrs. Wallingford quit her chamber, and soon afterwards, Mrs. Pembroke, the servant of her aunt, knocked at her chamber door, and upon entering, informed her that Mrs. Wallingford desired to know whether she did not feel disposed to come down to breakfast, as she was very anxious to see her, and know how she was; "and," added Mrs. Pembroke, "Mr. Walter has also been making inquiries after you, Miss, and has more than once or twice inquired of me concerning your health; and when I told him that I believed you had not yet risen, for that I had not seen you, he seemed very uneasy."

Maria's cheeks were for an instant suffused with blushes as Mrs. Pembroke thus spoke, but the old woman did not appear to take any notice of it, and Maria quickly recovering herself, said that as she had heard no noise during the night, she supposed nothing had taken place.

"Why, miss," answered Mrs. Pembroke, "I believe that nothing particular has occurred; but I do not think that the matter will be suffered to drop very easily, for my master and Mr. Walter appear to be more determined than ever to endeavour to elicit the mysterious circumstance, and as soon as it was daylight, they both went to the shrubbery and examined it and the summer-house minutely, but they did not, as I hear, make any particular discovery, except the remnant of an old scarlet cloak, which seemed to have belonged to some gipsy woman, and to have been torn off her shoulders by violence. Thus, you see, after all, miss, some female must have been there, although my master tried hard to make Mrs. Wallingford believe that the screams were not those of a woman; besides, what surprises me more than all is, that I overheard him, but a very short time ago, strictly enjoin Mr. Walter not to mention a syllable of the circumstance of the cloak to his mother."

"Merciful powers!" cried Maria, "this is almost a corroboration of my worst surmises, that some cruel deed has been perpetrated; for doubtless this has been torn from some poor wretch, in her struggles with her infamous assailant, and——"

"That's just what William, the gardener, told me he heard my master say," interrupted Mrs. Pembroke, "and besides, he says that when it was found, he turned as pale as a ghost, and trembled all over like an aspen leaf. Ah, well, conscience is certainly a very powerful monitor, and when certain facts bring other certain facts to the recollection, they——"

"You astonish me, Mrs. Pembroke," observed Maria; "for goodness sake, what do you mean to insinuate? What has conscience to do with one of the individuals to whom you allude?"

Mrs. Pembroke shook her head significantly, and looked around her to make sure that no one was listening to her, when she looked very much confused, and seemed to repent having made use of the expressions her garrulity had given birth to.

"Why, miss," at length she replied, "for the matter of that, I can't—that is, I don't mean to undertake to say that the circumstance I have mentioned touched any person's conscience in particular; but, to be sure, the gardener and me, who you know were old

sweethearts some thirty years ago, often have a little bit of chat together about Mrs. Wallingford, though I can't say that it is altogether right; and he says, that is, William says, that no one who now looks upon Mr. Wallingford, stern, austere, and a strict moralist as he now is, would imagine for one moment that he had mingled in scenes of guilt and dissipation, and what is more, to make love to a gipsy woman, and afterwards to put her into prison, and to declare that he was not the father of the child! If it be true, I must say, Miss, that I think it was very cruel of him, for no doubt a gipsy, after all, has the same feelings as any other human being."

"Your opinion is perfectly just, Mrs. Pembroke," said Maria, seriously; "but who informed you of all this, which to me is entirely new?"

"Is it indeed, Miss?" returned Mrs. Pembroke; "well, that is rather surprising, too, because you see it is not much of a secret among any of the domestics that have been in the family for some time; and as for old Anthony and Jenny, they are acquainted with all the particulars of the story; as for me, I know no more than what I have gathered from William and the other servants, in hints and scraps, and such like. But, depend upon it, Miss, to this may be attributed the greater part of my poor dear mistress's unhappiness. Well, I was certain from the first that something heavy weighed upon her heart. I made up my mind to that, only after I had lived with her a very fews days; but you know she is not a woman to divulge her own private feelings to every body, therefore, for the life of me, I never could arrive at the exact truth of the matter; while Mr. Wallingford was such a sturdy moral man in appearance, that it was the last thing that would ever have occurred to my thoughts, that any acts of dissipation on his part could take place to cause his wife uneasiness. But it's the way of all the men, the only difference is, that some manage more artfully than others. Well, be that as it may, take my word for it, Miss Herbert, the grief my mistress feels at present is all owing to those confounded gipsies taking up their abode so near the Hall. I wish they had all been hung before they came here, that I do, for I'm sure it would have broken your heart, had you only seen her last night, when I attended her in her chamber; she cried bitterly for some time, and nothing seemed to pacify her; I could not bear to look at her and see her suffer in such a manner, for you know what a good mistress she is to all her servants; so kind, so gentle; no domineering, like some of them, but treating the poorest person in the world just the same as if they were her equals."

The manner in which Mrs. Pembroke related this, and the circumstances she had herself noticed in the conduct of her aunt, convinced Maria that the story was not without foundation, although she doubted not but that Mrs. Pembroke and the other servants had greatly added to it; and as she thought of this additional cause of uneasiness endured by that amiable woman, and, perhaps, the heaviest affliction of all, she felt the most acute regret at the fate which compelled her to leave her, and sincerely commiserated her sufferings. Her reflections were interrupted by the loquacious Mrs. Pembroke again asking her whether she would descend to the breakfast-room; and hastily endeavouring to combat her emotions, and to appear with as much of her usual equanimity as could be expected after her alarm the night before, she made her way down stairs, and entered the apartment in which the repast was prepared, where she found her uncle and aunt conversing earnestly together, while Walter was looking from the window on to the lawn, and his mind seemed so completely abstracted by thought, that he gave no sign of having even observed the entrance of his cousin.

Mrs. Wallingford looked almost worn out with care and anxiety, but when Maria entered she arose, and greeted her with her usual warmth of feeling, and which Maria having returned with equal affection, she seated herself in her usual place at the breakfast-table, and after a time, during which Mr. Wallingford had been steadfastly watching her countenance, he observed to her in a serious but softened tone, that he hoped the adventure of the previous evening would render her more cautious in future in selecting a more seasonable hour for indulging in her favourite rambles in the shrubbery.

Maria could not make any answer to these observations, but she bowed her head in token of her assent to his wishes, and at that moment she observed the eyes of Walter fixed intently and with an expressive look upon her countenance; she hastily averted her face with a crimson blush, unable to trust herself with the contemplation of his glances. After a second or two, Walter once more turned towards the window, and again appeared to be lost in deep meditation.

"Why, Walter," at last observed Mr. Wallingford, "you seem to be lost in the contemplation of something from the window, that you forget that the breakfast has been for some time upon the table."

"I beg your pardon, sir," returned Walter, coming to the table, and taking his seat, "but my attention has been arrested by a number of persons, who were coming in haste and confusion across the lawn, and notwithstanding that they were too far off for me to recognise them distinctly, they appeared to me like some of the wandering tribe who at present occupy so much of our mind. However, whether

I was right in my conjectures or not, I can no say, but they have now gone off in the direction of Rosemary Dell, where I am informed they were formerly accustomed to take up their abode.

While Walter was making these observations, Maria had been watching narrowly the countenances of Mr. Wallingford and her aunt, and from the evident emotion they betrayed, the tale told to her by Mrs. Pembroke was all but confirmed in some of its particular points, in her mind. Mr. Wallingford seemed greatly embarrassed, and her aunt turned ghastly pale, and apparently unable to conquer her feelings, a tear started to her eye, and she heaved a deep sigh.

Mr. and Mrs. Wallingford, however, did not exchange a single sentence together; and Maria became lost in conjecture as to whether or not Walter was acquainted with the narrative she had so imperfectly heard from Mrs. Pembroke. But then, she reflected to herself, if he had been, would he have been at all astonished at the alarm the appearance of the gipsies in the vicinity of Wallingford Hall had created in the minds of his fathers and mother? —No—of course, he would not; much less would he have been so imprudent as to mention them at all in the presence of his mother, when he would be aware that it must cause her so much pain.

"I would suggest, sir," suddenly observed Walter, turning from the window, "that prior to our going to Ashdown Wood, we should ride over to Rosemary Dell; for I am almost confident that I was not mistaken in imagining the persons I just saw to be of the gipsy tribe; moreover——"

A great confusion in the entrance-hall interrupted his speech, and filled them all with astonishment; and they could here the tones of a female voice, who peremptorily demanded an interview with Mr. Wallingford.

"Good God!" exclaimed Mrs. Wallingford, clinging to her husband, "it is Ela's voice!"

Scarcely had she given utterance to these words, when the door was thrown hastily back on it hinges, and into the presence of the terrified Mr. Wallingford, his wife, and the others, rushed Ela, the Outcast Ela, with her hair wild and dishevelled, and her countenance, which was haggard and ghastly, expressive of the wildest passions.

"My child! my child!" she shrieked in frenzied accents, and her eyes darting an expression truly fiendish at Mr. Wallingford. "Monster! villain! assassin! Restore to me my child;— reveal to me where you have placed her;—and what your cruelty has suggested you to do, or I will tear the secret from your heart!"

"Why do you thus assail me?" cried Wallingford, starting to his feet in astonishment and alarm: "what mean you?"

Walter drew nearer to his father, for he dreaded the fury of the wretched woman, who, of course, he could only imagine to be some unfortunate mad woman.

"Wretch! have you the effrontery to tell me you know not what has become of my poor child?—Can you have the boldness to assert that she was not carried away by you from the shrubbery last night, and the female her companion?—Did you not do this in the sight of those who lacked the power, though they had the will to protect them?"

"By all my hopes of mercy," cried Wallingford, "by my love of truth and justice I declare that——"

"Ha! ha! ha!" interrupted Ela, looking fiercely and disdainfully upon Mr. Wallingford, *"your love of justice and truth!"* Wretch! think not again to deceive me by such vile mockery; and as for the Heaven you appeal to—"

"This is complete madness," observed Wallingford, with constrained composure, addressing himself to Ela, though with the most bitter shame and degradation he marked the emotions of astonishment and sorrow that agitated Walter, "Once more I tell you, and finally too, that I knew nothing whatevr of your daughter. It is madness, I repeat, to accuse me of what you do, for what motive could induce me to take her away from you?"

"*My* daughter, Edward Wallingford," exclaimed Ela, with marked emphasis; "yes, she is indeed *my* daughter, and is she not *your* daughter likewise,—the child of sorrow, for whom you forfeited that truth and justice of which you shamelessly boast?"

"By heaven!" cried Wallingford, "this is more than I can tamely endure!" and as he said this his eyes rested on his wife, who was transfixed to her seat, pale and motionless, and then on his son, who was gazing upon him with looks of impressive meaning. Maris, who felt that her presence might be considered an intrusion, anxious as she was to fathom the mystery of the gipsy woman's visit, had quitted the room almost immediately after Ela had entered. "Mark me, Ela," continued Wallingford, with forced firmness, "till now I have quietly submitted to your frenzied ravings, and your insolent annoyance: but I will no longer bear with it! in my own house I will not submit to such insult, or to have the peace of my family broken."

"The peace of *your* family," repeated Ela, with a bitter sneer, "and who studied the peace of my family, when, like a serpent, he worked himself into it but to poison their happiness for ever, and robbed them of all they prized in the world?—Who broke the poor white-haired people's hearts, and made ten times more poignant the anguish of death by the knowledge of their child, their darling child's disgrace?—Who did all this, I say?—Was it not Edward Wallingford? And yet you talk to me thus. Your house!—Ha! ha! and if you are master am I not mistress?" Throwing herself into a chair, as though she had resolved that she would insist upon taking up her residence there. "Did you not declare that I was your wife?—Was it not by that means you achieved your base designs?—did not a clergyman, or one whom you declared to be so, join our hands, and now—"

"Cease, woman, no more!" cried the distracted Wallingford, "I will no longer listen to your mad revilings. Force her from the house immediately," he said, turning to the domestics whom he had summoned for that purpose, "I will see whether I am to tamely bear with this woman's wild vagaries, and to have my domestic quiet invaded."

"Keep off, da tard knaves, or you will repent it!" exclaimed Ela, as her eyes flashed with rage and determination; "Edward Wallingford, beware how you arouse the sleeping lioness! I will not—I want not to disturb the quiet of your family, but I will have my child, whom you have doubtless been the means of persuading to abandon her wretched parent."

"I tell you once more that I have not beheld her," said Wallingford.

"Oh, shameless falsehood!" observed the frantic woman; "but you——" she added, suddenly approaching the trembling and horror-struck Mrs. Wallingford, "you, perhaps, may have a heart to commiserate my sufferings; you have been a parent; answer me, what would you not feel if you were aware that your Christabelle was not dead, but was forced from your protection, and was probably instructed to treat you with scorn and hate?"

Mrs. Wallingford buried her face in her handkerchief as she faintly articulated—

"Alas! my Christabelle is no more; she has long since been taken to the arms of her Maker."

"'Tis false," cried Ela, "you do but deceive yourself: your girl, your Christabelle—"

"Ah! monster!—liar!—idiot!—what of my child? Where have you hidden her! Tell me, or I will force the secret from your polluted heart!" ejaculated the frantic Wallingford, as he darted upon Ela, and grasped her arm with distracted violence. But he was soon diverted to the alarming and pitiable condition of his wife, who clasped her hands together, uttered one heart-rending shriek, and sunk insensible in the arms of her son.

"My God!" cried the frenzied husband, as he released Ela from his grasp, and hurried to Mrs. Wallingford, "she is murdered; the shock has destroyed her! Wretch!—heartless hag! But let her not escape, Walter; you have all of you heard her admit her share in the abduction of my daughter, and by all my hopes, let whatever may follow, she shall dearly suffer for this. "Fellows!" he added, "why do you stand there looking on like fools? Away with her, I say, and see that she is safely confined until I have decided what way to proceed with her."

In spite of the vehemence with which the maddened Wallingford spoke, Ela seemed to be quite unconscious of his words, but gazed with an expression of sorrow upon the pale face of the insensible Mrs. Wallingford, who looked indeed as if her soul had fled for ever.

"Poor thing," she said, in accents of regret,

ELA PREVENTS BLOODSHED BETWEEN THE GIPSIES AND WALTER'S PARTY.

"I am sorry to have been the cause of this; I did not intend it; but would sooner have been convinced that her child had died the horrid death she was supposed to have suffered?"

"Horror! horror! I shall go mad!" cried Wallingford, raising his clenched hands to his head: Walter, if you have any regard for me or your unfortunate mother, force that woman away."

Walter advanced in a gentle, persuasive manner towards Ela. Let me beg of you to leave

this room with me," he said; "I know not
what may have given you occasion to use this
violence, but surely my poor mother could
never have harmed you either by word or deed."

"True, true," observed the Gipsy, "and
had I known that your mother was not certain
what really became of your sister, I——"

"And what really did become of her?"
eagerly interrupted Walter, as she signified by
a nod her assent to accompany him into another
apartment, and at the door of which they had
now arrived.

" Why do you question me upon the subject,
young man?" demanded Ela, as she fixed
her penetrating eyes upon his face, and seemed
as though she would dive into his very
thoughts."

"Do not your own words give me authority
to imagine that you know?" said Walter:
"but, for my own part, I never heard any
more than that she died when a child."

"And why should you not yet still believe
it?" asked the Gipsy. "Many thought it
was true at that time, and I among the
number."

"But you have since ascertained to the contrary?" eagerly rejoined Walter.

"How do you suppose that I should be able
to ascertain to the contrary, or why should I
take the trouble so to do?" replied Ela;
"but I suppose you are inclined to believe that
I can divulge the hidden secrets of the past and
future, and that——"

"Psha!" interrupted Walter, "you only
equivocate; and I am sorry to see *you* capable
of such an evasion."

"And for what reason should you regret my
being capable of what you call an evasion?"
said Ela, and she looked yet more earnestly
into the countenance of the young man; "why
should you not believe that the wretched, the
despised, the Outcast Ela; the heartless hag,
as your father called her, is all that is base, and
cruel, and despicable? What good can you
expect to derive from me?"

"Oh, much, much good, if you will only follow the dictates of your own heart," answered
Walter, with energy; "I know you are not
really base."

"Ah! young man," uttered Ela, in a melancholy tone, and shaking her head, "you know
me not; you talk of my heart,—I tell you
oppression, deceit, cruelty, have turned it to
rock; I have no heart, I have no heart!"

"Oh, say not so," said Walter; "indeed
you only deceive yourself: I'm sure you have
still a heart, and one that has the warmest
sympathy for the sorrows of a fellow-being—
I marked you well as you stood over the insensible form of my poor mother, and heard the
words of regret you spoke, which plainly convinced me that you are not dead to the feelings of humanity. Do not then abandon the

kind feeling I think you bear towards her; and
thus you may in some measure repay the injury
you have done."

"Injury," reiterated Ela, with offended
pride; however, this is quite irrelevant to the
business I came upon—I seek my child, whom
your father has deprived me of."

"Trust me, my good woman," said Walter,
"you are mistaken—I can answer for it that
my father is entirely innocent of that which
you suspect him. He is incapable of such
baseness."

"Incapable of such baseness! young man,"
said Ela, bitterly. "Oh, were you made acquainted with my melancholy history of wrongs,
you would not say so—he is—but no matter,
I will not repeat that for which probably I
should gain but little of your sympathy."

"I know not what provocation you may
have received for your strange behaviour,"
said Walter, "but I repeat, that in this instance you are in error. If you will pay attention to me I will make you acquainted with all
I know, and that, perhaps, may serve to unravel
the mystery of your daughter's disappearance."

"Proceed, young man," said the Gipsy,
eagerly, "I will listen to you."

Walter complied with her request, and
described minutely all that he had been able to
elicit from Maria about the strange men whom
she had seen lurking about the grounds of
Wallingford Hall, and the shrieks afterwards
heard by all the family, the inquiries which had
been made into the cause of the same, and the
discovery they had made in the summer-house,
which left them but little reason to doubt but
that some dreadful crime or outrage had been
committed.

Ely listened to these details with her eyes
fixed searchingly upon Walter's face, and the
heaving of her bosom, the hasty palpitation of
her heart, her knitted brows, and clenched
hands, shewed how intense was the agony she
felt. For several minutes after Walter had
concluded his narrative, she moved not, neither
did she speak,—she was as inanimate as stone.
The young man felt deeply the powerful anguish the wretched outcast and bereaved
mother at that moment endured, and the sin-
cerest pity and compassion filled his mind.

"Ah!" she cried at length, starting from
her lethargy, and the tones of her voice becoming painfully and impressively hoarse and
hollow, "the wolf has at length obtained his
prey; but I will never rest until I have had
full, deep, and bloody revenge upon him and
all his accursed race."

As she thus spoke, she made towards the
room-door, but Walter, who was determined not
to suffer her to depart until he had obtained
the consent of his father, placed himself before
the door, and intercepted her flight.

"Nay, I will not suffer you to leave this place until you have afforded me the information I know it is in your power to give."

"Rash boy!" exclaimed Ela, passionately, "you know not what you do—detain me here, and nothing can save the life of the daughter of your parents. I tell you that their fate and mine are so closely connected, that to destroy one, is to bring perpetual misery upon the whole. Even now I go to save the life of your sister; but if you obstinately persist in obstructing me, the evils that will fall upon you and your family will be more terrible than you can possibly conceive. I tell you that any attempt on your part to detain me here, will be futile, for at the slightest signal I can bring such a host about me as would instantly release me, and bring the vengeance of enfuriated and desperate beings upon you all. I give you timely caution; receive it if you think proper —I care not how it is." "But," she added, with less violence, "why do you now doubt me, when but a minute since you expressed such confidence in my truth? I tell you again, that without my exertions your sister will be lost for ever. But one hour's delay, and nothing can save her!"

Ela's words, and the earnestness and apparent sincerity of her manner, bewildered Walter; and he hesitated, undecided in which way to act. His father had so strictly enjoined him not to suffer her to escape, that he was at a loss what to do. Ela watched him for a moment or two narrowly, and not an expression of his countenance escaped the penetration of her large black eyes, but she seemed quickly to come to a determination what course to adopt, and had discovered in a short time in what way to effect her escape.

"Do as you please, sir," she observed, proceeding with perfect composure towards a chair, as though she had resolved to follow entirely what his inclinations prompted. The window was open, however, which descended to the lawn, and which she had no sooner gained, than a look of determination overspread her features, and turning towards him, with a ferocious air, she drew forth a knife from under her cloak, and brandishing the glittering blade in the air, she exclaimed :—

"Mark my words, headstrong boy!—Move but an inch to pursue me, utter the slightest sound to alarm the inmates of the Hall, and this shall draw forth the life-blood from my heart. Beware—I am determined. I value not my life; but if I die, the secret that surrounds your sister can never be revealed. If you suffer me to act as my own judgment dictates, she is safe, and may once more be enfolded to their bosoms. Oppose me, and take the consequences—they nor you shall ever see her more."

Thus she spoke, and as the last words fell from her lips, she placed her feet upon the window cill, and sprang forth on to the lawn; took the path which led to the gate, and ran with a precipitation that was scarcely credible.

Walter hastily advanced to the window, and there became transfixed in mute astonishment, watching the wretched outcast, as she darted along with the speed of lightning. She did turn round once, and even at the distance she was, the glaring of her black eyes met his observation clearly; and he could also perceive that she still held in her hand the knife with which she had threatened to destroy herself.

"Good God! How strange—how inscrutable is this," exclaimed Walter; "alas! how soon does guilt make a wreck of those who lucklessly fall into its snares."

Walter continued to watch her, until he saw her met by a number of Gipsies, who made their appearance from the different bushes, &c., where they seemed to have been concealed for some sinister design, and be ready, he imagined, in case Ela should need their assistance.

"It seems almost impossible," he observed, as he withdrew from the window, "that she who is now such an object of misery and degradation, whose passions partake more of the violence of a fiend than of a human being, could once have been capable of fascinating my father's heart, and tempt him to bring such disgrace and misery upon his head."

Thus reflecting, the young man walked from the apartment, and returned to the room in which he had left his father and mother. The sight he there beheld completely harrowed up his feelings and buried every other thought. His dearest mother had been but just that moment restored to animation, and was held up between the affectionate and agitated Maria, and the distracted Wallingford, who was in vain seeking by every persuasive term he could think of, to restore her to composure.

"Where is she?" she exclaimed, glancing wildly round the apartment, "where is that fearful, but much injured woman? Ah! I do not see her now, with her large eyes glaring upon me, as though they would kill me with their lightning. No, she is not here! But still her words ring in mine ears—yes, yes, I shall never forget them more! Where is my child?—I thought she had perished in that dreadful fire!—But no, no, no; she is not dead—she told me she was not, and I dare not doubt her; she said she still lived to scorn and hate me.—Did she not?"

For a moment the unfortunate lady clasped her burning temples, and seemed to be endeavouring to recall her recollection, and then with a wild laugh, which struck every person present with horror, she cried :—

"Oh, what a curious thing it would be if I should indeed find my Christabelle living! Ha! ha! ha!—It would be such a strange thing to hear myself called mother by some fair-haired, blue-eyed girl. But, in what place could he have concealed her so long?—and why deprive her fond mother of her? And has he not taken away the child of Ela as well —Ela, who was the first to whom he plighted his vows—ah!" she added, as a sigh swelled her bosom, and seemed to proceed from the very inmost recesses of her heart, "he plighted his vows to her, but he deceived her; he abandoned her to misery, to a life of shame and guilt; then, since he could thus behave to her who was the mother of his first born, what— what can I expect? But oh! it was too cruel to take away my child, my infant cherub."

Here the poor sufferer's voice was stifled with convulsive sobs, and the weeping Maria, whose sensitive bosom was completely racked by the heart-rending scene to which she was a witness, proposed that her aunt should be removed to her own chamber, where she would be much better than in the apartment they at present occupied.

"Would that we could prevail upon her to do so," answered the agonised Wallingford.

"Ah!" gasped forth Mrs. Wallingford, looking angrily around her, "you shall not take me hence; I will fight—I will struggle while I have life; no power shall remove me from this room until I have seen my child, my Christabelle, which she promised she would restore to me; but then, how can she restore the dead from their ashes?"

At this moment Doctor Hartley, who had called upon his customary morning visit, fortunately entered, and his presence appeared to have the momentary effect of somewhat restoring her to consciousness, but she looked at him with an expression amounting to almost absolute sternness.

"What, pray, has so disordered you, my dear madam?" said the amiable doctor, taking the unhappy lady's hand, and feeling her pulse. It was evident from his looks that he considered her situation extremely dangerous.

"Nothing, nothing, has disordered me," said Mrs. Wallingford, hastily, "there is nothing at all the matter with me; but here, here, you must not leave me until you have answered me two or three questions; aye, and answer them truly, too. I think I may rely on your sincerity."

"I trust, madam," answered the worthy doctor, "that you have never had cause to doubt it. I would not wilfully tell an untruth, and that is not what all my neighbours can say of themselves, I fear."

"Then you will not equivocate, but answer me truly, as far as your memory will permit you?" said the lady, in a tone of earnestness and composure, that Mr. Hartley was ill able to reconcile with her apparent dangerou indisposition.

"Most assuredly, my dear lady," answered the doctor, smiling.

Mrs. Wallingford paused and placed her hands to her head, as if to recall her scattered senses, and at length, in a clear, firm tone, she said—

"Mr. Hartley, you remember the night of the dreadful conflagration, when my child, my dear little innocent, fell a victim to the fury of the destructive element?—But no!—She is not dead! She is not dead!—No one shall again deceive me!—My Christabelle lives!"

"My dear madam," said the doctor, no one has deceived you; I can answer for myself at any rate, and as for Mr. Wallingford——"

"Ah! 'twas he then!" screamed the unhappy lady, "my suspicions are confirmed, 'twas he that robbed me of my offspring!— Yes, did he not deceive Ela, and she was his first love, and why should I, vain fool, have thought for a moment that he would not deceive me?—He has stolen from me the little angel in whose smiles my greatest happiness was centered;—and he also deprived the unfortunate Ela of her only joy, her daughter!"

"Amelia, beloved Amelia," exclaimed the agonised husband, "for Heaven's sake do not entertain such terrible, such unjust thoughts as these; what motive, in the name of God—"

"Terrible and unjust," she reiterated, with convulsive sobs, "yes, yes, so it is, but alas! alas! it is too true, it is too true!"

Having given utterance to these words, she again became insensible, and by the advice of Doctor Hartley, she was conveyed to her own chamber, and he moreover advised Mr. Wallingford, until she was somewhat recovered, and more composed, to keep out of her presence, which would be the only means, it was evident, of saving her from those fits of delirium which were so violent, and might be attended with fatal consequences. What a painful alternative was this to the wretched husband, and never did he feel so lowered, so thoroughly degraded in his life.

Doctor Hartley having given this advice, departed from the Hall, and Walter and his father were left alone. Neither, however, for a time, seemed disposed to speak, but sat in moody abstraction. At length, Mr. Wallingford, who had been waiting for his son to speak, suddenly turned to him, and said—

"Walter, I wish to know whether that unhappy woman is still in custody, or if you have suffered her to depart?—But you——"

Mr. Wallingford stopped abruptly, and seemed incapable of concluding the sentence, so Walter, who noticed his confusion, answered—

"I did not think it at all prudent, sir, to prevent her departing, but had I been so inclined, I am bound to acknowledge that she completely eluded me."

Walter then detailed to his father all the particulars that had transpired between him and Ela at their interview, and the way in which she had escaped from his custody; he also added, that she was not, as might have been imagined, unprotected; far from it, and that if he had attempted to frustrate her designs, they would no doubt have been attacked by the whole gang of Gipsies, and that even if they had been able to defeat them, the whole of the unfortunate business would have gained publicity, and thus expose them to inconceivable annoyance and disgrace.

Mr. Wallingford frowned, and his face coloured at the candid manner in which his son expressed himself, and which very plainly showed that he felt the disgrace his father's misconduct had brought upon him and his dear mother, most keenly. But when Wallingford looked in the face of Walter, and beheld the deep expression of sorrow that was upon it, he could no longer bear to contemplate it, but paused for a few moments, partially covered his face with his hands, and for awhile indulged in the violent anguish that agitated his mind.

"I cannot hit upon a single idea how to alter the present melancholy state of things," said he at last; "in vain I rack my brain, I cannot conceive the most advisable plan to pursue."

Walter could not but take this as an appeal to his advice and aid, but he immediately answered, that not knowing much of the affair, it was impossible for him to give an opinion upon it.

"Right, right, Walter," said his father, eagerly, "it is proper therefore that you should know everything, and I will detail the circumstances to you. My motive for not having made you acquainted with them before was, because I had entirely despaired of ever being able to fathom out the mystery that involves the fate of your sister, and that therefore it would be imprudent, if not cruel, to make your mind uneasy, by telling you the fatal particulars. Oh, my son, need I describe to you, with what intensity of anguish, with what unceasing sorrow, I have reflected for many, many years, upon this dreadful fact; fearful and restless, owing to the apprehension I was under, that you would some day or the other become acquainted with it, and by your questions renew all your mother's agony, which originally was so near bringing her to her grave. Alas! never did I dream the being who was destined to strike the fatal blow; but I deserve it all, for the indiscretion of which I was guilty in my youthful days, and which has embittered my subsequent life. Oh, Walter, reflect for ever upon your father's humiliation at present, and let it be the cause of restraining your passions, and stimulating you to follow undeviatingly the paths of virtue."

The expression of Walter's countenance was quite sufficient evidence of the impression this admonition had made upon his mind; and, indeed his emotion was so great, that he was obliged to turn away his head to conceal his tears, that, in spite of all his efforts to the contrary, burst forth from his eyes. Could he behold this humiliation in that father whom he had ever reverenced, and whose example it was his greatest pride to follow?—No, he must have been indeed insensible if he did.

But if Walter was affected, how much more severely did Mr. Wallingford feel this self-abasement;—it must indeed have been a trial for a father to humble himself in sight of his son.

Neither of them could speak for some time after this; Mr. Wallingford appeared to be entirely absorbed in melancholy reminiscences of the past, and Walter held his sorrow in too great respect, to presume to interrupt it. Besides, if he spoke, would it not appear as if he was ever anxious to elicit from him an explanation which must be so painful to him.

However, at length, Mr. Wallingford having apparently somewhat battled with his emotions, began the melancholy story, and passed as briefly as possible over the events which followed the first appearance of the unfortunate victim of his unruly passions in the vicinity of Wallingford Hall, and the fatal secret which it had been the means of divulging to Mrs. Wallingford; but he expatiated more largely upon the several endeavours he had ineffectually made to claim the unfortunate Ela and her daughter, and to remove them from the life of shame in which they were placed. He next came to the particulars of his meeting and interview with the Gipsies, the attack they had made upon his life, and the narrow escape he had made;—the awful revenge they had taken by burning down the nursery of the Hall, and the supposition that followed of the poor little Christabelle having perished in the flames, but the circumstances that afterwards came out which led them to conjecture that the child was saved and still lived, which the recent admissions of Ela sufficiently confirmed.

This strange narrative was listened to with the greatest interest by Walter, and its varied incidents excited in his bosom alternate feelings of astonishment, incredulity, disgust, and horror. The terrible vengeance the Gipsy tribe had taken filled him with the most unqualified abhorrence, and it seemed almost impossible that such atrocious deeds should have been perpetrated in that place, which he had always been induced to look upon as the chosen retreat of every happiness and innocent enjoyment. It appeared to him also unaccountable that his parents, whom he had always heard spoken of among the de-

Pendants upon the estate, and the inhabitants of the neighbourhood, with the utmost esteem and veneration, and whom he had ever looked up to as the most virtuous and happiest of human beings, should be the objects thus selected for the persecution of these lawless people.

CHAPTER XIX.

" A blight has fallen on her senses,
   Her reason's sight has set in darkness,
   And all before her mental vision
   Is gloom and empty space."

ANON.

THE almost insupportable tortures of Wallingford's mind were increased tenfold, and the misery of the whole family rendered most exquisite, when it was discovered that Mrs. Wallingford, on recovering from the state of insensibility into which she had fallen after the disclosure made by Ela, was labouring under aberration of intellect, and that her ravings were truly awful and lamentable to hear. What even made it the more distressing was, that she seemed not to know one of the family, and her son and Maria, the gentle, the attentive, the ever affectionate Maria, she would not suffer, if she could have helped it, to approach her bedside; but in appalling accents, she declared that they were all combined to render her wretched, that they had robbed her of her little darling, and now, with demoniacal cruelty, still withheld her from her arms. These wild deliriums, however, did not last long, her strength was unable to bear up against them, but the state of absolute idiotcy which succeeded to them was not less heart-rending. It was awful to gaze upon that countenance which had once been so gently beautiful, and which even care and years of sorrow had been unable to destroy, now disfigured and repulsive; to behold those eyes that erst beamed with every expression, and kindness, and intelligence, now wild and vacant; and to hear occasionally from her an idiotic laugh, which would be succeeded immediately by torrents of tears, that flowed, as it were, unconsciously from the suffering lady's eyes.

Oh, how anxiously, how attentively, with what untiring assiduity, did Maria sit by her bedside, and watch the countenance of her unhappy aunt, and how often were her hopes raised, and did she imagine that she discovered the signs of returning reason in the expression of her eyes, and too soon, alas! were they again crushed when she beheld them again assume the same afflicting vacancy. It was a melancholy duty, and it is astonishing the gentle and delicate nature of Maria was enabled to bear up against it.

Walter, too, was unremitting in his atten-

tions by the sick couch of his beloved mother, and in vain tried every device that he could think of to recall her reason. But, alas! all his efforts were ineffectual, whatever he said to her she seemed perfectly unconscious of, and probably answered only by a vacant stare and a stupid laugh. Wallingford, too, with the aid of the good Doctor Hartley, sought hard to arouse the mind of his wretched wife from the horrible state of torpidity into which it had fallen, and when the unfortunate though guilty gentleman beheld the utter uselessness of all his efforts, he groaned in mental anguish, and clasped his hands to his forehead, and rushed out of the apartment, unable to endure the soul-harrowing sight, in a state of distraction too powerful to be described.

Amid all these painful calamities, however, which had thrown a complete blight upon the whole family, Walter never, for a moment, forgot his singular interview with Ela, and the strange acknowledgment she had made to him, and he determined to lose no opportunity of eliciting all the particulars he could, in the hope that it might ultimately lead to the recovery of the long lost Christabelle. Thus resolved, Walter seized upon the first spare hour to ride over to Ashdown Wood, the retreat of the Gipsies; but he saw nothing there to satisfy his curiosity. Ela was not in the encampment, and they also pretended not to know anything at all of the circumstances which had recently occurred. They, however, admitted that part of their gang had lately quitted them, in consequence of a misunderstanding that had arisen between them, and after some trouble, they also confessed that Ela and her daughter, whom they said was not known among the tribe by that name, had accompanied them; but they declared most positively that they had not the slightest knowledge of the place they had gone to, neither would they disclose it; notwithstanding Walter tried all his powers of persuasion, threats, and bribery, he was unable to induce them to divulge what had been the nature of the quarrel.

Walter next looked eagerly among all the young females who were in the encampment, but he saw nothing but a set of bold-faced, coarse, impudent girls, and looked in vain for the object of his anxiety, and the men all declared most firmly that these were the only young women who were in the tents or belonged to their party.

Dissapointed and vexed, Walter finding that any attempt to elicit more than the Gipsies had already told him would be unsuccessful, he returned towards the Hall, and on the way his thoughts naturally wandered into that channel, to which the recent events directed them, and he felt most bitterly the miserable life of shame, of poverty, and degradation into which Christabelle had been plunged ; the scenes of crime in which she had most likely for years mingled, and he could not but feel how dreadfully cruel had been the vengeance taken by the Gipsy tribe. Again he could not help reflecting with astonishment upon the circumstance of Ela, who had once, according to the accounts he had heard, been all that was gentle, innocent, and intellectual, becoming so far lost to all sense of shame, so thoroughly abandoned as to become one of that degraded and wretched class of wanderers, and that voluntarily too, at least so his father had informed him; and, moreover, that she had firmly and fiercely resisted every attempt that had been made to prevail upon her to abandon the Gipsy's life, and not only to quit it herself, but would not listen to any persuasions that were offered for her to resign her daughter to the care of those who would have-nurtured her with care and tenderness, brought her up in the paths of rectitude and virtue, and finally, provided for her in the most liberal manner. This obstinacy on the part of the wretched mother, Walter could not help thinking the most heartless of all, inasmuch as she thus condemned her daughter to the same life of infamy that she herself pursued.

These reflections, and the disappointment he had experienced in his interview with the Gipsies, rendered Walter very melancholy, and he sought his father and made him acquainted with the failure of his attempt.

Mr. Wallingford, however, did not express so much disappointment as his son anticipated he would, for he observed that he knew too well from experience the utter inutility of attempting to gain any intelligence from these people, for their subtlety, artfulness, and faithfulness to each other, were notorious, and they must only look to chance, and the probability of Ela's fulfilling the promise she had made to Walter, for any unravelment of the mystery which involved the fate of Christabelle.

"But alas!" exclaimed Mr. Wallingford, with a deep sigh, " should we again enfold the ill-fated girl to our bosoms; will she be all that fond parents could wish for in their offspring? Oh, no, no, I dare not hope so ! The bare thought maddens me. Has she not been brought up to a life of profligacy and licentiousness ; inured, probably, to almost every species of crime, and taught to look upon virtue as the cant of fools and old women ?"

" Nay, sir, pray do not let your fancy draw so frightful, so revolting a picture," observed Walter, although he could not but feel that the substance of his father's apprehensions was too painfully probable ;—" It may turn out far better than you anticipate ; Christabelle may not always have been placed among the Gipsies, or, if she has even, surely Ela—who once, you say was, good and virtuous—cannot be so entirely lost to all sense of feeling as to taken a part in leading the poor girl astray."

" Ah, Walter," answered his father, shaking his head despairingly, " how little do you know of that unhappy outcast, or you would not speak so."

As Mr. Wallingford reflected upon the scene he had once witnessed among the Gipsies in Rosemary Dell, and the prominent part that Ela had acted in it, a scene of profligacy and riot, which he could never forget, he felt that he had too much reason to make the observations he had done to Walter, and to entertain the doubts that at present occupied his mind. Had not Ela eagerly mixed in the scene of debauchery, and swallowed with evident pleasure the intoxicating beverage ? To one then so lost—so depraved, who could look up to for anything but baseness, and beneath her tuition, what could be expected of the unfortunate girl? Every way Wallingford looked, despair closed around him, and he longed for, yet dreaded the restoration of his daughter, fearful to have his worst ideas and apprehensions verified.

Several more days of misery had elapsed, and still the lamentable condition of Mrs. Wallingford remained unchanged; still did she continue in that awful state of mental torpor, which was so piteous to behold. Neither had Walter or his father been able to learn anything more upon the subject which so deeply engrossed their attention ; nothing to solace them under the heavy afflictions with which they were at present visited.

Neither did poor Maria suffer less poignantly than her uncle and her cousin ; for who could behold the awful situation of the amiable Mrs. Wallingford unmoved ;—more especially one whose heart was so brimful of kindness and affection, as Maria's ?—Nothing could prevail upon her to leave the couch of her aunt for any length of time together, and Walter, who was fearful that her health would suffer from this incessant watching and anxiety, had the greatest difficulty to persuade her to take such rest as was absolutely necessary. Nor was Mrs. Wallingford the only object of her anxious thoughts ; from Walter she had heard the avowal Ela had made, and she frequently inquired of him whether anything had been ascertained which might lead to a hope of Christabelle's recovery.

To her also, Walter imparted the sad apprehensions his father encouraged of Christabelle, if she was restored to them, being inured to vice, and rendered such a being that her relations would be ashamed of ; and in such moments as these, how deeply Maria regretted the oath she had taken, and but for which she might have disclosed to him that she had seen and spoken to the unfortunate girl, and that if anything could be judged from delicacy and beauty of face, the silvery sweetness of her tones, the intellectual expression of her eyes, and the exquisite playfulness and innocence of her demeanour, that she was all that the fondest parents could wish for in a daughter. How did she wish, we repeat, that she could have told him so much, what a weight would it not have taken from the minds of both him and his father.

"I feel confident I am not mistaken," she replied, "and that the beautiful girl to whom I spoke in the summer-house, and who her companion called by the name of Esther, was no other than the long lost Christabelle. The alteraton in the name was not at all remarkable, for it is not at all unreasonable to suppose that the Gipsies would call her by one by which she would soon have been discovered by her friends."

That the girl that Walter and her encountered in the summer-house, was the daughter of Ela, the ill-fated Fanny, she had not the least doubt, and Walter, when this circumstance was recalled to his memory by Maria, could not help admitting that he was struck with the extraordinary likeness she bore to Ela; and when he also remembered the words she had made use of on that occasion, and which he had at the time treated with so much indifference, he acknowleged conveyed a meaning that subsequent circumstances had fully explained.

"Yes, dear Maria," said Walter, "it was indeed as you say, the daughter of Ela, who, as well as Christabelle, is entitled to my love; for is she not the daughter of my father, who has so much right to receive the same attention and be called such, as the poor girl whom we are so solicitous to be restored to us? Oh, if I could once more behold her, and prevail upon her to abandon the wretched vagrants and outcasts with whom she is at present associated, and to place herself under the care of my father, nothing could afford me more infinite gratification. I feel convinced that vice is not natural to her mind; there was something so innocently expressive in her countenance, so intelligent, so gentle in her whole deportment and behaviour, I will not believe that it would require much persuasive eloquence to make her a bright ornament of society, and source of happiness to us. Would to heaven these fond hopes could be realized."

"And why, Walter," observed Maria, "should not your anticipations be equally sanguine with regard to Christabelle?—Can you not believe it possible that she should be equally worthy and virtuous as Fanny?—Indeed I cannot believe any otherwise than that she really is all you can wish."

"God send that your prognostications may come true, my dearest Maria," said Walter, "but I know not now it is, still I cannot for the life of me, encourage the same idea; though for what reason she should not be so, I cannot imagine. And yet it is not probable that Ela would be sure to bestow all the care that was possible upon her own offspring, and that her revengeful spirit would induce her to corrupt the heart and disposition of the other as much as possible, so that if fate should ever ordain her to be discovered by her parents, she might prove to them a curse instead of a blessing? Alas, Maria, you cannot but acknowledge that there is too much probability in this conjecture to be rejected."

Maria could no it but coincide with this opinion, but expressed a hope that their idea of the vindictive feeling of Ela might prove erroneous, and Walter, without making any further observation, left her, and attended his father, to consult with him on the most advisable method of proceeding with this intricate and unpleasant affair.

Nothing deserving of particular mention in these pages, occurred for nearly a fortnight; the situation of the inmates of Wallingford Hall remained in precisely the same state, and Mrs. Wallingford, in spite of the unremitted attentions of Dr. Hartley, and the assiduous care of her affectionate niece, continued in the same melancholy state, seldom speaking, and when she did in such incoherent sentences that they imparted no hope of her being restored to sensibility.

The Gipsies had once more altered their encampment in Ashdown Wood, but they did not appear at all disposed to retire from the neighbourhood altogether. Their movements were closely watched by Walter, and he soon discovered that they had only removed to about two miles further into the wood, although one circumstance surprised them, and which they could only attribute to a desire on their parts to appear innocent of having any connection with the transactions that had occurred of late, or from motives of defiance and curiosity, several of them had frequently been met in the immediate vicinity of Wallingford Hall, and seemed to have no desire to avoid observation, having in many instances actually solicited employment of the servants in the different trades they followed. The servants frequently endeavoured to gain something from them by putting questions relative to the late events that had so disturbed the quiet of the inhabitants of Wallingford Hall, but their answers were always characterized by caution, and never afforded the enquirers any more information than that which they already were in possession of.

Notwithstanding all this precaution on the part of the Gipsies, their actions were watched with the utmost jealousy by all those interested in the mysterious business, and sufficient was elicited to give them cause for suspicion.

One evening, when Walter had just dismounted from his horse, and given it into the care of James, his groom, the latter seemed anxious to communicate something, which his master perceiving, questioned him as to the subject of the intelligence he wished to impart.

"Why, sir," replied James, bowing, "it may not turn out of much importance to be sure, but, as I know you are anxious to learn every little that may be the means of bringing to light the doings of these confounded fellows the Gipsies, I will make bold to tell you what

ELA, BEWAILING THE LOSS OF HER MURDERED DAUGHTER.

these suspicions are. You, perhaps, do not know, sir, that they have again been seen lurking about the Hall, and, whenever that is the case, there is sure to be some evil brooding. The deuce take the hang-gallows rascals, sir, say, asking your pardon for making use of

such bold words, but I would no more mind turning executioner to about a dozen of them this very minute, than I would in mounting my horse. Their very sight is odious to me, and yet to see the impudence and indifference of the varlets; notwithstanding the rough words we give them, nothing can make them keep away from the Hall. I was only speaking to Robert, the coachman, yesterday, upon the subject, and it is his opinion that there must be some rich booty hidden in some parts of the grounds of this Hall, with which they are acquainted, and that it is to find an opportunity to obtain it that they thus persist in hanging about this place. I must say I am also of opinion, though my simple ideas may not go far to be sure, that they would not be so anxious apparently to get into the grounds, if they had not some object or the other in view; only you see, as you've taken the precaution to have your men keep the walls and fences in proper repair, the rascals are thwarted in their designs."

"Your observations are perfectly just, James," replied Walter, "and deserve attention. The conduct of these men is certainly very suspicious, and as you have just said, it does appear as if they were anxious to take something off the premises, for fear it might lead to some discovery of the crime which we imagine has been committed by them. This is a subject that ought to be scrutinized without delay; and were it not so late, we would immediately set about it. However, to-morrow I shall expect you to attend me as soon as day breaks, and then we will prosecute a careful search in every part of the grounds."

The subject thus suggested to Walter's mind by James, was one of such importance that he could not sleep the whole of the night for thinking upon it, and, although it might only prove an erroneous idea after all, there was too much probability in it for him to reject it altogether. The first blush of day, however, had scarcely tinged the horizon, when, so eager was he to put his plans into execution, he arose from his couch, and proceeded to perform the duties of his toilet by himself. He had scarcely completed this when James made his appearance, and was ready to attend him; but Walter, recollecting something that they might require to assist them in their search, sent for it, and desired him to follow him to the summer-house, and to arouse the gardener on his way, and bring him with him also.

Walter walked forth from the hall, and proceeded across the lawn to the summer-house, using the precaution to beat well the bushes on his way, to make sure that no one was concealed therein.

Not having encountered anything to excite his suspicion, he walked on and entered the summer-house, in the arrangement of which he did not perceive any alteration since the time he had last visited it, on the morning after the mysterious event which had caused such a sensation at the hall.

The morning was dull and cold, although only in the early part of autumn, and from the heavy clouds which hung over the summits of the lofty hills in the back ground, Walter anticipated a violent storm. The wind blew briskly, and the faded leaves were blown about in all directions. Walter looked at the signs of some violent outrage having been committed, and which remained exactly in the same state as when he and his father had first discovered them, and as he thought upon the dreadful crime that had in all probability been perpetrated, and that upon the person of his sister, an involuntary shudder passed through the current of his veins.

With his arms folded, Walter gazed over the lake, now overhung by a grey, unwholesome mist, and thought upon the many happy moments he had passed with his fair cousin in that place, and in contemplation of the clear pellucid waters glittering in the golden rays of a bright summer sun. While he was thus occupied the noise of approaching footsteps coming along the path startled him. It was not the path by which he had come from the hall, but one at the back of the summer-house, and which led to a small boat-house at some distance, where for the purpose of pleasure a boat was constantly kept moored.

Walter was not at first surprised at the sounds, for he supposed it was his groom and gardener, but he was soon undeceived, and he was not a little surprised, when, looking forth in the direction of the path, he beheld two men hurrying along in the direction of the lake. The speed with which they advanced, and their evident agitation, frequently looking back to see that they were not observed, was quite sufficient to excite suspicion, which became stronger in the mind of Walter, when he recognised, from their dresses, that they were two of the Gipsy gang.

Had they looked towards the summer-house, they must immediately have observed Walter; and cer ain now that there was something wrong, and that his determination of the previous night would not go unrewarded, he hurried inside the building, and placed himself in a position where he could watch all their actions, but where they could not, by an any possibility, observe him.

Walter was all trembling with anxiety to see the result of this, and his curiosity was very soon satisfied. When they had gained the margin of the water, they proceeded in the direction of the boat-house in great haste. Here they suddenly stopped, and then the tallest of them stooped down, and seemed to be engaged in endeavouring to reach something which appeared to be entangled among the weeds.

Walter's heart throbbed with suspense, and he thrust forward his head as far as he could without running any risk of being seen, should they turn round, so that he might watch their motions more narrowly. On his way to the summer-house, Walter had seen in the shrubbery the two men with the dogs, who had been employed since the night of the alarm, to keep watch in the grounds, and had sent them to their rest; and he had not the slightest doubt but that the two Gipsies having been lurking about, had watched them leave the place, and immediately hastened to put into execution the design they contemplated, whatever it might be, before any of the family was stirring.

The man who had been stooping over the lake, at length arose, and appeared to commune with his companion for a few moments, during which they frequently looked around, and seemed to be at a loss for something to assist them in their purpose. At length Walter observed the tallest man point towards the boat-house, and the other one, immediately nodding his head, as if in assent to his proposition, he hastened towards the boat, and in a very short time returned with the boat-hook.

Having obtained this, the man again knelt down on the bank, and the other assisted him. They seemed to be pulling at something which was very heavy, and Walter became more and more anxious to ascertain what it was they were doing. He did not have to wait much longer; but language must fail to do adequate justice to his astonishment and horror when he saw them draw to the bank a human form, and looking again he plainly distinguished that it was the body of a female.

Walter trembled with emotion at this unexpected sight, and he was fixed motionless to the spot, unable to utter a word. Here then was a confirmation of a dreadful crime having been committed; here at once the cries they had heard, and which had so much alarmed them, were fully accounted for. But what monsters! — God! could such wretches be suffered to live another hour to contaminate society, after such a sanguinary deed as this?

Walter continued with his eyes fixed upon the men and the corpse alternately,—they had dragged the body from the water, and were doing something to it, which, in consequence of the attitude of the ruffians, Walter was unable to make out, but he suspected they were examining the pockets. He was aroused to a sense of the necessity of his immediately taking some steps to secure the wretches; James and the gardener did not come, and he was at a complete loss to account for their delay. In their absence, he knew not what could be done, for to venture to attack them alone, and without any means of defence, desperate villains as they doubtless were, would be madness, and attended with inevitable destruction, and should he hasten back to the hall and alarm the inmates, most likely before he could return they would have effected their escape. While he was still deliberating what

was best to be done, he beheld James and the gardener coming towards the summer house, by the other path, and beckoning them to approach cautiously, he kept his eyes fixed upon the men, resolved that they should not escape apprehension if possible.

James had provided himself with three stout sticks, which were the only implements of defence he could lay his hand on, and Walter having grasped one of these, and desired them to be cautious, but firm, he hastened from the building, and with silent footsteps, hurried towards the spot where the men were still stooping over the corpse, and seemed to be either engaged in tying or untying something from the neck. When, however, they had got within a few yards of them, one of them happened to turn round, and uttering a loud exclamation they stood and confronted Walter and his companions.

" Forward !" exclaimed the latter, brandishing his stick in the air, " on to the villains, and drag them to justice."

As the young man uttered these words, he darted forward with an air of determination towards the Gipsies, followed by James and the gardener.

The fellows were at first apparently thunderstruck at this unexpected discovery, but they very soon recovered from their confusion, and, putting on a scowl of defiance, they stood with a firm air, and waited the attack; at the same moment drawing from under their coats each a long knife, which they grasped tightly in their hands, and appeared to have made up their minds not to yield without a desperate struggle.

Fortunately, neither James or the gardener lacked their full share of courage, or the sight of these destructive weapons, and the well-known character of the ruffians, might have alarmed them, and afforded the Gipsies an easy conquest ; but no sooner had Walter given them the command, than they were prepared to put their plans into execution at all hazards.

" Fools !" exclaimed one of them, who appeared to be much older than his companion— " Fools ! stand off, or by the infernal host the earth shall drink your warm blood. No power on earth shall take us alive, and we will not sell our lives cheaply. We give you timely caution, my masters ; avail yourselves of it if ye like. We wish not to injure ye, reckless and desperate as we are—no, the blood that has already been shed is too much. This deed is not ours ; but if we are taken, with such damning evidence of guilt, we know that the gibbet will be our portion—which shall not be. Hear me, then ; retire from this place, and leave us to depart without interruption ; for if you do not——"

" Heed not the villain's words," interrupted Walter, addressing himself to his companions,

as he led them on ; " let not the wretches escape. The blood of a fellow-creature is yet
reeking upon their hands, and we must secure
them from the perpetration of further atrocities.
—On, on to the miscreants; the Almighty
Judge will not desert us in such a struggle !"

Again Walter hastened forward a few paces
in advance of James and the gardener; and,
worked up to the utmost pitch of determination,
he was about, in spite of the apparent muscular
power of the Gipsies, and the deadly weapons
with which they were provided, to rush upon
them, when he was startled by a loud rustling
among a cluster of trees close by him ; and the
next moment Ela, with her hair wild and dishevelled, her eyes darting fury, and her whole
demeanour expressive of the most desperate
resolution, rushed in between them, and presenting a couple of pistols at the two Gipsies,
held them at bay.

"Rash boy !" she cried, speaking to Walter, "are you mad? Would you thus tamely
sacrifice your life and that of your companions?
Hold, I say !"

"It is the old hag herself," cried James,
who placed himself before her, with the idea
of preventing her joining her companions ; "we
will secure her, and then we shall, at any rate,
have the principal cause of all the trouble."

"Idiot !" answered Ela, as she looked disdainfully on the groom, " think you that such
a reptile as you could conquer Ela, were she
disposed to struggle against ye ? But I came
not here for that purpose—no, the old hag, as
you term her, is here to render you all the
assistance in her power. Behold ! I carry in
my hands that which will quickly make the
wretches yield. They shall be secured in a few
minutes !"

Thus speaking, Ela continued to level the
weapons at the heads of the two ruffians, who,
surprised, terrified, and aghast, were now fixed
motionless to the spot, and seemed to quail
beneath the looks of vengeance and detestation,
which Ela fixed upon them.

"Mark Darwin," said Ela, in a hoarse voice,
speaking to the eldest of the two fellows,
"Mark Darwin, at length your career of crime
and bloodshed is drawing to a close; and my
eyes will yet glut upon your corpse, as it swings
in the air like that of a dog, unless you save
the executioner the trouble, and plunge your
knife into your black heart—the knife which
cut short the days of your innocent victim.
Maniac ! you thought you had deceived me—
that my suspicions were not awakened, and
that the perpetrators of the hellish deed would
remain unknown. But what can shield the
murderers of my gentle offspring from the retribution of her mother? Did you imagine that
I could not penetrate the spacious mask you assumed? Fool ! Nothing could hide it from me ;
and I have been close at your side all the while,

although you thought you had secured me, by
sending me off many miles in the country on a
false errand. Yes, I have pursued you like your
very shadow, and will continue to do so until the
hangman does his duty. Not a movement of
yours, since the loss of my poor girl, has
escaped my observation. I braved every danger,
suffered every vicissitude, to accomplish my
purpose ; I have gone for days without any
food, but such as the bushes afforded me, and
the water from the brook has slaked my burning thirst; but Heaven, to which I dare still
appeal, has given me strength and resolution to
combat all—it has heard a mother's cry for
vengeance on the murderers of her only child ;
and it will be my task to bring to justice a fiend
in human form, whose bones should have been
bleaching on the gibbet years ago ! Yes, Mark
Darwin, I shall have the gratification of seeing
the hangman perform his office upon thy hated
carcase ; I shall witness and exult in your
agonized death struggles, a prelude only to the
eternal torments that await your soul hereafter.
I cannot, will not die, until my every wish is
accomplished ; until your name shall exist only
in the hatred of mankind, and your polluted
accursed race shall be extinct. Think not that
the gallows shall not have its full due; yes,
your infernal brood shall all swing upon the
same tree. Now then, on to them—seize the
wretches ; but remember, although if they resist, you may maim them—break their limbs—
the hangman must not be cheated of his victims !"

The man, it appeared, from the words of
Ela, was the father of Mark Darwin and
Rupert, who have been frequently alluded to in
this narrative ; and although it was evident
that more than fifty years had passed over his
head, he was still a powerful robust man, and
his countenance bespoke the utmost coolness
and determination. Mark, his son, who was
with him, was a tall, strong man, and evidently
a ruffian capable of performing any deed.
However, seeing that any attempt at resistance
would be useless, as Ela was so well armed,
he threw down his knife, and in a voice of
mingled scorn and wrath, he said :—

"It would be madness to attempt to contend
with ye ; but if we are treated fairly, I am
certain nothing can prove us guilty, although
this maniac would condemn us unheard. Her
brain has been turned for years past.

"Aye, but even if it be so, that shall not
preserve her from the fate she merits more than
us," said the old man, as he fixed his eyes,
blood shot, with implacable detestation upon
the countenance of Ela, and compressed his
livid lips, as the groom and his companion
proceeded to bind their arms with some rope
which they found in the summer-house. "Ela,
think not that me and mine will go alone to
the scaffold; for you, yes you, shall be our

companion. Nay, do not mistake me, or think that I talk idly. You know not the plot which has been laid to secure this consummation, and that even now it is matured, and no power on earth can save you from a fate to which you think you have condemned us. Think you I was that blind fool not to see that as soon as your girl, who you instructed to treat my sons with contempt and insult, was deprived of life, that me and them would be the objects of your deadly vengeance; but I repeat, the plot is matured, and you cannot escape from the snare that is laid for you. At any rate old Mark Darwin will not die unrevenged!"

"Wretch! monster! I laugh your threats to scorn; I spit at, I despise you!" answered Ela, with a fiendish hysterical laugh. "You cannot touch the soul of the bereaved mother more than you have done already."

During these words, Walter's eyes now wandered from the form and features of the wretched woman, for whom, in spite of her violence, his deepest sympathy was excited, to the ghastly and mutilated remains of her unfortunate daughter, which were stretched at her feet; the awful sight created a feeling of horror in his breast, and he could not help shuddering. The quick eye of Ela instantly observed his emotion, and turning from the two Gipsies, who were now secured, with their hands bound tightly behind them, she laid hold of his arm, and looking at him earnestly, and with an expression that fixed his whole attention upon her words, she ejaculated—

"I see this deplorable, this revolting sight even excites *your* sympathy, *your* horror; and what, then, think you must be the agony of that wretched woman who bore it?—Young man, when you think of this hellish deed, remember that your father was the origin of it all; the blood of the murdered girl rests upon his head, the head of her *father*; yes, her *father*, I repeat, as well as yours. Poor girl; it was in seeking an opportunity to behold that unnatural parent, whom she loved, though I bade her hate, despise, curse him, and to gaze upon you, her brother, whom I also instructed her to detest, because he inherits that fortune and rank, which by rights belonged to her;—it was in doing this she met her dreadful, her untimely death!—My poor butchered girl, my only one; alas! alas!"

"Impossible!" ejaculated the youngest Gipsy, "this tale must be false; Fanny surely was not the daughter of Mr. Wallingford, and the sister of this youth?"

"You have heard me say so," said Ela, with a look of scorn, "but I say it not for your gratification, miscreants!—You ——"

"Fiends of Hell, seize the wretch that so deceived me!" cried Mark, as he fixed his angry eyes upon his father, who contracted his brows, and held down his head, with conscious guilt; "did you not deceive me by the story you told me, of Ela having bartered to Mr. Wallingford what I in vain had been suing for!—Answer me; did you not say so?"

The old man shrunk from the scrutinizing look of his son, and remained silent for a moment or two; at length, however, regaining his self possession as quickly as he had lost it, he said—

"Psha! Mark!—Why talk now upon the subject, if even I did say so? It would be bad policy for us to quarrel at such a time as this;—be silent."

His son turned away sullenly, and made no reply to this; but he fixed his eyes upon Ela, who was on her knees by the side of the disfigured corpse of her ill-fated daughter, and had seemingly been unconscious of all that was passing around her. It was truly a pitiable, a melancholy sight, to behold the fond mother, with her eyes fixed intently upon the ghastly blood-stained features of her offspring, and with her hands clasped together, breathing in murmurs so low, that they could not reach the ear, an earnest prayer. There was no tear in her eye; not a muscle of her face was disturbed; but it was evident from the convulsive heaving of her bosom, that her heart was bursting.

Walter was wounded to the quick at this sight, and approaching the wretched outcast in a voice of gentle persuasiveness, he tried to prevail upon her to quit the soul-harrowing spectacle, and to accompany him into the Hall, when he would see that the remains of the poor girl were properly taken care of.

"Ah! you shall not tear her from me!" shrieked Ela, as she threw her arms over the corpse, and looked up fiercely at Walter; "no power on earth shall again separate us, now that I have once more beheld her, until her remains are placed in the cold, cold grave, in which, after I have witnessed the infliction of retributive vengeance on her demoniacal assassins, I pray to the God of mercy, I may be laid. My poor gentle girl, all so lovely to me, even in the ghastliness of death, and disfigured by the fiendish hands of your murderers;—they shall not force your mother from your cold remains. No, no, take the wretches into safe custody, and then, if you like to return to me, I will give ear to your proposition."

Walter could not but obey this mandate, and fixing upon Ela a look of the utmost pity, he quitted the place with his companions, and guarding the prisoners, who proceeded in silence towards the back of the house, where not wishing to create any confusion, which this strange affair would be likely to do among the servants, he bade James and the gardener to convey them to the stable for the present, and gave them the pistols which Ela had resigned to his care, in case they should make any attempt to escape. He then went into the Hall, and sought his father, to inform him of what had taken place, and to consult with him what was best to be done.

Mr. Wallingford had not yet left his chamber, when his son requested an interview with him, and on his entrance, the perturbed state he was in, and the paleness of his countenance, convinced the former that something important had occurred to disturb him.

"Walter," he eagerly inquired, "you are agitated; I can perceive it. What has occasioned this?"

"I am indeed, agitated, sir," answered Walter, "for I have this morning met with an adventure of the most awful and afflicting description."

"This morning?" repeated his father, "and so early too; why I thought you had scarcely risen."

"I have been up since daylight, sir," said Walter, "for an idea struck me, that by searching more minutely the shrubbery and the summer-house, I might make some discovery which would lead to the disclosure of the secret which at present so deeply occupies all our minds, and——"

"Did you succeed?" hastily demanded his father, trembling with suspense and dismal foreboding. Walter replied in the affirmative.

"And what is the nature of the discovery you have made, Walter?" asked Mr. Wallingford.

"Ela and her daughter——"

"Ah! what of them? Speak, answer me; do not keep me any longer in suspense. Good Heaven! shall I never know peace? are they, till my death, destined to be my curse?"

"One at any rate, sir," replied Walter, with much solemnity, "has no longer the power to torment you——"

"Is then, Ela no more? Oh, tell me quickly!" gasped forth Wallingford; his whole frame trembling with agitation and impatience.

"Ela is not dead," answered Walter, "but her daughter's corpse is watered by her tears."

"Ah! said Wallingford with much emotion, "and is it indeed so? you mean the girl—Fanny, do you not?" Walter bowed, and his father, after a pause, continued in a melancholy tone. "Poor unfortunate—poor girl—and yet it is a mercy that it is so; and my prayers are at length heard, and she is at rest in the grave, which is far better than for her to live and continue in the career of guilt to which her wretched mother had initiated her. But, tell me, in what way did it occur, and how did you become acquainted with it?"

In a voice of the deepest emotion, Walter detailed to his father all the distressing particulars; but how shall we describe the feelings of horror and fear with which the unhappy

gentleman listened to him! He smote his forehead, and groaned aloud.

"God of Heaven!" he cried, "when will my earthly torment cease? and you say that the corpse is still there, and Ela, too, with it? My brain is distracted! I know not what to do. Walter, you have acted very wrong not to compel Ela—or see that the body of the unfortunate girl was removed from the premises. Ela will now——"

Walter quickly interrupted the finish of this observation, and it was not without considerable difficulty that he could repress his real feelings on the subject. The idea to him was completely revolting and disgusting, to think that his father could so easily pass over the frenzied agonies of the bereaved mother, as she knelt and watched over the mutilated remains of that girl in whom her all of earthly happiness was centered, that he could so easily erase from his mind the violent death that poor girl had met with; the agonized cries which he himself had heard, and which must have been at the time her assassins were committing the horrid deed; the violent struggle, from the marks in the summer-house, which she must have had; how desperately she must have fought for life, and prayed for mercy to them whose hearts were callous to pity; none of these harrowing thoughts crossed his mind—his whole ideas were centered in one point, and that was the fear that Ela would think and insist upon her right of having the corpse brought into the Hall, and acknowledged as the remains of his daughter. O yes, there was another subject that tormented him, and that was the apprehension of the disgrace the examination and trial of the prisoners, and the consequent disclosures which would be made of his former life, would bring upon him.

"Indeed, sir," said Walter, after a brief pause, "your fears, as regards Ela, I am certain are groundless, and she will not give you any more trouble than possible. The body, you are aware, sir, cannot be removed far from the spot on which it was found, until a coroner's inquest have sat upon it. I was going to suggest that it be placed in the summer-house, where, most likely, the dreadful crime was perpetrated. The distracted parent has expressed a determination to remain by the body of her ill-fated daughter until it is laid in the grave; and, of course, she must not be suffered to stay there without being provided with——"

"Do as your judgment dictates, Walter," added his father, "my mind is too ill at ease to form any plan, and I will, therefore, leave it entirely with you. Let no comfort be wanting —but I must request you will not bring me into it any more than is indispensably necessary."

Walter bowed his acquiescence, and he then inquired of his father, whether he would take charge of the supposed murderers, to which that gentleman replied in the affirmative, and stated it to be his intention to send them to Squire Darlington's immediately, and get him to commit them to prison, adding that he felt so much indisposed, with anxiety and care, that he did not wish to be seen in the affair any more than could possibly be avoided.

Walter did not venture to make any reply to these observations, although he by no means approved of his father's plan, and could not imagine what could be his motives for sending them to such a distance, when he himself, being a magistrate, could have committed them to the county gaol forthwith. Besides, the taking of them to such a distance might be attended with the utmost danger, as the Gipsy tribe were spread in all directions over the country, and should a rescue be attempted, a terrible loss of life would no doubt be the result. He was, however, fully aware of the reason of his father's conduct, and he did not therefore presume to offer an opinion to him upon the subject.

Walter having quitted his father, returned to the summer-house, in which, as we have before stated, he had left Ela kneeling over the ghastly remains of her darling child. He paused at the door, and contemplated the wretched sufferer for a few moments in silence. It was truly a heart-rending sight to behold her, seated on the damp earth, with the head of her poor murdered child, which was still streaming with water, pressed to her bosom, in all the frenzy of despair, while she gazed wildly upon the marks of violence which disfigured the once handsome features of the deceased. So absorbed was she in this melancholy task, that she did not hear Walter enter, and it was not till he spoke that she was conscious of his presence. There was a large stone and a handkerchief at the feet of the corpse, to which Ela directed Walter's attention, and that of the men he had brought with him to assist, and the female who was to attend upon her.

"Behold here," she exclaimed, "here is damning proof of the villains' guilt, although they thought it would have saved them from detection. That handkerchief I can swear belongs to the elder Mark; the monster used it to fasten the stone to the poor girl's neck, thinking it would sink the corpse, and that his hideous crime would be hidden from the eye of justice; but an all-searching eye was fixed upon him, and detection overtook him sooner than he had expected. Young man, you cannot form any idea of the care, the sufferings, to which I have been exposed, since from your lips I obtained a clue to the discovery of the monsters who murdered my poor girl. For hours have I thrown my poor body in among the tall grass and laid concealed, near the place of the Gip-

sies' encampment, in Ashdown Wood, until I could ascertain where the villains had secreted themselves, for they were afraid to meet the lioness when they had robbed her of her cub. The other portion of the gang sought to lead me astray, and to shield them from the vengeance they knew I should not rest until I had obtained. They declared that Mark Darwin, and his two sons, having quarrelled with them, had quitted them, and gone they knew not whither, though they had since heard that they were with another party of Gipsies at ———, about thirty miles from this place. But they could not deceive me; too well I knew the base lies they were capable of uttering; when I heard it hinted by one of them, that my Fanny had accompanied them, I could have buried my fingers in her throat, and pressed her life out, for suggesting such an idea. Then, convinced that they had told me false, I swore that I would never rest more until I had accomplished my wishes, and hunted the fiends to destruction. I have kept my word, and my triumph is yet to come. But you would remove the corpse of this unfortunate girl.

Walter having informed her of his wishes, she offered no objection, and at the same time he assured her that all that could be done to alleviate and assist her should be performed, and that the servant was ordered to be in constant attendance upon her, to procure anything she might require, and also to see that her privacy was not intruded upon by those who were only stimulated by idle curiosity.

Ela shook her hand, and did not return any immediate answer, but as Walter was about to retire, she said, in a tone of satisfaction—

"I seek not that which you have mentioned; —hear me, this is what I ask, and which surely the heir of Wallingford Hall will not refuse to his father's eldest child. I crave of you a place of shelter for this cold corpse;—a winding sheet, a coffin, and a small space of ground for its final resting place, where I may be permitted sometimes to visit the spot that encloses the ashes of one, by whom I hope I may soon, very soon be laid."

"You shall have everything that you may require," said Walter, "but come, I beg you will retire with me from this melancholy scene for a short time, until——"

"Ah, no! it shall not be; no power shall induce me to stir from this spot for an instant!" said Ela resolutely; "I will be with her, never leave her, until the earth is heaped upon her."

With these words Ela beckoned the woman to bring forward the sheet that they might cover the corpse, and make her decent before she was removed to her final resting place.

The woman shuddered at the task, and

trembled so violently, that had not Ela's mind been entirely engrossed by the one all-absorbing thought, she must have observed her. But Ela was cool and collected, and evinced the strength of her love towards the senseless ashes of her murdered child. She raised the corpse, folding it ardently in her arms as she did so, as if she thought she could warm it into life again, and helped to place the covering around her, apparently taking little or no notice of the revolting and decomposed state it was in, from its being immersed in the water so long. As her eyes rested upon the frightful wound in her side, she laid down the corpse, and pointing to it, she exclaimed in a voice that was hollow with the intensity of her emotions—

"Ah! see here, this frightful wound;—it still gapes!—From this issued the life's blood of her for whose sake I have endured so many years of suffering, to have preserved whom, I would willingly have encountered years more, nay, have laid down a life which to me was of no other value than to protect her's. Yes, here the murderer plunged his fatal weapon. Oh, demon! demon!—would that I had you now in my power, and could use you at my own discretion! Hell's torments should be nothing compared to those I would contrive to torture you with, but my vengeance will yet be satiated—Yes, I shall see you on the scaffold, trembling and quivering at the thoughts of death, as my eyes once beheld you—but there will be no mercy shewn you now; no—you will swing high; and I shall watch with greedy eyes the agonized writhings of your body in the last struggle that consigns your black soul to perdition."

"Indeed, say you then that this man has once before been accused of a crime for which his life would have been forfeited to the laws of his country?" inquired Walter.

"Before accused of crime!" repeated Ela, emphatically, "oh, how little do you know of the villain, or——but enough for the present; at some future period I may divulge more upon this subject."

By the time this conversation was over, the melancholy duties had been completed upon the corpse, when it was put upon a sofa that was in the summer-house, and Ela having placed herself by its side, Walter gave Bridget, the female, strict injunctions to pay every attention to her charge, and then, attended by the men he had brought with him, he left the place, his mind deeply impressed with the horrible spectacle he had witnessed.

———

CHAPTER XXX.

"She weeps her first, her only born,
    Her only joy, her only care;
Her breast with bitter pangs is torn,
    And all around is dark despair."

WALTER was most anxious that the dreadful events that had recently taken place, and the discovery he had made, should be kept as secret as possible, fearing that the precipitation and general wrong-headedness of the domestics, if they should become acquainted with them, might be the means of bringing them to the knowledge of his mother, and thus the result might be too fatal to contemplate. To let them remain, however, an entire secret from the household, would be impossible, and therefore his principal object was to let it cause no more consternation than could be possibly helped. He, therefore, cautioned them all, and exacted from them a solemn promise, that whatever might be their own feelings, they would not give way to them, more especially when in the presence of Mrs. Wallingford.

But, notwithstanding these promises, the servants had found it utterly impossible for them to combat their dismay entirely, and a vague account of the shocking events reached the ears of Maria, who continued with unabated, zeal and the most sedulous care, her attendance upon her unfortunate aunt; and threw her into a most dreadful state of alarm, and anxiety to be made acquainted with the particulars.

No sooner had Walter gone to his mother's room, to inquire after the state of her health, than he found his cousin pale and agitated, and drawing him aside, although the poor lady remained precisely in the same state of unconsciousness, she exclaimed eagerly—

"Oh, Walter, what horrible tale is this I have heard? Has it then come at last to bloodshed; and that too—but tell me, is it true that only the daughter of the wretched outcast, Ela, has been found?"

"It is indeed Ela's daughter that is found," answered Walter, "the poor hapless Fanny, whose——"

"Oh, God!" interrupted the agitated Maria, "what then became of the other girl? was she saved from the awful fate of her companion; —or did she too fall beneath the murderer's knife?"

"Your mind is bewildered, dear Maria," said the astonished Walter. "what can be the meaning of your words? To what other person do you allude? Somebody has been telling you an erroneous story, and——"

"Oh, no, no, no!" ejaculated his cousin eagerly, "it is not so?—till now I have been foolish: nay, I know not whether it does not deserve a harsher term, in keeping confined to my own breast all that I know relative to this awful catastrophe—I—I—but still I am not

—I cannot be to blame, for I was bound by a solemn vow not to divulge the secret ;—the death of the poor girl releases me from my oath, and gives me full liberty to reveal everything I know."

"Maria," observed Walter, who was alarmed at the violent emotion she betrayed, " your words fill my mind with apprehension ;—to what do they allude? Tranquillize your feelings, my dear girl, I implore you."

Walter was not only fearful that Maria had been terrified by some wild story which had

WALTER MAKES A DISCOVERY THROUGH THE SAGACITY OF "CARLO."

en told to her by Mrs. Pembroke, or one of e other loquacious servants, but he also began imagine that the unusual exertion the poor had lately undergone in her constant attendance upon his mother, and in witnessing distressing malady, had worked upon her mind, and he therefore once more implored her more earnestly than before, to endeavour to compose herself, and not to dwell upon anything that might harass her feelings. But Maria, who heeded not his observations, and, in fact, did not understand them rightly, without any further remarks, detailed with as much composure as she could, her adventures on the night of the fatal deed, her meeting with the two Gipsy girls, and the conversation that had passed between them. Maria, who did not wish to wound the feelings of her cousin any more than they were at present, did not hint to him even what she too strongly suspected, that although the youngest one was called Esther, she was, in fact, the long-lost Christabelle Wallingford. But although she did not mention this suspicion, Walter seemed to read her thoughts, and the same idea occurred to him in a moment, and for some time he was completely petrified to the spot with wonder and consternation.

" Merciful Heavens !" he reflected, " surely it cannot be—the idea is too dreadful to encourage—Christabelle also the victim of the assassin's knife? And why should it not be? Ah ! should she have indeed perished, perhaps at the present time her cold corpse lies beneath the waters of the same lake from which I watched them drag the body of the ill-fated Fanny !"

A cold tremor seized his frame as this horrible thought darted like an electric shock through his brain, and he resolved directly to hasten to Ela, and endeavour to force her to reveal all she knew about Christabelle. He excused himself to Maria ; begged of her to calm her terrors as much as possible, so that she might not add to the dreadful distress and suffering which his father already endured, and hurried from the Hall.

He had not proceeded far, however, in the direction of the place where he had left Ela, when he met Bridget, who was returning to the Hall. Surprised at this, he hastily inquired what was the reason she had quitted her charge, when he had laid such strict injunctions on her to the contrary.

" Oh, sir," replied Bridget, ' I could not help it—in spite of all I could say or do in the way of persuasion, she would not suffer me to remain with her. After we had laid the unfortunate girl out, it was quite heartrending to behold the poor thing sitting down to watch by her, and strewing upon the cold corpse the choicest flowers she could find. She bade me leave her, and declared she would be alone ; and she strictly enjoined me to see that no persons who did not belong to the household should be suffered to enter the shrubbery. It is my firm belief, sir, that she apprehends that some of the gang are likely to surprise her : but surely, monsters as they are, and as this bloody crime proves them to be, they could never be brutal enough to interrupt that unhappy woman, while engaged in the melancholy duty of watching by her daughter's cold remains."

Walter was horrorstruck at the idea which the servant suggested, and it seemed too pro ble for him easily to reject it. What de however diabolical, were not these wretc capable of perpetrating.

" Return to the house, Bridget, for present," said he, " I will myself have interview with the unfortunate woman, and after that, I see any just ground to fear further outrage from the Gipsies, we m take care to be prepared to frustrate the desi of the ruffians."

With hasty steps Walter hurried tow the summer-house, the door of which he fo was closed. He was just going to kno and request Ela to admit him, when her vo in the most strange and melancholy acce vibrated on his ears. This not a little tonished him, for as Bridget had left h who could she be conversing with ?—He pau and listened with breathless curiosity, but was soon changed to a sentiment of gratificat and sympathy, when he found that Ela offering up a prayer to heaven by the side the corpse. But even this feeling was suffered to continue long, for the wretched man suddenly changed her tone, and in l accents she implored the Almighty to aff her the means of speedy and terrible vengea upon the heads of her enemies, the murder of her daughter.

" Oh, that she had continued to pray pardon for her own offences," soliloquised W ter, " and patience and resignation to bear heavy calamity that has befallen her."

Ela suddenly ceased, and Walter could h her sob hysterically ; but that did not last ma moments, and then all was again still as t grave.

Walter, who had before forborne to in terru the unfortunate woman, now opened the d and entered. He found Ela seated by the si of the corpse, but an air of perfect composu had taken the place of that wild demeanour a frantic grief which had before agitated h She arose when Walter entered, and express to him her thanks for the kindness and attenti he had bestowed upon her ; informing him th his orders had been strictly attended to, and th she had received everything she could wish f as regarded refreshments, &c.

" Indeed had I not had them," continu Ela, " I could not have survived many day longer ;—my strength fought against it as lo as it could, and it was the only hope, the thir of revenge that supported me ; but I am grat ful to Heaven for permitting me to live, whic I trust I shall do to see the fiends who han robbed me of my child expiate their crim upon the scaffold."

" And I trust also," said Walter, " that yo will not fail to do all in your power to repa the injury you have done to others."

Ela turned a keen glance upon him when sh

heard these words, and returned no answer for a few moments, but at length in an emphatic tone she observed—

"Injury, young man; you know not what you talk about; who is there can accuse Ela of doing them harm?—Point them out to me, and no one will be more willing than Ela to give them all the reparation in her power. Recollect, that if I retaliate upon those who have injured me, it is sanctioned by every law of justice."

"But call you that justice, where the guiltless have to suffer as well as those who are guilty?" demanded Walter.

"It is," answered Ela hastily; "or if not, why is not that law which condemns a robber to the scaffold considered unjust, because it brings misery and disgrace upon his unoffending family?—However, enough of this at present; it is not worth while to waste time upon a subject it is doubtful we should ever agree upon. I guess the purport of your words, and as I can have no interest whatever in the concealment of one fact, I tell you, solemnly assure you, that your mother was not robbed of her child by me, nor did I know anything about it at the time, for I was not near the spot, and it was not for some time afterwards, when it would have been useless to interfere, that I was made acquainted with the circumstance, and then——"

"You sought not," added Walter, "to quiet the grief and stay the sufferings of the wretched parents, by revealing to them what you knew?"

"True it is, I did not," replied Ela, "it would have been madness in me to attempt it at that time, for I was narrowly watched, by those who were ready enough to cast suspicion u on me, and had I given them the least cause to doubt my fidelity, my own life would have been the certain forfeit. More than once I made up my mind afterwards, that I wou'd make an attempt to divulge the secret, but there was always something or the other that occurred to thwart me. The last time I was near succeeding, and should have done so, for I gained access to the Hall, but owing to a misunderstanding on my part, I was led to believe that both your father and mother were dead, and I had a very narrow escape with my life in making the attempt."

"Now, at any rate," hastily observed Walter, "you have nothing that can induce you to keep the secret;—you have torn yourself from the tribe, and therefore, I implore you, for the sake of my poor distracted mother, and——"

"You have behaved kind to me, young man," interrupted Ela fervently. "and on that account, and for your sake alone, I promise to do all that is in my power. Your sister Christabelle is still alive—I have watched over her for years, and she was the favourite companion of my poor child, with whom she was, on the night she was so barbarously assassinated."

"Ah!" exclaimed Walter impatiently, "you say she still lives; oh, tell me then, and do not keep me in suspense, what has become of her now, and how did she escape the murderer's blade?"

Ela shook her head and sighed. "You ask me questions, young man," said she, "that I cannot answer. I know not where she is at present, for the villains have secreted her for fear she should divulge their crime, and the bloody perpetrators of it. Unhappy girl, I do, indeed, feel for her situation, for I have understood that she is accompanied by old Morna and Rupert, who are such heartless monsters, that they look upon murder as nothing, if by it they can save their own necks from the halter."

"God protect her!" cried the distracted Walter; "and have you no idea of the route the wretches have taken, and how we might be able to trace them?'

"I have not," answered Ela, "what I have already told you, I overheard from the lips of Mark, in talking to his son, by accident, or I should have imagined that she too was murdered by the insatiate demons."

"But do you not know all the places which the tribe visit?" demanded Walter.

"And what of that?" returned Ela; "oh, young man, you know nothing of the rules and dispositions of the wretches, if you imagine that my imparting to you where to find your sister, would be of any avail to you No, it would not; they have the means to elude your utmost vigilance, and of thwarting all your schemes. Besides, if they thought that there was any chance of the girl getting into your power, and that she would betray them, they would immediately have her life. Look on this mutilated corse, and doubt not that they will shrink from committing the most hideous crimes; and have I not in the many, many long and weary years that I have been their companion, learnt too well what they will do, when they are provoked to it. But I promise you my assistance—I will exert myself to the utmost, to accomplish the object of your ardent, your anxious wishes. I will but tarry till the earth receives the remains of my poor murdered child, and the interval that will elapse before the trial of the miscreants, shall be devoted by me to the task of endeavouring to find out the place where they are secreted. I want but another witness to convict Mark and his two sons, and I will not rest until I have obtained that; for my soul is thirsty for vengeance against all of their accursed race.—But sufficient proof of their guilt cannot, I am afraid, be established without Esther—Christabelle Wallingford I mean—for she, no doubt, was a

witness to the perpetration of the horrible crime.
You will thus see that I have sufficient reasons
of my own to induce me to use every means in
my power to track the wretches to their lair, to
discover where they have hidden her. My own
life may be the forfeit of my daring, indeed it
is certain, should they find out that I am pursuing them for the purpose of betraying them—
but I do not fear it—such I know will be my
fate one time or the other, and what matters
how soon it comes, so that I am permitted to
escape until I have seen the murderers of my
child swinging from the gallows!"

Walter betrayed considerable emotion. Not
only was he distracted by the critical and
awful situation in which his sister was involved,
but he was filled with the most sincere regret,
to see that hatred and revenge were still the
predominant passions that reigned in the
breast of Ela. In fact, almost every good
sentiment seemed to be stifled in her mind,
and she appeared to look upon the restoration
of Christabelle, more as the means that would
afford her the gratification she sought in the
destruction of Mark Darwin and his family,
than with the view of making her parents
some reparation for the evil she had so frequently brought upon them, or from any sympathy that she experienced in Christabelle's
fate. She did not show the least symptom of
remorse for the heavy affliction she had been
the cause at the present time of bringing upon
Walter and his parents, but if her feelings could
have been clearly defined, it is not at all improbable that her determined hatred against
Mr. Wallingford made her feel a spirit of
exultation at the anguish he was enduring.

Neither of them resumed the conversation
for several minutes after this, and Ela once
more turned her whole attention to the corpse,
and soon became apparently unconscious of
everything else around her. The wounds
and scarifications about the body she had
concealed as well as she could with a quantity of flowers, and as Walter watched her,
and recollected what she had told him concerning the implacability of the vengeance of her
former associates, he became satisfied that it was
no longer prudent or safe to suffer her to
remain where she was, and he tried to think of
some plan by which her safety might be secured,
and all suspicion of the facts hidden from the
knowledge of the Gipsies. As these ideas
occurred to him, he determined to broach the
subject to Ela, and hear what was her opinion;
accordingly he enquired whether she did not
think it probable that some of the ruffians were
lurking in the vicinity, who were anxious to
know what would be the result of the detection
of their comrades.

"It is not likely," replied Ela, "for I
know that they have now taken up their abode

some miles distant from Ashdown Wood, and
Mark and his son were only lurking about
here for an opportunity to secure the body of
their victim, and as they thought thus prevent
all discovery of the deed they had committed.
Their associates, therefore, are yet unacquainted
with their apprehension; and when it does
come to their knowledge, so far from seeking to
rescue them, or trying to obtain vengeance for
them at present, they will immediately fly the
spot, with the utmost precipitation, for fear
that they should also be apprehended as accessaries in the crime. When it arrives at the
worst, and the fate of their comrades is fixed,
they will not dread to rush out, and make a
a bold effort for their rescue; but the idea of
confinement to them is worse than death,
which they feel confident they would be condemned to if they were to be apprehended."

"Think you then," said Walter, " that any
others but the two men at present taken were
concerned in this dreadful deed: or do you
suppose that if they were taken into custody
they could add any links to the chain of evidence already against them?"

"Young man," returned Ela, with a bitter
smile, " you know little of our people if you
imagine that whatever their knowledge might
be, they would ever divulge it, when the lives
of their associates were placed in jeopardy. I
tell you that if they were so inclined, they
dare not do it, for they know full well that
nothing could save them from the vengeance of
some of the tribe, if they were to do so. They
are bound together by ties of which you cannot
form the slightest notion, and no danger do
they consider too great for them to hazard, if by
it they can see a chance of saving each other
from anything that may threaten. No, I do
not believe that anybody but Mark Darwin and
his two sons were concerned in the assassination
of my daughter, although old Zelta and Morna,
the former the mother of the eldest wretch, and
the latter, a fiend who is the very terror of all
the tribe, were made acquainted with it as soon
as it was committed; for Esther was too candid to conceal it, and for that reason they have
borne her far out of the way."

"The Gipsies, then, whom you mention as
having removed to some distance from Ashdown Wood, you think are not acquainted with
the atrocious crime at all?" interrogated
Walter.

"I do," answered Ela, " I indeed have my
suspicions, and besides, there is one being who
—but still I can scarcely imagine that—no
matter, she cannot live many years longer, and
then she will be called to a terrible account by
that Almighty Judge to whom all her crimes
are known. But is she not the stock from
whence came the whole detested race; and
shall she be suffered to escape?—Yes, I will
leave the old wretch to her fate, and we shall

soon see whether those who believe in her caba-listic art, will have their opinions corroborated; if she possesses the power, they attribute to her, she will assuredly save Mark and her grandsons from the fate that must otherwise be theirs. Often has she annoyed, insulted, and persecuted me; but the time is coming when she will tremble at my power, and see me exult over her misery.—Yes, yes, my triumph is at hand."

"What is the meaning of your words?" enquired Walter, whose curiosity was excited by her manner, " to whom do you allude ?"

"The old hag I have before mentioned," answered Ela, " Zelta, the mother of the elder Mark. She is nearly eighty years of age, and most of our people place implicit reliance in her boast of being able to dive into the secrets of futurity. One of her prognostications is said to allude to me, and she has predicted that I am to cause the ruin of the whole tribe, and in order to bring down upon me the hatred of the rest, she is continually seeking to make them understand that I am the person whom in her prophecy she meant.—In this she is backed and aided by old Morna, her sister, and one of my bitterest foes; but although I was subjected to constant annoyance, I always contrived to set their efforts at defiance."

"But if you really believe that this old wo-man is implicated in the murder," observed Walter, " why should you wish to see her escape the punishment which is due to her crimes ?"

"Because of her age," answered Ela, " and besides, by so doing I should exasperate all those who are now friendly disposed towards me, into my greatest enemies; and they would not rest until they had hunted me to destruction. I will leave her alone, and the torments of her own conscience will be a far greater punishment to her than death. The old wretch will weep blood when she sees the whole of her brood in the hands of the hangman."

"Then do you not think that there is a neces-sity for your removing for safety, from this place;" asked Walter, " do you not believe you need be under apprehensions of an attack from the ruffians?"

"That I cannot take upon myself to answer," replied Ela; " at any rate, it will perhaps be as well to be prepared for the worst; and there-fore I must beg of you to use such precaution as you may deem necessary. I would not for a moment, believe me, shrink from a fate which I well know, sometime or the other, is inevitable, were my task fully accomplished; but should I fall before the miscreants are brought to trial, they might escape that retribution, with which their crimes so well deserve to be visited. As I said before, my fate is certain; for there never was, and it is utterly impossible for any Gipsy to escape the vengeance of their tribe, if he has turned traitor to their cause. One of their

most solemn oaths relates to this, and they are sure to fulfil it, even though many years may elapse before they may meet with an opportunity to accomplish it. But I do not think we have much cause to apprehend their appearing just yet, for they will soon be far enough off, when they learn that Mark and his son are in custody; and before they will venture again in this neighbourhood, they will be pretty well assured that they can do so with safety."

"Forgive," said Walter, wildly—"forgive me if I am becoming tedious and tiresome by the number of my interrogatories; but you will perceive that my principal wish, in so doing, is to ascertain the best means of protecting you from any danger that may threaten. And have you any idea where the other son, who you suspect was connected in the murder with his brother and father, Rupert I mean—I say, have you any idea where he can be found?"

" That suggestion is a good one," eagerly uttered Ela—"that had escaped my thoughts : he certainly may be dreaded, and with good reason. I have not the slightest knowledge of what has become of him. 'Tis true, I did imagine at first that he was one of those who had concealed Esther; but this morning I over-heard his father make use of some observations that satisfied me he was not even aware of the place of his son's retreat; but then he said he had acted as a cowardly churl, not to remain with them in completing the awful task they had allotted to themselves. But still," she continued, as a look of scorn passed over her pale features, " what have I to apprehend from him? He dare not try to harm Ela alone, for well does he know her power, which he has felt long since. And then, what if he should ? Have I not these, wherewith to pro-tect myself?"

As Ela uttered these words, she pointed to the brace of loaded pistols which she had lent to Walter when he took the two ruffians into custody, and which he had brought back with him on leaving the Hall.

" These, certainly, may afford some protec-tion to you," observed Walter, " and if you do not know how to use them with advantage to yourself, the report of them will instantly bring those whom I shall keep on the alert to your assistance."

" Right," returned Ela, " these pistols be-longed to Mark, and when his back was turned this morning, I robbed him of them, having designed to have had the villain's life, and after-wards to have terminated my own wretched existence, rather than die an ignominious death upon the scaffold; for I felt certain that I should be deemed and sentenced as a murderess, although it was only an act of justice to destroy the life of a fiend who had robbed me of my child."

"Heaven be praised that saved you from the

perpetration of such a dreadful deed !'' ejaculated Walter sincerely.

"I should have exulted in it at the time," said Ela, "and thought not that I had committed any crime. But I am not sorry now that I did not do it; no, for my eyes will behold my poor girl's cold remains receive the rites of burial, my tears will moisten the clay which covers them, and—Young man, I have another request to make; promise me that you will perform what I ask of you, and Ela, the Outcast Ela, will then be prepared to meet her fate, let it come whenever it may."

"What is it you would ask of me ?" demanded Walter, moved by her manner, "if it is in my power, or consistent with propriety, I am indeed, not only ready to promise, but to swear to fulfil any request you may have to make."

Ela attempted to reply to this, but her feelings apparently choked her utterance, and Walter beheld her for the first time weep; while her brilliant eyes were fixed upon him with an appearance of kindness, that rendered her still handsome features remarkably interesting. Walter was deeply affected, and did not venture to interrupt her. At length, however, she seemed gradually to recover somewhat of her usual firmness and self-possession, and wiping away the tears which had flowed down her cheeks in abundance, she said, in a voice whose tones were so totally different to what they generally were, that Walter could not help listening to her with the deepest interest, which was increased by the subject she alluded to—

"Heaven be thanked that you are not like your father !—No, I see you have your mother's gentle disposition ; there is the same kind demeanour, the same placid features—I therefore will trust you, though, if you were like her—But," she suddenly remarked, as she beheld the expression of emotion which Walter betrayed at the words she had uttered, "this is not right of me to say anything that may hurt your feelings. It is ungrateful of me."

"I wait to hear what it is you request me to do," said Walter, conquering his feelings, and speaking to her in a tone of kindness.

"True," answered Ela, "this then it simply is;—that you will see my cold remains, when I am dead, placed in the same grave as those of my Fanny."

"Indeed I will," said Walter, much affected; "but do not give way to those thoughts, —indeed I hope that it will be long ere that event may overtake you."

"Young man, you know not what you say," returned Ela; "if you are that tender-hearted youth I believe you to be, you will rather pray to heaven that the time may be near which shall release me from my misery! Oh, for many, many years have I been doomed to groan beneath the almost insupportable burthen, and which must speedily have borne me down but for one hope, centered in the angelic being they have bereaved me of. Had you but been acquainte with the disposition of my unfortunate Fanny she could not have failed to have won your warmest regard. She was my saviour from many wicked crimes, to which the ungovernable strength of my vengeance would have led me—but I cannot dwell upon those things now ! The time may not be far distant when Ela will open her heart to you, and then, much as has been said to her prejudice, and wretch, and wandering friendless outcast, as she is, you will learn that she has once been worthy of your esteem, and that—"

The unhappy woman could not proceed any further—the violence of her anguish overpowered her, and choked her words; and Walter, after gazing at her for a few moments with the greatest sympathy, told her he would see her again shortly, and in the meantime that he would take every means to secure her from danger or interruption, he left the place.

<hr>

CHAPTER XXXI.

"Oh ! could not her innocence withhold
The murderer's cruel blade ?"

WHEN Walter returned to the Hall, he sought out James, the groom, and inquired of him whether Mr. Wallingford had sent off the two prisoners for examination and committal, to Squire Dorrington's' James seemed to be vexed and confused, and he slowly replied—

"Why to be sure, sir, master did send 'em to the squire's, but——"

"But what ?" demanded Walter, when he perceived the perplexity of James; "why do you hesitate ? Did you go with them ?"

"No, sir," answered James, "that's where it is ; if I had gone with them, it would have been right enough, I'll be bound, and what has taken place, I'm certain would never have happened."

"Well, what has happened, do you think ?" inquired Walter, impatiently. "You don't suppose that the fellows have escaped ?"

"That's the very thing I do suspect, sir," returned James—"it's my belief, the wretches have got away sure enough."

"Is it possible ?" exclaimed Walter, with evident vexation; "why do you think so, James ?"

"Why, I'll tell you, sir," answered James; "you see, master did not think there was any necessity for me to go up before the squire to give evidence, because he thought that the gardeners would be quite sufficient, and therefore, as he wanted me for something at home, he only sent Robert, the gardener, with them, and that old fool, and busy, intermeddling Jackanapes, Knobbs. the constable, who never undertakes anything but he is sure to make a mess of it. I am surprised that master, (begging your pardon, sir, for my boldness,) should have thought him fit to be employed in any such business, for he is as great a cur as ever stepped in two shoes, and no more fit for such a job than a child."

"Well, and so, between them, they have let the prisoners escape?"

"Why that's the plain truth of the matter, sir," answered James, "at least so I think, for it's a chance if the villains will be taken again in a hurry, for they are here and there, and everywhere, in no time at all. I did think I should have had the pleasure of seeing their necks stretched."

Walter made no answer to this, but, exceedingly vexed at the probability of the thought, and blaming the imprudence of his father—first, for sending the men to the squire's at all, when he could have examined and committed them himself; secondly, for not sending more efficient persons with them; and, thirdly, for keeping so material a witness of the villains' guilt, as James, away. He was about to seek his father, when a thought struck him, and turning to the groom he said—

"Saddle Rocket directly, I will myself go to Squire Dorrington's, and see what is to be done, and know whether your suspicions are confirmed."

"And may I be permitted to accompany you, sir?" asked James, who seemed to be very anxious for his request to be complied with.

Walter would willingly have had him with him, but recollecting what his father had said, he reminded James that his master had told him he could not be spared, and that, therefore, he should be compelled to ride over to the squire's by himself.

James was evidently vexed and disappointed at this, as his looks sufficiently testified; but, nevertheless, he set about obeying the order that had been given him with the utmost alacrity, and soon brought Rocket round to the hall-door in readiness for him. Walter only waited to give some necessary orders, as regarded Ela, visited the chamber of the invalid, and uttered a few sentences of kindness to Maria, and then he hastened down stairs, and prepared to mount his horse.

"I beg your pardon, sir," said the groom, "but don't you think you had better take Carlo with you?—It's not very safe for a person to go about now, when who can tell whether or not some of these rascally Gipsies are lurking in the bushes. I am sorry that I cannot be with you; however, I would not go without the dog, for he is a faithful creature, and he has such an antipathy to the gang, or any set of rogues, that

they are sure to feel the sharpness of his teeth if ever they cross his path."

Walter could not but approve of the suggestion of his faithful servant, and therefore Carlo accompanied him.

The road he had to travel was a gloomy one, and was well adapted for any dark purpose—the branches of the trees formed a complete canopy over Walter's head, and almost totally excluded the light of day; but any apprehension of danger never once entered his mind; and indeed his thoughts were fully occupied with the occurrences of the morning, and would not give way to anything else. Suddenly, however, he aroused himself from his lethargy, and looking round, was surprised to find that the dog had left him.

Walter paused, and reflected. Surely Carlo, who was so attached to him, could never have returned home again? Oh, no, he could not believe that he would so readily have forgotten his duty.

"This is very singular," said Walter, "and I cannot make it out. Carlo! Carlo!"

Quick at the sound of his voice, the dog forced his way through the neighbouring hedge, in which was a large gap, but he did not come to his master, but looked up in his face with an imploring expression, remained upon the spot, and whined piteously two or three times.

Walter again called the dog, but all to no purpose; and after having repeated the whining noise, he ran back to the same place from which he had emerged.

"For the life of me, I cannot understand this," said Walter. "Carlo! Carlo! come here, sir, I say!"

The dog did present himself in the same place, and made use of the same demonstrations he had done before, running back after a moment, as though he was inviting his master to follow him.

Walter being now confident that all was not right, or the faithful animal would not behave in such a singular manner, dismounted from his horse, fastened it to a tree, and grasping a pistol he had taken the precaution to bring with him in case of danger, he sprang up the hedge, and thrust his body through the gap before mentioned, into the field, the dog waiting for him below, and wagging his tail as if in approbation. He looked around him, and soon discovered the occasion of Carlo's strange behaviour, for the first object his eyes encountered was the prostrate body of Robert, securely bound, and gagged so as to prevent him from raising any cry for aid in his awkward dilemma.

Of course Walter had no occasion to inquire the cause of his finding him in that situation; it was clear enough that the surmises of James were verified, and the Gipsy, Mark, and his son had effected their escape. Walter immediately released the man, and having allowed him sufficient time to recover himself, he inquired of him where his companion, Knobbs, the valiant constable was, who in all probability had been served in the same manner as Robert, to prevent him from creating any alarm, until they had made good their retreat. Robert was, however, so much alarmed, that it was no very easy task to elicit anything like a distinct explanation from him. The gardener was never very courageous, neither could he boast of much sense, but what little he really had, had now completely vanished, and all that Walter could get from him was, innumerable solicitation for him to get away from the spot as expeditiously as he could, for the rascally Gipsies were coming back to take his life; they had told him they would do so.

" For goodness sake do not delay, sir," said the poor frightened fellow, " for depend upon it they will keep their word, they always do. They threatened me that if I did make the slightest attempt to escape, or make a noise, they would be on the watch, and cut my throat immediately. Oh dear, oh dear, do not stay a minute, sir. Lord bless me! what's that? Oh, it is them."

The cause of Robert's alarm was a noise in the hedges which seemed to proceed from the immediate proximity of the spot they were then standing upon; and his face became ghastly pale, his knees knocked together, and his teeth rattled like a pair of castanets. Walter endeavoured to quiet his fears, but that was no easy task, until he had discovered that the noise only proceeded from his horse; then his alarm was a little pacified, and he could not but admit the reason of Walter's observations, namely, that it was quite improbable that the Gipsies would venture to return to the spot, and thus run the risk of being retaken. He therefore regained sufficient firmness to make him acquainted with what had happened.

He informed Walter that Knobbs had consigned the eldest of the prisoners to his custody, and previously the most special care was taken that he should be securely handcuffed, so that resistance would be impossible; moreover, for farther protection, the gardener had taken with him a loaded pistol, and the constable, who had also taken the like precaution, took charge of Mark's son.

"Well," continued the gardener, after he and Walter had got into the high road, and the former could imagine himself in safety, "away we went with 'em, and quiet and sullen enough they wur, for some distance; and not a word could Master Knobbs get out on 'em, although he tried hard enough. So I thought it would be all right, and that we should get 'em to th' squire's wi'out much trouble. Hows'ever, I soon found out my mistake, for although we went on remarkably comfortable for more nor a mile, when we got to th' hill, I found that Knobbs and his prisoner wur a great way in advance of me and my fellow. So in course I did not feel altogether satisfied, for, to tell the truth, I have a mortal hatred and dread of the Gipsies, although no one is more courageous than I am, upon anything else, which I dare say you know very well, sir. So I was about to call out to Knobbs, and tell him to slacken his pace, for the old man was puffing and blowing like a broken winded horse, and I thought he was so bad that I should never be able to get him along, much more to ascend the hill, when at the very moment I looks behind me, and I sees a man dressed in a long smock frock, who looked like Farmer Fallowfield's carter, long Robin as they calls him; so I thought it was all right, and that he had come in very good time, if my customer should take it in his head to ride obstropolous, for two to one must succeed all the world over; therefore I did not care a straw then, how quick Knobbs went on with his prisoner, and as I did not call to him, away he went, and was soon out of sight; he took that part of the road yonder. I have no doubt my prisoner knew very well that the customer I have mentioned was close at our heels, for he kept turning and twisting, and seemed to be so fidgetty like, which rather excited my wonder at the time; but then I thought what fear could there be, when he was so well secured, and the man was a friend of mine; however, he soon undeceived me, for no sooner had we reached this place, than down falls the old Gipsy, accidentally as he pretended.

" There, up wi' you again," said I, " and come along, you haven't hurt yourself, so there's no harm done."

" You are very feeling, ain't you?" replied the fellow, looking at me as if he could swallow me at a mouthful; " if I had broke my neck you wouldn't have cared."

" Oh, yes, I should," answered I, " because that would have been depriving the hangman of a job. But get up."

" Then why the devil don't you lend me a hand?—How am I to get up by myself, secured as I am?"

In the meantime, while we were thus talking, up comes Long Robin, as I took the man in the smock frock to be, so thinking myself all safe, I stoops down to comply with the Gipsy fellow's request, but Heaven save me! I had no sooner done so, than the man in the smock frock gives me a blow at the back of my head with his fist, which was almost as big as a sledge hammer, and he floored me like as if I had been a bullock, and then put his knee upon my chest, and twisted his hand in my neckerchief in such a way that I thought to be sure must have choked me. I then stared stedfastly into his villanous face, and knew him in a moment to be one of the rascally Gipsy gang. He was not long in getting the pistol out of my hand, for what power had I to resist, pinned in as I was? And clapping the muzzle of it to my head, he said: "If you only utter a sound, I'll blow your brains out!" Lor' bless you, sir, I couldn't have spoken if I had had a *fortin* depending on it; I never was in such a flusteration before in all my born days, and that's the whole truth of the matter, for you see, sir, I was entirely in his power," and, in this gloomy place, what chance was there of anybody coming

ELA'S HORRID OATH ON HEARING OF THE ESCAPE OF OLD DARWIN.

to my assistance? So I made signs to him that I would do as he requested, and glad enough I confess I was, to accept of the terms he offered; and I scrambled up, and as he ordered me, I made my way through the gap into the field in which you found me, and I thought they had made up their minds to murder me, to prevent all further trouble. I should certainly have gone down upon my knees, and begged of them not to take my life, for how is a poor wretch like me prepared to die just yet? But Mark and him having exchanged a few words in a language I know nothing whatever about, the fellow in the smock frock, who I imagined—"

"Keep your imaginations to yourself," interrupted Walter, impatiently, "to sum it all up in a few words, you let your prisoner slip through your fingers."

"Why, sir, how could I help myself?" said Robert; "you see they had got me as snug as a bug in a rug, and if I attempted to ride any way restive, they would certainly have murdered me there and then. So the chap in the smock frock bound and gagged me, as you found me, and then he had the handcuffs off the other in no time, and away they both scampered, but I can't say whether or not they went after Knobbs and his prisoner, though I think it is most likely that they did; for in course the old man would not let his son be taken if he could help it, and two such fellows as him and the smock frock gentleman were enough to conquer half a dozen such men as Knobbs. "But pray, Mr. Walter, do not leave me here alone," implored the timid fellow, when he saw the young man making preparations to remount, and to pursue the road which the constable had taken. Walter, however, informed him that he certainly was, and reproved him for his cowardice, so that he was at last shamed into returning to Wallingford Hall by himself, more especially as he had no other alternative than either to do that, or to remain where he was until his young master's return, or to attend him in pursuing the prisoners, which latter presented the most awful terrors to his imagination. No sooner was he convinced that he must do one or the other, than he put himself into a running condition, and perhaps never performed a feat of the kind with so much agility before, for he was in an almost inconceivable short space of time out of sight; and Walter made the best of his way to the house of Squire Dorrington.

Walter was, however, gratified to find, on his arrival at the house of the magistrate, that Knobbs and his prisoner were there. Knobbs, for once, had acted with unusual sagacity, and when he found that the gardener was lingering behind, his suspicion was excited that all was not right; so, not choosing to wait to see whether his surmises would be realised, and thinking it best to make certain of the customer he had in his custody, he drove him on at a quick pace, holding the pistol very close to his head, and being prepared to act in a moment on the defensive. Knobbs had never been known to display such remarkable courage and presence of mind before, but it must be admitted that he did not forget to take an ample share of credit for the same. When he had got a certain distance with his charge, he met with a waggoner whom he knew, and who required very little persuasion to assist him. Into the waggon, therefore, the prisoner was hoisted, and in that manner the journey to Squire Dorrington's was completed.

Knobbs having enlisted a number of men into his service, just as Walter arrived at the magistrate's house, was preparing to make his departure with a desperate determination to rescue Robert the gardener, and secure the other Gipsy, but as Walter informed him of what had happened, and that the gardener had returned to the Hall, of course he was stopped in the achievement of such a hazardous and valorous exploit.

Mr. Dorrington, knowing the state of Mrs. Wallingford's health, and consequently how anxious Walter must feel to have the business despatched, did not delay a moment longer than was possible, and the culprit was accordingly brought into his presence.

The Gipsy, although stern and sullen, was yet, it might easily be perceived, very much agitated. When he was placed before Mr. Dorrington, he looked eagerly round the room, and took in the persons of every one present at a glance; but when he perceived that his father was not present, a grim smile of satisfaction passed over his swarthy countenance, and he stood firm, and apparently fully prepared for the worst. Satisfied that his father had effected his escape, he was quite indifferent to his own situation, and looked round as carelessly as if there was nothing at all the matter. In spite of the dreadful crime of which Walter could not help believing him guilty, he could not help feeling the deepest interest in his fate. There was something, too, so peculiar in the features of the man, which, once beheld, left an indelible impression on the mind ever afterwards.

The task which Walter was called upon to perform was a most revolting one, but he shrunk not from it, anxious as he was to bring the perpetrators of the horrible crime to justice. He was the principal witness against the Gipsy, and he proceeded to a minute detail of all he knew of the shocking catastrophe. How his heart shuddered, when in the course of this statement various ideas connected with the hellish deed rose upon his memory; how cool and deliberately must the abominable wretches have committed it. He could not but reflect, with the most intense anguish upon the untimely fate of that poor girl, who but a few days before he had seen in all the rosy freshness of youthful health, and over whose mangled remains, the wretched, the bereaved mother now wept, and his feelings were harrowed up to the utmost state of detestation against the villain, who stood, unmoved, awaiting the decision of the magistrate, and seemingly quite callous as to the result.

The Gipsy replied to these questions that were put to him with the utmost coolness and indifference, and evinced a shrewdness and sagacity which threatened to baffle the magistrate and the witnesses very severely. He protested his ignorance of the manner in which the body he had aided in rescuing from the water, had got in there; and that he knew not whether she had been murdered or had destroyed herself. He had, he said, merely gone with another man to fish in the lake, when they perceived the body in the water. Common humanity, he said, of course prompted them not to let it remain where it was, and accordingly they dragged it to the bank, and while they were performing what they considered a meritorious action, they were pounced upon by the young squire and his servants.

"Was not the man who accompanied you your father?" asked Walter.

"I decline answering that question," returned the Gipsy.

"You say that humanity prompted you to take the body out of the lake," observed Walter, "but can you call fastening a stone to——"

"Ah!" interrupted the Gipsy, and his eyes glared upon Walter as if they would penetrate to his very soul; "but how can you prove that I did so? I defy you to swear it was me. Did you not, when you left the spot, suffer a woman to remain with the corpse—a woman whose violence of disposition, and whose hatred to me and mine, is well known? Deny this if you can—but no, you cannot; and how then can you swear that she was not the person that attached the stone, prompted by feelings of hatred and revenge, to bring me into this dilemma? Walter Wallingford, that is your name I believe, I would warn you to be cautious what you say or do; you are endeavouring to screen and protect a fiend in female form; a monster, who would not shrink from any crime, however revolting, for the purpose of gratifying her demoniacal vengeance; nay, I defy you to disprove my words; but what is the use of my troubling myself to assert my innocence? Will my word, that is of a poor man, be taken in preference to that of a gentleman's! I care little what you do to me, I am not the only innocent man who has been accused wrongfully, and if I am hung, I doubt much whether upon your death-bed you will have a very clear conscience, when you reflect that you were the cause of bringing a poor fellow to an ignominious death, merely to screen from justice a guilty, an infamous woman."

Notwithstanding the strong proofs there appeared to be of the Gipsy's guilt, the firmness with which he had uttered these words, for a moment or two raised a doubt in Walter's mind. He looked earnestly at the man, and the perfect calmness with which he returned his glance, bewildered and confused him.

"Heaven forbid that I should wilfully wrong you!" exclaimed Walter, energetically, "but

I have only to speak to the facts that have come under my own observations, those facts I have declared, conscientiously, impartially declared, and I now leave the charge in thy hands of the magistrate, without making any remark of my own, that might in any wae prejudice the case. Mr. Dorrington will, I am convinced, act as justice and truth only prompt him."

"I have heard quite sufficient," said that gentleman, "to induce me to commit him for trial."

The magistrate then gave the necessary instructions to his clerk to make out the committal of the Gipsy for trial at the next assizes, which the man heard with the utmost composure and firmness, and stood with a bold mien, gazing sternly, alternately, upon Mr. Dorrington and Walter.

While the clerk was making the necessary preparations to write out the committal, a profound silence pervaded the room, and the Gipsy never altered his position in the least.

"Who does the prisoner stand charged with the murder of?" demanded the clerk, suddenly breaking the silence, and looking up at the magistrate.

"Charged with the murder of a person unknown," returned Mr. Dorrington.

"It is not so," ejaculated the Gipsy, smiling exultingly and maliciously upon Walter, "Mr. Wallingford can, if he likes, bear me out in what I say; he has a perfect knowledge of who the deceased is."

It would be impossible to do adequate justice to the emotion which Walter betrayed upon this; a cold tremour ran through all his veins, and he would have given the world to have been at that moment away. Mr. Dorrington expressed the most unfeigned astonishment.

"What does the man mean?" he observed, "Mr. Wallingford, can you explain this? We must be particular in these matters. Did you know the unfortunate deceased?"

"Know her, sir," exclaimed Walter, in a confused tone, for the manner in which the magistrate had spoken seemed to convey an insinuation that aroused his indignation; "I cannot be positive that I have ever seen her before, unless it is the same young Gipsy girl whom I saw a few days since, when me and my cousin, Miss Herbert, were together. Indeed I am inclined to think that she was the same individual."

"And where did you then behold the female you mention?" inquired the magistrate.

"In my father's grounds," answered Walter; and he then gave a particular account of the manner in which himself and his cousin had encountered the girl, and the mysterious and hasty manner in which she had taken her departure, without so much as asking for any emuneration for the prognostications which she had uttered: and he concluded by observing that he was strongly of opinion that the girl he had seen, and the murdered person was one and the same.

"And what meant you, man, by stating that Mr. Walter Wallingford knew the unfortunate girl?" inquired Mr. Dorrington, looking at the Gipsy.

"I spoke nothing but the truth," returned the man; "I say again, that he was well acquainted with her, although he tries to evade any explanation by equivocation. It is not my business to inquire what is his reason for not wishing it to be known that Fanny Beranzio was the daughter of his father; were he inclined to be a little more communicative, he might probably inform your honour by what means she came into the grounds of Wallingford Hall, and why she was prevented from claiming her parent. Oh, it would have been a sad disgrace to have acknowledged the Gipsy girl to be the offspring of the proud master of Wallingford; but he need not fear now, although those that removed the obstacle are not yet detected. But murder will out, and the real assassins meet with their just reward. Instead of harming the girl, I would have laid down my life for her; no one could feel for mortal a more powerful regard.

How shall we describe the agony of Walter while the Gipsy was giving utterance to this explanation?—Mingled emotions of shame, rage, and horror at the meaning it seemed meant to convey to the prejudice of Mr. Wallingford, struggled in his bosom, and crimsoned his cheeks; his indignation was about to find vent in reproaches against the prisoner, for thus basely endeavouring to inculpate an innocent person, when Mr. Dorrington interrupted him—

"In private, sir, I must request that you will talk further to me upon this subject; but the respect I entertain for your father and——"

"Nay, sir," exclaimed Walter, proudly, "I shun not an open explanation. I am inclined to believe that the girl of whom the prisoner has spoken, *was* the daughter of my father; but I do not see that what he states is at all relevant to the charges which I have brought against him. I charge him with being accessory to the murder of the deceased; but if the evidence adduced is not sufficiently satisfactory, sir, I can bring forward still stronger. Miss Herbert, my cousin, was in the shrubbery on the evening when the dreadful crime is supposed to have been committed, and she there beheld the ill-fated girl, attended by one——"

Walter's emotion overcame him, and he could not proceed for a moment or two; but he then, in broken accents, informed Mr. Dorrington what Maria told him.

"I must have an interview with Miss Her-

bert, sir," said Mr. Dorrington, formally; "such affairs as these require to be treated with the greatest caution."

This vexed and annoyed Walter more than all, for what would be the pain which Maria would feel, he thought, when subjected to such an investigation; and besides, her anxiety would, he was certain, be almost intolerable to be thus taken from the chamber of his mother, who so much needed every moment of her attendance! He felt it most keenly, likewise the exposure of his father's frailties, which such an examination was sure to make public. However, he could not raise any objection to anything that Mr. Dorrington required in the execution of his judicial duty, and the prisoner being safely secured, Walter re-mounted his horse, and hastened on his way to comply with the request of the magistrate.

CHAPTER XXXII.

"Come, fell revenge!
    How dear art thou to one who thirsts
    To make the author of his misery
    Taste of the poisoned chalice he
    Has often placed to other lips."
                            THE HOMICIDE.

WHAT had taken place before the magistrate occupied the mind of Walter all the way, as he rode on to Wallingford Hall, and he was racked with feelings of anguish, horror, and indignation. The conduct of Mr. Dorrington was far from satisfactory to him; he thought he had seemed to show an undue leniency towards the prisoner, and to receive his evidence with too cold a cautiousness. At this he was the more astonished, for Mr. Dorrington had gained an unenviable notoriety for the harshness with which he had ever treated any poor offender that might happen to be brought before him, and his name had become proverbial among the lower orders as a heartless tyrant, who exercised the power entrusted to him with unjust severity; but here he acted in decidedly a contrary manner, and that Walter conceived most inexplicable, inasmuch as the evidence against the Gipsy was undoubtedly sufficiently strong to show that he was either the murderer or an accomplice, and yet he hesitated to commit him, and seemed resolved to tamper with the charge, by making enquiries into subjects that were totally irrelevant to it. "Surely, too," thought Walter, "there cannot be any necessity for so much precaution, when, if he were proved to be innocent, he would only have been subjected to a few weeks' imprisonment, and, had the man been brought before him as a vagrant only, the magistrate would, without any hesitation, have inflicted a severer punishment."

But Walter was not acquainted with the

actual object which the magistrate had in view. Mr. Dorrington was related to the Earl of Harlington, and his lordship and him entertained an uncommon friendship for each other. The occurrence at Wallingford Hall had been the cause of much excitement in the vicinity, and various were the rumours that were circulated, all of which, however, being to the prejudice of Mr. Wallingford. Of course, the family of the Harlingtons felt a more than common interest in the matter, but, in spite of their most strenuous exertions, they had hitherto failed in eliciting the truth of the matter. Mr. Dorrington was aware of the anxiety his relatives felt upon the subject, and accordingly was highly pleased with the opportunity which now presented itself of gratifying their curiosity. Accordingly, no sooner had Walter left his house, than he despatched a messenger to the earl with a note, requesting him to attend him immediately, having planned that he should be present during the second investigation, and the examination of Miss Herbert.

Among other ridiculous stories circulated by the busy and the loquacious, and the one which reached the ears of Mr. Barnell, of Woodbine House, was the following, namely :—that a discovery had been made through the means of one of the Gipsy tribe, that Miss Herbert, who had so long been known only as the niece of Mr. Wallingford, was in reality his own daughter, by the Gipsy aforesaid. Moreover, the report went on to state that Mr. Wallingford, to prevent the truth being known, had managed to get the mother of the girl out of the country, but, that having now returned, she demanded the restoration of her daughter, and being refused, she had made an attempt to assassinate Mr. Wallingford, in his own house, and while his wife was present, which had the effect, aided by the discovery of the passion of Walter Wallingford for Maria, who, of course, had been in ignorance of their close consanguinity, had taken such an effect upon the unhappy Mrs. Wallingford, that she had become completely deranged.

Mr. Barnell heard this tale with all the credulity that might have been expected, and he was in a complete hurricane of wrath and insulted dignity, to think that Mr. Wallingford should try to induce him to marry his illegitimate daughter. It was really horrible to think upon such a thing ; that he—a gentleman with an income of fifteen thousand a year, the master of Woodbine House, and with every prospect of a title, to be thus attempted to be trepanned ; he never felt so indignant before in his life, and, in the heat of it he despatched a letter to Mr. Wallingford, in which, after upbraiding him in no very choice words for the trick he had endeavoured to play him, he stated his determination to hold no future correspondence with him or any of his family. As his

Mercury was leaving the house, however, a thought struck him that he would first pay a visit to Lord Harlington, and hear his opinion upon the subject. He therefore did not send off the letter at present.

Mr. Barnell had, prior to this, very seldom visited Harlington Castle, for what reason the reader may probably guess ; therefore, although they received him with the utmost politeness, there was not that warmth in the greeting which bespeaks friendship. The early part of the interview was passed away by Lady Harlington making to their visitors an ostentatious display of the improvements which owed their origin to her ingenious taste, and which so easily convinced Mr. Barnell how admirably calculated she was to form the mind of her daughter in the proper way, and more than ever raised her in his good opinion ; as for Euphemia, she was dressed plain and simple, and was occupied in revising the housekeeper's bill, thus showing, beyond a doubt, how well she had profited by the example of domestic economy and management which her mother had set her.

The Harlingtons, of course, did not believe the absurd tale thus circulated, neither did they attempt to make Mr. Barnell believe it, although they did not seek, on the other hand, to do away with the impression, and so artfully did they manage the business, throwing out, in many insinuations and hints, that they convinced Mr. Barnell before he departed from the castle, that he had been a most fortunate gentleman to have escaped the plans which had been laid down to entrap him into a marriage with Maria.

But, in spite of this conviction, it was no easy task for Mr. Barnell to erase from his mind the lovely image of Miss Herbert—Euphemia certainly had many charms, but what were they when compared with those of Maria ? And was she not the daughter of a peer, and only to think of the honour to become the son-in-law of a lord !

Mr. Barnell had a strong contest with his feelings for the whole of one night, but by the morning he had so far succeeded as to form a determination to renounce Miss Herbert, and to make immediate propositions for Miss Bamford. He had heard so many additional particulars of the transactions at Wallingford Hall, that he shuddered completely at the idea of entering such a family ; so he *did* send off the letter he had written to Mr. Wallingford, and then hastened back to Harlington Castle, where he made a formal declaration of his love to Euphemia ; and her parents, although they did not give him a positive answer, but referred him to Euphemia, left him no room to think that they would scruple to break the promise already made to Mr. Wallingford, or to say sufficient to convince him (Mr. Barnell) that they would not ultimately accept him as a suitor to their daughter.

Lord Harlington only wanted a reasonable excuse for breaking off his negociation with Mr. Wallingford, and that opportunity was soon afforded him. He lost no time in attending to the note which Mr. Dorrington had sent him, and upon his arrival at that gentleman's house, he was not a little gratified to hear from him the particulars of what had taken place at the examination of Mark Darwin the younger, and what had been his motive for sending for him.

Walter's astonishment and mortification may be easily imagined, when on his return to the magistrate's house with Maria, he found Lord Harlington seated by his side. He saluted the young man with haughty politeness, which the other returned with equally cold formality, and Mr. Dorrington then commenced a strict examination of Maria, in which he was assisted by Lord Harlington. Walter's blood boiled with indignation, and he could with difficulty restrain the expression of his feelings, when he listened to the questions put by them both, and the comments which they made upon the poor girl's evidence, which was delivered in a clear and distinct manner, and without anything that could in the remotest degree be construed into prevarication.

"You say that the men of whom the two females spoke, and expressed such fear, you did not see ?" said his lordship.

"I did not," answered Maria.

"And did you not hear them mention any names ?"

Maria replied in the negative.

Lord Harlington did not speak aloud again for a few moments, but turning to Mr. Dorrington, they consulted together; after which the latter gentleman said—

"Had you, prior to this, seen any person in the shrubbery ? I would impress upon your mind, miss, the necessity of being cautious in answering this question, as it is one of the greatest importance. Take time to collect your thoughts. Are you confident that you did not, previous to the time you have mentioned, see any person in the shrubbery—no one of the establishment?"

"Certainly not," replied the astonished Maria, "my cousin was the only person I saw near the shrubbery, and him I met just at the entrance, and returned with him into the road."

"Then you do not think it likely," said the magistrate, "that it was your cousin, Mr. Walter Wallingford, of whom the two girls expressed so much apprehension ?"

"Walter ?" repeated Maria, with much surprise. "Oh, impossible ! The girls mentioned two men, and spoke of one as being younger than the other."

"I recollect you said so," said Mr. Dorrington, emphatically.

"The one who was called Fanny," continue Maria, "uttered her fears that they should b surprised by the whole tribe, and probabl murdered, for that they would think they ha come there for the purpose of revealing thei designs."

"Why, how is this, Miss Herbert ?" interro gated his lordship hastily, and fixing upon he a piercing look. "This is the first we hav heard about the tribe; why did you not men tion it before ?"

Maria could not reply directly, for the look of, and the manner in which Lord Harlingto put this question confused and bewildered her As for Walter, his heart swelled with rage and he fixed a glance upon his lordship whic that nobleman could be at no loss to understand

"Let us be certain that the word tribe wa not mentioned before," said Mr. Dorrington addressing himself to his clerk, "refer to th notes of the proceedings."

The clerk scanned over the papers befor him, and then replied that he found no mention of such a word.

"Ah! I thought you would not," said Lord Harlington, with an air of triumph, which the more exasperated Walter. He looked to Maria, and found by the expression of her countenance what was passing in her mind. Having, however, regained her composure, she turned to Lord Harlington, and said—

"Had I been permitted, my lord, to have proceeded with my detail, and not have been interrupted by, I must say, I think unnecessary questions, I should undoubtedly have stated that——"

"Oh, very well, Miss Herbert," interrupted his lordship, evidently chagrined, "proceed, pray, with your statement, then, in your own *peculiar* way."

"I believe that I have stated nearly all that I know," replied Maria. "When I heard the screams which I have before mentioned, my terror overcame me, and I fainted, and was insensible to everything that afterwards took place."

"Very well, then," said Mr. Dorrington, "then we have no more questions to put to you, Miss Herbert, I believe."

Walter, upon hearing this, bowed haughtily to Lord Harlington, and knowing the state of Maria's mind, he did not wait to hear whether the man was committed, but conducting her to the carriage, they were driven away to the Hall.

As they returned home, Maria could not help expressing her astonishment to Walter at the strange observations that had been made, both by Lord Harlington and Mr. Dorrington, and the singular formality, almost approaching to insult, with which they had behaved to them. Lord Harlington, in particular, was cold and distant, not even so much as making any inquiries as to the family, and confining himself entirely to the business of the examination.

"And then," continued Maria, "do you not recollect the strange question they put to me about you, Walter? What could be his motive for that, and so earnestly as Mr. Dorrington seemed to put it; and the emphatic manner with which his lordship followed it up by other questions of an equally remarkable description?"

"Do not think of it, dear Maria, it is unworthy of attention," ejaculated Walter, whose anguish of mind was almost insupportable, when he reflected upon the insinuations that both Lord Harlington and Mr. Dorrington had thrown out, by which he could plainly perceive that they were inclined to suspect that it was his father that had been seen by the ill-fated Fanny, and thus give an aspect of probability to the villanous hints of the wretch Mark, that Wallingford was the assassin of his daughter.

Maria, who saw his emotion, though she knew not the exact cause, did not question him farther, and regretted having unconsciously given him occasion for a moment's pain. They did not hold any further converse until they arrived at the Hall, when Maria broke the silence, by observing that her uncle was anxiously watching for their return from the parlour window; and at the same time, she expressed her pleasure at observing him there, as she was convinced by that that Mrs. Wallingford was no worse.

"Dear Maria," exclaimed Walter, "surely you will hasten to my mother's chamber immediately?"

"Undoubtedly, Walter," answered she, with some surprise at the question.

"Then before you do so, my dearest girl," added her cousin, taking her hand, and looking earnestly in her face, "before you do so, let me beg of you, not upon any account to mention to any one, not excepting my father even, the strange conduct and observations of Lord Harlington and Mr. Dorrington. Oh, Maria, had not your innocence prevented you from so doing, you would have perceived the dreadful insinuation these observations conveyed; and if they were again to be mentioned——"

"They never shall, dear Walter, by me!" cried Maria, hastily and fervently, for she now at once saw the truth. "Nay, I am willing to swear that never shall a sentence escape my lips! Good God! how base must be the mind that could look upon my uncle's care-worn face and encourage such a suspicion!"

At this moment Mr. Wallingford came from the house to meet them, and Maria fixed upon him an inquiring look, which he understood and immediately replied—

"My good girl, all is as well as can be expected. Your unfortunate aunt is no worse,

and she has been totally unconscious that you have been away from her bedside. Well, Walter, I have been impatiently waiting your return. The examination has been a lengthy one. How has it terminated; by the committal of the man charged with the horrid crime?"

"Why, sir," returned his son, "I do not see how it could possibly be otherwise."

"It is rather a matter of astonishment to me that Mr. Dorrington should think it at all necessary to have the evidence of your cousin," continued Mr. Wallingford, as they walked into the house. "Were there any more magistrates than Mr. Dorrington present?"

"Yes, sir," answered Walter, "Lord Harlington was present, and took part in the proceedings."

"Lord Harlington!" repeated Wallingford, colouring; "and how did he seem to—did he make any inquiries after me or your——"

"He did not, sir," interrupted Walter, "he made no inquiries but such as were connected with the investigation."

"Can it be possible? And did he not mention the ladies?" exclaimed Mr. Wallingford.

"He did not, sir," answered his son, "and my mind was too much occupied with the painful business I had gone upon, to think to ask after them."

"I cannot account for this," exclaimed Mr. Wallingford, "the ladies, I think, cannot be at the castle, or his lordship surely would have mentioned them."

"I really think they were at home, sir," said Walter, who saw that his father still entertained a hope which he was anxious at once to crush; "for, on my way to Squire Dorrington's, you know I was compelled to pass the castle, and just as I did so, I saw the carriage of Mr. Barnell drive out from the court-yard, and I beheld him bow to some one at the windows, which, no doubt, was either Euphemia or her mother, as Lord Harlington was at that time with Mr. Dorrington, where I found him when I got there."

Mr. Wallingford took two or three hasty strides across the apartment, and then muttered to himself in a tone of vexation :—

"The contemptible wretch; this, then, explains the paltry, ignorant letter I received from him this morning. Well, be it so, he may have this illiterate minx if he pleases; I value him not, the knave; but the fellow had better be cautious how he takes liberties with my character, or he may have good cause to repent."

These observations excited the curiosity of Walter, and he would have liked much to have been made acquainted with the meaning of them. The predominant passion in his bosom, however, was indignation against the insignificant booby, Barnell, for presuming to make his father's conduct the subject of his aspersions;

and he also felt the most unqualified pleasure to find that Maria would no more be annoyed by his hated attentions. As for himself, he had fully determined beforehand that nothing should ever force him into an alliance with the family of Lord Harlington, and that as he questioned much the authority of a parent in an affair where the future happiness or misery of their offspring depended, he was resolved that so far from acting the hypocrite, he would make a candid confession of the truth, and declare his hatred to a match so completely obnoxious to his feelings. But he was the more gratified that the match was broken off, without putting him to the painful necessity of acting in any way contrary to his wishes.

"And what passed on the examination of the supposed murderer?" inquired his father, after a pause, during which he had been pacing the room, wrapt in deep meditation. Walter started when this question was put to him, and he shuddered at the thoughts it recalled to his memory, the most prominent of which was, that it was to this dreadful event he was indebted for his release from the projected match with Euphemia, and that it was likely to bring such sorrow and disgrace upon their family, by exposing the misdeeds of his father, whose fame even now was freely mutilated by the vulgar and envenomed tongue of slander. He was not only publicly pointed at as a seducer, and deceiver of maiden innocence, but now the voice of suspicion accused him of being a murderer. These distressing thoughts almost drove the youth to madness, and he felt both ashamed for himself and his father, for he knew that the opprobrium would fall upon him equally as severe.

He now turned his thoughts to the situation of the bereaved mother, the unfortunate Ela, who, although the clouds of night were fast descending, still watched alone by the ghastly corpse of her murdered child. He ascertained that no one had found sufficient courage to venture into her lonely retreat, while he had been away from Wallingford Hall, for the servants entertained almost a supernatural dread of her, and firmly believed that she was performing some wild incantation over the remains of her child to recall her to life.

Imagining that Ela, notwithstanding she had evinced so strong a desire to be alone, might think that, as he had promised to visit her shortly, his being so long away might be deemed by her neglectful, when he quitted his father, he bent his way to the summer-house in the shrubbery.

On his entrance, he was astonished and pleased to find her more calm and collected than he ever remembered to have seen her before, and she had been engaged in writing during his absence, he having, at her request supplied her with pens, ink, and paper.

"Young man," she observed when Walter entered, "you see I have not been idle during the time you have been away; I have been engaged in a melancholy, a painful task, that of recording the early sorrows and miseries which have brought me to the wretched state I am now in. I have not hidden the least fault, nor glossed over any indiscretions of which I may have been guilty. No! I have written only the truth, for I would scorn to tell a falsehood to shield myself from the world's opprobrium. What is the world's opprobrium to me?—I value it not; I have endured it too long, and yet I have not sunk beneath it, though Heaven knows my trials have been great, but none, not one that could equal this in severity. My motive for recording my early history, was that it might serve to warn my Fanny to shun the snares into which I had been so basely entrapped. The mother hesitated not to humble herself, with the hope of rescuing her daughter from the fate into which she had fallen. But what occasion was there for me so to do? None at all! no, for innocence and purity were my Fanny's principal characteristics, although surrounded by every vice, and breathing the air of contamination. But wither am I rambling? This theme cannot be to you at all interesting, and I will change it.—Let me see—what was I going to ask you?—This dreadful calamity, alas! has strangely benighted my recollection."

Ela paused for a few moments, and placed her hands to her temples as if endeavouring to recall her scattered thoughts, then suddenly turning her full black eyes with an inquiring glance upon Walter, she said—

"Oh, I know now what it is I would have said;—what of the villain Mark Darwin and his son, are the wretches in safe custody?"

"The youngest is secure enough in prison," answered Walter, "but his father contrived unfortunately to effect his escape from those who had charge of them to convey them before the magistrate."

"Escaped!" screamed Ela, starting suddenly from her seat, and looking wildly and inquiringly in the countenance of Walter; "fools! that they must be to suffer the old fiend to escape from their clutches!—But he shall not long elude me; no, I will search for him in the remotest corner of the earth, and I will not rest until he is again in my power!—Why do I hesitate?—Let me instantly be gone!"

"Pray be calm," said Walter, who was startled by the wildness of her manner, and thought, with dread, upon the danger and trouble the precipitancy and impetuosity of her disposition might lead her into.

"Talk not to me of calmness, boy," replied Ela, with all her former haughtiness of demeanour, "can I be calm, think you, and hear that the principal wretch has escaped? Recall your words if you would appease me, and tell me that you did not mean what you said.   Old Mark escaped—in what manner was it effected ?—answer me now; how—when—and in what place ?"

In as few words as possible, Walter related to her such particulars of the escape of the Gipsy as the reader has been made acquainted with, and informed her further, that she might rest assured that if there were any possibility of re-taking him, it would be done, and that persons had already been despatched in various

WALTER DISCOVERS MYSTERIOUS AND OMINOUS VISITORS

directions to scour the country in pursuit of the villain.

Ela did not suffer Walter to proceed further, but poured forth such a volley of disgusting and horrible execrations and threats, that he trembled to hear her.

"But I deserve this," she continued, "1 merit it all, for being so foolish as to quit him for a moment until I had seen him safely secured within the strong walls of a prison, for his infernal cunning rendered it an easy matter for him to escape from the idiots to whom he was entrusted. The monster, in fact, should never have been removed from my sight; no, not even in a prison, for fear that he should have been able to elude the vigilance of strangers. I ought to have watched him to the gallows, and not have left him until I had witnessed his last convulsive throe of dying agony. And his rescuer—oh, too well do I know the villain! It was Rupert, the other partner of their guilt; no one else but he would have run the hazard, neither could they have effected it so easily. But why do I waste time here in useless complaints? I am the only one that can track the wretches to their lair, and death alone shall prevent me doing so."

When Ela had thus spoken, she turned suddenly towards the cold remains of her ill-fated daughter, and, after gazing upon them for a moment or two, with the most intense emotion, she clasped her hands together, and raising her eyes towards heaven, seemed to be breathing a silent but earnest prayer.

Walter did not offer to interrupt her, for he hoped that this would be the means of restoring her to that calm which she had evinced previous to his making her acquainted with the escape of Mark Darwin; but at length she paused, and, after looking at him earnestly for a second or two, she took a knife from her bosom, and falling on her knees by the side of the corpse, she raised her hand in the air, and in a voice rendered hoarse by the anguish of her feelings, she thus ejaculated:—

"Hear me, just Heaven, and if the vows of the wretched Ela are still permitted to reach thine ears, bear witness to the one I now make; that I will not rest by night or by day, and that I will search every corner of the earth, while life sends its purple current through my veins, until I have discovered the wretch, Mark Darwin, and been the means of delivering him to justice."

She arose from her knees, returned the knife to the place from which she had taken it, and then, turning to Walter, she resumed—

"And now, Walter Wallingford, I must entrust this precious charge to you. I must not delay a moment, and the morning's dawn must see me many miles away from this spot. Would that I were not compelled to quit the body of my poor girl until the grave receives it, but it cannot be helped. Let me, however, intreat that you will delay the interment until the very latest moment, in case I should return. It is quite uncertain when that may be; a few hours only may separate us, and we may not meet again for weeks, nay, months—for no distance shall be too great for me to travel to accomplish my wishes. The monster shall be discovered, and Ela will yet live to see him and his detested race swing high upon the gallows tree!"

She ceased, and, as she did so, she folded her cloak closer around her, and, without giving Walter time to make a single observation, or to persuade her from attempting such a wild design, she quitted the summer-house, and made her way towards the garden-gate with the utmost precipitation.

After she had gone, Walter was so bewildered by what had taken place, that he stood for a few minutes without being able to move. When his eyes rested on the ghastly corpse of the unfortunate Fanny, with which he was now left alone, he shuddered, and a feeling of horror came over him, which he found difficult to suppress. While Ela had been speaking, evening had come on apace, and it was now nearly dark; and the gloominess of the place was by no means calculated to dissipate those feelings with which his mind was at that moment imbued. Feeling uncomfortable and melancholy after the wild imprecations and curses which he had heard Ela utter, he left the place and walked towards the garden-gate, from which he imagined she had emerged. When he had proceeded some way towards it, he was astonished to hear her in strong altercation with the man who was placed there to keep watch, and who, it appears, had refused to let her pass out. We say that Walter was astonished, but he was still more disgusted at the revolting language which Ela was making use of, and which he could scarcely have believed one of her sex could have been guilty of uttering, especially a woman who possessed a mind so superior to anything of the kind. He, therefore, hurried on to put a stop to the dispute, but ere he had arrived at the gate, all was perfectly quiet; and thinking, therefore, that Ela had overcome the man's scruples, he was about to make his way back to the Hall, when a low murmuring sound met his ear, and arrested his attention, so he hurried to the spot, fearful that the rage and impatience of Ela might have urged her to do the man, with whom she was contending, some injury. He was not a little satisfied, however, when he found, on arriving at the gate, that no such event had taken place, for Roger, the man, was keeping watch as usual, only he was grumbling most lustily at what had transpired between him and Ela.

"Well, Roger," said Walter, who had been looking at him, unobserved, "something seems to have displeased you;—what is it?"

"Mr.— Mr.— Mr. Wal—Walter," stammered out the man, "oh, is that you, sir? I am very glad you have come."

"Why what has been the matter?"

"Matter enough, sir, I can tell you," observed Roger; "and I hope you won't be angry, sir; but I couldn't help it. You must know, sir—that is, sir, I——curse me if I like to tell you, sir, and that's all about it."

"Nonsense, you foolish fellow," said Walter; "tell me at once, or I shall be very angry with you."

"I'm afraid you will when I do tell you, sir," replied Roger; "but, however, if I must, I must. Well then, that horrible Gipsy woman whom you——"

"What about her?—Has she been doing anything?"

"Yes, sir—she has *done me*, that's very clear," answered the man; "for she's gone away, although I did my best to prevent her, and told her that your strict order to me was, not to suffer any person to pass that way: but oh, if you had only heard what she said to me, it would have made your very hair stand an end—that I'm sure it would; she cursed me, and called me such names, that she made me tremble in my shoes again; and as for trying to force her back, I soon found out that that was no use, for she pulled out a long knife, and looking at me as savage as a tigress, she told me that she would bury it in my heart if I offered to *mislest* her further; so, in course, I did not want to lose my life by such a wretch as that, and therefore I took my hands off her very quickly, and before I had time to say another word she rushed out of the gate with the speed of lightning. I am sartin sure, sir, she be one of Satan's imps, for if she wasn't, she could never have made use of the language she did to me, and utter such dreadful wishes against all belonging to me; take my——"

"Ridiculous, Roger!" interrupted Walter, "I would never have believed you were half so silly. Why, you must indeed be a coward if the nonsense uttered by a woman thus frightens you."

"I beg your pardon, sir," said Roger, "but there you're wrong; I was not frightened by a woman; no, no, I don't call her one, for I am certain that she is nothing less than a devil incarnate, and that's what I will maintain to my dying day. And you would have said as I do, sir, if you had only heard what she said, which I'm sure was quite shocking."

"If she did so, Roger," said Walter, "I regret it very much; for I could scarcely believe one whom I wish to be treated with the utmost kindness capable of saying such things."

With these words Walter turned away, and Roger pursued his sentinelship, but muttering to himself when his young master was out of hearing—

"Treat an old hag like that with kindness, indeed—a very pretty thing. I wonder what we shall be told to do next; pay our respects to the devil, I suppose, and treat him as a gentleman. I don't know what's come to this family of late, and God knows what will be the finish of it. I do really think they have all gone crazy like my poor mistress. One

day here's master going to hang all the gang if he can, and the next one of the worst of them is taken into the house under his protection, and Mr. Walter Wallingford desires that she should be treated with kindness; a black-guard, dishonest, old fortin teller, who deserves to be burnt at the stake, and who should be, too, if I had my will. Well, arter all, I never will believe but that there is more in that story about master and the Gipsy woman than many folks think. Well, what a disgrace for a gentleman like him to have anything to do with such a party. I couldn't have believed that he ever could have even been guilty of such a thing, especially after the lecture he gave me, when Susan swore the little child to me, and I was compelled to marry her, or else he vowed he would send me to prison if I refused. Well, to be sure, these great folks think nothing of doing that which they consider very shocking indeed in us poor people. If justice had been done he would have been made to marry the Gipsy woman, the same as I was obliged to do with my Susan."

Thus communing with himself, Roger continued to walk backwards and forwards, and the only kindness he resolved to show the Gipsy woman, was to take especial care, if she returned, not to admit her upon any account whatever, and if she became obstinate, to call Mr. Walter to his assistance.

But Ela came not back, and therefore honest Roger's courage was not at that time put to the test. Walter was now obliged to see to the safety of the corpse, and he therefore made enquiries for some person who would undertake the task to sit up to watch it. This he found by no means easy, for every one to whom he mentioned it shuddered with horror at the bare idea. At last, however, by the dint of argument, the most forcible part of which was the promise of a good reward, he did persuade two women to undertake the task, and if they did not fail in their courage the first night, it was settled that they should continue there until such times as there had been a coroner's inquest held upon the body, and to endeavour to ascertain by what means the unfortunate girl came to her end; after which Walter would see her placed in a coffin, which he had already ordered to be made.

The business of the inquest was proceeded with without the least possible delay, and the jury that were empanelled, being principally composed of the tenants of Mr. Wallingford, and, consequently, perfectly acquainted with him, Walter could not entertain the slightest suspicion that his feelings would have to undergo another trial by hearing uttered again those dark hints which had before been uttered by the Gipsy, on his examination by Mr. Dorrington and Lord Harlington. But how soon was his heart wrung with agony and apprehension, when he found what he was before ignorant of; namely, that among those who were summoned to give evidence. were Maria, his father, Ela Beranzio, and Mark Darwin, the younger, whom he thought had been committed for trial not many hours prior.

This will show how ignorant was Walter of the forms of law; but Knobbs, who prided himself greatly upon his knowledge in that way, explained it to him as well as he was able, the consequence of which was, that Walter was very little wiser after he had given his explanation than he had been before; he, however, contrived to elicit that the custom invariably was to detain the person who might be suspected in prison, until after the coroner's inquest was over, when, according to the verdict of the jury, he would either be liberated or committed to take his trial at the assizes.

"Oh, God!" ejaculated Walter, as he hastened to impart the information he had obtained to his father and Maria, "will this torment never cease?"

He found Mr. Wallingford in his chamber, he having retired there for the purpose of making it appear that he was indifferent to the proceedings. Walter had, as soon as he returned to the hall, informed him of Ela having quitted the place, which he heard with much gratification, as he hoped by that means, that not only would his Christabelle in all probability be retored to him, but that also the public exposition of his own former conduct be avoided. After having indulged in these hopes then, it may easily be judged with what pain, disappointment, and indignation, he heard that his attendance at the inquest was indispensable, to state all that he was acquainted with throughout the whole of the affair.

"Oh, Walter," he ejaculated, with a look which penetrated to the heart of his son, "this will certainly be my death-blow. But I never can obey the summons; I should expire in the room; I am so ill, so shocked, so careworn. But send for Doctor Hartley immediately; he will be the means of saving me this awful trial, for he can prove the illness under which I at present labour, and how unfit I am to undergo the torture of an examination. Besides, what more have I to tell than what can be gathered from the evidence of any of my domestics? I am determined that I will not obey the summons; so go, you, Henry, and tell Mr. Hartley that I request to see him immediately."

"Doctor Hartley is at present with my mother, sir," said Walter, grieved beyond expression at the emotion of his father, and thoroughly convinced, from his haggard and ghastly appearance, how true had been his observations as regarded his being ill; "and as I am going there for the purpose of informing my cousin of

the necessity of her attendance at the inquest I will desire the doctor to come to you."

As Walter proceeded to his mother's chamber he hastily reflected upon the painful circumstances; and notwithstanding all that his father had stated, he could not help hoping that Mr. Hartley would use his influence to persuade him to attend the inquest; for if he were absent himself, Walter could not help suspecting that some malicious persons might throw out an insinuation that he was afraid to have his conduct investigated, and suspicion might increase its venom.

Walter, however, did not mention these thoughts to Doctor Hartley, but contented himself by informing him that his father wished to see him.

"I will attend to your father presently, Walter," replied Mr. Hartley, who, on the entrance of the former, was engaged with Maria in deep conversation; "presently, I say, although it is really quite useless, for I have told him repeatedly that it is only air and exercise that will do him any good, and yet he will persist in keeping to his bed-room; which is so close and confined, that it is surprising, in his present state, it does not kill him."

Walter here explained the purpose for which his father desired to see him. The doctor's countenance changed, and he shook his head hastily two or three times, which was a great habit of his, when he disapproved of anything.

"It's out of my power to do anything of the sort," he said, at length, candidly; "and, moreover, if it were in my power, I would not do it upon any account. I should not be acting as a friend to your father if I did; no, no, instead of doing that, I will do all that is in my power to persuade him to go; nay, I was almost about to say, that I would absolutely compel him to go, and that without a moment's delay."

Walter could not help turning an inquiring glance upon the doctor's face, he had never heard him speak so emphatically before, and his astonishment was therefore excited.

"Are you then acquainted, sir?" said he.

"No matter with what I am acquainted, my dear Walter," interrupted the worthy doctor, impatiently, "the whole of it is, I shall undoubtedly go directly to Mr. Wallingford, and use all my influence to persuade him to go without any more hesitation, as it is nothing more than his duty, from which, if he were to shrink, there is no knowing what might be the aspersions cast upon his character."

Walter was surprised to hear Mr. Hartley so readily adopt the same ideas as himself, and he was therefore the more anxious that he should succeed in his errand.

"Oh, Walter!" ejaculated Maria, when th doctor had quitted the room, "pray do explaie to me what all this means?—Why has the doen tor been interrogating me concerning all that took place before Mr. Dorrington and Lord Harlington, and why should he take such particular pains to caution me to be careful that I did not differ in one tittle of the evidence which I should have to give this day?—When I informed him that I certainly should speak nothing but the truth, he shook his head solemnly, and replied that he knew that, but that he had no doubt from what had already taken place, that there were those who were anxious to put a wrong construction upon everything, and to so twist and impugn facts as to make them appear falsehoods. He therefore repeated his entreaty for me to adhere as closely as possible to the manner of my stating what I knew at the examination. Had you not interrupted our conversation by your entrance, Walter, I should have requested Mr. Hartley to have spoken more explicitly; for I am convinced he would never have tried to frighten me without some very powerful motive dictated his conduct."

"Upon my word, my dear Maria, I do not perceive what occasion there was for Mr. Hartley to seek to alarm you," observed Walter, whose heart throbbed with agony as he listened to her words. How he reflected, could he ever make her acquainted with the dreadful truth, namely, that his father was actually suspected by certain persons of having assassinated his own daughter, and that from her evidence they sought to elicit something that might give confirmation to their base suspicions.

Maria, although she had not the slightest idea of what was passing in her cousin's mind, could not help noticing the agony he evinced, and fearful, therefore, that her questions might pain him, she did not pursue the subject farther.

CHAPTER XXXIII.

"Now comes the painful ordeal
Oh, Heaven, support me in this hour of need!"
ANON.

IN a very short time after Walter's interview with his cousin, the coroner arrived. Walter was anxious to speak to his father, yet was he in a state of dread and anxiety to know how the conference between Mr. Wallingford and Doctor Hartley had terminated. He had no doubt that the statements which the good doctor would find it necessary to make in order to urge the unavoidable necessity of his father's being present at the inquest would terribly shock him, and he trembled as he contemplated the result; he was, however, destined to be agreeably disappointed; for, shortly after the coroner had arrived, Mr. Wallingford descended from his chamber with Doctor Hartley, and, although, of course, his illness made him pale and weak, Walter could see from the composed expression of his features that he

was prepared to undergo the scrutiny with becoming fortitude.

The inquest was held in a large and commodious room in the Hall, wherein Mr. Wallingford generally performed his magisterial duties, and when he entered, supported by Dr. Hartley the jury, he found, were all assembled, and Walter was also present.

As Mr. Wallingford entered the room, a dead silence pervaded it, and then every eye became fixed upon him, and they exchanged looks of amazement among one another, for they had never thought that he would have been summoned. Mr. Wallingford bore this vulgar scrutiny with total indifference, and finding that the coroner was an old friend, he held a brief conversation with him on common-place topics until the business was ready to be commenced, when he took a seat close by, and seemed to take no interest whatever in the proceedings which were about to begin.

But although this assumption of calmness might have deceived the other persons present, it could not Walter, who could plainly perceive that his father was suffering the most intense mental anguish. Mr. Wallingford, who, at a glance, read his son's thoughts, averted his head, and took particular care not to look at him, or to hold any conversation with him.

The jury having been sworn, they were just about to leave the room, for the purpose of going to view the corpse, when their purpose was arrested, and the curiosity of all present was excited by Mark Darwin, the Gipsy, being led in by Knobbs, the constable, and another man.

The whole appearance of the man had undergone an extraordinary change during the short time he had been confined, and it was evident that his anxiety and suspense had been very great. His face was very pale, and he turned away his head, apparently abashed, when his eye met that of Walter.

From the Gipsy, Walter turned his gaze upon his father, and he was not at all astonished when he beheld the unfeigned emotion he betrayed as he looked upon the suspected assassin of his unfortunate daughter. The Gipsy, however, took no notice of him, and seemed either not to know, or pretended that he did not know, that Mr. Wallingford was the person on whom he had endeavoured to fix the foul stigma. A low murmur ran through the persons assembled, and they exchanged significant looks with one another. After this, there appeared to be an unusual excitement among the jurymen.

Walter had been minutely scrutinizing all that took place; and, at first, he thought that this was nothing more than the preliminary bustle common on such occasions, and that they were merely making some observations upon the appearance of the prisoner; but the real cause was very shortly explained to him, for the foreman of the jury, who was a farmer, suddenly arose, and addressing himself to the coroner, said—

"Sir, it is the wish of myself and my brother jurymen that the individual who is accused of the murder shall accompany us to view the body of the unfortunate person."

"Certainly, I can see no reason to object to your request;" returned the coroner.

"Well," said the farmer, addressing himself to Mark, "are you willing to attend us?—I should think you cannot refuse, if you are confident within yourself that you are innocent of the dreadful crime laid to your charge. You will not hesitate, I presume, to take a look at the corpse of the murdered girl?"

"What care I, guilty or innocent?" cried Mark, fiercely, "if I had even been the murderer I should not have been afraid to gaze upon the work of my hands. But am I the only person on whom suspicion rests?—Is Mr. Wallingford in the room?"

"He is;—I am he!" exclaimed Mr. Wallingford, rising from his chair with a firmness that astonished everybody present, and fixing his eyes steadfastly upon the countenance of the Gipsy. Mark was evidently not prepared for this, and he was for two or three seconds apparently somewhat disconcerted; however, his confusion soon subsided, and he said—

"Oh, then, you are Mr. Wallingford?"

"Have I not told you so before?" said Mr. Wallingford, "why do you ask the question?"

"I think I have good reason," returned the Gipsy, "is it you who accuses me of the murder of this girl?"

"I accuse no one,' said Mr. Wallingford, hastily; "of you I know nothing more than——"

"Nay, Mr. Wallingford, excuse me," said the coroner, interrupting him, "but this I consider is quite irrelevant, and is only delaying the inquiry."

Mr. Wallingford bowed, and resumed his seat, while the jury proceeded towards the door for the purpose of going to examine the body. But ere they could leave the room, Mark Darwin again spoke in louder tones than he had before done, and which immediately arrested their steps—

"I have a request to make," said he, "which I do not see why you should refuse to grant to me."

"What is it?" inquired the coroner.

"Why," returned the Gipsy, with an insolent sneer, "it is that Mr. Wallingford should also attend us; of course he as well as me cannot have any objection."

"Wretch! monster!" muttered Walter, scarcely able to restrain his feelings from an open demonstration of his indignation; but his father by an expressive glance quickly silenced him; and the latter, then turning with apparent indifference towards the jury, said—

"If it is the wish of the gentlemen of the jury that I should accompany them, I am very ready to comply with their request."

Notwithstanding the composure with which Mr. Wallingford uttered this, it was very evident that he was suffering all that mental agony which could well be imagined, and his limbs trembled violently.

In reply to his question, there were some persons who expressed their dissatisfaction at the proposition, and who could not perceive any necessity for Mr. Wallingford's presence, but it was very easy to be understood from the looks of the majority, that they were in favour of the request which had been made by Mark Darwin, the Gipsy; and, at length, one officious booby remarked that, "it would perhaps be quite as well, and give satisfaction to all parties if Mr. Wallingford did just walk with them as far, and most likely it would not put him to much inconvenience." Thereupon those who had before "seen no necessity" for such a thing, joined unanimously in the opinion of their companions; Mr. Wallingford therefore bowed, and taking the arm of Walter, proceeded with the jury, while Mark Darwin, with a look of malignant exultation, passed out before them, in the care of the constable and his assistant.

"Pray do not hurry so, my dear sir," said Doctor Hartley, following at their heels, "I wish to be with you. The miscreant!" he added, in an under tone, as he took the other arm of Walter; "what will be the result of this painful business? And the ignorant clowns, to pay any attention to his suggestions; they ought to have seen his motives in an instant."

"There, my dear sir, I am not of your opinion," said Mr. Wallingford, "unless they have more sagacity than I can boast of. For my part, I am totally at a loss to see through the villain's malice. What can be his object, and why should he indulge a feeling of revenge against a man whom he has evidently no knowledge of?"

"Perhaps the murdering hang-dog," said Walter, "imagines that his villanous malignant hints may serve to impugn the mass of evidence that will be adduced against him; but he is deceived, and——"

"Silence, that's a good fellow," interrupted the cautious doctor; "a still tongue makes a wise head, you know. And as Mr. Hartley said this, he winked his eye, and pointed significantly with his thumb over his shoulder towards several of the men who had been most urgent for Mr. Wallingford to accompany them to the summer-house, who were lurking close to their heels, as though they were anxious to overhear what they were talking about.

"Not so fast, not so fast, Mr. Wallingford," said the doctor, when they had got near the place where lay the body of the unfortunate Fanny. But Wallingford either did not hear what he said, or otherwise he paid no attention to it, and before any one else had even got up to the building, he was standing by the corpse of his murdered daughter, and gazing upon it with looks of the most undisguised pity and horror.

The struggle which Wallingford had with his feelings, wrung the heart of his son with the most poignant anguish, and he could scarcely refrain from an open expression of his powerful emotions, but at that moment Mark Darwin entering with the others, aroused him, and fixed his whole attention upon him.

The Gipsy cast an eager glance around the place as he entered, and when he perceived that the object of his search (Ela) was not present, his chagrin and disappointment were quite apparent. His brows became contracted, and his lips moved as if he were muttering some complaint to himself. After a second had elapsed in this manner, he raised his eyes, and, perceiving Walter looking intently upon him, he frowned, and fixed his eyes sternly upon his countenance.

"How is this," he murmured; "why is not the parent watching by the cold remains of her offspring?—Unfortunate girl, you——"

"Hold, fellow!" cried the doctor, in a commanding tone, "we have something else to do than to attend to your observations. Now, gentlemen, are you all contented?" he added, addressing the jurymen, who surrounded the corpse, and had neither of them uttered a syllable.

The foreman, upon the doctor putting this question to them, turned round to him and said—

"It is the unanimous wish of me and my companions, sir, that you would give your opinion as to whether the hapless young woman was murdered previous to her being thrown into the lake, and——"

"Most assuredly," interrupted the doctor, "there cannot be any question upon that subject; behold, it was this frightful wound which occasioned her death!"

The worthy doctor removed the covering from the bosom of the corpse as he spoke, and revealed the still-gaping wound to the horror-stricken spectators. They all uttered a cry of pity, disgust, and indignation at this appalling spectacle, but Wallingford and the Gipsy uttered not a word, but the ghastly countenance and livid lips of the former showed plainly how dreadfully he suffered; as for Mark Darwin, he seemed to be completely unmoved.

"If I mistake not," said the foreman of the jury, "a knife or dagger was found in this place?"

"True," returned the doctor, "and that can be produced, and will, I am informed, be easily proved to have belonged to——Walter, I believe the knife is in your possession?"

Walter replied in the negative; and, after a moment's pause, he added that it was then in the possession of Ela Beranzio, the mother of the murdered girl. Upon this answer, Walter observed a malignant smile pass over the countenance of the Gipsy.

"And this Ela Beranzio," asked the principal juryman, "of course you have secured her—have you not, sir?"

"I have not, sir," answered Walter; "she left here last night!"

"But you knew whither she has gone?"

Walter once more replied in the negative.

"That is strange," said the foreman; and then he looked round upon his companions, who all whispered together, and shook their heads, and afterwards more openly gave vent to expressions of astonishment and dissatisfaction. Walter noticed those demonstrations with much uneasiness; but, above all, his attention was drawn to Mark, who, when he mentioned the circumstance of Ela leaving, although he tried to stifle his agitation, turned ghastly pale, and his lips became compressed.

"But," continued Walter, after he had suffered the excitement in some degree to subside, "I can safely undertake to say that when her evidence is required, she will not fail to be present; circumstances of a peculiar nature, and which I do not consider myself at liberty just now to disclose, have compelled her to be away."

"No doubt," sneered Mark, with a look of contempt and defiance, "it would be very inconvenient, I dare say, for her to come forward at this time!—Ha!—ha!—It is no more than I expected, the old hell cat——"

"Wretch, miscreant! monster!" cried Wallingford, in a voice that made every person in the place start, "by the Almighty power that made us both, I will no longer tamely endure your taunts and insults!—I swear that if you dare apply such a vile epithet to the name of that ill-fated woman, I will rob the gallows of its due, murderer, and——"

"Oh, it is very brave, very manly, most heroic, forsooth," interrupted the Gipsy, ironically, "to offer such threats, especially when you are surrounded by your friends, against a poor devil whose hands are manacled, and who is therefore deprived of the power to defend himself; but the time perhaps will come, when we may meet again, Mr. Wallingford, under different circumstances, and——"

"Silence, fellow!" exclaimed the doctor, indignantly, "we have had enough of this. Gentlemen, I believe we have nothing more to do here; therefore we had better adjourn to the inquest room, instead of listening to the disgusting ravings of this hardened scoundrel."

"Not just yet, if you please, Mr. Hartley," remarked one of the men who were on the jury. "One thing, you know, has not been done, which I believe was our principal reason for wishing the prisoner to be present here; what I mean is this here, that we should make those here as is suspected of having assassinated this unfortunate girl, place his hand upon the body; 'cause yer see, doctor, it is a very well known fact, that if ever the real murderer does that 'ere, the wound is sure to burst out a bleeding again."

Doctor Hartley looked at the man who uttered this, and he with much difficulty could refrain from expressing his pity and contempt for his ignorance; but he saw that the greater portion of the rustic jurors placed a firm reliance in the absurd superstition, and therefore he knew it would be useless to attempt to argue the point with men who had previously made up their minds not to be convinced. So, after a moment or two's silence, he observed—

"There is no law to enforce this senseless test; but if the man does not object to such a trial, why, of course, I have nothing to do with it."

"I will comply this instant," ejaculated Mark, as he advanced towards the corpse, with not the least apparent fear; "that is, if another person will submit to the ordeal."

"Who is it?" demanded several of the persons eagerly.

"Wallingford!" replied the Gipsy, fixing his eyes firmly upon that gentleman, as he gave utterance to his name.

Mr. Wallingford returned no answer; but, after looking at his torturer with an expression which could not be mistaken, he walked from the place where he had been standing, removed the covering from the wound, and placed his hand upon the cold forehead of the poor, murdered girl.

We cannot do adequate justice to the feelings of disgust with which Walter viewed this sickening proceeding, and the abhorrence he felt for the senseless bigotry which had prompted such a ceremony, and the revengeful ferocity which had fixed upon it as a pretext for the furtherance of its diabolical designs, namely, to torture the mind of his wretched father to the very utmost. With the utmost difficulty did Doctor Hartley prevent him from giving the most unmeasured expression of his opinion upon the subject; but unable to endure the sight of the degradation to which Mr. Wallingford was thus unfeelingly exposed, he turned away, and looked from the window into the garden, while the others all gathered round the corpse, and watched with anxious eyes the result of the ordeal, which they seemed firmly to believe was infallible.

But Walter had not been so occupied a second, when he was startled by hearing a loud outcry from the people who were standing near the corpse, and, hastening from the window, his consternation may be easily imagined when he beheld his father stretched on the floor quite insensible, and his countenance frightfully distorted with convulsions.

"Good God! he is dying!" cried the distracted Walter; "fiends of hell, his death be upon your heads!"

"You are wrong, Mr. Walter," said Mark Darwin, as he forced his way towards the place where Walter was supporting his unfortunate father, and fixing a steady look upon the blackened and disfigured features of the suffering gentleman; "it is the power of a guilty conscience that has effected this. Ah! behold!" he suddenly exclaimed, with demoniacal exultation, and pointing to the corpse, "the black blood is flowing from the wound—the real assassin stands confessed—it is Wallingford, the unnatural wretch, who abandoned his child when——"

"Merciful Father," exclaimed Walter, with the most impressive earnestness, "surely you will not believe this?—Can you be so cruel or so unjust as to believe the foul aspersions uttered by this miscreant against my father? —Fools! idiots! You are so blinded by bigotry and superstition, that it is worse than madness to appeal to you."

But many of them seemed to pay very little attention to what he said, so fully were they occupied with looking at the corpse, and the awful miracle, which they firmly believed. Two or three of them shook their heads doubtfully, and others raised their hands and eyes, which indications were meant to convey a due sense of their horror, and a strong suspicion that what Mark Darwin had asserted was not without a very strong foundation.

"Walter Wallingford," at length, said Mr. Hartley, who had been engaged in trying to restore Mr. Wallingford to his senses, "I must entreat that you will not utter any more of these expostulations, but devote your attention to your unhappy parent instead;—it is but a waste of words to attempt to argue with people who are so grossly ignorant, that I almost blush to call them men. If they will not be convinced by reason, why e'en suffer them to believe in the miracle they imagine has but now taken place; for, fortunately, the fate of your unfortunate father rests not in their hands. Mr. Fallowfield, and Mr. Christopher, will you assist Mr. Walter to bear his father into the Hall? Be careful how you carry him:—there —that's it. See that he is immediately undressed and placed in bed, and then I must bleed him."

Having thus spoken, Mr. Hartley followed those who were carrying Mr. Wallingford into the Hall, after having first bestowed a look of pity and contempt upon the ignorant group of rustics, who seemed completely petrified to the spot.

When Doctor Hartley and the others were gone, however, the party above alluded to gave free indulgence to their opinions upon the mira-culous events that had taken place, and they did not confine themselves to any very measured comments upon the different actors in the scene. But on Wallingford was heaped the principal load of their calumny and suspicion, although there were several, in spite of all the others

WALTER REMONSTRATES WITH ELA FOR USING A PRECIOUS OPIATE.

could say, or the arguments they could advance, who strongly advocated his cause; but unfor-tunately the circumstance of the last few minutes had worked an extraordinary revolu-tion in the opinions of those who had before entertained no suspicion of Mr. Wallingford, and firmly believed that the Gipsy was the murderer, and they were now of opinion that the former was the actual perpetrator of the dread-ful deed.

Mark Darwin stood by, and with folded arms, and steadfast gaze, scrutinized minutely the expression of their features, as they consulted together, appearing by that to think that he could read what might be his probable fate. At length, however, finding that none of them seemed inclined to put any questions to him, he thus remarked—

"I know that all the words that a poor devil like myself can say will be of very little avail, because everybody is prejudiced against me, and imagine that I was one in the crime; but I can swear that many years ago I have heard Mr. Wallingford mentioned as the parent of that poor murdered creature. Nay, more, I know also that, years ago, he wished to get her in his power, and it was the firm belief of the mother that he wished to put her away, so that his treachery and shame might never be revealed to the public."

"Ah! that is a very just observation," said a thick-headed farmer, who laboured under the singular delusion that he was one of the most sensible and sagacious fellows in the kingdom. "It seems to me very probable that such might have been the case; and don't you see, now, they have managed to put the mother where she is not to be found. And then, too, don't we all very well know that it was something very bad and mysterious that induced Mr. Wallingford to leave his native country, and be away from it for years; and the Gipsies had a finger in that pie as well, for in course you must all recollect what a piece o' work there was in searching every hole and corner after 'em, and there was nothing else talked about at that time but them."

"To be sure, we all know that there was a great sensation about them at the period you are speaking of," observed one of the partizans of Mr. Wallingford; "but what was the occasion of it? Why, I can tell you. It was strongly suspected, and, I think, not without a very good reason, that they were the monsters who set fire to the nursery, where poor little Miss Christabelle was burned to death."

"And what good, think you, our people could have got by that?" inquired Mark Darwin. "Would it have brought them any benefit?—No. You must not think that the Gipsy tribe are fond of running the risk of placing their necks in the halter, when they have no object in view to reward them for their pains."

"Come, come, neighbours," said one of the jurors, "this is wasting time that ought to be occupied in more important business than in raking up old tales, about which we none of us know very little; so I think it would be as well if we were to return to the inquest room, and see about settling this melancholy duty."

As none of the others could offer anything against this proposition, they left the summer-house, and the inquest commenced. We should become tedious were we to endeavour to detail all the particulars of that investigation; there was nothing transpired with which the reader has not been made acquainted, but, notwithstanding the evidence against the Gipsy was clear and conclusive, and the innocence of Mr. Wallingford was equally apparent, yet there were two or three of the senseless dolts, who were on the jury, whose prejudices and suspicions could not be done away with. They contended that the wound bleeding afresh, when Wallingford touched the body, was quite sufficient proof that he was the perpetrator of the crime, and nothing should persuade them to the contrary. All that reason and common sense could accomplish, Doctor Hartley endeavoured to do, but without success, such was the implicit reliance they placed in the imagined miracle. He proved clearly that there was nothing at all remarkable in what they had seen, which he could easily account for, namely, that the coagulated blood had been dissolved by the heat of the room, and when Mr. Wallingford pressed his hand upon her forehead, and afterwards fell against the body, it very naturally caused the blood to flow.

However, nothing could alter their opinion, notwithstanding they paid the utmost attention to Doctor Hartley's observations, he being a great favourite with every one in the village, It was very fortunate that the majority of the jurors were in favour of Mr. Wallingford, and they argued the point with their obstinate companions most powerfully, showing them that to suppose he was the assassin was absolutely preposterous, as it was clearly proved, upon the evidence of all the servants, that he was in the house at the time the cries were heard, and had not been absent from it for several hours before, and that he did not leave it until he went with them to endeavour to ascertain the meaning of what they had heard, and that he had used the utmost vigilance, and most untiring assiduity, to endeavour to unravel the dreadful mystery.

Finding that they still obstinately adhered to the ridiculous opinion they had formed, they resolved that they would not easily yield their point, and consequently they were locked up until they should come to a decision.

What a trial of suspense and anxiety was this to Walter? Indeed, his anguish was so intense as to baffle every attempt at description. He was compelled to leave his father in the charge of Doctor Hartley, as he was obliged to attend before the coroner, and repeat the statement he had made on the examination of Mark Darwin before Mr. Derrington and Lord Harlington, and how torturing it was to him to find, from the manner in which he was interrogated, that the ignorant suspicions entertained by the vulgar people who were sitting to decide upon his father's fate, were also encouraged by the majority of the other persons present, and those who were engaged in the investigation.

"Great God! he will never be able to support this dreadful trial!" he murmured to himself, when he went once more to the bedside of his father, and marked the ghastly and death-like appearance of his countenance.

Doctor Hartley, whose impatience was almost insupportable, eagerly inquired what was the result, and Walter briefly informed him that they had not yet come to any conclusion, and that they were locked up in consequence.

"Alas! that my father's fate should be placed in such hands as those ignorant and superstitious beings," he continued, in accents of the most ungovernable grief. I dread to hear the verdict, for I know it will be one that will——. But I cannot finish the horrid sentence; the words would choke me!"

The unhappy youth covered his face with his handkerchief, and burst into a paroxysm of grief, and was entirely deaf to the expostulations and consolation which Mr. Hartley was himself in so bad a condition to impart. In the midst of this despair and sorrow, however, a ray of consolation did dart upon Walter at that moment, for his father, who had hitherto been insensible, felt the benefit of the skilful doctor's attention, and gradually recovering, he opened his eyes, and observing Walter, he beckoned him towards him, took his hand in his, and in a voice, calm but feeble with suffering, he thus addressed him—

"Walter," said Wallingford, in an affectionate but melancholy tone, as his son took his hand, and pressed it fervently within his, "do not, I beseech you, give way to the grief that this blow must inflict, but endeavour to meet the worst as becomes a man, and with patience and resolution. Of my own fate, I am now quite careless, but it is for you I am concerned, and for the sake of that name, which I have no doubt you will be able to restore to all its former honour, that I pray to heaven to save me from the opprobrium of such a verdict as I fear those ignorant men will return. I say again, my own fate is to me a matter of indifference, for nothing can wound or afflict me more than I am at present."

"Psha! stuff! nonsense!" exclaimed Doctor Hartley, impatiently, "I am surprised at you, Mr. Wallingford; but this moment you recommended your son not to give way to grief, and to meet the worst as becomes a man, and is this the way you take to teach him his lesson? And, after all, I should like to know what cause you have for apprehension, and thus giving way to despair? I admit your sufferings have been great, that they are now intense, but if you thus weakly give way to despair, you will continue to suffer. I repeat that you labour under apprehensions for which there is no foundation; who, think you, of common sense, will be prejudiced by such a set of brainless clowns, let them come to whatever decision they may?

But they cannot come to but one decision if they dare not fly in the face of facts that are so notorious to every one. Now, with regard to your health, if you can depend upon my assertion, I assure you that you are quite out of danger; and, only have to keep yourself still, and your mind calm and composed, and, no doubt, you will very soon recover. So let me beg of you, not to give way to this melancholy; we shall all be better soon, I know we shall; and Mrs. Wallingford, too, she is now decidedly considerably better, and will continue to amend with care; therefore remember that on your firmness depends——"

"Ah! my wife, my dearest Amelia!" ejaculated Wallingford, with an expression of delight; there is magic in that beloved name; yes, yes, for her sake, poor afflicted one, I will conquer my own sufferings:—oh, what would I not undergo, to restore her to health and happiness?"

"My words have had the effect I wished them to have, Walter," observed the worthy doctor, in a low tone of pleasure and triumph to the former;—"now we shall do—we shall do, my dear boy;—be careful that nothing is communicated to him which may cause the least agitation, and the result will, I hope, be all that we could desire. Nay, I guess what you would observe, Walter, but upon that point you may rest perfectly content; they cannot give any other verdict than such as the evidence adduced will authorise, and therefore what occasion is there for the slightest apprehension?"

Walter departed to do as Mr. Hartley had suggested, with a mind more elated with hope than it had been for some time before.

While this was going forward, the sufferings of Maria were full as poignant as those fo her cousin, and a thousand times she blamed herself for preventing, by her terrors, Walter from entering the shrubbery, on the evening she had encountered the two Gipsy girls, which would perhaps, have been the cause of frustrating the diabolical crime of the monsters, who had secreted themselves there. She had deeply regretted that she had not revealed to him the fact of her having seen the two girls, and of what they had uttered concerning their fears of being discovered by the Gipsies who were lurking in the shrubbery, before it was too late to save the unfortunate Fanny from the dreadful fate which she had suffered. Even the recovery of Mrs. Wallingford, singular as it may appear, was now a source of pain to her, for with the restoration of her reason she would be awakened to a knowledge of the tenfold misery which had descended upon them, and the shock, she feared, would be more than her frame, reduce as it was, could support.

What a mixture of pain and pleasure did it yield to the affectionate girl's heart, when Mrs. Wallingford spoke for the first time since he reason had wandered, and called upon the names of her husband and Walter, and enquired where they were.

"They will not be long, dearest aunt, before they are here," replied the delighted girl; and she immediately sent for Dr. Hartley, and informed him of the sudden change which had taken place. But at that time the good doctor was unable to attend, being at the bedside of Mr. Wallingford, and whose situation was so precarious, that he was almost fearful he should not be able to restore him. And Walter was at the same time engaged in the inquest room, and subjected to all the tedious and ridiculous interrogatories of the ignorant persons who composed the jury.

The moment he could make his escape, he flew to the chamber of his mother. But when she had several times inquired with deep emotion after Wallingford and her son, and expressed her astonishment that they should treat her with such neglect, she fell into a profound slumber, which Mr. Hartley hailed as a happy omen.

Maria watched by her while she slept, with the most painful anxiety and suspense, and she really dreaded her waking, for she was confident that the first person she would enquire for would be Mr. Wallingford, and what answer could she make her—how evade her questions as to the cause of his non-appearance, and how poignantly would the absence of her husband afflict her already deeply lacerated bosom. But this subject, tormenting and distracting as it was, was completely trivial when compared with another, which occupied Maria's mind.

The result of the investigation in the summer-house, had reached her from the rumours of the servants, and as may be well imagined she was completely paralysed and astounded, equally as much with the ignorant and disgusting superstition of the men, and the dreadful situation in which their suspicions placed Mr. Wallingford. Who could feel sufficiently disgusted with those, who, actuated by an absurd superstition, would place the life of their fellow beings in jeopardy, and that man too, who was celebrated for urbanity, philanthropy, and humanity, and who had been a kind benefactor to most of them, who were now so ready to attach obloquy to his name? The agitated countenance of Walter, and the earnestness of Mrs. Pembroke, from whom she received the greater part of the information, served to increase her uneasiness, and her mind became in a state of torment and suspense, actually almost insupportable.

Mrs. Pembroke was in a mood by no means calculated to soothe the terrors of Maria.

"Alas! Miss Herbert," she exclaimed with upraised hands, "I tremble to think upon this shocking circumstance ;—what if the boobies should return a verdict against my master, and he should be sent to prison?—oh, I'm certain

it would be the death blow to my poor dear lady, that it would !"

Maria felt too keenly the probability of this prediction being fulfilled, to make any reply; and she wrung her hands in silent agony, and looked the very picture of despair.

The day passed its slow length away, and twilight yielded to the deeper shadows of evening, but still the jury had not come to a decision, and the excitement and suspense of every member of the establishment, and of those who resided on the estate, may be readily conceived.

The sleep of Mrs. Wallingford continued calm and unbroken, and Maria was thankful that it was so, as she knew not what to say to appease the poor invalid's anxiety to see her husband.

Mr. Wallingford, in the meantime, had become calm and resigned, and appeared to await the result of the inquest with a firmness, almost amounting to indifference. His principal care seemed now to be the agitated state of Walter, and he used all the arguments in his power to tranquillize his feelings. But this was a task that was not very easy of accomplishment, for Walter could not view with anything but indignation and impatience the manner in which they protracted a business which might have been rationally disposed of in five minutes.

The suspense of Walter became quite intolerable, and feeling the heat of the room, in his agitated state, very oppressive, he left the Hall, and paced with uneven steps before the window of the room in which the jury were sitting. But not long could he remain there even, for his ears were tormented by the observations and prognostications of the servants, and the grave aspect of their countenances caused him the utmost anguish ; he also learned from what they said, that the persons inside had not yet come to any decision, so his patience being quite exhausted, he walked forth into the garden, as he thought the change of situation might afford him some relief.

It was a dull sultry evening, and not disposed to walk, he took a seat beneath the wide spreading branches of a chestnut tree, which reared its tall head at no great distance from the Hall, so that he might not be out of hearing when the jury might break up their deliberations on this most tedious and painful business. Thus elapsed nearly an hour, during which interval Walter's mind had been fully occupied in reflecting upon every event connected with the murder, and all the circumstances which had been the means of bringing such overwhelming sorrow and affliction upon his parents.

So deeply occupied was he in revolving those painful circumstances in his thoughts, that a storm had commenced before he had noticed its approach. It was very dark, and the murmur of distant thunder vibrated on the air, followed by heavy drops of rain, which pattering among the leaves above his head, aroused him, and showed him that it would be complete folly to remain there any longer, when he might so soon seek shelter in the Hall. Accordingly, he was about to quit his seat, when his purpose was arrested by the sound of voices, which seemed to proceed from some persons at no great distance from him. He looked eagerly in the direction, but the darkness for a second or two prevented his being able to distinguish any objects, but at last he was enabled to discern two figures, standing a short distance off, but whether male or female, he had no means of ascertaining. They remained so still and inanimate, that if it had not been for the circumstance of his having heard them speak, he would have been doubtful whether or not they were human forms. Certain, however, that they had some particular object in view, or else they would not have chosen such a secret manner to approach the place, as he had not heard the slightest sound of a footfall upon the ground, he was resolved to watch them narrowly, and with caution.

After a second or two, during which Walter remained with his eyes steadfastly fixed upon them, and scarcely venturing to breathe, they parted, and one of them walked up towards the Hall, and placing his head to the window, seemed to be watching and listening to the proceedings of the inquest, while the other remained behind, on the same spot where Walter had first seen them both, and appeared to be keeping a look-out, in case they might be surprised.

Walter's curiosity and anxiety increased, and he was unable to come to any immediate decision as to the best way it would be for him to act to prevent one or both of them from eluding him. He, therefore, kept still more concealed in the seat, and he being now unable to see the man who had made his way to the Hall, he kept his eyes firmly fixed upon the other one who had remained behind.

The storm, so far from abating, increased every moment in violence, and the thunder rolled, and the lightning flashed terrifically, and by a vivid sheet of the heavenly fire, casting its broad glare right upon Wallingford Hall, he beheld the man standing in the same position he had at first taken, namely, by the window of the room in which the jury were assembled; and by the attitude in which it stood, there could be no doubt but that it was listening to the business which was going forward, and endeavouring to scrutinise the interior of the room, through the cracks in the window-shutters, through which the rays of the light from the candles might be distinguished.

His astonishment, however, was not a little augmented, when he discovered that they were women, but for the purpose of disguise, as he imagined, they had on long top coats, and their heads were surmounted by men's hats. He could also discover that they were Gipsies, and his heart throbbed with emotion, as Ela and Christabelle darted upon his memory, and he watched them still more earnestly, to see in what manner they proceeded.

He was not kept in this manner long, for the one who had been watching at the window, a short time afterwards, turned away, and walked back to her companion, who had never, in the least, altered her posture. They seemed to exchange two or three words, and then, much to his surprise, they walked towards the very place where he was concealed.

Walter now made ready to pounce upon them and seize them both, for it appeared to him that they were about to seek shelter from the rain beneath the thickly interwoven foliage of the chestnut tree; but in that supposition he was most strangely disappointed, for instead of coming directly along the path, they turned off suddenly, without taking any notice of him, and stopped immediately behind the tree.

And now was the propitious moment, Walter thought, to become acquainted with their designs, so he remained as silent as possible, hardly venturing to respire, for fear they should discover him, and thus frustrate his wishes. He listened, and was enabled to catch the following words, although not without considerable difficulty, for they were uttered cautiously, and in a very low tone—

"He is not among them," observed the one who had watched at the window, "I am certain he is not among them; for I had a clear view of the faces of all who were assembled, and if he had been there, I should have known him in a minute."

Walter listened anxiously for the answer to this, but he was disappointed, it was couched in language that was totally incomprehensible to him, and which was in common use with the Gipsy tribe at that period, as we believe it is now; but Walter could not help surmising, from a word or two which dropped here and there, that it was the belief of the other that the person about whom they expressed such curiosity, could not be any great distance from the spot, and she was not going so easily to give up her design, but would make another effort, which might, in all probability, be attended with better success.

"At any rate," said her who had spoken first, "it is nonsense to remain here; Rupert will be anxious to know.—Ah!—the conference has broken up, and see the jurymen and the others are all coming out."

It is not by any means a matter of astonishment that at such a moment as that Walter should be confused and bewildered, for not only did he feel a strong desire to inquire immediately into the verdict which the jury had returned, but also was he most anxious, after the trouble that he had taken, that the women should not escape him. He therefore lost for a moment his presence of mind, and stood hesitating in what manner he should proceed; but he was not long permitted to remain so, for the noise he had made in suddenly rising, had either apprised them of his being so near, or otherwise they were apprehensive that they should be discovered by some of the persons coming from the Hall, for looking along the gravel path, Walter beheld them running with the speed of lightning, and the darkness of the night rendering all chance of his overtaking them hopeless, he bent his steps towards the house, very well satisfied with the important information he had obtained of Rupert Darwin, the brother of the person accused of the murder, and who was not only supposed to be deeply implicated with him in it, but also to have been the person who had rescued the old man, being in the neighbourhood. Yes, Rupert was in the vicinity of Rosemary Dell, and might, consequently, yet be taken and brought to justice. When he had reached the Hall, he hurried into the room wherein the jury had been assembled, but was forced back by the number of persons who were at that moment emerging from it, he stepped back into the garden, and had scarcely done so when the Gipsy Mark, heavily fettered, and in the custody of the officers, passed out with a firm step, and Walter's horrible doubts and fears were in a moment set at rest, for he was convinced how the verdict had gone, and that justice had at length prevailed over the minds of those obstinate and ignorant men, who had dared to entertain a suspicion of his unfortunate father.

As the Gipsy passed the place where Walter stood, he made a sudden stop, and he fixed upon him such a demoniacal look that made him shudder, and then, with the same undaunted step, walked on without uttering a word.

In spite of the monstrous crime of which Mark was accused, and the happiness he felt that the decision of the jury had saved his father from a punishment worse than death, Walter (who had never been known to glut on the miseries of a fellow enemy) could not help for a moment looking upon the culprit with a sensation of pity; for it was a dreadful situation for any unhappy wretch to be placed in—to be accused of the monstrous crime of murder—to be incarcerated, perhaps, for many weeks in a dungeon—to undergo a painful trial, and then, probably, to suffer a horrible and ignominious death, the death of a dog! All these ideas passed rapidly in the mind of Walter, and after returning the prisoner's savage look with one of compassion, he entered the Hall, and pro-

ceeded towards his father's apartment, eager to inform him of the happy termination of the prolonged and tedious inquest. But his father had already been made acquainted with it by Dr. Hartley, who was in attendance upon him.

Mr. Wallingford received the information with perfect composure, which the worthy doctor was very happy to see, and Walter having been informed by him that all his father required was to be kept as still as possible, he left his chamber, and hastened to his beloved Maria, to mingle his expressions of delight and thankfulness with her.

CHAPTER XXXIV.

" Where art thou gone? We look around,
But where is she in whom such joy we found?
Alas ! 'tis universal sadness drear
In our once happy home;—thou art not there!"

WALTER found Maria kneeling by the couch of his mother, with her hands raised towards heaven, and her eyes streaming with tears of rapture and gratitude. Mrs. Wallingford was in a calm slumber, and her features, though pale, now wore an expression of perfect composure. Walter ventured to press his lips gently on her cheeks, and then, beaming a look of the utmost affection upon Maria, he expressed in glowing language his transport at the result of the inquest, and that his father was spared the misery and disgrace which would have been sure to have fallen upon him had they returned a different verdict.

Finding that Mrs. Wallingford did not seem likely to awake just yet from her refreshing sleep, and, although the events of the day and the state of incessant excitement he had been kept in, had wearied and exhausted him, not at all feeling inclined to seek his pillow, he whispered a few words of affection to his cousin, and smiling sweetly, with her consent, they walked to the window of the chamber, from which they had an extensive view all over the gardens, and seating themselves before it, they watched the bright career of the silvery lamp of heaven, which had now taken the place of the heavy clouds, and was imparting a mellow and beautiful tint to the green foliage of the shrubbery and the emerald carpet of the earth.

" How beautiful does the shrubbery look, Walter, now the tree tops are silvered by the moonbeams," remarked Maria, " but after the dreadful events that have lately been enacted there, I am afraid that I shall never have the courage to enter it again; and yet what joyous hours, what moments of innocent happiness, have we there passed together."

" And when those dark clouds that at present obscure our happiness have passed away, shall we not do so again, dearest Maria?" said

Walter, in a tone which showed at once to the blushing damsel that his heart, his sentiments were still more ardent than ever. The words, which Walter had uttered, in a moment aroused her to all the recollection of the past, and which the late melancholy circumstances had only temporarily banished from her mind. In vivid colours she took again a retrospective view of the past, of all the anguish she had endured, the insults to which she had been subjected ; the manner in which she had been treated by by Mr. Wallingford, and the resolution she had formed to escape from it. Notwithstanding what had taken place, her position was precisely as it was before ; she was still the poor, despised, and humble dependent on her uncle's bounty, who had been considered presumptuous in daring to aspire to the affections of the heir of Wallingford Hall, and was she not now acting in direct opposition to the commands of Mr. Wallingford, by allowing this indulgence to Walter? She felt her heart sink at these reflections, and she was about to upbraid herself for giving way to it, when she was suddenly aroused from her thoughts by an exclamation from Walter, and directing her gaze towards the spot whither he pointed, what was her astonishment to behold standing in the path, and looking up towards the window, the figure of the hideous hag, who had several times appeared to them, and whose prognostications were always so fatally verified. The light of the moon beamed full upon her frightful face, so that her features were plainly discernible, and Maria was positive that it was the same. She uttered an ejaculation of terror, and clung to Walter.

"Be not alarmed, my dear Maria," said her cousin, " this is doubtless an accomplice of the Gipsies, and her apprehension may lead to such discoveries as may forward the ends of justice ; she must not be allowed to escape. Stay here, where no harm can come to you, and I will soon return."

"Oh, no, for heaven's sake, Walter, do not venture ; you know not whom she may have at hand, and should you—"

But Walter had hurried from the chamber before his cousin could finish her supplication, and meeting with a servant in the hall, bade him accompany him.

On emerging from the house, he beheld the woman still standing in the path, at only a few paces from him, and she did not appear to have altered her position in the least, but seemed to be awaiting his approach.

"Seize her! away with her!" Walter exclaimed, as he darted forward, followed by the domestics ; but quick as thought the woman bounded from the spot, uttering a wild derisive laugh, and defying the utmost speed of Walter and the others in pursuit, was soon out of sight. Walter felt that it would not be prudent to follow her in the shrubbery ; so, vexed and dis-

appointed, that the mysterious woman had escaped him, he returned to the chamber of his mother.

Here a circumstance had occurred during his absence, which for a while completely banished all other thoughts from his mind. He found Maria at the bedside of the invalid, who had awakened. As soon as he entered the room, she recognised and called upon the name of her son. With extatic delight, Walter flew towards her, and taking her thin fingers in his, he bent with the fondest affection over her.

" My son, my dear, dear Walter," she ejaculated, in a voice which breathed all the tenderness of an affectionate mother, " I do again behold you, then ; but your father ! oh, why does he not come to me, now that I feel I am dying—yes, dying ?"

"Oh, my adored mother, my ever fond parent, do not rack me with such a dreadful thought," cried the distracted Walter ; " you will be better, I know you will be better : do you not feel——"

"Happy, my son, very happy," added Mrs. Wallingford, with calm resignation ; " and I shall soon be much happier, when I slumber beneath the cold turf. Such strange visions have haunted my imagination, but they are past now, and I am contented and at rest."

"But you will recover, dear mother," said the anxious Walter, as he marked with almost uncontrollable agitation, the heaving of her chest, and the difficulty with which she seemed to breathe, and which gave such a positive contradiction to the wishes he had breathed. " You will be happy, I know you will."

" I am happy, my poor dear boy," murmured his mother, " very, very happy, but I shall be happier still before long. Ah, my dearest Maria, pr'ythee raise me up—you are too kind, my poor girl, too kind—there, I am better now. Oh, Maria, what a debt do I owe you, for your attention. But my husband—your father, Walter—say, what does his absence mean? Does he refuse to visit me ; shall I not be permitted to behold him once more ?"

Unable to return any answer, with his heart bursting with anguish, Walter hurried from the apartment, and as he did so, Mrs. Wallingford, who had been raised in the arms of her affectionate niece, reclined her head on her shoulder, and murmured—

" What a while have I been bad, dear Maria, and you have been in attendance upon me all that time ? Oh, you must have suffered much from fatigue."

"Oh, no, no," replied the agitated girl, " I have not suffered any fatigue ; and what could I not have endured, sustained by the hope to see my beloved aunt restored to health !"

Mrs. Wallingford pressed her hand, and looked up into her face with an expression that sunk deep into her heart ; she then passed her hand across her forehead, as though she was endeavouring to recall something to her memory, and said—

"But it was all a troubled dream! I cannot recollect—my memory still wanders; and I have been trying to think, but in vain, in what way I was taken ill, and how long I have remained so. Let me reflect——"

"Nay, my dearest aunt," answered Maria, "let me beg of you not to distress and harass your mind by thinking anything about it. We shall soon be restored to happiness again; you will be——"

"Ah!" ejaculated the sufferer suddenly, "I have it now—yes, yes, it darts across my brain! 'Twas Ela! Did she not tell me that my child—my darling was not dead? Yes, she did; she said my Christabelle did not perish in the flames, and——"

—"For the sake of those who love you, my dear aunt," ejaculated the weeping Maria, "I implore you to compose yourself. Ela did not tell you false. Christabelle *does* live; I have beheld her, and so will you, if you will only struggle against this violent agitation, not only for the poor girl's sake, but for all of us."

Maria had acted upon the impulse of the moment, thinking this information might be the means of raising the mind of the sufferer from that state of melancholy which in her fast sinking state was so alarming; but little was she prepared for the effect it had upon her. With a strength which seemed absolutely impossible, reduced by long suffering as she was, she started up in the bed, and looking piercingly into the face of her alarmed niece, she exclaimed—

"Tell me, Maria—do not attempt to deceive me! Repeat those words! You have beheld her—did you not say so? But when—in what way, and how did you meet? But as—no—it is not true;—my mind is not yet clear. Ah! but should my Christabelle indeed survive! Survive! 'tis madness to think of it, for if she did, who should keep her from the arms of her mother? Who would be monster enough to keep her from the dying embrace and blessing of her who brought her into the world? No, no! It is all a cruel fabrication. I shall never on earth again behold my daughter, though in heaven our souls will once more be shortly united."

The distracted Maria was completely paralyzed at the effect her words had caused, and gazing vacantly upon the ghastly features of her aunt, was unable to utter a syllable. She was also afraid to utter another sentence, lest by so doing she should only increase the suffering she had already so innocently occasioned. While she still remained in this state of agitation, the door opened, and Mr. Wallingford, looking like the tenant of a tomb, supported by his son, and attended by Dr. Hartley, entered the chamber. The sight of her husband had a strange and powerful effect upon the unfortunate invalid, and holding out her arms to embrace him, in a voice that showed too plainly that her words were fated shortly to be realized—

"My husband, my Edward," she said, "I am going to eternity."

The next instant the agitated husband was locked in the arms of his expiring wife, and weeping scalding tears of agony upon her cheek, he implored her, in a voice broken with the intensity of his emotion, not to despair, but to pray to Heaven to spare her, for his sake, for the sake of Walter, for Maria, for all that she loved, by whom she was so fondly beloved.

"Edward," she answered, earnestly, and fixing her eyes with expiring affection upon his countenance, "it is the will of Heaven that I should be taken from you, I feel that it is, and, therefore, why should I wish to encourage a hope which must be too soon blighted? But I have no wish to remain longer in this painful world—painful indeed it has been to me; the grave is now my only goal of happiness. Pay attention, Edward, to what I am about to say to you. No sooner did I hear the history of the unfortunate Ela, than I felt as though I was an intruder upon those affections which another had a previous claim to, and which I seemed to feel was cruel and unjust in me to usurp from her. Those affections I had before fondly considered were enjoyed by me alone, and when the veil was torn from my eyes, my heart became like a barren desert, where nought more could spring to give me happiness and enjoyment. Hark you, Edward, an instinctive voice seemed to whisper in my ear that I had no longer any business in the world, since I was merely an intruder upon the rights of that woman, who had a prior claim upon your heart. I felt something like a degraded being, as I reflected that I was taking the place of one who, in the sight of Heaven, should be your wife, and who, by everything sacred, was entitled to that name. Think you, Edward, that I could calmly endure these racking thoughts? No, they haunted my disordered imagination sleeping or waking. There was no rest for me. Ela—the wretched, the deeply injured Ela—was constantly before my eyes, and her voice breathing curses upon me, for usurping those rights which belonged to her, constantly rung in my ears. Ah! I know what you would say. You would upbraid me for taking such a view of the subject; you would tell me that I did myself an injustice by coming to such a harsh conclusion; that what had taken place was no fault of mine, and that before the painful facts had come to my knowledge it was out of my power to remedy what had taken place. But alas! that cannot be reconciled with my ideas. Ela was a wretched, wandering outcast, while I——"

"For the love of God!" interrupted Wallingford. "For the love of God, my only love, my Amelia, oh, do not pursue such a subject at a moment like this. Why—oh why—should they so deeply occupy your thoughts?"

"Because," replied Mrs. Wallingford, "I cannot longer indulge the delusion which before veiled the unhappy truth from my reason. For your sake (for to see you suffer was worse than all the torment I could myself endure), I have, when you have been present, stifled my real feelings, and endeavoured to persuade

WALTER AND MARIA DISCERN UNWELCOME VISITORS IN THE SHRUBBERY.

myself that I formed a wrong conception of the subject. I sought to conceal from you how poignantly I felt the truth, that there was another being to whom you had first plighted your vows, and who had a just claim upon those affections I wholly monopolized; af- fections which she flattered herself—fondly flattered herself—and which you positively declared she was the mistress of, long, long before those vows you had pledged to me. But my struggles were in vain; my lacerated heart convinced me how deeply the words of

Ela had sunk into it. I had drained the poisoned chalice to the dregs, and my happiness was gone for ever. But it is at an end now, Edward, it is at an end—I am dying."

Quite overpowered with the exertion she had undergone, the poor suffering invalid fell back on her pillow, and her husband, almost choked with the poignancy of his feelings, covered his face with his handkerchief, and sobbed like a child.

After a moment or two occupied in this melancholy manner, Mrs. Wallingford once more opened her lips, and gave utterance to the following words:—

"But I have much more to say, and my time is short; oh, let me not lose a moment, before my soul takes its external flight:—my son, Walter, my dear boy, come hither—your hand—my eyes grow dim; death is approaching me with rapid strides."

"Dearest mother, I am by your side; it is my arm which now encircles your neck," answered Walter, who had flown to her support, while his cousin was completely absorbed in the most overwhelming grief, with her head buried in the pillow.

"Oh! this is my own Maria, is it not?" said the poor dying soul, as she pressed her damp hand over the head of the weeping girl, who with a burst of anguish which she found it impossible to restrain, replied—

"Beloved aunt, it is indeed your poor girl."

"Oh, this, this affords me real happiness," said she; "this is what my fondest wishes have longed to see; Heaven smiles upon the sight and approves of it; Maria—Walter—I have had frightful visions—they told me that you were torn from each other—and I believed it too: but, thank God, it was only a delusion. Walter, promise me, solemnly swear that you will be a kind, an affectionate protector to Maria, while you have life; set my mind at rest upon that point, and——"

"Dearest mother," exclaimed the agonised youth, "you know my heart;—I do indeed pray that if I do not obey your wishes, the wrath of Heaven may descend upon my head."

"Nearer, my son, nearer,—nearer still," said Mrs. Wallingford, stretching forth her arms, "let me look into your beloved face, let me trace those lineaments for the last time. Ah! darkness is closing around me; Edward,—my son; Maria—I cannot see you. Wallingford, endeavour to make reparation to Ela for the injuries you have inflicted on her, and shield her from——"

An expression of anguish from some person, who was concealed by the bed curtains, at that instant vibrated on the ears of those present in the death chamber, and ere they had any of them time to give expression to their astonishment, Ela appeared at the foot of the bed, and darting towards the side of Mrs.

Wallingford, she sunk on her knees, pressed the hand of the poor dying sufferer to her lips, and in a paroxysm of grief, she exclaimed—

"Dear lady, the unbounded gratitude of the wretched Ela, be yours; but your intreaties are now too late, nothing can repair the injuries she has received. It is not the innocent, noble minded, generous, and affectionate Ela Beranzic that stands before you, that Edward Walling-ford once knew—no, no, no, look on this miserable form; this careworn visage; this troubled breast, which has long been a stranger to the softer passions; and ask yourself if you can trace in the picture the image of that fair and timid maiden, who captivated the proud master of Wallingford Hall! Oh, no, she lives but in recollection! But say, lady, can you, will you pardon me, for the many troubles and afflictions which I have occasioned you; convince me, in this solemn hour; for the Almighty ruler of all events knows how severely have my prayers and imprecations been visited upon myself. Give me but this assurance, and Ela will be more content. Oh, that I was placed in the situation that you are now in, what a blessing it would be to me; that with the serenity and resignation of a christian, I might meet my end, my dying couch surrounded by ———. But I dare not mention the word, there is not a being in the world to whom the fate of Ela possesses any interest, or who would shed one tear over the green sod that will cover her mouldering remains; the sigh of regret will never be given to the despised, the degraded outcast's memory.'

The dying lady raised her eyes towards Ela, and tried several times to speak, but it could be seen clear enough from the expression of her countenance that she had heard and compre-hended all that Ela had uttered. Doctor Hartley tried once or twice to prevent Ela proceeding with her observations, and to expostulate with her upon the imprudence of her entering the chamber in such a moment as the present; but Mrs. Wallingford, who seemed to understand what he wished to say, waved her hand disapprovingly, and tried also to raise herself in the bed; so the good doctor forbore to persevere in his well meaning intentions.

It was a moment of intense, of solemn anguish, such as those only who have been in the death chamber of a dear relation can form any idea of. It was so silent that the slightest motion in the chamber might have been heard. The dying lady bent her head slightly forward, and put forth her hands, and they were eagerly clasped by the distracted Wallingford and Ela. Every eye was fixed upon her with harrowing agony. They saw her lips move; but the sentences they uttered were unintelligible. She pressed the hands of her husband and Ela together, and raising her eyes towards Heaven, was evidently breathing a dying prayer for their future happiness. Calm and peaceful was the expression of her features—death, though near at hand, was disarmed of its terrors—it was the dying moments of one to whom sin had been unknown, and who could look forward to eternity with confidence.

Another moment, and the clammy hands relaxed their hold—the eyes became glazed with the film of death—the lips no longer moved, but a heavenly smile was upon her countenance. The next moment her head fell on the shoulder of her son, and the spirit of Mrs. Wallingford had departed to its native heaven.

We will pass over the scene which followed; we feel how inadequate we are to the task of describing it. It was not 'till some time after this melancholy event, that any inquiries were thought of being made as to how Ela had gained access to the chamber of the deceased lady, at such a painful moment, when Walter interrogated the servants closely about it; but the information he received was anything but satisfactorily; no one could tell him more than that Ela, having come to the Hall, demanded most earnestly to see Walter on immediate business; and notwithstanding she was informed of the situation of Mrs. Wallingford, and that therefore it was impossible she could have the interview she requested, she was so determined, that they had the greatest difficulty in the world to persuade her to leave the Hall until her wishes had been complied with.

There was scarcely, however, a word of truth in this statements, for the servants were fearful to explain the circumstance to Walter as it had happened, thinking that they should meet with a severe reprimand; the fact being, that they were so alarmed by the appearance of Ela, whom they had set down as a fiend in human shape, at least, that so far from offering any opposition to her wishes, immediately that she had demanded an interview with Walter, they had scampered away as if the devil had been at their heels, and thus she was enabled to gain access to the chamber of death, and concealing herself behind the curtains at the foot of the bed, overheard nearly all that passed, and which had been described.

"And what has now become of her?" inquired Walter, when he had listened with what patience he could muster, to the account the men had given.

"I really cannot tell, sir," replied the man to whom the question was put; "though I do think it is not unlikely that she has hastened to the summer-house, to the corpse of her unfortunate daughter; at any rate she so frightened Job Reuben and his wife, that they would not have stayed another moment in the place if they had even been rewarded by the whole kingdom. Ah! dear me, sir, what a sad day it was for us all when she first made her appearance in this place, for she never

shows her face but we are sure to be visited by some calamity or the other."

"And think you she is in the same place now, James?" inquired Walter.

"Why, sir, I think it's very likely, seeing ss she has not shown herself to any person since," answered James—"that is to say, since she left the Hall here a short time ago."

"It is very early, is it not, James?"

"Yes, sir—it is nearly break of day," replied the man.

"Come, or send for me, if my father should ask for me, James," said Walter; "I shall be in the shrubbery."

"Bless my soul, Mr. Walter, surely you will never run such a risk as to enter that dreary place (which is not only haunted by ghosts, but by human devils as well) at such an hour in the morning as this?"

"Psha!" said Walter, impatiently, "what is there to apprehend? There, don't frighten yourself, man; and, upon second thought, do not inform any person where I am gone. Come, come, James, what a coward you are to frighten yourself in this manner, after telling me that it is your belief that the unfortunate woman is sitting alone by the remains of her murdered daughter, and yet you are fearful that I should go thither by myself."

"Oh, as for her, Mr. Walter," returned James, " she has nothing to fear from any one wherever she goes, for folks are too much afraid of her; for my own part, I wouldn't walk in her way for all the gold in the nation, for her very look is sufficient to frighten any person into fits, and that's the truth of it."

Walter could not help breathing a sigh as James thus spoke, for it recalled to his imagination the image of Ela when in all the charms of youth and innocence, such as she must have been to captivate his father's heart. What a pang he felt when he reflected upon the wreck, the deceit and perfidy of his father had made. That woman, who was at one time the theme of admiration of both sexes, was now looked upon with abhorrence and horror by those menials whom she was evidently born to command.

Walter, therefore, gently corrected James, and informed him that he entertained a wrong opinion of Ela's character; and then, without waiting to receive any answer, he walked from the Hall towards the shrubbery.

When he arrived at the summer-house, he perceived a faint light twinkling from amidst the honeysuckle that covered the window, and he was thus enabled to view, but indistinctly, the objects that were inside, and was certain that Ela or some other individual was there, and keeping watch over the corpse. He was, therefore, not inclined to interrupt them, whoever they might be, by making his appearance too suddenly. He knocked gently at the door.

No answer was however returned, and all was silent as the grave. Walter felt a strange awe stealing over him, but nothing daunted, he gently turned back the lock, and walked into the place. The light beamed so faintly on the surrounding objects that when he first entered the summer-house he could not perceive anything, but, after a second or so, he found that his conjectures had been right, for a female form was reposing beside the murdered remains of the unfortunate Fanny, and certain was he that a mother only would have chosen that for a resting place.

A second glance convinced him that it was Ela, and advancing towards her, Walter found that she slept calmly and soundly, indeed, so soundly that, finding she was not likely to awaken, a sensation of horror smote his heart, and chilled his blood, as the thought darted across his brain that perhaps she was no more, that death had again been at work, and that her soul had rejoined that of her murdered daughter in eternity. Another idea, more alarming than the other, occurred to him, which was that, notwithstanding the firmness which the wretched woman had evinced, she had been so afflicted by the violence of her grief that she had, in a moment of insanity, deprived herself of existence.

He trembled with terror at the idea and the probability of it, and in a moment he snatched up the lamp, and held it above his head over the place where Ela was laid, upon whose countenance its light flashed, and he discovered with much gratification that she was asleep. The light for a moment disturbed her repose, and she partially unclosed her eyes, but without looking at anything, she turned on her side nearer towards the corpse of her daughter, and once more closed her eyes, and became insensible to everything around her, or that any person was in the room.

Walter paused and gazed upon her with the most intense interest for a few seconds, and then murmured,—

"Alas, unfortunate woman! this calm, this unconsciousness is a blessing to you; from such a forgetfulness of your miseries how cruel would it be to awaken you."

As he thus spoke, Walter walked gently across the room, and after replacing the lamp in the recess, where it had before stood, he walked forth in the gardens until she might awaken, when he thought he would return, and learn from her the particulars of what had befallen her after she had left the hall, in search of the elder Mark Darwin.

A rich perfume scented the morning air, fresh from the bosoms of the opening flowers, and the mists of early morning were slowly dispersing from the summits of the trees.

Walter walked towards the lake, and gazed across it, and as he did so, all the dreadful occurrences of the last few days darted with redoubled force upon his memory. After he had occupied himself in this manner for nearly half an hour, he returned to the summer-house, and listening at the door, he was convinced that Ela had awoke, and was pacing the apartment. He gently raised the latch, and walked in. Ela started on his entrance, and fixed upon him a look which almost led him to imagine that she considered his appearance at that time an intrusion.

"I beg pardon," observed Walter, "perhaps I have disturbed you; I observed that you slept when I first came here, and therefore walked into the garden for awhile, and——"

"Do you not marvel," interrupted Ela, "do you not marvel that sleep should fall upon my eyelids, and in such a place as this; where lie the cold remains of my poor girl?—But it is no matter of surprise; exhausted nature must have rest, and here, at any rate, I knew that I might seek it without fear of interruption. Perhaps you will ask me how I can repose, when such tormenting thoughts rack and harass my mind. I will tell you—this is the precious opiate which never fails to give me transitory forgetfulness. I do not, however, apply to it, unless it is absolutely necessary, for it causes me much suffering afterwards. Last night the quantity I took was more than usual, and but two or three more drops, and the wretched Ela would have slept for ever."

As Ela spoke, she took a small phial from her bosom, and held it up before Walter's eyes, who shook his head, and remonstrated with her on the danger of using such a remedy. He could plainly perceive that the opiate had had a most powerful effect upon her, and that her frame was weak and troubled.

"You talk to me, young man," said Ela, "as though life was dear to me; as though my earthly career was full of happiness, my path strewn with roses;—what need have I to care whether—but no matter; I will quit this subject; I have something to tell you of more importance. I came hither for that purpose, for, notwithstanding, my heart yearned to be once more with this lifeless form; I should not have come here yet, had it not been with the design I have informed you of."

The opiate seemed to have taken effect upon her memory, for she paused for several minutes, and passing her hand across her temples, seemed to be endeavouring to bring the circumstance she wished to impart to her recollection. Walter waited for her to speak with much impatience, and at length said—

"Have you been successful?—Have you made any discovery?"

"I have," returned Ela, "and this it is, that Esther, or Christabelle, has slipped through the fingers of the wretches who had the charge of her; that they have rejoined their companions, and that they are all in a terrible state of apprehension, thinking that she will be able to elude their vigilance, and most likely be present at the trial of Mark Darwin and his infamous sons,"

" God send that it may be so !" exclaimed Walter, earnestly ; " but," continued he, after a pause, " may you not be mistaken ?—Is it not probable that this may be only a stratagem of the Gipsies, and that they have taken care to remove her, fearful that should she——"

" To be sure, her evidence could not fail to convict them, and that they know," said Ela ; " but I am convinced that what I have informed you of is correct. I have taken especial care to ascertain the truth. I have secreted myself in their haunts, concealed among the long grass, and listened to their conversation. Last night only, for more than one hour did I thus conceal myself, when I overheard them amongst themselves relate the whole circumstance, and utter the heaviest maledictions against her, and swear that they would either frustrate her designs or perish in the attempt. Had it not been that my attention was called to others, who I heard were to go to the assistance of old Darwin, who was in the vicinity, if it were required, which made it necessary for me to watch them narrowly, I might in all probability have gained more information. But the persons were led astray, and took a different path to that which the villain Mark had gone, and when I found that he was too far from them for me to entertain any fears that they could go to his rescue, I made the best of my way back here again."

Walter here informed Ela of the two females he had seen lurking in the grounds, and watching at the window of the apartment in which the jury were sitting.

" Ah! that corresponds with what I have told you," said Ela ; " those women were Morna and her daughter, and they were trying to ascertain whether or not old Mark were present. They knew very little about the proceedings, and they imagined, at least, so it had been reported to the women, that the old fiend was still in custody, and that after the deliberation of the jury, he would immediately be acquitted, or else sent to the county prison. They therefore set off to the village, where they supposed Mark was in the custody of the constable ; and when they had gone, immediately after, in fact, I, who was watching close upon the spot, saw the prisoner, young Mark, brought out, fettered as the wretch ought to be, and saw him borne away in a cart, in another direction to the one they had taken."

" But I heard them mention the name of Rupert," remarked Walter.

" Very likely, for he was with the party."

" And could you not have given the villain into custody ?" inquired Walter.

" I could, but deemed it not prudent," answered Ela ; " but when it is, I can in a moment give him into the hands of justice, for, encouraged by his fancied security, and not dreaming that he will be charged as an accomplice in the murder, he takes but little precaution. I cannot swear that he was an accessory ; but if he were, it would be a bad policy to apprehend him at present. But it is his father I would secure, the old hell-hound ! Could I but see that monster fettered as his son, and without any chance of escape from the hands of the executioner, I should be content, but never till then can I know rest ; my heart yearns to gloat upon the miscreant's misery."

" All this is useless, and only a loss of time, which had much better be devoted to the furtherance of our designs," remarked Walter, who was shocked at the continued violence of her manner, and the savage spirit of revenge she seemed to entertain. " I need much your advice ; in the first place, what had we best do towards finding the place where Christabelle is concealed ?"

Ela returned no answer to the question of Walter for a few seconds, and leaning her head on her hand, seemed in deep cogitation, during which time Walter watched her countenance with much interest and anxiety. At last she raised her head, and after looking him steadfastly in the face, she said—

" The particulars of her flight I am at present unacquainted with ; but when her escape was discovered by those who had the charge of her, as I learned, they took to flight immediately, no doubt fearful that she would cause their apprehension if they stayed. I was unable also to ascertain in what neighbourhood it took place, but I elicited sufficient to convince me it was a great distance from home. I shall resume my inquiries this evening, and very probably I shall at the same time be able to learn where the old villain Mark is hidden. But it is daylight, and yet do I loiter here. I must away, for if they should discover that I am here, all my plans would be rendered abortive. At present I have contrived to deceive them, by leading them to suppose I had taken another course, and that I am at present a great distance from this place. After I had quitted you, I did not sneak about in the hedges, or hunt my prey in secret ; no, I put a bold face upon the matter, (for fear has become a stranger to the breast of Ela), and went to one of those places where I knew some of the gang would be almost certain to resort, and there I saw several of them, but none of them that I sought. I have before informed you that I have many friends in the tribe, but my foes by far outnumber them ; there are two or three hypocrites, who appear kind and friendly to my face, but whose serpent hearts I am thoroughly acquainted with, and keep a watchful and cautious eye upon them. It was one of those wretches who tried to lead me astray with regard to the road which the elder Mark had taken; but ere I could fall into the snare, I remarked the expression of the eyes of another, whose sincerity I could place confidence in, and it was enough. However, I did not let the one who had attempted to deceive me know that I was convinced of her hypocrisy; no, I pretended to seize upon the information with avidity, and the fools are no doubt now rejoicing at the manner in which they fancy I have been misled, and imagine that I am far away from this neighbourhood on the wrong scent."

"And in what direction do you purpose now bending your way?" inquired Walter. I cannot help thinking it is complete folly for you to think of leaving this place, where you certainly must be as safe, if not more so, than anywhere else."

Ela looked around her for a minute or two, and she seemed to reproach him for his observations, for she shook her head.

"Nay," observed Walter, "do not mistake my meaning; I do not, certainly, expect that you could stop in this dreary place, but that you should remain in the house, where your safety and comfort could be properly looked after."

Ela gave a melancholy smile, and shaking her head, said—

"It may not be, young man, you know not what you say; think you the wretched outcast Ela is a fit guest for the noble Halls of Edward Wallingford?—Think you I could cross the threshold of that house, where, by the cold remains of that unfortunate woman, whom I—but did she not offer up a prayer for me? For me, the despised wanderer; with her dying breath did she not implore of Heaven for mercy for me?—Yes, she did, and she was good and virtuous. and surely her voice would reach the footstool of the Most High. Alas!—headstrong fool that I was, not to have paid attention to her gentle voice, when she would have taken my hapless child under her fostering care. I should not be gazing upon her ghastly corpse. What better am I than an assassin, for had it not have been for my obstinacy, would not the life of my unfortunate Fanny have been saved? —Yes, she might even now have been living in all the bloom of youth and jocund health, to heap blessings upon the head of her now forlorn and wretched mother, who, although she could never have claimed her, would not have been deprived of the felicity of sometimes beholding her, and clasping her to her bosom. But enough of this; reflection comes too late, and I must forget that ever I entertained such sentiments. I must become indifferent to everything, but that for which I now only wish to live, revenge upon the murderers of my poor girl."

"I would that you would endeavour to divest yourself of those revolting feelings," remarked Walter; "they are alike disgraceful to your good sense and to your sex. Besides, think you that the violent death of those whom you suspect have injured you——"

"Suspect have injured me!" reiterated Ela, fiercely; "but it is useless to talk to you, if you think so lightly of the injuries Ela has sustained from these monsters."

"I do not doubt that they have persecuted you severely," returned Walter; "and for the sake of justice we should use our utmost exertions to bring them to punishment, if they be found guilty of the crimes which are laid to their charge. Society, in fact, demands it."

"Society;" repeated Ela, contemptuously —"I hate the very name—it is mockery to mention it to one who has nothing to do with it, and who has been hunted from it like some wild beast, and from which she has never received aught but contumely and cruelty. Walter Wallingford, you see me as I now am—the wretched, outcast, wandering, bereaved Ela— such have I been for years; and during the whole of that time, the only act of philanthropy and Christian kindness that I have received from any one was bestowed by your mother— her whose soul was far too pure for this world. 'Tis true I have received ample payment for prognosticating titles and wealth to a set of locusts, who disgraced the air they breathed; and I have also received goodly sums for promising to prevent the occurrence of those calamities which their own weak minds foreboded, but I never received one act of pure benevolence from anybody but your mother in my life; on the contrary, I have received nothing but the most degrading insults and cruelty."

"Ah! I can perfectly well imagine what your sufferings have been, and how unfortunate you have been," said Walter, endeavouring to soothe her from her violence; "but let me entreat that you will endeavour to change the current of your thoughts. The dullness of this place serves to disturb your mind, and if you were to——"

"Psha!" interrupted Ela, "this is absurd. What difference can change of scene make upon my mind? None!—Think you that anything can erase this dreadful sight from my thoughts? No!—let me be where I may, it will ever remain present to my mind's eye; and, therefore, what difference can it make to me, to contemplate it in reality? Hark you!—even while wandering amid the fertile fields and green woods, I was blind to the beauties of nature, and saw nothing since I quitted you but the ghastly, mangled corpse of my poor girl. I thank you, Walter Wallingford, for your kindness, but I will not leave this place."

Finding that her mind was fully made up, Walter did not attempt any further to persuade her ; but one thought occurred to him, which was, that the body of the unfortunate Fanny had better be interred with all possible expedition, so that Ela might have the opportunity of following her ill-fated daughter to her final resting place, and of satisfying herself that nothing was neglected in the melancholy ceremony which she could have desired. And besides, it would be the means of doing away with the excitement which at present prevailed, and would be likely to prevail as long as the corpse remained upon the building; consequently, Walter, after having weighed this in his mind, in the brief space of time that was allotted to him, he mentioned the same to Ela, at the same time assuring her that every preliminary for that melancholy ceremony was arranged, and leaving it entirely to her decision.

Ela made no answer for a few moments, but, resting her head on her hand, she seemed lost in thought ; at length, as a sudden idea seemed to strike her, she turned to Walter, and said—

" I have determined. This evening the dismal rites shall be performed."

" This evening !" said Walter—" is it not a strange time to select ?"

" No," replied Ela ; " when it is dark I should not be so likely to be known—besides, so dark a deed should be ended in darkness."

She fixed her eyes upon the corpse as she spoke, and her bosom heaved with emotion. At length, clenching her hand, she added, as she raised it in the air—

" This concluded, Mark Darwin, your fate shall soon be sealed."

" For awhile, then," observed Walter, who could not bear to listen to the violent expression of her revengeful feelings, " for awhile I must leave you. I know not whether or not I shall be able to see you again before the time you may fix for the melancholy ceremony to take place, but you have only to give your orders to the person whom I shall depute to attend upon you, and I will take care that they are punctually obeyed."

" There is nothing I require," said Ela, resuming something of her former disdainful air and tone ; " nothing more than that the corpse of my poor girl may be deposited in its last cold home with becoming decency and respect, with a respectability, mind you, that the station she was born to fill commands."

" You may depend upon it that all you can desire shall be complied with," answered Walter, who felt, however, somewhat piqued at the haughtiness of Ela's manner. " I will take especial care that nothing shall be omitted, consistent with propriety, and becoming the character of the unfortunate deceased. I will myself attend the funeral, and, therefore, I trust you will rely——"

" Attend the ceremony ! what you—you !" interrupted Ela, in a tone of evident surprise

and delight. Her bosom heaved ; her whole frame became violently agitated—she tried to speak, but for a few moments utterance was denied her, until at length, bursting into a passionate flood of tears, she grasped the hand of Walter eagerly, and pressing her lips fervently upon it, she exclaimed, in a voice broken by sobs—

" Oh ! Walter Wallingford, what shall I say how shall I plead for your forgiveness for the' manifold injuries I have done you and your family ? Pardon me, I beg of you—but how can I make reparation ? Here," she continued, as she took a roll of paper from the recess where the lamp had stood, and presented it to Walter ; " take this ; it is a faithful narrative of Ela's early history, from which you will perceive that she might have been honoured, revered, admired; that her dereliction from the paths of virtue was not her fault, but that of—No matter, enough has been said upon that subject ; take the manuscript and peruse it carefully ; the remainder of my story you are too well acquainted with, for I feel that the sequel to it is fast, fast approaching."

Walter looked in Ela's countenance with the deepest interest, as he took the manuscript from her hand ; but he did not return her any immediate answer. He was deeply affected by the tone and purport of her speech, and in the state in which his mind already was, from excitement caused by other painful circumstances, rendered him incapable of enduring more for the present; he, therefore, repeated his promise to attend her at the time she had fixed on, and then, avoiding all further conversation, he hurried from the summer-house, and bent his steps to the Hall, where he gave orders to the female domestics to supply Ela with such nourishments as she might require, and to be sure not to neglect to perform anything which she might wish, and which might seem necessary to her comfort.

When he had completed this part of the business, he retired to his chamber, to try to seek that rest which he so much needed, with the consolation of having performed all that he could think of, and that was in his power to alleviate the afflictions of others, notwithstanding he was himself almost borne down with the weight of sorrows which the Almighty had been pleased to heap upon the head of him and his unhappy father.

Heavy, indeed, was the blow inflicted by the death of his beloved wife, upon Mr. Wallingford ; doubly so, shaken and impaired as his spirits had previously been. Yet did he, in spite of his intense inward sufferings, keep them as much as possible concealed from the observation of others, and outwardly bore all the semblance of fortitude and resignation.

" She was too good for me," he remarked to the worthy doctor, as they retired from the chamber in which the remains of his wife lay. Alas! I was every way unworthy of her; and, therefore, I ought not to repine now that she is taken to her native Heaven."

This was the very state to which Dr. Hartley wished to confine the feelings of Mr. Wallingford, and he therefore expressed a reciprocal sentiment upon the melancholy subject, although in his heart he could not help deeming it one of the heaviest afflictions that could have happened; for no one knew better the worth of Mrs. Wallingford, or esteemed her more than did Mr. Hartley; in short, she was revered by all who knew her, and to the poor especially, her demise would prove an irreparable loss.

CHAPTER XXXV.

"Fiends! monsters! cannot e'en the grave
Protect the dead from your insatiate fury!"
                                    ANON.

WE must now return to the unhappy Maria, whose sufferings under this awful calamity, was, perhaps, even more poignant than that of Walter and Mr. Wallingford;—at any rate, she was unable to support the bereavement with that resignation which they did, and it was many hours before the vehemence of her grief abated. And it must be admitted, that she, poor girl, had quite sufficient cause for sorrow; for had she not, in Mrs. Wallingford, lost her kindest friend, and, she might say, her only protector; the only one to whom she could unbosom her thoughts; the guardian of her childhood; and the preceptor, adviser, and companion of her after years?—And whom was she now left dependent upon?—why, upon that man, who, by his conduct towards her, had entirely destroyed all that esteem and confidence she had formerly bestowed upon him; whose tyrannical pride would so lately have sacrificed her to a man, whom to know was but to hate, whom she viewed with the most unmitigated abhorrence, and whom, she was convinced, was viewed with contempt by Mr. Wallingford himself.

Had not Maria of late been so closely confined to the chamber of her aunt, and likewise had she not have possessed the utmost aversion to listen to the idle tittle tattle of the servants, she must have become acquainted with what had taken place so recently, between Mr. Barnell and Mr. Wallingford, by which all further idea of the proposed suit was entirely broken off; and thus, upon that point, her mind would have been partially set at rest.

Independent of the causes of grief which we have mentioned, she felt the utmost apprehension that, before many weeks had elapsed, Mr. Barnell might again urge his odious passion, and Mr. Wallingford become the over-bearing intercessor of his suit, than which, the contemplation of any other affliction was comparatively insignificant. But suddenly another idea presented itself to the damsels imagination which was too much in accordance with her own generous nature for her easily to reject.

"But very likely, now my poor dear aunt is no more, it may soften his feelings towards me; he may become more kind, more considerate, and view me with that commiseration, which surely one so every way forlorn and friendless deserves. Or, perhaps, he may think it too much trouble to interfere at all, and—" a deadly chill rushed through her veins at the thought which suggested itself to her mind—"deem me an intruder here;—no matter," she added, while a blush of pride mantled to her cheeks; "if he should think so, I well know the course to adopt; my plans have been before laid out, and I shall have no other alternative left than to put them into execution; and I shall have no reason to regret having separated from not one person, who will breathe a sigh for my departure."

But scarcely had this idea entered into Maria's mind, than the image of Walter started before her mental vision, and seemed to reproach her for her unkindness. Yes, yes, she felt that she had done him an injustice, whose mind would be racked to distraction, should she be compelled to do as she contemplated; yet was she not forbidden to confide in one whom she was taught to believe she was unworthy of?

"Alas!" she soliloquized, "I am but too well acquainted with what the heart of Walter and my own disposition might prompt to; before his mother's death, the fear of adding to the sufferings of her whom he so fondly loved, made him more submissive to the haughty will of his father; but now that he has no such motive to restrain him, I know full well, were I to confide to him the idea I have formed, what he would urge; and could I refuse him?—Oh, no, I feel that my weakness would not allow me to refuse him!"

She was interrupted in the midst of these reflections by the entrance of a domestic, who had been sent to her by Walter, to inquire whether she felt sufficiently convalescent to attend at tea with him and Doctor Hartley; to which she returned an answer that she would join them in a few minutes.

Having stifled her feelings as much as possible, Maria hastened to comply with the request of her cousin. Since the death of Mrs. Wallingford, they had never before met, and the countenances of each showed plainly how deeply they had suffered.

Walter arose immediately on her entrance, and, advancing towards her, took her hand in his, and trying ineffectually to give utterance to a few soothing expressions, he led her to a seat. Nor was the good doctor—although he seldom yielded to sorrow—much less affected than they were; and he was several times troubled with a short cough, which rendered an application to his pocket hankerchief indispensably necessary.

This scene lasted several minutes, and neither of the three could utter a sentence; but at last Doctor Hartley broke the silence, by inquiring at what hour the funeral of the unfortunate Fanny would take place.

The mention of the murdered girl caused Maria to start, and occasioned a complete revolution in her mind; for the illness and death of

MORNA'S FURIOUS ATTACK UPON GORDON.

Mrs. Wallingford had driven every other subject from her memory; but now the inquiry of Doctor Hartley recalled all the painful events of Ela and her murdered daughter with vivid force to her thoughts, and she eagerly asked of Walter whether Ela were still near the place.

"The wretched woman is still an inmate of the Summer-house," replied Walter, "the constant watcher of the corpse of the ill-fated girl."

"And did you not say that the funeral ceremony of the poor girl was to take place to-night?" asked Maria.

"I did," returned her cousin, "and Mr. Hartley has been so kind as to offer to accompany me to follow, as is my duty, her remains to the grave. One thing has displeased and afflicted me very much, which is, that Mrs. Pembroke should absolutely refuse to attend with the unfortunate parent, who, in a mournful moment like that, may, perhaps, so much require the attendance and soothing voice of one of her own sex ; but, I presume, she considered that such a condescension on her part would have been too degrading. I forbore to ask one of the more menial domestics, for fear that Ela should consider it an insult to her pride, and thus——"

"Should you deem it prudent—and if you are willing that I should go—I will most readily be her companion on that trying occasion," said Maria, eagerly.

Walter could not help expressing by his looks his astonishment at this offer.

"Indeed, my dear Maria," he said, "I can scarce believe my ears. But do you think that you have strength sufficient for such an undertaking?—Do you not think that you are too ill to endure——"

"Oh," I do not fear anything," interrupted Maria, fervently ; "I have lately suffered so much, that—I have become inured to——" She could not proceed further, for her lips trembled, she looked very pale, and the tears, in spite of her efforts to repress them, chased each other rapidly down her cheeks.

"Well, we certainly do evince our courage in a most singular way," observed Dr. Hartley, trying to force a smile, which very badly corresponded with the tone in which he spoke, "however, as in my opinion Miss Herbert has made a proposition which reflects the most infinite credit on the humanity of her feelings, and being also confident that Ela will look upon it in the same way, and derive consolation from it, I must certainly second her motion, Mr. Walter."

Walter had nothing whatever to offer in opposition, he therefore signified his acquiescence by bowing his head, and soon afterwards Maria observed—

"But I am not provided with mourning to wear on this melancholy occasion, for never since the dissolution of my parents—" here she paused, and her emotion seemed quite apparent; but in a second or two she resumed—"but as it is usual to wear white at the funeral of young females, I will adopt that plan myself, and immediately hasten to make such preparations as may be necessary, for it is my ardent wish to convince her unfortunate parent how anxious I am to pay her poor daughter all the respect in my power."

"And every blessing attend you, my dear girl," said Doctor Hartley, as Maria left the room. "She has, truly, a noble and amiable heart. Oh, Mr. Walter, how thankful oug you and your father to be, that after the hea loss you have just sustained, this amiable g is supplied to you to fill up that blank whi must otherwise have been. Thus are those w bless others, in return blessed themselves."

Walter bowed his head assentively to t latter remark, but he could not help far fr feeling the same sanguine anticipations as garded Maria, for he knew too well his fathe disposition, and he felt assured that when t violence of his grief had in some degree su sided, he would feel inclined to consider th Maria's residence at Wallingford Hall no long necessary or desirable.

These misgivings, in spite of all his phil sophy, Walter could not help encouraging, a his thoughts were immediately drawn to t subject by the observations which Doct Hartley had made.

The preparations for the funeral occupi Maria but a very short time, and she soon r entered the room, in which Walter and t doctor were still seated together.

Walter was immediately aroused from the s reverie which he had fallen into, to a conte plation of his cousin, whose appearance dre forth his most fervent admiration, and, indee never did he imagine she looked half so lovel Her dress was entirely white, and a veil of t same was thrown over her head. Her hair w no longer in ringlets, but instead was parte across her ivory forehead ; and, in fact, he whole appearance was such, that she migh have been mistaken for

"Some gentle spirit of far happier spheres."

She looked so lovely, that she could not fail t excite the warmest admiration, both from Walter and Doctor Hartley, the latter of whom, suddenly rising, said that he would only jus hasten up stairs, to the chamber of his patient, Mr. Wallingford, and give some further instruc tions to those who were attending upon him, and then he would follow them ; for, as it wanted only twenty minutes to the time ap pointed for the funeral to take place, it woul be much better for them not to delay their de parture by waiting for him.

"Should I not reach the Summer house i time to start with the procession, I will be sure to join it at the gate of the church-yard," he added ; and then quitted the room.

Walter and his cousin left the hall, and bent their steps towards the shrubbery ; but their walk was a dreary one, and both of them main tained a melancholy silence. Notwithstanding all her efforts to the contrary, Maria's frame trembled with alarm and horror, when they came to the fatal spot in which she had last seen the unfortunate Fanny and Esther, and re called to her memory the terror they had so justly evinced on that occasion.

"Look!—look!" she said in a tremulous voice, shrinking still closer towards her cousin, and directing his attention to what she was talking about ;—" there, in that gloomy place, in the midst of that cluster of trees, I am certain the men lurked !"

" Can it be possible that they would venture so near the hall ?" exclaimed Walter with astonishment ; " then it is very certain that they had contemplated some desperate deed, in which they were frustrated by the appearance of the girls."

The terror of Maria increased and prevented Walter from making any further observations upon the subject. The wind was very high, and, as it swept through the foliage in hollow gusts, Maria felt such a sensation of dread come over her, that she almost repented that she had undertaken to attend the funeral, and wished she was once more safe in the hall ; and Walter himself regretted that he had permitted her to accompany him. He remonstrated with her, and endeavoured to dissipate her fears.

" It is only a nervous feeling which oppresses me for a moment, caused by the recollection of the past," said Maria in reply ; " and when we have left these gloomy walks it will pass away."

Walter made no answer, but increased his speed, and they very soon arrived upon the grass plat, and in the full view of the silvery lake which it bordered. They looked towards the Summer-house, and there saw lights glimmering from the windows of the room, which had been converted into a chamber of death.

" No doubt they are waiting our arrival, only, to proceed to the church yard," said Walter, as he urged his companion to increase her speed. Upon entering the room, he found that his surmises had been correct, for they were all in readiness to depart to the church yard. Even at such a moment as that, the ridiculous prejudices and nonsensical superstitious fears of those who were employed to perform the funeral rites, could not be subdued, and they remained outside the house, all gathered together, and left Ela alone with the corpse of her daughter, for no one could possibly shake their belief that Ela was possessed of some supernatural power, and could, if she thought proper, visit those who gave her offence, with some dreadful calamity.

About the most cowardly of these blockheads, was a sort of village factotum, yclepod Dobson, the carpenter, undertaker, &c., &c., &c., whose limbs had been trembling, and whose teeth had so chattered with the terrors his own imagination conjured up, that his companions, having caught the infection, their teeth chattered in concert, until it could be compared to nothing else but a dirge of castanets. Dobson was a long, spare man, in body something like a corkscrew, and his nose, which was none of the smallest, was remarkable for its always possessing a very blue aspect. When this man, or rather the apology for one, perceived Walter, his countenance rose at least fifty per cent, and he perpetrated something of a grin of [satisfaction, which imparted to him the appearance of a death's head upon a tombstone, and walked towards him.

" Well, sir, I be so pleased to see you," said the courageous undertaker, " for now we may go into th' place, and none of my men would venture to do so before, though they want to screw the coffin down, for they say, and I do think wi' very good reason too, that if that shocking woman should only fix her evil eyes upon them, something very dreadful is sure to happen to 'em."

" Ridiculous !" said Walter ; " and is it possible, Mr. Dobson, that you are so weak as to place any reliance in such nonsense as that ? —Psha ! I am ashamed of you."

" Why, to be sure, sir," said the undertaker, rather ashamed at the tone in which Walter spoke, " to be sure, I don't see why she should wish to hurt those who never harmed her, and that's what I told them. But I can assure you, Mr. Walter," continued he, with a bad attempt to make a show of offended dignity, " I can assure you, sir, that I am not one of those persons that believe in such nonsense, as you are pleased to call it ; but one cannot shut one's eyes against facts, and, to say the least of it, her looks are quite sufficient to——"

Walter did not wait to hear the conclusion of the undertaker's speech, but, with Maria, passed into the room. The latter tried every effort to repress her apprehensions, but her heart throbbed quickly with emotion at the idea of meeting the wretched, bereaved mother at such a time as that ; but no sooner did she enter the room than her fears evaporated, and the most heartfelt compassion and sympathy took their place.

By the side of the coffin, which was not yet screwed down, Ela was seated with a calm and collected demeanour, and seemed resigned and prepared to encounter anything which might follow, with the utmost exemplary fortitude. Her eyes were sunk and melancholy, but when she raised them and beheld Walter, a ray of pleasure and gratitude beamed suddenly in them, and she bowed her head in token of welcome. She had not at first noticed Maria, who had drawn timidly behind her cousin, but when her eyes encountered her, and quickly rising from her seat, her emotion was very visible, as she said—

" Oh! this indeed is kind ; this is really more than I had a right to expect, or for a moment anticipated. Young lady, Ela thanks you, sincerely, from her heart, thanks you. Alas ! had you but known my poor girl, could you have became acquainted with her, you—"

Her powerful emotions choked her further

utterance, and Maria, whose mind was keenly susceptible of the grief which afflicted her, and who knew that words seldom imparted consolation under such circumstances, refrained from attempting to make any answer; but, taking her hand in her own, she pressed it fervently, which spoke, more than language could have done, and kindly led her back to the chair in which she had been seated.

Walter's presence having somewhat emboldened the men, they entered the room, and proceeded to perform their melancholy duties. When they appeared, Walter glanced earnestly at Maria, and his look conveyed the meaning that it would be prudent and proper, if they could, to prevail upon the unfortunate Ela to retire from the p'ace, while the men screwed down the coffin which contained the remains of her murdered daughter. Maria understood him, and sought, by gentle persuasion, to remove the unhappy mother, and to urge her to accompany her into the open air for a short time; but Ela shook her head, and declined complying with the request so kindly made.

"I cannot leave the spot until I have had the melancholy satisfaction of knowing that her mother's eyes were the last that looked upon her mangled remains," she replied, in tones that went to the heart of the affectionate Maria; "no—no; let me not quit her for a moment in this last struggle."

What could Maria urge against this?—Nothing. Deeply sympathising with the unfortunate woman, she returned no answer, and once more resumed her seat.

But in spite of the fortitude the wretched Ela had hitherto displayed, and the calm and firm manner with which she seemed determined to act, when the men proceeded about their sad duty, the cool and reckless manner in which they performed it were more than her feelings could endure;—drops of perspiration stood upon her forehead;—she gasped for breath;—and, after making an ineffectual attempt to speak, she hastily seized the hand of Maria, and darted out of the place. The latter followed her almost immediately, and then beheld her, on her knees, with clasped and upraised hands, imploring of Heaven that she might be enabled to support this heavy trial with fortitude and patience.

This sight imparted the utmost gratification to Maria, who from it anticipated the very best results, and hoped that it would change the mind of Ela, and soften it down to a proper feeling, instead of suffering it to indulge in those wild and revolting flights and insatiate thirst for vengeance, which had before characterised it, and lead her to bow with Christian submission and resignation to the will of that Almighty power, whose decrees what presumptious mortal shall dare to question? She trusted that it would lead her to penitence, to com-

punction for the many evils and afflictions, of which she had been the principal cause.

"Maria did not offer to interrupt her during the time she was praying, but when she had concluded, she approached her, and Ela, taking her hand, in a calm, melancholy tone ejaculated—

"My prayers, yes, even mine have prevailed, and I feel renewed strength; but mark me, young lady, you will not again be witness to a weakness of this kind in me."

"I sincerely hope to God I shall not," said Maria, earnestly; "in God alone is your only hope of consolation, in this hour of tribulation."

"True, true," answered the poor mourner; "and to Him I now raise my supplication with confidence, for there is an angel spirit there who will not plead for me in vain."

At that moment Walter appeared upon the step of the door, and beckoned for them to approach.

"They are ready, I suppose," observed Maria, "and only wait for us; let us return to the house."

Ela made no reply, but taking the arm of Maria, returned to the room, and, with a composure that surprised every one, she put on her large, dark cloak, so that her person was entirely concealed from observation. She did not, however, offer to arrange her long black hair, which fell far over her shoulders, until Maria suggested the propriety of her wearing the usual black silk hood; and then, when the undertaker offered it to her, she said with a look of ineffable scorn—

"What want I with your ridiculous garb? Think you the wearing of that can express the grief I feel? No, I will not wear it."

Here Maria, in a tone of gentle persuasiveness interposed, and Ela, who felt that she owed her every esteem, immediately assented, and put away the hat which she had previously worn, and which imparted to her such a romantic appearance. The coffin was now raised upon the shoulders of the bearers, the torches were lighted, for the way to the village church was through a dark and narrow lane, and it would have been impossible to have proceeded without them, and the melancholy procession was soon formed. Immediately behind the coffin, Ela and Maria took their places, and Walter followed next, by himself. They had no sooner quitted the grounds of the Hall, than Doctor Hartley, who had been waiting, joined them.

Although Walter had taken every possible precaution to keep it a profound secret from the persons in the neighbourhood, and the lateness of the hour, they found a considerable number of people assembled at the gates and along the road they had to take; and as soon as it had issued from the grounds, joined the procession, and seemed determined to follow it to the place of interment. When they arrived at the church, Walter and Maria were astonished and vexed. to find a still greater concourse assembled, but it was so very dark, that had it not been for the red flashes which the torches, carried by the men, emitted, they would scarcely have been aware that any persons but themselves, and those engaged in the funeral, were present.

All was silent as the grave, in which the mangled remains of the poor girl were about to be deposited ;—not a sound could be heard At the gates, which opened into the church-yard, they paused for a few minutes, to await the arrival of the clergyman, who had gone into the vestry to array himself in his surplice, and, during this interval, Walter could not help noticing, with some surprise and uneasiness, that there were several persons, who seemed most unbecomingly curious, and who pressed forward with impudent determination, and appeared to devote their whole attention to Ela and Maria, and were anxious to recognise who they were ; but in this they were unable to succeed, for both of them had taken good care to conceal their features entirely from observation.

But if the eyes of the others had been unable to penetrate through the sombre gloom of the night, Ela had immediately discovered that the principal portion of the congregation was composed of the Gipsies, and those whom she had the most cause to dread. Their eager eyes, as they tried to penetrate through the dark hood, which she had let fall completely over her features, had immediately been observed by her ; but she was convinced that they were unable to satisfy themselves that she was the person they thought her to be, and, notwithstanding, she knew full well the dangerous situation in which she was placed, she felt exasperated and disgusted at the presence of those who were connected with the murderers of her daughter. She had the greatest difficulty to keep her feelings within bounds, for she was well aware that the slightest sound, the least sign on her part, would confirm their suspicions, and she was also most anxious to keep her own agitation from the observation of Maria, lest she should be unable to control her fears.

The church was lighted up dimly to receive the corpse, and it was borne into it. Ela and Maria entered the pew nearest to it, and Walter took his seat in the one which belonged to his family. Only two or three individuals, except those connected with the ceremony, entered the building, and the restless behaviour of Ela did not escape the observation of Maria, and excited, in no small degree, her astonishment. She could not remain quietly in her seat, but kept on, every now and then, rising, and looking eagerly round the church, as if she expected to see somebody she knew ;—and then her eyes would wander to the door, and narrowly scrutinize every person who entered.

But although she made these observations, Maria had no idea of the truth, and could only attribute the emotion evinced by Ela to the effect which the solemn service which the clergyman uttered, made upon her mind. But she beheld her partly unclose her hood, and then the wild vacancy of her eye struck her with the idea that her mind was wandering, and that she was perfectly unconscious of, or inattentive to, the impressive rites of religion.

The service was over, the coffin was once more raised upon the shoulders of the bearers, and the procession moved along the aisle into the church-yard. Walter had given instructions about the grave, which had been strictly attended to, and it was consequently dug as near as possible to the vault appropriated to the family of Wallingford. This vault was at the further end of the burial ground, and a low, and much broken brick wall only separated it from the country beyond. There was a wide expanse of land adjoining this place, and the view in the day time was very pleasant ; but now, being only partially illumined by the light from the torches, it had a gloomy and cheerless appearance.

Maria could feel Ela tremble as she walked up to the final resting-place of that unfortunate ill-fated girl, whom she had so fondly loved in her life time, and to whom her very soul clung, with undiminished affection, in death ; and, in spite of her own feelings, she endeavoured to be firm, and followed the example which was set her by her cousin, who took up his station on one side of the wretched parent, and she on the other, and the solemn funeral rites were begun.

And now the mournful rites were concluded, and they proceeded to shovel the earth upon the coffin, and while the strained and aching eyes of Ela took a last eager look into the grave, in which was deposited all that she had valued on earth ; suddenly, every person was startled, by hearing a murmuring, confused noise among the crowd that had got as near the mourners as possible, and they pressed so hard upon Walter and those who were with him, that it was with the utmost difficulty he was enabled to preserve his equilibrium, and he was just in the act of turning round to expostulate with them, when the uproar and confusion commenced, by the torches being torn from the hands of those who had carried them, and trod under foot, and before another second had elapsed, bludgeons were wielded in all directions, and Walter found himself completely hemmed in, and unable to get near Maria, from whom he was, in fact forced away, and impelled towards the gates of the church yard.

It was very evident, however, though Walter was in too great a state of agitation about his cousin to notice it, that the men did not wish to assault him, for they only flourished their bludgeons above his head, and did not strike him. Their object was manifest, for they so surrounded him, that every effort on his part to get to Maria proved ineffectual, and he was forced right back to the church yard gates, and into the road.

Seeing that it was the intention of the fellows to prevent his returning, by closing the gates upon him, Walter rushed desperately forward, and got inside before they could accomplish their design, and there he resolved to make a firm resistance. Several of the fellows seized hold of him and endeavoured to re-open the gates, but he resisted all their efforts manfully, although opposed to such unequal odds, for he was confident, that should they succeed in getting him out at this place, as the wall was considerably higher there than at any other part, it might be some time before he should be able to find a place which he could scale; but at length the Gipsies muttered some words to one another, and in an instant the gate was forced open, and they fled in the direction of the village; and those persons who had been engaged in the ceremony, and the others who had merely come to see it, now came rushing towards the gate, with consternation depicted in their visages.

"Tell me where she is!—Take me to my Maria!" exclaimed the young man, with the most intense anxiety, as he forced his way through the crowd. But every one was too much engaged with their own terror to take any notice of him, and he flew with the speed of lightning, calling loudly upon her name as he proceeded, and endeavouring to distinguish her white dress through the almost impenetrable gloom. Suddenly his foot caught against something, and he stumbled and fell.

"Halloo! Mr. Walter, for God's sake are you going to kill me outright?" said a voice close to his ear. Walter looked up with surprise, and recognised the worthy doctor, who had been knocked down in the skirmish, and over whom Walter had fallen.

"Ah!" exclaimed Walter, breathlessly, "tell me, have you seen her?"

"Seen who?"

"Maria!—where is she? Tell me if you know, for this horrible suspense will drive me mad!"

"No, I have not seen her," answered Mr. Hartley. "But pray assist me to get upon my legs again, and I will accompany you in search of the dear girl."

"Light the torches!—light them immediately!" cried Walter, to some of the men, who were running, completely panic-struck, past him; "for Heaven's sake do not delay a minute, but light them at the first house you come to, and rest assured that you shall not go without being handsomely rewarded. Maria! Maria! oh, where are you?"

"Here is a female form stretched upon the ground," said one of the men, "and I don't know whether she lives or not."

Walter leaped to the spot in an instant, and raised the insensible form of the woman, with frenzied haste, in his arms.

"Good God!" exclaimed he, "it is Ela, and she is as cold and insensible as death!" Walter could not help feeling a sensation something like disappointment, and turning to the man he added—

"But Maria!—what has become of her?—Has no one seen her?" and he looked anxiously around him, to see if he could discover her he was inquiring after.

Doctor Hartley, at that moment, entered the place, he having followed Walter as fast as the shock he had received would permit him to do; and the latter committed Ela to his care, at the same time, saying—

"Whether she has become insensible through terror, or has been ill-treated by the ruffians, I cannot tell; but pray see to her recovery, while I go in search of my cousin."

He rushed about the ground, leaping over tombstones and graves, at the imminent hazard of falling, and calling in a voice of distraction upon her name; but it was so dark that he could not see many yards before him, and the men whom he had requested to get the torches lighted did not return. Oh, how he cursed the delay, and his distress became almost insupportable, when at that moment he beheld the light of the torches flashing among the foliage, and immediately afterwards a large concourse of persons, nearly every soul the village contained, the men bearing every variety of implement but the right, and the women, not content with the torches only, but also carrying candles, turned into the dark avenue, and made towards that spot where Walter was so anxiously awaiting them. But when they reached the gate, they made a dead stand, and had not the courage, either of them, to advance further. The impatience of Walter, however, being quite exhausted, he rushed to the gate, and snatching a torch from one of the men, called them all fools and cowards, and declared that there was no cause for their terrors, as the Gipsies had all taken to flight. This, together with the remonstrances of Doctor Hartley, who requested some of them to lend him their aid to support the insensible Ela into the house, prevailed over a small portion of them, who entered, and presently afterwards the rest, shamed into compliance, and seeing that no harm had befallen their companions, followed them.

The search was now begun with the utmost vigilance, and there was not a part of the churchyard, even to the grave of the murdered Fanny, which was not carefully scrutinised by Walter and the others. But it was all useless; Maria was nowhere to be found.

The distraction of Walter may be conceived, but cannot be properly described, and he was giving himself up to a paroxysm of grief and despair, when suddenly the light from the torch he held above his head, reflected upon the windows of the church. A thought darted like lightning across his brain.—He recollected that after the funeral had left the church, the door had not been closed, and might not Maria have sought refuge there? His heart palpitated more quickly at the thought;—with the speed of an arrow he rushed forward;—but what was his disappointment to find that the church doors were closed? In the midst of this perplexity, the idea of the vestry struck him, and hastening thither, he found the minister and several more, who had fled there for security; but as the eyes of Walter glanced hastily from one to the other, they rested not on the object of his search, and without a moment's delay, he hurried back to the place where he had seen her for the last time.

By the time that Walter had returned to the spot, Ela had shown some signs that she still existed, and, at the suggestion of two or three persons, she was conveyed into the vestry, and after the lapse of a moment or two, some restorative having been administered to her, she opened her eyes, and breathed a deep groan.

"Are you hurt?" eagerly inquired Mr. Hartley, who had at first thought that her insensibility was merely caused by terror, but who now suspected that she had been ill-used.

Ela opened her lips, and several times tried to speak, but being unable, she placed her hand to the back of her head, and again groaned.

The worthy doctor examined the part to which she had directed his attention, and then declared that she had received a very severe blow, and must be suffering great agony.

"The miscreants!" cried he; "then murder was their design; not contented with the blood they have already shed. The blow has been a very violent one, but I hope to God it will not prove to be mortal. She must be removed to some place where she can be properly attended to, without a moment's delay. Dame Jenkins, have you not got a spare room where you can accommodate the poor thing?"

Dame Jenkins turned up her eyes when he said this, in evident terror.

"Lor' bless you, sir," she answered, "what could I do with a sick person?—I haven't got a single necessary thing to 'commodate one with;—as for my pillow cases and sheets, they are all wet and hanging out to dry, and—"

"Stuff!" angrily interrupted the doctor, in a tone which shewed that he was quite determined; "that need not be any obstacle, for you can have whatever you require for her accommodation from my house; and, therefore, I cannot listen to any of your ridiculous objections. Do not be afraid, you shall not go unrewarded for your trouble, I will take good care of that; so come, come, bestir yourselves, for while you are considering about it, this poor woman may die."

Dame Jenkins was like, as it were, hemmed in a corner, by the doctor's peremptory manner, and although she did not like the job, she knew not how to refuse. Not that she doubted for an instant but that the doctor would handsomely keep his word, as regarded the remuneration he had promised to make her, for the generosity of that worthy man was proverbial all over the neighbourhood; but then, the very idea of giving shelter, and being under the same roof with a woman, who was believed to be a witch, by the generality of people, was too horrible a subject for her to think upon, and she heartily wished that Doctor Hartley had been in the bottomless pit, rather than to have had the chance to select her for the office of nurse and landlady to such a suspicious being. These thoughts she could not help communicating, in a whisper, to one of her garrulous neighbours, and it was a very great relief to her when one of the old gossips proffered her services to the doctor instead.

While this altercation had been going forward, a litter had been hastily formed out of the boards and cushions of the seats, and the unfortunate woman being lifted upon it, was conveyed to the cottage of Goody Robinson, who had volunteered to take her in charge, and Mr. Hartley, attended by Mr. Clements, the minister, went in search of Walter, who, while this was going forward, had, they were informed, to their great alarm, gone into the woods, attended only by three or four of the most courageous of the villagers, who would not have accompanied him, had it not been for the promise of a handsome reward which he held out to them.

"I fear," continued the man, from whom they derived this information, "I fear there is too much reason to believe that these suspicions are just, as regards the poor young lady, whom, I thoroughly believe, has been carried away by some of the wretches, although I cannot guess what can be their object for so doing, unless it be to assassinate her. I was within only a few paces of her, when the ruffians darted upon her like so many savages, and although I attempted to oppose 'em, lor', what was the use of it?—I was knocked down in a twinkling, and——"

"My good fellow, if you can tell us anything relating to this unfortunate affair, pray do so at once, and explicitly," interrupted Mr. Hartley, impatiently.

" Well, Doctor Hartley," returned the man, somewhat picqued, " so I was going, as fast as I could, but you will not give a person time. But the whole of the matter is, perhaps I saw no more, and probably not quite so much as the rest of you. I only beheld three or four of the villains scale the wall, while the rest of the gang drove the people out of the church yard, by the gate ;—that's all I saw, for just at that moment I received a blow on my head, which felled me to the ground, and stunned me for a few minutes, and when I came to myself, there was'nt a Gipsy to be seen."

Doctor Hartley had not the least doubt but that the man's surmises, as regarded the abduction of Maria, were quite correct ; but he could not, for the life of him, conceive what object they could have in view, unless it were to prevent her from coming forward to give evidence on the trial of their companion, Mark Darwin.

Mr. Clements, the minister, had not been many weeks in his present office, and not having resided in that part of the neighbourhood before, he was totally unacquainted with the events which were connected with the outrage of that night, and was, therefore, incapable of giving an opinion. He, however, apologized to Doctor Hartley, for having sought refuge in the vestry with such precipitation.

" My dear sir," replied the doctor, " there needs not any apology whatever, for I do not deny that I should also readily have availed myself of the same opportunity had it been afforded me. There is nothing in an encounter with these wretches to render it at all agreeable, as I know by former experience ; and when they rushed upon us with their savage, unearthly cry, I made sure that their intention was to murder us every one, although what could prompt them to such a deed' I am at a loss to imagine.'

" And so am I," said Mr. Clements

" I am speaking of Miss Herbert," said the doctor.

" Miss Herbert !—Mr. Wallingford's neice ! —is it possible !—why I never supposed for an instant but that it was a sister, or some other relative, of the ill-fated deceased."

" I repeat, sir, positively," said the doctor, " that the young woman in white was no other than Miss Herbert, the neice of Mr. Wallingford."

Mr. Hartley felt rather astonished to perceive the interest of Mr. Clements so suddenly excited, for he had before remarked a certain coldness, nay, frigidity, in his manner, which far from prepossessed him in his favour. But now he evinced an interest in the affair, that excited the doctor's astonishment, and questioned narrowly every person they met on the way to Goody Robinson's cottage, whom he thought it was at all likely they might elicit any intelli-

gence from, and put a thousand questions about the Gipsies, and seemed so willing to render all the assistance he was able, to rescue Maria from the power of the Gipsy tribe, that Mr. Hartley could not help gradually warming towards him, although his former indifference had somewhat prejudiced him.

They were not long in arriving at the cottage of Goody Robinson, which was remarkable for its neatness, and on entering the small, but compact and clean bed-room, the doctor was pleased to find that, although her memory evidently wandered, Ela had regained the use of her speech. But when she beheld the doctor, and heard the questions he put to her, gradually everything was brought fresh again to her recollection, and she said—

" I have had a narrow escape, doctor ; for the blow was a severe one ; but the wretch who aimed it was disappointed ;—but tell me— did I rescue her ?—was she saved ?—or did the monsters at length succeed ?—Why do you not answer me ?—Why do you stare at me in that strange manner ?—Tell me—what has become of her ?—and Walter Wallingford, where is he ? —Oh, God ! my worst surmises, I fear, are realised !—my heart chills with horror at the thought !—They tore her away from my side, when I sought to shield her from their fury !— But, for the love of Heaven end my doubts !— do not tell me that she has also fallen a victim to——"

" I pray you, my dear soul, be more calm," said the compassionate doctor, whose heart at the same time sunk within him, as he thought upon the too great probability of Ela's suspicions being correct. " Perhaps it is not so bad as you anticipate ;—at any rate, let us hope that it is not, though, as yet, no one can form any idea of the truth, as nothing more is known than that she is nowhere to be found."

" Great God ! then my worst ideas are confirmed !" cried Ela, in a tone of the utmost distraction, and clasping her hands violently ; " she is lost !—In the hands of such wretches, such fiends, all hope is at an end ;—and to me may be attributed all this ;—I—I have worked this frightful devastation ;—I have brought this most horrible of all afflictions upon the heart of that youth, whose nobleness of soul is beyond all praise—whose benevolence is unlimited ;—I have been the sole cause of this dreadful catastrophe ;—have I not first deprived him of his angel mother, and now of that fond girl who— but what's the use of talking now ?—The moment is past.—I ought to have saved her.—Yes, it was in my power, but it was my own selfish fears that withheld me. Did I not watch them narrowly, and knew that they were determined upon some act of desperation ?—Yes—yes, I did ;—but still, was I to blame ?—No ;—I did not suppose that it was against any one but me they meditated their foul designs, for how could

I suppose for a moment that they could think of harming her?—Yes, and the poor girl shrieked to me for help, and begged of me to rescue her; —and God knows how hard, yet vainly, I tried. —I held her arm, and tried to shield her from the villains' bludgeons, but at that moment, a blow was aimed at my head with a stick from behind; it was a sure mark; I was struck to the earth, and my senses left me; the rest that followed is unknown to me. But I will not remain here any longer!—let me arise?— where is Walter?—I will pursue the monsters!

HATFIELD THE HIGHWAYMAN.

—I can conduct him to their secret lurking place!"

"My dear, good creature," said the doctor, kindly, "pray compose yourself, or the most serious consequences may be apprehended. Walter has already departed in pursuit of them, and has the best wishes of all his friends for success in his undertaking."

Ela tried to make a reply to the observations of Doctor Hartley, but at that moment the pain of her head became more intense, and rendered her submissive to his wishes. She bestowed upon him a faint smile of gratitude for the commiseration he expressed in her sufferings, then, closing her eyes, once more sunk back on the couch.

CHAPTER XXXVI.

"The demon, Danger, stalks around
His head encompass'd by fierce hissing snakes;
His eyes darting the lightning of revenge!
But she, sweet maiden, strong in virtue's mail,
Escapes unscathed and free."

WE must now return to Maria, who, after the ruffians had seized her in the manner which Ela had described to the doctor, recognised in the swarthy features of those who held her, the Gipsies who had already caused so much mischief in that neighbourhood; and no sooner had she made the discovery, than her heart sunk with terror and despair, for she then imagined that their power was most unquestionable.

It would be complete folly to attempt to describe the consternation of Maria when she made this discovery, and looked eagerly around after Walter, to endeavour to ascertain whether he had likewise recognised the Gipsies: but, before her eyes could rest upon him, there was a shrill whistle given as a signal, and immediately afterwards she was forced from the arms of Ela, who was endeavouring to shield and save her, and was screaming loudly for help, and in an instant she found herself closely enveloped in something coarse and heavy, so that she had the utmost difficulty in breathing, and she was lifted in the arms of some persons, and carried along at a rapid rate, in what direction she had no opportunity of judging.

Ere they had proceeded far, she was certain that some one was struggling to rescue her, and her heart sunk with terror as she thought that it was Walter, and of the peril in which he was placed, exposed to the vengeance of such a number of remorseless and blood-thirsty villains. She tried, but in vain, to utter a cry, to warn him of his danger, and to beg of him to secure his retreat, but she could not articulate a syllable, and, completely overpowered by the strength of her emotions, she became unconscious of everything.

She recovered, but how long she had remained insensible, she had no means of ascertaining; neither had she an opportunity of forming any conception of what had taken place during that time. She found herself lying upon the emerald carpet of the earth, and the wind was playing gently and refreshing among her glossy tresses. It was a great release from the confined state she had been before placed in, and she did not offer to rise for several minutes, completely regardless of any danger, and wholly wrapt in the enjoyment of the delightful change. But this state of unconsciousness was not permitted to last long; all that

happened to her returned with full force upon her recollection, and she shuddered when she thought of the dangerous situation in which she was placed.

The murmuring of voices now vibrated on her ears, and with the utmost caution she raised her head, and looked in the direction from whence they seemed to proceed. Some few yards off only, she beheld several of the Gipsies, men and women, seated upon the ground, and engaged in earnest conversation; and, at first, their discourse was quite unintelligible to her, but at length she was enabled to overhear sufficient to understand that it was of her they were speaking. She listened with breathless anxiety, but for some moments was unable to catch more than a broken sentence here and there: but what she did overhear filled her mind with the utmost terror and apprehension. She could not but think they designed to assassinate her, or for what other purpose could they have borne her away in such a violent manner, and why bring her to that dreary and unfrequented place?—But then, again, surely if they had determined to murder her, would they not have taken the opportunity to perpetrate the deed while she was insensible, rather than have awaited her recovery, so that she might not raise any outcry or alarm?—Besides, what advantage could they gain by depriving her of existence?—Surely she could be no obstacle to their views, without, indeed, they were resolved to destroy all those whose evidence might lead to the conviction of Mark Darwin and his miscreant companions, in the hellish deed of which they were suspected. But although at first she could not help entertaining this horrible idea, upon mature reflection, its probability caused her to reject it; for, desperate and callous as the Gipsies were, it seemed to be out of all reason to suppose that they would try to prevent the detection of one crime, by committing many others of the same black dye, and again her despair partly evaporated, and she began to indulge a hope that she might yet be saved from a fate so dreadful.

The voices of the women now swelled into a louder tone, and it was evident that they were growing warm upon the subject of their discussion. Again Maria scarcely ventured to breathe, for fear that she should not be able to catch the subject of their discourse; but at length the following words, spoken by one of them, were heard by her—

"It is always your fault if we run in error, for you are so obstinate and headstrong that there is no controlling you. Did I not tell you as soon as I saw her that it was not Esther?— Her figure is like her's, to be sure; but Esther is not so tall by a good deal; but you are like Mark Darwin; and he, by his rashness and fool-hardiness, has brought all this trouble upon us, and caused us to be hunted like wild beasts. The prognostications, the curse of Mabel upon our tribe, is coming true, and ere long, our race will be totally exterminated, or we shall not have a place in the world where we can fly for refuge!"

"Silence, fool!" cried one of the men, in a passionate voice; "if this is all the consolation you can afford us, hold your peace. It comes well from your lips, Morna, thus to speak, when thee and thine have brought so much trouble upon the tribe, and we have risked so much to serve thee. Had it not been for our taking the part of thee and thy blood-thirsty crew, we should now have had nothing to fear, but might have been enjoying ourselves as we were wont to do, in our tents, and quaffing the goodly contents of our kegs. But mark the difference;—here have we been for these two hours, traversing this wild part of the country, over a confounded bad ground, with a heavy burthen, and the prospect of dangling upon the first tree we come to, should we be pursued and overtaken. Morna, you have ever been——"

"Hold! croaking raven!" interrupted Morna, furiously; "am I for ever to listen to your infernal tongue? Why do you upbraid me for crimes which have been occasioned by you, and others of the same description?—Why bring to my memory that which should be blotted from recollection? Hark ye, Gordon, was it not you that first introduced to us, her that has proved the bitter curse of our tribe?—Was it not you that introduced the pale-faced woman and her infants to our people? And what has been the result?—Why, misery and trouble to all of us. We have to thank you for all; yes, you, and not Morna, as you would—"

"Hell-cat, you lie!" ferociously interrupted the man; but the words had scarcely escaped his lips, when Morna flew upon him with the fury of a tigress just aroused, and grasped his throat with extraordinary strength, tearing and scratching his face with the other hand, notwithstanding, he made a desperate effort to release himself from her, dealing her the most tremendous blows, to which she seemed totally indifferent, but continued, at the same time, to pour forth upon him a volley of the most disgusting epithets that her passion could suggest.

"Off! off! damned hag!" cried the ruffian; "take her from me, or by all the infernal host I will stretch her a corpse at my feet!"

Fearful that Gordon would put his threat into execution, the other Gipsies now interposed; but they had some difficulty in accomplishing their object, for Morna was like a complete fury, and the more they tried to appease her rage, the more did it increase. The expostulations of the females were alike lost upon her, and the men were at length compelled to drag her forcibly from the throat of Gordon, or she would undoubtedly have strangled him; but still, in spite of all, she would renew the combat, till at last, two of the men flew upon

her, and forcibly held her arms, while one of them said—

"A murrian light upon you and your accursed race, you furious hell-bird;—see, your noise has put them upon our track; for, by the blaze of the lights among the foliage yonder, they are coming this way. Curses light upon you for this. There must be much blood spilt, ere we shall be able to elude their clutches."

The words of the man changed the current of affairs, and they all gazed in the direction to which he pointed, and where the red glare of the torches was plainly to be seen among the tall trees on the left of a hill, near which the Gipsies were seated. They seemed to be very much alarmed, and a hasty conference ensued among them, the subject of which, Maria soon discovered, was not the manner in which they should themselves escape the threatened danger, but in what way they should act with regard to her. It was a moment of terrible agony and suspense to the poor trembling maiden; her heart throbbed quicker, and a stream of fire seemed to pass through her throat; but yet her presence of mind did not forsake her, and closing her eyes, she pretended still to be insensible to what was passing around. Another moment, and two of the women came up to her, and bent over her form; they then arose again, and returned to their companions, and another hurried consultation ensued.

"She is still unconscious of everything," said one of the women who had made the investigation, "so what have we to apprehend from her? Leave her where she is, and when her friends find her, they will, most likely, stop all further pursuit of us."

"But are you sure her insensibility is not feigned?" said one of the men, suspiciously.

Maria's agitation had been wrought up to such a pitch, that she could plainly hear every throb of her heart; but still she endeavoured to maintain the same apparent insensibility, and remained quite motionless, but listening with the deepest attention and eagerness to what was said among the Gipsies.

"Certain," replied the woman, to the man's question; "what! think you we are both fools? If you suppose that you possess more sagacity than anybody else, go and satisfy yourself;—but I would have you be quick, for, in a few minutes, they will be upon us."

The ruffian acted upon the woman's suggestion, and it was with the utmost difficulty that Maria could controul the agony and agitation of her feelings, as he approached her, with a knife in his hand, and stooping down, bent over her for a second or two.

"'Tis well!" she at length heard him utter, "'tis well!—but if I thought that——"

He did not finish the sentence, but walked away. How shall we describe the relief which this was to Maria; the wretched culprit reprieved on the scaffold, could not have felt more ; but still her feelings had been excited in such a powerful manner, that she was totally incapable of listening to, or comprehending what now passed among the Gipsies, but uttered an heart-felt prayer to the Omnipotent power for protection.

In this manner, several minutes elapsed, and Maria could not now hear a sound. Every moment seemed more than an hour to the poor girl, in that painful, that trying situation; but still she did not venture to move—nay, scarcely did she venture to respire—so great was her apprehension that the Gipsies would again approach her with caution, and that, if they should discover she had been deceiving them, her life would have to pay the forfeit. Still the deep and death-like silence remained unbroken, and encouraged by its continuance, Maria did at last venture to open her eyes, and to gaze around her. Her heart bounded with joy and gratitude to Heaven when she found that the coast was clear, and that the Gipsies had gone and left her to herself. Completely overcome with feelings of unspeakable delight and gratitude, Maria threw herself upon her knees, and, with upraised hands and eyes, poured forth her thanks to the Almighty ruler of all events, for her preservation from a fate so horrible.

But she was soon roused to action; she arose upon her feet and cast her eyes anxiously round, to endeavour to ascertain in what part of the country she was. It was so dark that she could not see far, but she was enabled to trace, beyond a doubt, that she was in a place where she never remembered to have been before. She looked towards the avenue of trees the men had mentioned, to see if she could discover anything of the lights, which she fondly hoped proceeded from her friends, who had come in search of her ; and then, when her eyes rested on the hill, she was certain that she was in the immediate country which surrounded the romantic estate of Wallingford. But she was disappointed ; there were no lights to be seen, and she heard not a sound but the whistling of the wind, as it swept through the long avenue of pine-trees, which led to the hall. Her alarm now greatly increased, for she well knew at what a distance she must be from the hall, and she was such a stranger to the immediate spot, that she had but a slight knowledge of the way she ought to proceed, and road there was none, and only a very faint and irregular track upon the grass.

The night was cold, and the unwholesome dew seemed to cling around Maria like a mist, —she felt ill, too, from the excitement she had undergone ;—and before she might be enabled to reach a cottage where she could gain shelter for the night, her fatigue and consternation might overcome her, or the Gipsies returning, might once more get her into their power. Terrified

by these thoughts, but more especially the last one, she was urged into action, and the moon now emerging from the dark clouds, which had hitherto obscured it, pointed out to her what she considered to be the way to Rosemary Dell, to which, as well as her trembling frame would permit her, she proceeded.

She had not gone far, when the well-known bell from the village church, chiming forth the hour of one, convinced her that she was going in the right direction, and at the same time added to her alarm, for by it she ascertained that she had been away from her friends for more than three hours, and she was well aware that they would be in a most horrible and almost insupportable state of suspense and consternation, and she lost all thoughts of her own fears, in her anxiety to relieve them from their apprehensions. The way she was now going, led direct to the village, and although it was the furthest way to go to Rosemary Dell, she knew that she should there be certain to find friends, and also ascertain what had become of her cousin.

Had not Maria accustomed herself to seek recreation in the open air, and to look upon other difficulties with indifference, she would have shrunk with fear from attempting to make her way over the rough and uneven ground ; and as it was, she could not do so without putting herself to much pain and inconvenience. But her fear of the return of the Gipsies overcame every other thought, and she pushed on with as much speed as she could, but not without frequently looking back, to make sure that there were none of the persons she so much dreaded, at her heels. But there was no cause for her fears ; nothing appeared to intercept her flight, and, as she gained rapidly upon the village, she became more assured, and the prospect of speedy assistance reanimated her spirits ;—but then, the idea of Walter being perhaps in a similar situation to that from which she had just escaped, darted across her imagination, and interrupted the pleasure she might otherwise have felt, at the prospect of her being so soon placed once more in safety, and under the protection of her friends. Having returned exactly in the same direction which the people had taken who had forced her away, Maria soon found herself by the village church, upon whose white walls and tall spire the moon's rays fell, and showed distinctly every tomb and moss covered grave, which covered the mouldering bones of many, who had, perhaps, been the pride of the village, and of those who oft made the welkin roar again with their boisterous mirth.

Maria sighed, as a feeling of awe came over her, and she could not help pausing to contemplate the solemn scene. But her eyes quickly wandered to the grave of the unfortunate Fanny, and tears of sincere compassion and regret stole down her pale cheeks. From the grave of the ill-fated Gipsy girl, the eyes of Maria wandered to the magnificent mausoleum of the Wallingford's, and when she reflected upon the occupant it was so shortly to receive, her tears flowed fast and unrestrained, and it was some moments ere she had the power to proceed. At length, however, as the bell from the old church tower once more gave her warning of the rapid flight of time, she hurried on, and soon afterwards found herself in the village.

All was as still as the churchyard she had just quitted, and, looking up the little hamlet, Maria could not perceive the least signs of a light in any of the cottage windows; but it was not at all likely that any of the humble peasants, tired as they were with their hard day's toil, would be up at that unseasonable hour; but yet, wearied as she already was, by the unusual fatigue and excitement she had undergone, the distance to Rosemary Dell, she felt confident, was too much for her to accomplish, without resting and refreshing herself. She walked on, now completely exhausted, and not knowing what to do, until turning a corner, she suddenly came upon the house of Mr. Clements, the minister; and her spirits revived when she beheld lights in the rooms, and caught the figures of different persons moving about, which told her that the inmates were still up.

Maria approached the gate, and laid her hand on it, when she again paused and hesitated; but why she should feel tenacious under such circumstances, to claim the assistance of the pious proprietor of the house, she was at a loss to imagine. However, her weary limbs did not allow her much time to reflect, and she pulled the bell. Before the door could be opened, she heard the footfalls of persons on the lawn, and in a paroxysm of fear that the wretches from whom she had so recently escaped had been pursuing her, and had tracked her to the house, she once more pulled the bell with a violence which her terrors prompted, and the door was immediately opened by a female, who, alarmed at what she thought, no doubt, was an apparition, from the white robes which Maria wore, and the ghastly paleness of her countenance, uttered a scream, and was going once more to shut the door, when, wound up to a pitch of desperation, Maria forced herself into the hall, and, overcome by the agitation of her excited feelings, dropped down upon the bench and fainted.

When she recovered, she found herself supported in the arms of Walter, while Doctor Hartley, Mr. Clements, and two of the female servants were standing by, and watching her with the deepest interest and anxiety.

"Father of mercy, receive my heartfelt gratitude for the preservation of this dear girl!" exclaimed the delighted Walter, as Maria once more opened her eyes, and gazed affectionately upon him, and with grateful looks upon those who surrounded her. She was in a handsomely furnished apartment, Mr. Clements seeming to think that no attention he could bestow was sufficient for her; but the great difference there was between that and her recent situation, when she was not only exposed to the damp and unwholesome air of the night, but to all the terrible apprehensions which we have described, made her feel still more unwell, and the heat of the room seemed to be oppressive.

The solicitude of Walter after her health was most earnest; but they were both of them too much agitated to enter into any explanation of the circumstances that had happened to her for some time. Mr. Clements had, immediately after her entrance, ordered coffee to be got ready, thinking it would refresh her, and when she recovered, she partook of it with much pleasure. But now all her anxiety was to return to the hall, and she begged of Walter to hasten their departure.

"Think not that my anxiety is unreasonable," she said, "but the events which have occurred to me within the last few hours have seemed to endear that home to me more than ever; for never, oh, never again did I expect to behold it."

"What, then, Miss Herbert," said Mr. Clements, who seemed to be particularly curious upon the business, "I presume, from what you say, that they thought you had been one of their own degraded, wretched people?"

"They, doubtless, mistook me for one, sir, who was once compelled to be their associate, but whom, I now earnestly pray, has escaped from their power," replied Maria.

The countenance of the clergyman evinced the astonishment he felt at the fervour with which Maria spoke upon the subject; but he was, notwithstanding his anxiety to know all about it, possessed of too much good sense and politeness to urge a question which she did not seem willing to answer. He had heard from Walter rather a straggling account of the Gipsies, which only served to increase his curiosity, and he was more anxious than ever to have a full explanation of an affair, which seemed to possess so much interest, and to be wrapped in such deep mystery. All idea, however, of pressing his inquiries, if he had even been so determined, were put an end to, by Maria again begging that they should hurry their return to Wallingford Hall.

This, however, Mr. Clements strongly opposed, and would not, by any means, suffer her to depart (as he was certain she could not walk), unless she would accept of the use of his chaise, and being compelled to yield to this request, it was brought from the stable, the horse put to, and Maria departed, in the company of Walter and the worthy doctor, whose gratitude for her preservation had frequently been evinced, not only by words, but by an affectionate embrace, which Maria ardently returned.

Everything had been managed with the utmost propriety at the hall, so that Mr. Wallingford had not been made acquainted with the occurrences of the night, and entertained no other idea than that both Walter and his cousin were safe in their beds.

Mrs. Pembroke heard the sound of the wheels of the chaise which had brought them to the hall door, and beheld the return of Maria with much delight; but was evidently all upon thorns to be made acquainted with what had happened to her, and what had been the object of the Gipsies in bearing her away; but the good doctor, as he passed into the house, having read her thoughts and wishes, shook his finger at her, and enjoined her to silence, adding—

"Your curiosity shall be gratified to-morrow, Mrs. Pembroke; but to-night Miss Herbert cannot be pestered with questions."

Walter was now about to say something, but the doctor, who seemed to understand what he would have said, prevented him, and observed—

" My dear fellow, let us have no long rigmarole speeches to-night, but as I am certain both you and your cousin require rest, and my services can be dispensed with, I shall take the liberty of returning home in Mr. Clements's chaise, and advise you both to get to your chambers without any more delay. Good night, my dear children, may God watch over you, and speedily terminate all your sorrows."

With the utmost sincerity did Walter and his cousin reiterate this wish, and after bestowing again upon one another the expressions of congratulation at the manner in which Maria had been so fortunately saved from the terrible fate which had at first threatened her, they separated, and instantly sought their chambers.

CHAPTER XXXVII.

" A melancholy joy she felt to trace
The woes from memory she would still efface."

THE desperate nature of the outrage committed by the Gipsies, and the fatal consequences it might have been productive of, caused an universal feeling of indignation in the neighbourhood of Rosemary Dell, and every person expressed a wish that the parties might be apprehended and brought to justice, and were willing to render all the assistance they could. In consequence of this, not many days had elapsed, when ten men and women of the Gipsy tribe were taken up, on suspicion of being some of the parties concerned in the riot. But of their conviction, so far as the evidence of Maria would go, was not at all likely, as she was unable to swear to their identity, and such had naturally been the state of terror and confusion into which she had been thrown, on the night of the occurrence, that she had not so

much as taken any notice of the number of them that had borne her away.

Ela, however, whose anxiety to bring to punishment the delinquents, did not suffer her to think of the pain she was still suffering from the wound she had received in the riot, but she left her chamber to come forward against them. But her chagrin and disappointment may be readily conceived, when she found that there were only four of them that she could identify as having been present at the scene of outrage, or who had been her former companions; for the others, although of the Gipsy tribe, were unknown to her, and she, therefore, did not wish to charge them with an offence of which they might be innocent. Although these were her thoughts, she could not help surmising that they were likely enough to have been connected with the others in the affray; for it was not an unusual thing upon such an occasion, for them to summon the aid of distant tribes, they being all sworn to assist each other, and to be ready and willing to aid their people in cases of emergency.

Among those, however, whom Ela recognised, she could swear positively to two of them, as having been the most determined in bearing Maria away, and in forcing Ela back when she attempted to rescue her, and the other two she could swear to having seen them force the torches from the hands of two of the men that bore them, and taking an active part in the riot and violence. This evidence was deemed sufficient by the magistrate, who inflicted the severest punishment he was empowered to do, and the remainder were committed as rogues and vagabonds to gaol.

Ela had been in hopes that among the people taken, she should find her bitter enemies, Mark Darwin the elder, and his son Rupert, therefore, her vexation and disappointment may be readily guessed, and what rendered it still greater was, that the violence of the blow she had received, and her consequent confinement to her chamber, had been the means of rendering her entirely ignorant of the least clue to their haunts. It could not likewise escape the observation of Walter, notwithstanding the firmness which she had hitherto displayed, that Ela was now fully sensible and apprehensive of the danger in which she was placed, while the villains were at large, and she did not hesitate to give expression to her sentiments upon that subject.

" I have not the least doubt," said she, " that, some time or other, it is my fate to perish by the hands of these miscreants, for they have long marked me for a victim, and, notwithstanding all the precaution we may use, we shall not always be able to frustrate their designs. They never break their oath, and that oath binds them to take the life of any one who may abandon the tribe, and betray them to their enemies. But think not that I dread the fate ;—no, only let me live to see the murderers of my poor girl brought to condign punishment, and I care not how soon the other event may happen."

"Do you not think, then, you are secure in your present situation ?" eagerly asked Walter, who could not but notice the intense anxiety which was depicted in her countenance, and who felt convinced that she did not give utterance to all she thought.

"I do not think that I am safe," replied Ela; "but I am at a loss where to seek an asylum. Mark Darwin, the younger, will not be brought to trial for this two months yet, and a dreadful feeling of dread comes over me, that before that period can have elapsed, the old monsters, Mark and Rupert, will find some means to accomplish their bloody purpose, and effectually prevent my giving evidence at the trial. Even if they should lose their own life in the attempt, it will not deter them from it."

Walter could not help feeling the utmost horror as Ela thus spoke, for he was too well convinced, from the earnestness of her manner, that her fears were not unfounded, and he had himself seen enough of the relentless disposition of the Gipsies, for him to doubt the truth of what she said, as regarded the determination with which they would pursue her to destruction. As these ideas gained more strength upon his mind, Walter became very uneasy, and he held a conference with Doctor Hartley upon the subject, and to know what it would be best to do with Ela, so that she might be secure from the vengeance of the gang, at any rate, until the important day, on which her presence was of such consequence, after which, they had no doubt but that they could devise something for her future protection and provision. They thought of various plans, and rejected them as soon as they had crossed their minds ; in fact, it was a very difficult point to decide upon, and they were no forwarder than when they began, until Ela herself settled it, and suggested that the best place for her to seek refuge in for the present, would be the metropolis, for she had not been there for a long time, and there were few, if any persons, who would be likely to know her.

Mr. Hartley and Walter agreeing to this arrangement, and the former having a friend in town, no time was lost ; a man servant was deputed to attend her, and Ela was soon on her way to London ; and so secret was their departure, that no one in the village or neighbourhood knew anything about it for some hours afterwards—not even Goody Robinson, in whose cottage, as we have before stated, she had been residing since the night of the riot—and she was not at all surprised, as she only imagined she had rejoined her former associates, and did not wish any one to know the exact time of her departure. She never for a moment thought either Walter or Doctor Hartley knew anything at all about the affair, any more than herself.

"Ah !" said the old woman, the following morning, when she saw the doctor, "it is quite foolish to think of altering that wretched woman. She has become so used to the rambling vagabond life, that she could never exist out of it. Noise and riot, and everything wicked, has become a part of her nature, and she will never be good for anything again, if ever she was. During the time she was with me, she couldn't rest comfortable in my cottage, though I know there is not a cleaner or more comfortable one in the village ; her chief delight was, when she was sick in bed, to talk of the green fields, and long to be once more among them ; and when she got about a bit, she would always be either at the door or window. Well, I did think how it would be, and now my ideas have come true. What's bred in the bone will never come out of the flesh, as the saying is ; and it is not a very honest thing for her to walk off in this " clandecent " manner, and not even to thank Mr. Walter for the beautiful mourning dresses he had made for her. And what is more strange than all, only to think that she troubled herself to take all her old rags with her also, for she has not left as much as you could wrap round your finger behind her. That frightful hat she has also taken away, which I often said that no real Christian or female would wear ; and several times I wanted her to destroy it, and all the rest of her fantastical rags ;—but it was no use talking to her ;—she had another object in view, and it's plain enough now what that was. Depend upon it she hasn't got any of her new clothes left by this time ; they are all sold, I dare say, and she has resumed her old gear. However, it's no fault of mine, and, therefore, I have no occasion to trouble my head about her. I'm sure nobody could have tried more than I did, to make her something like a reasonable being ; but it was all to no purpose, and I dare say she has returned to all her former ways."

Mr. Hartley could not help smiling at the warmth with which Goody Robinson spoke ; but so far from endeavouring to undeceive her, as regarded the surmises she had formed, on the contrary, he rather encouraged her to keep thinking the same, and appeared to see at once the force and probability of the conjectures she had formed, by which the old woman felt very highly flattered, and much better satisfied, when the doctor made her a present of a few shillings more than he had agreed to pay her for lodging Ela ; and she hobbled away with a much lighter heart, being very well pleased to get rid of a person who was likely to give her so much trouble, and whom she could not help regarding with suspicion and abhorence.

Ela having left the country, and there being

nothing very particular to divert their attention the grief of Walter and his cousin for the death of Mrs. Wallingford suffered no interruption; there was no circumstance to draw their thoughts from it for a moment. But heavily as they were afflicted, agonizingly poignant as was the sorrow which racked their bosoms, it was trifling when compared with the anguish, the ceaseless, the bitter anguish of Mr. Wallingford, who accused himself of having been indirectly the cause of her death; for, if he had never so fatally erred, she might still have been alive to bless him with her angelic temper, and shed happiness around him. In vain did he try to erase from his recollection the dying scene—the words she had uttered, more especially those words, which convinced him that the knowledge of his indiscretions had broken her heart. He remembered also every sentence she had spoken as regarded Ela, and the protestations she had made, that her first meeting with Ela, and the maledictions, the dreadful maledictions she had given utterance to, had never been absent from her thoughts, and had been preying upon her mind, until it could no longer support the burthen of heavy care with which it was oppressed. And oh! how fatally had the curses of Ela been fulfilled, as regarded the distracted Wallingford? Had it not brought his wife prematurely to the grave, and his child—his Christabelle:—alas! to what a dreadful fate had she been doomed, by those who had been the cause of their other miseries?—But she might yet be saved—she might yet be restored to that station, from which she had so long and unjustly been torn, and a father's, a brother's love, bestowed unboundedly upon her, might make up for what she had suffered. But then again, had she not been made the associate of a set of wretches, whose revengeful dispositions would lead them to do all that was in their power to corrupt and vitiate her mind, and should he not be ashamed to acknowledge her as his daughter?—Would it not bring disgrace and mortification upon his head? Would not his conduct become the theme of every idle babbler's conversation, and would they not look upon the Gipsy girl with scorn? More than all did Mr. Wallingford feel this, for it touched his most predominant passion—pride.

Far different were the thoughts and feelings of Walter. He thought not of the disgraceful life which his sister had been doomed to mingle in, he only prayed for the moment that would give the poor girl to her friends—to that moment, when he could enfold her to his bosom, and assure her of a brother's warmest, fondest regard. He thought of the unfortunate Fanny, and then pictured to himself that she was like her—all beauty, gentleness, and intelligence—for such he could not help thinking the latter, in spite of the disadvantages under which he had himself beheld her. If, indeed, she was like that hapless girl, he felt assured that the

task would be an easy one, to render her all that a person could require. Besides, would not Maria readily become her preceptress, her adviser, her friend, companion, sister? and what an amiable, a lovely being she must become with such a one for her companion.

These thoughts often served to while away the heavy hours which Walter passed when alone, and previous to the last mournful obsequies being performed to the remains of his mother, after which, he determined that no exertion on his part should be wanting to find out the retreat of Christabelle, and to restore her to her rights in society.

At length the melancholy day of the funeral arrived, and the body of Mrs. Wallingford was conveyed to the family vault, with all that pomp which the pride of Mr. Wallingford prompted, attended by the latter, who, to the amazement of his friends, sufficiently conquered his emotion for that purpose. The last ceremony was over, the corpse was deposited in the vault, and the procession was about to move from the churchyard, when Mr. Wallingford paused, as his eye fell upon the grave of the ill-fated Fanny, which had been made near it; and the expression of his countenance plainly showed that even in such a moment as that, and when it might have been expected that all other ideas would have given way to the intensity of his grief, his unconquerable and selfish pride reigned paramount in his bosom, and he hastily demanded of Walter whose grave it was.

"Fanny Berauzio," said Walter, with deep emotion, and speaking in a low tone of voice, while his bosom swelled with disgust and indignation at the feeling displayed by his father at that trying moment, and in the dreary precincts of the dead. Had a thunderbolt at that moment struck Wallingford, he could not have started more; a dagger seemed plunged into his heart, and a heavy groan escaped his lips. Covering his face with his cloak, he staggered away, murmuring as he went—

"It is a just punishment for my pride; it is a just retribution for my crimes. Were they not both the victims of my cruelty and injustice, and in death they should not be divided."

No one could hear these sentences but the wretched Wallingford's son, and bitterly did he feel them, for he saw that his father suffered more from mortification at the idea of the exposure he was doomed to undergo, than from any compunction that he felt for the numerous errors he had committed. His mind, distracted as it had been for many years past, and the manner in which his spirits had been broken by sickness, had all tended also to sour his disposition, and he was frequently in a state which was truly pitiable, and which Walter could not bear to contemplate. But it was not to be wondered at;—what consolation could he find in retrospection, and what was the present but a source of every misery to him?

No sooner had they returned from the funeral, than Mr. Wallingford shut himself up in his apartment, and would not see any of his family, being determined to give uninterrupted indul-gence to his grief; and for several days he would not even admit Walter into his presence. Hoping that this seclusion, and the consequent meditation it would lead to, would be produc-tive of good results, Walter did not offer to break in upon his silence; but recollecting the

THE MURDER OF THE FARMER BY HATFIELD

manuscript which had been given to him by Ela, and taking it from the drawer in which he had deposited it, he commenced reading it.

Of course we shall not mention anything of the early part of Ela's history, as the reader has been already made sufficiently acquainted with it, but proceed at once to that period when she was absolutely driven into a connection with the heartless and unprincipled Rackett.

"Lost, degraded, hateful to myself, abandoned by him to whom my warmest love was devoted, and sold to the man whom I abhorred and despised, what a revolution was caused in my mind. I began to dread to look upon the past, and to banish retrospection, determined to give up everything for the gratification of the present. Rackett and myself, both alike reckless and thoughtless, rushed madly into the giddy vortex of extravagance and dissipation, and it would seem as though we were endeavouring to outrival one another in the nature of our folly. But very different were the motives that stimulated us to this conduct; in him, vice, licentiousness, and debauchery had been ingrafted from his earliest days—indeed they had become portions of his nature—but mine was the madness, the phrenzy of a mind diseased—the wild delirium of a seared heart—my conscience told me how grossly I was sinning, and that ruin must be the termination of it—but it was the oblivion of forgetfulness I sought, and therefore did I continue the giddy career, and daily increased in the extravagance of my conduct.

"Rapidly, indeed, came destruction—more rapidly, even, than my worst fears had anticipated. I had been led by Rackett to imagine that he had ample means to support the improvident career we were pursuing; but false in that as in everything else, too soon I found that he had deceived me, and that from the very pinnacle of wealth, fashion, and luxury, we were precipitated to the lowest abyss of misery and penury. Our furniture, carriage, horses, plate, and every article of property came under the auctioneer's hammer, having been seized in execution, and we were driven from that home, where we had been living in such show and splendour.

"Luckily, I had had sufficient notice, so as to save my own little property—such as jewellery, clothes, &c.—and Rackett had taken a mean apartment, in a low neighbourhood, to which I repaired to await his arrival. Bitterly, indeed, did I feel my own abasement, when I entered my new lodgings, and compared it with the magnificent apartments I had just quitted; my heart was wrung to madness.

"I waited in vain for Rackett's appearance, but he came not; and when the night had passed away, and he was still absent, I became uneasy, and set out to inquire after him. It was not long before I gained intelligence of him, and then I learned that he was the inmate of a debtor's prison. Shocked at his altered condition, my heart throbbed—fool that I was—and with pity and commiseration, I hurried to the Fleet, in which he was confined. Many were the protestations of eternal love with which he received me, and of gratitude for having so soon come to him, and I was weak enough to believe him, and to credit his asserverations, when he declared that on me alone he depended for hope and consolation, under his present misfortunes, from which he saw no prospect of being able to

extricate himself. Yes, pity for the man, whom in his prosperity I had despised and detested, whom I had looked upon in his true light, namely, un unprincipled, debauched scoundrel, now that he was in difficulties, entered my bosom. I buried all remembrance of his errors in oblivion, and assured him that I would never desert him, that I would never leave him to his misery, but that I would partake with him his adversity, and share with him his prison. He pretended, the base hypocrite, to be unbounded in his gratitude, and lavished upon me every expression of affection that the most ardent imagination could conceive. But the villain, as he had always done before, deceived me; and his conduct became base, cruel, and revolting, as my little property gradually diminished, and I was compelled to curtail the means of his indulgences. He never bestowed a word, a thought, a care, upon me or my poor infant; selfishness and brutality were his predominant passion;—nay, more, when at last my little funds were almost exhausted, and I could not comply with his extravagant demands, he even struck me!—yes, blows he gave me several times! Good God! how my blood boiled at this indignity!—I felt, as it were, estranged from every gentle feeling, and often times, had I had a knife about me, I am confident I should have plunged it in his heart! Think not that I wish to expose all his faults and to hide my own, by setting myself up as a pattern of female patience and resignation.—No; my temper rebelled against such treatment, and I returned it with equal violence at last; and, in revenge, I neglected him at every opportunity in the prison, and launched into such scenes of dissipation and pleasure as chance threw in my way. At length, I quitted him entirely, and took a miserable room in Charles Street, Drury Lane, for my money was now almost entirely gone. I never visited Rackett, and but seldom sent to him.

"It happened that, in the same house, there were lodging a young couple, with whom I suddenly became acquainted; for the female particularly drew my attention to her, from the kindness she evinced to my little Fanny, whom she was continually taking out, and frequently buying her presents. This was frequently a great release to me, and I was quite prepossessed in favour of the apparent kindness of disposition in the young woman, and so there was something like a friendship sprung up between us.

"Her husband, who was then from home, she informed me, was a commercial traveller, and I was foolish enough to credit what she said, although the obscurity and poverty of the lodgings she had chosen, and other circumstances might, if I had given it a moment's consideration, have convinced me that she was telling me that which was untrue. Her manners and habits, however, at that time assimilated with my own, for she was prone to every sensual extravagance. She used frequently to have plenty of money, and I was her partner in all the indulgences which it could procure; and when it was gone, we would, perhaps, be reduced to the most pressing necessity, and be obliged to pledge our wearing apparel to procure us a scanty means of subsistence. But her spirits were always volatile and buoyant, and she prevented me from thinking, if even I had been so inclined, until I at last endeavoured to copy her exactly, in which I too readily succeeded.

"Her husband, whose name was Hatfield, at last returned from the country, and my astonishment was not slight, to behold in him so different a man to what I had expected. She had given me the most glowing description of her beloved Richard, and I had, therefore, expected to find it realized; but, on the contrary, I beheld a vulgar, low, ill-mannered man, about the middle age, and whose principal ambition seemed to be to appear thoroughly acquainted with all the slang phrases and cant terms of low life, and he was evidently a man who had mingled with the very refuse of society, and whose origin had been of the same low nature. To me, however, he put on his best behaviour, and took much notice of Fanny, and played with her, and she soon became as much attached to him as she was to her Aunty Hatfield, for by that name she had instructed the child to call her.

"Mr. Hatfield made a profuse display of the cash he had brought with him, which was a considerable sum, and seemed to take no more care of it than his wife did, launching forth into the same scenes of folly and improvidence. We were now more than ever together, and I made them both acquainted with my early history, not concealing anything from them. They expressed, in no very measured terms, their opinion of the treatment of Rackett towards me, and often urged me to abandon him altogether to his fate, and not to submit to the ill-treatment of such a scoundrel, who entertained, evidently, no sentiment of affection towards me.

"Base as Rackett had treated me, I could not, for some time, make up my mind to act upon this advice; but, at length, having been to visit him one day, and not being able to take him what he wished, he so savagely ill-used me, that, when I quitted the prison, I took a vow that, from that time, Rackett and me should be strangers. This determination I imparted to Hatfield and his wife on my return, and they seemed to approve very much of it, and promised to assist me all that laid in their power, assuring me, that while they had the means, me and my child should be welcome to partake with them, so that I was completely overwhelmed by the kindness of persons who, I might say, were almost strangers to me.

"To prevent the annoyance of any one coming to me from Rackett, they advised me to take another lodging without further delay. The idea of going among those who were strange to me, made me feel uncomfortable; but as Hatfield and his wife both pointed out to me the necessity of it, I could not do otherwise than to comply. A lodging, more decent and comfortable than the one I was at present in, was soon procured for me, and the day after I had removed to it, Mrs. Hatfield joined me, telling me that her husband had been again called suddenly into the country, and that, as it was miserable and dull remaining in the house, without the company of myself and my dear little Fanny, she had determined to come and lodge with me.

"I was very glad to hear this, as without her society I should have been miserable, so, as she had no furniture to remove, she took up her station forthwith.

"Hatfield had nearly exhausted all his money before he left London, so that he was not able to leave her much, though she said that in the course of a week or two he would remit her more, so that I might make my life happy, as we should be comfortable enough, and should not want for anything.

"As I had not a penny in the world, nor the means of procuring one, I was compelled to be under an obligation to Mrs. Hatfield for my support, which she dealt out as liberally as her limited means would permit her, and with all the freedom which had ever characterised her conduct towards me, and when our funds became every day alarmingly less, she would not suffer me to give way to any depression of spirits, but endeavoured to lead me to hope that we should very soon be better off.

"At length, one day, a letter arrived, addressed to Mrs. Hatfield, which she eagerly took and opened. I could see that she had no sooner read the contents, than she was very much agitated and disappointed, and that she had received some intelligence which she did not expect. The letter, as I guessed, was from her husband, and she informed me that he had not sent her any money, but that she expected he would be in town that evening, and she was desired to go and meet him. We were in a pitiable condition on that day, for having pledged the last article that would fetch us a penny, we were unable to procure food with the exception of a little bread and milk, which I had given to Fanny.

"Mrs. Hatfield left me early in the afternoon, to go to the place where she expected to meet her husband, and not having broken my fast all day, I felt very ill, and quite exhausted. Fanny having gone to sleep, I put her to bed, and sat up in the most disconsolate mood to await the return of my companion; but when hour after hour elapsed, and still she did not me, I became apprehensive that something had happened to her. The hour of twelve had struck, and yet she did not return, and, weary with thinking, I threw myself on the bed, but was too agitated and too hungry to sleep. I was at a loss to form any conjecture, as to the cause of her not returning, but as it was now two o'clock, I gave up all hopes of it. No rest could I gain all that night, for the distracting thoughts that racked me, I arose early in the morning, and, in a state of mind I need not attempt to describe, I traversed the room with my child in my arms, who was now screaming with hunger. In the midst of this misery, I was suddenly aroused by hearing the rumbling noise of some vehicle coming up to the door, and the next moment there was a loud knock. I looked out of the window, and, with a delight which none can imagine who have not experienced the same, I beheld Hatfield alight from the coach, and presently afterwards hand his wife out. The next moment I heard them on the stairs, and they entered the room, followed by the coachman, who was loaded with bandboxes, &c., and Hatfield was also covered with dust, as though he had been travelling a long way outside a vehicle, and had with him two carpet bags, well filled, while Mrs. Hatfield carried a bandbox in her hand. Hatfield seemed to be more than usually elated, and his countenance was flushed as if he had been drinking. His wife, however, seemed very much confused and distressed.

"'Ah! how do you do, my old lass?' said Hatfield, in his usual unceremonious and vulgar way;—'glad to see you;—I dare say you thought my missus was never coming back again. But I've no time to tell you the reason just now—and it's no matter; here we are with all our kit, and we must make the best shift we can here for the present. I don't suppose you'll have any cause to grumble at your extra lodger. All right, now;—done the trick up this time, and no mistake. If we don't have a jolly day of it, say my name ain't what it is. Nance', go and get something good to eat; for I dare say Ela's hungry—ain't you, old girl?—And, damme, let's have a bottle of brandy? I mean enjoying myself, so that's all about it.'

"The behaviour and the words of Hatfield astonished me, and I could not make any reply. What had happened to him, and how could he have come by all this in such a hurry, were ideas that naturally occurred to my mind in a minute; but I could not form anything like a satisfactory conjecture; and as for enquiring of Hatfield, I could not for the present, lest he might consider my inquisitiveness impertinent. I never, however, recollected to have seen him in such capital spirits; and having taken Fanny from my arms soon after he had entered the room, they were gambolling together in the

most boisterous manner, and the screams of laughter which the child uttered, showed how delighted she was with her play-fellow.

"Mrs. Hatfield now made her appearance with the refreshments, which I beheld with greedy eyes; and without waiting to stand upon any ceremony, I commenced a very hearty meal, which I speedily despatched. I also partook of the brandy; and Hatfield swallowed it in large draughts, and his spirits became more elated with every libation.

"That day passed.—The whole truth had been imparted to me. I had learned the whole secret;—and horrible indeed were my reflections, when I recovered from the effects of the liquor I had taken, and recollected what I had been told. Hatfield had confessed to me that he had lived by thieving;—that he was a determined housebreaker;—and that he had, for some years past, been concerned in some of the most desperate robberies. He added, that it was sometimes his plan to get a situation by means of a false character, and then to rob his employers, and that the goods he had brought with him was the produce of his last burglary. He made this declaration with a sort of pride, as if he had been performing one of the most meritorious actions; and he detailed, with much laughter, the various schemes he had devised to accomplish his nefarious deeds, and the stratagem he had made use of in this, his last robbery.

"I now saw very clearly what had induced him more than all to persuade me to change my lodging;—it was for no other purpose than to secure a place of concealment for himself and his booty.

"You may form some idea of the anguish of my feelings, when I became acquainted with these particulars. I was stung with shame, terror, and remorse. But what could I do?—How could I escape from it? I had no one to look to but Mr. and Mrs. Hatfield; and could I tamely perish, or, what was more, see my poor little one expire for want? No; I could not. And, besides, they were ardently fond of her, and they seemed willing to render me all the assistance in their power, but it must be in the same dishonest manner that I have already described. Oh, God! it was a dreadful trial; but I had no other alternative, and was, therefore, compelled to stifle the voice of conscience as well as I could by drinking, and submit to it.

"While the money which Hatfield had got in so nefarious a manner lasted, we were never sober long together; and I shudder now as I look back upon the scenes which we passed together. As I was now forced regularly into a connection with them, the ill-gotten property was left entirely to me to dispose of; and I was afraid to refuse, although every time I did so the most awful apprehensions of being detected fil|led my mind; and I was well aware that if that were the case, I should be certain to suffer with the others, for being connected with the robbery, in the shape of an accessary after the fact.

"Thus passed away a month, and Hatfield remained secure, although we knew that they were instituting the most vigilant inquiries after him, and a large reward was offered for his apprehension, for they had made out several other robberies against him, and there could not be the slightest doubt of his conviction, if they succeeded in taking him into custody.

"He was not able to stir out at all, and at length he formed the resolution to make as much money as he possibly could, and go down to Yorkshire, where, he said, he had some friends, who might feel inclined to assist him, and put him in some way or the other to elude the hands of justice. This proposition was in accordance with my own wishes, for I was heartily tired of remaining where I was, and I flattered myself with the hope that, perchance, something might occur to remove me from the dangerous and degrading life I was then in. There was now property to full the value of two hundred pounds to dispose of, and he having mentioned to me such places as they were likely to buy it at, I, for the last time, run the risk, and sold them for less than one fourth of their real value.

"We now consulted upon the method of our travelling, and at length it was arranged that he should start first at night, and walk about twenty or thirty miles on the way, and that we could, on the following evening, go off in the mail, and meet him at any place he might appoint; but that we were not to seem as if we were acquainted with him; and if we should happen to become acquainted with any circumstances that should give rise to our suspicions, we should apprise him of the same by a signal agreed upon, and then we could pursue our journey without him, and leave it to chance whether he found us afterwards.

"Accordingly, the next evening, as soon as it was dark, Hatfield departed on his adventurous journey, and the agitation of his wife at parting was most powerful, for she had many good traits in her character, and was most devotedly attached to her abandoned and guilty husband. For my part, my emotion was scarcely less poignant than her's, but it was of a very different nature, and I prayed to Heaven that something would occur to release me from my present situation, and to prevent my being ever again connected with Hatfield.

"He had left us fifteen pounds out of the money which I had got by the sale of the property, which was to pay for our journey, and to provide for us until such time as he could join us with safety; but, fearful that something might happen to render it necessary that we should not expend any more money than it was absolutely necessary, instead of taking our places by the mail, Mrs. Hatfield acted upon my advice, and we took a coach to where we had appointed to meet him, knowing, that if we saw that there was no cause for fear, we could then take the mail, and proceed on to the end of our journey.

"Now it happened that the village where we expected to find Hatfield, was, when we got there, a scene of much gaiety, for a fair was held there; and it was a good job that we had gone in the way I have described, for Hatfield was not there according to his appointment. As the mail had not yet arrived, we waited. But he did not make his appearance, and we hesitated whether we should go in search of him, or where we could look for a place or lodging for the night, if we should not meet him. Mrs. Hatfield, as may be supposed, was in a state of great uneasiness at not seeing her husband; and, unable to rest longer, she saw me and Fanny to the inn at which the mails stopped, and hastened on her hopeless errand, among the different booths and public-houses, in the hopes of finding him. She had been gone above an hour, and I had engaged a bed for the night, when I heard a loud noise in the front of the house, and, alarmed lest something serious should have happened, I hastened to the spot, and there saw Hatfield and his wife, who both appeared to be terribly excited, the former especially, who was uttering the most dreadful expressions imaginable, and the most horrid imprecations against some parties, who, I soon made out, deep as he was, had succeeded in duping him out of all the money he had with him.

"Thus were we placed in a most awkward dilemma, with not quite fifteen pounds in the funds. The prospect was a dreary one, and I shuddered even to think of it. Villain as Hatfield was, this event appeared to have increased the baseness of his character. He was, in fact, nearly mad, and declared, with a terrible oath, that he would be revenged on some one, and make good his loss, even at the hazard of immediate death. And there was a desperation, a determination in his manner, that convinced me he meant what he said. Good God! how shall I describe my feelings, my shocking feelings and terrors at that moment? Even now I feel as though I were engaged in the same scene once more, and all the horrors of it rise vividly on my recollection! For many days, for many weeks, did we continue to ramble from place to place, uncertain what to do, whither to direct our steps, and kept in a continual state of fear and suspense, from the oath which aHtfield had sworn. He had given up the idea of going where he had first proposed, for he would not show himself among his friends, now his means had become so limited, and thus our money soon became expended, and we had nothing to subsist upon but such trifling sums as we could obtain by selling different articles of our wearing apparel. So terrible is the punishment awarded to guilt.

"You may form some idea of what I endured during that time, but I cannot do adequate justice to it in words. As for the temper of Hatfield, it had become completely savage, and we trembled even to speak to him. The gnawings of want seemed to add to its ferocity, and often did he utter the most dreadful curses against that fate which had so over-burthened him. I was oftentimes half driven to madness when I heard him, and I dared not now pray to that Heaven I had so greatly offended, to interpose to release me from it. But his fondness for little Fanny suffered no diminution, and for that I overlooked the rest. His unfortunate wife, too, lavished upon it the same affection, and was willing, at any time, to go without herself, rather than see her want for anything. I could not see this kindness to one that was so dear to me, without feeling grateful to them, and thus was I induced to overlook many errors, which would otherwise have appeared so revolting to me.

"And now the most terrible moment arrived, when we had spent even our last coin, and we had been walking many weary miles, tired, foot-sore, and hungry. It was a very stormy day ; the rain descended in torrents, and we were half drowned ; and, to render our situation still more awful, we knew not where we could find a shelter for the night, to rest our weary limbs, for we had not the means to procure even the most humble lodging. As we proceeded along, a burly, cheerful looking, middle-aged man, who had the appearance of a farmer, overtook us, and when he came up with us, it was evident from the manner in which he walked and spoke, that he had been drinking.

"He was a jovial, free-hearted sort of man, and made no hesitation in entering into conversation with us; but still there was something particularly bold and vulgar in his behaviour towards Mrs. Hatfield, who, I should have before told you, possessed considerable personal attractions.

"I could not help noticing the awful and ominous looks with which Hatfield observed him, and as though I had the presentiment of what was about to take place, I could not look at him without involuntarily shuddering with horror. He appeared to wish his wife to hold out every encouragement to the man's familiarities, and yet I could see that his blood boiled with indignation, and I thought every moment that he would press his fingers to his throat, and thus punish him for his audacity.

"The farmer, for such we found he was, had missed his way, and as we found that he was going our road, he did not want any pressing to continue our company. We walked on in this way for about three miles, and I could plainly see, by the mysterious expression of Hatfield's countenance, that he had determined upon committing some outrage on the man ; but whatever plot he might have meditated at that time, his designs were frustrated for the present, for he perceived that we were at no great distance from a village, and within sight of a little road-side public-house, although we had imagined that we were many miles away from anything of the sort.

"'Confound it all !' exclaimed Hatfield, 'I have taken the wrong road !'

"'Well, never mind, my lad,' said the farmer, 'I dare say they will find us refreshment and rest in that house yonder.'

"'But it's so unfortunate,' observed Hatfield, 'I haven't got a farthing of money with me; I've only got a cheque upon the banking-house at B———, and I suppose they wouldn't like to cash it for me there. Dear me, it's the most cursed job that could have happened, for these poor women and the child are so tired, that I'm afraid they will drop in the road, if we should attempt to proceed to the place of our destination.'

"'You shall not go another step further than that public-house, if I know it,' returned the man ; 'don't put yourself in a flurry, for I have got more money here than can be exhausted for one while, I'll be bound.' As the farmer thus spoke, he pulled a long leathern purse out of his pocket, and shook it at Mr. Hatfield. 'Damme, I wouldn't care a rush about spending five guineas out of it, if that pretty lass would not look so cross at me.'

"These words were addressed to Mrs. Hatfield, who said not a word, but looked very miserable and melancholy, and very likely entertained a full idea of what her guilty husband was meditating against the farmer. The latter supposed me to be Hatfield's wife, and Mrs. Hatfield his sister, he having introduced us as such to him.

"Hatfield acted his part too well ; and after an apparent deal of reluctance—for he knew well how to play the hypocrite—he accepted the offer of the farmer, telling him that, early in the morning, he would go to the banker's he had mentioned, get the cheque cashed, and return him the money which he might spend with us. With this promise the free-hearted farmer was perfectly satisfied, and, accordingly, we entered the public-house, and, after having had such refreshments as we required, we began to drink freely, and, in a few words, we passed the evening in all that noisy revelry which was consonant with the farmer's disposition. Hatfield was a jolly companion, who happened just to hit his taste, for he could sing well, and he had an ample store of those anecdotes with which the illiterate rustics endeavour to amuse each other. The farmer listened to him, and particularly his wife, who was also an excellent singer, with much pleasure; and Hatfield, taking good care to push the glass round to him pretty often, he soon became more communicative, and imparted to us that he had a considerable sum of money about him, which he had been to London to draw.

"We did not, unfortunately, think of inquiring about our beds until it was time to retire, and then we found that they were all engaged; but, as it was impossible for us to proceed any further, after a minute or two's consideration, the landlord informed us that, if we liked to make shift with it, he could supply us with some blankets and pillows, if we would only make our bed for once in a way, on some clean straw, in an out-house attached to the building.

"Weary and harassed as me and Mrs. Hatfield were, the offer was particularly welcome to us, and accordingly the good woman immediately set about arranging everything for our accommodation.

"A bed was easily contrived at the further end of the place, for Hatfield and the farmer; and me, the child, and Mrs. Hatfield were separated from them by some old boards, which the out-house contained.

"We left Hatfield and the farmer still drinking together, when we retired to rest, and the noise of their entrance waking me, I could find, by the stumbling noise which the farmer made, that he was very much inebriated; but when Hatfield urged him to allow him to help him to undress, he refused to permit him with much obstinacy. No doubt he had some idea of what Hatfield meditated. He stretched himself on the straw in his clothes; and, when I heard Hatfield take his place by his side, I could not resist a deadly chill and trembling that came over me.

"Mrs. Hatfield still slept, and so did Fanny, soundly; but I was so tired I could not, and I lay watching the strange shadows, which the faint glimmering light from the lanthorn, which was suspended from the ceiling, threw upon the wall opposite. The place, too, was very much broken and dilapidated, and the wind being rather high, moaned in hollow gusts in at the different apertures, which, combined with the loud snoring of the farmer, imparted anything but a pleasant feeling to my mind, which was still tormented with many horrible doubts and apprehensions.

"In this manner I lay till long after I had heard the midnight hour chime from the old bell of the village church, and every body in the public-house had evidently gone to bed, for there was not a sound to be heard, except, at intervals, the distant barking of a dog, which sounded hollow and solemn at that silent and dreary hour. At this moment my feelings were wrought up to an inconceivable pitch of horror

and excitement, for which I found it impossible to account. I trembled violently, and would have given anything to have had some one to whom I could speak; but I could not think of Mrs. Hatfield, who, like myself, needed rest; and, at last, determined once more to compose myself, I covered my face with the blanket, and endeavoured to sink into forgetfulness. Suddenly, a rustling noise at that end of the barn where the farmer and Hatfield were lying, aroused me, and I listened with eager and breathless attention. It did not last any great while, and then I thought I heard the farmer murmuring, as though he was talking in his sleep. A thought instantly struck me, which was, that the noise was occasioned by Hatfield endeavouring to rob the farmer, and with horrible anxiety, I arose from my recumbent posture, and, from between the old boards by which we were separated from them, I had a distinct view of what was going forward.

"The conjectures that had entered my mind were verified, for on the straw I beheld Hatfield kneeling, and trying, but in vain, to turn the farmer (who was a very heavy man) over on his other side, for it was in that breeches pocket he had seen him put his purse, which seemed to be well filled. The farmer was too intoxicated and half asleep to be able to make any resistance, although the words he muttered convinced me that he was notn etirely insensible to what Hatfield was attempting.

"Hatfield ceased for a few minutes, and stood looking at the farmer with a ghastly expression of countenance, which filled me with horror and dread, and the savage glare of his eye plainly showed that his determination, strengthened by opposition, was worked up to the very highest pitch imaginable. The farmer had once more gone off soundly to sleep, and he snored still more loud than before, but he had not turned, so that Hatfield was unable to get at the coveted purse.

"Suddenly an irresistible impulse seemed to arouse Hatfield, and he jumped up, and feeling in his coat pocket, he pulled out, what I shuddered with horror to behold, a large clasp knife. He opened it, and passed his thumb across the edge of it. Good God! how shall I describe my emotions at that dreadful moment? But I was unable to move a limb, or utter a sound, and sat, with distended eyelids, gazing upon what occurred. A deadly chill fell upon my heart, and large drops of perspiration stood upon my temples, when I beheld the villain bend over the sleeping farmer with the knife in his hand. Another moment, and the farmer uttered a groan, and jumped upon his feet; I saw his eyes staring wildly upon his murderer, and the blood gushing from a wound in his throat! Still he made an attempt to grapple with Hatfield, who directly seized a hatchet which was standing just by his feet.

I closed my eyes—I attempted to scream—but I could not. Another instant, the sound of the fatal blow—followed by a groan too terrible to think upon—and my senses left me!

"I recovered, and by the dim light which was emitted from the lanthorn, I beheld Hatfield on his knees, and rifling the pockets of the man he had so barbarously murdered, and his wife was sitting up by my side, with her face covered with her hands, and her body swaying to and fro—evidently from the effects of the great mental agony and horror she was suffering. I turned and groaned, but I could not utter a word.

"Hatfield continued at his revolting work for some moments, when he came to she side of the place where we had been lying, and, with a dreadful oath, exclaimed—

"'Come, enough of this foolery;—I'll not have any more of it. We must be off directly, before anybody is stirring; so up with you, without any more delay, and put on your clothes; this womanish squeamishness is just the way to get me a hempen cravat.'

"We dared not, we could not make any reply to this speech; but in a state of agitation too powerful for description, we did as he commanded, and hurried our clothes on with all the expedition that we could. But in vain did I try to look in a contrary direction to that in which lay the horribly mangled corpse. The ghastly, blood-stained face of the unfortunate man petrified me with horror; and even now it arises to my mind's eye with all the terror with which I then beheld it. Hatfield could not help noticing the deep expression of my horror at the sight of the dreadful spectacle, and he hid it from my view by covering the blood-stained, ghastly face, with some straw, which had formed part of the ill-fated man's bed."

Here Walter was unable to proceed any further with the manuscript, for the present, so deeply were his feelings excited by the horrible recital. He felt faint and sick; and, placing the papers securely in the drawer, from whence he had before taken them, he walked from the house, and took the path which led to Rosemary Dell, anxious to inhale the fresh air.

He had not proceeded far, when he perceived a couple of figures advancing towards him, which excited his deepest pity and sympathy. It was the form of a man, leaning on a staff, and supporting the attenuated figure of a blind woman, who appeared to be completely bent double with age and infirmity. Her dress was clean, although covered with patches, and her countenance, which was very much wrinkled, possessed a certain resigned and urbane expression, which immediately excited the interest of all who can feel for the cares and misfortunes of their fellow creatures.

The man seemed to be about the middle age, and, although sorrow had made the deepest impress on his features, they still bore the remains of what had once been handsome and manly. We say that he leant on a staff; but his form, although wretchedly attired in the ragged remains of a soldier's suit, still retained a portion of that nobleness and grace which had formerly characterised it.

They approached but slowly, for the aged woman's steps were so feeble, that the man, whose attentions seemed of the kindest description, had a great difficulty in getting her along at all. Walter's heart, which was ever alive to charity and pity, was sensibly touched by this sight, and he paused until they came up to him.

When they reached the spot where Walter stood, the man raised his eyes towards him, sighed heavily, and, without saying a word, was passing on, when Walter addressed him.

"Stay, my good man," said he, "you appear in terrible distress; and this aged woman?"

"Ah! gentle sir," said the man, sighing again, "if it were not for this poor soul, my aged mother, I would not care; it is to protect her, and to do what little I can to supply her wants, that alone makes me wish to live; for, in early youth, all my hopes, all my wishes were blighted, and since then, happiness has been a stranger to me."

"Oh! sir," said the poor old woman, in a feeble tone, and turning her sightless eyes towards the young man, "did you but know what my unfortunate son has endured for his friendless blind parent, how greatly would it draw your pity towards him. Alas! he has suffered much, very much indeed; but though, God knows, he has quite enough to sour his temper, nothing could make him forget his love to me."

"But have you not been a soldier?" inquired Walter, looking at his dress.

"I have," answered the man, "and many years have fought hard for my king and country, and was a stranger to my friends and my native home; but they took the paltry advantage to discharge me a few days before the time of my servitude had expired, and left me a miserable pittance, which they think a sufficient reward for the perils and dangers I have encountered. I am worn down with illness and suffering, and I am even willing to work; but who would employ me? They look upon me and my aged parent with scorn, and call us vagrants, beggars. Since yesterday we have not broken our fast, and then we divided a crust of bread between us, and slaked our thirst at a stream."

Walter looked still more earnestly in the man's countenance, for there sat candour and truth, while the deep traces of care were plainly perceptible, and showed that there was no attempt at imposition. Deeply moved to compassion, he put his hand in his pocket and, drawing forth his purse, placed several pieces of silver coin in the man's hand. As he did so, he saw a tear tremble in his eye, and, for a moment or two, his emotions were too strong to speak.

"Heaven bless and prosper you, dear young gentleman, for this aged woman's sake, who, but for this, could not have held up much longer!" he at length said, in tones that showed his sincerity. "God will reward you for your kindness, and to Him my voice, humble as it is, shall be raised for a blessing on your head. Farewell!—farewell!"

DISTRESSING SCENE IN THE OLD MANOR HOUSE.

The old woman tried to speak, but her grateful feelings choked her utterance, and her silence spoke more than volumes of words could have done. After the man had repeated his thanks with yet more vehemence than before, he pressed his mother's arm with a look of in- expressible feeling, and was walking away quicker than they had approached, when a sudden thought seemed to strike him, and, turning back, he bowed respectfully to Walter, and said—

"I would ask, young gentleman, if you do

not consider me too bold, to whom you stately mansion belongs?"

"It is called Wallingford Hall, and is the seat of the family of that name," replied Walter, wondering at the question.

He had scarcely uttered the name, when he perceived the countenances of both the old woman and her son change most remarkably, and the man exhibited, in particular, the most dreadful emotion.

"Wallingford! did you say?" he repeated, eagerly, "and the—the squire—does he still live?"

"My father is still alive," answered Walter; "but what is the meaning of your asking this question?"

"Your father!—you—you—the son of——" gasped forth the man, in a hoarse voice, and looking intensely in the countenance of Walter. "Good God! And have I lived to receive charity at the hands of the offspring of that man who—— Take back your money, boy; take it back, or I shall go mad!"

"What can be the meaning of all this?" inquired the bewildered Walter, more and more astonished at the words of the man, and the violent agitation of his demeanour.

"Ask me not—ask me not, lest I make you as wretched as I myself am!" he replied. "Oh! my God! that it should come to this! —Take back your money, or I will throw the accursed coin to the earth!"

As the man thus spoke, he hastily thrust the money into the hand of Walter, and turning away from him, took the arm of the old woman, and walked away, without so much as turning round once to look back. Walter was so completely thunderstruck with the adventure, that he was transfixed to the spot for some minutes, unable to move or to utter a word. At length, however, somewhat recovering himself, he looked around him, and perceiving that the man and woman were gone, he hastily pursued the path along which they had departed, but he could not see anything of them, and he returned, surprised and disappointed, towards the hall, not being now inclined to pursue the walk he had before thought of taking.

In vain Walter racked his brains, to endeavour to unravel the mystery of the man's words and behaviour; but he was unable to come to any other conclusion, than that he was either a madman or an impostor. But yet, had he been the latter, it was not at all probable, Walter reflected, that he would have returned the money he had given him; besides, he could not believe that such misery and distress as they appeared to be in, could have been assumed. His mind was disturbed with these conflicting thoughts, when, suddenly, he looked up, and discovered that he had entered the hall, and was standing by the door of his father's apartment. Not having seen him since the day

before, he knocked, and it was presently opened by Mr. Wallingford, whose countenance, though calm and dignified, showed plainly the deep mental anguish he had been enduring. He received his son with a faint, melancholy smile of welcome. Walter seated himself by his side, and entered into an affectionate conversation with him, in the course of which he ventured to remonstrate with him on the injury he was bringing on his constitution by the life of seclusion he was leading, and in giving way to the silent indulgence of grief, without affording himself any opportunity of receiving consolation.

"Oh, my dear father," concluded Walter, energetically, "let me beg of you no longer to give way to this weakness, but leave your gloomy chamber, and once more mingle with the world."

"And what have I now to do with the world?" replied his father, with a bitter and contemptuous sneer; "what is there in it to charm me, or who among its inhabitants has any regard for me?—Have I not disgraced the proud name of Wallingford? and think you I would mingle with the world to be looked upon with scorn, as being almost beneath contempt? —No! If I have tarnished the brightness of my name, let me remain alone to the degradation of my own thoughts; but I cannot endure the mockery of those who cannot appreciate my sufferings. This seclusion is a punishment for my errors—errors which I trust the future brightness of your conduct, my son, will serve to obliterate from the recollection of every one. No—no, I do not wish to leave here; I have no hope beyond this silent chamber; besides, you ought not to wish it, seeing that I might be the means of interrupting the delightful intimacy and affection which is no doubt now encouraged by your cousin, Miss Herbert."

Walter was heartily pained to see that no circumstance whatever, not even after the incessant attention she had paid his poor dear mother in her tedious illness, and the affectionate care she had taken of her, reckless alike of her own health, and struggling against fatigue, could induce him to change his foolish and sickening sentiments of pride towards Maria. He, however, stifled his feelings as well as he was able, and declared to his father that he was labouring under a most mistaken notion, to suppose that they had indulged in any more affectionate intercourse than such as might have been anticipated from their relationship, and that, so far from Maria wishing to act contrary to his will, she had taken particular care to avoid his (Walter's) society as much as possible, when there was no other person present.

Mr. Wallingford made no reply, but it was evident, from his manner, his suspicions were not in the least abated by the assertions of his son. Walter read his thoughts, and knowing that would be folly to continue a subject upon which they could not agree, he changed it, and informed Mr. allinford of the plan which he had devised, by which he hoped the discovery of Christabelle might be effected, and whose restoration might yet be the means of regaining his father's tranquillity. Mr. Wallingford sighed and shook his head.

"Alas!" said he, "how different are your opinions and mine, Walter?—in fact, I dread the event of which you appear so sanguine, for it will be but to increase my shame and misery."

The astonishment of Walter upon hearing these words 'may be readily conceived; but he felt it would be useless to endeavour to penetrate into the cause of this opinion; but poignant indeed was the anguish it caused him then, and for hours after, and he could scarcely bring himself to believe that he had heard such words fall from his father's lips: and then, again, he could not help imagining that his mind wandered, and he knew not what he said at the time.

CHAPTER XX VIII.

"Oh! when shall the grave hide for ever my
  sorrow ?
Oh! when shall my soul wing her flight from
  this clay ?
The present is hell, and the coming to-morrow,
But brings, with new torture, the curse of to-
  day."

BYRON.

THE following morning, Walter resumed the manuscript of Ela, which he found went on as follows—

"Not more than twenty minutes could have elapsed, at the furthest, from the perpetration of this dreadful crime, ere we quitted the outhouse and were making our way from the neighbourhood with the greatest precipitation. We took the same road which we had pursued with the farmer the night previous, and as we proceeded, the most terrific thoughts haunted my imagination. I could almost fancy, at every step I took, that I saw the unfortunate murdered man start up before me, with his healthy, jovial countenance, as it had appeared when we first met him; and the wind seemed to carry to my ears the boisterous laugh, as he enjoyed the jokes, with which Hatfield amused him on the journey. But it would be a fruitless task for me to attempt to describe the horrors I endured after the perpetration of that sanguinary deed, and the remembrance of which I have never succeeded in erasing from my recollection.

"Suddenly, I happened to raise my eyes, and then I perceived that Hatfield was not with us! I tried to mention his name, but I could not, the very thought of it carried a feeling of disgust and horror to my mind. It fearfully

alarmed me, and my companion soon understood what I meant, for she whispered to me, in an almost inarticulate tone, 'that he had most likely forgotten something, and was gone back to fetch it.' She had scarcely spoken the words, when I heard the hasty tread of some person behind, and the next moment Hatfield rejoined us. My heart seemed to sink within me when I again saw him, and I would have given the world at that moment, could I but have escaped from him altogether. His savage countenance bore an expression of fiendish triumph, and he did not seem to entertain the slightest terror or remorse at what he had done.

"'Now then. we must use our best speed,' said he; 'I have finished the business, and, if we only manage right, we may be far enough away before ever they will find out anything at all about the affair. I have got the plan in my head for us to travel, though I forget the names of the different places, in the confusion of the moment. We must get into the high-road after we pass through B——, and then we shall most likely meet with a coach, which will take us to where I think of going, and then we shall be safe enough.'

"It was an horrible thing to hear the wretch, who had but just committed so foul a crime, speak so indifferently about it; but we did as he had planned it, and we never stopped until we had got far away from the scene of the shocking transaction.

"We continued to travel on, after a very short stay to rest and refresh ourselves, until we arrived at a little obscure village. where Hatfield thought it was not likely we should have any occasion to apprehend any danger, and here we proposed to rest for a day or two. Upon examining his booty, after we had got to some distance from the place, the murderer was greatly disappointed and enraged to find there was not near so large a sum as he had anticipated; but that circumstance did not induce him to limit his expenses, and he went on in the most profuse and extravagant manner; but he sometimes expressed his regret that he had put himself into such a situation of danger for a sum so trifling, and that was the only sentiment he appeared to entertain upon the atrocious crime.

"We had taken up our lodging at a public house, which I thought, at that time, was very bad policy, but as we had not yet heard a word about the subject, which was continually in our minds, I suppose the murderer had begun to think himself entirely secure; but very soon was he undeceived.

"The time we had been lodging at the house, Hatfield had become quite a favourite among the guests who frequented it of an evening, and to whom his ample fund of song and anecdote was a source of much amusement. The account he gave of himself was, that having had a small legacy bequeathed him by the death of a relation in the country, he was on his way thither to settle the business ; and this story he told in such a plausible and off-handed manner, that they could not, by any possibility, suspect the truth of it. The reason of our staying at this place so long was easily accounted for, by the illness of me and Mrs. Hatfield.

"And now the critical moment was about to arrive. They seldom saw a paper in this obscure place, but, as it happened one morning, a traveller stopped there to refresh himself who had got one of the London journals, of a day or two old, and as everybody in the place was anxious to hear it read, the stranger began. But what was our horror and alarm, when the first paragraph he fixed upon gave a full account of the very murder which Hatfield had committed !

"Judge of our terror at that moment !—I could perceive the countenance of Hatfield change ; first, to a deadly pale, then to a feverish flush. But our agitation and alarm was still greater, when the man went on to say—

"'Well, I only hope the wretches may not escape, for a more barbarous murder I never heard of ;—however, there is no doubt but that they will soon be apprehended, for I see there is one hundred pounds reward offered, and the promise of a free pardon to any accomplice in the crime, but the person who actually committed it, if he or she will come forward, and give such evidence as may lead to the conviction of the assassin. Here is a full description of their persons ;—there was a man, and two females, and one of the latter had an infant. She was——'

"Before the reader of the paper could proceed any further, we had, one after the other, glided slyly out of the house, and taking the most unfrequented way, were soon a considerable distance off.

"Our sufferings were now dreadful ;—we were obliged to wander in bye-ways, with a scanty supply of victuals—only what we could beg from the inmates of a solitary cottage, for we were afraid to venture into a town to purchase anything, and we did not like to ask for food at a cottage, and then present them with money for it, lest it should arouse their suspicions ;—hunted like wolves from place to place !—fearful of the light of day, and trembling at the gloom of night, a very fair idea may be formed of the tortures to which we were subjected.

"Hatfield himself did not betray so much terror as might have been expected ; but his temper became hourly worse, and he seemed to look upon both me and his unfortunate wife, not only in the light of burthens, but with eyes of suspicion ; yes, he more than once hinted his doubts of our not betraying him ; and, in such momenas, his looks and words convinced us that he would not hesitate to perpetrate

another murder, for the purpose of concealing the first.

"We had been one whole day and a night without food, for we had been unable to meet with any habitation where the inmates could afford to supply us, and hunger and fatigue drove us nearly to madness. Being completely exhausted, we concealed ourselves in the thick covert of a wood, and sought to drown the recollection of our miseries in sleep ; but sleep was denied to me and Mrs. Hatfield ; and the murderer not only slept soundly, but snored so loudly, that we were afraid, if any one should happen to pass that way, he would be the means of betraying us.

"Towards dark he awoke, with all the raging and intolerable gnawings of hunger and thirst upon him. It was quite horrible to hear his oaths and curses, and to see the almost demoniacal expression of his blood-shot eyes, as he raved for food, and swore he would have it, if he swung for it the next moment. We tried our best to appease him, but all attempts of the kind only made him the more outrageous. There was a town, he said, two miles from the place were we then were, and he was determined to venture into it, and procure what he wanted at all hazards. We knew it would be in vain for us to attempt to dissuade him, but I ventured to advise that, at any rate, we should not all three enter the town together, but to separate, lest we might excite the curiosity and suspicions of the inhabitants ; but Hatfield would not hear of anything of the sort, for he dreaded to see us out of his sight, doubtful whether we should not return with the officers of justice. We were, therefore, compelled to comply ; but it was with many apprehensions that we did so, and we started at the sound of the whistling among the leaves, and the very least noise we heard we thought to be the track of our pursuers, and that we should be given up to the hands of justice. We did reach the town, and the first thing that met our eyes was a large bill, giving a full description of our persons, and offering the reward I have before mentioned for our apprehension ! Good God ! how my heart trembled ! and it was with difficulty I could support myself. Hatfield, who marked my agitation and terror, frowned significantly, and I endeavoured to subdue my fears as much as possible. Once more, however, I whispered to him the propriety of our departing, and offered myself to procure what little necessaries we wanted, if he would make his way out of the town as quickly as possible ; for I could not help imagining that more than one person had their eyes fixed upon us, and that they seemed half inclined to speak. Hatfield assented ; but he insisted upon my child remaining with him, as he said that was his only security, by which I too quickly perceived that he meant to convey his doubts of my remaining faithful to him. I was forced to give up my infant to him, which I did with a shudder, and it having been appointed where we should meet again, he put the money into my hand, and then hastened away, concealing his face as much possible, and altering his gait. Mrs. Hatfield went in another direction, and had another portion of the money to procure some other part of the provisions; and I then made my way stealthily into such shops as I fancied they were less likely to suspect me at. Into one where I went they were talking of the murder, and execrating the atrocious perpetrators of it. I thought I should have sunk in the shop, and it was wonderful that I could recover myself sufficiently to procure what I wanted, without betraying, by the agony of my manner, how painfully, how awfully interested I was in the subject of which they were discoursing.

"We did get what we wanted in safety, and rejoined each other at the appointed place, where we appeased the cravings of our hunger, and afterwards appeared a little more refreshed, though still harassed with fatigue.

"Thus did we pass away many wretched days—nay, weeks—and our fear of apprehension hourly became more acute and intolerable. We were, indeed, in a miserable condition, not daring to enter any house till after dark, and then we would be away again by the first dawn of day, for fear somebody should know us by the description in the bills, which were posted in all directions.

"During this time, Hatfield several times hinted his suspicions of my turning traitor, and of his determination to make the life of my child the sacrifice for my doing so; but such an idea, I declare positively, never entered my mind, although I would have given the world to have been able at the time to escape from the dreadful course I was now pursuing; but my nature revolted from betraying to punishment that man who, despite of his many faults, had been a friend to me in the hour of necessity.

"At length we had not a farthing of the ill-gotten money left, and shocking was the condition in which we then found ourselves. We had nothing to eat, but what we could steal on the way, and such as we could find in the produce of the hedges and fields; and our resting place was either a wretched barn, a haystack, or some uninhabited hut. Heaven knows, had it not been for my poor child, my darling Fanny, I should have prayed that my sufferings might have been ended by death, for the human mind can form but a faint idea of our bitter miseries.

"In this truly pitiable condition we had been for several weeks, and so reduced were we, that we fully expected death was rapidly approaching us, when at last Hatfield suddenly started up (we having been all huddled together under an haystack), and said that he would either procure some relief, or die in the effort. To

this desperate course he was further urged by having seen the signs of what he imagined was a Gipsy encampment not far away—such, for instance, as seeing the broad blaze of a light among the trees, and hearing loud sounds of hilarity and boisterous mirth proceeding from the same direction, and he, therefore, resolved to venture among them, and solicit their assistance. He was successful;—they did not turn a deaf ear to his melancholy tale of distress, but told him to bring us to the camp. We were assisted thither, received with a kindness which we never expected from the wandering tribe, and had both food and clothes given to us.

"Hatfield had before changed his name to Milford, and before the night closed he had promised to become one of their companions;—in fact, he seemed to be a man so well calculated for what, in the Gipsy phraseology, is called a "Romany," that they received his proposition with evident satisfaction. He proposed the same to me;—I shuddered at the idea of becoming one of these wandering, degraded, and abandoned people;—but alas! what other alternative had I?—what was to become of me?—and what was still more precious, what would become of my child?—how could I support her? This thought dispersed all my doubts, and put an end to any further hesitation on my part. That very night I accepted the offer made to me, and became one of the wandering tribe.

"Thus, at last, my fate was settled, and I was as low and degraded as I could be. Fate had worked its worst for me, and I was accursed and wretched. But trifling was my sorrow at my own degradation, but to think that my child, my Fanny, was condemned to such a career, was almost too much for me to endure.

"Several weeks elapsed, and nothing occurred worthy of particular notice. It was the finest season of the year: all Nature was apparelled in her best, and, to a mind at ease, even the life we led wandering about from one fair to another, and obtaining the easy living we did, would have been delightful. But my thoughts were always occupied with the dismal prospects of my child, and the horrible scene of which I had not long since been a witness, to feel anything like peace.

"Soon did Milford begin to express discontent and restlessness, for he did not consider the paltry thefts of which the Gipsies were guilty sufficient for him; he wanted something more important, and having watched an old man at one of the fairs, who, by some means of other, he had ascertained had a good sum of money about him, he persuaded two of the youngest of the gang to join him, and rob the old gentleman, which they imagined could be done without scarcely any difficulty; but the gentleman was a stout, hearty man, and did not yield so quietly as they expected he would have done; for having a stout, thick stick with him, he began to lay it about them in good style, and would, no doubt, have succeeded in making his escape from them, had it not been for Milford, who, with a dreadful imprecation, gave him a terrible blow, which brought him to the ground, and falling with his knees upon his chest, he would quickly have terminated his existence by cutting his throat, had it not been for the interference of his associates, who declared that they would not become the participators in the shedding of human blood.

"'A murrain seize you for your chicken-hearts!' exclaimed the sanguinary wretch;—"would it not be better to silence him altogether? If he is suffered to live, perhaps, before long, he will bring you to the gallows for your trouble.'

"'I think that blow you gave him has already settled him, remarked one of the others; 'this shedding of human blood is quite unnecessary.'

"'At any rate, I have his gold,' said Milford, drawing forth his purse.

"'Hark!—some one is approaching!' said one of his companions; 'we shall be taken now, if we do not make the best use of our legs.'

"In a moment the three leaped the hedge, and scampered away as fast as they could; but the person whom they had heard beheld them. A loud hue-and-cry was set up, and immediately they went in pursuit of them. One out of the three made his escape, but Milford and the other were taken, and were soon conveyed to prison, heavily ironed.

"The sorrow of his unfortunate wife at this circumstance, notwithstanding his frightful crimes, and the blood-thirsty disposition he, upon every occasion, evinced, was the most poignant which could be imagined; and in spite of the remonstrances of every one, nothing would induce her to abandon him now in his confinement; but to visit him in prison was her determination, and as I could not bear the thought of deserting her who had ever behaved to me with so much kindness, I also intimated my intention of accompanying her. But what was my astonishment and exasperation, upon making known my intention, to discover that I was no longer permitted to do as I thought proper, and that the generality of them opposed my leaving the camp most determinedly, some of them asserting, as a pretext for the same, 'that I could not be spared,' and that, moreover, they could not think of acquiescing with my request, not only because I could not possibly be doing any good there, but because it had been prognosticated by Jabella, one of the eldest of the female Gipsies, that my venturing to the place whither they had taken Milford, would be sure to be the cause of the greatest possible trouble and ruin to the whole of the gang.

"Jabella had opposed, most strongly, our being admitted members of the tribe, and, for what reason I cannot imagine, had ever shown the bitterest enmity towards me. And even, it is said—but how that could be I cannot say—several days before we made our appearance among them, she had predicted that event, and had warned the tribe that danger threatened them from 'such a circumstance; but yet, in spite of all this, and the reliance they placed in the words of the old woman, they admitted us, and it was that opposition to her will most likely which made Jabella my enemy.

"This old beldame took every opportunity to annoy us, but especially me; and often was my temper aroused to an almost insupportable pitch, by the virulence of her spleen and malevolence. Therefore, when I proposed accompanying Mrs. Hatfield, and sharing with her sorrows and her fate, she was the most determined of those that opposed it, and observed, that if I was allowed to quit them, destruction was inevitable to all the party. She added, that already was the curse which I had brought upon the tribe beginning to be realized in the most awful manner, and, therefore, it behoved us, if we would save ourselves, to use every effort in our power to avert the evil which threatened us.

"The persuasive arguments of Jabella prevailed, and they sternly refused to let me go, so that the unfortunate woman, who had been my companion in so many troubles, was compelled to depart alone; which gave me more bitter anguish than anything else they could possibly have inflicted.

"My situation, to which I had, prior to this, in some degree made up my mind, was now made absolutely hateful, detestable to me, and life itself became a burthen; my soul revolted from the shame and degradation to which I was subjected by wretches who were loathed and despised by every one; but alas! my heaviest afflictions were yet to come, and I soon found that the Gipsies only acted prudently in not permitting me to follow Mrs. Hatfield to the place in which her husband was confined.

"In a few days after her departure, one of the tribe, who had returned from the neighbourhood in which the gaol was situated, informed us that Mrs. Hatfield had no sooner made application to see him, than she was also taken into custody, and was now a prisoner.

"No sooner was this dreadful intelligence imparted to me, than I started upon my feet, and in a voice of the deepest anxiety, inquired whether he spoke the truth, and for what she was detained.

"This man was Mark Darwin, who had but recently buried his wife, and who had ever tried to seek my approbation since I had been admitted into the tribe. His two sons were then boys, and his brother, Rupert, after whom one of the former was named, was also a continual source of annoyance to me. Another brother, named Achbet, younger than the other two, was at present confined with Milford on the charge of assisting him in the robbery and attempt at murder.

"' We must confer together, Ela,' said Mark, 'in private it must be, though, for I have got something very particular to impart to you.'

"I hesitated whether to comply with his request, for well did I read what were his wishes as regarded me, and I had always shun-ned talking to him alone as much as I could; but he gave me such a significant look, that I could not help thinking that he really had some-thing particular to impart to me, and my anxiety to be made acquainted with the nature of it, overcame all my scruples. I therefore walked out of the camp, and when we were out of hearing of the others, he looked intently in my countenance, and in a low tone of voice observed : —

"' Ela, I have no doubt that you will feel at all surprised at the detention of Nance, when I inform you it is for that job of the farmer in——'

"My heart rose to my throat—my limbs were palsied with horror—a dreadful giddinesss seized my brain—and an icy cold ran through my veins, when he told me this, and I should have fallen to the ground had not Mark prevented me.

"' Be not alarmed,' said he, 'you are safe enough at present, that is, if they only keep their own counsel, and you think they are to be depended upon: for my part, I don't see that they could reap any benefit by playing you false. Now you will no doubt admit that our people did not act imprudently when they opposed your accompanying Nance.'

"' Oh! indeed—indeed I do!' I gasped out, and with the most grateful feeling for having escaped from such a horrible calamity. But, suddenly, I paused, for I saw Mark's eyes fixed mysteriously and searchingly upon me, and I felt confident that I was speaking too fast, and that I was all but expressing an ac-knowledgment of my participation in the dreadful business; so my presence of mind immediately supplied me with words more pru-dent, which I added—

"' But what should the guiltless apprehend? I had nothing to do with the dreadful crime which you have mentioned, and you may be certain that poor Nance would never harm anything.'

"' But you cannot deny that you were both with Milford on the very night, and at the time, for did you not all sleep in the out-house together? The house in which you lodged, was afterwards destroyed by fire, and the very same man keeps a public-house in the vicinity of the prison, into which Nance unfortunately went, after she had been to see Milford, and

was immediately recognized; and was taken too much by surprise to attempt to deny that she was the person they suspected her to be, and in the course of the questions put to her, it was elicited that you were his wife, and he was the brother of Nance.'

"Mark uttered this with an insolent sneer, which I could not help understanding the meaning of, and determined not to let him long indulge in his thoughts, I said—

"' You have heard what is untrue; it was to suit Milford's purposes, that he pretended I was so on that awful occasion.'

"Mark did not appear to notice my obser-vations, but proceeded as follows :—

"' It did not take them long to discover the facts of the case ;—they knew that Milford was already in custody on a capital charge, and the next question that was naturally put was after you. The way I learnt this was by happening to be in the house at the time it took place, and overhearing all that passed; indeed I was there waiting for Nance, but when she found what had happened, she had the presence of mind to take no notice of me, as if I were an entire stranger to her, and you may be certain I would not know her, but I could not make up my mind to leave the place until I had seen ther termination of it. When they put the question about the other woman who had the child with her, and whom they called the wife of Milford, I was fearful that you would be lost, Ela;—but Nance observed the expression of my countenance, and she remained unshaken in her assertion, that she was entirely ignorant what had become of you. She said you had deserted them some time before, and she did not know whither you had bent your footsteps. If she remains firm in that story,' Mark went on to say, ' and Milford asserts the same, in all probability you may be safe ;—but I thought I should not be acting right if I did not tell you of the danger you stood in at once, so that if anything afterwards should come of it, the shock might not fall too heavily upon you.'

"' And what if it should not pass off, how am I to escape the threatening danger?' I? asked;—' I am conscious of my own perfect innocence—and that if it had been in my power at the dreadful moment, I—' I checked myself and made a sudden pause ; for the countenance of Mark convinced me that I was acknowled-ging more than I ought to do, and that should I place myself in his power, I had everything to dread. But were I not firmly in his power already !'

"' Come, come, Ela,' said he, as he plainly penetrated to my thoughts, ' this is worse than useless; why should you try to conceal any-thing from me? It will answer no purpose. You had much better make a friend and con-fidant of me, I can tell you. I do not intend to say that you had any hand in assassinating the farmer, but were you not present at the time the murder was committed, and did you not share in the money of which he was plundered I tell you, woman, that there is no distinc‑ tion in the law, without you were positively the wife of Milford, when the law holds that a woman, being under the jurisdiction of her husband, is not guilty.'

"Here Mark stopped, and gazed earnestly in my face, as though he would read all my thoughts at a glance; but I made him no reply —terror rendered me incapable of speaking— terror at what he had said. It was the first time that such a dreadful view of the case had been presented to my mind. I knew that I was innocent of having anything to do with the horrible crime—nay, that I would have given the wealth of kingdoms, had they been mine, to have been able to save the unfortunate man from his horrible fate; but after the crime was committed it was only the fear that I should lose my own life, that kept me silent. To be sure, I might upon the first chance which pre‑ sented itself, be induced to save myself from all danger by betraying the assassin, and becoming evidence against him, but what besides saving my life could I have gained by that? What other good would it have effected? Could it have recalled to existence the murdered farmer? And what would have been my reflections after having betrayed to a dreadful and ignominious death those who had not only protected me and my child, but had given to us food in our great‑ est extremity, and had even gone without themselves that my girl should have it? Could I ever have been happy? Could I ever again have held up my head? Would not life have been a hell to me? And should I not have been reprobated, hated, and despised by every‑ body?

"These were my arguments—I knew that they were weak, they were wrong—for the duty I owed to society at large ought to have stifled every feeling; but if I erred, it was not from badness of heart; no, it was ignorance, and a mistaken sentiment of gratitude that made me do so, and the circumstances in which I was placed, over which, at that time, I had no con‑ troul."

Here Walter again laid down the manu‑ script, being anxious to visit his father. The narrative had deeply interested and moved him, and while he could not help sincerely commi‑ serating in the misfortunes and vicissitudes that had attended the writer, he equally blamed her errors, and the weakness which so easily rendered her the dupe of others, and the participator in their vices.

Upon knocking at the chamber door of his father, he was surprised to receive no answer, and repeating the knock with no better success, he gently opened the door and walked in, but Mr. Wallingford was not there. More asto‑

nished than ever, he enquired of the servants, and ascertained that their master had been seen to leave the house two or three hours before, and had taken the direction of Rosemary Dell. This information increased the surprise of Walter, who wondered what motive could have induced his father to quit that chamber, to which he had lately kept himself so entirely secluded, and moreover to walk to the Dell, which he had never since the last adventure with the Gipsies in that place, been in the habit of doing. Anxious to have his curiosity gratified, Walter took up his hat, and quitted the hall, turning, after he left the gardens, into the path which led to the dell, thinking he might in all probability meet his father on his return. He walked on at a quick pace, and it was not long ere he arrived at Rosemary Dell, where he stood and looked eagerly around him him, but he could not perceive anything of his father.

While he still remained in the same position he was startled by hearing a strange, unearthly sort of laugh from behind him, and turning hastily around, his astonishment may be well imagined when he beheld standing and grinning maliciously upon him the form of a frightful hag, whose very appearance was enough to ex‑ cite the utmost terror in the strongest breast.

Walter remained with his eyes fixed upon her for a second or two, during which time her eyes appeared to glare with a supernatural lustre, and there was something in her figure and countenance altogether, which to a person even not prone to superstition, would have pro‑ claimed her a being not of this world.

Walter remembered hearing his father and Maria speak of the mysterious being which had appeared to them at different times, and he had not the least doubt in his own mind that this was the one; and when he remembered that she had in every instance been the harbinger of evil to their family, he could not help shud‑ dering violently. This emotion seemed to be observed by the disgusting looking being with increased exultation, and again she laughed more awfully than before. It was then that Walter recovered his self-possession and he demanded in a firm voice—

"Who are you, woman, and what would you with me, that you appear to me in such a sus‑ picious manner?"

"Walter Wallingford, hear me!" replied the harsh voice of the mysterious being, as she leant with one hand upon the long staff she always carried with her, and placed one of her long, bony fingers upon his shoulder.

"I am the harbinger of woe,
A curse on mankind I bestow,
Though e'er so armed against all fear,
They quail and quake when I appear.

In sorrow and misery I revel.
At my command is ev'ry evil.
Beware—your troubles are not o'er,
There's many a grief for thee in store;
He who first caused the fell disgrace,
Has brought a curse upon his race;
Son of the guilty one beware,
For cause for anguish now is ne ar."

"Base, guilty impostor, I'll hear no more !" exclaimed Walter, as he made an attempt to seize the Sybil, but he grappled at empty air; in a moment the awful being had vanished, in what manner Walter could not imagine ;— her fiendish laugh still vibrated hollowly in his ear, but not a glimpse could he catch of her fleeting form.

ELA BERANZIO IN HER PROSPERITY.

CHAPTER XXXIX.

"Spirit of evil avaunt !
  Hast thou not yet gratified thy spleen,
  'Gainst me and my unhappy race ?"—ANON.

FOR a minute or two, Walter was so much surprised and bewildered by his adventure with the hag, and the prognostications she had uttered, that he could not move from the spot, but stood looking around him, wondering in what manner she could have vanished so suddenly. He was not in the least inclined to be superstitious, but there was something so unnatural in the event, that he was at a loss to form any conjecture upon it. Then her sudden disappearance—but a second before she had been addressing him, and gazing into his countenance with an earnestness which, in spite of all his efforts, made him tremble, but although he had never removed his eyes from her, she had gone, evaporated, "melted into thin air." It was strange, it was inscrutable, and unable to satisfy his mind upon the subject, he walked on, anxious to know what had become of his father.

Having crossed the dell, he looked up, and found himself near the old Manor House, which the Gipsies had once sought shelter in. He had not stood there more than a second or two, when he beheld the figure of a man issue hastily from beneath one of its porches, and on his raising his eyes, Walter was thunderstruck to recognize his father, pale, trembling, and evidently much excited.

"My dearest father," exclaimed Walter, "for heaven's sake, what is the matter with you? What has happened to cause this agitation?"

"Ah! Walter!" exclaimed Wallingford wildly, "follow me; this way, come and witness a scene of misery."

As he thus spoke, he laid hold of his son's arm and urged him into the ancient fabric he had only a minute or two come from. They passed hastily along the hall, when the most piercing cries burst upon the ears of Walter, accompanied by wild hysterical peals of laughter.

"Good God! what is the meaning of this?" demanded Walter, more and more astonished and alarmed; "from whom do these cries proceed?"

Mr. Wallingford returned no answer, but forced his son forward, until they stopped at a low wooden door, which he opened, and there a scene burst upon the young man's view, which smote his heart with horror.

Upon a heap of straw in one corner of a miserable apartment, lay stretched the corpse of the poor old blind woman whom Walter had seen but a day or two before; and kneeling over her, with his eyes wild and glaring, his hair dishevelled, laughing madly, and shrieking alternately, was her wretched son, who was evidently now in a state of insanity! When they entered the room, he was in the act of holding a dry crust of bread to the lips of the corpse, and imploring her with frantic gestures to eat, and then he would upbraid her for her obstinacy, and burst forth into such lamentable cries, that it was quite awful to hear him. Suddenly he became conscious that somebody was present, and fixing his eyes upon Mr. Wallingford, he shrieked out—

"Ah! what have you come again to mock me in my misery? Dare you, with all the load of crime upon your head, venture to approach the chamber of death, to gaze upon the corpse of her who knew no sin? But you have come to mock me! Yes, to laugh at me! Oh, wretch, wretch! Was it not enough to rob me of my first—my only love—to break her parents' hearts—to drive me from my once peaceful home, and to be the cause of reducing the old blind woman to want and misery, but that you must come at this time to laugh at and revile my sufferings? Away, I say, the curse of the broken-hearted parents of her you so cruelly betrayed is upon your head!"

The distracted Wallingford uttered a deep groan, and covering his face with his hands, turned away his head.

This circumstance can soon be explained. Mr. Wallingford feeling tired of the confinement of his chamber, and thinking that the fresh air would do him good, determined to take a walk; accordingly he left the hall, and quite careless whither he bent his steps, he sauntered towards Rosemary Dell. Having crossed this place, being too deeply buried in thought to notice where he was going, he was suddenly aroused from his lethargy by hearing loud and dismal cries, and looking up, he found himself standing before the entrance to the old Manor House. He paused and listened, the cries were repeated, and the first impulse of Mr. Wallingford was, ill as he was, and in spite of the danger there might be attending such a proceeding, to enter the ruinous building, and endeavour to ascertain the occasion of these cries of distress. He walked fearlessly on in the direction from whence they proceeded, and perceiving a room door open, he entered, and there he beheld the poor blind old woman expiring on the miserable bed of straw, and her son kneeling by her side, alternately pressing her cold and bloodless lips, and then bursting forth into a loud wail of bitter anguish.

When Mr. Wallingford first entered the room, the man's back was towards him, and he had but an imperfect view of the dying woman's features, but suddenly the man turned, upon hearing there was somebody in the room, and how shall we do adequate justice to the overwhelming astonishment and emotion of Wallingford, when he recognized in the miserable attenuated object before him, the once handsome and happy Edwin Hartfield, the lover of Ela, and in the features of the poor expiring creature over whom he knelt with such intense affection, his mother, poor blind Alice?

We will pass over the scene which followed this recognition; the remorse, the shame, the degradation which Mr. Wallingford felt, as the unhappy Edwin recalled to his recollection his early, his ardent, his honest passion for Ela, and how he had stepped in like a fiend to rob him of all he prized on earth, and had brought infamy and disgrace upon her he loved so fondly.

We will not repeat the repeat many reproaches, the bitter reproaches, Edwin heaped upon the wretched Wallingford, who, conscious how richly he merited all that could be said, remained silent, while the violence of his agony almost choked him, and he groaned aloud. The poor old woman was at her last gasp, and in the midst of the painful scene she suddenly clasped the hand of her son with the convulsive vehemence of death, and without a sigh or a moan, yielded up her soul to eternity. It was in that dreadful moment of trial that the senses of Edwin fled, and he became a raving maniac. Unable longer to endure the soul-harrowing scene, Mr. Wallingford rushed out of the house, and that moment met his son, as has been related.

The history of these unhappy people can be related in a few words :—After the abduction of Ela from her home, by Wallingford, Edwin Hartfield remained for some time in a state of absolute distraction, and shut his ears to all endeavours at consolation. At length he did recover, but he was an altered youth. He no more mingled in the scenes of rustic mirth which he had been wont to do with such alacrity, and he shunned all his former companions, going about in a state of the most pitiable melancholy.—Even the gentle pleading of his little sister Rosa, and her fond endearments, failed to make any impression upon him, and were, in fact, entirely unheeded. He neglected his work, and had it not been for the little that Rosa could earn at her needle, they must have been brought to the most abject poverty and distress. But nothing whatever could arouse him from this painful state. He would wander about the country to some distance, and, wrapped in the gloom of his own meditations, did not seem to take any notice of anybody.

It was in one of these fits that a recruiting sergeant got hold of him, and with very little difficulty persuaded him to enlist. No language can do adequate justice to the anguish of his friends when they became acquainted with what he had done, but it was out of their power to rescue him, and in a very short time afterward she was sent abroad with the regiment. There he remained for several years, enduring the greatest hardships, and was finally discharged, without receiving any pension. He came to England—sought out the cottage in which he was born ; a stately mansion was erected on the spot where it had stood. But few of the persons who had formerly inhabited the village remained ; but from one of those who did, heart-rending was the narrative which he received. After his departure, little Rosa had strove night and day to support, by the labour of her hands, herself and her mother ; but at length the poor girl's health suffered for it, and she was brought to a premature grave.

Without any means of support, poor blind Alice was brought to the parish poor-house where she had remained ever since. In the midst of all his calamities, it was a source of indescribable delight to Edwin that his mother was still alive, that he might still receive her blessing ere she closed her eyes in death ; and he immediately hastened to the house. The meeting of the blind mother and son was such as no pen could pourtray, though the mind may form a faint conception of it. It was wonderful that the violence of the poor old woman's emotions did not cause her immediate death. Having some few pounds saved by him, Edwin insisted upon taking his mother out of the poor-house, and took a small cottage as near as possible to where the one they had once been so happy in, formerly stood. Here he tried to get employment, but in vain ; the vicissitudes he had endured abroad had so emaciated his frame, that no one would engage with him ; the little money he had brought home with him, although he had laid it out with a most frugal hand, soon became exhausted, and illness pressing upon his frame, the utmost distress stared them in the face ; but still Edwin could not endure the thought of his mother again going to the poor-house, and he himself was determined rather to perish in the streets than to submit to it.—It was a foolish pride, but he could not conquer it, and although poor old Alice entertained no such very delicate scruples, she could not bear the idea of being again separated from that son whom she had never expected to embrace again.

We will pass over the sufferings they underwent for several months, reduced to beggary, as has been shown ; until completely worn out with hunger and fatigue, and the old woman being unable to walk further, they sought refuge in the old Manor-house, where blind Alice died of exhaustion, as has been already described in the foregoing pages.

Seeing the distracted state of mind the event had thrown his father into, Walter, in the best manner he was able, tried to soothe the unfortunate Edwin, but it was all to no purpose ; he every moment became worse, and at length finding that to remain longer there would make Mr. Wallingford worse than ever, he forcibly led him away, having resolved that he would send some persons to remove the corpse, and attend to the wretched survivor. These resolutions of Walter were fulfilled, but that same night Edwin Hartfield breathed his last.

This unexpected event caused Mr. Wallingford a relapse of the most dangerous description, and at one time there were very little hopes of his recovery. The meeting with Edwin Hartfield and his mother, under such melancholy circumstances, had revived many bitter thoughts that he had before contrived partially to erase from his recollection, and again he sought the seclusion of his chamber, and remained even closer confined to it than before, seldom admitting his son, and when he did so, with evident reluctance.

CHAPTER XL.

" He died the death that villains die,
  And left no one behind to drop soft pity's
     tear."

AT the first opportunity which presented itself, Walter resumed the manuscripts that had been given to him by Ela, which went on in the following manner :—

" From this state of unconsciousness I was immediately aroused by what Mark had said to me, and with horror I beheld the abyss of destruction, upon the very verge of which I was standing, and from which I knew not in what manner to escape. On my associates I could place but very little reliance, for I knew that they had it in their power to rescue me from the fate I dreaded ; but their looks, their dark hints, answered that most of them liked me not, and would rather exult at my misery, than try to lessen it, or save me from it altogether.

" ' Great Heaven assist me !' I exclaimed, clasping my hands in despair, ' this is indeed a dreadful, a heavy blow, and never can I support it.'

" ' Nay, do not give way to any idle fears, Ela,' observed Mark, for with us no harm can befall you. Nothing can ever induce our people to turn traitors to each other, and if Nance and Milford only act in the same manner, the job will be settled well enough ; however, you can quite secure your safety, if you will comply with what I shall mention.'

" I inquired what he meant, although my heart at the same time suggested what he wished, and my worst surmises were realized. He proposed for me to accept him for my husband, and directly after that we would hasten from the present place, and join another portion of the tribe, who were at a considerable distance off, and where we should be perfectly secure.

" ' How can I consent to what you wish, Mark,' said I, calmly, ' when I have already informed you that I have a husband living ?'

" I had told them this story when I joined them, as I conceived it would do away with the disgusting importunities of both Mark and his brother Rupert.

" ' Very well,' replied Mark, in a savage tone, ' then if that is the case, apply to your husband for assistance, and see of he can save you.'

" It was with the utmost difficulty I could repress the sentiments of disgust and abhorrence which I entertained towards this man ; but it was to my interest, to my safety, to make him a friend instead of an enemy if possible, and it was therefore politic in me to stifle my real feelings, at the same time not to say anything that might lead him to imagine I encouraged his suit. I tried all I could, but my endeavours were not attended with any successful results ; he felt indignan. at the answer I had given him, and he left me without condescending to hold any further conversation with me.

" I cannot describe the deep, the corroding anguish I endured for hours afterwards ; I was very well aware that many of the party viewed me with jealous eyes, and revengeful and heartless as they were in disposition, what could I hope for at their hands ? Was it not more than probable that they would, the first opportunity which presented itself, denounce me as the associate of the murderer, and give me up to a dreadful and ignominious punishment ? Alas ! despair encircled me around. But I did them an injustice by this supposition, and I should not have done so had I been as well acquainted with them as I am at present. Whatever may be their own private quarrels, and jealousies, and hatreds, they are so opposed to the law, that they forget them in their endeavours to save their companions from the power of it. But I was not long suffered to remain in my fancied security ; the Gipsies had remained too long in this quarter, and at length discovery was made that the prisoners had been associated with them, and one day, when we had never anticipated such an occurrence, the officers of justice arrived at the camp, and myself, two other females, and Mark, were taken up on suspicion of being concerned in the foul deed.

" Fortunately for me, that day I had entrusted my child to one of the women, who was not in the tent at the time the officers came, and to that circumstance I firmly believe I may only attribute saving my life. The person who had before recognized Nance, had no recollection of me ; and forsooth I do not marvel that he could not, for sad was the havoc that suffering and fatigue had made with me.

" They said that they were certain they should have known the child again, for it was such a pretty little thing, but they could not see that any of the women before them resembled the mother in the slightest degree. God knows how I conquered my terrors sufficiently not to betray myself, while undergoing their minute scrutiny ; but my heart throbbed with gratitude to Heaven to think that my darling Fanny had not been made the innocent means of bringing her unfortunate parent to the gallows. Fanny resembled her father, and I had a right then to be thankful to Heaven that she did so, for had she been like me, from the manner in which they scrutinized me, they must most assuredly have discovered me.

"The Gipsies, too, behaved with their usual coolness, courage, and self-possession, and gave so feasible an account of the place where they were when the murder was perpetrated, and Mark so unflinchingly asserted that I was his wife, that they could not do otherwise than suppose I was with them, and so, after we had been detained for a few days in custody, we were discharged.

"Thus it will be seen, that to these people I was a second time indebted for the preservation of my life, for that I must have died with hunger and fatigue there cannot be a doubt, in the first instance, and in this they could, if they had been so disposed, have set themselves at liberty in a minute, and consigned me to a shameful death ; but my life I only valued for the sake of my child.

"But I had now another difficulty to surmount, which caused me much painful thought. Mark Darwin, by keeping so firmly to his asseveraions that I was his wife, imagined that he indisputably entitled himself to my favour, and therefore renewed his importunities with tenfold more vigour and determination than before. Indeed he made sure that it was quite out of my power any longer to refuse him, and although my soul recoiled from such a proceeding with disgust, apprehensions haunting my mind that if I offended them, they would yet betray me, I was compelled to dissemble and receive his attentions with some little degree of courtesy, and to lead him to hope that he might yet succeed in eradicating my repugnance to his suit.

"I had, however, a very good excuse to rid myself at present of so much of his disgusting society, in the sorrow and suspense it was natural to suppose that I should feel at the awful situation of Milford and his wife, and Rupert having joined his party, also rescued me from his persecution.

"At length the assizes came on, and the fates of the prisoners were decided; Milford was condemned to suffer death, and Achbet was sentenced to banishment for life, which mitigated penalty was passed upon him in consideration of his having interposed to prevent the shedding of blood in the case of the highway robbery. Poor Nance! her fate was also sealed—the dreadful death of her husband, to whom she had been so strongly devoted, was too much for her to support, and only one hour before the time appointed for his execution she expired of a broken heart. Poor, ill-fated but misguided woman, even at this distance of time, I cannot help shedding a tear to her memory. My feelings overpower me—I must pause awhile, ere I conclude my melancholy narrative. * *

"I will not trouble you with an account of the various scenes of revolting depravity in which circumstances had so unfortunately placed me, and in which I was compelled to take an active part. My object in writing thus far has not been to mask my many errors, but to show that I was not a willing participator in those vices which have made me an object of scorn and hatred to the world. But there are still some events which probably may require an explanation, and I will do so as briefly as possible. I will not dwell upon what I suffered from the determined assiduities of Mark Darwin and his brother, for at length I became so inured to the manners of these people, that I learned the way to pay them out in their own coin, and to exhibit the same ferocious and ungovernable spirit as they themselves did. But imagine not that my sufferings were any the less on that account ; oh no, on the contrary, they were rather increased by them, for seeing my obstinacy, their full enmity was aroused towards me, and especially of those whose influence over the tribe was paramount. Scarcely a day was suffered to elapse without the spleen of Jabella, Morna, and Zelta, and others, being exhibited towards me in the most violent manner, and which all served to add fuel to the fire of my temper, which now grew more intractable every day. Besides I had now increased annoyance in the persons of the two sons of Mark, who had all the temper of their ruffian father, and who seemed to think it their duty, a duty they owed to him, to persecute as much as was in their power, one who ever evinced such a dislike to their parent. All these annoyances daily practised upon me, added to the fierceness of my temper, and at times I was really in a state bordering upon frenzy. But it was then, my beloved Fanny, that thy wretched mother found a temporary relief in thy gentle and angel spirit ;—yes, thy sweet voice, imparting words of consolation, abated my fury, or otherwise, many a time should I have been forced into acts of vengeance that I now shudder to think upon. Had it not been for thee, my child, thy unhappy parent would have stained her hands in the blood of her fellow creatures.

"I will not dwell upon my first introduction to Mrs. Wallingford, and the circumstances that immediately succeeded it ; it is also useless for me to mention the tempest of passions that raged in my bosom for many months afterwards ; it was long ere I could regain anything like a state of calmness.

"We left Rosemary Dell, and I had indulged the hope that we might never more return to it ; but I had not now a will of my own ; my fate was in the hands of those with whom I had become indissolubly connected, and my hopes were doomed to be disappointed. After a long sojourn in various parts of the country, I was given to understand that the party to which I was attached were about once more to take up their old quarters in that neighbourhood which had now become to me so hateful. I deter mined directly that I would not accompany them; and I was not a little astonished when I found that the Gipsies did not wish me to make one of their party, so I was permitted to go in a different direction, taking only Fanny with me.

"The beauty and interesting behaviour of my child had always succeeded in getting me friends and encouragement wherever I went, and I therefore made up my mind that I would take the same course which I had in the preceding spring travelled with my companions. Oh! how happy should I have been, could I have left those whom I hated and despised, never more to return to them! I would have purchased such a liberty at almost any cost, save sacrificing the life of my child. I would gladly have submitted to continue to do what I was now doing, namely, beg for my living and her's, but there was no hope of that; I was ordered to rejoin the gang at a particular spot, on a certain day, and death would be sure to be my portion if I neglected to do so.

"One consolation, however, I had in the midst of this trouble;—I was no longer persecuted by the elder Mark, who was married to a woman belonging to another party, which he had consequently joined.

"But to proceed with my dismal narrative. I was true to the very hour in which I had been ordered to rejoin the gang, and I made sure that I should find them punctually at the place of appointment; but I was disappointed; day after day elapsed, and yet I saw nothing of them, and a hope that I was relieved from them for ever began to spring up in my mind; but I was not long suffered to indulge in it, for I accidentally learned the outrages they had committed at Wallingford Hall.

"Me and Fanny had been sheltered in a barn for the last week or two, owing to the kindness of the farmer's wife, whose fortune I had several times told, and who placed great reliance in my prognostications, for one good reason—that they promised riches and all the other good things of this life in abundance. The farmer, too, being a kind-hearted man, and much pleased with the engaging ways of Fanny, raised no objection to his wife's kindness; but he used to lecture me occasionally by saying that a young woman like me ought to feel ashamed to lead the life of a vagabond, when I might get a respectable living by honest industry, and be esteemed in the world. I felt the justice of the old man's observations, and would have given worlds, had they been at my disposal, to have been able to do so. The kind farmer also permitted me to sit by the kitchen fire, to eat the humble repast which his wife always provided for me and Fanny before we retired to rest; and he, moreover, would frequently have my child to dinner with them, and I had every reason to suppose, from the hints

which they threw out, that if I would have consented to resign her altogether, they would provide for her, for they had no children of their own.

"Here it was that I was made acquainted with the evil transactions of the Gipsies of my party at Wallingford Hall, in a conversation which ensued one night, while I was seated in the company of the honest farmer and his wife, by their fireside.

"'I tell thee what, young woman,' said the farmer, 'it be a nation lucky job for thee that thou hast not been wi' th' rest o' thy vagabond tribe, down at a place they call Rosemary Dell, lately, for they have been making sad doings there, for which they all desarve to be hanged, if they had got a hundred necks each. They have been setting fire to people's houses, an' burning persons in 'em too—at least, so it is reported, and I have no doubt it is true enough, for they don't care what they do, I know, when the devil spurs 'em on. Then they do say that they made an attack on some great squire down there, and have nearly killed him, so I think you have very good cause to rejoice that you was not with the rascals, for you may depend upon it some of 'em will have their necks stretched for it. Do you know whereabouts the fellows be now?'

"To this, of course, I replied in the negative, but I was so surprised, and in such a state of anxiety, owing to what I had heard, that I could not get any rest the whole of the night for reflecting upon it, and the suspense I was in to know the particulars may be easily conceived. It was not long before my anxiety was satisfied. Two of the females belonging to the party contrived to meet me, and from them I learned the real facts of the case. They also informed me that the whole of the gang had sworn the most deadly vengeance against Wallingford and his family; and at that time, though I blush to own it now, I was quite as inveterate in my denunciations against him, and exulted in what they had done, which I considered was only a just punishment for the misery he had brought upon me.

"From the women I learned that Mark, who had rejoined the party for that purpose, was the concoctor and executer of the diabolical scheme. He had gained access to the room in which the infant Christabelle was sleeping, by climbing up to the window, and afterwards set fire to the place, by the means of a dark lantern which he had with him. The flame having spread very rapidly, it was miraculous how he had contrived to escape.

"I cannot deny, and I acknowledge so with shame, that this account made me quite wild with exultation, and impatient to be certain of the truth of it. That very night I took my departure from the place where the worthy farmer and his wife had treated me with so much kindness and hospitality, and made my way to where I understood old Zelta and the child were concealed. A thousand horrible ideas at that moment disturbed my mind, which I now shudder to think on ;— but yet I was perfectly undecided what I was going to do, though I was in a perfect transport of exultation. Heaven be thanked, who arrested my frenzied design, or what shocking deed might I not have to answer for ?— But how could I longer indulge such wicked thoughts, when I beheld the beauty and innocence of Christabelle ?—My sentiments were in a moment changed towards her, for in her I beheld the very counterpart of my own darling girl, and I could almost imagine that I again gazed upon my beauteous Fanny in infancy ; I reflected upon the dreadful, the bitter anguish the mother of so sweet a babe must endure at the loss of it, and an emotion of pity entered my bosom. I could not think of this, and gaze upon the countenance of my daughter, without a feeling of terror. The wild and almost ungovernable passions that had before distracted my brain had vanished, and I no longer thought of Wallingford as the father of that sweet infant, though every lineament of his features was so strongly impressed upon her countenance ; but all other ideas were banished from my mind, by the one which now solely occupied it, which was, how I could restore to her mother the little innocent babe. This would be a bold, hazardous attempt, and if it were found out by my companions, I was well aware that all the violence of their wrath would descend upon my head. But great as was the danger, it would not induce me to abandon my project, and I therefore resolved that the attempt should be made without further delay.

" My scheme was well contrived. In order that none of my associates might for a moment imagine that I was seeking to deprive them of the child, I ever, in their presence evinced the utmost hatred towards it, and old Zelta, who had the sole care of her, never seemed to suspect that my aversion was feigned, but she would not suffer the child to be away from her. However, I did not doubt but that I should be able to accomplish my purpose in spite of her, and I adopted the proper method to put her off her guard.

" It having been considered by those of our tribe who had the ruling of us that it would be better for our party not to remain together for some months, but that each should take the road they thought best, making an appointment to meet together at a certain time, we were about to separate. So this was an opportunity I determined not to let slip ; accordingly, I contrived to insinuate myself into the good graces of Zelta on that evening, and under the pretext of drinking towards the success of our peregrinations, and wishing we might all meet safe

again, I plied her so well with the beverage she was most accustomed to drink, that she became inebriated, and thus my design was very soon accomplished. She became quite unconscious, and without any difficulty I got the child in my power.''

From this part of Ela's narrative, it appears, that the account which old Zelta gave Doctor Hartley was not correct ; for here nothing was mentioned about the screaming of the infant, or the marks of blood, and these she had probably invented for the purpose of giving her story a greater probability, and thus making the worthy doctor more readily believe her, and imagine that Christabelle was no more. This, too, the old woman doubtless thought would be more likely to excite the utmost detestation and revenge against Ela, for whom she had a mortal hatred.

We will now return to the story of Ela.

" I had at first resolved that I would proceed direct to Wallingford Hall with the child ; but my design was quickly rendered abortive, when I understood that old Mark was in the neighbourhood of Rosemary Dell, he being on the look out to see what steps Wallingford and the others would take after the recent occurrence. I was then at a loss, for a few minutes, to know what I could best do, when suddenly I remembered Farmer Hodges and his wife, where I had so lately been, and to them I resolved to repair. I was certain that none of my associates would ever think of looking for me in such a place as that, because they never, themselves, returned to any quarter which they had visited, until a certain time had been allowed to elapse. This rule was by no means a strange one, inasmuch as they invariably remained in any neighbourhood they might choose for their encampment, until they had either tired out the patience and philanthropy of the inhabitants, or committed some offence, which rendered their departure unavoidable.

" I did not find it a very hard matter to impose upon the credulity of Mrs. Hodges, and to quiet any suspicions that might enter her mind upon my so soon reappearing with another child. What furthered my wishes was, that one of my prognostications to her, she declared, had just been verified. It was a regular hackneyed prediction with which me and my companions learned to delude the ignorant and the superstitious ; however, on the same day I got back to the farm, something occurred which coincided with it, and the poor woman received me graciously, for she firmly believed that I was possessed of supernatural powers.

" The tale I invented was a most pathetic one, and was readily credited by the farmer and his wife. I pretended that Esther (for so I called her) was the child of my sister, who had died suddenly, and it was thus left an orphan. The good people were moved by the manner in which I detailed this narrative, and the infant's likeness to Fanny convinced them that, as far as consanguinity was concerned, I had told nothing but the truth.

"'Why, young woman,' said Mr. Hodges, 'any one would take you to be the mother of the child, for I never saw two faces so much alike as her's and little Fanny's in my life. It is a sweet little creature;—let me kiss it—dang it if I should mind being the father of such a bairn as that mysen.'

"The last words of the farmer furnished me with a new idea, and I immediately resolved to endeavour to put it into execution. Previous to this, it had been my determination to return the child to her father and mother; but now my ideas were materially altered;—here was an excellent home for her, where she would be sure to receive every attention and affection, as if she were with those to whom she belonged; and this would afford an opportunity of awaiting a time when I might accomplish her restoration to her parents without hazard; so, without any more reflection, I set about effecting my object.

"'Ah! God help me!' I observed, 'and this poor baby too, for I'm sure I don't know how I shall provide for it and my own child too, for people are not all so charitable as I have found Mr. and Mrs. Hodges. I am sure it would be an act of real charity if some kind individual would release me from the burthen.'

"The infant, at that moment, who had been sitting on the farmer's knees, looked up in his face, and smiled innocently, at the same time that she played with his whiskers.

"'Well, dang it, I don't know whether I should be doing right or not,' he observed, 'but if I was certain that you have really told us the truth, and that the poor baby has no parents, I wouldn't mind becoming it's protector.' As the farmer thus expressed himself, he looked earnestly at his wife, who, from her looks, seemed by no means averse to the proposition.

"'It's the sweetest and innocentest little darling that ever I clapped my two eyes on,' said that worthy woman. This was quite sufficient to satisfy me that the business was all but settled. I had procured kind protectors for the child, and my mind was at rest. I did not, at that time, urge the subject any further, and it was not long before I found that I had acted prudently, for the next morning they informed me that they had been weighing the subject over in their own minds after they retired to bed, and they had come to the determination that they would take the child off my hands if I would consent to part with it.

"'Consent,' said I, 'oh, cheerfully will I, and every blessing light upon you for your kindness. Dear me! what a wicked woman to the poor child I should be, if I were to refuse to resign her to those who are so much better able to take care of her than I am; but you will allow me to come and see her now and then, will you not?'

"'You may come as often as you think proper, young woman,' said the farmer, 'and you shall always be received in the same manner that you have been; and I only wish you'd be persuaded by me to leave off your vagabond life, and then I might be inclined to see what could be done for you.'

"I expressed to him in unmeasured, but sincere terms, my gratitude, and when I quitted them my heart felt all the lighter, for I was not yet entirely without a friend in the world who would receive me with a welcome. And great was the consolation this afforded the poor outcast, who for so many years had been without a resting place, and had been the hunted and despised of mankind.

"Perhaps I may be blamed for deceiving the good farmer and his wife, so far as encouraging them to imagine that I had entirely resigned the child to them, if it was my design that she should, at some future period, be restored to her father and mother; but I had thought of a scheme to prevent their being disappointed or taken by surprise, by prognosticating that Esther was destined to be a lady, and the poor credulous people would not have presumed to discredit me for the world.

"'At any rate,' said Mrs. Hodges, 'let her fate be whatever it may, I hope she will not be so ungrateful as to cease to remember those who will protect her in her early years; and nothing would afford me greater delight than to see my poor little Etty become rich and great.'

"I cannot find time to recount all the circumstances that occurred subsequent to my quitting the house of Mr. and Mrs. Hodges, and which entirely precluded the possibility of my letting Mrs. Wallingford know of the existence and present retreat of her child.

"Many years now elapsed before I again went to Rosemary Dell—years of the most bitter anguish, privation, want, and disgrace to me. Oh! how it wrings my heart, as I recall them to my memory! Would that I could obliterate them for ever from the tablet of my recollection; but alas! I cannot;—they rise so vividly to my mind's eye, that all other thoughts are absorbed in the remembrance of them. Far, far did I travel during that time. There was not a spot in the kingdom which I did not visit. Often was I so tormented with the pangs of hunger that I laid myself down by the road side, and prayed for death to put a termination to my sorrows. At others, when fortune crowned my vagrant endeavours, I revelled in coarse extravagance and dissipation. Sometimes, too, I was the inmate of a gaol for months, often for sleeping in the open air;—not unfrequently on suspicion of having committed offences, of which I was completely innocent;—and sometimes for crimes to which I was driven by dreadful necessity and want.

"But, in the course of that time, think not that I abandoned the child. No; my thoughts and anxiety were constantly with her, and two or three times I had paid a visit to Farmer Hodges, for the purpose of seeing her. Esther (as Christabelle was now called) was daily becoming a lovely girl, and whenever my Fanny and her saw each other, they evinced the strongest affection for one another. They were made acquainted with the manner in

JABELLA.

which they were supposed to be related, and the parting between the two poor girls was always affecting in the extreme.

"Nearly six years had now passed away since Esther had been under the protection of Farmer Hodges and his wife; but great indeed was the change I found in her situation when I paid my last visit to the farm. I found that the farmer's wife had died suddenly, and after remaining a widower only a few months, the farmer took another wife in the person of a coarse, vulgar, ignorant girl, who had formerly been servant to him, and who, whenever I visited the farm, always looked upon me with an eye of jealousy; but why she should do so, I could not conceive. To the outrageous delight of the honest farmer, she had just been delivered of a fine boy, and the farmer, who had never anticipated such an event, was so overjoyed, that it drove him half out of his senses. The death of my former friend, and the substitution of this ignorant woman in her place, caused me to be received very differently to what I had been used to. Mr. Hedges, himself, did not abate any of the heartiness of his usual reception, but as for his present wife, she not only treated me with the utmost disdain, but told me, without any disguise, that 'she would not have her place made a 'ceptacle for such like cattle. I might lodge in the barn for a night or two, if I thought proper, but she was not a going for to give any encouragement to a set o' warmint who was too lazy to work, and who tried to impose upon them as would.'

"Dismal was the tale poor Esther told me of her own altered condition; formerly she was the pet, the very delight of the family, and was granted every possible indulgence that it was possible she could wish for; but now, she was not only made the fag of the house, but was huffed and abused by the farmer's new wife, and told that she had no business there, and that she didn't even so much' as earn salt to her porridge, and that she was cut out for nothing else than the life of vagrancy from which Hodges's first wife had been so silly as to take her.

"Esther, as I have before said, was a very fine girl, and looked much older than she was, being little more than nine years old. Her intelligence and sensibility were far beyond her age, and she, therefore, felt this greatest the more acutely. Her tears flowed fast, as she hung upon my neck, and related to me these particulars.

"'Indeed,' she added, 'there is nothing I would not rather endure with you and Fanny, than to remain where I am, to be driven about and nearly starved, when I know that I merit such different treatment. Mr. Hedges (for I am no longer permitted to call him father, as I used to do) behaves as well to me as his wife will permit him; but he is quite afraid of her, she has got such a temper, and he is, therefore, compelled to do as she orders him, and not as he would wish. Oh! I cannot endure this treatment much longer, indeed I can't. No; rather let me accompany you and Fanny, and crave public charity, than to remain where I am, in a place which is now becoming so hateful to me.'

"While poor Esther was thus speaking, I had been meditating upon how it would now be the most prudent and advisable for me to act; and it was now that I deeply regretted not having persevered in putting that plan into execution which I at first devised—namely, to restore the poor girl to that home and those friends, from whom she had been so cruelly torn; but as we were not about to revisit Rosemary Dell, I resolved that I would not delay it any longer. I therefore endeavoured to soothe Esther as well as I could, and begged of her to put up with her present miserable situation for a very short time longer, as I had a plan in my mind which I had every reason to hope would be productive of a great change to her; but I impressed upon her the necessity of remaining as quietly as possible at the farm, until I had time to put my designs into execution, when she would be sure either to see or to hear from me.

"'But,' said the affectionate girl, as the tears still trembled on her cheeks, 'you will not desert me in this misery?—if you are unsuccessful in what you at present contemplate, say, oh! only say that I shall become the companion of you and Fanny, and whatever misfortunes may attend us, believe me, I shall be content—be happy.'

"'You shall, my dear girl,' said I, kissing her fervently; "now—now, cheer up, and do not despair but that happiness is yet in store for you.'

"With these words we separated.

"I journeyed to Rosemary Dell, and you may judge of my anguish and regret when I found that Wallingford Hall was no longer occupied by its owners.

"The jealousy which my associates had always entertained towards me, especially as regarded the Wallingford family, daily increased; for they suspected that I received money from the members of it, and concealed it from them; and I told them many stories, which were only fabrications, for the purpose of misleading them with respect to the real motives for my conduct. I say they suspected that I received money which I did not make known to them, and consequently their enmity towards me every day became stronger. Frequently, when enraged, I would upbraid them in unmeasured terms for the shameful, the atrocious outrage they had committed upon Wallingford and his family, and I not only reproached them for their conduct, but even ventured to betray them to that punishment they merited. In consequence of this, now that we were again in the neighbourhood of Rosemary Dell, they kept a strict watch upon my conduct, lest I should put my threats into execution, and they followed closely my footsteps wherever I went. Notwithstanding all this precaution, however, my cunning was too great for them, and I managed to elude their vigilance, and with my unfortunate daughter, Fanny, got to the hall; but alas! my hopes proved abortive, there was no one in the house, with the exception of a few domestics, and from what I elicited from them, I was led to imagine that Mr. and Mrs. Wallingford were dead.

"Despair and misery now took paramount possession of my mind, and with a bursting heart, I was about to retrace my steps towards our miserable retreat, but, with all the care which I imagined I had taken, I soon found that my designs had been discovered, that I had been watched to the hall, and immediately afterwards I was in the power of my villanous associates, at the head of whom was Mark Darwin, who now looked upon me with the most inveterate detestation.

"Believing that I had gone to the hall for the purpose of divulging their secrets to Wallingford, they treated me with the utmost barbarity, and it is only astonishing that they did not sacrifice me to their brutality and vengeance. The treatment I received at their hands, the blows the villains dealt me with their bludgeons, and the kicks which I received from them while I lay helpless on the ground rendered me unconscious of all that was going forward around me, and in that wretched condition they conveyed me to the encampment;—but not there, even, did my tortures cease. Doctor Hartley came to enquire after me, but my poor child, my Fanny, was compelled to tell an untruth, and to deny her mother, although at the time the worthy gentleman was speaking to her I was lying not many yards from him under the tent. When the good doctor left the spot, I was forced from the tent, and dragged away by the miscreant Mark; and several of his companions, to prevent all possibility of a discovery being made, should the doctor return with the officers of justice, and insist upon making a minute search over the encampment.

"'Your tricks shall be put a stop to, you treacherous cat,' said the ruffian, Mark, 'I'll take good care of that.—There, in with you; this is the fittest place for such as you; and I'll remain with you until you are able to travel again; and I'll warrant you sha'n't have a chance of revealing our secrets to the gentlefolks about here. No—no, no more of your deceit, you vixen; only think yourself lucky that your life has been spared you.'

"With these words, Mark and the others dragged me into an out-house, which place, communicating with the old Manor House, they thought would be the fittest for their design.

"That I had carried away the child from old Zelta, was very well known to the gang, but in spite of all their artifices, their cunning, and their threats, they failed in making me reveal in what manner I had disposed of her, or whither I had taken her. When in their moments of rage, they vented their spleen upon me, they never failed to upbraid me with my treachery, and said that they had not the

least doubt but that it was my intention, at some period or the other, to return her to those to whom she belonged, for the purpose of getting the reward, which, there could be no doubt, would be gladly given. It is, therefore, not to be wondered, that with that impression upon their mind, they should firmly believe that, when they found I had gone to the hall, it was my design to put this into execution, and, moreover, to betray the whole of my associates to their enemies. Nay, more, what in no small degree strengthened their suspicions, was the circumstance of Doctor Hartley being found by Mark in the out-house, from whence they had not long before removed me, or the worthy doctor would doubtless there have discovered me, as I had been there lying on a pallet of straw, nearly dead from the effects of the brutal treatment I had received. The alarm of the gang at this was so great, that they would no longer remain at the Manor House, and, therefore, they left their retreat, and joined me and the wretch Mark at the place to which he had hurried me, notwithstanding the agony I was in.

"Old Zelta was left behind, to endeavour to find out whether it was the intention of Mr. Wallingford and the others to pursue us; and if it were so, to contrive to put them on the wrong scent. In two or three days, she made her appearance among us, and then, from what I could understand, informed my associates that they need not be under any further apprehension of my betraying them, as she had taken good care to invent a story that would set all my future attempts at defiance, and only recoil upon myself.

"As for me, I knew, at least I suspected that all hope of my now doing so was at an end, since I imagined that the parents of the child were both no more. And now, indeed, did I reproach myself for not having restored her at the time I first thought, which, probably, would have saved Wallingford and his wife from a premature grave.

"Many, many dreary months of bitter suffering and anguish intervened, ere I again beheld poor Esther, during which time, the treatment I received from the gang was monstrous, and it is only wonderful to me that I did not die under it; but Providence preserved me for my child and Esther.

"At length I did once more behold the poor girl, and the meeting may be easily imagined. It was one of the utmost affection on both sides, for there was nothing on earth that shared so large a portion of my affections as Esther, except my own ill-fated daughter. With a bursting heart she threw herself upon my bosom, and prayed that I would not again leave her to the misery she now endured at the farm. Every day, she informed me, it had become worse and worse, until it was really now intolerable, and she felt that any suffering would be preferable to what she endured from the detestable temper of that ignorant and brutal woman.

"Notwithstanding this appeal, situated as I was, and the wretched life I must lead her into, made me tenacious of removing her from any place of refuge; but it was decided by the farmer himself, who had at length yielded to the wicked inventions of his wife against the girl, and believed her to be "an ungrateful little hussy" (so he called her); so that he no sooner saw me, than in a spiteful and harsh tone he expressed the pleasure he felt at seeing me again, since they should get rid of one whom they had fed, clothed, and protected too long.

"This manner of speaking very justly aroused my indignation, and I replied with warmth, saying that I would not believe that the girl was deserving of such an epithet, and that it only originated in the jealousy and malevolence of his wife; but that it was of very little consequence, as I had come with the express purpose of taking her off their hands. But Mr. Hodges would not be convinced of this, for he had, doubtlessly, been very artfully prejudiced against Esther, by her bitter enemy, and, in extenuation and exculpation of the latter, who, he said, had "behaved like a mother to her," he proceeded to recount a number of delinquencies, of which, he said, Esther had been guilty —mere fabrications of his wife, for the purpose of gaining her ends, and getting Esther away from the place. But, in spite of all he said, it was no very difficult matter to discover that his heart was not yet dead to her, who had once been his little favourite, and whom he had taught himself to look upon as his own offspring, and especially when he saw the poor girl, with her bundle in her hand, about to leave the house with me, and, in doing so, drop him a curtsey, while a tear trembled in her expressive eye. He could no longer resist his real feelings, but following her out of the house, he thrust a purse of silver into her hand, and hastily re-entered the house, for fear that he should encounter the wrath of his termagant wife.

"The tale I told to introduce her among the tribe, succeeded; but there were many who firmly believed that she was the child which I had abducted from old Zelta; still the great likeness that existed between her and Fanny, in some degree silenced their suspicions, and made them the more readily believe that they were cousins; I having told them the same story as I had to Farmer Hodges and his wife, and Esther needed scarcely any injunction from me, not to reveal any of the circumstances of her early days; indeed, a more sweet, intelligent, or prudent child, I never beheld.

"She also possessed a firm and vigorous mind, that made her smile at difficulties which others would have sunk under; and never did I hear her repine at the many privations to which, in our precarious life, we were frequently subjected. Mild and compliant to those who treated her with kindness, she could not possibly have enemies; no one was jealous of her, no one disliked her, no one suspected her, and possessed with a buoyancy of spirits that would not permit her to indulge in sorrow or regret, but which always prompted her to submit with patience to circumstances, it was not long ere she became contented with those manners, from which, at first, her heart had recoiled with disgust.

"Soon womanhood, fresh, blooming, and enchanting, crept upon her, and the beauties of her spotless mind expanded. In the midst of all that was base and wicked, still did Esther and Fanny remain uncontaminated. They were so strong in spotless virtue, that nothing could blemish its purity; they were compelled to yield to the necessities of their situation, but yet did they not suffer the slightest error to sully their minds, and in the communication of thought, formed for each other a source of inexhaustible enjoyment and instruction.

"I now draw near the conclusion of this melancholy narrative—the final scene; and much I fear that I shall not be able to do adequate justice to it. When we returned to our old quarters at Rosemary Dell, we had not the slightest idea that Wallingford Hall was inhabited by any of its former occupants. I say we, but in that I am wrong; I knew it, although the rest of the tribe were entirely ignorant of it—and I cannot adequately describe my feelings when I discovered that those whom I had thought no more were still in existence, and I determined to seize the first chance which presented itself to make my way to Wallingford Hall, and endeavour to learn the truth or falsehood of the report. It was not long before I found an opportunity, and without any companion I and found my way to Rosemary Dell, and soon did I ascertain that what I had been told was true. The Wallingfords again inhabited the place, and there I saw him looking as calm and contented as if he had never known what guilt was, and had never diffused anything but happiness around him, instead of bringing irretrievable misery and disgrace upon one whose only fault at that time was in loving him too fondly.

"He was imparting instruction from a book which he held in his hand to a lovely girl on one side of him, and a handsome lad who stood upon the other. My heart throbbed violently as I gazed upon him, and all the injuries he had done me rose in forcible colours upon my recollection. For a moment my fiercer passions gained the ascendancy over my reason, and I could scarcely forbear starting before him, and upbraiding him for his perfidy; but at that moment a circumstance took place which I have every reason to believe made my presence known to him. A man who happened to be near the spot, and who noticed me, looked at me with an eye of suspicion, as these abject hinds always do at our people, and asked why I was lurking about that place, and whether I wanted to beg.

"'Beg!' I ejaculated in a tone which completely frightened the rustic; 'beg of that wretch? ha! ha! ha!——'

"I laughed in a derisive tone, which made the very place re-echo again, and hastily left the spot. I had seen enough, I had my doubts verified; Wallingford and his wife still lived, and without waiting for anything more, I made the best of my way to the place where I had left Esther and Fanny until I came back."

At this part of the unfortunate Ela's narrative, Walter put down the manuscript, and reflected upon the circumstance which it had just related, and which came as fresh upon his memory as if it had only taken place the day before; and likewise did he recollect the state of agitation into which it had thrown his father, and the singular thoughts and doubts it had excited in his bosom. For many years had Walter and Maria known no other preceptor than Mr. Wallingford, and few indeed were so well calculated for such an office. The time to which Ela had alluded in her manuscript, the affectionate father and his son and niece, were seated in the summer-house, and he was just about to begin his lecture, when he was prevented from doing so by the sudden appearance of one of the servants at the farm, whose manner and countenance expressed much perturbation.

"What is the matter, Humphrey, and what have you come here for?" demanded Mr. Wallingford.

"Oh, dear sir," stammered forth the man, "would you have believed it,—that there confounded Gipsy woman has again made her appearance; I saw her with my own two blessed eyes not two minutes ago."

Mr. Wallingford evinced no little emotion and alarm upon receiving this intelligence, but with that self-possession which was one of the most remarkable traits in his character, he requested his son and Maria to return immediately to the hall, and then he demanded a full explanation from Humphrey of the circumstance of which he had made mention. But what transpired, Walter was never made acquainted with, for both his father and mother took the most sedulous care that nothing should be imparted to him which might serve to prejudice him against the man to whom he was indebted for his existence. Therefore, in vain had Walter tried at that time to conjecture the cause of his father's strange agitation, and for what reason

himself and his cousin had been enjoined upon no account whatever to walk in the grounds for for some days afterwards, and Mr. Wallingford did not give them his evening instruction, as he had usually done, for some time after this event had taken place. Now Ela's narrative fully explained the cause of all this emotion on the part of his father, and he could not wonder at it.

The story which the man had told to Mr. Wallingford, being much exaggerated, had indeed very much alarmed him; but upon more mature reflection, Mr. Wallingford, recollecting that Humphrey was notorious for his lying propensities, discarded all thoughts of the truth of it from his mind, and accused the man of having sought to impose upon him, by inventing an impudent falsehood; but as Humphrey strongly protested his innocence, and declared again and again that he had seen the Gipsy woman, Mr. Wallingford ordered every minute inquiry into the truth or falsehood of the same, but after a strict investigation nothing could be obtained; no one in the vicinity had seen a woman answering the description given of Ela, and Mr. Wallingford, therefore, became satisfied that his suspicions of the erroneousness of what Humphrey had stated were correct, and read him a severe lecture for his impudence, and told him that if he ever heard of doing such a thing again, he would that instant dismiss him from his service.

CHAPTER XLI.

"Though many years may run their course,
    E'en midst life's gayest throngs,
The mind of feelings sensitive
    Can ne'er forget its wrongs."—ANON.

THE narrative of Ela went on as follows:—

"After having ascertained the truth of what I had been told, I did not remain in the neighbourhood a moment longer than possible, but hurried away for many powerful reasons, the principal of which was that I was apprehensive of being known. Dreadful, too, was the state of my mind—my brain was racked to torture. While I was labouring under the delusion that Wallingford was mouldering in his tomb, I had tried to forget the injuries, the injustice he had heaped upon me, and I felt the greatest possible compunction for the trouble I had brought upon those so dear to him, by the revengeful nature of my disposition; but when these surmises were dissipated, and I once more saw him alive and apparently in good health, and in the possession of every happiness and luxury; at the same time to judge from the placid appearance of his countenance, he seemed to have driven from his mind all thoughts of the cruel and perfidious manner in which he had behaved towards me, all my most malevolent passions were again aroused towards him, and I became the same violent being that I had been years before. And wherefore should I be ashamed to acknowledge these sentiments towards a man who has brought me to disgrace, infamy, and the most abject misery?—I will not endeavour to deny the truth:—I will not seek to deny the rancorous feelings that were revived in my bosom. —Is he not a wretch deserving of every misfortune that can befall him?—Did he not hurl me from the pinnacle of happiness and innocence to the lowest depths of misery and guilt?— Was it not he who crushed all my early prospects, made a desert of what was before a way of flowers and beauty?—Was it not he who broke my parents' hearts, and brought them to an untimely grave?—Was it not he who drove an honest and industrious youth, who sincerely loved me, first to madness, and then to abandon his poor blind mother?—Yes, he is the guilty wretch who has caused all this, and yet on me alone, Ela, the wretched outcast, all the degradation and opprobrium are thrown. But was it my fault that I sinned? Oh, no,— Heaven knows that I was pure and innocent, and never harboured a thought of wrong. It was no lascivious creature, who willingly took the path to lead to her own ruin. No; in the first place, I was hurried clandestinely from my home, and afterwards thought I was legally, lawfully made his bride!—Was I to blame?— No!—But oh, I was indeed a fool that I could not see through the villain's deceit and treachery!—But let me erase it from my thoughts; it drives me to distraction, when I recall it to my memory.—My brain whirls round and frenzy seizes upon my memory, when I think upon that moment that the mist was driven from before my eyes—when I was told that I had been deceived—deceived by him whose mind I had thought was the seat of truth and sincerity; when I learned that I was not his wife, but a poor, degraded, ruined wretch.—Yes, Ela Beranzio, the descendant of a family whose name had never been sullied, was now the object of scorn and disgust.—The despised of her fellow creatures—and—oh, God! blot it out from my recollection altogether!—Wallingford—bane of my peace— never—never can I pardon you—the dying curse of my parents speak against it!—Yet have I not been avenged?—Oh, yes, yes, I have—and my mind wanders—I know not what I write—oh, would that I could gain a sweet oblivion to all these agonizing reminiscences, and that all might end amicably."

Walter was again compelled to lay down the manuscript. Deeply did he sympathize in the sufferings and injuries Ela had sustained, and the eternal disgrace which the misconduct of his father had brought upon himself and his family. Yet was he terribly shocked at the violence, the unquenchable malevolence of the feelings which Ela entertained towards him, and sincerely reciprocated her wish that all might yet terminate peaceably; although much he dreaded that there was yet much more trouble in store for them, he resumed the narrative:—

"Distracted as my mind is with bewildering and tormenting reflections, I have wandered from my subject, and almost forgotten with what intention I sat down to record these melancholy incidents. I would not give a moment's anguish to the son, by making any remarks that may sound harsh and severe, or by exaggerating circumstances; no, I have related nothing but facts, and in justice to myself it is necessary that it should be made known, first, to convince the world, or those who take any interest in the subject, that Ela was not the culpable party she may have been considered, and that she has had sufficient to excite her to these acts of violence that have been productive of such unhappiness to all of us.

"I have informed you that Fanny and Esther progressed alike in personal and intrinsic loveliness, and indeed never were a more beauteous or intelligent pair seen. I was induced to keep the secret now, which I had before thought of revealing, because Fanny could not bear the idea of being separated from Esther, which such a discovery must, of course, occasion.

"'Since it has so far gone, and the parents have, no doubt, by this time become reconciled to the loss of their child,' I reflected, 'I will keep silent. Yes, let their fates be alike, and never shall Esther know that she has any other relations living, who are entitled to her affections.'

"My alarm was not a little excited when I was made acquainted with the determination of my associates to pay another visit to Rosemary Dell, after they had been away from it for such a considerable time; and I had another reason for consternation. The two sons of Mark Darwin, who had been away at a distant part of the country for several years, now rejoined us; they had become men, and no sooner did they behold Fanny and Esther, than they were captivated by their charms. I have before said that they had always evinced the same spirit of enmity towards me as their father had done; and as may very readily be imagined, Fanny and Esther looked upon these two wretches with contempt and abhorrence. How could it ever be supposed for a moment that they could give the slightest encouragement to their attentions? on the contrary, they took every opportunity of convincing them that they did not, and Fanny had even gone so far as to assure Mark that it was her determination to remain single, consequently he must not for a moment encourage a sentiment towards her which she could not return. This she said with the utmost mildness, and told him that she was not prompted to give him such a decisive answer in consequence of any personal dislike she entertained towards him. As for Esther, she adopted a different plan, and made it no secret from Rupert that she thought she should be degrading herself by any connection with one of the Gipsy tribe.

"'You are aware, Rupert,' she has several times remarked, 'you are aware that I am not a member of the tribe, and that I have such an aversion to it, that I will never be persuaded to become one. I am for liberty, and liberty is now my right, and never will I resign it; you may send me from among your people, but nothing shall ever induce me to be made one of them.'

"But Rupert in secret only smiled at the delusion she was labouring under—at the idea she entertained of her freedom;—but as there was not much chance of her being able to leave them, he did not take much notice of what she said that time, and flattered himself that time would effect wonders in making her yield to his persuasions.

"I thought, I was in hopes, that when we returned to Rosemary Dell, Fanny would have erased from her memory all those scenes and incidents which I was so anxious for her to forget;—but I was deceived—no sooner did she behold it, than every circumstance arose fresh in her memory, and her sentiments underwent a change, which caused me much pain and anxiety. She acknowledged to me that she longed once more to behold her father—that guilty father, who had abandoned her in her infancy, and by his treachery condemned her and her mother to a life of suffering and disgrace.

"'Dear mother,' she pleaded earnestly, 'do not refuse to comply with my wishes; I have set my mind upon it, and shall be wretched if you do. But I give you my solemn promise, that I will not reveal to him by word or deed who I really am, nor for what purpose I force myself into his presence. If he does indeed behold me, believe me that he shall never know me in any other character than that I now bear, and which I have been made by him.'

"Perhaps, Walter Wallingford, you may wish to know whether my designs as regarded your sister Christabelle were changed? To which I answer in the negative. It was still my wish to put into execution my first intentions, but I had not an opportunity; whichever way I turned—whatever I did, I was sure to be narrowly watched by my companions; they viewed me with eyes of suspicion and jealousy, more particularly since the affair when they suspected that I had gone to the hall for the purpose of betraying them.

"I cannot say by what means the elder Mark had excited the suspicions of his two sons—what stories he had told them, or what their designs might be — I say of these I was entirely ignorant, all that I can say in regard to the disappearance of Fanny and Esther, on the night of the murder, is, that I had been away from the camp for nearly the whole of the day, and when I returned I was informed that they had gone to another part of the locality with some of the tribe, and Fanny was detained a prisoner by Squire Wallingford.

"Alas! too soon—too fatally was the veil torn from my eyes, and I was awakened to a knowledge of the dreadful truth—and how shall I describe my terrible suffering, when I ascertained beyond a doubt, that I was bereaved of that dear girl, for whose sake alone I clung to a life which had long since become burthensome to me. Let me hasten to drop this subject, lest madness seize upon my brain!

"My only thought—my every wish—my constant prayer, from the moment I learned this dreadful truth, was vengeance on the murderers of my daughter. Mark Darwin, when Ela beholds thee and thy hated race brought to the ignominious punishment you merit, then, and not till then, will her only wish in life be fulfilled."

Thus ended the manuscript.

CHAPTER XLII.

" So great the change, my lord,
From misery to splendour, that
Methought some strange delusion had
Of my brain taken possession.
In truth she was passing fair,
And noble too withal to look upon."
                    THE LIBERTINE.

THE scene in the old Manor House, the death of Edwin Hartfield and his mother, and the melancholy and harrowing circumstances these events recalled to his mind, had a great effect upon the spirits of Mr. Wallingford, and in spite of the remonstrances of his son, who was in his chamber as often as he possibly could be, he gave way to the most violent grief, which the latter was fearful would have a serious effect upon his constitution, shaken as it had been before, by the other painful events; but the near approach of the day of trial, the day upon which the thoughts and the deepest interest of every person were excited, aroused him from his frame of mind, and absorbed every other thought in it.

The day before the time appointed for the trial of Mark, Walter was standing in the gardens of the hall, when he was surprised to behold a post-chaise drive up, and more so, when from it descended Ela Beranzio, elegantly attired.

Walter had only just returned from the house of Doctor Hartley, whither he had been for the very purpose of making inquiries of him, as to whether he had heard anything of her, and he was very much astonished, and greatly displeased, when he saw the manner in which she had chosen to make her re-appearance at the hall. He could not help thinking that she had acted very imprudently indeed in making her return so public, which was running the risk of throwing herself into the power, and of meeting with the vengeance of her enemies; and these opinions he made no hesitation in candidly expressing to Ela herself, but she returned no immediate answer, and there was an expression of exultation in the glance of her eye, which convinced him she had more to impart than he had at first anticipated.

Ela was dressed most splendidly, and her fine, graceful, and noble figure was sufficient to make an indelible impression upon all who beheld her. Who would have imagined for an instant that she and the despised wandering vagrant, Ela, were one and the same person. If her appearance was changed, no less so were her manners, and Walter was completely bewildered by the extraordinary metamorphosis. She advanced towards him eagerly, as he entered the parlour, into which she had been shown by the servants, and would have embraced him warmly, but he shrunk back from her and looked upon her with an expression of coldness which he had never before assumed towards her.

"Nay, do not look so disdainfully upon me, Walter Wallingford," said Ela, proudly, "though perhaps I may be to blame in making this display. You no longer address the poor wretched outcast, Ela, but Ela Beranzio, the wealthiest heiress this country contains. Yes, tell your proud father, tell the haughty and contemptible deceiver, that she whom he despised and thought not worthy of his hand, is now in a condition to purchase all his boasted wealth with the same ease as she could before buy a loaf of bread. Tell him that the outcast —the degraded—the abandoned, is wealthy —and that in her veins flows the blood of royalty, quite sufficient to sink the boasted name of Wallingford into miserable insignificance !"

These words caused a blush of wounded pride to mantle in the cheek of Walter, but he stifled his indignation, and instead of giving expression to the feelings Ela's observations had at first aroused, he looked upon her with pity, for he construed her conduct into insanity, caused by long suffering and in giving way too much to the violence of her passions.

Ela seemed perfectly well to comprehend what he was thinking about, for she almost immediately observed :—

"You look upon me with eyes of pity, Wal-
ter Wallingford?—wherefore do you so? have you not seen the person I sent to apprize you of what has taken place ?"

"I have seen no person purporting to come from you," replied Walter, "neither did I expect it, as this is the time you promised me and Doctor Hartley that you would return from the metropolis. I must, however, confess that your not going to Doctor Hartley's direct, and your coming here in this very public, and I will add, extravagant manner, not a little astonishes me moreover, that you should be yourself, the first to break through the injunctions which you urged the necessity of complying with."

"I do not wonder at your surprise, young man," returned Ela, "since you have not seen my messenger ; but you entertain an erroneous opinion as regards my return to this neighbourhood. Had I come back here the poor, miserable, abject wretch that I have been usually seen, I should have been recognised immediately; but who would think of finding me in this splendid gear, and with all this show of wealth—which is no more than I can now well afford.—Ah! your surprise seems to increase, and I do not wonder at it, especially as you are yet ignorant of what has happened ; but, if you will pay attention, I will make you acquainted with every particular."

Walter drew his chair nearer to her, and, with breathless attention listened to the story she related, which was so remarkable, that he could scarcely credit that it was true, and thought that the mind of Ela was still labouring under some singular delusion ; but as she proceeded, there appeared such a connection and consistency in the narrative. that he could no longer doubt.

We will proceed at once to explain the strange events that occurred to Ela, since she had left the neighbourhood of Rosemary Dell, and those which led to a wonderful alteration in her condition.

We have, in the early part of this narrative, informed the reader that the real name of Gilbert Sherwin, as he chose to call himself, was Angelo Beranzio, and that he was, by birth, an Italian gentleman. He was descended from a very ancient house, and his father was immensely rich; but he offended him by marrying against his will, and, in consequence, he turned his back upon him, and after a year or two passed in his native country, in vain endeavours to bring about a reconciliation, finding that he had nothing to hope, he made up his mind to go to England, with the scanty remains of a little property which had been bequeathed to him by a maiden aunt, and see if he could not contrive to get an honest living without being under any obligation to his inexorable parent. A few months afterwards his father died, and carrying his animosity to the grave, he bequeathed the whole of his princely fortune to Nicolo Beranzio, his nephew, who was established as a merchant in England.

It will be quite unnecessary for us to enter into any more minute detail, as this is quite sufficient to show how Beranzio was situated at the time of the commencement of our story, and that there had been no alteration in his fortunes up to the day of his death.   From that time, Ela had never taken the trouble to recur to the melancholy and unfortunate circumstances of her father's early history, nor had ever deigned

ELA BERANZIO GIVING HER EVIDENCE AT THE TRIAL OF MARK DARWIN.

to think upon those proud and heartless relations who had refused to render them the slightest assistance, in the time of their greatest need.

Of her history, the person to whose care Doctor Hartley had consigned her in London, was quite ignorant, and was not given to understand more than that she was a lady, who enjoyed the warmest friendship of Doctor Hartley, and that peculiar circumstances rendered it necessary that her place of residence in London should be kept as secret as possible. Not being of an inquisitive disposition, Mr. Goodwin (for such was his name) did not attempt to make any further inquiries, and had not even requested to know her name, but when he addressed her, called her " Madam," only.

Mr. Goodwin and his wife, however, were very agreeable people, and although they never made themselves officiously busy with the affairs of others, they were not, by any means, taciturn upon their own, and Ela, therefore, without seeking it, soon became acquainted with their history. She was informed by them, that Mr. Goodwin had, from boyhood, been a confidential clerk to a merchant in London, who, when he died, having left him a very liberal bequest, together with what he had, by his own sober and industrious habits been able to save, he retired, and had, ever since, been living on his income. These particulars, which, no doubt, the good people thought were mightily interesting, were listened to by Ela with the utmost indifference; but it was about to bring round a discovery in which she was deeply interested and which she had never expected, or even thought of hearing alluded to again.

It happened one day, that Mr. Goodwin had been addressing her in his usual manner, by the title of "Madam," when Ela, tired of a title so unfamiliar to her ears, said—

"My name is Ela, sir, and by that I would much rather you would address me in future."

"Ela!" said Mr. Goodwin, with apparent astonishment ;—"that is a curious name, and I never remember to have heard it but once before.—Pray is your——"

"My name is Ela Beranzio," interrupted Ela, hastily, guessing what the old gentleman was about to enquire.

"Ela Beranzio!" repeated Mr. Goodwin, with increased astonishment of demeanour ;— "surely you are not a native of England, at least I never heard of a person of that name who was not of foreign——"

"Italy was the birth-place of my father," again interrupted Ela, rather vexed at the unusual inquisitiveness of Mr. Goodwin.

Mr. Goodwin started upon this, and looked more earnestly in the countenance of Ela, while his wife left off the needle-work which had previously occupied her attention, and gazed at her with an expression of astonishment which was equal to that evinced by her husband.

"I hope you will excuse the apparent liberty I am taking," said the former, "but I assure you that I am not prompted to make these inquiries by idle curiosity. Pray was the name of your father Beranzio ?—That is, you——"

"My father's name was Beranzio—Angelo Beranzio," was the answer.

"Ah! and your relations—had you any in England ?" earnestly asked Mr. Goodwin ;— "did you ever hear of an uncle that was——"

"My father had an uncle and a cousin both here," replied Ela, " who were established as merchants. His cousin, Nicolo Beranzio, enjoyed that immense fortune, which, had justice been done, belonged to my father."

"That is true—'tis perfectly true, Miss Beranzio," returned the old gentleman. "Oh, this is a happiness that I had despaired of ever meeting with. Madam (for I can no longer doubt that you are the person after whom so many enquiries have been made), I am glad—I am delighted to be the herald of good news to you, to inform you that you are heiress to the princely fortune which should have been your father's many years ago. His uncle was my employer, and for nearly half a century I passed my life in his service. Nicolo, his son, I need not inform you, came into possession of that wealth to which your father was entitled by birthright; the mercenary son, however, was much blamed by his father for taking the property, and when Nicolo persisted in taking advantage of the unnatural wrath of your grandfather, and went over to Italy for the purpose of taking possession of the property, my master refused to hold any further communication with him.

"The son had, as you will suppose, previously withdrawn himself from all connection with the business of his father, which he now considered was degrading to his dignity, and the rank he was enabled, by his great accession of wealth, to fill in society.

"His father, however, did not quit the business in consequence of this circumstance, and to me he entrusted those responsible duties that had hitherto devolved upon Nicolo.—He could confide in me, for many years had I then been in his service, and we had known each other from childhood. From him I learned that 'twas his determination to bequeath the fortune he had accumulated, at his death, to your father, if he could find him out ; but he had not been able to learn anything of him since he had left Italy."

"No," said Ela, proudly, "my poor father possessed a noble and independent spirit, and resolved, since his father had cast him off, he would endeavour to forget that he belonged to the family, at any rate, he would not sue to them. He changed his name, and with the residue of the money he possessed, purchased a farm, where, by honest industry, he gained sufficient to make him happy, and he sighed not for that abundant fortune which his cousin so unjustly enjoyed."

"I cannot but admire the noble independence of your father, madam," said Mr. Goodwin, " still, I much regret that he did not come forward, as it would have saved my good master much care and anxiety. Many were the advertisements he put in the daily papers for your father to come forward, but without success. It caused my master much uneasiness, eager as he was to befriend his ill-used nephew; and he was most sincerely grieved, when, some time afterwards, he was made acquainted with the death of him and his wife, and that his daughter was gone, no one knew whither. Not long after this, Nicolo was accidentally killed, and my master, of course, became the inheritor of his wealth. Again he renewed advertisements for the daughter of his nephew to come forward, but with as bad success as before, notwithstanding he offered a handsome reward to any person who could supply him with any information which might lead to a discovery of her retreat. But every effort he made to that effect was met with disappointment.

"My master did not live long after the demise of his son, and, as you will readily suppose, he bequeathed (with the exception of a legacy to me and others) the whole of his fortune to you, should you be alive, and if it were ascertained that you were no more, then it was to be disposed of in such charitable ways as he had ordered in his will. Need I tell you, madam, how delighted I am to think that you are at length discovered, and therefore, if you please, we will hasten directly to the executors, and make them acquainted with the fortunate circumstance."

Thus did Ela conclude her narrative to Walter, adding with a sigh—

"Alas! my whole career has been one of misfortune, and in this instance, it was more painfully exemplified than in any, for had I but seen the advertisements in time, I should have been saved from crime and sorrow. But what is gold to me now but useless dross?—for her, for whose enjoyment and future prosperity I alone wished it, is now mouldering to dust beneath the sod."

She paused, and her bosom heaved with agony as these thoughts harassed her mind; and then, turning once more to Walter, she continued—

"We proceeded forthwith to the executors, and the affair was speedily settled without any difficulty, for I with ease established my claim, and proved that I was the person who had been so long sought after. Then followed the congratulations, and sickening adulatory ceremonies, that such a circumstance was sure to give rise to. Need I tell you with what disgust I received these demonstrations, for I knew that the same person who now bowed to me as the wealthy heiress, would, but a few days before, have despised, insulted, and recoiled from me, as the wretched outcast—the wandering Gipsy beggar, and, probably, been anxious to consign me to the walls of a prison."

Walter could not but duly appreciate her observations, for he well knew them to be correct; yet, on the other hand, he could not help considering that she had to attribute the scorn and hatred of the world more to her own vitiated

temper, and the extreme violence of her behaviour; for if she had acted with propriety and perseverance after her first misfortunes, she might still have been rescued from a great deal of the misery and degradation into which she was afterwards plunged.

While these reflections were passing in the mind of Walter, Ela was evidently in a state of much anxiety and excitement. She walked hurriedly to and fro across the room, and several times turned to Walter, apparently with an intention to speak, but as hastily checked herself. At last, however, she said—

"Tell me, Walter, for I am all anxiety and impatience to know—have you anything more to say upon the important business which has brought me hither?—Has anything else transpired regarding the murderers, or have you yet been enabled to gain any clue to the place where Esther is concealed?"

"I have not, neither have I anything more to tell you upon the subject which at present occupies so much of our attention," answered Walter, hurriedly, for the sudden mention of his sister had caused him much pain, and many conflicting and agonising reflections. As he contemplated Ela, he shuddered, and turned away with a feeling of disgust, for he could not help considering that she was the primary cause of the loss of that unfortunate girl she now pretended to regret, and that, had it not been for her, his poor mother might still have been alive. He could not help viewing Ela now with very different feelings to what he had before done. Before, he had pitied her for the troubles in which she was placed, owing to the cruelty and enmity of her base and guilty companions; and when he had beheld the heavy affliction which had been brought upon her by the violent and untimely death of her daughter, and saw her mourn the bereavement with such bitter anguish, his heart melted with compassion, and he forgot all her errors, and the troubles she had brought upon his family. But now the case was very different;—the recent circumstances had made an alteration in the conduct and general bearing of Ela, which Walter could not help noticing and viewing with feelings of disgust. She seemed, in spite of all her assertions to the contrary, to exult in the change in her circumstances, and, with all the pride inherent in her nature, to look forward with delight to that which would enable her to resume a station in which she might triumph over Mr. Wallingford, and exact the homage of those individuals who had heretofore despised her.

Such were Walter's ideas, but he did Ela an injustice by them, and entirely misunderstood her feelings, which were solely occupied with the trial, and in her anxiety to see the murderers of her unfortunate child brought to punishment, and the disappointment she experienced to find that the wretch Mark, the elder, had yet been enabled to elude the vigilance of the officers of justice. Her anxiety was also intense as regarded the situation of Christabelle, or Esther, as she was commonly called, and she trembled with horror when she reflected that, perhaps, she had shared the same fate as poor Fanny ; for well did she know that the miscreants would not hesitate to perpetrate such a crime, if they entertained the least suspicion that she would betray them if she had an opportunity.

We must not go so far as to say that all the interest which Walter had formerly taken in Ela was banished from his mind ; but now that he saw her elevated suddenly to rank and wealth, and apparently exulting at her altered condition, and the means it would afford her of triumphing over his father, when she no longer appeared as an object of commiseration, his ardour was considerably cooled, and he viewed her with just the contrary sentiments that the world would do generally ; namely—instead of treating her with more respect since the change in her condition, he looked upon her with not half the regard and interest that he did when she was the wretched outcast.

At length she arose, and said that she would go to Doctor Hartley, which Walter heard with much satisfaction, for he now felt uneasy while she was present.

"After I have seen the good doctor," continued Ela, " I shall proceed at once to ——, where the assizes are held, for I think it would be more prudent for me to get there before my late companions, the Gipsies, who are sure to be hastening in there to-morrow and the next day, to be present at the trial ; and, indeed, if no such circumstance were about to take place they would not fail to be there, as this is their time for visiting that town."

"I hope you will use discretion," said Walter, when he beheld all signs of her late pride and exultation had yielded to an expression of the deepest sorrow and affliction, pitied her ;— "I repeat, I trust you will not lose sight of discretion in the manner in which you act, and be careful that you do not betray yourself to them."

Ela made no reply. and did not seem to understand what he had been saying. Her hands were clasped together, and she was buried in a deep and agonizing reverie.

"Discretion !" she at last ejaculated, starting from the deep lethargy into which she had fallen ; "oh! do not fear that I shall, by any imprudence of . mine, discover myself to my enemies, until I have seen my wish accomplished ; then let them do as they please, for life will no longer be valued my me."

Again she paused for a minute or two, and dropped into meditation ; then suddenly looking up, she said—

"Walter Wallingford, when I am no more,

when fate has done its worst, and my sorrows are at an end, you will find that Ela Beranzio, whatever may have been her faults, had not learned to be ungrateful to those who were kind to her !—alas ! language must fail to express as I should wish, the sense I have of the kindness with which you and your gentle cousin, Maria Herbert, have behaved to me."

The tone in which Ela gave utterance to these words, sank deeply into the heart of Walter, and succeeded in banishing from his mind all those thoughts to her prejudice, that had a short time before only occupied it.

"Heaven send that many years may elapse ere that event takes place," exclaimed he, fervently, "and I sincerely pray that the danger you seem to apprehend may be wended for you."

Ela made no answer, but she shook her head and seemed to have determined to close her breast against all consolation, and only to indulge the most melancholy ideas and apprehensions. She then in a hurried manner bade Walter adieu, and returning to her splendid vehicle, was driven off in the direction of Doctor Hartley's.

"Adieu, Walter," were the last words she uttered, "adieu till the day of trial, and then my anxiety will be at rest."

In spite of his endeavours to the contrary, Walter could not resist the melancholy feeling which came over him at the solemn manner in which Ela uttered these words, and at the strange and ominous demeanour she assumed, and so dull did it make him, that he felt unhappy for the remainder of the day, and the thought even followed him to his pillow at night, and haunted him in dreams of the most agonising description.

CHAPTER XLIII.

"God! am I sane ? Has not reason fled
  The terri'ory of my brain? Can the grave
  Yield up its dead ? No,—'tis her !
  Well do I know her features, she
  Is rescued by some miraculous agency."
                                        ANON.

THE night preceding the day of trial, was one of very little rest to any of the inmates of Wallingford Hall, more particularly those connected immediately with the painful and important affair, and as soon as daylight had dawned, Mr. Wallingford, his son, and Maria, met together in the parlour. They had not been together for more than a month before, and neither of them looked so well as they had done.

An early breakfast had been ordered to be

got ready for them, prior to their departure to the place where the assizes were held.

Walter had been led to hope that his father would not have been required to attend the trial, as he imagined that the state of his health would be admitted as a sufficient excuse for his not being present, but this hope soon evaporated, when a short time before the day of trial arrived, he told him that he was determined to attend upon that occasion, and added with peculiar emphasis, which showed that he was sincere in what he uttered—

"I will not give my enemies an opportunity of saying that I was afraid to meet the scrutiny of the public. No—I will let them see that I do not shrink from meeting its most searching gaze. I will appear fearlessly before them, and show the pitiful wretches who have impugned me, that I hold them in superlative contempt and defiance, that I despise them for their villanous, ungenerous endeavours to place this foul deed upon a man whose mind could never contemplate so dreadful a crime. Doubtless, there is sufficient evidence to convict the persons accused, without there being any necessity to call upon me, but if they should require it, I shall be fully prepared to give it. As a magistrate, leaving all other considerations out of the question, I think it my bounden duty to be present."

Walter would fain have persuaded his father from this, but he saw no reasonable motive that he could advance to object to his determination. He was fearful that it would be productive of the most fatal results, in the debilitated state of health, to which Mr. Wallingford was reduced; such a scene being, of course, every way calculated to cause an unusual excitement.

They met in a most gloomy silence, and everybody's thoughts seemed to be intent upon the important business in which they had soon to take such active parts; however, when Mr. Wallingford did address himself to Maria, Walter had the gratification to notice that he spoke to her with much more kindness than he had been in the habit of doing.

But could it be wondered that his interest and affections should be aroused towards that beauteous damsel, who had risked her own life, to sooth the dying sufferings of his wife, and whose once roseate cheeks, now pale as alabaster, sufficiently told the fatigue she had endured,—the injury her health had sustained by the exertion. Her spirits, too, which once were ever buoyant, had suffered in a similar manner, they were broken, and her countenance was expressive of every melancholy feeling.

"You are much altered, Maria," said Mr. Wallingford, who had been intently observing her, "you are now thin, and your countenance betokens illness."

These words were spoken during the absence of Walter from the room, who had gone to see about the carriage.

Maria's heart throbbed with strange emotions, and she held down her head in confusion, for she knew not what reply to make to these observations.

"Wallingford Hall," continued he, "is a melancholy abode for a young girl of your temperament, my dear girl. After this trial is over, if nothing happen to me, I must endeavour to see if I cannot make some alteration as regards you."

"Oh, my dear sir," eagerly exclaimed Maria, "I am very well as I am at present situated, and have no wish to alter my abode—that is, sir, I do not like changing after I have become used to a place."

Maria paused, and blushed deeply, for she was afraid she had spoken too candidly. And the conduct of Mr. Wallingford, and the change that came over his countenance, proved that she was not mistaken in the idea she had formed.

"That may be your opinion, Miss Herbert," said he, "but you will probably allow those who have had more experience in the world, to know better. For my own part, I think that we have already acted with great imprudence, for the benefit of all parties, in not having made an alteration ere this, and I will see that a change be speedily effected, as soon as ever this painful business has terminated."

With these words, Mr. Wallingford quitted the room; Maria was left to her own reflections on the subject. Poignant indeed were her feelings, at the observations which her uncle had made, and which plainly convinced her that she had deceived herself, by imagining that his sentiments as regarded her had suffered any change. She beheld in him the same haughty, sordid, imperious man he had before shown himself to be, in his harsh treatment to her; who looked upon her as an intruder, and who watched all her actions with jealousy and suspicion. As these thoughts crossed her mind, the full misery and degradation of her situation appeared more forcibly to her, and she could not restrain her tears; but suddenly checking herself, as her bosom swelled with becoming pride and indignation, she exclaimed—

"But he shall find that I am not the mean, despicable, passive being he thinks I am ;—I will no longer be the humble dependent on his bounty.—No, when this painful trial is over, I will, at all hazards, put that plan into execution, which I before devised."

Many a bitter pang did it cost her, to think that she should at last be driven to this painful alternative, but she was aroused from her melancholy ruminations by the entrance of Mr. Wallingford and Walter, to inform her that the carriage was waiting for them. She immediately arose, and endeavouring to assume as great a look of composure as possible, she timidly gave her arm to Walter, who led her from the house.

The journey was a dreary one, for each person seemed to be too much engaged with the business they were going upon to feel disposed to talk. As they got near the place where the assizes were held, the road presented a scene of unusual bustle, which plainly showed that a circumstance of more than ordinary interest was about to take place, and that the curiosity of the public was much excited. The road was thickly thronged with passengers, and Maria shuddered with terror, when on looking from the window of the carriage, she recognised in the black and piercing eyes, and swarthy complexion of many of them, their enemies, the Gipsies, and remarked that they watched the carriage with the most intense curiosity. Suddenly the crowd appeared to increase, and flocking into the middle of the road, the carriage was only enabled to proceed at a walking pace. Mr. Wallingford grew impatient, and thrusting his head from the window, he demanded of the coachman the reason he did not drive faster.

" Please you, sir," replied the coachman, "I would if I could, but here are these confounded Gipsies, all in the middle of the road, and if I attempt to do so I must drive over some of them."

Mr. Wallingford now beheld that the coachman spoke the truth, for he remarked several of the men watching him narrowly, and perceiving that they were all armed with stout bludgeons, he began to be apprehensive that they intended to commit some outrage. He felt far from comfortable in his situation, but he did not mention his suspicions to Walter or Maria, fearful that he might unnecessarily alarm the latter.

But what attracted the attention of Mr. Wallingford more than any other object, was the decrepid and loathsome form of the ancient sybil who had so many times appeared before him, and whom he was now convinced was connected with the Gipsies. He shuddered with an involuntary feeling of horror when he saw her, and remembered the different prognostications she had uttered against him, and how they had almost invariably come true, and his heart sank, as, in spite of the discredit he placed on the supernatural, a foreboding of some additional evil crossed his mind.

She was seated with two more Gipsies in a cart, and her appearance was remarkable in the extreme. Her form, quite different to what it had been whenever she had appeared to Mr. Wallingford, was now enveloped in a huge cloak, or rather a series of cloaks, so that no one could imagine that it was a human being, and, indeed, her whole appearance was awful and supernatural in the extreme. Full a hun-

dred years had evidently passed over her head, and her dark skin, now parched, hung loosely about her face, and gave her the aspect of a mummy more than a being of life and sense. Her lips, which were thin and black, were closely compressed, and her prominent nose, and long thin chin, made her look particularly hideous and revolting.

At the time when Wallingford first beheld her, he thought she was sleeping, for she held down her head, and did not appear to notice any of the objects around her; but he was soon undeceived, for as the carriage slowly went past the cart, one of her companions nudged her, and directed her attention to the former, and in a moment the old hag raised her head, and before Mr. Wallingford could draw up the window blinds, she glanced towards Walter and Maria, and her eyes beamed with an expression that was sufficient to strike terror to the most hardy heart. The next moment her lips moved, and she appeared to be muttering something (which, as she held forth her long bony finger towards them,) they judged to be a malediction, and they could at the same time hear the supernatural croaking of her voice, but they were unable to distinguish a sentence that she uttered.

Appalled at the sight, and observing the many fierce eyes that were fixed upon him, Mr Wallingford again desired the coachman to drive on, and then sank back in the carriage to avoid those looks he dreaded to encounter.

" Surely, Thomas," said Walter, who now began to get out of all patience, "surely, Thomas, you are doing this for the purpose; why do you not do as you have been desired?"

" Pardon me, sir," said Thomas, "but I have already stated my reason; these fellows will persist in obstructing the way, and, as I said before, I can't drive over the devils, although it is no more than they richly merit, and that's the truth."

Walter again looked from the carriage window, and beheld that the men still stood in the road, and seemed resolved that the carriage should only proceed at the rate they thought proper, and only that the imprudence of such a step was so glaring at that time of the day, when, as there were so many persons passing, their plans must have been thwarted, and themselves got into trouble, he would have thought that they certainly had determined upon committing some outrage or the other, but he was soon convinced that they had no other motive than to prevent the vehicle from proceeding, until the aged crone had delivered herself of her curses and imprecations. In this object they succeeded, for they had so contrived it, that the carriage was brought nearly to a stand-still, and the cart which contained the hag and her companions was brought close by the side of the window, so that she was enabled to thrust her head into the vehicle.

She extricated her long parchment looking arm from the mantle with which it had been covered, and as she uttered the following curse, she shook it menacingly at the objects to whom she addressed herself—

" Woe to the haughty Wallingford,
Woe attend both his bed and board,
There's many a curse for him in store,
That will pierce his heart to its inmost core.
Woe and misery, foul disgrace,
Attend the accursed traitor's race.
May peace ne'er in their path be seen,
And nought from sorrow their bosoms screen !
May their hopes all fade, all sad, all drear,
Around them close anguish and despair ;
May they live in scorn, in misery die,
And ne'er gain a tear from pity's eye !
Woe to the haughty Wallingford,
Woe attend both his bed and board !"

Thus spoke the sybil, in tones that made a lasting impression upon the minds of those who heard them, then suddenly dropping her head upon her chest, she became apparently unconscious of all around her. The women pulled the hood of the cloak over her head, and her revolting features were hidden from the sight.

Walter had no doubt that this was Jabella, whom Ela had mentioned in her narrative, and he involuntarily shuddered when he thought of the terrible denunciations she had uttered, and the frightful gestures and expressions of ferocious malevolence with which they were accompanied. He looked at his cousin ; she was very pale, and had drawn herself into one corner of the carriage, apparently unable to gaze upon the demoniacal features of the hag. He endeavoured by a look of the utmost kindness to reassure her, but as the carriage was now suffered to proceed without any interruption, and was soon out of sight of the cart which contained Jabella, she again revived, and as the town appeared in sight, she became more composed and assured of safety.

The vehicle was not long in arriving at the place of destination, which was a small, but handsome house, in a retired part of the place, and which Dr. Hartley had taken especial care to have in readiness for them against their arrival, and there had been everything that could possibly be obtained in so short a time, for their convenience. But the first part of the Sybil's curse seemed to have commenced its operation, for they had not been there many minutes, before they were convinced they had come to the very locality (notwithstanding it was so retired), in which the Gipsies, their bitterest foes, had taken up their temporary residence. This circumstance caused them a considerable deal of uneasiness, and what added

to it was, that the greater portion of the gang had put up at a low public-house almost immediately opposite to the house in which Mr. Wallingford and his companions were lodging.

It was Maria who first made this discovery, for happening to go to the drawing-room window, what was her astonishment and dismay, to perceive at that moment, being assisted out of the cart, which stood at the public-house door, the form of old Jabella, and several more of the gang peeping through the window of the tap-room, and advancing towards the house. Filled with terror, she left the window, lest they should observe her, and communicated what she had seen to her uncle and Walter.

They both expressed their regret that they should have been so unfortunate as to take up their abode in a place so near their enemies, but as it could not be helped, they must endeavour to make the best they could of it, and to use all the caution it was possible, to prevent themselves from falling the victims to any act of villany they might have in contemplation.

Unwilling that the public should receive an impression that he was afraid of meeting their gaze, Mr. Wallingford, accompanied by his son, several times in the course of the day, went to the court, and thus Maria, being entirely left alone, could not forbear endeavouring to ascertain what were the motions of the Gipsies opposite to her, and it was not long before she elicited from the little loquacious servant girl some further particulars concerning them.

This servant was particularly civil and attentive, and frequently entered the room to see that everything was comfortable, or whether there were anything which Maria required, and upon one occasion she happened to observe that the persons who were located over the way did not appear to be any of the most respectable ; to which the girl, apparently very glad to think that some license was thus given to her loquacity, replied—

" You are right, miss, they are a very strange lot of people, sure enough, and for my part, I think Mrs. Radcliffe must have been out of her wits] when she suffered such a set to enter her house, for they will ruin the respectability of it altogether. You would not think it, I dare say, miss, from the low appearance of the house, but I can vouch for the truth of it, for having lived servant there, before I got my present situation, that it always bore a very creditable character, but when such riff-raff as these people are suffered to enter it, and take up their lodging in it, what can they expect will be the consequences ? Still, after all, I have a great hankering to see that old woman, who they call the Gipsy Queen. They have hired a room on purpose for her, and they do say she's such a horrible looking being, not at all like anything human, and more than that, she is so aged, they say above a century."

"It is strange—what could induce them to bring the poor old woman such a distance?" observed Maria.

"Bless your soul, miss," replied the girl, "the landlady of the public-house has informed my mistress that the Gipsies could not make more fuss with her, or pay her greater homage, if she were a queen in reality, and they do not venture to do anything without first consulting her; they are guided by her advice in all their transactions, and they firmly believe that she can prophesy all that is going to happen to them, and the place is like a fair with them hurrying into the house to ask her what will be the fate of their companion, and how the trial will terminate; I mean the trial of one of their gang, who, they suspect, has 'sassinated some poor young woman; but I dare say you know all about that, miss, as well as I can tell you."

Maria did not make any verbal reply to this question, but she nodded her head affirmatively, and the girl then went on to say—

"The landlady has tried very hard to get something out of them, but it's all to no purpose, for they are very secret, and know how to keep their own counsel; but still she can judge, by the expression of their countenances, that they are quite low spirited, especially the old woman, who, they say, is the prisoner's grandmother, and she is quite inconsolable, but she was in good spirits when she came here, about a week ago, and said that she was confident there was no evidence to convict him; but since the old Gipsy Queen has been consulted, she thinks very different, and, indeed, has said that it is now his fate to meet with a shameful death upon the scaffold."

The girl now retired from the room.

"Surely there cannot be any persons so superstitious as these people are represented to be," she observed; "I can scarcely credit that they can place that implicit reliance on their own powers of divination. They must have become acquainted with some additional evidence, which it is intended to bring forward, and is likely to lead to the conviction of this wretched man."

Maria remained at the window until darkness enveloped the earth, and was enabled to watch the actions of the Gipsies without being herself observed, for she was concealed from view by the window curtain. Her fears increased as she beheld that the Gipsies were accumulating rapidly, and that every few minutes fresh numbers of dark-eyed, swarthy visaged men and women flocked into the house, for she had no idea that their numbers were so great.

When the darkness deepened, and she was prevented from clearly distinguishing what was passing in the street, the gratification of her curiosity was by no means diminished, for the room in which the old Sybil was seated was lighted by the red glare of a fire, and two candles, the latter being placed upon a table in the centre of the room.

Maria stretched her head more forward, and endeavoured to observe them more narrowly, but for some time she could not accurately distinguish the objects in the parlour, for the house was a very old-fashioned one, and the windows were composed of small diamond squares of glass, which were by no means remarkable for their cleanliness; but as the fire burnt more clearly, and cast a broader glare upon the persons present, which was rendered more effective from the deep darkness without, the frightful and corpse-like countenance of old Jabella, who was seated in a high backed chair at the head of the table, became more visible. The Gipsies seemed to be watching her with the most intense interest and anxiety, as ever and anon she raised her eyes, that seemed to gleam like coals of fire, and directed them towards the casement in the front of which she was sitting.

From what Maria could perceive, the room was very poorly furnished, or rather it was not furnished at all, unless an old stump bedstead in one corner of the room, the table before mentioned, and two or three chairs were deserving of that title. Men and females were seated upon the floor, both sexes smoking immoderately, while in other parts of the room they stood in small groups, and were apparently discussing some deeply interesting and important subject. Many seemed, from the uneasy motion of their body, to be completely overwhelmed with grief, and one woman especially, whose head drooped upon her chest, and whose hands were vehemently clasped together, seemed to be in a state bordering upon distraction.

The interest and curiosity of Maria was now more than ever aroused, and she strained her eyes to discover all that was passing in the room. She could now discern what had before escaped her observation, namely, that on the table were chalked a number of mysterious characters and hieroglyphics; and on either side of Jabella was an hour glass, and a small white wand.

The astonishment of Maria was excited to the utmost degree when she beheld all these remarkable symptoms of the ignorant bigotry of these wandering people, and she could not at the same time repress a feeling of awe, which gradually stole over her. A few minutes elapsed in this manner, and then several other men and women came in, and they gathered around the table, at which the old woman was seated.

Once more the old hag raised her head, and her eyes seemed to beam with more lustre than ever; even at that distance their supernatural brightness was clearly distinguishable to Maria, while the impressive vehemence of her whole demeanour, as she grasped the wand, and at times raising her thin withered hands energetically above her head, particularly struck her.

The expression predominant in the countenances of those who were listening so attentively to all she uttered, was that of the deepest melancholy and despair. It was very evident that something had occurred to give rise to their worst forebodings as to the result of the trial. But Maria was suddenly aroused from the contemplation of these persons, by the entrance of Mrs. Patterson, the landlady of the house, followed by Betsey, bringing in the tea utensils, and the former carrying a couple of lighted candles.

Mrs. Patterson proceeded to make many apologies to Maria for not having brought the lights before, and hoped that she would not forget to make herself quite comfortable during the time she was in her house, as she should feel a pleasure in doing everything that was in

WALTER ACCOMPANIES MARIA TO THE CARRIAGE ON THE DAY OF TRIAL.

her power towards making her "at home" while she remained there, and she was certain there were very few places that were much more confortable than her's.

Having thus expressed herself, Mrs. Patterson proceeded to fasten the shutters, so that Maria's view was entirely excluded, and the transactions of the Gipsies in the public-house were hidden from her further observation. This vexed Maria, whose curiosity had been aroused by what she had seen, to an almost unsupportable degree, but, of course, prudence withheld her from speaking what she thought, and almost immediately afterwards Doctor Hartley entered the room, and was followed by Mr. Wallingford and Walter.

The former kind-hearted gentleman met her with the same unaffected regard which he had ever evinced towards her, and then the party entered into a discourse upon general topics, which for awhile made her forget the transactions of the Gipsies, which she had lately observed. Mr. Wallingford, however, did not seem in any mood to converse, but was uncommonly agitated and melancholy. Maria was at a loss to imagine what had occurred to increase the depression of spirits her uncle had for some time been labouring under, and she looked to Walter for an explanation, but there was no necessity for it, for Mr. Wallingford very soon revealed the cause himself. He had, it appears, been cordially received by his brother magistrates at the court, with the exception of Lord Harlington and Mr. Ashburne, who merely greeted him with a cold and formal bow. Mr. Barnel, Lord Harlington's intended son-in-law, too, was also present, and looked as contemptuously upon Mr. Wallingford as such a booby was capable of doing; as for the females belonging to the family, they seemed to think of nothing else than getting into the most conspicuous places for displaying their finery and gew-gaws, and when Walter and his father saluted them with becoming politeness, they did not deign to take any other notice of it than by a most stiff and haughty inclination of the head, and moved on, as though they were anxious to avoid giving them an opportunity of addressing themselves to them again.

Walter, far from considering this a circumstance to feel vexed at, was very well pleased that it had occurred, for it would be the means of preventing any further intimacy between the families, and would save him from a great many annoyances and unpleasantries; but it was very different with his father, his pride received a severe wound from it, and when he beheld that all his hopes, as far as regarded an alliance with the family of Lord Harlington were at an end, he found it utterly impossible to disguise his indignation.

Not wishing the others to notice his emotions, he excused himself when the tea was over, and retired to the chamber which was allotted to him, where he gave unrestrained indulgence to the expression of that chagrin, with which his mind was up to that time harassed.

Doctor Hartley, Walter, and Maria, being now left alone, the latter proceeded to relate all she had observed from the window of the drawing-room, and the singular behaviour of the Gipsies, to which the good doctor and her cousin listened with the deepest interest.

"Well," observed the doctor, "it certainly is a delusion for which I am at a loss to account, for any person would naturally suppose that in the present enlightened generation there could not possibly be any one who could be so foolish and so superstitious as to think themselves capable of reading the Book of Fate, and to foretell future events, but yet 'tis nevertheless

the fact, as your detail, Miss Herbert, proves; and, in fact, I need not go further than Ela, with a mind like she possesses, who, when I came out, was engaged in the performance of some strange and mysterious ceremonies, which she imagines will enable her to learn what will be the termination of this important business."

At the mention of Ela's name, a variety of strange and exciting ideas and reflections occurred to the mind of Maria, and she was all anxiety to have her curiosity gratified. Walter had only given her a very slight sketch of the remarkable events which had befallen her in London, and of the means by which she had suddenly and in such an extraordinary manner, become possessed of her present enormous wealth, and now that he was more at his leisure, and they were alone, he detailed minutely every circumstance exactly as he had it from the lips of Ela herself; and it was with no little astonishment that she listened to a narrative too replete with interest to all who knew that unfortunate woman. The discussion, too, which afterwards took place between Walter and Doctor Hartley, upon the subject, and of the chance there was, whether or not Ela would make a proper use of her wealth, could not fail to engage Maria's most profound attention, and she listened to them without presuming to interrupt them by any observation of her own.

"I am fearful," remarked the doctor, "that Ela will not find her happiness much increased by this acquisition to her wealth, for what has she now endearing to her in the world, for whose sake it could render money valuable? Had not her unfortunate daughter met with the dreadful fate she did, had she still been alive, to have the fond affections of her mother lavished upon her, and soften the violence of those passions that often rise beyond control, she might yet live to become once more a bright ornament to society, and to make all the reparation in her power to those, upon whom she had been the means of bringing so much misery and trouble. It is only the excitement caused by the approaching trial which, in my opinion, keeps up her energies, and I am very fearful, when it is over, her reason will sink beneath the weight of the many racking thoughts, and cares, and vehement passions, that have for some time inhabited her breast. Should also the murderers of her daughter escape punishment, there cannot be a doubt but that the rage and disappointment she will experience must prove fatal one way or the other."

The words of the good doctor excited much anguish in the mind of Maria, more especially his latter observations. The passion of revenge, or cruelty of any description, was so repugnant to her nature, that even the wretches who had been the assassins of Fanny, richly as they merited the severest punishment that could be inflicted, she could not help viewing with pity, and breathing a hope that they might be brought to a full sense of the crime they had committed, and be suffered to repent of it, and seek the forgiveness of the Almighty and Supreme Being they had so terribly offended. These sentiments she expressed, but she was not a little astonished to find that neither Doctor Hartley nor Walter coincided with her in opinion, more especially the latter, whose humanity was always evinced in such a conspicuous manner.

"For my part," said Doctor Hartley, "they have reason to thank their lucky stars that I have not the power, for if I had, I should think it an act of justice to hang one half of the rascals up like dogs. Nay, miss, I understand your looks, but they cannot alter my opinion, which is, that such miscreants, to whom the shedding of human blood and every other crime is familiar, are totally unworthy of compassion."

Maria did not attempt to make any answer to these remarks, although she still could not bring her mind to receive them, and she thought that in many cases the wandering tribe were treated with an undue severity, and that there were many excuses to be offered for some of their errors, when the state of ignorance in which they were brought up was taken into consideration, and when it was also remembered that from their childhood they were looked upon as the outcasts of society, and almost entirely precluded the possibility of swerving from the path of vice in which their destiny had placed them.

Deeply interested by the subjects they had in discussion, the time passed rapidly away, and it was nearly eleven o'clock before Doctor Hartley thought of rising to depart, saying, as he did so, that he ought to have gone before, for it might not be altogether safe walking out so late, when they were surrounded by such desperate characters.

"I must not suffer you to go alone, my dear sir," said Walter, suddenly recollecting that the observations of the doctor in all probability were very just. The doctor, however, firmly opposed this offer, for he considered that the appearance of Walter might be calculated to do more harm than any good he could render him, should the Gipsies attempt any outrage. Besides, he and Betsey had previously made an arrangement, to the mutual satisfaction of both, which was that she should proceed with him to the door of his lodgings with a lantern, as it was a very dark night, and he did not know much of the way, and a young man who was courting her, was to follow behind, so that he might be ready to escort the girl home again after she had performed this office. He therefore rang the bell for the attendance of the servant, who came all ready prepared for the short journey, and after having urged upon Maria and her cousin the necessity there was for their retiring to rest without delay, so that they might be ready for the tedious and painful

business they had to perform the following day, he bade them both good night, and followed Betsey down the stairs. Maria not feeling at all disposed for further conversation, took the opportunity at the same time of bidding good night to Walter and the doctor, and hastened to her chamber.

Sleep, however, Maria did not feel the least inclined to seek, for she was in a strange place, and everything around her, although it was very neat, clean, and comfortable, had an appearance of loneliness to her. It was the first time for many years that she had ever reposed in any other apartment than the one allotted to her at Wallingford Hall, which was very romantically situated, and was endeared to her by many fond recollections. The time of the year was rather mild, yet to Maria's imagination the room had a cold and comfortless appearance, and the girl who acted as under servant to Mrs. Patterson observing her shiver, seemed to guess her thoughts, for without saying a word she piled up the fire, and it soon emitted a cheerful blaze, which made the place appear more comfortable to Maria, and having dispensed with the further attendance of the girl, she gave her mind up to meditation, previous to her retiring to her couch.

Very different was the situation she was now placed in to that she had occupied at Wallingford Hall; there at night reigned a profound silence, which was seldom or never broken,—but here she was frequently startled by the sound of footsteps or voices in the street, and, totally unused to such interruptions, it was some time before she could conquer the alarm she felt when they met her ear.

The noise of the voices, however, convinced her that the same objects could be viewed from the windows of this chamber as she had seen from the sitting room, and as soon as the thought occurred to her, she unfastened the shutters, and drew aside the curtains, but before she did so, extinguished the light in the lamp, so that the persons whose actions she was so anxious to watch, might not observe her, although she could not think that it was very likely, so late as it was, that they would still be there. In this opinion she found, however, she was mistaken, for the same objects were still to be seen, with the exception of old Jabella; but after a short time Maria discovered that she was also in the room, but that she was lying upon the rude pallet in the corner of the room.

Maria had now a much better opportunity of observing their actions, for she was a story higher, and consequently everything in the room she could distinguish without the slightest trouble. It was, notwithstanding, a long time before anything took place to gratify her curiosity, and her patience was almost exhausted, for during the space of three quarters of an hour, the whole of which time she did not remove her eyes from them, they never in the slightest degree altered their position, and any individual might have imagined they were inanimate. Maria therefore conjectured that they had done with all those mystic rites in which they had before been engaged. She was therefore upon the point of giving over watching, and once more putting to the shutters, when just at that moment the women seemed to move as if by some sudden impulse, and Maria's curiosity was more than ever aroused.

She watched them narrowly, and had not been many minutes so engaged, when she saw one of the females advance, and having opened the casement she fixed her eyes upon the sky, as though she was watching for the appearance of some particular star.

At first Maria was apprehensive that they had seen her, and that she was the object upon whom the woman was gazing, but her fears were speedily quieted, and upon mature reflection she was confident that there was not the least possibility of their observing her, from the place where she had stationed herself, and the darkness of the room, with the exception of the light emitted by the fire ; so, gaining fresh courage on this conviction, she once more took up her position at the window, and waited eagerly to see what would be the result of this strange meeting.

The woman who had first approached the window was soon joined by several others, who, by the manner in which they thrust their heads forward, seemed most anxious to gain a sight of some particular object. It was not long before Maria discovered that they were all gazing upon a brilliant star, which sparkled in the deep grey sky above, alternately with greater brightness, and then hidden behind the dense clouds that passed over it, and foreboded that a storm was not far distant. The voices of the women now sounded in Maria's ears, apparently expressing their opinions upon the object which engaged their deep attention ; and after one party had gratified their curiosity, they retired, and were as speedily succeeded by others, until there was not an individual in the room who had not gazed upon it, with the exception of old Jabella, who still remained stretched upon the bed, and seemed to sleep soundly. But it did not last much longer, for suddenly she raised herself on her elbow, and looked around her, and then several of the persons in the room drew the chair she had lately been seated in to the bedside, and placing her in it, they wrapped a blanket around her, and brought her to the window, so that she could have a clear view of the planet which had engaged their attention for the last few minutes.

As near as Maria could discern the features of the ancient Sybil, which was very indistinctly, there was an expression of the deepest interest upon them, and she noticed in particular that her eyes, which glowed with supernatural brightness, were fixed intently upon the same bright star at which the others had been so earnestly gazing, and the persons who surrounded her seemed to be awaiting to hear her opinion with the most painful anxiety and impatience. At lenth Jabella extended her arms, and turning to her companions, appeared to speak something in the most energetic manner, whereupon she was hastily carried from the window to the table, on which the mystic characters were inscribed, and on which, Maria now perceived, when they brought in two more candles, that there was a large volume, which was opened and placed before the old woman.

And now her hideous and revolting countenance was plainly distinguishable to Maria who could not help shuddering as she gazed upon it, and noticed its unearthly expression.

"Can it be possible that such disgusting ignorance and superstition can exist," said she, unable any longer to repress the expression of her feelings?—"Good God ! enlighten these unfortunate beings' minds, and bring them, to a proper sense of the sinfulness of their doings."

More eagerly did both women and men now appear to listen to some words that this repulsive object was muttering, and they all flocked around her with as much anxiety as if the fate of a nation depended upon her decision. And it was not long ere the troubled looks and altered behaviour of the persons present plainly showed that they were disappointed in whatever they had anticipated ; for the Sybil addressed them no more, but sinking back in her chair, seemed not to have strength to utter another syllable; and immediately afterwards loud sounds of sorrow broke from the others, and the extravagance of their demeanour plainly showed that they were suffering all the tortures of intense grief.

The scene lasted for a few minutes, when suddenly their exclamations of sorrow and despair ceased, and the room was involved in complete darkness. Again the window was opened, and one of the women appeared at it, and seemed to look from it very eagerly, and what was the terror of Maria, when at that moment she beheld several men approaching towards the public-house, and carrying what had the appearance of a corpse. The woman at the window and the men exchanged two or three words together, and directly afterwards the street door was unfastened, and they entered the house. A light was once more seen in the room, and the men entering, Maria beheld them deposit their burthen on the floor, and directly the lights were again extinguished, and she could behold no more.

Completely horror-struck by the idea which

her frightened imagination had conjured up, her heart throbbing violently against her side, and the blood seeming to freeze and stagnate in her veins, Maria staggered from the place where she had been standing, and dropped, overcome with terror into a chair. Perplexed, bewildered, astonished, at what she had seen, she was unable for some time to gain her self-possession sufficiently to arrange her thoughts, and although her mind was far from 'prone to superstition, so powerful a hold had fear got of her faculties, that, as she glanced hurriedly around the room, she almost imagined that she beheld some ghastly and appalling vision.

But how was she to act in this business? Was it not wrong for her to remain thus inactive, when, by raising an alarm, she might be the means of detecting the wretches in their iniquities, and in bringing them to punishment? Was she not doing decidedly wrong in not seizing the opportunity of revealing to the world the dark deeds of which the monsters were the perpetrators?

But then again how could she be certain that what she had seen the men carry into the house was really a dead body. She had, however, no reason to doubt that it was a human form, and the form of a female, for she had plainly distinguished that, as they entered the house, it was enveloped in a cloak or mantle. But then she had [no proof that it was not a living woman, and might she not after all be ill, and one of their own party? And then if she should raise an alarm without any occasion, it might be attended with the most fatal results, for the Gipsies being thus exasperated, would, in all probability, seek to revenge themselves, and commit some desperate outrage or the other. Besides, she could not help involuntarily shuddering when she thought of the danger which might arise from her making an alarm. Walter, she was confident would be the first to rush in upon the wretches, and, probably his own life might be the sacrifice. She, therefore, determined not to say anything, and once more she ventured to approach the window, and to peep from it, thinking that she might be enabled to discover whether there were any just cause for her suspicions. All, however, was now buried in complete darkness; so thinking it useless longer to watch, and feeling also fatigued with the anxiety and excitement she had experienced, she finally closed the shutters and retired from the window, concluding that the Gipsies had separated for the night.

"Good God!" she ejaculated, as she prepared to go to her couch, "what wretches they must be; and yet to calmly, after such crimes, retire to repose! Repose!—surely miscreants like those can never sleep!"

She went to bed, and tried to sleep to forget what she had seen, but it was all to no purpose, her mind was too much occupied with the re-

collection of the different mysterious and impressive circumstances, to suffer her to succeed in these endeavours; she lay tossing and tumbling about, and her brain was completely bewildered in endeavouring to conjecture what could be the meaning of the form she had seen conveyed into the house. She tried to put the most favourable construction upon it, and to persuade herself that it was not a corpse, but some female who had sunk with illness, fatigue and exhaustion; or, considering how addicted they were to acts of intemperance—but no, she could not erase from her mind, in spite of these ideas, the impression which had first taken possession of it, namely, that it was a lifeless form; for she had noticed how motionless it was, and then the men had carried it in a manner which fully confirmed her worst surmises.

From these reflections her thoughts wandered to old Jabella, and the strange reliance the Gipsies evidently placed in her powers of divination. She recollected, too, the times she had appeared to her, and her awful predictions, which had been so fatally verified, and the sudden and mysterious manner in which she had disappeared from her sight; and all those circumstances combined, served to increase her anxiety and perplexity.

At length, completely wearied out with harassing thoughts, sleep pressed upon her eyelids, but slumber did not grant her any reprieve; and frightful dreams tormented her till the morning's sun peeped in at her chamber window.

She was vexed when she found that it was a considerable deal later than her usual time of rising; and on descending to the breakfast-room she found Dr. Hartley had already arrived, and had been awaiting her appearance with much patience.

"My dear Miss Herbert," said the doctor, "this is breaking through your regular rules of early rising with a vengeance; and were it not that your looks convince me that rest has not been your companion during the night, I might feel inclined to call you a sluggard. Ah, I see you have not attended to the advice I gave you last night, or else you have been endeavouring to gratify your curiosity, and indulge in your taste for the marvellous, by scrutinizing the actions of the Gipsies opposite."

"In the latter conjecture," replied Maria, "I must admit that you are quite right, sir, but——" and she looked round the apartment to be certain that nobody but themselves were present, "but I have something to tell you that will, no doubt, astonish you more than any of the supernatural discoveries I have made."

"Indeed!" said Doctor Hartley, with a smile, "what new wonder have you to tell me now, Miss Maria?—Truly this the age of marvels and excitement."

Maria looked serious as she said in an under tone of voice, "I must request, my dear sir, that you will not impart what I am about to tell you, to my cousin Walter, for he——"

"I understand, my dear," hastily interrupted the doctor, "and I think you are very prudent for having come to such a determination; but pray be quick, for Walter will be here directly, and then you will not have an opportunity of speaking to me on the subject for the remainder of the day."

Maria obeyed him in as few words as possible; and when she had concluded, the good doctor appeared to be perfectly paralyzed, for he stood aghast and silent, and stared at her with astonishment, doubt, and incredulity.

"Impossible!" at length he exclaimed, "you must have been deceived, or have been dreaming all that you have told me. To me it appears so perfectly improbable, that the fellows would venture to bring a corpse through the streets, that I cannot bring my mind to credit it. In the opposite, too, you say you saw them take it?"

"I assure you, sir," said Maria, earnestly, "I assure you that what I have told you was no idle chimera; I was as wide awake as I am at present, and I am confident my eyes did not deceive me. There," she continued, as she advanced with the doctor towards the window, "I am positive those are some of the very men, who were engaged in the mysterious affair, especially that stout powerful looking man, I am certain he was one of them."

Doctor Hartley looked in the direction whither she pointed, and beheld several of the Gipsy tribe assembled outside the public-house, disposed of in various groups, some engaged in discussion, and others smoking. He watched the expression of their countenances as narrowly as the distance would permit him, but he saw nothing in them to give him any cause to believe that the suspicions of Maria were correct. True, they seemed melancholy, and their minds appeared to be occupied with thought, but yet their demeanour altogether was so composed, that he felt it impossible to suppose that they could so recently have committed murder, and be so near the corpse of their victim.

"She must have been dreaming," murmured the doctor to himself, as he resumed his seat; "the recent dreadful occurrences have so shocked her, that her imagination has become disordered. The female, if such it was, was very likely ill, or else fatigued with travelling, or perhaps (which is the most likely) had taken more than her usual quantity of drink. That must be it, and yet I was simple enough to imagine for awhile—— However," he continued aloud, addressing himself to Maria, "pray let us have the breakfast; and endeavour, if possible, to divest your mind of these wild phantasies: God knows we have enough to combat with this day, in reality, without giving way to sickly fancy."

Maria could not help feeling in some degree that the doctor's observations were just, but still she was chagrined to think he should imagine that she was deluded by some wild phantasy. She, however, made no observation upon the subject, and did as the doctor desired her, and the repast was nearly over, when Walter entered the room, as his father, with whom he had been, had chosen to breakfast alone, not feeling disposed for company.

"Maria will entrust herself to my care, I hope," remarked Doctor Hartley, "and therefore, as time is precious, you will be so good as to prepare yourself for our departure immediately, my dear miss. Mr. Wallingford and Walter will not be long after us, I dare say."

Her mind completely absorbed by other thoughts, Maria scarcely had any recollection of what the business of the day was to be, or whither they were about to go; but of course, she did not offer the slightest objection to the good doctor's proposition, and having quickly put on her bonnet and shawl, she gave her arm to Mr. Hartley, and in a minute or two they had emerged from the house, and her terror was not a little excited, when on looking up she discovered that they were being narrowly scrutinized by the Gipsies, who were still standing outside the house, and of whom the number was considerably augmented.

Maria trembled, for she was conscious that they were the objects of curiosity to every one as they passed on to the place of their destination; but Doctor Hartley, who had also observed the members of the tribe, and noticed the evil glances they fixed upon them, put on a look of such indifference, and walked on at a pace that showed them he felt not the slightest alarm, that she at length became more firm, and by the time they had got into the more frequented street, she became quite re-assured, especially as it was thronged with passengers, which was quite sufficient to convince her that they would not be so rash as to attempt to molest them.

But although her fears for her own safety were at an end, when she thought of the danger which Walter and her uncle must run in passing by their bitterest enemies, her terrors were again aroused with redoubled force. Ever and anon did she turn to look back, to ascertain whether they were coming, and fearful that they would be exposed to some outrage from the ruffians. Often, too, she imagined that she heard the shouts of exultation from the gang, and the cries of assistance from those attacked; but an end was soon put to her anxiety, and Mr. Hartley, who had been noticing her agitation, although he did not pretend to do so, remarked—

"Now, my dear girl, I hope your fears are all over, for see, Walter is approaching, and if we may judge from his countenance, he is quite as uneasy about you, as you have been for this quarter of an hour about him."

Maria blushed; but the satisfaction she felt at seeing Walter, did away with every other feeling. She soon learned that the doctor's motive for urging her to depart so hastily, was that she and the other witnesses against Mark the Gipsy, were to go before the grand jury as soon as convenient. Doctor Hartley placed her in a part of the court where she could have an excellent opportunity of observing all that passed, without being herself much noticed in her turn, and then contrived to divest the time considerably of its tediousness, by instructing her in the ceremony she was about to take a part in, and in explaining to her every particular which it was necessary she should know as to the forms of a court of justice.

But notwithstanding Doctor Hartley called all his force of rhetoric into operation, and left no stone unturned to impart to her sufficient confidence to support the ordeal she had to pass, Maria felt a dreadful sinking at her heart, and she could not stop herself from trembling with agitation, which was the more increased when her name was called in a loud, sonorous tone, and immediately afterwards she was ushered into the presence of the grand jury, who all fixed their eyes upon her countenance with looks of the most searching inquiry.

Maria, however, shortly regained a large portion of her self-possession, for the gentlemen seemed to sympathise with her situation, and the modest timidity of her manners, and what questions they put to her they did so in tones of mildness and kindness, so that Maria speedily recovered her equanimity, and stated every particular of the shocking affair, with which she was acquainted, so clearly, that it appeared to give the gentlemen of the jury the utmost satisfaction. She was the more encouraged, when on looking round she perceived amongst them, many gentlemen who were on terms of intimacy and friendship with Mr. Wallingford, and she now began to feel a degree of confidence, which she never expected she should have experienced, prior to her entrance into the court. This feeling, however, was but brief, and she felt considerably disconcerted on beholding present, and eyeing her most minutely, Lord Harlington, Mr. Ashburne, and the detestable Mr. Barnell. The latter individual was observing her with remarkable earnestness, and there was an expression in his vulgar countenance which quite abashed Maria. It was very evident, notwithstanding he had broken off all pretensions to an alliance with her, that his admiration was as warm as ever, and that it had increased

rather than abated. Lord Harlington could not but notice the conduct of his intended son-in-law, and it was very plain to be seen that he far from approved of it.

Maria's emotion might be plainly discernable to everybody present, although of course, they would not be able to conceive the cause, but fortunately, she was soon released from the awkwardness of her situation, for she having answered all the questions that the jury put to her, she was allowed to leave the room, and leaning on the arm of the Doctor Hartley returned to the Court, there to await until, she should be required to give her evidence.

There was a trial going on when she came back, and Maria soon became completely absorbed in the interest of the proceedings, although it was upon a charge of a very trivial description. She noticed the proceedings in this case with the utmost attention, and when she observed the many attentive eyes and curious ears that were fixed upon the different witnesses, and the abrupt questions that were put to them, and remembered that in a short time she should be placed in a similar situation, she shuddered and wished it was all over.

Much to her satisfaction, however, the prisoner in this case was acquitted, and certainly upon what she considered to be very clear evidence, and she could not help noticing the change which in a moment came over that countenance which had only a short time before exhibited such ghastly symptoms of terror and despair. She had not much time given her to reflect upon this circumstance, when she perceived an unusual bustle in the Court. A general murmuring might be heard, and people were seen to be rapidly entering the place, so that in a short time every part of the building was crowded to suffocation. Another pause—a silence like that preceding the departure of the soul from its tenement of clay, and then Maria plainly distinguished the name of Mark Darwin, the Gipsy, and she was therefore convinced that the moment of trial was come.

Maria had been seated in the gallery, and therefore had an excellent view of all that was passing below, and she beheld with considerable surprise, that nearly two-thirds of the persons seemed to be of the Gipsy tribe, at least their dark flashing eyes, and olive complexions showed them to be so, and it was evident from the expression of their countenances, and the anxiety which they evinced, that they were in some way connected with the wretched man who was about to be put upon his trial.

It was not long though, before she was aroused from the intensity with which she had been observing them, by the prisoner being brought into the Court. Not a muscle seemed to quiver with fear, his eyes beamed with intrepidity, and with a firm step he walked into the dock, and a gaoler took his station on either side of him.

Maria had a full view of the Gipsy's countenance, for the place where she was seated was exactly opposite to him, and she remarked, that although his pale face showed plainly that he had suffered considerably from his incarceration, it still bore every outward sign of boldness and courage; and indeed there was nothing in his appearance that was repulsive, on the contrary, rather the reverse, and such as might induce a person to think him guiltless of the heinous crime he was charged with.

During the short interval which elapsed before the commencement of the trial, Mark Darwin looked around upon the individuals who surrounded him, and with much boldness and nonchalance bowed to those among the dense mass, whom he knew, and smiled encouragingly upon his own people.

Having satisfied himself with scanning the faces of the persons below, Mark looked up towards the spot in which Maria was seated, and trembling with fear, and terribly shocked, as she imagined his dark and piercing eye had singled her out, she drew herself back as far as she could into an obscure corner, where she thought his eyes could not penetrate. She had scarcely done so, when the attention of the prisoner was diverted from her to another object. This was Mr. Wallingford, who, evincing evident signs of the ravages which grief had made upon his frame, but with a look and general behaviour which plainly showed that he was fully prepared for the worst which might happen, entered the court, and without seeming to notice any person present, walked to the bench and took his seat by the other magistrates.

Maria was extremely shocked as she gazed upon her uncle, and noticed his pale visage and attenuated form, which had once been so muscular and graceful. It presented a strange and melancholy contrast to the stout and hearty forms of the country gentlemen in whose company he was seated, and never had Maria before taken such particular notice of it. While she was wrapped in these reflections, she suddenly heard her name spoken in a whisper from behind, and turning round, she perceived that Walter was the person who had uttered it, and that he was at her elbow though it was not without considerable trouble, he succeeded in getting a seat by her side, so densely was the gallery, and in fact every place in the court crowded, by persons anxious to hear the important trial. After a short time passed in conversation, in the course of which Walter tried all in his power to impart confidence to his fair cousin, they were given

to understand that it would be better for them to go below, where the other witnesses were waiting, so that they might not be detained by the crowd when their name should be called upon; and seeing at once the truth of this, Walter proceeded, but not without great difficulty, to get her from the gallery, and conduct her down the stairs, which were even more crowded than the former, persons struggling every way to get up them. Maria was so hot and faint with the confinement, and the sickly feverish smell of the different breaths, that it was with the utmost difficulty she could keep herself from sinking; but her agitation was increased to terror, when they had got below, and upon raising her eyes, they encountered the revengeful glances of the Gipsies, by whom they were surrounded on every side; and to add to her confusion and alarm, she found that she was an object of the most intense curiosity, and men and women exerted themselves to the utmost to obtain a view of her countenance.

Hemmed in on all sides, until Maria could scarcely breathe, and then the pressure every moment becoming greater, they were kept in this situation for several minutes, in spite of the powerful efforts of Walter to extricate her. While he was still struggling to press through the crowd, there was a strange muttering and buzzing sound in the court, which seemed to set all the proclamations for silence at defiance, and Walter felt confident that something particular had taken place, in which opinion he was confirmed, by the increased suspense and anxiety depicted on the countenances of the Gipsies.

It is more than probable that Walter and his terrified companion would have been some time longer before they could have succeeded in pressing through the crowd, had they not been observed by one of the officers belonging to the court, who spoke to another, and by the dint of their staves and other forcible arguments, they did at last manage to get Walter and his almost fainting charge to the witness box, in which they found Doctor Hartley and the other witnesses for the trial.

"Good God!" exclaimed Doctor Hartley, "what can be the cause of Ela not having arrived yet?" surely no accident can have befallen her on the way. Oh, how she would gloat upon this sight. I cannot account for her tardiness in coming."

The tone and words of Doctor Hartley astonished and attracted the attention of Walter and his cousin, and looking up and in the direction that he was gazing, which was the dock where the prisoner stood, language cannot give utterance to their astonishment, their almost incredulity, when there they beheld standing by the side of his son, Mark Darwin the elder! —His deeply marked, and rugged features had an expression of the most undaunted villany, and he gazed upon the bench where the judge and the magistrates were seated, with the greatest contempt.

"Wonderful!" ejaculated Walter; "what is the meaning of this? It is the father of the prisoner, and suspected of being the principal in the murder."

"It is true," said Doctor Hartley; "not many minutes since he gave himself up to the officers, and stated that he was ready to be put upon his trial. They have some deep-laid

WALTER WALLINGFORD RESCUES MARIA FROM THE IMPORTUNITIES OF BARNELL.

sign in view, depend upon it; but what that can be I am perfectly at a loss to conjecture."

The doctor was prevented from saying any more, by there being another proclamation for silence, and then they (that is, the persons so immediately interested) fixed their earnest attention upon the proceedings. The silence, however, which had been obtained, was once more broken by a noise and unusual bustle. The next moment the bar of the witness box was raised by the officers, and a woman, whose appearance was very humble, and who appeared to be scarcely able to walk, so greatly did she seem to totter from the ravages of time, entered. She had on an old cloak, and the hood covered her head, so that her features were not visible, more particularly as her chin was buried in her chest.

She tottered to a seat beside Maria, and did not seem to take any notice of what was passing. The persons in the witness-box were surprised, and looked at each other with inquiring glances.

"Who is this, and what business can she have here?" thought Maria and her companions. But they had not many minutes allowed them for useless conjecture, when they were called to pay immediate attention to the trial.

"Walter Wallingford!" exclaimed the officer of the court; "Walter Wallingford," he repeated, in a louder tone than before, and the instant after he had called the first time, notwithstanding, Walter, of course, had paid immediate attention to the summons, and stepping forward, stood before the prisoners. A low murmuring sound was heard in the court for a second or two, and a death-like silence prevailed, and the attention of every person was fixed upon the evidence which Walter gave utterance to.

We need not recapitulate particulars with which the reader has already been made acquainted; suffice it to say, that Walter gave his evidence most distinctly, and readily answered to the questions that were asked him, though they were not many, one of the most important being, whether he could swear to the identity of the elder prisoner as being one of the two men whom he had seen take the body out of the water, to which he unhesitatingly answered in the affirmative. The judge then inquired of the prisoners whether it was their wish to interrogate the witness.

"Yes, my lord," replied the elder Gipsy, firmly, "I do." Then turning to Walter, he fixed his eyes steadfastly upon him, and addressing himself to him, said—

"It is my wish to inquire of you, Mr. Walter Wallingford, whether you are positive it was the young woman Fanny Beranzio, whom you say you saw us take out of the lake in the gardens of your father's mansion?"

"I did not know her at that time," answered Walter, "but I afterwards learnt it, from the words dropped by her distracted parent."

"But you were acquainted with the deceased, were you not?" inquired Mark, with great emphasis, and fixing his eyes still more intently on the countenance of Walter.

"I cannot conceive the necessity for that question," said the latter, impatiently.

"Of course you have no motive in not wishing to answer it?" observed the prisoner, with a look of sarcasm.

"I have no motive," returned Walter, calmly. "'Tis true, if my memory serves me right, that I have seen her before—once only, I believe; but at that time, of her name I was entirely ignorant, likewise of any particulars of her history."

"Recollect yourself, Mr. Wallingford," said the youngest Gipsy, sharply, "did you not make an assignation with her in the grounds of Wallingford Hall?—And did you not there meet, night after night, and was——"

"'Tis false!—'tis false!" interrupted Walter, with warmth, and all the energy of truth.

"Neither did you ever make an agreement to meet her mother, I suppose?" observed the elder Mark, coolly, and glancing fiercely towards Mr. Wallingford.

"Until after the murder of her daughter, I knew nothing whatever of the unfortunate woman of whom you speak."

The elder Mark smiled ironically when Walter returned this answer; and then remarked—

"I have no more questions to put to you, sir."

Walter descended, and returned to his seat, and then the name of "Ela Beranzio" was called out in the same loud tones by the officer of the court. A thrill of expectation seemed to run through the immense throng at the mention of the name, and Doctor Hartley started up with consternation, thinking that Ela was not there;—but an instant, however, when all were in breathless anxiety awaiting—when not a sound disturbed the sepulchral stillness,—the seeming aged female, who had taken her seat by the side of Maria, started up, and throwing back her disguise before the astonished eyes of the assembly, her eyes sparkling with the vehemence of her anxiety, and her bosom throbbing with emotion, there stood Ela Beranzio, and confronted her deadly foes.

Powerful was the sensation which ran through the court at this unexpected sight, and deadly was the malice and bitter hatred which flashed from the eyes of Ela and the prisoners, as they fixed them upon each other. The expression of the old man's countenance was that of contempt and undaunted courage, but the younger Mark seemed completely thunderstruck, and nothing near so firm.

"My prayers are heard—the moment so long wished for has come at last—the moment for which alone I wished to retain life," said Ela, as she fixed upon the elder Mark a look of exultation, which he returned with one of defiance; she was about to proceed, but she was prevented from doing so, and ordered to pay due respect to the court, and to give such evidence as she had to offer, without adding any irrelevant remarks of her own. Ela turned away for a moment from the prisoners, curtseyed respectfully to the court, and then seemed with impatient haste to await while the oath was administered to her. During this time the silence was unbroken by the slightest noise, and every person seemed to await the evidence with the most breathless anxiety.

The first question put to her was, when she last beheld her daughter living. An instant only, and she seemed to tremble, and a deadly paleness overspread her features,—but the emotion was transient; she overcame it, and then proceeded to reply to the interrogatory, and mentioned the morning preceding the night of the murder; at least on the evening when Maria had encountered Fanny and Esther in the shrubbery, and the screams that had afterwards been heard from that direction.

"On that fatal day," Ela went on to say, with the utmost composure of tone and gesture, "we were sent in different routes, and it was arranged that we should meet on a particular spot at a certain time, and return to our tents. My memory fails to furnish me with the cause, but it happened that I was detained, and I did not go, in consequence, to the place appointed for us to meet at, neither did I arrive at the encampment till long after midnight, and then my daughter was not in the tents. When I eagerly inquired where she was, they informed me that she had come back at an early hour in company with a young girl who went by the name of Esther;"—here her lip again for a moment quivered, and she fixed her eyes upon Wallingford, whose countenance was ghastly pale, and who with terrible anxiety was listening to all she uttered. Ela, after a brief pause, continued : "To my eager inquiries they replied that Esther had quitted my child, in order that she might accompany another portion of the tribe, and that Fanny had returned very much vexed, and would not consent to go out any more that day. Then did the wretches seek to impose upon me, and to quiet my suspicions by an infamous invention, the improbability of which must be apparent to any persons of penetration. They said that the two girls were missed from the tents at the time of supper, and furthermore that these two miscreants, the prisoners at the bar, had gone in search of them in the gardens of Wallingford Hall, which they said was a place of frequent resort by my ill-fated girl; and maniac, idiot that I was at the time, they gained such an influence over my credulity, I say, that I believed that they spoke the truth, and imagined that Wallingford, the proprietor of the hall of that name, had taken from me my daughter;—but too soon did I find my error, when it was, alas, too late to save the dreadful catastrophe which had taken place. I quickly discovered who were the

monsters that had assassinated my poor, gentle, and unoffending girl, and from that moment I never rested, no, not either day or night, until I had found out the place where they had hidden her mangled remains."

This harangue had been two or three times attempted to be interrupted, but there was something so fascinating in the words and manner of Ela, that seemed to cast a spell upon every person present,—for although she had been several times told of the informality of the detail she was giving, and that she must not tell them of what she thought, but that which had come under her observation, she paid no attention to what they said, but went on with a story, which no one for a moment disbelieved. She then minutely detailed the way in which she had followed the two Gipsies, until she tracked them to the lake in the gardens of Wallingford Hall, and beheld them take from it the corpse of her unfortunate daughter. Having recapitulated these facts, she brought forward the handkerchief which had been found in the summerhouse, tied round the throat of the murdered girl, to which was attached a weighty stone, no doubt, with an idea of concealing their guilt by sinking the body in the dark waters of the lake.

"Strange events bring about the punishment of the guilty," continued Ela, looking fiercely and triumphantly upon the elder Gipsy, "and so has it proved with you, Mark Darwin. That handkerchief, you would not let me rest until I had marked it with your name, and now it is brought forward as a damning proof of your guilt, and, if justice is to be obtained, will be the means of consigning you to the death of a dog."

"Do you then mean to swear," was the question put to her, "do you mean to swear, that the handkerchief, which you say was found around the neck of the deceased, is the same which you marked for the elder prisoner, and that it is his property?"

"Undoubtedly I do," she answered;— "many years have elapsed, for the wretch, his son, who is now with him charged with this bloody crime, was at the period I am speaking of, an innocent boy. I was the only one among the tribe who was expert at my needle, and Mark Darwin was quite delighted when I had wrought it. He placed a peculiar value upon it, and never used it only on particular occasions; but when has there been an occasion of such importance as this?"

This being the whole of Ela's evidence, the prisoners were once more asked whether they wished to put any questions to her.

The youngest Gipsy merely signified a negative by a shake of the head, but his father looked at her for a moment with a mysterious expression, and then said that "He had no questions to ask her then, but that presently he should require her to prove that he was not guilty of the crime which was laid to his charge!"

These words caused an extraordinary sensation in the court, and expressions of astonishment were freely uttered by the persons present, which, in spite of the efforts of the officers, could not for several moments be silenced; meanwhile Ela was apparently completely paralysed, and stood staring vacantly upon the prisoners, until she was told to retire, but not to go from the court.

"Oh, you need not fear that I will withdraw from this place until I hear——" She was not permitted to proceed in what she was about to give utterance to, and she resumed her seat by the side of Maria, but she had scarcely done so, when the former was called upon to give evidence, and with more confidence than might have been expected in one naturally so timid and retiring, she stepped forward.

It was soon visible that the prisoners paid particular attention to the evidence of Maria, more so than they had to either of the other witnesses, and it was very evident that the manner in which she related all she knew of the horrible affair, made them feel much more doubtful of the result of the trial than they had previously done. Her testimony was such as to prove beyond a doubt, that there were two girls, one of whom she knew to be Fanny, she having beheld her once before near the same place where the murder was supposed to have been committed. She described, in the most clear and distinct manner, the alarm which the two girls had evinced, the conversation she had heard between them, by which it was evident they had seen men lurking about in the shrubbery, and then the observations which one of them made in allusion to the countenance of the old man, and everything she stated; in fact, the agonised shrieks she had heard, and which had for awhile deprived her of her faculties, all appeared to be such confirmatory evidence of their guilt, to which was added their attempt to carry away the corpse, that no person in the court could see the slightest chance of their being able to rebut; and it was very evident that the elder prisoner, who had eluded the vigilance of the officers of justice for some time, had never imagined that such proof of their criminality could have been adduced, and although all along a hitherto reckless confidence had been discernible in the expression of his countenance, it was now very clear he began to despair.

He betrayed great agitation during the time she was speaking, and large drops of perspiration might be seen standing upon his temples, and even after she had concluded her evidence,

he seemed completely petrified, and could not remove his eyes from her, as though he expected every instant she would give utterance to some fresh proof of their guilt.

The usual question having been put to him, he replied:—"No; I have no questions to ask the last witness;—in fact, how is it possible I can have anything to say to her, when all that she has taken such pains to detail, is perfectly unknown to me?—I say again, that I am as ignorant of it as the judge upon the bench."

But although the elder Mark declined interrogating Maria, his son did not; and apparently with all the revengeful feelings of his heart, he immediately put a number of questions to her which were only calculated to involve her in confusion and perplexity. And he also tried all that his ingenuity and consummate artfulness could suggest, to make it appear, that instead of himself and his father, it was Mr. Wallingford and his son who were in the grounds at the time she mentioned, and who alarmed the ill-fated Fanny and her companion.

"Do you not think it probable," said he, "that two outcast people of the Gipsy tribe, who had no right to be found in the private grounds of a gentleman's mansion, would have been less likely to be alarmed at seeing their own associates, than at the appearance of the masters of the place?"

Mark had evidently studied this question, and he put it with such vehemence of tone and gesture, that he doubtless considered it would cause a very great sensation, and occasion a turn in the balance of their fate. Maria, however, answered him with perfect composure and propriety, very much to the ruffian's disappointment apparently.

"Such an idea never once occurred to me," replied Maria, "indeed my terror was so great, that I had not an opportunity of reflecting upon who had been the occasion of alarm; and even had such a thought entered my mind, it would have been immediately dismissed, when, in the path leading from the house, I met Mr. Walter Wallingford, who——"

"Ah! that will do," interrupted the fellow with an insolent frown, "you have well studied your part."

When these expressions escaped him, there was a burst of indignation against him from many of the persons in the court; for no person could have given their evidence more dispassionately, impartially, or with greater reluctance than Maria did; and quite overcome by his manner, and the insinuation he had uttered upon her veracity, she staggered from the place, and sunk pale and overcome on the seat by the side of Ela.

The other portion of the evidence did not occupy much time to go through, and the most important part of it, was that given by Mr. Wallingford, who did not come from the bench

Mr. Wallingford made a deep impression upon everybody present, by the manner in which he recited the particulars of the melancholy event with which he was acquainted, and so calm and collected was he throughout, that it could never have been imagined, only by such persons as knew the particulars of his early history, that he was himself so deeply and immediately interested in the whole of the circumstances, and how poignantly, how bitterly he had suffered.

However, the prisoners' spirit of diabolical hatred and revenge urged them to inflict upon him all the agony that was in their power, and the first question which the elder Mark put to him rendered it impossible for him to help admitting that he had every reason to believe the murdered girl was his daughter, which caused such a burst of astonishment in the court, that a few seconds elapsed before it was possible to resume the proceedings. To this feeling was added one of the deepest horror, for every word that the two villains gave utterance to, was to endeavour to fix the perpetration of the dreadful crime upon Mr. Wallingford.

"And is it possible," said the youngest prisoner, "is it possible, that when you saw the body of the deceased, you did not immediately recollect the features of her you had been long seeking to get possession of, your daughter Fanny, by the Gipsy woman, Ela Beranzio?"

"Certainly I did not," answered Mr. Wallingford; "how is it to be supposed I should, when it was so many years since I had before seen her, not indeed since she was a child?"

"Bright example of parental affection," exclaimed the fellow, ironically; "however, I have no more to say to you—at any rate, not just yet."

The countenance of Mr. Wallingford spoke more than words could even have done. His bosom swelled with indignation, and he felt himself a miserable, debased, and degraded being. But the behaviour of the prisoners, so far from having the effect they desired it should, only served to excite their sympathy towards the object at whom their malice was aimed, and in the hope of having retribution for his wrongs, and seeing his base slanderers brought to justice, he overcame his feelings as much as possible, and resumed his seat.

Shortly after this, the case for the prosecution being closed, the prisoners were asked whether they would call any witnesses for their defence.

"Yes, my lord," answered the elder Mark, "I will take the liberty of calling two witnesses, one of whom is Ela Beranzio."

Ela started from her seat when Mark thus had spoken, and fixed her large black and brilliant eyes upon him with the most indescribable astonishment.

"Villain! what mean you?" she demanded.

"You shall know soon," he answered, with a triumphant smile; "answer me—have you not sworn, positively sworn, that your girl, Fanny Beranzio, was assassinated?—that her corpse was found in the lake, in the grounds of Wallingford Hall?—and do you not suspect me and my son are the persons who have perpetrated this crime?"

"Suspect!" reiterated Ela. "Oh! Mark, do I not know it too well—am I not certain that——"

"Let the name of Fanny Beranzio be called, if you please!" interrupted Mark, without waiting to hear the conclusion of her speech, and speaking to the crier of the court.

Had a sudden earthquake at that moment have shaken the building to its foundation, it could not have caused a stronger feeling of surprise and consternation among the persons present, than did the words of the Gipsy. Not a whisper, not a sound could be heard throughout the densely crowded building; and Ela was fixed as a statue on the spot—her eyelids distended, her bosom heaving, and every feature giving evidence of the intense, the almost insupportable anxiety she was suffering. But another second, and the eyes of every person were attracted to the door at which the witnesses entered, and there tripped into the place a light and beauteous form, which seemed not like an inhabitant of this earth, and who having reached the place where Ela stood, was lifted up and placed by her side, and the bewildered woman stared upon it, as if something supernatural met her eyes.

"Gracious Heavens! Has thy angelic spirit been allowed to revisit this earth?" she at last was enabled to ejaculate; and had she not held the bar of the witness-box, she must have fallen to the ground.

There was scarcely the lapse of a second, when the lovely girl, whom the voice seemed at once to arouse from the state of stupefaction in which she was wrapped from her first entrance into the court, with a faint scream rushed into Ela's arms, and ejaculated—

"Speak to me, mother!—embrace your poor girl! Dearest mother, it is me—it is your own, your darling Fanny!"

With these words she fell upon her bosom, and became completely insensible.

In an instant, Walter, Doctor Hartley, and Maria rendered their aid to the unfortunate woman, and so deeply engaged were they in trying to restore her to recollection, that the business of the trial proceeded without their taking any notice of it.

The prisoners now evidently thought their acquittal certain, and they replied to the further questions that were put to them with the utmost insolence and effrontery. Having, however, been reprimanded in severe terms by the judge, they altered their tone, and though their answers were naturally bold, from the confidence they entertained of their innocence being admitted, they were couched in respectful language.

"I repeat, my lord," said the elder Mark, "that in that girl you behold the very Fanny Beranzio, of assassinating whom we have been accused; and we therefore trust you will gladly acquit us of the terrible charge which has been maliciously brought against us. It is very clear that this has been a base plot against the lives of two innocent men; but we have triumphed, and the shame and disgrace our enemies thought to bring upon us will recoil upon themselves."

Before, however, the judge could pronounce a verdict of acquittal, it was indispensably requisite, according to law, that there should be some person come forward who could prove, beyond a doubt, that this was really Fanny Beranzio, the young woman whom they had been charged with having murdered, for the wild exclamations of Ela, and the bewildered state of Fanny, rendered it impossible, at present, to take their evidence; and, indeed, they were both in such a frantic state, that it was found necessary that they should be immediately taken from the court, and receive medical attendance.

Notwithstanding the unexpected issue of the trial, and the remarkable events that had taken place, Doctor Hartley exhibited none of that confusion and lack of presence of mind, which it might have been expected he would, and took the liberty to express to the judge his opinion of the danger to which Ela and her daughter would be exposed, if they were to attempt to take them through the dense congregation which was assembled in the court, and which was, moreover, principally composed of their enemies, the Gipsies. The judge immediately saw through the reasonableness and propriety of the hint, and, therefore, ordered a strong body of officers to guard them from the place to Ela's carriage, which had been brought round to the court by her orders, after her arrival, so that no person might have a knowledge of whom it belonged to—which was done with safety, and Doctor Hartley, Walter, and Maria, took their places in the carriage also, which, by the express orders of the former, was driven to the house at which he was lodging.

They had not, however, got far, when Walter remembered that he had forgotten his father.

"Gracious Heaven! what could I be thinking about to do this?" he exclaimed, when he had made the discovery.

"It was, indeed, very thoughtless of you, Mr. Walter, observed the doctor, "but I cannot be thinking for you all, you know;—however, you had better go back again directly, and see your father in safety to the house, for, of course, I cannot leave the females, who may need my attendance. I will be with you as

early as possible; but if there should be any necessity for medical assistance, send for it without any delay, and do not await my arrival."

With the utmost apprehension that something had happened to his parent, and blaming himself a thousand times for his thoughtlessness, Walter retraced his steps to the place he had so recently left; but upon his arrival there, he was most agreeably disappointed when he beheld his father with more composure of demeanour and cheerfulness of countenance than he had seen him display since the fatal occurrence which had caused him so much unhappiness. making some remarks to the court, which seemed to be listened to with the most breathless attention and sympathy by every person present.

Walter heard only the concluding part of the address, and his father having seen him approach, made a respectful bow to the court, and left amidst the most earnest manifestations of condolence from the persons who still thronged the place. Walter took his arm, and then made his way through the crowd towards the door by which they had entered into the building.

"Let us make what haste we can to Mrs. Patterson's, now Walter," he remarked, "I stand much in need of repose, which having obtained, I trust that the all-merciful God, who has this day brought about this strange event, will enable me to bring to condign punishment the assassins of my unfortunate Christabelle!"

"Christabelle!" gasped forth Walter, with a look of horror. He had never thought of this;—so completely had his ideas been occupied by the remarkable occurrences of the day, that even when his father mentioned the name of his sister, he could not exactly form an idea of the full force of his meaning.

"Christabelle!" he repeated, looking at his father aghast for an explanation.

"Is it possible, Walter, that the idea has not occurred to you, that the unfortunate girl who was really assassinated was your sister, whom Ela, in the confusion of the moment, mistook for her daughter?"

The horror and astonishment—the consternation and the sudden shock occasioned by this conviction, appeared for a while to fetter all the faculties of Walter, and he was transfixed to the spot like a statue, and stared upon his father in stupified amazement. It was several moments before he recovered sufficiently to see the impropriety of delaying their departure from the spot, where he could still perceive the dark flashing eyes of the Gipsies fixed upon them; and without uttering another word, he hurried his father to the carriage, following after him himself, and it drove away quickly in the direction of their lodgings.

They conversed not at all on their way home,

and it was not until the following morning, that Mr. Wallingford gave him the particulars of what had taken place after he had left the court with Ela and Fanny.

It appeared that several of the Gipsy women came forward, who having stated that they had known Fanny from infancy, fully convinced the jury that she was the absolute person whom Mark and his son had been charged with having murdered, and upon this being clearly established, the judge without any further hesitation directed the jury to acquit the prisoners.

The uncontrollable exultation and delight at this termination was clearly visible on their countenances, as was also the most intense anxiety to hear their acquittal pronounced; this sensation also seemed to communicate itself to the Gipsies who were yet in the court, and all eyes were fixed on the jury, who, acting upon the direction of the judge, immediately pronounced a verdict of "Not Guilty!"

A burst of triumph and applause was uttered by the Gipsies when the verdict was returned, and they pressed forward towards the dock, from which Mark and his son, without any further ceremony, were endeavouring to get out. And indeed the people were so excited by the extraordinary events of the day, and at the sudden appearance of the female who had been supposed to have been assassinated, that they took no notice of the behaviour of Mark and his son, whom they, in fact, pitied for the awful situation in which they had apparently been so unjustly placed. They were, therefore, about to leave the dock; another instant, and they would have been carried off in triumph by their eager associates, when their progress was suddenly arrested by a voice which commanded them to stop, as there was another charge against them.

Immediately upon hearing this, the officer who was about to set them at liberty, removed the key from the lock, and Mark and his son turned their ghastly and enraged looks upon Mr. Wallingford, who was the person that had spoken.

"I have yet a serious charge to bring against them," said Mr. Wallingford, in a firm tone; "I accuse them of having murdered Christabelle Wallingford, the child of whom I was robbed by them in its infancy, and whom they initiated into their disgraceful and lawless life under the name of Esther. It can be proved that she was in company with Fanny Beranzio on the night that the dreadful crime was committed, and I shall be able to adduce sufficient evidence to establish the fact that the unfortunate girl fell beneath their hands. Fanny Beranzio, who, in the late trial, proved the means of their acquittal, will, in this instance, be enabled to prove their guilt : there is not a single circumstance of that fatal night, of which she can be ignorant."

A mingled expression of malice and contempt passed over the features of the elder Mark, when Mr. Wallingford gave utterance to the latter remarks ; but it gave place to the most indescribable wrath, when he was interrupted in the midst of a speech which he attempted to make in reply to the second charge brought against them, by the judge telling him that he had better reserve anything he might have to offer in proof of his innocence, for his trial. His lordship then inquired of Mr. Wallingford whether he had his witnesses in readiness, to which the latter replied in the affirmative, requesting at the same time that the trial should be postponed till the following day, when he promised faithfully to produce such evidence that could not fail fully to establish the guilt of the accused.

The judge without any hesitation granted Mr. Wallingford's request, and ordering the gaoler to look carefully after the safe custody of his prisoners, postponed the trial till the morning.

It would be a useless task to endeavour to describe the sensation which was exhibited in the court upon this unexpected change in the proceedings; the Gipsies by execrations expressed their rage and disappointment, while Mark and his son seemed completely aroused to a full sense of the terrible situation in which they stood, and, passive as infants, they were loaded with fetters, and removed from the dock to the prison, in the custody of the gaoler and a strong body of the officers.

CHAPTER XLV.

"My heart is sad, my hopes are gone,
    My blood runs coldly through my breast ;
And when I perish, thou alone
    Wilt sigh above my place of rest."
                                    BYRON.

THE feelings of Ela may be better imagined than any language can pourtray them, when she became fully conscious of the fact that her daughter, her own darling Fanny was alive, and that she pressed to her bosom the form of her whom she had imagined was now mouldering in the silent grave. With the most impassioned feelings that could move the human breast, she looked into the pale countenance of Fanny, parted the hair from her temples, and then turned her glances towards Doctor Hartley and Maria, who were in the apartment, as if she required some further corroboration of the truth.

"Oh, why are you so silent ?" she at length ejaculated, "why do you not speak to me, that I may be convinced I am not dreaming, that this is all reality ?—But no, it cannot be a delusion ;—it cannot be any ideal occurrence —for did I not behold Mark Darwin and his son;—did I not hear the old serpent command Fanny Beranzio to come forward—and did she not appear? Yes, she came, like a celestial spirit, the moment the words escaped his lips. Surely he could not make the dead rise from their graves at his bidd ng, and yet did I not gaze upon the mangled corpse of my child?"

" 'Tis there where you was mistaken," returned Doctor Hartley, who found that if he allowed her wild imaginings to have full scope, it might be attended with the most serious consequences. "Your haste and imprudence has in a great measure caused all this misunderstanding, and brought the suffering upon yourself and others. You, of course, best know what motives you had to believe, in the first instance, that Mark and his son, were the murderers of your daughter; but it is very evident that your having received that impression, made you less careful, more particularly in examining the features of the ill-fated victim, who was dressed exactly like your daughter, or you would have discovered that it was Esther who——"

"Good God!" exclaimed Ela. "I see it all now;—idiot that I must have been. Yes, it was indeed the unfortunate Esther, or Christabelle, more properly speaking, that fell a victim to the wretches!"

These words aroused Fanny, who, opening her eyes, looked affectionately in her mother's face, as she placed her small white hand on her lips, and said, in a voice of evident alarm—

"Silence, for Heaven's sake, dear mother; any name but that of Esther; that you must not again venture to breathe."

The solemnity and wildness of her manner, impressed all who were present that her mind wandered, and the deepest sympathy was excited in their bosoms in consequence. But Ela, after having looked intently at her for a minute or two, seemed suddenly to understand the truth, and exclaimed :—

"Ah! I see how it is. The villains, the miscreants have been playing their fiendish deeds upon my poor girl; they have forced her to take their stupifying and destructive drugs, and her senses are disordered."

"Surely it cannot be so bad as you say," replied the doctor, who, notwithstanding, could not help noticing the strange alteration which had taken place in the unhappy girl within the last few minutes.

At length her eyes became heavy, her recollection seemed to leave her, and she appeared not to be aware of what was going forward, so that Ela's suspicions were too strongly confirmed, and each person was struck with horror and consternation.

"Do not give way to any useless alarm," said the doctor, with much solicitude in his manner, "she may yet be recovered." His countenance was sufficiently expressive to show that he

uttered what he scarcely dared believe himself. "You must endeavour to awaken her from this state of apathy and unconsciousness," he continued, as he pointed to Ela to remove the head of poor Fanny from her shoulder, where she had languidly laid it. "Talk to her as much as you can, no matter however repugnant the subject may be to your feelings; the excitement will probably arouse her from this lethargy, and in the meantime I will see and prepare her something to take, which I trust will do her good, and conquer the effects of the deadly drug which has evidently been administered to her."

Completely horror-struck at the situation of her daughter, who had so lately been restored to her, as it were from the grave, Ela obeyed the worthy doctor's injunctions, and aroused poor Fanny from the posture in which she had been reclining by her side on the sofa, and notwithstanding she evinced every disinclination to be disturbed, traversed the apartment with her.

The eyes of Fanny were several times raised towards her mother's face, but it was with a stupid, vacant stare, which sh wed that her senses wandered. Ela spoke to her, and she appeared to listen, but to be unable, though she tried, to understand what she was saying to her. Her heart told her who it was that spoke, but the words she was quite incapable of understanding.

"You say then, my dear girl," said Ela, thinking by the means of a more exciting subject, to arouse her dormant faculties, "at least you are aware, that it was poor Esther who fell beneath the knife of the assassins? Was you not a witness of the horrible deed, Fanny?—did you not behold——"

"Oh, for the love of God, do not agonize me with such questions," answered the unfortunate Fanny, with every symptom of the most violent anguish and terror, at the same time her eyes wandered round the room, as though she was fearful that some one was watching them: "oh do not, I beseech you, do not question me upon that dreadful subject."

"Nay, my child," answered Ela, "I must question you, therefore it is complete folly to solicit me to forbear. But why do you look around you so fearfully; there is no one here that will harm you, no one of whom you need be apprehensive. Come, my poor girl, let me beg of you to recollect yourself, and do not suffer the monsters who murdered your sister to escape the punishment due to their dreadful crime. Tell me, my dear girl, who dealt the ill-fated Esther the fatal blow? Was it the old monster or the young fiend?"

Fanny once more rested her head on her mother's shoulder, and appeared as if about to relapse once more into the state of unconsciousness from which she had been so recently aroused.

"Merciful Father," she cried, my blood seems to freeze in my veins at the terrible recollection:—but it was not my fault; God knows I would have saved her, but I could not; then——   But I must not divulge the dreadful truth:—no, no, mother, dear mother, I am bound by an oath,—that horrible oath, which we must not, dare not violate."

"Hark ye, girl," said Dr. Hartley, assuming an air of harshness and severity, which was quite foreign to his nature, "it matters not what oath you have taken; no oath can be

BARNELL ATTEMPTS THE LIFE OF WALTER WALLINGFORD.

binding which is extorted from an individual for the purpose of concealing murder. I warn you, Fanny, that in a few hours you will be brought before a judge and jury of your countrymen, when you will be sworn to speak the truth, and must do so, or you will be suspected most likely of being an accomplice in the barbarous crime. Walter Wallingford, whom I have just seen, has informed me to-morrow the prisoners will be put upon their trial a second time, charged with being the murderers of Christabelle, and upon the evidence of

No. 35.

Fanny, the issue of the trial principally depends."

The countenance of Fanny for a second or two became more animated than before, and looking earnestly in the good doctor's face, said—

"Christabelle—that name—what have I to do with her—I know her not, and therefore cannot give any evidence concerning her;—therefore——"

"Oh, yes, you can—you can, my child," hastily observed Ela; "it is of Esther you will be called upon to say all that you are acquainted with."

"Yes," added the doctor, solemnly, "and if you will not relate all the particulars, as far as your knowledge will permit you, as I before said, you will be accused of being connected with them in the murder, and arraigned at the bar with them; for it is very well known that you were in the unfortunate girl's company at the time, and can therefore reveal——"

"Oh, my dear sir," said the kind-hearted Maria, "pray do not speak to the poor girl with such severity; there is no necessity for it; I am certain, for I much mistake the character of Fanny, if she does not yield to the persuations of her mother or you, sir; she will not suffer justice to escape the guilty." Then she added in a low tone to Mr. Hartley—"Persuasion, I think, my dear sir, will be more likely to succeed than harshness;—if you will only allow her time to collect her thoughts, I am certain——"

"Which is the very thing that I should at present regret, Miss Herbert; but as you seem to knew so much better than me——"

"Oh, sir," eagerly interrupted Maria, "you cannot believe me to be so vain, I am sure you do not."

"Believe me, my dear girl," said Mr. Hartley, with all his accustomed kindness, "I do not; but your interruption at the moment, I must confess, vexed me. I must beg that you will leave it all to my discretion, and I feel confident that my judgment and experience will not lead me astray. It is enough that the villains have contrived to gain some ascendancy over the mind of the unfortunate girl, as well as they have tampered with her body, and it must be harsh, or apparently harsh measures alone, that can shake the influence they have acquired. If, for instance, we were to endeavour to persuade her, and suffer her to recall to her memory that she is somewhat obligated to them;—or the wild and illegal oaths they have administered to her, we should be certain not to succeed; for this reason, that the time is so brief, that her reason could never combat against the dense and heavy mass of superstition with which they have overloaded it. Instead of doing so, we must follow in some measure the course that the wretches themselves have adopted; for it is plain enough to be seen that intimidation has been one of the principal weapons with which they have fought her; they have preyed first upon her mind and constitution, by their infernal drugs, and then they have frightened her, by terrific representations, into a compliance with their wishes; and threatened her with more horrors than my imagination can conceive if she refused to do as they demanded; therefore as they have succeeded by frightening her, in making her silent, we must do our best endeavours by the same method to thwart their schemes, and bring her to a due sense of her duty again."

While the doctor was thus talking to Maria, Ela had lost no time in trying all the force of rhetoric which she was possessed of to endeavour to persuade her unhappy daughter to do as she was requested.

"My dearest Fanny," she continued, in reply to some observations which the latter had been making, "why do you persist in calling them our people, when I tell you once more they are no longer connected with us? You must learn in future to despise and hate them, for we are no longer bound to obey their laws, or to yield to their customs. Hark you, my dear Fanny, your mother has wealth now, wealth, aye, in abundance, and we are therefore secure from the effects of their vengeance. Think of them no more, only as wretches beneath your contempt even. Do not, for a moment, encourage the idea that they possess any power over our destiny; but if they enter your thoughts at all, let it be only accompanied with a sense that it is your duty to bring them to justice for the crimes of which they are guilty."

Fanny made no reply, but it was very evident from the expression of her countenance, that all the arguments made use of by Ela had not succeeded in bringing to her mind a conviction of their truth. They had, however, the satisfaction to perceive that the effects of the potion she had taken was fast evaporating, and that she was gradually being restored to reason. Seeing the good effects of the first dose he had given her, Dr. Hartley administered a second, and she had not long taken it when a portion of her natural colour was restored to her cheek and her lips, and her countenance by degrees began to re-assume all its natural loveliness, although even in insensibility its beauty was most impressive.

Ever and anon did Fanny remove her eyes from the countenance of her parent, to gaze upon the other persons in the room. First she fixed her eyes upon the doctor, and she as quickly removed them to Maria, and placed her hand to her forehead, as if she was endeavouring to recall something to her memory. From Maria her eyes wandered with eager curiosity to the apartment, and the handsome furniture it contained, and she appeared to be completely at a loss to know by what extraordinary means she had become the inmate of a place, the appearance and comforts of which were so new to her.

"I cannot stay with you any longer at present," said Doctor Hartley, after he had been engaged privately with Maria, for a few minutes, in conversation, in which he strongly urged her to do all that was in her power to prepare the mind of Fanny for the trial; "in a short time, however, I dare say I shall be able to rejoin you, and in the meanwhile I shall leave you under the care of a capital nurse, in Miss Herbert, whose wishes I beg that you will strictly attend to."

At the mention of Maria's name, Fanny started, and passing her hand across her temples, seemed to be endeavouring to recollect something—

"Herbert," she said at length, fixing her bright and expressive eyes upon the countenance of Maria, "surely that name is——"

"Oh, yes," eagerly added Maria, "you have heard it before, and this is not the first time we have met; the last time we were together, was under circumstances that no distance of time will ever be able to erase from my memory. Do you not recollect the night when we encountered each other in the shrubbery, and had it not been for the warning you gave me, my life would——"

"Oh, well do I remember now!" Fanny interrupted, hastily, and her bosom heaved with emotion; "yes, it is the same—the cousin to him who—of Walter!—eternal gratitude to the Almighty, who saved her life from the assassin's blade!—Oh, my poor brain has been so distracted since that awful, that fatal night; and such frightful visions have tormented my imagination. Sometimes I thought that they had murdered her as well as the unfortunate Esther, for she had scarcely quitted the spot, when the villains rushed in to perform their fiendish work. My God! I wonder that I did not expire at that moment! They were like savages, or beasts of prey. But since then all has appeared like a vision upon my mind, and often has the horrid idea occurred to me that they had been lurking there for the purpose of murdering the whole family—for I was well aware how inveterate they were against them, and I was confident that they would not hesitate to do anything for the purpose of gratifying their vengeance; but after all, our people——"

"That hated title again," interrupted Ela, "it is abhorrent to my ears, Fanny, why then do you persist in making use of it?—I hope that this is the last time I shall hear you give utterance to such a word. Have I not already informed you, my dear girl, that all connection

between them and us is at an end, and that in future my Fanny will not be attached to that life of crime and misery, which the villany of her father in the first instance consigned her to; and I trust that she will never forget that——"

"Oh, my dearest mother," interrupted Fanny, joy, hope, and astonishment imparting unusual animation to her features, "and has my father then at length relented, and does he at last do us that justice which has been so tardy?—Shall I at last have a place that I can call my home, and be allowed to make use of the dear—dear name of brother?—and will you, miss, now that I am no longer the wretched wandering Gipsy Girl, be——"

"Dear, dear Fanny," interrupted Maria vehemently—for she could perceive from the lowering brow of Ela, that she was about to make some harsh and severe answer, and she was anxious to prevent her—"believe me, my dear girl, that in me you shall find a sister, friend, everything. Yes, yes, I am certain that happiness is in store for us all, and I know that the pleasure of Walter Wallingford will be fully equal to our own."

"Walter Wallingford—my brother," said Fanny, with emphasis, and then a sigh escaped her gentle breast, and she cast her eyes towards the floor, and for awhile seemed lost to any other but that one endearing thought.

This was an excellent opportunity, it occurred to Maria, to put into operation the injunctions of Doctor Hartley, and to make Fanny acquainted with the trial that was forthcoming; she therefore observed—

"He is your brother, Fanny, and you must not forget that the unfortunate Esther was also his sister, and therefore he has no other person save you to look to, to depend upon—for the purpose of bringing to that retribution they have incurred, those wretches who inflicted upon her so untimely a death. Come, Fanny, let me, in terms of mildness but persuasion, address myself to you," she went on to say, not paying any serious attention to the repeated attempts on the part of Ela to interrupt her; for she felt confident that the method the latter adopted to endeavour to elicit the particulars from her daughter, was more calculated to effect harm than good;—"pay particular attention to what I shall say to you, and I will immediately shew you the manner in which you and I, and others are situated, and of the absolute necessity there is for you to act in the manner you are advised; I am confident that you will only need to be told that, to be induced to try every effort in your power to perform what you have been asked to do."

"Oh, yes, I will listen to you, young lady," answered Fanny, eagerly, "I will pay attention to your words, for you speak so kind, so gentle. But I assure you, even now, my brain seems so confused that I scarcely know what I say or do. Alas! how should I, after what I have seen, what I have endured?—All—all is dark and mysterious to me—I cannot imagine where I am—or how I was brought here;—indeed I cannot imagine how it is that I am still alive when I thought the shocking draught they compelled me to take was to seal my fate; and there did I lay, stretched upon the bank and cold grass, in the gloomy cave, with the frightful and hated Morna, and another wretch, a man, to keep watch over me;—it seems as though it were not possible for it to be reality —I mean this sudden, this singular change;— from the most horrible wretchedness, I am awakened to see around me kind and sympa- thising looks, and to hear words of gentleness uttered, by those whom I had thought would ever despise the unfortunate Gipsy girl. Oh, how I should make you shudder, were I to attempt to describe to you the sufferings I endured, and the many terrific visions of demon looks, and murderers' knives reeking with blood, that haunted my imagination;— and it was Zelta that compelled me to take the dreadful vow!—oh, never shall I forget her dreadful visage as she forced me on to my knees, and insisted upon me repeating the terrible oath.—But what am I saying?—I did not mean to be so garrulous, but to listen to what you had to say, miss."

As Fanny thus spoke, she smiled faintly upon Maria, and prepared herself to listen to what she had to say.

Maria did not keep her long in suspense, but detailed, in as few words as possible, what had taken place since the dreadful night on which the cruel crime had been committed, and from the moment she had quitted her (Fanny) and Esther in the shrubbery, until Mark and his son were acquitted on the charge, when it was found that she was still alive. It would be impossible to describe as we ought to do, the deep impression which Maria's descrip- tion of the discovery of the corpse, and the firm belief of Ela that it was the body of her child, and the dreadful, the bitter anguish she had suffered subsequently. Fanny's heaving bosom and trembling limbs fully evinced the powerful emotion she was enduring, and the deep horror which the recital had excited. She tried to speak, but utterance was for awhile denied her, but with enthusiastic fondness she pressed her mother to her bosom and gazed intensely in her face, as if she dreaded all was a delusion, and that she was separated from her for ever. At length the power of speech was restored to her, and then she was about to to make some eager inquiry of Maria, but the latter placed her fingers significantly on her lips, and prevented her, and again she resumed the narrative, and at length arrived at the con- clusion without any interruption.

Notwithstanding, Ela could not help imagin- ing that Maria might have laid more emphasis on many of the particular passages, she did not seek by any remark to interfere with the deep interest which her narrative had evidently ex- cited in the bosom of her daughter, and the cir- cumstances of which so clearly explained to her the position she stood in, and what it was her paramount duty to perform.

"Time will not permit me for the present to explain to you by what singular circumstances that ill-fated girl, whose dearest friend and com- panion you was, instead of being Esther, the name you had always known her by, was no other than Christabelle Wallingford, and therefore connected by the same ties of consanguinity as you, to my cousin, to one whose father is yours also."

"My father!" exclaimed Fanny, emphati- cally, and with clasped hands, raising her eyes towards Heaven.

"But I know your affection for poor Esther, as a sister even, was ardent and sincere," ob- served Maria, "and therefore you cannot, you will not refuse to be the means of bringing retribution upon the heads of her barbarous assassins."

"I will be guided by you and my dear mother in everything," replied Fanny; "but yet do I shrink with terror from so doing, for I fear my conscience will only upbraid me for it, and not only that, but that I shall by it sacrifice my own life, and that of my mother, to the vengeance of the tribe."

"Oh, my love," said Ela, straining her daughter to her bosom, "do not let any appre- hension for me prevent you from doing your duty;—do not fear either for me or yourself, dear Fanny; for I have now the means to elude their vigilance, and to transport us far beyond the reach of their power, and in a short time after the trial is at an end, we shall both be where their penetrating eyes even cannot find us. In a foreign clime, far away from these wretches, we may partake of every enjoyment and comfort money can procure. I see you are asto- nished by my words, but at present your curiosity cannot be gratified; but of this, rest assured, that your poor unfortunate mother, but lately the wandering, the despised outcast, is now possessed of wealth almost unlimited, and need no longer fear the scorn of the despicable world, whose adulation, whose respect, whose homage, riches can at all times command, no matter how worth- less the object; yes, the world, I say, will no longer be able to trace in the wealthy heiress of Signer Angelo Beranzio, any signs of the wretched Gipsy, Ela, the Outcast."

Fanny was evidently in doubt as to the state of her mother's mind, and imagined that it was only the effects of a disordered brain; she first fixed her eyes upon Ela's glowing countenance, and then removed her gaze to Maria, the expression of whose eyes, however, and the smile of confirmation she bestowed upon her, quickly convinced her that her suspicions were wrong, and that the assertions her mother had uttered were not merely the ebullitions of frenzy.

An interval of silence now prevailed;—and each seemed to be too deeply engaged by the thoughts that inhabited their minds, to be disposed to break it. Fanny, it seemed certain, was ruminating upon some agonising subject, and Ela also appeared to be entirely absorbed by thoughts of a painful and conflicting description. All in a moment, however, her eyes sparkled with more than usual animation, and her cheek became pale, and her lips seemed to quiver, as a thought appeared to strike her suddenly.

"Good God!" she exclaimed, with the utmost terror depicted in her features and demeanour, "Can it be possible that I did not remember it? Alas! my memory seems to be a complete wreck.—Oh, mother, may I venture to inform you—dare my tongue give utterance to the horrible story they told me, to induce me to take their wicked oath?—Indeed they could not prevail upon me directly; no, I made a long resistance, and even suffered every insult—mocked their dreadful threats:—but at last, when they found that they had completely failed in all these endeavours, they tried another scheme, in which they too well succeeded. They swore that if I continued obstinate, and refused to comply with their wishes, your life should be the forfeit of my obstinacy. I dared no longer refuse—I took the oath they demanded."

"And did they then threaten your mother's life?" said Ela: "come, my dear child, be not afraid to speak all you know; Miss Herbert is our friend, and who would do anything but what would promote our welfare. She is also acquainted with all the worst passages of your unfortunate mother's life, and if she even was not, I should place the utmost reliance in her secrecy."

"Oh, my mother," said Fanny, her countenance ghastly pale with the violence of her horror, "they even threatened much worse than your murder, if it were possible. They told me that many years since, when you were first admitted among them, you had been accessory to a dreadful crime of bloodshed, which had been perpetrated by that man, whom I even now remember I used to look upon and call my father; that you were secreting yourself from the hands of justice with him and his wife, whom I also recollect I was in the habit of calling my aunt Nancy; that you was endeavouring," I say, "to elude the officers of justice, who had been some time on the look-out for you, there having been a great reward for the apprehension of you all three. Oh, mother, surely it could not be true——Oh, do not convince me that it was so. And yet, your

cheek is pale—your lips quiver. But no; I will not believe the horrid tale."

"Fanny," answered Ela, impressively, and regaining in a moment her former composure, "no deed of blood is yet upon your mother's conscience; neither, amid all the sufferings and vicissitudes she has encountered, did she ever become the heartless wretch that could deliberately concoct a design of cruelty or injustice towards her fellow creatures. However, proceed, my child, and make me acquainted with all that the wretches, the monsters, have invented for the purpose of bringing you to a compliance with their brutal desires."

Fanny once more rushed into her mother's arms, and burying her face in her mother's bosom, sobbed aloud, and her tears fell fast, but they were tears of joy, to hear her mother so emphatically, and as she imagined satisfactorily, deny the terrible charge which had been brought against her by the Gipsies.

"They said," she continued, "they said that Milford paid the penalty of his crimes by an ignominious death on the gallows; that his wife would doubtless have shared the same fate, had not the excess of her grief broke her heart, a short time after the sentence was passed; and that you, yes, my dearest mother, you would have met with the same awful and untimely death, had it not been for the kindness of the Gipsies, who, at the risk of their own safety, and utter contempt of every temptation held out, concealed you. But alas! I have not yet come to the most dreadful part of what they told me; they told me that the witnesses who were the means of convicting Milford, were still alive, and that they would be prepared to swear to your identity; and the villains added, that so sure as I offered to betray them, so surely would they consign my mother to the scaffold."

An ashy paleness, like that of death, overspread the features of Ela as her daughter gave utterance to these words, and she was obliged to cling to the back of the chair to prevent herself from sinking to the earth. It was very evident from the convulsive movement of her body, that she was undergoing the most dreadful internal agony, and as Maria gazed upon her, and reflected within her own mind whether there was any probability of the Gipsies' accusations being true, she felt exceedingly shocked. But she had not much time given her for reflection.

"Oh, mother! beloved mother!" exclaimed the frantic Fanny as she beheld the terror Ela betrayed, "for Heaven's sake do not look so awful, and thus violently clasp your hands! Surely you have no occasion to fear them, for I am certain that everthing they have uttered is false, and, therefore, why should we——"

"Alas! my child," interrupted Ela, "little do you think that—but if I could only now have an interview with Doctor Hartley or Walter, so that I might advise with them what it would be best to do in this emergency; my own mind is so distracted, that I cannot collect my ideas, and at such a time as this, when I know not what a danger may be hanging over my head, I must stand in need of advice and consolation."

"But are there no means of sending for either of the gentlemen?" said Fanny anxiously, "surely neither of them would refuse to come?"

"Oh, no, I am confident that both of them are too good to refuse," said Maria, warmly; "and as for Walter, there is nothing he would consider a trouble, in which he could render himself a service to you."

"A moment's delay may be fraught with danger," said Ela, as her eyes glanced fearfully and hastily round the apartment, but at the same time doing all in her power to regain her former composure; "it would not be safe for me to venture to either of them, and then, if we entrust such a message to a servant, they may make some blunder in delivering it, and we may be just as far back as ever."

"Well then," said Maria readily, "to settle the matter, I will myself go to Walter, and then there is sure not to be any mistake. Of course I shall require the attendance of one of the servants."

With these words, Maria rang the bell, which was quickly answered by the domestic. Upon putting the question to the young woman, however, they found themselves placed in a dilemma, which they had none of them ever contemplated, for it so happened that the name of the street in which Mr. Wallingford was at present residing, had never been heard by either of them, and the girl seemed as stupid as a person could be when the name of Mrs. Patterson was mentioned to her; and, with an ignorant grin, she remarked that " Mrs. Patterson was quite a common name in that place—there was Mrs. Patterson, the miller's wife; then there was widow Patterson, who had only one eye, and Dame Patterson of——"

"Nonsense!" interrupted Maria, impatiently, "you have not mentioned any of the persons I wish to see. I must request of you to endeavour to recall to your memory. You cannot, of course, forget that Doctor Hartley was accompanied home by a female servant last night; did you know her?"

"I can't say," replied the girl with an ignorant simper, "I might, though, if I had only have happened to have seen her."

"I see I shall never be able to make you understand," said Maria; "for goodness sake request your mistress to do me the favour to step here for a minute."

"Missis be'ant at whoame, miss," was the reply of the simple rustic.

"Well, then, request your master." The girl now laughed outright.

"Measter! I ha' gotten no measter, as I know on," said she; " but they do zay——"

"There, there, that is enough," said Maria, hastily, and pitying the poor girl for her apparent ignorance and simplicity. They were in the midst of a consultation upon what was best to be done, when the girl once more made her appearance, and, to the agreeable astonishment of them all, announced the name of Mr. Walter Wallingford, who had come to them on a visit.

Ceremony, of course, was completely out of the question at a moment like this, but when he spoke in words of the utmost tenderness to Fanny, she could not help regarding him with blushing timidity. He quickly, however, removed his glances to Ela, and when he beheld the deep sorrow and terror imprinted on her features, his curiosity became excited to an uncommon degree.

"Why do you look so pale, and so alarmed?" he enquired eagerly; "pray inform me whether anything else has occurred?"

"Alas! yes," replied Ela, "much more than you can form any conception of; my life is at this very time in jeopardy, and perhaps the delay of a few hours only, may snap the thread upon which it hangs. Will you venture to attend me to Doctor Hartley's?"

"I am at your service as soon as you like," said Walter, readily.

"I have one more favour to ask of you, Maria," said Ela, turning to the former; "perhaps, if I were to put on your cloak, bonnet, and veil, I might not be so easily recognized."

"By all means," answered Maria, preparing to get them, "the idea is an excellent one."

"But surely, my dearest mother," exclaimed Fanny, clinging round her parent, and her countenance expressive of the utmost alarm; "surely you will not, you cannot leave me in this manner.—And oh, if the wretches should be watching for you, and recognize you——"

"Do not, I entreat, give way to this violent alarm, my dear Fanny," said Ela; "pray endeavour to compose your feelings, and do not meet danger half way. You will be quite secure from all danger, with Miss Herbert, until I come back;—nay, my child, do not attempt to oppose me, for you know not how dreadful may be the consequences to us both, should I procrastinate my visit to Doctor Hartley. Hear me, Fanny—I call upon you to prepare yourself to give such evidence as may lead to the conviction of the murderers of poor Esther to-morrow, instead of giving way to this dangerous and useless alarm. Should I not return all night, be not alarmed, for circumstances may render my absence unavoidable. Again I tell you—I enjoin you, to act as becomes you on the trial to-morrow; let no foolish ideas, no groundless apprehensions, prevent you from telling all that you know of this dreadful affair. Mark me, and believe me, I am serious when I say so, that if you deceive me, and do not speak the truth, from that moment I discard you—from that moment you are no longer the daughter of Ela Beranzio; she will disown you for ever."

As Ela thus seriously gave utterance to her determinations, she forcibly released herself from the ardent embrace of her daughter, and hastened from the room, accompanied by Walter Wallingford. As for poor Fanny, the violent language which her mother had addressed to her caused her to repress, as well as she was able, the deep anguish which laboured in her bosom, but the pain caused by the effort overcame her when Ela quitted the room, and she sunk on the floor in a state of insensibility, from which Maria had some difficulty to restore her.

"Come, come, my dear Fanny," said Maria, in her kindest tones, "you must not, indeed you must not give way to this weakness. If you persist in so doing, how can you possibly do what your mother has so strictly enjoined to-morrow? And surely it is your duty to do all that lays in your power to comply with her wishes. To-morrow morning, at an early hour, we shall again be compelled to make our appearance in the court, and if you thus indulge in grief, how can it be expected that you will have firmness enough to support, perhaps, a tedious and protracted trial? How will you ever be able to find strength sufficient to re-count those terrible events of which you was the witness, and that too, in the presence of so many persons? Recollect, that you will be subjected to the buffetings, and questions, and cross-questions of counsel; and the revengeful looks of our enemies, and that, therefore, you will require all the fortitude, caution, and self-possession you can gather, to support you through the trial, and if you continue thus to give way to the violence of your fears and anguish, it cannot be expected that you will be able to acquit yourself as it is necessary you should do on this very important occasion. If, then, you should not succeed, and that, owing to you, the murderers should escape that punish-ment which is due to their crime, oh, Fanny, recollect, how frightful then will be your situa-tion; remember the warning your mother gave you, remember that if you fail, she has ex-pressed her determination to renounce you for ever."

"Oh, yes, it shall be so," sobbed forth Fanny, "your gentle words, dear lady, have recalled me to reason; pr'ythee, give me your hand, and help me to rise; I will be obedient to your wishes and to those of my mother. She shall not be disappointed in her hopes;—I

will divulge all the dreadful secret, though in the effort I should go mad."

Maria was delighted to hear the change her persuasions had worked in her, and with most soothing words, and all the affectionate care of a fond sister, she raised her from the floor, and succeeded in reviving her, so that Walter was not a little surprised, when, in a short time afterwards, he returned, followed by Doctor Hartley.

Fanny was evidently alarmed when she perceived that her mother was not with them, but the good doctor, reading her thoughts, ad-vanced towards her, and kindly taking her hand, said—

"Be not under any apprehensions, my dear girl, that your mother has not returned—she is where no harm can come to her; which you cannot doubt, I am sure, when you are told so by your best friends. She will not, however, be home to-night, and probably it may be late before you will see her to-morrow; prudence and peculiar circumstances have rendered the adoption of this plan indispensable. But calm your feelings, I pray, and let us hope, that ere long you may meet again in happiness, a hap-piness which nothing may have the power to interrupt."

"The Almighty grant that it may be so," said the beauteous girl, as she raised her clasped hands towards Heaven, and her countenance beamed forth an expression which deeply affected all who beheld it.

"And now, my dear girls, as it is arranged that Miss Herbert shall remain here to-night," added the doctor, "let me entreat you to seek that repose you stand so much in need of for to-morrow. Good night—God bless you, my children. Come, Walter, it is late, and you had better, therefore, see about departing."

Walter seemed very reluctant to go, but the doctor becoming more urgent, he bade Maria and Fanny an affectionate adieu, and departed. Soon afterwards the lovely females retired to the chamber allotted for their repose.

CHAPTER XLVI.

—— "Save me! spare me!
I dare not meet the fate my crime deserves!"

THE following morning Maria and Fanny arose at an early hour, and on descending to the breakfast room, they found Doctor Hartley already there, and shortly afterwards Walter Wallingford made his appearance. Fanny looked pale, but her manners were more com-posed, and to the questions which Doctor Hart-ley put to her, she replied in a tone which con-vinced him that she had in a great measure conquered the fears that had before inhabited her bosom.

The repast was a hasty one, for they were all too fully occupied with the business they were going upon to eat; as soon as it was over, the doctor arose, and addressing himself to Fanny and Maria, observed—

"We had better now depart immediately, for the business of the court commences early, and the carriage is now awaiting to convey us to it; the streets are so thronged with people, that it would have been almost impossible to——"

These observations of Doctor Hartley caused Fanny for a moment to turn more pale than she had been before, and she trembled so violently, that she was obliged to lean upon the arm of Maria to support herself. She, however, tried all in her power to vanquish her terrors, and immediately set about preparing herself for her departure, and put on the Gipsy hat and short cloak, in which she looked so lovely and interesting, the time having been too short for any alteration being made in her dress, and to get apparel more suitable to the change which had taken place in her condition.

Maria also arrayed herself with equal expedition, putting on Ela's black bonnet and silk cloak, which she had left behind her, having, as we have before stated, borrowed those belonging to the former, and Walter could not help smiling at the singular change effected in her appearance by the matronly fashion of the different articles of apparel she had assumed.

They were vexed and surprised when, on reaching the street, they found that the carriage was surrounded by several people, who seemed to watch their appearance with the utmost curiosity; and Maria's courage began to fail, as she marked the rude and flashing eyes that were fixed upon her, and the eager manner in which many of the persons pressed forward as her and Doctor Hartley approached the vehicle, and who seemed resolved to discover who she really was.

They had, however, only a few steps to proceed to the carriage, into which Maria was soon handed, and then Fanny followed, leaning on the arm of Walter, and trembling with fear and emotion; she was handed in, but although it was done with great haste, it seemed it was not before she had been recognized by those who were anxious to discover her; and just at the moment that she had placed her foot upon the first step, a tall, savage-looking man, evidently a Gipsy, darted past them, and in a threatening tone he uttered in her ear —

"Girl, beware! break not the oath you have taken, or your mother swings on the gallows!"

"Wretch!" cried Walter, turning hastily towards the spot from whence the voice proceeded; but the ruffian had escaped in the crowd, and Walter and the doctor prudently hastened into the vehicle, and endeavoured to compose Fanny, after so severe a shock to her feelings.

The crowd was so great, that, notwithstanding the distance of the Justice Hall was nothing scarcely, they found the greatest difficulty to proceed, and as they did so, their ears were frequently assailed by groans and hisses, which they could perceive proceeded from the Gipsies, who followed and were in advance of the carriage.

At length they did reach the hall, and entering it, they discovered that it was thronged more densely even, if possible, than it had been the day before. The officers, who saw them enter the court, instantly cleared a passage for them, and the trembling girls were led to the place allotted to them until such time as they should be called upon to give evidence. Walter placed Fanny between himself and Maria, and each of them taking one of her cold hands, in whispers endeavoured to convince her that she had nothing whatever to apprehend; but she had not courage sufficient to look around her, and with her eyes cast down, she remained, and scarcely seemed to breathe, so anxious was she to avoid meeting the scrutiny of the persons in the court.

It would not only be tedious, but a waste of time, to detail minutely all the proceedings on the second indictment of Mark Darwin and his son, as the facts, many of them, adduced were exactly the same as on the previous trial, so far as regarded the dying cries of the murdered girl, the discovery of the corpse, &c. Of course the name of the person they were charged with murdering was altered in the indictment from Fanny Beranzio to Christabelle Wallingford, commonly called Esther Darwin (which name the tribe, to suit their own purposes, had thought proper to give her).

The change in the looks and behaviour of the two prisoners, from what they had been the day before, was visible to every one. The elder Mark in vain endeavoured to conceal his real feelings under a show of carelessness and courage, sometimes, too, forcing a laugh; and his son fruitlessly tried to appear totally indifferent to the proceedings; nothing could hide from the observation of every person present the intense agony, the almost insupportable anxiety they were both suffering, and the suspense and eagerness with which they marked the statements of the different witnesses. Their faces, too, were as livid as if they had been corpses, and their eyes were extremely wild, and wandered round the court with a restlessness which showed the bitter torment which harrowed up their hearts.

When Maria and Walter were giving their evidence, Fanny listened with the most breathless attention, and when they came to the particulars that they knew concerning the night of the murder, her heart was smote with horror, and it required all the perseverance of Doctor Hartley to prevent her from suffering her emotion to overpower her; no sooner, however, did she hear the officer of the court, in his usual sonorous tones, call on the name of Mr. Wallingford, than all her former feelings seemed to vanish in a moment, and her eyes sparkled with animation, as she arose from her seat, and with flushed cheeks, and an expression of the greatest affection, looked upon that parent whose fond embrace she had never known.

Wallingford, too, beheld her conduct;—he

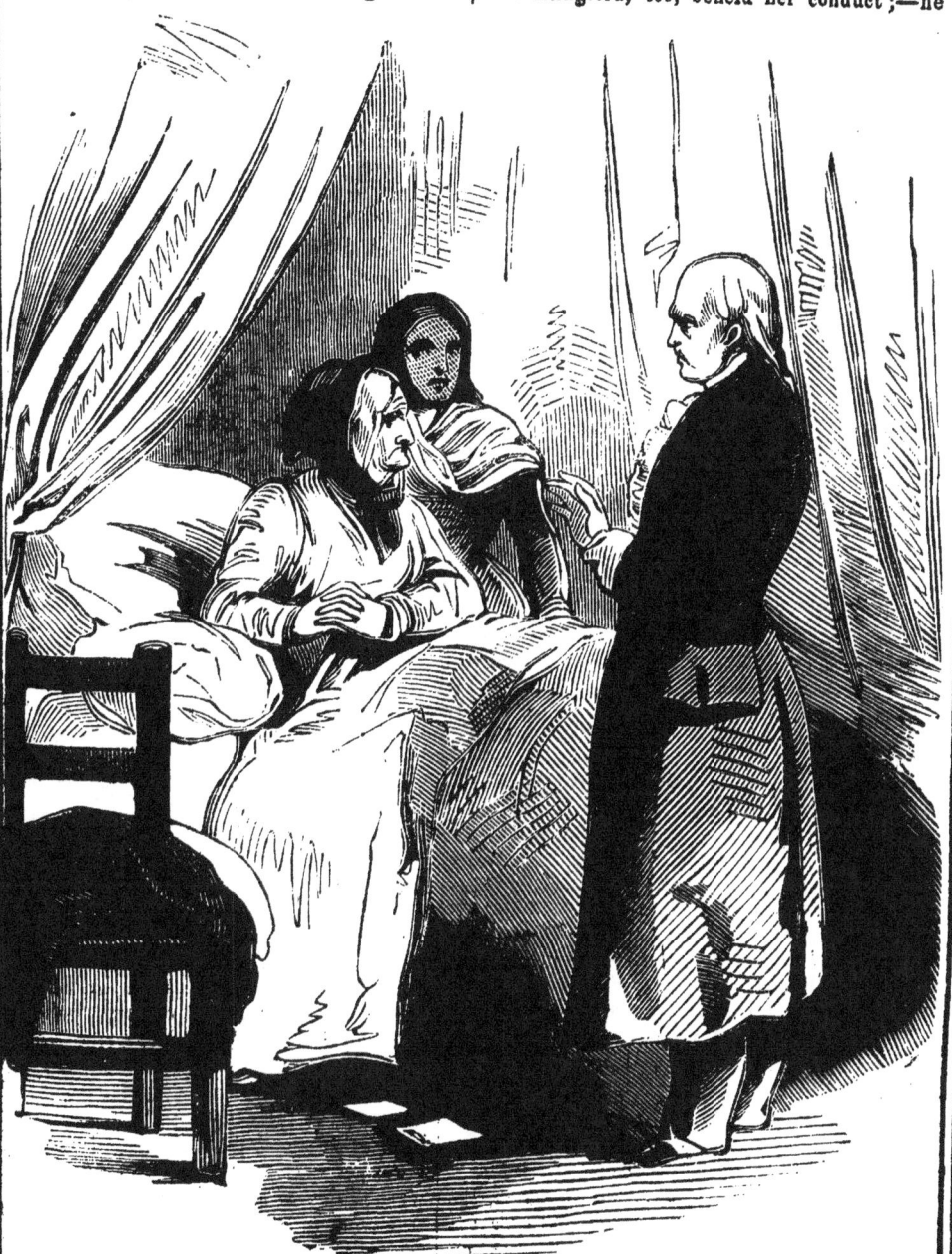

DOCTOR HARTLEY SOOTHING THE LAST MOMENTS OF MRS. WALLINGFORD.

was placed in a situation which made it impossible for her to escape his observation, and for an instant his attention was drawn to the lovely features and intelligent glances of that beauteous girl of whose being he was the author. But the sensation was only brief—his still handsome countenance was again enveloped in that aspect of pride and dignity which he had accustomed himself to, and in a calm and collected manner, he gave exactly the same evidence as he had done the day before, not prevaricating in the slightest degree.

This over, "Fanny Beranzio" resounded through the court. She came forward;—not any of her former trepidation was now apparent;—she had gained a complete triumph over her fears, and her thoughts were entirely fixed upon the purpose for which she had gone there !—the importance attached to the evidence she had to give, and the warning her mother had given her on parting with her; and she stood with a firmness and self-possession that completely astonished her companions. Notwithstanding, however, that she had thus far succeeded in conquering her emotions, she could not find sufficient courage to encounter the glance of the prisoners in the dock, who, the moment she made her appearance in the witness box, fixed their blood-shot eyes upon her, and their bodies were convulsed with the most powerful emotions.

Every precaution had been taken by Mr. Wallingford, and other influential persons, to have Fanny so completely guarded by officers that there was not the slightest danger of her being exposed to any insult or interruption in giving her evidence, from the Gipsies, of whom the greater portion of the vast congregation in the court was composed, but, notwithstanding all this, which precluded the possibility of their getting near her, all the most strenuous efforts of the officers could not prevent them from giving vent to the expression of their feelings, which was exhibited in the most violent and strong demonstrations of rage and disappointment, especially when they beheld the calm, cool, and collected manner in which she stood, prepared to give her evidence when called upon. Neither was the poor girl deaf to the hisses, groans, and curses, which for awhile set order at defiance—but she still remained firm in her purpose, and only mentally offered up a prayer to Omnipotence for its almighty protection in this important hour.

At last, after considerable difficulty, the officers of the court did succeed in gaining silence, and the usual oath was administered to Fanny, after which the question was put to her as to what she knew of the deceased, Christabelle Wallingford, alias Esther Darwin?

"Oh, we were sisters in affection," answered Fanny, with a sweetness and simplicity that went home to the hearts of every person present, with the exception of the Gipsies. "Many, many years had the same tent sheltered us, the same rude couch formed a resting-place for our weary limbs. Nothing could ever part us, until the dreadful deed which separated us for ever."

Tears here prevented her from proceeding for a second or two, but after a pause, she wiped the glistening drops from her pallid cheeks, and then went on as follows:—

"On the evening that the dreadful crime was committed, Christabelle, or Esther, as we always called her, proposed that we should, as my mother was absent from the camp, seize upon the opportunity to pay a visit to the grounds belonging to Mr. Wallingford. It was merely a whim on her part, but I had stronger motives, I confess, to induce me readily to acquiesce in her wishes, and for making me attached to the spot."

Here the cheeks of Fanny became flushed, and she paused.

"We at first only went into the shrubbery," she went on to say, "but at length being urged on by curiosity, we entered where some palings were broken, and then made our way towards the summer-house, which I knew to be the favourite retreat of some of the family."

Here she related, what the reader has already been made acquainted with, namely, that Esther had made a discovery that some of the Gipsies were lurking in the shrubbery; in addition to which she stated, that Esther had, prior to this, informed her of her suspicions that Mark Darwin and his sons had some secret and desperate undertaking in hand, and after discovering them endeavouring to conceal themselves in the manner she had described, it occurred to her imagination that they had in contemplation an attack upon Wallingford Hall, and some outrage to the inmates.

"After Miss Herbert left us," continued Fanny, "we remained in the summer-house, and consulted with each other what we had better do under such circumstances as those I have mentioned; when suddenly we were startled and alarmed by hearing persons speaking near the window. Previous to this, we had taken the precaution to bolt the door, and with the utmost horror and breathless consternation we listened to hear if we could distinguish what they were talking about. At length, the voice of the younger Mark Darwin met our ears, and we heard him make use of these words—

" 'What's the use of your endeavouring to persuade me that I was mistaken, I am positive they are somewhere about the grounds, for I watched them enter, and I know also that he is there; I heard his faithful dog bark, and therefore I was confident that his master was no distance off. I consequently secreted myself in the hedge on the opposite side of the way, for I knew he must pass along the lane. However, I was not mistaken; it seems the dog smelt scent of something, and they suddenly stopped short, and by the light of the moon, I could plainly see the shadowy form of a man enter the door-way in the garden wall.'

"After a moment or two," continued Fanny, "I again heard the voice of the younger prisoner, and he was then vowing dreadful vengeance on us all, meaning, as I believe, myself and the deceased, and the person whom they seemed to suspect formed one of the party which I should imagine, from the manner which he spoke, they took to be Mr. Wallingford. The threats of the prisoners filled us with the greatest terror, and we embraced each other with the utmost horror. Unhappily, the fears of poor Esther overcame her, and she could not suppress a faint scream, but not so low but that it caught the ears of those we dreaded to encounter."

"'Ah! they are in the summer-house,' exclaimed the voice of the elder prisoner. 'I will swear that scream proceeded from some person concealed there.'

"In a moment we heard them trying the door, which we had fastened inside, and against which we piled all the furniture we could possibly find, thinking that if we could only prevent their entrance until we had alarmed the inmates of the house, we should be safe. But alas! we were mistaken. What could two weak girls do, opposed to the united strength of three powerful men?—Our efforts were like the lamb opposed to the lion, or like that of a child trying to snatch the prey from the jaws of the tiger. The door was burst off the hinges, and the assassins came upon us with terrible fury. I am positive that it was me they intended to make a victim of, but in the darkness they made a mistake, and seized upon the unfortunate Christabelle; both Mark and his father held her in their grasp, and with horrible curses and imprecations vowed they would instantly murder her if she hesitated to inform them where——" Here Fanny paused, blushed deeply, and cast her eyes towards the ground, then added in a voice more faint than before —"where the man was with whom she had made the appointment. I cannot recollect what reply she made, neither am I certain that she answered them at all;—another instant, however, and her terrific shrieks rent the air, and filled me with horror. Rupert had forced me from the summer-house, and the light of the moon showed him that they had made a mistake.

"In the name of Astaroth, stay—stay 'your hands," he cried, "you have butchered Esther."

"With these words he dashed me from him, and falling on my head, my senses left me, and I know nothing of what happened afterwards. When I was again awakened to consciousness, I was many miles away from the place."

With these words, Fanny ceased speaking, and made a humble curtsey to the judge and the other official members of the court.

"But what was your reason for concealing these circumstances from the officers of justice so long?" was the next interrogatory put to her.

"They kept me strictly confined, and I was narrowly watched by Rupert Darwin, and other Gipsies," replied Fanny.

"Do you observe any of the individuals, who held you a prisoner against your will, present?" demanded the court. "Look narrowly at the persons present, and see if you recognize any of them."

Fanny shuddered as she gazed fearfully around, and met the threatening looks of the Gipsies who were present, and, therefore, not taking much trouble to do as she had been told, she almost immediately turned her eyes towards the judge again, and observed, "That she could not perceive any persons there whom she could recognize as the parties."

Every witness had now been examined but one, and that was Ela Beranzio, whose name was presently called.

There was a loud murmuring, and a strange movement among the Gipsies, when they heard it, and the prisoners underwent a most extraordinary change. Fanny left the witness-box and resumed her seat by the side of Maria, while the crier repeated the name of her mother twice more, in louder tones than before.

The remarkable change in the countenances of the prisoners struck Walter with astonishment, and he could not help gazing upon them. The elder Mark appeared to feel a sentiment of hope, mingled with a feeling of gratification, and his eyes flashed with more animation than heretofore; while expectation and exultation were plainly distinguishable in the countenance of his son. But soon was disappointment and depression once more distinguishable upon their features. Several times was the name of Beranzio called, but all to no purpose, for no person answered, and at length it was concluded that she had not attended the court, the counsel for the prosecution remarking that her absence was of no material consequence, inasmuch as her evidence could not have strengthened the testimony which the court was already in possession of, and as his case was closed, he called upon the prisoners for their defence. But they seemed totally unconscious of what was being said, or what was passing around them, and the question was put three times before either of them appeared to understand it; fury and hatred filled their breasts when they discovered that Ela was not present. Their design was now manifest; and it could not be doubted by any person who was acquainted with the circumstances, that it had been their intention, as soon as Ela had given her evidence, that several of her old associates should start forward, and charge her with being the accomplice of Milford and his wife in the murder of the farmer, which they imagined was not yet forgotten by many persons; and Fanny immediately saw that the persons who had been chosen to make this accusation were some of her mother's most inveterate enemies; for she knew them by the eagerness with which they pushed towards the witness-box, to be ready at the moment Ela should make her appearance. The officers would have persisted in keeping them back, had they not assured them that they had some information of importance to give the court, which would possibly prove the innocence of the prisoners. When, however, Ela did not appear, their rage and disappointment plainly showed that all their deep laid stratagems were thwarted, and despair was visible upon their swarthy countenances. They had also imagined that the drugs which they had administered to Fanny would have had a more powerful effect, and that before she could have recovered sufficiently to disclose to Ela the scheme they had concocted to destroy her, they would have been tried and acquitted, and their victim's fate securely sealed; besides they also fancied (so fondly, so fervently attached to her daughter did they know Ela to be), that even if she had recovered, the latter would never suffer her to quit her presence so shortly after she had been restored to her in such a miraculous and unexpected manner.

The consternation and dismay of the prisoner and their associates every moment became stronger, as the certainty of their fate rushed upon their brain, and curses and deep mutterings might be heard on all sides.

"By Astaroth, the wretch has outwitted us, and escaped the doom we had marked out for her;" murmured the elder prisoner to his son, while he gnashed his teeth, and contracted his shaggy eyebrows; "but do not, boy, let them imagine that we tremble at the fate in store for us. No, there are those left behind who will avenge our death, and rest not until they have inflicted a terrible punishment upon the hell-cat through whom we have been brought to this. Did I not always warn you that Ela and her hated offspring would bring us to destruction?"

"And why be so ready to give that advice which you did not follow you rself?" said the son, fiercely;—"did you notdeceive me, and tell me such tales about her, that I was nearly frantic; and would I not fain have stayed the spilling——"

"Silence, Mark, silence," interrupted his father, "I will not act unjustly by you;—I am reckless what they do with me, but you are young and——"

"Prisoners at the bar, have you anything to say in your defenem.?" was the question once more put to hteec

"Nothing," replied the younger prisoner boldly, "no further than to protest that I am not guilty of the crime with which I am charged. I would sooner have forfeited my own life than have injured either of the girls, of which she swill aware who has this day borne false witness against me."

As the guilty wretch gave utterance to these assertions, Fanny arose hastily from her seat, and fixed her eyes steadfastly and piercingly upon his countenance; terms of reproach were rising

to her lips, which Walter perceiving, pull her forcibly back, and by a significant gestu enjoined her to silence. She immediately sa the folly of which she was nigh being guilt and once more listened with breathless attenti to the words of the unhappy culprits at t bar.

"I repeat, in the words of my son, n lord," said the elder prisoner, "that I a not guilty, and I maintain that this is a bla and base conspiracy against us, for the purpo of taking away our lives; but what is the u of poor despised wanderers like us, attemptir to confute the statements of these who hav wealth and power?"

As the villain said this, he darted a look malice and revenge towards Mr. Wallingfor who, however, met his gaze with the utmo indifference and contempt, and he then pr ceeded in the following words—"You ma take our lives—doubtless they will be sacr ficed, upon the false-swearing of those wh have been brought as witnesses against us, bi if we are hanged, we shall be murdered, whil those who were actually the perpetrators of th crime, will go unscathed and free."

A murmur of indignation ran through th court when the prisoner had thus expresse himself, and even the Gipsies themselves, wh were assembled, were abashed by the marke demonstrations of displeasure that were s unequivocally evinced; the elder Mark, how ever, was perfectly callous to everything of th sort, and he went on to say—

"My lord, I claim your attention for a fev minutes. I am placed in an awful situation and therefore I think there ought to be som licence given to my tongue."

"The court is very ready to hear anything you may have to say in your defence; but the; cannot listen to subjects irrelevant to the mat ter," answered the judge.

"What I want to say, my lord," resumed Mark, "is, that had Ela Beranzio come for ward to-day, there is little doubt but that the actual murderer of the daughter of Mr. Wal lingford would not long have remained con cealed; doubtless, he imagined, that he was for ever released from that girl who——"

"Prisoner," interrupted the judge, hastily, "what you are now giving utterance to, not only has nothing whatever to do with the case, but is calculated to prejudice the minds of the jury, by betraying the malice you entertain in your heart against an individual, upon whom suspicion cannot possibly descend."

"Then I have nothing more to say, my lord," said the Gipsy, in a firm tone, "except that if Ela Beranzio had answered to her name to-day, I could have proved that she is a murderess. Nay, I speak the truth, and there are plenty of persons present who could prove her to have been an accessory to the assassination of Mr. Wilmot, the farmer, some years ago, for which a man of the name of Milford—at least, by such name only I knew him—was tried and executed."

"Ah!" said the judge, evidently surprised, "this is strange ;—but it must be thoroughly investigated," he added, speaking to some of the magistrates who sat near him. "However, prisoner, I wish to impress upon your mind, that even if it were in your power to prove this witness guilty of the crime alleged, still it cannot serve you in the least, as it would not have the effect of throwing discredit upon the powerful evidence which has been adduced against you. However, if you have anything more to add to what you have already said, in giving it my most earnest attention, I shall feel great pleasure."

For a moment Mark paused, and his lips quivered ;—it was plainly visible in his blanched cheek, and the restless wanderings of his blood-shot eyes, that the firmness he had before seemed to possess, was fast evaporating ; and he seemed to despair entirely of being able to save himself or his son from an ignominious death.

"I have done, my lord," at length the elder prisoner observed, as he made an effort to conceal his face (which exhibited great emotion) from the observation of the persons present.

But how shall we describe the situation of Fanny, after the horrible accusation which the Gipsy had brought against her mother ? Her features, which had before been so remarkable for their gentleness, underwent an immediate and extraordinary change, and Walter and Maria gazed with astonishment upon the demeanour she assumed, and which rendered her resemblance to Ela most striking. While Mark had been speaking, her large eyes seemed to flash fire, as she leant forward, and endeavoured to catch the prisoner's eye ; and her exultation, as despair more rapidly closed around the poor wretch, was plainly discernible in the half smile of satisfaction which took possession of her countenance.

But Maria's emotions were of a very different description during this awful moment of suspense and doubt. The jury had now, after having heard the judge's summing up, retired to consider their verdict. This did not take them many minutes, but it was very clear to be seen, that in that short interval the prisoners suffered the most violent mental agony, and in a manner of speaking, Maria might be said to endure a portion of their torment. Her heart throbbed violently, and her whole frame trembled, as though her very existence depended upon the decision of the jury : and had it been in her power, how readily would she have made any sacrifice to have rescued them from the dreadful fate their heinous crime had

merited. Many were the mental prayers that she uttered, that mercy might be extended towards them, but it was all to no avail ;—the jury returned into the box; silence was proclaimed ; all eyes were turned upon them in breathless anxiety; the prisoners fixed upon them one searching glance, in which they seemed to read their fate. All was now as still as death—the slightest breath, the lowest aspiration might have been plainly heard ;—the question was put to them in the usual manner, and the next instant the awful words—

"Guilty, my lord," decided the unhappy wretches' fate.

"Heaven be thanked !" ejaculated Fanny fervently, and in a tone which might have been heard by many of the persons in the body of the court ; but Maria covered her face with her handkerchief, fearful to behold the features of the culprits in that awful moment.

"Dear Walter," she exclaimed, earnestly, "do not let us remain here longer ;—let us return home, I pray."

But Walter appeared to take no notice of her, and seemed indeed not to understand what she was urging, and having waited for a second or two, expecting an answer from him, she said in a tone of reproof—

"From you, Walter, I did not expect this ; surely to persist in remaining here any longer evinces a morbid taste, and——"

"Pardon me, dear Maria," said Walter, "but you really do me an injustice by entertaining for a moment such a supposition ; if you will look around you, and notice the dense manner in which the hall is crowded, you will perceive that any attempt to leave at present would be futile, and might be attended with danger. We shall be compelled to remain here, I am afraid, until it is all at an end."

This was a most painful alternative to Maria, and how she shuddered with horror, and tried to stifle the sense of hearing, while the judge proceeded to pass upon Mark and his son the awful sentence of the law. She could not help feeling something like repugnance towards Walter and Fanny, for the gratification the sentence on the unhappy prisoners seemed to afford them.

The solemn business was at last concluded, and the judge arose from his seat, which was the signal for a simultaneous movement throughout the court, but the next moment the deep attention of everybody was arrested, when they heard the tones of the elder Mark, who implored earnestly that the judge would suffer him to address a few more words to him.

"My lord," said he, "since it has come to this, I see that no good can be effected by my any longer concealing the facts. I own, then, that I am guilty of murdering the girl ; but I solemnly protest that it was not premeditated and that it was done in a moment when my reason was overpowered by rage; as for this unfortunate boy, my son, he is not at all guilty. He was not aware, indeed, that I had any weapon in my hand at the time; and so far from assisting in the perpetration of the crime, he tried to rescue her, and in so doing he himself received a wound. He imagined that it was Fanny Beranzio, and he would sooner have suffered a thousand deaths himself, than have done her any harm. Therefore, I trust your lordship will view his case with a merciful eye. You may do as you like with me—I care little about it—and if I must swing, I must: we must all go some time or the other, and I don't know whether we might not as well go that way as any other; but I have been injured, wronged——"

The judge motioned to the officers to remove them, and interrupted his speech; and this mandate being obeyed, the business was over, and the people began to depart. Mr. Wallingford quitted the Hall, in the company of the judge, by a private door; but it was a considerable time before Walter and his companions saw any chance of their being able to effect an egress, for the Gipsies loitered behind, and their feelings were so exasperated against them, particularly Fanny, that they were apprehensive they would be bold enough to attempt to commit some outrage upon them; indeed, they made no secret of their sentiments, for many of them who lurked behind were heard to utter threats of vengeance against the whole party who had been the means of bringing to conviction Mark Darwin and his son. But, of course, the principal portion of their wrath was bestowed upon Ela and her daughter; and Walter, at the same time that he was pleased in the idea that Ela was far from the threatened danger by this time, was puzzled to conceive in what manner he should be able to save Fanny from the fate with which they had threatened her.

As for Fanny herself, she did not appear to give a thought for a moment to this circumstance, and was probably indifferent at that time to the danger in which she was involved. To know that her mother was secure from the insatiable revenge of her terrible foes afforded her such infinite delight, that it entirely excluded every other thought from her bosom, or if indeed she did indulge for a moment in any other idea, it was but to utter her gratification at the result of the trial, and to exult in the fate which had at last fallen upon Mark Darwin and his son.

In a short time after this, however, the persons who had been instructed by Walter to look out, informed him that the coast was nearly clear of the Gipsy tribe, who seemed to have been suddenly summoned away; so they arose to leave the court. They had, however, scarcely descended from the gallery in which they had

been seated, when, as if it had been planned, a stream of people poured in at two or three different avenues, and pressed so closely upon them, that they found the greatest difficulty imaginable to proceed. Maria looked around her with consternation, and although this only occupied a second, after having thus satisfied her curiosity, her terror and confusion may easily be imagined when she found that her friends had been separated from her, and had been driven on, and she had no idea by which door they had gone forth. She was, however, compelled to move with the throng, and at length found herself outside the hall, but she could not see anything of the carriage, and she therefore concluded it was round at some other side of the building, for she could not for a moment suppose that her friends would go on without her. She went round to the entrance where she expected to find the carriage, but it was not there, and she was very much alarmed when she beheld a number of the Gipsy tribe, who were standing in different groups in the very direction which she wanted to go, apparently engaged in earnest conversation upon some important subject. She dared not venture that way, for to go in amongst them in their present excited state would only be to rush upon certain death. She therefore took the contrary direction, thinking, by a circuitous route, to be able to reach home, and avoid the Gipsies.

She ran rather than walked, but in the course of a few minutes, instead of discovering any signs of being able to to make her way home in that direction, she found herself in a woody dell, with which she was, of course, entirely unacquainted. Knowing that it would be useless for her to proceed in that manner, and thinking that most probably the Gipsies, of whom she was so much in fear, had dispersed, she turned to go back into the town, pulling her veil over her face as much as she could, to conceal her features from observation. She had no sooner done so, however, when she was alarmed by observing a man running towards her, with whose person she was certain she was not unacquainted, although she was not near enough to recognize exactly who he was. For a second, she was so bewildered that she scarcely knew how to act, but when the man called upon her by name, she knew his voice in a minute, and was not a little astonished and terrified, after the disgusting familiarity of his looks towards her on the day before, to find that it was Mr. Barnell.

"Stop! stop! Miss Herbert," he exclaimed, as Maria turned away, and sooner than encounter him, flew with precipitancy into the wood, thinking to find some outlet by which she might be enabled to avoid him. Her agitation was very great, especially when she noticed that he persisted in his pursuit of her, and continued to call upon her name, and desired her to stop. Mr. Barnell's clumsy, awkward figure did not suffer him to proceed with any great speed, and under anyo ther circumstances Maria would have found no great difficulty in outstripping him; but now her alarm was so strong, that it impeded her progress, and at length, completely exhausted, she was obliged to lean against a tree to recover herself. Mr. Barnell took advantage of this, and by dint of much exertion, he redoubled his speed, and at length came up to the spot where Maria was standing, pale and trembling. He had evidently been drinking, for his unmeaning, vulgar countenance was much flushed, and his eyes were more than usually dull and heavy.

"So, I have caught you at last, have I, Miss Herbert?" said he, as he insolently endeavoured to seize her hand; "well, I never saw such a little devil to run in all my born days. Why, any one would think that I was something very disgusting or frightful, by your scampering away from me in such a manner."

Maria looked upon the idiot with an expression of pity and contempt, and having partially recovered herself, she said, in a voice of indignation—

"By what authority came you here to insult me, or why you should take the liberty to pursue me, sir, I am at a loss to imagine; but if you really wish to be considered a gentleman, you will no longer attempt to detain me."

"You are very pretty, Miss Herbert, after all," said Mr. Barnell, attempting to smile flatteringly upon her;—"upon my word, I have seldom seen a prettier pair of eyes. Come, come, what do you look so cross at me for? —You know there is no occasion for us to be bad friends, although I have declined marrying you."

"Sir," said the indignant Maria, with a look of offended delicacy and pride, "if you have a spark of feeling for an unprotected female, I beg you will leave me, and suffer me to proceed unmolested on my way."

"Stuff, nonsense; what have you got to be afraid of, my dear?—Why, bless your soul, there is no harm at all in me. But I saw you n the Justic-Hall yesterday and to-day, and I confess that I could not help admiring how pretty you looked, and so to-day l watched you out——"

"Unhand me, sir, I command you!" cried Maria, who was now seriously alarmed by his manner, for he had forcibly taken her hand, and encircling her waist with his other arm, was endeavouring to draw her towards him; "this outrage, you may depend upon it, shall——"

"Pooh, pooh, nonsense!" interrupted Barnell, "how very squeamish you are;—but I don't care, I have followed you all this way;—I have had a rare race to overtake you, and before I will let you go, I am determined to have a kiss from those ruby lips."

"With these words the odious fellow attempt-

ed to put his threat into execution;—Maria screamed;—the next moment a rustling was heard among the foliage, and a voice exclaiming—

"Hold! presumptuous hound!"

Before Barnell had time to defend himself he was felled to the earth by a violent blow from the double fist of the enraged Walter.

"Maria, nearly fainting, threw herself into the arms of her cousin, who stood over his prostrate antagonist with his fists clenched, and his eyes flashing glances of deep resentment.

"Unmanly ruffian!" exclaimed Walter, in a voice almost choked with wrath, and half inclined to inflict summary punishment upon one who had so grossly insulted her to whom his fondest affections were devoted; "contemptible, beggar-bred clown; were you not beneath even my chastisement, you should dearly repent this; —get up, and leave the place immediately, lest I forget the years that have passed over your head, and correct you upon the spot."

Mr. Barnell bit his lips, and slowly gathered himself upon his feet; he was evidently greatly exasperated, not only at the interruption, but at the blow he had received from what he considered to be a mere stripling; but his courage being rather of a questionable character, he was afraid to resent it, and looking savagely upon Walter and Maria alternately, he said, as he turned upon his heels—

"Mr. Walter Wallingford, you shall suffer for this insult offered to a gentleman; as for that puny girl, who——"

"Impudent scoundrel!" passionately cried Walter, rushing towards him—"dare you insult her——"

"Hold, Walter, I beg," interposed Maria, "he is not worthy of your serious attention."

But Barnell, who always considered that "discretion was the better part of valour," had been prudent enough to make a hasty retreat as soon as he had given utterance to his threat, and was quickly out of sight.

"The insolent booby!" observed Walter, as he led Maria towards the town; "and yet my father could think of uniting that odious mass of ignorance to his fair, his gentle niece. But, for goodness sake, my dear Maria, how did you get separated from us? You cannot form any idea of the state of alarm we have all been in, for we made sure that you had fallen into the power of the Gipsies, who have not yet left the neighbourhood, and doubtless will not, until after the execution of Mark Darwin and his son. It was a fortunate job that I thought of coming in this direction, and thus saved you from further insult from that detestable fellow, Barnell."

Maria explained to him how it had happened as they proceeded, and having got once more into the town, she beheld the carriage containing Dr. Hartley and Fanny waiting, and surrounded with officers to prevent any outrage which the threatening looks of the Gipsies, who were in large numbers near the spot, prognosticated. We need not attempt to describe the pleasure of the doctor and of Fanny when Maria was brought back to them, and having seated herself by the side of Fanny, the carriage was driven off in the direction of the doctor's lodgings.

"Your father will think it strange, Mr. Walter," said Dr. Hartley, "that you should leave him to go home by himself."

"Why, my dear sir," observed Walter, "he certainly will pardon the apparent neglect on my part, when he is made acquainted with what has happened."

Mr. Hartley felt convinced in his own mind that it would have quite a contrary effect, but he did not make any reply.

"But, my dear sir, I should like to ask you how it will be advisable now to act?" inquired Walter.

"What do you mean?" demanded the doctor.

"Why," returned Walter, "in regard to the females—for my part, I should have been pleased to have taken poor Fanny home with me and my cousin, but without my father's consent, of course——"

"And you must not forget that your father is also the father of this poor girl," interrupted the doctor, sharply; "but it is of no consequence, as I happen to have arranged all that myself. I promised her mother that I would give her shelter and protection until she could be restored to her, and, of course, I shall fulfil it, however great may be the danger which I shall probably incur by so doing."

"But when shall I again behold my mother?" eagerly demanded Fanny; "did you not promise me that I should be restored to her in a few hours, and surely you will not distract me by breaking your word?"

"My good child," remarked the doctor, kindly, "your mother is, I have not the least doubt, perfectly safe, and at some distance from this spot; but if the affection you profess for her is really sincere, and you wish to be secure from the power of her enemies, you will compose your anguish, and be grateful to Providence that she has been preserved, and not regret, however long the time may be, before those who really are your friends, and who are the most competent to judge of the circumstances, may think it prudent and safe for you to meet her again."

Fanny could not make any reply—the violence of her grief choked her utterance, and covering her face with her hands, she gave free indulgence to her tears.

"But you will, too, leave me?" she, after a pause, interrogated, looking up affectionately at Maria.

"Not for the present, my dear girl," observed the latter, soothingly, "that is, if I can only intrude upon the kindness of Doctor Hartley."

Mr. Hartley smiled kindly upon her.

"Of course, my father will think it strange, nay, imprudent," remarked Walter, warmly, "if you do not return to him, Maria."

"Rest yourself contented upon that point, Mr. Walter," observed the doctor; "though I see what it is, you are fearful of losing the society of your fair cousin; I have not the least doubt that Mr. Wallingford will readily agree to Miss Herbert's remaining with Fanny, especially as she will be under my protection; at any rate she will sleep with her to-night, and in the morning I will consult him upon the subject."

"Of course, if Maria is agreeable to this arrangement, I can have no right to object," said Walter, evidently very much chagrined at the proposition, and looking reproachfully at his cousin, as though he suspected that the plan was a premeditated one between her and the doctor; "but I must confess——"

"Tut, tut, tut," interrupted the doctor, drily, "I know what you would say—you must confess that you think I am an impudent old fool for my pains; however, prudence points out to me which is the best course, and I have no doubt Mr. Wallingford will see it in the same light that I do."

The carriage had now arrived at the house in which Mr. Hartley was lodging, and the conversation was dropped for the present. After they had partaken of some refreshment, Walter, who was anxious to release his father from any apprehensions for his safety, arose, and was about to depart, when the doctor, assuming a smile of forced jocularity, placed his hand on his shoulder, and said—

"Stop, Mr. Walter, I have thought better of it, and there is nothing like striking the iron while it is hot: I will not delay my visit to your father until the morning, but go to him at once. Don't you see, if I leave you to speak to him first, there is no knowing what the eloquence of love might persuade him to do; so you can stay there, and keep Fanny and Maria company till I come back."

"There is no necessity for your using this precaution, sir," said Walter, somewhat piqued at the levity of Mr. Hartley; "my cousin is, of course, her own mistress, and therefore——"

"There—there, that will do, now," said the doctor, hastily; "I am off. But, I say, Walter, before I go, I would warn you to be cautious, and be sure you do not suffer any person whatever to see Fanny, for when you least expect it, there might be an attempt made upon her life. We have certainly a right to abide by the decision of your father upon this subject, and, therefore, to obtain his advice, I am now going to wait upon him ; in the mean time, I repeat, be on your guard in respect to Fanny ;—at the same time, rest assured, that however unseasonable my raillery may at present appear to be, I have, and will continue to have, the best interests of yourself and Maria at heart."

Walter readily took the proffered hand of the worthy doctor, and pressed it warmly between his own, to assure him that he was convinced of the sincerity of his words, and the doctor, taking his hat and stick, departed in the direction of Mrs. Patterson's.

FARMER HODGES

CHAPTER XLVIII.

WALTER and his companions were astonished at the quickness with which Doctor Hartley returned from his consultation with Mr. Wallingford, and it was very easy to be seen, from his looks, that he had not been disappointed as to the result of the interview.

"I guess that my uncle has acceded to your proposition, my dear sir," observed Maria, as he entered the room.

"It is, indeed, as you suspect," replied the

latter, seriously: "of course, you could not presume so far as to imagine that Mr. Wallingford would refuse to grant my request? To-morrow morning you return to Wallingford Hall, Mr. Walter."

"Of course you will accompany us, my dear sir," said the latter, eagerly.

"Of course I shall do no such thing," replied the doctor. "I have particular reasons for wishing to remain where I am for a few days. But I had almost forgotten to tell you that your father desires to see you as soon as possible."

Bewildered, vexed, and astonished as he was, Walter immediately rose to obey, and hastily left the house, hardly giving himself time to bid his cousin and Fanny good night.

Doctor Hartley had, in fact, found no difficulty in persuading Mr. Wallingford to resign Maria to his protection. It had occupied his thoughts for some time. There was another circumstance, also, which greatly changed the current of his thoughts, and endued him with more determination and vigour; this was the discovery that it was his own Christabelle who had been assassinated by the Gipsies, and that the daughter of Mr. Bernazie was still alive. If he was not actually rejoiced to hear this, it is very clear that he felt very well satisfied, as it removed from his breast a number of fears that had formerly occupied it, that he was doomed to be disgraced by his having to acknowledge, as his own child, a girl who had been brought up in the midst of vice and depravity, and who was, doubtless, as vitiated as her abandoned associates. But now that he was assured that Christabelle rested under the cold turf, his mind was comparatively at rest, for she had gone thither unconscious of the station she had a right to fill in society, and ignorant of the enjoyment which riches can bestow. With reflections such as these he tried to content himself, unmixed as they were, and, indeed, he considered that she was rather to be envied than compassionated, forasmuch as all her troubles were at an end, and she had escaped all those sorrows and afflictions that seemed like a spell to pursue all the members of the proud house of Wallingford.

Nor could he often help bringing the beauty of Fanny to his mind, and reflecting on her with kindness; but he shrank from the idea of acknowledging her as his daughter, and admitting her to his house.

It was, therefore, no wonder that the good doctor so easily succeeded in persuading him to leave both Fanny and Maria under his protection; in fact, he said he had partly made up his mind to travel, for it was necessary Walter should see something of the world; at any rate he did not intend to remain at Wallingford Hall long, for which place he should depart in the morning.

This intelligence Doctor Hartley imparted to Fanny and Maria, to the latter of whom especially it gave the most poignant sorrow; the bare thoughts of a separation from Walter gave her the keenest anguish, and she heartily dreaded the time to approach. It was only by the determined persuasions of Mr. Hartley, that either of them was induced to partake of supper.

"Come, come," said he, "I will not have anything of this:—I do not want you for patients, because you would be most unprofitable ones to me, consequently, if you feel indisposed, the only way you must do, is to eat yourselves into convalescence again. After a hearty supper, I should advise you to go to bed, for after the fatigues of the two last days, I am sure you must require rest."

But if Maria or her companion were incapable of eating much, the doctor made up for all the deficiencies on their part, and very soon decreased the appearance of the cold fowl which had a few minutes before been placed on the table. After this he made Maria make him his nightly allowance of punch, which she had always done at the hall, and then he would have persuaded them to retire to their chamber, but Maria, having shaken off all appearance of fatigue, begged the doctor to inform her more minutely, what had taken place between him and Mr. Wallingford at their interview, and whether he had resigned her, or had hinted at what he intended to do at a future period, particularly in respect to Fanny.

"Well, well, I do not see the utility of keeping anything from you," said the doctor, "for you have too much sense, my dear girl, not to receive the information I shall give you as becomes you. I will therefore candidly acknowledge to you, that I found not the least difficulty in the business, for, so far from Mr. Wallingford waiting for me to make the proposition, he made the request himself, and, indeed, he seemed as if he had been for some time puzzling his brains to know in what manner he should be able best to dispose of you. As I told you before, he intends to return to Rosemary Dell to-morrow morning, where it is not his intention to remain many days—at least, no longer than is necessary for him to arrange his affairs for going upon the continent; he, therefore, very willingly gave me permission to hold you under my protection, until one or both of us get tired of the bargain; so the whole of it is, my dear, we will remain here for a short time, when you let me know whether you will be ready to attend me and Fanny to the metropolis."

"And shall I be thus torn for ever from Wallingford Hall—that place in which I have passed so many—many happy hours?" cried Maria in melancholy tones, while heavy sighs escaped her bosom at the thought.

"Nonsense!" exclaimed the doctor, "to be

sure you will. Indeed, I think you pay but a bad compliment to Walter, by such a supposition."

In spite, however, of the remonstrances and apparent coolness of Dr. Hartley, Maria felt it impossible to stifle the deep grief which assailed her, and sitting down, her tears flowed fast and unrestrained. Fanny, with a smile of sweet persuasiveness, took her hand, and tried to soothe her, while Mr. Hartley seemed to take more notice of the punch before him, than her sorrow.

"Well, I must say this is a very pretty sample of the gratitude I am likely to receive, for sacrificing my comfortable home; my worthy housekeeper, and——"

"Oh, sir," suddenly interrupted Maria, recollecting herself, and chasing away her tears, she pressed the hand of Mr. Hartley warmly, as she added, "forgive me, if I appeared unmindful of your kindness; but I was unprepared for this sudden shock. I confess that I did not expect to hear that my uncle would so readily abandon me; and that I shall not go back to that place, which is endeared to me by so many happy remembrances."

"Nay, my dear girl," said the kind-hearted doctor, "do not give way to this violent grief. Providence is kind, and no doubt you will yet live to pass many more happy hours in Wallingford Hall. Think not of Mr. Wallingford abandoning you; or if, indeed, he has, it shall be my constant study to convince you, that in losing an uncle, you have found a father, at least, if you will only submit——"

"Submit!" eagerly repeated Maria, in tones of gratitude, and embracing the old man, she wept upon his shoulder.

While they were still in this position, they heard a footstep on the stairs, the next moment the door was thrown open, and Walter appeared, his whole demeanour denoting extreme agitation.

"Is it really true, sir," he cried, "that you have treated me so unfairly, so unkindly, as to do your utmost to persuade my father to adopt such plans as will tear me and Maria asunder? I could not believe it when my my father told me so, and now call upon you to confirm or deny it."

"My dear girls," said the doctor, turning to Maria and Fanny, "take my advice, and retire to rest; for the occurrences of the day have been quite enough to fatigue you, without your witnessing any more. Heaven protect you, and may sweet sleep light upon your pillow."

Fanny did not offer to raise any objection to his wishes, and Maria was also about to accompany her, when Walter suddenly placed his back against the door, with a look of determination, and impeded her progress.

"Nay, Maria," said he, determinedly, "you shall not quit this room until I have heard you

positively, unequivocally avow your designs—your resolutions—if it is true that you could thus callously resign the companions, the friends of your youthful days, and to discard—"

"Walter," interrupted Maria, energetically, "you mistake me. I resign—I discard no one—but—" she checked herself as she was about to say, "but it is I who have reason to complain of being resigned, discarded;" but knowing that it would but increase the misery of her cousin, to see that she felt the unkind treatment of her father so keenly, she continued—"I cannot combat with circumstances, but I trust that, although I exchange the protection of one friend for another, I shall never forget the gratitude and affection due to both."

"Very sensible observations, my dear Miss Herbert," said Dr. Hartley, "and now I hope that Mr. Walter will be satisfied; however, there is no necessity to detain you any longer from your couch, I will arrange this affair with your cousin;—good night, my dear; good night."

Notwithstanding the decisive manner of the doctor commanded submission, Walter plainly showed by his looks that he was not at all pleased with this arrangement, and he could not help thinking that his old friend was acting with unnecessary cruelty towards him; but still, though he felt such treatment severely, he did not venture to offer any observation or opposition to the will of the doctor, and Maria accordingly retired to rest.

Rest—no; not to rest did Maria retire, for although she had struggled with her feelings so as to put on an appearance of calmness and composure, she felt an emotion which was nothing short of that experienced by Walter. The greatest consolation that she had, was the conviction that his passion was fervent and sincere, and that it would not evaporate with absence. But then again, had not Mr. Wallingford taken the surest way of obstructing their wishes by separating them so far from each other?—and might not time work its effect upon the mind of Walter, and cause him to remember her only as the companion of his younger days? Besides, was it not his father's intention to make him mingle in the busy scenes of life?—and to what temptations might he not be exposed?—what other females might he not encounter, who, holding out all the soft blandishments of their sex, might win his affections, and whose beauty might completely put into the shade the rustic charms of which she only could boast? Then again, was not the wealthy alliance of his son the chief subject which occupied the heart of Mr. Wallingford?—and how could it be supposed that Walter could long continue to resist the wishes of his father, when beauty, wealth, and accomplishments were added to the glittering bait? Alas! it was vanity in her for a moment to imagine that she could hold the supremacy over his affections: it was to his interest to endeavour to forget her, and she could not doubt but that the persuasions of his father and the influence of rank, beauty, and fashion would tempt him to do so.

As these thoughts, too cogent, too reasonable, crossed the maiden's mind, she found it impossible to restrain her emotions, and therefore, after she had left the object that gave rise to them, she gave herself up to the free indulgence of her grief, and wept abundantly. Fanny exerted herself to the utmost to impart consolation to her afflicted companion, and at length she partially succeeded, and upbraiding herself for her weakness, she wiped the pearly drops from her cheeks, and endeavoured to appear more calm.

"But surely this weakness is excusable," she observed, "for what can impart more poignant anguish to the sensitive mind, than to have to separate from those dear friends with whom our whole happiness has been passed, and to know that henceforward I must be estranged from those scenes in which I have passed so many blissful hours?—to be torn from the members of a family—the ancient servants to whom I am so fervently attached, and who have ever been such generous, attentive, and affectionate friends to me. And talking of that, I cannot help wondering whether or not Mr. Wallingford will keep up his establishment, or if he will dismiss his domestics. But should he do so, I know that they will find a warm, a liberal friend in Walter, who will take good care they are amply provided for;—oh, Fanny, you cannot form any idea how generous, how kind, how charitable he is; if you could you would not think it a matter of astonishment I shall dread the hour that shall separate him from me."

"My dear Maria," said Fanny with much archness, "indeed I can fully appreciate your feelings, and I am positive that if we were to change places, I should be ten times more wretched than you are."

Maria coloured up and evinced the greatest confusion, for she felt convinced that she had disclosed too much of her real sentiments as regarded Walter; and she could not help thinking herself somewhat lowered by being looked upon by Fanny with an eye of pity as a poor love-sick maiden, despairing of again seeing the object of her affections; she therefore tried all that she possibly could to regain her usual equanimity, and endeavoured to change the topic of conversation.

But as if she had made up her mind to confuse her still more, and as though she delighted in witnessing the embarrassment of her companion, Fanny would not be diverted from the subject, and would not take any part in a discourse in which either Mr. Wallingford or Walter did not figure as principal characters. Of her father, in particular, she seemed as if he should never be tired of talking, and the questions she put to Maria were enumerable, and the particulars which the latter gave her concerning Mr. Wallingford's ways and peculiarities, appeared but to sharpen her curiosity to hear and know more. Maria, however, was particularly careful that she did not utter a sentence which might prejudice Fanny against the author of her being; his errors she cautiously avoided mentioning—his merits she placed in the most prominent position, and eulogised in the most glowing terms, so that nothing that she had divulged to her could create a breach in that love and veneration, with which the mind of the poor girl was inclined to look up to him. Indeed it was only the recent harshness and haughtiness of his behaviour towards her, that Maria could possibly have to complain of, and as she proceeded with her animated description, the eyes of her attentive auditor sparkled, and her bosom heaved with extacy.

"Ah," she exclaimed, "would he but suffer me an interview—would he but call me daughter, and allow me to call him by the title of father, what happiness would be mine!" and as the poor girl thus spoke, with an energy which showed the sincerity of what she said, she clasped her hands fervently together, and the big tear of sensitive affection trembled in her eye.

"I cannot account for the feeling, my dear Miss Herbert," Fanny resumed, after a pause, "but in spite of my mother's fierce expressions of indignation towards him, the name of Mr. Wallingford never arose to my thoughts but with a sentiment of the most enthusiastic reverence and regard, and I felt that he could not possess any faults that would be sufficient to prevent me loving him as a father, if he would allow me that dear, that inestimable privilege. But I do not mind remarking to you, Maria," she added, in a lower tone, as though she was fearful that some one might be listening to her, and that she was anxious so impress upon the mind of her companion that she did not put too harsh a construction upon her mother's conduct. "I do not mind remarking to you, that I ever considered my poor mother was too prone to think everybody was all that was good and estimable, or that they were all that the blackest vice could make them;—although there were, alas! not many who deserved the former opinion whom she knew, or was connected with; and it was this which I have no doubt made me believe that my father was not so bad, not so guilty as she painted him." She again paused for a minute, and then continued; —"Certainly, with all the events of Mr. Wallingford's connection with my mother, I am not acquainted, and therefore I must not, I cannot believe but that he treated her with much cruelty and deception; still I could not close my heart against him—no ;—it suggested to me that there might be some extenuating causes for him, which I was ignorant of, and never have I been able to erase from my memory the time when I first beheld him, and many years have elapsed since then, for at that time I was quite a child ; his urgent entreaties for my mother to resign me to his care, are still as fresh in my recollection as if they had been uttered but yesterday. I could not have abandoned her certainly," she continued, sighing deeply. "Oh, no, never, not for all the wealth, all the grandeur which the world could afford ; nothing could have tempted me to leave my poor, wretched, out-cast mother, notwithstanding in after years, when my reason was more matured, and my sensibility was more awakened—when I experienced all the wretchedness, privations, scorn, and sorrow, to which our tribe was subjected—the despised of all—the objects of derision and persecution of the vulgar and the brutal—suffering all the miseries attendant on our precarious life, then—oh, yes,—would the name of my father arise upon my thoughts, and the idea of the different situation in which I ought to move, and in which he had exhibited such anxiety to place me, came vividly upon my mind, and in such moments I felt that my love towards him was all that the fondest child could feel for the author of its being. Could I hate him ? No, no, no ! My heart revolted from the idea—I prayed, I yearned once more to behold him, to assure him that he still occupied my thoughts, and that I had never ceased to entertain a proper sense of the kindness he had intended towards me. But these thoughts, these feelings, I was compelled to keep locked within my own bosom—I dared not state them to my mother, and it was to this unhappy circumstance I may attribute all the fatal consequences that have taken place, for when an opportunity presented itself, I was in the habit of hastening from our tents, to wander in the grounds of Wallingford Hall, in the hope of seeing my father. It was with that object in view, I went to the shrubbery on the fatal night of the murder. It was in one of those stolen visits that I first beheld you and Walter, and you will not be surprised at the terror I evinced on that occasion, and the abruptness of my departure, when I inform you that I saw Mark watching me from behind a tree, and it was that circumstance which first disclosed to me the bitter animosity he entertained towards the family of Wallingford, although I was at a loss to conjecture what motives he could have for his hatred. The fiendish look he gave me then, is still fresh in my memory, and filled with apprehension. I

hastened after him, to endeavour to chase from his mind the opinions he had evidently imbibed towards me, and above all, to entreat him to keep my visit to the shrubbery a secret from my mother. Never shall I forget the rude, the brutal insinuations, and bitter sarcasms he heaped upon me ; and to induce him to silence, I was compelled to give him all the little store of cash I had in my possession. Alas ! little did I then imagine what would be the termination of it. Unfortunate Esther —ill-fated, murdered girl," she added, as the tears flowed from her eyes in torrents, and she wrung her hands in the agony of her feelings —" never shall I forgive myself for being, by my imprudent conduct, the cause of bringing you to so terrible a fate."

The violence of Fanny's grief became almost insupportable, and Maria therefore interrupted the expression of her feelings, and with gentle, soothing accents, persuaded her to seek that rest and refreshment which her couch would afford her. Fanny, who seemed to look upon her companion as a gentle monitor, whose will it was her duty to obey, required very little persuasion, and having retired to bed, exhausted with the cares and fatigues of the day, she soon fell into a sound sleep.

But it was far otherwise with Maria ; she was unable to compose herself to rest; her thoughts were of Walter, and she listened with breathless attention, as his voice every now and then reached her ear, and the loudness of its tones occasionally led her to suppose that the worthy doctor and him were engaged in an argument of unusual warmth.

But at length she heard the bell ring, and soon afterwards the opening and closing of the street door, convinced her that he had departed. Notwithstanding, however, that she had listened most anxiously, she could not hear him wish the doctor good night as he retired, and this circumstance led her to imagine, that not only had they separated bad friends, but that he was filled with an uncontrollable feeling of melancholy and despair.

"Alas !" she sighed, as she reclined her head upon the pillow, after having heard the closing of the street door, "alas ! perhaps we have met for the last time ; I may be doomed never more to behold him!"

But Maria was mistaken in her ideas regarding the result of the interview between Walter and Dr. Hartley. The latter had entered willingly and candidly into a thorough explanation of every circumstance, and of his designs as regarded Maria ; and although, of course, it was no easy task to make Walter view with anything like patience a separation from his cousin, he could not help feeling redoubled admiration and gratitude towards the doctor for the fatherly interest he took in the affair. Doctor Hartley had also taken especial care to show to him the present awkward position in which Maria was placed, when Mr. Wallingford seemed to entertain so sordid and ungenerous a prejudice against her; and of the advantages which most undoubtedly would ultimately accrue to both him and Maria, from his scheme, for had she been left to the caprices of her uncle, he might have forced her on strangers, and thus have been the means of parting them for ever.

"On the contrary, Walter," continued the doctor, "as long as she remains under my protection, her friends can always communicate with her; but I must impress upon you at the same time, the necessity of my prohibiting any correspondence between you and your cousin as lovers, until your father may change his opinions, or circumstances transpire to render such a course no longer necessary. Mind you, I do mean to say that you shall not communicate with each other, as friends, as relatives—but of course Maria will have more prudence, I know she will, than to attempt to carry on a correspondence which her uncle does not approve of!"

"How cold, how freezing, is that word prudence," murmured Walter; "oh, if she had ever loved with anything like the ardour of the passion I feel for her, she could never be induced to yield so readily to its rules."

Doctor Hartley having been engaged at this time in mixing up another strong glass of punch, did not, or affected not to hear all that Walter last uttered, and after having completed his task, and tested its quality, which he pronounced to be excellent, he resumed the conversation.

"Do not suppose that I have formed this design only from a brief whim, which a short time may tend to make me repent, for you would be doing me an injustice, of which I will convince you presently. I will impart to you a secret, which would never have escaped my lips were you not inclined to be so sceptical;—that is, that to Maria I have bequeathed, at my death, the whole of the property which I have it in my power to dispose of:—as for the house which I have inhabited for so many years, and the land which is attached to it, that is left to a worthless, spendthrift man, who I am ashamed to call my nephew, but whom I have not beheld for more than twenty years, and I sincerely hope that he will never present himself to me again. All the rest, as I before said, I have made Maria heiress to, and that will be sufficient to secure her from penury and distress, if (which is very unlikely) she should never be united. Therefore, Mr. Walter, after this candid explanation, I trust that you will not be so lavish in the little compliments you have paid to my motives, such as sudden favouritism, whims, and a variety of other insinuations; for by referring to my will, you will find that I formed this determination directly after your father showed that he was averse to the passion you and Maria had formed

for each other, and which my reason told me would be the occasion of much sorrow to her, and throw her into many awkward embarrassments."

The heart of Walter prompted him to have given expression, in the most unbounded terms, to the feelings of gratitude which he felt for the doctor's disinterested kindness, and to have apologized for the injustice he had done him, for supposing for a moment that he could possibly have been urged by any other feelings than those of pure kindness, in his conduct towards Maria; but Mr. Hartley, who saw what he would say, interrupted him.

"I need no apology, Walter," he observed, "all that I require is sincere friendship and confidence between us; I will not keep any secrets from you, and I trust that you will act in the same spirit of candour towards me. Of this you may rest assured, that as regards your fair cousin, she shall always be treated by me with the same care, affection, and attention, as if she were my own child; of the sentiments of friendship that I entertain towards you, you must be well aware; therefore you cannot doubt but that I shall always have your interest; as well as Maria's at heart; let me therefore beg you will, for the present (as it is your imperative duty so to do) submit to the will of your father, hoping that time and circumstances may change his views, and that happiness may yet be in store for you and her to whom you are, I know, so fondly and sincerely attached."

"But shall I not have a parting interview with Maria, before we leave to-morrow, my dear sir?" inquired Walter, eagerly.

"I scarcely know indeed," remarked Mr. Hartley, "whether I should not be acting imprudently by acceding to your desire—but upon this particular occasion I will yield to your request. To-morrow morning I shall be happy to see you with me at breakfast; but remember we breakfast early, and likewise that, as your father will probably not think of making his departure late, if you are not in good time, your interview must of necessity be a brief one; therefore, remember, I have cautioned you, and it will be your own fault if you do not act upon my advice."

"Oh, I shall be sure to be here as early as you will want me," observed Walter with a sigh, "for I know that I shall rest but little, if any, to-night."

"Although this arrangement has been made between your father and me," resumed Doctor Hartley, "he did not give me any decisive answer, but has promised to furnish me with it in the morning, and perhaps, therefore, you will bring it with you. He had not made up his mind what provision he would make for Maria, but whatever it is, I shall accept it; not that I want it, having quite enough to provide for her in every way that her wishes or her comfort can require, but it is from a feeling that he has an undoubted right to do something for her, and because I think that she herself would feel more contented at not being entirely dependent on a stranger. Whatever he settles on her, she may find a use for, be it ever so small, as pocket money."

Walter returned no answer to this, for he could not believe his father to be the mercenary being which the good doctor seemed to suppose him to be, and after a few more brief observations, he left the house.

When he arrived at home, he found that his father had retired to rest, and he appeared to take so little interest in his interview with Doctor Hartley, that he had not even left a word for him in the shape of a message with William, who had accompained them from Wallingford Hall. Walter hastened to his chamber, followed by William, but his mind was too much occupied to suffer him to feel the least inclination to sleep, and William seemed very well pleased at the opportunity which was thus afforded him of indulging his loquacity, and broke the ice by remarking—

"Why, sir, I was quite astonished, I declare, when master informed me a short time ago, that it is his intention, as soon as he has settled his affairs at the Hall, to travel to Switzerland."

"To Switzerland!" repeated Walter, hastily, this being the first time he had heard any hint of the ultimate destination of his father, and feeling surprised and vexed that that information should first come to him through the means of a servant; but quickly checking himself, so that William might not perceive his real thoughts, he added—

"I suppose you will accompany us, William?"

"I am to follow you, sir," replied William, "at least so master told me; and from what he informed me, he has arranged all his plans as far as regards the establishment, and very excellently too, I think; he says that all the old servants, who think proper, may remain for a year at the hall, and receive the same wages and board wages as they have always done, or if they prefer it, they may leave as soon as they like, and he will give them just the same money as their expenses would have been, had they remained in the house; moreover, they are all at liberty, if they think proper, to enter his service again, if he should return to this country, with the exception of Mrs. Pembroke, who is to have a handsome annuity. Old Anthony and his wife, assisted by their son-in-law and daughter, are to be left in the care of the hall, and I am to follow after you, in a month, with the horses."

"Well, certainly," remarked Walter, "nothing could have been arranged in a more systematic manner, truly; but I can never believe

but what it must have been some time in contemplation."

At this moment two letters lying upon the table met the eye of Walter, and going up to them, he found that they were from his father, and were addressed, one to Doctor Hartley, and the other to his cousin. A feeling of indignation crossed his mind as he took them up.

"And can this really be the conduct of my father," he observed to himself—"that father whom I ever believed was all nobleness, generosity, and kindness? Can he with such recklessness, such insulting callousness, abandon her who has ever acted towards him as a daughter, and whom it was his duty to protect?—If his own heart could not prompt him to a different course, surely the memory of my poor mother, whose darling she ever was, and who experienced from her such affectionate, such assiduous, such untiring attention, when on her death bed, should have been more than sufficient to have prevented him from so cruelly, so heartlessly turning his back upon her, and to treat her with less respect even than he would one of his domestics."

William had not overheard what his young master had said; but he had been observing the deep emotion he appeared to be suffering, and he, although he could not form a very clear idea of the nature of his feelings, felt sincere regret.

"Master told me, sir," said he, "to take those letters early in the morning."

"There will be no necessity for you to do that, William," returned Walter, "for I am going there myself first thing, and will therefore take them with me."

"I hope you will excuse what I am going to say, sir," remarked William, after he had been standing musing, apparently for a few minutes; "I hope you will not think I am impertinent, or take too many liberties about things that don't concern me, but I cannot, for the life of me, imagine what will become of Miss Herbert; master did not 'say anything about her, only that in all probability she would send instructions by me to Mrs. Pembroke, about her apparel, and——"

"My cousin is to be placed under the protection of Doctor Hartley, William," interrupted his young master; at the same time the deep anguish of his mind was clearly legible upon his countenance.

"Ah! indeed?" uttered William, "oh, that will be much better than I expected, after all—for I was terribly alarmed lest Miss Maria should——" Walter fixed upon him a look of astonishment, which he observed, and continued; —"I hope you won't be offended, sir;—my words may sound rather bold, but I am sure I meant no offence—but don't you see, I being acquainted with the design which Miss Herbert had in view at one time, I was fearful that she might now be about to——"

"What mean you, William?" hastily interrupted Walter, with an expression of the most unfeigned astonishment. "Designs!—designs formed by Maria. And how came you to be acquainted with them, and what were they?"

William paused and hesitated for a moment or two, but he evidently seemed to think himself a person of some consequence, now that he was acquainted with a secret, of which his betters were ignorant, for he pursed himself up not a little, and he did not immediately condescend to return any answer to his young master's question; at last he said—

"Why, sir, the truth is, what I am about to tell you is a secret, and therefore I hope you will not mention it to anybody, but above all not to Miss Herbert. You must know that old Jenny told it to me, the wife of Anthony I mean; well, she told me that on that very night the murder took place in the shrubbery, Miss Maria had concerted a plot with Anthony and his wife, to fly to London, and to go to take up her residence with Jenny's sister, who, you know, had been Miss Maria's nurse."

Walter could scarce believe his ears, and made William recount every particular of the affair, which excited the most unbounded surprise in his mind, and he was at a loss to imagine the reasons that could have induced her to think of such a design as the one his servant had been describing. William having told him all he knew, his young master dismissed him, and then retired to his bed, but the story he had just heard, in addition to the other thoughts that had before so much annoyed him, prevented him from sleeping, and as soon as it was daylight, he arose and walked from the house.

It was a very fine morning, and thinking it was yet too early to go to the doctor's, Walter turned towards the woody dell, where he had lately rescued Maria from the power of Barnell. The birds were warbling their most mellifluous notes, and all around was radiant with the first golden tint of the sun; but that which, at any other time, would have afforded him such infinite delight, and called forth his warmest admiration, was now unheeded by him. He walked on, buried in gloomy meditation, until he was aroused by a rustling among the foliage, and ere he had an opportunity to ascertain the cause, he was startled by the report of a pistol, and a shot passed so close, that he was completely stunned by it. In a moment afterwards, however, he recovered his self-possession, and then his eyes followed the direction from whence the smoke issued, to see if he could perceive the miscreant, who had evidently aimed at his life. He started towards the spot, and passing through an opening in the trees, he beheld running from the place at some distance, Mr. Barnell.

"Cowardly villain!" exclaimed the exasperated Walter, as he rushed after him in pursuit; but he had got too far a-head, and making his way towards a deep cluster of trees, he became lost to the view of Walter altogether.

Walter's heart swelled with indignation at this outrage, and had he been able to overtake the villain, he would most assuredly have chastised him on the spot. He determined, however, that at the very first opportunity he should meet with the punishment he merited.

"And yet, my father could think of sacrificing Maria to such a fellow as this," he ejaculated; "a poltroon, a cowardly ruffian, who would commit murder in the dark. But in spite of his money, and his powerful friend, Lord Harlington, he shall not escape receiving a full and ample punishment at my hands."

It was strange, Walter thought, that so early in the morning, Barnell should be lurking apparently in ambush for him; but it was clear he must have dodged him from the house where he was lodging, or else he had some secret spy or the other upon his actions. He did not, however, suffer the affair long to occupy his thoughts, which quickly reverted to Maria, and the short time which must elapse before they parted, perhaps for ever. Above an hour having now elapsed since he had quitted home, he thought it was most likely that Maria had arisen, he therefore made his way towards the residence of Dr. Hartley.

Walter had a wish to see Maria by herself, and thought it was probable, that being so early he might be able to do so, and having rung the bell, the slovenly looking female domestic made her appearance, and expressed by her gestures no very great pleasure at being disturbed so early.

She led the way to the breakfast-room, and muttered in tones loud enough for Walter to hear, that "she was sure it was a very fine hour to come to breakfast, before a person had even time to light a fire, much more to clean up the room for the reception of company."

Walter, however, soon found a talisman to dissipate the cross looks and cross words of the soubrette, by slipping into her palm a shilling or two, and accompanying the same with an apology for having put her to such inconvenience, and he then ventured to request her to inform his cousin that he was all impatience to behold her, and to entreat that she would attend him in the breakfast room as quick as possible, he having got a letter to her from Mr. Wallingford!—which, of course was added for the purpose of doing away with the wonder of the servant at the anxiety he expressed.

But Walter was doomed to be disappointed, for Maria, after having passed a restless night, completely worn out with thinking, had just sunk into a sound sleep, and Fanny, therefore, had quietly retired from the bed, so that she might uninterruptedly indulge in refreshing slumber, until the latest moment before the breakfast would be ready. Fanny was just about to leave the chamber, when the servant made her appearance to deliver the mes-sage which had been entrusted to her by Walter.

"Hush!" said Fanny, "do not disturb Miss Herbert; I will attend Mr. Walter."

In a moment she left the room, and stepped lightly down the stairs, but not so softly but

FANNY BERANZIO COMPELLED BY RUPERT TO LOOK ON THE CORSES OF THE MALEFACTORS.

that her footsteps met the eager ears of Walter, who, with the door open, had been listening attentively for the approach of his lover, and making no doubt that this was her, he ad-vanced with a buoyant heart to salute her.

If he were disappointed at not beholding Maria, the mild and sparkling eyes that met his, quickly dissipated his agitation, and when she informed him of the cause of Maria's not being able to attend him just yet, and why she had not awakened her, he expressed him-self perfectly satisfied. What, upon any other occasion, would have caused him the deepest regret, now afforded him consolation—we mean that Maria, as well as himself, had passed a miserable night.

"I am not then indifferent to her," he murmured, as if he had forgotten that Fanny was present, and that she was watching him with the most penetrating looks, "she cannot think of the hour of parting without sorrow."

"Sorrow!" ejaculated Fanny, with emphasis, "oh, Walter, you do her an injustice to imagine for a moment that she could think of your separation without the most poignant anguish. Poor girl, it was quite piteous to behold how bitterly she suffered all the night; it grieved me sadly to hear her; and just now, as I left the chamber, I heard her murmur your name, coupled with accents of love, and therefore it is evident, that sleeping or waking, you are the constant subject of her thoughts."

The heart of Walter bounded with a mingled feeling of love and gratitude towards Fanny as she gave utterance to these words, and he had never before contemplated her with so deep an interest. Her words fell like balm upon his heart, and chased away a great portion of the heavy burthen of sorrow which had before oppressed it.

"My own fond Maria—my sweet Fanny," he exclaimed with ecstacy, "oh, how shall I express the love I feel for you both?—my heart is divided between you;—but oh, tell me, dearest Fanny, will you not, when I am away, recall me to her memory sometimes?—Will you not impress upon her mind, that there is still one in the world who loves her even more fondly than he does his own life, and who, to know that she forgot him, must expire?"

"I will, indeed, dear Walter," answered Fanny, eagerly, "it will be our greatest enjoyment; but why should such apparent doubt harass and torment your mind, my brother?—How can you imagine for a moment that Maria could cease to remember him to whom her heart is devoted?—Oh, no, she can never, never forget you, Walter."

At this moment Doctor Hartley made his appearance, and consequently all further conversation upon this deeply interesting subject was prevented; and Walter took care, by significant glances at Fanny, to warn her not to allude to anything about which they had just been discoursing.

"Will you be so good, Fanny, as to give this to Maria, when she awakes?" he said, putting into her hand the letter from Mr. Wallingford.

"Zounds!" cried the doctor, "methinks the little slut is turning sluggard, if she has not arisen yet."

"I dare say my cousin was tired, sir," observed Walter; "besides, it is early yet, I think I was rather before the time at which I

promised to come. But here is a letter for you sir, from my father."

Mr. Hartley took the letter which Walter presented to him, and in the meantime Fanny hastened to Maria, whom she found awake and in the act of performing the duties of her toilet.

"I have brought you a letter, Miss Herbert," Fanny said, in a tone of sadness, "it is sent to you by my father;—alas!—will he ever address himself to me?—shall I ever trace the beloved characters inscribed by his hand, in sentences of affection to me? Oh, would that this fond hope could be realized, would to God he would write me a few brief words, if it was only to call me his child; then, indeed, I should be happy, I should be satisfied; but no, I never once enter his thoughts; he treats me with cold indifference, as if I were a stranger, instead of his own offspring, and as nearly related to him as child can be to parent."

"Certainly, my dear Fanny, you have no reason to be envious of his remembering me," replied Maria, who had perused the letter, and which contained only a cool adieu, and expressing a wish for her future health and welfare. In respect to the arrangements he had made about her, he referred her to her present protector, and he concluded by telling her, that if there was anything else which she required, and he had not thought of, or any alteration she wished him to make, he should be happy to accede to her wishes, if it were possible, and if she would send a communication to that effect to him to Wallingford Hall; but she must do so in the course of a week, for at the end of that time, at the very latest, they would have left the neighbourhood of Rosemary Dell for Switzerland.

As Maria perused this epistle, the tears gushed to her eyes, and her sobs of anguish almost choked her. Her sorrow, however, was that of affection and not of wounded pride, which the formal letter of her uncle was every way calculated to excite. To Mr. Wallingford she had ever looked up with the utmost tenderness and reverence; in fact, had he been her father, she could not have behaved with more affection than she had done towards him; and in spite of the manner in which he had lately treated her, which would have chilled the warmest regard, she could not help feeling this moment, when she was about to leave him, and perhaps never to behold him again, as deeply afflicted as if he had ever behaved to her with the most unexampled kindness.

Fanny remarked, with the deepest interest and solicitude, the sorrow of Maria, but fearful of adding to her grief, she forbore to put a single question to her as to the cause; but to her father she could not help attributing the whole of Maria's grief and her own. And yet was she willing—nay, ready to love and honour that father who had occasioned this. She resolved, however, henceforth never to afflict Maria by recalling the name of Mr. Wallingford to her memory :—and she would also endeavour to erase him from her thoughts, for did it not appear that it was the farthest from his wishes or inclinations to acknowledge her for his daughter?

But did Mr. Wallingford feel no anguish, no regret at parting with his niece ?—Oh, yes, in spite of his excessive pride, which overwhelmed all his better feelings, he found it impossible to come to the determination he had, without many a severe pang. Notwithstanding he had behaved so harshly and coolly towards her, he had ever loved Maria, as if she had been his own daughter, and now that the time had arrived when he was about to separate from her, perhaps for ever, all the many amiable qualities which she possessed arose more vividly on his recollection—the deep, the ardent, the sincere affection, she had ever evinced for him—her assiduous and unremitting love for his late wife—the willingness with which she attended her in her illness, night and day—all recurred to him, and for some time he could not help thinking that his deserting her was unjust and cruel. These thoughts, however, were quickly combated by others of an opposite description. This was the time when he must be firm and determined in checking the passion of Walter and Maria, which could only be effected, he imagined, by separating them, and if he did not do so, the result would, he was confident, be what his worst fears apprehended. Every day, he foresaw, would add fresh strength to the affection which his son had imbibed for Maria, while she was constantly in his presence, and he could not doubt but that they would get united, and thus at once would all his ambitious hope as regarded him be annihilated. Walter would content himself by leading the inactive life which he himself had done, and then where would be all that senatorial glory, which he had foundly hoped he would ultimately acquire ?—The thought was unendurable, and he resolved that such an event should never happen. Would it not be the worst of folly to suffer such a noble youth as Walter, with such brilliant oratorical powers, and with such powerful talents, altogether, to sacrifice himself to a simple rustic beauty like Maria, when rank, fame, and riches were only waiting for his grasp ?—Yes, it would, and the very idea that he would passively submit to such a sacrifice, was preposterous.

" Had there been a proper restraint put upon my passions in my youth," soliloquized Mr. Wallingford, " what misery it would have saved me—what a different sphere I might now have been moving in. Am I not then justified in seeing that my son does not become involved in the same dilemma ? Yes, and it shall be so, let the world say what it likes of me, and call

me cruel and severe, and tyrannical and unjust. I should be unjust to myself and Walter too, did I not oppose those inclinations, which would be the means of destroying all the hopes and wishes I had formed for him."

It was thus that the mind of Mr. Wallingford was occupied, and it was in this manner that he sought to excuse the severity of his conduct and his abandonment of his niece: but yet his gentler feelings would obtrude in spite of all his efforts to the contrary, and fearful of betraying a weakness of which he was ashamed, he avoided having a parting interview with Maria. As for Fanny, his thoughts were frequently upon her, but he shuddered at the idea of acknowledging one as his child, who had, he doubted not, been brought up from childhood to curse and abhor him.

The persons assembled at breakfast at Doctor Hartley's were all absorbed in the utmost gloom, and the thought of their speedy separation, perhaps for ever, was sufficient to afflict them most poignantly. Doctor Hartley, although unused to the melting mood, could with difficulty repress his feelings ; although he made several attempts to joke as usual, they were in truth melancholy and wretched attempts, and failed to draw the attention of his guests.

The worthy doctor, however, could not help expressing his admiration of the manner in which Mr. Wallingford had provided for the pecuniary wants of his niece, which he had done very handsomely. He gave the letter which Mr. Wallingford had addressed to him, to Maria, and requested to have her opinion upon it. Maria glanced over its contents hastily, and the tears fell fast from her eyes as she perused them, then returning it to the doctor, she sobbed forth that her uncle had been too liberal, that she had never anticipated such generosity, and neither did she by any means wish for it. Maria spoke with sincerity, when she said it was more than she required, and indeed her heart revolted from receiving any favours of a pecuniary description at all from that man, whose pride had driven her from his home, in which she had ever expected to find a shelter; and who she could not help thinking was prompted more by motives of pride in making this provision for her, than by any feelings of affection or liberality. She would freely have declined it, but Dr. Hartley strongly opposed such a thought, and designated it as one of the most absurd description; therefore, feeling the delicacy of her situation, and fearful that Dr. Hartley would think her foolishly obstinate and unreasonable to reject an offer which would render her more independent, she no longer raised any objection.

At length the moment arrived—the painful, the long dreaded moment of parting :—it wanted but about half an hour to the time at which the chaise would be waiting to convey

Mr. Wallingford and his son to the hall. We find ourselves inadequate to the task of describing this sorrowful scene as it ought to be, and will therefore drop a veil over it. The good doctor, however, endeavoured to soothe the violence of Maria's anguish, by observing, that in all probability they would yet see each other again, as it was his intention to return home in a few days to prepare for their journey to London, and most likely that Walter and his father would not by that time have quitted Wallingford Hall.

Maria returned to her chamber in a paroxysm of grief, and it was some time ere the gentle persuasions and soothing accents of Fanny could prevail upon her to rejoin Dr. Hartley down stairs again.

CHAPTER XLVIII.

" Let mercy plead, when the fierce law
    Hath done its worst;—carry not revenge
    Even to the dead;—mangle not my kindred's
        cold remains !"   ANON.

WHILE the good doctor was still engaged in endeavouring to administer consolation to poor Maria, there was a gentle tap at the room door, and the next moment Matthew, the faithful and long-tried servant of Mr. Hartley, presented himself, and who, to judge by his countenance, had not very pleasant news to impart.

"Now, Matthew, my good fellow," said his master, kindly, " what is it pray?"

"The confounded Gipsies again, sir," replied Matthew, shrugging up his shoulders.

Maria and Fanny turned very pale.

"The Gipsies!" repeated the doctor, starting from his chair, " how—where—what do you mean?"

"Why, sir," said Matthew, "there are two females of the tribe now at the door, and they desire to see you directly. I told them that you was engaged, but they wouldn't be satisfied with that answer, and said they must and would see you, and that if it was till to-morrow night, they'd wait for you. So with that, sir, they sat themselves down at the door, as if they were resolved to keep their promise in downright earnest; so I thought it was best to come to you, and let you know all about it."

While Matthew had been speaking, Fanny had evinced the most violent fear and agitation; her cheeks were ghastly pale, and she clung for support to Maria, while she eagerly awaited to hear what answer Doctor Hartley would make to the message.

"Request an interview with me," he observed;—"this is very strange, I cannot conceive what they can possibly wish to see me for. But, however, as they seem so obstinate over the matter, I suppose I had better get over the business at once, see what they want, and

despatch them again. Mary and Fanny, do not stir from here, my dears, until I come back."

" Surely, my dear sir," gasped forth Fanny, with evident alarm, " surely you are not going to run the risk of an interview with them ? For Heaven's sake, if you do, be upon your guard ; for you cannot form any idea of the cunning and subtlety of these people, and by what deep laid schemes of treachery they effect the objects they aim at. It is to revenge themselves upon me, I fear, that they have come hither, and asking for you is merely a plan to——"

" Nonsense ! my dear child, " interrupted the doctor, affecting to laugh at her fears, " do you entertain so poor an opinion of my sagacity as to imagine that it is not able to compete with that possessed by the same two Gipsy women ?—They will not outwit me, I am positive, let their cunning be ever so great. There, my dears, do not fear, stay where you are, and I will return to you in a few minutes."

With these words the doctor left the room, and Fanny, sinking into a chair, remained in a dreadful state of suspense and apprehension until Mr. Hartley came back, which was in a very short time.

" My dear girls," said he, " I have been requested to attend the humble pallet of a poor person who is supposed to be dying, and, of course, it would be cruel in the extreme of me, were I to refuse ; however, rest yourselves perfectly content during my absence. Matthew, and the man servant of the house, will remain with you, to guard you against any outrage that might be attempted upon you, but such an occurrence is highly improbable in the broad light of day, and in the vicinity of the justice hall, from whence a force could in a few seconds be obtained, sufficient to repel them."

" But, oh, my dear sir," said Fanny, " should this be only a stratagem to effect some object —what will become of you ?—How will you escape from their power— and——"

" There, there, quiet all your doubts and fears upon that point, my dear child," interrupted Doctor Hartley, "you may rest assured that I shall use all proper caution, and that I shall not be so fool-hardy as to venture into any place with them, where I think there is the least danger. The women told me that it is a public-house they wish me to go to, the sign of which I forget, but from what I can make out, Maria, it is the one in the same street where Mr. Wallingford lodged ; and by the description, the aged woman, who they say is——"

" Ah ! my suspicions are confirmed!" exclaimed Fanny, hastily, " it is the old prophetess, Jabella, they mean, and this is all a dark laid scheme, concocted by her, Morna, and Zelta, to entrap us. For the love of heaven! let me implore you not to venture near her, for who can withstand her serpent-like cunning? Jabella is the great grand-mother of Mark Darwin, and is urged to some deed of blood, for vengeance upon those who have been the means of bringing her kindred to so ignominious a fate;—her power no one can find limit for; she is sure to accomplish that which she sets her mind upon, and she can foresee——"

"'Psha! this is ridiculous—and I am sur-prised that a girl of your good sense should betray such superstitious weakness," interrupted the doctor: "what think you can be the extent of the power of this old crone? But it is useless wasting time, neither do I feel disposed to argue the point with you—the women are, no doubt, impatiently expecting me below, so I must begone. Mind, and do precisely as I have directed, and you need not be under the apprehension that I shall thrust my nose into danger myself."

Doctor Hartley having thus spoken, quitted the apartment, and Fanny turned to her companion, placed her head upon her shoulder and wept bitterly, thinking still that there was some terrible plot concocted by which the whole of them would fall victims to the insatiable vengeance of the Gipsies. Notwithstanding the doctor had affected to treat her belief in the supernatural power of Jabella with such derision and scorn, it had not the power to shake the credulity of Fanny, and even Maria was half inclined to listen seriously to the accounts which her companion was prepared to give her of the several miracles that Jabella had performed, and of the remarkable prognos-tications she had at different times given utter-ance to, and which she protested were almost invariably fulfilled.

What rendered Maria more ready to believe the stories that Fanny told her, was, that she herself had been an eye witness to her conduct in the room of the public-house, on the evening before the first trial, and the supernatural appearance which the old woman bore; in-dependent of which, had she not appeared to her, and other members of the Wallingford family, several times in a most mysterious manner, and had not her predictions always come true some time or the other, as they could too well prove from woful experience? As she recalled these facts to her memory, Maria could not help feeling a sensation of horror, and in spite of trying all her powers of reason, she could not divest her mind of the impression.

In the meantime, the good-hearted Doctor Hartley set forth with the two women who had called for him, to perform the Christian office for which they had stated his services were required. His conscience was clear of hav-ing wilfully done injury to any mortal being by word or deed, therefore did he feel not the slightest fear, although it must be admitted that he considered the errand he was going upon rather a hazardous one, considering the des-perate character of the persons he would have to deal with, and the animosity they bore to all those who had been in any way connected with the recent trials. But the story which had been told to him by the two women had won upon his humanity, and he did not hesitate a moment, after he had heard it, to accompany them.

"Old Zelta," they said, "who was the daughter of Jabella, had desired them to assure him that she had not forgotten the time when he kindly befriended her, and had saved her, not only from becoming an inmate of a gaol, but had also rescued her from the hands of the fellows by whom she was being so roughly treated, and by whom she would probably have lost her life. And she had also requested them to state to him that she had long entertained the highest respect for him, knowing, as she did, that he had ever been a good friend to the tribe, instead of hunting them like so many wild beasts. She had therefore been tempted to request him to attend the couch of the expiring Jabella, to receive a request which that ancient sybil had to make to him, as well as to endeavour to soften her passage to the grave. to which she was certain she was fast descending."

Doctor Hartley, who had no ambition to have his merits thus vaunted, was glad when they came to the conclusion of this harangue, and which referred to circumstances, which, had it not been for the connection which they had with the Wallingford family, would have been entirely blotted from his recollection. But the patience of the worthy doctor was to be again tried, for the woman who had been thus prolix in her communication, after a brief pause. thus resumed—

"What I have already told your honour, is not all that Zelta requested me to say. She bade me endeavour to bring to your recollec-tion the time when you made the present of the gold, to add to what she had already laid by her, as she told you, to provide a grave for herself, but which was, in reality, to place her mother, or any of her kindred, beneath the green sod. She desired me to tell you, that for that deed alone, you were entitled to, and had the gratitude of the whole tribe, and that she would not forget it, notwithstanding you assisted in bringing home a conviction to her kindred, which condemned them to die the death of dogs, but he said no more, they be-lieved, than such as truth prompted him. She therefore added, that now death had set his hand upon her aged mother, whose soul would have quitted its mortal tenement by the time Mark Darwin and his son were led to their ignominious fate, she wished to see him, that she might say something to him, which she would not say to any other person but him, and which he only had the power to assist her in, and then would the ancient woman calmly resign herself to the cold embrace of the grim destroyer."

The woman who had thus spoken paused for a brief interval, and then added—

"Thus have I done as I was bid; I have faithfully delivered the message of Zelta and Jabella to you, and tell me, then, if you will now hesitate to accompany us?"

"I am ready to attend you," replied the doctor, "but before I go, you must convince me that I shall be free from all danger in so doing. I am not speaking of my own personal safety, for that I feel is secure enough, but then, of course, you are not ignorant that I have others under my protection, who——"

"For the present they are secure," answered the woman, with a malicious scowl, "their fate is not yet decided on, at least their time has not yet come, if you allude to Ela and Fanny. Come, come, I see you doubt me," continued the woman, when she beheld the doctor pause, and look earnestly at her, "but you have no occasion, for may the sun set this evening upon my corpse, if I do not speak the truth."

Doctor Hartley did no longer doubt her, for the expression of the woman's countenance seemed to carry an assurance of her sincerity along with it—but still he was upon his guard, if they should attempt to deceive him.

He soon found that he had been right in his conjecture as to the house to which he was going, which he perceived was the public-house which had been the receptacle of the Gipsies during the recent trial, and where she had witnessed the remarkable doings that had so excited her wonder and consternation.

As the doctor approached the house, he observed that there were a number of swarthy-looking fellows gathered around the door, and no sooner was he seen advancing, accompanied by the women, than words and nods were passed from one to the other, until the information seemed to be conveyed into the house, and no sooner had Mr. Hartley and his companions arrived at the house, than several men and women issued forth, who appeared to scrutinize him with much curiosity and interest, and some of them even bowed to him approvingly as he passed. There was nothing, however, said, and the doctor feeling even more than ever assured by the manner in which he had been received, he followed the two females into the house, and up a dark staircase, until they had arrived at the door of the chamber in which the venerable invalid was lying.

When Doctor Hartley entered the room, he perceived four females, who looked at him

respectfully, and then retired, and he was left alone with the dying woman, and the females by whom he had been attended from his lodgings. Mr. Hartley fixed his eyes upon the humble pallet on which was stretched the squalid form of that ancient woman whose long pilgrimage was now fast drawing to a close. She moved not, but her thick heavy breathing alone indicated to him that she still lived. The woman advanced towards her, and having whispered something in her ear, Jabella moved her head and opened her eyes, which she immediately fixed upon the countenance of Doctor Hartley.

"Ah!" she hollowly observed, "you have complied with my request then;—oh, yes, I knew you would not refuse me—for you have more humanity than most of your pale-faced people. Orilla, I told you he would visit me. Pr'ythee lend me your hand to raise myself, and that I may impart what I wish without delay. My time in this world is short—is short."

The skeleton form of the old woman was raised in the bed by Orilla, and then she fixed her eyes upon the countenance of Mr. Hartley with unearthly fierceness of expression, which struck him with awe. The pangs of death had imparted a still more ghastly aspect to her corpse-like face, and it was difficult to recognize in her whole appearance anything human.

"Well, the hell-cat has triumphed at last," she said, "and to-morrow will witness the death of three of our race; to-morrow three of our ancient race will be destroyed, to satiate the vengeance of a fiend in the form of a woman, and to gratify the malice of a base man."

"What mean you by three of your race?" demanded the doctor, who was led almost unconsciously to make this inquiry, although it touched upon a theme he was determined to evade.

"Aye, three," repeated Jabella, "am I of no consequence? Are not those who are to forfeit their lives to the savage laws of your people, not my descendants? and think you old Jabella will survive their disgrace?"

As she thus spoke, her eyes glowed yet more fiercely.

"We must not, dare not question the will of the Almighty, my good woman," said Doctor Hartley, "yours has been a long life, and——"

"I know what you would say," interrupted Jabella, "you would tell me that I have lived too long—well, be it so; think as you like—it matters not to me—but aged as I am, I tell you that it is the brutal laws of your people that have murdered me—had it not been for the fate of my children's children, I should not yet have finished my earthly career—but now I know that my end is fast approaching, and that—but why should I talk to you in this manner? Why should I upbraid you, who have always been so ready to endeavour to ameliorate the sorrows and sufferings of the poor? I would ask you a favour—it is my dying request, and if you will but comply with it, the last few moments of my existence will be passed in peace."

"Tell me," said Doctor Hartley, "what is it you would ask of me?—If there is aught that I can serve you in, rest assured that——"

"I am given to understand," said the old woman, "that you have the means of obtaining what I require; but of your laws I am ignorant. The savage vengeance of what you call justice, I am told, is not to be appeased by dooming human beings to the death of dogs, but they attempt to glut it more upon the inanimate corpse. The principal wish which now inhabits my breast is, that the same spot of earth should enclose the remains of me and my children's children—and I have ample means, with the aid of my tribe, to purchase for myself and them a decent resting-place. Ah! there was a time, many years ago, when our people needed not the yellow gold to——"

"This, my good woman," interrupted the doctor, "is foreign to the subject, and is what I cannot enter upon."

"True—true," observed Jabella, "and I should not speak to you upon the subject, for what have you to do with the cruelty and oppression that have been heaped upon our race? I am convinced that you are too good for that, and therefore I will at once make known to you my petition. I was led to suppose, at first, that after my children had suffered death, their bodies would be hung in chains, for the birds of prey to banquet on, and had it been so, I should have been content, for well do I know that my people would never have rested until they had removed them; but now, by an alteration in your laws, it appears, instead of leaving the bodies of your victims to blanch and moulder in gibbets, they are consigned to the knife of the surgeon; tell me, am I rightly informed?"

"You are," replied Doctor Hartley, "the law now orders the bodies of murderers to be given up for dissection; and it is not at all probable that the culprits you speak of will be made an exception."

"Doubtless you are right," remarked Jabella, "for we have not the yellow lucre by which any favours may be obtained; if it was a man of wealth and estate, even if he had been convicted of a murder more monstrous than ever was heard of before, his friends would find very little difficulty in getting that part of the sentence remitted, and of burying him as they might think proper. Nay, it is useless your attempting to deny the truth of what I say, for I am positive that such would be the case. I

know that such has been done, and my earnest prayer is that it may once more be done, and I know that if you possess not the power, no other person that I know of, does."

"Upon my word, my good woman," said Mr. Hartley, "you give me credit for much more than I can perform; indeed I have no power—no influence."

"Nay, you speak not the truth," hastily returned the ancient woman, "I am certain that you have sufficient interest, and that if they were your own sons, you could without much difficulty, get the favour granted you, which I now entreat of you to obtain for mine."

The doctor felt confused and agitated at the resolute manner of the old woman, in these her dying moments, and scarcely knew in what way to reply.

"My good woman, you are now speaking extravagantly," at length he said; "were such the case, in all probability I might be able to get the favour granted you speak of, but as it is, I do not see the least chance of my succeeding if I were to make the application."

"Oh, tell me, will you only make the effort?" quickly interrogated the poor old woman, as she rose herself up in the bed with incredible strength, and gazed upon the face of the doctor with an intensity which seemed as if it would penetrate the inmost recesses of his soul; "oh, only make the application, and whether you succeed or fail, you shall receive the blessing of me and my people for ever."

The doctor reflected, that if he were to consent, the application would be sure to take him at least two or three hours, and Maria and Fanny would be dreadfully alarmed at his protracted absence, and would most likely be apprehensive that some harm had befallen him.

"But then," he muttered in a low tone, not sufficiently loud to catch the ear of Jabella or her companion, "I can easily call round at home, and inform them what I have been doing, and where I am going, and thus set their minds at rest."

While he was thus deliberating, the dying woman had never removed her eyes, with all their intensity of expression, from his countenance, and when he looked round, and observed her, he found it impossible longer to hesitate.

"Well, my good woman," he observed, "at any rate I will make the effort; although I cannot help thinking that I have very little chance of success; but now I wish to know exactly what you want me to ask."

"I will do so in a few words," said Jabella, "I pray the authorities to give up to my people the bodies of my ill-fated descendants, so that they may be buried with me on that spot which I have long since selected. There will be no disturbance; their cold remains will be placed in coffins, and with me will be conveyed away in as private a manner as possible."

"I certainly will make the application," mentalised the worthy doctor, as he departed from the house, "I certainly will make the application, and should I not succeed, it will be no fault of mine, and I shall only have sacrificed an hour or two in the cause of mercy. But if they should grant my request, it may be the means of securing to me the grateful feelings of the Gipsies, and may perhaps save Ela and her daughter from their vengeance, which I tremble to think will sometime or the other else overtake them."

The doctor went about his task with a determination to strain every nerve to accomplish it; but he had, notwithstanding, a very hard matter to succeed, although he was held in such high estimation by the gentlemen who were in the same profession as himself. Indeed the application was a most extraordinary one, coming as it did from the intimate friend of the Wallingford family, and they at first doubted whether he could really be in earnest. But at length he convinced them that he was indeed serious, and urged his request with such energy that they yielded; and delighted with his success, certain as he was, what pleasure, what consolation it would impart to the mind of the dying old woman, he hurried from the place, and soon once more arrived at the house at which the Gipsies were staying. He entered the chamber of death; all was silent as the grave to which the old woman was fast descending, but Orilla continued to watch by the side of her couch, who told him that during the time he had been away Jabella had never moved or uttered a syllable.

"I am apprehensive, then, that it is all over, and that my errand has been too long delayed, although I used all the expedition I could," said the doctor, who, as he fixed his eyes upon the withered and inanimate form of the old woman, really thought it impossible that she could still be in existence, when she had not received the least sustenance for so many hours. Evening had now come on, for he had been detained longer than he had even anticipated, and was anxious to return once more to Maria and Fanny. Several other persons had now entered the room, and appeared to eye the doctor with much curiosity and suspense.

But the doctor was soon convinced that the spark of life still lingered in the frame of the poor old woman, for no sooner did she hear him speak, than it awakened her from the deep lethargy into which she had fallen, and opening her eyes, she fixed them upon the face of Mr. Hartley with the deepest earnestness; a second afterwards, and a half murmured expression of joy escaped her, and she made a sign to Orilla and the other females, to come and assist her to rise; supporting herself upon her pillow, she exclaimed in a hasty tone—

"You have not failed—I see you have not?"

Mr. Hartley nodded his head affirmatively.

"Oh, I was certain you would not do so;" she went on to say, "I knew that you would exert yourself to the utmost to serve the poor dying old woman, and oh, may every blessing that life can afford, light upon your head for it. May no care or sorrow ever cross your path; may happiness ever be yours, and may your last moments be calm and painless, for this kind action. Admit them now, Orilla, admit them, for my moments are numbered, and I have something to say to them before I go. I would, before I die, show to them he who has this day stood so great a friend to our despised and oppressed people."

Orilla needed no second order, but opening the door gave admittance to a number of the Gipsy tribe, who flocked around the couch of the dying woman, and listened with breathless attention and suspense to the words she gave utterance to, and that they might receive the last injunctions of the ancient sybil of their tribe.

When the doctor perceived these persons enter, and understood for what purpose Jabella had summoned them, he began to hope that he should be able to elicit from them a promise that they would not harm Ela or her daughter; for the old woman was bound in gratitude to make some return for what he had done, and he was certain that whatever she enjoined them to do, especially at such a time, they would strictly obey. But when he gazed round upon the grim and repulsive faces of many of them, his hopes were somewhat damped, and he hesitated to broach the important subject. At length, however, conquering his doubts, he was about to speak, when Jabella began to address them in that slang which was quite unintelligible to him, and her impressive manner seemed to have a due effect upon her auditors, for they ever and anon turned upon him looks of the utmost kindness, which convinced him that the service he had recently rendered Jabella formed the subject of her observations to them; and at the end of her address they gave open demonstrations of their gratitude towards him by various expressions of thanks.

Old Zelta, who had seated herself by the side of her dying mother, seemed to be particularly interested in what she said, and when she had concluded, she turned towards Doctor Hartley, and said, in tones that bespoke her sincerity—

"For this, the blessing of the branded race descend upon thee and thine;—no matter in what clime—no matter the spot; be it night or day, storm or calm, the Gipsy tribe must hasten to assist you, should you stand in need of their aid; they are bound to protect you, at the hazard of their own lives, from all danger; and when death shall close your eyelids, deeply will our people have cause to regret your loss —the loss of that real friend, who was prompted by no feelings of interest in the act of kindness he rendered them."

"Now was the time to make an impression," thought Mr. Hartley; so turning to Zelta, he said aloud—"You really give me credit for more disinterestedness than I can lay claim to, which you will probably say, when you hear the obligation I am about to ask at your hands; the obligation will be great, and cost you nothing, but the resolution to do away with wrong senti-

THE GIBBET SEEN BY FANNY BERANZIO.

ments of malice and revenge, which cannot effect you any good, and would be the means of bringing much misery upon him you are pleased to recognise as your friend. Grant me the favour I shall ask of you, and I shall ever consider myself your debtor, instead of you being under any obligation to me, for what I have done, or all that I can ever accomplish to aid your people."

The doctor ceased to speak, and he glanced earnestly and with eagerness around upon those present, and he could tell in a moment from their gloomy looks and lowering brows, that they read what was passing in his thoughts, and what he was about to request of them. They exchanged glances with one another, and some of them divided themselves into groups, and seemed to be conversing together upon the subject, although what they said, being spoken in the language peculiar to the tribe, could not be understood by Doctor Hartley; he could perceive, however, that a great change had come over their countenances, and they glanced towards him with all their usual malice and ferocity, so that the hopes he had first begun to indulge in, were quickly crushed.

Disappointed, and uneasy at this result, he removed his eyes from the persons assembled in the room, and fixed them once more on the countenance of old Jabella, but in that he saw only one denial to his wishes. He could not, however, but remark that she seemed to be most violently combating with her feelings, sensible, as she no doubt was of the debt of gratitude she owed to Mr. Hartley, and the spirit of vengeance, which even then, when she was on the verge of eternity, burned in her bosom against Ela. She did not raise her eyes, but seemed to be completely absorbed in agonizing thought.

At last, however, when Mr. Hartley found that none of the other persons seemed inclined to reply to his observations, he determined to push his request to Jabella, which he did in the following urgent manner,—" Jabella, you stand upon the margin of the grave; a few minutes more and you will be numbered with the dead, and you will have to stand in the presence of your Almighty Judge, who will deal with you according to the actions you have performed in this world. To you, then, do I earnestly appeal; nay turn not away, for if you are not the means of extending mercy to others, how can you expect mercy from Heaven? I know the power you possess over your tribe is almost supreme," he added, in a tone of voice which could reach her ear alone, " I therefore beg of you to endeavour to persuade them to swear to you that they will forget their malevolent and revengeful feelings against Ela and Fanny, and suffer them in future to go in safety."

" You could not ask me a single thing it is in my power to consent to, which I would not grant," replied Jabella, looking at him with a bewildered expression;—" I should be ungrateful to refuse you, after the inestimable service you have rendered me, but you now request that in which my influence is of no avail. Ela has broken the laws of our tribe, and those laws sentence her to death; over them I have no control, I could no more save her, than I could rescue my own kindred from the fate which awaits them, and yet greater, far greater have been her crimes than those for which they are

unjustly deemed to suffer a violent death. I see that you are inclined to treat what I say with contempt, but I tell you that we have laws more powerful than those of your people, and which no one yet disobeyed and lived. By those laws has Ela been doomed, and nothing can save her from the fate to which she is condemned."

" Impossible !" exclaimed Doctor Hartley, with emotions of the utmost terror, " they cannot be so dead to all sentiments of mercy."

" What mercy does your people show to the branded race ? Hang them up like dogs !" said Jabella fiercely.

The doctor could not help feeling the deepest horror at hearing such words escape from the lips of a woman who was just upon the margin of another world, and he turned his head away for a moment in disgust.

" Well, but Fanny," he observed, after a pause, " inexorable as they may be, they certainly will not——"

" I would warn her to avoid our tribe, while the recollection of the misery she has brought upon us is most vivid," returned Jabella, whose voice was gradually getting weaker ;—" time often effects wonders, and there is no knowing what it may do in her case,—she has youth and all—But I need not explain to you—" and she spoke in tones scarcely audible, apparently fearful that those who were around her would consider that she was giving him too much reason to hope for the safety of Fanny, " I need not explain to you, but you must be aware from what I have already said, that it is only by her not crossing the path of those whom she has so deeply injured, that even she can hope to escape the fate which her treachery so richly merits, at any rate, until time has worn away some portion of the hatred and vengeance she has excited. Deeply at this moment do I regret that such is the fact, and that it is out of my power to aid you; believe me, if I could, most willingly would I do it. Were Fanny your girl or nearly related to you, I might have it in my power, or were you even to take her under your protection, and adopt her for your daughter, I firmly believe that I could persuade the tribe to give you the required promise, but as——"

" Nay then," interrupted the worthy doctor, joyfully, " you have the opportunity of gratifying your inclination, if such is the nature of it, for know that Fanny Beranzie is now my adopted daughter, and has no other protector but me, for Ela has left for a foreign country, and is no doubt by this time a considerable way on her journey."

Upon the mention of this, the rage and disappointment of most of the persons in the room was clearly discernible, and curses and execrations against Ela were freely bandied from one to the other. Then a dead pause of a second or two followed, after which they appeared to be holding a deep and earnest consultation wi h one another, which they carried on in their own language, and in which those persons who possessed more influence than the rest of the tribe seemed to take a most active part, and in which Jabella appeared to exert herself with astonishing energy.

Doctor Hartley watched them with considerable anxiety and suspense, and endeavoured to read by the expression of their countenances what would probably be the issue of the conference. At last Jabella turned her eyes once more upon the doctor, and thus addressed him—

"I have prevailed upon them to promise that they will not interfere with Fanny, while she continues to be protected by you, or is parted from Ela. This is much more than I ever expected they would do, for Fanny has not only betrayed us, and acted with base ingratitude, but she has also disregarded our oath, which is the most solemn offence of all. Does this satisfy you?"

"Then all hopes of Ela——" commenced Doctor Hartley, but he was not suffered to proceed, for no sooner did he mention her name than several of the Gipsies became outrageous in her exclamations, and he began to fear that he had excited them too much, for to his no little consternation, they uttered a variety of threats, which he could not at the time exactly understand whether they were meant for himself or Ela; and one of the men, a tall, powerful, dark-looking ruffian, leaped forward towards where he was standing, and flourishing a long knife in his hand, with demoniacal gestures exclaimed—

"This shall be buried in Ela's heart whenever Rupert and her again meet, though he suffer all the tortures that your pale-faced people can inflict for it the next moment; by his kindred who lives, and those she has basely sacrificed, he swears it, and never did he break his oath. Bitter cause have we to heap curses upon that moment which introduced the tigress to us, for she immediately caused discord and trouble amongst us. Did she not make a madman of me by her haughty scorn, and by the contempt and insult which she heaped upon my father? How often has she nearly occasioned murder amongst us, and did she not at last drive me from my kindred, to another part of the country, and a strange encampment? Was she not always taunting and upbraiding us, and prognosticating destruction to the tribe? Had it not been for her, we should have probably never beheld the wretch Milford, by whom my youngest brother was led to ruin, and is now a manacled slave? And did not yon dying aged woman often predict that she would bring ruin upon us; a

prediction which all the misfortunes that have since fallen upon us, sufficiently prove she was correct in?"

"Yes," observed Jabella, "and how frequently did I caution our people against the poisonous adder they were cherishing, and intreat them to cast it from them? But no, they were obstinate; they disregarded the words of her who was never yet known to be wrong in her prognostications; some foul spell must have been upon them; they suffered her still to remain in our tents, and this has been the way in which she has repaid us; sorrow, disgrace, and death have accompanied her."

"By Eblus, nothing can satiate the vengeance her treachery has engendered; not all the blood in her veins can wash out her guilt!" ferociously exclaimed Rupert; "can her single life repay the destruction she has caused? My constant prayer is that I may have the means of gratifying my revenge, at the very moment when she believes herself in security. I have been told that she has become the possessor of great wealth. I hope the report is true, for then will my vengeance be more complete, and her death more poignant, since she has the ample means of enjoying life in all its sweetness."

"Methinks, young man," remarked Doctor Hartley; "methinks you make use of rather bold words, thus openly to avow your determination to become an assassin; you cannot be ignorant, I should imagine, that for these expressions you could be sent to prison, and detained in safe custody until you found security for your good behaviour."

"And what if I were?" cried Rupert, scornfully, "think you that that would save the life of Ela? No—there are a hundred or more who are sworn to sacrifice her life, and nothing can protect her from it. She may try to elude us if she pleases, but I only wish to caution you."

"I will hear no more of this," ejaculated the doctor, as he made his way towards the room door, but should anything happen to Ela, the threats you have this night uttered will——"

"It was but a few minutes since that you said Ela had left England for a foreign land," interrupted one of the Gipsies, who had been a silent but apparently deeply interested observer of all that had taken place, "if that be true, the best advice you can send her, is to continue there, and then she will be out of the threatened danger."

"Psha! are you mad, Morna?" cried the ruffian, fiercely, "do you not know that there is no land in the world that can shelter Ela from our revenge?—Bah!—What care I for your cautious looks, Morna? I am not afraid to speak boldly out what I mean—she is cendemned, and nothing shall save her from a painful death."

It was no easy matter for the doctor to make his way to the door, through the crowd of persons who thronged the room, and who being now excited by the words of the ruffian Rupert, eyed him with looks that tended in no small degree to excite his alarm; but before he could leave the room, the woman who had been his conductor to the house, begged of him to return, as Jabella wished to speak with him before he went. Doctor Hartley accordingly returned, and the people fell back at a motion from Orilla, and made a clear passage for him to approach the bed.

"Do not leave me in wrath," said the old woman, "do not leave me in wrath;—but—but pr'ythee mark what I say;" and with a violent effort of strength, she raised herself so that her feeble voice might reach his ear, and then added, "mark my words—Ela is not doomed to become the victim of Rupert's vengeance—she will escape—if she shuns——"

She sunk back on the bed, and strove, but in vain, to finish the sentence which the doctor was listening for with the most anxious attention, notwithstanding his scepticism, as regarded superstition and witchcraft. Again and again did her black and skinny lips separate, and she tried to give utterance to the warning she had commenced: but nature was exhausted;—the veil of death was descending upon her; her eyes became glazed; and the doctor turned away with a feeling of horror, as the moans of the persons around convinced him that the old woman's last mortal struggles were over.

CHAPTER XLIX.

"Girl! think not to escape,
No power, nor time, nor fate, nor space,
Can crush the spirit of our revenge.
E'en wert thou buried in the earth's deep bowels,
Vengeance, vengeance should be ours!
'Tis that alone for which we wish to live,
That gratified, we do not fear to die!"
OLD PLAY

THE scene we have just described in the preceding chapter made a powerful impression upon Doctor Hartley, and the ferocious threats and implacable hatred of the villain Rupert filled him with much uneasiness and apprehension. Notwithstanding the promise which had been exacted from him by Jabella in her dying moments, with such violent passions as Rupert possessed, what might he not be induced to perpetrate? seemingly alike reckless of everything, he might treat the injunctions of Jabella with contempt, and think only of the gratification of his insatiable cruelty.

Of one thing he felt convinced, that, as the Gipsies still continued in the town, and com-

pletely surrounded them, it was not safe for them to remain there, consequently he quickly came to a determination that he would leave there on the following day, and immediately went to give the necessary orders for their departure.

Upon his entering the sitting-room to apprize Maria and Fanny of his intention, he beheld them both in a melancholy attitude; Maria wrapt in deep meditation, while tears trembled in her eyes, and Fanny was gazing upon, and kissing alternately, some bauble which had been given to her by her mother. They were both so absorbed in reflection, that they did not notice Mr. Hartley's entrance until he spoke.

"What, sad and sombre as usual, children?" said he: "how silly you both are. I shall positively be vexed with you if you persist in giving way to this weakness. But I have come to a determination that will perhaps afford you some satisfaction; to-morrow morning we leave this place, and return to my house until I have made the necessary arrangements for our trip to London."

"Then I shall again behold Rosemary Dell," ejaculated Maria, in a tone of delight.

"And I shall once more see my—my father, and Walter," exclaimed Fanny with equal earnestness. Maria blushed deeply, and hid her face while she awaited anxiously the good doctor's answer.

"Why," said he, "I cannot, of course, answer for that, although I do not think it probable that Mr. Wallingford will be able to leave the Hall so soon as he at first had thought of, as he was very much indisposed after the trial, and the fatigue attendant upon his journey home would unquestionably incapacitate him for travelling. Mr. Wallingford has become so fickle minded of late," continued the doctor, "that it is not at all impossible he may relinquish his idea of going to Switzerland, and indeed his mind is so changeable that I do not consider there is the slightest dependence to be placed upon him."

A ray of hope and joy beamed upon the bosom of Maria, but it was transitory, for what indeed had she to hope, from one who had coolly and deliberately discarded her, and who would doubtless take especial care that her and her cousin should never meet again? Emotion the most powerful took possession of her breast as this thought occurred to her, and it was augmented to an almost insupportable degree, when she recollected the dreadful fate that Mark Darwin and his son were destined to meet with on the following day, and to which she had in some measure been instrumental in bringing them. She shuddered, and was almost overwhelmed with the sickening sensations these reflections occasioned her.

Fanny felt little less emotion than Maria, but still could not but feel confident that they fully merited the punishment they were going to receive, and when she recollected the many persecutions and annoyances to which her mother and herself had been subjected by them, she could not help feeling a sentiment of gratification at the certainty that they would thus be released from all fear of them.

Doctor Hartley, perceiving the deep melancholy which was creeping over them, made a powerful effort to arouse them from it, and tried all his skill at joking, but in vain, and the afternoon passed off with even more sadness than the morning had done. Immediately after supper, the good doctor, finding that all his endeavours to make them cheerful were ineffectual, desired them to retire to their chamber as he said it was his intention to commence their journey at an early hour, before the concourse of people which might be expected on the occasion of the tragic scene, which was about to be enacted, had begun to assemble, and he trusted that there would not be anything take place to prevent his putting his intentions into execution.

The night passed gloomily away, and almost as soon as daylight had dawned, Maria and Fanny had descended to the breakfast-room, and eagerly awaited the appearance of Doctor Hartley; but they were doomed to be disappointed, for shortly after they had left their chamber, Matthew, the old coachman of Mr. Hartley, came to them with a most sombre-looking aspect, and informed them that his master felt so much indisposed that he could not leave his bed, but that he hoped by the afternoon he should be able to undertake the journey.

"I'll tell you what it is, miss," continued old Matthew, "and I knows it well, too, that master is shortening his days as fast as he can by all this bustle and exertion, to which he has been so unused. I am sure that he will kill himself; and how can he expect to do otherwise, when he goes out of his regular steady course—bothering this way and that way—and what is it all for?—why, all to look after business that don't concern him, and what it's a chance if he gets any thanks for taking such an interest in. I declare I never saw any one so dreadfully worn out with fatigue as he was last night when he went up stairs to his chamber, and he acknowledged to me that he has, for the last few days, undergone more exertion and harassing than he has done before for the last twelve years, and I should very much like to know what it is for, after all."

Maria could scarcely resist a smile, at the consequence old Matthew assumed in his tone and manner.

"It is to be regretted, Matthew," said she, "that your master should suffer for doing that which his humanity and benevolence prompt him to; but when we have got over our journey to London, we shall, no doubt, not be exposed to this disquietude, and then he will not be compelled to break through the steady and regular habits he has been accustomed to."

"Ah, you may think so, miss," said Matthew, "but for my part, I am not quite so certain as to that matter; and you must recollect that master is not a young man, and that it is not altogether safe for a person of his years to tamper with his constitution, however strong it may be. To talk about being quiet in such a wild place as London is ridiculous, and more particularly when he has got a couple of giddy young girls tied to him, and to endeavour to keep in good temper."

Matthew made use of these words as he quitted the room, and he continued to mutter as he descended the stairs—

"Well, let him take his fling; it's no use my saying nothing, I can't prevent it. I have no objection to his doing what he did last night, namely, call in the assistance of another man to take some of the labour off my shoulders, for at my time of life that is no unpleasant thing, but as sure as I live, this London business will be the death of him. Ah! the foolish old gentleman! It's not pleasant for an old man like me to be as a servant to two children, as these girls are. Miss Herbert, I do not so much care about, because she has some claims to having been lady-bred, and all that, but as for that daughter of the infamous Gipsy woman, who has caused so much mischief, notwithstanding she is remarkably good-looking and full of fun and good temper, when she is in the right mood, it does not suit my palate to be at her beck and call. And then, although, as I have said before, she is very pretty, nay, I may say handsome, she often reminds me of her mother, for she can put on that haughty tyrannical look, and then her eyes too, are enough to pierce any person through. Well, after all, I cannot look upon either of them, although Ela is now said to be the mistress of great riches, as anything else than vagabonds."

With this amiable opinion of the Gipsy girl, old Mathew grumbled his way into the kitchen, where he endeavoured to drown his spleen in a jug of excellent ale, and he succeeded tolerably well.

Although the opinion of old Matthew was ungenerous and erroneous in many respects, it must be admitted there is some truth in it, for instance, there were times when an innate feeling of pride would break through Fanny's usual gentleness of demeanour, and there was an expression in her tone and manners which seemed to convey an impression to the minds of the beholders, that she considered herself superior to every one else. But this was to be attributed more to the life which she had led from childhood, and for the want of another example than that which her mother had set her.

Maria was not blind to this defect, but she thought if Fanny mingled in the busy and varied scenes of life, it would soon be obliterated, and she would shine forth in all the perfection which can be seen in the female, and to which the failing we have mentioned formed the only blemish. Doctor Hartley, however, had a very different opinion, and he entertained a keen sense of all the disadvantages, in spite of her many charms, under which Fanny would appear in the world, and he therefore took especial care to impress upon her mind the drawback which her past life would be to her, and urged her most earnestly to exert herself to the very utmost to rise superior to this disadvantage, and he invariably checked her when she assumed the haughty demeanour to which I have alluded ; and when, as she often did get into conversation about her former companions, and reverted to the scenes in which she had mingled with them, he always addressed her in a tone which was calculated to make her look back upon her early days with feelings of disgust and horror.

" Nonsense, Fanny," he would observe, why will you persist in even bestowing a thought upon a set of rascals and vagabond wretches, whom it is your greatest misfortune to have known and associated with ; I say you must endeavour to banish them from your recollection, instead of speaking of them as you do, and seeming to look upon them as an injured race, and the children of liberty, whom no laws have a right or power to confine."

" This generally had the effect which the worthy doctor had desired it should, although the expressive eyes of the damsel frequently seemed to denote a dissentient opinion. There were times too, when Fanny experienced very different feelings, and she appeared to lose all her pride and dignity, in an opinion of her having been degraded by the set of wanderers and vagrants, among whom she had been brought up ; and took the remarks of Doctor Hartley, however well they were intended, sadly to heart, as may be seen from the observations she upon one particular occasion addressed to Maria.

" Oh, Maria," she said, " how can you disgrace yourself by becoming the friend, the companion, of the vagrant Gipsy girl—one of those despised beings who are a pest to society, and who are abandoned to every nefarious act ? Yes, it was so he designated them."

" Fanny, dear Fanny," said Maria with astonishment, " what strange idea has gained possession of your brain now ? Who would venture to call you by such opprobrious epithets ?"

" Who—why did you not hear the words which Doctor Hartley made use of ?" inquired

Fanny with a blushing cheek, and eyes sparkling with a momentary feeling of indignation ; " did you not notice the contempt in which he evidently holds me, or else why say that there was no difference among any of the Gipsy tribe—that they must all be base and vicious, and that nothing but evil can spring from such a source of contamination ? Oh, Maria, did this not include me ?—Yes, he made no exceptions, and therefore——"

" Hush, Fanny ; I must not, will not suffer you to do the kind doctor such a palpable injustice," said Maria, " he did not class you with the rest, for he was well aware that the greatest care was bestowed upon you by your mother, and that, although you were compelled to mingle in the same wandering life, you had never been guilty of any of those criminal practices of which the others might be accused. You ought to know that the esteem in which he views your mother——"

" An esteem no more than she deserves," interrupted Fanny energetically, at the same time that tears filled her eyes, and her bosom throbbed with anguish ; " oh, what praises could any one bestow upon her which she does not merit ? My mother, my beloved mother, to you alone am I indebted for everything ; you only know the heart of your poor girl."

Maria did not attempt to interrupt the vehemence of Fanny's grief, for she knew that when it had subsided, she would see the injustice with which she had spoken of Doctor Hartley, and benefit by the reflections it would give rise to.

The circumstance of Doctor Hartley's indisposition caused Maria much regret, not only on account of the doctor himself, but for the delay it caused in their journey. Every moment they now stayed in the town became more painful to her and Fanny, and they had hoped to have been away from it before the enactment of the awful drama which was that morning to take place. As the noise of the crowd passing through the town to the place of execution vibrated on their ears, mingled with the shouts and rude observations of the ignorant beings who could find enjoyment in such a revolting spectacle as the violent death of two wretched fellow creatures, their hearts sunk with horror, and a sickening sensation came over them, which they struggled, but in vain, to vanquish. They sat together in gloomy silence, and only by looks evinced the mutual pain they were suffering.

The increased noise in the street, and the hurried manner in which they could hear that the crowd pressed along, convinced them that the fatal hour for the termination of the murderers' career was fast approaching, and it would be no easy task to attempt to depicture the real state of their minds as this idea occurred to them. An unusual noise in the street urged them to approach the window, and the novel scene completely rivetted them to the spot. Every town and village for miles around seemed to have been deserted, and all to have centered in the dense mass that moved forward to the place where the gallows was erected, and any person unacquainted with the fact, would have imagined that it was some particular fair day, instead of one devoted to such a dreadful and revolting circumstance.

Suddenly, Fanny uttered a faint scream, and grasping hold of Maria's arm, with pale cheeks and distended eyelids, directed her attention to some object in the street. Maria gazed whither she pointed, and standing on the step of a door opposite to them, stood the tall and masculine form of a Gipsy woman, who with her arms folded seemed to have fixed her eyes steadfastly upon the window at which they were standing.

"'Tis Morna," said Fanny, in a voice of horror, as Maria led her away from the window and hastily drew the blinds, "it is Morna, I knew the expression of her evil eye in a minute; oh, Maria, depend upon it the vengeance of the Gipsies will pursue us to destruction for the part we have taken in this affair."

Maria tried to calm her fears, but in reality she as much needed consolation as her companion, and she could not think of their journey from the town now, without the greatest apprehensions for what might befall them on the road. They hurried from the room, and entering their chamber, tried to beguile the time by reading until the appearance of Doctor Hartley should announce to them that the vehicle had arrived which was to convey them from town. But they were doomed to be still further vexed and disappointed; the doctor certainly did contrive to leave his bed at dinner time, but he felt himself still too much indisposed to venture to travel, so their departure was thus unavoidably postponed until the following morning.

It was in the course of that afternoon that Doctor Hartley had made use of those observations we have before mentioned, and by which he had unconsciously so wounded the pride of Fanny; but the good doctor, never intending that his words should have the effect they had upon her sensitive mind, never noticed any change in her manner, and he therefore endeavoured to enliven them in his usual jocular manner, and entered into an animated picture of the busy metropolis to which they were shortly going, and the pleasures and recreations in which they should of course mingle.

"You talk, sir," suddenly observed Fanny, "as if I were going to participate in those pleasures and recreations of which you speak, but I trust that my mother will shortly take the burthen off your——"

She could not proceed, for the keen and penetrating eye of Doctor Hartley was fixed earnestly upon her, and shrinking abashed at what she had given utterance to, she could no longer repress her emotion, but wept and sobbed on the shoulder of Maria.

"Tut, tut, tut!" said the doctor, in his gentlest tones; "silly girl, what is the cause of this strange weakness?" He paused a moment and looked kindly in her face, then added —"Certainly, my poor child, I do not wonder that you should feel a painful anxiety to behold your mother once more, and it is my fervent wish that circumstance will ere long take place; but, in the meantime, I can assure you, that it would sincerely grieve me if I was aware that you looked upon yourself as an intruder upon me; nay, so far from that, I can only say that I am delighted that you and Maria are together, for were not such the case, I am fearful that her and me would pass rather a melancholy time of it together. Come, come, child, let me see no more of this, I pray."

"Ay, dear Fanny," observed Maria, with gentle persuasiveness, and fixing upon her a look, the meaning of which she could not but comprehend. "I am sure you cannot help observing that you formed a very ungenerous opinion of the motives of our kind friend."

Fanny made no reply, but her looks, and the abashed manner in which she turned away, expressed much more than words could have done, and the vexation which she had by her petulant conduct created in Maria's bosom, was soon dissipated. The temporary clouds that had obscured their peace had now passed over, and Fanny's sweetness of behaviour soon convinced Maria that she had banished from her mind all recollection of the thoughts that had occasioned it.

The day passed heavily away, and by daylight the following morning the chaise was at the door, and as the doctor felt himself considerably better, they commenced their journey.

The morning was lowering and cheerless; dark and heavy clouds obscured the horizon, and they had not proceeded far, when a violent storm came on: Heaven's artillery ever and anon seemed to shake the earth to its foundation: the lightning darted along the sky, and it rained a perfect deluge. They were on an extensive common, where there was not a tree or a shrub, nor the sign of a human habitation for miles, so that they were compelled to proceed. This increased the deep melancholy which hung upon the travellers' spirits, and they were too sad to enter into conversation even. But the storm at length abated, and at last entirely subsided; the murky clouds no longer obscured the sky, and the sun bursting forth in golden majesty, gave omen of a lovely day.

"Ah! we shall have a glorious day after the storm," at length said the doctor, for the first time breaking the silence, "and so let us hope it will be with us, my girls, and that a glorious sunshine may succeed the storms of adversity we have all had to encounter. If I am not mistaken, there are a number of persons just ahead of us, but my eyesight does not improve with age; look out, Maria, and tell me whether or no I am right in my conjecture."

Maria did as Dr. Hartley desired her, and it was soon evident that her astonishment and alarm were not a little excited, for she continued to look in the direction which the doctor had pointed out with great earnestness, and gave utterance to nothing but a few disjointed sentences, that were quite incomprehensible to the doctor and Fanny.

"Come, my dear, do you see anything?" demanded the doctor at length, tired of waiting.

"Yes, sir," replied Maria, "I do perceive a number of persons who are walking on at a slow pace exactly in the road we are pursuing; they are yet too far off for me to determine—but—ah, I am positive now; it is—it is the Gipsies, sir, for there is the same cart in which I saw them convey old Jabella into the town we have just left."

With these words, Maria, whose countenance bespoke her terror, drew in her head with much haste, and Fanny, overcome with consternation at the idea of the Gipsies being so near at hand, uttered a shriek, and trembling all over, drew herself into the most obscure part of the vehicle. Dr. Hartley was so surprised, that for a moment or two he lost his self-possession, and did not say a word.

Before any of them could recover themselves the chaise stopped, and Matthew who had been behind, descended, and approaching the window, with alarm depicted in his countenance, said—

"Oh, sir, we are in a very nice hobble, and I only wish we may get out of it, that's all; there's them confounded Gipsies, the whole gang of 'em, I'm certain, just ahead of us, and if they don't insult us, we may think ourselves lucky."

"Nonsense, Matthew," said his master, petulantly, "why, you are worse than an old woman; what if the Gipsies are there, has that anything to do with us?—As for insulting us, that is a most ridiculous idea, for do you think they have no more to do than to create broils where they are uncalled for? At any rate, I see no cause for fear, so desire the postboys to keep on, though not so fast as they were going before, and not to notice them. It is rather unfortunate that this has taken place," he continued, addressing himself to Maria and Fanny, "but notwithstanding, I do not think we have any cause for fear; they are, I dare say, on their road to some distant place or the other, and will doubtless not observe us."

"Oh, no, no," ejaculated Fanny, in a tone of the greatest terror, "that is not it, too well I know it is not ;—they are carrying their dead to its final resting place, and if they should recognise me, my life would be certain to be sacrificed."

"Nay, my dear child," said Mr. Hartley, "indeed you have no cause for such serious alarm; they will not attempt to annoy or obstruct us, for it was Jabella's dying injunctions to them, and they all promised solemnly to obey her, that they would not harm you while you continued under my protection."

"Ah !" gasped forth Fanny eagerly, "did they indeed promise that ?".

"They did."

"Then I am safe," said Fanny, "they will not venture to break their word to her, however great their wrath may be towards me. But see, they have stopped, and seem to be waiting for us to get up to them. I fear now that if they see me they will insult me, if even they do not attempt to commit any outrage upon me. There is no knowing what the savage nature of the ruffian Rupert may urge them on to, and of course, he is with them."

"I cannot conceive," said the doctor, "what the grand jury could have been about to have ignored the bill against that fellow; for I cannot help thinking that he as richly merited being arraigned at the bar as an accessory to the murder, as the younger Darwin. He is a desperate villain."

"Oh, he is, indeed," said Fanny, with a shudder, "and I cannot even look at him without horror. Severe and many have been the insults and persecutions to which my mother and myself have been subjected by him, and much do I fear that some time or the other he will succeed in accomplishing his vengeance."

"But I tell you again," observed the doctor, "that Jabella exacted an oath from them in her dying moments not to harm you; of course you can best tell whether they deserve to be relied on."

"Yes, yes, I repeat it, if they really did promise old Jabella, I am secure from danger," cried Fanny.

"You cannot suppose, my dear girl," observed Doctor Hartley, "that I would tell you that which was not true, especially in such a case as this; and so confident do I feel that they will keep their word, that I am resolved to proceed; I know there is nothing to apprehend, more especially in such a solemn moment as this, when their minds are occupied with the solemn business they are going on, that is, if they have with them the cold remains of their former companions, and those of her in whose power they placed such confidence."

"You are right, my dear sir," said Fanny, making a desperate effort to vanquish her terrors, "I have no occasion to fear them: they will not break their word."

Notwithstanding Fanny expressed this opinion, she found it perfectly impossible to regain her composure, and she could scarcely support herself, she trembled so violently.

"How foolish I am," she added, after a pause; "there cannot be any fear, for well do I know that not one of them, however desperate, would venture to disobey the mandates of Jabella; but never did I imagine that to her I should be indebted for my security; her, who was one of the most inveterate and implacable enemies that me and my mother ever had."

FANNY ATTACKED BY THE GIPSY "MORNA."

"It was the last thing she did in this world," said Mr. Hartley, "she did it at my request, and in return for the services I had rendered to her and the rest of the tribe, and the oath she made them take to obey her injunctions was administered in the most serious manner."

"Then I have nothing to fear; I am certain I have not," said Fanny, regaining her former equanimity; "but still it is my opinion that, to prevent all chance of any thing unpleasant taking place, and in order that neither you nor Miss Herbert may suffer through m o, that I should endeavour to conceal myself."

To this Mr. Hartley yielded, and the poor girl crouched down in one corner of the carriage, and being covered by the doctor's mantle, and the skirts of Maria's cloak, she was completely hidden from observation. Her shawl and bonnet were also concealed, and they thought there was not the least danger of her being seen by any one.

A short time elapsed only, before they arrived at the place where the Gipsies were standing, and seemingly in consultation with one another, for they frequently pointed towards the vehicle, and Maria trembled with apprehension, notwithstanding Fanny had expressed her belief, after all, that there was no danger, when she beheld them using the most menacing gestures and indications towards them. She also observed, before they had got quite up to them, that there was another cart with them, which seemed to be of a stronger description than the one she at first noticed. But fearful that the Gipsies might perceive her watching them, she once more drew her head in hastily, and trembled violently, but no longer was she permitted to indulge in these speculations, for very soon after her attention was wholly occupied by subjects of more immediate importance, and she removed her eyes from the vehicles, which, doubtless, were appropriated to the removal of the bodies of Mark Darvell, his son, and old Jabella, when she saw the fierce and eager glances of several of the tribe scrutinizing her with an expression of mingled astonishment and detestation, and in spite of the assurances of Mr. Hartley, that they had nothing to apprehend, she was unable to struggle against her terrors, as she recalled to her memory the many dreadful events that had happened through their guilty machinations, and when she remembered that they were even now surrounded by those wretched people, from whom they had experienced so much misery.

Having arrived at the place where the solemn cavalcade was pausing, the coachman endeavoured to drive past them, but could not succeed, for the road was not wide enough. The Gipsies, however, having apparently only been doing something to one of the vehicles, and not having, as it seemed, seen Doctor Hartley yet resumed their journey at a slow and measured pace, and the post boys who drove the chaise were compelled to follow them behind, at the same miserable rate, very much to the annoyance of them all, but more especially to Matthew, whose looks expressed anything but pleasure at their proximity to the gang.

Doctor Hartley did not alter his position in the carriage, and although he did not, of course, court observation, he sat perfectly composed, being in no fear of what might take place, but at the same time on his guard in case the conduct of the Gipsies should call for the exertions of his energy and determination.

They proceeded for a short distance further, and no one seemed inclined to interrupt their slow and tedious course, and when she saw this, Maria gradually felt her courage reviving, and she proceeded to take a more minute observation of the Gipsy tribe.

She could not help noticing, however, more particularly the behaviour of one of the men, who kept away from the other party, and walked on slowly, and in sullen silence. Ever and anon, his eyes, which were otherwise bent upon the earth, were fixed with an earnest gesture on the cart, which Maria perceived was considerably larger than the other, and when she could catch a glimpse of his dark countenance, she shuddered at the expression of vengeance which characterized it.

Under any other circumstances, and if she had been in ignorance of his really diabolical character, Maria could not have helped gazing upon this individual with a feeling of the deepest interest, mingled with admiration, for there was something in his whole appearance, which savoured more of a character in a romance, than a being of life and reality. His form was athletic, but graceful, and his demeanour was such as to impress the beholder with wonder and awe. From time to time, when his dark eyes became fixed upon the cart before mentioned, he raised his clenched fist in the air, and seemed to be breathing a curse, or threatening revenge upon the head of some person, and Maria trembled, as fear once more began to take possession of her bosom.

"Surely this must be Rupert," she said, mentally, "oh yes, who can be mistaken in the man, after the description which Fanny has given of him."

As these thoughts crossed her mind, she shrunk with disgust, with repugnance from the contemplation of such a wretch, and inwardly ejaculated a prayer that the carriage would be allowed to pass without receiving any interruption from him. But her hopes were not to be realized, for the next minute the carriage had reached the place where he was walking, and raising his head, he immediately recognized Mr. Hartley. An expression of savage anger, mingled with satisfaction, enveloped his features at this recognition, and the next instant he came to the side of the vehicle, and fixing his eyes fiercely on the doctor, ejaculated—

" 'Tis well we have met; I longed again to behold you, so that I might deliver to you the thanks of those whom your laws have murdered, and which in their dying moments they requested I would impart to you. They met their death with undaunted courage, and they commissioned me to complete the scheme of vengeance which their wrongs call for. Your people fulfilled the promise they had made to you, and at the hour of midnight the remains of my kindred were delivered over to us, and since that time we have been on our way to the place which we have fixed upon for their spot of burial, there to rest by the corpse of the ancient mother of our tribe. Never did she imagine, that when she used to enjoin Mark, that when her time should come, she should be consigned to no other place than the spot which she herself selected, that he and his son should at the same time be committed to it."

"And it was a good job," observed the doctor, " it was a good job she had no presentiment of the kind, that she did——"

Rupert hastily checked himself, for he immediately perceived the error he had made, and tried to rectify it :—

"She might not have had a presentiment of that, to be sure ; but often did she predict that one of your pale-complexioned people would bring ruin and misery on her family, oft did she prognosticate that, I say, long before Ela was introduced to us."

"Is there anything else that you wish to say to me, my friend ?" demanded Mr. Hartley, for he was anxious to proceed, and Rupert, he noticed, seemed not at all willing to let the vehicle move on its way again until he had given full expression to his thoughts. His hand he had placed on the handle of the carriage door, and his eye glanced fiercely in at the window, as if he suspected that there was some other object which was studiously concealed from his sight.

Maria at first turned her head away from him with abhorrence, but she afterwards reflected, that if she thus openly demonstrated the hatred and repugnance she felt towards him, it might exasperate him into the committal of some outrage, and she therefore discontinued to avert her eyes from him, although it was with the greatest difficulty imaginable that she could restrain her feelings, while she gazed upon the visage of that man, who she was certain would not shrink from the perpetration of any crime, however revolting it might be.

Doctor Hartley was a second time obliged to put the interrogatory to him, before Rupert appeared even to be aware that he was addressing himself to him. His eyes still appeared to be narrowly examining the interior of the vehicle, and Maria, who suddenly felt conscious what his thoughts and suspicions were, tried more effectually to conceal from his notice the form of Fanny, who remained in a state of breathless anxiety and trepidation, and listened with feelings of horror to the words which Rupert gave utterance to.

"I do not want to appear to be imposing upon good-nature," at last remarked Rupert, "we have experienced much kindness from you; but, of course, I could not have the face

to appeal to your generosity again. However, if I mistake not, and she has a heart which corresponds with her looks, this young lady is feeling and benevolent; we have still many weary miles to journey, ere we shall reach the place of our destination ; and we have but sad hearts to help us on the road ; besides, as you may perceive, our women and children cannot ride now, as that vehicle, which was once used to convey them in, is now occupied by the cold and lifeless bodies of our kindred."

Maria needed no further hint, but immediately taking out her purse, she was about to place it with the whole of its glittering contents in his hand, when she caught the eye of the doctor, which rebuked her for her misplaced liberality; however, she drew forth a piece of gold, which she gave to him, and at the sight of which the Gipsy seemed overjoyed.

"Ah! this is a goodly sight," he exclaimed, "a goodly sight, and which not often gladdens the Gipsy's eyes. The yellow metal is seldom taken from the purse of the wealthy to relieve the necessities of the wandering vagabond. Lady, receive my thanks, they are justly your due, and——"

"Here is another guinea for you," observed the doctor, offering him one, which Rupert however, turned away from. "What nonsense,' he continued, "why should you refuse? You will not find the money any too much among you all."

The eyes of Rupert glowed with a peculiar expression as he thus answered—

"Nay, put up your money. I will have none of it. Already am I under too many obligations to you—curses on the circumstances that have made me so; for it deprives me of the gratification which I might otherwise now have. Nay," continued he, in a voice hoarse with the fierceness of his passions, and fixing his eyes on the cart, and directing the attention of the doctor to it : "had my will only been consulted, sooner than have lost the opportunity of revenge which I have done, those cold forms should have been left to blanch and moulder in the open air, sooner than thus allow the object of my hatred to escape due punishment, at the very moment when I have the power to gratify my wishes."

"Ah! dare you?" exclaimed the doctor, in a determined and fearless tone and manner—"but no matter—I am only wasting time by bandying words with you. At the same time, whatever may be your thoughts or intentions, you must remember that this is a poor return for the services I have been the means of rendering; a strange way of requiting me by threatening, and alarming——"

"It is not my desire to threaten or alarm you," cried Rupert, "no ;—but let not that girl, the trembling betrayer of her friends, let her not, I say, endeavour to hide herself from me—

she shall come forward, and moreover she shall gaze upon the work of her treachery—No danger can happen to her—and of that she is well aware;—for we have sworn—and nothing can ever induce us to break our oath. Fool!—who can deceive Rupert Darwin? much less Fanny Beranzio. Nay, I will see the frightened wretch. Reveal yourself, I say;—forward, and let me show what your treachery has been the means of accomplishing. Doctor Hartley," he went on to say in a still more peremptory and determined manner, by which it was plain to be seen that he was resolved not to be trifled with—"Doctor Hartley, you have nothing to fear;—we will not forget our promise to you. If we could be guilty of such a thing, never could we expect to prosper again. I repeat that she shall not receive the least injury from any of us; but she shall not continue to hide herself from our sight. I am resolved, and nothing shall prevent her from presenting herself, and gazing upon the misery she has wrought."

"But I am equally as determined that she shall not be subjected to any insult, or be forced to do anything which is repugnant to her feelings, while I have her under my protection," retorted the doctor with indignation and equal firmness. However, the point was soon decided by Fanny herself at that moment starting form her place of concealment, and with quivering lips, and ashy cheeks, she said—

"I come at your wish, Rupert: I am not afraid to do as you command, for I know that you will not deceive me."

"Do you? The same at one time did I think of you," he answered.

Before any one could again speak, the other Gipsies had all approached, and having got round the carriage, they rent the air with shouts, execrations, and every other demonstration of fierce wrath against Fanny. Doctor Hartley addressed himself to them; but notwithstanding he spoke in loud tones, it was some time before his voice could be heard, and they seemed half inclined to make a rush upon the defenceless girl, in spite of the promises of Rupert. The doctor, who never for a second lost his firmness and self-possession, at length managed to get a hearing, and in a voice of command he exclaimed—

"Rupert Darwin, remember your promise—remember the dying injunctions of her whose corpse lies now in yonder cart, and by your esteem for her, and the thanks she expressed for the favour I was fortunate enough to succeed in obtaining for her, I command you—I adjure you not to suffer this poor girl to be treated either with insolence or violence."

"Back, back, I command you!" cried Rupert, addressing himself to his companions, and waving his arm authoritatively. No sooner had the mandate issued from his lips than they obeyed

it, and the noise which had at one time been deafening, gradually subsided into peace.

"You see my power," said Rupert: "that skulking trembler knows it well."

"I do—I do indeed," hastily remarked Fanny, who seemed to be in a dreadful state of agitation, and eager to appease the wrath of the ruffian, and that the dreadful business she was forced into should be finished with all possible despatch. "I also know that Rupert will keep his word, and that he possesses too good a heart to—— He will not fail to do all that he undertakes and gives his word for."

A sardonic grin overspread the deep-lined countenance of the ruffian as Fanny gave utterance to these words, and he answered—

"Bah! you think to conciliate me by that, do you? But your effort will not succeed; no, you would say the same words to any other person who was placed in a similar situation to that in which I am to you; to those whom you have brought to a savage and ignominious death: but no matter;—as I before said, I will keep my word, no power can ever tempt me to break it; you have therefore nothing to fear at present."

Encouraged by this assertion, Fanny arose, and advanced towards the door of the carriage, but no sooner had her eyes fallen upon the dense mass of people that surrounded the vehicle, and encountered the ferocious glances of of the men, and the no less malevolent and savage looks of the women, than her courage failed her, and she trembled; and Maria, completely overcome by the alarm she exhibited, laid hold of her frantically, and in accents of terror ejaculated—

"Oh, for the love of heaven, do not venture among them——Surely, sir, you will not suffer her to run this terrible risk, and—but are there no means of saving her from being exposed to their——"

"Saving her, girl," cried Rupert passionately, "what mean you? Have I not passed my word that she shall be secure, and what has she then to fear?—Doctor Hartley," he continued, turning to that gentleman, "let me advise you no longer to suffer the girl to tamper with the patience of my people, or you may all have cause to repent, as it might arrive at a pitch which even I should not have the power to quell."

"Oh, Rupert," cried the distracted Fanny, "do not let me go in among them while they are in this state of excitement; for mercy sake do not——"

"Mercy," repeated the Gipsy, scornfully, "what have you to do with mercy? Look on the work of your tongue, and then repeat the question."

"Do say something to them, Rupert," sobbed the poor girl; "tell them that you have promised to protect me, and I will no longer hesitate."

"You deserve it not at my hands—but I will say a few words to them that will save you from the fury of their just wrath."

As he thus spoke, he turned to his associates, and proceeded to address them with emphatic gestures, but in the language of their tribe, which was, of course, quite incomprehensible to Doctor Hartley and Maria—but Fanny appeared to listen to it with the most profound attention, and they guessed from the expression of her countenance that the replies that were given to the harangue of Rupert afforded her satisfaction.

But a few seconds did this conference last, when Fanny in earnest tones, speaking to Maria, said—

"Pray do not detain me, Maria—there is nothing to be afraid of, I am thoroughly convinced of that now, but we may exasperate them by my any longer delaying to comply with their wishes. It will not last long, and why should I be afraid to gaze at those who have only suffered a just punishment for their enormities?"

With these words, which were spoken in too low a tone for Rupert to comprehend the meaning of them, Fanny released herself from the hold of Maria, and opening the door, stepped out of the carriage with a firmer step than might have been expected, and delivered herself to the custody of Rupert.

This was a moment of painful doubt, fear, and suspense to Doctor Hartley and Maria, and they expected every instant to see the Gipsies attempt some outrage upon her; but they were very much astonished to perceive that they did not offer to stir from the place where they had at first gathered; neither did they attempt, either by word or deed to express those feelings of hatred and revenge that their looks plainly evinced were passing in their bosoms.

Rupert laid hold of her arm, and urged her towards the spot where the cart was standing. "Quick, traitress!" he said, "I am all impatience to shew you the effects of your fidelity to your friends—your companions—I am eager to shew you what credit you may take to yourself for having, with that gentleness and humanity so becoming in your sex, brought two of your fellow-creatures to a frightful death; and who, had it not been for you, might for many years have continued to enjoy the pure air, and the green fields, and unbounded liberty; but now look into what a narrow space have you been the means of confining them; behold, I say," and he pulled down the back of the cart which revealed to her two shells placed side by side, in which were the remains of Mark Darwin and his son. "There, wretch, gaze and glut your fill, at your triumph, if you think it

so; look upon the frightful distorted features of him who behaved to you as a father, and has many a time carried you about with him, fed you when you was hungry, and clothed you when you was naked, and for all was looked upon with scorn and hatred by your viperous mother. But what else had she a right to do —what other treatment did the poor Gipsy deserve from the mother of the bastard of the proud Mr. Wallingford, and——"

"But why upbraid me for this, Rupert?" interrupted Fanny, mildly, for she saw that his rage was fast increasing, and she trembled at the thoughts of the excesses into which he might be led; "surely I could not be accountable for my mother's conduct."

"But shall I not upbraid you for being the cause of this?" demanded the ruffian, fiercely, as he took off the lid of the coffin, and revealed to her the disgusting spectacle of the discoloured and swoln features of the elder Mark Darwin, which, even while he was alive, she could never contemplate but with a feeling of the utmost terror and abhorrence.

"There, look on that," continued the wretch, in a tone of savage exultation, as he marked the feelings of disgust and horror that evidently agonised her bosom; "is not that a pleasant, a gratifying sight? Aye, gaze your fill, and may the recollection of it haunt your mind until your dying day. May that blackened, distorted visage, with his glazed and starting eye balls be present to your imagination in the darkness of night and in the light of day. May it rise up before you in your moments of pleasure, and startle you from sleep in frightful visions. May all your moments be made miserable, as you have been the cause of making the remaining kindred of this, the victim of your treachery. Nay, this is not all, you must not go from hence until you have seen all," he continued, as the horror-struck girl, with a burst of anguish, covered her face with her hands and endeavoured to shut out the revolting sight from her observation. "I will now exhibit to you the other victim to the sanguinary laws of the white-faced people, the son of him upon whose ghastly corpse you have just now gazed. That youth, whose beauty was the universal theme of admiration, and who, in spite of his being one of the branded race, made many a gentle heart throb. Look upon him, I say, and exult in the change you have made."

The villain grasped her arm as he spoke, and drew her nearer towards the cart, then taking the lid from the second coffin also, he pointed with the look of a demon at the awful face of the corpse, which, if possible, presented a still more disgusting appearance than the other.

"Oh, mercy!—have mercy! Rupert!" she shrieked, as she turned her head away, and sought to release herself from his hold.

"Mercy to you!" cried the ruffian, "and the

eyes of my murdered brother and father looking up to me for vengeance all the time?" But Fanny had become insensible, and throwing her over his shoulder, he returned to the carriage,

"There," said Rupert, when he returned to the carriage, in which the worthy doctor and Maria had been waiting with the greatest anxiety and suspense; "there, sir, I now resign her once more to your care, and may your kindness be bestowed upon one who never may have the ingratitude to repay it in the same manner in which she has done that of her former companions and friends, and by whom her and her mother were saved from an awful death. But the time will come when we shall once more encounter each other, and then, Fanny Berauzie, tremble," and he clenched his fist, and shook it at Fanny, who still remained in a state of unconsciousness;—"our next meeting," he added, "will be to settle the debt of vengeance which I owe you. Think not that it will ever be forgotten—no—it may be procrastinated, but it shall surely happen."

As he thus gave expression to his savage feelings, the villain gnashed his teeth, once more shook his fist, and with compressed lips and contracted eye-brows, he turned from the vehicle and rejoining his companions, the mournful procession moved on, and turning a corner, when they had emerged from the narrow road, they were soon hidden from their sight.

CHAPTER L.

"What fresh trials am I reserved for?—
What means this cruel outrage,
Am I to be made the sport
Of brutal men?—Nay, touch me not,
Thy sight is odious to me,
And though I possess but woman's bodily
          strength,
I am strong enough in virtue
To render thee powerless."
                    THE LIBERTINE.

"It would be advisable for us to make our way to the Imperial Hotel, my dear," remarked Doctor Hartley to Maria, as he perceived that Fanny began to give some faint symptoms of returning sensibility; "it is not any great distance from here, if I mistake not, and it is very evident that poor Fanny will not be in a condition for us to continue our journey to-day; neither do I consider that it would be at all proper, after what has happened; for should we again encounter these desperate people, there is no knowing what might be the consequences. We will, consequently, put up till to-morrow at the inn."

Of course Maria could not but coincide in this opinion, for her terrors had almost been as great as Fanny's, and the bare idea of once more coming in contact with the Gipsies was sufficient to increase her alarm tenfold. They, therefore, turned off in the direction of the hotel, and shortly after they had done so, Fanny recovered.

The poor girl glanced wildly round, but when she beheld she was really safe, and in the company of her friends, her tears gushed forth unrestrained;—but they were tears of gratitude and joy. Suddenly, however, she passed her hands across her burning forehead, as if endeavouring to collect her scattered thoughts, and then in a tone of melancholy wildness, she said—

"But it was not reality!—It could not be. —No, no, no, it was only some frightful vision. But yet I am deceiving myself; I have not been dreaming;—they did come here, and Rupert— oh, God! all the horrible circumstance rushes forcibly on my memory now."

She covered her face with her hands, and convulsive sobs choked her further utterance. Maria, who was deeply affected at the agitation of the poor girl, would have attempted to soothe her, but Doctor Hartley made signs for her not to interrupt her grief, and she forbore to do as her feelings prompted her.

"Let her give free indulgence to her sorrow, my love," said he, in a low tone, "it will relieve her over-charged heart, and no doubt but that, in the cheerful place to which we are going, we shall soon be able to obliterate from her recollection this painful circumstance."

Fanny could not help expressing some surprise when the carriage stopped at the door of the hotel, but she quickly comprehended what had been the good doctor's intentions for so doing, and her heart overflowed with gratitude to her friends for their kind consideration, which she expressed in such simple yet forcible language, that it drew their hearts more closely than ever towards her, and rivetted their deepest interest.

"Of course, the strange event had not failed to make a due impression upon the minds of all three, and it was not at all likely that it would be so easily effaced as the doctor had predicted. The remainder of the day passed off miserably dull, and in spite of all his endeavours to the contrary, Mr. Hartley could neither rally his own spirits, nor those of his companions. The doctor was more dull than Maria had ever before seen him, and it was very evident that he was recalling the threats of the villain Rupert to his memory, with the most painful apprehension.

But Maria did not exactly comprehend the nature of the doctor's thoughts. He was pained at what had happened, and he could not help reproaching himself for what he considered, upon mature reflection, could only be denominated weakness, in suffering Fanny to be exposed to the brutal threats, imprecations, and ruffianism of Rupert, and in passively allowing the wretch to expose the poor girl's feelings to such a terrible shock. He had not acted up to the character of her protector, which he had voluntarily taken upon himself, or he ought to have determinedly opposed the wishes of the Gipsies at every hazard.

These were the ideas that harassed the doctor's mind, as he gazed upon the ghastly features, the heaving bosom, the trembling frame, and restless wandering eye of Fanny, and which so clearly evinced the mental torment she was suffering; and how vividly all the dreadful images which had been so brutally forced upon her, were stamped upon her memory. But still, when he reflected on their numbers, and the inutility it would have been to have offered any opposition to them, he felt that he had only acted as prudence had dictated, and that, had he not done so, they must have brought down upon them the vengeance of the whole gang, and most probably their lives would have paid the sacrifice. He, therefore, after some time passed in these thoughts, became more composed, and ultimately was convinced that he had only acted as circumstances had compelled him, and which, had he resisted, would have undoubtedly brought destruction upon them all.

Terrible was the night which Fanny and Maria passed together after these events. Sleep was a stranger to them, and the latter in vain tried to divert the thoughts of her companion from the awful images that now pressed upon them. The threats, the curses of Rupert, still seemed to vibrate in her ears; and still did she imagine that she saw his fiendish looks fixed upon her, as he predicted the horror, the misery she would in future undergo. It was a great relief to them both when the morning dawned, but Fanny was too ill to rise, and in consequence they were again compelled to delay the resumption of their journey till the following day.

The incessant soothing observations and affectionate attentions of Maria, and the arguments and exhortations of Doctor Hartley, however, at length had a due effect upon the mind of Fanny, and by the evening she was so much composed, as scarcely to leave any traces of the former violent agitation which had tormented her, and to assure Mr. Hartley of her feeling competent to resume the journey the following morning.

The remainder of the journey was performed without anything occurring worthy of particular notice, and Doctor Hartley felt sincerely glad when he once more trod the chambers of that comfortable house which had formed his habitation for so many years.

Maria, too, felt more composed than she had done for some time, when she found herself under the roof of her benefactor; but still there was one thought, one anxious thought, which was ever present to her mind, and which must be gratified ere she could rest. This was, as the reader has most probably guessed, whether Mr. Wallingford and Walter were still at the hall. A melancholy foreboding of disappointment pressed upon her heart, as the thought darted across her brain, and she could not help sighing as she reflected upon the hard fate which had thus divided her and her cousin, and upon the probability there was that they would never be permitted to meet again. Mr. Wallingford's plans seemed to be so systematically arranged that she could not doubt but that they had long been in contemplation, and had only been delayed being put into operation in consequence of the events which had recently occurred.

"Well, my love, I see what you are moping about in this manner for," said Doctor Hartley, the morning after their return, "but if you will promise me that you will make up your mind for the worst, I will take a ride over to the hall after breakfast, and see whether the objects of your thoughts are or are not there. But I do not promise you that you will not be disappointed; for as I have before observed, Mr. Wallingford is so changeable, that it is not by any means improbable that he made his departure from the dell almost immediately after his return to it."

Maria sighed as the doctor made use of these observations, for she was well aware how possible it was that his ideas would be realized; in fact, they were in unison with her own, and it was with a hopeless and heavy heart that she saw him leave the house on the errand of inquiry he had undertaken.

The interval during his absence passed heavily away between Maria and Fanny, each of their minds being fully occupied by their different thoughts, of which it could scarcely be said which were the most painful and bewildering. Fanny's ideas were fixed upon her mother, the uncertainty where she was, and likewise that they might never meet again; and as she thus reflected, her grief became so intense as to be almost insupportable.

"Surely to me, her daughter, there ought not to have been so much secresy observed as to the place of her destination," she reflected, "it is unkind—'tis unnecessary, and only exposing me to that anguish, created by uncertainty, which might have been avoided. And could my mother thus readily abandon me, without so much as leaving me a message when it would be likely that I should be restored to her bosom, or what were her future motives and intentions? I cannot believe that she would willingly do so; oh, no, her anxiety for her poor girl would not permit her to act in such a manner."

These thoughts led Fanny to suppose that Doctor Hartley had acted in a strange inconsistent manner, and that the secresy he maintained on these points were not only absurd but unfeeling, and she could not in spite of all her efforts to drown these thoughts in the recollection of the kindness and disinterested conduct of Mr. Hartley.

The doctor was absent about three hours, which to the impatient Maria seemed like a month; she sat at the parlour window, which looked upon the high road, and watched every form that approached with eager curiosity, and at length she was gratified at beholding the doctor riding towards the house. He was going at a very slow pace, and seemed to be buried in profound thought. As he entered the parlour Maria hastened towards him, and looking eagerly and searchingly in his face, observed—

"My worst surmises are verified—I see by your serious looks that they are ;—they are not at the Hall?"

Mr. Hartley nodded his head affirmatively, and Maria averting her head, burst into a paroxysm of tears.

"Nay, my dear," observed the doctor in gentle and soothing tones, "did I not tell you that I would not promise you that you would not be disappointed, and I therefore thought that you had made up your mind to the worst. It is useless thus giving way to weakness; the more commendable virtue is to endeavour to show a becoming firmness against such afflictions, and to anticipate at some future period a change of fortune. There now, my dear girl, compose your feelings;— you will again behold your cousin, never fear, and when time may have changed the ideas of Mr. Wallingford in your favour."

Maria wiped the tears from her eyes, and raising her hand towards heaven, uttered a mental prayer that the predictions of Mr. Hartley might be verified.

"I must say," resumed the latter, "that in my opinion the conduct of Mr. Wallingford is most strange and unaccountable, and I am fearful that it will have a dangerous effect upon his health, so impaired as his constitution is already, and so totally unfit as he must be to encounter the fatigue of travelling. It seems, however, that this plan had been premeditated, for old Anthony informs me, that during the two days which they only remained at the Hall, he watched Walter with the most scrupulous care, and would not permit him out of his sight a minute. All the arrangements were completed, even before Walter had any idea of the time which his father had fixed upon for his departure, and the travelling carriages were at the door, before the former had been apprized of Mr. Wallingford's intentions."

Maria wrung her hands, and once more the tears started in her eyes.

"Not a word, not a line at leaving, either," she sobbed; "alas! am I then also so easily forgotten by him who——"

"Not so, my dear child," interrupted the good doctor; "I have before told you that Walter was so narrowly watched by his father, that he had no opportunity of writing to you; but he has left a verbal message with Anthony and his wife, accompanied with some little memento of his affection, which they will not deliver only to yourself."

"And shall I, then, be permitted to visit the Hall?" ejaculated Maria, looking up, at the last words of Doctor Hartley, while a ray of consolation beamed through her tears. "Shall I be permitted to wander once more through those delightful scenes, in which I have passed so many happy hours, and every spot of which will recall so many pleasurable associations to my memory?"

"And many, many equally as melancholy," said Mr. Hartley.

Maria sighed. "Alas! 'tis too true," she said. "Oh! my poor aunt, had you been alive, I should never, perhaps, have been estranged from that sweet spot."

"Well, my love," remarked the doctor, finding he had touched upon a tender chord and one which might bring reminiscences to the mind of Maria it would be better for her to bury in oblivion; "well, my love, during the time we remain here, and I find that I cannot complete my arrangements for the journey to London under a month, you can, if you please, pay daily visits to old Anthony and his wife, who have the care of the hall; but I would, at the same time, caution you to return home early of an evening, for I understand that the fellow Barnell has returned to the neighbourhood, and from the manner in which he has already insulted you, it is plain that you have everything to apprehend from a recontre with him. I know not whether Lord Harlington is acquainted with the behaviour of his intended son-in-law, but I should think he would not be inclined to take the conduct of this man as paying any very flattering compliment to his daughter. At any rate, I shall take the liberty of calling upon his lordship, and making him acquainted with the business, and likewise cautioning the booby Barnell that such insolent behaviour to a person under my protection, if repeated, shall not go unpunished."

"Oh, no, for goodness sake, my dear sir, do no such thing," said Maria. "It is much better to let the affair rest where it is, and no doubt he will not repeat it. If you should make a complaint to Lord Harlington, prejudiced, as I am convinced he is, against any portion of the Wallingford family, there is no knowing what view he might take of it, and the tongue of malice can too often effect an injury against even the most guiltless."

The good doctor shook his head, but made no reply, and soon afterwards he changed the theme of the conversation, and the discourse became more general. But Maria was ill-disposed to converse, although the doctor tried all that he could to exhilirate her spirits, and he was in one of his most cheerful and jocular moods;—her mind was fully occupied with subjects of a more, a far more important nature, than anything else he could mention, and feel-ing quite incompetent to the task of replying to him, she made an excuse to retire, and in the solitude of her own chamber, gave unre-strained indulgence to the dismal train of thoughts which the doctor's information had given rise to.

GRAYLING THE HIGHWAYMAN.

The die was then cast, Mr. Wallingford had put the so long anxious wish of his heart into operation, and Walter and her were separated, perhaps never to meet again; or if they did, under what far different circumstances it might be;—Walter's affections might be estranged from her; he might look upon her with cold-ness and indifference; in other climes, he might have seen those who had taught him to look upon his poor simple rustic cousin with feelings only of cold respect; or (and how she shuddered at the thought, and a deadly chill fell upon her heart) he might have become the husband of another. But could he ever forget the vows he had so long made to her? Could he let another take possession of that heart which he had many a time so solemnly sworn was irrevocably her's, and her's alone? Oh, yes; he was but young, and had seen nothing of the world—he was now bursting, as it were, for the first time into life, and in its giddy vortex might lose all remembrance of her and his promises. Wealth, rank, and beauty would be set to ensnare him; and to them would be added the incessant exhortations of his father, and was it to be supposed that he could struggle against all these temptations? Oh, no, it was impossible. But then again, she reflected, to suppose him capable of acting in this manner, was to deny him the possession of every principle of truth and honour; and she upbraided herself for doing him the injustice to suppose him capable of such conduct.

Thus was she tossed about on a sea of conflicting thoughts; one moment goaded on by fear, doubt, and suspicion, the next buoyed up with hope, love, and courage. She could not have believed that she loved her cousin half so fondly as she did; but absence makes known the full strength of the mainsprings of the heart's affections; and what before was warmth of esteem, is expanded into all the effervescence of ardent passion.

Doctor Hartley, when she descended to dinner, had the greatest difficulty to persuade her to defer her visit to Wallingford Hall until the following morning, so eager was she to hear the message which Walter had left behind for her; but at length, feeling the truth of the doctor's remarks as to the danger of going to the Dell at that hour, as it was nearly dark, she gave up the idea, and the evening passed away more comfortably than might have been expected. Fanny had, by the persuasions of the doctor, conquered her grief at her continued separation from her mother, and her uncertainty where she was, so much as to appear quite composed; but in her heart still reigned that agony and anxiety, which nothing but the gratification of her wishes could remove.

The next morning came, and as soon as the breakfast was over, Maria left the house of her benefactor to go to the Hall. It was a fine morning, the sun shone brightly upon the rich and variegated scenery with which that delightful part of the country was surrounded. In spite of the weather, however, and the enchanting prospect which was spread before her, Maria's heart felt sad and heavy, as she recalled to her memory under what different circumstances she had traversed that spot the last time she was there. Then was Walter the companion of her rambles, and no prospect of their being separated was before

them. Now she was like a poor isolated being, with not a friend in the world, and depending upon the kindness of one who might be said to be a stranger to her, for protection, while he on whom her whole heart was immoveably fixed, was far away, and despair whispered to her that their separation was for ever.

So deeply was she wrapped in these reflections, that she did not take notice of anything around her, but suddenly she thought she heard a footfall on the ground, and looking back, she was alarmed to behold a man following her. He was a low, dirty looking fellow, and for the moment she supposed him to be a Gipsy. On seeing her look back, he suddenly stopped, and looked earnestly at her for a second or two, and then turning into another path, immediately disappeared.

Maria was greatly relieved when she saw him depart, but she was seriously alarmed at the circumstance, and was half inclined to turn back; but upon reflection, she considered that there was equally as much danger in that as in proceeding on her way, and she therefore took courage and went on. She, however, looked carefully around her as she proceeded, but saw nothing more to increase her fears, and she began to think that she had probably been alarmed without sufficient cause, and that the man after all might not have been watching her, for if he had, and his design had been robbery, he would surely have endeavoured to effect his object in the place where she had at first observed him, which was every way fitting for such a purpose, and there not being any one near at the time. These thoughts, and the circumstance of her not seeing anything further to excite her fears, re-assured her, and she therefore hastened on her way more boldly.

Wallingford Hall, with its noble masonry, and magnificent architecture, now burst upon her view, and she paused a few moments to gaze upon it, and to indulge in the mingled feelings of joy and sorrow which the sight of it excited. While she yet stood, a faint scream vibrated on her ears, and made her start, and turn her eyes in the direction from whence it seemed to proceed, but she could see nothing, and imagining that she had probably been mistaken, she once more hurried on her way, and at length arrived at the door of the garden wall, which surrounded the hall, and with eager haste, which her fears gave rise to, she pulled the bell, and the gate was soon after opened by Anthony.

"Ah! my dear young lady," said the poor old man, in a voice of joy. "Oh, how delighted I am to see you again, and so I'm sure will Jenny be; we have done nothing but talk about you ever since master and Mr. Walter left the hall, and we have been all impatience for your return from the unpleasant business you have been upon. Pray walk in, my dear young lady, pray walk in."

Maria had not waited to hear this request, but having warmly pressed the hand of her old friend, she had passed on, and was now half way across the lawn which fronted the hall. She found old Jenny waiting at the door for her, and when she saw her, she tottered forth to meet her, as well as age and infirmity would permit her, and greeted her with all that simple sincerity which her heart prompted.

"Oh, my dear miss," said the old woman, "I guessed it was you; my heart told me it was. But, goodness me, how ill you look; I hope nothing has happened to you."

"Nothing, my good Jenny," said Maria, "nothing of any importance; but I have scarcely got over the fatigue of my journey yet, and perhaps that may make me look pale."

The old woman led the way to the parlour, and here Maria requested that her and her husband would be seated, and eagerly inquired of them all that happened since she had been away.

"Ah! miss, there have been sad doings," observed Jenny, with a sigh, "and I never thought to have lived to see such a change as this in Wallingford Hall. But, to be sure, master is a strange gentleman—a very strange gentleman, and there is no such thing as accounting for the whims he takes."

"He is indeed," returned Maria, in a melancholy tone, "but pray proceed, Jenny."

Jenny complied, but she was rather more prolix in her narrative than suited the impatience of Maria, and which, if we were to relate it in the manner she did, would be extremely tedious to our readers.

"Ah, miss," continued old Jenny, "I am sure it was enough to break any person's heart, only to see how poor Mr. Walter did take on, when master and him returned to the hall; he would sit and mope by himself for hours together, unless when he could get an opportunity to come and talk to me and Anthony, which he seemed to be very fond of doing, because we used to speak of you, miss."

Maria blushed deeply, and the garrulous old woman proceeded—

"Yes, miss, I am certain, though perhaps you may think I am very bold for so saying; I am certain that young master loves you as dearly or more dearly than he does his own life, and I think, though to be sure it is not my duty to talk in that manner, it was very cruel of Mr. Wallingford to separate——"

"Jenny, Jenny," interrupted Maria, who never liked to encourage menials in tattling about the domestic affairs of their superiors, "I must not listen to any remarks of this kind; my uncle, doubtless, had strong motives for

taking the step he has done, and however severely I may feel the separation from my cousin, I do not think myself justified in questioning his conduct."

"Well, to be sure," said old Anthony, "I cannot but think it is all very correct what you state, and that it was wrong in dame to speak in the manner she did; but she did not mean any harm by it, for you know that no person could ever have your interest more deeply at heart than me and Jenny. Besides, she says very true, I'm sure it was quite pitiful to see the poor young gentleman how melancholy he did seem."

"Yes, and what sweet things he used to say of Miss Herbert too," added Jenny, "and then he would sigh so deeply, and——"

"Pray, my good Jenny," interrupted Maria, who, much as her heart throbbed with ecstacy at all that the old woman told her, which showed that Walter's sentiments towards her were sincere, she felt confused to hear them so warmly allude to it; "pray, my good Jenny, inform me what could be the reason of my uncle so soon leaving the Hall after his return to it?"

"Why, miss, as for that matter, I can't tell you," replied the old woman, "for I don't believe that anybody knew it but himself, indeed I am sure my poor young master did not, it was all done in no time at all; the affairs were settled, Mr. Walter was ordered to get himself ready, and the next morning the post-chaises drove up to the Hall door, and away they went."

"Strange!" ejaculated Maria; "this conduct is the most abrupt and unaccountable I have heard of in my uncle—but," she added, in a louder tone, these observations being uttered in a voice too low for Jenny and her husband to understand her, "but Mr. Hartley informed me that you had a message to deliver to me, and——"

"Ah!" said Jenny, with a look of delight, "I told the good doctor it was a message only, because I did not know whether you would like him to be made acquainted with the truth in this instance; but the fact of it is that I have a letter for you!"

"A letter!" reiterated Maria, unable to conceal the pleasure she felt at this information.

"Yes, miss, a letter, which poor Mr. Walter slipped into my hand a few minutes before his departure," said Jenny, "and that was not all, miss—but not to keep you any longer in suspense, I will go and fetch them for you."

The old woman here tottered out of the room, and during her brief absence, which seemed an age to the impatient girl, her heart palpitated hurriedly with emotion and expectation. At length Jenny returned, bearing in one hand a letter, and in the other a miniature, the latter of which she held with an expression of extreme pleasure, and Maria immediately recognised the features of Walter.

With the utmost delight she flew towards the old woman, and took them both from her hands. She gazed upon the likeness with a feeling of rapture almost uncontrollable, and scarcely could she refrain from pressing it to her lips in the presence of Jenny and her husband. It was admirably executed, the limner had evidently applied all his skill to the task, and so correct was the resemblance, that Maria could almost have imagined that her cousin lived and breathed before her.

But her attention was speedily diverted from the miniature to the letter, and with trembling hands she broke the seal, and perused the contents. Her heart swelled, and the tear, in spite of all her efforts, started to her eye as she proceeded. It breathed expressions of the most impassioned, the most enthusiastic fondness; vowed eternal constancy, and declared that whatever might be the consequences, he would never consent to pay his addresses to another. He begged of her to endeavour to seek consolation even in their separation, and to depend upon it that it would not be for long, for that something whispered to him, ere long circumstances would transpire, which would re-unite them, never more to part. He concluded by praying her to accept of the accompanying miniature, and when she gazed upon it, sometimes to bestow a thought upon him whom time, nor distance, nor mortal event could alter.

The tears flowed from Maria's eyes as she perused this affectionate epistle, and pressing it first to her lips and next to her heart, she mentally uttered a prayer for his welfare, and that his predictions, as regarded their shortly meeting again, might be verified.

Anthony and his wife marked her emotion with the deepest interest, and exchanging glances, the tears chased each other down their furrowed cheeks. For Maria, the poor honest creatures felt as much affection as if she had been their own daughter, and there was nothing which could come within the scope of their power that they would not willingly do to promote her happiness.

Again and again did Maria read the dear characters traced by the hand of Walter, and as she did so she felt a ray of consolation beam upon her heart, which she had thought it impossible that anything could impart to her.

Jenny would have continued to converse upon Walter, all the afternoon, and Maria would never have been tired of listening to the honest but simple encomiums which she passed upon him, but Anthony, who was fearful that dwelling too much upon the theme would render Maria more uncomfortable than she was already, changed the subject, and talked about

the journey to London, which Anthony, who had once been there, described in his own simple manner, pourtraying it as " a mortal gay place, but as full of temptation and vice, as a bush is full of blackberries."

Maria, after talking some time to the good old people, took a stroll over the hall, visited every apartment which recalled to her memory former scenes of happiness, and pondering with a mixture of pleasure and melancholy upon the numerous and strange events connected with them. Many a pang did her bosom feel when she entered the library, and took up the volumes that Walter had been fond of perusing, in many of which he had written his name, and other poetical lines, called forth either by his admiration or censure of the author. The chamber in which Mrs. Wallingford had breathed her last, was the next she entered. It seemed scarcely altered since that melancholy occasion, and as she glanced towards the bed, she could almost imagine that she could see the form of that amiable lady stretched upon it, and looking upon her with a placid smile of resignation and Christian fortitude, as she did in that moment when her soul winged its flight to eternity.

"Angel of bliss, for such, my dearest aunt, you are now," she exclaimed, raising her hands towards Heaven, " by the love I know you bore to me while living, I beseech you look down upon me, direct my steps, and protect and guide me from the dangers and the sorrows with which my passage through life seems intersected."

She felt more composed after uttering this prayer, and left the chamber. Every spot so dear to her did Maria visit; the garden, the shrubbery, the summer-house, the lake, all so powerfully interesting to her from circumstances which nothing could ever erase from her memory. At length, warned by the approach of dusk, she prepared to return to the house of Doctor Hartley, promising to visit the hall every day while they remained in the neighbourhood.

Anthony would have accompanied her part of the way back, but Maria, considering his age, would not suffer him, but the altercation between them on this point was soon decided by the entrance of Giles, their son-in-law, who very readily undertook the task which Anthony had proffered, and they left the hall together.

"You are later than you ought to be, my dear," said Dr. Hartley, on her entrance, "but where is Fanny ?"

" Fanny !" repeated Maria.

"Yes," returned Mr. Hartley, " has she not returned with you ?"

" Why, my dear sir," said Maria, with an expression of astonishment at the question, "you know I left her here with you, when I departed for Wallingford Hall, and I have not seen her since."

"Not seen her?" exclaimed the doctor, starting from his chair, with astonishment and alarm depicted in his countenance; "why, what can be the reason of that? Something must have happened to the poor girl; how foolish it was of me to yield to her request."

"What do you mean, sir? pray tell me?" solicited Maria.

"Why, scarcely five minutes after you left the house," said Doctor Hartley, "Fanny expressed a wish to accompany you to the hall, and so earnestly did she urge her request, that I could not refuse her; so she followed after you, and I made sure, as she did not return all day, that she had overtaken you, and that you were both together. Good God! surely something must have happened to her——. Should any of those wretches who——"

"Ah!" interrupted Maria, shuddering with horror and apprehension, as she recollected the man she had observed, and the female shriek which she had afterwards heard, "my heart forebodes the worst; oh, my dear sir, for the love of heaven, do not delay a moment, but send persons to search in the direction to which I shall point out your attention."

"For goodness sake, Maria, what do you mean? Has anything happened that——"

In as few words as possible she related to him what had occurred to her, and the shrieks she had heard.

"Alas! 'tis but too evident that the poor girl has got into some danger," observed the doctor, with extreme agitation, as he hastily pulled the bell to summon the servant to his presence; "this is all through my confounded folly, in suffering her to go out at all, so soon after our return home; should anything have happened to her, I shall for ever blame myself as the indirect cause."

"Nay, my dear sir," said Maria, " do not too hastily alarm yourself; after all, Fanny may be safe, and has only been tempted to ramble f.r.her than she had probably anticipated, by the beauty of the scenery."

The worthy doctor shook his head, and again pulled the bell more violently than he had before done, as the servant did not appear so promptly as his impatience looked for.

The doctor's horse was quickly harnessed, and giving orders for one man to accompany him and two more to go a different way, he started off at full speed in the direction which Maria had described.

The time of their absence was an interval of the utmost anxiety and suspense to Maria, who sat watching at the window, thinking to see them return with the object of their search, until darkness completely enshrouded the earth. But three hours elapsed, and neither the doctor nor the domestics returned, and Maria gave herself up to despair, and anticipated the worst. She had no doubt but that the man she had

seen was one of the Gipsy gang; that Fanny had mistaken the path which she (Maria) had taken, had fallen into the hands of the miscreants, and that the shriek which she had heard had proceeded from her.

Another half hour of the greatest agony elapsed, when Maria heard the bell ring, and hastily descending to the hall door, as soon as the old housekeeper could get there, she beheld the doctor just dismounting from his horse, pale and breathless.

"My worst surmises are almost confirmed," he exclaimed, as he walked into the parlour; —"we have searched in vain for the poor girl, in the direction you sent us, but by the light of our lantern, we could perceive that the grass was much disturbed, near the spot from whence I imagine you heard the shriek, as if there had been a struggle, and examining a little further on, we picked up this comb."

Maria looked at it for a moment, and then ejaculated—

"That comb belongs to Fanny, and I know she had it in her hair this morning."

"Good God!" cried Mr. Hartley, "then it is but too true, the unfortunate girl has fallen into the hands of her enemies, and has doubtless fallen a sacrifice to their blood-thirsty vengeance, through my imprudence."

"It may not yet be too late to save her," said the terrified Maria; "surely you do not mean to give up the search?"

"Give up the search!" answered he, "no, I only returned to see whether the other two men, whom I despatched in a contrary road, had been more successful than we have, and will instantly renew it; I called at Mr. Ashburne's, and made him acquainted with the circumstance, and he promptly sent out two or three constables, and several of his dependents; but I much doubt whether or no they will prove successful, for the Gipsies concert their plots with such skill and sagacity, that it is almost an impossibility to detect them. It was very wrong of me to suffer her to leave the house while we were in this neighbourhood."

While Doctor Hartley was thus speaking, the other two men who had been sent in search of Fanny, came back, having met with no better success than the doctor and his companion; and without any more delay, they all remounted, and started off different ways upon their hopeless errand.

Maria had conjectured right when she thought that Fanny had mistaken the path. After leaving the house, she tripped swiftly along, thinking to overtake the former, but after pursuing what she thought to be the right path for a few minutes, she found herself in a narrow lane, which was completely overshadowed by the thick foliage of the trees on each side. At the entrance of this lane she paused, having discovered her mistake, and scarcely knowing which way it would be best for her to proceed, or whether she should turn back.

While she still hesitated, a rustling among the branches in the hedges startled her, and in an instant two ruffianly-looking fellows, armed with thick cudgels, jumped into the lane, and, seizing her roughly by the arms, dragged her forcibly forward. Fanny screamed, but the men immediately forced a handkerchief into her mouth, and with horrible threats and imprecations, dragged her after them.

Terrified as Fanny was at this unexpected circumstance, it was some relief to her to perceive that the men who had seized her were not of the Gipsy tribe, but she had not many seconds allowed her for thought. Upon emerging from the lane, she was thunderstruck at beholding a travelling carriage, which seemed to be waiting for some one, towards which the men hurried her, and without saying a word, opened the door, and forced her into it—gave some directions by signs to the man who drove it, and, taking their places on each side of her, it started off with great rapidity.

Overcome with terror, Fanny was no sooner placed in the carriage than she fainted away. When she recovered her senses, she found that the coach was still proceeding with the utmost velocity, but the carriage windows being closed, and the blinds down, she was unable to tell whether it was night or day, or how long they had been travelling. The handkerchief had been removed, so that her tongue was at liberty, but the ruffians, seeing her about to speak, scowled frightfully upon her, and gave her other significant hints that she had better remain silent; so her lips closed, and sinking back, she gave herself up to all the horrors of thought.

In vain did she rack her brain to imagine who were the authors of this outrage, and what motives could prompt them to it ; besides the Gipsies, she knew not of any enemies that she had, and she was perfectly well convinced, both from the appearance of the men, and the manner of her seizure, that she was not in their power. The uncertainty she was in, and the agony which she well knew her strange disappearance would cause her friends, filled her breast with the most poignant anguish, and she wrung her hands, and gave free vent to the tears which chased each other rapidly down her cheeks.

The ruffians who guarded her never conversed, and the vehicle rolled on in gloomy and awful silence for about another hour, when it suddenly stopped, and the driver alighting and opening the door, helped Fanny out, and she then, as well as the darkness would permit her, discovered that they were stopping at the door of a red brick house, which appeared to be an inn, but it was in a wild and apparently unfrequented place. A faint ray of hope, however, darted across the poor girl's mind, when she saw that it was an inn, for surely she should be able to interest some persons in her favour, who would endeavour to rescue her from a power into which she was so mysteriously thrown. This, however, was soon overclouded upon entering the house, which had a dirty and gloomy appearance, and on encountering the landlord, who was a coarse, surly-looking man, and by the significant nods and winks which passed between him and the ruffians by whom she had been brought thither, Fanny was soon convinced that they knew each other very well, and consequently, he being most likely a party in the plot, from him she had nothing to hope.

As the fellows upon a sign from the landlord, took her along a dark passage, and up a steep staircase, loud peals of rude and boisterous laughter frequently burst upon her ears, which seemed to proceed from a number of men.

"Good Heaven!" she thought, "surely I am in a retreat for robbers? What will become of me ; and for what purpose can they possibly have brought me hither?"

Reason, however, was opposed to this idea, and after a second or two she gave it up, and became lost in a chaos of doubt, misery, and perplexity.

After ascending two flights of stairs, the men stopped at a door, which having opened, they led her into a room, which was rendered comfortable in appearance by a good fire which was blazing on the hearth. Here they did not stop a minute, but beckoning her to silence, retired and locked the door after them.

Fanny paced the room with disordered steps, and wrung her hands ; to cry for help when none was nigh, would be useless, and doubtless only draw down upon her the vengeance of those in whose power she was ; she therefore gave up the idea, and gave way entirely to the indulgence of her thoughts, and in vain speculations as to what could be the motives of those who were at the bottom of this plot, and for what purpose they should have seized her.

She was aroused from thought, by hearing footsteps upon the stairs, and directly afterwards the following words, in a man's voice—

"Which is the room do you say she is in?"

"The one before you, sir," answered another. Fanny trembled violently, as she listened to these words, and heard the key turning in the lock, and the next instant the room door was thrown open, and a stout, unprepossessing, but well dressed man, whom she never remembered to have seen before, entered the room, but almost immediately started back again, apparently with great amazement, on beholding her, and exclaimed—

"Why, who the devil have you brought here?"

"Why, the young girl you wished us to bring, Mr. Barnell," replied one of the men who had seized Fanny. Mr. Barnell!—she remembered the name: it was the one she had heard Maria mention, and the truth was now evident; the latter had been the person upon whom the outrage was to have been committed. Her mind by this discovery was relieved from a load of terror and care, for she was not in the power of her terrible enemies, the Gipsies, and by the mistake which had taken place, she had been the means of saving Maria from the danger which had threatened her.

"The devil!" cried Mr. Barnell, in a tone of vexation and disappoinment, "this is not her whom I wanted;—this is not Miss Herbert. Why, you must have been very stupid, after all the trouble I took several times to point her out to you."

"Well, and I am certain that whenever you did so, this female was always present, so that we mistook her for the one you, it seems, meant," answered the fellow.

"There, get about your business," said Barnell, "I must talk to this young woman."

The men left the room upon this order, and Fanny trembled when she found herself alone with Mr. Barnell, whose hateful character she had so frequently heard described.

He stood looking at her for some moments in silence, and with a bold air of admiration, then advancing familiarly towards her, he sought to take her hand, and looking with what he meant to be a smirkish expression in her face, he said—

"This is a rum start, a—very rum start;—and who are you, my dear?"

"One, sir," replied Fanny firmly, and with indignation,—"one sir, who ought not to have been here, and who demands her instant restoration to her friends."

"Humph!" returned Barnell, somewhat abashed at the dignity and chilling coldness of her manner, "very pretty, and very heroic too;—but it's no use being cross about the matter, you know; the whole of it is, it has been a little bit of a mistake of those damned fellows, but it can't be helped, and so we had better make the best of it. You are a devilish fine girl, that you are; rather dark, but as bright an eye as——"

"Cease this disgusting strain," interrupted Fanny, with increased wrath, and her bosom swelling with offended delicacy,—"and tell me by what right you have had me brought hither, and why you seem so determined to detain me?"

"Why, as I said before, my little black-eyed Houri," replied the idiot, "in the first instance, it was a mistake, which I do not know that I have any particular cause to regret; in the next case, you are a long way from home, and it is very late; so at any rate you must stop here all night, but you need not be out of temper, for that matter, for I have no doubt we shall be able to make ourselves very agreeable to each other. By Jove! you are excessively pretty, and I must have a kiss from those ruby lips, which seem to invite to——"

"Stand off, sir,—stand off!" exclaimed Fanny, her eyes seeming to flash sparks of indignation, as she snatched up a knife, which she at that moment discovered accidentally lying on the table, and brandishing it in a threatening manner;—"if you dare to approach me, or pollute me with your disgusting caresses, I will plunge this to your heart!"

Mr. Barnell started back with evident amazement and incredulity at the manner of Fanny, and the air of resolution which was pourtrayed in her whole demeanour, and for a while stood looking at her, unable to utter a word—

"How soon the angel can be converted into a devil," at length he said; "why she is a perfect fury, I declare. But come now, my dear, this is very ridiculous, and quite uncalled for; I should like to know what harm there can be in a kiss, especially from a perfect gentleman, which I am."

"Your conduct has proved you to be an un-manly ruffian," said Fanny, with unshaken firmness, "but I know you, Mr. Barnell."

"Know me, do you?" observed Mr. Barnell, apparently taking it as a compliment to his popularity;—"well I should not be surprised neither, for there are very few but what have heard of me; why, I am as rich a man as there is in the country, and——"

"I want not to listen to this harangue, sir," interrupted Fanny contemptuously, "it is sufficient for me to know that you have committed a gross outrage; although it was not intended for me, the insult was directed towards my friend, Miss Herbert, and therefore——"

"Your friend,—Miss Herbert your friend?" —repeated Barnell with astonishment, "can it be possible? But, by Jingo, now I look at you more earnestly, I have some recollection of your features, and—why, ain't you the young Gipsy girl who convicted——"

"Sir," exclaimed Fanny, with almost insupportable wrath, "have you one spark of manly feeling about you?"

"Oh, as for that," returned he, "I always had the character of being a very good man; I did not mean to offend, because if you was a Gipsy it was not your fault, and then, if reports speak true, you have some rich blood in your veins, that is, on your father's side."

"Heartless, unmanly wretch," ejaculated the poor girl, completely worn out with the insults she had received, "why am I to be subjected to this insolence, and from a perfect stranger?—You have dragged me from my friends, and now you have found out your mistake, the least you can do is to take steps to restore me."

"You are a cross, provoking little thing," said Barnell, with a supercilious grin, which in all probability was meant for a smile, "but after all you are devilish pretty; however, as it seems you and I can't be friends, I will leave you for to-night, and talk about business to-morrow. There is a couch in the anteroom when you like to retire to repose. Good night, my love, and pleasant dreams to you!"

As the fellow said this, he impudently blew a kiss from his hand towards the disgusted damsel, and made his exit from the room, taking care, however, to lock the door after him.

Fanny threw herself into a chair, and gave way to a paroxysm of grief, which was occasioned by the boldness of the vulgar and illiterate brute who had just left her; and she felt that she was placed in a situation of the utmost danger, from which she saw no chance of escape. Retire to rest, she could not think of, for ever and anon the rude laughter of many coarse voices, convinced her that a party of men were carousing below, who no doubt were the associates of Barnell, and she shuddered when she reflected upon the danger to which she was exposed, confined in a house, in that lone place, with a parcel of vulgar roisterers, who probably gloried in insulting that sex it was their duty instead to protect. More than once she could distinguish the voice of Barnell high above the rest, and his speeches were occasionally interlarded with oaths that made even her tremble, who had from childhood been used to the most horrible language, from the lips of those whom fate had thrown her among. Fanny listened with the greatest fear, expecting every moment that the noisy revellers would hasten up-stairs; and as these thoughts crossed her mind, and she knew her helpless and unprotected state, her terror may be easily conceived. From the master of the place she felt confident she had nothing to hope, for she had no doubt, from the looks of familiarity he had exchanged with the ruffians who had brought her there, that he was in some way or other connected with them, and that he had been paid by Barnell for the part he had to play in this nefarious transaction. From the noise they made below, she was certain they were all inebriated, and the language which shocked her ears, would have disgraced the lowest pot-house. Singing, bawling, and swearing predominated, and above all the rest

she could hear the voice of Barnell appeared to take a principal part in the proceedings. How disgusted was she with the ignorant wretch, and could not help thinking that it was a pity Providence should bestow wealth upon such a blot upon society, when there were so many deserving objects who were forced to eat the bread of poverty.

From her own situation, her thoughts reverted to that in which the worthy doctor and Maria were placed; the state of agitation and alarm into which her strange disappearance would throw them, and the various conjectures they would form as to the cause of it; and she became truly wretched.

To attempt to sleep would have been madness, nor would she venture to retire to bed. She walked to the window, and found it was unfastened; so she gently pushed it up, fearful that they might hear her below, and fancy she was attempting to escape. She looked out, and although the idea of liberty had at first dawned upon her mind, when she perceived the height it was from the ground, she turned away in despair. The room she occupied was at the back of the house, and immediately beneath the window was a ditch, which to her imagination entirely precluded all chance of her escape, if she should even have the courage to attempt it. The wind blowing keen, she closed the window again, and returned towards the fire-place. She listened—all was now perfectly still in the house, and she doubted not but that, overcome with the deep libations they had taken, Mr. Barnell and the others had fallen asleep. All at once a strong smell of smoke, which seemed to proceed from below, almost suffocated her, and she was forced to rush to the window again, to endeavour to get some fresh air. No sooner had she thrown it open and looked out, than to her horror she beheld flames pouring forth from the back parlour window (the room in which she imagined the revellers had been assembled), and which were ascending with fearful rapidity. Doubtless one of the senseless wretches had knocked down the candle, and thus set fire to the premises.

"Good God! what will become of me?" cried the distracted Fanny, wringing her hands—"I am lost!—Escape this way is utterly impossible; and here then must I perish!"

In a paroxysm of despair the wretched girl screamed aloud, and called "fire!"—but no one heard the alarm, and the flames had now reached the window, and her death seemed inevitable. With frenzied haste she seized hold of a heavy poker, and directing all her strength against the room door, after repeated efforts, she succeeded in breaking one of the panels, through which she crept on to the landing place. Here the smoke was so dense, that she was nearly stifled, and she was unable to distinguish any objects through it. The burning timbers crackled fearfully, and it was very evident that to attempt to escape down stairs, would have been attended with certain death. There was very little time for hesitation ;— with much difficulty she groped her way through the smoke across the landing, and her hand came in contact with the handle of a door ; she turned it and the door yielded. With a precipitation increased by the imminent danger in which she was placed, she rushed into the room, and ran to the window. She opened it, and perceived that there was a pos-

DOCTOR HARTLEY ROBBED BY HIS NEPHEW, RICHARD GRAYLING.

sibility of her effecting her escape, for it was not so lofty as the room in which she had been confined, and the flames were not raging with such fury at the back part of the house. Imploring the protection of Providence, Fanny resolutely flung herself from the window, think-ing she should be able to reach a ledge beneath, which projected over the shop front, but her feet would not reach it, and she hung by her hands for a second or two to the window sill before she could venture to jump, for fear she should fail in the attempt and be precipitated to the earth.

The fire had now gained to a frightful ascendancy, and the flames had reached the front room, and were pouring like the lava adown the volcano's side, towards the window from which Fanny was hanging. There was not a moment to be lost; she let go her hold and fortunately reached the ledge in safety. From this place it was a very short distance to the ground, and she accomplished her descent without much inconvenience. With a mingled feeling of horror at the awful situation in which she had been placed, and gratitude for the providential escape she had made, Fanny rushed from the spot, and flew along, she knew not in what direction, with the precipitation which fright had caused her, and she had proceeded for some distance before she ventured to stop; she looked around her—all was pitchy darkness; she had emerged from the wood, and found herself standing on a barren wild, across which the bleak wind was blowing, and sent a deadly chill into her veins, which seemed to curdle up her blood. She looked in the direction from whence she came, and beheld the sky still illumined with an ensanguined hue, from the reflection of the fire she had so fortunately escaped from. Notwithstanding the horrors of her situation, she could not help shuddering when she thought upon the fate of Barnell and his debauched companions, for she had not the least doubt but that they had all perished in the flames.

She was soon aroused to the sense of the dangers of her own situation, and wrung her hands in the intensity of her agony. Of what part of the country she was in, she was perfectly ignorant, and which way to proceed she knew not.

"Almighty God direct me!" she exclaimed fervently, and then leaving her fate in the hands of that Supreme Being she had invoked, she took a narrow footpath to the left, for at that moment the distant sound of a church bell which was borne across the air from that direction assured her that she should find a town or village if she proceeded that way.

The darkness of the night now increased —the wind ceased for a while, and presently the rain began to fall with much violence. This was succeeded by loud claps of thunder and flashes of lightning, which played across the sky like so many fiery serpents. Fanny's dress, which was very thin, was soon drenched through, and what with the terrors she had lately undergone, the fatigue of her escape from the scene of conflagration, and the despair which now seemed to close around her on every side, she was almost ready to sink to the earth.

"The pitiless pelting of the storm" still continued, and Fanny walked on as well as she could, quite unconscious whither she was going, and without encountering any place which could afford her the least shelter. She had paused a moment to look around her, when a rattling sound, like the clanking of chains, sounded in her ears, and looking up, God! what a sensation of horror darted through her veins, when she beheld swinging in the night wind, the ghastly spectacle of a human skeleton, suspended in a gibbet. With a groan of agony she covered her face with her hands, and fled from the spot with all the rapidity which her strength would allow.

Revolting as this sight was, at such an hour, and on such a spot, it imparted some relief to the anxiety and suspense of Fanny; for she knew well in what part of the country she was, for many a time, while with the Gipsies had she crossed that heath, and she was certain she was not far from a village. But what of that. Could she expect to gain shelter at such an unseasonable hour, and without any money in her purse? Still there was a ray of hope, in the knowledge that she was near some place of human habitation, and she determined, at all events, to try the humanity of one of the cottagers. She had a small trinket with her, she recollected, which would sufficiently reward any person for the favour she required, and she therefore hastened on her way with renewed courage.

In about another quarter of an hour, she emerged from the heath, and came to the village she had expected to find, and just as she did so, the church bell chimed the hour of two. Not a light was to be seen in any of the cottages, but Fanny—rendered more bold by the desperate situation she was placed in, as she was many miles from Doctor Hartleys residence—knocked loudly at the first cottage she came to. She waited for a few minutes, but no answer was returned; so she repeated the knocks still more loudly than she had done before. In another second she heard the casement thrown open above, and by the voice, an old woman, whose tones were none of the most pleasant, demanded who was there.

"A stranger!" replied Fanny, in a tremulous voice;—"I have but just escaped from a fire —and being many miles from home, I request of you to afford me shelter till daylight, and I will reward you for your trouble!"

"A fire!" repeated the old woman, with peculiar emphasis, "where, girl?"

"At the inn across the heath," answered Fanny.

"Ah!—a pretty house truly for a young girl to be in," croaked forth the old woman; "you can be no good, I'm sure."

"It was against my will," said Fanny, beginning to despair; "for the love of Heaven, do not refuse my request; I am drenched with rain, and care not what inconvenience I put up with, so long as I can obtain shelter."

"Well, well," said the old woman, after a pause, during which she had thrust her head out of the window as far as she could, so as to enable her to scrutinise the applicant more narrowly; "it is indeed a rough night, and as you do not seem to be what I at first thought you was, if you do not mind putting up with an old mattress, in my back room, I will comply with your request."

"Oh, anything, anything," exclaimed Fanny, eagerly.

"Very well, stay there a minute then," said the old woman, "and I will let you in."

With these words she closed the casement and retired. The interval that succeeded appeared an age to Fanny; but presently she heard the clicking of the flint and steel, and shortly afterwards saw a faint light glimmering from the casement above, which disappeared, and then Fanny heard a footstep descending the stairs.

The door was opened by a feeble-looking old woman, who was in her night gear; her cheeks were very much furrowed, and her countenance, though grave, was far from unprepossessing. She eyed Fanny narrowly from head to foot, and then being apparently satisfied, desired her to walk in. She complied with this request, and the old woman placed a chair for her in the chimney corner, and proceeded to place some more wood on the fire, which was not quite out.

"Dear me, child, you are in a miserable plight, sure enough," said she; "but sit a few minutes and warm yourself, before I show you to the humble mattress, which is all I can accommodate you with."

Fanny sincerely thanked her for her kindness, and the cheerful blaze in a short time revived her, and she mentally returned thanks to the Almighty for her escape from the fire, and for the shelter which she had thus so fortunately obtained.

The old woman, seeing how fatigued Fanny looked, did not ask her many questions, and a short time afterwards, she having sufficiently warmed herself, requested her to follow her, and taking the lamp in her hand, led the way up a narrow flight of stairs, into a back room, which was remarkable for its cleanliness. In one corner of the room, on a stump bedstead, was a mattress, with a clean rug over it, and which seemed to be put in readiness for the reception of some person.

"There, young lady, that is the only way I can accommodate you in," said the old woman. "I had prepared it for a young woman, who is about to leave her situation, and intends to remain with me until she gets another; I expected her here this evening, but it was a fortunate job that she did not come, or else you would have had to walk long enough, no doubt, before any one would have felt inclined to have given you shelter. There, you had better go to rest

at once, for in another hour or two it will be peep o' day;—good morning."

With these words, the old woman having lit another lamp, which was on the table, left the room.

Fanny locked the door, and was about to undress herself, when she was alarmed by hearing a loud knocking at the door below, accompanied by the voices of men, demanding admittance. She trembled, and her heart throbbed so violently against her side, that she could scarcely sustain herself. She approached the room door, and listened with the utmost alarm. Her terrors conjured up a thousand fears and fancies, and her fear was increased, when the knocking was repeated, and a gruff voice, with a terrible imprecation, commanded the old woman to open the door.

"Well, well, don't be in such a pucker, Charley," said the old woman in reply, "I'm coming as fast as I can; but I think you might have stayed till daylight before you came to disturb me in this manner."

The door was now opened, and Fanny could hear the heavy footsteps of two or three persons.

"Why, mother," exclaimed the voice of a man who had first spoken, "I thought you would never let us in; and yet you had such a light in both rooms, that we could see it half-way across the heath. But," he added, in a lower tone, "it is not half such a light as we have kindled to-night at——"

"Hush!" interrupted the old woman.

"Oh," returned the man after a pause, "it is the young woman you expected, I suppose."

The old woman answered in the affirmative, and Fanny's mind was relieved of a dead weight.

"We did the job nicely," Fanny heard another male voice remark, after a pause, "the drink went round freely, and the gent took his full share—we were down upon him—the money—fired the place—all perished——"

Thus in broken sentences did the affrighted Fanny learn that the fire from which she had so fortunately escaped, was the wilful act of an incendiary, and she was under the same roof with the wretches who had committed such an atrocious crime!—Her safety now only depended upon the old woman, and when she heard her remonstrating with her sons, for such they appeared to be, on the enormity of their conduct, she was more at rest. The conversation was now conducted in such low tones that Fanny was not able to catch a word for some time; but at length one of the fellows with an oath exclaimed—

"If I thought so, she should never leave this cottage alive!"

At these words, her terrors were increased tenfold, and she breathed thick and short; but shortly afterwards all was still, and she began to think that they had gone to sleep.

Fanny, in the midst of the terror and alarm which these different thrilling adventures caused her, could not help thinking with a feeling of horror upon the shocking fate of Mr. Barnell and his guilty companions, and which appeared to be so singular and awful a proof of the retributive wrath of the Almighty. At length, however, all remaining perfectly still in the cottage, she threw herself on the humble pallet, and fell into a deep sleep, from which she did not awake until the old woman aroused her at an advanced hour of the morning.

Fanny could perceive the deep traces of heavy care in the old woman's furrowed countenance, and she had evidently been weeping, for her eyes were inflamed and bloodshot. Fanny could read her history in a moment; she saw that she was unfortunate in having two wild and abandoned sons, who, despite all her remonstrances to the contrary, were determined to pursue the path which must lead them to destruction, and from her heart she could not but pity her.

She had prepared a frugal repast, of which she invited Fanny to partake, with much earnestness. The latter complied, and after a hasty meal, returned her thanks to the old woman, and offered her the bauble, which was all she had about her, for the trouble she had been at.

"No, my child," said the old woman, "I wish not to be paid for the trifling services I have rendered you, put up your trinket, and I am sufficiently repaid in the satisfaction of having been the means of saving you most likely from insult and shame. God knows, had those wretched boys—but enough; good bye, child, and Heaven speed you on your journey. But I would have you keep out of the high road, for there is a fair close at hand, this day, and no doubt the road will be infested with Gipsies, some of whom, seeing you a young woman, and alone, might be tempted to insult you.

"Gipsies!" gasped forth Fanny, turning very pale, and trembling.

"Aye, child," answered the old woman, "and they are a bad lot, who care very little what they do. This neighbourhood has been sadly pestered with them for the last few years, and the farmers dread their coming, for they never fail to take all they can lay their hand on."

Fanny knew full well that the old woman spoke the truth, for several times had she been with the gang there, and their depredations were shameful. However, she made no observation in reply to what she said, and once more earnestly thanking her for her kindness, she left the cottage.

She struck out of the high road, and pursued her way with a palpitating heart, and the utmost trepidation, for she knew that if she should encounter any of the Gipsies, her death

would be inevitable. She had, before she received this information, been in hopes of meeting with a stage that was going to the town where Doctor Hartley resided, but the way she was compelled to travel precluded all chance of that, and increased her apprehensions, for she knew she was above half a day's journey from home.

She travelled, however, a considerable distance without encountering a single individual, for it was a most unfrequented way, and as she approached nearer and nearer towards the place of her destination, her courage revived, and she proceeded with redoubled celerity. And now she had arrived so near the town, that she could see the spire of the church, and observe the smoke curling from the different chimney pots, and her heart began to leap with joy and gratitude to heaven, which had saved her unhurt from the danger by which she had been surrounded; when, just as she had reached a woody glade, which was not more than a quarter of a mile from the town, she was alarmed by hearing a harsh and commanding voice calling upon her to stop. She looked back, and her terror may be readily conceived, when she beheld two Gipsy women in rapid pursuit of her, in one of whom she recognized the person of the hated Morna, and from whose vengeance she had so much to dread. With the utmost precipitation, or as well as her trembling limbs would permit her, Fanny hurried on, hoping to be able to reach town before her enemies could come up with her, and who she was very well aware would then abandon their pursuit; but her strength gradually failed her, and the Gipsies were fast gaining ground upon her.

"Stop, girl!" shouted Morna, in a fierce tone, "you cannot escape us—stop, I say!"

"Good God! protect me!" exclaimed the despairing girl, as, completely exhausted, she was compelled to hold by a tree to support herself, and to regain her breath; she could not proceed another step, and the next instant the two women got up to her, and seizing her fiercely by the wrists, glared in her countenance with the fury of demons. Fanny screamed.

"Wretch! traitress!" exclaimed Morna, pressing her wrist with a Herculean gripe, "you scream in vain—here no help is at hand; no person to interpose between me and that vengeance which your treachery has excited. Ah! well may you tremble to encounter me! Vile spawn of the hag who has brought such misery upon my race—I could tear your polluted heart from your breast, but the hour for the gratification of my revenge has come, and——"

"Oh, Morna!" exclaimed the terrified girl, as she beheld the fiendish looks with which Morna and the other Gipsy contemplated her; "spare me, spare me!"

"Spare you!" replied Morna, in a voice hoarse with rage; "wretch, dare you ask mercy from those whose kindred you have murdered? I have you now in my power, and this hour shall seal your fate!"

"Ay, death to the traitress who has brought wailing and weeping upon our tribe!" said the old woman, as she pressed the wrist of Fanny more tightly.

"It shall be so," said Morna, at the same moment drawing a knife from beneath her cloak, and brandishing it above the head of Fanny; "prepare yourself, girl; this moment is your last!"

"Beware," gasped forth the distracted girl, in vain struggling to escape, "would you break your oath to Jabella? Did you not swear to her in her dying moments that you would not harm me while I was under the protection of Doctor Hartley? Remember, Morna, and hesitate ere——"

"I care not," interrupted the woman; "even my oath am I ready to break, and to take the consequences of the same, rather than lose the chance of gratifying my revenge! Fool! think you that we are going to let both you and your mother escape us? No! it shall not be; prepare, I say again, this moment is your last!"

"Hold, miscreants!" cried a well-known voice, which struck confusion and terror into the breasts of the women, and they relaxed their hold of the astonished Fanny, as there suddenly darted before them, with a pistol in each hand, the form of Ela! Fanny uttered a wild shriek of surprise and delight, and forcibly releasing herself from the now feeble hold of the women, rushed into her mother's arms. Morna, who seemed to be completely paralyzed to the spot, gazed upon Ela with a mingled expression of fiendish hate, disappointment, and incredulity, while the latter fixed upon her a look which was sufficient to strike awe into the most stubborn breast.

"Fiends of hell!" she ejaculated, "your diabolical thirst for revenge is thwarted; the mother is still at hand to protect her child, and to tell you she hates—she despises you. Even now could I stretch you lifeless before me—but I want not to spill your blood! Away, wretches, and be grateful for the mercy I have shown you!"

"Mercy!" reiterated Morna, her eyes rolling wildly in their sockets, and her form trembling with almost ungovernable rage, "mercy from Ela, the curse, the bane of our tribe! Perdition's fires blister the tongue which spoke the accursed word. Zarah, heed not her threats! On to her, and let the tigress and her cub both fall a sacrifice to our just vengeance!"

"Advance but a step, but an inch towards me, and I will discharge the contents of each of these pistols to your brains," cried Ela, in a determined voice, as Morna and her companion, brandishing their knives with fierce gestures, were about to spring upon her. Fanny clung fearfully to her mother's bosom, while the latter presented the weapons at their enemies, and by her looks showed that she was resolved to put her threats into execution.

Morna and the other, evidently alarmed by her determined demeanour, started back a few paces, and looked at her and Fanny, with eyes bloodshot with the violence of their rage and disappointment; while Ela, still presenting the pistols at their heads, slowly retreated backwards, Fanny fearfully clinging to her.

"A murrain seize thee and thine!" exclaimed Morna; "but you shall not long triumph thus—the vengeance of our injured tribe shall yet overtake you, and Morna before she dies will have the satisfaction to behold the consummation of her wishes. Beware!"

Ela replied to these threats with a scornful laugh—and shaking her fist at her, Morna and her companion quitted the spot, and they were speedily out of sight.

It would be impossible to describe, as we ought to do, the sensations of delight and astonishment that filled the bosom of Fanny, as she looked up in her mother's face, and felt herself pressed with the most impassioned fondenss in her arms. But Ela seeing her about to give vent to her feelings in words, by a significant look checked her, and taking her arm, hurried her on towards the town, fearful that more of the Gipsies were near the place, and that they might fall victims to their vengeance; and they soon arrived at the house of Doctor Hartley.

CHAPTER LI.

"Let me glut mine eyes, and have
My ample share of blood and vengeance;
Oh, 'twill delight me to see them writhe,
And groan, and shriek—in agony!"
ANON.

INDESCRIBABLE had been the agony of Doctor Hartley and Maria, when all their endeavours to discover any traces of Fanny proved unsuccessful, and hour after hour was added to the time of her absence. They now entertained the worst fears, and thought that the unfortunate girl had really fallen a victim to her bitter enemies—but yet, in all their researches, none of them had seen or heard of a Gipsy having been in the neighbourhood subsequent to the trial of Mark Darwin and his son.

Mr. Hartley became perfectly distracted—for what could he say to Ela, if he ever beheld her again, or how write to her upon the awful subject? She would accuse him of neglecting her, of being careless of the charge which he had voluntarily taken upon himself; and indeed he could not help upbraiding himself for having suffered her to leave the house by herself, so soon after the trial, and when there was every cause to apprehend danger lurking about.

The night passed dismally away, and the morning brought with it no ray of hope. The doctor had offered a large reward to any person who could discover Fanny, or gain any clue to what had become of her, and at an early hour parties resumed their search in different directions. Doctor Hartley, completely worn out with fatigue and agitation, had just returned home and had thrown himself in despair in a chair, by the fireside, when he was aroused by hearing a female voice, the tones of which immediately struck him as being known to him, seemingly in angry altercation on the stairs with old Matthew, and directly after the door was thrown passionately back on its hinges, and, much to the astonishment of Mr. Hartley, Ela Beranzio stood before him.

"So then," she exclaimed, in a haughty tone, "I have succeeded in discovering you, after all; this fool either would not, or could not reply to the simple questions I put to him. My child, my Fanny, where is she?"

Matthew looked daggers at Ela, for the epithet she had bestowed upon him, and was evidently about to make some reply which would have been anything but harmonious to her feelings, but his master looked at him significantly, and he took the hint, held his peace and quitted the room.

"Where is Fanny?" repeated Ela with greater eagerness than before, for she had probably noticed the agitation which Doctor Hartley evinced when she put the question. Mr. Hartley paused, and scarcely knew how to reply, or in what manner to break to her the painful intelligence of her daugher's mysterious and suspicious disappearance; he never felt so embarrassed before, and when he attempted to speak, his tongue faltered, and he trembled violently.

"Do not be impatient, I beg of you," he at last said, handing her a chair, "I will tell you all you wish to know directly; but really you have acted very imprudently I must say, to venture into this neighbourhood so soon after the trial and ignominious death of your enemies, Mark Darwin and his guilty son."

"You know little of the disposition of Ela Beranzio," she replied, "if you imagine that she would have seen her vengeance but half completed before she quitted the country. Think you that anything less than the gratification of enjoying my success would have contented me? No, to have the opportunity of exulting over my foes, has been the hope which has raised my spirits, when all else would have been dark despair. How meanly

must you judge of me, to suppose that any apprehensions of the hazard I might run would prevent me from attempting to gratify my wishes. 'Tis true, I did not divulge to you or Walter Wallingford the exact scheme or resolution I had in contemplation, because I was certain you would only treat it as the determination of a mad woman. Although I left B,——merely to make you believe that I had done as you advised, I returned by another way immediately, being determined to be present at the death of those who had so frequently exulted in my misery, and whose fate I had so often predicted.

"Explain yourself—I do not understand you," said Mr. Hartley, who shuddered at the idea of the revolting answer he expected she would return him.

"Explain myself," said she, "aye, that will I, and in a very few words. At the foot of the gallows, which was erected for the execution of Mark Darwin and his son, thirsting to witness their dying anguish, there stood I—yes, I the woman who has so frequently had to endure their brutal treatment. Yes, and I did behold their execution—I did, with gloating eyes, mark their blanced cheeks——their quivering lips—their trembling forms—their wildly despairing eyes, as they glanced up towards the fatal beam, from which they were in a few seconds to swing like dogs. I marked how they trembled at the approach of death;—and could scarcely repress the laugh of exultation that rose to my lips as I gazed upon their agony, and thought how, in spite of all their artfulness and subtlety, they had been at last caught. But my triumph was not yet complete, —no,—I had not half accomplished my wishes;—I was determined that they, the wretches, should also see me, and know that I gloried, I delighted in their suffering and exulted in their fate.—And well did I perform the task I had taken upon myself;—they did see me;—yes, they beheld me smile in triumph, and saw that what I had so often said was verified, namely, I saw them with the halter round their necks, and triumphed in the agonies they were enduring,"

"Most horrible! most disgusting!" remarked Doctor Hartley, "and yet for such a revolting purpose, what dangers have you hazarded?"

"You say true," answered Ela, in a subdued tone, "I have indeed ran many risks, but they were nought when opposed to my anxiety to gratify my vengeance to the fullest possible extent. But I have more methods of eluding the vigilance, and deceiving the eyes of my foes, than you can possibly have any idea of; which, however, I will not now trouble you by explaining. I could have saved the son, I know, for he was not so guilty as his father, and there were many extenuating circumstances which the Jury upon the trial seemed half inclined to weigh in his favour, and I was confident that I could urge other things which would have enabled me to have gained him a mitigation of punishment;—but no, I would not;—I wished the destruction of the serpent and the whole of his brood, and therefore did I look as eagerly for his death as that of his father, and amply was I gratified."

Doctor Hartley could not help turning away with a feeling of disgust and abhorrence, from a woman who could thus express such brutal, such inhuman sentiments;—but Ela was too much absorbed in her own thoughts to take much notice of him, and after a brief pause she added, with a look of impatience—

"But Fanny—why have you not informed me where she is?"

Now was the moment of trial, and the doctor shrank with terror from it—but he knew it was useless to defer that information, which must be imparted to her, and therefore, in as few words, and as calmly as possible, he related to her the painful truth.

It would be impossible to describe the emotion which Ela evinced during this recital, her bosom heaved convulsively—her countenance first became red, then ghastly pale—her frame trembled—and she had scarcely sufficient patience to wait till the doctor had concluded, when turning suddenly round, she exclaimed fiercely—

"Fool! idiot that I was!—it is what I ought to have expected, by trusting her to the care of strangers. I ought never to have suffered her to have quitted my presence. Alas! my poor girl, if anything has happened to you, I shall for ever consider myself your murderess. But no, the wretches dare not have committed so foul a deed! Her innocence must have disarmed even their wrath! I will this instant away in search of her—a mother's anxiety will not fail to discover her, and let those who shall attempt to harm her tremble!"

As she thus spoke, she took a couple of pistols from beneath her cloak, and was making towards the door, when Doctor Hartley started before her, and said—

"But surely you are not going to be so rash as to venture on this melancholy and dangerous errand alone?"

"Nay, do not detain me," said Ela, forcing her way to the door, "I want no one to accompany me—they would only baffle me in my endeavours to find my poor girl. As for danger, I do not apprehend it—something whispers to me that I shall succeed in finding her, and that I have nothing to fear; at any rate these two good pistols, which I have lately always carried about me, will serve me well, and make a couple of my enemies pay for their crimes! Fanny, my poor girl, your mother flies to save you, or perish also!"

With these words she rushed from the room, and flying down the stairs, quitted the house, and was soon far enough away. It has been seen how her footsteps were providentially guided to the very spot where her daughter was placed in such imminent peril, and at the very moment when her life was threatened. But oh, what feelings of transport and gratitude rushed to her heart as she returned towards the house of Doctor Hartley, accompanied by that girl, whose safety was far more precious to her than her own life?—One moment she could have laughed deliriously, and the next the tears were ready to gush from her eyes. The astonishment and joy, too, of both the worthy doctor and Maria, on the unexpected restoration of Fanny, may be readily imagined; and they embraced her with the utmost transport. They all heard with astonishment the account which Fanny gave of her abduction, and her miraculous escape from death; and Ela's looks sufficiently expressed her indignation, when her daughter related the manner in which she had been insulted by Barnell.

"But the poor wretch has paid the full penalty of his offences," she said, "and I will therefore endeavour to pardon him."

Maria shuddered when she thought on the shocking fate Mr. Barnell had met with in the midst of his iniquities; and she could not help feeling a sentiment of pity for the fate of a man, whose errors were perhaps more of the head than the heart.

Mr. Hartley was afraid that Fanny would relate to her mother the whole particulars of the affair with Rupert Darwin, and the shock his brutal conduct had given her; knowing that Ela would upbraid him for not having endeavoured to prevent that which was completely out of his power. But he was much gratified when he found that she remained silent upon the subject; and during the interval of her mother's temporary absence from the room, he took the opportunity of mentioning to her the propriety of not saying anything at all about it. Fanny readily promised to comply with his request, and Maria was also cautioned not to give the slightest hint of what had happened, though her own prudence would have suggested that course if she had not been.

But it was very clear that Ela, from some cause or other, had a suspicion of the truth, and it was not without considerable trouble and caution that they were enabled to evade her questions.

"But why should I suspect such a thing?" she murmured in a low tone, "I am certain they must have passed through the town at a late hour of the night, when there was no one to observe them but their own people, and therefore it is not at all likely that she should see them. And what if she should behold them?—surely the spirit of her mother is not so dead within her, that she would not rather have exulted at the fall of her foes, than to have felt any emotion of pity or of terror."

Of course, Maria could not but easily guess what Ela meant by these observations, and to whom they hinted—but with that cautious prudence for which she was so remarkable, she affected not to have overheard the words Ela made use of; and Ela soon afterwards became apparently completely absorbed in deep rumination, and paid no attention to the conversation that was going on.

Maria could not help dwelling with a feeling of the utmost horror upon the circumstances that Ela had narrated, and the savage, the revolting spirit of revenge she had exhibited towards her foes. But oppressions, which from being constantly heaped upon her, had rendered her heart callous, and quite overclouded all those gentle feelings that had at one time held such paramount sway in her bosom. There was a time when Ela Beranzio would have felt the same sentiments of disgust and abhorrence, at the bare idea of witnessing such a spectacle as the one she had been describing, as Maria now experienced; and when her gentle bosom was ready to melt at the least appeal to her sensitive feelings. But, alas, time, circumstances, and bad examples, had strangely altered that mind which erst might have been held up as a bright pattern for others of her sex to copy and emulate. But happy was the change which their restoration to each other had wrought in the bosoms of Ela and her daughter, and it would have been a difficult matter to have discovered which were the most powerful. They gave free expression to their sentiments, and it was a circumstance which caused the good doctor no little astonishment, when he discovered that Fanny, in reality, was the same passionate, violent, and hasty being as her mother; and as they separated for the night, and he left them both together—being accompanied by Maria—he could not help saying to her before he left her, that he felt very happy to think that it would not be long first, before Ela would take a deal of care and anxiety off his mind, by removing her daughter from his charge, who would require a considerable deal more trouble and kind attention than at his time of life he could be expected to afford.

Satisfied as the doctor might be at this idea, Maria experienced a very different sensation. The sweetness of Fanny's disposition, and her intrinsic qualifications, had made a deep impression upon her heart—and besides, there was another and yet more powerful cause for her feeling for her a sentiment of the warmest affection; she was Walter Wallingford's sister. The likeness, too, she bore to

him was most remarkable, and at times, as Maria gazed upon her, she looked so much like him, that the tears would insensibly steal to her eyes, and she felt her love for the Gipsy girl daily and hourly gaining strength. Then their sentiments, their feelings, their ideas were so much alike, that they had scarcely a thought which was concealed from one another. Often did they converse about Walter, for no subject could be so dear to Maria as that; and who could feel more pleasure in listening to it than the delighted Fanny? It need not, therefore, be wondered at, that she should contemplate a separation from her without the deepest regret, and therefore her anguish may be very easily conceived, when the doctor added to the observations he had before made use of, the following remarks:—

"Thank God I shall not be plagued with these wild women many days longer;—Fanny will, no doubt, not be tempted to leave her mother again, and indeed Ela will not, I am confident, think of travelling without being accompanied by her. Of course, as I do not think it is safe for them to remain in this neighbourhood any longer than possible, I shall urge them to make their departure as early as it is convenient. They will be constantly in danger it is very evident, while they remain in this country, that is, if they have not exaggerated the accounts they have given me of the Gipsies' implacable disposition, and of the trouble and patience, and the determination with which they prosecute their schemes of vengeance, and the indefatigable manner in which they pursue the footsteps of their intended victim, until they have found them out; consequently, the sooner they hasten from England the better. Indeed, I shall be terribly uneasy myself, until I hear that they are in a place of security."

"And shall me and Fanny never more meet?" inquired Maria in a tone of melancholy.

"It is a matter of great doubt, my love," replied Mr. Hartley, who sympathised sincerely with the feelings her manner expressed,—"but there are many circumstances which render you and Fanny meeting again very improbable."

Maria sighed deeply at these observations, but she made no reply, and the doctor having paused a short time in meditation, resumed—

"Still, my dear, I would not have you give way entirely to despair upon the subject, for there is no knowing what strange events may take place to bring you together once more: one circumstance, although it is a melancholy one to think upon, but which must happen some time or other, this one circumstance in particular, which is the death of Mr. Wallingford, might bring about the event for which you are so solicitous. Walter would then, no doubt, with all a brother's regard (being entirely his

own master), eagerly renew his intimacy with Fanny, and then of course—but I see, my dear girl, that you are getting out of patience in listening to what appears to be mere vague suppositions, and so I will no longer detain you, only to add, that, in my opinion, such may be the result before long, and that, after all, your being once more restored to the company of Fanny is not at all unlikely."

"Heaven send that your words may prove true, my dear sir," said Maria, once more heaving a sigh, and then they separated for the night.

RICHARD GRAYLING AND HIS COMPEER AGAIN IN SEARCH OF DR. HARTLEY.

CHAPTER LII.

"Stop! stop's, the word all dread to hear,
　Your gold and your gems resign;
With my pistols cock'd, nad my looks severe,
　For a desperate life is mine."

SEVERAL days had now elapsed since Ela had resided in the house of Doctor Hartley, and in that time it was astonishing to behold the alteration which had been wrought in her general behaviour. She had apparently quelled, if not entirely subdued, those violent passions which had before so distorted her real character; and the quiet, gentle, and insinuating manners of those with whom she was, had the effect of making her seem quite another being. The

excitement, the painful excitement under which she had so long suffered, had now entirely abated, and the natural good qualities of her character shone forth with almost all their pristine brilliancy. She seemed to have resolved to efface all recollection of the events that had taken place from her memory, and talked with calmness and prudence upon the plans she had devised for the regulation of her future conduct. She did sometimes mention the Gipsies, but then it was only to express her determination to use the utmost caution to avoid falling into the snares there would doubtless be to entrap her and her daughter, and to be prepared to resist the gratification of that deadly, that unquenchable spirit of vengeance, which she felt confident would exist in their bosoms as long as one of the race remained alive.

At times, too, it was plain to be seen that these thoughts caused her the deepest anguish and melancholy, and was the cloud which alone obscured the bright sunshine of her happiness.

"Alas!" she would remark, "I may strive, I may rack my brain—try all my deepest ingenuity, and though for awhile I may be able to elude them, yet may the slightest accident, the most trifling and momentary lack of caution, make known to them my place of retreat, and then what can protect me from them?"

Doctor Hartley knew it would be the most advisable plan for him rather to encourage than to endeavour to dispute these apprehensions, for they would be the means of causing Ela to use more caution than she might probably have done otherwise, and would thus not only expose her to the insatiable revenge of the Gipsy tribe, but also Fanny; but although he did not hint such a thing to Ela, he could not divest his mind of the opinion that she by far overrated the ingenuity, power, and perseverance of the Gipsies, and he therefore did not believe that she would have anything to fear after she had quitted England; still, fearful as he was that he should make her careless, he could not help imparting to her something in the shape of comfort.

"On your own prudence," he observed, "depends everything: you have now the means to prevent the intrusion of any one but those you well know upon your society, consequently you have no occasion to fear that the Gipsies can easily gain access to you. I would have you, by all means, use every precaution, but at the same time there is no necessity for you to embitter all your moments of pleasure by continually thinking upon these powerless and abandoned people."

Ela shook her head, and a deep sigh escaped her bosom. She had paid the greatest attention to the good doctor's observations, and it was very clear that she was most anxious to receive consolation from what he said: but her own terrors and the knowledge she had of those people, who, he would persuade her, were weak and obscure, rendered her slow to be convinced, and after a pause, she said in a tone of the deepest melancholy—

"God grant that your ideas may be verified, but alas! my heart cannot receive any such hope—something whispers that, some time or the other, I shall surely fall a victim to their revenge."

"Psha! this is ridiculous! it is preposterous," said Mr. Hartley, who could not help feeling a sentiment of vexation that she should so obstinately cling to the opinion she had first formed; but the entrance of Fanny at that moment, put a stop to all further conversation upon the subject, and Ela, resuming her former composure, entered upon the subject of their departure from England, and the time was at length fully fixed for it to take place. It was settled that Ela and her daughter should depart with all the privacy that they possibly could to the metropolis, where they were to remain no longer than was absolutely necessary to arrange their affairs with Mr. Goodwin, who had been the means of bringing her to wealth, and who she had appointed her agent; and when these affairs were settled, it was planned that they should immediately take their departure for the continent, Ela having fixed upon Italy as her final residence.

Ela flattered herself that the Wallingfords and Doctor Hartley were the only individuals who would be acquainted with her future intentions and her early history, but a circumstance soon afterwards occurred which convinced her that she was fated to endure still more vexation than she had hitherto experienced.

That she had been connected with the Gipsies, of course, Mr. and Mrs. Goodwin were aware; but the manners and habits of the former, and the care they took not to make any person acquainted with the secrets of their own tribe, rendered it very unlikely that they should come to the knowledge of anything further.

"I care not," said Ela, when speaking upon this subject, "I care not for myself, for I am callous as to what the world may say or think of me, but I am fearful that my poor child should suffer by the exaggerated tales promulgated by the lovers of idle gossip, and which might ruin and obscure her prospects in life. I would wish that the painful events of the past should be forgotten, and that the future happiness of the heiress of Angelo Beranzio should not be clouded by the envenomed tongue of scandal, envy, and malevolence; or that she should have to suffer the world's contumely and scorn for those views and indiscretions for which her mother is alone accountable."

She had no sooner given utterance to these observations, than she took up the morning paper, which was lying on the table before her, and, judge of her chagrin, sorrow, and indignation, when her eye accidentally fell upon the following paragraph, which was headed "Extraordinary circumstances connected with the Heiress of the late Nicolo Beranzio :—

"'The heiress of the princely fortune left by the late Nicolo Beranzio has suffered a most extraordinary reverse. For many years advertisements were inserted in the public journals, but all traces of her were for some time lost, until she was discovered among a tribe of Gipsies, in the most abject poverty and vice, with whom she had been connected for a number of years, and, as it is stated, had mingled with them in all their nefarious practices, and was several times placed in situations of a *peculiar* nature, and which are of common occurrence among beggars and vagrants of this description. We have no doubt that we shall very shortly be favoured with a circumstantial account of this *lady's* exploits, which will be read with much avidity by the public." '

"Peace and me are for ever strangers!" exclaimed Ela, as she threw the paper on the table, and her countenance evinced the most violent mortification and despair; "alas! who among the few persons to whom my unfortunate history is known, could have been so cruel as to thus try to blight the hopes I had encouraged that the past would have been buried in oblivion, and that henceforth my poor girl might have gone through the world without reproach and shame?"

This was a question which Ela was totally at a loss to answer—Mr. and Mrs. Goodwin, Ela knew, were totally incapable of such a thing, and as for Doctor Hartley, or any of the Wallingford family, she could have answered with her life. She clasped her forehead in agony of grief, and traversed the apartment with disordered steps.

But although Ela or Doctor Hartley could not form the slightest idea as to who was the author of this cruel and obnoxious paragraph, the origin of it may be easily explained, though neither of the party became acquainted with it for some time afterwards.

Mrs. Goodwin had brought up from childhood, with the care and affection of a parent, the orphan daughter of her sister, whose name was Elizabeth. She was a modest, gentle, and interesting girl, and when Ela took up her residence with her benefactors, she became very much attached to her, and after she had come into the possession of her property, made her many handsome presents, which she did not only out of respect to her, but by way of a trifling recompense for the kindness she had experienced from Mr. and Mrs. Goodwin.

Elizabeth had never been one of the party, when Ela was talking to her friends, about her private history, or her future intentions, and, of course, she never, for an instant, imagined

that Mrs. Goodwin would divulge to a mere girl, a secret of so much importance. But such, nevertheless, was the case ; the old lady, being rather of a garrulous disposition, and very fond of her niece, had imprudently talked with her upon the subject when they were alone together, and consequently every circumstance became as familiar to one as the other, although Mrs. Goodwin never failed to make use of the common-place caution of all tattlers, that "she was to be sure not to say a word to any other person on the subject," which Elizabeth promised to obey, but kept her promise no longer than she saw her sweetheart, who generally paid her a visit every evening.

This young man was a lawyer's clerk, but having a very scanty income, and a taste for literature, he used occasionally to earn a few shillings by supplying dreadful accidents and other striking paragraphs to the newspapers ; and, therefore, it may very well be imagined, he listened with no small degree of pleasure to the story which Elizabeth told him, after strictly enjoining him to secresy, which he as faithfully promised to preserve. The circumstances, however, were of that extraordinary description that were not to be met with every day, and the consequence was, that he wrote the paragraph, which caused so much pain to Ela, and got it inserted in the paper, which she so unfortunately laid her hands upon.

This circumstance caused as much astonishment to Mr. and Mrs. Goodwin as it did to Ela and the others, for Mr. Goodwin never imagined for a moment that his wife would be so imprudent as to make Elizabeth the depository of the secret, and the old lady, for her part, could not think that her niece would ever betray the confidence which she had thus reposed in her, or that the young man, who she knew was paying his attentions to her, was in any was connected with such a source of public information.

Many were the pangs this circumstance occasioned Ela, and her mind, which had before been tranquil and satisfied, was now rendered the abode of suspicion, fear, and anguish. She began to doubt whether or not she would be acting prudently by doing as she first intended; for the same person who had been so ready to circulate this paragraph to her prejudice, might also communicate her designs, and thus render all her schemes of peace and security, from the power of her enemies, abortive. But after a considerable time spent in rumination on the subject, she could not think of anything which seemed more likely to prove successful, so she at length determined not to abandon the project. To this resolution, however, she did not come, after she had consulted Doctor Hartley, and who advanced arguments so strong in favour of it, that she immediately adopted his views, and agreed to be guided by the advice of him and Mr. Goodwin in her future conduct. That the latter had read the paragraph which caused her so much disquietude, she had no doubt, for he regularly took the same paper in, and was one of those zealous newspaper readers, that seldom suffer a line to escape their perusal.

There was another circumstance which Doctor Hartley often thought of, and which rendered him the more anxious that Ela should leave the country with the least possible delay. This was the charge which the Gipsies had brought against her of being one of the parties connected with the murder of the unfortunate farmer, and he was in a state of alarm, apprehensive that it should be discovered that Ela was the woman who had been accused. Hundreds of persons, who resided in the immediate vicinity, had recently seen her in the court of justice, and it was not to be supposed that a woman of her peculiar features and remarkable deportment could be easily erased from their recollection. But, in spite of this, she had ventured to the very spot in which all the danger rested, and only a short distance from the very place where the charge of being a murderess had been brought against her, and where she might be said to be in the very hotbed of her deadliest foes.

But not so much most likely would Doctor Hartley have marvelled that Ela should have so much hardihood, had he been acquainted with the extraordinary abilities which Ela possessed in the art of disguising and transformation. She could assume any character at will, and with such infinite ability, that it was almost an impossibility to detect her. To this she had had recourse on her late visit to the town of B——, to witness the execution of her enemies, Mark Darwin and his son, being on that occasion dressed in male apparel, and so thoroughly disguised, that it was utterly impossible for her most intimate friends to recognize her.

Ela had, however, avoided mentioning this fact to Doctor Hartley, when she related to him the particulars of her adventure at the revolting spectacle above mentioned, and he had no opportunity of inquiring by what means she had eluded detection on that occasion since.

But it was now evident that every moment she stayed there was fraught with danger, and therefore was Mr. Hartley most anxious to see her and Fanny depart. Ela, however, did not appear to give this subject a moment's thought. The death of Mark and his son seemed to have removed all apprehensions from her breast, and flattering herself that the Gipsies were far away from the neighbourhood, as she knew from the time of the year where it was customary for them to be, she thought, in consequence, that she could not be more secure than in the place where she was at present.

Strange as it may appear, notwithstanding her encounter with Morna and the other woman, no suspicion entered her mind that her place of retreat would be guessed, or that any of the tribe whould be lurking in the vicinity; in fact, the circumstance which had lately caused her so much mortification and anguish, seemed to have driven it entirely out of her mind; but it was soon to be recalled to her memory in a manner which she had never anticipated.

Buried in deep and corroding thought, she was standing at the drawing-room window, which descended from the ceiling to the floor, when happening to cast her eyes in the direction of the lawn, judge of her astonishment and consternation when she beheld Morna standing immediately underneath the window, and gazing full upon her. It was very evident she recognized her, for immediately when she observed her look up, she shook her fist in a menacing manner towards her, and then, with a look in which was expressed all the revengeful feeling of her soul, she hurried from the spot.

"I am lost!—I am lost!" gasped forth Ela, with a look of greater terror than the doctor had ever before seen her assume. She staggered to a chair, and sunk into it. Fanny flew towards the door, with the utmost alarm depicted in her countenance, and Doctor Hartley, who was very much astonished at her conduct and the words she had uttered, hastily demanded what was the occasion of her terror—

"I have seen her!—the wretch I have so much cause to dread," answered Ela.

"Seen her? Who do you mean?" asked the doctor, eagerly.

"You must have been mistaken," said Mr. Hartley.

"Oh, no, no, I am not so easily deceived; I tell you I saw her ferocious eye fixed upon me, and she shook her fist at me in a manner which too plainly told her meaning. My retreat is now known, and in a short time we shall have the whole gang down upon the house, like hungry wolves seeking their prey."

"Nonsense!" said the doctor, "how know you that the remainder of the gang are near this place?—Besides——"

"I care not for myself," interrupted Ela, "for, as I have before said, I know that some time or the other I shall fall by their hands; but it is my poor child here; oh, are there no means of escape from this threatened danger?"

"Nay, nay, quiet your fears, I entreat you," said Mr. Hartley, "and learn to be a little more reasonable. It is not, to my thinking, at all likely that the Gipsies, even supposing them to be in the neighbourhood, would make an open attack here in the broad daylight, where there is plenty of assistance so near at hand, and a defeat would be inevitable."

"It is not a little that will make them fearful," returned Ela, "especially at a time like the present, when their feelings are so excited."

"That may be all very true," observed Mr. Hartley, but at any rate you may quiet your apprehensions as regards your daughter, for they are sworn not to harm her while she is under my protection."

"But did not Morna and Zarah but lately make an attempt on her life?" said Ela, "therefore you may judge how little dependence is to be placed on their oaths, when they are urged on by the powerful incentive of revenge. Alas! I know not how to act. Flight would only be attended with equal danger as remaining here."

"Besides, whither could you fly?" asked the doctor; "come, come, calm your terrors; I do not think there is so much cause for them as you seem to think. However, that we may be prepared for any exigency, I will send Matthew to Mr. Ashburne's, to apprise him of the circumstance, and to request his assistance; we will bar all the doors and the windows, and there is no possibility of their getting near you."

"Heaven send your words may prove true," fervently ejaculated Ela, as the doctor rang the bell for Matthew.

Fanny still clung to her mother, and her cheeks were pale with terror, but her fears were more excited on her mother's account than her own, for the promise which Rupert had given her assured her that she was safe.

Matthew was not long before he returned, for in truth he did not much fancy the errand he was sent upon, being afraid that he might encounter some of the Gipsy tribe, and he therefore redoubled his usual speed. He informed his master that Mr. Ashburne, immediately on his delivering the doctor's letter to him, gave instructions to some officers to go by different routes to the vicinity of Mr. Hartley's residence, so that they might not excite suspicion, and that they had also enlisted the services of a number of stout rustics, who were ready enough to oppose the rascally Gipsies, to whom they had a mortal dislike, and that they were now in the immediate neighbourhood, and at the first touch of the alarm bell, would be ready to come forth and give their enemies perhaps a warmer reception than they might calculate upon.

"Well, for my part," muttered old Matthew, as he descended the stairs, "for my part, I positively think master must have taken leave of his senses, here at this time of life to take all this trouble and danger upon himself, for people whom he has not the slightest right to take any interest in. But this last business is worse than all; getting his place besieged by a gang of villains who are likely enough to murder us all in cold blood, and all merely to take the part of that wild woman and her daughter, who, although they may have money now, were once as bad, if not worse than any of the gang. Dear me! dear me!—I can't imagine what has come to people now-a-days. I verily believe there are half of them gone quite crazy."

Thus, grumbling all the way he went, the old man descended to the kitchen, where he determined to keep secure as long as he could, if the Gipsies should make the attack which had been apprehended.

Two hours passed away in this manner, and nothing happening, Ela became more calm, and the fears of Fanny had almost entirely vanished. The afternoon was now far advanced, and the whole party were seated around the table, and the conversation was becoming more free, when they were suddenly all startled by a loud ringing at the bell, followed by a murmuring of many voices. Ela and Fanny jumped from their seats and their countenances turned very pale.

"They are here!" exclaimed Ela, "and my worst apprehensions are fulfilled. Hark! they ring again, and the tumult outside increases—they will force their way into the house in a minute, and then nothing can save me and my poor child from destruction."

"Do not give way to any unnecessary terror," said the doctor, "we have but to ring the alarm bell to bring plenty to our assistance."

He approached the window as he spoke, and beheld a number of Gipsies, male and female, armed with bludgeons and knives, and with the villain Rupert at their head, standing on the lawn, and by their ferocious gestures, seeming to be in a most excited state.

"I will go out and speak to them," said the doctor, "and then if they will not quietly disperse, Matthew can ring the alarm bell, and we must see what can be done to compel them."

"Oh, my dear sir, do not venture, pray," ejaculated Maria, when she saw the doctor unfasten the window for the purpose of going out on to the balcony, "you know not what danger you may run, for in their present excited state it is evident they are perfectly reckless what they do."

"Nonsense, child," said Mr. Hartley, "how silly you all are, they will not harm me." Having thus spoke, he walked forth on to the balcony, and being immediately recognised, the Gipsies raised a loud shout, which rent the air and lasted for several seconds. The doctor stood perfectly calm, and looked firmly down upon them, only making a sign with his hand two or three times, as if he wished to be heard.

At length, Rupert, in a peremptory tone, commanded them to silence, and obedient to the same, they all became still, and afforded Mr. Hartley the opportunity of speaking, which he sought.

"What is the meaning of this uproar," demanded the latter, "and what is it you seek?"

"Vengeance!" cried Rupert, in a ferocious tone, and brandishing a knife above his head, "vengeance for our murdered kindred—vengeance on that accursed wretch, who is now sheltered beneath your roof."

"Know you not the punishment you incur by this outrage?" said Mr. Hartley. "Depart, and no notice shall be taken of it, but if you remain, you may repent your rashness."

"Never will we depart," returned the ruffian, "until you have given Ela up to that fate to which she is doomed by our laws, and which her crimes have fully merited. Nay, Doctor Hartley, it is useless for you to refuse—she shall be ours!—We would not harm you, but if you obstinately persist in sheltering her, we will pull your house to the ground, and sacrifice our victim before your eyes!—We will not wait :—say, will you give her up or not?"

"I will not!" replied Mr. Hartley, firmly, as he retired from the balcony, and closed the window. "The alarm bell; ring the alarm bell!" he shouted to the servant, and the next moment it was rung loudly. Thi was followed immediately by the loud shouts and yells of the marauders outside, and then they commenced endeavouring to beat in the door, and break the windows.

"Good God! they will surely force an entrance, before any assistance arrives!" said Ela, as she pressed the form of her daughter more closely in her arms. The next moment the hammering at the door ceased, and the ruffians appeared to be diverted from their object by something or the other.

Mr. Hartley ventured once more to the window, and beheld the Gipsies warmly engaged wtih the officers and rustics, who had drawn them from the immediate spot, and had made a bold, and resolute attack upon them. The shouts, yells, and imprecations of the Gipsies were dreadful to hear, and it was very plain to be seen that they were determined not to be thwarted in their nefarious designs without powerful effort. The contest was maintained with equal courage and skill for some time and it was extremely doubtful which would prove the conquerors: but, at length the Gipsies began to give way, and their antagonists taking advantage of this, followed up the combat with redoubled energy, until the former were completely worsted, and took to flight in all directions, pursued by the officers.

As soon as Doctor Hartley had informed them of this fortunate circumstance, Ela, completely overcome, threw herself upon her knees and in the most fervent terms poured forth her gratitude to Heaven, in which she was joined by Fanny and Maria.

"But now it is necessary that we should, without any more delay, adopt some plan to avoid the danger which may threaten us from the return of the Gipsies in large numbers," observed the doctor; "I have been thinking that if you and Fanny were to disguise yourselves, while the officers are now driving your enemies before them, you might be able to effect your escape to Wallingford Hall, where they would not think of looking for you, and there you might remain until your departure, which can and must be done with the greatest privacy."

"An excellent thought," said Ela, eagerly, "it shall be done—and I am confident that I shall be able so to metamorphose myself and Fanny, that we may defy the most critical inspection."

"Let it be done quickly," said Mr. Hartley, "for there is not a moment to lose."

Ela motioned her daughter to follow her, and they quitted the apartment. They were not gone many minutes, but when they returned, so great was the change in their appearance, that had not the worthy doctor and Maria been aware of their intentions, they could not possibly have known them.

Ela was attired in an old livery suit of Matthew's, and with the addition of a pair of spectacles, and a stoop in her gait, looked the feeble old man uncommonly well; and Fanny was dressed in a gown, bonnet, and cloak belonging to Mr. Hartley's old housekeeper.

In spite of the anxiety of his mind, and the pressing nature of the occasion, the worthy doctor could scarcely resist a smile, at the outre and grotesque appearance whi ch they made.

"It will not take you long to reach the hall," said the doctor, "and heaven send you may arrive safe there. Myself and Maria will drive over there to-morrow to bid you farewell."

Ela, with much earnestness of demeanour, pressed first the hand of Mr. Hartley to her lips, and then embraced Maria, and Fanny followed her example, with the same fervour. Their silence spoke more than words could have done. The doctor first went out on the balcony to reconnoitre, and finding that the coast was quite clear, and that everything was still around, Ela and her daughter departed from the house. Maria and the doctor, from the balcony, watched them as far as the darkness would permit them, and they proceeded with the feeble slow pace of the old people they represented, and so well did they act their parts, that it was evident that should they even encounter any of the Gipsies, they would not excite the least suspicion.

A short time after their departure, some of the officers and their assistants returned to the house, and informed the doctor that they had pursued the Gipsies to some distance from the town, that several of them were very severely wounded in the conflict, but that they had not succeeded in taking any of them prisoners. The doctor thought it prudent that they should remain in the house during the night in case of any second attack, and accordingly they went down below to refresh themselves after the fatigue they had undergone, which in truth they much needed.

Mr. Hartley was very much surprised and alarmed at this daring outrage committed by the Gipsies, and which fully confirmed the truth of all that Ela had related of their desperate and fearless character. He was very fearful that ultimately, if Ela and her daughter did not succeed in getting speedily out of the country, they would contrive to gratify their implacable revenge, and he was extremely anxious for the arrival of the following day, which was fixed for their departure to the metropolis.

Maria was extremely shocked at what had taken place, and saw with a feeling of horror, the dangerous position in which Ela and Fanny were placed; she was likewise fearful that the resolute manner in which Doctor Hartley had protected them, might bring down their vengeance upon him, and she should feel in a continual state of dread until they had quitted the neighbourhood.

Doctor Hartley and Maria sat up later than they usually did, but nothing occurred to create any further alarm, and when the latter retired to her chamber, all round the house was as quiet as if it had been the abode of the dead. But sleep would not visit her eyelids, her mind was too fully occupied in reflecting upon the strange and alarming events of the day, and his dwelling upon the perilous situation in which Ela and her daughter were placed. It was very evident that the Gipsies would not be frightened by any peril, from the gratification of their blood-thirsty vengeance, and as much as Doctor Hartley seemed to despise what he called the superstition of Ela, Maria could not help being of her opinion, namely, that they would not rest until they had accomplished their object, and that sooner or later she was doomed to fall by their hands.

The slightest gust of wind, the least noise in the house, alarmed her, and her fears suggested to her that the Gipsies had renewed their daring attack upon the house, and this apprehension entirely excluded sleep from her pillow, and rendered her miserable the whole of the night. The idea of her being separated from Fanny, too, to whom she had become as much attached as if she had been her own sister, also preyed upon her spirits, and she firmly believed that she should never behold her again.

"Alas!" she said, "what circumstances may occur to prevent our ever again meeting; divided by many, many miles, and with so many obstacles in the way, such an idea is quite hope-less. Where, then, shall I seek for a companion? Where find one of my own sex to whom I can confide my thoughts? Mine is, indeed, rendered an untoward fate."

She could not restrain her tears as these melancholy reflections crossed her mind, and for some time they so entirely engrossed her attention, that all other ideas were entirely excluded from her thoughts.

At length the rosy tint of morn came to her relief, and she descended to the sitting-room, but although it was so early, she found the worthy doctor already there and breakfast ready upon the table.

"You have risen early, my dear," said he, advancing kindly to salute her, "and if I may judge from your pale face and sunken eyes, you have experienced but little of the benefits of sleep. But it is very silly, child, for you to give way to such extreme terror. Certainly the affair of yesterday was sufficient to alarm any one, knowing the desperate characters of the Gipsies, but after the signal defeat they met with, and finding us so well prepared for them, I do not think it is at all likely that they will be in any hurry to renew the attack. Besides, the officers are gone in search of the rascals, and no doubt many of them will be safely lodged in gaol in the course of the day. We must make a severe example of some of them, or we shall never be secure from these scandalous outrages. The law must tell them they are not to carry on their nefarious tricks with impunity."

Mr. Hartley, however, was wrong in the opinion he had formed that the Gipsies would so easily be apprehended, for in spite of the most diligent search for miles round the neighbourhood, not the least trace of them could be seen. They had evidently taken advantage of the night, and fled from the locality.

The doctor was very well pleased to hear this, for it removed all apprehensions from his mind concerning the danger of Ela and her daughter, and he doubted not but they would be able to prosecute their journey to London with perfect safety and without suspicion. Maria also felt more at ease, and prepared to accompany Mr. Hartley to Wallingford Hall with alacrity.

To prevent any person surmising whither they were going, the doctor chose a circuitous route, and they arrived at the hall without seeing the least signs of the Gipsies on their way.

They found Ela and her daughter waiting most anxiously to see them, and the latter no sooner beheld Maria, than she rushed into her arms with the utmost affection, and embraced her warmly.

Ela looked very pale, and had evidently been suffering a great deal of alarm during the night, but her countenance suddenly brightened up, when, in reply to her anxious questions, the doctor informed her of the unsuccessful efforts made by the officers to find the Gipsies and to apprehend them.

"For the present," she said, "we are safe; they are, no doubt, far away from hence, and will not be inclined to return to this neighbourhood for some time, not till they imagine that the excitement of this affair has blown over."

"Still," observed Doctor Hartley, "I would persuade you to leave this place as early as possible, for you cannot be certain that even now some of your enemies may not be left behind to fulfil the wishes of their villanous associates."

"True," replied Ela, with a serious expression of countenance, "but of that I have before thought, and intend to provide against it. This evening, it is my intention that we depart for London, and, in order to prevent all possibility of a discovery, I purpose going by the mail, and disguised."

"I commend your caution," returned Doctor Hartley; "when you have such desperate characters to fight against, it is necessary that you should always have your wits keen."

During the time this brief dialogue had been going on between Ela and Doctor Hartley, Maria and Fanny had been discoursing upon the melancholy subject of their separation, and interchanging expressions of regret at the painful necessity which compelled them to it—

"Alas! I fear me we shall never meet again," sighed Maria, "and then shall I be without a companion in whose bosom I can repose my thoughts and wishes."

"Nay, I know not that," said Doctor Hartley, who overheard what she said, "I shall not be long before I shall have completed my arrangements here, and then we shall go to London, and we may therefore probably see Ela and Fanny again before they depart on their continental journey."

"Very likely," observed Ela, "for I shall have a good deal to settle with Mr. Goodwin relative to my property, and I may therefore be detained there for some time."

The doctor and Maria remained at Wallingford Hall the whole of the day, and Anthony having booked the places of Ela and Fanny, the former attended them to the coach office, and saw them start safely on their journey, when, grateful for their preservation from the danger which had so recently threatened them, they returned home, and found that nothing had occurred during the day to create any alarm, and it was therefore very evident that the Gipsies had left that part of the country.

We will now pass over an interval of a month, during which time Mr. Hartley had completed his business, and he therefore appointed a period for their departure to the metropolis. The doctor had received a letter from Ela, informing him of their safe arrival in London, and Maria had one also from Fanny, couched in the most

affectionate terms, and expressing to her how dull she felt, even in that gay city, deprived of her society. Maria kissed the letter a thousand times, and looked forward with the utmost impatience and anxiety to their meeting again.

In two days from this period, all the preparations being complete, the doctor and his fair charge departed on their journey, resolving to proceed by easy stages, for the weather was beautifully fine, and the country through which they had to travel was romantic in the extreme.

On the evening of their departure, however, night overtook them in a gloomy part of the country, and the postilion missed his way, so that they became entangled in the mazes of a thick wood, from which they did not perceive any chance of quickly extricating themselves. While they were still in this dilemma, the sound of a horse's hoofs smote their ears; soon afterwards a gruff voice in a commanding tone, called upon the postilion to stop, and before the doctor could inquire what was the meaning of it, a man rode up to the side of the vehicle, masked, and thrusting his head and hand (the latter of which held a pistol) in at the window, demanded his money or his life.

The alarm of Maria at this unexpected circumstance may be better imagined than we can find language to describe it; but Doctor Hartley, who retained all his usual coolness and self-possession, being unarmed, did not offer any resistance, but immediately delivered his purse to the highwayman.

"Your watch," demanded the fellow; "come, be quick about it, for I am in a hurry."

The doctor started.

"Ah!" he exclaimed, "that voice!—Its tones are familiar to me."

"Known!" cried the ruffian; "who are you? let me see."

With these words, he thrust his lantern into the face of Doctor Hartley, and immediately said in a tone of astonishment—

"By hell, it is my uncle!"

"I was right, then," observed Mr. Hartley; "oh, Richard Grayling, have you indeed come to this?"

"There, no preaching, it won't do for me," answered the ruffian; "had it not been for your parsimony, I should not have been what I am. Young fellows must see life and enjoy themselves, but you old fellows would have them all be as steady as a set of hermits. However, it's no matter, I have chosen my course, and I must take the consequences I suppose, some time or other, unless you feel inclined to advance me a hundred or two. But come, we have not met for some time, so I think you can come down with something more handsome than this, uncle."

Doctor Hartley was so shocked at the situation of his unfortunate and guilty nephew, and the recklessness of his conduct, that it was some seconds before he could make any reply to him, and in the meantime the highwayman had removed the mask from his features, and gazed with a bold and daring air upon the doctor and his trembling companion.

Maria had thus an opportunity of scrutini-zing the man's features. He was apparently between thirty and forty, and his countenance might once have been reckoned good-looking, but it was now blotched and swollen with dissipation. He was seemingly a very tall and powerfully made man, and there was some-

MARIA WATCHING THE BODY OF DR. HARTLEY.

thing in his whole deportment which Maria could not gaze upon without an involuntary shudder of horror. She felt severely for Doctor Hartley, for it was very evident that he was greatly hurt at the degraded situation of his nephew, and that he noticed his re-appear-ance as the forerunner of much trouble and misery to himself. Maria removed her eyes from the ruffian with a sentiment of the utmost disgust, when she beheld him contemplating her with an impudent smirk; and immediately afterwards he said — addressing himself to the doctor, and weighing the purse in his hand—

"The contents of this is no great deal, uncle, after the many years it is since we have met."

"Would that we had never met again," retorted Mr. Hartley.

"No doubt you have been very glad," said Richard Grayling, sarcastically, "for that is the way with all you old curmudgeons that have got plenty of the yellow, towards your poor relations. However, old boy, you see I have deceived you, and I shall often pay my respects to you. Off to London, I suppose; I should have called upon you before now, but you see I have been a little way *out of town* for the last few years back, not at home exactly, understand, eh?—Ha! ha! ha!"

"Drive on!" exclaimed the doctor, his heart swelling with disgust, shame and indignation; "drive on, postilion, directly."

"If he only makes the attempt," said Richard Grayling, in a determined tone, as the man cracked his whip, "if he only makes the attempt to move an inch from the spot, I will stretch him a corpse upon the earth. Mr. Hartley, I warn you to be careful how you offend me, for you know that I am not a man tamely to brook an insult, and who never fails to keep his word. I must have money; this is but a trifle, and——"

"I have no more," interrupted the doctor.

"'Tis false!" observed the ruffian, with an expression of rage; "I know you have, and I must have it. This lady's watch, too, and that diamond ring, they look very handsome. I'll just take care of them for her, if she pleases."

"Shameless scoundrel!" returned Mr. Hartley, "leave me!"

"When you have given me more money," said Grayling. At this moment the sound of horses' hoofs, and which seemed to be approaching in the same direction as they were proceeding, vibrated in their ears, and appeared to alarm the highwayman, for turning upon Mr. Hartley, he said—

"Mr. Hartley, we shall meet again; and then you and I will have an account to settle, which you may not be very well pleased to hear mentioned. Beware."

So saying, the highwayman scowled threateningly upon Mr. Hartley and Maria, and clapping spurs into the sides of his horse, he rode away in a contrary direction to that which the persons, whoever they might be, were coming, and was shortly out of sight. Our travellers immediately pursued their journey, and it was several seconds ere Maria could sufficiently recover from the terror into which the adventure had thrown her to speak.

"Alas!" said Doctor Hartley, "I fear this meeting with that unhappy man is but the harbinger of some heavy affliction to me.

Should he by any chance find out whither I am going, he will be continually annoying me by his presence, and extorting money from me, and he knows full well, that for my own sake, and from the fear of bringing disgrace upon my name, I will not seek that means to prevent him which the law would afford me."

"But there is not much chance, I should imagine, my dear sir," said Maria, "of his finding us out, and therefore your fears are groundless."

"Would to Heaven that your ideas may be verified, my love," returned Doctor Hartley, "but of that I fear there is very little hope; depend upon it, he will leave no stone unturned to accomplish his wishes, and then his principal delight will be to annoy me, and endeavour to render me miserable. Alas! my poor sister, what bitter anguish would have been yours, had you been living to behold the disgrace of your son. Even now, after all that I have hitherto done for him, I am willing, nay, I should be delighted to give him anything, could I but reclaim him; but of that there is no hope."

Maria endeavoured to soothe her kind protector, but her efforts apparently met with but very indifferent success, and the doctor sunk into a state of melancholy silence, while the vehicle continued on its way; and she gave indulgence to the thoughts which the various adventures she had met with lately, crowded upon her memory. They had just emerged from the wood, and the lights that proceeded from the different houses of the town where the doctor purposed to put up for the night burst upon their sight, when the fore wheels of the carriage came in contact with the stump of a tree, and it was immediately upset. Providentially, neither the doctor or Maria were particularly hurt, being only slightly bruised, and finding that the vehicle was too much damaged by the shock it had sustained to proceed, they left it in the care of the postilion, and walked to the inn, and received every accommodation.

Refreshment somewhat recruited their strength, and they sat talking for an hour or two on the subject of their unfortunate meeting with Richard Grayling, before they thought of retiring to rest.

A good night's rest had entirely recovered Maria from the state of fatigue which their first day's journey had caused her, and she was very glad to observe that Mr. Hartley had in a great measure recovered his composure and his spirits, and did not mention a word about his scapegrace nephew; consequently, having noticed the pain it had caused him before, Maria avoided mentioning the subject, and only questioned him concerning the way they had to travel, and the place to which they were going. At the idea, too, of once more beholding Fanny, a sensation of pleasure filled her mind, and she looked forward to the meeting with the utmost impatience.

The doctor ascertained, on inquiry, that the carriage had received so much damage, that it would be impossible for it to be got in a condition for them to resume their journey until the following day, and as they could not at that time be accommodated with another vehicle, they would be compelled to remain at the inn during that period. This caused them some vexation, but as there was no alternative, they were obliged to make up their minds to it.

The inn immediately faced the high road, and during the day the doctor and Maria amused themselves by sitting at the window and watching the coaches, and the different people that passed. Suddenly, however, the doctor uttered an exclamation of surprise, and the astonishment of Maria was quite equal to his own, when she beheld, riding up to the door, the person who the night before so much alarmed them, Richard Grayling. He beheld them at the window, and with an air of the most consummate impudence bowed to them, while they could perceive a smile of triumph upon his countenance.

The doctor withdrew from the window with an air of vexation and alarm, and in a melancholy tone observed—

"My surmises are verified already; the villain has found us out, and it is a chance if I shall be able to rid myself of him in a hurry. What is to be done? There is no chance of avoiding him; but how he has been able to discover us, I am at a loss to imagine, for after leaving us last night, he pursued quite a contrary route, therefore he could not have been watching us."

But the manner in which Grayling had tracked them might have been better explained. It appears, that having committed another robbery, he left his uncle, and being apprehensive of a discovery, he had resolved to make his way to London, and had therefore started at an early hour in the morning. On arriving at the spot where the accident had occurred, he observed the postilion who had drove Doctor Hartley, assisting the workmen to remove the carriage into the workshop. He instantly knew him, but the postilion had no recollection of him, for he was differently dressed, besides, he had been masked on the night before.

Grayling stopped upon seeing him, resolving to question him, and after he had returned from the shop, he went up to him and said—

"There has been an accident I suppose, young man, but I trust nobody has been hurt?"

"Why, for the matter o' that," answered the man, "th' only thing as is hurt partic'ler is th' carriage; but it is very lucky that we happened to be so near the inn, or we should ha' had no very pleasant job to walk all the way from that dreary wood."

"You are right," answered Grayling, well satisfied at having made the discovery, and adding that he was glad to hear that no one had suffered any material injury, he rode on.

A few minutes after they had observed Grayling enter the house, a servant made his appearance and informed Doctor Hartley that a gentleman requested to see him below.

"It is he," said the doctor to Maria, in a low tone; "retire, my love, for a short time; we must confer alone, and I will see what persuasion and argument can accomplish with the wretched man.—Desire the person to walk up stairs," he added, speaking to the servant.

Maria looked at him earnestly, and was loth to leave him alone with such a ruffian as his nephew, but he, seeming at once to comprehend her thoughts, said—

"Nay, my dear girl, you need not be under any apprehensions on my account—reckless although I know him to be, and capable of committing almost any crime, he will not venture anything here. But hark, I hear his footsteps on the stairs now, my love."

The doctor, as he spoke, pointed to a door which opened into an ante-room, into which Maria hurried, just as the door opened, and Richard Grayling entered into the presence of his uncle.

Mr. Hartley received him calmly and with perfect composure, and Grayling, without any more ceremony, placed himself in a seat, and looked impudently and exultingly up into the the former's face.

"So," said he, "you see I have soon found you out again—I promised you at parting last night, that it would not be long before we should once more meet, and I have kept my word—though I have no doubt you consider the visit is much more free than welcome."

"Richard," answered Mr. Hartley, in a voice of kindness, "had you but rendered yourself worthy of my esteem and friendship, heaven knows what pleasure it would have afforded me to behold you once more after so long an absence."

"Why, yes," returned the other, with a sarcastic grin, "it is rather a long while, some fifteen or sixteen years I know, and in that time I have seen some strange ups and downs, and met with many curious adventures."

"Doubtless you have," said the doctor, "and mingled in scenes of depravity and crime I shudder to think upon. And what do I now behold you?—a——"

"Hush!" interrupted Grayling; "I know what you would say, but that name must not be mentioned here, for we know not who may be listening, and I can't say that I have any particular wish to be known among the people of the inn. Who made me what I am? who drove me to the desperate life I now pursue? You, who refused me aid when I wanted it."

"Richard," replied Mr. Hartley, "you

wrong me, and you know it. My poor sister on her death-bed made me promise to be a friend, a protector to her only child ; that promise I faithfully kept, and I may say I felt for you the same anxious care as if I had been your father, until your intemperance and dissipation became intolerable, and I was forced to send you from beneath my roof. But I did not abandon you, although your behaviour to me was that of a blackguard and a ruffian. I supplied you with sufficient money to enable you to hold a respectable footing in society ; but when I found that you only squandered it away with the vile and the abandoned ; when I saw that unless some stop was put to it, you must ultimately bring me to ruin ; when I found that you scorned all my good advice, expostulations, and exhortations, then, of course, in justice to myself, I felt that I should no longer continue to supply you with the means of indulging in your fatal vices."

"And by that harsh measure you plunged me into the lowest abyss of crime," retorted the highwayman ; "I became penniless ;—I applied to you ;—I promised to reform—I firmly believe that, had you acceded to my request, I should have kept my promise—but you refused me. I became desperate ;—for a while I joined a gang of sharpers and black-legs, but meeting with bad luck, we separated, and I fell in with some fellows who were in the habit of frequenting fairs and races, and made a considerable booty, by robbing the simpletons who are to be found generally in abundance at those places. At last me and my associates agreed to break into a house belonging to a wealthy man, in a certain place in Suffolk. We did so, robbed the place to a great amount, and were about to make our escape with our booty, when the gentleman, whose chamber we were compelled to cross, awoke and raised an alarm. The old fool paid for his temerity with his life !"

"Great God ! are you then a murderer, also ?" ejaculated Doctor Hartley, with a shudder of horror.

"No," answered Grayling, "I did not shed the old man's blood, but I saw it done. Enough, he died ;—me and my companions were apprehended and tried for the crime ;—two of them suffered the full penalty of the law, but my sentence and that of the others was commuted to transportation for life."

"How is it then I see you here ?" demanded the doctor, with astonishment.

"For one very good reason," replied Grayling ; "because I contrived to escape."

"In what manner did you effect that ?"

"It matters not," said the highwayman, "here I am. It would take me too long to detail the particulars of that event, neither have I any particular wish to recall it to my memory. After the most unparalleled vicissitudes I reached my native shore, from which, if I have good luck, it will be some time before I shall depart again. To this I was brought——"

"By your own base disposition, and nefarious practices," added Mr. Hartley.

"'Psha ! this is always the cant of you humbug moralists, sooner than you will draw your purse-strings. However, I have found you out, and I do not intend to leave you again until we have come to a little better understanding."

"What do you mean ?" demanded the doctor ; "what would you of me ?"

"Cash."

"Villain !"

"Better language, 'uncle," said Grayling, jeeringly.

"Think you to intimidate me

"I expect to compel you to comply with my demands," said the fellow, with a determined air.

"What if I were to denounce you for a——"

"Ah ! you dare not," returned the wretch, "for that would only be to bring disgrace upon your own head."

"I will be detained no longer," said the doctor, advancing towards the bell ; "quit my presence."

"Hold !" exclaimed Grayling, fiercely, and placing himself between his uncle and the bell ; "I will not go until you have granted my wishes. I must—I will have money !"

"Scoundrel !—ruffian !—extortioner !" cried the exasperated Mr. Hartley, as he once more attempted to pull the bell.

"Will you give me money ?" was the fierce interrogatory.

"I will not," answered the doctor resolutely.

"Then, though I swing for it to-morrow, force shall drag it from you !" exclaimed Grayling, as he seized him with an Herculean grasp, and hurled him to the floor, and he was then about to rush upon the prostrate old man, when Maria, who had been a terrified listener to the discourse which had been carried on between them, darted into the room, and placed herself before the ruffian, who drew back at her appearance in confusion and rage, just as the room door was thrown open, and several persons who had heard the uproar, entered, and demanded to know the meaning of it.

"Take the villain from the room," said Mr. Hartley, as he rose from the floor, much hurt and bruised by the brutal violence of the fall.

"Let any man lay a hand upon me if he dare, and he shall dearly repent it," said Grayling, with a look of determination—"I will leave the house ; but, soon again I will cross your path, and then beware !"

"Do you not hear him threaten me ?" ejaculated Doctor Hartley, "the wretch is——"

"Hold ! as you would save yourself from

infamy and disgrace," cried Grayling ferociously.

"Oh, suffer him to depart," said Maria in fearful accents, and clinging to the doctor.

"Suffer me to depart!" repeated the villain with a contemptuous laugh, " let the fellow who is bold enough to obstruct me, stand forward. Stand aside—uncle, for the present I leave you, but mark me, it shall not be for long."

As he said this he shook his fist menacingly, and the persons who had entered the room being evidently daunted by the boldness of his demeanour, and the fierceness of his looks, fell back, and he retired from the place, and immediately left the house.

Mr. Hartley was completely overcome by this meeting with his abandoned nephew, and even the mild consolations and persuasive arguments of Maria for awhile failed to have any effect on him.

"The villain," he said, "now he has found me out, will hunt me to death, and I have no means of escaping from his oppression without bringing disgrace upon myself and the memory of my poor sister. If I were even to yield to his demands, it would only give fresh encouragement to his extortion, and he would never cease to persecute me until he had brought me to ruin."

"But surely there may be some means of eluding him, my dear sir," observed Maria; "and particularly in such a place as you describe London to be."

"Alas! I am doubtful too of that," answered Mr. Hartley, "he will no doubt pursue us thither, and he will be sure to try every method to find us out. Besides, a fellow like him will adopt such methods to accomplish their wishes, that we should never for a moment think of."

"At any rate let us hope for the best," said Maria, "and do not let the empty threats of such a man alarm you."

But in spite of what she said, Maria felt the most intense uneasiness at what had taken place, for it was very clear that a ruffian like Richard Grayling would not stick at anything, nay, even the murder of his aged relative, to obtain his ends. She shuddered with horror as this idea occurred to her, and was the more anxious to get away from the place where the accident which had occurred to their vehicle had compelled them to stop. This she urged to the doctor, who seemed likewise to partake of her apprehensions, and again sent down to the people who were repairing it, to know whether they could not get it done before the time specified; but the answer was that they could not get it ready before twelve o'clock the next day, and therefore they had no other alternative than to make up their minds to the inconvenience.

CHAPTER LIII.

"Darkness veils the earth, and now
    Through the dark gloom and silence stalks
    The guilty forms of rapine and of murder."

THE day passed away without anything more occurring to alarm our travellers; and they kept themselves confined to a private room, not feeling disposed to join the company of any of the inmates of the inn, who would naturally look upon them with curiosity, and that suspicion which ungratified inquisitiveness never fails to engender, after the circumstance which we have just detailed in the previous chapter. Neither would the doctor venture to leave the house, for fear Grayling should be lurking in the neighbourhood, and he knew, particularly now his wrath was aroused by his (Mr. Hartley's) firm refusal to comply with his demands, that he would not hesitate at anything, let it be ever so desperate, to gratify his vengeance and accomplish his designs.

At an early hour he and Maria separated for the night, and the former being quite fatigued and tired with the events of the day, retired to his bed immediately, and soon went off to sleep. But still he was disturbed by frightful dreams, and he frequently started up in bed, under the impression that somebody was in the chamber. But everything was still in the house, and it was evident that the inmates had all retired to rest. He looked around the room—the light was just dying away in the socket, but feeble as were its rays they enabled him to see that there was no person in the place. He threw himself back on his pillow, closed his eyes, and once more went to sleep.

How long he had remained so, he had no means of ascertaining, but he was awakened by a cold breeze being wafted to his face, and looking up to ascertain the cause, he was astonished to behold the window (which looked upon the yard at the back of the house, and was only surrounded by a low wall) wide open. He was confident he had closed it before he went to bed, and besides, it was not open when he before awoke. Another moment and he was certain he heard some one moving in the room. He was alarmed—for his imagination suggested that the intruder could be nothing but a robber, and unarmed as he was, what means had he of defending himself against any attack he might make on him ?—He crouched down in the bed, and scarcely dared to breathe, for should he do so, and the supposed thief find that he was watching him, he had not the least doubt but that he would take his life, to prevent all chance of his being detected. Again he distinctly heard the tread of some person in the room, and he ventured to peep towards the spot from whence the sounds seemed to issue. There, as well as the small portion of light would permit, he beheld the figure of a man, who with one knee bent to the ground, was rifling the contents of his portmanteau. At that moment, in spite of all his efforts to repress it, Mr. Hartley coughed, and the man jumped upon his feet, and after looking around him for a minute, walked on tiptoe towards the bed. The horror of the doctor at this moment may be easily imagined—but still he had the presence of mind not to move, and to feign sleep. The man came to the side of the bed, and opening a dark lantern which he had brought with him, passed it several times across Mr. Hartley's eyes.

"I could have sworn I heard him cough," he muttered in an under tone—the doctor knew his voice in a moment—it was the villain Richard Grayling ; " perhaps it would be better to despatch him at once," he continued; "still I cannot make up my mind to shed his blood, and as he sleeps soundly, I may make my escape before he awakes, or has any opportunity of giving an alarm."

Having once more passed the light across his eyes to be certain that he was not deceiving him, Grayling retired from the side of the couch, much to the relief of Mr. Hartley, and having secured the property out of the portmanteau which he wanted, he walked towards the window, and in a moment afterwards disappeared from it. Unable longer to restrain his excited feelings, Mr. Hartley jumped out of bed, and rushing to the window, beheld a ladder fixed against the wall beneath it, from which his villanous nephew was just descending. Acting only upon the impulse of the moment, Mr. Hartley seized the ladder, and dashed it into the yard, at the same time exclaiming—

"Miscreant! thief! I know you!"

Richard Grayling was near the bottom of the ladder when his uncle did this, so that although he was precipitated to the earth, he was not hurt, and quickly gathering himself on his feet again, he raised his eyes towards the window at which Doctor Hartley was standing, and with a dreadful execration discharged the contents of a pistol at him—and bounding over the wall, fled from the spot with the utmost precipitation.

The shots whizzed past the head of Doctor Hartley, and lodged in the wainscot, but he was unhurt. The report of the pistol had alarmed and aroused the inmates of the inn, who now rushed from the different apartments to ascertain the cause; by this time the doctor had hastily thrown on his dressing gown, and immediately explained what had happened, pointing to his ransacked portmanteau, and the ladder in the yard, in proof of the truth of his assertions. A pursuit was immediately set on foot, but all traces of the ruffian were entirely lost.

In the meantime, Maria, terrified by hearing what had happened, rose from her couch and hastened to join Doctor Hartley, and the other guests in the coffee room, where they had assembled, and were discussing the subject of the late robbery, and putting innumerable questions to the worthy doctor, to not one of which did he think it prudent to return an explicit answer.

The doctor drew her aside, and in a few words detailed to her what had happened, and who was the robber. Maria was terribly shocked when she was made acquainted with the atrocious villany of Ricard Grayling, and she could scarcely bring her mind to believe, but that he had been deceived by some frightful dream, until Doctor Hartley taking her to his chamber, showed her the unquestionable proofs of the truth of his statement, in the ransacked portmanteau, and the different articles that were scattered about the floor, which the robber had in his hurry and confusion dropped. The wretch had plundered him of a considerable sum in gold, and other property, but fortunately, a pocket book, containing a large quantity of valuable notes, etc., had escaped his observation. But the good man did not grieve so much about his loss, as he did to think that his own nephew, he, whom he had fostered with parental care, and sought to guide in the paths of rectitude and honour, should be the thief; nay, that even the thought of taking his life, should enter his head.

"Wretched, wretched man," he exclaimed, "heaven turn you from your evil ways, ere 'tis too late, for an ignominious death alone can follow the course you are now pursuing."

The morning was too far advanced, and the inmates of the inn were too much surprised and alarmed, by what had taken place, to seek their chambers again, so they congregated together around a good fire in the coffee room, talking upon the robbery, until the sound of the bugle summoned them to the coach.

The doctor and Maria kept to their own room till the time, so impatiently looked forward to by them arrived, and the post-chaise was brought up to the door, and they were unable to pursue their journey.

As nothing that would be of any interest to the reader, occurred to them for the remainder of the way, we shall pass it over, and set them down in London, at the residence of Mr. and Mrs. Goodwin, which was in Devonshire Street, Portland Place. But here they were doomed to meet with another subject of vexation and disappointment, Mr. and Mrs. Goodwin, with Ela and her daughter, had left for Bath two or three days before.

To Maria this indeed was a sad disappointment, for the hope of once more meeting with Fanny, had been the only thing which had sustained her during the journey, and London now, had she been so disposed to have been pleased with its gaieties and amusements, would appear as a complete desert to her, totally devoid of any means of enjoyment.

Ela and Fanny had left letters to the doctor and Maria, in which they gave them the warmest assurances of their affectionate regard; and expressed their regret, that particular circumstances had compelled them to depart from London before their arrival, but they hoped to see them yet before they quitted Bath, although they did not wish them to go there yet, for particular reasons, which they did not think proper to mention at that time.

The epistle of Fanny was couched in the most affectionate terms, and Maria perused it with a sensation of the greatest pleasure, still she could not imagine what reasons they could have, strong enough to induce them to throw any obstacle in the way of her and Doctor Hartley rejoining them. She knew, that, placed in the peculiar circumstances Ela and her daughter were, it was necessary that they should act with particular caution, but she could not imagine what occasion there was for their present strict behaviour, especially towards her and her benefactor.

Mr. Goodwin had also left a letter behind addressed to Mr. Hartley, who was an old and particular friend of his, in which he earnestly requested that he would use his house the same as if it were his own, during his absence from London, and gave him many assurances of the continuance of his esteem and friendship.

Maria immediately sat down to reply to the letter of Fanny, which she did in a manner which her feelings prompted. She, however, at the request of Mr. Hartley, refrained from mentioning anything about their adventure with Richard Grayling.

For the first few days after their arrival in the metropolis, the novelty of everything she saw;—the number of streets—the variety and splendour of the shops—the bustle of the passengers—the number of carriages passing to and fro—the costliness of the equipages—the different bazaars—public lounges, and places of entertainment, amused Maria, and partially diverted her mind from other thoughts; but the charm soon evaporated, and she became nauseated and tired of that which had previously afforded her so much gratification. Ever used to the tranquil pleasures of a country life, and to the social comforts of the domestic hearth, the noise and bustle, and unsteady joys of London were little calculated to make a lasting impression on her mind, and she longed once more for the peaceful shades and rural beauties of Rosemary Dell.

In the midst of all the gaiety, too, which surrounded her, she felt miserably dull and lonely, for she was, as it were, alone in the world, having no female companion, into whose bosom she could pour her thoughts. Mr. Hartley did all in his power to make her happy, and insisted upon her accompanying him to the threatres, and other places of amusement; and having shaken off the melancholy and terror which the unexpected re-appearance and brutality of his nephew had occasioned him, he assumed his former general jocular behaviour, and endeavoured all in his power to arouse Maria whenever he perceived her drooping.

In the course of a week after they had been in London, they received other letters from Ela and Fanny, which afforded them much satisfaction. They informed them that they were going on very well, that every arrangement both for their comfort and their safety had been made by Mr. Goodwin, and that in a very short time they should be in a condition to go on their projected trip to the continent. The latter information, although Maria felt uneasy while they remained in England, and thus ran the hazard of encountering their bitter enemies, imparted to her a sensation of sorrow, when she thought, that in all probability she should never behold them again. But from this passage of the letter she turned to another in the epistle of Fanny, which caused her the most infinite delight and astonishment; it went on in the following words—

"And now, my dear Maria, I have got some news to impart to you, which will, I doubt not, afford you both gratification and surprise. Yesterday morning, just after I had sat down to write to you these few lines, I was suddenly interrupted by hearing a knock at the room door, and before I could possibly give the order for the entrance of the person who applied for admittance, in came Elizabeth, the niece of Mrs. Goodwin; who, I must apprise you, I am not much prepossessed in favour of; for there is a cunning and artfulness in her behaviour, which makes me very tenacious of entrusting any secret to her, although she is very inquisitive, and always listening to the conversation that is going on, but never appears to be taking any notice of what is said;—but stop, let me see—I had almost forgot what I was going to write to you about—well, in came Elizabeth, and with an expression in her countenance of wonder and eagerness, informed me that a gentleman had just come to the house and was enquiring for me. Of course, I need not tell you, dear Maria, how astonished I was when she told me of this, and I was rather alarmed too into the bargain, for I was at a loss to imagine who it could be.

"'A gentleman, Elizabeth,' said I, 'surely you must be mistaken—what gentleman? What name did he say? What business has he come upon, and where does he come from?'

"I was the more terrifed, because there was no one in the place but me and Elizabeth, for my mother, and Mr. and Mrs. Goodwin, had gone to transact some business in the city. As for this silly girl, I could not elicit anything from her, no more than he was one of the most beautiful young men she had ever seen, and quite the gentleman too ; and he had requested that I would go to him immediately, as he was waiting in the parlour.

" ' Why, bless your soul, you have no occasion to be so fearful, miss,' said Elizabeth, seeing me still hesitate and trembling—for I could not imagine that it was any other person than Rupert, or one of the Gipsies—' you have no occasion to be so alarmed, and as for me, you may fully depend upon my sincerity, I am an excellent one to keep a secret, and wouldn't divulge a sentence about any young girl, if it were to save my life, and it was for that very reason I popped him into the parlour as sly as possible, so that Peggy, the servant, might not see him, and because I imagined that if you——'

" I cannot express the mortification I felt at the observations and the behaviour of Elizabeth, Maria, and therefore, at all hazards, I determined to proceed to the parlour, and see who the gentleman was, and I also resolved to take her along with me, that the ideas she had formed might be contradicted ; but then she made such a bother about making proper preparations to attend me, that she fairly tired out my patience. First, her hair was out of order, and then her dress was not the thing, and a deal more which made me quite vexed, for I could not conceive, if her suspicions were just, that the gentleman was a sweetheart of mine, what she wanted to take such pains for ? And if, on the contrary, she surely could not expect that she would captivate him at first sight.

" At last, however, my dear girl, we did make our way to the parlour, and when I opened the door, I could scarcely believe my eyes, when Walter, dear Walter, rushed eagerly forward to meet me !"

At this passage, Maria put down the letter in the greatest possible surprise, and gasped for breath, so much had she been struck by the unexpected information. Walter in England, when she thought him far away on the continent ? Could it be possible ? And what could be the occasion of such a singular and unlooked-for circumstance ? With a throbbing heart, and trembling with wonder, doubt, and anxiety, she once more took up the letter and read as follows—

" Nothing could exceed my astonishment, dearest Maria ; and at first, although I am by no means given to superstition, I must confess that I was half inclined to believe it was his fetch, instead of he himself ; however, he soon convinced me that he was real flesh and blood, by rushing into my arms, and pressing me to

his heart, to the no small amazement of Elizabeth, who stood gaping at us completely stupified.

" ' Elizabeth,' said I, ' you need not be surprised—in this gentleman you behold my brother ; at the same time I expressed in as significant a manner as possible, that I should not be at all offended if she would retire ; but my looks were quite unavailing, for I had strictly enjoined her before we came down stairs, to keep close to me, and on no account to leave me, and she seemed resolved that she would obey me to the very letter.

" Walter then asked of me the particulars of what had happened to me and my mother since he had last seen us, and what had occurred to us since we left the neighbourhood of Rosemary Dell for London, and from London to Bath ? He also informed me in a few words, that his servant had accidentally seen me walking the day before, and not presuming to speak to me, but thinking that his young master might wish to have an interview with me, had watched me home, and given the information, to which circumstance, of course, I must attribute our meeting.

" Upon arriving at the end of this explanation, Walter paused, and looking inquiringly upon me, beckoned me to the other side of the room, where he asked me in a low tone who Elizabeth was ?

" Of course I was not long in satisfying him upon this point, and likewise whispered to him a sentence or two, the dangerous character I thought she was, upon which he turned round, and with an air of politeness which could not possibly offend any person of common sense, he told her that as he had something of a private nature to say to Miss Beranzio, he desired that they should be left alone.

" But notwithstanding the manner in which Walter spoke, when Elizabeth retired from the room, she darted upon me such a look that convinced me, although she was so mild and affable in her manners at times, that she really possesses a revengeful mind, and would not hesitate to retaliate upon me for the disappointment she had met with, and the manner in which her inquisitiveness had been baulked, by any act of spite that she could be guilty of towards me. But after all, I cannot imagine what has come to me, that I should take so much notice of what this girl says or does, and more particularly, why I should occupy so much of this letter about her, when I am certain you will be all impatience to be informed of all that Walter spoke to me about ; whether he looked well, and how he behaved during the interview.

" Well, my dear Maria, I will no longer keep you in suspense, and to begin, I must say that I never saw him look more handsome or interesting in my life ; and as for the other questions which I have imagined you would put so eagerly to me, it will probably satisfy you when I inform you that you were the only subject upon which he talked, upon which he seemed to care to listen. When I informed him that you and I had been companions for some time, his pleasure was unbounded, and when I told him what a warm, what an ardent, what a sincere affection for each other, in that period, had sprung up between us, his transport was increased tenfold, and he again and again embraced me, and called me his dear sister !—

THE ABDUCTION OF FANNY BERANZIO IN MISTAKE FOR MARIA.

Oh, Maria, these were the most felicitous moments I ever experienced !—It appeared that his father, after they had left Wallingford Hall, never imparted to him his real intentions, and he fully expected that they were going direct to the sea-port at which they were to embark for the continent; how surprised was he then, when, instead of that, they went to London, where they only stayed two days, and then travelled on to this place, but never expected the pleasure that was in store for him, in meeting me here.''

"And now, Maria, I come to something which more immediately concerns you, and which you will no doubt learn with mingled feelings of surprise and hope! My——but no, I must not call him my father now, for it is very clear that he has no regard for me, although Walter says that it is impossible he can help loving me,—but that is foreign to the subject I was going to write upon. Well, you must know, that it is Walter's firm belief that Mr. Wallingford will not go abroad after all; and that, after a provincial tour for a few months, he will once more take up his residence at Rosemary Dell, and resume all his former quiet ways and domestic habits. Walter says, that although he at first affected to treat it with indifference, it is now very evident that the loss of female society has a great effect upon his spirits, and his temper has become still more peevish and morose. Besides, since they have been away from the Dell, they have encountered several vexatious circumstances to give him ample cause to regret that he ever quitted Wallingford Hall, where, he observes, he had never any cause to complain of mismanagement; and had a sympathising friend in Doctor Hartley (whose loss he sadly feels), in whom he could confide, and whose advice was always ready to direct him under any difficulties which he had to contend with. In fact, my dear Maria, he seems out of temper with the world altogether, and will probably retire from its busy scenes, so ill adapted to his tastes and wishes, in a short time. Indeed Walter assured me that he should not at all be astonished if, in a few days, he should come at once to the determination of returning to Wallingford Hall, and that with the same haste as their departure from it had taken place, for Mr. Hartley said very true, when he spoke upon his changeable disposition.

"But my mother is of a different opinion, for before Walter took his departure she returned home, and by that means satisfied Elizabeth that I had spoken the truth, and that her impertinent ideas were entirely wrong; although I must say that Elizabeth's observation afterwards was reasonable enough, although it was no business of her's,—that of course she had a right to doubt whether I had a brother or not, when she had never heard any allusion made to him. She is really a very forward girl, and takes a considerable deal more upon herself than she has any right to do ;—but, bless my soul, what a troublesome tedious girl I am, to be sure ; here am I tiring out your patience with remarks upon an individual who is not of the least consequence to either of us, and who is really unworthy of a thought. Well then, I was going to say, that it is my mother's opinion, that it will not be long ere Mr. Wallingford will meet with plenty of his old friends and companions to reconcile him to England, and she does not think that he will go abroad, and

certainly not return to Rosemary Dell. But I sincerely hope that her ideas may not be realized in this instance, and for many reasons, one of the most powerful of which is, according to the description she gives of his former acquaintances, they are not at all likely to improve his condition, or to add to the peace of himself or Walter; and then again I am convinced that all Walter's hopes of happiness are centered in returning to Rosemary Dell, which I earnestly hope the Almighty will direct, before Mr. Wallingford can come in contact with those persons, of whom my mother has given so indifferent a character."

The heart of Maria responded most fervently to this wish, but her hopes were not fated to be realized. In two days more Walter Wallingford himself sent her a letter. It was the first she had received from him since the one he had left for her with Anthony and Agatha, and it was with a feeling of the utmost delight and awakened hope that she broke the seal and glanced her eye over the contents; but disappointment and sorrow fell upon her heart as she perused them, notwithstanding the caution which Walter had used in the inditing of his epistle, and not to write anything which might occasion her anguish. The style in which he wrote convinced Maria that his ideas, his wishes were frustrated, and that Ela had formed too correct an opinion of what would be the ultimate determination of Mr. Wallingford. They had removed from Bath, and gone to Cheltenham, "where," Walter went on to write, "my father, as he imagines, has formed that which he failed to meet with either in London or Bath, namely, a friend. In the two latter places, he seldom met with anything but cause for vexation. Those friends, as he designates them, and who he thought would welcome him in the most enthusiastic manner, received him with the most freezing coldness, and thus crushed all the hopes he previously formed of meeting in society an oblivion to the heavy afflictions which have rendered his life one continual round of misery for so many years. Some he found had left town, and no one could inform him of the place of their destination ; others had retired from the busy scenes of public life, and become staid and domestic beings, and who looked upon him with eyes of anything but welcome, and seemed by no means anxious to renew his acquaintance, or to bring to their recollection what they had experienced together in the days of their youth. Another class looked upon my father with eyes of suspicion, in consequence of his appearing to be solicitous to renew the intimacy he had himself been the cause of breaking off in the first instance.

"Thus was he subjected to continual annoyances and vexatious disappointments for some time, and he became disgusted with both the metropolis and Bath; what induced him to come here, I knew not, but the resolution was taken with his usual apparent haste, and without for a moment consulting me upon the subject. At the hotel where we first put up when we entered the town, my father met with a Mr. Chesterton, with whom he had been on terms of intimacy in former days. This gentleman, a person would suppose to be a jovial, blunt, sincere sort of personage, and he *appeared* deeply to lament the reception my father had met with from his former associates; to sum it up in a few words, they have renewed all their former intimacy, my father has abandoned his project of going to Switzerland, and has made up his mind to reside for the future at one of the fashionable watering places, or in London. I must inform you, my dearest Maria, that he has not thought proper to let me be the companion of his visits to the said Mr. Chesterton, but for particular reasons, and from what I have heard of his character, from persons on whose veracity I can depend, I have very good reason to doubt that he is sincere in his professions of friendship, especially as he is far advanced in years, and as he has a large family of grown up sons and daughters; who, according to his (Mr. Chesterton's) description, must all be complete specimens of perfection, and therefore cannot be at any loss for society. But my father was very differently situated, and therefore hailed with avidity the slightest prospect of the means of escaping from the dull monotonous life he was leading. But really I should have thought that Mr. Chesterton, at his time of life, would have been rather tenacious of forming intimacies out of the immediate circle of his own family. I cannot help thinking, that, with all his fine and plausible professions, he has some sinister object in view; but I sincerely hope that I may find I have done him an injustice by these opinions. However, whether or not it may turn out as I expect, I cannot say, but this I know, that my father seems to have formed such an enthusiastic attachment to this Mr. Chesterton, that he seems determined all but to take up his residence at his house, for since they have met, he has scarcely been a couple of hours, with the exception of night, away from his house; and because I have always declined going with him, he never fails, whenever we meet, to complain that I am cold and disagreeable, and that I am very little better than a misanthrope altogether. In excuse. I have said that I was indisposed, and that my spirits were depressed; but these excuses were of no avail, for my looks contradicted them, as I assure you, my dear Maria, that I never felt in better health, neither did I ever look better than I do at present, as long as I can remember; and, moreover, my father has a powerful argument, which he never fails to make use of in refutation of this excuse, which

is, that he has even in this short time immensely improved, through his going into company; and really, I do feel astonished at the change which it has wrought in him; consequently, I cannot reasonably long expect to be excused from accompanying him, although nothing can be more repugnant to my feelings, anxious as I am for tranquillity, and the indulgence of my own thoughts. Oh, my dearest Maria, what misery does this thought cause me; for my only enjoyment (a melancholy one, truly) was in recalling to my memory the reminiscences of those hours of pleasure which in former days we have passed together."

"Alas!" sighed Maria, as she folded up the letter, "he will soon cease to remember those happy hours, or to look upon them with regret, and will look forward to the future with very contrary views to those he has hitherto formed."

A pang shot through her heart upon this reflection, and the tears started to her eyes; but soon did she upbraid herself for having for an instant entertained such ideas, which she felt confident were unjust to her cousin. Walter did not seem to read the motives of Mr. Chesterton, in his anxiety to secure the friendship of Mr. Wallingford, but Maria too readily unravelled them, at least so she imagined, and her conception was too plausible for her easily to reject it. It was the daughters of Mr. Chesterton that aroused every fear in her bosom, and revealed that which to Walter seemed such a mystery. Doubtless, from the hint which he had thrown out in his letter, they were complete paragons of beauty and accomplishments; and, with such powerful temptations, would it be surprising if they enamoured Walter's heart, and made him cease to dwell on the name of his unpretending cousin with any other sentiments than those of indifference? These painful imaginings stamped themselves so forcibly on her mind, that, notwithstanding she read the letter over and over again, and upon each perusal was the more certain that Walter had no idea of Mr. Chesterton's object, still she could not but imagine that one of the daughters of that gentleman was marked out by fate to be the bride of Walter.

In the course of two or three weeks, Maria received several letters from her cousin, but still, although there was nothing in them to lead her to suppose that she had come to a right conclusion, they breathed a tone of melancholy which, notwithstanding he evidently tried hard to conceal, assured Maria and Doctor Hartley that his mind was oppressed by some serious grief.

A letter arrived also from Ela, which stated that all her arrangements being complete, in the course of a week from that period it was their intention to leave Bath, for the purpose of hastening to the sea-port where they purposed embarking, and that, therefore, if the worthy doctor or Maria wished for an interview with them before they departed, they must expedite their departure from London. Doctor Hartley had no preparations to make, so the next day him and his fair charge were on their way to that city, in which they arrived, without anything occurring to them on the journey worthy of receiving any notice in these pages.

We will pass hastily over the meeting which took place between Maria and Fanny: it was possessed of all that same warmth of feeling as if they had been separated for years, and no doubt was strengthened by the knowledge that they would, in the course of a few days, be parted, and left in a state of uncertainty as to when, if ever, they should meet again.

Ela was looking better than Mr. Hartley had seen her for some time, and she expressed, in terms of the most ardent sincerity, her gratitude for the deep interest and trouble he had taken in her affairs, and entered into a minute detail of the arrangements which she had made with Mr. Goodwin as to her future course, with which he expressed himself satisfied.

" Let me but see you once on shipboard, and on the way to the place of your destination, and much as I shall have reason to regret the loss of the society of yourself and your charming daughter, I shall think you are safe, and shall, therefore, be happy. In a foreign land you may rest in peace, and without any apprehension of your old and inveterate enemies, the Gipsies."

Ela shook her head.

" Well may you call them inveterate, sir," she replied ; " they are truly so. Depend upon it, as I have often before said, although you have derided me for what you would say was sheer absurdity and superstition, they will not suffer any distance to obstruct them in the gratification of their vengeance, and that, some time or other, I am fated to fall a victim to it."

" Still must I say that such an idea is, in my opinion, superlatively ridiculous," said Doctor Hartley; " and I am really astonished that you will persist in indulging in it."

" Well, well," replied Ela, in a melancholy tone, " time will show—time will show."

Mr. and Mrs. Goodwin were also very glad to see once more their old friend, Doctor Hartley, and expressed their sentiments very cordially. It was many years since they had met, and their friendship had commenced in such a manner, that there was no fear of it ever abating but with life.

After the usual interchange of sentiments among their friends, Maria and Fanny were permitted to retire, and, descending to the parlour, the former eagerly entered upon the subject of Walter, about whom she could never have grown tired of listening, or Fanny of talking. Every word he had uttered, and which was carefully treasured up in the memory of Fanny, she repeated a dozen times, and expa-

tiated, in glowing terms, upon the state of his feelings, which were made evident by the manner in which he spoke of her. She described the poignant misery he was enduring at being separated from her, and at the ambiguity and uncertainty of Mr. Wallingford's conduct, which rendered it utterly impossible for him to judge what were his designs, and whither would be his ultimate place of destination—whether to go abroad, or to remain in England : in fact, he was of the firm opinion that his father did not actually know himself.

Maria sighed when she remembered the last letter she had received from Walter from Cheltenham, and recollected what he had said concerning the intimacy which had been established between her uncle and the family of the Chesterton's, and, in spite of everything else, nothing could erase from her mind the idea which, at the time, had taken possession of it.

She showed the letters to Fanny, who perused them with much interest, but strongly combatted the opinion Maria had formed, certain, as she said she was, that her image was too firmly engrafted in his heart for any other object to remove it, and she gently reproached Maria for the injustice she did her cousin by the imputation she had cast upon him. Maria appeared to yield to her opinions, and they were still engaged in discussing the matter when they were startled by a rattling at the parlour window, and on turning their eyes in that direction, they were both alarmed and surprised on seeing a dark-visaged, ruffianly-looking man standing before it, and looking into the room as though he had an inclination to force his way into it, and take French leave with some of the contents of the room. Maria could not repress a scream, upon which the fellow, doffing a crownless hat, affected to bow, and said, in anything but an agreeable voice—

" Oh, you need not be alarmed, young ladies, I only came to ask you to relieve a poor fellow who is in great distress."

Fanny looked at Maria, as much as to ask whether she should venture to open the window and relieve the man, but she not having the power to answer her, the former, seeing that there was no chance of his leaving the window without, timidly approached, when looking more narrowly in the fellow's face, she shrieked loudly, and running back to Maria, in a voice of extreme terror exclaimed—

" Oh, heavens! it is one of the ruffians by whom I was seized at Rosemary Dell in mistake for you!"

The ruffian seemed to recognize Fanny at the same instant, for he knit his brows, shook his fist menacingly at her, and uttering a dreadful execration, fled from the place.

Overcome by terror, Fanny and Maria were for a short time unable to move or to utter a syllable, but Fanny was the first that regained self-possession enough to advise that they should immediately retire to the room in which their friends were, and make them acquainted with what had happened, with which suggestion Maria immediately complied.

The doctor and Ela were very much astonished at the circumstance, as they had reason to believe, according to the account which they had received from Fanny, that Mr. Barnell and his infamous associates had all perished in the fire which had taken place at the inn, but here was a proof that one of them was living, and that accordingly Mr. Barnell might be living also; and that, if the late event had not tired him of such pranks, they would, in all probability, be subjected to more of his annoyance. But yet, upon more mature deliberation, Mr. Hartley could not help thinking that these apprehensions were groundless; as Barnell, being certain that his villany was made known, would, with good reason, imagine that any future action of the kind would be visited with such punishment as the law afforded. After a while he succeeded in soothing the fears of Fanny and Maria, more particularly the latter, and the subject was dropped.

Three days elapsed and nothing more occurred; and as the time approached for Ela and her daughter to leave the place, the melancholy of Maria and Fanny increased. We will pass over their parting, which the reader will find no difficulty in imagining, and leave the doctor, Maria, and Mr. and Mrs. Goodwin still in Bath, they having resolved to stay there for some months, the doctor and his charge occupying the same place which Ela and her daughter had recently left. Maria had received several letters from her cousin, and the tone of the language in which they were couched convinced her that he was still suffering under the deepest depression of spirits, from which nothing but a restoration to her society could relieve him. They were still at Cheltenham, and his father continued his intimacy with Mr. Chesterton and his family, and it was very clear to Maria, although he tried hard to conceal the fact, that he suffered some most painful annoyances from that circumstance.

But she was soon fated to have her attention drawn more immediately to other events of far more paramount interest, and which were calculated to fill her bosom with fresh cause for sorrow.

About three months after Ela and Fanny had quitted England, as she was with Mr. Hartley just coming past the principal inn, and returning towards home, they were somewhat alarmed by the rearing of a horse in a gig, and the doctor, seeing that the driver seemed rather to enjoy it as a rich joke, than to try to curb the restive animal, was about to remonstrate with him on the folly of his conduct, when, looking up, he uttered an exclamation of surprise and alarm, and pressing the arm of Maria, he directed her attention to the person, or rather persons (for there were two) in the gig, and her wonder and terror may easily be guessed, when, in the person of one of them, and that one the man who was driving, she recognised Richard Grayling.

In the momentary glance she was permitted to take of him, she could not help noticing the remarkable change which was effected in his personal appearance. He was attired in the first style of fashion, and really being a very handsome man, and exceedingly gentlemanly in his appearance, could not be looked upon, by any one who was acquainted with his real character, with anything but a feeling of the deepest regret. The man who accompanied him was also most elegantly dressed, but he was a coarse vulgar-looking person, with whom vice and dissipation (if his countenance were an index of his mind), were familiar.

The doctor had the presence of mind to enter a confectioner's shop, which was on the spot, and the vehicle soon after dashed off, as he hoped without his graceless nephew having observed him.

This circumstance caused both him and Maria considerable pain, for it not only recalled to their memory all the horrors of the past, but put them into an excessive state of fear, lest he, being in the same place, should once more find them out, and renew his gross annoyances.

"Alas!" said the doctor, after some consideration on the subject, and when they had left the shop, and were making the best of their way towards home; "alas! it is a sad thing to be induced to pray for the dissolution of any one'; but that I have done so in regard to that wretched man, I must fain acknowledge. But I pray to heaven that his stay here will only be transient, and that he may again depart without becoming acquainted with our being in the neighbourhood."

This prayer, however, to which Maria heartily responded, was not fated to be realised, for just at that moment they looked back, and perceived the gig returning the way they were going, and almost close up to them.

"It is no use to avoid him," said the doctor, in despair, "he has evidently seen us, and I must, therefore, endeavour to bear the meeting with as much firmness and self-possession as I can."

Scarcely had the doctor done speaking, when the gig was driven close up to them, and giving the reins to his companion, Grayling jumped out, and with the greatest effrontery and *nonchalance*, as if, in fact, nothing had happened to interrupt their friendship in the least, he grasped his hand, and shaking it violently, said—

"Well, curse me if I didn't think it was

you, uncle; upon my word this is a pleasure I had not anticipated so soon, although I was on the look-out after you."

"And is it possible that you can be so dead to all sense of shame, sir?" said Mr. Hartley, indignantly, but at the same time in tremulous tones, that bespoke his emotion; "is it possible, I say, that you can be so dead to all sense of shame, as even to dare to meet me—to look at me—to speak to me, after your infamous conduct when last we met?"

"Psha!" returned Grayling, "what a one you are to recall old grievances; let that be buried in oblivion, I was driven to it by necessity, but have repented it ever since;—quite reformed;—I have, by Jupiter!"

"Would to Heaven your words were true," said the doctor, emphatically.

"They are, I assure you, upon my *honour*," returned Grayling, with an impudent smile, and for the first time acknowledging the presence of Maria, with a low bow and a smirk; "but come, come, say no more about it; it was all caused by the impetuosity of youth, and what is done cannot be undone, you know. I have got much to tell you about my change of life, and so to finish the business in a tangent, I shall dismiss my friend in the gig to the inn, and be the companion of you and this young *lady* home."

Doctor Hartley sighed, and his heart swelled to his mouth, but he felt incapable of making any answer, and he knew it would be useless to offer any objection to Grayling's decision, which would only be productive of some very unpleasant explanations in the street. As for Maria, she felt a strange feeling of dread and disgust at the presence of the villain, and boldness of his behaviour towards her, and the insinuations which his half hints, and sarcasm, seemed to convey, filled her bosom with shame, mortification, and alarm.

In the meantime, Richard Grayling turning to his companion, said——"

"Well, Ned, you may as well return to the inn; and do not leave the place until I come back, in case the party we expect should come, and we might not have the opportunity of *plucking the goose* to-night."

The latter part of this speech was uttered in a low tone, that it did not reach the doctor's ear, and if it had, it is very doubtful whether he would have understood the *elegant* technicality which his nephew had made use of. There was an expression in the person's countenance spoken to, which Maria thought most horribly revolting, and which seemed to indicate that every bad passion reigned predominant in his mind; but she turned from him with a shudder of disgust, and after waving his hand majestically to the trio, he dashed off with reckless speed, to the imminent hazard of everything and every one he encountered in his way.

"Now, sir, I am at your service." said Grayling, turning towards his uncle; "I am very well assured you do not thank me for my company, but I have not the least doubt, after I have explained something to you, you will be inclined to look over the past, and to think very different of me."

"Most happy should I be, Richard, if you could give me good cause to do so," replied the doctor seriously, and shaking his head in a doubtful manner; "but after what has taken place, how can I depend upon your words? Ought I even to speak to you,—to suffer you near me; to consider my life even safe when——"

"'Psha!" interrupted Richard, with some confusion and shame; "That was never intended;—it was only—however, you have nothing to fear now, and so——let's talk of something else."

The doctor remained silent, while Grayling, with the greatest coolness and indifference imaginable, changed the topic of conversation, and talked with much eloquence upon a variety of subjects, in which he displayed considerable learning and natural ability.

Maria could not but listen to him with a mingled feeling of surprise and regret; while Grayling several times tried to elicit from her some remark, which might enlighten him upon the subject of the intimate terms with which she seemed to be with his uncle.

At length they arrived at the house, and upon old Matthew opening the door, he seemed to be completely thunderstruck by the reappearance of his master's nephew, and stood gaping upon him, completely deprived of the use of speech for a few moments.

"Yes, you see I am here, old fellow;" said Grayling, "it is some years since you and I spoke to one another."

Matthew returned no reply, but glancing compassionately at his master, endeavoured to read his thoughts, at this unpleasant, this painful meeting; but Mr. Hartley, who, doubtless, read the old man's thoughts, and did not wish to encounter his looks, stepped into the sitting-room, followed by his nephew, and Maria hastened to her own apartment, in a state of great uneasiness at the probable issue of the interview between Grayling and the doctor. She recalled to her memory the scene which had taken place on the occasion of their last meeting at the inn, and when she thought upon the savage, the ruffianly behaviour of the former towards his uncle, she shuddered and anticipated the worst results for the future. Two hours elapsed, and Maria (whose chamber was immediately over the room in which were the doctor and Grayling,) could frequently hear their voices, which were apparently raised in anger, and particularly that of Grayling, who seemed to be making some demand, which his uncle was peremptorily refusing.

Another half hour passed slowly away, and still did the altercation appear to increase in warmth, and at last overhearing Grayling give utterance to some violent threats, and fearful, after what he had previously done, that he would put the same into execution, she flew down stairs, resolved at every hazard to enter the parlour, and interpose between them. She had but just descended the stairs, when she was terrified by hearing a noise, resembling that of the heavy fall of some person on the floor, and at the same time Matthew ran up the kitchen stairs with consternation depictured in his face, and just as both he and Maria rushed simultaneously towards the door, the bell was rung with great violence.

"Oh, this is as I feared it would be;—oh! my master, my poor master, he is killed, he is killed!" cried poor old Matthew, when he beheld Grayling supporting Doctor Hartley in a chair, having apparently just before raised him from the floor.

"Killed!" ejaculated Grayling, in evident alarm, notwithstanding he tried all that he could to conceal it; "old idiot! how dare you make use of such an observation as that?—My uncle has fallen from his chair in a fit; why don't you run for medical assistance, instead of standing there staring at me?"

The extreme agitation which Grayling now exhibited, the willingness with which he assisted his uncle, and the anxiety he expressed to obtain medical aid, all served to make Maria believe that he spoke the truth, and that Mr. Hartley had really been attacked with an apoplectic fit; therefore, in spite of the disgust she felt for the being with whom she had by such singular and unlooked-for circumstances been drawn into connection with, she willingly aided him in attending to the unfortunate gentleman, until Matthew came back with the doctor, who, upon seeing Mr. Hartley, instantly confirmed the assertion of Grayling, and added, candidly, that he was very doubtful whether it was possible for him to survive.

Alas! the doctor's worst fears were verified, for although Mr. Hartley did survive the fit, he did not regain his senses for some time, and knew no person near him, not even Maria, who, distracted with grief, could not be induced to quit the side of his couch for a minute, nor Richard Grayling, who, whatever his faults might have been, evinced on this occasion much anxiety and sorrow. Speech was also denied the unfortunate sufferer, and there he lay in a state of stupefaction, that was even more afflicting than death.

CHAPTER LIV.

"He was a man——man did I say,
By Heaven 'tis a libel on the name :—
He was a wretch, to whom the blackest deed
Was food unto his guilt athirsted soul!"
ETHELBERT.

SEVERAL days did the doctor continue in this lamentable condition, and Richard Grayling had taken up his residence at the house, and exercised the authority of its master; at which poor old Matthew was not a little chagrined and disgusted, and had the greatest difficulty in the world to behave to him with anything like common civility.

"Ah, Miss Herbert," he observed to Maria, upon one occasion, when they had been conversing upon the subject, "you need not be surprised at my opinion of him, and I'm sure you will not, after I tell [you what I know of his doings, and what he has been."

But Maria needed no such information; the conversation she had overheard between him and Mr. Hartley, on the day that he made the ruffianly attack on him at the inn, convinced her that he had been connected with almost every species of vice, and that he had been a convict, but Matthew persisted in going through all the particulars with which he was acquainted, and she was obliged patiently to listen to him—

"Yes, miss," continued the old man, "I can assure you this is all true, and there are many more instances of his villany I could relate were it worth while; ah! my poor master has suffered a great deal through him, and it has ended as I always expected it would. It was the ill-conduct of this bad man that drove him from London, where he had a most extensive practice, and thinking to escape from his annoyance, he took the house which he inhabited near Rosemary Dell; but that was all to no purpose, and he continued to visit him and extort money from him, until he was transported; yes, miss, I have heard for a positive fact that he was transported; and that accounts for Mr. Hartley not hearing from him for so many years. But what makes it more vexatious than all, is, that my poor master has not a relation living, except this fellow, and consequently he is the heir to his property, and if he should not get over his present illness, why—but I am certain that he made a second will some short time ago, though what his motives were for doing so I cannot say—but he told me he had done so, and at the same time observed, that by that means he had prevented the chance of your being bothered by Richard. But there is one circumstance which it is necessary we should ascertain, and that is, whether my master has been so silly as to make away with the old will before the new one was made; although I should think it is not very probable he would do so without consulting his solicitor—however, this can soon be ascertained—you know where the key of the iron chest is always kept, and you can therefore very soon learn wheter the old will is still deposited therein or not. If it should happen to be, we may snap our fingers at Mr. Grayling; for I know the second will is made in your favour, and therefore he can only enter an action against you, and cannot turn us both into the street withott a minute's warning, which he would no more care about doing than he would at drinking a glass of wine."

It was with the utmost horror and despair that Maria contemplated this dreadful picture of the situation she was placed in; she would be left as it were almost in the power of the villain, and without a friend near at hand to whom she could fly for assistance or protection (Mr. and Mrs. Goodwin having returned to London,)—and the idea of the same filled her mind with the most poignant and uncontrollable anguish. But what alarmed her still more, and rendered her completely wretched, was a suspicion which she coud not confide to poor old Matthew, and which was, that the *kindness* which Grayling had for the last few days exhibited towards her, was much more to be dreaded than his anger.

Indeed from the first moment that they had encountered each other, she had noticed with feelings of the most inexpressible disgust, the freedom of his behaviour towards her, and the opportunities he had taken to show her that the beauty of her face and person had made some impressions on him. He had also taken every means to make use of observations to her, which sufficiently explained his thoughts, and though she had at the time they were uttered treated them as they merited—namely, with the most superlative contempt—when he now at the time of his uncle's critical situation, ventured to repeat them, she could not but view them with the utmost detestation, and despise and abhor the person who could make use of them.

But Maria's heart shrank with abhorrence from availing herself of the proposition of Matthew, to ascertain the fact concerning the will. It seemed to her as if it was casting a doubt on the generosity of him, to whom she had lately looked as a father, and who had certainly behaved with sufficient kindness towards her to merit that name; besides, was it not looking forward to his demise, at the bare idea of which her heart shrunk with horror; and, again, might not sordid avarice be then said to be the motive of her actions? All these ideas she mentioned to old Matthew, who heard them with evident indifference.

"For my part, miss," said he, "I do not see why you should be so very particular and so tenacious, especially under all circumstances, for are you not in danger of losing the means

which have been provided for your support, and I should like to know, miss, whether you or I are very well qualified to bustle through the world without money?"

Maria could not help blushing for a moment at the freedom of the old man's words, and at the equality on which he seemed to place himself and her; but these thoughts occupied her mind but a short time, and she could with difficulty prevent the anguish which she felt gaining vent at her eyes, when she reflected that Matthew had drawn but a faint picture of the melancholy situation in which she would be placed if the demise of her benefactor took place.

"And yet, Matthew," she at length gently observed, after a minute or two's reflection; "I do not see what use it will be to make the examination you suggest; for instance, should the will not have been destroyed, it is doubtless secure in the chest, and if it *has* been destroyed——"

"Then I shall know what steps to take, miss," interrupted the old man, and he shook his head, and winked his eye with much affectation of sagacity and penetration; indeed, miss, I am only urging what is strictly right, and that which I am sure my poor master would also approve, were he in a condition to be consulted upon the matter."

Maria did not answer him—old Matthew was so urgent in the business, that she could not bring her mind to oppose his wishes, yet were they quite contrary to her own ideas and inclinations.

"Well, Miss Herbert," at last he said, after a pause, "if you'll only agree to what I propose, I'll soon settle the business, and take all the weight off your shoulders—only just trust me with the key of the iron chest for awhile, which will be doing nothing wrong you know, as my master has frequently done so, and desired me to get him money out of it, at the same time that he was almost entirely ignorant what sum there was deposited therein. Well, you can do as you please—I will not press you—if you do not think me trustworthy, of course you will refuse me, but if the contrary, you will not hesitate. I will not detain it many minutes, and after I have made the investigation, I maintain we shall be in a better condition to meet any exigences that may follow, as we shall then know what we have to depend upon."

Of course, Maria could no longer refuse to accede to what old Matthew requested, as in doing so, she must have cast an imputation of want of integrity upon him, by declining to give him the key of the iron chest, but it was far against her own will and judgment that she delivered it up to him.

She was aware that the place in which the iron box stood was a cabinet, in an ante-room, which the doctor had used as his study since their residence in Bath, and having delivered to him the key, Matthew left her, and made his way to the said room, to make his examination. In the meantime Maria hastened to the bedside of her benefactor—the discourse we have just related, having occurred in the library—whither Maria had wandered for a few minutes, the patient having fallen off to sleep, for the purpose of taking a hasty repast.

Doctor Hartley was still wrapt in slumber, and as she contemplated by the alteration in

THE ABDUCTION OF MARIA HERBERT BY MR. BARNELL AND HIS MYRMIDONS.

his looks, an apparent certainty there seemed to be of his approaching dissolution, her thoughts were entirely abstracted from what had recently taken place between her and Matthew, until she was suddenly arroused from the deep lethargy into which these dismal thoughts had thrown her, by a female servant entering the room, and in accents of alarm, ejaculating—

" Oh, miss, there is such a noise down stairs, and I verily believe that Mr. Grayling is murdering poor old Matthew, for I heard him call out to that effect just this minute."

Maria waited to hear no more, but rushing down the stairs with the velocity of an arrow, she darted into the library, and there beheld the old man struggling in the grasp of the ruffian Grayling. who having seized him by the throat, seemed determined to strangle him at the same time he was uttering the most intemperate and revolting language, such as could only be used by the lowest and most abandoned persons.

Maria immediately darted forward, and on seeing her, he released his grasp, and stood looking at her in amazement and confusion.

"How now, sir," she exclaimed, "what is the meaning of this outrage, this violence against a feeble old man?"

The scoundrel spurned the poor old man from him with violence, so much so, in fact, that he almost hurled him to the floor, and after a moment or two passed in quelling his passion, he answered—

"I hope I have not given you any uneasiness, Miss Maria, but I have just discovered that grey-headed old wretch in the very act of robbing his master; no doubt he is an old thief, although he has before escaped detection, and no doubt has brought many an innocent person into the scrape; but he may reckon his nefarious career over now, as sure as my name is Richard Grayling."

Maria turned away with a feeling of contempt and disgust from a wretch railing against dishonesty, who had not long since himself returned from transportation, who had stopped his own uncle and benefactor on the highway, and robbed him, and had not only afterwards repeated the crime, but had actually made an attempt upon his life. Grayling evidently read her thoughts, for he turned away his head in confusion, and could not look her in the face; after a short pause, in which she endeavoured to conquer the thoughts that occupied her mind sufficiently to keep her tongue within the limits of prudence, Maria said—

"You say this old man has attempted to commit a robbery;—where is your proof?" This question she put with a dignity that appeared somewhat to abash the ruffian.

"Where is my proof—miss madam?" he replied, after a brief pause, with something of contempt in his manner;—proof positive—as I said before, I detected him in the fact—I had entered this study about an hour ago, and was perusing some private documents behind this screen, when I heard him enter. Of course, I suppose that he had no idea there was anybody in the room with the exception of himself. He entered the room stealthily—looking cautiously around him, to ascertain that he was not watched, and unlocking yonder cabinet, I beheld him place the key in the lock of the iron chest, where, of course, the money of my uncle is deposited; I suffered him to raise the lid, but my patience could endure no more,

and I darted upon the old villain, and seize him."

"Your suspicions of this poor old man's dishonesty," replied Maria, indignantly—"a entirely unfounded, sir, for it was from me received the keys of the cabinet and of the iro chest, and he acted upon my orders when I went there."

"Yes," returned Matthew, who now had part ally recovered himself, "you say true, miss it is only he, who would wish to conceal hi real motives—his conduct only will not be investigation. He wanted to get the keys his possession, so that he might know whe the cash was deposited;—if I had resigne them easily, there would be nothing at all this calumny uttered by him;—but he coul not dupe me—his character was too well know to me—too well known to me for years before and had it not been that I——"

Richard Grayling, whose countenance wa pale with passion, did not suffer the old man conclude his speech, but rushing upon him attempted to fell him to the earth. Mari interposed between them, and receiving th ferocious blow on the head which had bee intended for Matthew, sunk insensible on th floor.

When she regained her sensibility, sh shuddered with disgust and abhorrence to behol herself supported by the villain Grayling, an spurning him from her in the manner h deserved, thanked by her looks the person wh had rushed into the apartment, (all the house hold, in fact,) who were using their be endeavours to restore her, and who, (with th exception of some old woman, who had latel been engaged,) by their looks, sufficiend expressed their reprehension of his conduct.

"Well, for my part," said the old woman above alluded to, "other people may say as the will, but I never will believe it, and certainl nobody, in their sober senses, can do so, th young master, would ever think of doing an injury to a female, especially to a young lady like Miss Herbert."

"To be sure not," returned Grayling, in fierce tone, and looking ferociously round upo every person present in the room; "who wil have the hardihood to accuse me of such a thing I should like to know?" He then approache the place where Maria was seated, attende to by the domestics, and with a well assume air of regret, said—

"But I am certain that Miss Maria wil also acquit me of having intentionally harme her—nothing can afford me more poignan regret, I do assure you, than the thought tha I have been so unfortunate as to do so."

"You have unmanned yourself, sir, by you savage violence," replied Maria; "I know that the blow was not meant for me, but bein aimed at a feeble and innocent old man, th offence possesses equally the same magnitude in my estimation."

As Maria spoke, the countenance of Grayling presented an expression of the greatest rage and mortification; but he stifled his feelings as well as he could, and in his former tones of dissembled regret, observed—

"I will not endeavour to maintain that I acted right, miss; but if you were aware what a many reasons I have to hate that hoary-headed old hypocrite, who has always been my greatest foe, and has studiously endeavoured to embitter my uncle towards me, you would excuse me; he would not conceal any of my youthful indiscretions, but on——"

"Youthful indiscretions," repeated old Matthew, "yes, a trifling youthful indiscretion, undoubtedly that was, when he contemplated the murder of his uncle and myself, after we had retired to rest, and——"

"By hell, I will not endure this!" cried Richard, foaming with rage, and once more endeavouring to inflict summary vengeance upon Matthew; but the persons who were now present held him back. "Am I to be calumniated by this old viper, whom I have not long since detected in an attempt to commit a robbery, to plunder that master to whom he has pretended to be faithful for so many years?"

"Again I tell you that you utter a falsehood, sir," exclaimed Maria, firmly; "Matthew, I say, acted only by my orders, and he received the keys from me."

"And if I may make so bold, Miss Herbert," returned Grayling, with an expression of half sarcasm and assumed humility, "if I may make so bold, who authorised you to take upon yourself the custody of the keys, while I, the only relative and heir of my poor uncle, am in the house?"

For a second or two Maria was so disgusted, that she was unable to return any answer, but at length fixing upon him a look of proud scorn, she said—

"To you, sir, I shall not take the trouble of offering an explanation of my behaviour; thank Heaven, your uncle is still alive; and it is the earnest prayer of my heart that he may continue so, so that he may bear witness to how much he is indebted for your duty and affection."

"At any rate," replied Grayling, "these keys shall not again pass from my hands until such time as my uncle is capable of managing his own affairs."

As the fellow thus spoke, he very deliberately locked up the iron chest and cabinet, and scowling defiance upon Maria, quitted the room.

Maria, having now partially recovered from the effects of the violent blow which Grayling had dealt her, left the room also, and reascended to her own apartment, followed by old Matthew, who informed her that the will was in the chest—that he had seen it as soon as he

raised the lid, and that he was just in the act of removing it for the purpose of inspecting it, when the ruffian darted forward, as has been described, and seized him.

"Ah," continued the old man, "I know that has been his principal object ever since he has been in the house; he wished to ascertain where the money was deposited, and I dare say he had come into the study for that purpose, when, hearing me come into the room, he had concealed himself in the manner which has been disclosed, in the hopes of succeeding in his object."

"Probably your idea may be correct," replied Maria, and I do not doubt but that it is so; however, I would most seriously caution you not to get in the way of Mr. Grayling any more than you can possibly help."

Maria had scarcely entered the room, when she was surprised by the nurse coming to her, and informing her that within the last hour Doctor Hartley had evidently regained his senses, although he was incapable of speaking, but he had by many significant expressions evinced an anxiety to see her. Maria immediately hastened with all possible expedition to the chamber of her suffering benefactor, whom she found awake, and who, by the expressive glances which he fixed upon her, convinced her that the nurse was right in the conjectures she had formed, and that Doctor Hartley knew her. He also signified in a manner which she could not misunderstand, that he had heard the noise which had taken place down stairs, and showed the greatest anxiety and pain upon the subject, which the pale cheeks and trembling form of Maria were by no means calculated to allay.

The good doctor tried hard to raise himself on his elbow, and made several ineffectual attempts to speak, doubtless with the intention of enquiring into the cause of the disturbance, and Maria therefore, to compose him, went over to the side of the couch, and taking his hand, said—

"Pray, my dear sir, tranquillize yourself, and I trust that you will soon be better; as for the —the noise which probably may have reached your ears, it is not so serious as you seem to apprehend; it is only a trifling mishap which has befallen me, that's all; nothing more, sir, and no doubt I am not so much hurt as I am alarmed."

As she spoke, she attempted to smile; but the doctor shook his head impatiently, and then, after a very powerful effort he said, in a faint voice—

"It is the villain Richard, who——"

"There, miss," observed the simple nurse, "you see that you might as well save yourself the trouble of trying to make him believe anything but the facts of the case; the whole of the matter is, as soon as he regained his senses, he overheard the voice of Mr. Grayling, and——"

She would have proceeded further, had it not been for the glances of disapprobation and anger which Maria fixed upon her, but the unfortunate Mr. Hartley had heard quite enough, and looking compassionately upon Maria, he uttered a groan, and fell back in the bed.

Nature was completely exhausted; although Doctor Hartley had recovered his sensibility, it was, as it often occurs in cases, but the prelude to death, and in less than two hours after what we have related had taken place, his soul had fled to the realms of bliss to receive that reward which his exemplary and innumerable virtues so justly entitled him to.

Need we attempt to describe the sorrow, the bitter, the intense sorrow of Maria on this melancholy occasion? She was completely inconsolable, and, alas! plenty of cause had she for grief. She had now lost the only friend and protector she had in the world, and whither could she look for happiness? where could she even seek an asylum? To remain where she was any longer than the remains of Doctor Hartley were consigned to the tomb would of course be impossible, and she even trembled at being under the same roof as the ruffian Richard Grayling, even at that time. As for all claim which, by the will of the doctor, she might have upon any portion of his property, she was very willing to resign it; for she was not, owing to the liberal provision which Mr. Wallingford had made for her, placed in any pecuniary difficulties.

She kept herself closely confined to her own chamber for three days after the demise of her beloved benefactor, and for that interval Richard Grayling had fully established himself as master of the house, and by his brutality and unnatural conduct, Maria could not help thinking Mr. Hartley's death had been expedited. He, however, never offered to disturb her, and she was therefore left to the free indulgence of her grief, and for which she was extremely grateful.

At the critical moment, she had at first hesitated to make Grayling acquainted with the real situation and danger of his uncle, for she was fully confident that the latter wished not to see one who had inflicted upon him so many injuries, and who, by his base misconduct, had totally estranged from his (Mr. Hartley's) bosom all those feelings, which the ties of consanguinity might naturally be expected to engender. She knew that it would only torture and disturb the few short remaining minutes the good doctor had to remain in this world, and therefore did she forbear to send for him, until she was satisfied by the medical attendants that he could not survive many minutes, when she thought that she would not be acting with propriety, if she did not let Richard know the truth, so that he might attend if he thought proper; consequently she sent a servant to the apartment which he had chosen for his sleeping room, to summon him; but upon her knocking repeatedly at the room door, and not receiving any answer, she opened it, and found that it was vacated. Richard Grayling had immediately left the house after the affray, and remained the whole of the night in drunkenness and debauchery with some of his infamous associates at a neighbouring tavern, and to whom he expressed his anxiety to "see the end of the business," and that "the old boy would not linger much longer, keeping him in suspense."

When the servant informed Maria that Grayling had left the house, a transient ray of hope darted across her mind, that he did not intend to return again. She was fully aware that the iron chest contained a large sum of money, for she was present at the time that the doctor deposited it there, and she was in hopes, that this having satisfied the villain's cupidity, he had taken himself off, and would not come back again, at any rate, until that sum was exhausted; but she was very soon doomed to be disappointed in this hope, for the old nurse, who was constantly peeping and prying into everything, and minding everything but her own business, informed her that Mr. Grayling had taken care not to leave either the key of the study or the street door behind him, and added—

"No doubt, miss, he has acted with this caution, in case you might happen to have another key to the iron chest in your possession."

"Silence, I beg of you," observed Maria, hastily, for she was afraid to disturb the patient, who was now in a state of unconsciousness, and was fast sinking, and alarmed lest any sentence in allusion to his worthless nephew might be overheard by him, and render his few brief moments those of agony. But happily the poor doctor heard them not, and in a few minutes afterwards he opened his eyes, and fixed them affectionately upon Maria, his lips moved, as if invoking a blessing upon her head; she pressed him in her arms, and dropping his head on her bosom, resigned his spirit into the hands of his Creator.

It was morning, and Maria still sat by the side of the corpse, not all the arguments which the attendants could make use of, being able to prevail upon her to quit the chamber of death, when she heard the street door opened loudly, and some person stagger into the passage, which she had no doubt was Grayling returned home from his night's debauch; and she was soon convinced of the truth of these surmises, for she heard him apparently with much trouble stumble into his chamber, which was in the immediate vicinity of the one in which she now was, and where lay the lifeless body of that good old man, towards whom he had behaved with such unexampled villany.

Maria trembled with consternation, when

she heard him stumble up against the room door, and alarmed lest he should force himself into the chamber, (now tenanted by the dead,) while he was in that disgraceful condition, she begged that the old woman would go to him, and inform him that his uncle was no more, but that he could not enter the room for the present. The nurse obeyed, and Maria listened in breathless anxiety, to hear how he received the intelligence, and what answer he would make to the message. He did not keep her long in suspense, for almost immediately afterwards she heard him in his usual revolting tones observe—although she could distinguish no other feeling than gratification in it—

"All over!—A pretty start this, and not to say a word to me about it before I went out last night. You could not be ignorant that his end was aproaching."

The nurse made some reply, by way of an apology, but Maria did not hear what she said, and to which the heartless miscreant returned the following answer—

"Never mind;—it's not of much importance—what would have been the use of me?—I couldn't have helped him, and I don't imagine that he fretted much after me. Didn't he inquire about me?"

"No, sir," replied the nurse, "and for one very good reason, poor dear gentleman; he had not the power to speak a word."

Richard Grayling made no reply to this, and the mind of Maria was much relieved when she heard him enter his own chamber and close the door after him.

At the expiration of the three days we have mentioned that Maria kept herself confined to her chamber, a servant came to her with a message from Grayling, who had taken everything under his management and superintendance,—in which he desired that she would favour him with an interview for a short time, as he had something to say to her of importance.

Maria heard this request with vexation, and was for some time in doubt whether or not to comply, but upon more mature reflection, knowing that she must some time or other have an interview with him to settle the painful business between them, she mustered all her courage, and hastened to the room in which Grayling was waiting to meet her.

When she entered, he arose and saluted her with much affected grief and sympathy, and commenced a long tirade upon "the melancholy and deeply-lamented demise of his uncle, an, the very great, and, in fact, irreparable loss they had both of them sustained by the same."

Maria looked at him as he spoke, and she could not conceal the utter disgust and abhorrence she felt at his hypocrisy, which, in her opinion, was by far more revolting than his usual reckless conduct and demeanour. He saw what she thought, and he appeared somewhat confused, but soon afterwards, with the utmost coolness and effrontery, as if he himself had always been a most exemplary character, he proceeded to lavish upon her a string of the most fulsome compliments for the kindness and attention with which she had behaved to the late Dr. Hartley;—but turning away from him with a look of contempt and aversion, she begged leave to be made acquainted with the nature of the business upon which he had requested an interview with her, and not to detain her any longer than necessary.

"Well, by Jupiter, you are the most singular person I ever encountered, Miss Herbert—I understand that is your name," said he, evincing no little chagrin at the haughtiness and repulsiveness of her behaviour.

Maria did not condescend any reply to these observations, and Grayling continued—

"I have been for some time anxious to know, Miss Herbert, in what way you and my late uncle were situated; and I was not at all disposed to listen to the assertions of the domestics, who insinuated that you were in no way whatever related;—or, in other words, that I cannot have the extreme felicity of claiming any relationship with you,—notwithstanding, I must say, when I heard you call my uncle your papa, I was rather a little surprised;—but I have since been given to understand—"

"Doubtless you have been given to understand what is perfectly correct, sir," interrupted Maria, her bosom swelling with indignation at the base insinuations, and the bold conduct of the villain Grayling!—"I was not in any way connected with Dr. Hartley, and had no claim upon him, but what he in his liberality awarded me."

"Well, come," said Grayling, "it is not so bad as I expected, and I am not at all sorry that it is so; for, if I must speak the sentiments of my mind, I should not have been very well pleased to have discovered that you was the daughter of my uncle, although, I confess, there was a strong impression on my mind at first that the old boy had been after— —"

"I have nothing to do with what your ideas upon that subject might have been, sir," interrupted Maria, hastily, "and, therefore, if this is all you sent for me for, our interview is at an end."

As she thus spoke, she moved towards the door.

"Oh, I hope you will excuse me, Miss Herbert," he said, "I confess that for the moment I had unconsciously strayed from the subject I wished to speak to you upon, and indeed if I did forget myself, surely there is nothing to marvel at, when in the presence of so beauteous a female as yourself; but to come at once to the point, I am anxious to inquire whether you have any request to make regarding my poor uncle's funeral—and if, as you have apparently been his confidant, he has at any time informed you whether he should like to be interred in any particular spot, or anything else which he may have mentioned to you. You will find by this that I am not a bad fellow, and although he did not behave so well to me as he might have done, while he was living, I don't want to do anything but to repay good for evil, now he has gone to his last account."

Maria had a hard struggle with her feelings to prevent her giving vent to her indignation at this infamous untruth ; but after a moment's pause, she said—

"What your poor uncle desired, you will find mentioned in his will, sir ; for I am aware that all his wishes he fully expressed in that document "

"Mentioned in his will !" exclaimed Grayling, starting, and with well affected astonishment ; "this is certainly the first time that I ever knew that he had made a will. However, I dare say you can inform me where it is concealed, if there is any such document—I have made a diligent search among all the papers that have come under my notice, and——"

"Had you looked in the iron chest, sir," interrupted Maria, " the key of which you obtained in a forcible manner, you would have seen it there ; at least, I know it was there at the time you took possession of the key."

The countenance of Grayling changed, and he fixed upon Maria a piercing glance, as he muttered—

"Ah !—will you take your oath to that?—No—I did not mean to say that, exac'ly," he added, in a very confused manner ; "what I wished to ask was, whether—that is—if you are positive that the will was in the iron chest at the time that——"

"I mean to say," interrupted Maria, firmly, "that at the very instant when you forcibly possessed yourself of the key, the will *was* in the iron chest."

"Oh," returned Grayling, "you are quite certain of that ?—And pray, when did you last behold it ?"

"Your interrogatories are rather singular, sir," said Maria, " and as you seem to doubt what I state, I should advise you at once to satisfy yourself by looking in the chest."

Maria said this in as composed a manner as possible, and Grayling was seemingly quite thunderstruck at her coolness and courage. He looked at her for a minute with much earnestness, and then apparently recollecting himself, he assumed his usual levity, and replied—

"As for searching the chest, that would only be a waste of time, for there I know very well I should not find anything of the sort ; I, as you may be certain, had a thorough search there ; it was only to see that none of the cash deposited in it had escaped my observation, and if there had been such a document there, it

would have been sure to have fallen into my hands."

"And do you mean to persist in asserting that the will was not in the chest at the time you forcibly took possession of the keys ?" demanded Maria, with astonishing firmness, and fixing upon him a look, which evidently bewildered and abashed him ; but his confusion was only transient, and resuming all his former coolness, and boldness of manner, he replied—

"Most decidedly, I maintain that there was no such document in the chest."

" 'Tis false, sir," answered Maria, "and I can prove it to be so."

The firmness and unflinching calmness of her demeanour again abashed him, and he once more hesitated for a moment, ere he made any reply.

"You can prove what I state to be false, Miss Herbert," at length he said ; "methinks you make use of rather bold assertions. However, I imagine you have some better means of proving what you say, than that hoary-headed scoundrel, whom I detected just——"

"Shame on you, sir," interrupted the indignant Maria, "to repeat what you knew to be a gross libel ; you have been told, and I repeat it again, that Matthew received the authority——"

"Of whom ?" cried Grayling, scowling upon her, and in a tone of irony, "who authorised him to go to the chest of his master, and attempt to purloin its contents ?—Was it you, madam ?—Know you not, that if I thought proper I could accuse you of being colleagued with him ?—And who authorised *you*, pray ?—And can you prove, too, that these keys were not taken from the deceased ?—Now, young lady, I suppose you see by this time, that I am not the man to be trifled with ; so I think we had much better come to an amicable understanding at once, and you will find that I am not a bad fellow, but am ready to do the thing that's right, and all that. I dare say you anticipated, and very likely it was the old boy's design to have remembered you, if he had happened to have made a will ; but as he didn't, it cannot be helped, you know. Come, come, don't be so out of temper about it," he continued, as Maria, completely disgusted at his conduct, and the baseness of his heart, as evinced in his words, tried to leave the room ; "now, now," taking her hand forcibly, "I cannot bear to see anything of this sort, and I am sure it would be much better for us both to be on friendly terms, than to wrangle in this manner. You entertain a very wrong opinion of Richard Grayling, I can tell you, if you imagine he could act otherwise than as a gentleman towards one of the fair sex, and especially such a lovely sample as yourself. Only just tell me what you desire, and if I don't accede to your wishes, 1 wish I may be hung."

"I scorn to accept anything of you, sir," said Maria, as she with difficulty disengaged her hand from his grasp; "I will no longer remain here to be an obstacle to you, but instantly quit the house, and return to those friends who will gladly receive me."

"Stay, stay," Miss Herbert," exclaimed Grayling; but Maria had hastened from the room, and was rapidly descending the stairs.

Completely overcome by what had happened, Maria, scarcely knowing what she did, hurried out at the back of the house and into the garden, and was walking on, unconscious of what she did, towards the gate, when her hand was once more forcibly seized, and turning round, she beheld that it was the wretch Grayling, who had followed her.

"Dear Miss Herbert," he said, "why will you be so confoundedly provoking, as to treat me in the manner you do?—You say you will go to your friends, but I was informed that you had not a friend in the world; and, therefore, why should you think about leaving this house, because you and I have had a few words, which, after all, amounts to nothing?— Dear girl, believe me, I will prove to you an affectionate, an ardent, a sincere friend, and do everything I can to render you happy. So, pray dissipate all these dark looks, and the scorn with which you have hitherto treated me; throw aside your icy coldness, and make this your home, and me your slave. Beauteous girl, hear me, while 1 declare that your charms have made an indelible impression upon my heart, and that I love you beyond any other woman that my eyes have ever beheld! I am ready to worship you, to throw all my fortune at your feet, and every moment of my existence will I readily devote to the study of making you happy; give then your consent, my angel, to become mine, and we will, with the least possible delay, hasten from this dreary horrible spot, and——"

"Release me, sir, I command you," ejaculated Maria, her heart swelling to her mouth, and her limbs trembling with anger and alarm; at the same time she struggled all that was in her power to get away from the ruffian.

The more her fears, however, increased, so seemed to do the determination of Grayling.

"You little gipsy," he exclaimed, "how can you be so obstinate, and look towards me with such freezing coldness?" and as he spoke, he threw his arms round her neck, and forcibly imprinted a kiss upon her cheek.

Maria screamed, and again tried more violently than before to release herself. "Help! save me!" she cried in the utmost alarm; "monster, is it thus you pay respect to the dead—to the ashes of your uncle? Unhand me, villain! I insist upon it!"

"What is the meaning of this?" demanded the voice of old Matthew, sternly; confused and enraged, the ruffian released his hold, and turned his gaze upon the old man with the greatest fierceness.

Matthew looked still more sternly towards Grayling, and drawing Maria aside, repeated his question as to the cause of the disturbance.

"We must hasten away, Matthew," sobbed the deeply-agitated girl, "we must immediately hasten from this house, where I have been subjected to insults of the grossest kind; oh, let me not stay in it another hour."

We have before stated that Grayling was confused and abashed at the sudden appearance of the old man, but he soon recovered himself, and looking fiercely upon old Matthew, he said—

"What right have you here; and how dare you presume to ask such a question as you have? I say, what mean you by questioning my private conduct?"

"Your *private* conduct, Richard Grayling," returned Matthew, sarcastically, "but I do not marvel that you should feel tenacious of of its being questioned; it is rather unpleasant for some people to——"

"Old viper!" exclaimed Grayling, passionately; and clenching his fist, he approached Matthew in a menacing attitude, but the coolness and contempt with which the latter treated it, had the effect of arresting his arm, and he started back with evident amazement, and almost uncontrollable rage.

"Vile epithets from such as Richard Grayling," answered Matthew, with bitter sarcasm, "are a compliment to the party against whom they may be levelled. However, I will talk with you by and by, sir. Miss Herbert, if you please, I will immediately attend you from this place to one of security, to one where you will not be subjected to such ruffianly violence."

Richard Grayling was almost choked with rage; his eyes flashed vengeance, and it was wonderful that he could withheld from darting upon Matthew, who, however, looked at him with the most ineffable contempt. At length, after a very severe struggle with his feelings, he sufficiently subdued them to make the following answer to Matthew, in an assumed tone of scorn—

"Doubtless you pride yourself on your sagacity, but it may be as well to remind you, that of this place, I am now the master, and, moreover, I am determined that neither you nor Miss Herbert shall quit the house until I am satisfied that all the property which has been entrusted to you both, is safe. Of Miss Maria, although she assumes so much, and seems to entertain such a good opinion of herself, I know nothing, at least only as the companion and housekeeper of my late uncle, and until I am satisfied that neither of you have abused your situations, I am determined that you shall not leave this house. Your sagacity will not out-general me," he continued, winking his eye, and looking frightfully malicious; "I am acquainted with more upon this subject than you probably suspect, or than may meet with your approbation, and therefore I caution you to beware, and endeavour to cultivate my friendship, for my enmity may be productive of worse consequences than you probably surmise. Miss Herbert is at liberty, if she pleases, to retire to her own room; I have no inclination to interrupt her, and if I did cause her any fear just now, because I was a little too free probably, I did not mean any harm, and I trust she will therefore think no more about it, more especially, as I have never before met with such a cool reception from young, handsome and susceptible females, although they perhaps might not think proper to make any exhibition of their real sentiments."

Maria did not condescend to return any answer to this bold and insolent speech, but the look of ineffable contempt and detestation which she turned upon Grayling, expressed more than language could have done. The manner in which he spoke;—the cool and insolent tone in which he couched his language, she felt more keenly and indignantly than anything that he had before addressed to her, and it was with the greatest difficulty that she could restrain the full expression of her feelings. The only part of his speech, or whatever he might think proper to call it, which she heard with anything like pleasure, was that in which he permitted her to retire to her own apartment, and at the same time the promise that he would not make any attempt to molest her. However, before she even availed herself of this *gracious* permission, she looked at her venerable protector, to know whether by so doing she should be acting prudently, and it was very clear that Matthew comprehended her meaning, for he said—

"Yes, Miss Herbert, I think you had better retire to your own room for awhile, and I will take good care that you are not intruded upon by any one; in the meantime, I must have a few words with Mr. Grayling, which perhaps may not be very pleasant to his ears; however, it may cause a better understanding between all parties."

The old man uttered these words in a tone, and with an expression of countenance, that fully evinced his sentiments as regarded the villain Grayling, but the latter only replied to them by a loud laugh of scorn; and Maria, without waiting to hear any more, immediately hastened to her chamber, where she secured the door on the inside, by locking and bolting it, and then in a paroxysm of grief, she covered her face with her handkerchief, and wept abun-

dantly. This having somewhat abated, she threw herself upon her knees, and supplicated protection from the Allwise and supreme being, and almost immediately afterwards felt composed and tranquillized, such are invariably the benefits resulting from the performance of this sacred duty.

She could now sit down calmly and dispassionately, and reflect upon all that had occurred to her, and also endeavour to think of some scheme for the future; some plan by which she might instantly be delivered from the villain's power who seemed so determinedly and so unjustly bent upon assuming an authority over her.

Never did she more painfully, more severely feel her lonely, her friendless situation ;—Mr. Wallingford and his son were away, and for what she knew, in a foreign land, and therefore to whom could she appeal for protection? Had her uncle been near her, she felt assured, that notwithstanding his behaviour towards her, and the indifference he had lately evinced, he was too susceptible to the feelings of honour and humanity not to see immediately that she was released from such a dangerous and degrading situation, and likewise to seek retribution upon the head of the villain who had behaved so shamefully towards her. But, of course, there was no chance of that now, for she had not received any letter of late from Walter, and she therefore could not be certain whether or not Mr. Wallingford was still in England, and it would be useless to send them any account of her situation, for travelling from one place to another, as they might be, it would very likely not only be many weeks, but even months, before the communication would fall into their hands, and then what assistance they could have rendered, would be of no avail, and only cause Walter, at any rate, the greatest uneasiness, to know how she had been situated, and what she must have suffered, without his being able to rescue her from the unmanly wretch who had exercised such an undue authority over her.

"Alas!" she soliloquised, while the tears flowed fast down her cheeks at the thought; "alas!—I must erase them from my memory, although to them only have I a right to look for protection—they are taken from me ; probably I shall never more behold them, and therefore I have no one to depend upon but myself ; —upon my own individual exertions only, can I rely to escape from the dilemma in which I am placed."

There was one circumstance which rendered her indifferent to the conduct of Richard Grayling, in regard to his monopolizing, or rather usurping the property which she was convinced Doctor Hartley had bequeathed to her, and that was the handsome and generous manner in which Mr. Wallingford had provided for her, and which amply secured her independence ; and she was also placed in no difficulty by the death of her kind protector, as the money, she had been made acquainted, was made payable either to the doctor or herself.

After some time longer spent in deliberation, she determined to return to Rosemary Dell, and seek the advice of old Anthony and his wife, as to her future conduct, as soon as she could find an opportunity to effect her escape from her present place of confinement, for in that light, and that only, could she view it.

Notwithstanding her apprehensions of the

MARIA TRIES TO REFUTE BARNELL'S MISREPRESENTATIONS TO MOTHER MUGGERIDGE.

villain, Grayling, she felt convinced, however daring he might be, that he would not, that he could not long persevere in putting any restraint upon her, or denying her full liberty to leave the place; but even though her confinement were but to last for a brief interval, and that interval only an hour or two, she shuddered at the thoughts of the insolence she might be subjected to; and she was fearful of insisting upon leaving the house, or to do so secretly, for fear the menaces he had held out to her of bringing a charge of attempted burglary against her and old Matthew, he should put into execution.

Maria, it is known, was a complete novice to the ways of the world, or she would not have given the threats of the villain Grayling a second thought, or if she had done so, it would only have been that of the most superlative contempt. To effect her escape from the house was all she had any occasion to care about ; for once out of his clutches, she was immediately safe, and he dared not repeat his insults only on the pain of punishment. But of this, of course, Maria was ignorant, and therefore at the idea of the disgrace which would be heaped upon her and Matthew, should he make such a charge against them a he had threatened, she trembled with consternation; nay, more, she imagined that Matthew himself felt the danger of their position, and that she had remarked the utmost horror and fear depicted in his countenance when Grayling made use of the threats.

But Maria had another motive for not wishing to leave the house at present, and that was, that it contained the remains of her benefactor, Doctor Hartley, which she felt it was a duty incumbent upon her, to see consigned to its final resting place. Indeed she considered that while those cold remains were in the house, reckless and insensible as Richard Grayling was, she felt convinced that he would be prevented from any further outrage on her feelings, even though he might threaten. She, however, determined to make certain upon that point, and, therefore, after some time occupied in rumination, she formed the singular resolution that for the rest of the time which she continued in the house, she would pass it in the chamber in which the corpse of Doctor Hartley was, for surely Grayling, with all his guilt, could never be so brutal as to dare to intrude upon the chamber of death for the purpose of giving utterance to his base, his revolting passion.

Having come to this determination, she immediately hastened down the stairs, the key of the room she having retained possession of ever since the melancholy event had taken place, and indeed Richard Grayling had never expressed a wish to enter it, having thought he had done quite enough in having given some orders respecting the funeral, and probably, although on every occasion he acted with such bravado, not having the courage to look at the cold remains of him to whom he acted the part of a villain, and whose memory by his base conduct he was now outraging. In fact, there had been no person except Maria and Matthew, who had entered the room since the corpse had been placed in the coffin, and, therefore, Maria feeling confident that there at any rate she was secure from the intrusion of the man she so much dreaded, fastened the room door, and then removing the lid from the head of the coffin,

with the most poignant feelings of sorrow and regret, gazed upon that countenance which had never beamed with anything but kindness and benevolence towards his fellow creatures, and which had so often dwelt upon her with the affection of a fond father. Language could not do adequate justice to the emotion she felt while thus dismally occupied, and the tears flowed rapidly from her eyes as she looked upon the placid features of him who was the only protector she had left in the world. Alas! how terrible was her present situation; to whom could she now look for that solicitude and kindness which she had ever experienced from the good doctor? She was a lonely, isolated being, without a friend in the world—without any individual into whose bosom she could pour her sorrows, and who would sympathize in her situation. For some time did she remain weeping over the coffin, and the longer she gazed upon the pale features of the corpse, she became more tranquillized and composed, for she imagined they beamed upon her with kindness and hope, and at length the violence of her grief was entirely dissipated.

"Spirit of my benefactor," she ejaculated, as she returned the lid of the coffin to its place, "look down upon, watch over, and protect her whom, when alive, you loved with even more than parental affection."

After this solemn aspiration, her mind being restored to comparative peace, she took her seat by the window, and gazed upon the scenery which it overlooked. The dreary thoughts that had previously pervaded her bosom, were entirely soothed, and she no longer felt that melancholy which in the chamber of death any person might be expected to feel. At length, hearing the female servant, Susan, ascending the stairs, no doubt to take the tea to her apartment, she left the room and followed her.

Susan could scarcely credit her senses when she beheld Maria, and saw her make a sign for her to bring the tea equipage into the apartment in which the corpse was.

"God bless my soul, miss!" she exclaimed, with a mixture of terror and astonishment depicted in her countenance, "is it possible that you have chosen such an awful place as this, and that you are going to remain here, and that too alone?"

"Alone," repeated Maria, in a melancholy tone, and pointing towards the coffin, "no, Susan, I am not alone; I am in the presence of one, in whom I feel more peace and safety than I could experience from many persons who are alive."

Susan shrugged up her shoulders, and seemed quite horrorstruck.

"Gracious me!" said the simple girl, "you must not have a heart like too many in this wicked world, and your conscience must also be very clear, or you could never have the courage to act so, miss. I am certain that it would be a long while before Mr. Grayling could follow your example: no, I don't think he could do it for all the money in the kingdom. I took notice of him last night when he was going up stairs to his bed-room, for he did look so pale, and trembled so when he reached the door of this apartment, and he hurried past it as quickly as possible; and well he might, after the manner which he has behaved to his poor deceased uncle. I am certain that he could no more venture to put his head into this room than he could fly."

"I sincerely hope that your words may be verified," answered Maria, "and it is with that idea that I have resolved to take up my lodging in this apartment, while I remain here."

"Goodness gracious!" cried Susan, with unaffected terror and amazement, "you surely cannot be serious, Miss Herbert?"

"Certainly I am," returned Maria.

"Why, bless my soul! you really cannot mean to sleep here, to stay in this dismal chamber by yourself all night!" ejaculated the girl.

"Most assuredly that is my intention, Susan," replied Maria, "I will sleep on yonder bed, where my poor friend breathed his last, and on which I shall feel more at peace, and in greater safety than anywhere, or on anything I could repose."

"Mercy on me, it makes the blood run cold in my veins," said Susan shuddering, "the bare thoughts of it are quite sufficient; but I must say, miss, that I think you are quite right in supposing that Mr. Grayling will not venture to intrude here."

Maria perceiving that the poor girl's fears increased, and having no occasion for her services, dismissed her, after she had first, however, ascertained from her, that Grayling had had a long and apparently angry interview, but that after the altercation had lasted for some time, they had separated, and apparently on much better terms than they had met; and Susan added, that Mr. Grayling had dispatched Matthew with a letter to some person or the other, but she did not know who, who it was said was to come there, and make all the arrangements that were necessary for their settling the business in an amicable manner.

"When Matthew left the house," continued Susan, "he informed me that he should be back in a short time; howsomever, he's not come back yet, and he has been gone nearly three hours, so I don't know what he considers a long time; as for Mr. Grayling, he went out soon after Matthew, and has not returned home yet; but I suppose he will be home to tea presently, and as to Matthew, I have been puzzling my brains, and all to no purpose, to

endeavour to imagine what has become of him, and what can have detained him so long."

Maria felt a strong emotion of terror, when Susan mentioned the protracted absence of the old man, and she was in a state of apprehension, lest the villain Grayling should have devised some scheme or the other to put out of the way a person who was a source of so much annoyance to him, and who frustrated all his nefarious designs.

She, however, kept her thoughts confined to her own breast, and contented herself with asking Susan, as she left the room, to desire Matthew when he did come back, to come to her—if she had not retired to rest, as she wished to speak with him. She then told the good-hearted but simple girl, that she did not want her any more, and that she might rejoin her fellow servants in the kitchen, which intimation she was extremely glad to hear, and scampered out of the room, after having first solemnly promised Maria that she would not let a word drop to any of them about what they had been saying, or that she had changed her apartment.

As the time passed on, and still Matthew did not return, the uneasiness of Maria became more intense, and she formed a variety of fruitless conjectures as to the cause, the whole of which were rejected almost as soon as they had entered her imagination. Soon after Susan had quitted her, a double knock at the front door announced to her that Grayling had come back, and she soon heard his voice upon the stairs; but still she heard not the footsteps of the old man, and the suspicions that gradually stole upon her mind were of a terrible description. She could not for a moment think that Matthew absented himself of his own accord, but that he had become the victim of some dark plot contrived by Grayling to get rid of him, was firmly impressed upon her ideas.

In the midst of these harrowing thoughts, she heard a loud knocking, and the bell pulled violently. This rather startled her, for it was getting late, and she could not imagine who would call at such an unreasonable hour, unless it was some one connected with the subject which filled her bosom with so many fears. In a moment she forgot all the precaution she had resolved upon making use of to conceal herself from Richard Grayling, and before Susan could open the door, she had descended nearly into the hall, when she heard the strange tone of a man's voice inquiring after the former, and soon afterwards she rushed up the stairs again with noiseless steps, when she heard the parlour door opened, and the voice of Grayling utter the following words, in reply to the questions of the man—

"Ah, Ned, my lad, demme, I'm glad you've come; walk in—if you had not come here to rouse my depressed spirits, I really think I should have been dead with the blues before to-morrow."

Having given utterance to this speech, the parlour door was closed with a loud bang, and Maria concluded that it was one of Grayling's dissipated and abandoned associates.

Completely exhausted with the anxiety of her mind, Maria now re-entered the silent chamber, where she threw herself in a chair, and gave way to the most fearful conjectures, occasioned by the mysterious absence of poor old Matthew. Ever and anon the loud laughter and boisterous mirth of Grayling and his companion vibrated on her ears, and made her shudder with horror as she listened to these disgusting sounds of riotous revelry, while the dead was in the house. Her candle now burned dim, and as its faint rays fell upon the coffin which contained the ashes of him who had endured such misery and anguish through his heartless nephew, tears of agony once more chased each other down her cheeks.

The noise, however, soon ceased, and Maria heard the parlour door opened, and Richard Grayling and the other fellow quitted the house together.

This was a relief to the overcharged heart of Maria, and as she heard the street door closed upon them, she felt a sensation of gratitude to Omnipotence, and her fears were appeased. However, to be certain that they had both gone out, she left the dreary apartment, and descended the stairs. She ascertained that they had really left the house, and she then sought out Susan, and eagerly inquired of her whether anything had been heard of Matthew.

"Why, miss," replied the girl, "I declare I am not at all easy upon that subject, and it puzzles me to understand it. There is something wrong, depend upon it; or else——"

"Why, what do you think has happened to the poor old man?" inquired Maria with much emotion.

"As to that, miss," returned Susan, "I can't say, and I should be very sorry to judge anybody wrongfully, but certainly it looks very suspicious."

"And do you think that Mr. Grayling knows anything as to the cause of his long absence?" demanded Maria.

"Why, I'll tell you, miss," said Susan, "Mr. Grayling told me that me and the other servants had no occasion to sit up for him, as he had taken the key of the street door with him, and could let himself in; and when I asked him if he knew what time it was likely that Matthew would return, he only laughed, and said, that I had better mind my own business instead of thinking about the old man, who he thought was almost old enough to take care of himself. Then he winked at his companion and his companion winked at him in return,

upon which they laughed so loud that I'm sure you might have heard them half way along the road."

Maria wrung her hands, and with a look of the most intense grief, exclaimed—

"Alas—alas! my worst surmises are confirmed, and the poor old man has fallen into some snare laid for him by the villain Grayling, and I am deprived of that humble but honest friend."

"Oh! no, miss, indeed you are not quite friendless," said the kind-hearted Susan, "for I'm sure, as far as my humble abilities go, you may freely command me. There is nothing I would think too much trouble if it was to render you a service. Do tell me, I pray, if there be anything that you require of me."

Maria, in hearty terms, returned her acknowledgments to the poor girl for her kindness. A thought at that moment crossed her mind, but she was almost fearful to communicate it to Susan, lest it might involve her in the same trouble. She was determined to escape from the house at every hazard, and that at an hour when there was no one stirring; but she was fearful that if Grayling was to suspect that Susan was privy to her escape, and had assisted her in it, she would certainly be exposed to his vengeance, and there was no knowing to what violence his indignation might lead him. In spite of all her efforts, she could not divest her mind of a foreboding which took possession of it, and which whispered to her that she should be placed in the most imminent danger if she remained in the house that night, and she was almost resolved that she would take the present opportunity, and hasten away while there was no person at home to prevent her. But alas! she was placed in a situation which made her tremble to think of it even, for if she was to leave the house, whither could she go —where could she seek a shelter—to whom could she appeal for protection? She was a perfect stranger in the place, and knew not even in what direction to turn her steps;— besides, at such a time of night, what chance was there of her obtaining any place of shelter? The only chance that she had at all of exciting the sympathy of any person in the place, was in the breasts of the two or three persons with whom she had dealt for different trinkets and articles of wearing apparel: but then that was all an uncertainty, and when it came to the point, they might not be disposed to run any risk of a quarrel with Grayling by assisting her. Another thing—it was now night, and so little did she know of the place, that she doubted very much whether she should be able to find their houses now it was dark.

Hour after hour elapsed in this melancholy way, and Maria heard the clock strike twelve: and now more and more uneasy, and feeling confident that the old man would not return that night, she returned to the gloomy chamber of death, being resolved to venture to trust herself there for a few hours more, until the morning should dawn, and she could quit the house without any apprehension. She entered the dreary room, and after once more offering up her prayers to Heaven for its protection, she threw herself upon the bed, and endeavoured to compose herself to rest.

CHAPTER LV.

"Oh! when, alas! will cease my care?
When shall the coming morrow
Bring me the balm my heart to cheer,
And chase away my sorrow?"

ANON.

SILENCE now pervaded the house, and it was evident that the servants had all gone to bed. Another hour passed away without any changes, but, by degrees, the anguish of Maria became somewhat appeased. She felt confident that Richard Grayling had gone upon one of his night debauches, from which he never returned till the morning, and, therefore, from any interruption from him she was quite safe, and had it not been that she was so uneasy as to what had befallen poor old Matthew, and whether her conjectures and suspicions as regarded him were safe, she could have become comparatively calm; but as it was, she gradually became so much composed, that she sunk into a sound slumber, and thus gained a transient oblivion of her cares and anxieties.

It was, indeed, but transient, for soon she was aroused and alarmed by hearing the street-door unfastened, and immediately afterwards Mr. Grayling staggered into the passage, uttering a shocking oath as he did so. Maria trembled with fear, which was increased as she heard him stumbling up the stairs, and he fell against the door of the room in which she was, as he went past to his own chamber. She listened breathlessly, and at length heard him enter his own apartment; but her terror was excited to a considerable extent, when he left it almost immediately, and she heard him plainly go towards the room which she had been so fortunate as not to remain in. Still did she listen with the utmost trepidation, and a silence like that of death reigning throughout the house, the sound of his voice vibrated on her ears, and the next moment she heard him mention her name. A pause of a moment or two succeeded, and then he once more mentioned her name in a louder tone than he had before done; some other words reached her ear, from which she learnt that he was endeavouring to prevail upon her to open the door, as he wanted to speak with her about something particular. Receiving no answer, his patience became exhausted, and he became more peremp-

tory in his tone, assuming an air of command, and insisting that she should grant his request. At first his accents had been very low, so that he might not awaken the servants who slept up stairs; but when he found that he could not obtain any answer, his indignation was evidently aroused, and he spoke in much louder tones than he had before done, so that every word he uttered was heard by Maria, who trembled with fear as she listened, though at the same time she could not but think herself secure in the chamber she had so prudently taken possession of.

"What's the use of being so d—d obstinate, Miss Herbert?" said the wretch: "I tell you I must have a few words with you. I have something very particular to communicate to you. It's respecting old Matthew. Do you hear what I say? The old scoundrel, he—— But when you open the door I will tell you all about it, and not before, I am determined. I will not keep you long—only a few moments; and while you are dressing, if you will promise to see me, I will retire to my own room."

Need we attempt to describe the agitation of Maria as she listened to the words of the villain?—but how much more violent would have been her terror had she really been in her own apartment?—but she had fortunately locked the door, so that Grayling could not directly ascertain that the room was deserted. Again there was an interval of silence, but it was very brief, for not receiving any answer, his rage seemed to burst every restraint, which, added to his state of inebriation, urged him on to still more desperate measures, and she heard him shake the door with a violence which was enough to burst it off its hinges.

At length she heard one of the servant's room-doors opened, and presently the voice of Susan spoke as follows—

"If you please, sir, has anything happened, or what do you want?"

"Why the devil don't you mind your own business?—What right have you to ask such a question?" returned the ruffian, in savage accents, "get to bed with you, you impudent slut."

Susan did not obey him; she seemed to have more courage than Maria had given her credit for, and presently afterwards she heard her make the following reply to the foregoing speech of the villain Grayling—

"I am minding my own business, sir; at any rate, I don't know it, if I am not speaking about that which don't concern me; this I do know, that Miss Herbert has been worried and worried, until it has made her very ill; she was very bad when she went to her chamber, and I must say that I consider it is a scandalous thing, to go for to disturb her at such an hour as this here, half-past three o'clock in the morning."

"A little less of your impertinence, Sukey Scrub," answered Grayling, in a tone that partook of displeasure and ridicule; "if you don't go to bed again, and that directly, I shall just take the trouble to come and escort you."

Maria hearing him move from the door, had not the least doubt that he was going to suit the action to the word, but Susan hearing him beginning to ascend the stairs, darted into the chamber like lightning, and fastened the door after her.

Grayling now again returned to the door of the chamber Maria had deserted, and in still more peremptory terms repeated his commands for her to open it, and give him an audience. Finding that he was still unsuccessful, he assumed a more softened and coaxing tone, but finding that also failed to obtain him his object, his passion arose beyond all limits, and at length he threw himself against the door with such violence, that it gave way, and he was apparently precipitated into the apartment. Maria's fears increased when she heard him gather himself up, and walk heavily two or three times across the room, and utter loud and most revolting execrations, which were increased tenfold, when she heard him run from the room on to the landing, giving vent to a volley of imprecations, and the most horrible language, no doubt excited by disappointment in not finding her there. The principal portion of his abuse and vituperation was lavished upon Susan, who had been all the time listening to him, and when she heard him make such free use of her name, she had the boldness to speak, and demanded in rather pert terms, what was the matter now, and what in the name of goodness he wanted, making such a terrible noise.

"No trifling with me," he cried in a furious voice, "you had better not attempt to tamper with my feelings;—where is she gone—what has become of Miss Herbert?—It's no use your saying you don't know, for you are at the bottom of all her secrets, I know. Is she up in your room, eh?"

"God bless me! is not Miss Maria in her own room?" ejaculated Susan, with well assumed astonishment.

"To be sure she's not, and you are aware that she is not, perfectly well, I'm certain," said the ruffian; "come, you lying impertinent jade, no more of your nonsense and hypocrisy, if you conceal her five minutes longer, I'll——"

"Gracious me!" said the housekeeper, who now popped her head out of the door, "but is it really true that Miss Herbert has left the house?"

"I tell you that she is not in this room," said Grayling, "and you know all about it—it's no use any of you pleading ignorance."

"Lauks a daisy me, sir, how you do 'stonish me," returned the housekeeper; "as for me a knowing anything about it, or that she had left in a clandecent manner, you sartainly ingers my karracter by such a hidee. I seed her in the parlour the last place as I seed her in, but that was at the very time as you and t'other gentleman left the house together, but I'm sure I can't say whether she went up stairs arterwards or not."

This hint was enough for Grayling, and immediately afterwards, Maria heard him descend the stairs in great haste, she did not doubt but with the design of seeing whether she was still in the parlour, but he was so intoxicated that he could not keep his equilibrium, and when he reached the first landing, his foot slipped, and he fell with such violence against the door of the very room in which Maria was, that he burst it open.

The terror which Maria felt was almost past all endurance. She had retreated behind the bed curtains, and so fearful was she that she should be discovered by him, that she did not venture to breathe scarcely, at least there was no sound escaped her lips that could have reached the most attentive ear. Fortunately, in his fall, the candle which he had borne in his hand, was thrown upon the floor and the light extinguished, or he must have seen her, and he was now making every effort in his power to get up again, which, after considerable difficulty, he accomplished, and immediately made use of the most revolting and horrible execrations, which made Maria shudder as she heard them. Now was the moment that her fears were at the utmost pitch, for she expected that he would not leave the room until he had examined it, and then he must discover her; but how greatly was she relieved, and how grateful was she to the Almighty, when, after glancing towards the coffin, he uttered an exclamation of horror and staggered out of the room as fast as his fears, and the effects of the wine he had been drinking, would let him.

"You, girl!" exclaimed the wretch in a hoarse thick voice, from the bottom of the stairs, "come and shut this d—d door, that I have accidentally opened; do you hear?"

Susan hastened to obey this mandate, and when she had reached the door of the room in which Maria was, she thoughtlessly and imprudently exclaimed—

"Why, God bless my soul!—I declare that Mr. Grayling has forced open the door of the room in which the corpse of the poor doctor is. What could be his reason for doing that? Certainly he could not have been so silly as to suppose that Miss Herbert had concealed herself in there."

The worst apprehensions of Maria were aroused when she heard the simple but well-meaning girl make use of these observations, for she was fearful that it would suggest the truth to the mind of Grayling, and that he would repair himself to the chamber in which she was concealed: but in this idea she was happily disappointed, and she doubted not that it had either not been heard by him, or that the suspicion of which she was so fearful had not entered her mind, for he did not offer to obtrude himself upon her; but his vows of revenge when he should have discovered her, did not fail to reach her ear, and they gradually became more violent, until he had apparently pretty well exhausted all the abuse and black-guardism in his vocabulary, and became rather more quiet.

The females after a few minutes returned to their beds, but Grayling still continued up, and another hour elapsed in this manner, and Maria could not think of attempting to go to sleep again. But as she imagined that now she had no reason to be fearful that he would prosecute any further search after her for the present, she threw herself upon the bed, busied in ruminating upon what had recently taken place, and what it would be better for her to do for the future. How to effect her escape in safety she was yet at a loss to conceive, and she racked her brain in vain for some time. Most poignant was her regret and sorrow to think she was compelled to abandon the ashes of her benefactor, and as she once more removed the lid of the coffin, and gazed upon his pale and marble-like features, she mentally supplicated forgiveness of his spirit with all the same earnestness and energy as if he had been still alive and conscious of all that was passing.

At length the first red streak of day appeared in the eastern horizon, and was welcomed by Maria, who now knowing that any further delay would render all her attempts hopeless, listened attentively, and hearing Grayling snore loudly, she was convinced that he was asleep, and therefore that she was secure from any interruption on his part, she with a light and cautious step ascended to her bed-room, where she equipped herself in her bonnet and cloak, and secured a change of clothes in a small bundle, and then in a state of mingled fear, doubt, and hope, her heart beating violently against her side, and her limbs trembling with agitation, she hastened down the stairs, having determined if she could only emerge from the house, if he should awaken and pursue her, she would claim protection of the first passenger she encountered.

When she came to the parlour door, the thick heavy breathing of Grayling convinced her that he was still wrapped in sleep, and she soon gained the street door without any impediment. But her hopes were at once crushed, when she found that the door was locked, and the key not there, and her dismay

may be readily imagined, when just at the moment she made this discovery she heard Grayling yawn, and soon afterwards he moved, and she was certain that he was awaking.

The terror and suspense of Maria may now be easily imagined, but she stood on the mat at the door and was unable to move, and scarcely to breathe, for fear Grayling should overhear her. She was not kept in this state of agitation however many minutes, when the parlour door was opened, and out came Gray-ling, gaping, and apparently half asleep, so that he never once turned round, but made his way to the staircase, and ascended the stairs, no doubt with an intention to retire to his own bed and complete his slumbers, instead of remaining on the sofa in the parlour exposed to the cold. She heard him ascend to the door of the chamber, open it, enter, and close it after him, and clasping her hands, she thanked Providence that she was once more safe.

Still was she at a loss what plan to pursue, and how to effect her liberation. At last she bethought her of the parlour window, and she immediately entered that apartment. But here she was once more doomed to disappointment; she tried her utmost strength to open them, but in vain, and even if she had been able to have done so, she knew there was a deep area in front, which she could not possibly get across. She was completely at a loss what to do.

At last, casting her eyes around the room, they fell on a door at the left hand side, which she remembered opened into another apartment of smaller dimensions than the one she was in, and was made no other use of than to keep umbrellas, cloaks, hats, &c., in.

Her hopes again revived, for she knew that there was no area beneath the windows of that room; so, hastily entering it, she lifted up the windows without any trouble.

Once more she paused, and her heart failed her. Several times did she raise the sash, and look out, but the people who were passing, and whose inquisitive looks seemed to convey suspicion, made her shrink back, and hesitate whether or not she should venture. Indeed she had not the courage to appeal to the coarse labouring men and women, who were passing, to assist her, and despair began to seize upon her. For more than half an hour she remained in this manner; although she was often on the point of addressing herself to one of them, there was something in their looks or manner that prevented her, and disheartened her, and she was afraid to make the attempt herself, lest their curiosity should raise an alarm, and the villain Grayling thus be apprised of her situation.

Quick elapsed the time, and yet did Maria continue in the same manner, and afraid to make the effort, she heard the servants descend from their chambers, and Susan also, who came to the hall door and attempted to open it, and when she found it was fastened, she expressed her indignation that Mr. Grayling should take upon himself to hold her in confinement. But Maria imagined that it would be as well not to make known to her where she was, so, that she might not implicate her any more than possible in her flight.

At length she heard a neighbouring church clock strike seven, and the impatience and anxiety of Maria increased, but notwithstanding, she had not the courage to put her wishes into practice.

The road now became clearer, for the persons who had before passed along it, had gone to their daily labour, and it was not much frequented in the day time. Suddenly, Maria beheld a young woman, clean but meanly clad, approaching that way, and to her she determined to appeal. When she had got beneath the window she looked up at our heroine, and by the melancholy expression of her countenance, seemed about to ask charity, but Maria did not wait to hear her, although she comprehended what she was about to do, and throwing her half-a-crown, ejaculated—

"Pray render me your assistance, I am detained here against my will, and am anxious to make my escape from it; will you do as I request of you?"

The young woman made no reply, although it was evident from the expression of her countenance that she was very much surprised; however, she immediately took the bundle from Maria, and then lending her hand, Maria without much difficulty alighted from the window into the road.

Unable to speak, she made a sign to her to walk on with her as fast as she was able, and notwithstanding the agitation she was in, there was something in the young woman's countenance which was very familiar to her, although it was so pale and careworn, that she could not call to mind where it was that she had seen her before.

"I am a stranger here," at length she said, "I have no friends to whom I can go, in Bath. Do you reside here?"

"Yes," answered the young girl, "I do reside here, and have a home, such as it is, perhaps better than I deserve, but still it is too poor for such as Miss Herbert to go to."

At the mention of her name Maria started, and scrutinised the features of the young woman more narrowly, but still, although she was confident she had seen her before, she could not call to mind where it was, and under what circumstances. A tear started to the young woman's eye, and she sighed deeply.

"No wonder you do not recollect me, Miss Herbert," she said, in mournful accents, "and I ought to feel ashamed, after what has

happened, to remind you who I am. Oh, you cannot form any idea of the hardships, the cares, the anguish, the privations me and my poor unfortunate sister (who has a baby) have endured since you last saw us; but we have deserved it all."

Maria again looked at her companion, and she instantly knew her, and exclaimed—

"Why, surely it is Emma Sherwood?"

"It is, miss; me and my sister Rose were the scholars whom you and Mrs. Wallingford took so much notice of, at the school in the village, of which you were the benefactresses," answered the young woman. "Alas! miss, see what disgrace and trouble we have brought upon ourselves by straying from those paths of rectitude to which we were always directed."

Maria looked at her compassionately, and pressed her hand in a soothing manner. She was already in possession of the melancholy story of her and her sister's downfall, and she was gratified to find that she was brought to a sense of her shame and degradation, and apparently repented of her error. Emma and Rose had both fallen victims to the seductive arts of two gentlemen, who had afterwards deserted them. Their mother had died broken-hearted, and it had never been known whither they had gone, although it was strongly suspected, that, driven to despair, they had committed suicide.

We say that Maria knew all this, and knowing that they were not so much to blame as those through whom they had fallen, she sincerely pitied them.

"But how do you live, and in what manner have you managed to exist all this time?" demanded Maria.

"Exist," returned Emma, "God knows, I can scarcely tell you, miss. When our seducers abandoned us, ashamed to return home, we tried to get into service, but could not; but we did get a little needlework, which brought us in a few pence, scarcely enough to keep body and soul together; we have been for days, and have had nothing to eat but a crust of bread and a few potatoes. To add to our misery, my sister proved to be in the family way, and with what horror did we look forward to the period of her confinement, and to the misery to which the poor infant would be born. We prayed to heaven that it might not be suffered to live; but our prayer was not heard. I cannot describe to you the horrors, the miseries that followed, it is wonderful that we did not sink beneath the weight of it, and rush into eternity with all our sins upon our heads; but we did not. To add to our wretched condition, we lost the trifling work we had previously had, and had nothing whatever to depend upon. What could we do? We had no one near to assist us, so at last we were driven to beggary. Rose has been ill for the last two or three days, and therefore, we have both had to depend upon my individual exertions. Oh, miss, what a degrading life it is, but it is a just punishment for those who break through the laws of virtue."

Maria was extremely shocked at the account which Emma gave of her and her sister's sufferings, but she was very glad to hear, if it might be judged from her words, that they were so penitent.

Maria's courage increased as they got

THE BRUTAL INSOLENCE OF BARNELL TO MARIA.

farther away from the house which contained Richard Grayling, but still she continued to walk with great speed, and, in fact, Emma had a difficulty in keeping up with her, for want and sorrow had so reduced her strength.

"But surely you cannot think of entering my wretched dwelling, miss?" said the poor girl, as they proceeded.

"I certainly do, Emma," she replied, "at least if you will permit me to do so. As I before told you, I am a complete stranger in Bath, and know no one, and I require a few hours' repose and reflection before I can fix upon a plan for my future pursuit. Never mind the wretchedness of the habitation, my poor girl, I have it in my power to assist you to improve it, and I have not yet forgotten to be charitable and kind to those who are in distress."

Emma's eyes filled with tears, but there was an expression in her countenance which spoke more than words could have done, the gratitude she felt for the kindness of Maria. Her spirits and her hopes were raised, and she seemed to have imbibed new life, for she redoubled her speed, and no longer seemed to feel that fatigue which her emaciated frame was so characteristic of. She seemed anxious to conduct Maria on the way, but ever and anon, she would repeat her remarks upon the wretchedness of her abode, and express a fear that Maria would find it far more miserable than she anticipated, and likewise her regret that she could not accommodate Miss Herbert in a better manner.

Maria endeavoured to quiet her fears, and at length they arrived at the place. Maria certainly was not, even after all that Emma had said about it, prepared to find so much squalid poverty as the hovel (for it deserved no better title), in which the two unfortunate girls resided, presented. The appearance of it, so cold, so cheerless, so dismal, so utterly destitute of anything in the shape of comfort, completely chilled her heart, and she shrank back for a moment, from its entrance, with a sensation of disgust.

It was a miserable hut, which seemed incapable of sheltering a human being, situated at the top of a long, narrow, and dreary lane, which led on to a barren heath; and the timber in many parts had completely rotted away, affording no protection from the inclemency of the weather.

The interior of this place presented even a more cheerless aspect than the exterior. It consisted of no more than one apartment, extremely low, without ceiling, nothing but the bare tiles and rafters; no flooring to cover the naked earth, and the walls, which consisted only of lath and plaster, were broken in many places, and gave free admittance to the wind and the rain. The casement was very small, and did not contain more than three or four pieces of glass, the other portions being covered with paper, or stuffed with old rags. Such was the wretched tenement, and the furniture (if it deserved the title) was in every way worthy of it. There was no grate in the fireplace, but a few bricks piled up, and a bar of iron across, was made to answer the purpose, but it looked as if it and the fire had for some time been unacquainted.—There was a dilapidated chair, an old stool, and a ricketty deal table. In one corner of the place was a straw mattress, upon which was seated Rose Sherwood, the picture of squalid misery, who was hugging with parental fondness a chubby-faced infant boy to her bosom when Maria and Emma entered.

The shame, the astonishment, and grief, yet mingled with a feeling of hope, which poor Rose experienced on seeing Maria, may readily be conceived, and were evidently not affected, and she was for some moments totally incapable of speaking; Maria, in the meantime, who was much moved by all she saw, in the most affectionate manner endeavouring to impart consolation to her.

"Oh, this is a miserable place, Miss Herbert," at length she said, "this is a miserable place for you to come to, but here me and my poor sister have been more contented and happy than anywhere else that we have been, for we may say that it belongs to us; the rent is but a trifle, and that, the good woman to whom it belongs suffers us to work out at my needle, which is as much as I can do, ill as I am. Alas! what would have become of me and my poor baby, had it not been for Emma? And she to be reduced to the degrading life that—— But why should we complain? We have no right to do so—we have both of us erred, wickedly erred, after the good advice we received, and we deserve to be punished. Oh, what punishment is adequate to the misery that has been occasioned by our misconduct?—Did we not break our poor old mother's heart?—Did we not—— But," she added, seeing the strong emotion Maria evinced, "I will not rack your feelings, miss, with a recital which must fill your gentle bosom with horror. Emma will hasten and procure some coals, and kindle a fire, and perhaps she will be able to borrow Mrs. Merton's tea-kettle, who lives at the other end of the lane, for she is a good soul, and ready to do everything that lies in her power to help us; though, God knows, that is not much, for she is almost as bad off as ourselves, poor creature."

"You had better purchase one, Emma," said Maria, putting some money into her hand, "and also get such little necessaries as may tend to your present comfort."

Emma and Rose, with tears in their eyes, were about to give expression to their gratitude, but Maria stopped them, and said—

"Nay, nay, I need no thanks. While you are gone, Emma, and you have no occasion to hurry yourself back, I will lay myself down by the side of your sister, and endeavour to gain that rest of which I stand in so much need. But I must caution you not to give the slightest hint to any one that you may meet, that I am your guest, or that you know anything about me—unless," recollecting herself, "you should meet old Matthew, Doctor Hartley's servant, whom you know very well. To him you may mention everything, but not in the hearing of any other person, and desire him to come to me immediately, or, at least, as soon as he can, without exciting any suspicion."

Of course, Emma promised implicit obedience, and immediately departed on her errand.

Rose made many apologies to Maria, for the humble pallet she only had to offer her, but Maria impatiently put an end to them, and assured her of her perfect content with it;—indeed, although it was poor, it was particularly clean, and to Maria, to whom rest had been a stranger for a night or two, it was most inviting;—she, therefore, w thout any hesitation, stretched her weary limbs upon it, and with the assurance of being out of danger, and the length of the walk she had had, being sufficient of itself to tire her, she soon sunk into a deep refreshing slumber.

How long she had slept she knew not, but she was suddenly aroused by some person shaking her arm, and looking up, she beheld Emma standing over her, and by her countenance it was evident she had something important to tell her.

"I beg your pardon, miss," she said, "for arousing you so abruptly, but when I went into the town to purchase the things I wanted, the very first person I met was Matthew, and he is now outside, waiting to——"

"Oh, I am instantly ready to receive him," exclaimed Maria, jumping up joyfully upon receiving this intelligence, and feeling an indescribable relief, when she found the poor old man was safe. The next moment the door was opened, and Matthew presented himself before her. His countenance was pale, and he had every other appearance of being ill and violently agitated, and Maria eagerly inquired what had been the matter, and how it was that he had been so long absent.

The indignation of the old man almost choked his utterance, and that of Maria was equal to his own, when he related the particulars she had requested of him.

It appeared that the villain Grayling had preferred a charge of robbery against him, but the proofs of his entire innocence were so glaring, that he was immediately discharged by the magistrate, and Grayling censured by the former, for charging him with so heinous an offence on such trivial grounds. He had, therefore, hastened back to the house, and there heard of Maria's flight, Grayling raving like a madman and vowing that he would get her once more in his power or die in the attempt. Of course, he (Matthew) could not form the slightest conjecture whith r she had gone; however, he immediately packed up his things, and ordering them to be left for him at one of the taverns in the city, left the house, and had scarcely

done so when he was so fortunate as to encounter Emma.

Maria heard the old man's story with the utmost indignation, and entertained a feeling of still greater abhorrence against the villain, Richard Grayling, who, it was very evident, would not hesitate to do anything, no matter how base, to gratify his malice and revenge, or to forward his nefarious views. She was very much concerned to see Matthew so ill, as he evidently was, more especially at that time, when she so much needed his assistance. Matthew himself expressed his regret at the circumstance, as he considered that it would be advisable for Maria to leave Bath as soon as possible, and he could not bear the idea of her doing so alone. He, however, trusted that he should be better the next day, which Maria had fixed for her departure to Rosemary Dell, and, anxious to see what effect rest would have upon him, he did not remain long with her, but departed to the house of a friend, where he intended to visit while he remained in Bath.

Contrary to his wishes, however, and in accordance with the apprehensions of Maria, Matthew found himself so much worse the next day, that he could not leave his bed, much to her regret, as she was thus deprived of the aid and advice of her only friend, and, fearful of encountering Grayling, she could not herself venture to visit him. She, however, sent Emma, by whom the old man returned a letter, in which he stated that as it was quite uncertain when he should be able to accompany her, every hour she remained where she was, was fraught with danger, and he advised her, by all means, to leave by the coach that day, and that, as soon as he found himself in a condition to travel, he would follow her.

Maria had taken her place in the coach, so she followed this advice, and towards evening, after bidding adieu to the unfortunate sisters, and giving them the means of temporary relief, she made her way towards the coach-office, trembling all the way she went, fearful that she would meet her oppressor or some of his myrmidons.

Before she could reach the coach-office, she had to pass by the house in which she had so recently resided, and where dwelt the object of her fears, and it was with a palpitating heart that she approached it. With a hurried glance she looked up at all the windows, but the place was buried in complete darkness, and it was very evident that Grayling was away from home. Maria felt greatly relieved, when she had got past the house, and had entered upon the field which she had to cross before she could reach the inn from which the coach started, and where the trifling luggage which it was necessary for her to take with her, had been deposited by Emma, in the morning. It was now quite dark, and Maria had proceeded to some distance, when she heard a person approaching her, who with stentorian lungs was bawling out a portion of a popular song, and seemed to be, what is technically called "pretty fresh," which translated, means pretty considerably intexicated.

She trembled, and paused, not knowing how to act, whether to advance or retreat; her heart foreboded some danger, yet she had not the strength or the energy to attempt to avoid it. There was something, too, in the tones of the voice which were perfectly familiar to her. While she thus stood hesitating, the very object she dreaded staggered up to her, and perceiving it was a female, was about to address her in a rude manner, when suddenly he started back with amazement and evident pleasure, and judge of the terror of Maria, when she found herself in the presence of the very man she wished to avoid, the wretch, Richard Grayling!

The unexpected meeting seemed to sober him directly, and hastily catching her round the waist, he exclaimed with a look, and in accents of triumph—

"By the devil, it is her very self! So—so, my runaway miss, you thought to escape me altogether, did you? Ha—ha—ha! Do Richard Grayling, and you have only got another to beat; no, no. You have given me a bit of a puzzle, and I had almost given it up for a bad job, though I was resolved to search every nook and corner of Bath, but I would find you. Damme, only to think that I should fall in with you in such a manner; well, we'll not part company so soon this time, I'll warrant."

"Villain, have you not already sufficiently insulted and outraged my feelings, but you must now add to the offence?" answered Maria, with more spirit and firmness than might have been expected, and fixing upon Grayling a look of the utmost dignity and resentment; "do not seek to detain me, or you may have reason to repent it. Release me, I say!"

"Not so fast, my little queen," said the fellow, with the most disgusting boldness, and still forcibly retaining his hold of Maria's hand, and, in spite of her resistance, pulling her towards him; "come, now, what's the use of being so devilish cross?—I don't want to be bad friends with you—quite different, so just return home with me, and I will not say another word about your having left me in the shabby manner you did. Lor' bless you, I'll be bound that we shall very soon understand each other, and then you will find me as nice a fellow as any young girl need wish to have."

"Miscreant!" cried the indignant damsel, still making the most violent efforts to release

herself from his hold, while the expression of his countenance filled her with the utmost alarm, "unhand me, or my cries shall speedily bring those to my assistance who may cause you to repent this unmanly, this brutal insolence."

"Ha—ha—ha!" laughed Grayling, scornfully, "you might cry here as long as you liked, but there is no one near to hear you, besides, if there was, I could soon find the way to stop your tongue. But what is the use of all this nonsense; I'm sure I have not done anything to make you take such a thorough dislike to me, and I can only tell you, that many a finer girl than you even, have been proud to acknowledge the attention of Dick Grayling. I must have a kiss of those pouting lips! Nay——"

"Villain—wretch!" exclaimed the exasperated maiden, as Grayling attempted to press her lips, "unhand me!—Oh, help help!"

"No squeamishness!" cried Grayling, rendered more determined by her resistance, "a kiss I am determined to have, and then we can talk other matters over when we get home."

"Help—help! for Heaven's sake, help!" again screamed Maria, and completely exhausted, her feelings overpowered her, and she fainted; and Grayling raising her in his arms, fled with her precipitately across the field towards the house.

CHAPTER LVI.

"And though unequal is thy fate,
　Since title deck'd my higher birth;
Yet envy not this gaudy state,
　Thine is the pride of modest worth."
　　　　　　　　　　BYRON.

WE will now return to Ela and her daughter, who arrived safe at their place of destination, after having passed some time in travelling to different parts of the continent. Ela took an elegant house, and in one of the most pleasant spots, being on the margin of a beautiful lake; and feeling, as it were, quite secure from their bitter enemies, at any rate, for the present, Fanny and her mother became more tranquil than they had been for some time. The beauteous and ever sunny clime of Italy had a wonderful effect upon the spirits of Fanny, and Ela felt a degree of pride and pleasure upon treading the land of her forefathers, which she had not for many years experienced.

But it must not be supposed that they had no other thoughts but those of satisfaction, that melancholy reflections were entirely excluded from their minds; no, they deeply lamented the necessity which had compelled them to separate from their friends, and Fanny sadly missed the affectionate attentions and society of Maria. She took the earliest opportunity of writing to her, and giving her every particular of what had happened to them, and how they were then situated, and expressed in glowing language the continued affectionate regard which existed in her bosom towards her, and which must increase instead of diminish with time. Ela also sent letters to Dr. Hartley and Mr. Goodwin, which teemed with the most enthusiastic assurances of her friendship, and expressed the due sense she entertained, and always should entertain of their kindness, and the services they had rendered her, trusting that they might at some future period meet again. Alas! little did Ela think that one of her best friends, Dr. Hartley, at the time she wrote this, was no more, and of the change which had been caused in Maria's circumstances.

The surprise and alarm of Ela and her daughter may be readily conceived, when, after waiting patiently for some time, they received no answer from their friends. They racked their brains in vain to endeavour to account for it; surely nothing serious had happened to them, and yet if they had not, they felt confident they would have been too overjoyed at hearing from them, to have delayed sending an answer immediately. Perhaps, however, they had left Bath, but then if they had, the letters would certainly have been forwarded to them. They were quite at a loss what to think, and became very uneasy, and in the midst of this perplexity, a letter arrived for Ela (addressed to her under a fictitious name, as she had requested). It was from Mr. Goodwin, and how afflicting to Ela and Fanny was the information the letter imparted; Mr. Goodwin informed them of the melancholy circumstance of the death of Mr. Hartley. the behaviour of his villanous nephew, and added that from what they had been able to ascertain, Maria, under the impression that she would be in more security, had departed to Rosemary Dell, intending for the present, at any rate, to take up her residence with Anthony and his wife in Wallingford Hall.

Fanny was very uneasy on hearing this account of Maria, but she thought, under the melancholy circumstances which had been retailed to them, she acted very wisely in taking up her abode at Wallingford Hall. Of Mr. Wallingford and his son, Mr. Goodwin wrote scarcely anything, but informed them that they had left England for Switzerland, he believed, although there was nothing positive known upon the matter. Fanny sighed when she came to this passage, and tears came to her eyes, as she said—

"I shall never see them again, neither my——Mr. Wallingford or Walter; but will they—can they feel that regret at the certainty which I do? Oh, yes, there is one, Walter, I know, will experience all the sorrow, all the anguish which I now feel; I will not do him

the injustice to suppose he can feel otherwise."

Fanny immediately set about writing a second letter to Maria, which she addressed to Wallingford Hall, and feeling now more easy, she endeavoured to wait with patience until she should receive an answer.

The beauty of Fanny, and the elegance and apparent wealth of the mother, soon attracted much attention and admiration among the gentry in the neighbourhood where they resided, and their acquaintance was much sought after; but Ela, who was averse to society, and who did not choose to let her daughter mingle among the gay, unprincipled, and dissipated young men who thronged the fashionable circles, respectfully declined all the invitations she received, and kept no society at all, being entirely secluded in their own house.

But Fanny required no other companions than her dear mother, her own thoughts, or a book, and in the contemplation of the beautiful scenery by which they were environed, she found ample means of gratification and delight.

One of Fanny's principle enjoyments was in equestrian exercises, she having taken great pains to become a good horsewoman, since they had settled in Italy. She would frequently ride out for some distance, and unattended by any servant—for she had an infinite dislike to ostentation, and, in fact, she felt more real pleasure in this exercise than in anything else.

It happened upon one occasion, Fanny had extended her ride farther than usual, and was just about to return, when her horse shyed, and started off along the road at a most furious rate. Fanny kept her seat remarkably well, but her terror may be easily imagined, for she found it impossible to restrain it, and the spirited animal rather increased than abated his frightful velocity. The road which he was pursuing with his terrified burthen led to an awful abyss, and of this Fanny was aware, and as the distance from it became every instant shorter, and the certainty of a terrible fate rushed upon her mind, her fears became more terrible than can be described. And now she had arrived to within a few yards of the yawning gulph, and her fate seemed to be inevitable, when at that critical moment, and when all hope appeared to be at an end, a young man elegantly attired, on horseback also, dashed from behind a cluster of trees at a turning in the road, and riding up towards her, at the imminent hazard of his own life, seized the bridle, and stopped the horse, just as she had arrived to within only a few paces of the abyss, and another plunge they must have been precipitated to the bottom.

Fanny was so terrified at her narrow escape, that it was several moments before she could speak a word, but at length, with a deep blush, she raised her eyes towards her preserver, and in accents of sweetness, expressed her thanks to him for what he had done, and begged to assure him of her gratitude.

If Fanny blushed when she addressed the stranger, she felt still more confused on beholding him gazing at her with looks of the most ardent admiration. He was young, tall, graceful, and remarkably handsome. His features bespoke him to be an Englishman, and the kindness and urbanity of his looks immediately prepossessed the beholder in his favour.

To the thanks of Fanny he replied in the most appropriate manner, and in words which seemed to bear a conviction of their sincerity along with them. He said that he felt more than rewarded by the pleasure it afforded him of having been the means of preserving her from so shocking a fate as that which had threatened her; and added that he should ever consider that the happiest period of his life. Fanny's cheeks were suffused with blushes, and she in vain endeavoured to make a reply, but when he further requested that he might have the honour to escort her home, she kindly thanked him, but assured him that she was not under any apprehensions, and therefore she would not put him to so much unnecessary trouble. The gentleman, however, who seemed to have made up his mind, would take no denial, and therefore Fanny was forced to yield to his request, and turning their horses' heads, they rode slowly on towards the residence of Fanny and her mother.

On the way thither, the gentleman conversed upon different topics, but principally remarking upon the beauty of the scenery, and the various objects they encountered as they went along, with an ease and elegance which shewed that he possessed a refined taste and highly cultivated mind. Fanny could not help listening to him with a degree of pleasure she had never felt before, except in the society of Walter; and he seemed no less delighted with the answers she returned, which plainly evinced the excellent abilities with which nature had endowed her. They were both so well pleased with one another, that the time seemed to pass away doubly quick, and they had arrived at the mansion of Ela before Fanny had taken any notice scarcely of the way they were proceeding. The gentleman was one of those individuals, who, from the first moment of introduction, create confidence and esteem, and even in the few short minutes that Fanny had been in his company, she felt as intimate as if they had been acquainted for years.

The astonishment of Ela may be easily guessed, when she saw Fanny ride up to the house, attended by a young and handsome stranger, but upon being made acquainted with what had happened, she expressed in the warmest manner possible her thanks, and invited the gentleman in. He very readily availed himself of the in-

vitation, and the next moment beheld the two seated in the library, and conversing as familiarly as if they had been many years in each other's society.

It appeared that the preserver of Fanny's life was an English nobleman, of the title of Lord Halvendon, who with his mother had been residing for some few months past in Italy, and not far from the house of Ela. He was an only son, and was devotedly attached to his amiable parent, who was a lady of the most eminent virtues and accomplishments, and had bestowed the utmost care and attention upon her son, who she hoped would hand down with increased honour to posterity their ancient name.

Ela was completely charmed with the young nobleman's behaviour and manners, and he prolonged his visit as long as the rules of etiquette would allow him to do, and then seemed very loth to depart. When he requested that he might be permitted to call again, and that Signora Beranzio and her charming daughter would honour his mother with a visit, Ela paused. She could not refuse, and Lord Halvendon took his leave evidently much delighted, while, on the other hand, Ela and her daughter had experienced no less pleasure in his company.

When he had gone, Ela and Fanny entered into a conversation upon the events of the morning, and Ela eulogised in the warmest manner the elegance of behaviour and apparent urbanity of disposition which the young nobleman possessed. Fanny listened to her with evident satisfaction, and she could not help giving utterance to her most unqualified coincidence with all her mother had remarked about him. And indeed Fanny spoke sincerely, for she felt so deep an interest in Lord Halvendon, that she could not erase him from her thoughts, but recalled his features to her mind's eye the whole of the day, and at night when she retired to rest, visions of the most pleasing description flitted before her imagination. She felt an anxious wish to see him again, and awaited his second visit with much impatience. Already had the penetrating eye of Ela discovered that Fanny felt a more than common interest in their new acquaintance, but she was not displeased, and was fully resolved that she would not exercise any tyranical authority over her affections, reserving to herself the task of advising her for the best, as she was well assured that she would never fix her choice upon an unworthy object.

Three days elapsed before they saw or heard anything more of Lord Halvendon, when Ela and Fanny, who were seated at the parlour window, were suddenly surprised to see a splendid carriage, on which were the armorial bearings of a nobleman of ancient family, drive along the principal walk, and soon afterwards it stopped at the door, and from it alighted Lord Halvendon, assisting from it an old lady, of dignified air, but whose countenance was exceedingly mild and affable. In a few moments more they were ushered into the presence of Ela and her daughter, Lord Halvendon introducing his companion as his mother, Lady Halvendon.

Lady Halvendon exactly resembled her son in her amiable disposition and the affability of her manners, and she therefore made an immediate favourable impression upon Ela and Fanny, who received her with much cordiality, and in a short time all the diffidence which accompanies a first meeting was dissipated, and they soon became all immersed in the pleasures of a most delightful conversation, which was carried on with equal spirit and eloquence on all sides.

Lady Halvendon was a woman of vast information, and with a mind highly accomplished. She hated and despised the frivolities and gaeties of fashionable life, and entered no more into society than was absolutely necessary for the benefit of her son, and to qualify him for the rank he was destined to hold in the world. She seemed very much struck with the melancholy dignity of Ela's behaviour, and the beauty and natural intrinsic charms of her daughter, and she was not at all surprised that her son had eulogised her so warmly, so enthusiastically as he had done to her.

Lady Halvendon was not an inquisitive woman, but there was something so peculiar in the manner of Ela, that convinced her that her career had not been an ordinary one, and she longed to be made acquainted with it; she was certain that she had experienced her full share of sorrow, and that thought already excited her sympathy for her, which she was anxious to express.

The visit of Lady Halvendon and her son was a long one, and they separated with evident reluctance, though not before her ladyship had obtained from Ela a promise to pay her a visit the following day.

"Well, Frederick," observed his mother, as they rode home, "I must confess that you possess a most excellent taste upon the subject of female beauty and accomplishments. This Fanny is one of the sweetest girls that I have seen for some time."

"I am glad to hear that your ladyship is of my opinion," replied her son, warmly, "she certainly is a charming girl, adding as she does to a fascinating simplicity and modesty of demeanour, natural accomplishments which would render her an ornament to any station of society."

Lady Halvendon smiled.

"I am afraid, Frederick," she said, "that this fair damsel has made an impression upon you that will not very quickly be forgot."

"*Afraid*," repeated the young nobleman; "supposing your idea to be correct, my dear mother, surely there cannot be much cause for fear in the circumstance."

Lady Halvendon made no reply to her son,

and the subject dropped for the present, although it was very evident that it still continued to occupy both of their minds above every other.

We shall not enter into a minute detail of all the visits which passed between them, it is sufficient to say that a most fervent intimacy sprung up between them, and it was very soon discovered that Lord Frederick and Fanny had imbibed for one another a sincere and ardent passion. They could not long keep this fact concealed either from their parents or themselves;—but why should they? Surely there was no harm in encouraging a virtuous passion? And were they not worthy of each other? Yes, they were; — their parents thought so too, and when they found that they loved each other, they readily sanctioned their vows, and the time was even appointed for their nuptials to take place, but circumstances were about to happen to interrupt their joys, and to fill them with the most unbounded alarm.

There was only one drawback upon the peace of Fanny, and that was the mystery with respect to Maria, who had never written to her yet, and about whom Mr. Goodwin remained silent whenever he sent any letters to them. That something had occurred to her, it was very certain, and her mind was racked with anguish and anxiety when she endeavoured, and ineffectually, to imagine what it was. This often rendered her very miserable, and her mother was unable to afford her any consolation, for she was as much perplexed as herself, to conceive what could be the cause of it. Sometimes she thought of the Gipsies, and that they, finding herself and Fanny had escaped from them, had resolved to wreak their vengeance on Maria, for the part which she had taken in proceeding against them. These ideas, however, she kept confined to her own breast, for she was afraid, if she mentioned it to Fanny, it would cause her much agony, without being able to effect any good, and after all perhaps it might turn out to be erroneous. But she could not succeed in banishing the thought from her mind, and it caused her many an hour of the most poignant anguish.

CHAPTER LVII.

" Again the poison'd cup I drain,
    Again grief's potent sway
Rules in my breast, distracts my brain,
    And drives all peace away."

WE will now return to Maria, who we left being borne away in a state of insensibility by the villain Richard Grayling.

Upon recovering her senses she found herself in the chamber she had formerly occupied at the house belonging to Doctor Hartley, and the disagreeable old housekeeper supporting her in a chair, and bathing her temples with vinegar. Grayling was standing by her side, watching attentively the proceedings, and when he beheld her open her eyes and look around the room, he evinced much satisfaction, and said in a coarse brutal tone—

"Ah! it's all right, I see, she's not dead this time. What strange animals these women are, only just put your lips to theirs, and they faint in an instant. See to her, old woman, and you know what I told you about the other business."

"Oh, yes, sir," answered the old jezabel, who seemed to glory in the office she had been commissioned to perform, "I will take good care to manage everything to your satisfaction, and no doubt it will go on right enough, now you have got rid of that impudent minx, Susan, and that officious old fellow, Matthew."

"Yes, it only requires caution, but I must be off, for you know where I have got to go to," observed Grayling, moving towards the door. "Good night, Miss Herbert; no doubt you think me rather harsh in making you my prisoner, but you know it was all your own fault, for——"

"Villain!" interrupted Maria, indignantly, "by what right do you make a prisoner of me; what authority have you over my actions?"

"Oh, never mind that," returned he, "I have not time to stand arguing that point with you just now, and if I had, I do not suppose we should ever come to a satisfactory conclusion. Here you are, and here I mean to keep you, too."

"Wretch! this treatment shall not go unpunished; you shall yet be taught that a defenceless female is not to be insulted with impunity."

"'Psha! what the devil's the use of talking in that manner," said Grayling, "I tell you it's your own fault, because you will be so obstinate. I should like to know if any female besides yourself would feel offended because a man wanted to make a lady of her. But it's only a waste of time talking upon that subject at present; I have no doubt we shall be able to agree better by-and-by."

"Can any man be so lost to all sense of feeling?" exclaimed Maria, with disgust, "even while the corpse of your uncle is in the house, to——"

"Perhaps you might be mistaken as to that," interrupted Grayling, with a revolting grin, and winking at the old housekeeper, who returned it with one which was meant to be equally as knowing. "However, I must go; you can have everything you may want for your comfort; Mrs. Crabley has orders to that effect from me. Good night."

Before Maria could make any reply to this insolent speech, Grayling had quitted the room, and descending the stairs, she heard him leave the house and close the street-door with a loud bang. No sooner had he gone, than the old woman locked the room-door, and deposited the key in her pocket, and then, seemingly ashamed to meet the reproachful glances of the indignant maiden, she pretended to be busying herself by doing something or the other in the chamber.

"Old woman," said Maria, at last, in a stern voice, "are you not ashamed to be seen in an abominable affair of this description; to become the panderer to a villain, and to aid him in the persecution of one of your own sex, that one, too, a young and defenceless girl?—Shame on you—shame on you!"

Mrs. Crabley was evidently abashed, and for a minute or so remained silent, playing with one corner of her apron; at length in a whining tone, and with several "a-hems," and short coughs, she said—

"Lawks, miss, I'm sure I never thought as how I was a doin' anythink unproper; indeed, as young master says he loves you, and as you have no friends, I thought——"

"You thought!" interrupted Maria, with strong marks of resentment depicted in her countenance, "let me hear no more of these disgusting hints. You have subjected yourself to punishment as well as the villain you call 'your young master' for this outrage, and depend upon it, unless you immediately unlock the door and suffer me to leave the house, you will be dealt with with all the severity which the law will allow."

"Me let you quit the house, and at such a time of night too?" ejaculated the old woman; "gracious me! why you must think I have taken leave o' my senses; 'sides, as for punishment, I hope young master an' you will settle matters in a better manner than that arter a bit."

"Mrs. Crabley," observed Maria, indignantly, "do you intend to do as I say without any more bother? I command you to open the door, and no longer try to confine me against my will."

"But indeed I shall do no such thing, don't you think it," returned the old woman, pertly; "I'm not to be frightened by fine words off a weak stomach, not I; and for the matter of that, if you become obstropolous, there is a gentleman down stairs as can manage you if I can't."

"I will not be detained," said Maria, determinedly, "if you refuse to let me depart, my cries shall bring assistance."

"That would be quite as useless, young lady," replied Mrs. Crabley, with a sardonic grin; "do you suppose that young master would not be sure to provide against that there?"

Finding it was useless to endeavour to intimidate the old woman by threats, Maria next tried the force of persuasion, and in impressive language appealed to her feelings, and offered to remunerate her well, and never reproach her afterwards, if she would suffer her to escape. But in this she was equally unsuccessful; the old woman was callous to all feeling, and it seemed indifferent to reward, or else she doubted the truth of what Maria promised, and having proceeded so far in the business, thought it would be useless to abandon the

MARIA'S VISIT TO THE TOMB OF DR. HARTLEY.

designs of her " *young master,*" as in the event of Maria proceeding against them, her punishment would be sure to be equally severe.

"But la !" said she, continuing a long senseless rigmarole she had given utterance to, in answer to Maria, " what is the reason you will be so foolish as to refuse the offers of Mr. Grayling, miss? He has got plenty of money now, for I dare say old master was very rich, and I'm sure no one can say but that he is a fine looking young man, and would no doubt make a very good husband. For my part, I can't tell what's come to a parcel of girls now-a-days, they have such strange fancies, and are so very hard to please."

Maria made no reply, but looking scornfully at the old woman, she covered her face with her handkerchief, and for a few minutes gave way to the violence of the grief which distracted her bosom. Mrs. Crabley did not offer to interrupt her, but sat in a chair by the fireside, and pretended to be busily engaged at needlework. After some time passed in this manner, Maria sufficiently recovered herself to come to a determination not to show any further weakness, and accordingly she wiped her eyes, and assumed all the former dignity which had ever characterised her manners. She knew that it would be impossible for Grayling to detain her long; but, alas! what could she do in resistance to his villany, destitute as she was of a single friend near at hand? Matthew, while in the house, in spite of the bravado of Grayling, had kept him in awe, and prevented him from going to extremities, but now he was gone, and, according to the hint thrown out by Mrs. Crabley, Susan had also been discharged, as had likewise, no doubt, all others that had been obnoxious to him; so that she was left entirely at his mercy, and was surrounded by his myrmidons. She learned from the old woman that Grayling, who had been indefatigable in searching after her, had seen Emma address herself to Matthew, and then walk off together, and following them at a distance, he saw them enter the hut, and had no doubt that Maria was there concealed; he had, therefore, formed a plan with one or two of his vile associates to seize her by force that very night, and was going home to meet his friends for that purpose, when he was "so lucky" (so the old woman expressed herself,) as to meet her.

There was one thing which particularly troubled Maria, and made her for a short time forget her immediate troubles, and that was to know whether the remains of her kind benefactor were still in the house, although from what Grayling had said, she imagined that they had been removed, and she was willing to believe him, even villain as he was, not so bad as to behave in the shameful manner he had, while the corpse of his relative was in the house. She was soon convinced that her conjectures were right, for from what the old woman stated, Grayling had ordered the body of his uncle to be removed in the afternoon of that day, and it was then on its way to the former residence of Doctor Hartley, near Rosemary Dell, where Grayling had proposed joining the funeral procession before it was consigned to its final resting place.

Maria shuddered with horror and disgust at this account. That any person could so coldly dispose of the remains of the dead, especially of those who had been so kind to them as Mr. Hartley had been to his abandoned nephew, seemed so unnatural, so revolting, that she would fain have believed it impossible for humanity to become so debased.

Finding that all remonstrances, and solicitations, were alike unavailable with the old woman, Maria abandoned any attempt, and mentally consigning herself to the care of Providence, relapsed into silence for about an hour, when Mrs. Crabley requested to know whether she felt disposed for supper, and arose, apparently with the intention of going to fetch it, when she received the answer of Maria. At first, the latter, who felt not at all disposed to eat, declined, but upon reflecting that the absence of the old woman from the chamber for a short time would enable her to ascertain whether or not there was any probability or chance of her being able to make her escape, she assented, and the old woman left the room without saying any more. As soon as she had gone, (she having taken care to lock the room-door after her,) Maria proceeded to examine the room, and tried the windows, and to her great joy she discovered they were not fastened; and that, at any rate, there was a hope of her being able to escape, if it was ever so slight. The time was too short for her to make the attempt before the old woman returned, and if she should persevere in remaining in the room with her all night, every chance of her effecting her object would be rendered futile. She determined, however, to dissimulate before the old woman, for she saw it was useless to use harsh measures, or to threaten her, for if she did, she probably might not be afforded the opportunity she sought, as Mrs. Crabley might persist in remaining in the same room with her all the night.

Before she had time to think of more, Mrs. Crabley returned, bringing in the supper, which she placed on the table before her, and requested Maria to eat. The latter, although not much disposed, complied, and partook but sparingly of the repast.

"Ah, that's right," observed the old woman, "what's the use of fretting, or putting yourself in a fever about nothing at all; you and Mr. Grayling will soon be friends, I'll be bound, and much better for you both. To be sure, I dare say it vexed you to be seized in the *clandecent* manner as you was, but then I know that young master does not mean you the least harm, only in course it's nat'ral that he should want a companion, and it seems you have taken his fancy. Why, you might be as happy as the days are long, if——"

How far the old woman might have suffered her garrulous tongue to proceed, there is no knowing, had not Maria (who, we need not ay, was thoroughly disgusted with all she said), interrupted her, and hiding her indignation as much as possible, she said—

"I feel very tired and far from well, and as it appears I must make up my mind not to leave here, I wish to retire to bed; but how am I to know I am safe, after the manner in which Mr. Grayling has behaved to me?"

"Oh, as for that, miss," replied the old woman, who appeared to be very well pleased at the alteration which had taken place in the behaviour of Maria, "as for that, you need not be at all alarmed, for Mr. Grayling will not be home to-night, of that I'm quite certain, and if he was, you need not fear but that he would act as a gentleman towards you. I shall sleep in the next chamber, and the slightest tap on the wainscot will arouse me in a minute. Shall I assist you to undress, miss?"

Maria, in order that she might not arouse Mrs. Crabley's suspicions, assented, and the old woman, after wishing her good night, retired, and Maria heard her enter the adjoining chamber.

Maria was sorry that her ancient enemy was so near, for she was fearful that she would overhear her, and frustrate all her attempts, before she could have an opportunity of putting them into execution. However, she determined to wait patiently for some time, until she thought the old woman had gone to sleep, when she could make the attempt without any fear of interruption.

She continued to lie in bed and listen, but although at first she could not hear the old woman moving in her room, all was now silent in the house, and she therefore concluded that the old woman had either retired to bed, or that she had fallen asleep in her chair.

During the interval we have described, Maria had concocted the method of her escape, and having passed another short space of time in listening, and hearing the old woman snore, she was convinced that she was right in the conjectures she had formed, and therefore got hastily out of bed, and slipped on her clothes; she first went to the room door, thinking it not at all improbable that Mrs. Crabley had forgotten to lock it, but she was mistaken, it was perfectly fast. She next went to the window, and with as much caution as possible, lifted up the sash, and when she had done so, she again walked on tiptoe to the room door, and listened, but the snoring of the old woman was all she heard, and encouraged by that, she offered up a prayer to Heaven for its assistance and protection, and then again went to the window, and looked out. It was a beautiful starlight night, and all nature was wrapt in a serenity that was particularly charming. Below, was the garden attached to the house, and the descent was somewhat considerable. Maria shuddered when she contemplated it, but the risk

was not so great as that of remaining where she was, exposed to the brutal insolence of Grayling, and she therefore soon recovered her resolution, and set about putting the plans she had formed into execution.

She removed the sheets off the bed, together with the blankets, and tying them together, secured one end to the bed-post, and throwing the other from the window, she found that it reached to within a very short distance of the earth. Once more she prayed for the protection of Omnipotence, and then standing upon a chair, and closing her eyes, she seized hold of the sheets, and sprang from the window. She reached the earth in perfect safety, and looking up at the windows at the back of the house, she did not perceive a light, with the exception of the one she had left burning in the apartment she had just quitted, and all was perfectly still around.

Fearful that delay might be attended with danger, she took the path which she knew led to that part of the wall which was the lowest, and which she might contrive to scale.

As she hurried along with noiseless steps, she frequently turned her head, and looked back to see if any one was following her, and two or three times her excited imagination led her to suppose that there was some person in pursuit of her; but there were no signs of it, and at length she had got within a few paces of the wall, when, to her extreme horror, the savage growling of a dog met her ears, and a dog which had only been brought there that morning by Grayling, and which was secured by a chain of some length, flew out upon her, and had she not retreated a few yards back, it must have caught hold of her, and would, no doubt, have brought her to the earth.

Terrified at this unlooked-for circumstance, Maria stood for some moments aghast, and was unable to move a step, while the savage dog continued to bark so loudly that he made the air re-echo again, while at the same time he gnawed at the chain which held him, with almost uncontrollable fury.

At length regaining somewhat of her presence of mind, and knowing that there was not a moment to be lost, as the dog would undoubtedly arouse the inmates of the house, and her escape be prevented, she hastened, as fast as her terrors would permit her, towards the low part of the wall, which she found without much difficulty, and had very little more in getting over it into the fields beyond.

The moon was shining full upon the house, which she could see through the long avenue of trees along which she had fled, and she then plainly beheld lights moving hurriedly in the different rooms, and as the dog still continued barking, she had no doubt that the persons in the house were alarmed, and that there would soon be a chase after her.

Goaded on by her fears, Maria fled with precipitation across the fields, but in what direction she scarcely knew. She wanted to get into the city, for then she considered that she would be perfectly safe, as she could claim the protection of the proper authorities, but, by some means or the other, in the confused state of her feelings, she took quite a contrary direction, and did not find her mistake until she was too far to retrace her steps; besides, such a plan would be fraught with danger, as she might, in doing so, encounter her enemies, and then, in that lonely place, she would be completely in their power.

She was now compelled to pause to take breath, and looking around her, she perceived that she had got far away from the house, and, before her, could see nothing but a succession of fields for some distance. She was tired with the extraordinary exertions she had undergone, and she could fain have laid herself upon the grass, and there rested till the morning. It was now about ten o'clock, and Maria having aroused herself, proceeded on her way, thinking she might arrive at a village before it was too late to obtain a shelter for the night. For some distance further, however, did she proceed, without perceiving any signs of a human habitation, and she began to despair. She sat herself down upon the fallen trunk of a tree, to rest herself, and to give a few moments to reflection upon what course it would be best for her to pursue, and she saw no alternative but to proceed or to remain in the fields all the night; the latter of which, of course, would not bear a moment's consideration. With a heavy heart, therefore, she once more arose, and, as well as her exhausted limbs would permit her, walked on her way.

At length, after she had travelled at least five miles, the scene changed, and shortly afterwards she came to a low stile, which opened upon a road, and by the side of which were a few straggling cottages. Maria rejoiced at this circumstance, although she knew not at present whether she could obtain any shelter in them, for they seemed to be all involved in utter darkness, and the inmates of them had, doubtless, long since gone to bed.

But in this supposition she was mistaken; for, at length, she reached one of them, from the parlour casement of which a light glimmered, and she perceived the shadow of some one on the palings which surrounded the little garden in front.

Rejoicing at this circumstance, Maria, without a moment's delay, gently raised the latch of the gate, and stepped up to the door, at which she tapped, and then, in breathless anxiety, waited for some one to answer it. As soon as she had knocked, she heard sounds like the movements of more than one person in the room, and the next moment a female voice, whose tones it struck Maria she had heard before, said—

"Oh, it is only Jem, I dare say; he is rather late though, and ought not to keep such unseasonable hours as this."

"Why, it is excusable," answered the voice of another female, which seemed to belong to an old woman, "it is excusable when people are courting; but open the door, for goodness sake, or else you'll put the lad out of temper."

The first speaker made some laconic reply to this, and the door was then opened by a young girl, who no sooner fixed her eyes upon Maria, than she screamed, and started back into the cottage as if she had seen a ghost, and Maria's astonishment was quite equal to her's, when she recognised in the young girl, Susan.

The old woman, who was doubtless her mother, for there was an extraordinary likeness between them, looked first at Susan, then at Maria with astonishment, and seemed most anxious for an explanation, but the latter was the first to recover herself, and stepping into the cottage, addressed herself to the elder female, and said—

"Pray do not be alarmed, your daughter (for such I presume she is,) and myself know each other very well. Although I was not aware that she lived here, whither by some miraculous chance my footsteps have been directed, and when we both recognised each other, I was upon the point of asking you to grant me shelter for the night."

"Gracious me, Miss Herbert," exclaimed Susan, at length, partly regaining her composure, "is it possible that it is you?—who would have ever thought that——This is the young lady, mother, who I have told you so much about. Oh, miss, how delighted I am to see you;—sit down—how tired you look, and so flurried——Dear me; but where have you been since you made your escape from that most abominable villain, Richard Grayling, as he is called,—and how did you find me out?"

"I will tell you everything by-and-by, my good girl," said Maria, whose surprise at such a singular circumstance, and whose agitation combined, rendered it impossible for her to satisfy Susan so quickly as she desired, "but, tell me, can you allow a poor wanderer to sit up in your parlour till the morning?"

"No, indeed, I will not," said the old woman, "I should indeed be ashamed of myself if I suffered any one to sit up when I have got a clean and comfortable bed for them to lie upon, although, miss, I dare say it is not so good as what you have been accustomed to. My daughter has told me all about you, miss, and I am sure if there is anything in my humble way, I can do to serve you, I will most readily do it, that I will."

Maria returned her thanks to the good woman, and then expressed a fear that she should put them to an inconvenience by remaining there, particularly as she had understood by what she had overheard when she knocked at the cottage door, that they expected another guest.

"Oh, miss," replied the old woman, "that is only my son Jem, who is courting a farmer's daughter a few miles off, and who often, when it gets late, stays at the farm till the morning, which, no doubt, he will do to-night. Besides, if he was to come home, it would make no difference, for he sleeps down here; and I in the back parlour, as I always like to have a bed to myself. The bed I spoke to you about is upstairs, and is slept in by Susan, but if you do not mind sleeping with her, I——"

"Don't mention it, my good woman," hastily interrupted Maria, "I am not particular, and I am so weary that I thought I should have laid down in the fields as I came along. Susan and I can sleep very well together. But"—she added, as a thought seemed to strike her—"should he discover my retreat."

"Oh, do not be under any apprehensions, miss," observed Susan, "for he does not know where I live, neither does Mrs. Crabley, who, I know, would tell him in a moment if she did, and glory in doing so."

"I am satisfied," returned Maria, "and now, if you please, I will retire to rest, for I must be up at an early hour in the morning."

Susan waited not to hear any more, but taking up a candle, lighted their unexpected guest up stairs to a neat little chamber, which contained, in one corner, a bedstead, on which was placed a bed, remarkable for the cleanliness of everything about it.

Susan's impatience to be made acquainted with the circumstances that had brought Maria to the cottage, and the events that had happened to her since her escape from the power of Richard Grayling, could scarcely be restrained, and she put several questions to Maria while she was assisting her to undress, which she returned no answer to than if she (Susan) would wait till the morning, she would furnish her with all the particulars. With this, of course, Susan was obliged to appear satisfied, and Maria having retired to bed, soon fell into a deep slumber, and did not awaken until she was aroused by Susan, by the first peep of day in the morning; she excused herself for this, however, upon the account of the wish which Maria had expressed the night before, that she might not be suffered to sleep late in the morning.

Susan had slept but little during the night, so much was her curiosity excited, and so eager was she to have it gratified. Maria did not keep her long in suspense, but related in as few words as she could, the manner in which she had first escaped from the house, her subsequent secreting herself in the habitation of Emma and her sister, whom she had met with in so singular a manner, and at the critical moment when she so much needed assistance;—her interview with poor old Matthew, his illness, and finally, her re-seizure by the villain Grayling on her way to the coach-office, and the means by which she had effected her liberty a second time.

Susan listened to her with the greatest astonishment, and when she had concluded, she said—

"Well, to be sure, that Grayling is a bad man, and no good will come to him, depend upon it. You ought to be very thankful to think you have a second time so fortunately escaped from his clutches. I'm sure, miss, I never thought we should meet again, for I could not form any idea where you had gone, though I was certain you would make your escape from Bath as quickly as possible. Mr. Grayling was in a terrible *quandary*, to be sure, when he found you had escaped, and we thought he would have gone mad; for you see, miss, he discovered that you must have been hidden somewhere in the house when he first missed you, for he was in the parlour himself at a late hour, and then the window was closed. Dear me, how he did stamp and storm, and swear, and rage, to be sure, and nothing for awhile could pacify him. That hateful old woman, Mrs. Crabley, who never liked me, and God knows that there was not much love lost between us, at length threw out a hint that I must have known of it, and that I must have assisted you in your flight. Gracious me! miss, you should have seen how he flew at me then; any one would have supposed that he was going to murder me.—He seized me like a tiger, and he looked so fierce and savage at me, that it was quite frightful to see him. And then he called me such dreadful names, that it makes me shudder to think of them; I will not shock your ears, miss, by repeating them. He accused me of having been connected with you, and that I had assisted you to escape, and he threatened me with, I don't know what, if I didn't immediately tell him all I knew, and whither you was gone. In vain I declared I knew nothing at all about it, and that I was not aware that you had left the house even, until he had himself announced it. He swore it was a lie, and that I should pay dearly for deceiving him. In a few minutes, however, he rushed out of the room, and from the house, as I supposed, in search of you. I did not await his return, but hastening to my own room, I packed up my clothes in a great hurry, and leaving the house, even before the old housekeeper was aware of it, I returned home. And I think, miss, that, take it altogether, I acted by far the wisest plan, for who knows what such a ruffian as Grayling would mind doing?"

"I perfectly agree with you, Susan," returned Maria, " and I am very sorry to think you should have been put to such trouble and inconvenience through me."

" Pray, miss, do not mention that," said the good-natured girl, " for I'm sure if it had been twice as much trouble, I would not have minded encountering it for your sake. But I am so rejoiced to think you have got away from the villain ; ah ! miss," she added in a melancholy tone, " I suppose we shall never meet again, when we part this time."

" Oh, yes, Susan, I dare say we shall," observed Maria, " but," she continued, after a pause, " I have been thinking that, as I have been the indirect cause of your losing one situation, I should also endeavour to supply you with another. Should you like to become my companion, Susan ?"

" Should I, miss," replied the latter, while her eyes sparkled with delight, " there is nothing I should like half so well, indeed there is not."

" I am going to return to Rosemary Dell," observed Maria, " and should you like to accompany me, I shall be happy of your services."

" Oh, miss, I am overjoyed at the thought," ejaculated Susan, and her looks evinced that she did not exaggerate.

" But do you think your mother will consent to what I propose ?" asked Maria.

" I am certain she will be as well pleased as I am myself, miss," replied Susan ; " why shouldn't she, indeed ? And what can she have to object to ? But when do you think of departing ?"

" This very day," said Maria, " and if we agree about terms, as I, of course, cannot expect you to attend me at a minute's notice, you can follow after me as soon as you like, or, at any rate, as soon as you can make it convenient."

" Oh, no, miss, there is no necessity for any delay, for my things are all ready, and as I should not, I'm sure, like to see you go that long journey by yourself, whenever you are ready to depart, I will accompany you."

" Well, well, be it so," returned Maria, " but we must first ask the consent of your mother."

" Of obtaining that," said Susan, " you need not be under any apprehension, miss, for I know she will grant it willingly."

Mrs. Hutchings, although she would have been glad of her daughter to remain with her a few days longer, as they seldom met, was very ready to give her consent to the proposition, and Susan immediately set about preparing for the journey.

" There is a coach passes this way at three o'clock in the afternoon," said Susan's mother, " so you had better prolong your departure till that time, and then you will not run any dan-

ger of meeting with your enemy in going to the coach-office."

Maria assented to this, and, in the interim, made such preparations as were necessary, and got Jem, the son of Mrs. Hutchins, to carry a letter to Matthew, in which she gave an account of what had happened to her on the night before, where she was now, and what was her determination for the future. She also requested him to write to her or rejoin her as soon as possible. This letter she despatched immediately, thinking that Jem would have been able to have got back with an answer before the coach arrived, but hour after hour passed away, and still he did not return ; and at length, hearing the sound of the guard's bugle, they bade farewell to Mrs. Hutchins, entered the vehicle, which was driven off, and they were soon far away.

There was only another person inside the coach, and that was a gentleman, who was seated in one corner, and his face was half concealed in a huge travelling shawl. At first, when Maria and Susan entered the vehicle, he seemed to be dosing, but suddenly rousing himself up, he fixed his eyes upon them, and uttering an exclamation of surprise, hastily came and placed himself on the seat by the side of Maria, and attempted to take her hand.

Astonished—indignant—Maria shrunk back and withdrew her hand.

" What ; don't you know me ?" said the man with a half laugh, " well, now, that is remarkable."

As he spoke he took off the shawl, and the astonishment and alarm of Maria may be easily imagined, when she recognised Mr. Barnell.

The shock was so sudden, and her terror was so great, that Maria almost fainted, and Susan, who noticed her alarm, though she knew not the cause, drew herself close to the side of Maria, to prevent the insolent importunities of her persecutor.

" Well, dash me !" exclaimed the ignorant fellow, with a stupid look of pleasure and exultation ; " well, dash me ! who'd have thought of this ? What a devilish lucky fellow I am, after all, to meet with you in such a singular manner, after the many disappointments I have had ; nay, more, even after having nearly lost my life once. Ah ! that was a mistake ; but this slice of luck, and so unexpected too, amply repays me for all.—By Jupiter ! I am delighted to see you, Miss Herbert ; you are rather pale, but looking as pretty as ever !"

For a few moments Maria was so thoroughly alarmed and disgusted, that she could not speak, and Mr. Barnell continued—

" What, won't you give me a word ? This is rather uncivil of you, I must say, especially after all the trouble I have taken to shew you how much I admire you, Miss Herbert. Well, we shall perhaps get better friends by the time we get to Rosemary Dell, for I presume you are going there; though I know all your friends have gone from there. By-the-bye," he continued, looking significantly at Susan, "by-the-bye, it's a bad plan to make too free with servants;—should always make them ride outside of the coach—it's very awkward, two's company you know, but three's none! Ha! ha! ha!"

It would be impossible to describe the feelings of Maria, as she was forced to listen to this ignorant and insolent speech, and saw the consummate effrontery and boldness of Barnell; but at length, fixing upon him a look that even abashed him, she gave utterance to the following words—

"Mr. Barnell, this behaviour to an unprotected female is disgraceful to you, as a man and a gentleman, as you would wish to be thought, but do not think that I will submit to be insulted with impunity; cease your insolent language, or I will claim the protection of the other passengers; I dare say there are some of them that would have the spirit not to see a a female's feelings thus outraged without chastising the offender."

"Why, what a fiery little vixen it is, to be sure," replied Barnell; "can't speak a word, or do a little bit of gallantry, but you are off like a cracker. Lor' bless you, my love, I have no wish to insult you; and there are many young ladies, Miss Herbert—yes, a great many young ladies who would have been ready to have jumped out of their shoes with joy if I had said half so much to them as I have to you."

Maria scarcely knew whether to laugh or not at this absurd piece of self-flattery, but she fixed upon the idiot a look of the most ineffable scorn, and did not even deign him any reply.

"Do you usually treat your menials with such familiarity, Miss Herbert?" he added, looking with the greatest contempt upon Susan, who had been listening with the most painful impatience to the observations of Barnell, and, as she afterwards expressed herself, her fingers itched to have a claw at him. But the last-mentioned insult was more than she could brook; she coloured up, and darting a look of resentment upon the offender, said—

"Perhaps, sir, those menials as you calls 'em are more superior in point of sense and behaviour than many folks who calls themselves gentlemen and ladies. It's not fine clothes or money that makes the gentleman, but the heart, at any rate; I never heard before, sir, that it was very gentlemanly conduct to wound the feelings of a woman."

"Bah!" exclaimed Barnell, with an affectation of contempt, although it was very evident that he was not a little chagrined and disconcerted by the pert and pointed remarks of Susan. "I cannot bear to be in the company of such low people."

"Low people, indeed," returned Susan, with increased anger, "well, I'm sure, and I dare say it has only lately come to the turn of some folks whom I could mention to——"

Maria, seeing no likelihood of where this unpleasant wrangle might end, or to what length the wrath of Susan might carry her, here interrupted her, and turning a look of superlative contempt upon Barnell, ejaculated—

"This young girl, sir, is my companion, and the inside of the vehicle, which is a public one, is as free for her as anybody else; if being in proximity with such a person is offensive to your dignity, you can indulge your aristocratic spirit at the next stage by having a post chaise, and removing from the coach."

Mr. Barnell was so abashed at the pointed sarcasm of Maria's manner, that he could not return any answer for a short time; but he pulled up his shirt collar as high as it would go, and was troubled with a short cough, until he at last managed to make the following reply—

"Why, upon my word, Miss Herbert, you do take one up so sharp, that there is no knowing how to deal with you. I didn't mean any harm, bless your soul, no, and as for offending the young woman, why I had no idea of it. The fact of it is, miss, I want to say a few words to you alone, and——"

"You can have nothing to say to me, sir,' interrupted Maria, indignantly, "which it can be any more improper for this young woman to hear than myself. Besides, I do not understand the reason why you should take the liberty of addressing your conversation to me at all."

"Lor', Miss Herbert, replied he, with a stupid, vacant look, "how can you say so, when you know we were to have been sweethearts, and should have been so too, had I not found out that Mr. Wallingford had deceived me."

"If my uncle led you to imagine that I would ever encourage your addresses, sir," returned Maria, with the utmost abhorrence expressed in her countenance, "he did indeed deceive you. However, that is immaterial to me, I will not converse upon a subject which I loathe."

"Nonsense, Miss Herbert," said Barnell, again sidling up towards her, "you can't mean that, I know. Come, come, do not be cross—what is the use of it? I have the best wishes towards you, I assure you, and as for insulting you, I would not do so for the world. Who knows but we might be sweethearts again?" continued the ignorant fellow, winking his eye as if it was

"A consummation devoutly to be wished;" "and then, you know, miss, it would not do to be always wrangling and jangling as we are at present. Did you but know the regard I have for you, I am certain that——"

"Will you persist in talking in this sickening, this disgusting strain, sir?" interrupted Maria, swelling with the most ungovernable indignation; "if you do, I must alarm the people outside the coach, and request their assistance."

"What stuff!" he returned, "what nonsense it is to get so out of temper, because we are merely having a little chat together. But never mind, you'll get over this by-and-by, and I shouldn't wonder if we ain't the best friends in Christendom. Why, you are in mourning, I perceive," he continued, noticing her melancholy dress, apparently for the first time; "dear me, I hope you have not lost a very dear friend."

The tears gushed into the eyes of Maria, and convulsive sobs almost choked her utterance, as she replied—

"Alas! I have indeed lost a dear friend, and a protector, or I should not be thus exposed to the brutal insolence of a man, who is evidently callous to every feeling of shame!"

Barnell coloured up, and did not make any immediate answer. He seemed to be ruminating for a second or two.

"Oh, I see, miss," he at length said, "I see; it's the old doctor; he was a stern old chap, but I dare say he was a good hearted man enough. At any rate, I imagine he was always very kind to you."

Barnell uttered the last words in such a significant tone, that it made Maria shudder, deep blushes of shame and resentment suffused her cheeks, and she was incapable for some minutes to utter a word.

"I have no doubt it is a very bad job for you," resumed Barnell, taking no notice, or affecting not to take any notice of the emotion he had caused Maria; "and then you see you have been abandoned by your uncle, which was not altogether right, so that I suppose you have not a friend in the world?"

"My God!" ejaculated Maria, wound up to a pitch of almost insupportable indignation, "must I tamely submit to this? Mr. Barnell, if you have one particle of feeling or manhood in your composition, you will not persevere in wounding the feelings of one who has never offended you by word or deed, and who has not the slightest right to be subjected to your impertinence."

"Why do you not raise an alarm, miss?" said Susan;—"I wonder that you have had patience to endure it so long as you have."

"Hold your tongue, you saucebox, will you?" observed Barnell; "I dare say your mistress and me can settle this business without your interference. As for alarming the people of the coach, that would all be of no use, I am too well known here. Ha! ha! ha!—it couldn't

have happened better; but how confounded singular that we should meet in the manner we did. But, come now, Miss Maria, we have had quite enough of this; what's the use of being so cross? That will never get you a husband, I'm sure. If you will only just humour my ways a little, you will find me a capital friend to you, and you know I have plenty of money. You have lost all your other friends, now make one of me, and you will have no reason to repent, I'll warrant. I have got a snug little box, which I have just purchased, about forty miles beyond Rosemary Dell, whither we will go directly, if you like, and your maid can accompany us. There, you'll be as happy as the days are long, be sole mistress of the place, and have money at your command. Come, come, short reckonings make the best of friends, come let's e'en seal the bargain at once. One kiss from those pretty lips, and it's done. Nay, it is no use, I am determined to have one."

As the vulgar wretch thus spoke, he threw his arms round the neck of Maria, and forcibly endeavoured to do as he said; she screamed aloud, and resisted him all that she was able, while poor Susan did her best to rescue her mistress, by calling aloud for help, and endeavouring to pull Mr. Barnell away. At that moment the vehicle stopped at the door of an inn, and the guard, opening the door, demanded what was the matter.

"The matter," said Mr. Barnell, "why bad enough for me I think. Would you believe it now, to look at her," pointing to Maria, "so innocent and simple as she seems to be, that she is an adulteress?—It's a fact. Unfortunately she is my wife; six weeks ago she eloped from me with a military officer, and here have I met with her in the most miraculous way in your coach. I'll take good care to hold her fast this time, though. Yes, yes, no more running away from your husband, madam; we will try what effect confinement, and a little harsher treatment than you have hitherto been in the habit of receiving, will have upon you."

Thunderstruck, speechless, at this unparalleled piece of audacity, and at the coolness with which he spoke it, Maria was rendered completely motionless, and stood looking upon the gaping individuals (who, having heard the latter part of Barnell's speech, now gathered round the door of the vehicle,) with a vacant stare; and Susan (who was quite unprepared for such a circumstance) was scarcely in any better condition. At length, when she saw from the expression in the countenances of those around her, that they actually believed what Barnell had said, and were beginning to indulge in various rude remarks, laughing, and passing upon her no very high compliments, she regained the power of speech, and clasping her hands together in a distracted manner, said—

"By Heaven it is an infamous, a base falsehood, and he knows it. I am in no way related to him, neither has he any claim upon me, I therefore throw myself upon your mercy, and beg your protection, from a villain who would force me away against my will, and from whose outrages I have more than once before suffered. My servant here can corroborate what I have said."

But Susan was so completely bewildered, and thunderstruck by the impudence of Barnell, and the tale he had so readily invented, that she

LORD HALVENDON RESCUING FANNY FROM HER AFFRIGHTED HORSE.

was unable to speak a word; and to the horror of Maria, she observed that the people seemed to place reliance upon the story of Barnell, and to treat what she had said with incredulity and indifference, and he was so delighted at the success of his scheme, that he followed it up with redoubled boldness, and even ventured to lay hold of Maria and force her into the house, while as he did so, the deepest sympathy was manifested for him, and they were not at all sparing of the observations of abuse which they made against her.

In scenes like these, the mind becomes so perplexed, confused, and terrified, that the object of the persecution very often assumes that appearance and demeanour, which by a superficial observer might be mistaken for a proof of guilt; and so it was with Maria on this occasion. But how dreadfully shocked were her feelings at the strange and fearful situation in which she was placed; it was wonderful how she could support it. To attempt to fly, would only make the appearance of the truth of Barnell's asseverations the stronger, and to appeal to the persons present was evidently useless, for they were prejudiced against her, and nothing that she could say would convince them to the contrary, but that she was the runaway wife of the crafty villain Barnell. It seemed as though she was never to be released from trouble, only a few hours as she might say, she had made her escape from Grayling, and now she had fallen into the hands of another of her enemies, who, she was thoroughly convinced, was equally as much to be dreaded as the other, if not more, for he had more power as regarded wealth and abettors than Grayling.

"Get into the house, madam," said Barnell, sternly, "unless you wish me to expose you more fully to these good people. There, in with you; as for you, you slut, you can go into the kitchen, or about your business, which you like."

"I will not leave this much-injured young lady, you have the impudence to call your wife, an inch," exclaimed Susan, resolutely. "My good people do not believe him; he has stated that which is abominably false, and he knows it. She *his* wife! The very idea is laughable." And she looked with the most supreme contempt on the coarse features and person of Barnell, and then by another expressive glance at the persons present, appealed to them whether it was at all likely that such an assertion should be true. They first seemed inclined to relent, but it was only for a moment, and their offensive observations were renewed with redoubled severity.

"You see how well the maid has been tutored,' observed Barnell. "This girl, I have every reason to believe, has been the principal abettor of my unfortunate wife in the furtherance of that plot which has been the means of destroying my domestic quiet. But I will be determined; away, with you, girl, and think yourself lucky that you have got off in the manner you have."

Barnell now once more attempted to force Maria into the inn, and Susan interposed to prevent him, but Maria's strength was completely exhausted, and her feelings so shocked by the circumstances that had occurred that she fainted.

When she recovered, her terror and surprise may be easily conjectured when she found herself in a post-chase, with the hated Barnell and two other men. The chaise was going at a most furious rate, and apparently not over very even ground, for the vehicle jolted most terribly, anh Maria felt the effects of it in a most painful manner. Barnel, and the two other men appeared to have been wrapped in earnest conversation during her insensibility; but they dropped it when the perceived her recover, and Barnell seemed to be prepared for the observations which it was natural to suppose Maria would make to him.

"Good God!" exclaimed the terrified girl, looking wildly upon the three men, who met her glances with the greatest unconcern, "whither am I going, and what has become of Susan? Tell me Mr. Barnell by what authority you seize me in this manner, and what are your designs with me?"

"Oh, that you will learn soon enough," said Barnell, smiling, "as for authority, I have none that I know of, no more than that I have taken a great fancy to you, and thought that I might as well have you as any body else. 'Faint heart never won fair lady,' and by Jingo I have had trouble enough in this business, but I dont care, for I have succeeded at last."

"Mr. Barnell," said Maria, earnestly, "you think me friendless, and therefore take a cowardly advantage, which any man, and much more one who calls himself a gentleman, would despise; but do not deceive yourself, I have still those who will look after me, and will not see me taken advantage of; beware, then, how you behave, for most assuredly will you have to answer for what you arenew doing at the bar of justice."

"Nonsense!" said Barnell, "what a strange thing it is you cannot, or will not, perceive that I intend you no harm, but on the contrary to make your fortune for you; but you will be so very perverse."

"Wretch!" cried Maria, "this audacity is unbearable; whither are you taking me? Tell me, I command you."

"There now, don't get out of temper, my love," answered Barnell, "you will be quite delighted with the place when you see it, I know; it is situated in one of the most romantic parts of the country, and is a perfect little palace. There you may reign supreme, and I will be your slave at command."

"Villain!" ejaculated Maria, her feelings so excited that she found it impossible to control them.

"Nay, nay," said Barnell with a course, vulgar smile, which made his low-looking features still more unprepossessing; "better aames, my love; that title came not at all pretty from lips like yours. Let this seal our friendship for the future, and let us bury the past in oblivion." And, even in the presence of his two companions, Mr. Barnell attempted to imprint a kiss upon the cheek of Maria, but she spurned him from her with a look of the greatest disgust, and exclaimed—

"Off, wretch!—Your touch, like your presence, is odious to me!—Good Heavens! am I to be continually the victim of unmanly ruffianism? Will no one step forward to save an unprotected female from the danger which threatens her? My voice shall raise the——"

"You may save yourself the trouble, and spare your lungs the unnecessary exertion, my dear Miss Herbert," said Barnell, with the most provoking coolness. "for here it would be entirely useless, of which you can convince yourself."

As he said these words, he removed one of the blinds, which enabled Maria to look out, and she then, to her utter anguish and despair, discovered, as well as the darkness would permit her to do, that they were travelling through a wild and unfrequented part of the country, with not a house or habitation of any sort nigh. Alas! what would cries avail her there? And when she thought upon her situation, even worse than the one she had been placed in with Grayling, she wrung her hands, and gave herself entirely up to despair.

The night was uncommon dark, and the wind was very boisterous; and as it howled dismally over the dreary waste across which they were travelling, it increased the terrors which had already taken possession of her bosom. The companions of Barnell, during the time the conversation we have been describing was going on, seemed to enjoy the adventure vastly, and they frequently winked at each other, and laughed. They were two low, blackguard-looking fellows, who appeared as if they would not be very particular as to what they would do, and who were evidently two wretches whom Barnell had picked up to aid him in his nefarious transactions.

The vehicle still proceeded with great speed, and Maria, finding it was useless to remonstrate, covered her face with her handkerchief, and sunk into a deep and melancholy meditation, from which Barnell did not offer to disturb her, but entered into conversation with his companions, in an under tone, the subject of which she never attempted to ascertain.

Harrowing in the extreme were the thoughts that passed in rapid succession over the mind of Maria, and distracted her brain. Alas! what an untoward fate was her's! No sooner was she out of one dilemma, than something transpired to place her in another. She seemed to be destined to incessant misery and vexation, and whichever way she turned, she could see no place to which she could fly for peace or hope. Never did she more painfully feel her wretched, unprotected state—never did she more poignantly feel the irreparable loss of her kind benefactor, Doctor Hartley. As his name

arose to her memory, her tears gushed forth with redoubled impetuosity, and a pang shot through her quivering temples which for a few, moments rendered her almost unconscious of everything. Besides, how great would be the distress of Mathew when he heard of her second disappearance, and in such an unaccountable manner, and the information he would be compelled to forward to her uncle of the uncertainty of her fate. What would be the suffering of Walter when he heard of it? How would Mr. Wallingford reproach himself for having exposed her to such danger, by withdrawing from her the protection he had before so long afforded her? And then, again, more terrible than all, what fate could she expect, fallen as she had into the power of a man destitute of feeling or principle, and who would, doubtless, sacrifice anything to the gratification of his evil passions? She felt that the situation she was placed in, was truly pitiable, and she gave herself up to despair.

She had been unable to elicit from Barnell what had become of Susan; but if she was at liberty, then did Maria feel that she had a prospect of being extricated from the danger by which she was surrounded; for Susan would, of course, take the earliest opportunity of making her friends acquainted with what had happened, and they would take immediate steps to restore her to liberty, and bring the scoundrel Barnell to punishment for the daring outrage he had committed. But, alas! before that could be accomplished, what misery, what shame, what degradation, might she not have been exposed to!

She was aroused from these thoughts by the vehicle suddenly stopping; and soon afterwards Barnell whispered something to the two men, upon which, they took their places, one on each side of Maria, and Barnell left the vehicle; at the same time she caught a glance of what appeared to be a road-side public-house. A transient ray of hope again darted across Maria's mind, but it was only momentary, for she recollected too-well the scene at the inn, when she was borne away, and she knew how useless it would be to attempt to move the feelings of the people here, and which might probably only cause a similar occurrence. She therefore remained quiet, though she shuddered beneath the looks of the ruffians by whom she was guarded, and who took such particular care of their charge.

Barnell was not gone many minutes, when he returned to the vehicle with some wine, and a slight relish, which he requested she would take, and apologised for not letting her leave the post-chaise, stating, as his excuse, that there was no accommodation.

Maria turned away from Barnell when he addressed her, and did not even deign him an answer; so after drinking the wine himself, and supplying his companions with brandy at their request, he returned to the carriage, and it proceeded on its journey.

It was now evidently very late, and Maria wondered how much farther they could have to go, but she made no further inquiries, and relapsed into the same train of thought she had indulged in prior to the vehicle's stopping.

The more Maria ruminated on the horrors of her situation, the more distracted did her mind become; more especially as she saw no chance of her escaping from the power of Barnell very easily; for if even Susan should make Mathew acquainted with the circumstance, they would be entirely ignorant of whither he had taken her: besides, what assistance could old Mathew render her, ill as he was; and before any of her friends could have time to interfere, she might have suffered the worst that her fears could suggest. Fast did her tears flow, when she thought upon this, and despair rested like a dead weight upon her heart.

"The horses are so jaded, that we shall be compelled to put up at 'The Swan,'" observed Barnell, at length breaking the silence which for a few minutes had prevailed: "they know me well there, and therefore it will be all right. We cannot be far from it now, I think."

"Let me see," said one of the fellows, drawing the blind, "we are on Black Downs, now; no, ten minutes more will bring us there."

Maria's hopes once more revived, when she heard them mention about stopping at an inn for the night; surely she might find there some person of humanity who would sympathise with her, and interfere in her behalf, or something might providentially occur to afford her an opportunity of releasing herself from the power of the villain Barnell. But when she thought upon the significant manner in which Barnell had made use of the words, that "they knew him well, and that therefore it would be all right," her hopes were once more crushed, for by that she was at no loss to understand that the persons belonging to the inn were no good, and that Barnell had it in his power to induce them rather to aid him in his project, than to pity and to interfere in the behalf of her.

Barnell, who had not spoken to her for some time, now turned towards her, and with a look which he meant to be very agreeable, and apologetic, he said—

"I am afraid, Miss, that you will feel very much fatigued with your journey, but it could not be helped;—it don't do to loiter in such matters as these, lest the pursuers should get upon your scent, and there then might be an end to the sport. The inn we are going to is a very good one, and they have excellent accommoda-

tion; but I warn you before you enter it, that it will be useless your making any appeal to the people there; they know me too well; it is not the first time I have done business with them, and they have often felt the full weight of my gold."

"Villain, are you not ashamed to talk with such effrontry upon a subject which redounds only to your unmanly and brutal discredit?" said Maria, in accents that would have made any other individual, but the insensible being to whom they were addressed, shrink abashed: —"your behaviour throughout this unlawful affair has been characterised by everything that is base; but depend upon it, you will yet be thwarted in your diabolical schemes, and be richly punished for the offence you have so shamefully committed."

"Oh, as for that, Miss Herbert," observed Barnell, with a grin of exultation, "I have not much fear of that; they will not find you out in a hurry; besides, nobody will have the least suspicion that you are in my power, as I was not known to be in the neighbourhood were we so strangely met."

Here one of the men whispered something in his ear, upon which he changed countenance, and said—

"By Jupiter!—I never once thought of that: how foolish I must be; if I had brought the girl with us, all would have been safe; but no matter. she has not got Doctor Hartley or Mr. Wallingford to fly to now."

"If I have neither of those friends here," said Maria, and her eyes filled with tears at the mention of Mr. Hartley's name, "you need not think to escape with impunity; I have others who I knew will immediately see to my restoration to that liberty of which you have so unjustly deprived me, until such times as my uncle can take steps to bring you to an account for your infamous conduct. The spirit of him, too, who was to me so kind a friend and protector on earth, will, I am confident, look down upon me from heaven with a watchful eye, and shield me in the hour of danger. To that blessed spirit I now appeal, and defy your power."

"It's all very fine, Miss Herbert, talking in that manner," said Barnell; "but you know, 'a bird in the hand 's worth two in the bush.' But, for my part, I cannot see what you have to complain of; you are not the first young lady that a gentleman has thought proper to run away with; and if the worst comes to the worst, they can only make an action of it, and make me drop a few cool hundreds:—a newspaper paragraph, and then the matter's settled. But you will get your temper better by-and-by, when you see how I behave to you. You will find me a man of *honour*, Miss, I assure you."

"A man of *honour*!" repeated Maria, with bitter scorn; "disgrace not the name by applying it to yourself; is it the action of a man of honour to force a defenceless female from her friends—to insult her, and ——"

"Psha!" interrupted Barnell, impatiently, "I am sick of listening to this rubbish, and it can effect no good. At any rate, as I, have ventured so far, it's no use my retreating, for I should be placed in just the same situation of danger. I will treat you with kindness, Miss, I have told you repeatedly I will; and I dare say you will soon forget this resentment when you find how I behave."

"If you have a spark of feeling left," said Maria, in softened tones, and looking imploringly in his face, thinking that probably entreaties might better prevail than threats, "if you have a spark of pity left, pray abandon your project, which can do you no ultimate good, but may be productive of more unpleasant results to you than you have at present any idea of, and suffer me to depart, and I am ready to promise you never to mention to any one what has happened, and also to ——"

"We have got to the inn," said Barnell, interrupting her. "I am sorry, Miss Herbert," he added, "that I cannot comply with your request; I have no doubt that you would do as you say, though; but then you see, I have formed such a very strong attachment towards you, that now I have got you, I do not like to part with you. But it's no use standing talking here; remember what I told you; it's no use making any fuss here."

Barnell having alighted, went into the house, and was absent for about five minutes, leaving Maria in the charge of the two men; —when he returned he offered his arm to Maria to assist her out of the vehicle. A gawky, stupid-looking lad, with straight red hair, and holding a lanthorn in his hand, stood yawning on the step of a door, and Maria, who now saw that her case was entirely hopeless, suffered them to lead her into a comfortable parlour; where a young girl was putting some more fuel on the fire, and who, upon her entrance, turned an inquiring look upon Maria, and the latter thought that, mingled with her curiosity, there was a sentiment of gentleness and pity, and that she seemed to judge by the appearance of Maria, and the deep melancholy which was expressed in her countenance, that something was not right, and that she was against her own will, detained in the power of Barnell. This idea was a relief to the anguish of Maria; for under such circumstances as she was placed in, the most trifling event affords a feeling of momentray gratification. In a few minutes, a cross-looking old woman entered the room, bringing some refreshments with her, and a bottle of wine, which she placed on the table; and after exchanging a few words with Barnell, and gazing at Maria with an expression of countenance that was anything but prepossessing, she was about to retire again,

when Maria, in spite of the looks of the old woman, driven to a state of desperation by the danger of being left to the mercy of the villains, Barnell and his companions, in that lone house all night, rushed forward, and falling on her knees, with looks of earnest supplication, implored her protection—

"You are a woman," she exclaimed, "perhaps you have daughters of your own; to you, then, I earnestly appeal, and implore of you to save me from these bad men. I am brought here against my will."

"Against your will?" repeated the old woman, in disagreeable tones, and with a grin which filled the bosom of Maria with disgust, "yes, my lady, I have no doubt it is very much against your will to be forced away from your paramour; but you ought for ever to feel grateful to your *guardian*, for the trouble he has taken to save you from destruction; and to feel sincere regret for the pain and anxiety you have caused him. I have not got any daughters of my own, and I am glad of it, for, after all the trouble you may take to bring them up properly, perhaps at the very time when they ought to be the greatest blessing to you, they will turn out to be your bitterest curse."

"Oh, this is cruel," said the agonized Maria, still grasping the skirt of the old woman's gown, and forcibly detaining her; "Mr. Barnell has told you false, indeed he has; it is a story of his own invention, merely to further his own designs. I am in no way related, or connected with him, neither has he any authority over me. For heaven's sake, do not turn a deaf ear to my entreaties; exert you influence, and take me under your protection till the morning, and I will ever remember you with feelings of unbounded gratitude."

"There, there," said Barnell, "get along about your business, Mother Muggeridge, and do not pay any attention to what this silly girl says; of course, it is only natural for a person in her situation, and after suffering the disappointment she has."

"Indeed, you need not fear me," replied the old woman, "I am not to be deceived so easily; and, thank God, my heart is made of a little better stuff than to be touched by such nonsense as this. The young lady seems to know how to act her part very well, but it wont do for me."

Maria turned away from the woman with a sentiment of disgust and abhorrence; and after the utterance of such an unfeeling remark, she could scarcely believe she was one of her own sex.. She now turned her looks upon Barnell, who had seated himself, with the utmost indifference, at the table with his associates, and was preparing to dispatch the contents of the bottle.

"Mr. Barnell, once more to you I appeal;

you know that you have stated nothing but what was abominably false, and that you have no power to detain me. I give you again the chance which I before offered you, namely, to pardon the outrage you have already committed, if you will abandon your present wicked project, and suffer me to depart."

"To your chamber you are at liberty to go," answered Barnell, "but as for the other part of your request, you know it is all a waste of time to urge anything of the sort. Kitty will show you to the room allotted for your repose, and I should advise you to lose no time in retiring, for we must start from here by the break of day."

"Good God! what will become of me?" cried the distracted Maria, wringing her hands; "I am lost, I am lost!"

"There, there, that's enough of that," said Barnell, hastily; "you have nothing to fear, no one will disturb you in the night; obstinacy will not avail you anything here."

Maria's feelings were wound up to the utmost pitch, and throwing herself into a chair, she covered her face with her hands; convulsive sobs heaved her bosom, and a flood of tears gushed from her eyes. Kitty approached her at a motion to that effect from Barnell, and gently raising her, Maria, so deeply absorbed in the violent grief which racked her bosom, as to be almost unconscious of what she was doing, suffered herself to be led away by the girl; and ascending two flights of stairs, they entered a back apartment, in which was a bed, and a few other decent articles of furniture.

"There, Miss," said Kitty, who seemed to behold Maria with feelings of compassion, "you see, there is a fire in the room, and——"

"Oh, my God!" interrupted Maria, in tones of distraction, "will no one interpose to rescue me from this danger? Am I to be left here alone, and exposed to the violence of the villain Barnell? My good girl, you do not seem like that spiteful-looking old woman below; and surely, you will not aid them in their nefarious practices, especially against one of your own sex?"

"I do, indeed, pity you, Miss," said the girl, in low tones; "but it is out of my power to aid you; what cou'd I do to——"

"Alas!" ejaculated Maria, "then am I indeed lost! Oh, my uncle, if you knew the critical situation of her who has a claim upon your protection, you must bitterly reproach yourself for the manner in which you have acted."

"I cannot stay, Miss," said Kitty kindly, "but, rest assured that you have nothing to dread while in this house. If it will be any relief to you, I will endeavour to persuade them to let me sleep with you."

"Oh, do, I implore you," exclaimed Maria, gratefully, "this kindness I shall ——"

The shrill, disagreeable voice of Mrs. Mug-geridge, calling impatiently to Kitty to come down stairs, and demanding what she was doing there all that time, interrupted Maria; and Kitty, looking significantly at her, and placing her finger on her lips to enforce silence, hastily quitted the apartment, and Maria heard her lock the door after her.

Despair now completely superseded every other feeling in the bosom of Maria; and seating herself on the side of the bed, she gave herself up to the distracting thoughts that tormented her mind. What was to become of her in the power of such wretches?—what outrage was there that they would hesitate in committing? The idea was too horrible to dwell upon. To retire to the couch, she could not for a moment think upon; and when she heard the noisy revelry of those below, and frequently had her ears shocked by their intemperate expressions, her fears increased, and she expected every moment to hear the footsteps of one of the wretches upon the stairs. Barnell's voice might have been heard above the rest, and it was very evident that he had been drinking to excess, and was now inebriated.

Thus hour after hour passed away, and the noise of the persons below increased; and as Kitty did not make her appearance, Maria was fearful that she had not been able to succeed in gaining the consent of the old woman to sleep with her, and all hope of the slightest relief even, from the misery of her situation, was banished from her mind.

Not knowing to what extremes (mad as he now appeared to be) he might be tempted to proceed, Maria, aroused by a sudden impulse into action, placed the table against the room-door, and piled such articles of furniture as the room contained, and which she could lift upon it; and then, breathless with the exertion which she had undergone, she returned to her seat, and once more listened attentively to hear what was going on below. All was completely still, and she was therefore about to conclude that Barnell and the others had either retired to rest, or had fallen asleep from the effects of the deep potations they had taken, when suddenly she heard a room-door open, and presently afterwards the noise of some person or persons ascending the stairs. Terror almost overcame her, and she trembled violently as she held by the bedpost, and awaited in the most agonizing suspense the result of this adventure.

At length, through the crevices of the door, she saw the rays apparently emitted from a lamp; and shortly afterwards she heard the key turning in the lock, and then somebody tried to push the door open, but finding that some obstructions from the inside prevented them from doing so immediately, she heard the voice of old Mrs. Muggeridge grumbling out some expressions of displeasure, followed by the proceeding observations—

"What the plague has the jade been doing inside? I cannot push the confounded door open; do you hear, girl? Open the door, directly, and don't keep me waiting here a month."

Maria made no answer, but her agitation was so great, that she could with the utmost difficulty, only, sustain herself. There was a muttering outside; and presently afterwards, a gentle voice exclaimed—

"Pray do not be alarmed, Miss; you have no occasion to fear; it is only me, Kitty, and I have come to sleep with you."

Re-assured by this, Maria removed the furniture from the door, and Mrs. Muggeridge, looking frightfully cross, and followed by Kitty, entered the room.

"What the devil have you been about?" said the former, "and what was you so frightened about? Did you suppose that anybody was coming to murder you? I think it's almost time you were in bed; but I suppose you think this bed is not good enough for you."

Maria made no reply, but covered her face with her hands, not only to conceal her anguish but to shut out the disgusting features of the old woman.

"There," said Mrs. Muggeridge, after a pause, "I have complied with your wishes, young woman; but let me have no talking; it's time everybody was in bed now. Recollect, Kitty, what I have told you."

Kitty nodded her head in reply, and locked the door after her. Maria listened to hear her descend the stairs; and when she heard her enter her own room, she turned upon Kitty a look of gratitude, and said—

"Thanks, my good girl, for this kindness; situated as I am, it is doubly estimable. But, I can see that you do not possess a hard heart, and——"

"I hope, Miss," interrupted the girl, "I hope that I shall never live to become insensible to the misfortunes of my fellow-creatures; and I feel confident that you are deserving of every compassion."

"You do me no more than justice, I assure you," returned Maria; "you surely will not believe me to be the abandoned wretch the villain Barnell has represented me to be?"

"Speak low, Miss," said Kitty, "for although Mr. Barnell and the other two ruffians, are snoring soundly asleep in the parlour below, there is no doubt, but that the curiosity of that bad woman, my mistress, might tempt her to listen, and I should have a terrible life of it afterwards. What I have to put up with already from her hateful temper, is bad enough, but it would be ten times worse if she was to hear me talking to you, in disobedience to her orders."

"Do you know anything of this man, Barnell?" inquired Maria, who suffered Kitty to assist her to undress, although she despaired of being able to gain any repose.

"Oh, yes, we know him very well," replied Kitty, "and therefore, we knew that what he stated about you was false, although my mistress pretended to believe him; but she is a thorough bad one, and I really believe she would not care what she did to get money. I only wish I could get another situation, and I have often thought of running away; but then, where could I go to, for I have not a friend in in the world!—Mr. Barnell has been here frequently; and I have heard it said, that Mrs. Muggeridge is related to him, for he was poor and humble enough once, I have heard, although he has lately been so very fortunate. A worse man, or a more vulgar, ignorant one than he is, I am sure there cannot be."

"Alas! too well do I know it," ejaculated Maria; "oh, what will become of me, in the power of such a villain?"

"Do not despair, Miss," said Kitty, in accents of the warmest compassion; "there is no knowing what may occur to release you. I wish it was in in my power to assist you to do so, for your looks convince me that you possess a good and virtuous mind. But pray, Miss, how did you get into the power of Mr. Barnell?"

Maria now, as well and in as few words as she could, related to Kitty that which she was anxious to know, and when she had concluded, the poor girl said—

"Well, Miss, you certainly have been unfortunate, and again I regret that I cannot do anything to assist you. But talking about Rosemary Dell, why I was born near that spot and knew Mr. Wallingford's family well. Are you, indeed, his niece?"

Maria replied in the affirmative, and she then inquired if she was far from Rosemary Dell?

"Lor' bless you, Miss," replied Kitty, "more than sixty miles, and quite in a contrary direction. I imagine it is the intention of Mr. Barnell to take you to Willoughby Lodge, which he has lately bought, and which is more than fifty miles from this place."

"Good Heaven!" exclaimed Maria, "I know not what to do;—the thought is enough to rack my brain to madness."

"Do not give way to despair, I beg, Miss," observed Kitty, "he will not dare to proceed to the violence you fear, knowing as he does that you have so respectable a friend as your uncle, Mr. Wallingford, who he might rest assured would not fail to punish him to the fullest extent of the law for such an outrage."

Maria shook her head.

"Alas!" she said, "what could ever recompence me for such a terrible occurrence; could any punishment that might be inflicted upon him be a sufficient retribution for the heinous offence? I feel myself standing upon the brink of ruin and degradation, from which I see no chance of escaping. Almighty God, assist me in this trying moment; without Thy supreme intervention, nothing can save me from destruction."

"But," said Kitty, after a short pause "have you no friends in England to whom you could make known your situation, and solicit their interference to rescue you from the power of the man who unjustly detains you?"

"Ah! a lucky thought," returned Maria; —"Susan, of course, if she is at liberty, would take care to make known my seizure to Mathew, who would, if his health permitted him, take immediate steps to release me; but then she had no knowledge of whither Barnell would take me; and therefore, while the time was occupied in endeavouring to obtain the necessary information, all the danger to be apprehended might have take place. I have my pocket-book here; I will therefore write a few lines, and if you could contrive by any means to get it conveyed to Mathew, I shall owe you a debt of gratitude, nothing can ever sufficiently repay."

"I will do so with pleasure, Miss, and without any loss of time. As for gratitude, what more is it than doing as I would be done unto, towards my fellow creature. Directed from this place, it will give your friend some clue to what part of the country you are in, if even I should be wrong in the conjecture I formed as to Willoughby Lodge being the place of your destination."

"There is but very little doubt but that you are correct in your surmises," answered Maria, "for now I remember that the villian Barnell did mention something about going to some lodge; but I was so agitated, that if he mentioned the name, I did not take any notice of it."

Maria then took out her pencil, and tearing out a leaf or two from her pocket-book, hastily wrote a few lines to Mathew, describing what had happened, and whither she was being taken; and she requested him to take such immediate steps to enforce her restoration to liberty, as should seem to him most prudent.

This she delivered to the good-natured Kitty, and endeavoured to induce her to take a guinea, as some little acknowledgment for the service; but Kitty firmly refused to accept of it, and Maria was forced to return it to her purse:

"And now, Miss," said Kitty, " let me persuade you to get an hour or two's sleep; it will so refresh you, and prepare you for the fatigues of the day, and you know Barnell said that it was his intention to resume his journey at an early hour to-morrow morning, doubtless to avoid being observed much by the passengers."

Maria, who saw that Kitty was evidently tired, endeavoured to comply; and having ceased to talk, the good-natured girl was very soon soundly asleep; but painful thoughts kept Maria awake for nearly an hour, when she also yielded to the influence of the drowsy god, and gained a temporary respite from her cares and terrors.

She was awakened in the morning by some one shaking her violently; and looking up, she beheld the disagreeable old woman standing by the bed-side.

"Come," said she, in her usual harsh and croaking voice, " are you going to sleep all day, I should like to know?—Here is the post-chaise been waiting at the door this quarter of an hour, and I believe you will want some refreshment before you depart, for I don't suppose you will stop at many places on the road. You, Kitty, you lazy hussy, get up, I tell you, or you and I will fall out, that's very certain."

Maria turned away from the disgusting old woman, with a look of the utmost abhorrence; and without saying a word, she and Kitty arose from the couch, and proceeded to dress themselves, Mrs Muggeridge remaining in the room, grumbling all the time. When they had done, Maria, with a trembling step, followed the old harridan down the stairs, and Kitty went to another part of the house, after having taken an opportunity, when her mistress was not observing her, to exchange an expressive glance with Maria, which the latter perfectly understood.

Upon entering the parlour, she found Mr. Barnell and his two companions there; and their looks convinced her that they had not yet recovered from their previous nights debauch. Her heart sunk with terror at the thoughts of being compelled to ride in the same vehicle with three such abondoned wretches; but she thought it more prudent to endeavour to conquer her fears as much as possible, and to assume a determination and firmness she was far from, in reality, experiencing; thinking that if she betrayed any particular weakness, Barnell might be inclined to take advantage of it.

When she entered the room, Barnell rose from his seat, and approaching her with insolent familiarity, attempted to address her; but she turned from him with a look of ineffable scorn, and seating herself in a remote corner of the room, she awaited in silence the time of departure. She declined partaking of any refreshment, for her heart was too full to allow her to eat; and after Barnell and his companions had satisfied the cravings of their appetite, which, even at that early hour in the morning, seemed to be most voracious, for they ate quite enough for any moderate six persons, she was led hastily to the chaise, which was waiting at the door, and Barnell and his companions handed her in, and the vehicle dashed off at full speed.

Frequently did Barnell attempt to get her into conversation, and endeavoured to excuse the step he had taken, pleading the violence of the sentiments he entertained towards her, and which impelled him to use violent measures.

"Indeed, Miss Herbert," continued he, "my conduct may appear very cruel to you, but I can assure you, my motives are far from being so. I never was of a cruel disposition in my life, and particularly towards a female ; no, no, damme, I like the sex too well for that. But when a man's desperately in love, and the object

ELVIRA AND INEZ.

of his love is so terribly obstinate, that she will not scarcely deign him a look, what is he to do? You see, Miss, me and Lord Harlington have quarrelled, so that the proposed match with his daughter is broken off. And if it had not been for your having no fortune, I should have had no objection to have made you my wife;—however, as it is, we may live very happily together after all, for what is marriage but a mere ceremony?"

"Insolent, unmanly wretch!" exclaimed Maria, unable to controul the burning indignation which swelled her bosom at his observations, "have you not one spark of virtue left within your bosom, that you thus brutally insult a female, who never gave your hateful addresses any encouragement, and then to attempt to justify your infamous actions ? Think not, although I am now in your power, that your triumph is secure;—no, I shall speedily be released from your power, and you will, when too late, have reason to repent your villanous conduct towards me."

"That I must leave to chance, Miss Herbert," returned Barnell, with a smile of exultation, "but I rather think that your friends, if you have any, will not so readily find you out as you seem to imagine. But if you will endeavour to get rid of your delicate scruples, and not behave with such scorn and detestation towards a man who is so able and willing to make you happy——"

"Cease, sir," ejaculated Maria, "your words are as disgusting to my ears, as your person is odious."

"Well, you are a strange little devil," observed the vulgar, ignorant fellow; "however, it's no use quarrelling over the business; we shall see what time and my most assiduous attention will effect; I do not despair of effecting a reformation in your sentiments."

Maria fixed upon him a look of contempt and detestation, but made no answer; and Barnell, turning to his companions, entered into conversation with them, and suffered Maria to relapse into thought. They stopped to change horses; but Maria was not suffered to leave the vehicle, and even had she been permitted to do so, she despaired of meeting with any success, if she appealed to the people of the inn, after what had taken place on the day before, on her attempting to do so. What refreshments they had, were brought to the carriage; but it was only once that Maria could be prevailed to partake of them, and then it was but very sparingly.

Frequently, on the way, Barnell endeavoured to get her to converse with him, but she resolutely evaded him, and remained silent during the remainder of the journey.

It was towards the afternoon, that Mr. Barnell put up one of the blinds; and looking out at the scenery beyond, exclaimed—

"By Jingo! I did not think we were so nigh; we are now at S——, and another half hour will bring us to Willoughby Lodge!"

Maria trembled with emotion, when she heard of their being so near to that place which was, for the present, destined to become her prison; but by a violent effort she appeased her agitation, and did not appear to take any notice of what Barnell had said. The remainder of the journey was performed in silence, and at length the vehicle stopped, and Maria heard a bell ring, soon after which, a pair of heavy gates were thrown back on their hinges, and the carriage passed into what she imagined to be the ground surrounding the lodge.

For what reason Willoughby Lodge had obtained the latter insignificant title, we are at a loss to conceive, or what Mr. Barnell meant by calling it a "box," inasmuch, as it was a fine old Gothic spacious mansion, covering a large space of ground, surrounded with extensive and romantic gardens. It had more the appearance of an ancient abbey, and had, we believe, in former times, belonged to the order of Cistersian Monks. Many parts of the fabric had been so modernised, as to retain very little of its pristine aspect, but upon the whole, it had a most venerable and interesting appearance. It had come into the possession of Barnell at a sum considerably beneath its actual value, its former owner having dissipated a princely fortune away in gambling, and was compelled to sell the estate.

When the gates had closed upon them, Barnell, having let down the blind, Maria was enabled to have a full view of the noble and ancient pile; and she was completely astonished at the size and magnificence of the building, (having expected to have seen nothing more than a small villa, from hearing it designated the lodge). The beauty, too, of the gardens, and the exquisite taste with which they were arranged, particularly struck her, and she was so taken by surprise, that for a few moments her thoughts were completely estranged from her own troubles, in the contemplation of the many attractions which surrounded her.

She was soon aroused to recollection, however, by the chaise stopping at the entrance to the fabric, where a tall, foppish, smirking-looking young man, in livery, and whose appearance was anything but in accordance with the appearance of the edifice, was already standing to receive his master. Before Barnell assisted Maria to alight, after apologizing in the best way he was able, he placed a large mantle over her, so as completely to conceal her person from observation; and having been lifted from the vehicle, she was carried into the mansion; and after ascending, apparently, several flights of stairs, they stopped, the mantle was removed from her head, and Maria beheld herself in a spacious and elegant apartment.

The room, which was one of a suite, was very lofty; the wainscot was of chesnut, elegantly carved, and was decorated with numerous paintings (landscapes and portraits) and large mirrors. The floor was richly carpeted; and the furniture which the room contained might be said to be gorgeous,

Maria was completely astonished as she looked around her, and could not help feeling the utmost astonishment and admiration of everything which she saw. Barnell evidently noticed her, and perceived the thoughts that were passing in her mind, for he smiled exultingly, and said :—

"This suite of apartments, which any one must acknowledge are magnificent enough for a palace, I intend to appropriate to your service, beauteous Miss Herbert; and here every comfort you can wish for, every enjoyment, shall be yours at command. True, I must put a little restraint upon you, until you shall be pleased to see the propriety of yielding to my wishes, when you shall have full liberty to range where you please ; but until then, I must not suffer you to quit these rooms. In the next room you will find a library, and no doubt a choice collection of books, for the late possessor of this place was a gentleman of the most refined literary taste, as they call it. The room beyond that, opens upon a terrace, where you can walk whenever you please, and which commands a beautiful view of the country. You shall also have the attendance of a maid, who, no doubt, will please you, for she is a young girl, who was much esteemed in the family which lately belonged here. So you see, Miss Maria, that I have determined to do all in my power to make you happy ; and, now, pray reward me with one of those smiles of approbation which make you look so irresistibly charming."

Maria replied to this long and fulsome speech with a look of superlative contempt; but when Barnell took her hand, and endeavoured to press it to his lips, she forcibly withdrew it, and with a look of apprehension, exclaimed :—

"Stand off, sir, dare not to approach ;—insulted pride and wounded modesty will add double energy to my woman's strength, and I will make my voice heard by those who will stand forward in the defence of an insulted female, and punish her oppressor."

Barnell smiled ironically, as he replied :—

"Your cries here would be useless, Miss Herbert—in this place you are so secluded from the world, that you are——"

"And by what right do you detain me, sir ?" interrupted Maria, with the deepest resentment depicted on her countenance. "Think you that your conduct will always remain concealed, and that you will be suffered to go unpunished?"

"Why, as to that matter," returned Barnell with cool indifference—"I must take my chance, and I do not feel very qualmish about it. At any rate, the risk you seem to think I run, ought to prove to you how powerful must be the regard I entertain for you, to tempt me to hazard it. But you will consider better of this affair, and of me also, I am sure, dear Maria, when you see how kind I behave to you ; and I am not without hope, that the time is not far distant when you will admire me full as much as you now appear to dislike me."

"Consummate idiot !" was upon the lips of Maria, but she repressed the expression of her feelings, and turning away from him with a look of abhorrence, made him no reply. After a pause, Mr. Barnell resumed :—

"Well, Miss Herbert, to show you that I do not wish to tease you, I will not intrude upon you again to-day, but I will send your maid to you. Perhaps, by the time we meet again, you will be able to receive me with a little more civility. Good-day to you, Miss."

With these words Barnell, with an ignorant smile, much to the gratification of Maria bowed himself out of the room, and secured the door by locking and bolting it. When he had gone Maria threw herself on her knees, and in earnest terms implored the Divine protection, after which she felt more composed and seemed to be imbued with double fortitude to resist the danger which threatened her. The words and the behaviour of Barnell assured her that she had no occasion to fear that he would take any immediate step to force her to comply with his infamous desires ; and in the meantime Mathew would become acquainted with her situation, and take such steps as would enforce her restoration to liberty.

This hope revived her, and she determined to collect all the energy and equanimity she was possessed of, so as to be enabled to meet with all necessary resolution and resistance any contingency that might take place.

After once more looking round at the costliness of the furniture in the apartment, and admiring the taste with which all its arrangements were conceived, she walked into the adjoining room, which was not quite so large as the one she had first left, but equally elicited her admiration. She found, as Barnell had informed her, that this room was appropriated to a library, and the books, which were numerous and fancifully arranged, were all in handsome bindings, and were the works of the first authors.

"Here," thought Maria, "I can, at any rate, beguile some of the tedious hours, before I regain my liberty ; and in the precious works of genius, gain a short respite from care."

She passed on to the third room, which was handsomely fitted up as a bed-room, and presented every comfort that a person could desire. She walked on to the terrace, and was delighted at the lovely prospect commanded from it. Hills rising on hills, meadows, pastures, and vallies of emerald green, and here and there a meandering rivulet, gave a pleasing variety to the romantic scene. To the right, could be seen the umbrageous foliage of a deep forest, the summit of whose lofty trees seemed almost buried in the clouds :—and, to the left, was an open champaign country, which presented innumerable charms to the admirers of the beauteous and stupendous works of Nature.

This view was from the back of the building, the front being occupied for several acres of land, in the extensive garden, and surrounded by a very high wall, which, however, as the abbey (for such we shall call it) stood upon an eminence did not prevent its proud turrets from being seen for many miles around.

The sun was now in full meridian glory, and the magnificent scenery, illumined by its golden beams, had an effect most grand and imposing. Maria, in the contemplation of this scene, forgot her cares, and became for awhile completely absorbed in the admiration and sublime feelings which it inspired in her bosom. She was, however, suddenly aroused by hearing a female voice behind her, and turning round, she beheld standing in the apartment, a good-looking, good-tempered, and neatly dressed young woman, who, with a polite courtsey, introduced herself as the maid deputed to attend upon her, and who intimated that her name was Clara.

"I hope, Miss," said Clara, "that you will be satisfied with my behaviour, for I am sure there is not anything which is in my power that I would not do to serve you; and I am very sorry to see you placed in such a situation that I am."

"Are you, indeed sorry, for me, my good girl?" said Maria, who was much pleased with the appearance and behaviour of Clara, and was greatly prepossessed in her favour— "then, if you really are sincere in your expressions you will readily assist me to escape from the power of the man who so unjustly detains me."

"Ah, Miss," replied Clara, "that indeed would I freely do, but I have not the power. In the first place, if I should permit you to leave these apartments, and assist you in quitting the mansion, before you could escape into the open country, you must cross the garden, and the old porter at the gate, who is never found napping, would take good care to prevent you from proceeding any further."

"But," exclaimed Maria, catching eagerly at the words of Clara, "surely I might climb the garden wall in some part where I should not be observed."

Clara shook her head.

"That would be impossible, for it is so high," answered she, " in fact, it is more like the wall of a prison, than that surrounding a gentleman's mansion."

" But is there no way at the back of the building by which I might escape?" eagerly inquired Maria.

"None," answered the girl.

Maria sighed, and traversed the room for a few moments wrapt in thought.

"I am surprised, Clara," at length she said, "that a young girl like you, and apparantly possessed of such goodness of heart, should remain in the service of such a man as Mr. Barnell."

"Why, Miss," answered Clara, "I was brought up in the family of Lady Willoughby, whose husband, Sir James Willoughby, was the late possessor of this estate. Lady Willoughby was an amiable woman, and much attached to me; but, poor dear lady, she was fated to experience much trouble. Sir James became very gay, and used to gamble very much, until he lost such large sums of money that he was all but ruined. I have heard say, but, of course, I cannot vouch for the truth of it, that Mr. Barnell won money to an immense amount of him at the gaming-table, and afterwards took advantage, when Sir James was driven to desperation and despair, to get this abbey from him for a mere trifle in comparison to its actual value."

" But what has this to do with the question I asked you, Clara?" said Maria.

"Why, Miss, I was going to say that Sir James and his lady had it not in their power to retain any of their old servants, or to take them along with them, for they went on the Continent, and when Mr. Barnell came into possession, as he expected to be married shortly, and said that I should be just the young girl, he was certain, who would suit his intended lady for a maid, he offered to keep me in his service, and I consented to stop. I confess, though, that I had no good opinion of my master, and if it had not been that I have a poor sick mother to support, I would not have accepted his offer ; however, depend upon it, I will not remain here any longer than I can get another situation."

Maria was satisfied with this explanation, and highly applauded the affectionate attention which Clara bestowed upon her helpless parent. She deeply sympathised with the misfortunes of Lady Willoughby, brought on by the imprudent conduct of her husband ; and the hint which Clara had given her of the behaviour of Barnell, filled her with increased detestation for his character, and rendered her still more wretched at the thought that she was in his power.

In the society of Clara, however, Maria soon became more tranquil, and she partook more heartily of the repast which was provided for her, than she had done for some time. The first day passed away without anything particular occurring, and at night Maria retired to rest and slept pretty comfortably, Clara sleeping in the same chamber.

———

CHAPTER LVIII.

"Oh, let me not die in the midst of all
The iniquities with which my mind,
My conscience is so loaded. Stem the red tide
That drains my veins, and oh, in pity snatch
My soul from that eternity it dreads to meet!"
THE PENITENT.

THE next morning, soon after Maria had taken breakfast, the door of the apartment in which she and Clara were seated, was thrown open, and Mr. Barnell entered, and advanced towards Maria, who felt an emotion of disgust as she beheld him, and averted her face.

"Leave the room," said he in an authorative tone to Clara. The latter courtseyed and obeyed, and Mr. Barnell, after a few short coughs and attempts to draw the attention of Maria, said—

"Why, my dear Miss Herbert, do you persist in looking upon me so coldly, especially when you see that my only study is to make you happy?"

"If you really had a wish to see me happy, Mr. Barnell," said Maria, "you would no longer detain me prisoner, but show your compunction for the offence you have committed by allowing me to depart, and never again seeking to annoy me by insulting my ears with the utterance of sentiments which can only excite my abhorrence and disgust, and which are utterly disgraceful to any person laying claim to the title of a gentleman and a man of honour."

"What nonsense," answered Barnell, "this is only the silly talk of neglected prudes, who are either too old or too ugly to create any sentiment of love in the heart of the other sex. But I am sure such a fine, handsome and sensible young lady as yourself, Miss Herbert, will——"

"Silence, sir," interrupted Maria, "I must not, I will not listen, to language like this. Leave me, I beg of you."

"Oh no, Miss, I am too fond of your sweet society to comply with your request; although I can assure you I do not wish to offend you; besides, you must allow me to pass an hour or two with you this morning, as I have just received a letter—the contents of which will compel me to leave here this day, and it will probably be three or four days, or a week, before I shall be able to return."

Maria could scarcely help expressing the delight this information imparted to her; Providence had heard her prayers and interfered for her deliverance, and her heart overflowed with gratitude.

"You will have every means of making yourself comfortable during my absence, which happens very unfortunate just at this time," continued Mr. Barnell, after a brief interval of silence, during which time he had been gazing on the lovely countenance of Maria (now animated with revived hope) with looks of the most intense admiration; "whatever you may ask for, for your amusement or enjoyment, Clara, will receive instructions from me to supply you with; in short, my dear Miss Herbert, I have made in my study to give you no cause to complain of my want of attention or courtesy. Willoughby Lodge, you see, is a perfect palace, and there are very few noblemen in the land who can boast of such an estate. I hope to find you, when I return, perfectly reconciled to your lot; which, allow me to to say, Miss, there are many young ladies in the world would feel absolutely delighted with."

"Think you, sir," said Maria with much warmth, "think you, sir, that senseless show and empty splendour have any charms for me, or can have the power to lure me from those paths of virtue from which I have never yet deviated? A palace becomes a prison to the truly good, when it becomes the receptacle of vice, while the humblest cottage possesses inestimable blessings to those whose consciences cannot accuse them of acting in any way contrary to the dictates of virtue and morality."

Mr. Barnell made no immediate answer; in fact, it is extremely doubtful whether he scarcely understood a word of it; for beyond that knowledge which a low, vulgar, and debased mind imbibes, he could not be accused of soaring.

"Well, I dare say that's all very pretty in its place," at length he said, "but I confess that it is a subject I have never paid any particular attention to myself , and I do not think it is likely I shall commence just now. But if I must give my candid opinion, I do not see that wedlock, which is only a ceremony, can render our connection with one another any the more virtuous."

"Are my ears still to be poluted by your shameless, your revolting observations?" exclaimed Maria, while blushes of shame and resentment suffused her cheeks; "shame on you, sir, if your heart is not entirely callous to that sentiment."

"Really, Miss Herbert," answered Barnell, "you are a most provoking, interesting, obstinate, and fascinating little creature, and that's speaking nothing but the truth; I cannot say anything to please you, and yet I don't know how it is, for in my time I have been a very great favourite among the ladies, who were extremely happy when I was in their society."

Maria felt alarmed at the increased boldness of Barnell's manner, whose passion, the more she evinced her disgust, seemed to gain strength. What could she do to oppose him if he continued determined to urge his hateful suit? Was she not completely in his power? and who had she near her that could render her the least assistance in the hour of need? She trembled with terror as these thoughts flashed across her brain, and she was unable to give utterance to a sentence for several minutes. Mr. Barnell did not offer to interrupt her—in fact, he very probably had exhausted all he had to say, and was endeavouring to think of something else to address to the object he wished to captivate. He sat gazing at her with a bold and ignorant expression of countenance, and whistling the burthen of some popular melody.

At length an idea occurred to Maria that it would be best to dissimulate, although her nature revolted from anything of the kind, and accordingly turning to Mr. Barnell with a calm demeanour, and in dispassionate accents, she said—

"Mr. Barnell, let me beg of you, at any rate for the present, not to persist in urging your suit, but to leave me for a few days to recover myself from the shock which this unexpected occurrence has occasioned me, and the illness under which I am labouring from the fatigue of the journey; recollect that kindness and compliance with the wishes of those you affect to admire, is the surest way of conciliating their esteem."

"My dearest Miss Herbert," ejaculated Mr. Barnell, apparently quite elated with the change in the behaviour of Maria; "these are the most delightful words I have ever heard you utter, and I should indeed be unworthy of your esteem did I refuse to assent to your desires. Yes, Maria, I will this instant leave you, and as I shall not return for a few days, I hope that period will effect the happy change in you I am so anxious to see. Farewell, sweetest—nay, you must, at parting, allow me to kiss your fair hand."

Maria in vain endeavoured to withdraw her hand from the hated being's grasp—he persisted, and raising it to his lips, kissed it vehemently several times, while the bosom of Maria was filled with sentiments of almost insupportable disgust and indignation. At length, extricating herself from him, she rushed into the adjoining apartment, and hastily closing the door after her, locked it on the inside. She heard Barnell repeat the word "Farewell," and immediately after she heard him quit the room, and fasten the door after him; and relieved from the weight of excessive terror that had filled her bosom, she sunk upon her knees, and once more poured forth her gratitude to the Almighty disposer of all events.

The departure of Barnell was a most fortunate circumstance, and she hailed it with delight, for if Kitty, the servant at the inn, had been faithful to her promise, in forwarding her hasty scrawl to Mathew, he would have re-

ceived it before now, and would, no doubt, before the return of the former, be enabled to adopt such plans as would insure her immediate liberation from his power.

She walked into the room she had lately quitted, and soon after Clara rejoined her, with pleasure depicted in her good-tempered countenance.

"Oh, miss, I didn't know whether master said anything to you or not," said she, "but you will, I'm sure, be very glad to hear that he has left the abbey this moment on horseback, and from what I heard him say to those two cross-looking men who accompanied him when you was brought hither, I do not think it is his intention to return again for two or three days."

"He has told me all about it, Clara," replied Maria, "and, indeed, it is a great relief to me; Heaven send that in the meantime something may take place to release me from the thraldom in which he so cruelly and unjustly holds me."

"God grant it, Miss," said Clara, fervently; "but something convinces me that your prayers will be granted, and that you have nothing to apprehend. At any rate we can pass two or three days in peace, and you must live in hopes that all will turn out as you desire."

Thus did the kind-hearted and sensible girl endeavour to tranquillize Maria's feelings; and having partially succeeded, she sought to divert her thoughts from the painful subject which had before occupied them, and conversed upon different topics, in which Maria freely joined her. Several hours were passed in this agreeable manner, and the time appeared not to hang half so heavily on Maria's hands. When tired of discourse, Maria and Clara walked on to the terrace, and watched the beauty of the scenery spread before them, in which Maria described a thousand remarkable charms, which would have escaped the eye of a superficial observer.

At length, Clara, recollecting that she had some domestic business to perform, left Maria for a short time, which interim the latter tried to pass away in the library; but although the books she laid her hands upon were the productions of some of her favourite authors, she could not compose the thoughts that crowded on her brain sufficiently to allow her to read; and, at length, tired of making the attempt, she replaced the books on the shelves, and awaited the return of Clara (whose artless simplicity and kindness of manners had much interested her) in the sitting-room.

Clara was no great while absent, and the afternoon passed away as comfortably as could be expected. Maria learnt, with satisfaction too, that the two ruffians who had assisted in bearing her away, had also departed soon after Mr. Barnell left the abbey, and there were no persons but the domestics remaining in the place.

Evening set in, and still Maria and Clara sat together, engaged in conversation, when all at once their attention was arrested by hearing a strange noise, which seemed to proceed from below, and sounded like the hubbub occasioned from a number of voices all speaking together.

Maria and her astonished companion listened attentively, and presently thought they heard groans, and from some person in great agony.

"Good gracious! what can be the matter?" exclaimed Clara.

"I am certain it is some person groaning," answered Maria. "Hasten, pray, good Clara, and see if you can ascertain what is the cause of the disturbance."

Clara, whose anxiety was equally as great as Maria's, did not wait to be requested a second time, but immediately left the room, and hurried down the stairs. In her haste she forgot to fasten the room-door after her, although she had been strictly enjoined to do so by Mr. Barnell before he quitted the place; and Maria, who now heard the groans more loudly than before, could not resist the temptation she had to follow her, and ascertain the cause. She did not wait a moment to deliberate, but, quitting the room, she descended the stairs, while a mingled feeling of fear, hope, and doubt filled her bosom. When she reached the bottom of the last flight of stairs, she was astonished to behold drops of blood on the marble pavement, and there were several strange persons standing at the parlour-door. Presently afterwards Clara rushed out of the parlour, pale and trembling; and perceiving Maria, she made a sign for her to return to the rooms above, which the latter, in a state of great trepidation and curiosity, complied with.

When they had got into the apartment, it was some moments ere Clara could sufficiently recover her breath to answer the eager interrogatories of Maria, as to what had so terrified her, and what was the meaning of the confusion below.

"Oh, Miss!" at length exclaimed the horrified girl. "Oh, Miss! such a dreadful catastrophe! Dear me—I shall never get it out of my eyes! Surely it is a judgment upon him for his wickedness!"

"What do you mean?" demanded Maria; "for goodness' sake do not keep me in this painful suspense. What dreadful catastrophe do you allude to? Who is it that is hurt?"

"Oh! Miss—Mr. Barnell!"

"Ah! what of him? Has anything happened to him?" inquired Maria, with eager haste.

"He is murdered!" answered Clara, with a shudder of horror, and placing her hands across her eyes, as if to shut out some frightful and terrifying object from her sight.

"Murdered?"

"Oh! yes, Miss; he is murdered—poor, wretched, unfortunate, gentleman! I saw him in the parlour, covered with blood; and he looked so awful, that I am certain he is dying."

"Great God! is it possible?" cried Maria. "How has this dreadful event taken place?"

"Oh! do not attempt to go and look at him, I beg, Miss," said Clara, seeing Maria move towards the door, as if for that purpose; "it will strike you with such horror to see him. He has been shot in the side; and from what I could gather from the persons who assisted to bring him home, it has been done in a duel."

"Done in a duel!—by whom?" inquired Maria, hastily.

"That, of course, I know not; but whoever it was, he has escaped."

"God of mercy!" exclaimed Maria, " thy retribution is just, though terrible."

She had scarcely made use of these words when a female servant made her appearance, and requested her, in the name of the unfortunate man, to grant him an interview.

With trembling steps she accompanied the woman, and entered the parlour, where the unfortunate Mr. Barnell was reclining upon a sofa. The doctor and several other persons were in the room. The hemorrhage had been stopped, but he was evidently dying. His countenance was ghastly pale, and his lips lived, and he was, apparently, suffering the most excruciating agony. When he saw Maria enter the room, he motioned her to approach him, which she did, trembling violently. He took her hand.

"Miss Herbert," said he, in faint tones, "you need not fear me now—my career of guilt is over, and in a few minutes I shall cease to be. Too surely it was the hand of an offended God that dealt this retributive blow! —Richly do I merit it all; but, oh! that I had been permitted to live a short time longer to repent of my many crimes."

Maria, who, horror-struck at the dreadful spectacle, in a moment forgot her own wrongs in her pity for the hapless dying wretch before her, attempted to utter to him some words of consolation, but he waived his hand and prevented her; and then, after a brief pause, he continued—

"I know what you would say, but I cannot —dare not hope; you, whose heart is all gentleness and Christian charity, may forgive me for the injuries I have done you, but——"

"I do, indeed, forgive you," eagerly ejaculated Maria, "and may the God of mercy, in His infinite goodness, do the same."

"Oh, do not mention His name," said the dying wretch, with a shudder of the most inconceivable horror and despair; "a wretch, a monster, a murderer—yes, you start, and well you may, but I repeat I am a murderer! Even now the blood-stained victim of my hideous crime rises before mine eyes, and points to perdition as my certain doom!—Hide him from my sight!—do not let him approach me!—Back!—back!—Oh, how hard it is for a guilty being like me to die!"

Mr. Barnell, again exhausted, paused, and his horror-struck listeners looked at each other with the most unfeigned expressions of amazement and terror. At length, the attendants having, in obedience to a sign he gave them, gently raised him, he motioned the doctor and Maria to draw nearer, and in accents that were scarcely audible, he thus spoke:—

"My time in this world is short, and, therefore, let me make the best use I can of it while I am here. The relation who had left me in his will all he possessed, died by my hands. He was taken ill, and I having offended him, he threatened to make another will, and bequeath his property to a nephew whom he had previously discarded. Alarmed at this, my brain was worked up to a pitch of madness. There was no one in the room at the time he made this declaration, but himself and me. In a moment a hellish thought flashed upon my brain, and I jumped up with a determination, at all risks, to perpetrate it. I sprang upon the poor, feeble, helpless, dying old man, and, cowardly monster that I was, I buried my fingers in his throat, and pressed the small portion of life remaining out of him. Oh, God! methinks I see the poor old man now, as he fixed his glazed eyes upon me with a look of dying agony and reproach, and made a feeble—a futile effort, to remove my ruffian grasp! Ah, see!—he is there!—I see his blackened face, his blood-shot eyes, his frightfully-distorted features! Horror!—horror!—Take him away—take him away! Hark, he speaks!—What is it he says? Ah!—I hear it now!—oh, these terrible words! 'No mercy for the murderer!' I feel the torments of the damned already upon me!—A thousand fiends are worrying at my heart! I burn! I burn!—Water! water—Ha! ha! ha!"

Maria turned away from the awful sight with the most intense horror, as she heard the doctor, in a low voice, observe—

"It is all over."

Completely overcome by what she had seen and heard, Maria hastened from the chamber of death, and flew up stairs to the apartments that had been allotted to herself, where she found Clara awaiting in the most anxious suspense to hear the result of the interview and the fate of Mr. Barnell. It was several minutes before Maria could speak, but when she did, she informed Clara that Mr. Barnell was no more, and briefly informed her what had taken place, and the dreadful confession which he had made.

Clara was not less surprised and horror-struck, when she heard the particulars, than Maria was herself.

"But what do you mean to do, Miss, under these shocking, but to you fortunate, events?" interrogated Clara; "surely you cannot think of staying in the house after such a terrible occurrence, and with the corpse of a murderer in the place? For my part, I would not remain for all the *inges* of gold!"

"But whither can we go?" demanded Maria; "I am a complete stranger in this part of the country, and it is now getting late."

"Why, I'll tell you, Miss," answered Clara, "my mother lives only a short distance off, and if you do not mind putting up with a little inconvenience, for once in a way, you can stay there until you feel yourself fit to travel, and I know my poor mother will make you as welcome and comfortable as she can. God bless my soul, to remain in this Gothic-looking edifice with——"

"You shall not be put to any such trial," interrupted Maria, "I agree to your proposition, and am ready to depart as soon as you are."

"Oh, I am so glad to hear you say so," replied Clara; "it will not take me many minutes to pack up my things, and as for the wages that are owing to me, I do not care if I never receive a penny of them; ill-gotten money never does any person any good."

With these words, Clara hurried out of the room, and Maria was left to herself. In a few minutes the medical man requested to see her, and she admitted him. After having informed her, that he understood the circumstances under which she had been brought there, he took the liberty of inquiring what she intended to do. Maria informed him, when he said he had come with the intention of offering her an asylum at his house, until her friends could be made acquainted with situation.

Maria thanked the doctor for his kindness, and assured him that she should have been most happy to have availed herself of his offer, but, having already arranged with Clara, to repair to the mother of the latter, she would rather not alter that plan. The doctor, finding her so resolved, did not urge her further, and was about to leave the room, when Maria inquired of him if he knew by what means the fatal catastrophe had taken place, which had filled their bosoms with such horror.

From the doctor's account, it appeared, that Mr. Barnell, after departing from Willoughby Lodge, met with one of his gay and dissipated companions, who prevailed on him to go with him to an adjacent hotel, where they met with several more gentlemen, to whom they were known, and sat down to have a game at hazard.

By some means or the other, a quarrel ensued between one of the gentlemen and Barnell, and the latter had become so excited by the wine he had drunk, and the provocation he had received, that he jumped up and gave the gentleman a violent blow. Upon this, the latter demanded immediate satisfaction, which was granted, and selecting their seconds, they left the hotel and went to a field near Willoughby Abbey, where the duel took place, which ended so fatally for the unfortunate Mr. Barnell.

In the confusion that prevailed, the gentle-

MARIETTE.

man and his second made their escape, and no one could tell in what direction they had gone. This was the brief history of the fatal tragedy.

Maria could not help admiring the wonderful ways of Providence throughout this affair, and while she returned her fervent thanks for being delivered from the danger that had surrounded her, she offered up a prayer for forgiveness for the miserable wretch who had been the author of the sorrow she had lately suffered.

The doctor having quitted the house, Clara shortly afterwards entered the room, all ready prepared for their departure, and Maria, glad to escape from the place, immediately took her arm, and they hastened on their way to the house of Clara's mother. On the road, the thoughts of Maria were occupied with the melancholy and appalling events that had recently taken place, and the awful death of Barnell was impressed upon her mind in characters too vivid for her readily to efface them. But her providential escape, when so environed by danger, excited her most grateful feelings; and now that she was once more restored to liberty, she seemed to breathe the pure air with redoubled pleasure, and walked on with the kind-hearted Clara with the utmost avidity.

"Oh, Miss," said Clara, as they walked on, "what a shocking fate for Mr. Barnell to meet with, in the midst of all his sins; but what a dreadful wretch he must have been (God forgive me for speaking ill of the dead), for murdering the poor old man, his relation."

"Indeed he must," said Maria, with a shudder of horror; "but do not say any more upon the subject, there's a good girl, it make's my blood run cold to think of it. Heaven pardon him for his crimes, as I can readily forgive him for the uneasiness and inconvenience he has put me to."

"How astonished your friends will be, Miss," said Clara, "when they come to hear what has happened to you, and what a narrow escape you have had."

"They will, indeed, my good girl," said Maria; "but your kindness I shall, believe me, ever remember; and should you ever want a friend, and need assistance, that friend you shall find in Maria Herbert."

"Oh, Miss," returned Clara, "you are too kind; but, indeed, this is more than I merit. I have done nothing more than what every well-disposed person would feel a pleasure in doing, and it is unworthy of so many acknowledgments. I am sure no one would have felt a greater pleasure than I should have done to liberate you, had it been practicable; but I knew it was not, and sincerely grieved I was, to think that my wishes were so frustrated."

"Believe me, my good girl," observed Maria, "I could read your wishes, and duly appreciate them; they will deserves as much gratitude as if you had the power. But, are we far from the cottage of your mother?"

"It is only about a mile across the fields, Miss," answered Clara; "it is a very fine evening, and the walk will do us both good. Oh, how surprised my poor mother will be, to be sure."

"I am afraid she will consider me an intruder," said Maria, "and that I shall put her to great inconvenience."

"Oh, pray do not mention it, my dear Miss," replied Clara; "I am sure my poor mother will be sincerely glad to serve you in her humble way, and will readily do all that lies in her power to make you comfortable."

"If she resembles her daughter, I am certain she will," said Maria.

Clara expressed by her looks and a low courtesy, her gratitude for this compliment, and they now walked on in silence, until at length, after traversing a lane, they came in sight of the cottage of Clara's mother, from the casement of which a light was glimmering. The exterior of the cottage, as far as Maria could see, had a very neat and pretty appearance, and the honey-suckle entwined around the casement, and overhung the door-porch.

Clara tapped gently at the door, which, after a pause, was opened by a cleanly-dressed, middle-aged woman, who seemed to be reduced to premature feebleness, rather by illness than her years. Upon beholding Clara, she uttered an exclamation of surprise, and started back, which was not a little increased when she saw Maria standing behind her.

"Dear mother, do not be astonished," said Clara, "it is me. I have come to stop with you, and I have brought this young lady with me, who needs an asylum until such time as her friends have arrived to take her under their protection."

"I am sure the young lady is quite welcome to all the asylum my humble roof can afford her," said the woman, in a kind voice; "pray walk in, Miss; Clara will see to your comfort, for I am so ill, that I have a great deal of trouble to move about at all. But, bless my soul, child, what can have happened to have made you leave your situation so abruptly?"

"I will tell you all presently, mother," answered Clara, "but, pray do let me assist you to your arm-chair, while I prepare supper."

"I am afraid, Miss," said the good woman, "you will find what I have to offer you but sorry fare; but humble as it is, it is given with a free heart, and a sincere regret that I cannot furnish you with better."

"My dear woman," said Maria, "do not, I pray, make any apology; for your kindness I am extremely grateful, and shall not readily forget it. If you can, without materially inconveniencing yourself, accommodate me with a shelter beneath your roof, until such time as my friends arrive to receive me, I shall esteem it as a great favour, and will reward you as far as lies in my power, for your trouble."

"Oh, pray Miss," said Mrs. Jackson, (which was her name,) "pray do not mention anything about reward, for the humble service it is in my power to render you. The accommodation I afford you is poor, but clean, and to such as it is, you are heartily welcome."

Maria once more thanked Mrs. Jackson, and then, seeing how impatient she was to learn all the particulars of the cause of her daughter's sudden and unexpected return home, she related all the circumstances of her own abduction, and the awful events that had since taken place at Willoughby Abbey. Mrs. Jackson listened to her with the strongest demonstrations of astonishment, and she frequently interrupted her by an exclamation of indignation against Barnell for his villany; butwhen Maria came to the conclusion of her recital, and mentioned the appalling fate of the unfortunate man, and the dreadful confession of his dying moments, she clasped her hands together, and raising her eyes with an expression of horror, she ejaculated—

"Good God! what a monster! to murder the poor dying old man; and then my child, my Clara, to live in the service of such a wretch. Oh, how glad I am that she has left, and that she did not wait to receive the wages due to her; for I am sure I should have fancied every coin was stained with the blood of the old man! Heaven have mercy on his soul!"

Maria sincerely responded to Mrs. Jackson's prayer, and by this time Clara, who had been bustling about in making such preparations as were necessary for the accommodation of Maria, had now spread the humble repast upon the table, and they sat down to supper.

Simple as was the fare, Maria could not help thinking that she had never partaken of anything more sweet; for under the painful circumstances to which she had been subjected lately, she never knew what it was to enjoy a meal, and even the most sumptuous repast under those circumstances, is sickening and nauseous.

During the meal, the trio discussed the strange and startling events that had taken place; but the supper being over, Mrs. Jackson was unable to sit up any longer, and Clara, having assisted her to bed, she and Maria retired to one prepared for them.

The room and the bed were remarkable for cleanliness, and Maria could not help admiring the neatness with which everything was arranged.

"Ah, Miss," said Clara, while a tear glistened in her eye, in answer to some observation which was made by Maria, "we were not in such humble circumstances when my poor father was alive. He had accumulated a great sum of money in business, which would have been sufficient to have supported my mother in comfort for the rest of her days, but just before his death, he was unfortunate enough to lend a person, whom he thought his best friend, the greater portion of his money; the borrower went abroad, and we never heard anything more of him afterwards."

"And so you were at once reduced to poverty?" asked Maria.

"Yes, Miss," replied Clara; "and soon afterwards my poor mother was attacked with a paralytic stroke, and has never been well since. As I once before told you, I had been brought up in the family of Lady Willoughby, with whom I was a great favourite, and my mother had then only me to depend upon; but Lady Willoughby was very kind to us, and built us this cottage, and paid the doctor's bills—making me many handsome presents, independent of my wages; so that I was enabled to keep my mother pretty comfortable."

"But has your mother no one to attend upon her in your absence?" inquired Maria: "in her debilitated state, she ought to have some person constantly with her."

"Why, so she ought, Miss," returned Clara, "certainly; but then, you see, the neighbours are very kind to her, and any of them are ready enough to come and render her all the assistance in their power."

Thus did Clara and Maria continue to converse with each other for some time after they had retired to bed; but at length the former fell off to sleep, and Maria was left to the undisturbed indulgence of her thoughts.

She entered into a review of the many singular events in which she had moved so conspicuously for the last few months, and dwelt with no small anxiety upon what she was probably fated yet to undergo. Her prospect was dreary enough, and the contemplation of it caused her much pain. She was, she might say, left almost alone in the world, without any one to protect her, unless it was such feeble aid as poor old Mathew could afford her; and she shuddered with horror when she reflected that, probably, ill as he was when she parted from him, death might have taken him from her. As the memory of the good, the kind-hearted, the benevolent Doctor Hartley came fresh upon her, her tears flowed fast, and her heart felt so heavily oppressed, that she could scarcely support herself. From him her thoughts reverted to Mr. Wallingford, who had so coldly abandoned her, and who, if he had continued his protection to her, could have saved her from the many sufferings she had so lately endured. Surely, she thought, he must upbraid himself, did he but know under what circumstances she was placed, and to what insults, oppressions, and degradations she had been exposed. But yet did it seem that he never bestowed a thought upon her; otherwise, could he have left England without so much even as sending her a few farewell lines? Oh! no: it was clear that his inordinate pride had completely steeled his heart to every kindly feeling. Walter, too!—oh, what a pang shot through her heart as she dwelt upon his name! Was she destined never to behold him again?

—Had he also forgotten her ?—Had change of scene and the society of other damsels entirely estranged her from his heart?—Did he never bestow a thought upon her to whom his tenderest vows and asseverations had so often been pledged ?—In whom he had avowed repeatedly, and with an enthusiasm which did not leave her room to doubt, his whole soul was centred?—No, no, perish such a thought; rather let her die than believe that Walter had deceived her ; that he had ceased to remember but with the cold sentiment of friendship !—And yet, surrounded, as he doubtless was, by every glittering temptation and allurement, too strongly did her reason convince her of the probability of the suspicion.

"Oh, Walter !" she exclaimed, "my first, my only love ; even if you are false to me—even should you despise me, disown me, still my heart's latest throb will be for you ! Never can the image of any other man take possession of that poor girl's heart, which is all your own !"

Again a torrent of tears gushed from her eyes, and bedewed her fevered cheek ; and she was so completely absorbed by this agonising thought, that for a time she forgot everything else.

At length, completely exhausted, and worn out with grief and rumination, sleep came to her relief, and gave a temporary balm to her sorrows.

CHAPTER LIX.

" Seize her, drag her from the light of day,
And rake her mind to torture, 'till
The secret we require shall
Have passed her lips."—ANON.

NEARLY a week passed away, and still Maria remained at the cottage of Mrs. Jackson, without hearing anything of Mathew. She felt the utmost alarm at this, and began to think that either Kitty, the servant at the inn, had neglected to send him the note she had written, that the old man was either too ill to render any assistance, or that he was probably no more. But then, again, she could not imagine that the supposed neglect of Kitty could be the cause of this procrastination, as she had herself written to Mathew the day after she was liberated from Willoughby Abbey, giving him an account of all that had occurred, and where she was at present, informing him that she should remain there until she received his advice how to act. She was surprised not to receive any answer to this letter, and knew not to what cause to attribute it.

At length, unable any longer to endure the torturing suspense, she made up her mind to take the coach herself to Wallingford Hall, where she could, at any rate, be sure of an asylum, until she could communicate with her uncle, who surely would not suffer her any longer to be exposed to those dangers and heavy trials from which she had so recently escaped.

With this design in view, she bade farewell to Mrs. Jackson, insisting upon leaving her some token of her remembrance of the kindness with which she had behaved to her ; and accompanied by Clara, who was quite melancholy at the thoughts of parting with her, she bent her steps towards the coach-office.

They were not long in getting there, and were just about to enter the booking-office, when a stage-coach drove up, and from it alighted several passengers, and with a frantic exclamation of joy, the eyes of Maria almost immediately rested upon the person of him she had so long been anxious to see, namely, poor old Mathew.

The faithful old man, who still looked very pale and weak, was so overjoyed at the meeting, that he could not speak, and Maria kindly taking his arm, they walked into the coffee-room.

After a few minutes, Mathew having recovered, and mutual congratulations of joy having passed between him and Maria, he expressed the agony which the first account that was brought to him by the brother of Susan caused him ; but he was then so ill in bed, that he was unable to be removed. Learning, however, that she and Susan had taken the coach to Rosemary Dell, he had flattered himself that they were safe, and immediately despatched a letter to Wallingford Hall, giving her his advice how to act, and informing her his intention to follow her as soon as his health would permit. His alarm and astonishment may readily be conceived, when the next day Susan came to him in a state of great trepidation, and made him acquainted with Maria's meeting with Barnell in the coach, and what had subsequently taken place. What to do he knew not, for Susan had no idea in what direction the post-chaise was going, and if even she had known, so ill as he was, he was not in any condition to do anything to endeavour to save her, and he had no one whom he could entrust with such an undertaking. He, however, received the note which Kitty had faithfully forwarded to him, and he was now furnished with a clue as to the place of her destination ; but still he was in the same awkward predicament, and could not devise any plan which offered the slightest prospect of assisting him in his vexatious dilemma. In this way several days elapsed ; and, from the effects of his illness, he was, during the greater part of that time, in a state of unconsciousness. With returning sensibility, however, he fortunately, in a great measure, recovered his health, and in a day or two was able to leave his chamber. He then received the letter from Maria, and lost no time in making preparations for joining her; but his illness had so weakened him, that it was considered dangerous for him to travel, and that had caused the delay which so surprised and alarmed Maria.

In addition to this, Mathew had other news of importance to give her. He informed her that the villain Grayling, only a few days after her escape from him, had been recognised as a runaway convict, and two other charges of highway robbery had been brought against him; and upon searching the house, in the expectation of finding some stolen property, they had discovered the will which Mr. Hartley had made, and in which he bequeathed to her the greater portion of his property.

The latter portion of this information afforded Maria very little gratification, no more than that it would enable her to remunerate those kind individuals who had befriended her in difficulties; but she could not help again admiring the wonderful ways of Providence, which in a signal manner had delivered her from another of her enemies.

"The villain will now meet with his deserts," observed Mathew, "and retribution will at last overtake him for the injuries he has done to others."

Maria made no answer to this; and after remaining there some time, and partaking of some refreshment, she lent old Mathew the support of her arm, and they moved on towards the cottage of Mrs. Jackson. On the way Mathew acquainted her with his plans, which were that they should proceed with the least possible delay to Rosemary Dell, where they should take up their abode for the present, until she could forward a communication to Mr. Wallingford, making him acquainted with past events, and soliciting his advice as to their future operations.

Mathew made Maria acquainted with one circumstance which particularly pleased her, and that was that he had sent Susan to Rosemary Dell, the day before he started, and that she would be at Wallingford Hall to receive them.

Maria was much gratified to hear that Mathew had so well anticipated her wishes in this respect; to Susan she had taken a great fancy, from the generous simplicity of her disposition, and she was confident that the poor girl was very much attached to her; so that having a companion in whom she could confide, she hoped to be able to banish much of that melancholy which her solitaryness would otherwise engender.

"Besides, Miss," observed Mathew, "you must not forget that this change in the affairs of Richard Grayling will make a vast difference in your fortune; in fact, you will have a very handsome independence, and be in a condition to keep proper persons to attend to you without being beholden to any one."

Maria felt the full force of the old man's observations, and a deep blush mantled in her cheeks as she reflected:—

"Alas! what a poor dependant creature have I always been; and even now I feel myself beholden even for the means of subsistence, which is allowded me by that relation who has denied me his protection."

She could scarcely resist a tear, as these reflections passed over her mind, but anxious to conceal from the old man her real thoughts, she assumed as much calmness as possible, and said—

"But do you think it is likely, Mathew, that this unfortunate man, Grayling, will be convicted of the crimes with which he stands charged?"

"There is not the slightest doubt but that he will, Miss," replied the old man, "the evidence that will be brought forward on his trial, it is said, will be so strong that nothing can save him."

"And should he be found guilty, Mathew?" asked Maria, in a tremulous tone.

"Why, then nothing can save him from the gallows, Miss," answered Mathew.

"Poor wretch!" exclaimed Maria, with a shudder of horror.

"Ah, Miss, you may well say wretch," observed old Mathew; "he was a most heartless scoundrel, and has richly merited hanging years ago; he does not deserve the slightest feeling of pity."

"Mercy and pity for our enemies, is one of the brightest attributes of Christianity, Mathew," said Maria, reprovingly, "and, however they may have injured us, that sentiment should ever be paramount in our bosoms."

"I know it should, Miss," returned Mathew, "but when I think of all the villanies of which Grayling has been guilty, my wrath overcomes my better feelings, and, God forgive me, I was going to say that I could almost exult in his downfall. Look at the many years of suffering he caused my late poor dear master; and did he not ultimately break his heart? at any rate, his violent conduct was the cause of hastening his death; and did he not even insult his cold remains, and send them to their final resting-place with no more ceremony than if they had been those of a complete stranger to him? But we could not expect that he would respect the remains of that being to whom he had so shamefully behaved while living."

"Alas! my poor benefactor, my ever kind and benevolent friend," exclaimed Maria, while tears filled her eyes, "happy indeed art thou that thou didst not live to see the disgrace which this misguided man has brought upon your name."

"Yes, Miss," responded Mathew, "it was indeed a blessing, and God knows my poor master had suffered enough before. But retribution is sure to fall upon the guilty sooner or later, and Grayling, whom it has overtaken just at the time when he thought himself most secure and fortunate, is a terrible example of this."

"He is, indeed," returned Maria, with a shudder; "but still I do hope that his life may be spared, to give him time to think upon his iniquities to repent."

They had now arrived at the cottage, and Clara, having hurried on first to apprise her mother of Maria's return, and who her companion was, Mrs. Jackson was prepared to receive them. Mathew no sooner beheld her, than he recognised in her the widow of his old friend, Mr. Jackson, with whom, some years before, he had been on terms of intimacy, and Mrs. Jackson, after a short time, remembered him, as he used to be a frequent visitor to their house formerly. They were very glad to meet each other, and the day passed cheerfully away, in conversation upon old times, and in relating various anecdotes of the kind which old people usually like to indulge in.

Mathew, however, did not fail deliberately and carefully to discuss with Maria the plans which he thought it would be advisable to adopt, and it was finally arranged that they should depart the next day for Rosemary Dell, and for the present take up their residence with Anthony and Jenny at Wallingford Hall, until they should hear from Mr. Wallingford, and know his wishes upon the subject.

In the confusion occasioned by the meeting, and the many matters they had to talk about, old Mathew had forgotten to inform Maria of one most important circumstance, which was, that he had received letters through Mr. Goodwin, directed to her from Ela and Fanny, which, as he saw the eagerness and anxiety that was depicted on her countenance, he immediately delivered to her, and, with a palpitating heart, Maria broke the seal of that one which bore the characters of Fanny first. With eager delight did she peruse the contents of this letter, and her tears flowed fast at the generous and affectionate sentiments it contained.

"Dear, dear Fanny," she cried, as she pressed her epistle to her lips, "you then are unchanged—you still are my own fond Fanny, and even though so many miles divide us, still do I feel as if you were now present to me, and speaking to me. Yes, each sentence here written, is a portrait of yourself, which is, and ever must be, engraven on my heart!"

Again she kissed the letter, and then proceeded to finish reading it. With the deepest interest she read that part which gave an account of Fanny's meeting with Lord Helvendon, and her glowing description of the perfections of his mind and person.

"And now, my dear Maria," continued Fanny, in her letter, "I dare say, by this time, you will be ready to put my letter by with a heigho! and 'alas! poor Fanny, your heart is no longer your own, I can plainly see!' Well, be it so; and do you know, if such is the case, you never imagined anything more correct in your life. And why should I deny that I love this Lord Helvendon, when I am convinced he is in every way worthy of my affections, and certain as I am that he feels a mutual passion? Oh, Maria, I should like you to see him; so handsome, so noble, so generous, equalled only by dear Walter, of whom he is a complete prototype. This will be sufficient to give you an idea of what he is.—Can you, then, my dear Maria, wonder that I should love a being like this? What delight would it afford me if you were here, beneath these ever-sunny skies, to share in the pleasures of our society; indeed, that is the only desideratum I have now at heart; and often do I think, with the most painful feelings, upon the distance that parts us, and of the uncertainty when we shall meet again."

"Dear Fanny," ejaculated Maria, when she came to this passage,—"most mutual are our sentiments upon this subject, and it is that painful uncertainty which often causes me some hours of the most poignant suffering. But you are happy, happy in the man of your choice, in one who loves you, and there is no one to oppose your affections; while I——'

The thoughts of Walter came so powerful'ly upon her memory, that her emotion checked her further utterance, and she was unable to proceed with the letter for a few minutes. It was a very long epistle; indeed, Fanny had apparently taken especial pains not to omit any particular which she knew, however trivial, would be important and interesting to Maria. All that she had thought, all that she had done, everything that had happened to her since they had parted from one another, was related in that letter, and nothing could be a stronger proof of the sincerity of Maria's attachment to her, than the avidity with which she perused it; and having once read, commenced it again, and re-perused it with as much care as if she had never seen a syllable of it before. In writing of Mr. Wallingford and Walter, there was evidently a marked change in the manners and style of Fanny; the former she merely inquired after with the coldness of a slight acquaintance, and of the latter she seemed to write with diffidence, although it was very clear that beneath all this assumption of indifference, there remained all that ardent feeling with which her heart had ever yearned towards them.

The letter of Ela was equally kind and

affectionate, but as regarded the particulars of what had occurred to them since they had left England, and how they were at present situated, was a mere repetition of what Fanny had so minutely detailed in her letter.

Knowing how anxious Ela and her daughter would be to hear from her, and how uneasy and surprised they would be that her answer should be so long delayed, Maria took an opportunity of retiring early, that she might write to them without any further delay, and Mathew, having made an arrangement with one of Mrs. Jackson's neighbours to pass the night in his cottage, retired.

The task which Maria had allotted to herself occupied her for a couple of hours; and delightful it was to her, when she could divulge all her thoughts, pour fourth all her sorrows, impart every secret of her heart, to a congenial soul; to one who would sympathise so sincerely with her, and who, she could almost imagine, was at that moment with her, and that she heard her gentle voice in soothing accents, breathing in her ear. It seemed to relieve her mind of an immense weight, and when she had done, she felt more tranquil than she had before for some time; and Clara having entered the chamber, they retired to rest.

Clara, however, could not sleep, for the thoughts that Maria was about to leave the next day were quite sufficient to keep her awake. The urbanity of Maria's manners never failed to make a deep impression upon hearts susceptible of kindly feelings; and so it was with poor Clara, who, from the first moment she had seen Maria, became so strongly prepossessed in her favour, that there was not anything she would not willingly have undertaken to have done—there was no risk which she would not have run to serve her.

"What are you sighing so heavily for, Clara?" asked Maria, after they had been in bed for some time, "why; any one to hear you would suppose you were in love."

"Ah! Miss," replied Clara, "it is not that; but I am afraid you would think me bold, and chide me for my rudeness, if I were to tell you what it is that makes me so sad."

"Why should I chide you, Clara?" observed Maria,—"I am certain you would not willingly do anything which should deserve censure; but tell me what is the matter with you?"

"Oh, Miss," said Clara, blushing, "I am ashamed to tell you, that I am."

"Silly girl!" ejaculated Maria, rather impatiently, "what have you got to be ashamed of?"

"Why, I do not know, Miss," answered Clara, "I do not know whether I ought to be ashamed. To be sure, one can't help one's feelings, and that's all about it."

"Ah! I see how it is," remarked Maria, smiling; "you are in love."

"Then it is with you, Miss Herbert," returned Clara, "for I declare I have taken such a fancy to you, that the whole and sole cause of my present melancholy is the thought that you are going away to-morrow, and the idea, the almost certainty, I may say, that we shall never meet again. You will, perhaps, excuse me, Miss, for the freedom of my speech, but you are so kind, and so familiar, that I feel towards you in a way which I cannot describe: but I only know this, Miss, that if you was in the same station of life as myself, I should not hesitate to say that I love you as well as if you were my own sister."

Maria was moved by the simplicity, yet evident sincerity, of the kind-hearted girl. "Those upon whom I have a claim by the ties of nature and consanguinity, abandon me," she reflected, "but among strangers, I find hearts that warm towards me, and who are ready to put themselves to any inconvenience to serve me."

"My good girl," she at length said, in reply to Clara, "I thank you for your opinion, which, I trust, is no more than my due, and that I shall ever deserve the character; but it is silly of you to take to heart a circumstance which is unavoidable; as to meeting again, that may happen, and very shortly too; but I assure you that, should we not, I shall ever remember with gratitude and esteem the services you have rendered to me."

"Oh! pray do not talk in that manner, Miss Herbert," said Clara. "I am sure I have done nothing that deserves praise or gratitude; but if you will sometimes condescend to think of me, I shall be so happy."

"You are a good, warm-hearted girl, Clara," exclaimed Maria, ardently, "and I am confident you will never do anything that will render you undeserving of my esteem and respect; therefore be assured that I will not forget the promise I have made you."

"Oh, thank you, Miss," eagerly ejaculated Clara, in tones that evinced her delight, "that is indeed kind, but no more than I might have expected from you."

After a short time longer, the conversation dropped, and Maria soon after fell off to sleep, when busy imagination presented to her fancy happy visions of Fanny, and all that she had so particularly described in her letter. It was blissful respite from her sorrows to be enabled, if only in ideality, to enjoy the society of her dearest friend again, and to feel a repetition of those pleasures they had, amidst all their many cares and trials, so frequently shared together. But sad was her disappointment when she awoke to a sense of her loneliness.

A good night's rest had tended greatly to recruit her strength, which had been much reduced by the recent trials she had been subjected to; and she arose to prepare for the journey with better spirits than she had for some time before experienced. She was also much gratified to perceive that old Mathew looked considerably better than he had done the day before, and he said that he now felt very little of the effects of his recent indisposition, and would, no doubt, in the course of a day or two, be completely restored to a state of convalesence. They had no arrangements to make for the journey, and and consequently they took their departure by the first coach.

As nothing of any importance occurred to them on the journey, we shall not occupy the time of the reader by recounting the particulars of it, but set them down without impediment or accident at Rosemary Dell.

How Maria's heart throbbed with mingled feelings of melancholy delight, as the noble towers of Wallingford Hall once more burst upon her view, and those scenes which she knew so well once more came upon her sight with all their former freshness. But, alas! what a change was there, since last she had trod that spot; then she was blest with the society of her friends, of Mr. Wallingford, of Walter, of Doctor Hartley, and of Fanny;—alas! where were they all now?——Doctor Hartley was an inmate of the silent tomb, and from the others she was divided by many, many miles; and it was quite uncertain whether or not she should ever behold them again. She was left alone, abandoned, deserted, and miserable!

The delight of honest Anthony and his wife upon once more beholding Maria, may be better imagined than we can find time to attempt to pourtray it; the account of the troubles she had undergone since she had left the Hall, had filled them with the most sincere regret, and they were in a terrible state of consternation when they heard of her having been seized and forced away by Mr. Barnell; but when Susan made her appearance, (who had arrived two days before,) everything was explained, and they were in raptures when they were informed that she was once more safe, and in a few days they might expect to see her at the Hall.

"Oh, Miss Maria," said Jenny, "I can assure you we have passed many a miserable hour since you have been away, thinking of you; and when we heard of the death of that good gentleman, poor old Doctor Hartley, and knew that you were once more left without a protector, we were completely wretched."

At the mention of Doctor Hartley, Maria sighed, and a tear started to her eye.

"Alas! my good Jenny," said she, "I did indeed loose a friend, a father, everything in that excellent man; oh, where, how can I ever replace the loss?—It is irreparable."

"Nay, my dear young lady," observed Anthony, "do not give way entirely to despair.

Providence is kind, and will not desert you while you continue to merit its protection. But I have something to tell you, which may not afford you much satisfaction."

"What is it, Anthony?" hastily inquired Maria;—"are there any fresh troubles in store for me?"

"I hope not, Miss," replied the old man; "but I do not like the present aspect of affairs; them confounded wretches, the Gipsies, whom I thought the late events, and the well merited and ignominious punishment of two of their abominable associates, would have effectually driven them from this quarter altogether, are once more in the neighbourhood of the Dell!"

"The Gipsies once more here?" reiterated Maria, turning very pale and trembling.

"Yes, Miss, they are, I assure you," returned Anthony; "they have taken up their quarters at the old Manor House; and so we may expect them to remain here for the winter. Some of them have even had the impudence to come here and ask for charity, and I gave it them, too, glad enough to get rid of them, and fearful if I did not, they might feel inclined to besiege the Hall, and murder me and Jenny; for we know very well from woful experience, that they do not care what they do to gratify their revenge."

"Good God!" ejaculated Maria, "am I never to be released from danger?"

"Do not fear, Miss," said Mathew, who was present when this conversation took place; "I am of opinion that they would not attempt to harm you; what object could they have in doing so?"

"Revenge," answered Maria. "Do you think that they have forgotten that I was one of the principal witnesses against their ill-fated comrades? and now when they know I am deprived of the protection of my friends, and that Doctor Hartley is no more, there is no knowing what they may be tempted to commit."

"One thing is certain," remarked Mathew; "which is, that it will be necessary to use every possible precaution to avoid the danger you apprehend. Your return to the Hall must not be made known any more than you can help; and I would advise you not to walk out alone to any distance from home. Anthony may be mistaken in the idea he has formed, that they will remain here all the winter, and in the interim you may hear from your uncle, who will be able to instruct you better how to act."

"That is very true," observed Anthony. "I am of your opinion, Mathew, and I do not think there will be much to dread from these people, that is, if Miss Herbert does not make her being here too-well known."

"And after all," said Mathew, "I do not think they would offer to interfere with her, if even they knew she was at the hall; the vengeance of the Gipsies is principally directed against Ela and her daughter; and now they are far away from their power, the cause of their revenge may be said to be in a manner in abeyance. As for Miss Herbert, they never, that I have heard of, exhibited any particular vindictive feelings towards her."

"Why, that is true," returned Maria, "but then we cannot say what effect their disappointment in the escape of Ela Beranzio and Fanny may have had upon them, and they may

RUPERT DARWIN THREATENING VENGEANCE TO LORD HELVENDON.

be ready to wreak that vengeance upon those who were connected with the late painful affair, and who are in England, to make up for those who have escaped them."

"At any rate," remarked Mathew, "it is no use meeting troubles half way; I think the safest plan for us to adopt would be, to make the magistrates acquainted with the proximity of our old enemies, and they no doubt will use the necessary precautions to prevent a breach of the peace."

"Then that is decidedly what I would not

No. 53.

do," said Anthony, "for if the Gipsies were not inclined to disturb us, that would be the very thing that would exasperate them into doing it, in my opinion; whereas, if we take no notice of them, and do not appear to suspect them of any bad intentions, all may pass off quiet."

"I am certainly of Anthony's opinion," said Maria, "and would therefore advise you not to do anything that may tend to excite the Gipsies."

"Of course I shall be guided by what you say, Miss," returned Mathew; "and after all, upon more mature reflection, I do not know but what Anthony's suggestion is a good one."

Here the subject for the present dropped, and Maria walked into the gardens of the hall, and wandered on towards the summer-house, in which she and Walter had passed so many happy hours, but which had at last been the scene of such tragical events. With a sigh she entered this now deserted place, and seating herself on that spot on which she and Walter had so often sat together, her thoughts became completely engrossed in reminiscences of the past, and in reflecting upon the probability of what other remarkable circumstances were in store for her. Alas! what a change had taken place since last she entered that summer-house; what a revolution had there been in the circumstances of the Wallingford family, and those connected with it.—And where was the companion in whose society she had passed so many happy hours; the companion of her childhood; the friend, the lover of her riper years?—Alas! fate had separated them, and she feared that separation was for ever!

Deep was the melancholy which took possession of her bosom, as thus she reflected; and unable to endure the horrors which the place excited, as she recalled to her memory the murder of the unfortunate Christabelle, she quitted it, and walked for a few minutes on the margin of the lake. With this, too, was associated many dismal ideas; and finding it impossible for her to shake off the heavy depression of spirits which the contemplation of all around created; she left the gardens, and walked once more into the hall.

She endeavoured for a while to divest her thoughts from the dreary subjects which had before occupied them by reading; and going to the library, she took a book from one of the shelves, and soon became so enchanted with the beauties of the author, as to gain an oblivion to the sorrows which had previously tormented her.

In Susan, Maria found a simple, but interesting, kind, and sincere companion; and she felt pleased to think that she had secured her services. Susan had become so devoted to Maria, that she would have done anything rather than incur her displeasure or censure.

Thus passed away three days, and nothing occurred to interrupt the peace of the inmates of Wallingford Hall, when intelligence reached Mathew of the self-destruction of Richard Grayling. It appeared that the unfortunate man had been committed to take his trial for the crimes with which he stood charged, when the same day that he was taken to the goal, he was found in his cell with his throat cut and quite dead. The razor with which he had done the dreadful deed was lying by his side; but how he had contrived to conceal it about his person, no one could imagine, as he had been strictly searched when 'he was brought to the prison.

"Heaven have mercy upon the unfortunate man," exclaimed Maria, fervently; "such is ever the reward of crime."

"And now, Miss Herbert," observed old Mathew, "the house and the whole of the property of the late Mr. Hartley are yours, and it is necessary that you should see to making some settlement about it."

"I will leave that entirely to you, good Mathew," said Maria; "that is, if you will not consider the job of too much trouble."

"Trouble, Miss?" answered Mathew, "oh, I think nothing of that; what trouble ought I to think too great for she who was beloved as a daughter by my poor dear master? But in regard to the house, how will you manage about that?"

"Why, I scarcely know," said Maria, "let me see;—ah! I have it—I will make a proposition to Mrs. Jackson and her daughter Clara to live in it and take care of it, and thus I shall be able to make them some little remuneration for the trouble they were put to for my sake, and to gratify the wishes of poor Clara in being near me. I will immediately write to them."

"There is no necessity for that, Miss," said Mathew, "because I shall be compelled to go to Bath to settle affairs there, and see after the property which is left in the house, and which now belongs to you; and I can, therefore, call upon Mrs. Jackson and talk the matter over with her."

"But I am afraid at your time of life, to attempt to go such a long journey again; it may be too much for your strength to bear," observed Maria.

"Do not mention it, I pray," said Mathew; "I feel fully competent to the task, for my health is now quite established, and I am not one of the weakest at my age. I like your plan respecting Mrs. Jackson and her daughter very much; she is a worthy woman, and I don't know any one who is better qualified to do what you wish."

After some further discussion, therefore, it was settled that Mathew should do has he said; and the following day accordingly, he left the hall and got inside the coach for Bath, with full authority from Maria to act as he thought proper, and as his judgment dictated.

Hitherto Maria had kept herself confined to the hall ; but at length, as she heard nothing more of the Gipsies, and thinking that there was no danger, she was at last tempted to venture to take a walk, although Anthony and his wife endeavoured to dissuade her from doing so. She was, however, accompanied by Susan.

They walked on for some distance, without anything occurring to alarm them. It was a very fine morning, and the air was reviving, and Maria and Susan were so well pleased with their walk that they did not think of returning.

Suddenly they found themselves near the village church. A thought immediately struck Maria ; it was a melancholy one, but still she could not resist the temptation which she had to indulge in it. It was to enter the church-yard, and gaze upon that tomb which contained the ashes of her late benefactor, Doctor Hartley.

She was not long in finding it. It was a plain tomb, on which was merely inscribed his name, and the day of his decease. Many were the tears Maria shed, as she gazed upon this dismal resting-place of him from whom she had, while living, experienced such unexampled kindness and disinterested affection.

"Blest spirit of him, whose mortal career was one of uninterrupted virtue and philanthropy," she ejaculated, "if you are permitted to watch over the beings you loved while living, oh, look down upon me, and protect me from those dangers to which I have lately been exposed, and give me strength and fortitude to support any other trials that may be in store for me !"

She uttered this prayer with much fervour, leaning over the tomb, with clasped hands and Susan responded to every sentence she spoke. After this, she continued in silent meditation for some minutes, and then taking the arm of Susan, she quitted the church-yard.

They now bent their steps towards the hall, but had not proceeded far, when Susan uttered a faint scream, and laid a firmer hold of the arm of Maria, at the same time looking round her with much apparent consternation.

"What is the matter, Susan ?" demanded Maria, with astonishment, "what has alarmed you."

"Oh, Miss, did you not see them ?" said the girl, once more looking back, and trembling with fear ; "ah ! they are gone now."

"For goodess' sake, what do you mean ?" said Maria ; " of whom are you speaking, who and what have you seen, to cause this alarm ?"

"Oh, Miss," answered Susan, " just as we came past the copse yonder, I am positive I saw two or three frightful-looking men peep from behind the trees as though they were

watching us, and when they saw that I observed them, they frowned so at me, and one of them shook his fist in a threatening manner at me."

"Surely you must have been mistaken, Susan," said Maria, who now partook largely of her fears ; " but let us hasten on our way home ; we shall soon reach the hall."

They now quickened their pace, but still Susan kept looking back every now and then, and it was very clear that her alarm was very little, if any abated.

"Oh, my God ! Miss," she suddenly exclaimed, "there they are again ;—look—look—they are coming this way ;—they are following us ! —Oh, dear."

Maria now looked behind her, and to her great consternation, beheld the confirmation of the words of Susan ; for pursuing them with rapid steps, were three or four ruffians, whom Maria immediately knew to be Gipsies.

When they saw that Maria looked back after them, they motioned her to wait until they came up, and the foremost one, in a loud and authoritative voice, commanded them to stop.

"Good heavens !" cried Maria, trembling with the utmost horror,—" what can they want ?—what will become of us ?"

She endeavoured to quicken her pace, and completely dragged Susan after her, but her limbs soon refused to perform their office, and breathless, leaned with terror against a tree to prevent her from sinking to the earth, while Susan was quite immovable. Before they could recover themselves, the fellows had come up with them, and Maria recognized in their swarthy features, and dark piercing eyes, some of the Gipsies belonging to the same gang as that which she had every reason to dread.

"It is her" said one of the men ; " seize her, and let us away !"

In a moment two of the ruffians grasped her arm violently, and attempted to drag her away, while Susan wrung her hands and screamed loudly for help.

"Stop that screech-owl's noise," exclaimed the man who had before spoken ; " stop her cries, I say."

No sooner was this order given, than one of the unmanly wretches raised his fist, and with a violent blow, felled the poor girl senseless to the earth.

"Away with her," said the man, to those who had hold of Maria, (who was so overcome with her terrors, that she could not move or utter the least outcry,) "leave this girl behind, we don't want her."

"Oh ! in mercy tell me, what would you with me, and why am I seized in this violent manher, " at length Maria found strength to utter. "Let me go, for the love of heaven."

"Psha ! do not heed her nonsense," said the fellow, who seemed to have the command of the party, "you know our orders and therefore if she does not go quietly, we must try whether we cannot make her."

" Save me ! save me ! oh, help !" shrieked Maria, as the ruffians dragged her away, and completely exhausted with struggling and her fears, she fainted.

When she recovered her senses, she rubbed her eyes, and looked fearfully around her ; at first, she could not distinguish any particular object ; but at last became sensible that she was reclining on some straw, and that she was covered with a coarse rug. With an emotion of the utmost consternation, as the events which had recently occurred to her rushed upon her recollection, she raised herself hastily, and by the red glare of a fire which was burning at the farther end of the place, and round which were gathered several men and women, who were evidently of the Gipsy tribe, she beheld herself in a lofty cavern, which seemed to be dug out of the bowels of the earth.

" Gracious heaven !" exclaimed the affrighted maiden, " where am I ?"

" Ah ! she has recovered," cried the harsh voice of a female, and the next moment one of the men, taking up a lamp from the table on which they had been carousing, several of them advanced towards Maria, and her terror may be readily imagined when she found herself in the presence of Rupert Darwin, Morna, Zelta, and several others of the Gipsies, who had ever been most violent.

" So," exclaimed Rubert, while a look of savage exultation passed over his features, " we have you now safely in our power, young lady ; and deprived of the protection of Mr. Hartley and your other friends, you will have no chance of obtaining your liberation, or of saving your life even, without you comply with our commands."

" Good God ! cried Maria, in despair, " am I for ever to be the victim of cruel destiny? What would you with me, and whither have ye brought me ?"

" You shall know that anon," said Rupert ; " let it suffice that here you are secure, and no one would ever think of looking for you here."

" Oh, for mercy's sake, keep me not in suspense," implored Maria, " tell me what are your designs with me, and what do you require me to do?"

" Ah ! you can suffer now," said the ruffian, fiercely ; " you know what it is to feel ; what think you then must have been the sufferings of the kindred of those unfortunate men, whose lives you assisted to swear away? What think you must have been the torments, the hellish torments of their kindred on the morning when they were led forth to a public scaffold, and there hanged like dogs, in the gaze of mocking hundreds of your pale-faced people? Think you the Gipsy tribe have no sense, no feeling ?

Think you they have no love for those in whose veins flows the same blood as in their own? Yes, they have, and yet you, you who have lent your aid to bring misery and sorrow upon them, think to excite their pity, their forbearance."

" Such pity as she gave to ours, will we grant to her," cried Morna, in a savage tone, and her large black eyes seemed to sparkle with more than mortal brightness. " What pity did she bestow, when she shamelessly came forward to swear away the lives of the father and his son ?"

" Oh, for mercy's sake spare me," exclaimed the terrified Maria, who marked with terror the revengeful and ferocious gestures of the Gipsy woman, and expected every minute to see her plunge her knife into her breast ; " I only spoke the truth, and entertained no vindictive feelings towards the unfortunate men. Why then should you seek to prosecute me ?"

" You appeal to me in vain," said Morna ; " insults, oppressions, degradations, the common lot of our wandering tribe, have steeled my heart against all such feelings, and to see you suffer, adds pleasure to my breast. Ah, I would have thee and all those concerned with thee in that affair which robbed us of our kindred, suffer greater torments than the mind can conceive, or the tongue give utterance to. It would be all too little to gratify my vengeance. Had it not been for the mad weakness of Jabella, long since should the murder of Mark Darwin and his son have been satiated in the blood of all their enemies. Fools that we were, to suffer them to escape us, when they might have been easily secured in our power. But if Ela and her daughter have escaped us, we have——"

" They have not escaped us," said Rupert, fiercely ; " they shall not escape us ; this girl knows perfectly well in what part of the country they are, and she shall either divulge it to us, or never more quit this cavern alive."

Maria averted her head in despair, and covering her face with her hands, groaned with the intense anguish of her mind.

" There, girl, thou hearest what Rupert says," ejaculated old Zelta, " and thou knowest that he will keep his word ; thou wilt, therefore, if thou art wise, consult thine own safety, by immediately revealing where the wretch Ela and her daughter are concealed."

" Never !" exclaimed Maria, in a sudden tone of determination ; " rather let me die, than be the means of sacrificing the lives of them."

" Ah ! say you so, young lady ?" cried Rupert, ferociously, as he brandished a knife, and seemed half-disposed to make use of it ; " but, methinks, you will say very different, when the moment of trial comes. But of this be certain, that unless you yield to our demands, a death of the most lingering torture shall certainly be your fate. Think not that we shall be afraid to commit the crime, for fear that we should afterwards be brought to justice, for we do not hesitate to perform any desperate deed, though we should be certain that we should swing for it the next moment. We are not to be intimidated;—death has no terrors for us, when we have the gratification of our revenge at heart. However, we will give you time to reflect upon it, and then, if you do not act according to our wishes, depend upon it, I will not fail to carry my threats into effect. Here you are secure from discovery; no one can form the least idea of where you are concealed; and no person can have any suspicion of where you are confined, or that you are in the power of our tribe. Follow me."

As the gipsy spoke, he took up a lamp, and motioned her towards a low archway, which seemed to lead to an inner cavern; but, once more bound up to a pitch of almost insupportable agony by the ruffian's words, she threw herself on her knees, and with streaming eyes and clasped hands, she implored him to relent, and take pity on her.

"Oh, do not turn a deaf ear to my supplications," she exclaimed; "I implore you to do so; as you hope for mercy hereafter, do not put your dreadful threats into execution, but release me, and I will readily promise you not to disclose to any person the circumstance of my seizure by your people."

"You know the terms," replied the ruffian; "you have only to reveal to me the place where Ela and her daughter are at present concealed, and you shall be at immediate liberty to depart."

Maria turned away in despair, and wrung her hands, and seeing it was no use to appeal to him, she followed him into a smaller cavern, in which was spread a pallet of straw, and which, with an old stool, was all the furniture the place contained. It was secured from the other cavern by a wooden door, and which had the means of fastening on the outside. Rupert placed the lamp on the damp ground, and then turning once more towards Maria, he said—

"Remember my words, and as you would save your life, obey me."

With these words, he quitted the place, and Maria was left to herself.

It would be a fruitless task for us to attempt to describe the feelings of Maria, when Rupert had retired; and when she found herself left to the mercy of the wretches whom she had so much reason to fear, with no means of making known to her friends her perilous situation, and completely in the power of Rupert and the others, she had, indeed, good cause to fear the worst; yet she was determined to suffer death rather than divulge to the villain Rupert the place where Ela and Fanny were at present. The damp of the place struck an icy chillness

to her heart, and she trembled violently as she crouched down upon the straw, and looked with a despairing eye upon the dreary cavern in which she was confined. The untowardness of her fate racked her mind greatly; no sooner had she escaped from one danger than she had become involved in another, and seemed as if she was to be perpetually the sport of Fortune.

"My God!" she cried, "I once more pray Thine Almighty aid and protection; and if it is Thy will that I should perish by the hands of these wretched people, grant me fortitude to meet my fate, rather than be the means of betraying to their insatiable vengeance those friends to whom my heart is devoted."

Frequently did the ribald and intemperate discourse of the gipsies reach her ears, and made her tremble, while, at the same time, she thought every moment to hear one of the ruffians enter and offer her some insult. But although they were evidently carousing and enjoying themselves, they did not offer to interrupt her; and, at length, they gradually became silent, and Maria, worn out with painful thought, stretched herself on the rude pallet, and, in spite of the misery which oppressed her mind, gradually sank of to sleep.

CHAPTER LX.

"Beware! link not thy fate to one
Who will prove to thee a curse,
Bringing upon thy devoted head
Misery incessant and insupportable.
Beware, I say: this goodly warning scorn'd,
Thou will have ample cause for regret,
When no mortal power can lend thee aid!"
THE CURSE.

IN the meantime, while all the events which we have been been describing in the preceding chapter were taking place, Ela and Fanny were restored to comparative happiness, and had even began to find an oblivion to the many afflicting circumstances which they had formerly encountered. The affection between the latter and Lord Helvendon increased, as every day brought to their knowledge some fresh virtue which they each of them possessed; and they thought upon the time which was destined to unite their fates with impatience, and anticipated the pleasure which would doubtless be the lot of two individuals every way so well formed to meet together. There was only one circumstance which at all damped the spirits of Fanny, and often interrupted her in her most joyous moments; this was her separation from Maria, and the uncertainty of what had become of her.

"Oh, how supremely blessed should I have been," soliloquised the kind hearted girl, "could but that dearest friend of my heart have been present on this auspicious occasion; what delight it would have afforded her to see me happy in possessing the affections of a man so deserving as my dear Frederick, and what rapture she would have experienced to have been one of the bridesmaids on the day of my nuptials."

These thoughts filled her gentle bosom with the most intense uneasiness, and she tried, but in vain, to shake it off. Walter, too, could he be made acquainted with her situation, and see the object of her choice, what unfeigned delight would it afforded him, and how ready would he be to acknowledge Lord Helvendon as a brother.

These thoughts gave rise to another of equal importance in the mind of Maria, and that was the change which her marriage with that young nobleman might cause in the bosom of her father. He might be no longer ashamed to acknowledge her, and yet, when she reflected that this would not be exacted from him by any increase of affection, or compunctious feelings of justice, but rather occasioned by pride, she felt that consumation would be anything but a source of pleasure to her.

In this manner, many weeks passed away, and nothing occurred to Ela or her daughter worthy of being mentioned in these pages; when, to the no small delight of them both, they received the letters from Maria, which she had forwarded as soon as she had arrived at Wallingford Hall. With the deepest interest did they both peruse the contents of these letters, and it may easily be imagined how sincerely they sympathised with Maria in her afflictions, and the manifold troubles which had attended her since their separation.

"Oh, that she was with us, dear mother," said Fanny; "here she would be perfectly free from all danger, and she would find that home and protection which her uncle has so heartlessly denied her. Lord Helvendon and his noble mother, I am sure, would be enraptured with her, and I know that you would look upon her with the same affectionate care as if she were your own child."

Ela made no reply to these observations for a few minutes, but she seemed to be buried in deep reflection; and at length, turning to her daughter, she said—

"This idea never occurred to me, Fanny, but I must confess that it is one which pleases me much; poor Maria is now, as we may say, left alone in the world, while here, beneath this lovely clime, and surrounded by every rational enjoyment, and by friends whose attachment she cannot doubt, she might soon be completely happy. Besides, what a delightful companion she would form to us both; and as Lord Helvendon and his mother appear to have made up their mind to settle in Italy, and I do not feel disposed to leave it, there is no cer-

tainty of our ever meeting again unless adopt this plan. You shall, my love, immediately return an answer to the affectiona letter of Maria, and make the proposition her."

With the utmost transport, Fanny set abo her task, delighted at the ready coinciden of her mother with her plans; and in a sho time, she had written one of the most affe tionate letters which had ever emanated fro her pen, and which, enclosing one from El was immediately despatched to England.

Fanny felt like a dead weight taken off h mind when she had completed this task, an she was extremely happy in anticipating th answer which Maria would return to the epistle Alas! little did she dream of the fresh trouble in which her unfortunate friend was involved or those which awaited her and her mother.

The next day Ela and Fanny, having bee on a visit to Lady Helvendon, at her house were returning in their carriage, accompanie by Lord Helvendon, when just as they reache the garden gates, the latter, who had been look ing out of the window very earnestly for some time, as if something particular had attracted his attention, suddenly exclaimed—

"This is very remarkable, certainly."

"What do you mean, my lord?" asked Ela and Fanny, both in one breath.

"Why, for the last mile that we have come," returned Lord Frederick, "I have observed strange, tall, rough-looking man, with dark and swarthy features of a Gipsy, apparently following the vehicle; and as soon as he saw it stop at the gates, he stopped also, and yonder he is standing, with his gaze fixed earnestly upon us, and to judge by his looks, with no very good feelings inhabiting his bosom at the present time."

"A Gipsy!" gasped forth Ela and Fanny together, and turning very pale.

"Yes, he certainly looks like one," returned Lord Helvendon; "but judge for yourselves See, he is standing there yet, with his arm folded across his chest, and he does not seem to have altered his position in the least."

With trembling haste, Ela and Fanny both looked from the carriage window at the same instant, but the man had turned round, an was then walking rapidly away. He was too far off for them to recognise him; but from what they could see of his person, they were strongly impressed with the idea that the had seen him before, and from the manner his dress, they were convinced that he was on of the Gipsy tribe.

"Good God! they have discovered our place of retreat," exclaimed Ela, sinking back i her seat, as the man disappeared from their view, "and even at this distance pursued u doubtless bent upon our destruction. Alas there is no escaping from their insatiate ven-geance."

"Oh, pray do not alarm yourself," said Lord Frederick, tenderly, as he took the arms of Ela and Fanny and led them into the house; "your supposition is too improbable to be entertained for a moment. Besides, if it should be as your terrors suggest, what have you to apprehend, when any attempt on the part of the wretches would be sure to be attended with punish-ment?"

Ela shook her head with a gloomy smile, as she returned—

"Alas! how little, my lord, do you know the desperate character of these people, or you would not have made the observations you have just given utterance to. To gratify their ven-geance, they are ready to run any risk, even to the forfeiture of their own lives; and their stratagems are always conducted in so secret and subtle a manner, that they very seldom fail in their undertakings. But it is no more than I thought, secure as we began to imagine ourselves in this place. It is no more than I said at first, that no distance could long pro-tect me from their vengeance, and that some time or other I should most assuredly fall by their hands."

"Oh, my dear madam, for Heaven's sake," expostulated Lord Helvendon, who was dread-fully uneasy at the apprehensions which Ela seemed to entertain.

"Nay, my lord," interrupted Ela, "this is no idle presentiment, of that I feel as confident as that I am in existence at this very moment; but it is not for myself I fear—for I have so long been prepared for such a result, and been so buffeted about by the world's misfortunes, as to become perfectly indifferent to it; no, it is for my poor girl, my Fanny, on whom they will not fail also to wreak their deadly hatred; oh, I cannot think upon that without a shudder of horror."

"You certainly must place too much confi-dence in the power of those wretches," said Lord Helvendon; "I can never persuade myself that, with all their determination and cunning, they would have the hardihood to attempt the desperate deeds you seem to be so apprehensive of."

"Alas!" said Ela, "you can form but very little idea of what they will not venture to do; I know what they have done, and what they will be ready to do again. They are all sworn to have the lives of me and my daughter, and they will not rest until they have accomplished that oath; and if one fails, there will be another ready at a moment's warning to supply his place. They are not so easily daunted as you appear to imagine they would be; and I am as certain that I, if not Fanny, shall fall by their hands as if the assassin's knife was at this moment entering my bosom. Oh, God, pro-tect my poor child, and for my own fate I care not."

"Pray appease your fears, my dearest mo-ther," ejaculated Fanny, whose countenance evinced the deepest emotion, occasioned partly by her own terrors, and the anguish of Ela: "let us put our trust in the Supreme Being, and He will assuredly avert the catastrophe we apprehend, and render futile all the designs of our enemies."

Lord Helvendon had been for the last few moments silent, but it was evident that his mind was experiencing the most painful agita-tion, and that he, in spite of what he had said to the contrary, partook largely of the terrors which Ela had so strongly expressed. At length, as a sudden thought seemed to strike him, he turned to Ela, and said—

"But, my dear madam, even admitting that you are correct in the desperate character you have given to these miscreants, you have no proof that the man we have observed was one of them, or that he was attracted to the spot by anything more than mere idle curi-osity."

"Why, my lord," hastily returned Ela, "you said yourself, that the man had the ap-pearance of one of the Gipsy tribe, and that he had the dark, swarthy features of one of that class of wanderers; and although I did not see his face, I am convinced that he was a Gipsy, and it strikes me forcibly, one that I have too much reason to fear."

"And who is that?" inquired Lord Helvendon.

"Rupert Darwin," replied Ela.

"Rupert Darwin, the son of——"

"The same," interrupted Ela; "and now, after what I have already related to you, my lord, concerning the blood-thirsty and des-perate character of this ruffian, can you won-der that I should be so alarmed; although my own safety is of the least consequence in my thoughts?"

Lord Helvendon, in spite of his affected scepticism, could not help shuddering, when Ela mentioned the name of that determined villain Rupert, and he again became silent for a short time, and seemed to be revolving in his thoughts the different observations which Ela had made upon the subject; at last, however, he remarked—

"But even admitting your conjecture to be right, as regards the identity of this fellow, I do not see that you have any occasion for all this violent alarm, as we can take proper steps to guard against any attempt which he might have the audacity to make. I will take care that nothing shall be left undone to frustrate any plan which he, or his infamous associates, may have in contemplation; I will not delay it at all, but use such immediate precautions as may be deemed most prudent under these circumstances. In the meantime, endeavour to banish your fears, and all may yet be well. I will immediately send home for three or four of my servants, who will remain in the house with you, in case, if there is more than one, they should have the audacity to make an attack upon the house; and above all, you must not walk out again, except in the garden, until you imagine that everything is secure, and I myself will not fail to be as constantly with you as business will permit.''

Ela and Fanny thanked him for the lively interest he took in their safety and happiness; but it was evident, from the melancholy tone in which they spoke, that they were far from being so sanguine upon the subject as himself; and after some further time spent in conversation, and in arranging their plans for security, his lordship very reluctantly took his departure.

Notwithstanding the incredulity with which he had pretended to treat the fears of Ela, he was in a great state of uneasiness from the circumstance; and as he slowly returned home, he reflected deeply upon what had taken place, and the assertions of Ela, as regarded the desperate and guilty character of the Gipsies; and from what he had hitherto heard of their doings, he could not be off placing great reliance in the truth of the same.

"Good God!'' he replied, "what misery has the unhappy connection of Ela and her daughter with these guilty people involved them in, and how terrible may be the result of it. At any rate, I will use every means in my power to prevent the wretches from gratifying their diabolical revenge.''

He made the best of his way home, and immediately despatched six stout men to the residence of Ela, well armed, and with instructions how to act in case of any danger. He also instructed several persons to endeavour to find out whether the Gipsies, any of them, were in that neighbourhood, and if they could descover a person answering the description of the man who had followed the carriage, and who Ela imagined was Rupert Darwin; if they did, they where deputed in secret to watch narrowly his actions, and to give him immediate notice when they saw anything to excite their suspicions.

When Lord Holvendon had made these arrangements, he felt a little more easy, but still his thoughts were wholly occupied with the strange and perplexing event, and, unable to rest while in such a state of doubt and uncertainty, he in the evening again rode over to the house, where he found everything quiet, although the fears of Ela and Fanny were evidently very little abated. He endeavoured to reassure them all that was in his power, but they profited very little by his arguments, and the evening was passed away in a very dull manner.

Ela now saw the folly of encouraging the least hope of being happy again in this world; and many were the bitter pangs she endured, as she anticipated the herrors that were yet in store for her and her ill-fated daughter. But, for her own part, she cared very little (although, for her daughter's sake, she wished to live), but it was the probability that that daughter would also fall a victim to the barbarity of the wretches, who seemed determined to hunt them to death, which tormented her, and racked her bosom more than all, and she was unable—in spite of all the efforts of Lord Helvendon, and the strength of the arguments he made use of,—to erase from her mind the impression that the crisis of her and her daughter's fate was approaching, and that they were both fated to fall by the hands of the Gipsies. But, how had they discovered the place of their retreat, after the many precautions they had taken to prevent discovery? She was quite at a loss to conjecture this, and at length gave up the task in despair, and endeavoured to regain somewhat of her tranquillity, and to resign herself to the will of Heaven. In this attempt, she, at last, partially succeeded, and likewise contrived to pacify the fears of Fanny, who upon the bare mention of the name of Rupert Darwin, felt a deadly chill run through her veins, and the blood appeared to congeal around her heart.

One thing, which tended more than all to urge Fanny to do her utmost to endeavour to conquer her emotions, was the grief it seemed to cause Lord Helvendon, and the anxiety she felt not to cause him to experience one moment's uneasiness, which it was in her power to alleviate. She, therefore, assumed a degree of composure when in his society and that of his amiable mother, which she was far from really feeling; and, in some measure, Lord Frederick was deceived by her, and had began to indulge in the hope that all would yet pass off well.

In this hope he was the more encouraged when three days passed away after they had seen the man who had occasioned them so much alarm, without anything particular taking place; and Lord Helvendon, rendered more confident, once more endeavoured to persuade Ela that she had been mistaken, and that the man could not belong to the Gipsy tribe, or, if he did, he was not one whom they had any occasion to fear.

"Oh, no,'' answered Ela, "my eye is not easily deceived; I am confident I was not mistaken; the person of the villain Rupert Darwin is too firmly stamped on my recollection for me not to know him again, although I had no opportunity of observing his features. It was most assuredly he; and though they may at present have particular reasons for not attempting to put their designs into execution, depend upon it, they are in secret only ripening the plot, and the storm will burst over our heads when we least expect it."

Lord Helvendon felt a renewal of all his former anguish and anxiety, when he heard Ela still so obstinately persist in her first opinion, and he was quite at a loss what steps to pursue; in fact he did not know anything more that he could do, to be prepared to resist any outrage which might be attempted to be committed, than that which he had done already.

LORD HELVENDON.

It was with a heavy heart Lord Helvendon walked from the residence of Ela and his betrothed on the evening of the fourth day; in fact, he felt more than usually depressed, and he had never felt so loath to quit them. Several times he walked back to the house and walked round it, watching whether there was anything which ought to raise his suspicions; but he saw nothing whatever; and at length, he slowly bent his steps towards home.

His way lay along one of the public promenades, and he had only proceeded a short distance in that direction, when, by the light of the moon, he beheld the shadow of a human form upon the ground, and looking up, he was rather startled and surprised to see the tall figure of a man, with folded arms, standing across his path, and, apparently, awaiting his approach.

Coming so unexpectedly upon him as this circumstance did, Lord Helvendon did not, at first, know what to do, and paused suddenly; but seeing that the man did not offer to move, he walked boldly up to him, and, as the reader may guess, his astonishment was not by any means diminished, when he recognised in him the very fellow who had caused all the alarm which, for the last few days, had occupied the minds of Ela, Fanny, and himself.

He was a determined, ruffian-looking man, and, in every respect, answering the description which Ela had given of Rupert Darwin. In this lone spot (for it was getting late), and quite unarmed, he felt himself anything but comfortable.

The man seemed to observe his confusion and alarm with exultation, and putting on a satirical grin, with the utmost effrontery and familiarity, he thus addressed himself to Lord Helvendon.

"You are late from your lady-love's, my Lord Helvendon; the gipsy's brat, the wandering outcast's offspring, it appears, has the magnetic power to detain you in her company; she will not have it long, though."

More and more surprised and bewildered by the man mentioning his name, and the singularity of his words, Lord Helvendon was, for a moment or two, unable to reply to him; but at length, seeing that the fellow's boldness was likely to increase, from the effect which he could not but observe that his words had taken upon him, he hastily overcame his confusion, and assuming all his former dignity, he demanded—

"Who are you, fellow, who use my name so familiarly: and how dare you obstruct my path?"

"How dare I?" repeated the ruffian, scornfully? "ha! ha! ha!—It is not a trifle that I am not prepared to dare; and, at any rate, I am not to be intimidated from my purpose by such as Lord Frederick Helvendon, although he possesses title and wealth. The path here, at any rate, in a foreign land, is as free for me as it is for you, and I shall not budge an inch to accommodate you, depend upon it. It may be that the time is not far distant when the fellow, as you have been pleased to call me, shall have food for exultation, and when Lord Helvendon may think upon him with dread.

"Villain!" cried his lordship, aroused by his words, "am I to be insulted thus? Tell me, I command you, who and what you are,

and what is your purpose in stopping me; is robbery your aim?"

"Robbery?" reiterated the man, with another contemptuous laugh? "oh, no; had that been my purpose, I could soon effect it. But I will tell you who I am, and be sure you convey the same to Ela Beranzio, and she you have chosen to be your bride; doubtless they will be delighted to hear it; that is, if they have not, since they have come into the possession of plenty of the yellow gold, become too proud to acknowledge their old acquaintances; tell them you have seen Rupert Darwin; that he has discovered their retreat, in spite of their secrecy and their ingenuity, and that he has come all the way from England with the determination of wreaking that vengeance on their heads which the blood of his murdered father and brother calls aloud for. Tell them this, I say; and add, although they imagine themselves secure in the protection of you and those you employ, that nothing shall prevent me from ultimately gratifying that revenge which I have long contemplated.'

"Wretch, daring miscreant!" exclaimed Lord Helvendon, wound up to the highest pitch of desperation by the insolent threats of Rupert, "stand back and let me pass, or——"

"Hold, my lord!" interrupted Rupert, drawing forth a long-bladed knife from underneath his coat;—"unless you would rush on death, you will not attempt to proceed further. You have a desperate man to deal with, and one who values not his own life, to satiate his hatred and revenge."

The gipsy brandished the knife as he spoke with menacing gestures, and Lord Helvendon, who was quite unharmed, and in point of muscular strength totally unable to cope with him, involuntarily stepped back, and gazed at Rupert with a mixture of astonishment and irresistible dread.

"You have acted wisely to do as I bid you," said the gipsy.—"Had you not, this knife, ere now, would have been buried in your heart. Tell Ela and her daughter, that Rupert Darwin sends to them his curses, his bitterest malediction, and swears not to rest night or day, until he has died his hands in their blood. Mark me, Lord Helvendon—Fanny Beranzio will never be your bride;—there is a fate between you and her, which renders such an alliance hopeless. But surely the proud Lord Helvendon does not soar much, when he seeks to wed one of that wandering, oppressed, scorned, and degraded race, whom he affects to despise."

"Am I to stand here to be taunted and insulted by a wretch——"

"Did I value a name a breath of wind, you might repent this language, my Lord Helvendon," said Rupert;—"however, it is not with you I would seek to quarrel, unless you attempt to thwart me in my purpose, and then you must take the consequences. Remember my message to Ela Beranzio and her daughter, and bid them, from me, tremble !"

Before Lord Helvendon could make any reply to this speech, the ruffian had turned upon his heel, and hurrying from the spot, was very soon out of sight.

Lord Helvendon stood for some moments after his departure so much amazed at the adventure, that he was unable to move ;—but at length, acting upon the impulse of the moment, he determined to return to the residence of Ela and her daughter, and put them on their guard, and also to make preparations (for he had, no doubt, not attempted the accomplishment of his bloodthirsty design alone) against any attack he might contemplate making. Before, however, he had proceeded far, he changed his mind, and fearful of throwing them into alarm, and which might be attended with the most serious and fatal consequences, he turned back, and once more made his way towards his own house, deeply reflecting upon all that had taken place on his meeting with the gipsy, and the menaces which he had given utterance to, and which, from the apparent determined character of the man, he had no doubt he would make every effort to put into execution.

The meeting with the miscreant Rupert served Lord Helveldon with the subject of much harrowing reflection, and he had but little sleep that night. To his mother he imparted what had taken place, and she expressed an alarm equal to his own; but still upon more mature reflection, she said, that she could not imagine but that, by using proper precaution, they might set the threats of the gipsy ruffian at defiance. She advised her son, by all means, not to let Ela or her daughter know what had taken place, as it would so terrify them, in all probability, that they would be prevented from using that proper nerve and caution which would be necessary for them to maintain under the circumstances.

Lord Helvendon could not but acknowledge the propriety of this advice, and promised strictly to follow it. He waited impatiently for the morning, and at an early hour he walked over to the house of Ela, anxious to see whether all was safe, or if anything had occurred to give him cause to apprehend any immediate danger ;—having previously given orders to several more men to hold themselves in readiness to act at a moments notice, should there be any occasion for their services, and to watch near the place. He was anxious that they should, if possible, get the villain Rupert in their power, which effected, he was in hopes that the danger to be apprehended would be trifling, if any.

Upon reaching the house, everything appeared the same as when he had left it the night before, and Ela and Fanny in rather better spirits than usual. They were astonished at his visiting them so early, but he made an excuse by saying that the fineness of the morning had tempted him to walk forth sooner than was his ordinary custom, and he knew no better place where he could walk to, than the house which contained the object of his dearest affections.

Fanny blushed, and cast her eyes to the ground at this compliment; but she made no reply.

Notwithstanding all the efforts, however, of Lord Helvendon to conceal his agitation from Ela and her daughter, they were not long in discovering that something more than common disturbed him; and at length Ela questioned him about it. He was confused, and at first sought to evade the question and affected to smile; but that would not do for Ela, who again urged her question, and was aided by Fanny, who felt considerable uneasiness at the paleness of Lord Frederick, and at the restlessness of his manner. Interrogated so closely, he scarcely knew how to answer; but at length he said that he had been rather indisposed all night with a violent head-ache, and it was probably that which made him look pale and ill.

Ela shook her head incredulously; and after a short pause, said—

" This, my lord, I fear is only an evasion. Something has occurred which you do not wish us to know ;—but my own mind can suggest to me the cause, as well as if you had already divulged it. You have seen *him* !"

" Seen *him* ; – who ?" interrogated Lord Helvendon.

" Rupert Darwin," answered Ela, and she fixed her penetrating eye with searching earnestness upon his countenance.

Lord Helvendon started, and his confusion was greatly increased.

" Ah, my lord," continued Ela, " I see I have guessed rightly, and it is useless for you longer to deny it. I was certain it was him we saw, and I was as conscious of the way he would proceed in his dark and villainous plot, as if he had himself made me his confidant. It is the wretch's delight to see his victims writhe in agony before he strikes the final blow. Now, tell me, for it is useless longer to deny it, where saw you the villain, and what said he to you?"

Lord Helvendon saw that any evasion he might now attempt to make, would have no effect, and he therefore, with much reluctance, related his meeting with Rupert Darwin, but did not state the precise words as he had spoken them to him. Ela and Fanny listened with the most breathless attention as he proceeded, and the terror of the latter was so great that she seemed, with great difficulty, to prevent herself from sinking to the floor.

"Yes, I knew it was so," said Ela; "I knew well that it was he, my bitterest foe, who will not rest until he has completed his blood-thirsty purpose. Ah! Rupert, you need not have sent your threats to me and mine; it was quite sufficient to mention your name; that alone carries death along with it."

"Oh, God!" cried Fanny, weeping—"what will become of us?—How shall we avoid the threatened danger?"

"It is unavoidable, my poor girl," said Ela, in tones of despair.

Lord Helvendon paced the room with hasty and uneven steps, in great agitation.

"But, surely, there is some means of escaping from these wretches?" he said. "If you think it advisable not to come into collision with them, could we not by secretly quitting the country, avoid them, and remain concealed until we could bring them to the bar of justice, and prevent them from making any future attempt at annoying us?"

Ela shook her head.

"Where can we fly that their cunning would not find us?" said she "Did you not and our friends imagine we were secure when we came hither? but you see they have been deceived. No one can form any adequate conception of the craftiness of those people, but those who have had any connection with them; and, indeed, so singular is at times the manner in which they accomplish their ends, that they might really be imagined to possess that power of divination to which they lay claim."

Lord Helvendon tried all the force of the eloquence he was possessed of, to console and appease the fears of Ela and Fanny; and after considerable pains he did partially succeed; but the day passed away in the most gloomy manner, although nothing occurred to cause them any alarm.

His lordship could not be persuaded to leave the house until a very late hour at night, and he then did so with the greatest reluctance.

It was midnight by the time he reached one of the principal streets which led to his own residence; and he was so deeply wrapped in thought as to take no notice of surrounding objects; but just as he arrived at the corner, he was startled by hearing a rustling sound, and the next moment a man, wrapped in a huge mantle, and masked, rushed upon him, and attempted to plunge a poniard into his breast. Fortunately, however, he caught the bravo's arm, before he could effect his diabolical purpose; and after a brief but desperate struggle, he succeeded in wresting the murderous weapon from his hand, and immediately plunged it into his body. The man uttered a deep groan, and rushed away from the spot, while Lord Helvendon was so surprised and thunderstruck at the circumstance, that he was unable to pursue him, and he soon disappeared in the darkness.

Having recovered in some measure from the confusion into which this occurrence had thrown him, Lord Helvendon thought it was advisable to make the best of his way home, lest the bravo might have some accomplices, who might rush suddenly upon him, and effect the crime which he had failed in.

He reached his residence in safety, where he found Lady Helvendon still up, she being so anxious to hear if anything had happened to Ela or Fanny.

Fearful of seriously alarming his amiable parent, he disguised his agitation as much as possible, and concealed from her the alarming adventure he had just met with, and she attributed what emotion he exhibited to the agitation which his anxiety about Ela and Fanny occasioned.

Lord Helvendon retired almost immediately to his chamber, and then gave himself up to the most serious reflections upon the last event which had occurred to him. Who the individual could be who sought his life he could not imagine, for he was totally unconscious of giving any one the slightest cause for enmity. Could it originate in Rupert Darwin, who might be anxious to take his life, for the purpose of more fully gratifying his revenge against Ela and Fanny, or with the design of depriving them of his aid or protection? But still he could not make up his mind to that conclusion; and the most probable conjecture that he could come to at last, was, that the ruffian had mistaken him for some other person in the darkness of the night; and this idea greatly allayed his fears. He, however, resolved to use the utmost precaution for the future, and never to venture out again without having the means of defence about him.

A fortnight elapsed, and nothing transpired to create any apprehension, and they gradually became more composed. But Ela, although, for the sake of her daughter, put on the semblance of tranquillity, her bosom was the abode of the utmost anguish, and she viewed this calm only as the prelude to the storm which she dreaded was about to burst over them. Too well did she know the character of Rupert to imagine for a moment that he would abandon his project; and if he were even to do so, were not all the others sworn to do the deed, or perish in the attempt?—Oh, yes, they were, and the fate of she and her unfortunate child, she felt was certain. It is useless to attempt to describe the intense agony which racked and distracted her bosom, as she thus reflected; but it was not her own fate that she so trembled at, could she have been certain that the vengeance of the gipsies would be satiated by her death alone. For her own part, she had been so buffetted about in the world's troubles, that she had little reason to wish to remain in it, any further than to be the comforter of Fanny. She would shortly be united to a worthy man; and could she secure her from the malice of those who had proved their greatest enemies, she could leave the world without regret; for she would then be confident that Fanny, in the society of her husband, would be happy. There was a hope, indeed, which would occasionally dart upon her mind, which was, that by some accident Rupert would be prevented from making the diabolical attempt he had in contemplation for the present; and that, during the delay, they might contrive some means of leaving the country privately, and thus avert the apprehended evil for a time, at any rate, if not altogether; for every delay gave room to hope that something might occur to render the plans of the gipsies abortive altogether.

Lord Helvendon had not made Ela or her daughter acquainted with his adventure with the bravo, for he knew it would only seriously alarm them upon his account, and that they could not assist him by any advice in the matter; and it was very prudent that he did so, for it saved them an immense deal of anguish and fear; and they had already almost more than they could find fortitude to withstand.

To add to the uneasiness of Ela and her daughter, although more than sufficient time had elapsed since they had written to Maria, they had not received any answer from her, and they could not imagine what could be the reason of it. Something particular must have happened to her they were certain, or she would not have neglected writing; she must be ill, or some accident had befallen her.—Perhaps, however, they reflected, the letters had miscarried? A thousand ideas occurred to them, which were rejected almost as soon as formed; but the latter one seemed to be the most probable, and they therefore determined to write again immediately, telling her the particulars that had happened to them, and requesting her to answer them with the utmost despatch, and inform them of everything about herself, and in which she knew they were so deeply interested. They also wrote a letter to old Mathew, in case anything should have transpired to have rendered an answer from Maria impossible, and in which they urgently requested him, at any rate, to write to them immediately on the receipt of theirs, and to make them acquainted with all those particulars they were so anxious to hear. This done, they felt more at their ease; and as nothing more occurred at present to alarm them, they regained, in a considerable degree, their former tranquillity.

Lord Helvendon, too, became more composed and satisfied that something had occurred to cause the gipsies to abandon their designs, and that it would yet be in their power entirely to defeat them. He also felt convinced that his idea as regarded the bravo having made a mistake as to the identity of his person, was correct, for he had received to further interruption, neither had he ever heard, in the remotest manner, anything at all alluding to the affair.

Another month passed away, in the same quiet uninterrupted manner. Nothing had been heard of Rupert Darwin or his associates; and could Fanny have heard from Maria, and been assured that she was in safety, she would have been comparatively happy again. She and Lord Helvendon had resumed their customary rambles; and once more the day for their nuptials was appointed, and they anticipated it with sentiments of delight and impatience. Very little preparations, however, were made for the joyful occasion, for it was the intention of them all that the ceremony should take place as privately as possible, as that it should be solemnized in a little private chapel, which Lady Helvendon had had erected on the grounds surrounding her house, for her own devotions. After the ceremony, it was planned that the new-married couple and their friends should all depart from the place as secretly as possible, and their return to it be guided by circumstances.

This plan met with the approbation of all parties, and they hoped from it the best results; but, still the great drawback upon the certain happiness of Fanny was the continued silence of Maria.

At length, however, they received a letter from Wallingford Hall. It was in the handwriting of Mathew; and as soon as Ela and Fanny saw it, their hearts sunk within them, and they felt certain that something particular had happened to the poor girl, or it was very clear that she would have written herself. The contents of the letter confirmed their worst surmises, and filled their bosoms with the most insupportable anguish. Poor old Mathew informed them, after several prefatory remarks, expressive of the sorrow he was at that time labouring under, that Maria had suddenly disappeared from the hall, and not the least clue could be gained to the place of her concealment, or in whose power she was, although it was very strongly suspected that the gipsies had carried her away, as they had taken up their residence at the old Manor House at the time, and immediately after her disappearance they had also left the place, and they had been unable to gain any information as to the direction they had taken. The old man added, that every effort had been used to discover Maria, but without success, and that he had written to Mr. Wallingford upon the subject, but had not, as yet, received any answer.

Terrible, indeed, was the distress that this intelligence imparted to Ela and Fanny. They were for some time, as it were, completely paralysed at the news. When, however, they could more deliberately reflect upon the painful subject, they were of the opinion of old Mathew, namely, that she had fallen into the power of the gipsies, who, they feared, would not fail to wreak their vengeance upon her head, for the part she had taken on the trial of Mark Darwin and his son. Their horror at this idea exceeded all bounds, and many were the tears of bitter anguish which they both shed for her unfortunate fate. Perhaps, already she had fallen by their hands, and her mouldering remains were now mouldering in the earth.

"Alas! alas! poor girl!" cried Fanny, wringing her hands, "and who is it that has brought you to all this misery—who is it that must be blamed as the indirect cause of your death, if you are indeed murdered, but my wretched mother and myself? Oh, God! surely a curse attends us, for we bring misery, and sorrow, and shame, wherever we appear!"

Almost immediately after they had read this melancholy epistle, Fanny wrote an answer to Mathew, in which she fully described the anguish and sorrow into which his information had thrown them, and requesting him to prosecute his inquiries with increased spirit, and also to offer a large reward to any one who could give them any intelligence upon the fatal subject. By the instructions of her mother, too, Fanny gave him some minute directions as to the most probable method of tracking the gipsies, and the different places they were in the habit of frequenting, and desiring him to lose no time in writing and letting them know how he proceeded, and whether his efforts had been attended with anything like success.

Soon after they had despatched this letter, strange doubts and perplexing ideas crowded upon their minds. If Maria had been seized by the gipsies, was it before Rupert had left England or since, and had he now quitted Italy and rejoined his associates? Upon this subject they found it impossible to come to any reasonable conclusion, and they at length abandoned it in despair. Had Barnell or Richard Grayling been still living, they would have been inclined to have thought that she had again fallen into the hands of one of them; but as it was, it was very evident that she was detained somewhere against her will, and who could they suspect but the gipsies?

In this state of doubt, agitation, and uncertainty, they could think of nothing else, and the wedding was postponed until they had obtained positive information concerning the place of concealment, or the fate of the unfortunate girl; and they waited with the greatest anxiety until they could again hear from Mathew.

While they were still immersed in this painful state of perplexity, their astonishment and delight may be more easily imagined than language can pourtray it, when they received a letter, the superscription of which they immediately knew to be in the handwriting of Maria. With trembling and eager haste, they broke the seal; and the first sentences took a dead weight off their hearts; Maria was once more safe, and at Wallingford Hall!

A spontaneous exclamation of thanksgiving to Providence for this, immediately escaped the bosoms of Ela and Fanny, and it was several minutes before they had sufficiently recovered themselves to be able to finish perusing the contents of the letter. After warmly expressing her sentiments as regarded them, and her terror at the circumstance of their being again pursued by their old and savage enemies, the gipsies, she proceeded to furnish them with the particulars of everything that had happened to her since she had before had an opportunity of writing to them. With her seisure and subsequent confinement in the cavern, the reader is already acquainted. We shall, therefore, give the account of what she afterwards suffered, and by what means she had been permitted again to go at large, in her own words.

"I need not describe to you, my dear friends," she writes, "the dreadful anguish of mind I endured after Rupert Darwin and the others had left me to myself. My anguish was so great that it was wonderful I did not sink under it. Well did I know the character of the heartless wretches in whose power I was, and fully confident was I that what they said, they would not fail to put into execution; and nothing but a terrible and untimely death stared me in the face; for what was the alternative they offered me?—the betrayal of you, my dear friends, into their power!—Oh, no; a thousand deaths would have been preferable to that!—You may form an idea of the suffering to which I was subjected through my firmly and determinedly refusing to comply with their desires; insults, upbraidings, threats, and maledictions, were hourly heaped upon me, by Rupert, old Zelta, Morna, and the others. Two or three times the former seized me in his ruffian grasp, and brandishing a knife, threatened me with instant death if I any longer remained obstinate; but still Providence gave me strength to resist all, and most miraculously always interposed to save me from the fate with which I was threatened.

But it was the consciousness of the rectitude of my own conduct which sustained me throughout all these trials, and I determined to lose my life sooner than be the means of betraying you, my dear friends, to your implacable enemies. God knows, I had little to wish to live for, pursued by misfortune as I had ever been, with no other prospect around me; I was alone in the world, separated by many miles from those who I knew sincerely loved me, and life had become, as it were, a blank to me. But yet to die by so violent a manner, I shuddered with horror, and my blood froze in my vains at the idea. I remembered the dreadful death of the unfortunate Christabelle Wallingford, and my terror was greater than I can describe, when I reflected that probably, alas! I was doomed to meet a similar fate. Yet I was resolved, however horrible it might be, to encounter it, rather than reveal to the wretches the place were you were concealed.

"Zelta and Morna were, if possible, more savage in their conduct than the ruffian Rupert; and frequently did I expect that they would themselves have buried their knives in my breast; and they would, too, of that I am convinced, had they not been withheld from doing so by the inteference of Rupert.

"The place of my concealment I afterwards found was a cavern which communicated with one of the subterraneous passages underneath the old Manor House, whither I had been conveyed during my insensibility. You may judge, my dear friends, how great must have been my despair, when I reflected upon this circumstance, and the improbability there was of my friends, or any person who might feel disposed to interfere in my behalf, ever having any suspicion of the place of any incarceration; nay, they would not, most likely, imagine that I was in the power of the gipsies. A better retreat, or a place more adapted for the perpetration of their iniquities, they could have selected. Oh, my dear Fanny, need I tell you how often my thoughts were fixed upon you and your mother, and how I trembled at even the most distant apprehension that the wretches who held me in confinement should, by some accident, become acquainted with that which I was so firmly resolved not to divulge, namely, the place in which you were concealed? Alas! alas!— those apprehensions were too fatally realised, and perhaps, even now, my beloved friends, while I am addressing this epistle to you, the monster Rupert may have accomplished his diabolical purpose, and you may rest beneath the cold sod.

"Frequently, when left to the indulgence of my thoughts, I would trace through the long vista of by-gone years, the sunny scenes of childhood, and picture, in fancy's mirror, the home of infancy and youth; that home with its evergreen porch, and its little parteree—with its orchard and woodbine, its village church, and its long green lanes—with its meek-eyed minister, and honest-hearted pedagogue—its lounging villagers, and a long line of laughing running, gambolling school-boys—all glowing and glad in the vesper beams of a summer's sun. Or, when the hills had put on their mantles of snow, and the winds of winter whistled in fitful gusts through the naked branches of the leafless trees, it is a relief, my dear friends, when we are in the midst of care, and all around is cold and drear, to fancy oneself back again near the hearth of our childhood—to see the blazing faggot, and warm fire-side—the Christmas group, with its sparkling, bubbling cheer—to hear once more the fairy legend, or the awe-inspiring ghost tale;—these, with a thousand similar tender reminiscences, all deeply interwoven with a memory of the past, bring before our mental vision the elysian days of childhood. Even though age may have dimmed the eye and palsied the step, in imagination we are still the same merry, careless, light-hearted creatures—buoyant with hope, ruddy with health—as we were sixty years ago. The past is but a name; all, all his present;—childhood, adolescence, and maturity, seem but the flitting of a thought. That which was, is now, and will be, so long as memory holds her empire over the soul.

"But I am straying from the subject, and I am fearful you will begin to think that I grow tedious. These were, however, frequently the subject of my thoughts, and they alone had the power to estrange my mind from the certainty of my present misery; but alas! how transient was this relief; how quickly would the wretchedness, the horror of my situation, burst upon my mind, and then my grief would seem to have acquired redoubled power.

"Three days and nights of horror passed away without any decrease of my suffering.— I shall, I know, my dear friends, harrow up your feelings, when I inform you all I suffered; and yet, by a fatal accident, all my good intentions were rendered abortive. On the fourth day, Rupert came to me, and again endeavoured to make me reveal to him the place where you were concealed, but in vain; threats, imprecations, were alike fruitless, for I remained firm, and he was so exasperated at last, that he struck me a violent blow, which rendered me insensible."

"Unmanly, brutal ruffian!" exclaimed Ela and Fanny, in a breath, when they came to this passage in the letter of Maria, and Fanny was so agitated, that it was several moments ere she could compose herself sufficiently to proceed.— At length, however, she did resume, as follows:—

"When I had recovered my senses, the villain Rupert again made his appearance before me, and he then informed me, that he should only give me to the following day to reflect upon it, when, if I did not comply with his commands, I might expect to die. I heard this resolution with more fortitude than I had imagined I could have evinced, and the wretch retired. Indeed, I had, I may say, made up my mind for the worst, and left my fate in the hands of Omnipotence, who, I knew, would not desert me in the hour of danger. Yet, to die without one friend near to sooth me in my last moments, or to shed the pitying tear at my untimely fate—to die so young, and such a death!—these were, indeed, horrible reflections, and I shrank from them with an innate feeling of disgust and terror. All that night I passed in offering up prayers to the Almighty, and imploring His protection to you and Fanny. And there was another too,—oh, I need not mention his name, a name that I am forbidden to think upon; but which, in spite of the stern decree of his father, would rush upon my memory, in all the vivid colours which my fondest, my most enthusiastic admiration pictured.— Need I say that one was Walter? My imagination recalled all the manifold graces of his mind and person to my recollection, all the many blissful days we have passed together; days when we were unconscious of sorrow, and dreamed not that we should ever experience it. Alas! were those days never again to return? Were we fated never again to behold each other? How often, I ruminated, in the wildness of unfettered youth, had we together bounded over the summits of my native hills.— Often, for me, had Walter chased, with shouting and clapping, the gambolling squirrel, as it leaped from branch to branch, and tree to tree, until, wearied by the violence of the exercise, and the glowing heat of a meridian midsummer's sun, we have seated ourselves upon a bed of mountain heather. There, canopied by the bright blue sky, glowing and still, without a cloud to dim the transparency of the deep etherial void, would we sit, gazing upon the sea, whose mighty water—with scarcely a wave to dimple the serenity of its peaceful bosom—stretched silent and deep in the far, far west. Oh, with what rapture have we gazed upon each little bark, as its massy hull, with sails set, followed its trackless course to leeward; growing smaller and fainter as it receded from the straining eye, until nothing was seen but a small white sail, floating, like a sea bird, on the surface of the waters, which gradually sank in the misty distance. These were the thoughts that continually haunted my imagination, and, oh, my dear friends, need I tell you what anguish they caused me? Oh, no, I am certain I need not. Alas! such happy scenes, such joyous moments, as those I have been depicting, were gone never to return again; myself and Walter were separated never to meet any more;—he might never know the fate of she who had so fondly loved him. And would he ever bestow a tear upon her memory? —Oh, yes, too well did I know the heart of my beloved cousin to doubt his constancy.—

And what would be his torments, when he was made acquainted with my mysterious disappearance? Alas! when I thought of the dreadful sufferings he would endure, my own misery was redoubled, and it was only by the most resolute exertion that I was enabled to preserve anything like fortitude under the painful, the trying, the apparently hopeless circumstances.

"But again I grow tedious. I will now come to the point where all my praiseworthy determinations were rendered completely futile. On the fourth morning, after having indulged in such ruminations as I have described above, I took out the letters which I had received from you and Fanny, and which I had carried in my bosom ever since I received them, and began once more to retrace those characters which had imparted to me so much pleasure.— With the most intense melancholy did I peruse their contents, and dwelt upon every sentence with that eagerness, which the melancholy situation I was placed in occasioned. I could almost imagine that you were present, and were bidding me farewell, and expressing the grateful sense of the resolution I had formed. I could, in fancy, hear you bless me for that resolution; and as I did so, my courage increased, and I prepared myself for the interview with Rupert, which I expected would take place every moment.

"I was just beginning to fold the letters up again, when I heard some one behind me. The next instant they were snatched from my hands. I turned round with terror, and judge my consternation, distraction, and confusion, when I beheld Rupert standing in the cavern, and his eyes glaring upon the letters with looks of fiendish triumph and exultation. I uttered a loud scream, knowing that your address was affixed to the epistles, and made a futile effort to snatch them from the villain's grasp; but he laughed at me scornfully, and in a voice which bespoke his exultation, exclaimed—

"'Ah! by Astaroth, it is their hand-writing. I know it well;—and see, here is that revealed, which you have so obstinately refused to impart to me. 'Tis well for you, young lady, that it is so, for it has saved your life! Now, Ela and her brat shall feel the vengeance of Rupert Darwin and the gipsy tribe. You shall see that neither time nor distance shall tempt him to abandon the design which he would run any risk to put into execution. Let me away to my companions to exult in my success.'

"Thus speaking, Rupert Darwin, with the letters open in his hand, was proceeding to leave the cavern, when, driven to phrenzy and despair, I threw myself on my knees before him, and implored him not to act up to his threats, but rather to take my life than sacrifice those of my dearest friends, whom I had so fatally been the innocent cause of betraying.

He was deaf to my supplications, and quitted the cavern, and I could hear, by the loud exclamations of savage delight which shortly afterwards proceeded from the outer cavern, that he had made known the discovery of your retreat to the other wretches.   My God! what feelings of horror and distraction then racked my brain, and do at the present time, when I am uncertain whether or not they have put their threats into execution.   I paced the place of my confinement with the most agitated steps, and gave vent to the power of my emotions in

MARIA AND EMMA'S VISIT TO ROSE SHERWOOD.

heavy groans and cries of despair.   At length, becoming more calm, I implored the interposition of Providence, and prayed that He would protect you from the diabolical vengeance of Rupert Darwin, and his vile associates.   This somewhat reassured me, and I prepared to await the issue of this adventure with a great deal more composure.

"All was now so still in the outer cavern that I began to think the gipsies had quitted it, and in this conjecture I was all but confirmed by the continued silence.   A sudden idea urged me to try the door, and my surprise was not a little increased, when I discovered it was not fastened. I ventured to open it gently, and peeped into the cavern beyond, which I perceived was entirely vacated, and the gipsies seemed to have gone altogether, for they had not left behind the least thing. After listening attentively to ascertain for certain that there was no one lurking near at hand, I stepped from the place of my confinement, and cautiously across to the outer cavern. A lamp, still lighted, was suspended from the roof, which enabled me to find my way to a door which was on the opposite side, and which I could perceive was partially open. It showed me a dark passage beyond, which, like the caverns, was cut out of the bowels of the earth. Along this, with difficulty, I gropped my way, and I thought it would never come to a termination, so great was its length. At last, however, I felt my toe come in contact with something, which, upon feeling, I found to be a step, and a faint ray of light was perceivable above my head.

"I found no difficulty in ascending the steps, which were in very good repair, and having arrived at the top, I found myself in a large vaulted apartment, which evidently belonged to some building or the other. It seemed very clear to me that the gipsies had gone the same way that I was pursuing, for every door that I encountered was left standing open, so that there was nothing whatever to step my egress from the place.

"I passed from a door in one corner of this apartment into a kind of court, which I crossed hastily, and entered a low gateway in the wall opposite. Frequently, however, did I pause and look back, fearful that I might be pursued, and I felt convinced that if any of the gang should discover me in that situation, they would not hesitate a moment in despatching me. But my fears were all groundless, and I traversed my way without interruption.

"I need not detain you, my dear friends, by relating the different apartments and passages I passed through ; suffice it to say, that at length I succeeded in emerging into the open air, and I then, to my astonishment, discovered that the building with which the caverns were connected was the Old Manor House.

"Overjoyed, almost driven out of reason, by my unexpected escape, I ran forward with all the rapidity in my power, towards Wallingford Hall, being anxious to set the fears of my humble friends there at rest as soon as possible. It was now twilight, and all around seemed as still as death. When I arrived at the gate of the grounds that surrounded Wallingford Hall, I paused to take breath, and to regain my composure. I reflected on the surprise my sudden and unexpected appreparance would have upon my friends, and I therefore determined to use all the caution I could. With a trembling hand I rang the bell, and soon afterwards the gate was opened by Anthony. Upon seeing me, the old man started back with as much amazement and apparent terror, as if he had encountered a spectre ; and it was not until I had extended my hand to him, and spoken, that he could believe the evidence of his senses.

"'Good God, Miss, is it possible?" he exclaimed, while tears of joy actually filled his eyes ; "'do I indeed gaze upon our dear young lady? Oh, where have you been, and what fresh troubles have attended you ? We have all of us been half dead with terror.'

"I made a sign to the good old man to refrain for the present, and that I would afterwards gratify his curiosity ; and seeing me so pale and faint, he lent me the support of his arm, and led me across the grounds to the Hall.

"I will pass over the meeting between me and Jenny, and poor old Mathew, who had been in a state bordering on distraction at my mysterious disappearance, as he could not now form any conjecture in whose power I was, as my two persecutors Barnell, and Grayling, were no more. He had used every endeavour to ascertain what had become of me ; and Mr. Ashborne, the magistrate, had sent officers to different parts of the country, but without success. They had searched the Old Manor House, thinking I had been borne away by the gipsies ; but they could not discover the least traces of the gang, and they therefore supposed that they had abandoned their retreat, and they set out in pursuit of them, thinking it now very likely that they had me in their power. No person was acquainted with the secret of the caverns that communicated with the Old Manor House, and thus the gipsies, when they retired, were quite perfectly safe, especially as they never ventured out of their hiding-place until after dark, and then carefully avoided any place where they might be known. Thus might they have murdered me with impunity, and there would have been some difficulty in detecting them. When day after day elapsed, and still I appeared not, and they could not obtain any tidings of me, the alarm of Mathew and the others was almost insupportable, and they really began to think that some dreadful fate or the other had befallen me.

"Only the day after my disappearance, letters had arrived at the Hall to me, from my uncle and Walter ; but Mathew, anxious to give them timely notice of what had happened, immediately sent off another letter to Mr. Wallingford, apprising him of the painful and alarming circumstance.

"You may guess, my dearest friends, with what eager haste I broke the seals of these letters, and perused the contents. My uncle's letter was more than usually affectionate.

He condoled with me on the many misfortunes I had met with, but more particularly the lamented demise of Doctor Hartley, in whom he had also lost such an excellent friend and able adviser;—and regretted that circumstances had rendered it necessary for him to quit England, and thus deprive me of his protection. He, however, did not expect he should remain much longer in Switzerland, when he should return to Rosemary Dell, and would make such arrangements as would, no doubt, afford me satisfaction, and prevent those annoyances by which I had been so frequently tormented. In the meantime, although he quite approved of my residing at Wallingford Hall, he thought it would tend more to my safety, and likewise afford me society, if I would seek the protection of Mr. and Mrs. Goodwin, who, he felt certain, would very willingly grant it to me, until his return to England. This, however, he left entirely to my own pleasure and discretion.

"Oh, my kind friends, imagine with what transport I perused the contents of my cousin's epistle. It was one expressive of the most unbounded affection and grief, that we should be separated, and at the many troubles to which I had been subjected. It was very clear that absence had made no change in his sentiments; it was evident that I still held the same paramount situation in his heart which I had ever done, and that our separation, if possible, had added strength to the ardent love which glowed within his bosom. I could not doubt his sincerity; his noble, his generous, his constant nature breathed in every sentence, and I could almost imagine he was before me. Oh what a weight of care, of painful and bitter thought, did this remove from my heart; and, how did I upbraid myself for having for an instant done him the injustice to doubt the fidelity of his love.

"In the most unmeasured terms of indignation did Walter express himself at the unmanly and brutal treatment I had experienced at the hands of Barnell and Grayling, and regretted that he had not been near to rescue me from their power, and to bring upon their heads the punishment they merited for their crimes.

"My first action, after perusing these letters, was to write in reply, and despatch them directly, as Mr. Wallingford and his son would, no doubt, be in a great state of alarm when they received Mathew's letters, informing them of my disappearance, and I was therefore anxious to put an end to their anxiety, by relating to them my safety, and the circumstances that had happened to me. I also wrote to you this long letter immediately afterwards, hoping that if the gipsies should not reach the place where you are staying before it, you would have an opportunity of securing your safety by flight. God grant

that this may not be the case; I cannot, I dare not, think otherwise: it would drive my mind to distraction were I to do so. Oh, heavens! should the wretch Rupert have arrived where you are at present, alas! even now he may have accomplished his cruel purpose, and Ela and her daughter may be no more. At the thought my blood seems to chill in my veins, and I tremble with apprehension. And this, too, to take place when my dear Fanny has every prospect of happiness, in her union with the man of her choice, and who appears to be so worthy of her. I pray to God that my fears may prove without foundation, and that the gipsies will either abandon their design, or that something may take place to frustrate their attempts, and to place them in a situation in which they will never again be able to molest you.

"You express a wish for me to come to reside with you? I need not tell you how delighted I should be were it practicable or prudent for me to do so; but even had not subsequent events of so painful and alarming a nature taken place, I could not have availed myself of your affectionate offer, for my uncle would not most probably have approved of such a course, and I ought to regard his wishes. For the present I shall remain at Wallingford Hall, where I think I shall be more comfortable. I should indeed be very happy to possess the society of Mr. and Mrs. Goodwin, but they are living in London, and the noise and bustle of the metropolis would not agree with my present state of mind.

"And now, my dear friends, I implore you to write to me immediately on the receipt of this; I shall await your reply in the most dreadful state of suspense and anxiety, and shall, if I do not hear from you, conclude that my worst fears have been realised, and that the wretch Rupert has accomplished his blood-thirsty purpose. Heaven forbid that such should be the dreadful result. But if you have not heard anything from your implacable enemies the gipsies, previous to your receiving this letter, let me entreat that you will immediately consult your safety by leaving the country, and seeking some place of refuge where they will not be able to discover you."

With a few observations of minor importance, Maria concluded her communications to Ela and Fanny; and the deep, the painful interest with which they perused them, requires no difficulty to imagine. Everything was now fully explained as to the means by which Rupert and the other gipsies had become acquainted with the place in which they were residing; and they earnestly commiserated the sufferings to which Maria had been subjected on their account, and rejoiced in her escape from the power of the wretches, who, they had no doubt, would not in future seek to annoy her, unless it were to accomplish some object of a similar nature.

Their fears for their own safety were, however, increased, for they were confident that the villain, Rupert Darwin, and his associates, (for it was not at all likely he would come alone) would not suffer any obstacle to interrupt them in the gratification of their deadly and inhuman revenge.

The affectionate resolution with which Maria had resisted all the threats of the gipsies, and refused to divulge the secret they were so anxious to obtain, choosing rather to lose her own life than be the cause of betraying them to their enemies, filled them with the most unbounded gratitude and admiration, and redoubled the affection they had ever experienced towards her. The tender solicitude which she expressed in their fate, and her eagerness for them to get away from the place which contained their foes, all made a deep impression upon their minds; and even hopeless as they considered such a project to be, after what had taken place between Lord Helvendon and Rupert Darwin, they resolved to lose no time in consulting the former upon the subject; and accordingly despatched a messenger to him, requesting his attendance immediately.

Lord Helvendon lost no time in making his appearance ; and, upon being shown the letter of Maria, and the request she so strenuously urged, he reflected for a few moments upon it, and then said, that, although he did not believe that it was at all probable Rupert Darwin would make the attempt he had threatened, as he (Lord Helvendon) had taken such precautions to be prepared to meet him, and frustrate him in his designs, it would, perhaps, be as well to guard against every possible chance of danger ; he would, therefore, reflect what, in his judgment, it would be best for them to do. In the meantime, he advised Ela to give such orders to her domestics, with strict injunctions to secresy, that they might be in readiness to depart at a minute's notice.

Ela and her daughter approved of this advice, and the former immediately gave the necessary directions, which were shortly complied with, and it was also their determination to take with them the whole of the domestics they had now in their service, to prevent the possibility of any discovery of their place of destination being made known by that means. Ela and Fanny both lost no time in answering the letters which Maria had sent them, and assuring her of their present safety, and their resolution to act according to her suggestions, should they be fortunate enough to do so with safety. They also promise to send her further intelligence in a few days. These letters they took the precaution to write in disguised hands, and took especial care to do so under fictitious names.

The next morning Lord Helvendon met them at an earlier hour than usual, and informed Ela and Fanny that he had already arranged everything, and only awaited their assent to put his plans into immediate execution. His mother was most urgent for them to leave Italy without the least possible delay, and did not mind putting herself to any inconvenience to accompany them. She proposed travelling to Spain, where she had a distant relation, by marriage, residing, and who would be very happy to receive them. It was, therefore, settled that they should leave their houses, and what they contained, in the charge of trustworthy agents, stating that it was their intention to return to England, and that it depended on particular circumstances when they might revisit Italy again ; and they might depart at night, when no one would be likely to observe them, and make the best of their way to the nearest port, where they could embark for Spain.

These propositions met with the ready assent of Ela Beranzio and her daughter, and they were most anxious for the time to arrive when they might put their plans into execution. The following night was proposed for making the attempt, and finally agreed to, and they waited with the utmost impatience for its arrival; for they felt every moment they remained in Italy they were involved in still greater danger.

The next day passed away without anything particular occurring, and exactly at ten o'clock, a good look out having been kept for the last hour or two, to ascertain whether or not the coast was clear, without anything being seen to excite surprise, Lord Helvendon, having been in the house all the afternoon, speaking a few words of confidence to Ela and Fanny, took an arm of each, and conducted them to the carriage, which had been waiting for them in readiness at the back of the premises ; and handing them in, stepped into it himself, and it was driven off by the most obscure ways to the place where they had agreed to meet Lady Helvendon. They arrived at the place of appointment at the same moment, and Lady Helvendon, having left her own carriage, entered theirs, and the former was immediately taken possession of by the domestics, and they drove off without any interruption, with the greatest rapidity, in the direction they wished to go, and before daylight they were safe on board a vessel which was going to Spain, and for the present, at any rate, entirely free from danger, or, at least, the danger which had been threatened by Rupert.

The vessel, however, had not got any great distance from the port, when a violent storm arose ; heavy clouds obscured the horizon, the wind blew a perfect hurricane; the lightning flashed awfully, and the ship was tossed about on the mountainous billows like a straw, and every one expected that she must very quickly founder. It was with the utmost difficulty that Lord Helvendon could keep the terrors of Ela, Fanny, and his mother within bounds, while their emotions were considerably increased by the piteous cries and lamentations of the other females on board, and the coarse observations and shouts of the sailors, as they gave their orders one to another amidst the raging of the storm. In fact the tempest was so terrible, that many a stout heart among the seamen, that had not trembled at meeting the daring foe, or in hours of great peril, now quailed, and they looked at one another with pale and ghastly countenances, and an expression that fully evinced the apprehensions under which they laboured.

One of the masts was torn away by the wind, and fell upon the deck, and the noise it made so alarmed Ela and her companions, that they thought the ship was going to pieces. It was a dreadful scene, and such a one as those only who have experienced under similar circumstances, can form the least conception of. Now, prayers might be heard from lips that had heretofore seldom given utterance to anything but blasphemy ; and those appealed to Heaven for mercy, who had never before admitted the existence of a Supreme Power.

" ————— Some part burst into tears,
And others, looking with a stupid stare,
Could not yet separate their hopes from fears,
And seemed as if they had no farther care ;
While a few pray'd (the first time for some years)."

Towards morning, however, the storm abated, and the ship went steadily on her course again, and all danger was entirely over.

Nothing more occurred to alarm them, and at last they arrived at the place of their destination in safety, and were overflowing with gratitude to the Almighty, who had favoured their escape from their enemies, and had protected them amid all the horrors of the tempest.

The Castello di Alancantaros was situated in a delightful spot, on the banks of the Guadalquiver. It was an ancient and noble edifice, which had withstood the storm of ages, and had been for centuries in the possession of the noble family it took its name from.

Don Ferdinand di Alancantaros, the present possessor, was a nobleman of about sixty years of age, and who had only two daughters living, out of a numerous family. He was a nobleman who bore an excellent character, and indeed he was urbane, benevolent and generous. Donna Alancantaros (who was an English lady, and first cousin to Lady Helvendon) was also a lady of very estimable qualities of heart, and she was much beloved by all who knew her.

The two daughters, Elvira and Inez, were no less celebrated for their beauty than their intellectual charms, and the sweetness of their disposition ; and they had many admirers among the young nobility in the neighbourhood where they resided, and for miles around ; but they looked upon none of them with a favourable eye, for they had not yet beheld any man on whom they could fix their choice as a partner for life.

Lady Helvendon, her son, and their companions, were received most cordially by the good Hidalgo and his family ; and when they were made acquainted with such parts of Ela and her daughter's melancholy story as it was thought necessary to impart to them, they expressed the deep sympathy which they felt in their misfortunes ; and Don Ferdinand offered them all the protection his castello would afford them as long as they thought proper to remain there.

Ela and Fanny expressed their thanks in the warmest manner, and they soon became as much at home there as if they had been on terms of intimacy for years before.

Fanny was particularly delighted with the charming behaviour and sweetness of disposition which the beauteous Elvira and Inez ever evinced, and they were no less pleased with her. They would sit for hours together upon the terrace of the castello, which overlooked the blue waters of the Guadalquiver, engaged in the most delightful conversation; and frequently Elvira would touch the strings of her guitar, while her sister sang to it notes, that were sufficient to fill the most insensible bosom with rapture. At others, they would ramble among the delightful scenery by which the neighbourhood was surrounded; and in admiring the beauties of Nature, improve and amuse their minds.

Fanny and her mother had taken especial care to send Maria the earliest information of their safe arrival in Spain, and how happily they were situated, and the latter communicated to them all the news which she knew they would be most anxious to hear. Nothing, she informed them, had been heard of Rupert Darwin and his infamous associates, so that it was not yet certain whether they had returned to England, and abandoned their designs, when they found that Ela and Fanny had once more eluded them; although it was very certain that they would not again make their appearance in the neighbourhood of Rosemary Dell in a hurry, as they would naturally conclude, that some steps would be taken to punish them for the outrages they were constantly in the habit of practising there.

To Maria, they were happy to hear, nothing of a painful description had happened lately.— She still remained at Wallingford Hall, and was as comfortable as circumstances would permit her to be. She had heard twice from Walter and her uncle since they had gone to Switzerland, and their letters, particularly the former, were a solace to her in her loneliness. As far as regarded Mr. Wallingford, Maria could not help expressing a hope that his sentiments had lately undergone a change in her favour. He wrote more kindly to her, and with less reserve, as regarded Walter. He never mentioned a word about the future settlement of the latter, neither did he put to her that cold, pedantic, and formal advice which he had formerly invariably made use of when he wrote to her.

From these circumstances, she was almost afraid to augur too favourable a conclusion, lest her too sanguine hopes, should be doomed to be crushed; but it lightened her heart, and made her feel more happy than she had done for some time before; and she divested herself, in a great measure, of that aspect of melancholy which the recent painful events had made her assume.

Among the few persons who visited the Castello di Alancantaros, was the Marchese Vivaldi, an Italian nobleman. He was a man about thirty, greatly accomplished, handsome, rich; but, withal, proud, austere, and overbearing. He was also a great gallant, and considerably vain of his conquests, seeming to think that no lady could behold without admiring him, and envious of those who were more fortunate in their amours than himself.

Don Ferdinand was far from admiring the character of this nobleman, and did not care how few and far between his visits to the castello were—but he could not decidedly refuse him, as his father was one of his most intimate friends, and had, upon his death-bed, requested him to continue that friendship to his son.

The Marchese Vivaldi had, at first, aspired to the hand of the beauteous Elvira, but she having positively rejected his vows, he, after awhile, did not press his suit, although it was very evident that he was chagrined at the circumstance, and with much difficulty stifled the open expression of his anger.

This nobleman, Fanny took a particular dislike to the moment she saw him, which considerably increased when she beheld him eyeing her with looks of such deep earnestness and attention, that it brought the blushes mantling in her cheeks, and filled her bosom with much confusion.

Ela watched him also with looks of suspicion, and frequently he observed her black piercing eye fixed upon him with a look of anger, upon which he would withdraw his gaze, evidently much abashed. When the Marchese was present, Ela usually managed, if possible, to engage her daughter in another way, and in this there was no great difficulty, as Lord Helvendon was most unremitting in his attentions to her, and his affection for her increased every hour; and now when they seemed to be secure from every danger which had before threatened them, their union was again spoken of, and the day was once more appointed.

The Marchese Vivaldi heard this with such feelings of anger, that he had the utmost difficulty in the world to conceal them from the observation of those against whom they were directed; but from that time, he did not come near the castello for several weeks, and no one knew what had become of him.

It is strange, that wary as was the love of Lord Helvendon, and bold as the conduct of the Marchese had been, the former had never noticed it, and he had not the slightest idea of it.—Neither Ela or her daughter had had the imprudence to mention the circumstance to him, which, in fact, was only bare surmise on their parts, and might lead to the most serious results; but now the Marchese had gone away, they were in hopes that they should see no more of him until after the safety of Fanny was secured by her becoming the bride of Lord Helvendon.

Time passed on,—three months elapsed, and the day appointed for the union of Fanny Beranzio and Lord Frederick Helvendon at length arrived.

It had been settled that the marriage should be solemnised after the Protestant faith, in the Chapel of the Castello di Alancantaros, and there were to be considerable festivities provided for the occasion, as they were not under the same apprehensions as those that had tormented them when they were in Italy. A great number of the Spanish nobility had been invited, and preparations had been making for some weeks before.

Never did the bride look more lovely than she did on that memorable morning; and every one who beheld her, were most enthusiastic in their admiration. Ela's commanding figure, and dignified features and mien, attracted much attention also; and, in short, all around seemed gladness and hilarity.

The two lovely daughters of Don Ferdinand di Alancantaros were the bridemaids, and nothing could be more charming than the appearance they made.

Lord Elvendon was all joy and expectation, and he saluted his blushing bride with a warmth that shewed that his whole soul, his every comfort, was centred in her.

And now the bridal procession moved towards the chapel in the castello, and the gladness that prevailed seemed to be universal. It reached the altar, the marriage rights had commenced, when suddenly Ela was heard to utter a piercing scream, and grasp the arm of her daughter; the next moment the report of a pistol was heard, and to the horror of all present, the bride sank bleeding and senseless into the arms of the distracted Lord Helvendon.

"Great God!" shrieked Ela, in phrensied accents, and leaning over the unfortunate Fanny. "My child—my Fanny—she is killed! The blow was meant for me!—It was the monster Rupert Darwin who did it.—I am certain I am not mistaken, for I saw him take deliberate aim, and when he had discharged the contents of the pistol, he made his escape by yonder door!—Oh, my poor girl!—she is dying!"

"Pursue the miscreant!" exclaimed the horror-struck Lord Frederick, addressing himself to the domestics present,—"a fortune shall be his who shall slay or take the villain! Fanny, my love; oh, open your eyes; look upon me, and convince me that the blood-thirsty monster has not quite succeeded in his infernal object."

But Fanny spoke not, and the blood was streaming fast from a wound in the neck; she was therefore borne to her, with all possible expedition, and medical advice immediately sent for. In the meantime, the domestics had flown different ways in pursuit of the assassin, and the guests, who were completely thunderstruck at the melancholy and unexpected event which had taken place, were unable to move from the spot for several minutes, and stood looking upon each other in stupified amazement.

CHAPTER LXI.

"Villains! why seek ye my life?
What harm did I do ye, that ye thus
Would send my soul, unprepared,
Into the presence of its Almighty Judge?"
THE FRATRICIDE.

THE reader is, by this time, no doubt anxious to hear what had occurred to Mr. Wallingford and his son, after this long interval of silence.

We have stated before how abruptly Mr. Wallingford quitted Cheltenham, and, accompanied by his son, took his immediate departure to the nearest sea-port, with a determination to depart directly for the continent. To this he was prompted by a certain restlessness and fickleness of disposition, which made him look upon anything, so long as it caused a change, with eager impatience. He had grown out of temper with everything in London, Bath, and Cheltenham;—everything seemed to pall upon his fancy. He acted from the impulse of the moment, at least, so he endeavoured to flatter himself;—but had he drawn a real picture of the sentiments of his mind, he must have admitted that it was his inordinate pride and ambition which prompted him

in everything. While he was in England there seemed to be a dread upon his mind that his wishes, as regarded his son and Maria, would be thwarted, and that the darling project which he had formed, as regarded the future settlement of Walter, and the rank in society his sanguine anticipation had already placed him in, would be defeated by some means or the other. But in change of scene and society; in the ranks of fashion, which it was his intention they should mingle in on the continent, a favourable change in the sentiments of his son might be effected. Amid damsels of rank, beauty and accomplishments, he might surely meet with one who could estrange his heart from the simple, unsophisticated Maria, and place herself in his affections; and in the charms of her society, Walter would soon forget that such a being existed, or remember her only one deserving his esteem.

Thus did Mr. Wallingford flatter himself, and in the selfishness of his own sentiments, never gave a thought to the anguish he was inflicting upon those whose happiness it ought to have been his most anxious study to promote. But could he have read the heart of his son (and yet he prided himself not a little upon his penetration) he would there have seen that Maria's image, her virtues, her innumerable charms, were there engraven too deeply for time to efface them. He would have discovered that Walter and Maria's souls were linked together; that it was those simple beauties, which his father affected so much to despise, that had principally captivated him, and that absence was only calculated to draw their hearts, if possible, more closely together. Affection once implanted in bosoms like Walter's and Maria's, can expire only in death. Walter could see no charms in any other of the sex, who, in the course of their travels, he was introduced to; no, Maria was constantly before his eyes, and they lost what pretensions to admiration they possessed in comparison with her. Frequently had his father rebuked him for what he called the cold stoical nature of his conduct, but it failed to make any impression upon his mind; and more than once he candidly confessed to Mr. Wallingford his real opinions, and assuring him of the utter impossibility of his ever being able to effect any change in his sentiments, and acknowledged the unbounded affection he entertained for his fair cousin, and the daily strength he found it gaining in his heart.

At such times as these, Mr. Wallingford would evince much anger, and give utterance to his indignation in no measured terms, and accused his son of a want of duty. But Walter could not perceive any dereliction of duty on his part by indulging a passion which virtue and propriety sanctioned. There were times, indeed, when he regretted he had been so easily persuaded to yield to the tyrannical caprices of his father; for in any other light he certainly could not view his conduct, in tearing him away from the companion of his youth, and abandoning her to the mercies of strangers, whom gratitude, if not humanity, for the sake of the late Mrs. Wallingford, ought to have induced him to shelter and watch ever with the most sedulous care; and when he reflected upon the wretched unprotected state Maria would be left in if anything should happen to Dr. Hartley, he upbraided himself for not having at all risks persisted in remaining nearer her.

In the hope that company would tend to remove his melancholy, and divert his thoughts from the subject which wholly engrossed them, Mr. Wallingford had taken him into society as much as possible, but it had failed to have its effect, and at length he determined to travel to the continent. But although he had strictly enjoined Walter and Maria in their correspondence not to make any allusion to the passion which inhabited their bosoms, he was convinced that the power of their attachment was so great that it had tempted them to break through the orders he had given them, and he was therefore determined that no letters should pass between them any oftener than could be helped. This was another circumstance which increased the melancholy of Walter, and excited in his mind anything but goodly feelings towards the behaviour of him he had been proud and eager to watch, that he might acquire those manly virtues which he imagined his father to possess in so pre-eminent a degree. But yet he could not make up his mind to disobey his father, however cruel he considered him in the manner he at present acted, and between the tumult of passion which raged in his breast, he became completely wretched.

Before they reached the port where he meant they should embark, Mr. Wallingford had never mentioned to his son that it was his intention to go to Switzerland; but to Walter it was a matter of indifference whatever place they travelled to, all was alike the same to him; his heart, his thoughts were with Maria, and every place they travelled to, when deprived of her presence, however romantic or lovely it might be, seemed like a desert to him, and filled him only with thoughts of sadness.

We will pass over the voyage, and ultimately set them down at Lausanne, in which delightful place they soon met with a handsome cottage, situated in a most pleasant spot, and which commanded a picturesque view, with the *Chateau de Chillon* in the distance.

The health of Mr. Wallingford soon became reatly recruited by the change of air, but he was still unhappy;—he was dissatisfied with his own conduct, which his conscience t ld him

was tyrannical and unjust.; and yet his pride was so great, that it would not suffer him to yield. The wild and beautiful scenery of the place, much as he admired it; the company of the persons with whom he associated, and he found many English and foreign families of distinction, to whom he got introduced; the gaieties into which they entered; all failed to give him permanent ease and content, and there were hours when he suffered most poignantly. He recalled to his memory the kind, the affectionate, the unremitting attentions which Maria had paid to his wife during her last illness, and his conscience could not but accuse him of having acted with ingratitude towards her.

Many an hour, too, did he reflect upon the situation of Ela and her daughter, *his daughter*, who was as much entitled to his love and protection as Walter. Alas! what had been his conduct towards that poor girl, the sorrows of whose unhappy mother, her shame, her degradation, he had been the originator of?—Had it not been characterised by the most disgraceful neglect and unnatural cruelty—a cruelty which was only equalled by that with which he had behaved to Ela in the first instance? Had he not absolutely shunned her, deserted her, been ashamed to acknowledge her, fearful that she should bring disgrace upon his name? And was this the conduct of a parent?—On, no! it was rather the behaviour of one whose heart was callous to every feeling of pity and affection.

Adjoining where Mr. Wallingford and his son had taken up their residence, there lived a gentleman about forty years of age, who seldom saw any visitors, and appeared to shun society. He was a man of elegant manners and address, and had evidently moved in the first circles, but a deep melancholy seemed to be praying upon his spirits, and a smile was seldom seen upon his countenance.

He was a Frenchman, and called himself M. De Monville, although that was supposed to be, by many persons, only a fictitious name. To this gentleman, Mr. Wallingford and his son contrived to introduce themselves, and there being an assimilarity in their manners and dispositions, an intimacy sprung up between them, and M. de Monville opened his mind to them more than he had ever been known to do to any other persons before.

To Walter, he seemed to take a particular fancy; and the latter soon became so well pleased with his new acquaintance, that he did not fail to make him the depository of the sorrows which tormented his bosom, and the opposition which was made to the passion which had sprung up between him and Maria by his father.

M. De Monville frequently sighed heavily during the time he was speaking; and when Walter had concluded, he said;—

"You think yours an unhappy lot, and doubtless it is. But alas! what are your troubles to those which I have undergone? I have loved, young man, and—but, if you will not deem me tedious, and have any wish to hear my melancholy story, now, as we are alone, I will detail it to you."

Walter, who was most anxious to become acquainted with the events of M. De Monville's early life, expressed his readiness to listen to

THE ABDUCTION OF FANNY BY THE MYRMIDONS OF VIVALDI.

him, if he felt himself competent to the task; and M. De Monville, having paused a few minutes to compose himself, and collect his thoughts, commenced as follows—

M. DE MONVILLE'S TALE.

"I am a native of the south of France, and am descended from a noble and ancient family. My real name I have particular reasons for wishing to conceal.

"About ten miles from Tours, there stands an ancient castle, whose noble appearance has for ages been the admiration of the traveller, and whose strong embattled towers, in former times, were considered impregnable. Moss and ivy, when I last gazed upon that revered pile, grew thickly around its small pointed casements, which just twinkled from amid the foliage in the moonbeams. Its court was deserted; the bat and owl had taken up their abode in its Gothic towers, and the tenantry around it had for a long time shunned the place; for report's busy tongue had attributed a supernatural story to the venerable structure, and the timid and credulous shuddered at the bare mention of a place which had once called forth universal admiration. Alas! how shall I describe the feeling which crept over my senses, as I gazed upon its walls, and paced its silent and vacated courts? Reminiscences of past happiness danced in golden panoply before mine enthusiastic imagination, and I had almost began to think myself what I had been, when a tide of recollections recurred to my memory, overclouded my momentary happiness, and brought with it remembrances of so cruel, so poignant a nature, that madness almost seized my brain.

"I traversed each well-known passage, gallery, and chamber, with the wild air of a maniac. I gazed myself nearly blind upon every article of furniture, now sinking rapidly to decay; and I laughed, shouted, and raved by turns, with all the fury of a demon. Where was the owner of this neglected fabric? Where the happy persons who once bounded joyously through its halls, or joined in the song or the festive dance? Where that angelic form, that once was wont to—but how am I wandering! Excuse me, sir; the remembrance of the past often leads me sadly astray; but you will probably bear with my tediousness, when you shall hear all I have to relate.

"The building I have been describing was the ancient seat of my ancestors, and about twelve years ago was occupied by one, whom I shall, for the present, call M. De Monville, who was rich, noble, brave, and generous. Oh, what words shall I find to describe, as his merits deserve, the virtues of that good old man? He was universally beloved, and his life had been one splendid scene of philantrophy, benevolence, and humanity, for mankind.

"Of this excellent gentleman, I am the only son, the last surviving heir to his titles and estates, yet you behold me here an exile, leading the life of a recluse, and hourly feasting upon the miseries that have befallen me. Oh, memory, bitter, painful memory! when will you cease to wound my deeply lacerated heart? When will peace and happiness smile upon the unfortunate Adolphe? When will the real guilt of his enemies be made manifest to the world? When will he be restored to his rights and rank in society? Alas! never!"

M. De Monville here paused, for his emotions completely overcame him; and covering his face with his hands, he gave way to the poignant anguish which afflicted him. Walter, who was much hurt, did not offer to interrupt him; and after a few minutes passed in this manner, the former apologised for his prolixity, and then resumed his narrative:

"My honoured mother died when I was a mere boy, and the care of fostering my youth, and instilling good precepts into my mind, of course devolved upon my father. He loved me dearer than his own life, and every indulgence that a parent could give his offspring, he lavished upon me. I had masters to instruct me in every department of literature, and I profited by their exertions, for before I was fifteen years old (without egotism I speak it) I was accounted a prodigy of learning and gallantry.

"Thus happily passed my youth; and when I was about nineteen, my wishes being to travel, my father, with much reluctance, and after a violent struggle with his feelings, agreed to my desires. Accordingly, I was well equipped, supplied with money, two faithful domestics, and a tutor; and I left my native place. Nothing particular occurred to me during my travels; and, after an absence of three years, I thought of returning, as I had received several letters from my father, urging me no longer to procrastinate my return, as his health was much impaired, and he was very anxious to to see me. This was quite enough to induce me to return to my home, with all possible alacrity, and in another month I again trod my native soil, and was hastening to my happy home. My heart bounded with joy as I neared the building, and I pictured to myself the transport of my beloved father at our meeting. At length, the tall turrets of the castle burst upon my view; but alas! a deadly chill beset my heart, for the ancient black banner of death waved mournfully above its towers, and told me that the general despoiler had been busy with its inmate.

"With feelings of mingled hope and despair, I stuck my spurs into the flanks of my spirited horse, and galloped along the avenue which led to the entrance of the castle. Henri, who was one of the oldest domestics, met me in the hall, the old man was attired in mourning, melancholy was upon his brow, and announced the dismal tale his quivering lips afterwards gave utterance to; my poor father was no more.

"I shall not attempt to describe my feelings on this mournful occasion, you, I am sure, sir, who possess feelings so susceptible, can best imagine what mine must have been. My father expired very suddenly, two days before my arrival. It was some time ere I could bring my mind to anything like composure after this severe and irreparable loss, and I wandered about the castle more like a spectre than a human being. At night, the solitude of the forest would frequently invite me to court its solemn shades, and there, seated beneath the wide spreading branches of some huge tree, I would indulge, unrestrained, in sorrowful reflection.

"It was a beautiful autumnal evening, when darkness had spread its dusky mantle over the earth, that I was reclining as usual in the forest, when I was startled by hearing the shrieks of a female, which seemed to issue at no great distance from me. Being aware that many ruffians were continually lurking in the wood for plunder and other base purposes I rushed towards the spot from whence the cries proceeded, armed only with a large stick.

"The moon had now arisen, and shed a pale lustre on the dew-bespangled foliage. The leaves danced in the silvery beams of Cynthia like emerald trinkets, and myriads of stars began to shed forth their twinkling influence. The screams of the female still vibrated in my ears; I bounded up an avenue of trees with the velocity of an arrow, and quickly arrived at a small inclosure, in which I beheld the graceful and delicate form of a female, struggling in the grasp of a tall ruffian of the most savage and revolting aspect. The strength of the female was nearly exhausted, and she was fast sinking to the earth; another minute, and she would have been lost for ever, when I rushed forward, and grasping the waist of the unfortunate object of my compassion firmly, with a well directed blow, I immediately felled the villain to the earth.

"My first care was to soothe the girl I had so happily rescued, and my pleasure and admiration were great when I found she was ravishingly beautiful, and evidently noble and accomplished. My eyes had never before gazed upon so much loveliness and fascination; alas! that I did not expire the moment I beheld her!—Oh, Mariette, Mariette, why were you born to make me so happy, and yet so wretched?

"As soon as the lovely maiden had sufficiently regained her composure, she returned her thanks to me in language so simple, yet so forcible, that my heart was completely fascinated. The tones of her voice thrilled to my very soul, and never had I listened to accents half so musical, or language so highly polished and eloquent. All night could I have listened to her, and then felt regret when she ceased.— There was an irresistible allurement in all she said, a captivating sweetness in her every action, and when she had given utterance to her gratitude for the risk I had ran in rescuing her from the power of the ruffian, I was so bewildered and entranced that I could not return any answer.

"However, I am fearful, my dear sir, you will consider me very prolix, therefore I will at once come to particulars.

"The lady whom I had saved from the grasp of the ruffian, proved to be the daughter of a nobleman, who I shall for the present designate, by the title of the Marquis Florida; who possessed immense wealth, and resided a few leagues from my castle. He was, however, at present, on a visit to M. De Chatres, whose mansion was not more than a league from mine, and who had been on the most intimate terms with my late father.

"Mariette had been walking in the forest to inhale the evening air, when, wandering too far, she became involved in its intricacies, and was endeavouring to find the right path, when she was seized by the ruffian from whom I was so fortunate to save her, and who might have succeeded in effecting his villanous design but for my timely arrival.

"I became the more deeply interested the longer I listened to Mariette; her surpassing loveliness, her youth, and the simplicity of her manners, had made a deep impression upon me. The damsel, too, I also imagined, seemed to eye me wish a sentiment of anything but indifference, and by the time we had arrived at the *Chateau* of M. De Chatres, to which, of course, I escorted her, after the adventure which had caused her so much alarm, we were as sociable as if we had been acquainted for years.

"Mariette invited me to enter the *chateau*, that I might see her father, and receive from him an acknowledgment for the valuable service I had that night rendered him. This invitation I was ready to accept, for I dreaded to leave the presence of that lovely being who had so infatuated me.

"It is needless to relate minutely the reception I met with from the father of Mariette, or the good owner of the *chateau*; let it suffice that it was one of the most cordial description, and that, pleased with the jovial manners of the Marquis Florida, the generous urbanity of M. De Chatres, and the enchanting converse of Mariette. I prolonged my stay till after midnight, and at parting, received a hearty invitation to visit, in future, daily at the *chateau*, an offer, as you may imagine, I did not raise any objection to.

"From that eventful night, therefore, I was a constant guest at the *chateau* of M. De Chatres, and (not to detain you by any unnecessary detail,) before the time had arrived that the Marquis and his daughter had resolved to stay at the *chateau*, I was admitted the chosen suitor of Mariette, and the time was even fixed for our nuptials.

"We were united! Oh, how joyous passed the first twelvemonth of our marriage;—a perpetual summer,—one uninterrupted sunshine

—one universal calm. Alas! that it should so soon be fated to be overclouded by one of the greatest storms of adversity that could befal mankind.

"In spite of our pressing invitations, the marquis was so attached to his native home, that he declined every inducement to stay with us at my castle; and only three months after our nuptials, the good old nobleman returned to his own *chateau*.

"About this time, an old companion of mine, whom I shall call the Count Montauban, and who had been my play-fellow, arrived from England, where he had been for several years, and accepted with pleasure, my invitation to remain a few months at my castle. He was a man of handsome exterior, and great mental endowments, added to which, he had an abundant flow of that trifling converse, generally so pleasing to the fair sex, denominated 'small talk,' at the end of his tongue; flattery, gallantry, and wit, were his *fortes*, in short,

'He had a tongue that could wheedle with the devil.'

briefly speaking, the count was an interesting and accomplished man, one who seemed to be cut out by nature to please the fairest of Adam's daughters, and to insinuate himself into the good graces of his own sex. He could argue, reason, pun, sing, dance, and, in fact, make himself generally agreeable. Curses light upon the fatal hour he crossed my threshold !

"A short time after the arrival of the count at my castle, the regiment to which I belonged, it being war-time, was ordered away, and I was compelled to leave Mariette for awhile.

"This was our first separation, and I need not attempt to pourtray to you the anguish we both endured. It was, indeed, greater than language can express. Trusting to the honour of the man, whom I really thought to be my friend, I left my wife in the care of Count Montauban, and with a heavy heart left the halls of my ancestors, never more to return to them a happy man.

"I was absent from home for six months; and, oh! how my heart bounded with joyful expectation, when our army was ordered to its native land. All the pleasures of home, the domestic felicities of my fireside, the fond endearments of my wife, the extasy she would feel in seeing me return safe once more to her arms, rushed to my mind, and I looked forward to our meeting as one of the happiest events of my life. How bitter was my disappointment —how dreadful the blow which was about to descend upon my devoted head !

"I was not long in reaching Tours, and made the best of my speed to my castle, but the meeting I encountered, was far different to the one I had expected. No sounds of mirth or revelry announced my arrival ; no festival w got up to hail my return ; in place of whic although my domestics did indeed come for to meet me, and greeted my return with joyf exclamations, they sounded to mine ears ho low and insincere, while an air of myst rious melancholy seemed to overshadow the brows.

"'What can this mean?' I exclaimed, di mounting from my horse, and advancing to th old gothic portal; 'Henri,' continued I, a dressing the old grey-headed domestic in voice of trepidation, 'where is your mis tress ?'

"The old man hesitated, and sighed.

"'Why do you sigh, and for what reason d you not return an answer to my interrogatory old man ?' I added impatiently. 'What is th reason that I meet with this strange and col reception, and where is your lady, and th Count Montauban, that they do not come fort to welcome me?'

"'Monsieur,' returned Henri, in a tremulou voice, 'several weeks have elapsed since m lady and the Count Montauban have been a the castle.'

"'Not in the castle?' I exclaimed, with the most undisguised astonishment; 'where have they gone ?'

"'To your estate at Orleans, monsieur,' answered the old man.

"'But surely they must have been aware of my intended return ?'

"'They were!'

"'Great Heavens!' I cried, 'what dreadful mystery is this ? My wife, my affectionate Mariette, absent from home at a time like this ? The Count Montauban, too?'

"A burning thought crossed my brain like a flash of lightning. 'Some treachery is in this!' I mentally ejaculated, and remounted my horse in an instant.

"'Follow me!' I exclaimed to my atten dants; and the next moment I was riding a a rapid rate far from the castle of my an cestors.

"Horrible surmises are worse than the torments of certain terrors, and thus it was with me as I rode along; my mind was dis tracted with the various and painful ideas which crossed my imagination, and I was ready to fall from my horse with emotion.

"We rode all that night, and in the morn ing, after changing our horses at an hotel on the road-side, we again pursued our weary journey. I will pass it over as hastily as possible, and come to the period when, as the last golden streak of day was fading away behind the western hills, I arrived at my estate, the *Chateau Montvilliers*. I paused to endeavour to regain my composure before I entered, and while I thus stood, a faithful servant, who had been in my family for half century, came from the *chateau*, and seeing me, started back in amazement.

"'Monsieur,' said he, turning pale, 'are you here?'

"'Speak immediately, Jacques,' I almost shrieked, 'is your lady, is the Count Montauban here?'

"'Alas! alas!' replied the old man, 'the dreadful secret must now come out, and ruin and desolation be spread around.'

"These words increased my alarm and horrible forebodings. 'Secret! secret!' I vociferated, while my blood ran cold to my heart, 'what is it you mean, Jacques? Why are you so terrified? What secret do you allude to? Tell me immediately, as you value my existence.'

"'I will! I will!' answered Jacques; 'but for the love of Heaven, do not enter the *chateau* until I have revealed to you what has happened. Oh, that I should live to see things come to this pass in the noble family of De Monville! Follow me alone, monsieur, I beseech you, to the forest, where we may talk without fear of listeners.'

"I bade the domestics enter the *chateau*, and followed the old man with a foreboding heart. When we had arrived at a deep enclosure, or forest-dell, the old man said to me, while a tear trickled from his eye, and rolled down his furrowed cheek—

"'I beseech you, my dear young master, to prepare your mind to receive a dreadful shock; I have bad news to tell you, but I trust you will receive it as a man, and not let it crush you in the flower of your youth.'

"'For Mercy's sake, old man,' said I, impatiently, 'do not torture me! My mind is on the rack. Reveal this dreadful secret at once; let me know the worst; I cannot suffer more than I do at present. Why is my wife absent from the castle, when she knew I was about to return home? Where is my friend, the Count Montauban? Oh, tell me all, or I shall go mad!'

"'Your *friend*,' repeated Jacques, with peculiar emphasis, and his countenance assuming a still more important expression, 'alas! alas!—my poor young master, sadly, cruelly have you been deceived!'

"'Deceived! what mean you?'

"'That you have nourished a viper in your bosom, to sting your peace of mind for ever.'

"'Be explicit, old man,' I ejaculated, in the greatest agitation, 'or you will drive me to frenzy.'

"'I will—I will; but oh, I fear to give it utterance!'

"My blood rushed hot and impetuous through my veins—delirium seized my brain—and not knowing scarcely what I did, I seized the venerable Jacques by the collar, and vociferated—

"'Tiresome, torturing old idiot, if you do not instantly, without more equivocation, reveal to me all you know, I will tear the secret from your heart!' But in a moment, recollecting myself, I released my hold of him, and apologizing for my violence, requested him at once to disclose all he knew.

"'Monsieur,' said he, 'I repeat, you have been betrayed! The *friend* you trusted, has deceived you!'

"'Of whom do you speak?' I eagerly inquired.

"'The Count, Montauban!'

"'Ah! what of him?'

"'He is a villain!'

"'How!—dare you?'

"'Nay, my dear young master, patience, I beseech; I say nothing, I make no assertions but what I can fully corroborate by painful facts. Alas! would that I could not. The Count Montauban, I say again, is a villain—a seducer;—and your wife——'

"'My wife!' I exclaimed, while anguish nearly choked me, 'coupled too with the name of the man whom you have called by such opprobrious epithets; what can you mean?'

"Jacques again paused and hesitated, but seeing my impatience increase, he made a powerful effort to stifle his emotions, and said—

"'Your wife, monsieur, is—is——'

"'What?' I exclaimed.

"'An adulteress!'

"I sunk senseless to the earth, as though struck by a thunderbolt.

"When I regained my senses, I found myself reclining on a clean but humble pallet in a cottage, with my faithful Jacques and an old woman anxiously watching me. I soon understood that it was the cottage of his aunt, and the joy of the poor old woman at my recovery was unbounded. My God! to what a consciousness of the horrors of my situation did I awake! My Mariette an adulteress! Could it, and I still exist? Why did not the dreadful intelligence strike me dead? I called upon Jacques to tell me everything he knew, as he valued his life; but the poor old man, fearful that the consequences might be fatal in my present state of mind, implored me to be calm and wait till the morning, when he would tell me the whole horrid truth. In the frenzy of the moment, I jumped from the couch, and grasping the arm of Jacques violently, I articulated—

"'Jacques, by all my hopes of mercy, here and hereafter, if you do not tell me all this very minute, I will tear the secret from your heart!'

"The ancient domestic, alarmed at my vehemence, saw it would be useless any longer to attempt to expostulate, and therefore told me all he knew. Oh, God! what a tale of

infamy and horror did I have to listen to!—
My wife was a base, depraved degraded
wretch; my *friend*, Count Montauban, one of
the most infernal of villains; who, not content
with wheedling from me the affections of my
wife, had usurped my estates, and concerted a
plot to ruin me for ever in the estimation of
my sovereign! — I was thunderstruck!—
Horror-struck!—A raging hell was burning
within my brain—a thousand furies gnawing
at my heart!

"'Say you that the guilty pair meet nightly
gardens of the *Chateau*, Jacques?' demanded
I, in a hoarse voice.

"'They do, Monsieur,' was the answer of
the old man.

"'Then this night shall my revenge be
gratified, and——'

"'Oh, hold! hold! my dear young master,'
interrupted Jacques, 'I pray you abandon the
thought; you know not the danger of that you
would undertake; the *chateau* is filled with
creatures of the count, who would be ready on
the spot, and your life would most assuredly pay
the forfeit of your daring. Return—hasten with
all possible speed to Court, throw yourself at
the feet of the king, and crave his mercy and
protection, and justice for your wrongs.'

"'Never!' I cried, 'think you then I can
thus tamper with my burning rage? No—no
—I must have vengeance—speedy, bloody
vengeance!—Follow me, Jacques, it is now
night, and the lamp of heaven will guide me to
the scene of retribution.'

"With these words, I grasped firmly my
unsheathed weapon, and throwing my cloak
hastily around me, I rushed out of the cottage,
and hurried with the wild air of a maniac to
wards the gardens of the *chateau*.

"Never was a more lovely evening; the
queen of night was riding grandly through an
ocean of fleecy clouds, and the earth, the foliage
of the trees, and all around seemed one placid
mass of silver. But heedless of these beauties,
which at any other time would have afforded
me such infinite delight, I still bent my way
with eager footsteps towards the scene of guilt.

"The distance of the *Chateau Montvilliers*
from the cottage of Jacques' aunt, was about
two leagues, and it was not long, therefore,
before its white walls burst upon my sight.
Having arrived at the garden walls, I paused to
recover myself from the state of agitation into
which I had been thrown by the speed I had
made, and here Jacques once more ventured to
beg of me to use caution, as Count Montauban
had spies in all directions. He therefore advised me to enter the garden of the *chateau* by
a secret door at the back, known only to a few
persons. I took his advice, and was soon
threading the flowery carpet of the gardens.

"'The spot! the spot! old man,' I cried
with impatience.

"'Yonder summer house;' answered Jacques, 'but oh! for mercy's sake, be not rash,
or we are lost for ever.'

"I stayed not to listen to his entreaties, but
was soon at the door of the summer-house, which
concealed me from the observation of any person who might be within. I heard voices—
tender words were uttered—sighs of the
utmost affection followed—my heart was
bursting—when the moon shone full into the
summer-house, and revealed to me a sight that
froze my blood with horror. I gazed again
upon the dreadful sight;—it was real—it was
too true—my wife—my Mariette, was fondly
locked in the arms of the villain, the Count
Montauban; who was languishing upon her
bosom, and imprinting warm kisses upon those
lips I had fondly imagined would never have
been pressed by any but myself!—Great God!
why did You not strike me a corpse at that
appaling moment?—Why was I left to know
myself the disgraced, the degraded being that I
now am? I was struck dumb at the guilty
scene, and was completely transfixed to the
spot with terror, grief, and confusion. Poor
old Jacques, who beheld my emotion, hurried
towards me, and laying hold of my arm, was
about to force me from the spot, when at that
moment, the villain, Count Montauban turned
his eyes towards the place where I stood, and
starting from the arms of my treacherous wife,
he exclaimed, instantly recognising me:—

"'Ah! by hell it is De Monville!'

"'Yes, base, deceitful, guilty wretches!'
I shouted, drawing forth my sword, and rushing
into the summer-house, 'it is indeed the injured,
the much wronged De Monville, who is a witness to your infamy, and is resolved to die in
avenging the wrongs you have done him, the
disgrace, the degradation you have heaped
upon him. Turn, vile sycophant, and meet
the man you have so cruelly deceived; and you,
disgrace to your sex, prepare to meet the vengeance of your unfortunate husband!'

"I was rushing upon Montauban with the
fury of a maniac, when he stamped loudly upon
the floor, and before my sword could reach his
polluted heart, I was surrounded by a dozen of
ruffians, who darted into the summer-house,
and quickly discovering me, bore me, in spite
of my futile attempts at resistance, and the
loud cries of Jacques, from the garden, and
dragging me forcibly to one of the wings of the
chateau, they opened a small door in the wall,
which was almost concealed from view by the
brushwood, and dragged me along several dark
and winding passages, till we arrived at an iron-
door, which they opened with difficulty, and
thrusting me into a dungeon, which formed a
portion of the ancient fabric which had formerly
stood on the site of the present *chateau*, closed
the door upon me, and left me in the dark to
my own dreadful reflections.

"I need not attempt to describe to you the state of mind I was thrown into by this catastrophe; the fates seemed to have conspired against me, and it appeared as if I were doomed to be the sport of fortune to my enemies. I raved—I stamped—groaned—and dashed myself against the damp and loathsome walls of my wretched dungeon, in a paroxysm of excessive agony, by turns, then I cursed Montauban, and called down the most dreadful maledictions upon the head of my wife!

"Thus passed away that night, and no one visited me, nor had I any means of resting myself but by lying on the bare earth, for there was not a a bed, stool, or the smallest article of furniture in the dungeon. This awful cell was dripping with unwholesome dews, and, when overcome by fatigue and grief, I threw myself upon the earth; the vermin crawled over my face, the poisonous toad spit at me with all his revolting venon. The horrors I endured that night were beyond all human conception, but the sufferings of my body were nothing compared with the intense agony of my mind, when I reflected upon the guilt and perfidy of those persons I had esteemed as my very existence. I could not distinguish the day from night in this wretched abode, for there was no casement, and not the slightest crevice through which the rays of the sun could penetrate. I beat my breast, and tore my hair in the most poignant misery, and called down the heaviest curses upon the head of my guilty wife, and her villanous paramour.

"In the midst of this phrenzy, I heard my dungeon door unlocked, and a man of the most forbidding visage entered the cell, carrying a small lamp, a coarse brown loaf, and a jug of water. He deposited the whole of them on the floor, and was departing as he had entered, when, overcome by emotion, and the horrors of the very idea of remaining in my present fearful situation, I threw myself at his feet, and implored his assistance in affecting my escape, and offered him a handsome reward at the same time for his trouble. I own this was a weakness, which I then could not conquer, but which at any other time I should have been ashamed to have evinced; but under all the circumstances, there was every allowance to be made for the state of mind into which so unexpected an event had thrown me.

"My supplications, however, made no impersrsion upon the fellow to whom they were addressed; he heard me not, and then, laughing ironically, he extricated himself from my hold, and retired from the cell, locking and bolting the door after him cautiously.

"Thus I passed three of the most unhappy days and nights of my existence; and the same ruffian daily visited me with a like scanty allowance of provisions. On the fourth morning of my confinement, the dungeon door was once more opened, and the next moment the villain Montaubon stood before me.

Had a demon crossed my path, I could not have experienced feelings of greater indignation and disgust; my brain whirled round with a variety of emotions, while my heart seemed to swell so as nearly to burst its tenement. All this time, the heartless wretch stood contemplating me with an air of the utmost scorn and exultation.

"'Miscreant!' I at length found power to articulate, and I advanced towards him, and fixed a glance upon him, which was enough to sink into his very soul. I tried to continue, but the words choked me, and I was bursting with the most uncontrolable rage. All this time, the sarcastic glances of Montauban mocked my anguish; at length he spoke—

"'Monsieur de Monville, better language will now best become your lips, since it so happens that I am master where you were wont to be.—Miscreant, too!—what, to yield to the embraces of an angel, whose only crime has been in preferring me to such a beardless stripling as you are?'

"'Heartless, unfeeling scoundrel!' I cried, 'have you not one spark of humanity ar manhood in your cold nature? By what right do you dare to usurp my place here, and why am I imprisoned and treated like a culprit?'

"'Simply because it pleases me so to do, Monsieur de Monville,' he replied, in the same unfeeling tone of irony; 'plainly speaking, your power and wealth are at an end. Mariette no longer loves you, she is mine. This *chateau* and all your estates, too, are mine, you are only known to your king now as a traitor, and, therefore, if you did escape from this place, which is utterly impossible, it would only be to meet an ignominious death upon the scaffold. Adieu, M. de Monville, your *domestic* will attend daily as usual, with your *sumptuous* repast. Adieu, I go to meet the fair, the lovely Mariette.'

"And with these words, before I had time even to make any reply, the villain quitted the dungeon, and I heard him laugh trimphantly as he secured the door after him.

"Two months longer did I pass in this wretched situation, without any alteration in my circumstances; my ruffianly jailor daily visited me, but maintained the same taciturn and austere conduct. Such was the dreadful state of mind to which my sufferings had reduced me, that I several times thought of committing suicide by dashing my brains out against the walls of my miserable cell; but Providence withheld me from perpetrating so rash and sinful a deed, and I was reserved for another fate.

"One night, when I judged it to be about the twelfth hour, I heard my dungeon door unbolted cautiously, a light streamed into it, and, the next moment, faithful old Jacques advanced towards me.

"I was about to express my astonishment at his appearance, when he whispered—

"'For Heaven's sake, my dear young master, say nothing, or we shall both be murdered. With extreme difficulty I have overcome the fidelity of the fellow who acts as your gaoler, and I have come to restore you to liberty. Be quick then,—while fortune favours us, let us escape from this dreadful place, and leave the future to the will of an All-wise Judge.'

"I was going to thank the good old man for his kindness, when he put his hands before my mouth and enjoined me to silence. He then threw a large cloak around me, and beckoned me to follow him cautiously.

"After much difficulty, time and danger, we succeeded in gaining the forest, and I was once more freed from the merciless fangs of my bitterest foes. Ah, how my heart swelled as I gazed upon the noble edifice which sheltered the woman I had so fondly loved, and who had so basely, so cruelly deceived me. It was now early in the morning, and already Aurora began to tinge the eastern horizon. Jacques hurried me from the spot, and in a deep enclosure of the forest, I beheld two horses waiting, upon which we mounted, and in a few hours were far from the scene of my sufferings and privations.

"Hitherto, I and my venerable companion had proceeded in silence, and I had not for a moment considered what course, in future, I should pursue. But I now enquired of Jacques whither he was conducting me.

"'Why, monsieur, answered the old man, 'it is necessary that we should seek some distant part of the country until the clouds of adversity, which now so dismally obscure the horizon of your days, may be blown over, and you may be restored to those rights which have been so unjustly wrested from you. I have a brother who resides at B——; thither I propose going, and I know he will receive the son of my honoured master with pleasure, and make him as comfortable as his limited means will afford. For my own part, thanks to the Almighty, I have been enabled to save a pretty round sum, which I doubt not will support us both frugally, for some time to come. So cheer you, my dear young master, and all may yet be well.'

"The words of Jacques sank deep into my breast, which was too full for me to express my gratitude by words, but I pressed his hand in silence, and we continued our journey with redoubled speed; we did not stop at any place oftener than we could help, and then only for a few minutes to bait our jaded horses, and to get some refreshment for ourselves. The whole of that day we travelled in the same manner, and at nightfall found ourselves enter-

ing the gloomy forest of R——, which at that time was infested by robbers, who carried on their lawless proceedings with perfect impunity. We had not proceeded far, when we were surrounded by a numerous gang of ruffians, who stripped us of all we possessed; and then, in spite of my prayers and supplications, had the barbarity to take the life of my ancient domestic, by hanging him to the branch of a tree. This inhuman act so enraged me that I scarcely knew what I did, and seizing the weapon of one of the robbers, I rushed frantically upon them, and dealt destruction around, till at last, covered with innumerable wounds, I fell senseless to the earth, and was borne to their secret haunt, which was in an old building in the interior of the forest, which every person was afraid to approach, even in the daytime.

"It was a considerable time before I recovered from my wounds, and then the shocking fate of poor old Jacques recurred to me in such vivid colours, that it threw me into a high fever, and my life was nearly despaired of.

"At length, my youth, and the natural vigour of my constitution, restored me to convalescence, and I demanded my liberty, of what appeared to be the captain of the lawless gang, but he only smiled at my request.

"'Young man,' said he, 'a person once entering this place, is never allowed to leave it again alive, unless he agrees to join our gang. You have, therefore, now only to make your choice, either to become our comrade, or to remain a prisoner in this place for the rest of your life; I will give you a week to consider of it, and if you are wise, you will prefer being the companion of as jovial a set of fellows as ever reigned masters of the bonny greenwood, to passing the rest of your life in a miserable dungeon, deprived of every comfort, and shut out from all intercourse with your fellow beings.'

"With these words the captain left me to my reflections, which, you may be sure, were none of the most agreeable description. I will not detain you any unnecessary time, by detailing to you what were my reflections during the week allowed me, but suffice it to say, that at last I thought it would be the most advisable for me to assent to the proposition of the robber, as that was the only chance I should have of effecting my escape. It was several weeks, however, before I had the opportunity I wished for, and during that time I was not sent out on any of their unlawful expeditions, but was left at home with two or three others in charge of the place of our retreat. At last, however, an opportunity did present itself to me, and as I had nothing of my own, I took care to borrow a considerable sum from the coffers of the robbers, with which I started on my hazardous journey.

"By the following day I reached the place, where I had understood, from Jacques, that his brother resided; but I was very much disappointed to learn that he had quitted there some few days before I had arrived, in consequence of the death of a relation who had left him some property, and that he had gone to reside for the future, at Lausanne, in Switzerland.

"I did not travel any more that day, but on the following I had come to the determination that I would go to Switzerland; for as I was then situated, all places were to me the same;

THE MYSTERIOUS HAG SHOWERING MALEDICTIONS ON MR. WALLINGFORD.

and at that distance from my native place, I was in hopes that I should be enabled to live unmolested by my enemies, until it should please Providence to work a change in my circumstances.

"Accordingly, I travelled hither, and was received by the brother of poor old Jacques with the same kindness as if I had been his son. He had formerly been in the service of my father, and when he quitted him, my father fixed upon him a handsome annuity, as a mark of his esteem for the old man.

"Jean Desperres had lately, as I have before stated, come into the possession of considerable property by the death of a relation, so that he was now in in comfortable circumstances. He deeply sympathised with me in my misfortunes, and sadly lamented the cruel and untimely death of his brother.

"Jean was a man of superior attainments for the station of life in which he had been brought up, and was of a studious turn of mind. He had an excellent assortment of books, from the pens of the most eminent ancient and modern authors; and, in perusing them, in his society, attending to the garden attached to his cottage, or climbing the steep and lofty mountains, I endeavoured to banish the recollection of my misfortunes; but alas! they were too heavily and too powerfully impressed upon my mind to render this a task very easy of accomplishing, and a settled and immoveable melancholy fixed itself upon me, which threw a blight over my youth, and overclouded the sun of my days. This was increased by the sudden death of my companion, which event took place after I had been residing there about five years. He had no relation in the world that he knew of, and the good old man had left all that he was possessed of to me, which is more than sufficient to keep me comfortably, if not in affluence.

"I have now lived here twelve years, and have recently heard of the demise of my guilty wife. Heaven pardon her for her crimes, and the misery and suffering she has brought upon me. The villain, Montauban, still retains possession of my estates, which he obtained by accusing me to the king of treasonable intentions, in consequence of which, I was left entirely at the mercy of Montauban, as instructions had been immediately given for my apprehension.

"However, I have recently been informed that Montauban no longer retains the confidence of his sovereign, and that circumstances have transpired which has nearly convinced the king of his treachery; and of the manner in which I have been so basely and unjustly accused; so that there is a chance of justice at last being done to me, and that I shall be restored to that rank and position in society from which I ought never to have been removed. Were it not that this calm and peaceful retreat is so endeared to me, I should ere this have ventured to have thrown myself at the feet of the king, protested my innocence, and having called for an investigation into my conduct, demanded retribution on the head of the miscreant, Montauban.

"Thus ends my melancholy narrative, and may you, my dear sir, never experience those misfortunes it has been my lot to endure.— You are the only person, except Jean Desperres, another confidential friend, who watches my affairs at Tours and the *Chateau Mont-*

villiers, to whom I have imparted the unfortunate events of my life; and I did so because I felt certain that you would duly appreciate them, and sympathize with me in my afflictions.

De Monville ceased, and Walter, who had listened to him with a feeling of the deepest interest, expressed, in earnest terms, his regret at the misfortunes he had undergone, and his disgust at the cold and deliberate villany of the Count Montauban, who he sincerely hoped would ere long be brought to that punishment which his crimes so richly merited.

Satisfied that he should meet with friendly advice from De Monville, Walter then disclosed to him his love for Maria, and the opposition it had met with from his father. De Monville heard him with great attention, and appeared to feel much for his situation, but he advised him for the present to endeavour to banish it from his thoughts, and he had no doubt, but that in the course of time, his father would vanquish the sentiments of pride which now inhabited his breast, and no longer withhold his assent to his union with the object of his affection.

Walter could not but approve of this counsel, which breathed his own sentiments and wishes, and he felt very well pleased that he had here found a person in whose bosom he could deposit his thoughts, and meet with that sympathy which was calculated to appease his anguish.

He had soon good reason to believe that De Monville was just in the calculations he had formed; for Mr. Wallingford behaved more kind to him; and seemed averse to entering into society. He never spoke to him upon the subject of his future settlement, and when the name of Maria happened to be mentioned, he evinced much emotion, and spoke of her with more affection than he had been in the habit of doing for some time. It was very evident that he reproached himself for the part he had acted towards her, and felt severely for the unprotected situation in which she was left, but more especially, when the news of the death of the good Doctor Hartley reached him and likewise the insults she had received from Grayling, his nephew, and Mr. Barnell.

"Poor girl, poor girl," he involuntarily uttered, after perusing the letter which imparted the melancholy information; but, suddenly recollecting himself, and that Walter was in the room, he resumed his silence, and a short time afterwards retired to his own apartment.

From all these symptoms, Walter could not help auguring the most favourable ultimate results, and his mind became more composed. But it would be useless to attempt to describe the violent agitation he experienced when the letter arrived from Mathew, informing them of the sudden disappearance of Maria, and the suspicions they entertained of her being in the power of the Gipsies, from the circumstance of its being known that at the time they had taken up their residence at the old Manor-house, and that immediately after Maria had been taken away, they abandoned it in a sudden and mysterious manner.

Walter was completely distracted, and it was not without the greatest difficulty imaginable that he could be prevented from immediately embarking for England, so that he might prosecute his inquiries after her. The anguish of Mr. Wallingford, also, was scarcely less than that of his son, and he traversed his apartment with hasty and disordered steps.

"It was cruel, it was unjust of me to desert the poor girl," he soliloquised; "had I not done so, all these misfortunes might have been spared her, and she might now have been happy. Gratitude ought to have prompted me to look upon her as my own child, especially when the dying request of my wife was that I should be a protector and guardian to her. In the power of those wretches, alas! what have we not to fear? Have we not had terrible proof of the appalling and desperate deeds they will not hesitate to commit? Oh, my unfortunate child! My poor murdered Christabelle, and shall I have to mourn the dreadful fate of another victim to the barbarity of the monsters who murdered you? Shall I have to blame myself for having been indirectly the cause of bringing her to an untimely end? Alas; reflection will drive me mad."

He beat his breast and groaned with agony as he thus spoke, and again he paced the room with an emotion which evinced the deep mental anguish he was enduring.

Walter was so distracted, that he would not listen with any degree of patience to the consolation which De Monville sought to impart to him, and there were moments when his imagination painted to him the situation of Maria, in such dreadful characters, that it was matter of astonishment how he could retain his senses. Both he and his father passed several of the most miserable days, after the receipt of Mathew's letter, which they had endured for some time, and the suspense and anxiety under which they laboured was utterly insupportable.

At length, however, much to their relief, they received the letters of Maria, announcing her safety. How were the feelings of Walter and his father harrowed up, as they perused the account which Maria gave of her seizure by the Gipsies, her subsequent sufferings, and the narrow escape she had had from a horrible death. But they had now a fresh source of misery, and that was in the unfortunate discovery which the Gipsies had made of the residence of Ela and Fanny, whom, they had not the slightest doubt they would pursue, and would

not rest until they had wreaked their vengeance in their blood. The agony of mind they endured when they thought of the perilous situation in which Ela and her daughter were placed and the little chance they now had of being able to escape from the implacable revenge of their enemies, unless they could be apprised of the circumstance of their having been discovered and leave the country before the arrival of Rupert Darwin, and his blood-thirsty associates. Justice they well knew the Gipsies scoffed at, for they had such subtle and ingenious means of eluding it, that it was but very seldom they were apprehended, or foiled in any guilty designs they might have in view. But circumstances shortly after occurred which for awhile engrossed all their attention, and filled the mind of Walter with the most serious alarm.

He had been sitting with M. de Monville, one afternoon, and the conversation they had indulged in together, was of such an interesting description, that they did not notice the lapse of time, and twilight had set in before Walter thought of rejoining his father, whom he had left alone. Suddenly, the sound of horses hoofs' smote their ears, and almost immediately afterwards they were very much alarmed by hearing loud groans. They rushed to the door of the cottage, and immediately beheld three men on horseback, and riding off at a most furious rate. But their attention was quickly attracted to another object, which smote their bosoms with horror. Stretched across the threshold of the door of his cottage, was the form of Mr. Wallingford, from which the blood streamed copiously.

Walter rushed towards him, and raised him him in his arms. He then beheld with great terror, that he had been stabbed in several parts of the body.

"Good God! who has done this?" exclaimed the distracted youth.

Mr. Wallingford who was still sensible, pointed in the direction which the men had taken, and immediately afterwards he fainted with the loss of blood. M. de Monville assisted Walter to carry his father into the house, and immediately dispatched a servant for the attendance of a medical man of great skill, who resided in the neighbourhood. On his arrival, he examined and dressed the wounds of his patient, which he pronounced to be very severe, but still not dangerous.

Walter was delighted when he heard this, but still he was quite at a loss even to imagine who had been the wretches who attempted the murder, and what could be their object in so doing. It was very clear that robbery had not been their design, for they had left Mr. Wallingford immediately after they had inflicted the wounds, and from their dress and general appearance, they did not seem to be anything connected with the lawless tribe, from whom Mr. Wallingford and his family had experienced so many annoyances and so much trouble.

The patient remained in too weak a state for two or three days to be questioned upon the subject, but when at last he was a little recovered, the account he gave of it, was, that while he was seated in the parlour, he heard a loud knocking at the door, and not having any servant in the house at the time, he went to the door himself. He had, however, no sooner opened it, than he found three men standing there, having just dismounted from their horses, which were standing close by, and without saying a word to him, he no sooner made his appearance, they each of them plunged a knife into his body, and remounting their steeds, escaped in the manner we have before described.

"That they were not Gipsis, I am convinced," said Mr. Wallingford, "for they did not resemble that wandering class of people the least in the world. Who they could be, and what could have urged them to the perpetration of such an atrocious crime, I am perfectly at at loss to imagine."

"It is strange," said Monsieur de Monville, who was present when this conversation took place, "such an offence is scarcely ever heard of in this quiet peaceable neighbourhood. But," he continued, seeing suddenly to recollect himself, "now, I remember, a day or two since, I received a letter from my friend, at Tours, cautioning me to be on my guard, for that Montauban had discovered the place of my retreat, and being fearful that I should throw myself at the feet of the king, and solicit an investigation into the unfortunate circumstance that had brought down upon me his displeasure, and which would, doubtless, be the means of bringing his villany to light, would, in all probability, employ some means of getting rid of me. These ruffians have no doubt been employed by the villain, and though their mistaking the exact place of my risidence, this unfortunate affair has taken place."

"It must be so;" observed Walter, whose mind was greatly relieved by this explanation, "for it is certain my father could not have created any enemies since he has been here, and it is equally evident that the object of the ruffians was revenge, and not plunder."

"This event at once decides me," said De Monville; "I will at once to court, seek an interview with the king, and by explaining all that has taken place, bring the wretch Montauban to justice, and gain the restitution of those rights he has so long and so unjustly witheld from me."

Both Mr. Wallingford and Walter highly applauded this resolution, and Monsieur De Monville shortly afterwards left to make preparations for his departure from Switzerland to his native place.

By the following day, all the arrangements of Monsieur De Monville were complete, and after many protestations of continued friendship towards Mr. Wallingford and his son, and an earnest wish that they might meet again, and their acquaintance be renewed under happier circumstances, he quitted Lausanne."

Mr. Wallingford recovered more rapidly from his wounds than might have been expected, but the circumstance had made a very great alteration in his mind. The place had no longer any charms for him, in fact he appeared to be miserable in it, and looked with an eye of suspicion and misturst upon every one. Walter was very glad to see this alteration in his manners, and he prognosticated the most favourable results from it. He did not fail to seize upon so seasonable an opportunity to press upon his father to return to England, which he did, backing it at the same time by all the arguments in his power. Mr. Wallingford listened to him with patience, and although he did not glve him any definate answer as to whether or not he would return to England, he said quite sufficient to satisfy Walter that his stay in Switzerland would not longer than he had completely recovered from the effects of the wounds he had received. It was about this time that they received information of the flight of Ela and her daughter from Spain, and of the subsequent attempt which had been made upon the life of the former, by the wretch, Robert Darwen, and which had so unfertunately been the means of the latter being so dreadfully wounded, that great doubts were still entertained of her ultimate recovery.

This circumstance, while it sincerely grieved Mr. Wallingford, still further urged him to depart from a foreign land, and Walter's pleasure may be conceived better than we could describe it, when his father informed him that he had at length come to the determination of returning to Wallingford Hall.

Walter no sooner received this announcement than, knowing the pleasure it would afford Maria, he immediately wrote an affectionate letter to her, and condoled with her on the unhappy event which had happened to poor Fanny. He then set about making preparations for their journey, which, it was intended, should take place as soon as his father was restored to convalescence.

CHAPTER LXII.

"My lord, 'tis true, I saw him with an eye of
    lewd desire
Gaze in the countenance of your lovely bride,
And as I read the lustful workings of his
    thoughts,
I could have struck my dagger to his heart for
    his presumption."

                    JEALOUSY.

THE horror, the consternation of all who had been present in the Chapel of the Castello di Alancantaros, when the fatal catastrophe occurred, which we have described in a former chapter, was excessive, and the grief of Ela and Lord Helvendon was more powerful than words can covey an adequate idea of. Ela hung over the couch of the unfortunate girl, while the medical man was examining the wound, and the despair which was stamped upon her countenance, and her anxiety to know the result of the doctor's investigation was strongly discernable in her features. Lord Helvendon, too, occupied an adjoining room and every few minutes was sending in a messenger to inquire how she got on.

It was a great relief to them both to hear that the bullet had not touched any vital part, and that with care, there was not much fear of her speedy recovery.

Filled with extasy at this information, Ela and Lord Helvendon dropped simultaneously upon their knees, and poured forth their gratitude to Heaven. The next thought, was to take such precaution as would render a recurrence of the affair, while they remained in the Castello di Alancantares impractible, but this was a task of no ordinary difficulty. How the villain, Rupert, could have gained access to the chapel, they were totally at a loss to conceive, and might not he or some of his infernal colleagues, be still concealed in some part of the fabric, and only waiting an opportunity to complete the hellish deed they had commenced? A strict search all over the castello was immediately instituted, but without success, neither had the persons who had gone in pursuit of Rupert Darwin, been enabled to gain the slightest clue which might lead to his detection.

The beauteous Elvira and Inez were unremitting in their attentions upon the patient, and their affectionate solicitude for her recovery, and the many kind things they said of her, tended in a great measure to alleviate her pain, and to expedite her recovery.

At length, by the great skill and attention of her medical attendant, and a naturally strong and robust constitution, Fanny was so far restored to health, as to be able to leave her couch; but her spirits were greatly depressed, for she trembled for the safety of her mother, and so

totally absorbed was she by this idea, that she lost all apprehension of danger to herself.

Ela, by the advice of her friends, had never once ventured outside the door since the occurrence had taken place, and a strict watch had been kept over the building, by the order of Don Ferdinand, to see that no strangers were, on any pretext, admitted. But nothing had since occurred to occasion any alarm, and Don Ferdinand expressed it as his opinion, that the villain, Rupert Darwin, imagining that he had accomplished his atrocious design, had left Spain with all possible expedition, to avoid apprehensions, and that it was not very likely they would be troubled by him again.

Ela and the rest could not but acknowledge the probably of this idea, and they, therefore, became more tranquillized, and Fanny's terrors gradually evaporated.

Several weeks passed away, and nothing further happening to disturb their peace, or to excite their fears, Ela and Fanny, attended by Lord Helvendon, frequently ventured to walk forth from the castello, and to enjoy the beauty and fragrance of the scenery which surrounded it.

As time elapsed, and they heard no more of Rupert Darwin, or the other gipsies, Ela and Fanny began to think that Lord Helvendon was correct in the surmises he had formed,—namely, that Rupert and his accomplices, having probably imagined that they had accomplished their object, had made their way out of the country, and that there would be no danger of their being troubled with them again. This idea gradually restored their spirits, and tended in a great measure towards the more speedy recovery of Fanny.

Again the day was fixed for the union of Lord Helvendon and Fanny, and they fondly hoped that this time nothing would occur to interrupt it. They, however, determined that the ceremony should be performed as privately as possible, although most of their friends and acquaintances were invited to be present.

They had not heard anything of the Marchese Vivaldi, since his abrupt departure, and both Ela and her daughter were very well pleased that they had not, and were in hopes that they would not again be annoyed by his society. But they were doomed to be disappointed. Only a few days previous to the one appointed for the nuptials, he suddenly made his appearance at the Castello di Alancantaros, and expressed the pleasure he felt at meeting again with his old friends, and his extreme regret at the outrage which had been committed on Fanny.

Both Ela and her daughter received the marchese with a very bad grace, and with the greatest difficulty repressed the expression of the sentiments which they entertained towards him; and Don Ferdinand, and his two lovely daughters also received him very coldly. However, he either did not, or would not take any notice of it, and had seldom seemed in better spirits.

Frequently at the dinner table did Fanny observe his eyes fixed upon her, with an expression which filled her bosom with disgust and indignation ; and she averted her face, which she felt glowed with the deep blushes of offended modesty.

She was surprised that Lord Helvendon, who watched over her with such affectionate attention, did not observe the boldness and assurance of the marchese, and the wrath of Ela was so great that she was several times on the point of taxing him with it, and demanding an explanation of his conduct before Lord Frederick, but fearful of the consequences that might follow, she restrained her feelings as well as she could, and made no observation upon the subject.

It was very evident that the marchese noticed what was passing in the minds of Ela and her daughter; but so far from being abashed at it, he seemed to exult in their distress, and behaved with the greatest possible nonchalance—talking boldly and fluently upon every variety of subject that was broached, and laughing heartier than any of the rest, if any joke happened to be uttered.

It was a great relief to Fanny when the dinner was concluded, and she could find an opportunity of escaping from the presence of the marchese, and walking out on the terrace of the castello with Lord Helvendon ; but she had some difficulty in tranquillizing her feelings sufficiently to conceal from her lover what had happened to disturb her. In fact, she felt uncertain whether or not she was acting imprudently by keeping the insolent conduct of the licentious noblemen a secret from him ; but in dread of the consequences which would be sure to follow, exasperated as Lord Frederick would undoubtedly be, she was deterred from doing so, and they continued their walk on the terrace for some time, and probably would have remained longer, had it not been for a message from Don Ferdinand di Alancantares, to inform them that their guests regretted their absence and requested the favour of their society. Of course they could no longer absent themselves, and indeed the evening air was getting cool, so they walked into the castello, and rejoined the company in the banquetting hall.

There were more guests on this occasion than were in the habit of assembling in the castello, and mirth was the reigning deity. A ball was got up in the evening, which gave a zest to the entertainments, and Fanny and the two daughters of their noble host joined in the fantastic and graceful movements of the dance with the greatest hilarity, whilst Ela and the elders looked on, and admired the ease and

elegance with which the three mentioned individuals stepped through its mazy figures. But still the conduct of the Marchese Vivaldi was as annoying as ever it had been, and, in fact, he seemed to exult in the confusion and agitation it excited in the bosom of the object of his persecution. It was in vain that Fanny sought to avoid his bold glances. Which ever way she turned his eyes were fixed upon her ; and whenever she approached him in the dance, she trembled with emotion, for once or twice he attempted to take her hand ; and the poor girl scarcely knew which to detest the most—his consummate impudence, or his obstinate annoyance of a female, whom he could plainly see beheld him with aversion. But the Marchese Vivaldi was a man who was so completely wrapped up in self-opinion and vanity, that he could not imagine it possible for any female long to resist him ; and he had not the least doubt within himself that, however Fanny might at present despise and hate him, he should shortly have the power to captivate her ; and he therefore, notwithstanding the near approach of her nuptials with Lord Helvendon, resolved to follow up his persecution with the most persevering obstinacy.

It may be asked whether he never once turned his thoughts upon this subject to Lord Halvendon ; he certainly did, but his sentiments towards him were those of the most superlative contempt, for the marchese was one of those reckless votaries, of what is called life, and, he therefore, in consequence made honour a foot-ball, and considered rectitude a bugbear. He looked upon the anger of Lord Helvendon, if he should become acquainted with his boldness to Fanny, as a mere trifle, that a pistol shot would settle, and as most fools of fashion, or "men of honour," as they call themselves do, he always calculated upon coming off triumphant in the affray. Possessing these sentiments and ideas, therefore, it is no wonder that the marchese should persevere in his designs with the utmost determination, and he resolved to run every risk to obtain the object he had in contemplation. Hitherto, however, his persecution had been confined to rude glances, but he had not sought a private interview with Fanny, although in the course of the conversation which passed among the different guests when they met together, he had ventured to throw out certain remarks and inuendos which she either did not or affected not to understand. It was indeed no easy matter too meet with Fanny alone, for when she was not attended by her lover, Ela was sure to be her companion, and, therefore, all his designs in that way were frustrated. Nevertheless, he detemined to adopt some plan or another to meet her alone, and to pour forth the base passion which was raging in his bosom and which was ready to burst through all the bounds of decorum, rather than miss the gratification of his wishes.

That Fanny could resist the honied flattery of his tongue, the marchese never expected for a moment; on the contrary, he considered it was absolutely impossible for any one to withstand his tender asseverations, and prudence he looked upon as a barrier which might be bounded with the greatest of ease.

Several days passed away, and yet the Marchese Vivaldi was unable to meet with the opportunity he was so anxious to obtain, although he never missed being at the castello every day. The delay in the achievment of his desires only added to the lawless passion he dared to entertain, and such a powerful impression had the beauty of Fanny made upon him, that he resolved to run any risk rather than be thwarted.

In the meantime, Ela had watched narrowly the behaviour of Vivaldi, and it was with the utmost difficulty she could keep her inidgnation within the bounds of decorum. The Marchese Vivaldi was a being so contemptible in her eyes, that she considered it actually degrading to come in contact with him: she looked upon him as one of tho e worthless reptiles, who flutter in circles of fashion until lost in the vortex of folly and dissipation, they sink to their native insignificance, and perish in obscurity and contempt. Nevertheless, when she perceived the impudent resolution with which he followed up his annoyance towards her daughter, she was at last determined that she would seek an interview with him, and demand an explanation of his conduct, and likewise a promise not to repeat such behaviour again. She was firmly resolved to make Lord Helvendon acquainted with it, and leave him to act as the case demanded.

Fanny would fain have persuaded her mother from doing this, but Ela had quite made up her mind, and when she had once done so, nothing whatever could move her from her purpose. The proud and hot blood of her native country prompted her to resent with full force, what she considered to be so gross an insult, and she was now all anxiety to put the plan she had devised into execution.

"What," she observed to Fanny, "shall I longer tamely submit to be insulted, and see my child insulted; by this contemptible, this despicable mockery of nobility?—No; were I to do so, he would ere long imagine that I truckled to his wishes, and would be ready to sanction his loathsome attentions to you, my child. Besides, it is cruel, it is unjust towards your betrothed husband, Lord Helvendon."

Fanny made no immediate reply to these observations; in fact, they were so reasonable, this to she could not but believe them to be so, that they were completely unanswerable; at length, however, she seemed to recollect herself and observed:—

"But, I pray you, my dear mother, to defer putting your plan into effect for the present.— In a few days I shall be united to the man of my choice, in the indissoluble bonds of matrimony, and surely he will not then dare to follow up his infamous annoyance; I shall have a sufficient protector from his insolence."

"And have you not the same now?" demanded Ela, quickly, "and does that prevent his behaviour?—No!—And think you then that because you have undergone the matrimonial rights, he will be deterred from following up his designs?—Your ideas are preposterous, Fanny, and I am determined that I will not lose any delay in doing as I have said I would. It is useless your endeavouring to persuade me to the contrary."

"But oh, consider what may be the consequences," observed Fanny, with much emotion; "reflect, dearest mother, what may be the shocking results, when Frederick is made acquainted with it. You know the courage and impetuosity of his disposition, and a duel would be certain to follow, in which, should he fall, the happiness of your poor girl would be crushed for ever."

"I have thought upon all these things," replied Ela, "and have been sufficiently able to combat them; for instance, there is no certainty of their occurring, and if they should, is it not as likely that Lord Frederick would escape unhurt as to the contrary? Besides, recollect, that to conceal anything of this description from your affianced husband, is highly reprehensible, and should the knowledge of it afterwards come to his ears, he might strongly reproach you, for not disclosing the circumstances to him in time, which might have rendered him an opportunity of averting the evil, and chastising the insolent villain who had dared to call a blush upon your cheeks, or raise an emotion in your bosom."

Fanny could not make any answer to this, and after a few more observations, which her mother addressed to her, and endeavours to appease her fears, and to reconcile her to the steps it was her intention to take, she left her.

Just as Ela was about to leave the castello, the Marchese Vivaldi entered the Hall, and bowing with the most studied politeness to the former, he was about to pass on, when Ela, who did not deign to acknowledge his obsequious attentions, fixed a stern look upon him, and said:—

"Marchese Vivaldi, I request a few words with you in private."

"With me, signora?"—ejaculated the marchese, colouring up, and betraying the greatest confusion and surprise.

"Yes, marchese," replied Ela, in a determined tone, "and I must have them. If it please you this place will do very well, but if you prefer it, I will accompany you to the garden, where we may confer with less fear of being interrupted."

The marchese betrayed even more confusion and astonishment than he had done before, and looking at Ela, with some symptoms of uneasiness, for her piercing eyes were fixed with an expression of anger upon his countenance, he stammered out,—

"Really, signora, this singular request, has quite—that is to say—I positively do not know—"

"Shall our conference take place here, Marchese Vivaldi?" demanded Ela, impatiently, "or shall we repair to the garden? I am neither in the humour, nor have I the time to waste in parleying here."

"I will attend you to the garden, signora, since you are so pressing," answered Vivaldi, affecting to smile; and Ela, without saying another word, led the way, the former following.

"And now, signora," said the marchese, when they had got to a retired part of the garden, and Ela, stopped, "pray, what would you with me?"

Ela fixed her eyes sternly upon the countenance of the libertine, as she answered—

"Marchese Vivaldi, I would demand of you an explanation?—I would insist on your explaining to me the reason that you still persist in annoying and persecuting my daughter, by your attentions, and rude, and insolent behaviour, when you know that she is the chosen of another; and that she only receives your apparent admiration with the disgust and abhorrence it deserves?"

"Oh, is that all?" exclaimed the marchese, with the most consummate and provoking nonchalance.

"All!" reiterated Ela, while her eyes sparkled fiercely with wounded pride and indignation; "and is all sense of honour and virtue dead in the bosom of the Marchese Vivaldi, that he thus affects to treat a most flagrant and infamous outrage upon them with indifference?"

"I never give explanations to women," said the marchese, with a look of mingled wrath and sarcasm.

"And who has more right to demand it than her mother?" asked Ela, hastily; "but if it agree not with your taste, marchese, you can be accommodated in the manner you prefer; namely, give an explanation to a man, and that man Lord Helvendon."

"Lord Helvendon!" repeated Vivaldi, with a bitter and contemptuous sneer; "but—"

"Enough, Marchese Vivaldi," returned Ela, her bosom swelling with rage; "you may, probably, have reason to repeat this insolence. I shall not fail to refer Lord Helvendon to you."

"Stay, signora, I beg. I have perhaps been too hasty in my observations, and beg leave to apologize. With regard to the explanation you have demanded, I can soon give it you. The fact is, I love your beauteous daughter—love her to distraction, and I would fain seek to raise a similar passion in her heart, and—"

"Hold, marchese," interrupted Ela, passionately; dare you speak thus, when you know that the object you have deigned to honour with your admiration, is the affianced bride of another, whose affections are centered in her, and to whom her heart is devoted?—This to me, her mother?"

"I was prepared to find you treat my behaviour as unpardonable," said Vivaldi; "but I cannot conquer my sentiments; and, tell me, where is the man who could behold your beauteous daughter and not admire—not adore her!"

"I cannot, I will not listen to such base, such unprincipled observations," returned Ela, indignantly. "Marchese Vivaldi, I demand from you an unequivocal answer. Is it your determination, or not, to persevere in your disgusting and dishonourable conduct towards my daughter?"

"It would be hypocrisy, were I to promise you that I would cease to evince by my conduct, the ardent passion I entertain for the lovely Fanny Beranzio," replied the marchese.

"Then our interview is at an end," said Ela, looking sternly upon the daring libertine. I immediately go to lay your conduct before Lord Helvendon."

She directly left the spot, her bosom glowing with rage, and firm in her resolution, hurried to the apartments of Lord Helvendon, whom she found alone. So much were her feelings exasperated by the obstinate and insolent behaviour of the Marchese Vivaldi, that it was several minutes before she could sufficiently collect herself to enter into the explanation she wished, and his lordship, who observed her agitation, was all astonishment and impatience, until she could satisfy his curiosity.

As Ela proceeded, the surprise and wrath of Lord Helvendon were so powerful that he several times interrupted her, and when she had concluded, he paced the room in a most violent state of agitation, and she almost repented having told him, for she plainly perceived that he would resent the behaviour of the marchese in the way which Fanny had apprehended he would, and the consequences might be as fatal as the worst fears of the latter suggested.

"The presumptuous villain!" exclaimed Lord Frederick, passionately, "can it be possible that he has been so daring? And, fool that I was, not to notice his base behaviour! But he shall repent his conduct; I will immediately seek him out."

In a moment Lord Helvendon rushed from the room, and before Ela could recover from her confusion, he had made his way to the saloon, where, however, not perceiving the object of his rage, he left the place in search of him, without saying a word to any person present.

As soon as Ela recovered herself, she hurried into the saloon, hoping to be in time to prevent the serious encounter, which she apprehended would take place between Lord Helvendon and the marchese, but seeing neither of them, and that her daughter was not present, she made her way to the apartment of the latter, where

WALLINGFORD PLACES THE HAND OF MARIA IN HIS SON'S.

she ascertained that she was not in the castello.

When her mother had quitted her, after the conversation had taken place between them, Fanny, never imagining that her mother would put her designs into execution, she left the castello alone, for a short time, in the hope of being enabled to regain her composure by a ramble among the beautiful and romantic scenery adjacent; for now all apprehensions of the gipsy, Rupert Darwin, were entirely vanished from her mind.

She had proceeded to some distance, when, finding the wind blow keenly off the water, she prepared to return to the castello. She had arrived in a lane which led up to the back entrance of the castello, when she thought she heard the voices of men in loud altercation, she listened again, and certain that she was not mistaken, she looked over into an adjacent field, from whence the sounds seemed to proceed, and to her consternation and horror, behold Lord Helvendon and the Marchese Vivaldi presenting pistols at each other, and evidently about to discharge their contents at one another.

With a frantic scream of terror, she sprang into the field, and with a precipitation which nothing but her alarm could have occasioned, she rushed towards the combatants, and darted in between them, just at the moment when they were about to fire, and arrested their intention.

"Hold ! for mercy's sake, hold !" she cried ; "rash men, would ye commit murder ?"

The Marchese Vivaldi dropped his upraised hand in confusion, while Fanny threw herself into the arms of her lover, and with looks of supplication, and tearful eyes, implored him to desist.

The marchese scowled frightfully, and gnashed his teeth with rage when he beheld this, while Lord Helvendon pressed the affectionate girl to his bosom and frowned defiance and wrath upon Vivaldi.

"Lord Helvendon," at length exclaimed the latter, "for the present, you may bless your lucky stars ; but we shall meet again, and then our account will be finaly settled."

Having thus spoken, the villain turned upon his heel, and was quickly out of sight, while his thoughts filled Lord Helvendon with such ungovernable rage, that it was with the utmost difficulty that Fanny could prevent him from inflicting summary vengeance on the marchese upon the spot.

"Oh, forbear, forbear," she implored, "for my sake, do not rush into danger—perhaps death !"

"And think you, Fanny," returned her affianced husband, "think you, that I can tamely brook the unmanly insolence of the marchese towards you ?—Never !—by all my hopes of mercy, he shall be made to pay dearly for this, and had you not unfortunately have appeared at the critical moment, his life's blood should at present have stained the earth."

"Thank heaven that crime has been spared you, my love," returned Fanny, while tears of gratitude streamed from her eyes ; alas ! it was wrong surely, of my mother to make you acquainted with the circumstance which has been the means of your running into so much danger. But if you love me, Frederick, you will endeavour to calm your feelings, amd to stifle

your revenge, and all will yet be well. The marchese will not again have the boldness to show himself in our presence."

Lord Helvendon shook his head.

"Do you suppose, Fanny, that he will so easily forget his animosity, or the manner in which he has been foiled ?" said he. "No, my love, depend upon it, he will seek some method of gratifying his revenge ; nor can I tamely suffer one who has dared to call a blush upon the cheeks of my Fanny, to escape with impunity. Oh, no, you much underrate my affection for you, if you can think thus of me."

"Oh, that it had been kept a secret from you, Frederick," said the poor girl, as her fears almost overcame her, "for then might those dreadful results which I now foresee have been avoided."

"And would you have me remain in ignorance of the villany of the marchese, when he had the audacity to look upon you with an eye of sinful passion, Fanny ?" returned Lord Helvendon, in a tone of gentle reproach ; "this would have been treating me with injustice, and I entertain too high an opinion of you, my love, to imagine for a moment that you could act with anything like deceit."

Fanny blushed, and after a few more observations they returned to the castello. The mind of Fanny was most painfully harassed when she took all the circumstances into consideration ; and the hint which Lord Helvendon had himself given utterance to, namely, that the marchese "would seek some method of gratifying his revenge," more than all excited her terrors, for she reflected upon the sanguinary and determined disposition of the marchese, and she had not the slightest doubt but that he would readily avail himself of the means of assassination, if every other scheme failed ; and perhaps he would prefer that to risking his own life in a duel with Lord Helvendon ; for she well knew that the greatest villains are generally the greatest cowards. She was filled with almost insupportable terror every time that Lord Frederick left the castello, especially if it happened to be late at night, and her mind was so disturbed that she could scarcely get any rest.

Ela also regretted that she had been so hasty in divulging the secret to Lord Helvendon, but on reflection, she considered that she had done nothing more than her duty, and she would ever after have reproached herself, had she kept his lordship in ignorance of the secret enemy, who was seeking to destroy the happiness of himself, and she upon whom his warmest affections were placed. Besides, might not the jealousy of the marchese have prompted him to have sought the life of Lord Helvendon, whether or not she had informed the latter of his behaviour ? and therefore his danger would have been the same; consequently, she became more composed, and was perfectly satisfied with her own conduct.

CHAPTER LXIII.

"Beshrew thee, damsel, I love thee for thy scorn,
Thy reproaches do but increase my passion's
  fire;
Each frown but adds to my infatuation;
And, methinks, I could bask contented in thy
  displeasure,
And love thee for the hatred thou dost bear
  me."   OLD PLAY.

LORD HELVENDON, on his return to the castello, after the circumstance which we have related in the foregoing chapter, made Don Ferdinand acquainted with all that had taken place. The honest hidalgo had scarcely patience sufficient to hear the recital out, so great was his indignation against the offender; and when Lord Frederick had concluded, he gave vent to his feelings in no very measured terms.

"The scoundrel—the daring villain!" he exclaimed; "he shall never come beneath this roof again; from this very time he and I are strangers; I will hold no further intercourse with him, and I only regret that I ever became acquainted with him. His base character renders him unworthy of that esteem I promised his father on his death-bed to bestow upon him. The villain!"

A week passed away, and nothing more was heard of the Marchese Vivaldi, and Lord Helvendon had now nearly erased him from his memory. Fanny, too, had become more composed, and thought that the marchese, finding, perhaps, that all his wishes were frustrated, and not choosing to risk his own life, had left the country to seek fresh pursuits and fresh acquaintances. It now only wanted three days to the time appointed for the nuptials, and each one began to look forward with joyful impatience to that auspicious event, although it was resolved, as we have before stated, to let it be conducted in as private a manner as possible.

"I trust there will be nothing to interrupt the completion of our happiness this time, my love," observed Lord Helvendon, when they were walking together on the terrace of the castello, which was their favourite promenade. "Nay, sweetest," he continued, "why do you sigh? Surely that is not an event to excite your melancholy?"

Fanny did, indeed, sigh, for at that moment a feeling of the most dismal foreboding, or presentiment of some approaching calamity, crossed her mind.

"No, dear Frederick," she replied, "it is not, but——"

"But what, Fanny?" inquired Lord Hel-

vendon, eagerly; "a sudden gloom seems to have come over you; tell me, I beg of you, what is it that has given rise to this change."

"Nothing, dear Frederick, nothing," answered Fanny, attempting to smile; "it was only a sudden pain in my head, but it is all over now. You will not walk out this evening, will you, my love?"

"I must, dear Fanny," answered her lover, "because I have particular business to transact in the city; but it shall not be late before I return. Why do you ask the question?"

Fanny, whose countenance had become very pale, again attempted to evade the question, but Frederick could plainly perceive that something or the other afflicted her, and almost immediately guessed the real cause.

"Nay, my love," he said, "why will you persist in giving way to this weakness? Indeed, you have nothing to apprehend; the villain Vivaldi, I have no doubt, is far away from hence at this time. Besides, if he even is not, I do not think he will now make any attempt to put his threats into execution. And probably he has by this time forgotten all about the affair."

Fanny again sighed and looked very uneasy.

"Could you not put off your business until to-morrow, Frederick?" she inquired, in a tremulous voice. "I know you will deem me weak, but surely you will not blame me for a sentiment which has its origin in my anxiety for you? I cannot—indeed I cannot help thinking that something is about to happen. Do, I pray you, postpone your journey till to-morrow."

"I cannot, dear girl," replied Frederick; "it is of the utmost importance, and to-morrow would be too late to transact it. But really I think you are fearful without a cause, and implore you to endeavour to conquer such superstitious ideas. I shall return quite safe, and then you will see the fallacy and folly of such surmises."

Fanny affected to be appeased, but it was very evident she was far from being so. They shortly afterwards re-entered the castello, and after the interchange of a few observations, in which Lord Helvendon sought to reconcile her to the necessity which compelled him to leave her, took his departure. Fanny once more walked on to the terrace of the castello, and with streaming eyes, watched his receding form, as well as the twilight would permit, until it was hid entirely from view, and she then returned to the apartment she had left, unable to shake from her heart the heavy melancholy which oppressed it. Her mother endeavoured all in her power to reanimate her spirits, but every effort failed, and she at last gave up the attempt, although she would not quit her daughter for a moment.

In the meantime, Lord Helvendon pursued his way to the place of his destination; but in spite of all his efforts to the contrary, he could not remove from his mind the impression which the words and fears of Fanny had made upon him. He reached the place, however, in safety, transacted his business to his satisfaction, and then made the best of his way back to the castello. He had reached the walls of the ancient building, when suddenly he beheld two or three long shadows on the earth ; and in a moment, before he had sufficient time to look around him, he was pounced upon by two ruffians, armed with stilettos, and a voice exclaimed—

"That's him! plunge your weapons to his heart!"

Lord Helvendon knew the voice in a moment. It was that of the villain Vivaldi, who now stood before him ; and ere he had time to offer the least resistance, the miscreants darted upon him, buried their stilettos in his body, and he sunk bleeding and insensible to the earth.

It was growing late, and Lord Helvendon being still absent, the fears of Fanny increased ; and it would be impossible to describe the state of mind she was in, the intense, the almost insupportable agony she endured. In vain did her mother seek to pacify her: in fact, she was herself in very little better condition than her daughter ; and in spite of all her efforts to the contrary, could not help partaking of the fears and presentiments which tormented the bosom of the latter. Don Ferdinand and the fair Elvira, and Inez, also began to fear that something had happened, as the time passed rapidly away, and still Lord Helvendon did not make his appearance at the castello, and Lady Helvendon was in such a state of excitement that it was distressing to see her.

At length, unable any longer to control his own fears, or to alleviate those of the others, Don Ferdinand despatched several domestics in different directions in search of him. The suspense—the dreadful anguish and anxiety which Fanny suffered during the time the men were gone, was more than she could very well support ; and, unable to remain in the castello, she walked on to the terrace, and endeavoured, by the light of the moon, to trace their progress over the country beyond, and to discover whether or not they had found him. Oh! how her heart throbbed as she looked in vain across the wide space of country which the terrace overlooked, in the hope of seeing her lover approaching. But alas! no signs could she see of him, neither of the men who were sent in search of him, and her worst surmises seemed now to be realised. While she thus stood in a state of breathless excitement, a deep groan smote her ears, and made her start with horror. She listened : it was repeated. It seemed to proceed from a spot immediately underneath the terrace where she stood. She stretched

her head over the pallisadoes ; but a deadly faintness came over her ; her heart rose to her mouth, and a thick mist appeared to float before her eyes. Had it not been for clinging to the pallisadoes she must have dropped, especially when the groans were repeated with yet deeper agony than before. At length they ceased, and a death like calm succeeded ; and Fanny, unable any longer to endure the extreme suspense and agitation with which she was tormented, staggered from the terrace into the castello, to endeavour to ascertain there what dreadful event had happened, though her heart foreboded too well what was the cause of the sounds of suffering she had heard.

No sooner had she entered the building, than the sounds were repeated ; and, pale and trembling, she tottered down the stairs towards the apartment from whence they appeared to issue. She paused at the door, and was so terribly agitated that she could not open it, although she could hear, from the noises which proceeded from the inside, that something of more than an ordinary nature had occurred.

At length the door was opened by one of the attendants, and the eye of Fanny fell immediately upon the terrible spectacle she had so forcibly foreboded.

Stretched upon a sofa, and supported by his distracted mother and Don Ferdinand, was the bleeding form of the unfortunate Lord Helvendon, who had recovered sufficiently to be conscious of his pain, but not of what was going forward, or to discern any one around him. With a frantic scream, which startled every one in the room, Fanny rushed towards the sofa ; and as her eyes gazed upon the pale and ghastly countenance of her lover, she fell senseless in the arms of her mother, who had entered the room a few minutes before her.

The poor girl was immediately conveyed to her chamber, were such restoratives as were requisite for her recovery were applied by the deeply agitated Ela and the two beauteous daughters of Don Ferdinand, who would insist upon being in attendance upon their favourite and companion.

In the meantime, Lord Helvendon having been undressed, and put to bed in the chamber which was appropriated to his use, the medical man—who had been immediately sent for, after he had been discovered by the men who had been despatched by Don Ferdinand—arrived, and examined and dressed his wounds, which he pronounced to be very severe ; but he hoped that, with care, and keeping him as quiet as possible, they would not prove dangerous.

Lord Helvendon passed a night of great suffering, and was attended by his unhappy mother, whom no argument or persuasion, nor any idea of fatigue, could induce to leave his side for an instant.

In the morning, however, his symptoms

became more favourable, and he was much easier.   He had so far recovered his senses, too, as to be able to give an account of the horrible transaction; and the just indignation of every one was excited in the utmost degree, when they heard that the crime was perpetrated at the instigation, and by the command of the villain Vivaldi; and intelligence was immediately forwarded to the proper authorities, and steps taken to apprehend the marchese and his creatures. But this was, of course, a hopeless task, for murder was at that time committed by hired assassins with impunity, and seldom any trouble was taken to detect them; and it was most likely that the Marchese Vivaldi had left the country immediately after the crime, and if not, his rank would protect him.

Almost the first thing Lord Helvendon did on being restored to consciousness, was to inquire for Fanny; but as the medical man had strictly ordered that he should be kept as still as possible, and by no means to be allowed to do anything which might strongly excite him, Lady Helvendon entreated him to submit for the present, and to endeavour to calm his feelings.

Frederick did submit; but it was with extreme reluctance, and only on the promise that he should see her the next day.

Poor Fanny remained insensible the whole of the night; and her distracted and wretched parent feared that she had received so severe a shock that she would never more recover. It is impossible to describe the anguish of Ela, as this idea crossed her imagination; and she was for some time deaf to all the arguments, expostulations, and soothing remonstrances of Elvira and her sister, who exerted all their power to arouse her from the keep despondency and state of despair into which she was rapidly sinking. Long suffering, and one heavy calamity following another in such rapid succession, seemed to have entirely broken up the energy of Ela's character, and the least trouble had a most remarkable effect upon her feelings, which she had the greatest difficulty of conquering. But in Fanny, her whole soul, her very existence was centred. She was, as it were, the only link which connected her with the world; and that link broken, eternity was the only goal of happiness she looked forward to.

It seemed, too, as though a dreadful spell, a horrible fatality, attended all those who became in any way connected with them; as if a curse rested upon the heads of all those who offered them amity and friendship. Alas! how many had they been the cause of bringing misery upon!—The catalogue was too painful for her to enumerate. The same fatality had attended Lord Helvendon since they had become acquainted with him and his amiable mother; and it seemed as if they were destined by fate not to come together. This was

the second time that some terrible event had happened to prevent their union, and it seemed as if Providence was offended with them, and that it was ordained they should not enter into the holy alliance of matrimony.   The first time the life of Fanny was almost falling a sacrifice to the villany of Rupert Darwin, and now only a few days prior to the time again appointed for the union, Lord Helvendon's life had been sought by the Marchese Vivaldi.

These reflections filled the mind of Ela with the most harrowing affliction, and it was some time before she could be brought to listen with any degree of patience to the consolatory observations that were addressed to her by the two charming sisters.

Towards morning, however, Fanny partially recovered, and when she was informed of the actual situation of Lord Helvendon, and that the doctor had expressed his opinion of the wounds he had received not being dangerous, she became more composed, and exhibited visible symptoms of being speedily restored. When she was informed that her worst conjectures were realised, and that it was the wretch Vivaldi who had made the attempt upon his life, she could not help admiring the wonderful ways of Providence, which had thus given her a presentiment of what was going to take place, and which would most likely have been the means, had Lord Helvendon taken her advice and attended to her earnest solicitations, of saving him from the catastrophe which had nearly deprived him of existence.

The anxiety she felt to see her lover, and to assure herself that he was not in that imminent danger which her fears would suggest, tended in a great measure to expedite the recovery of Fanny, but still it was thought advisable not to let their meeting be too premature, and in consequence, Fanny was persuaded, but with great difficulty, to wait until the following day.

By the following morning, Fanny was so far recovered from the shock her feelings had sustained, as to exhibit the utmost composure and fortitude, and Ela's prayers of gratitude to the Almighty, were offered up with sincerity to Heaven.

The next day the lovers met; but we will not endeavour to describe the interview. Nothing could more clearly prove the sincerity and the effervescence of the passion which inhabited their bosoms.   Day after day, attended by her mother, and Lady Helvendon, did the affectionate Fanny watch by the couch of her affianced lord, and nothing could prevail upon her to leave him. It was her presence which made the patient endure his sufferings with resignation and composure, and made him rapidly progress towards recovery; but yet it was very evident from the severe nature of his wounds, and the consequent weakness which must ensue, that it would be a considerable time before he would be thoroughly restored to convalescence.

While affairs were in this position at the Castello di Alancantaros, every effort had been prosecuted with the utmost vigilance, to detect and apprehend the Marchese Vivaldi and his colleagues, so that they might be brought to justice, and thus secure Lord Helvenden and Fanny from any further danger from the effects of his diabolical vengeance, but hitherto they had been totally unsuccessful. It was, therefore, at last concluded that they had quitted Spain altogether. It was not so, however, for the marchese still remained concealed at no great distance from the Castello di Alancantaros, and was thoroughly acquainted with all that was passing there. Several of the Alguazils knew of his retreat, but the gold of the marchese silenced them, and kept him secure from apprehension. When he heard that Lord Helvendon had been rescued from the death which he had thought his creatures had inflicted upon him, and was rapidly regaining health and strength, his rage and disappointment were unbounded, and with that increased his sinful passion for Fanny, and his determination, by some means or the other, to gain possession of her person. He had his secret spies about in all directions around the castello, to watch the motions of its inmates, and to bring him information of all that was passing, and he only watched for a favourable opportunity to bear her off to a place of security which he had in Italy, where he had resolved that nothing should prevent him from gratifying his licentious desires.

From having been a constant frequenter at the castello from childood, he was thoroughly acquainted with every portion of the building, and at last he recollected that there was a secret entrance in the left wing, which was known only to a few individuals, and could he but get possession of the key of this place, he might easily gain access to the castello, and by secreting himself and his myrmidons in the apartments of Fanny, bear her away without any danger of being obstructed.

At length, after endeavouring in vain for some time to hit upon a scheme to get the key of the secret entrance into his possession, which he did by bribing the domestic who had the care of it, and whom he bought over entirely to his service, and he now, therefore, made no doubt that he should soon have the object of his desires in his power. He felt the most demoniacal exultation, as these thoughts crossed his mind; and as he traversed his apartment, he exclaimed—

"Yes, proud, scornful beauty, soon shall you be mine, soon shall you be made to yield to my wishes, and to succumb to my desires. The man whom you have presumed to scorn shall

learn you to be humble and submissive, and ere long he will have you so completely in his power, that he will make you studious to gratify his most remote wish. I will not be foiled when once I form a resolution, and though for a time I may not be able to accomplish my views, success must and shall ultimately crown my projects. The knowledge of her hatred towards me, has but increased my desire to triumph over her, and stimulated me to attempt more desperate measures. Her lover, too, the hated Lord Helvendon, he who has escaped the death I intended for him, he shall never have her, or if he does, it shall be after she has served as the mistress of his rival."

Such was the soliloquy of the villain Vivaldi; and when he reflected upon the almost complete certainty there was of his being able to accomplish all these designs, his exultation was so great, that he could scarcely contain himself. He sent one of his emissary's off to Italy, to make such arrangements at his castle there, as would be necessary for the reception of Fanny, but which he had determined should be conducted with the utmost secrecy, and that no one should know the circumstance of Fanny's residence there, but those who might be concerned with him in the plot.

Three months elapsed, before Lord Helvendon was sufficiently recovered to leave his bed, and he remained uncommonly weak. Fanny was almost his constant companion, and in her society, he forgot his pain, and felt a degree of happiness which he had never experienced before.

Sometimes Fanny would sit and read to him passages from his favourite authors, in which occupation she highly improved and cultivated her own taste;—at others she would sing him the songs he had so often heard her execute with a degree of chaste simplicity which was truly captivating. Then she would engage with him in converse, and listen with eager delight to the forcible manner in which her lover expatiated upon any topic;—or they would draw in imagination a picture of happiness which they anticipated awaited them, notwithstanding the painful and alarming obstacles that had hitherto been thrown in the way of their union.

These were moments of the most extatic rapture; moments which they hoped would last for ever, but which were soon, alas! to be interrupted in a manner which at that time they had not the most remote idea of, otherwise they might have probably adopted some plan or the other to avoid it.

It was nearly midnight shortly after this period, before Fanny retired to her chamber for the night, and even then, not feeling disposed to sleep, she took up a book that was lying on the table, and began to peruse its contents, which were of a description to excite her utmost interest. Totally absorbed in the subject of the book she was reading, she took no notice of the lapse of time, until all at once, she was aroused by hearing a strange noise in the ante-room, and rising from her seat, she took the lamp in her hand, and went to the room, in order to ascertain, if possible, the occasion of the tumult. She had scarcely got to the door, when two powerful men, masked, rushed upon her from the interior of the room, and throwing a mantle over her head, which they drew so close as scarcely to allow her to breathe, she felt herself, to her horror, dragged forward, and presently afterwards descending a flight of stairs, which seemed to be narrow and uneven. At the bottom of these they stopped, and Fanny then heard the following words uttered in a voice, in the tones of which she immediately recognised that of the Marchese Vivaldi:—

" 'Tis well done, you have her safely now, and it is my turn to triumph. Hasten, follow me; in another hour we will be far away from the Castello di Alancantaros with our prize."

Completely overpowered at the knowledge of her being in the power of Vivaldi, Fanny had fainted away. The ruffians then took her up in their arms, and while the marchese preceded them with a light, exulting in the success of his stratagem, the ruffians followed with their senseless burthen.

They soon arrived at the exterior of the castello, (the inhabitants of which were all deeply wrapped in the arms of sleep), and the marchese, extinguishing the light, locked the door of the secret entrance, and putting the key in his pocket, told the fellows who carried Fanny to hasten as fast as they could towards the spot where he had a vehicle in waiting. But there was no occasion for this order, for there was not a person stirring about, and nothing could be more favourable to their infamous design.

Having reached the carriage, they placed the insensible maiden in it, Vivaldi jumped in and seated himself by her side, and the men, having taken their seats outside, the vehicle was driven off with the utmost rapidity.

Great was the satisfaction which the Marchese Vivaldi experienced, now that the unfortunate Fanny was so securely in his power, and as they quickly left the Castello di Alancantaros far behind them, he gazed with delighted eyes upon the beauteous countenance of the insensible damsel, as she laid by his side, and pressed his lips with transport on the twin rubies, which had so often excited his desires, and he felt that his triumph was nearly complete.

" You are mine, fair maiden," he exclaimed, " the man whom you hate and despise, has you, at last, securely in h s power, and will not fail to make good use of the transporting opportunity which chance has thrown in my way. Oh, this repays me for all the scorn I have experienced from you ; and the trouble I have had to obtain it, renders the prize doubly valuable to me. What glorious revenge it is for me to picture to myself, what will be the agony of Lord Halvendon and your friends, when they discover that yon are taken away from them, and they will be ignorant where to seek you, or know in whose power you actua ly are ? Cirenzio Vivaldi, you have a rich source of felicity now in your hands, and the most happy might envy you your fortune."

Thus did the villain rejoice in his iniquity, and as the carriage fast proceeded on the journey, he formed, in his own mind, plans for the persecution of his unoffending victim, and the indulgence of his guilty passions.

It was so long ere Fanny evinced any signs of returning sensibility, that even Vivaldi began to feel alarmed, lest she should not recover again. But at length, heaving a deep sigh, she opened her eyes, and fixing them on the countenance of the marchese, giving utterance to a scream of horror, she relapsed once more into unconsciousness. In consequence of this, Vivaldi ordered the men to stop at a posade, which was in an obscure part of the country, the proprietor of which was well known to him, and had frequently assisted him in similar diabolical stratagems, and here he resolved to remain until an early hour in the morning, and ordered a female attendant to see Fanny into a chamber and attend to her recovery.

This order was obeyed, and the marchese, after partaking of a bottle of wine, and other refreshments, also retired to a chamber prepared for him, ordering the men to have the carriage in readiness for their departure before the blush of day in the morning.

Vivaldi, however, was so delighted at the success of his scheme, that he found it impossible to sleep for thinking upon the means which was now afforded him for indulging in those wishes that had so long occupied his mind.

Soon after Fanny had been placed in the bed by the female, who was deputed to attend her, and who was remarkable for her repulvive manners and features, she recovered, and opening her eyes, she started around in wild amazement.

" Good God!" she cried, starting up in the bed, and fixing her eyes with increased amazement upon the countenance of the young woman, " where am I ? Why am I brought hither, and what has become of my friends ?"

" You had better be quiet," said the girl ; " it is no use making any disturbance here, for there is no one disposed to assist you, However, if you only act prudently, there is no one who will harm you."

Fanny shuddered with horror at the manner in which this was spoken, and at first, an idea that she was in the power of the gipsies occurred to her, but the moment afterwards her memory returned to her, and she recollected the words of the Marchese, so that the whole truth was evident to her, and filled her bosom with the utmost terror and despair.

"Merciful father!" cried the poor girl, clasping her hands, and raising her eyes piteously towards heaven, "what will become of me? What mercy can I expect from a wretch so insensible to feeling as the Marchese Vivaldi? Alas! alas! all—all is despair!"

Thus speaking, she groaned aloud with the intensity of her agony. The girl appeared to view the anguish of Fanny with anything but pity, and, in fact, frowned when the latter mentioned the name of her master, and looked more disagreeable than ever.

After having finished the arrangement of some of the furniture in the apartment, the girl retired, and Fanny was left to herself, and to the indulgence of the melancholy and dismal thoughts that beset her mind. Terrible indeed were they, as may be expected, for she apprehended the worst from the impetuosity of the sinful passion which existed in the bosom of the marchese, and without any person nigh who would sympathise and interfere to rescue her from her fate, what avail would be the opposition which she could offer? None, none,—and hopelessly wretched did she feel herself.

"My God!" she exclaimed, with a burst agony, "what will be the sufferings of my poor mother, what those of Frederick, at my mysterious disappearance, and at the uncertainty of the place where I am confined, and in whose power I am? Oh, give me strength to support these racking thoughts, or I shall go mad."

Again she clasped her hands, and rising from her seat, traversed the room backwards and forwards in the most violent state of agitation.

The suite of rooms she was in, were very elegant and commodious, and seemed to have been recently fitted up and re-decorated, but the mind of Fanny was too much tormented with the thoughts of the situation she was in, to allow her to take any notice of them, and at that time she could not have experienced any greater misery, had she been confined in the most dismal dungeon.

It was very certain that her friends would immediately conclude that she was in the power of the marchese, but yet they could not possibly have any idea whither he had borne her, so that her delivery seemed to be utterly impossible, and the fate she dreaded inevitable.

"Would that I had fallen by the hands of the gipsies," she ejaculated, "would that the miscreant, Rupert Darwin, had buried his knife in my heart, rather than I should have been reserved for such a fate as this! Oh, my poor mother! Your heart will be broken, when you hear what your unfortunate child has suffered. My love, my betrothed too! Great God! I cannot—dare not dwell upon the dreadful thought."

She was interrupted in the midst of these melancholy reflections, by some one unlocking the room-door, and immediately afterwards, the object of her thoughts and terrors, the Marchese Vivaldi, stood before her. An icy chill ran through her veins, and she could scarcely repress a scream, but quickly recollecting herself, she sufficiently regained her composure to assume an air of dignity, and offended virtue, which struck a momentary feeling of awe into the callous mind of the Marchese Vivaldi even. However, he soon conquered the feeling, and advancing to Fanny with his usual bold demeanour, and a supercilious smile upon his countenance, he extended his hand towards her, and gave utterance to the following words—

"Welcome, fair damsel, welcome to the mansion of the man whose whole soul is devoted to you, whose affections are held captive by the power of your charms. Here do I come to offer you my heart's adoration, to become your slave, your willing slave, anxious to do your behests, and to make any sacrifice to contribute to your happiness; anything but to suffer you to leave this place, over which you are destined to reign mistress. Come then, dearest, loveliest of women, throw aside your coyness, and the cold disdain with which you have hitherto treated me, and live alone for love and Vivaldi."

As the marchese spoke, he endeavoured to take her hand, but she shrunk back with disgust and horror, and fixing upon him a look of the most ineffable abhorrence, in a voice of dignity and firmness, exclaimed—

"Away, and no longer disgust me with your presence. For you, I have no other feelings than those of hatred and contempt, and while I have life, nothing can alter those sentiments. Dare you, who have outraged every feeling of humanity, violated every sacred law, and trampled upon the happiness of a female, talk of love?"

"Ay, indeed can I," replied Vivaldi, with the utmost carelessness, "and not only can I talk of love, but you will find that I shall soon become a thriving wooer. The irresistible force of your charms, sweet maiden, will impart eloquence to my tongue, and you —"

"Cease this bold and insulting harangue," ejaculated the indignant Fanny, her fine dark eyes glowing with more than their usual brilliancy, and her bosom swelling and throbbing with wrath, "such language cannot but increase the hatred I bear you, and render your presence more odious to me. Marchese Vivaldi, you may fancy that you triumph now, but a just God above will not fail to punish you for this brutal outrage upon one of that sex it is the bounden duty of every man to protect. My

friends, too, will soon become acquainted with the truth, and not only release me from your power, but bring you to justice for your offences."

The marchese turned upon her a look of scorn, and smiling ironically, replied—

"At any rate, fair maiden, you are at pre-

FANNY AND CLOTILDE IN THE SALOON OF THE MARCHESE VIVALDI.

sent securely in my power; neither do I fear any of those results you have thought proper to predict. You are now at a sufficient distance from all your friends, nor can they have it in their power to form the slightest conjecture where you are confined; and if they had, it

would avail them but little, for this building may be said to be impregnable, and might defy every effort they might think proper to make to obtain an entrance into it and liberate you. At any rate, I am determined that, let whatever may be the consequences, nothing shall thwart my plans, or prevent the gratification of my wishes. You hear what I say, Fanny Beranzio, and rest assured that I will not fail to act according to my promise; I am a man who will not be trifled with, or baulked in any darling object I may have fixed my mind upon. Banish then your scorn—divest yourself of that repugnance which you at present evince towards me, which can be of no service to you here, and may only serve to arouse my anger, and prompt me to act with a severity towards you, which is foreign to my wishes. Here, every pleasure you can desire shall be your's, and all that I ask for in return is your smiles, and a return of that passion which so fiercely glows within my bosom towards you. What need we care for the opinion of the world? Are we not secure from its frowns? Here let us throw off its trammels, and give up all for the unrestrained enjoyment of exuberant affection."

Fanny could not speak; her cheeks turned pale and red, alternately, with shame, disgust, and indignation; her limbs trembled violently, and she was compelled to grasp the arm of a chair to save herself from falling; and at length, her feelings completely overpowering her, she covered her face with her hands, and burst into a paroxysm of convulsive sobs and tears.

So far from feeling any emotion or pity for her distress, the Marchese Vivaldi gazed upon her with looks of the most unbounded admiration and sinful desire, and at length taking her hand (for the power of her grief had now rendered her weak and passive), he in a voice whose accents were softened to suit his purposes, thus observed—

"Why will the beauteous Fanny thus rack and torture herself, why give way to a grief which is as uncalled for as it is useless? It is true you are torn away from your friends, you are deprived of your liberty: but here you shall find those pleasures, those enjoyments, that shall leave you no cause to regret them. Here you may command all which can contribute to your happiness, and I will be your willing slave, subservient to all your wishes, studious to anticipate your utmost desires. Then, prithee, dearest girl, endeavour to dissipate this useless sorrow, and you shall find me kind, indulgent, solicitous only for your enjoyment. Now, on those ruby lips, which mine have oft so longed to press, let me——"

"Hold! unmanly ruffian!" cried Fanny, aroused by the insolence of his manner, and snatching suddenly from his belt a poniard, "hold! I say—for by Heaven, if you attempt to pollute me by your hated touch, I will plunge this weapon to my heart and die in your presence."

As Fanny thus spoke, she brandished the glittering weapon, her eyes seemed to flash fire, and her whole demeanour was so determined, that the marchese shrank back in as-

tonishment and terror, and stood gazing at her with a vacant stare, expecting every moment to see her put her threats into execution.

"Marchese Vivaldi," said the poor girl, in a firmer tone, "you may think to triumph over my woman's weakness, but you will find yourself deceived; by that Almighty Power which watches and guides all our actions, I swear, that the moment you attempt to approach me, this dagger shall be sheathed in thy bosom. Leave me; Fanny Beranzio can better die than she can listen to your detestible passion."

"Rash girl! what would ye do?" cried the marchese, who was now evidently alarmed; 'give me the deadly weapon."

"Never!" ejaculated the maiden, determinedly; "nay, Marchese Vivaldi, do not dare me to it; advance not an inch towards me, or you will see me in an instant a lifeless corpse at your feet. Think not that I will fear to put my threat into execution."

There was everything in the expression of the intrepid girl's countenance to convince the libertine that she would not fail to keep her word; and assuming as much composure as he possibly could, he turned to her and said—

"At present, I see you are in no mood to talk; I will therefore leave you, with a request that you will do nothing rashly, but reflect seriously upon what I have said, and the promises that I have made you, and which shall be amply fulfilled. Every happiness is offered to you, and you will be mad if you reject it. Farewell till we meet again."

He bowed obsequiously, kissed his hand, and immediately retired from the room.

"Yes," ejaculated Fanny, once more gazing on the poniard, with a look of satisfaction, "you, at any rate, will prove a true friend to me in the hour of danger, and should I see no other means of avoiding the fate with which the marchese threatens me, willingly will I end at once my terrors and my life."

She put the dangerous weapon carefully in a place of concealment; and she had no sooner done so, than the door opened, and the girl entered, the Marchese Vivaldi having given her strict injunctions never to quit her charge for a moment longer than she could help.

CHAPTER LXIV.

"We meet again, in joy we meet,
    After an absence full of pain;
Oh, may such moments blest and sweet,
    Ne'er cease to be our lot again!
May fate our hands and hearts unite,
    And ev'ry blessing be our share;
Our mutual constancy requite,
    And make us strangers unto care."
                                        ANON.

IN the meantime, Maria was still at Rosemary Dell, and had met with nothing to disturb her tranquillity, with the exception of the dismal thoughts her continued absence from her friends created in her bosom, and the uncertainty as to when she should see them again. She had received several letters from Fanny and her mother, in which they had made her acquainted with all that had happened to them; and as may be expected, she felt the utmost pain at the many unfortunate and alarming events that had occurred to them, and the different untoward circumstances that had happened to prevent the union of Fanny and Lord Helvendon, and felt afraid that it was their fate never to enjoy real and uninterrupted happiness. With the abduction of Fanny, she was, however, yet unacquainted, and she began to be somewhat surprised and alarmed at the length of time which had elapsed since they had written to her, and to be anxious to know the reason.

Nothing took place in the Dell to create any alarm in her mind—she had heard nothing more of the Gipsies, and it was not at all improbable that they would never again make their appearance there, since Ela and her daughter were not in that part of the country, and they would run the risk of being apprehended and punished for the outrages they had already committed. Thus was her mind set at ease entirely upon this point; and had all those she loved been near her, she felt that she could have been extremely happy. But circumstances were about to happen, which would completely change the current of her thoughts, and raise in her bosom a tide of joy she had never before experienced.

Walter continued to write occasionally, and we need not attempt to describe how eagerly she perused each fond epistle, every one increasing more and more in affection, and being characterised by less restraint in their style. The letters of Mr. Wallingford, also, were couched in language of unusual tenderness, and he seemed to take the most lively interest in her welfare, yet, notwithstanding, appearing to be still tenacious of impressing her mind with too strong an idea of his actual sentiments. Maria heard of his accident with the most unfeigned regret, and was very much delighted when she heard that it was not so alarming as they had at first apprehended. Many prayers did she offer up to heaven in the purity and sincerity of her soul for his speedy restoration to health, and regretted that she was not near him to attend to his sick couch.

Every letter that Walter sent her strengthened the hopes of Maria, that Mr. Wallingford would relent, and returning to England, would no longer seek to control the affections of his son, but at length give his sanction to their vows, and no more oppose their union. It was very evident, not only by what Walter himself stated in his letters, but from the tone and tenour of Mr. Wallingford's, that he was tired of being abroad; and soon all her hopes were perfectly realized, and all her doubts set at rest, when her cousin wrote to her and informed her, with many expressions of delight, that his father had at length intimated to him his determination to return to his native country immediately on his restoration to convalescence. All thoughts of the sufferings she had formerly undergone, were lost in the present transport the intended return of her uncle and Walter created; and with feelings of the utmost avidity she set about seeing after the preparations necessary for their reception. Under her directions, the old hall was soon restored to all its pristine elegance, and the gardens were arranged with all that taste which had formerly characterised them. The tenantry of Mr. Wallingford were delighted when they heard that that gentleman and his son were about to return to the ancient seat of their ancestors; for they had all most amply felt the blessings of their benevolence and philanthropy; they therefore determined to give them such a reception as the joyful occasion merited. Walter had also instructed Maria to make preparations for a festival at the hall to celebrate the return of his father, and to invite all the nobility, gentry, and tenantry to partake in its pleasure. This her cousin had taken upon himself to order, and without the knowledge of his father, for he considered that the occasion not only demanded such a demonstration, but that it might have the most beneficial effects upon the health and spirits of Mr. Wallingford, and lead him into that happy train of spirits, which would in time serve to dissipate entirely the melancholy which had overclouded his days.

We should not forget to mention that old Mathew had been to Bath, and arranged all the affairs that arose from the bequest of the late Doctor Hartley to Maria, and at the earliest opportunity he paid a visit to Mrs. Jackson, who, as well as her daughter Clara, were delighted to see him, and inquired most eagerly after Maria. When they heard of the proposition Mathew was entrusted to make to them, their pleasure exceeded all bounds, especially that of Clara, who felt for Maria the affection of a sister, and who had never got her out of her mind since they had been separated. We need not say that they accepted the offer of "their dear Miss Herbert" with avidity, and immediately set about making preparations for their departure with old Mathew, which were soon completed, and Clara and her mother (who felt so overjoyed, that she almost forgot her indifferent state of health, and became young again) stepped into the coach which was to convey them from Bath, as they believed for ever.

Maria was almost as pleased to see the kind-hearted Clara and her mother again as they were; and she felt at the same time the utmost gratification that it was in her power to place them in a situation where they would be comfortable, particularly as Mrs. Jackson and her daughter could be together.

From the late Doctor Hartley's house it was but a short distance, and Maria never failed, every morning, to pay it a visit. She felt a melancholy pleasure in rambling over those apartments which had been trodden by the footsteps of her benefactor; to gaze upon the different articles he had used during his life-time; and to peruse the books he had delighted to read. The most trifling thing brought back the recollection of the deceased so vividly to her memory, that she could at times almost fancy that he stood before her, and that she was holding communion with him. In moments such as these, the human mind becomes, as it were, estranged from the world, and associates with things celestial. It is a moment of inexpressible delight, a moment in which we are again united to those departed spirits we have loved so fondly while living.

The preparations for the return of Mr. Wallingford and his son, were now progressing rapidly, and every one was on the tiptoe of joyful expectation and impatience, when Maria received a letter from Walter, which informed her that in consequence of his father not having sufficiently recovered his strength to render him fit to undertake the fatigue of travelling, their return to England must be deferred for another month or six weeks. This letter very much vexed and disappointed Maria, for to her every day appeared like a week, so eager was she again to behold her cousin and his father; and every delay filled her mind with dread, for fear that anything should occur to cause the latter to change his mind, or prevent him from returning to England. The letter of Walter, however, was couched in the same affectionate language as his former ones, and he described his father to be still more anxious than ever to return to his native country, and that he was extremely vexed it should be so long retarded. Indeed, if Maria could have entertained any doubt of the truth of this, it must have been immediately dispelled on perusing the letter which her uncle had sent to her; which breathed the utmost tenderness towards her, and in which he stated that "he looked forward with the greatest anxiety and impatience to the time when they should again meet, he hoped no more to be separated until death." The altered tone of Mr. Wallingford (and his sincerity she could not doubt) was a source of the most unbounded delight to Maria, and filled her bosom with hope.

"Oh, surely," she soliloquized, "after such affectionate asseverations, he cannot, he will not stand in the way of the happiness of Walter and me?—That girl who is not unworthy of his love, must be deserving of the hand of his son. He will no longer deny his consent to our union; my heart assures me he will not; and our bliss will be rendered complete.—Dear, dear Walter, the few months we have been separated from each other, appear like so many years to me; what language can give expression to the ecstasy I feel at the prospect I have of once more beholding you, of listening to the tender accents of your voice; of hearing you repeat your vows of undiminished love, and assuring you of my constancy?—Heaven grant that such halcyon days may be in store for us, and that Providence may ordain that the many troubles we have endured, may be at an end."

These reflections served to increase the hopes of Maria, and she watched the progress of the preparations that were making at the Hall with the utmost pleasure and satisfaction. In the midst of this, however, she received a letter from Ela, the contents of which filled her bosom with intense grief. Ela, in terms which fully evinced her distracted state of mind, informed her of the sudden and melancholy disappearance of Fanny, from the Castello di Alancantaros, and of all the ineffectual attempts they had made to discover her retreat, although they had not a doubt but that she was in the power of the Marchese Vivaldi, though by what means he had affected his villanous design, or where he had concealed the unfortunate girl, they could not form the most remote idea. The agitation of Lord Helvendon, at the dreadful circumstance, she described as being so intense, that the excitement had thrown him into a high and dangerous fever, with which he was at that time confined to his bed, attended with the most anxious care by his amiable mother.

The tears of poor Maria flowed fast, as she perused this melancholy epistle, which imparted such painful intelligence; and it was some time ere she could, in the slightest degree, tranquillise her feelings.

"Alas! Fanny, unfortunate girl," she ejaculated, "when will your sorrows be at an end? What an untoward fate is yours, continually the victim of some terrible persecution; and yet, so amiable, so good, so virtuous—so worthy of every happiness. Born in sorrow, your whole life has been one of almost incessant suffering; and now, just at the moment when the cup of bliss is held to your lips, misery and guilt are at hand to dash it way, and hold the poisoned chalice in its place. Good God! in the power of a villian, such as he is described to be, what will become of her?—What a horrible fate may be hers! I shudder to think of it, and yet, what can avert it, if it is not already accomplished? Hapless girl, may the Almighty watch over and protect you, and defend you from, and frustrate, the diabolical designs of the miscreant who so cruelly and so unjustly detains you."

Again were her tears shed for the misfortunes of Fanny Beranzio, and sincerely did she sympathize in the distress it must occasion her mother, and her affianced husband; but, still, she could not help thinking it was very improbable that the Marchese Vivaldi should long be able to escape the vigilance of those who were endeavouring to detect him, and she hoped that Providence would render the efforts of the villain to accomplish his wicked designs futile, and bring him to the punishment he so richly merited, for the misery and suffering which he had been the guilty cause of.

It was about a fortnight within the time, at which Mr. Wallingford and Walter were expected to return to Rosemary Dell, that Susan appeared before Maria one morning, and informed her that two young women were waiting in the parlour below, and requested to see her.

"Two young women?" repeated Maria, in a tone of surprise; "did they not tell you their names, Susan?"

"No, miss," replied the other, "and I did not thing to ask them; but it strikes me very forcibly that I have seen them somewhere before, though, for the life of me, I can't call to mind at the present moment in what place it was. They are very pretty young women, and so much alike, that I should take them to be sisters."

Maria, without saying anything more, descended the stairs, and entered the parlour, where she was very much surprised to behold Emma and Rose Sherwood, who arose upon her entrance and courtseyed with humble politeness. They were both very cleanly and neatly attired, and were looking much better than when Maria saw them last. The roseate bloom had returned to their cheeks, and their countenances no longer bore that careworn appearance which they had recently done.

"Doubtless, Miss Herbert," said Emma, "you are surprised at seeing us here, and we hope you will pardon us for the liberty we have taken; but we could not resist the temptation of calling upon you the first opportunity we had, in order to return you our acknowledgments for the kindness which you were pleased to bestow upon us in our late distress."

"Do not mention it, my good girl," answered Maria; "I am very happy to see you again, and to notice the alteration in your appearance. But your child, Rose, say, how is he?"

"He is quite well, Miss, thank you," replied Rose, her eyes sparkling with maternal fondness, at the mention of his name.

"And have you come to reside in this neighbourhood?" Maria inquired.

"Yes, Miss," returned Emma, "though many a hard struggle had we with our feelings, before we could make up our minds to come to that neighbourhood where our disgrace was so well known. Ah! Miss Herbert, our situation is greatly altered from what it was when you met with us at Bath. God has been very kind to us; much better than we deserved after all our errors."

"Indeed?" said Maria; "I am rejoiced to hear you say so; but, pray, in what way has your condition changed?"

"Why, Miss," returned Emma, with a deep blush, "since we last saw you, we are married."

"Married!" reiterated Maria; "what, both married?"

"Both, Miss."

"You astonish me," observed Maria; "but to whom are you united?"

"To two of the best creatures in existence," said Emma;—"too good indeed for us. I am the wife of Arthur Dalton, the farmer's son, in this neighbourhood; and Rose is now Mrs. Mayburn, having married farmer Mayburn's son."

"Remarkable!" exclaimed Maria; "but pray, how was this happy affair brought about?"

"I will tell you, Miss," answered the poor girl; "you must know that we were playfellows together, and from childhood we called each other sweethearts, and looked upon ourselves as such. As we grew older, so did our affection for each other increase, and sanctioned by our parents, we paid our addresses to one another, and the time was even appointed for our union. Alas! in the interim, ill-fortune; introduced to our notice, the two villains who afterwards succeeded in triumphing over our virtues: we forgot our vows to the two poor youths who so ardently loved us, and brought misery, disgrace, and infamy upon our own heads, and nearly broke the hearts of those who deserved so much better a fate. You know, Miss, what followed, and the state of wretchedness we were in when you saw us in Bath. Shortly after you left Bath, going out one morning to purchase food for our frugal meal, I met Arthur and Henry—you may imagine the meeting better than I can describe it to you; they recognised me in a moment; pale, trembling, yet glowing with shame,—I sought to avoid them, but it was all to no purpose; they frantically held me, and would not release me until they had elicited from me all the dreadful particulars, and the awful manner in which we had been punished for our offences. They insisted on returning with me to the wretched hut we inhabited, but which your kindness had enabled us to make comfortable. The meeting between Henry Mayburn and my sister, was equally as affecting as that which had taken place between me and Arthur Dalton. The love that they had imbibed for us from childhood, nothing had been able to extinguish, and, if possible, the misfortunes we had undergone rather served to increase it than anything else, and from their hearts, they freely pardoned us for those errors, which our inexperience, and the natural weakness of our sex, had led us into, rather than from any vicious propensities. Their first care was to remove us from our present gloomy abode into comfortable lodgings, and they immediately wrote to their parents, to inform them of what had taken place, and the sentiments which they found still held so powerful a situation in their bosoms. In a few days they received an answer, which was all they could wish. Their parents warmly commiserated in our misfortunes, expressed their gratification at our contrition, and they left their sons to act entirely from the dictates of their own hearts and consciences, not seeking to bias or prejudice them on either side. The consequence of this was, that the generous young men once more avowed their ardent passion for us, and offered us marriage. It was some time ere we could make up our minds to suffer them to make such a sacrifice. We considered ourselves unworty of them, and shuddered at the idea of the remarks that might be made by the busy and the scandal-loving, after the circumstance that had taken place ; but at length they prevailed, and we were married. We have returned to this neighbourhood, where the business of our husbands compel us to reside, and we were therefore resolved to take the earliest opportunity of calling upon you, Miss, for we felt certain that you would be gratified at the happy change it has pleased Providence to make in our circumstances.''

"You are perfectly right, Emma," said Maria, when the former had given the explanation above, "nothing could afford me greater pleasure than to hear what you have been telling me ; and I hope that you will, by attention and affection towards the generous young men who have thus replaced you in a respectable position in society, prove your gratitude, and make all the atonement in your power for the indiscretion into which you have been led.''

"We shall never forget your kind, your excellent advice, Miss. Herbert, indeed we shall not," said Emma, the tears streaming from her eyes, while the emotion of Rose was so strong that she had not the power to speak ; "but will you allow us to call upon you sometimes, miss. to pay our respects to you?''

"Most assuredly," answered Maria. "I shall be very happy to see you and your sister at any time."

"Oh, this indeed is too good, too kind of you, dear Miss Herbert," said Rose ; "encou-

raged by you, we shall be secured from the foul breath of calumny and malevolence, which otherwise might be directed against us. But we are detaining you, miss, and——''

"Oh, no," interrupted Maria, "you are not; I am very happy of your company ; and as I have nothing to occupy my time, I shall be glad if you will remain with me for an hour or two longer.''

Rose and Emma accepted this invitation with many acknowledgments, and they walked into the sitting-room. The generous and warm-hearted nature of Maria, made her feel really very glad to see the sisters, who possessed natural endowments of no ordinary description, and would have embellished a far higher station in society than that which they had been born to. They sat together for some time in social conversation, upon various topics, and at length Maria said—

"I have never heard the particulars of the early part of your melancholy history, and, therefore, if you feel adequate to the task, I should feel obliged to you if you would relate it to me."

Emma sighed, and looked at her sister.

"What you ask us, my dear Miss Herbert," said she, "is a painful task, but we cannot refuse you anything. Our stories are so much alike, that by relating one it will be quite sufficient. But I must request some time to collect my thoughts and feelings ; to-morrow, with my sister's permission, and if it meets your approbation, I will, to the best of my abilities, relate the simple facts of the case, without exaggeration, or omiting anything which might serve to inculpate more than they merit, the villains whose wily tongues caused us to stray from the paths of virtue.''

Maria expressed her thanks, and after some further conversation, the two sisters departed.

The following day Emma and her sister came at an earlier hour than the day before; and after some preliminary discourse of no importance, the former commenced her narrative in the following words :—

EMMA DALTON'S TALE.

"OF the early passages of our lives, you have a sufficient knowledge, and they passed away in a manner very little different to that of other children ; unacquainted with care, and blessed with two excellent parents, whose sole study was to make us happy, and to inculcate such precepts in your youthful minds, as should render us worthy of that name they had borne without a blemish.

"They bestowed upon us a more liberal education than usually falls to the lot of children in the station of life we occupied ; and it is but fair to ourselves to state that we received it with an alacrity which was equal to their warmest wishes, and our dispositions were such as to give fair promise of virtue and integrity.

"It was while at school, Miss, that we first became acquainted with you, although we had known the amiable Mrs. Wallingford as long as we could recollect anything at all. It was in the performance of those noble acts of philanthrophy which always distinguished that good lady, that you were introduced to me and my sister : and many were the generous acts we owe to you an eternal debt of gratitude for. Heaven bless you for your kindness as you merit. I have told you before of the passion which our present husbands early imbibed for us, and of the affection we entertained for them in return, which we thought would have been sufficient to have prevented us from acting in the manner we did towards them ; I will not, therefore, trouble you by recapitulating these particulars, but come as quick as possible to that unfortunate event, which was the prelude to the misery and disgrace which afterwards befel us.

"Our parents, at this time, kept a small road-side inn, which was much frequented by travellers ; but afterwards their fortune changed, and sorrow and distress came upon them at the same time. My God! what have we not got to reproach ourselves with, for to our misconduct may be attributed all that happened to them !"

Here Emma was forced to pause, for her grief choked her utterance, and her sister mingled her tears, scalding tears of compunction with hers. Maria did not offer to interrupt them in their sorrow, for she knew it would relieve their minds ; and after some minutes passed in this way, Emma became more composed, and resumed her story as follows :—

"It was very late one night, in the depth of winter, when the wind howled dismally without, and the snow descended in large flakes, that we were alarmed by a loud knocking at the door, which not being answered immediately, was repeated with increased violence, and at length my father threw up the casement to ascertain the cause, and to see who it was that was knocking at that unseasonable hour. In answer to his inquiries, he was informed by the persons below, that a carriage had broken down close at hand, by which a gentleman was seriously injured, and that as it was impossible for him to proceed farther, they requested that he should be admitted into the house, and his friends and servants accommodated.

"My father did not wait to ask any more questions, being always as ready to assist those who needed it, as he was to have an eye to business ; so he quickly descended the stairs and gave admittance to a gentleman, who was supported by another, and a servant, and who appeared to be suffering most acutely. Neither me nor Rose had retired to rest when the knocking was heard, and prompted by curiosity and anxiety to see whether we could render any assistance, we entered the parlour into which the strangers had been conducted, and the wounded gentleman placed upon the sofa, while my father despatched one of his servants to town for the assistance of the late Doctor Hartley, who was, as usual, very prompt in his attendance.

"The gentleman who had met with the accident, and his friend, were both very young men, tall, and remarkably handsome ; and there was something in their appearance, independent of the circumstances under which they were introduced to us, which particularly excited our interest, at least it did that of mine and Rose, as she afterwards acknowledged to me. Alas! accursed for ever be that hour which brought them to our house, for ruin, misery, and destruction followed in their path.

"The stranger was put to bed, and it was found that he was so severely hurt that it would be impossible for him to be removed for several days. The gentleman, his friend, and the servants, were also accommodated, and every one in the house had soon retired for the night.

"Such was the impression the handsome countenance of the wounded gentleman had made upon my mind, that I could not erase him from my thoughts, and I laid awake for a considerable time conversing with Rose upon the subject of the accident, she being quite as ready to talk about it as I was ; and it was very evident to me, that if one of the strangers had made an impression upon me, no less effect had the appearance of the other had upon Rose, for she seemed as if she could sit and talk about them the whole of the night. Strange infatuation !—Unfortunate delusion ! Why were we selected for their victims, or why did not the Almighty enable us to conquer the sinful thoughts that had already taken possession of our minds ?—But it was our fate, and the weakness of our nature led us into the fatal error, which afterwards brought upon us so much and irremediable wretchedness.

"We soon learnt that both the gentlemen were men of rank and property ; the name of the gentleman who had met with the accident was Sir Charles Perceval, and his friend the Honourable Algernon Singleton, and they were returning from a visit they had been paying to a friend, when the event occurred which brought them to our house. It was soon found that it would be most likely three or four weeks before Sir Charles would be in a fit state for it to be safe to remove him ; and as we could not accommodate him according to his rank, the Honourable Mr. Singleton took apartments in the immediate neighbourhood, so that he might be near his friend; and he was a constant, and seemingly eager guest at our house. He was a gentleman of the most affable and insinuating manners, and he talked eloquently upon every subject. He did not seem to possess the least pride, and he treated my mother and father with marked familiarity, but to me and my sister (particularly the latter) he was very attentive, and I frequently observed him gazing at Rose with looks of the warmest admiration. She, too, received his attentions in a manner that was far from likely to abash him, and I was in no condition to offer her any advice, for from the moment I beheld Sir Charles, my thoughts had been continually occupied by his image, and that of my lover but seldom occurred to me.

"I was anxious to hear how he got on, and was solicitous too for him to be alleviated from his pain; yet when I thought of his recovery, and that he would then leave the house, a feeling came over me which I am pefectly at a loss to describe.

"Neither me nor my sister were strangers to each others thoughts, but we seemed as if we were at that time unconscious of doing wrong; a fatal spell appeared to be upon us, and to drive us headlong to destruction, and we did not awake from the fatal insensibility until it was too late.

"A fortnight passed away, and the recovery of Sir Charles was very slow, but at length he was able to leave his chamber, and walk down stairs. Never had I beheld a more interesting being; his manners were remarkably gentle, polite, and agreeable, and the whole was characterised by an air of gallantry, and gentlemanly bearing, that rendered him irresistibly charming. Alas! he was too dangerous for my peace!—Oh, that deceit should inhabit a form of such attractions!—But was I not unpardonably culpable, in raising my thoughts to one who being so far above me in rank and fortune, I might have felt assured could never be mine? —And where were all the vows I had plighted to Arthur Dalton? What had become of the love I had vowed so frequently to entertain for him?—Alas! I must have been mad!

"If I was charmed with the society of Sir Charles, no less delighted did he seem in mine, and he choose every opportunity of indulging in this pleasure, as did his friend also in that of my sister, and our parents, who, of course, could never entertain the most distant idea of such a circumstance, never looked upon us with any suspicion.

"Day after day passed away, and my ill-fated passion increased; yet such a strange hold had it taken of my affections, that I found it utterly impossible to release myself from it. The visits of Arthur became less agreeable to me, and I felt a restraint on my actions while in his company, which always made me ex-

perience a degree of pleasure when he left me. When I compared his simple, rustic manners with those of the highly polished, accomplished, and agreeable Sir Charles Perceval, they appeared rude, disgusting and boorish; and I often wondered to myself, how ever I could have experienced anything like affection for one who now appeared so unprepossessing.

"When Sir Charles talked about leaving our house, and expressed his regret that he should so soon be deprived of the pleasure of my society, never to enjoy it again, most likely; a pang shot through my heart of the most painful description, and I could not bear to think of it. More than once I could scarcely repress my tears; and upon one occasion, Sir Charles perceived me, and at that moment an expression of satisfaction illumined his countenance, and it was evident that the pleasure he felt was so powerful, that it was with the utmost difficulty he was prevented from giving utterance to it.

"Although he was now rapidly improving, he still kept making some excuses to delay his departure, and Mr. Singleton still remained in the apartments he had taken in the neighbourhood, and was a constant visiter at the house of my parents, upon which occasion, Rose placed herself in his society as much as possible; in fact she had openly declared to me her sentiments, and I had made a similar confession of mine. Good God! we must have been lost to all sense of reason, all sense of shame!

"But I will not dwell any longer than is absolutely necessary upon this painful part of mine and my sister's history. Six weeks having elapsed, and Sir Charles being perfectly restored to convalescence, he could no longer offer any excuse to procrastinate his departure. I must not attempt to describe the scene which passed between us, on the day previous to the one he had fixed on for leaving. Suffice it to say, that he had confessed his love (so he termed it) for me, and, in a moment of weakness, had drawn from me an acknowledgment of the real state of my feelings; and I was all but lost! The snare was laid to entrap me, and it was not long ere the designs of my seducer were accomplished. At the time fixed on, Sir Charles and his friend departed, and had our parents had the slightest suspicion, they must have noticed the deep emotion which was evinced by me, Rose, and our two admirers. For my own part, I felt as if it were like the separation of body from soul, and there was scarcely any sacrifice that I would have hesitated in making (which virtue could sanction) to have been able to have prevented his departing, and to have had him residing in the neighbourhood. My heart foreboded that we should never meet again, and the thought was so dreadful, that it is astonishing how I could prevent myself from giving the most violent expression to my grief. Sir Charles also showed the same agitation, and it was with difficulty he could so far master his feelings, as not to betray himself to my parents, who were standing by at the time. The affliction of Mr. Singleton and my sister appeared to be equally as powerful, and it was a great relief to all parties when the scene was over. I and my sister made an excuse to retire immediately to our chamber, where we unbosomed ourselves to each

FANNY DEFENDS HER HONOUR FROM THE MARCHESE VIVALDI.

ther, and gave the most unrestrained indulgence to our sorrow. Rose was of the same opinion as myself, namely, that we had parted, never to meet again; and nothing could impart consolation to her mind; nothing could assuage the violence and impetuosity of the tide of passions which rolled within her bosom, and imparted to her cheek the pallid hue of care.

"I have often since dwelt with astonishment upon the strange, the unaccountable infatuation which had thus taken possession of us both, and which, in so short a space of time, had, as it were, made every other feeling subservient to its will; and the more I reflected on it, the more perplexed I became, and sought, but in vain, to banish it from my mind. We must have been mad, for what could be the consequences of our fixing our affections upon two beings placed so far above us, and whose sentiments were probably only evanescent, and such as the sensualist alone indulges in ?—Would they ever marry us ?—No !—it was not at all likely that they would so far banish from themselves those prospects which their property, and the rank they held in society, entitled them to expect. Then what could we anticipate from the indulgence of this fatal passion, but ruin, misery, and disgrace ?—Oh, could we but have thought and seen this at the time, what many hours of wretchedness, what moments of horror, would it have saved us. We should have become the brides of Arthur and Henry, before we had known what guilt was, and our parents, our unfortunate, our affectionate parents, might have been still alive, instead of being the inmates of that grave, into which we must always accuse ourselves of prematurely hastening them !—Reflection, how bitter, how poignant art thou, to the mind where guilt has once gained admittance !—What sacrifice would be too great, could we but again be restored to that happy state of innocence we formerly were in !"

At this passage of her dismal narrative, Emma was again obliged to pause, and the grief of she and her sister once more burst forth with great violence, which Maria, as before, never offered to interrupt. It was very evident that their bosoms had received a wound from which they would not easily, if ever they would, recover, and the terrible effects of a self-accusing conscience, were most painfully exhibited in them. At last, however, after a severe struggle with her feelings, Emma conquered her emotion sufficiently to enable her to proceed with her story in the following manner :—

"Three weeks passed away, three weeks of the greatest anguish to me and Rose; we found it utterly impossible to conquer the passion which we had unfortunately imbibed, and the recollection of those we loved became more strongly imprinted on our minds than ever it had been before. Our only enjoyment was to wander from the house upon every opportunity we could meet with, and to stroll to a neighbouring wood, where we could give vent to the feelings which predominated in our breast, and entertain no fear of the searching eye of curiosity and suspicion being upon us.

"We avoided the society of our lovers as much as possible, and when we were compelled to be in it, there was a marked and freezing coldness in our behaviour towards them (although we struggled hard to disguise it), which it is not at all likely they could be off noticing. Indeed we were convinced that they did notice it, and that it caused the greatest unhappiness; and more than once they questioned us so closely, that we had the most difficult matter in the world to evade them. With what base ingratitude, with what shameful hypocrisy were we acting towards those kind-hearted young men, who were ready to worship us, and to whom we were the only source of hope and happiness !—Never, never can we think upon this without upbraiding ourselves for it.

"At length the misery we endured had such an effect upon our health, that we were confined to our beds, and our parents became alarmed, but yet they had no suspicion of the real cause, and attributed it to a fever. We were attended to with the utmost solicitude and affection, and after much trouble, gradually recovered; but although our spirits were rather more tranquillised, we had found it utterly impossible to erase the cause of our melancholy entirely from our minds.

"When we were getting better, it was our custom to walk out alone in the adjacent fields, for the benefit of the air, though often Arthur and Henry, much to our annoyance, would insist upon accompanying us.

"One afternoon, however, we happened to be alone, and had got to some distance from the house, when we heard hurried footsteps from behind us, and turning round, we beheld a man, in the livery of a groom, hastening towards us, and perceiving us look back, he made a motion for us to stop. Our astonishment was a great deal excited at this circumstance, and more so as the figure of the man appeared to be familiar to us. We involuntarily stopped, and the man soon came near enough to us to distinguish his features, when our amazement may be readily conceived, for in them we recognised those of Thomas, the groom of Sir Charles Perceval.

" 'My dear young ladies,' said Thomas, after he had come up with us, 'you have given me a rare run for it, and I declare I am quite out of breath; but pray how are you both ?'

" 'For goodness sake, Thomas,' said I, without answering his question, 'what brought you down here at this time? Have you left your master ?'

" 'Oh, no, Miss,' replied the man, 'he is too good for that, and I will never leave him while he will keep me.'

" 'But I thought your master was in London, Thomas ?' said I, and my heart palpitated in expectation of his answer.

" 'So he *was*, Miss,' returned Thomas; 'but at the present time he is not more than a mile-and-a-half from the spot we are now standing upon.'

" 'Is it possible ?' I exclaimed, and I could feel that I turned pale and red, alternately.

" 'And Mr. Singleton ?' eagerly ejaculated Rose, and I felt her tremble with anxiety for an answer to her question.

" ' Oh, of course he is with him,' replied Thomas,—' for they are so fond of each other, that they are complete inseparables. But here is a letter from each of them, which I have been entrusted to deliver to you, and likewise to request that you would return an answer by me.'

As the man thus spoke, he put a letter into each of our hands, and which we tremblingly received, scarcely knowing, in the confusion of the moment, what we did. Upon breaking the seal and looking at the first few words, the same infatuation which had lately taken possession of our minds, seemed to urge us on to peruse the remainder, and how our bosoms throbbed with mingled feelings of delight, wonder, and incredulity, as we did so !

" They were couched in the most ardent and affectionate language imaginable, and gave expression in the most glowing terms to the unbounded passion with which we had inspired them, the manner in which we had haunted their imagination since their absence, and how utterly impossible they found it to live out of our presence. They stated that they did not like to call at the house of our parents for particular reasons, which they would explain, and they entreated that we would meet them at a place named on the following day, when they had much to say to us, and many things to inform us, which were requisite to our happiness. They added, that if we assented to meet them, to signify the same as briefly as possible to Thomas.

" After reading these epistles, which we both did two or three time over, we looked at each other, as though we wished advice, but in a moment reading my sister's thoughts by my own, I returned a verbal and monosyllable answer of ' Yes,' and after bowing and looking very well pleased at the success of his mission, he hastily departed.

" I will not seek to describe our emotions at this unexpected occurrence, but delight was the predominant sentiment which presided in our minds, and we never once gave a thought to the imprudent step we had taken in giving our consent to hold a secret assignation with our admirers. On the contrary, we were all impatience for the time to arrive, and our bosoms throbbed with eagerness and anxiety once more to behold them, who had excited such a deep sensation in our bosoms. It served to occupy our thoughts and our conversation all the way as we returned home, and we slept little that night, our minds being too busily occupied with the reflections which the unexpected circumstance naturally gave rise to. Had we not been mad, or under some accursed spell, the very manner in which the appoint-

ment was made, and the circumstance of Sir Charles and his friend not making their appearance at the inn, ought to have created the strongest suspicions of their intentions in our bosoms. But no—so strong was the opinion we entertained of them, and so little doubt had we of the honour of their designs, that such an idea never once occurred to us, and had any person even suggested such a thing, we should have scouted it with indignation.

" But at length, the fatal day day arrived ; a day which will always be stamped upon our memories with horror, disgrace and shame. At an early hour we left the inn, and were at the place of appointment long before the time. It was in a woody glade, quite secluded, and which was not much frequented. With anxious and palpitating hearts, with alternate feelings of hope, doubt, and wonder, we waited, and at exactly at the hour stated in their letters that they would meet us, Sir Charles and Mr. Singleton made their appearance, and rushed joyfully into our arms.

" I should fail were I to attempt to describe the meeting ; no, rather, let me pass over it as quickly as possible : oh, let me not dwell upon that which racks my brain to distraction to think of ; let me not repeat the soft persuasions, the tender protestations, the insidious arguments they made use of to win me and my unfortunate sister to their purposes. Let it suffice that they but too well succeeded,—that we consented to elope with him ; that we could heartlessly, cruelly make up our minds to return no more to our once happy home, and in a short time we were travelling in a post-chaise and four, at a rapid rate to London.

Callous alike to all sense or feeling, alive only to the fatal passion which had so strongly got possession of our minds, we never once reflected on the guilty and unfortunate step we had taken, and the misery, the ruin it would bring upon our parents. We had ever been most sensibly alive to the feelings of affection, and were most studiously careful of not giving our parents the least cause for pain on our account ; and, therefore, was our present conduct the more strange. As we proceeded on our journey, we listened to sentiments of the most unbounded delight to the honied accents and tender vows of our companions ; and the farther we got from that home, which we had now made wretched for ever, the more did our happiness increase, and we yielded everything to love. Alas ! too well did our companions understand the art of flattery, and all the preliminaries which the libertine uses to the accomplishment of his diabolical desires, and they brought the full force of their eloquence to bear against us. They saw our weakest points in a moment, and it was there they assailed us with all the power of flattery and persuasion, and, to our shame, I own it, that both me and my sister were too ready to listen to them, and to believe what they said.— Simple, rustic girls as we were, certainly there was some excuse to be offered for us, when it is remembered that our companions were fully accomplished in the art of flattery and seduction, and that, although young, many were the unfortunate creatures, who, like ourselves, had fallen victims to their villany. But yet, the image of our parents should have been ever present to our mind's eye, and prevented us from taking any step which might be productive of sorrow to them, and bring upon their grey hairs disgrace and obloquy. Oh, how bitterly have we reflected upon this since, and bitter has been the anguish it has caused us; but can sorrow restore from the grave our broken-hearted parents? Can it remove the infamy which our dereliction from the paths of virtue has brought upon their name ?—Oh, no, I feel that whole ages of sorrow and repentance, could never wash out the guilt with which our souls are contaminated."

Emma was once more compelled to stop in her narrative, for the purpose of giving vent to the deep emotions which the stings of a guilty conscience excited in her bosom.

Maria tried to soothe her by offering all the consolation that was in her power to bestow ; and, after a time, she so far succeeded, as to enable Emma to proceed with her melancholy narrative.

"Hitherto, so strong was the infatuation under which me and my sister laboured," resumed Emma, " and we were so wrapt up in the tender endearments of Sir Charles and his friend, that we had not had the presence of mind to reflect upon the step we had taken, or what it was their intention to do ; but, at length, when the post-chaise stopped to change horses, and the rash and guilty offence which we had committed, rushed all at once upon our minds,—home deserted, our parents broken-hearted, our lovers distracted, came in a full tide of poignant anguish to our recollection, we burst into tears, and implored our seducers to let us know what they intended to do with us, and to suffer us to return home, and to crave the forgiveness of our parents. Oh, would to God that we had kept firm to that resolution, then might we have been again happy, and prevented that disgrace which afterwards descended upon us, and made our lives so indescribably wretched. But the villains knew too well how to act their parts ; they used all the power of rhetoric to sooth our anguish ;— assured us of their honourable intentions ;— that they intended to marry us as soon as we got to London, and that they would manage to obtain the forgiveness of our mother and father for the step we had taken, and henceforth the whole study of their lives should be to render us happy. Their affectionate, and "apparently

sincere asseverations, gradually re-assured us, and home and our friends were once more forgotten. In order to turn the current of our thoughts, they made some interesting remarks upon the scenery which we travelled through, and expiated most eloquently upon the gaities of the metropolis, and the pleasures which we might anticipate there, and they soon succeeded in tranquillising us, and in making us look forward with impatience to the time when we should arrive in London. Alas! had we not been completely senseless, had we but given their promises a moment's serious consideration, we should have at once detected their hollowness, and the treachery of those who gave utterance to them ; we should have felt convinced that our ruin was the sole object they had in view, and that once accomplished, all idea of matrimony, if ever they entertained such a thought, would be abandoned, and they would only laugh at our reproaches, and leave us to our fate. If their intentions—we might have reflected—had been really honourable, why did they not seek us in an honourable way ; ask the consent of our parents, and fulfil the engagement without any delay? Or, had they been possessed of one particle of honour, would they, knowing that Arthur and Henry were already our accepted lovers, have sought to estrange our affections from them at all? No, they would not ; they would much rather have made any sacrifice of their own feelings, than have brought misery and disgrace upon a virtuous family, or have blighted the hopes of two worthy young men. Had these ideas, I repeat, have crossed my imagination, and have struck my sister, the designs of the villains would have been speedily rendered abortive, and we should have returned spotless to our unhappy parents, and been received with forgiveness for our temporary error, and not have had at the present time that afflicting subject to reflect upon, which tends to obscure the sunshine of our happiness, which would otherwise so brightly illumine our pathway. But it was not to be ;—we were doomed to become the victims of shame and sorrow, and an accursed spell seemed to rest upon us, from which it appeared that we were never fated to escape.

"I will not detain you, Miss Herbert, by any unnecessary detail ;—rather let me pass over this guilty passage of our lives as quickly as possible. When I recal it to my memory, burning blushes of shame and self-degradation mantle in my cheeks, and I cannot, dare not give utterance to all I feel, and ever must.— That night we stopped at an hotel,—and before the morning dawned, me and my unfortunate sister were two wretched, degraded beings,— the triumph of our seducers was complete,

"How soon is the mind—not naturally

base—awakened to a sense of shame and compunction after it has erred, and how terrible are the first wounds of a guilty conscience! No sooner was our ruin accomplished, than the whole power of our misery rushed upon our brain, and drove us to distraction. We reproached Sir Charles and his friend with having murdered our peace of mind for ever—with having broken the hearts of our parents; and the paroxysms of our grief were so violent, that for some time we were quite deaf to all their entreaties and expostulations, and turned from them with a feeling of disgust and loathing, we thought it would have been impossible for us ever to experience towards them. All the horrors of our situation darted upon our imagination, and the deceit, the too successful deceit with which they had behaved towards us, and for a short time we were inconsolable, and could not behold them without giving full expression to our repugnance. But the wretches had got too strong a hold upon our affections, to suffer us long to continue this behaviour towards them;—they listened to our reproaches with apparent anguish, implored us to pardon them, for what the ungovernable passion we had inspired in their bosoms had urged them to commit; assured us that their love was more powerful than ever, and that nothing could ever eradicate it from their hearts; that they would still act honourably towards us, and as soon as we arrived in London, fulfil their promises, by giving us their hands. They also endeavoured to soothe our agony as regarded our parents, and to convince us that they should be able very soon to bring about a reconciliation with them, and that all would yet be well. They drew a flattering picture of the happiness which we might anticipate in a union with them, and how they would make it their constant study to render us comfortable. They spoke of their friends, and said, that, notwithstanding they should, no doubt, incur their displeasure for awhile, for having married without consulting them upon the subject, they were confident that they should soon be able to make some amicable arrangements with them, until which time they would be compelled to take lodgings for us, when they should feel the greatest pleasure in introducing us to them in the characters which it was their intention to bestow upon us.

"Suffice it to say, that they too soon succeeded in quieting our sorrows, and we forgave them, and gave ourselves up entirely to the passion which inhabited our bosoms.

"I will pass over the remainder of our journey, and satisfy myself by stating that we arrived in London quite safe, where we put up at an hotel, until such time as our companions could procure for us suitable apartments.— This was done in a day or two, and we re-

moved to a handsome little villa not far from Highgate, which was kept by an agreeable looking widow, who, with a female servant, was the only person besides ourselves who lived there.

"The villa was very romantically situated, and possessed every convenience. Mrs. Wallis, too, (which was the name of the landlady) was a very pleasant, affable, lady-like woman, and received us with much respect and attention. Our seducers, it appeared, had made her acquainted with the truth, and what it was their intention to perform, and she seemed very much to commiserate us, and promised us that she would do all in her power to make us happy. It was her conversation which, for awhile, had the effect of alleviating our sorrows, and we became, in the course of a few days, more reconciled.

"Sir Charles and Mr. Singleton visited us nearly every day, and there was nothing in their behaviour to lead us to suppose that their love had in the least abated. Indeed, if anything, it seemed more fervent than ever, and they appeared to be only happy when they were in our society. Sir Charles was an excellent musician, and Mr. Singleton possessed a beautiful rich tenor voice, and sometimes the latter would sing to us some of the most popular and beautiful songs of the day, accompanied on the piano or the flute by Sir Charles. These were moments of forgetfulness that were not fated to last long, and we were too soon to be aroused to an awful sense of the real misery and disgrace of our situation. At other times they would sit and read to us selections from the works of the most eminent authors, and explain to us passages which we might not be able altogether to comprehend. They certainly were most elegant and accomplished men, and formed in every way to conquer the female heart.— Would that we had never beheld them, then should we not now have had to reproach ourselves in the manner which our consciences dictate. But it is useless to repine; rather let us by our future conduct make all the reparation it is in our power for the past.

"We had now been a week in London, or rather in one of its suburban villages, and our lovers had not said anything about our union, but that did not surprise us, as we did not expect they could make arrangements immediately, and they had taken such strong hold of our affections, and seemed so attentive to us, that we could not for a moment doubt the honour of their intentions. Thus deceived, did we go on sinning, and was not awakened to a sense of our weakness until we found ourselves placed upon the verge of a precipice, down which we could not save ourselves from falling.

"Our admirers took us into the town frequently; and the size, the variety of shops, the number of streets, the dense masses of passengers, and the number of vehicles, astonished and delighted us, for we had never been in London before, and the novelty of everything we saw could not fail to excite our most especial wonder.

"Twice we had visited the opera, and that splendid edifice, the gorgeousness of the decorations, the splendour of the scenery and dresses, the talent of the different performers, and the remarkable effect of the whole entertainment, afforded us another means of forgetting for awhile the circumstances in which we were placed, and the condition of those we had so heartlessly abandoned.

"At the end of another fortnight, during which period I had heard nothing from home, although Sir Charles had promised to make every inquiry, they mentioned to us, that they were prosecuting the arrangements for our nuptials with all possible expedition, and they hoped in a very few days to be able to introduce us to their friends and relations. This satisfied us, more so, as it was spoken with such a semblance of candour and truth, that the greatest sceptic could not have doubted it. We never questioned them again upon the subject, placing full reliance in the truth of their assertions, and we were comparatively happy, more so than under the circumstances, the most callous persons ought to have been; but we were soon to be undeceived.

"Another month passed in this manner, and in the meantime Rose communicated to me that she was in the family way, a circumstance which I could not help hearing with a foreboding of misery, and regret filled my bosom.

"Sir Charles and Mr. Singleton had, day after day, made some excuse or other, for not fulfilling their promise, and such were the plausible stories they told us, that they never failed to impose upon our credulity. They were never absent from us any more than they could possibly avoid, but when they were, we were completely wretched, notwithstanding all the endeavours of Mrs. Wallis (who was a most accomplished woman) to exhilarate our spirits. The full extent of our guilt would dart across our brain; the sufferings of our fond parents, abandoned by those two children on whom they had bestowed so much care, whom they had ever treated so fondly, and to whom they had always granted every indulgence; the two young men who had been the companions of our childhood, who loved us with such fervour and sincerity, and whom we had often so ardently vowed to love in return; the ignominy which we had brought upon our once unsullied name; all these facts would rush like a torrent upon our memory, driving away all thoughts of happiness before its impetuous current. It was then that we would compare the noise and

bustle of town, its continual riot, its insipid pleasures, its many temptations to the innocent and unwary, with the calm, the happy tranquillity of a country life, and weak, puerile, evanescent did the former appear. At such moments as these, too, all the many little incidents that had occurred to us in our childhood, would rush back to our thoughts, and open a fresh source for sorrow and regret. It was then that we would sigh to be the same innocent beings that we were at that time, and upbraid ourselves for being so readily led astray from those paths of virtue and rectitude, which our parents had taken such pains to point out to us. Could we have heard from home; could we have been assured that we were forgiven, we could have been at peace; but still how could we presume to hope for such a consummation; had we not by our conduct rendered ourselves deserving of the most severe punishment? Yes, we had, and the present was but a prelude to the many sufferings it was our fate afterwards to undergo.

"At length, however, as week after week passed away, and yet Sir Charles and Mr. Singleton still continued to make the same idle excuses to us, our suspicions began to be excited, and I expressed my surprise that they should so long delay fulfilling their promises, more especially when they recollected the delicate situation of my sister.

"My question seemed to confuse them very much, especially Mr. Singleton; but at length, Sir Charles, affecting to smile, said 'I was a most impatient little creature, and expected our happiness to be completed in a moment. But,' he added, 'at present our friends are out of town, and will be so for a month or two, but when they return I have not the slightest doubt but that everything will be settled to your satisfaction.'

"I must say that this answer astonished me, more especially as they had been making a similar excuse ever since we had been in London, and I was far from feeling comfortable about it. They, however, took an opportunity of speedily diverting our attention from the subject, and chose a lively topic of discourse, which they kept up with unabated spirit until they left us, which was not till a late hour that night.

"The next day our lovers called upon us to inform us that sudden business of importance, rendered their journeying to Bath necessary, and that we might please ourselves as to whether we would accompany them, or remain in London until their return, which they added, was not exactly certain to take place for a month or two.

"I thought this rather a strange question for men to put to us, who had so often vowed that if they were only out of our presence for a single day they were miserable, and my surprise must have been visable in the expression of my countenance; however, I conquered my emotion as well as I could, and replied, ' that of course, we could not think of remaining in such a place as London alone; to be deprived of their company, and especially as they had stated that their absence was for an indefinite period; therefore we would most assuredly attend them to Bath.'

" I could not help noticing that there was an expression of disappointment, if not chagrin, when I stated this as our resolve; but they endeavoured to repress it, and telling us to hold ourselves in readiness to depart the following morning, they took their leave much earlier than they had been accustomed to do.

" Me and my sister passed anything but a comfortable night, for she, as well as myself, had noticed the difference in the behaviour, and the confusion of Sir Charles and Mr. Singleton, and melancholy forebodings and suspicions, for the first time, took possession of her mind, which she communicated to me. Although there was something which told me that we had both of us too much cause for mistrust, I would fain have persuaded myself that it was not so—and I, therefore, tried all I could to remove the fears from the mind of Rose, which I had some difficulty in doing, and I was then far from being satisfied.

" The night passed gloomily away, and in the morning, exact to the time they had mentioned, a post-chaise drove up to the door, from which our lovers alighted, and walked into the breakfast-room where we were waiting to receive them.

" They seemed in much better spirits than they had been the day before, and greeted us with all the ardour they had ever evinced; which speedily reassured us, and we forgot all the circumstances which had so shortly before excited our suspicions and alarm. We had made every preparation for our journey, and after partaking of a hasty repast, and bidding Mrs. Wallis adieu (who seemed much hurt at parting with us, although Sir Charles told her that we should, in all probability, return to London in a month or two, when we should not fail to renew our friendship) we took our departure.

" We arrived in Bath early the same evening, and took up our residence at the house of a gentleman, whom Sir Charles called his particular friend, and to whom and his wife, he introduced us with great ceremony. There was something in the manner and behaviour of Mr. Harding (for such was the name of the gentleman) which prejudiced me against him from the first moment I beheld him. He was what I may call disagreeably polite, and his protestations of friendship wanted the stamp of sincerity and warmth about them to cause them to be believed. His wife was a tall,

bony, mean-looking woman, and with a countenance which was, if not absolutely repulsive, anything but prepossessing. She also greeted us with much constrained politeness, but I soon perceived, or fancied that I perceived, beneath it all an expression which was anything but favourable to me and my sister.

" Somehow or other, I felt my heart sink upon entering this place, and a thought, for a moment, crossed my mind that our happiness was speedily drawing towards a close. Happiness I call it, but it was nothing more than mad enthusiasm—a dream from which we were shortly to be awakened in a manner we at that time little anticipated.

" Both Sir Charles and Mr. Singleton seemed to observe our lowness of spirits, and tried all they could to arouse us, but in that they only partially succeeded. Mr. Harding was very loquacious, but withal extremely vulgar, and very illiterate. His conversation consisted generally of a wretched attempt to re-animate stale jokes, and pass them off as his own; or if he at any time changed the tenor of his discourse, it was only to talk about prize-fighting, bull-baiting, &c., in which gentlemanly sports, according to his own account, he was highly accomplished. He was also very fond of boasting of the noble lords, &c., who formed the circle of his acquaintance—the wonderful exploits they had performed together at foot-racing, boxing, single-stick, and other equally fashionable amusements. Every resuscited pun which he gave utterance to he accompanied with a self-approving chuckle, and turned a familiar glance upon me and my sister, which was not at all pleasant, however he might imagine we might fancy it, or admire the exuberance or originality of his wit.

" Mrs. Harding was a woman who seemed to be completely wrapped up in admiration of the superior talents of her husband, in consequence of which she was always the very first to give utterance to a laugh, when she imagined he had said anything particularly good, and to applaud to the very skies the most trivial or ridiculous opinion which he ventured to offer upon any subject. She was also exceedingly jealous of him, and watched all his actions with the eye of a lynx. She was a woman not younger than forty-six, and had never, it was evident, been remarkable for personal beauty; yet it was very clear that she entertained a very high opinion of her charms, and was particularly fond, occasionally, of vaunting of the many conquests she had made before she knew Mr. Harding, and of the number of advantageous offers she had foolishly rejected for him. These kind of observations did not, at all times, come very palatable to her lord and master, and he would wax wroth. However, a single look from Mrs. Harding was quite enough for him, for as she was rather a bit of a termagant, he did not particularly wish to come to open hostilities with her. But you will, doubtless, consider that I am growing tedious; therefore I will drop this prolix description, and come as quickly as possible to the facts more immediately connected with my melancholy narrative.

"Sir Charles and his friend could perceive that we were far from liking our new acquaintances, but they endeavoured all they could to do away with our prejudice. They made themselves even more agreeable than ever they had done on the first evening of our being in Bath, and Mr. and Mrs. Harding, no doubt from having previously received instructions to that effect, did manage to divest themselves of some portion of their coarse and ignorant manners, and paid us both particular attention.

"It appeared that Sir Charles had a relation in Bristol, with whom he had some particular business to transact, and at whose mansion himself and Mr. Singleton would be compelled to stop, but that they would visit us daily at Mrs. Harding's, until they had settled their affairs, when they promised that they would take an early opportunity of fulfilling those vows which they had made to us. These asseverations silenced all our doubts, and we looked forward with impatience to that period which we fondly hoped would unite us to the men, for whose love we had made so great a sacrifice. Fools that we were to be so often deluded! how was it that we could not see through the deceptive masks which our seducers had assumed towards us?

"Sir Charles and Mr. Singleton called very regularly upon us for some weeks, and they appeared to be solicitous to pay us the utmost attention. But all at once they fell off in this punctuality, and would not visit us sometimes for two days together. Their manners also seemed to be greatly altered, and they did not behave to us with near that kindness which they had been in the habit of doing. When they were questioned as to the cause of this, their answers were evasive, and they seemed to be very much confused, and anxious to drop the subject; and it appeared very evident to us both that something occupied their minds which they did not wish us to become acquainted with at present. This behaviour once more gave rise to our suspicious surmises and apprehensions, and many an uneasy hour did we pass together.

"Placed in the delicate situation in which we were, it may be imagined that poor Rose felt this treatment much more severely even than I did, and the fear of being left destitute and unprotected, in the midst of our shame, it had a most serious effect upon our spirits, and brought to our recollection yet more vividly than it had ever done before, the many pangs we had doubtless caused our unhappy parents,

and those poor youths whom we had vowed to be constant to; and we could not help thinking that what we were at present suffering was only a prelude to that earthly punishment we should be certain to receive for our offences.

"We had not seen Sir Charles or Mr. Singleton for three days, and we had noticed a very great alteration in the behaviour of Mr. and Mrs. Harding towards us. Whenever they spoke to us it was in a snappish tone, and the servant girl, too, also appeared to wait upon us with considerable reluctance. There was a continual bustle in the house, as if something of importance was being transacted; and when we ventured to ask their opinion as to the cause of Sir Charles and Mr. Singleton absenting themselves from the house—which we did upon one or two occasions—they returned us some abrupt and evasive answer, and exchanged glances with one another, which attracted our attention from the singularity of their expression.

"All these circumstances served to cause us much uneasiness, and we avoided their presence as much as possible, keeping ourselves confined to our own apartments. At length, for a change, we walked from the house, and strolled into the city. We were so busied in the melancholy discourse which the subject of our thoughts gave rise to, that we did not take the least notice of anything that was passing around us, until we had arrived at the principal inn, when, suddenly looking up, we beheld the different stages coming in and going out; and from the outside of one of the former, which had just drawn up before the door, alighted a country farmer-looking man, whose person seemed to be familiar to us, at least it struck us so very forcibly. We were not far from it when the vehicle stopped, but the back of the traveller was towards us; a minute after, however, he turned his face in the direction where we were standing, and our astonishment and emotion may be easily conceived, when in the healthy, ruddy features of the traveller, we recognised those of Farmer Greenfield, who resided close by the house of our parents.

"Anxious as we were to hear all the particulars of our home, yet a feeling of shame rendered us eager to avoid the observation of Mr. Greenfield, and we were turning away for that purpose, when some remark of a rude description, alluding to us, was addressed by a man to a by-stander, and which drew the attention of the farmer towards us. He immediately knew us, and started back a few paces in evident astonishment.

"'Why, as I live, it is the two Miss Sherwood's!' ejaculated the farmer, in accents of surprise and pity,—'alas! alas! unfortunate, wretched girls!'

"'Mr. Greenfield,' I cried, in a voice almost choking with anguish, 'one word, in pity to our sufferings, tell us of our poor parents, and whether they—'"

"'Go search the old church-yard near that once happy home which you have now rendered desolate,' gasped forth the honest farmer, with a shudder of horror, 'they sleep there!—they sleep there!'

"He said no more, but covering his face with his hands, he turned abruptly from the spot, hurried away, and we never saw him after-

THE ESCAPE OF RUPERT DARWIN.

wards, until we came to live again in this neighbourhood.

"Poor Rose had no sooner heard what Mr. Greenfield had said, than she breathed a groan of intense agony, and sank senseless in my arms; and it was a matter of the greatest astonishment how I could support myself, for I trembled like an aspen leaf.

"'Dead! dead!' I cried, looking wildly around me, and imagining, for the moment, that I had experienced some frightful and hideous dream; 'my God! surely this cannot be true!

if it is, we are wretched and accursed for ever !'

"I was aroused from these reflections by the rude laughter of several by-standers and ignorant hostlers, who, in their superlative wisdom, seemed to be enjoying my emotion as a rich joke, and regarding the insensibility of my sister with looks which seemed to express an opinion that she was enebriated.

"Horror-struck, disgusted, I immediately beckoned to the driver of an empty vehicle who was near the spot, and with his assistance managed to place Rose in the carriage, and following myself, told him to drive with all possible speed to Mrs. Harding's.

"As the vehicle proceeded to the place of our destination, the mental torture I endured may be far better imagined by you than any language of mine could describe it. The enormity of the offence we had committed was at length made apparent, and I could consider us in no other light than as the murderers of our unfortunate parents !—Our abandoning them had broken their hearts, and we could never know peace again!—the dying curse of those parents, who had loved us so fondly, would ever appear to ring in our ears, and a guilty conscience would henceforth be a perpetual earthly purgatory to us. But could it be true? I could scarcely believe it was so; I feared to think so, or I verily believe at that moment I should have gone mad! Had Mr. Greenfield spoken the truth, or merely made the assertions he had done to harrow up our feelings, and bring us to a sense of the enormity of the offence of which we had been guilty? for, by the observation he had made, he seemed to have a full knowledge of how we had fallen. I was at first somewhat inclined to encourage the latter supposition, from the hasty manner in which he had quitted us; but then these words, which he had uttered so solemnly, were impressed upon my recollection so vividly, that I could not forget them, namely,—' Go search the old church-yard, near that once happy home which you have now rendered desolate : *they sleep there*!—they sleep there!' and my conscience told me that it was, alas! too true.

"It was wonderful that amidst all these soul-harrowing circumstances, and the neglect with which the destroyers of our happiness seemed now to be treating us, my reason did not leave me, but I sustained myself with a fortitude which I had never felt before, and have not experienced since, and the melancholy situation of my sister, who still remained in a state of insensibility, seemed to sustain me, at the same time that a copious flood of tears came to the relief of my overcharged bosom.

"The vehicle soon arrived at the house of Mr. and Mrs. Harding, but the driver had to pull the bell several times before any one appeared to answer the door. The window-blinds, too, were all down, and there was an air of mystery about the appearance of the house altogether, which excited considerable astonishment in my mind.

"At length, however, the door was slowly opened by Letty, the servant girl of Mr. and Mrs. Harding, who, upon seeing me alight from the vehicle, did not offer to come to render me any assistance, but on the contrary, stood staring at me with a look of stupid amazement, mingled with an expression of anger. This was not a little increased, evidently, when she saw the driver and me lift the insensible form of Rose out of the carriage; but she still stood with the handle of the door in her hand, and did not offer to move to render us any assistance.

"' What is the meaning of this, miss?' said the girl, pertly, as we reached the door, and offered to walk into the house, the driver carrying Rose in his arms; ' I don't know but that I shall be acting wrong to admit you.'

"' Are you mad, girl?' demanded I, in accents of astonishment; ' where is your mistress?'

"' No, indeed, I am not mad,' returned Letty; ' as for mistress, you won't find here, I can tell you; nor master either.'

"Thinking that, perhaps, the girl had been drinking, as she had been accused of doing so several times by Mrs. Harding, I pushed past her, and motioned the driver to follow me into the parlour, where Rose was deposited on a sofa, and I desired Letty to go for a medical man with all possible dispatch. At the same time, I could help noticing the altered appearance of the room, being nearly stripped of the handsome furniture it had lately contained, and all the pictures, glasses and ornaments.

"'As for going for a doctor, I cannot do any such thing,' said Letty, "for I must not leave the house. And I wish you would just take yourself and her somewhere else, for I can't be bothered with you here.'

"I was, as you may imagine, thunderstruck at the words and the impertinence of the girl; but without waiting for any farther ceremony, with the assistance of the driver of the vehicle, I placed my sister upon the sofa, and then requested her to send for Mrs. Harding to me. Upon this Letty all but laughed outright.

"' Send for Mrs. Harding, indeed," said she; "I think, young woman, you might send to some distance before you would find that person. The whole of the matter is, Mr. and Mrs. Harding, who were merely the servants of Sir Charles Perceval, have gone away; the gentlemen have found other mistresses; and as this house was only hired of my real mistress, the sooner you and your sister leave it the better. I can't stand palavering here with the likes of you all day; it's a bad job for you, no doubt, as the gentlemen have given you up, for no doubt they were very good friends to you; but you knew your business best, and I dare say it won't be long before you will be suited again. There's more men than parish churches.'

"I will not attempt to describe my emotion—my horror—my bewilderment at this brutal statement, and the manner in which the vulgar and ignorant Letty treated me!—I could not believe it was true—it was a dream, or some scheme of Sir Charles and Mr. Singleton to try our constancy; there could not surely be such monsters, such base, such heartless hypocrites in existence! It was not possible that they who had so often and so fervently vowed their adoration and promised eternal fidelity, could have abandoned us in the inhuman manner which it would appear they had done, by the statement of Letty! It was too horrible to believe it true, and yet every circumstance which had lately happened, too fully confirmed the truth of it. The coldness of the behaviour of our seducers towards us, their absence from the house, the bold and insolent manner in which Mr. and Mrs. Harding had treated us, all rushed at once upon my brain, and bringing home at once conviction to my mind, almost drove me to distraction. And then the information, the dreadful information which Farmer Greenfield had imparted to us, recurred to my recollection (alas! what can ever erase it from my memory?) and the ghastly faces of my broken-hearted parents at that time seemed to stare me reproachfully in the face, while their dying curses appeared to vibrate in my ears. I stood the perfect image of despair and horror, and was paralysed to the spot, gazing around me in stupified amazement. I tried to speak, but my tongue clave to the palate of my mouth. Every faculty seemed bound up in horror—the blood appeared to be frozen in my veins—while my brain burned like a furnace.

" Letty witnessed my agitation without any emotion; she seemed indeed to enjoy it, and a broad grin was upon her countenance all the time. I shall never forget that horrible moment; even now it comes more vividly fresh than ever upon my memory; I feel as if I were once more acting over the dreadful scene, and all my manifold sins and errors start before my mind's eye, and smite me with a feeling of horror, I find it impossible to describe. But yet the suffering I was then enduring, was not half the punishment the crime of which I had been guilty merited. The voices of my aged parents seemed to resound from the grave, and to heap maledictions upon my head. Oh, when shall I find an oblivion to my sorrows?"

Emma was so violently agitated in this part of her narrative, that she was again obliged to pause, and give vent to her sorrows, and Rose was also so dreadfully affected, that her sobs were quite distressing to hear. Maria, who was deeply moved at the melancholy story of the two sisters, once more used her best efforts to tranquillise them, and ere long, so far succeeded, that Emma was sufficiently restored to composure, to resume her narrative in the following words:—

"At length, I regained my reason sufficiently to inquire for Letty to implore of her, if she had the least spark of humanity left in her bosom, to inform me if what she had stated was the truth, that Sir Charles and Mr. Singleton had indeed deserted us, and whether they were not in Bath, or their relatives at Bristol.

" ' Why,' replied, who seemed rather to relent, ' you know very well, that neither of the gentlemen have been here for several days, and I know it for certain that they are not in England, having started for Paris. After all, I must say that it is not a right thing exactly, after seducing young girls, and taking them away from their friends under a promise of marriage, to leave them in such a manner ; but Lor' bless you, it is nothing at all to them; they are quite used to it, and they glory in doing it. You are not the first, by many, that they have served in this manner, and they keep this house for the very purpose of carrying on their intrigues. As for Mr. and Mrs. Harding, they are nothing more than myself; that is, as I said before, they are servants, that's all.'

" ' Good God !' I cried, in a tone of bitter agony, ' can it be possible that there can be such wretches in the world? can so much guilt and hypocrisy be enshrined in all the semblance of honour and virtue? Let me not be convinced of the truth of it—rather let me be taken immediately from the world, which I can no longer covet, than believe it.'

"The driver of the vehicle was a very feeling man, and seeming to pity my situation, he had not offered to depart, thinking, probably, that he might be able to render me some assistance or the other. He now took upon himself to remonstrate with Letty on her conduct, and which had a beneficial effect, inasmuch as she got some vinegar and other things necessary, and set about endeavouring to restore my sister to her senses with much assiduity. In the course of a quarter of an hour, she recovered her sensibility, and Letty then assisted me to convey her into a chamber, where, after saying she did not know whether or not it would make much difference (although it was against her orders, and would probably get her dismissed if it were known) if we remained there for a day or two until we had recovered ourselves a little from the shock which this sudden and unexpected occurrence had caused us, when it would be absolutely necessary for us to see about making some arrangements for seeking some other place of refuge. For this kindness, so unexpected from Letty, I was grateful; for had we been immediately driven forth, what could have become of us?—whither could we have gone?—where found shelter?—without friends; without a relation near at hand; complete strangers in the neighbourhood, and so situated as to be likely to excite the sympathy and commiseration of but very few. I thanked her heartily, and her manners, by degrees, became less disagreeable.

"At that time we did not make poor Rose acquainted with the awful circumstance I have been recounting, and it was a mercy that we did not do so, for the remembrance of what Mr. Greenfield had said was quite enough to distract her, and she continued to relapse occasionally into fits, during that night, and when she was sensible, she raved incessantly of her broken-hearted, and murdered parents. We had the hardest matter in the world to control her, and Heaven only knows how I so well supported the accumulated sorrows under which I then suffered. It is remarkable that my senses did not leave me. But Omnipotence was kind, and sustained me throughout the heavy trial, for had I sunk beneath it, what would indeed have become of us? We must both of us have died. Perhaps, it would have been better had we done so; we should then have been out of our troubles, and should have been spared all the future misery, to which this was but a prelude. But, even under the most heavy afflictions, it is a feeling inherent in most of us, to cling to life with extraordinary tenacity; and so it was with me upon that occasion. In fact, death presented such horrors to my imagination, that I shrunk from it with the most unutterable dread. How could I enter the presence of my Maker, with the load of guilt which was then upon my mind? Oh, no, rather let me live to repent, to endeavour, by compunction, to make what little atonement I could in this world, before I could think of entering another without a shudder of horror.

"By degrees, Letty became more sociable, and, at length, informed me all she knew about the matter; which was, that Sir Charles and Mr. Singleton, having expressed themselves tired of our society to Mr. and Mrs. Harding, intimated to them that it was not their intention to visit us any more, and that they were, therefore, to get rid of us in the usual way. These instructions, the base creatures of the libertines, I need not inform you, obeyed to the very letter, and the result was what I have related.

"It was some time before I could make up my mind to believe that what had taken place was reality, and I could not credit that two such cold-blooded, inhuman villains could bear the human form. But when I was convinced that it was no idle chimera of the brain, the ardent love which I had so lately felt for Sir Charles, was turned at once to hatred, indignation and disgust. I then viewed him in his proper character, and imagination could not paint him blacker than his own vices had already done. But to think that we should have been made the dupes, the victims of two such wretches!—That we should have been led from the paths of virtue, and to be the cause of bringing our parents to an untimely grave, as well as ruining the prospects, and blighting the hopes, of those two young men, who so sincerely loved us, for ever; and had voluntarily exchanged the certain happiness which was presented to our acceptance, for the disgrace and misery it was now our fate to experience;—it was that which racked and distracted my brain more than all. But I am fearful that I am growing tedious, Miss; my misfortunes lead me into reflections, which may suit the mind diseased, but to one who has never experienced such troubles, must seem remarkably prolix. And yet, to reflect, to repent, and to condemn my past conduct, is the only reparation I have it now in my power to make; and it seems to give my mind relief.

"I did not make my sister acquainted with what had really happened for two or three days afterwards, although she made frequent inquiries after Mr. Singleton, which I evaded in the best manner I possibly could. But when I did tell her, you may judge what were her emotions, by those I have described to you as having myself experienced. Suffice it to say, that she suffered a relapse, and for a week afterwards we despaired of her life. During this painful interval, I must do Letty the justice to say, she behaved with more kindness and attention than I thought was in her nature, and she was not, indeed, like the same girl. She said it was really a very shocking thing, and that she very much regretted it was not in her power to render us any assistance; but that she must obey the orders of her master, and it would be as much as her place was worth if it should be discovered that she had so far broken through the injunctions of Sir Charles. I thanked the girl, and told her that I should be very sorry to get her into any trouble, and that, as soon as my unfortunate sister was well enough to leave her bed, we would no longer intrude upon her, but would make our departure.

"Depart! Whither could we go? To what quarter could we direct our wretched footsteps; with not a relation or friend in the world to whose humanity we could appeal: Should we return to our native village? Alas! no, we did not dare venture to do so? we could not venture into the vicinity of that spot where the ashes of our parents reposed. To be pointed at by the finger of scorn, indignation, opprobrium, and reproach! We felt that we could sooner perish! Then where should we go? How in future support ourselves? Where find a home or shelter? Alas! we were now indeed two miserable outcasts—the degraded of society. And we must not again expect to shake the hand of virtuous friendship, or to receive pity for our errors.

"We had a few pounds left, but that would not last long. At length we determined to take lodgings in Bath for a time, and see whether we could not get a living by dress-making. I got apartments, and it was with heavy hearts, and many scalding tears, we left the dwelling in which we had so often listened to the vows and protestations of our seducers.

"The apartments I had taken were very comfortable ones, and were kept by a widow, who was a kind, motherly sort of a woman; and as I had thought it best to make known to her such portions of our dismal story as I considered necessary, she expressed much pity for us, and was ready to do all that was in her power to assist us. We did succeed in getting some needlework, but it was very little, and brought us in but a scanty pittance; however, it was sufficient partly to keep us, and to preserve the greater portion of the little capital we had by us to a future period.

"And now the time of my sister's confinement rapidly approached, and it may be guessed with what painful anxiety and dread we looked forward to that event, and reflected with bitter anguish upon the misery which the little innocent would be born to. There was also another source of horror to us, and that was the expense which we should be at, and that the few pounds we had by us would then be entirely exhausted. But at length, tired of thinking, we gave it up, and trusted to Providence for the issue.

"The time passed over better than we had anticipated, and poor Rose brought forth a fine boy, over which we both shed torrents of tears, caused by frantic joy and love for the little stranger. I will pass this circumstance over as quickly as possible, and arrive at the conclusion of my narrative with as little delay as I can help.

"Rose recovered sooner than might have been expected from the sufferings which she had lately endured, and, as I expected, our small stock of cash was entirely expended in the expenses attending her *accouchement*. To add to our misfortunes, likewise, the limited employment we had been hitherto enabled to obtain, was much reduced, and we could barely get sufficient to supply us with the common necessaries of life; and, indeed, many a time we should actually have gone without a meal, or a days victuals, had it not been for the kindness of Mrs. Woburn, the landlady of the house. Yet it pained me to take it from her, for she was herself very poor, and I knew far from able to afford it. She had one or two relations, who had much impoverished her, and it was no great while after we two had gone to lodge with her, that we discovered she was in very straitened and reduced circumstances. She daily became worse, and as our employment decreased in proportion, and we were unable to pay her any rent, the prospects of us all became hourly more dismal. The storm which had long been hanging over our heads, at length burst with full fury upon us. Mrs. Woburn had become involved in debt for rent, and her landlord being an arbitrary sort of man, distrained upon her goods, and we were all turned shelterless into the street. Mrs. Woburn, poor woman, was at last taken in by her cousin, until she could make some arrangement; but we were left without a home, or a place to put our heads in. Now, indeed, was the full penalty of our indiscretions coming most forcibly home to us despair and horror surrounded us on every side. Oh, how terrible is the judgment; which follows a dereliction from the paths of virtue!—What horrors are sure to succeed to those who suffer themselves to yield to vice! And had we not much to answer for, much to reflect upon?—Alas! yes; and when we recalled to our mind the misery we had caused, we could not but acknowledge that the retribution of the Almighty was just. But what punishment could be adequate to the guilt of those who had seduced us from the paths of innocence?—Surely they would not be permitted to triumph in their iniquity —they would have to suffer in this world, as well as their unfortunate victims!—Yes, we felt confident that they would; and when we reflected upon the untimely end of our broken-hearted parents, we could not help wishing that they might. But to return to ourselves, poor, houseless, friendless wanderers as we were; alas! you may easily imagine what dreadful agony we suffered. Our minds were in such a distracted state, that we were unable to devise any plan to relieve us from our immediate difficulties, and continued to wander about the city and the fields adjoining, the very images of despair, and quite undecided what to do, or whither to direct our footsteps. Mrs. Woburn, good woman, had been deeply affected when she quitted us, more especially as it was entirely out of her power to assist us, or to advise us in which way to act. Her relative was too poor, neither had she the convenience to afford us any shelter; besides, how could we expect assistance from a perfect stranger?—No,—even if she had the means, our hearts revolted from placing ourselves under an obligation to those upon whom we had no claim. And, alas! upon whom had we now any claim?—Who was there in the world to care about us?—Not one.—By our misconduct we had broken the hearts of our parents, and estranged from us those who had formerly been our friends. To return to our native village we could not bear to think upon for a moment; besides, even had we been so inclined, and had come to such a resolution, how could we travel in the weak state we were in, and without a penny in our pockets to obtain for us a morsel of food, or a night's lodging on the road?—And what could we do by remaining where we were?—What prospect of relief did Bath present to us? —None!—Our only hope appeared to be in death, and driven as we were to perfect frenzy, it is wonderful that we did not commit suicide!

"It was in the depth of winter,—the frost was very intense; the wind piercingly cold, and the snow was lying thick upon the ground. My poor sister's little one was crying with the cold, and Rose in vain tried to appease him, although she endeavoured to impart all the warmth she could to it, by wrapping it up in her cloak and pressing it closely to her breast. Every one we met seemed to look upon us with the same freezing coldness as the weather. No one appeared to behold us with feelings of compassion, although, wretched as we felt, we must have looked objects sufficiently miserable to have excited the pity and commiseration of the humane. We had wept until our tears could flow no more, and the icy hand of despair seemed to have become fixed upon our hearts.

"Unconscious where we were going, we had wandered as far as Marlborough Downs, where we felt the wind and the frost so severely, that we could proceed no farther; and it was with the utmost difficulty that we could support our tired and shivering limbs. Standing upon the heath for a minute or two, and looking round us with despairing eyes, hunger coming now keenly upon us, for we had eaten but little for the last two or three days, a thought suddenly occurred to me. I recollected that I had a small article of jewellery about me, which I might pledge or sell; and we, therefore, resolved to return to Bath again with all possible haste. The prospect of temporary relief somewhat tranquillised our spirits, and we walked on at a more rapid pace than might have been expected considering the condition we were in.

"We soon got back to Bath, where I disposed of the bauble, and having procured some food, we entered an obscure tavern in the outskirts of the city, where the landlady treated us with much kindness, and showed us into a private room. Here we cooked the victuals I

had bought, and having partaken of rather a hearty repast, felt more composed, and became sufficiently collected to discourse upon our situation, and to consult with one another what was best to be done in our emergency, but we were unable to come to any conclusion.

"We noticed that the landlady, frequently when she came into the room where we were sitting, would fix her eyes earnestly upon us, and then she would burst into tears; and this so moved us, that we felt a sentiment of gratitude and esteem for her, in a moment spring up in our bosoms, which we shall never forget. It was the first kind soul we had met with to sympathise with us; the first from whom we had received the feelings of compassion. Oh, sympathy, how soothing are you to the care-afflicted heart; it cometh like the gentle dew of charity, blessing those on whom it is bestowed, and those who give it!

"Our hearts immediately warmed towards this good woman, and she brought to our recollection the kind, the indulgent mother we had had: the many affectionate attentions we had received from her; the maternal fondness she had ever lavished upon us, and the base, the cruel, the heartless ingratitude with which we had repaid her; our agony became so intense, that we could scarcely support it. It seemed as if the poor woman read our melancholy history at a glance, and entered at once into the full depth of its misery. Alas! she did, and keenly, bitterly did she feel it; for we afterwards learnt that she had had a daughter, who, like ourselves, had strayed from the paths of virtue, and when recalled to a full sense of her shame, she died broken-hearted.

"Unable to think of any other plan at present, and the snow continuing to fall fast, we inquired of the landlady whether we could be accommodated with a lodging in her house for the night; to which she readily answered in the affirmative, and seemed happy to think that it was in her power to oblige us, without putting us to the necessity of again going out in such an inclement night. We were very glad of this, for independent of the uncertainty we should have been in of being able to procure a lodging, the pity she had evinced towards us inspired us with confidence, and created in our bosoms a feeling of regard towards her.

"We retired early to the chamber allotted to us, which was adjoining that of our worthy hostess, and was remarkable for its cleanly and comfortable appearance. Every thing around us reminded us of our once happy home, and brought with distracting influence upon our recollection, every circumstance of our childhood, and the change which had now come upon us.

"Fatigued as we were, notwithstanding

the anguish of our minds, we slept soundly till the morning, and arose refreshed and more composed. On descending to the parlour we found that the landlady had prepared breakfast for us, which she requested kindly that we would partake of heartily. Confident that the good woman spoke with sincerity, we readily complied with her request, and made a hearty meal. We had decided before we went to bed on the previous evening, that we would see Mrs. Woburn on the following day, and once more see whether she could advise us in what manner to proceed ; and, therefore, when we had breakfasted, we arose, and I asked the landlady what we were indebted to her for the accommodation she had afforded us, and the uncommon kindness with which she had behaved towards us. Tears filled the good woman's eyes as she pressed my hand expressively, and said—

"'God forbid, my poor girls, that I should take anything from you, when I am certain, or else I am very much mistaken, that you are not in a condition to pay anything, but, on the contrary, need assistance. You are heartily welcome to what you have had here, and Heaven send you better fortune than that which at present seems to attend you.'

"I was astonished at the good woman's penetration, but her words deeply affected me and my sister, and for some moments we had not the power to make any reply. She perceived our emotion, and pressed us to be seated again.

"I am extremely sorry, my good girls," said she, 'I am extremely sorry if I have said anything that may wound your feelings; but you have excited so deep an interest in my bosom, that I cannot help feeling anxious to know more about you. If I may take the liberty of asking, in what direction are you going when you leave here? Whither are you bound ?'

"Tears gushed from the eyes of Rose, and sighing deeply, I shook my head, and in a melancholy voice, replied—

"'Alas! we know not!—We have no fixed place of destination;—no home to go to; no friend to whom we can apply for shelter or assistance.'

"'Poor things, poor things,' observed the kind-hearted hostess, 'it is then as I suspected!—Oh, how I pity you, from my heart I pity you; at this inclement season of the year to be so situated, is dreadful. But what terrible misfortune can have brought you into such a condition ?'

"I felt that confidence in the landlady, and was so much moved by the kindness she had shown us, that in a moment I determined to disclose to her our dismal story; and, after an elapse of a few minutes, during which I contrived to muster up fortitude for the task, I made her acquainted with al that had occurred to us, not concealing from her any of our errors, not exaggerating any of the circumstances. She listened to me with the most profound attention, and was very much affected at what we had undergone. She evidently felt the utmost pity for us, and during the narrative frequently shed tears, and clasped her hands in the utmost apparent agony. The violence of her emotions very much astonished us, but our wonder was soon changed into commiseration, when we learnt from her that her daughter—her only daughter—had met with a similar fate. She had been seduced by a gentleman, who had insinuated himself into her affections, unknown to her parents;—she had eloped with him, had lived with him for some time, and like the wretches to whom we owe our destruction, he afterwards deserted her. The parents of the unfortunate young woman were unacquainted with the place of her retreat, and it was in vain that they had endeavoured to find her out, and nearly heart-broken, they had given her up for lost. Awakened to a full sense of her shame and disgrace, the poor young girl had not the courage to return to that home she had rendered miserable; and where she would have been received with kindness and forgiveness ; nor had she the fortitude to write. She died in a few days of a broken heart, and it was not till then that the wretched bereaved parents were made acquainted with the real circumstances attending the fate of their unfortunate child.

"When Mrs. Wilkinson (for that was the name of the hostess) had made us acquainted with this dismal story, we, of course, no longer wondered at the emotion which she had exhibited, and we mingled our tears with hers. She would not suffer us to leave her house that day, and could not have behaved with greater kindness to us if we had been her own daughters. Her husband was dead, and she had no incumbrances, and such was the singular attachment she had formed for us, that she would willingly have kept us under her own roof. But this, from a stranger, we could not think of accepting; no, we had a spirit above that, and were determined to endeavour to gain a situation, and to live by our own exertions. We, however, found it was impossible to help yielding to her request that we would remain with her for a few days, until we might hear of something, or make some arrangements which were likely to be of a permanent description.

"Nor did we forget to return our thanks to the Almighty for His goodness in thus providing us with a friend, in the midst of our most extreme adversity; which we felt was far more than we deserved.

"We were thus located at Mrs. Wilkinson's for a short time, and every comfort which her house could afford was bestowed upon us with a freedom, which showed us how willingly she assisted us.

"But the melancholy prospect before us was the constant theme of our conversation, and the subject of our thoughts when alone, and we saw nothing to give us the least cause to hope for anything but the most poignant misery. We saw very little chance of getting a situation, for the world is so censorious, and no one would, in all probability, think of taking us without a character. Could we get work of any kind, we were willing to do it; but that seemed equally hopeless to us. I had often reflected with regret on the circumstance of Mr. Greenfield hurrying away in such an abrupt manner, after I had met him at the coach-office, before I could ascertain from him any farther particulars as regarded the state my parents affairs were left in—for although they were in humble circumstances, yet I knew that my father, by industry and perseverance, had saved a little money, and it was only proper that I should how it had been disposed of. I had an uncle living not far from where my parents had resided, but hitherto I had been tenacious of writing to him upon the subject; however, at length, by the persuasion of Mrs. Woburn, who I saw every day, and Mrs. Wilkinson, I did at length make up my mind to write to him, and accordingly forwarded him a letter, in which I forcibly and feelingly expressed the deep contrition of me and my unfortunate sister, and begged an answer, with all the particulars we wished to know, as early as possible. A week elapsed, and no notice was taken of my letter, but at the end of that time, it was returned to me, inclosed in an envelope, without a word in reply. We have since, however, ascertained that our uncle contrived to get into his possession what little property our poor father had accumulated, and he has ever since refused to acknowledge us as his relations.

"To be brief, it was to the generous hearted Mrs. Wilkinson we were indebted for that humble cottage, wretched as it was, but not near so bad when we first went to it, and she assisted us all that was in her power, and seemed never to be so happy as when she could render us a service. We had been unable to procure a situation, but Mrs. Wilkinson got us a little needlework, which brought us in a trifling sum, and while this good woman lived, we were comparatively comfortable; but she died suddenly, and then indeed we might say we lost our best friend. A female cousin came into the possession of the property she had left, which materially altered our circumstances, for although she was not a bad sort of a woman, she had a heavy family, and could not assist us much, if she had been disposed so to do, which, of course, we could not expect, as we

were entire strangers to her. As her relation had felt such an interest in us, she also was inclined to continue that friendship towards us, and, therefore, although she charged us rent, she gave us needlework, which more than paid for it. She also, now and then, gave us what assistance she could, and showed us many other marks of kindness, which are entitled to our gratitude. But now our fate began once more to darken; we lost our employment, sickness fell upon the family of our new friend, and she was unable to render us that aid which she had done, and absolute hunger stared us in the face. To add to the horrors of our situation, Rose was taken very ill, and I could not obtain her any advice. I must pass over this awful part of our history as quickly as possible; whenever I recal it to my mind, I cannot help shuddering with horror.

"In a state of actual frenzy I left the hovel one morning, with a determination to obtain the means of food let whatever might be the consequences. I could no longer, in fact, remain in the wretched place and view the suff rings of my unfortunate sister and her child, without making a desperate effort to bring them the means of relief. For three days we had not a bit of fire in the place, although it was bitter cold, neither had we any food but a few stale crusts and a cup of tea, which we had obtained from the kindness of a poor neighbour, and we found it would be impossible to exist much longer in this manner—in this dreadful state of destitution. My frame was so weak, for the want of proper sustenance, that I could scarcely walk, and my countenance was the picture of hunger and despair. Having made away with every article of apparel which would fetch anything, my dress was also very miserable thought clean and patched.

"When I left the cottage, I had no idea as to whither I should bend my footsteps, for where could I go to seek that relief we needed? —Who was there whom I could ask to assist us?—Alas! I knew of no one, unless it was Mrs. Harwood, and from her we had already received so much, and she was herself so poor, what with a heavy family and illness, that I could hardly have the courage to ask it. However, the gnowing pangs of dire necessity urged me on, and, I therefore, directed my way towards her house.

"I had not proceeded any great distance, when I felt so weak and weary, that I was compelled to pause, and rest myself. I had only stood in this manner a few minutes, when an elderly gentleman, whom I now recollected to have noticed following me, came up, and before I was hardly aware of his presence, slipped something into my hand, and turning hastily on his heel, was out of sight in a minute.

"I was so much astonished at first, that I

scarcely knew what had happened, but looking in my hand, I was thunderstruck to behold a five-shilling piece !—I was so affected that the tears gushed from my eyes in torrents, and I turned it over and over in my hand for a few seconds, I could scarcely credit the evidence of my senses. It was like a fortune to me at that critical moment, and I fell upon my knees, and poured forth my gratitude to the Most High.

THE PEASANT DELIVERING A LETTER TO WALTER AND MARIA.

"This circumstance seemed to have imparted fresh strength to me, and I ran on with the most astonishing precipitation towards the city, and at the first shop I came to, purchased such necessaries as we required for our present relief; and, with a heart bounding with the joy occasioned by the event I have been relating, I returned with as much haste as I possibly could to the hut.

"My sister was astonished to see me return so soon, but when she saw the provisions, she could scarcely credit her eyes. In a few words

No. 62.

I related to her what had happened, and the manner in which she received the account did credit to her feelings of gratitude, which flowed spontaneously at the benevolence of the kind and disinterested strangers.

"I soon made a cheerful fire, cooked the victuals, and I and poor Rose both partook heartily, and had sufficient left us for two or three days more, in which interval we trusted that Providence would bring us some permanent relief. If the stranger had seen the happiness his benevolence had caused in the bosoms which had been so wretched and forlorn, he would have been amply rewarded for his charity.

"The next day and the succeeding one, I was out every morning early, to endeavour to gain some sort of employment; but the Almighty had ordained that our punishment should not be over yet. I walked until I was completely exhausted, and left not a place but what I inquired at; still no success crowned my endeavours, and each night I returned home, cheerless and despairing.

"The provisions which I had purchased with the money given to me by the gentleman, were now all gone, and we had no other prospect than the same state of suffering from which we had been temporarily released before our eyes. I could not think of it without almost going mad, and Rose was so ill, that I was fearful she would sink under it. When I looked upon her pale face and squalid form, which was daily becoming more attenuated, and then turned to the little innocent at her breast, and noticed the bloom of health gradually fading from its cheeks; the agony I felt for them entirely superseded my own, and I became the more determined than ever to strain every nerve to release us from the dreadful state of poverty to which we were reduced.

"I left the hut, and made my way towards Mrs. Harwood's, determining to ask her advice, if she even had it not in her power to relieve us. When I got to the house, however, Mrs. Harwood, I found, had been suddenly sent for from London, upon business of importance, and thus was my errand unsuccessful.

"With a despairing heart, I turned away from the door, and racked my brain to know what course I should next pursue; but all my efforts were fruitless. I thought upon the wretched hovel I had left, and the poor starving creatures it contained;—I pictured to myself my sister encouraging the faint ray of hope, and anxiously looking for my return, to give food to herself and child; and, in imagination, I saw her looks of despair and horror, when she should be made acquainted that I had nothing to give her, but that we must pass another night in cold, in misery, and hunger, without any change in favour of our circumstances. I say as I thought of all these things, a sudden idea darted across my brain, from which I at first recoiled with disgust and horror. But I overcame my feelings of repugnance sufficiently to put my design into execution. That night I returned to the wretched hut we inhabited with the benefits of my first day's mendicity. It was sufficient to afford us relief, and awful as was the alternative, it in some degree reconciled me to it.

"I have nothing more of sufficient importance to relate, but what you are already acquainted with, having informed you of the manner in which we met our present husbands, after our long separation;—how generously they pardoned our errors, renewed our protestations of love, and offered to marry us, and of our subsequently yielding to their solicitations; and therefore my dismal story is at an end."

Thus did Emma Dalton conclude her long and melancholy narrative, with which Maria was very much affected, and had listened to it with the deepest interest.

"And have you never since heard any more of Sir Charles Perceval and the Honourable Mr. Singleton?" inquired Maria.

"Never," answered Emma, "and I hope to Heaven that they may never again cross our path, for the sight of them would cause a renewal of all those horrors from which we have of late gained some relief.—If their consciences have been tortured as much as ours have been, God knows they must have been most severely punished."

Emma and her sister did not remain much longer at the hall, and when they departed they were filled with sentiments of gratitude and esteem towards Maria for the urbanity with which she had behaved towards them. They frequently afterwards visited Miss Herbert, and were always received by her with the greatest of kindness, and their past errors were never alluded to by her. Their husbands were two worthy and industrious young men, and they lived very happily together, and it was a pleasure to see so bright a specimen of repentance and reformation. Even those who had been most violent in their censure of them in the neighbourhood where they resided, now were glad to restore to them their friendship, and never in the slightest degree alluded to what had taken place. If ever the event which had occasioned them so much misery was broached in company, it was only to reprobate the heartless conduct of their seducers in the most unmeasured terms, and to express their pity for the sorrow it had been productive of to them.

CHAPTER LXV.

" Oh, the heavenly bliss of meeting,
    After suffering woes and cares ;
The fond embrace, love's warmest greeting,
    Repays us for our pangs and tears.
But to know the heart we cherish
    Still faithful beats for us alone,
To know its love can never perish,
    Transports us to joy's golden throne."

THE preparations for the reception of Mr·
Wallingford and his son were now completed,
and on a most expensive and magnificent scale
were they.   As day after day brought the
happy period nearer, the impatience of Maria
increased, and she pictured to herself the
change which the few months Walter had
been away from his native land had proba·
bly effected in his personal character.   She
anticipated all the improvements which had
taken place in him since last they had
met, and as she did so, her heart overflowed with joy ; but the principal cause of
her joy, was the assurance he had given her of
his love being unchanged, and in which assurance she felt positive he was sincere.   And
the favourable, the affectionate tone in which
her uncle had recently addressed his letters,
and the altered manner in which Walter had
stated he spoke of her, was another source of
the most unbounded pleasure to her, and hope
springing up in her bosom, made her look forward to happier days.   There was only one drawback upon her happiness, and that was the
dreadful uncertainty of the fate of Fanny, and
the trouble in which Ela must be placed at
her mysterious disappearance, and this she
reflected upon until she was almost ready to
go mad.   If Fanny had fallen into the hands
of the wretch, Rupert Darwin, or any of the
gipsy tribe, her fate would be certain, and
perhaps even now, while she was making preparations for joy, the mangled remains of the
unfortunate girl were mouldering in the earth.
She shuddered with horror at this thought,
and it was many hours before she could compose her mind ; but the same day it was
diverted to other subjects.   She received another letter from Mr. Wallingford, stating it to
be his intention to be at Rosemary Dell on the
following day.

We need not mention how delighted poor
Maria was when she received this news—in
fact, she could scarcely contain herself—long
had she been looking forward to this happy
event, but now that it was so near at hand her
feelings may be imagined, but cannot be accurately described.   She felt like the poor
houseless wanderer, who has been exposed to
the greatest misery and wretchedness that ever
fell to the lot of human nature, when restored
to home, friends, and all the joys of youth ; or
like the shipwrecked mariner, when cast upon

a desolate island, and his eyes are suddenly
gladdened by the sight of an approaching
vessel to rescue him from his sufferings, and
the terrors of a dreadful death.   With what
transport would Walter meet her again—what
delight would sparkle in his eyes—what
words of bliss would fall from his lips.   What
happiness would it be for her to notice the improvements which even the absence of a few
months only had wrought in his person ; to
hear him repeat the acknowledgment of the
intensity of his passion, and to know that their
love was sanctioned by his father ; for what
else could she judge from the tenor of Mr.
Wallingford's letters, and the hopes which her
cousin had held out ?   She anticipated uninterrupted happiness, after the many sorrows
she had experienced, and her heart felt
lightened of every care, except that which
was occasioned by the mysterious disappearance
of the unfortunate Fanny.

Poor old Mathew, and Anthony and his
wife, partook most largely of the pleasures of
Maria, and they awaited the next day with the
utmost impatience.   Indeed, there was scarcely
a person in the neighbourhood but what rejoiced at the circumstance of Mr. Wallingford's return, particularly the poor people—for
to them he was one of the kindest and most
philanthropic benefactors, and it was his delight to relieve their wants when represented
to him ; for though naturally austere and
haughty in his deportment, Mr. Wallingford
possessed, in reality, a most humane heart,
and had done an immense deal of good in acts
of charity and benevolence.

Soon after she had received the letter
announcing this joyful intelligence, Maria went
over the hall and the gardens to inspect the
preparations that had been made under her
directions, to receive her uncle and cousin, and
to see whether there were any alterations
which she could make by way of improvement ;
but she could not see anything, and she could
not but feel the utmost satisfaction with all
that had been done, and anticipated the gratification it would, no doubt, afford those whom it
was her most anxious wish to please.

Maria slept but little that night, and when
she did, dreams of the joys of the coming
morrow flitted before her busy imagination,
and afforded her a foretaste of the pleasures
she could not help thinking it was her fortune
to have to experience.

The next morning was ushered in by the
ringing of the old church bells, to welcome
back the lord of the manor to his native land,
and at an early hour the whole town was on
the stir, and the honest rustics, for whom a
repast was to be prepared on the lawn, were
seen to be bustling along towards Wallingford
Hall, all attired in their best, and quite elated
with the thought of the good things they

were going to partake of, and the joys they anticipated would take place on that day. Ever and anon, too, the carriages and splendid equipages of the different nobility and gentry, who had been invited, drove along the grand walk, and excited universal curiosity and admiration.

Before the arrival of Mr. Wallingford and his son, the hall and gardens were thronged, and Maria, who acted as mistress of the cheerful ceremonies, performed her task with the most bewitching sweetness and grace, and moved about the admired of all. Insensible indeed must have been the heart which could not be captivated by the elegant deportment of that lovely damsel; and many were the bosoms that felt for the first time the glow of love, as they gazed upon perfections seldom to be found concentrated in one object. Many returned home from Wallingford Hall that night, and left their hearts in the possession of Maria Herbert, hopeless of ever meeting with a return of that love which they felt could cease only with their existence.

At length, the loud shouts of the rustics proclaimed the arrival of Mr. Wallingford and Walter, and Maria's heart throbbed with a sensation too powerful for language to do justice to it, as she waited in the hall to receive them.

Another moment, and Mr. Wallingford and his son, in an open carriage and four, followed by the deafening shouts of those assembled upon this happy occasion, drove up to the door, and in another second Maria found herself locked, alternately, in the arms of Walter and her uncle, and felt the tear of rapture trickling from her eyes, and responded to in a similar manner by the tears of Walter.

We will pass hastily over the meeting; let it suffice that it was all that the warmest imagination could depicture it, both as regarded the behaviour of Walter and his father towards Maria; indeed, the latter was so overcome by the affectionate manner in which she was greeted by her uncle, that she had the utmost difficulty in supporting herself, and was for several minutes completely deprived of the use of her speech.

But what language could pourtray the joys of that meeting? How Walter and Maria gave free indulgence to their feelings—the many affectionate things they uttered—the tears they shed—the glances of adoration that passed between them—the unspeakable feelings of transport which swelled their bosoms, and often made their eyes more eloquent than their tongues.

Mr. Wallingford, too, often stood by, and seemed to admire their behaviour and to participate in their feelings. He dwelt with evident delight upon the improvement which even the short time which had elapsed had

wrought in her face and person; and when he recollected the manner in which he had behaved to her—the scorn, the insult with which he had treated her—a pang of the most poignant reproach and regret shot through his heart. He recalled to his memory all the reminiscences of Maria's conduct while she had been under his protection, and he could remember nothing but that which was irreproachable. It had been all that was amiable, gentle, affectionate, dutiful, and attentive. He reflected upon her behaviour during the illness of the late Mrs. Wallingford; the self-devotedness, the untiring care with which she watched by the side of her couch, night and day, and did all she could to alleviate her sufferings, with a total disregard of her own health; and more bitterly than ever did he upbraid himself for having so ungratefully rewarded her kindness, more especially when the dying words of his wife had committed her to his particular care. He was, however, now fully determined to do all that was in his power to repay her for the injustice which he had done her, and to make her future days happy.

These were the thoughts that passed rapidly in the mind of Mr. Wallingford on his return to the home of his ancestors; and contemplating the form and features of his lovely niece, who never looked more beautiful than she did on that joyous and auspicious occasion, he was determined that nothing should induce him to swerve from those resolutions.

Mr. Wallingford was looking very pale, but he stated that he felt in better health than he had done for some time, only being weak from the effects of the wounds he had received in Switzerland, and he certainly seemed to be much improved in spirits. Maria had ever loved him, in spite of the manner in which he had behaved to her, with the same affection as if she had been his daughter. He was the father of Walter, and that alone was sufficient to engage her utmost affections for him.—It was, therefore, with sentiments of the most unbounded gratification that she noticed the change in his spirits;—but how shall we speak of the transport she experienced at the marked, the happy change in his behaviour towards her—the mild, the gentle, and affectionate tones in which he addressed her, and the warm tenderness with which he regarded her? So great and so happy was the change, that she could hardly persuade herself it was real, and she felt as if she owed him whole years of gratitude and love.

But Walter; how shall we speak of him? His face glowing with manly beauty;—his form exhibiting every grace!—To Maria he appeared more noble and amiable than ever, and those beautiful little tell-tales, her brilliant eyes, the windows of a soul in which true purity was enshrined, spoke the unbounded love which inhabited her bosom, in language far more eloquent than the tongue could give utterance to. What hours of bliss were those which the lovers now enjoyed; how often did they seize the opportunity to escape from the gay revellers, and hastening to their old favourite retreat, the summer-house on the margin of the lake, give free indulgence to the expression of their love, and vow eternal constancy. Then they would recal to their memory everything that had happened to them, every hour of happiness they had passed together; and relate all that had taken place since they had been parted. In this manner the time passed away unheeded by them, and they remained longer away from the scene of festivity than they had intended. They anticipated the future, and formed the most sanguine hopes, from the evident triumph with which he had at last gained over those powerful sentiments of pride, that had been the principal blemish in his character all through life.

"He will no longer oppose our union, dear Maria," observed Walter, imprinting a fervent kiss upon the lips of his lover; "I am certain he will not now withhold his consent, and oh, how happy shall we be!—We will make it, my lovely cousin, our constant study to endeavour to repay him for his kindness, by all that gratitude and affection can dictate."

The noise of some one moving behind interrupted them, and looking in that direction, their surprise and confusion may be easily judged, when they beheld Mr. Wallingford (who had entered the summer-house a minute or two before) standing and gazing upon them in apparent admiration. Neither Walter nor Maria could speak;—but their blushes, and the tremour they evinced, showed the perplexity into which this unexpected adventure had thrown them. Mr. Wallingford fixed his eyes affectionately and feelingly upon them for a few moments in silence, then, with a bland approving smile, he approached them nearer, and in a voice of the deepest tenderness, he said—

"Rise, my children, rise, and receive the blessing of one, who has too long opposed the virtuous passion which glows within your bosoms."

He placed the hand of the astonished and deeply-blushing maiden into that of his son, and pressing them fervently together, continued, in tones that spoke the sincerity which prompted him to this act of justice and love—

"Walter, receive from the hands of your father a gift more inestimable than monarchs could purchase:—she is yours, my son. Glady do I accept her for a daughter, and may you, by every affectionate attention towards her, prove yourself worthy of that warm heart she has bestowed upon you. Bless ye, my children, bless ye!"

Mr. Wallingford raised his eyes towards heaven as he thus invoked a blessing upon their heads; while doubt, wonder, and perplexity, still chained their tongues. At length, however, the warm tide of their feelings rushed like a torrent to their hearts, and overflowed at their eyes; they threw themselves into the arms of Mr. Wallingford, and wept upon his bosom.

What pen could describe as it merits, the scene which followed this sudden, this joyful consummation of the fondest wishes of the lovers? How shall we portray the feelings that played around the heart of Mr. Wallingford at that moment?—Feelings such as he had never before experienced. Never before had such sensations of happiness and satisfaction glowed in his heart. He had suffered his better passions to overcome his pride, and made two beings blessed, whom his obstinacy would have otherwise doomed to endless misery.—Never had he felt more pure pleasure, and contentment of mind, than he did at that time. Such is the reward which ever follows a virtuous action. To the generous mind there cannot be a greater source of happiness, than in conferring happiness upon others;—in seeing those rejoice, who erst were sunk in sorrow, and to know that we have been the cause of their being rescued from the gulph of grief and despair. It bursts like sunshine upon the feelings, after they have been tossed and buffetted about by the storms of adversity, and we experience, as it were, a new life, in beholding the state of living death from which we have saved those it is our duty to love and endeavour to make happy.

Such, we repeat, were the feelings which Mr. Wallingford experienced as he pressed his son and the beauteous Maria to his heart, after he had pronounced his blessing, and he was assured that if his wife's spirit could now look down upon him, that she would approve of his conduct.

But the joy, the gratitude of Walter and Maria exceeded all bounds; it could not find vent in words, but their looks, their tears, expressed much more than language could possibly have done. Mr. Wallingford had made them the most blessed of human beings, and never had he appeared half so amiable, in their eyes, as he did at this moment. They could have worshipped him—they could have never ceased demonstrating their thanks—their love for the acquiescence he had yielded, though tardily, to their wishes. With bounding hearts, and a flow of spirits such as they had seldom ever known before, they rejoined the gay revellers in the hall, where the festivities were being carried on with all the spirit that joy and mirth could inspire. On every side, beauty and splendour were to be seen: rosy cheeks, sparkling eyes, and fascinating smiles met the gaze whichever way the eye was turned, and the gladsome strains of music vibrated on the air, and kindled fresh pleasure in the bosoms of those who had come with a determination of entering enthusiastically into all the sports of the day. Never had Wallingford Hall been a greater scene of revelry and joy: it was more like a festival of feudal splendour than one of modern times. But chief of all, amid the mass of beauty and nobility which thronged the hall, Maria and Walter were admired and eulogised by every one; and as Mr. Wallingford noticed the sensation they created, he felt a sentiment of honest pride glow within his bosom, which fully compensated him for all the years of care and suffeirng he had endured.

Nor must we forget the more humble portion of the guests, who were regaled with everything of the best, and whose honest mirth was suffered to have free vent, and not the least restraint put upon their festivity. Several times during the day, Mr. Wallingford, his son, and Maria, walked amongst them, and watched the manner in which they comforted themselves; and every time they did so, they were received by the most deafening and overwhelming shouts of welcome and gladness.

It was, indeed, a goodly sight, and such a one as would have cheered the saddest heart to look upon. Home, and his native land, never appeared half so dear to Mr. Wallingford as they did on this occasion, and he felt that in this world, and in contributing to the happiness of his son and Maria, he could find no greater pleasures. In that home would he settle for the remainder of his days, and endeavour to find that calm in the downhill of life, which he had long been a stranger to. What should have ever tempted him to roam—what business had he ever to have quitted his own country for a foreign climate?—His own conscience immediately answered the question. It was his pride, and the anxiety he had felt to wean the affections of his son from that virtuous, that amiable being upon whom they were fixed, which had caused it; but although he should for ever reproach himself for this, yet he felt so gratified in his own mind with the resolution he had at last come to, and the consent he had yielded to their union, and in witnessing the happiness he had conferred upon them, that he found an ample source for self-congratulation.

But in the midst of this joyous change, there was one painful thought which would obtrude itself; one idea which filled his bosom with the most intense agony, and that was the uncertain situation of Fanny, and the grief which Ela—Ela, who, with all her faults, he had been the cause of bringing so much trouble upon;—nay, he might say, he had been the origin of all her sorrows, all

her shame. Perhaps the poor girl had already fallen beneath the knife of an assassin, and where was he, her father, who ought to have had her under his protection ?—Still that he had not done so, he could not consider was his fault, as he had when she was but a child tried so frquently to attain that object, but without success :—the obstinacy, and implacable spirit of malevolence and revenge of Ela had prevented it, and thus it might be said that she had herself to blame for the subsequent misfortunes that had befallen her. He made a powerful effort to divest his mind of these melancholy thoughts, and at length succeeded better than might have been anticipated : but they were to be recalled in a manner, and by a circumstance which he was little prepared for.

The day went off merrily, and at night there was a grand ball given in the hall to the more distinguished guests, while the domestics, and rustic portion ef the company, amused themselves by dancing upon the green lawn beneath the silvery light of the Queen of Night. Mr. Wallingford contemplated with delight the persons of Walter and Maria, as they gracefully trod the mazy windings of the dance, and elicited the admiration of every one; and in the pleasures of the moment, forgot all the anguish which had recently tormented his bosom. Long did the dance continue, and the cheerful strains of the music floated along the hall, in tones sufficient to soothe the heart most heavily oppressed with sorrow.

Mr. Wallingford was standing at one end of the hall, and contemplating with pleasure the graceful motions of the dancers, when he heard his name repeated from behind, and looking round, his gaze fell with astonishment upon the dark features of a frightful old hag-like woman, whose head only protruded from behind a pillar, which supported the vaulted roof, and where she had concealed herself. He had some recollection of having seen her before, and doubtless he had, for a single glance would have convinced a person that she belonged to the gipsy tribe. He was so thunderstruck, that he was unable to move or utter a word, and the woman placing her long thin fingers on his arm, while her eyes beamed with a supernatural lustre, which was sufficient to strike terror into the bosom of the gazer, she said,—

"Think not thy trouble, proud sir, is o'er,
Many pangs yet are for thee in store;
Though now in thy bosom exists such joy,
There are griefs in store that will it destroy.
Many a care and many a pain,
Shall torture thy treach'rous heart again.
With death alone escape you can,
From the curse that's upon thee, the Gipsy's
    ban."

One look of dreadful meaning the Gipsy Sybil fixed upon Mr. Wallingford; the next instant she darted from the spot, and was lost amidst the numerous guests, before he could recover from the surprise and consternation into which the circumstance had thrown him.

"Close every door! secure the gates!" at length he vociferated, "and do not let the wretch escape."

This sudden exclamation, and the wild and agitated demeanour of Mr. Wallingford, put an immediately stop to the festivities, and all eyes were turned towards him for an explanation. Walter and Maria, alarmed at his behaviour, immediately flew to his side, and inquired what was the matter with him, but he only repeated his orders, in tones of wildness, and looked vacantly towards that part of the hall whence the gipsy had disappeared.

"Of whom do you speak, dear father?" inquired Walter, eagerly: "what has alarmed you?"

"Why, did you not hear her?—Did you not see her?" cried Mr. Wallingford.

"See her?—Who?"

"The gipsy," answered Mr. Wallingford, impatiently, "she was here not a minute since, and spoke to me;—yes, spoke to me words that—but, no matter!—Do not suffer her to escape!—she is, no doubt, somewhere concealed about the house, and as some base design in contemplation, which may involve us all in misery."

The guests were astonished, and Walter could not help imagining that his father was labouring under some sickly delusion, occasioned probably by weakness or unusual excitement; however, remarking the determined tone in which his father spoke, and seeing him rush away from the spot, he followed him, accompanied by several of the guests. Every one in the grounds was examined, and questioned strictly, but nothing satisfactory could be elicited. A woman answering the description given of the gipsy by Mr. Wallingford had not been seen by any of them. They also searched all over the house, but there they were equally unsuccessful, and finding it useless to continue the investigation, they gave it up, and could only come to the same conclusion as Walter, namely, that Mr. Wallingford's imagination had been wrought upon by weakness, occasioned by illness, the warmth of the room, and the excitement occasioned by the festivities, which were so far out of the course of his usual quiet and secluded life. Nevertheless, it put an abrupt stop to the sports, and the guests gradually dispersed, very much regretting the cause of the curtailment of those pleasures they had so amply enjoyed, until it had taken place.

When they were alone, Walter, more earnestly than before, questioned his father about it, and asked him whether he might not have been deceived.

"Deceived!" reiterated Mr. Wallingford, impatiently. "Walter, do you think I am mad?—I tell you again, I saw the frightful old hag as plainly as I behold you now!—She stood by the pillar I. pointed out to you in the hall, and the words she uttered made such an impression upon me, that I can repeat every one of them; listen:—

'Think not thy trouble, proud sir, is o'er,
Many pangs yet are for thee in store;
Though now in thy bosom exists such joy,
There are griefs in store that will it destroy.
Many a curse and many a pain,
Shall torture thy treach'rous heart again.
With death alone escape you can,
From the curse that's upon you, the Gipsy's ban.'"

Mr. Wallingford repeated the lines to his son without the slightest hesitation, although it was very evident that they had not failed to cause in his bosom considerable uneasiness, and to recal to his memory many sorrowful reminiscences he had hoped to have buried in oblivion.

"It is strange," said Walter, "but yet after all, why should the predictions of these wandering vagrants cause you any uneasiness or alarm?"

"And can you ask such a question as that, Walter?" said his father, "have we not had sufficient cause, all of us, to make us shudder with horror even at the bare mention of the name of that accursed tribe?—Have they not alone been our bane, our sole source of unhappiness? And, therefore, is not this circumstance, occurring, especially at a time like this, on the occasion of the day of my return to this neighbourhood, quite enough to make me feel miserable? Alas! I fear, Walter, that it is my fate never to be permitted to enjoy permanent happiness in this world."

"Oh! my dear sir," observed his son, "I beseech you do not give way to this despondency; I do not see that there is any particular cause for apprehension in this event, for if the gipsies are in the neighbourhood, we can very soon deprive them of the power to do us any injury, and secure them in prison. We must see to this immediately, although I don't believe there is much necessity for it, for it is not very probable, at least it does not appear so to me, that they will come to Rosemary Dell in a hurry again."

Mr. Wallingford shook his head, and then retired to his chamber, but not to sleep; no, the adventure with the gipsy-woman, and the prognostications she had given utterance to, occupied his thoughts too much to suffer him to do that, and in spite of all that Walter had said, he could not banish from his mind the idea that he was yet destined to experience more troubles, and, in fact, notwithstanding he was striving to make all the atonement in his power, that he was not fated to experience peace again in this world.

Walter, too, although he had disguised his real feelings from his father, was far from being so easy as he had pretended to be upon the subject, and he was fearful that the unconquerable hatred of the gipsies to his father, might urge them to do him some serious injury ultimately, and that the woman he had seen was the one who had been deputed by the tribe to commit the deed; from their black treachery and vengeance, who could escape? But if murder had been her purpose, could she not have easily done it on this occasion, and then have made her escape as well as she had done as it was? Yes, it was very clear she might have done so, and, therefore, all idea of such a desperate design was at once banished from the imagination of Walter, and he concluded that it was some idle person, and not a gipsy at all, who (knowing the events which had formerly occurred in the family) had assumed the appearance and composed the prediction uttered on the occasion, merely for a frolic. However, as it was as well to use every possible precaution, he, the next day, made every inquiry in the neighbourhood of Rosemary Dell, and the vicinity, to know if anything had been seen or heard of the gipsies lately, but not any signs of an encampment was to be seen, neither did any one know of their having been there since the time that Maria had been seized by them, when they took up their residence in a cavern which, as she had stated, was underneath the old Manor-house. Having heard this, Walter procured the assistance of some constables, and determined upon making a search over the Manor-house, and in the place mentioned, and, accordingly, the next day, accompanied by about a dozen stout men, they entered the deserted house, and examined every nook and corner in it, but they saw nothing to indicate that any persons had been there for some time. The doors remained open, and every thing in the same state as Maria had described she had left them, when she made her escape after her confinement in the cavern, or rather vault. They therefore proceeded to descend to the latter place, and see whether they could there discover any clue which might lead them to imagine there were any just grounds to suppose that the gipsies had recently inhabited it. They were not long in gaining this secret place, but there they saw nothing whatever to cause them to believe that the gipsies or any other persons had been there since the time when they quitted it in so abrupt a manner, as had been described by Maria. They retired from the place, and returned to the hall, Walter, now, feeling confident that the gipsies were not in the neighbourhood, and, in consequence, that they had nothing to apprehend.

Although this inquiry had been attended by the results which we have been describing Mr. Wallingford was far from being satisfied—so certain was he that he had seen the woman, and rejecting the construction which his son had put upon it, namely, that the woman was not a gypsy at all, but some person who had played the trick out of a frolic. On a former occasion they had taken the same view of a similar circumstance, and yet, how fearfully had his worst surmises been verified; and, therefore, had he not good reasons to be doubtful on the present occasion?

But the present joy they experienced soon drowned every other thought in the bosoms of Walter and his fair cousin; and in the anticipation of the consummation of that happiness which was now sanctioned by the consent of Mr. Wallingford, they formed a picture of future bliss, which they fondly hoped was not exaggerated. With light hearts and cheerful footsteps, they now daily wandered to their favourite haunts, and indulged in the utterance of those sentiments they had before been forbidden to encourage. Every spot seemed to possess a double charm, now that no care occupied their minds, and each scene they had been so happy in former days in contemplating, appeared to be endowed with fresh life and beauty. Every hour but served to increase the strength of their love, and to add to their impatience for the arrival of that time which should unite their fates for ever. Mr. Wallingford had intimated that it was his wish that the nuptuals should not take place in less than a year, and to the anxious lovers, that period would appear an age. With these joyful feelings, however, was mingled one of the most poignant anguish and regret, and that was the uncertain fate of poor Fanny.

"Alas!" exclaimed Maria, "how delighted would the poor girl be, could she but now be present, and witness our happiness, and know that we have at last gained the consent of my uncle, and that he feels a pleasure in seeing our love for each other daily increase?— What pleasure it would afford the kind-hearted girl to be our companion in our rambles, to share with us all our enjoyments, and to partake of our conversation. But where is she now?—Perhaps in the silent grave, the victim of some vile assassin!—I shudder with horror at the thought!—Oh, God! what a terrible fate is hers; and to happen, too, just at the time when she was about to become the bride of a man who seems to be every way so worthy of her!—Unfortunate Fanny, am I destined never to behold you again!"

"Nay, my love," said Walter, who was himself deeply affected, "do not entirely give way to despair; horrible as this state of uncertainty is, as regards the fate of my poor sister, it may not be so bad as we apprehend, and by some fortunate circumstance, she may be again restored to us, uninjured. At any rate, let us pray to Heaven that such may be the result. Of this, we are both certain, that Ela will not rest until she has made some discovery, and either got her daughter restored to her arms, or find out in what manner she has been disposed of, what has been her fate, and bring the parties who have injured her to punishment. What I principally regret is, that Ela being away from England, renders it impossible for us to afford her any assistance

ELA SEIZING VIVALDI.

but she is so indefatigable, that perhaps, she can accomplish it as well without our aid. There certainly seems to be a spell upon that unfortunate girl and her mother, for no sooner is the cup of happiness raised to their lips, than it is dashed away, and the poisoned chalice of sorrow substituted. But still, something convinces me that all is not so bad as we conjecture. I cannot bring myself to believe that Fanny is no more, but that we shall meet again. Oh, would that it were to-day, my happiness would then be complete."

No. 63.

Maria cordially reiterated the good wishes of her lover, and after some more conversation they dropped the subject.

The day after Walter and Maria had been talking upon this subject, a letter arrived from Ela, which was opened and perused with an eagerness which may be imagined, from the anxiety which they felt to know whether or not anything had been ascertained of the fate of Fanny. The letter of Ela, which was a very brief one, she seeming to be in a hurry when she wrote it, went on to state, after mentioning a few things of little importance, that although herself, Lord Helvendon, and the authorities, had been unremitting in their exertions to endeavour to find out the retreat of her unfortunate daughter, they had hitherto been unsuccessful, although of one thing they were certain, namely, that she was not in the power of the gipsies; but there was very little doubt that she was in that of the Marchese Vivaldi, from some particulars they had been enabled to collect of his having been seen lurking in the neighbourhood of the Castello di Alancantaros; but whither he was gone to, they had not been able to gather the least clue. Ela added that she was then about to depart once more in search of her; and it was her determination not again to rest until she had found her out, or learnt her fate; also who was the villain who had been the cause of so much misery to them. It was very evident from the whole tenour of Ela's letter that she did not yet despair of succeeding in her plans, and had hopes of recovering her daughter; but both Walter and Maria saw very little hope, from the reason there was to believe she was in the power of the Marchese Vivaldi, instead of the gipsies; for one was as much to be dreaded as the other. The Marchese Vivaldi, it was very evident, from the description which had been given of him, was a man who would not hesitate to run any risk for the purpose of gratifying his licentious passions,—and when tired of his victim, what crime might he not perpetrate to screen himself, and hide the knowledge of his villany from the world?—Alas! what might not be the fate of the wretched, the deeply persecuted girl?—Perhaps groaning beneath the weight of shame, and forced to endure the loathsome caresses of Vivaldi, or, likely enough, she had fallen a victim to the disappointed vengeance, or the fears of her persecutor.— View the case in whatever shape they might, it was equally bad, and their minds were perpetually tormented by reflecting upon these melancholy events, which were the only interruption to that happiness they would otherwise have indulged in, and made them the more miserable, as they were totally incapable of doing anything in it, or of advising Ela in what manner it would be best for her to act under such afflicting circumstances.

Mr. Wallingford was also very much aggrieved at the news they had received from Spain, and to learn that Ela and the others were still in a state of ignorance as to the fate of Fanny, and he would willingly, had it been of any avail, have made any sacrifice which might be the means of unravelling the mystery, and restoring peace to the already so deeply lacerated heart of Ela Beranzie.— This circumstance caused him to take a review of his past life, from his first becoming acquainted with Ela, when she was all purity, all innocence, and loveliness, of which he became the spoliator, and occasioned those years of bitter suffering, of shame, of degradation, and of guilt, it afterwards had been her fate to undergo. Every circumstance came so vividly before his mind's eye, that he could almost have imagined that Ela stood once more in his presence, endowed with all the loveliness and virtue, and simplicity of her youth, and which had first captivated him.— Then again he saw her after the false marriage, by which he had imposed upon her, and which obtained him the gratification of his diabolical desires; he heard her reproaches, when he told her the deceptive tale of his engagement with the late Mrs. Wallingford,— and when he swore to her that she was his wife, indissolubly his wife, and that none other should ever possess his heart. In imagination he beheld her when she received the brutal letter, in which he informed her she must not expect to see him again. Again he beheld her at the awful moment when she attempted to commit suicide on the bridge;—he saw her in the wretched abode where she had been compelled to seek shelter, with her infant nearly perishing at her milkless breast. He heard her tale of horror! the dying curses of her parents, and—but retrospection was too horrible, and he shrank appalled from it, exclaiming,

"All, all this have I occasioned; and shall I murmur that I am punished?—Oh, no, I deserve it all, and ten times more than that it has been my lot to endure, and for which I may be still reserved!"

He clasped his forehead with an air of intense agony as he spoke, and rushed out of the hall into the solitude of a neighbouring wood. He walked on at a hurried pace, heedless of everything around him, being entirely wrapped up in the horror of his own thoughts, and must have proceeded some distance, when he felt his arm suddenly seized with a firm gripe, and raising his eyes, they once more encountered the hideous features of the mysterious woman who had so much alarmed him on the night of the festival at the hall. She looked even more frightful than she had done before, and he was so much startled at first, that he remained as passive in her hand as an infant; but having quickly recovered, he demanded,

"Frightful old hag, who are you, and what is your purpose with me, that you thus a second time obstruct me?" he endeavoured to released himself. This, however, he found to be a much more difficult task than he had calculated upon, and although he struggled hard, the woman retained her hold, and laughed aloud with fiend-like exultation.

"Squire Wallingford," cried the woman, in a harsh croaking voice, "thou triest in vain; thou canst not release thyself from my hold until I choose, and that shall not be until I have thundered my curses in thine ears, and predicted the fate which will attend thee."

"Disgusting wretch! detain me not," cried Wallingford, in a voice hoarse with rage and terror, and still endeavouring, but in vain, to release himself from her grasp. "Why am I to be annoyed by your hated presence! I know you not, and cannot therefore be your enemy."

"Thou knowest me not, Edward Wallingford?" returned the woman, "ha! ha! ha!—But 'tis well,—it is sufficient that I know thee, know thee well! Art thou not he through whose vile means the blood of the gipsy has been shed upon the scaffold?—Answer me that, wretch; villain!—Didst thou not hunt the father and son to death, and exult in their suffering, and thinkest thou to escape the vengeance of their companions? No, by Astaroth, thou shalt not; and even now could I stretch thee a bleeding corpse at my feet!"

As the woman thus spoke, she drew forth a long knife from her bosom, and brandished it above her head, with fierce and threatening gestures, while her eyes flashed with an expression of fury, which gave her all the appearance of a supernatural being.

Mr. Wallingford exhibited no signs of fear, on the contrary, he appeared to treat the threats of the woman with the most ineffable scorn; while after a brief pause, during which she still retained her hold of Wallingford's arm with herculean power, she continued,—

"But no, thy life for a brief space longer is spared thee; the task is not allotted to me; there is one for whom it is reserved, who will not fail to effect his task. Tremble, Squire Wallingford; the curse of the gipsy tribe is upon thee. Thou art doomed by their laws, and nothing can save thee from the fury of their revenge. Tremble, again I say; twice more shall we meet, and then beware, for thy fate will be at hand. Tremble—tremble—tremble!"

As the woman thus spoke, she set up a frightful wailing cry, which re-echoed through the wood, and shaking her long, thin, bony fingers at Wallingford, and darting a fiendish look of terrific meaning upon him, she hurried from the spot, and before he had time to recover himself from the state of surprise and horror into which her appearance, and the words she had uttered, had thrown him, she had disappeared.

"Good God!" exclaimed Mr. Wallingford, in tones of distraction; "for what am I reserved? When will my troubles be at an end? Or, am I to be perpetually tormented by some painful circumstance or the other? Oh, how bitterly do I repent of the errors of which I have been guilty, and how ready am I to make all the earthly reparation that is in my power, but yet can I find no alleviation of my sufferings! Am I then cursed for ever? Are my sins too great to entitle me, by compunction and atonement, to forgiveness? But I rave! Why should the rabid threats and prognostications of this wandering vagrant alarm me? The wretch! But I will discover her retreat, and drag her and her infamous associates to justice. Yes, this moment I will pursue her, and though I fall in the endeavour to apprehend her, nothing shall daunt me. Death itself is preferable to this continual state of torture!"

And scarcely knowing what he did, Mr. Wallingford rushed forward in the direction which the gipsy woman had taken, but after pursuing the track for some distance through the wood, without perceiving anything of her, he recollected himself, and retraced his steps back again to the hall.

The adventure we have just related had a powerful effect upon the mind of Mr. Wallingford, notwithstanding he tried to view it with contempt, for there was something so earnest and supernatural in the woman's manner, that, in spite of all his efforts, he could not erase her from his recollection. He caused the search after this woman and the associates he imagined her to have at hand, to be renewed, but it was all without effect—not the least traces could be discovered, nor anything to conclude that the gipsies were near the spot, or had been there for some time; and Walter and Maria were fain to believe that the woman existed only in the imagination of Mr. Wallingford.

The unhappy malady under which he laboured, however, severely grieved them, and interrupted those joyful anticipations his consent to their union had caused them to indulge in. Both of them did all that the most affectionate attention could, to banish the thoughts of it from his mind, and to restore him to those spirits he enjoyed on his return from Switzerland; but although they did succeed in ameliorating his anguish, they found it utterly impossible to eradicate it entirely from his breast.

In witnessing the ardent passion which Walter and Maria felt for each other, and in beholding it daily increase, was the only source of relief Mr. Wallingford now experienced, and that he had been the means of making them happy, in granting his sanction to their passion, afforded him the greatest satisfaction. He often, too, pictured to himself the disgrace and misery he might have saved himself and others, had he indulged the same pure affection for Ela, and have made her his wife, instead of so basely deceiving her; by which means he had for years rendered her a complete outcast from society—caused her to herd with wretches to whom crimes of every description were familiar, and to bring up her child in the same wretched course of life, where it was only marvellous that her mind did not become as vitiated and base as those with whom she was compelled to associate. Besides, had he not created the most cruel and implacable enemies for himself, and Ela, and Fanny, who seemed determined to hunt them to death? Yes, all this he had been the cause of, through his accursed pride and ambition. But it could not now be recalled, or what self-suffering would he think too severe to do so? There was no anguish he would not willingly submit to, to be enabled to wash out the guilt of his past offences.

Notwithstanding all the endeavours of Walter and Maria, and his own efforts to conquer his feelings, the predictions of the gipsy woman continued to ring in his ears, and her hideous form was constantly before his eyes. Every precaution had been taken to prevent the occurrence of any such catastrophe as Mr. Wallingford apprehended, and persons were ever on the look out to apprehend any individuals of suspicious appearance who might be seen lurking about the hall; but nothing could appease the fears of Mr. Wallingford, although he made a powerful effort to appear more satisfied when in the society of his son and Maria.

Thus passed away several weeks, and the news from Spain was of the same alarming and melancholy description. The letters were sent by Lord Helvendon, who seemed to be bordering on distraction, for Ela had started in search of her daughter, of whom no traces had yet been discovered, although it appeared, from the confession of one of the men who were concerned in the plot, and who was taken before the Corregidore for another offence, that she was for certain in the power of the Marchese Vivaldi, but where she was confined, or where it was likely to find the marchese, he either could not, or would not, reveal. Lord Helvendon had himself adopted every means that he could think of, but without success;— every attempt at discovery seemed to be alike useless, and he had completely given himself

up to despair. His fears were also raised fo the safety of Ela, who, independent of the risk she ran in seeking to discover and rescue Fanny from the clutches of the villain Vivaldi, might fall into the power of Rupert Darwin, or some of the gipsies, in which case the sacrifice of her life would be certain.

The pain this intelligence caused in the bosoms of those so deeply interested in the fate of Ela and her daughter, was of the most bitter and poignant description, and many were the tears which were shed by the affectionate Maria, as she dwelt upon the probable miseries that were being endured by that unfortunate girl, whom she loved with all the fervour of a sister.

Her situation was too dreadful to think upon, and Maria turned from it with a shudder of horror and disgust, which it requires no great stretch of the imagination to conjecture. Perhaps she had fallen a victim to the licentious passions of Vivaldi, and was now mourning in all the intensity of shame and self-degradation. Or, to conceal the knowledge of his baseness from the world, and to save himself from the punishment which he might be certain would be sure to follow him, he had very likely murdered her. Maria's blood froze in her veins as she thought upon this—it appeared so probable, that she found it utterly impossible for her to banish it from her mind.

Walter did all that was in his power to appease her anguish, but his own apprehensions coincided too well with hers, to render his arguments at all forcible, and at last he relinquished the attempt, and tried, by broaching other subjects, to divert her mind from that painfully overwhelming one.

Of course, as might be expected, no one suffered more severely from this melancholy intelligence than Mr. Wallingford, and for several days it took such an effect upon him that he was unable to leave his couch, and Walter feared that he would experience a repetition of that dreadful malady under which he had so long suffered, and which had so reduced his constitution. With the aid of a skilful doctor, however, and the affectionate attention of Walter and Maria, fortunately these fears were not realized, and Mr. Wallingford was again rendered sufficiently convalescent to leave his chamber and take his customary walks, which since his meeting with the gipsy woman, had never extended beyond the gardens of the hall; but a deep melancholy seemed settled upon him, from which he could seldom be aroused.

Thus passed away several months, and still no tidings of Fanny, neither had Lord Helvendon heard anything of her mother for some time, until a letter arrived from her to him, informing him that although she had been most indefatigable and wary, resting neither n ght or day for any time together, she had not been able to trace the retreat of her hapless child, or the miscreant who had so surreptitiously gained possession of her. Still, she added, she felt convinced in her own mind that Fanny was alive, and something seemed to whisper to her that she would yet be restored to her ; and, in spite of what she had hitherto undergone, it was her determination not to abandon her search until she had accomplished her object, and wreaked her vengeance upon the head of the miscreant Vivaldi. At the time she wrote this letter she was in Italy, in which place she knew that Vilaldi was well known, and she hoped, therefore, that she might be able to gain some information which might lead to his detection.

And now the winter had set in and the snow was thick upon the ground. It was a very severe winter, and the frost had been most intense. To the poor on his estate, and for miles around, Mr. Wallingford behaved with a kindness that was most praiseworthy, and many a poor but honest heart was made glad, that would otherwise have been wretched, by the relief which he afforded them in that inclement season. The time of Walter and Maria was fully occupied in visiting the poor, looking out for distressed objects, and imparting to them all the comforts which they were enabled to do, from the philanthropy of Mr. Wallingford.

One evening Walter had been by himself across the Dell to visit a poor person, and did not return until night had come on. The snow had been falling heavily the whole of the day, and it was so thick in many places that the roads were rendered almost impassable. The wind blew very high, and the cold was so severe that Walter was almost perished. He hurried on as fast as he was able, and he felt very well pleased to think he had not brought Maria with him. The lights from the windows of the hall had just burst upon his view, when he was startled by hearing the groans of some person seemingly suffering most dreadfully. They appeared to proceed from a spot not far from where he was, and he was at length enabled to catch a glimpse of some object which was now moving about in the snow.

Not doubting but that it was some unfortunate person who was overcome with the cold, Walter hastened to their relief, and raising up the form which was writhing among the snow, he discovered it to be that of a woman, and apparently very meanly attired, as well as the darkness would permit him to see. She was perfectly senseless, and seemed to be dying fast ; but she was so heavy that Walter was fearful he should not be able to carry her to any distance by himself. He was thus placed in an awkward predicament, and knew not in what way to act, for that the poor woman must

die, if she had not some immediate relief, he felt certain.

While he thus stood consulting with himself what was best to be done, he heard some one approaching, who was whistling, and called to him to come to his assistance. The man was by his side in a moment, and it proved to be his own groom.

"Why, as I live, sir," said William, looking more closely at the woman, "as I live, sir, it is one of them confounded gipsy women."

"A gipsy!" repeated Walter, and another look convinced him his groom was right.

"Yes, sir," observed William, "it is, and I know her well too ; why, it is no other than that old devil Doctor Hartley had once in custody, old Zelta, I think they call her. If I had my will, she might remain here and perish for any assistance she should get from me."

"William," said his master, seriously, "humanity calls upon us to assist this poor wretch, and gipsy or no gipsy, friend or foe, it is no matter at a time like this, she must be saved if possible."

"Very well, sir, you know best," remarked the groom, very reluctantly rendering his assistance to convey the woman to the hall, "you know best, of course, and it is my duty to obey you, but I only hope this may not be the cause of something happening to occasion a repetition of those events that have already——"

"Psha!" impatiently interrupted his master, "how absurdly you talk—what harm can result from this poor, miserable old creature, think you? Let me hear no more of your ridiculous fears."

William said no more, but helped his master to convey the old woman to the hall, where they soon arrived, and the woman being taken into the servants' hall, was placed before a good fire and every means resorted to to restore sensibility.

Notwithstanding Walter had cautioned the servants not to mention anything of the circumstance to his father, it, by some means or other, reached his ears, and he came to the servants' hall to inquire into the particulars. Mr. Wallingford was horrorstruck as he gazed into the frightful countenance of the old woman, and immediately recognised in her features those of the gipsy who had some few months ago so alarmed him. It was Zelta, and the circumstance which surprised him more than all, was, that he had not recognised her features before.

Her cheeks were ghastly pale, and death had evidently set his icy hand upon her, and Mr. Wallingford shrank appalled from the sight; and when he recollected the curses she had heaped upon his head, and the prognostications she had given utterance to, in spite of his efforts to the contrary, he could not help evincing the terror she had excited in his bosom,

"Ah!" he exclaimed, the moment he cast his eyes upon her countenance, "it is the same hideous being who has two or three times crossed my path, and predicted misery to me and mine."

"If you had ever any reason to dread this unfortunate woman, sir," observed his son, "you have no cause now, for she is struggliug in the arms of death; and certainly is an object of pity, more than of terror."

Mr. Wallingford tried to make a reply to conceal his agitation, but he could not, and unable to look upon the countenance of Zelta, which was strongly convulsed, he covered his face with his hands.

By the strict application of such remedies as the doctor ordered, the violence of her pangs abated; her senses returned, and once more opening her eyes, she looked around the room with a vacant stare, and then upon those who were attending her.

"Where am I?" she cried, in hollow tones, "where have I go to, and who is it that I—— Ah! I see now!—Yes, there he stands; he who has been one of the principal causes of the destruction of nearly the whole of our tribe. I know you, Edward Wallingford, and breath my dying curse upon your head. Unhand me!" she continued, in a fierce strain, and bursting from those who were holding her, "I will not receive kindness from those I hate!"

With a supernatural strength, she made her way from the place whereon she had reclined, and staggering up to Wallingford, seized him by the arm, and while she gazed in his countenance with an expression which seemed as if it would penetrate to his very soul, she said—

"Squire Wallingford, when I am no more, there is but one of our wandering tribe left; but think not that you will escape the doom which has been awarded you, or that female fiend and her hated brat, who were the first cause of bringing misery and bloodshed into the gipy tent.—That one, nothing can daunt; there is no danger he will not risk to gratify the vengeance he has taken upon himself to accomplish alone, and no power can prevent his being able to put it into execution before long. Tremble!—Your fate is at hand, and but that Rupert Darwin wished to have the gratification of affecting the deed himself, you would, ere now, have fallen, fallen by my hands! I am dying; my eyes grow dim; the cold hand of death is upon my heart; but, ere I go, hear me again curse you, and tell you that whatever you may flee, in whatever place you may conceal yourself, no matter, however secure you may think you are, Rupert Darwin will not fail to find you out, and wreak his vengeance in your blood! This is the dying prognostication of old Zelta, and by Astaroth it will be fulfilled."

Zelta looked awfully upon the unhappy, the horrorstruck Wallingford as she spoke, and her features became frightfully distorted. Gradually she relaxed her hold, but still kept her eyes fixed upon Mr. Wallingford, until sinking back into the arms of two of the servants, she gave but one groan, and the next moment was a corpse.

Mr. Wallingford was, apparently, completely petrified to the spot, and stood with his eyes fixed upon vacancy, until Walter, laying hold of his arm, led him away, and conducted him to his own chamber, where the doctor attended him, and applied such remedies as he considered necessary.

It was several days ere Mr. Wallingford was sufficiently recovered from the violence of of the shock his feelings had sustained from the above related incident, to leave his bed-room; and in the meantime the remains of Zelta were deposited in a grave, by the orders of Walter. The circumstance afforded the latter and Maria much subject for speculation, and occasioned them much uneasiness on more accounts than one; not that the predictions of Zelta had any weight upon their minds, but while the villain, Rupert Darwin, still lived, they knew there was much to fear. Rupert was so crafty, subtle, and designing, that it was a difficult matter to guard against his machinations, and at the very time when they might imagine him far away, he would be probably just upon the spot, and ready to pounce upon his unsuspecting victims. That he would not hesitate to run any hazard to accomplish the sanguinary task he had allotted to himself, was very clear, from what they had already seen and heard of him, and even should he lose his own life in effecting his object, he would die with pleasure when he knew that those whom he had sworn to sacrifice, had not escaped his murderous hands. From these circumstances, therefore, both Walter and Maria felt that they had cause to be most seriously alarmed for Mr. Wallingford, and they scarcely knew how to act, or what steps to take to guard against the danger they apprehended. The only security they could see, would be in taking Rupert Darwin into custody; but they had not the least clue as to where they should find him, and he would be sure to take good care that they should not.

"I have always had a more particular dread of that man, than any other of the gipsies," observed Maria to Walter, when they were discoursing upon this subject alone, "and the impression upon my mind is, that his crimes are not ended yet, but that one of us, at least, is doomed to fall by his hands."

"Heaven forbid that it should be so, my love," replied her cousin,—"at any rate, it will be necessary that we use all the precaution we possibly can, to frustrate any plans which the miscreant may have in view. I will have some persons constantly on the look out, and as my father never leaves the hall any further than the gardens, I do not see that there is much cause for apprehension on his account. Rupert Darwin would not find it such an easy matter to gain access to the grounds."

"And why not, Walter ?" demanded Maria, "did not the gipsies formerly gain easy access to the grounds any time?—and, moreover, has it not been proved in the recent case of the gipsy woman, Zelta, that she not only got into the gardens, but gained admittance to the house?"

"Very true, my dear," said Walter, "but you will recollect that that was on the occasion of a festival, when the gardens were thrown open to any one who chose to come, and it would have been no difficult matter for any person to have forced their way into the hall in the manner of Zelta, when you bear in mind the number of individuals who were at that time moving about, and the little notice that would be likely to be taken of them."

"And what do you purpose doing to guard against the danger now, Walter?"

"Why, as I said before, I will have a number of persons constantly to watch the gardens, and as my father only walks out in the day-time, it is not at all likely that Rupert Darwin would make the attempt in the broad daylight. I trust that Ela will be able to elude him. I was hopeful that, as we had not heard any-thing of him for so long a time, some accident had taken place, to prevent the possibility of his ever having an opportunity of annoy-ing us again. But it appears that I was mis-taken."

"Zelta said that if she died, he would be the only one of the gipsies that was left," re-marked Maria. "I wonder if she spoke the truth ?"

"Perhaps not," replied Walter, "sho might only say so for the purpose of lulling us into fancied security, and thereby rendering us more likely to fall easily into their clutches. At all events it would be the best way for us to place no reliance upon such an assertion, which, to say the least of it, does not appear to be very probable."

Here the conversation dropped, but neither Walter nor Maria were near so easy in their minds as they pretended to be, and a cloud of fear and suspense hung over them, which rendered them very miserable, and that, at a time, when they had every other reason to feel the greatest pleasure.

Mr. Wallingford soon appeared in much better spirits than could have been anticipated, and the event was never mentioned, and, in fact, seemed to be almost entirely forgotten. But the same precautions were kept up, and

several men were constantly employed to watch the place ; but not the least signs of a gipsy had been seen since Zelta, and it really appeared to be true what she had said, namely, that their tribe, with the exception of Rupert Darwin, was extinct.

Two more months elapsed without any circumstance of importance taking place, Ela having as yet been unsuccessful in her endeavours to find her daughter, and despair of her ever being able to so, or to learn what had been her fate, began to settle upon their hearts. But this calm at Wallingford Hall was shortly to be interrupted.

Mr. Wallingford had been taking his customary ramble in the gardens, along the margin of the lake, and was returning to the hall, when, just before he reached the house, a man rushed into the walk, from behind a cluster of trees, and presenting a pistol at him, fired. Fortunately, Mr. Wallingford had the presence of mind to step a little on one side, and then suddenly closing with the ruffian, whom he had instantly discovered to be Rupert Darwin, a severe struggle ensued between them, in which Mr. Wallingford attempted to get possession of another pistol, which he per-ceived in the villain's bosom, and called loudly for help.

"Curses light upon it !" exclaimed Rupert Darwin, his eyes flashing fire with rage; "am I for ever to be foiled ? Hold your d——d tongue, or another moment may stop your croaking for ever !"

But the report of a pistol, and the cries of Mr. Wallingford, had not only alarmed Walter, and the other persons in the hall, but those who were set to watch the grounds, and the whole of them were seen rushing towards the spot where the gipsy and Mr. Wallingford were still struggling desperately.

The gipsy foamed at the mouth with rage, and at the dangerous position in which he was placed, and with a powerful effort of strength, he disengaged himself from the hold of Mr. Wallingford, dashed him to the earth, and turned hastily off to the right, where he saw a path was clear.

Walter, with the others, pursued the ruffian with all the precipitation they could, and several shots were fired after him, but without taking any effect. He far outstripped them, and gained the wall in safety ; and having climbed to the top, he stood erect, with a pistol in each hand, directed towards his pursuers, and laughed aloud in derision and defiance. He did not offer to move until they got very near to him, when he sprang into the road and disappeared.

"Follow the wretch !" vociferated Walter, to some of the men who had gained the wall first ; "do not suffer him to escape, but take him either dead or alive."

The men were over the wall in an instant, and Walter and his companions almost instantly followed their example, but their astonishment was, as may be expected, very great, when they found themselves attacked in the most desperate manner ley about twenty gipsies, with Rupert Darwin at their head, and who were armed with immense bludgeons and knives.

They were thrown into such confusion by this unexpected event, that most of them, in spite of the entreaties of Walter, scrambled over the wall again, and sought security in flight, while those who remained with Walter, had a difficult matter to escape with their lives; the gipsies, having grown daring by the panic they had struck into the bosoms of the men, scaled the walls again, and pursued them through the grounds, making the air resound with frightful yells of triumph. They would probably have made an attack upon the house, but fortunately one of the domestics, with great presence of mind, had run off to the town, on the first report of the pistol, thinking that there was more than one, and had just returned with a strong reinforcement of constables, and stout rustics, all armed. At the sight of these, the gipsies, in their turn, fled, and were pursued in the same manner as before. Several times was Rupert Darwin nearly taken, and the contents of one pistol seemed to have wounded him, by the blood which was seen to stain the earth, in the direction he was flying. However, he escaped into the road as well as the others; and, in spite of the rapidity with which the pursuers followed, they managed to elude them.

Walter and the others continued to follow, until all traces of the blood were lost to them, and they then reluctantly returned towards Rosemary Dell.

Upon returning to the hall, a consultation was held, when it was agreed that every inquiry should be made as to where the gipsies were located, when such steps should be taken as would appear most likely to effect their apprehension.

It will thus be seen that Walter had been perfectly correct in surmising that old Zelta had not spoken the truth, when she said that Rupert Darwin was the only one left of the gipsy tribe; and had it not been for the steps he had taken, in all probability the life of his father, as well as that of others, would have fallen a sacrifice.

This adventure renewed all the fears of Mr. Wallingford, and, in fact, Walter himself scarcely knew what to say to quiet them. Maria, too, was dreadfully alarmed, and all the endeavours of her cousin to soothe her, had very little effect. It seemed as if they were never to be released from the persecution of their old enemies, and that nothing could daunt their desperate character. They were in continual danger while they were near the spot, and it would not be safe for any of them to leave the house. So subtle, too, did the gipsies prove themselves to be, that there was no possibility of fathoming their designs, and at the very time when they imagined themselves in the fullest security, the greatest possible danger might be impending over their heads. Strict has had been their search, every part of the country, as they thought, they had scoured, which was likely to contain them, but without success; and yet that they had been secreted there at the time, and were still, was certain. Then, how were they to guard against them? What pains could they adopt for their self-preservation? Rewards they might offer for their apprehension, the strictest search they might prosecute after them, but yet did it seem as though they could fearlessly scorn the one, and elude all the vigilance used in the other.

There was one thing, however, very certain, since the recent attempt which had been made by Rupert Darwin, and that was, that Ela had been rightly informed, when she ascertained that Fanny was in the power of the Marchese Vivaldi, instead of having fallen into the hands of the gipsies; but alas! what consolation was there in that? Was not one as much to be dreaded as the other?

Mr. Wallingford had received so severe a shock, by the recent events, that he was unable to leave his chamber for a few days, and, indeed, his mind was too much occupied with the melancholy ideas that crowded upon it, to render him at all in a disposition to indulge in the society of his son or Maria even. But Walter would be with him all that he possibly could, and at such times he would endeavour to put a better aspect upon affairs than they really deserved, and to lead his father to hope that something would transpire to enable them to frustrate the evil machinations of Rupert Darwin, and his infamous associates. Mr. Wallingford however had received an impression which all the arguments and remonstrances of Walter failed to remove, and he gave himself up to a settled melancholy, which seemed likely to stamp his character for the future.

Yet did Mr. Wallingford's kindness and affection for his niece daily increase; her attention to him, her unremitting endeavours to soften his anguish, and the constant care she took to invent something which might tend to alleviate his sufferings, were irresistible, and never did he so forcibly feel the value of that gentle, that amiable girl's affections.

In the meantime, Walter was most indefatigable in his endeavours to secure them from a recurrence of a similar outrage to that we have just related, and to seek by every means, which integrity could devise, to discover the villains from whom they had already experienced so much annoyance, and whom they had so much reason to dread in future. The magistrates were all upon the alert, and persons were placed in all parts of the neighbourhood on the look out: but weeks passed away, and nothing satisfactory was discovered, and, as all remained tranquil, it was at last really believed that the gipsies had abandoned their designs, at any rate for the present, and had quitted that part of the country. Mr. Wallingford gradually became more composed, although he kept himself closely confined to

RUPERT SURPRISES MARIA AND CLARA.

the house. Walter and Maria seldom left the hall, and when they did, it was not to walk far, and then they used such precautions as were considered necessary to protect them from any sudden surprise. The persons in the neighbourhood of Rosemary Dell were most inveterate against the gipsies, and vowed to exterminate the whole race of them should they venture again to show themselves near the place, which entirely quieted all apprehensions upon the subject, although it created the greatest possible astonishment in the minds of all persons who were acquainted with the strict means that had been made use of to endeavour to find out the retreat of the enemies they so much dreaded.

It was about two months after the attempt which Rupert Darwin and his colleagues had made, that Walter, having had occasion to go to town on business, was returning at night to Wallingford Hall, when just before he arrived at Rosemary Dell, he suddenly beheld a volley of flames and a thick cloud of sparks burst into the air, in the direction of the old Manor House, whilst the report which preceded it, was as loud as the heaviest peals of thunder, and the earth appeared to shake under him. He was so surprised by the event, that he had not the power to move for a few minutes, but stood gazing with stupified amazement upon the lurid glare, the broad-red reflection which was left in the firmament after the explosion had taken place. The inhabitants near the spot were all aroused by the circumstance, and came rushing from their dwellings in the direction where Walter stood to endeavour to ascertain the cause. The point to which their attention was simultaneously directed, was the old Manor House, and Walter at their head, proceeded immediately towards that ancient fabric. Upon arriving there, a scene of devastation and horror presented itself, which they had little calculated upon, and which filled them with surprise and terror. The old Manor House was one heap of smoking ruins, and round about the place were strewed the mangled remains of men, from whose garb and features they were convinced were the gipsies of whom they had been in search, and who had so successfully baffled all their efforts to apprehend them.

"Good God !" exclaimed Walter, as he gazed on this terrible spectacle, " what can be the meaning of this?"

Immediate search was made, but not one of of the mutilated persons outside the building were found to be living. The fire having been subdued, men were immediately employed to clear away the ruins, and to examine whether there were any survivors, and, at length, they discovered one man, who, although much mutilated, and passed all hope of being ultimately saved, still breathed. By the orders of Walter he was removed with much care to the nearest dwelling, and medical men were in quick attendance, who used their utmost endeavours to restore him ; and by the morning succeeded so far as to enable him to speak, and to recognise the persons about him, and having apprised his father and Maria of what had taken place, he instantly fixed his dark eyes upon him, and exclaimed—

"Oh! you are the son of Squire Wallingford ? Come nearer to me, be quick, for I have something to disclose, and my time is short.'

Walter eagerly drew near the bed on which the wretched man was laid, who, after a long struggle to gain sufficient strength to speak, said—

"No doubt, after the daring attempt we made at the hall, and the vigilant search you have instituted against us, you will be surprised to find us in the old Manor House. But who shall fathom or elude the craftiness of the gipsy tribe? Even when your officers were in the old ruins, we were secreted in the caverns beneath. Mr. Wallingford, have you discovered any survivors beside me?"

Walter replied in the negative.

"Then," said the man, "all your apprehensions may be at an end, for not one of the tribe who were sworn to destroy your family, and Ela and her daughter, now live ; they are all destroyed by that terrible and devastating explosion.''

Walter could not help expressing his satisfaction at this information, but he quickly checked himself, and inquired how the catastrophe had occurred.

"I will inform you," said the man, and a malignant frown of disappointed revenge overspread his features as he spoke:--"We had devised a plot by which we hoped to destroy you all, without running any risk ourselves. The plan we had fixed upon was this—we had determined to blow up the old Manor House by gunpowder, and try a scheme to induce you and your friends to visit the place, under the impression that we were there, and might be easily surprised, and apprehended. For that purpose we had contrived to get several barrels of gunpowder into the caverns, preparatory to our placing them in a convenient place for our purpose, and where we might destroy our enemies, and escape uninjured ourselves. The gunpowder was disposed of in the ruins, and a train laid, which reached to the cavern, so that we might lay the spark to the train, and quit the cavern directly. By some accident, however—I suppose that one of us had dropped the lighted contents of a pipe upon the train as we quitted the cavern last night, for we had no sooner entered the ruins, than the explosion took place ; and as we were altogether, and as you say I am the only survivor found, there cannot be a doubt that all my companions have been destroyed."

"Was Rupert Darwin with you at the time?" eagerly inquired Walter.

"He was," replied the gipsy.

"Strange !'' said Walter, shuddering at the idea of the dreadful plot which the man had just related, and which had in so miraculous and just a manner recoiled upon themselves. "And yet no traces of his body have been discovered."

The man made no reply, and he soon afterwards relapsed into a state of insensibility and never recovered again. In two hours more he was a corpse.

There was only one circumstance which surprised and disturbed Walter, and that was the non discovery of the remains of Rupert Darwin, but yet it seemed impossible after the gipsy's statement, that he should have escaped. He, however, ordered a strict search to be made about the ruins, and everywhere where it was likely to find them, or, if in the event of his having escaped, every place he was likely to be concealed in. But they were not crowned with any success, and the only conclusion Walter and his father could come to at last, was that Rupert had been destroyed, and his features so much disfigured, that they were unable to recognise him.

CHAPTER LXVI.

"Stand off!—thy sight to me is odious,
Thy words are poison, and e'en thy voice
Is contamination!—Away! I say,
But think not so easily to gain your will,
For so strong am I in virtue, that
I laugh thy base attempts to scorn."

WE will now return to the unfortunate Fanny, who we left in the utmost misery, after her interview with the Marchese Vivaldi. With the utmost care she concealed the poniard she had discovered carefully in her bosom, and felt determined that sooner than the villain Vivaldi should succeed in his nefarious designs, she would plunge it, as she threatened, in her heart. Often she reflected upon the horrors of her present situation, and was almost inclined to believe that death would be preferable to it; but then the thought of the dreadful shock it would be to her poor mother, when she should hear of her fate, recurred to her memory, and she shrunk appalled from the deed.

The girl, whose name was Clotilde, and who spoke English fluently, relaxed considerably in the sourness of her behaviour, and had, no doubt, received instructions from Vivaldi to that effect, in hopes that she might conciliate her favour, and be the means of furthering his designs. But Fanny, in spite of all the girl's endeavours, could not behold her without a feeling of disgust, and avoided talking to her as much as possible. She retired into the next room, but Clotilde, having been so strictly enjoined by the marchese not to quit her for a moment, followed her, and thus Fanny could not gain a moment to herself. But she was become so deeply engrossed by her own thoughts, that she paid no attention to her, and was, in fact, almost unconscious that she was present.

The windows of the apartment she was now in, commanded a beautiful view of the surrounding country, rich in all the varied charms of nature, and embracing a vast expanse. But so occupied was the mind of Fanny with other thoughts, that the charms of nature were almost indifferent to her.

Some hours passed away in this manner, and although Clotilde had several times sought to engage Fanny in discourse, no conversation had passed between them.

"Dear me, Miss," said Clotilde, at length, "how silly it is of you to make yourself so obnoxious to the wishes of the marchese, who, I am sure, loves you, and that he would make you as happy as a queen. He is very rich, and in this place no one could be melancholy long. Besides, only think what a handsome man he is."

"The Marchese Vivaldi is a villain, and more hateful to my sight than the most odious of beings," ejaculated Fanny, her bosom swelling with indignation at the boldness of the speech Clotilde had thought proper to make; "but much as he may think he triumphs now, he may depend upon it that ere long I shall be rescued from his power, and he will be severely punished for the indignities he has heaped upon me."

"Well, I can't see why they should punish a man for loving one of our own sex, especially such a pretty one as you," observed Clotilde; "but I only know that if I were in your place, I would not act in the manner you do now. As for the marchese being a villain, I can tell you, you will gain nothing by calling him one, and if you continue your present behaviour, you will probably only exasperate him to acts of violence that he would otherwise not think of."

"This will protect me from the violence you have alluded to," exclaimed Fanny, as she exhibited the poniard; "while I have this in my possession I fear him not."

"Oh! Miss, do put away that frightful instrument, or suffer me to take it away," said Clotilde, "it makes me shudder to look at it."

"Never!" exclaimed Fanny; "this is my only guard against the villain who has so forcibly and brutally torn me away from my friends."

"Well, well, some people are certainly very blind to their own interests," said Clotilde; "but you will change your mind before long, or else I am much mistaken."

Fanny returned no answer to this speech, and in order that she might not longer be annoyed by the impertinent and ignorant remarks of Clotilde, she took up a book and pretended to read; but her mind was too much engrossed by the troubles that afflicted her, to suffer her to pay any attention to the contents, and Clotilde finding that it would be useless to attempt to engage her in conversation again, remained silent. As she thought upon the misery her mother and Lord Helvendon must endure, at her mysterious di appearance, her own agony was increased tenfold, and it was with difficulty she could support the accumulated weight of sorrow which pressed upon her heart.

As evening approached, she heard an unusual bustle below, and then followed the sweet strains of music, played with such admirable skill that it rivetted the soul of Fanny in attention. The air was plaintively beautiful, and accorded so with the melancholy state of her mind, that, overpowered by her emotions, she burst into tears.

"Lor', miss," ejaculated Clotilde, "what can you be weeping about? Surely it cannot be at the music, for that is the prettiest I ever heard. The marchese has a party every evening, at which many beautiful and accomplished females attend, to whom he has, on former occasions, paid his attentions. Hark! there is one of them singing now."

Fanny did, indeed, listen, and was so delighted with the lovely tones of the female's voice, and the melody of the air she was singing, that, for a few moments, she was completely entranced from her sorrows, and she listened with the most profound attention, fearful lest she should lose a single note. At length, the voice ceased, but still did Fanny listen, and, at length, a full chorus of harmonious sweetness vibrated on her ears, and added to the temporary pleasure which the novelty of the circumstance had imparted to her. She was completely astonished and bewildered by all she had heard, and could scarcely fancy herself in the mansion of one of the nobles of modern times ; but, in a moment, her sentiments were changed to those of disgust and terror. It was evident that the marchese was one of the most depraved of men; that he was a libertine, a debauchee, and a voluptuary ; and, solely in his power, what could she anticipate would ultimately be her fate? Could she be able long to resist his power? and unless by some fortunate circumstance, which she could not foresee at that time, she was rescued from his power, what could save her from destruction? Oh, yes, she had yet the means—the poniard! But to one so young, life was sweet; she thought of her mother, of her affianced husband, and she shrunk from the idea of an untimely death, with a feeling of horror too powerful for description. But yet she felt that, while she retained possession of the poniard, she might with safety repel the advances of the marchese, and keep him in fear of her putting her threats into execution, and therefore did she treasure it with the utmost care.

The music did not cease until a late hour, but at length, Fanny being tired, went to rest, Clotilde occupying the same apartment

with her. It was not, however, until some time after she had been in bed, that she could close her eyes in sleep, and then she was disturbed by frightful dreams which rendered her slumbers horrible to her. Frequently did she start from her sleep, and rise hastily up in bed ; she thought she heard some one in the apartment walking about; then she imagined she heard some one trying the door; and as the idea of Vivaldi darted across her brain, her terror may be easily imagined. But at length she was satisfied that it was only her own frightened imagination, and she became more composed. Clotilde slept soundly by her side, and everything remained the same in the chamber as when they had retired to bed. The lamp was still burning on the table, but the rays it emitted beamed but faintly on the objects around, rendering them very indistinct. A bell at that moment chimed the hour of four ; so Fanny once more threw herself back on the pillow, and tried to compose herself to sleep, which she at last succeeded in doing, and did not again awake until the beams of the morning sun darted in at the chamber windows.

She was surprised to find that Clotilde was not by her side. She arose, and looked in the next apartment, but she was not there either. Another thought in an instant flashed across her brain. She hastened to the place where she had carefully deposited the poniard the night before, previous to her retiring to rest, but it was gone! It was evident that Clotilde had taken it away during the night, and thus was she again left to the mercy of the villain Vivaldi.

This circumstance served to increase the distress of the poor girl in no small degree, and she burst into tears as she reflected upon the dangerous and pitiable situation in which she was thus placed. Nothing but ruin stared her in the face, and it was very certain that the marchese would not long submit to her opposition to his licentious wishes, and what opposition, in fact, could a weak, defenceless girl like her make to a man who held her completely in his power? What could she do to avert the misery, the horrors she dreaded? She had not a friend near at hand to interfere in her behalf, and indeed, her own friends were, she was afraid, entirely ignorant in whose power she was, and certain it was that they could not be aware whither she had been borne, or where to seek her. Well she knew that her mother and Lord Helvendon would use the most strenuous exertions to ascertain the truth, but the conclusion she imagined that they would arrive at, would be that she had fallen into the hands of the gipsies, and probably would not have any suspicion that the Marchese Vivaldi was the perpetrator of the outrage, especially as he had not been seen in the neighbourhood of the Castello di Alancantaros for some time before.

She was interrupted in these reflections by the entrance of Clotilde, with the morning's repast. The girl immediately met the reproachful glances of Fanny, and evinced much confusion; nevertheless, she quickly recovered herself, and observed—

"Well, I'm sure, miss, you ought to be very glad that I have taken that nasty instrument, in my opinion. What does a young girl like you want to make away with yourself for, I should like to know? Because a very handsome and gallant nobleman has fallen desperately in love with you, and all that he wants of you is to return his passion! Such an idea is absolutely ridiculous, and might do much better in a play, than in reality."

Fanny could not help bursting into tears.

"Clotilde," she exclaimed, "can it be possible that you, one of my own sex, can be so completely lost to pity, delicacy, and virtue, as to talk thus; to advocate the detestable passion of a libertine, a wretch without one spark of feeling in his composition? Shame on you, shame on you. I blush for you, indeed I do."

Clotilde was evidently abashed, and remained for some moments silent.

"But who knows, miss," she observed, at length, "who knows but that he might marry you?'

"Marry me!" repeated Fanny in a tone of disgust, "sooner than I would become the wife of such a being, I would suffer death. That would be far preferable to such a fate as a union with Vivaldi, who exults in his iniquitous successes; makes crime his constant companion, and whose delight is to trample on female virtue. Besides, he knew my heart was already engaged; he knew that I was affianced to another; he was told that I was averse to him, and if he had been a man of honour, would he, under such circumstances, have pressed his suit further? But no, honour is a stranger to the villain's breast, and to triumph over a woman's weakness is his chief gratification."

"Well, to be sure, miss," said Clotilde, "you do not appear to entertain a very amiable opinion of the marchese; but I would advise you not to be so candid in expressing your sentiments to him when you see him, and he intends to do himself the pleasure of having an interview with you to-day."

Fanny turned pale on this intimation, but she speedily recovered herself, and in tones of greater firmness and resolution than might have been expected, said—

"Whatever may be the ideas of the Marchese Vivaldi, and however indifferently he may think of my fortitude and resolution, he will find I am not that weak girl he may take

me to be, and that I will resist all his importunities to the last."

"And so you may, miss," remarked Clotilde, "but allow me to ask you what think you they will avail when opposed to the power of the marchese? Are you not here securely in his power? and is not every one, who you imagine could assist you, entirely ignorant of the place of your concealment? Of this I can assure you, that the Marchese Vivaldi is not one who will be trifled with, and who, having fixed his mind upon any object, will not be easily diverted from it, but will obtain the gratification of his desires at all hazards."

"The Almighty Father of all," said Fanny, solemnly, and with a firmness of tone which showed that she had not yet given way to despair, "the Almighty Father of all, who knows the virtuous sentiments of my bosom, will be my protector, and while I can so confidently put my trust in him, I do not fear the power of the Marchese Vivaldi."

"Ah, miss," said Clotilde, "I have heard others in the same situation as you are express a similar confidence, but they have been disappointed. But what a folly it is of you to be so obstinate, as to persist in pursuing a course, which can only be productive of misery to you. Let me advise you to think better of it, and not any longer to oppose the passion of the marchese. Depend upon it, you will never have cause to regret such an alteration in your behaviour, and——"

"Silence, girl!" interrupted Fanny, sternly, and her bosom heaving with feelings of the deepest resentment; "your words shock and disgust me; I will no longer listen to them. Leave me to myself—I feel uncomfortable while in your presence."

"Well, I'm sure," said Clotilde, tossing up her head, "some people do take a great deal upon themselves because they have got on in the world a little. It's not every gipsy vagrant, however, who is lucky enough to have a fortune left her. But we shall soon see some of that pride lowered, or else I am much mistaken. I wish you good day, miss, for the present, but I have no doubt you will have the *pleasure* of my company again before long."

With these words, Clotilde darted a malignant look at Fanny, which the latter returned with one of scorn, and then left the room in a great hurry, closing the door with a loud bang after her, and locking and bolting it securely.

When she was gone, Fanny once more gave vent to her grief and indignation in the most passionate terms. The boldness and indelicacy of Clotilde's behaviour had filled her bosom with the utmost disgust, and she felt her pride insulted, and her feelings outraged by the remark the girl had last made; but a short time served to remove that from her thoughts, as the source from which it had emanated was too contemptible to be worthy of any serious consideration. She endeavoured to muster up all her firmness to meet the marchese, but she dreaded his appearance. Hour after hour passed away, however, and still he came not, and it was evening before she heard the key turning in the lock, and expected that Vivaldi would present himself before her; but she was most agreeably disappointed when the door opened to behold Clotilde.

She seemed in a better disposition than she had been in the morning, but Fanny could not behold her without a deep feeling of repugnance.

' You are requested to follow me, miss," said Clotilde.

"Follow you!" said Fanny, in a tone of the greatest astonishment, "where?"

"To the saloon," replied Clotilde; "but you have no occasion to be in any dread—no harm is intended you; on the contrary, I can answer for it that you will be highly gratified with what you will behold there. This is one of the nights which the marchese appropriates to a gala, and he wishes you to witness the entertainment he gives."

"I will remain here," returned Fanny; " my mind is in no condition to indulge in the exhibition of vulgar mirth and revelry."

However, on a second consideration, a thought crossed her mind that, by assenting, she might secure the forbearance of Vivaldi, and that, by some means or the other, she might behold among some of the persons present, one, at least, who would pity her situation, and, perhaps—but the idea was preposterous that she was going to indulge in, for who was it likely among the marchese's guests, would take any interest in her fate?—Was it at all probable that any persons but those who were of the same disposition as himself, would associate with him?—She therefore rejected it in a moment, and as she really felt some curiosity to see the entertainment Clotilde had spoken of, she said—

"I am ready to attend you."

After traversing several elegant apartments and galleries, they arrived at a small room in which there were seats, and one side was covered with a crimson curtain. Clotilde desired Fanny to be seated, and after taking a chair by her side, she drew the curtain aside, and the astonishment of Fanny was indescribable, when she found that the room they occupied looked down upon a spacious and splendid saloon, which quite dazzled her eyes to gaze upon, and had more the appearance of some scene of enchantment, such as we read of in a fairy tale, than one of the nineteenth century. The marchese must have been immensely rich, and had displayed the most consummate taste; the arrangement of everything which Fanny

saw, and the place, would not have disgraced an Eastern sultan. The gorgeously fretted roof was supported by twelve massy pillars, round which, twisted fantastically, were wreathes of virgin gold. It was paved with pure white marble, whose delicacy seemed meant alone for fairy tread. Lofty mirrors glittered from all sides of the room—

" And vases sent forth their silvery clouds,
  Like those which the face of the young moon
    shrouds,
  But sweet as the breathe o' the twilight hour,
  When the dew awakens the roses power."

"Here we can sit, miss, and see all that passes, without being observed by any one," said Clotilde. "Is it not a beautiful place?"

But Fanny was too much surprised and bewildered to make any reply, and she sat gazing in mute admiration of all before her. The Marchese Vivaldi, and several of the male guests, were seated at a table at the further end of the saloon, but he frequently cast his eyes towards the place were Fanny was, and it was evident his thoughts were fixed upon her, and that he had adopted this plan merely from motives of jealousy, lest she should captivate the hearts of some of his companions; and more probable in order that it might not be known that Fanny was in his power.

But she felt greatly relieved to think that Vivaldi kept at a proper distance, and hoped that she would not be annoyed by his society all the evening. The novelty of everything she gazed upon for sometime estranged her thoughts from the melancholy situation in which she was placed, and she could not but look with the deepest interest upon what passed in the saloon.

In a few minutes after Fanny had taken her seat, soft music gradually swelled into the full brilliancy of perfection, from a distant part of the saloon, and as it seemed to approach nearer towards the place were Fanny was seated, the voices of several females arose in melodious tones to the various instruments, and floated in harmonious sweetness upon the air.

Fanny felt delighted; she seemed as if she were suddenly transported to fairy-land, and listened eagerly, fearful lest she should lose a single note of the dulcet and entrancing sounds; and the following words, sang with the most exquisite sweetness, were distinguished by her—

" Now let pleasure lend its powers,
  Let each bosom fill with joy,
  Mirth and pastime crown the hours,
  And all the cares of life destroy.
  Trip it gaily in the dance,
  And our hours of bliss prolong;
  Let music's charms our sweets enhance,
  Music, dancing, mirth and song

" Care was never meant for hearts
    That can feel the shafts of love ;
  Mirth a foretaste e'er imparts
    Of the joys of heaven above !
  Then trip it gaily in the dance,
    And our hours of bliss prolong ;
  Let music's charms our sweets enhance,
    Music, dancing, mirth and song !"

The voice ceased, but the music now changed to a gay and airy measure ; a pair of large folding doors were thrown open at the further end of the saloon, and six lovely females skipt lightly into the apartment, and danced with the most voluptuous and graceful attitudes before the Marchese Vivaldi and the other guests. They were attired in petticoats of thin muslin which descended just below their knees, leaving their beautifully modelled legs and gracefully turned ancles exposed to the gaze. 'Kerchiefs of thin gauze covered their bosoms, but was unable entirely to conceal their charms from the delighted observation ; and their brilliant black hair flowed in long and negligent tresses over their snowy necks and shoulders, like clouds of darkness chasing each other over the fleecy halo formed around the moon. Each held a silken scarf in their hands, which, in the course of the dance, they waved in a variety of fantastic forms. Sometimes they made a circle around the marchese, and those guests seated on each side of him, and joining their hands together above their heads, with their scarfs they formed a canopy of silken drapery over them, of which they seemed the statue supporters, like fairy figures standing beneath the gorgeous canopy of a magician's throne. Then, on a sudden turn in the music, they rushed to the extremity of the saloon, and erecting themselves each on one foot, they threw their scarfs over their shoulders, so that the gentle zephyrs caused them to expand in the form of wings, and in that attitude the beauteous damsels for several moments stood, having all the appearance of seraphs, just escaped from the abode of Elysian felicity. Every step was enough to inspire admiration—every attitude seemed sufficient to inflame the mind with the most voluptuous ideas.

" I will remain here no longer," cried Fanny, suddenly rising from her chair, as a feeling of disgust crept into her bosom ; " this is done to dazzle my senses, and to lure me from other thoughts. Show me back to the apartment we have not long since quitted ; I will not look upon the guilty scene."

" Surely you cannot mean what you say, miss ?" said Clotilde, who evinced much surprise at the words and conduct of Fanny ; " why the sports have but just begun, and I would not lose the sight of the whole of them for ever so much."

" I care not," said Fanny, resolutely. " I will not remain any longer, of that I am

fully determined ; I have seen quite enough to excite in my bosom feelings of disgust and indignation ; and to show me more plainly than ever that the marchese is a villain of the blackest dye. Will you do as I desire you ?"

Clotilde still hesitated, and once more tried to induce Fanny to alter her determination, but it was all in vain.

" You can do as you like," said Fanny, at length ; " but if you do not speedily comply with my wishes, I will present myself in the saloon, before the whole of the guests, and stating the circumstances under which I have been brought hither, demand my instant restoration to liberty."

Alarmed at this threat, and the resolute tone in which it was spoken, Clotilde very unwillingly arose, and Fanny followed her back to the apartments in which she was imprisoned ; and falling on her knees, she again prayed most fervently for the protection of Heaven, under the painful and dangerous circumstances in which she was placed ; while Clotilde muttered and grumbled, at having been, at what she considered to be a treat, so abruptly interrupted.

" Some people," said the pert girl, " have neither sense nor feeling for anything that is really excellent. It shows a vulgar mind though, which is incapable of appreciating anything out of the common way to which they have been brought up."

Fanny gazed upon her with a look of pity and contempt, but she did not deign to return her any answer ; and soon afterwards she quitted the room. She had not been gone many minutes, when the door was unlocked again, and the Marchese Vivaldi entered.

Fanny could not help trembling when she beheld him, notwithstanding she had previously made up her mind to meet him with firmness ; for, at the first glance, she was convinced that he was flushed with drinking, and she feared that, goaded on by his sinful passions, and the effects of what he had been drinking, he might be tempted to proceed to some excesses. He advanced towards her with an unsteady step, while his eyes sparkled with more than their usual fire, and he endeavoured to take her hand, but she resisted him ; and looking upon him with an expression which struck sudden awe into his bosom, although he endeavoured to treat it with as much indifference as possible, she said—

" Marchese Vivaldi, attempt not to pollute me with your hated touch ; for though you have deprived me of that weapon on which I depended as a friend in the hour of need, the God above will give me power to thwart your villanous designs, and to make them recoil upon yourself. Leave me, sir."

" Leave you, beauteous, too fascinating girl? Never !" exclaimed Vivaldi ; " to leave your presence, is to die: for what is life without the sight of your sparkling eyes?—a dreary waste; a moonless night.—Ah! frown not, sweet Fanny; and yet even in your frowns there is a spell sufficient to excite man's warmest admiration. Once more I come to offer you the homage of a heart sincerely devoted to you, and to entreat you to look down with an eye of favour upon my suit; suffer me to hope that I may yet hold a place in your affections, that I may ere long meet with a return of those sentiments which so fervently ——"

"Cease to give utterance to your guilty vows," interrupted Fanny; "they are an insult to me. Well do I read your real sentiments, ane despise as much as I abhor you for them."

"By Heaven, sweet girl," said Vivaldi, "you wrong me. The passion I feel for you is love—love, pure, ardent, and sincere."

"Disgrace not the sacred name of love by associating it with the odious thoughts that occupy your mind," said Fanny. "Marchese Vivaldi, it is a pity that Providence should bestow rank and power upon one whose breast is the abode of so much guilt."

"Sweet prattler," observed Vivaldi, "even your censure is music to my ears. But why do you entertain so bad an opinion of me?—I who would worship, who would adore you!—Pray, dearest girl, be a little more generous, and believe me, I will act towards you only as becomes a man of honour."

"Honour?" repeated Fanny, with a look of scorn; "the word honour from such lips as those of the Marchese Vivaldi?—Was it honourable to seek to supplant another in my favour; and one with whom you pretended to be on terms of the greatest friendship?—Was it honourable, after my mother had sought an explanation of you, and informed you that your behaviour was obnoxious to both her and me,—was it honourable, I ask, still to persist in such annoyance? Was it acting like an honourable man, when you engaged assassins to rob your rival of his life? Was it honoura ble afterwards to tear me from my friends and relations in the dead of the night, and afterwards to keep me here incarcerated against my will? Think you that it is by such base actions as these, that you are likely to create either love or esteem? No; say rather that every just-minded person must view your conduct not only with abhorrence, but horror."

"A very pretty sermon, and by a very pretty preacher, too," ejaculated Vivaldi, with a half laugh; "but again I repeat, you do me an injustice; all that you have enumerated was caused entirely by my intense love for you. The moment I beheld you, you inspired me with a passion which nothing can ever efface from my heart. Finding that you had bestowed your love upon another man, and that

he was you affianced husband, I struggled hard to vanquish it, but in vain; the more I sought to conquer it, the fiercer did it glow within my breast, until I was absolutely driven to a state bordering on phrensy, and scarcely knew what I was doing. Still did I seek to forget you, and to fix my affections upon another. Forget you? how fruitless was the task! Love another?—I had no eyes for any other female than you! All others appeared to me dull, senseless, insipid. I tore myself away (reluctantly, I confess,) from the Castello di Alancantaros, thinking, perhaps, when out of your sight, I should succeed in driving you from my thoughts; alas! every effort was alike fruitless!—Your image, dear girl, was constantly before my eyes. Sleeping, or waking, it was never absent from me! I found that I could not live out of your presence, so I hastened back to the castello. But powerfully as I loved you, I kept the secret confined to my own bosom. You can bear witness, dear Fanny, that I never once ventured to breathe a sentence in your ear, although I felt it knawing upon my vitals. Your mother alone drew it from me, and I must admit that the abrupt manner of her speech, elicited from me words in reply, which I afterwards repented having spoken, and gave rise to the hostile meeting between Lord Helvendon and myself, and which you fortunately came up in time to prevent, or some fatal consequences would, no doubt, have been the result. Once more, as you know, I left the neighbourhood of the castello, and again I sought to banish you from my thoughts, but my efforts were all, as before, ineffectual. What subsequently transpired you know, but however base, however violent my conduct may have appeared, it must be all attributed to your superlative beauty, dearest girl, and the seeming utter hopelessness of my ever being able to get possession of you, that caused me to act in the manner I have done. Here then do I crave your forgiveness, and beg you to look with condescension on my suit. Do not, I implore you, hastily reject those vows that indeed are now sincere, as they ever have been. Beauteous damsel, I am ready to do your bidding in a moment, if you will promise that you will become mine. No earthly happiness shall you want, if you will but consent; I shall live alone in seeing you blest, and the constant study of my life shall be to prevent you——"

"No more; no more!" interrupted Fanny, who had listened with feelings which may be much better imagined than we could pourtray them, to this harangue, so long, so tedious, so hypocritical; "each sentence which you utter, but increases my hatred for you, and shows your character in a more detestable point of view. If you would at all wish to alter my opinion of you, you will immediately make all the re-paration in your power for the misery you have caused them, by immediately restoring me to my friends, and abandoning your wicked pro-jects for the future."

"Ask me for my life, it is yours, freely, willingly yours," said the hypocrite, "but to ask me to resign you to the arms of my rival, now I have once got such secure possession of you, is to endeavour to exact by far too much from me !-- No, lovely maiden, anything but that, and I will not refuse you, ...

DEATH OF RUPERT

you to quit my sight, and to become the bride of another, that can I never assent to."

"Heartless, cruel man, who would thus rob the parent of her child," said Fanny, "bring her to a premature grave, and break the heart of him who never injured you, but who, until he was made acquainted with your black deceit, bestowed upon you his warmest friendship. How can you look her in the face whom you would condemn to destruction ?—But you shall not triumph ; no, there is a just God above, who views all our actions, and who, although He may suffer the guilty to succeed for a time, never fails to visit them with retribution; to Him I appeal, and I am certain that not only will He frustrate your diabolical designs against me, but most assuredly bring you to punishment."

"By Jupiter!" exclaimed Vivaldi, "any after punishment am I willing to undergo, rather than suffer you to leave me!—No, sweet girl, no earthly power shall again separate us; we will live only for bliss and one another; and thus on your lips let me again seek to press the pledge of my immovable, my unchangeable adoration for you!"

The marchese advanced towards Fanny as he spoke, and attempted to throw his arms round her neck, but burning with shame and indignation, she broke from him, and, acting on the impulse of the moment, she flew to the door, which was standing open, and bounded forth into the gallery beyond, and down the staircase at the end, with the speed of the affrighted deer. The marchese was so bewildered and astonished at this unexpected action, that he remained in the room for a second or two fixed to the spot, and gazing upon the door by which Fanny had fled, in stupified amazement. Soon, however, recovering himself, he pursued her with the utmost rapidity. She had got to the bottom of the staircase before he reached the top, and fearful that she would indeed gain egress from the house before he could reach her, and might be enabled to effect her escape from him altogther, he flew rather than ran down the stairs, calling madly upon any of the domestics who might happen to be about, to stop her progress. He was within only a few steps of the bottom, when his foot slipped, and he fell heavily to the floor.

In the meantime, Fanny had gained the outside of the house, and she was proceeding at a rapid rate across the garden, when she was stopped by two of the male servants, who had been aroused by the cries of their master, and who, in spite of the violence of her resistance, bore her back into the house, where the groans of the Marchese Vivaldi were now attracting the attention of the servants and others to the spot where he was lying. This caused them not to take so much notice of Fanny, and she was taken back to the apartments she had so recently fled from, and as they passed the place where the marchese had just been raised in the arms of his attendants, in order that they might convey him to his chamber, it was ascertained that he had severely fractured one of his legs.

Disappointed and grieved as Fanny was to think that she had not been able to effect her escape, she could not help being grateful to the wonderful interference of Providence, by which she had been saved from the brutal insult which the marchese had offered to her. The accident which had happened to Vivaldi, also, would secure her from a repetition of his visits to her for some time, and in the interim something might transpire to release her from his power altogether. The illness caused by the accident might also bring him to a sense of compunction, and he might himself voluntarily restore her again to her friends. Whichever way she viewed it, therefore, it gave her great cause for hope, and her spirits became somewhat lightened of the heavy care which had before oppressed her heart.

Fanny was now almost left entirely to the indulgence of her own thoughts, for Clotilde was seldom with her, and although her sorrow was very great, as may be imagined, when it is recollected how long she had been separated from those she loved, under such mysterious circumstances, and the uncertainty there was that they would ever meet again, yet it was in a great measure alleviated by the non-appearance of the marchese, who was very bad, and at one period it seemed as if it were likely to be attended with fatal results. Often did her thoughts wander to England, and she dwelt with the most sisterly affection upon Maria, and wondered what she was doing, and whether she was any happier than she was. But no, how could she be happy? Well assured she was that she could not; for doubtless, she had been made acquainted with her mysterious disappearance from the Castello di Alancantaros; and, oh, how wretched, she was certain, would that affectionate girl be at the uncertainty of her fate. Then, again, would the images of Walter and her father rush before her mental vision, and her bosom would become distracted with the most tormenting thoughts. Should she ever behold them again? Would they feel unhappy at the misfortunes, or shed one tear of compassion to the untoward fate which attended her? Oh, yes, one, at any rate, there was who would feel most poignantly the severity of her miseries, whose thoughts would be constantly upon her, and who would pray night and day that she might be restored to them unscathed, and never more be separated from them. That one, need we say, was Walter—her brother, and to whom her heart clung with all the enthusiastic fondness as if they had been brought up from childhood together, and been taught to look upon one another as brother and sister. Her father, too, surely he could not be so insensible to the feelings of nature and humanity, as to treat her fate with indifference? He must, in spite of all, sometimes think upon her, and there were moments when hope would be so strongly revived in her bosom, as to render her certain that the time was not very far distant when, in spite of the present gloomy aspect of affairs, they would all be restored to one another, and the misfortunes that had for so many years attended them, would be at an end. These reflections served not a little to lighten her woe, and to make her more reconciled to her present situation, although the misery which she was certain her mother and Lord Helvendon must be suffering, filled her bosom with the utmost agony. Lord Frederick, whose love for her was so violent, she felt confident must be quite distracted at the unaccountable way in which she had been taken away from them ; and should they not succeed in making out the place where she was confined, he would never see happiness again.

There was a good collection of books in one of the apartments to which Fanny had access, and sometimes she endeavoured to abstract her attention from her own troubles in the perusal of their contents. At others she would sit for hours together at the window, and contemplate the beautiful scenery, and sigh to think when she should again be at liberty to ramble, unrestrained, among its beauties.

Thus elapsed two long and tedious months, and still Fanny experienced no change in her circumstances. The marchese had not yet been able to leave his couch, and, therefore, she had suffered no interruption. But the time that she had been a prisoner was now so long, that she almost completely despaired of being ever restored to liberty again. It was very evident that Vivaldi had managed his plot with great ingenuity, and so secretly, that there did not seem to be the slightest suspicion attach itself to him.

Another idea now rushed upon the mind of Fanny, and filled her bosom with even more powerful emotions than had ever before tormented it. This was, the chance that there was of her mother having fallen into the hands of Rupert Darwin, or some of his gang ; or, perhaps, she had already become a victim to his implacable spirit of revenge, and she should never behold her again, or know the spot where her remains mouldered. This idea impressed itself still more strongly on her mind, for one reason, which was, that she knew that Ela would never rest night or day until she had found out some clue as to the place where she (Fanny) was concealed, or whether she still lived ; and in some of her ramblings, it was not at all improbable that she might have encountered some of the gipsies, who, it was very certain, would not suffer her very easily again to slip through their fingers.

The more the wretched girl ruminated upon this, the more feasible did it appear, until she could scarcely persuade herself but that it was true, and that she had actually received intelligence of it ; and her anguish now became more severe than any she had endured since she had been separated from them. Her incarceration now became intolerable, and she frequently raved in such a frenzied manner, that Clotilde often imagined her mad. Oh, that she

were possessed of a magician's wand, she would reflect to herself, that she might bid the doors of her prison to fly open ; how soon would she be at liberty.

Another week passed away in this manner, and Fanny daily became more miserable. The Marchese Vivaldi was able to quit his chamber, and he had sent word by Clotilde that she might expect a visit from him on the following day, which, of course, had greatly added to her mental uneasiness, and, altogether, she was in such an unhappy situation, that it was quite lamentable to see her.

It was the day that she had received this message from the detested Vivaldi, that, tired of thinking, she walked to one of the windows in her bed-room, which overlooked that part of the country at the back of the house. She had no sooner got there, than her eyes rested upon some object which seemed to be moving along a dark avenue of tall trees, and approaching towards the house. She could not, at first, distinguish whether the form was that of a man or a woman, or a human being at all ; but as it approached nearer, she saw that it was the figure of a female, rather tall, and who wore an old cloak, very much patched, and such as the gipsy women were in the habit of wearing ; but the person of the woman struck Fanny as being perfectly familiar to her, and so strong was that impression, that she kept her eyes fixed upon the woman, and watched her every action with the utmost interest. She moved cautiously along the avenue, and occasionally paused to see if there was any one watching her, and when she had reached an angle of the house, she raised her head, and seemed to be examining the windows. Fanny's eyes became fixed upon her countenance, and she uttered a faint scream, and sunk back in the chair with astonishment, for, notwithstanding her disguise, she recognised in the features of the woman those of her mother ! Yes, it was Ela ; and poor Fanny had, after so long a separation, once more gazed upon the features of that dear being who had borne her, and who her fears had imagined no more ! With frenzied eagerness, she once more looked from the window, but Ela was gone !

It would be impossible now to do justice to the agitation which Fanny experienced ; a tumult of mingled feelings raged within her bosom ; joy, doubt, and fear, by turns distracted her. Had her mother seen her ?—She was fearful she had not, for the time was so brief that she remained at the window, when she looked up, and the window was at such a distance from the ground, that she imagined it was almost impossible she could have recognised her. Still, however, she had no doubt that her mother, from the disguise she had assumed, would not be long before she would ascertain that she was confined in the house of the Marchese Vivaldi, and then her liberation would be certain to take place promptly, as Lord Helvendon and her mother's interest would compel the proper authorities to demand him to deliver her up, and he must hold himself responsible, in a court of justice, for the manner in which he had persecuted her. With streaming tears she fell upon her knees, and returned her thanks to the Almighty, who had hitherto protected her mother from harm, and guided her to the very place where she was suffering beneath the confinement of a villain, whose wicked schemes had hitherto been thwarted in a most miraculous manner, and from whom any future attempts would be completely futile, as, doubtless, the law would restrain him from them. Oh, how many, many hours of bitter misery and suffering must her poor mother have endured, previous to her reaching this place; what a multitude of cares must have racked her brain, and oppressed her heart. What alternate doubts, hopes, and fears, and terrors must have haunted her mind, in the course of the time Fanny had been so mysteriously taken from them; and what extatic joy would they both feel, when they were once more restored to each others arms. Her lover, too, was he with her? Doubtless he was near at hand, to render his immediate assistance when required.—Oh! what would be his transports at again pressing to his heart she who he must have imagined was lost to him for ever? The picture was so delightful that Fanny could not but continue to indulge in it, and so lost did she become to all other subjects, that she could scarcely believe but that it had already taken place.

She continued at the window the whole of that afternoon, in hopes that she might again behold her mother, and she did not retire until the last golden streak of the setting sun sank behind the lofty trees. With a lighter heart than she had for some time felt, she went to rest that night; but the unexpected circumstance which had taken place, had too much overjoyed her to suffer her to sleep. Visions of the most cheerful description flitted before her imagination—when slumber did, for a short time, close her eyelids, she already fancied that she was at liberty, and restored to the society and caresses of her friends. She was pressed fondly and fervently to the bosom of her mother, and they mingled their tears of ecstacy together. Then she was locked in the affectionate embraces of her affianced bridegroom, Lord Frederick, and never had his lips given utterance to such eloquent expressions of love, as she imagined they did on that occasion; never did he look half so handsome or amiable. Then, by a sudden change, common in dreams, they were instantaneously transported to England, and found themselves in Wallingford, and Walter, Maria, all and every

one, smiling affection and welcome upon them. In the midst of this pleasure, she awoke. We shall see, in due course, whether or not the visions of Fanny were fated to be realised.

CHAPTER LXVII.

"I am a man
So buffeted with misfortunes, tugg'd by fortune,
That I should set my life on any chance
To mend it, or be rid on't."—Shakspere.

THE ruins of the old Manor House were cleared away, and not a vestige of it was left behind. The vaults underneath were closed up, and thus all chance of their affording any place of concealment to any other parties was entirely done away with. Nothing more was heard of Rupert Darwin or any of the gipsy tribe, and it was therefore concluded that the whole of the wretches who had caused so much mischief in that part of the country for many years past, were destroyed, and that there was no farther cause for apprehension.

Although Mr. Wallingford and the others would have been much better satisfied if there had been any certainty of the death of their desperate foe, Rupert Darwin, yet the circumstance which had taken place, and led to the destruction of the old Manor House, and so many of their enemies, was sufficient to give great relief to their minds, and Mr. Wallingford, who, as we have before shown, was suffering under the greatest intensity of mental anguish, became so much tranquillised as to evince nearly as much composure as he had done on his first return from Switzerland to England. Had it not been for the gloomy letters they still continued to receive from Spain, and which left them very little hopes that the fate of Fanny would be discovered, they would have been comparatively happy. The sufferings to which Ela much be exposed, in the apparently fruitless search after her unfortunate daughter, sincerely grieved them; and the deep and inconsolable grief into which the melancholy circumstances must have thrown Lord Helvendon and his amiable mother, excited their utmost sympathy.— From the glowing colours in which Fanny had painted her lover, Walter was fully prepared to love him as a brother, and he was most anxious to see him, and from the description which the poor girl had given of him, in every letter which she had sent to Maria, she had fondly anticipated that the brightest happiness was in store for her, after the many years of suffering she had undergone; but this terrible event had o'erclouded all these hopes, and sadly did she fear that it was never her fate, nor those of her dear friends, to behold the poor girl again. This was the more lamentable, as the supposed extermination of all their bitter enemies opened a prospect to her mother of uninterrupted peace. But alas! it was useless to ruminate upon that dreary state of things, which she had it not in her power to alter; and all that they could do was to trust to Providence that it was not so bad as their worst fears apprehended.

In the moments when they could divest their minds of these dismal thoughts, Mr. Wallingford, and Walter, and Maria, talked of those happy days which they trusted that the union of the two latter would be productive of, and Mr. Wallingford, at such times, experienced more hours of serene enjoyment than he had done for many years. He had done, at last, his duty to his son and niece, and he was richly rewarded in the approval of his own conscience and their increase of affection towards him. Could he have imagined the happiness he would have brought to himself, how long since would he have done his duty upon this point, and thus have saved himself and them years of unnecessary misery, and most likely have prevented the occurrence of many of the afflicting circumstances that had happened to them.

But the troubles of the persons at Wallingford Hall were not yet at an end; another event was about to take place to renew their alarm, which we will proceed to relate.

We have before mentioned the attachment which had sprung up between Maria and Clara Jackson, and when the former did not visit the house of which Clara and her mother had the charge, she was warmly invited to Wallingford Hall. Clara was a very intelligent girl, and her manners, although simple, were rather superior to those of persons in her station of life; and Walter treated her with marked distinction; but, of course, every one whom Maria honoured with her friendship and regard, must be equally dear to him. Whenever anything called Walter away from the hall and the society of his lover, Clara was always her companion;—she made her the depository of all her little secrets, and she seemed partly to supply that vacuum which her separation from Fanny had occasioned.

Clara entertained a great horror of the gipsies, and could not persuade herself that they had all been destroyed in the explosion which had taken place in the old Manor House; but was inclined to believe that Rupert Darwin, as well as some others of his companions, had escaped, and were lurking about in some part of the neighbourhood, and only waiting an opportunity to gratify their diabolical vengeance.

In the latter opinion, Maria was often inclined to agree with her; and they had frequent conversations upon the subject.

"It has often struck me, miss," said Clara, one day, when they were seated together in the summer-house, and Walter had gone upon business to the town, "it has often struck me that the forebodings of poor Mr. Wallingford—though God forbid that my ideas should come true—will, one day or the other, be realised; and that even this last event, the destruction of the old Manor House, will not prevent it. I firmly believe that Rupert Darwin yet lives; and that the tale which the dying gipsy told to Mr. Walter was only partially true, and meant to lull him and his father into fancied security, until the opportunity should present itself for their putting their villanous designs into execution."

"I hope not, Clara," returned Maria, shuddering at the probability of the idea; "and yet it is not impossible that such may be the case, and it, therefore, behoves Mr. Wallingford and my cousin, to use the utmost caution."

"You say right, miss, it does indeed," observed Clara; "you recollect how you were deceived by the dying words of old Zelta, who said there was but Rupert left after her, and yet when he made the late desperate attack upon Mr. Wallingford, he was accompanied by numbers."

"True," said Maria, "there is no reliance to be placed on the words of such wretches."

"But is it not strange," continued Clara, "that Rupert Darwin should be able to elude all the endeavours to apprehend him so successfully, and actually seems to set at defiance all laws, and the power of those who have the enforcing of them? Any one would suppose that he had some dealings with Lucifer himself."

"The whole of the gipsy tribe," returned Maria, "are remarkable for their uncommon cunning, and their skill in being able to carry on their nefarious designs without running scarcely any risk of detection. Rupert Darwin seems to be a greater adept at this species of deception, than many of his infamous associates, and has, hitherto, been too successful; that is, supposing he be still living, which, I hope, for the peace of so many, that he is not. In fact, his success would tempt many persons to imagine that he was guifted with some supernatural power."

"So it really would, miss," said Clara, "and, indeed, I should not wonder at any one entertaining such an idea, after what has occurred. I only hope and trust, that we may not be disturbed by him again."

"What astonishes me more than all is," remarked Maria, "that he should appear to have abandoned his designs upon Ela and Fanny, at any rate, for the present;—or else why did he not pursue them after the last attempt he made upon their lives? His vengeance before this has principally been directed against them, and yet his re-appearance in England would lead us to infer that he had grown tired of persecuting them any further, and that he had resolved that my uncle and the members of his family should fall, to gratify that revenge he has been so unsuccessful in attempting to wreak upon Ela and her daughter."

"It certainly is strange, miss," returned Clara, "and I am at a loss to account for it; but there cannot be a doubt, if he is still living, that he will not abandon his cruel project, and is only waiting a more favourable opportunity of executing his villanous designs."

"Alas!" said Maria, "I cannot flatter myself with any more favourable opinion than you have just expressed, and something strikes me very forcibly, that we shall yet experience some trouble from the miscreant."

"Heaven grant that his intention may be frustrated," ejaculated Clara, fervently: "and I sincerely hope that poor Fanny may be still living, and once more be restored to happiness and her friends. That Marchese Vivaldi, as they call him, seems to be as great a wretch as Rupert Darwin, and equally as much to be dreaded."

"He does, indeed," replied Maria, "and I shudder with horror to think upon what the unfortunate girl probably has suffered, and is still likely to suffer, if it is true that she has been in his power all this time; and likewise the danger into which Ela may herself run, in endeavouring to find out the place of her concealment."

"I trust that Providence will protect the poor lady in her endeavours, and ultimately crown them with success," observed Clara; "what years of bitter misery she must have endured, miss, and her mind must now be almost distracted."

"It must, indeed," coincided Maria, tears starting to her eyes, as her thoughts became fixed upon the melancholy subject; "heaven alone knows when there will be a termination to it. She seems as if she were designed by fate, together with her daughter, and all who in any way become connected with them, to be the sport of fortune, and to endure a succession of sorrows sufficient to crush the stoutest hearts."

"Why, one really would imagine such to be the case, miss," replied Clara, "for I scarcely ever remember hearing of such an accumulation of miseries as have fallen to their lot;—it seems more like those wonderful and improbable adventures pictured in a romance than in reality. Lord Helvendon, too, his anguish must be very great, thus to have all his hopes of happiness blighted."

"Yes, he must, as you say, Clara, endure much torture at the disappearance, under such alarming and ambiguous circumstances, of her to whom he was apparently so devotedly attached, and upon whom all his hopes of bliss were fixed. Should they be unsuccessful in discovering the villain Vivaldi, and in rescuing Fanny uninjured from his power, he will, in all probability, never recover."

"Still, miss," said Clara, "as Ela is a native of Italy, you say, and it is imagined that it is there where the marchese and the victim of his persecution are concealed, I do not think it very likely that he will be long able to avoid discovery."

"Why, one would imagine that he would not, certainly," returned Maria; "but then it is not known for certain that he is in Italy, and if he even is, we cannot tell what schemes he may adopt to render discovery almost impossible."

"Very true, miss," said Clara; "but all that we can do is, to pray to God that the guilty may not triumph in their inquities, and that all may turn out for the best. I cannot, do you know, divest my mind entirely of the idea that Fanny still lives, and that she will, ere long, be restored to her mother and her friends. Something seems to assure me that she will yet experience every earthly pleasure, as a reward for the many heavy afflictions she has had to undergo."

"God grant that your surmises my be just," ejaculated Maria, fervently; "but——"

At that moment they were both startled by hearing a rustling noise from behind the place where they were seated, which was beneath the window of the summer-house, and turning hastily round, the reader may judge of their unspeakable astonishment and horror, when they discovered that the foliage had been forced aside, and their eyes immediately fell upon the savage features of Rupert Darwin, who was brandishing a knife, and seemed to be just in the act of plunging it into the bosom of Maria.

Clara and Maria both uttered a simultaneous shriek of terror, and springing immediately from their seat, rushed to the other side of the summer-house, where they became completely paralysed, and unable to make any attempt whatever to escape.

"Your cries are useless," exclaimed the miscreant, as he attempted to get in at the window, "this will soon silence you. There is no help at hand; you, therefore, shall be the first of my victims."

Thus speaking, Rupert Darwin had clambered to the window, and had placed one leg inside, when the report of a pistol was heard, and the gipsy with a dreadful oath, and a groan of pain, fell back and disappeared; almost at the same moment a second pistol was discharged, but Maria and her companion were so completely overcome with their terrors, that they remained fixed to the spot, and were still quite incapable of attempting to move. Maria was the first to recover, and hastening to the window, she sprang upon the seat which was beneath it, and in a dreadful state of agitation, looked forth from it, and to her infinite astonishment beheld the gipsy, although he was wounded, running with all the speed he could, and pursued by Walter, and several of the domestics. He reached the wall; but here, apparently quite exhausted with the loss of blood, placed his back against it, and flourishing the knife with the most menacing gestures, seemed determined to resist to the last moment, and rather to die upon the spot than be taken.

Maria watched the proceedings in a state of horror and anxiety which was almost insupportable, especially when she beheld Walter approach him first, he having somewhat outstripped his companions. She perceived, and she drew her breath short as she did so, and her heart seemed to rise to her mouth, that no sooner did her lover approach the villain, that the latter, with an effort of strength almost incredible, after the loss of blood he had sustained, flew upon him, grasped him by the throat, and raising his knife, was about to plunge it in his breast, when at that critical juncture some man who had been attracted to the spot by the report of the pistols, and the noise of the affray, appeared upon the wall with a stout stick in his hand, and just as the villain was about to put his hellish deed into execution, the man struck him violently across the arm, which made him not only drop the knife in an instant, but to release his hold of Walter. Directly afterwards, the domestics came up, and Rupert Darwin was secured and borne away to gaol amid the execrations of those who followed him.

"Thank God! the wretch is now safely in their power," exclaimed Maria, falling on her knees, and clasping her hands. Clara, who had by this time become acquainted with what had happened, followed the example, and tears succeeded to their other powerful emotions, occasioned by their own providential escape, and the improbability there was that Rupert Darwin would ever again be let loose upon society, so that all their apprehensions as regarded him would now be at an end.

Maria and Clara left the summer-house, and were proceeding towards the hall, to which Walter, the former had no doubt, would return, as soon as he had seen Rupert Darwin safely lodged in gaol, when they beheld Mr. Wallingford approaching rapidly towards them. He had been alarmed by the noise of the pistols, and hurrying from the hall to ascertain the cause, for he could not meet with any of the servants, he encountered his niece and the other, as we have been describing.

The surprise he evinced at the re-appearance, and the villanous attempt of the monster whom they had supposed to be dead, may easily imagined; but when he learnt from the lips of his niece that he was taken, his satisfaction exceeded all bounds. He raised his eyes towards Heaven, and it was very evident he was thankful to that all-wise Providence, which had thus arrested the arm of the murderer at the very moment when the accomplishment of his sanguinary design seemed all but certain.

They had not re-entered the hall many minutes, when Walter returned, and his first words were to inquire in the most anxious and affectionate manner after Maria, whose life he had been fortunate in saving at the imminent risk of his own.

Walter stated that soon after crossing the Dell, he was astonished to behold Rupert proceeding at a stealthy pace before him, and he determined to watch his motions cautiously, and by some means or the other, succeed in apprehending him. To do that, he knew he should want the assistance of others, for he was quite unarmed, and if he had been to the contrary, he felt himself to be by no means an equal match for the desperate villain he had to encounter with. He was, however, in hopes that he should meet with some persons who might be induced to aid and assist him, and then he doubted not but that he might be enabled to secure him. He was shaping his course towards Wallingford Hall, and he had not the least doubt but that he had some design or the other upon its inmates. He dogged him about for some time, until he came up to the cottage of one of his father's tenants, and still keeping Rupert in sight, he knocked at the door, intending to ask the assistance of the man who inhabited it. His wife opened the door directly, and to Walter's hasty interrogatory, replied that her husband was not at home. Walter's eyes immediately fell upon two pistols that were hanging over the mantelpiece, and he hastily inquired whether they were loaded. To this question the woman, with some expression of surprise and fear, answered in the affirmative. Walter then requested her to lend them to him, upon which her astonishment and apprehension evidently increased, probably thinking that Walter meant to commit suicide, or some other desperate deed; but he noticing that Rupert was almost out of sight, and fearful that he should lose him altogether, he darted hastily into the cottage, and snatching the pistols from the place where they were suspended, quitted the cottage before the old woman had time to recover from her astonishment and confusion.

He soon gained upon Rupert, but kept at a sufficient distance, so that he might have an opportunity of watching his actions, without being observed himself. In a moment he could have brought the miscreant a corpse at his feet; but then he was fearful that he might have accomplices at hand, who would be alarmed at the report of his pistol, and thus not only would his scheme be frustrated, but he should very likely himself fall a victim to the gipsies.

He saw him mount the wall, and as soon as he had cleared it, he followed him, and seeing that the direction he took was the summer house, he went along by another path, and came up with him just at the very moment when he had pushed away the foliage, and was attempting to get in at the casement. What followed has been already related, and the miraculous manner in which the life of Maria and Clara had been saved. Walter added that Rupert had received a severe wound, and it was very doubtful whether he would recover or not.

"Heaven pardon the guilty wretch!" cried Maria; "but oh, my dear Walter, how thankful we ought to be that our doubts are now at rest, and that the miscreant we have so long, and so justly dreaded, is in our power, and we shall have nothing more to fear from him or his colleagues."

Walter reciprocated her sentiments, and then having been assured by Maria repeatedly that she had quite recovered from the alarm which the sudden and unexpected appearance of Rupert had caused her, he hastened back to the gaol, to see that the prisoner had proper surgical attention.

A dead weight seemed to be removed from the heart of Mr. Wallingford when he heard of the capture and safe custody of Rupert Darwin; and he fervently uttered his gratitude to Omnipotence, who had thus interposed between him and a fate which his fears had foreboded would be inflicted by the hand of the gipsy.

In the meantime Rupert Darwin had been secured in prison, and a surgeon had been sent for to dress his wound. But he appeared to suffer more from disappointment and rage than from bodily anguish, and his oaths and execrations were truly appalling to hear. He actually foamed at the mouth with ungovernable passion, and they were compelled to strap him down to the bed, before the surgeon could proceed to examine his wound.

"Curses light upon the dastard knave who has thwarted Rupert Darwin in his darling schemes of vengeance!—But he shall not triumph! No, these walls shall not long contain me—mark me; secure as you think me now, the gipsy chief will yet regain his liberty, and live to shed the life's blood of those he mortally detests."

These expressions, however, were only looked upon as the wild ravings of a madman; and Rupert Darwin continued in that manner for several hours successively, and shocked every one around him. Upon the entrance of Walter, after he had left his father and Maria at the hall, the expression of the miscreant's countenance became dreadful, and for some seconds the violence of his rage choked his utterance, while so violent were his struggles that he almost burst the bandages by which he was secured to the bed.

"Eternal curses!" at length he exclaimed, fixing his blood-shot eyes fiercely upon him, while his lips were livid with passion; "eternal curses be your portion for this! May you and yours, if you escape the vengeance I have designed against ye, live only to endure an earthly hell—may your days and nights be those of horror—may your children, if you have any, live only to be a curse and a torment to you—may disgrace fall upon your name, greater than that even which has attended the villanous career of he who ha given you being; and may you at length end your days in the abject poverty in which those whom your have affected to despise, have so long lingered."

"Wretched man," observed Walter, in a tone of pity at the wretch's ravings; "spare your maledictions, for I heed them not. Your crimes merit the severest punishment, but your present situation is only deserving of pity."

"Pity, pity from one of the detested race of Wallingford?" almost shrieked the gipsy, and his eyes glared like balls of fire;—ha! ha! ha!—I scorn it; I will have no pity; I need it not;—think not that you will long detain me a prisoner, no, no, no;—Rupert Darwin is not fated to die thus, neither is he doomed to end his days until he has wreaked his vengeance at least upon one of his hated foes. He will yet live to triumph," he continued, in a firmer voice; "yes, he will yet live to accomplish his wishes, and to cause you tenfold more sorrow than has hitherto attended you;—mark me, the gipsy chief, the last of his kindred, tells you this, and, by Astaroth, his predictions shall be verified. Look to the fair damsel you expect to call your bride. Look to her, for I say, for she may not be so safe as you imagine. I live alone for revenge, for revenge for the death, for the murder of a father and a brother, and I am convinced that my eyes will never close in death, until I have effected my object."

In spite of the indifference with which Walter affected to treat the observations of Rupert Darwin, he could not help inwardly shuddering at his prognostications, and the vehemence with which he spoke. Too often had his family felt the weight of the persecution of the gipsy tribe, and although he was not naturally superstitious, there had been such a coincidence in the former prophecies of the gipsies, and what had afterwards happened to them, that, in spite of all his efforts to the contrary, he could not help feeling far from easy upon the subject. The gipsy evidently read his thoughts, for he smiled a ghastly smile of exultation, and then in a voice of triumph, exclaimed,—

"Ah! you tremble at my words, do you? Yes, I see that the gipsy chief, much as you may pretend to despise him, speaks the truth, and that his day of triumph is not far distant. Ela and her hated offspring may also think to escape me, but they shall not! No, they shall not; were they to bury themselves in the bowels of the earth, I would pursue them. They are only spared for a time; but time,

THE REUNION OF ELA AND FANNY.

nor difficulty, nor distance, shall finally save them."

"Unhappy wretch," ejaculated Walter, with forced calmness, "this is but the wild raving of despair!" and unwilling longer to aggravate him, in the presence of others, to repeat circumstances which he wished to be buried in oblivion, and which could only militate against the reputation of his father, he hastily quitted the prison, after requesting that every care should be taken of Rupert, and returned to Wallingford Hall.

Walter did not relate what had taken place at the prison between him and the miscreant, Rupert Darwin, to his father or Maria, and they were at length released from a heavy weight of care and apprehension, to know that their most desperate, and as they believed, their only enemy, was in custody, and without any prospect of being again set at large. But in spite of the apparent present security of Rupert, Walter, notwithstanding all his endeavours to the contrary, could not help feeling some misgivings as to his ultimate safety, and he was fearful that something would occur, when they were the least prepared for it, to aid him in effecting his escape from confinement, and accomplishing that diabolical scheme of vengeance he had threatened them with.

The sufferings and ravings of Rupert Darwin continued for several days with unabated violence, and the medical man almost despaired of his being able to survive. Walter Wallingford was a constant visitor at the goal, and was most anxious about the manner in which the wound of the gipsy proceeded; in fact, he would have been very happy if he had not recovered from it, for it would not only have set their minds at rest, but have saved them a great deal of trouble, in not having to prosecute him.

In the meantime Mr. Wallingford's apprehensions had been so much quieted by the detection of Rupert Darwin, that he mended space, and his spirits began to revive. He could now converse with Walter and Maria freely upon their present and future prospects, and formed ideal pictures of the happiness which was in store for them, and which his vivid imagination conjured up. The lovers listened to him with the most inexpressible delight, and in the anticipation of the future, they almost forgot their past sufferings. Indeed, had they been assured of the safety of poor Fanny, they would have been completely happy, but every now and then that mysterious circumstance would rush upon their minds with redoubled force, and threw a cloud of anguish over their pleasures. It appeared that fate was determined that this painful event should never be unravelled, but that the end of the unfortunate girl should for ever remain an inpenetrable mystery. They had not lately received a letter either form Ela or Lord Helvendon, and they began to fear that something had happened to them, in their endeavours to trace out the villain who was the cause of their misery, and to restore the poor girl they so fondly loved once more to liberty. This, of course, was an addition to their anxiety and unhappiness, and which they saw no prospect of being easily dissipated. They despatched letters to Lord Helvendon, earnestly resquesting that he would not delay sending them an answer, explaining the meaning of thier silence,

and whether there was any prospect of their succeeding in their efforts to discover Fanny and force her from the power of the Marchese Vivaldi, if it was indeed he who had thus villanously torn her from her friends, and that he had done so, there was very little doubt, if there was any reliance to be placed on the assertions of the man who had been taken before the Corregidore; besides, it was very evident that it could not be any other who had borne her away, as Rupert Darwin and the other gipsies, there had been proof, were in England at the time. Maria, in a letter addressed to Ela, made her acquainted with all that had happened at Rosemary Dell, since she had last heard from them; the attempts which Rupert Darwin had made, first upon the life of Mr. Wallingford, and then upon her's; the savage plot at the old Manor House; the way in which it had fortunately been foiled; the dreadful death of the gipsies, and the ultimate apprehension and confinement of Rupert; which, of course, would set all apprehensions of danger from him at rest, and would be a great source of relief to the minds of them all. Maria felt, at least, that under her present misery, this intelligence would impart no inconsiderable share of consolation to the bosom of Ela, although she was convinced that if Fanny were not discovered, life would be considered by her rather as a burden than a pleasure, and that she would pray to be rid of it as soon as possible, she would not care in what manner.

In the course of a few days the wound of Rupert Darwin took a favourable turn, and the medical man said that he would no doubt be completely recovered in about a month. Walter had visited him several times since the day of his apprehension, and he always received him with the same demonstrations of hatred, and poured out the same savage maledictions and threats. It was very clear that he firmly believed that he should effect his escape, notwithstanding all the precautions that were taken to secure him; and in that hope, he kept up the same spirit of bravado and indifference, which had characterised him from the first.

"And so," he observed to Walter one day, knitting his brows, and gnashing his teeth, as he he spoke, "so, you think that your dungeons will hold the gipsy chief;—that your locks and bolts, and letters, will secure him from that liberty which he has hitherto unlimitedly enjoyed?—Ha! ha! ha! you will be deceived!—Mark me, I tell you, you will be deceived; and when you think you have Rupert Darwin the most secure, that is the very time he will slip through your fingers, in spite of all your precautions."

Walter smiled contemptuously, but he could not help feeling deeply impressed with the gipsy's words notwithstanding; and the pre-sentiment which had before haunted his mind, that Rupert would by some means contrive to elude the vigilance of his keepers, still remained.

"Ah! you will smile, and scorn my words, if you please," returned Rupert, "but you will find that I am no vain boaster. The gipsies schemes are inscrutable to the pale-faced race, and impossible as it may appear to you, the accomplishment of that I promise will be an easy task for me. The soul of Rupert Darwin scorns confinement; nor was he born to die by the hands of man; no, mark me, son of Wallingford of the Dell, when I fall, one at least of those I hate shall fall with me!—I have said it, and the word of Rupert Darwin was never broken yet."

"You do but waste your breath in giving vent to those useless threats," said Walter, affecting to treat the words of the man with the most superlative indifference, although he really felt quite to the contrary; "here you are safe enough, and will so remain until you are brought to justice and punishment, for the many brutal outrages you have committed upon society!"

"What, you would hang me like a dog, as you and yours were the cause of murdering my father and my brother?" said the gipsy, with a fierce look; "but you will not, no, you shall not have that gratification. Rupert Darwin will outwit ye all; he tells you so again, and defies you to do your best to prevent him. Mark me, Walter Wallingford, and think not it is mere idle boasting, ere a month has elapsed, the gipsy chief will be again at liberty, and prosecuting that scheme of venge-ance he has so long contemplated."

"It would be much better for you to cease this fruitless boasting, and by repentance, hope to gain some mitigation of the punish-ment which is doubtless in store for you," ob-served Walter, calmly.

"Repent?" exclaimed Rupert, with a bitter laugh of scorn. "Fool! What have I to re-pent? Regret I do, but it is only that I have failed hitherto to effect that darling scheme of revenge, my soul has so long feasted upon. Re-pentance to the ears of a man like me, is sick-ening cant; I live only to shed the blood of those I hate, of those who have shed the blood of mine; that hope accomplished, I care not how soon there is an end of me! The gipsy chief knows not fear, and he can meet death as readily as he would smoke his pipe. It is only for the pale-faced tribe to fear death, such is unknown to the gipsy race. They are born in the midst of danger, they are inured in the vicissitudes and miseries of the world; they experience nothing but its scorn, its hatred, its contumely, and consequently they treat life as a mere game of chance; when luck is against them, like all good gamblers, they sub-mit to their fate without a murmur. All the inmates of the world, except their own asso-ciates, are their enemies; and when, there-fore, they have gained their revenge of the world, they care not how soon they leave it. I have not yet completed my vengeance, Walter Wallingford, although I have caused you and yours many years of misery, and I know I shall never quit this life until I have satiated my hatred in the blood of at least one of ye. Receive this from Rupert Darwin, and rest assured that his threats will be accomplished."

As the villain thus spoke, his countenance assumed an expression that was truly demo-niacal, and Walter, in spite of all his efforts, could not help showing the impression his words had made upon him. The gipsy's keen eye immediately detected his thoughts, and he laughed exultingly as the young man, ashamed of the weakness he betrayed, abruptly quitted the prison, and returned to the hall in a state of mind far from comfortable, although he had given the authorities connected with the gaol the most particular instructions as regarded the safe custody of their prisoner.

Walter did not impart to his father or to Maria what had taken place between him and Rupert Darwin at their interview, for he felt convinced that it was calculated to cause them great uneasiness, and occasion them to enter-tain fears which, after all, might be perfectly groundless. He was himself, however, very ill at ease, and, in spite of all his endeavours to the contrary, could not avoid the gloomy fore-bodings that from the first occupied his mind, that Rupert Darwin would, by some means or other, contrive to effect his liberation, and that his vengeance would fall, in a fatal manner, upon one or more of those upon whom he had fixed his hatred. Of the subtlety and untiring spirit of revenge against those who had offended them, the conduct of the gipsies had furnishd him sufficient proofs, and he had his doubts as to whether he was the last of his tribe, or why should he make so certain of the success of the scheme he had formed?—It was very evi-dent that he must rest his hopes upon the assistance of accessaries; for, closely confined as he was, if he had no accomplices, it was not at all probable that he could expect to find an op-portunity, or entertain a shadow of an idea that he would be enabled to effect his liberation. He must have friends outside, who were devising some scheme to secure his enlargement; and therefore, it behoved them to use the most wary exertions to endeavour to discover them. He consequently made known to the magistrates in the neighbourhood his suspicions, and a strict search was made, to see if they could discover any of the gipsies, who were supposed to be connected with the prisoner, and to apprehend and examine all persons of a suspicious character, who were found lurking in the locality. From this, however, nothing of any importance resulted; no person at all resembling the gipsy tribe, had been seen in the neighbourhood—with the exception of Rupert Darwin—since the time the latter made the attack upon Wallingford Hall, and it was, therefore, considered by the magistrates, that Walter was entertaining apprehensions that were entirely groundless, and they relaxed in their exertions. But not so Walter; on the contrary, he had, unknown to his father, persons continually on the look out, near the prison and the environs, and the least cause for suspicion was immediately communicated to him. As for Rupert Darwin, he was confined in what was considered to be the strongest room in the gaol, and heavily fettered, so that any idea of escape seemed to be quite preposterous. He had undergone several examinations before the magistrates, and was fully committed to take his trial at the next assizes for having made attempts upon the lives of Mr. Wallingford, Walter, and Maria, and there did not seem to be the least doubt but that there was sufficient evidence to convict him, and that he would receive a sentence of perpetual banishment at least; consequently, there did not appear to be the least cause for the fears and apprehensions which Walter entertained, and which seemed to astonish the magistrates to a no very inconsiderable degree.

Rupert Darwin, in his dungeon, maintained the same indomitable spirit of indifference and bravado which he had done throughout; and when the gaolers and others who had the charge of him, talked of his trial, he laughed in utter derision, and told them that he should quit their company long before that could take place. This they only treated as the wild ravings of a desperado, who felt that his career was at an end, and was resolved to act to the last with that appearance of contempt which had marked his character throughout his career. A short time, however, will show how far they were right in their conjectures.

Another month passed away in this manner, and the fears of Walter had become somewhat abated, for there appeared nothing whatever to give him cause to imagine that there was the least reason for them. Rupert Darwin was most securely watched, but his manner had changed; he seemed to have abandoned all the sanguine hopes he had previously entertained, and to have made up his mind for the worst. In fact, his spirits seemed to have drooped amazingly, and when he did engage in conversation with any person who visited him in his cell, his language and whole demeanour would lead them to suppose that he had given way to despair, and had made up his mind to meet the fate which his numerous offences entitled him to. But they little imagined the deep-laid scheme the villain had concocted, and which was mentally ripening into perfection.

The iron-grated window of the room which Rupert Darwin was confined in, and which was placed very high in the wall, overlooked an open space of country, and the main road branched off from the right of the gaol. This was called the strong-room, and Rupert was placed there because, being considered a most desperate character, it was thought to be utterly impossible for him to escape therefrom. The result, however, showed how much they were mistaken.

A few days only before the trial of the prisoner was to have taken place, the gaoler, upon entering the room in which he had been confined, was completely thunderstruck to find it empty. Rupert Darwin had escaped. The bars were wrenched from the window, and his fetters were left behind, having evidently been filed off. Rupert had tied the blankets and rugs together, with which he had been supplied for his bed, and had let himself down from the window. On the table was left a note, in which the following words were inscribed with a black-lead pencil:—

"Rupert Darwin told ye he would escape your power, notwithstanding your vigilance and fancied security. He has kept his word: the gipsy was never yet known to break it. Let his enemies tremble: he lives for vengeance!"

To describe the consternation and surprise of every person upon this unexpected discovery would be impossible; and it was in vain that they endeavoured to conjecture by what means Rupert Darwin had been able to obtain the means to assist him to gain his liberation. Walter was immediately apprised of the circumstance, and his astonishment and chagrin when he heard of it may be readily imagined. His worst apprehensions were then confirmed, and the villain Rupert was again at large, and would, no doubt, with the least possible delay, set about putting his diabolical scheme of vengeance into execution. He dreaded to impart the intelligence to his father, for he knew how much it would excite his alarm, which had been completely subdued by the supposition of the gipsy chief's safe custody; but the truth reached Mr. Wallingford's ears as soon as his son's, and his agitation was excited to such a degree, that he was compelled to keep his chamber. Long sickness, and the heavy load of troubles he had had to contend with, had so weakened the nerves of Mr. Wallingford, that the least shock reduced him to the most pitiable state of illness; and this was an event which was more calculated than any to produce a melancholy effect. All the apprehensions of the unquenchable vengeance of Rupert Darwin which he had formerly entertained were again aroused in his bosom, and he became completely restless and miserable. He was deaf to all the expostulations and soothings of Walter and Maria, and seemed to have made up his mind that, with Rupert's escape, the fate of himself, if not more, was sealed.

Although Maria tried all that was in her power to appease the fears of her uncle, and to calm his feelings, she could not help largely participating in them, and was inclined to believe that there had been some treachery on the part of some of the persons connected with the prison, or else, she thought, it would have been impossible for Rupert to have effected his escape. It was, however, very evident that he must also have had some friends outside, and thus it was evident that some of his colleagues were yet living, and that they would yet have good reason to fear any outrage which they might have it in contemplation to commit. Although she endeavoured to vanquish the display of her fears as much as possible, she could not quite succeed; and Mr. Wallingford clearly observed that, while in the kindness of her heart she sought to tranquillize his feelings, her own needed as much consolation.

Walter made the strictest inquiry into this unfortunate affair, but for some time was unable to elicit anything which could throw the least light upon this mysterious circumstance. The gaoler underwent a strict examination, but it was very evident that he was totally innocent of being concerned in the escape of the prisoner, as was also every person who had access to him. It was, however, very clear that some person must have supplied him with a file, by which he had ridded himself of his fetters; but who that individual could be they were for some time quite at a loss to imagine.

At last, however, it was remembered that, only the day before the prisoner's escape, a Protestant clergyman had requested to be allowed to see him, and to pass a short time with him in prayer, which was assented to, and the supposed holy man was shown to the room in which Rupert was confined. He remained with him for some short time alone, for, being supposed to be a minister, no suspicion was attached to him. After weighing this circumstance maturely in their minds, they had no doubt that the supposed clergyman was in reality an accomplice of Rupert's, and that, in that interview, they had devised that plan of escape which had met with such success. The imaginary reverend gentleman had, doubtless, brought Rupert the file, and all things necessary for him to effect the design he had in view; and thus, while suspicion had been hushed, the plot was ripening which was to secure Rupert Darwin his restoration to liberty.

No sooner was the flight of the gipsy chief made known, than persons were sent in different directions all over the country, to endeavour to trace him; but not the least clue could be obtained, although it was generally supposed that

he was lurking somewhere in the neighbourhood; but he had such methods of disguising himself, that he might almost defy detection in those who were well acquainted with him. Mr. Wallingford offered a large reward for his apprehension, or any of the gipsies who might be seen in the neighbourhood, but it was all to no purpose: Rupert Darwin was too cunning and watchful to be easily trepanned.

Mr. Wallingford was now in constant fear, notwithstanding Walter had taken every possible precaution to prevent any surprise; but a circumstance was about to take place which was calculated to divert their attention from every other subject, and to fill their bosoms with the most unbounded joy.

Walter and Maria could not help participating in the apprehensions that tormented the mind of Mr. Wallingford at the escape of Rupert Darwin, although they endeavoured as much as possible to conceal it from him, and sought, by every means in their power, to appease the fears in which he so largely indulged, and led him to hope that the ruffian who had caused him so much uneasiness would be speedily re-apprehended, and brought to condign punishment.

Mr. Wallingford, however, seemed to place but little reliance on the surmises of his son, and, in fact, he had given himself up entirely to despair.

"It is useless," he observed to Walter, "to seek to flatter me with hope. It appears evidently that Fate is against me, and that I am a doomed man. I am not superstitious, but so many circumstances have recently occurred, such frequent coincidences, that render it impossible for me to banish from my mind a presentiment that I am fated to fall by the hands of an assassin, and that that assassin will be no other than the villain Rupert Darwin.

"Pardon me, sir," observed Walter, "but this is a weakness which really surprises me; any one would imagine, who heard you speak, that you consider the gipsy endowed with a charmed life, or that he possessed some superhuman power which would render all the attempts of those he has so deeply injured to bring him to punishment totally ineffectual."

"Why, really," returned Mr. Wallingford, "any person, however sceptical they might be, would almost be inclined to be of that opinion. Hitherto, has he not evaded all the attempts that have been made to bring him to the bar of justice? and even now, when we thought him so secure in our power, has he not, accordingly to his threats, escaped, with apparent facility? Walter, you may call me a coward, but that it is a weakness, I am ready to admit, and one which I find it utterly impossible, notwithstanding all the efforts I have made, to relinquish. Depend upon it, ere Rupert

Darwin finishes his mortal career, I am doomed to fall by his hands; and my conscience assures me that it would be no more than a just retribution for the offences of which I have been guilty. Look at the misery, the irremediable misery I have brought upon Ela and her child! Is not the latter, even now, suffering, or, perhaps, has fallen a victim to a fate, from which, had I become her protector, as I ought to have done, I might have saved her? And is not her unhappy mother doomed to the greatest distress through my perfidy and treachery, for I cannot call them by any milder terms. I shall never forget the words of the Gipsy Sybil, and I feel convinced that some time or other her predictions will be fulfilled; a part of them have already, to my sorrow, been realized; these were the words, and they are too indelibly stamped upon my memory ever to be effaced—

"A curse shall attend the deceiver's race,
His reward shall be misery and disgrace,
On his home there shall fall a deadly blight,
That shall turn his days into dreary night.
The heart that his treachery sought to break,
Shall live a fell revenge to seek;
Sorrow and pain shall triumphant lord
O'er the proud house of Wallingford!"

These were her prognostications, and my conscience tells me that I may not treat them lightly."

There was too much truth in the observations of his father, for Walter to offer any immediate argument to rebut them, and he remained silent for a few minutes; but the reader may easily imagine his agony at the mental suffering his father was enduring, and the self-abasement to which he, in acknowledging his guilt, thus submitted. He would willingly have endured any pain almost, however poignant, to have been able to efface the gloomy ideas that were bearing his spirit down, from the memory of his father; but that, he knew, would be impossible, and he was thus left with the most gloomy prospects in contemplation, and knew not in which way to act. To use every precaution that security could suggest, seemed to be perfectly useless with the gipsy chief; for had he not before taken every step which seemed at all necessary, to apprehend him, and afterwards to keep him in safe custody, and yet he had contrived, and that without much apparent difficulty to himself, to escape? It was very evident, in spite of all that he had said, and that old Zelta, and others had asserted, that he was not the only one of the tribe who survived; he must have some accomplices; and so cunningly did they devise all their schemes, that there was no such thing as guarding against them, and at the very time when persons might imagine themselves the most secure, they might be within the very jaws, in a manner of speaking, of the

enemies they so much dreaded. They were so clever in disguising themselves, that they might even be 'in the immediate neighbourhood, and mingling amongst the other inhabitants, without any person having the slightest suspicion of them; and Walter well knew from experience, that the offer of any reward would not induce any of them to turn traitors.

With such dangerous beings as these to encounter with, how then was a person to act? —what steps could they take to avoid the evil which they dreaded? Walter racked his brain in vain to think of any scheme; and his uneasiness increased every hour, notwithstanding he very prudently tried, as much as he possibly could, to conceal his real thoughts when in the presence of his father. To Maria, however, he breathed his ideas; and she could not but coincide with them—and became very unhappy in consequence; for should anything occur to her uncle, would it not completely blight those prospects of happiness which she and Walter had indulged in the hope of experiencing? Alas! it would, and would throw a gloom across their path, which time could never disperse. With a powerful and praiseworthy effort, which Walter never imagined she could have accomplished, she, however, sufficiently subdued her own anguish to endeavour to impart consolation, and to tranquillize the feelings of Wallingford, and adduced all the arguments her gentle nature could suggest in support of her observations—but like Walter, all her efforts failed; although her uncle gratefully acknowledged the good intentions with which they were made, and evinced by his behaviour towards her how much his love for her daily—nay, hourly—increased.

Hitherto, all attempts to discover the retreat of the gipsy, Rupert Darwin, or the existence of any other of the tribe, had utterly failed, although Walter had offered a large reward to any person who could furnish him with any information upon the subject; and something soon afterwards occurred, which served not a little to increase the alarm of every one, and which convinced Mr. Wallingford and the others that their conjectures were perfectly right, and that Rupert Darwin was concealed somewhere in the neighbourhood, and was only awaiting a fitting opportunity to put his diabolical and blood-thirsty designs into execution. About a week after the escape of the gipsy chief, Mr. Wallingford received a letter, of which the following is a purport:—

"Squire Wallingford,—you may fancy yourself in security, but you are mistaken. The train is even now laid, which shall 'destroy you and yours. Think not to escape, or that the schemes of Rupert Darwin will be again thwarted; for nothing can save you from his vengeance. Tremble, for Rupert Darwin still lives for vengeance on all his hated foes."

The terror of Mr. Wallingford was increased tenfold on the receipt of this, and Walter's emotion was scarcely less. However, how to seek to avoid the threatened danger, he was at a perfect loss to imagine, and yet that some steps should be taken for that purpose, he saw was absolutely necessary. He could only increase the number of the persons who were employed on the look out, around Wallingford Hall, and in the neighbourhood of Rosemary Dell, and he then applied to the proper authorities, who redoubled their exertions to discover the place in which the villain was secreted, and to get him once more into custody; but these efforts were attended with no better success than their former ones, and not the least clue, not even the shadow of an idea could be obtained, which was at all likely to lead to the detection of Rupert, who was, however, they were thoroughly convinced, lurking somewhere in the neighbourhood. So great were the fears of Wallingford, that, notwithstanding they had taken especial care that every part of the hall should be safely watched and guarded, he was continually imagining that some one had forced an entrance into the house, and were approaching his chamber for the purpose of putting the designs which he believed to be formed against his life, into execution. He became daily more wretched, was deaf to all expostulations; even the affectionate attentions and endearments of Maria now failed to soothe him; and, in fact, he became what might be termed a perfect misanthrope;—avoided society as much as possible, even that of his son and niece, and seemed to look upon every one with an eye of suspicion. Walter was very much grieved at this, and tried every means in his power to dissipate his sorrow, but he saw too much cause to fear himself, to be able to make use of any arguments at all calculated to accomplish, the end he wished.

"And yet it is strange," he observed, one day, to Maria; "it is very remarkable that this miscreant should seem to set justice and every one at defiance, and to carry on his villany with impunity. It seems that neither bolts or bars are strong enough to hold him. He laughs to scorn every attempt to punish him. He is, certainly, the most daring villain I ever heard of, and great as are the miseries we have already experienced from him, I fear that my father has too much cause to dread his further vengeance!"

"Heaven forbid that your fears should be realized, dear Walter," exclaimed Maria, while her bosom heaved with emotion;—"but surely there must be some means of thwarting his diabolical designs, and bringing him to that punishment he so richly merits? The Almighty will not suffer the guilty wretch to triumph in his iniquity!"

"I trust He will not," replied Walter; "but hitherto the wretch Rupert has been so successful, that it is enough to make us give way to despair. It seems that whatever precautions we may make use of, he is able to overcome them, and so artfully are his designs laid, that there is no means of unravelling them, or even to find the least clue to the place of his retreat, notwithstanding it is very certain that he is lurking somewhere in the neighbourhood."

"The more we reflect upon this circumstance, dear Walter," observed Maria, "the more surprising does it appear; but let us pray to heaven to avert those evils which we so seriously, and with too good reason apprehend;—in the meantime we cannot do no more than is already done, namely, to see that the hall is well guarded, and to keep persons constantly on the watch in the gardens and the immediate vicinity."

"True," said Walter, "we cannot do any more, as you say;—as for my poor father, there is no fear of his leaving the house, since he has taken to seclude himself almost entirely within his own chamber; but I feel for you my dearest Maria, who will thus be made a complete prisoner for an indefinite period."

"But shall I not be blest with your society, Walter?" said the beauteous girl, her eyes sparkling with affection;—"in your company how can any place appear a prison to me!"

Walter kissed her fervently, and they then sought the presence of Mr. Wallingford, who they found rather more composed than usual, although his countenance was overshadowed with a cloud of melancholy which nothing seemed capable of being able to remove.

"I have been thinking, Walter," he observed, "that after all, the villain, Rupert Darwin, and his base companions, may not be so close at hand as we apprehend;—and that the letter which he recently sent me, was done more to intimidate us than anything else; and to make us miserable, by keeping us in a continual state of dread. I will not give way to such groundless fears in future; the wretch is not invulnerable, and should he make any attempt, I think we have adopted such means to foil him as must prove successful."

Walter and Maria were both delighted to hear Mr. Wallingford talk in this manner, and they did not fail to use all their endeavours to strengthen his hopes, and that day passed off more calmly and pleasantly than any they had experienced for some time. They again talked of the union of Walter and Maria, and ventured to anticipate future happiness, in spite of the clouds that at present obscured their mental horizon.

In the course of the day, Maria, at the request of her uncle, sang a song, which the late Mrs.

Wallingford used to delight to hear. She had a beautiful and melodious voice, and the words of the song were of that description, that so admirably corresponded with the plantive air to which they were set, that they could not fail to make an instant and lasting impression upon the heart. Mr. Wallingford listened to her with a feeling of melancholy rapture, and tears filled his eyes, as they recalled to his memory the image of her who was now at rest in the silent tomb; and whose death his unfortunate indiscretions had been the means of hastening. Conscience, that severe monitor, filled his bosom with indescribable agony; he turned away his head, and unable longer to restrain his feelings, burst into tears, and sobbed aloud. Walter and Maria could both well understand the nature of his thoughts, and therefore did not attempt to interrupt him in the indulgence of his grief;—it passed over, and Mr. Wallingford became more calm than might have been expected. Maria changed the subject, and endeavoured to divert her uncle's thoughts from that which had recently engrossed them. In this, with the aid of Walter, she was partially successful; and they sat conversing upon different topics, until it was time to retire to rest. They then bade Mr. Wallingford good night, and Maria not feeling disposed to go to bed just yet, accompanied Walter into the parlour in order that she might get a book which she had left there in the afternoon.

"I am happy, indeed, to see the favourable change which has taken place in my father, Maria," said Walter as she was about to retire, "and if he goes on in this manner, I have great hopes that we shall ultimately succeed in conquering all his fears, and in restoring him to his former spirits."

"Oh, sincerely do I hope we may, dearest Walter," said Maria, in reply, "and, indeed, I must say that my uncle has formed precisely the same opinion as regards the gipsy, Rupert, as I have; but hark! what noise was that?"

"Noise, my love?" said Walter. "I did not hear any."

"I am certain I heard a cry," added Maria, listening, "it seemed to proceed from up stairs, and——ah! there it is again. It is the voice of my uncle."

Walter did that time plainly distinguish the voice of his father calling for help, and the next moment the room door was thrown hastily open, and Mr. Wallingford, pale and trembling, rushed into the apartment, and grasping the arm of his son, exclaimed in a voice of the utmost agitation—

"Quick—quick, or she will have escaped; pursue her, I say."

"My dear father, what do you mean?" inquired Walter, "what has alarmed you, and to whom do you allude?"

"The Gipsy Sybil!" cried Mr. Wallingford, still grasping the arm of his son, and directing his attention towards the door; "the gipsy hag, she came to me in my chamber, I saw her as plainly as——but she will escape; why do you not pursue her?"

"My dear father, surely you must have suffered your fears to overcome you," said Walter, whose astonishment was excessive; "no person could obtain admittance into the hall without our knowledge."

"I tell you," passionately answered Mr. Wallingford, "I tell you that I was not mistaken, and that the gipsy woman came to me in my chamber, as I stated before, and gave utterance to threats, curses, prognostications, which I shall not easily forget. The latter are pratically stamped upon my recollection, they were these:—

"There's a cloud o'er thy head which shall burst ere long,
   Retribution shall come for each earthly wrong;
   Thou may'st hie thee to some distant land,
   But tremble, for know that thy fate is at hand.
   No power shall save thee the deadly blow,
   Which shall lay the fiend lord of Wallingford low."

As Mr. Wallingford gave utterance to the last words, a rude laugh vibrated in their ears, and seemed to proceed from somebody outside.

"Ah! see, she is there," hastily uttered Mr. Wallingford, directing the attention of Walter and Maria towards the parlour window. The moon was shining brilliantly, and objects for some distance beyond could be seen as clearly as at noon-day. The astonished eyes of Walter and Maria immediately fell upon the tall figure of a woman of frightful aspect and wretched appearance, who was gazing into the room with a look of the most diabolical exultation, and shook her long, bony fingers in a menacing manner at Wallingford and the others. There was something so peculiarly awful about the woman's appearance that she did not seem like a being of this world; and Walter was so surprised and bewildered that he stood for a second or two, and was totally incapable of moving.

"There is some infernal spell in this," at length he exclaimed, as he rushed towards the door; "I am determined that the mystery shall be unravelled."

"Oh, for Heaven's sake stay!" exclaimed Maria, who was almost fainting with fear, "you know not the danger you are rushing upon."

But Walter had fled the room before she could finish her supplication, and the woman had also disappeared from the window in an instant. Several minutes elapsed, and Walter did not return; but all was perfectly quiet outside. Maria was in a terrible state of suspense and consternation, and she and her uncle stood gazing upon each other in stupified amazement, without being able to utter a syllable.

After the elapse of a quarter of an hour,

Walter came back, with astonishment and agitation depicted in his countenance.

"This is a mystery," he observed, "which to me is perfectly impenetrable; I had no sooner got into the garden than the woman

FARMER FALLOWFIELD AND KNOBBS HANGING TO A TREE.

had vanished, and I could discover no traces of her. I made known the circumstance to those on the watch, and they all declared most positively that they had not seen any one enter the grounds, neither had they beheld any one leave the place. A strict search was imme-diately made, but all to no purpose; the wo-man could nowhere be seen, neither had any of the gipsies been seen lurking in the neigh-bourhood, or else, of course, they would have been immediately apprehended."

"Wonderful!" exclaimed Mr. Wallingford

"and yet you must be convinced that I was not mistaken in what I previously asserted. The woman must have some place of concealment about the gardens. But what security have we against the vengeance of the wretches, when they can thus so easily gain access at their pleasure to the hall, and even to my private apartments? It is very evident that I am not safe for a moment."

"Quiet your fears, my dear father," urged Walter, "and alarming as it may appear at present, I have not the least doubt but that we shall ultimately be able to discover the retreat of our bitter enemies, and frustrate their designs at the very time when they may probably fancy they are the most certain of being accomplished. We will strictly examine every part of the gardens to-morrow. What surprises me more than all is, that although it appears they can easily gain access to the hall, and even get into your presence without its being known, that if their object is your life, they do not put it into execution. Unprepared as you were, could not this gipsy woman easily have committed the deed, instead of wasting her time, and running into danger, merely for the sake of holding out threats, and giving utterance to a parcel of prognostications? There is an inconsistency and ambiguity about the whole affair, which only bewilders and perplexes me more, the more I endeavour to fathom it."

"It is indeed very mysterious," remarked Mr. Wallingford, with a shudder, "and God only knows how it will end."

"It is most unaccountable how the woman could have gained admittance to the hall, and afterwards effected her escape, without being seen by those whom you have employed to keep watch," said Maria; "are you certain that there is no treachery among any of them?"

"Ah!" replied Walter, "that is an excellent thought; they shall undergo a strict examination to-morrow; some of them may have been playing us false; but they will have good reason to repent it if they have done so."

They sat for some time conversing upon this painful and alarming subject, and, at length, the feelings of Wallingford became rather more tranquillized than they were at first, although he was still in a state of the utmost agitation, and the predictions of the gipsy woman appeared continually to be ringing in his ears, and rendered him very miserable. Before he again ventured to retire to rest, he insisted upon the hall undergoing a strict search, to see whether any of their enemies were concealed in any part of the building: but although every nook and corner which was capable of holding a human being, underwent the most minute scrutiny, there was nothing whatever discovered to excite their suspicions, or to increase their fears. Wal-

ter's chamber was adjoining that in which his father reposed, so that he would be ready to fly to his assistance in a moment, if anything should happen, and he had a rope in his apartment which communicated with the alarm-bell, so that those who were upon the watch, and the inhabitants of the house could be aroused in a moment.

Walter slept none that night, for his mind was racked in vain endeavours to conjecture who the gipsy woman was, and by what means she had contrived to gain an entrance to the hall. Mr. Wallingford did not offer to retire to repose that night, and Walter could hear him traversing his chamber with disordered steps, and muttering incoherent sentences to himself. The night, however, passed away, without anything more occurring, and they were all very well pleased, when the morning's sun beamed in upon their pillows.

According to his promise, as soon as he had partaken of his morning's repast, attended by several men, he commenced a very minute search in the gardens of the hall, but made no discovery to warrant him in encouraging the opinion that the gipsies had some place of concealment therein. He next called together all the domestics, and those persons whom he had employed to watch about the grounds and the neighbourhood, and questioned them narrowly, to see whether he could perceive anything that would authorise the encouragement of the suggestion which Maria had given utterance to, of the probability of some of them acting with duplicity. All their answers were perfectly satisfactory, and left Walter no room to doubt their honesty and fidelity; everything, therefore, remained involved in the same impenetrable mystery as it had been before, and they were quite at a loss what future steps to pursue. As for attempting to guard against any attack that might be made, seemed perfectly useless, as it appeared, from the appearance of the gipsy woman, that they could gain access to the hall whenever they thought proper; and they had no alternative left, but to leave it to the will of Providence, unless, indeed, they thought proper to remove from Wallingford Hall, until such times as affairs took a change, or Rupert Darwin and his associates should, perchance, have fallen into the hands of justice. The latter plan, Mr. Wallingford was almost inclined to adopt, but then in what other house could he be more secure, in that part of the country, than Wallingford Hall? and as for travelling, neither his health nor inclination would permit him to do.

The rewards for the apprehension of Rupert Darwin and his companions were doubled; and, in consequence of the extreme vigilance of the officers, Walter did not yet despair of their being ultimately able to succeed in detecting, and taking the ruffians into custody; but several weeks passed away, and nothing occurred to effect any change; all remained quiet at the hall, and nothing had taken place in the neighbourhood to give any reason to suppose that the gipsies were near the spot, or that they were likely to make their appearance again in a hurry.

As week after week, and month after month rolled away, and still they heard nothing more of Rupert Darwin or the other gipsies, the confidence of Mr. Wallingford, Walter, and Maria, increased, and they began to think that there was no further cause for their apprehension. Still they used the same precautions they had hitherto done, imagining, and very prudently, that if their enemies should happen to be in the neighbourhood, and should find them relax in their endeavours, in that respect, they would seize upon the opportunity of putting their long-concerted plot into execution. Mr. Wallingford's spirits upon this subject, revived, and he even ventured to leave the hall, occasionally, and walk forth to Rosemary Del, in the company of his son and Maria; and never met with anything to excite his fears, or to give him the slightest cause to suppose that he had any reason to dread that Rupert Darwin or his companions were lurking near the spot.

But now a more mysterious and painful subject than all, absorbed all their thoughts, and engrossed their whole attention. Two months had elapsed, the summer had advanced, and yet, during that period they had not heard from Ela Beranzio, or Lord Helvendon. They had written several letters to them, urging an answer as speedily as possible, to satisfy their doubts as to whether they had heard anything of the unfortunate Fanny, but hitherto they had not received any. The last letter they had was from Lord Helvendon, and then he informed them that he was at Milan, in which place Ela was prosecuting her inquiries with the most indefatigable perseverance; but that they had not then been attended with any favourable result, although he still entertained strong hopes that something would transpire, ere long, to bring about the discovery they were so anxious to obtain, and to restore Fanny once more to their arms. This letter, it will be seen, was couched in the language of hope; but since that one they had not received any.

To what cause, therefore, could they attribute this most unaccountable silence? Surely, something must have happened—some accident must have occurred to them, or they would never have kept them so long in that state of agonizing suspense. They must have failed in their efforts to discover the place in which the villain, the Marchese Vivaldi, had concealed Fanny, and had probably all of them fallen

victims to some deep-laid scheme of cruelty, devised by that nobleman, to rid him of the only obstacles to the full gratification of all his diabolical wishes; and Vivaldi had been enabled by his rank and influence to silence the affair!—Maria shuddered with an innate feeling of the most indescribable horror, as these ideas occurred to her; and so overcome was she by the strength of them, that she never paused to question the probability of them; otherwise, she would have been convinced, after a moment's reasonable reflection, that there was nothing at all likely in such suppositions, and that such a catastrophe could not occur without its becoming well known, neither could the perpetrator of such enormous crimes, however great his power and rank, be suffered to escape with impunity.

Walter combated the fears of his cousin with all the strength of argument he could make use of; but, in fact, he was so greatly at a loss to form even the most remote conjecture of the cause of this long silence, to render the reasons he advanced, in opposition to the opinions of Maria, very forcible or eloquent. His agony was nothing short of that which she experienced, although he endeavoured as much as he possibly could to conceal it from her and her father, the latter suffering all the anguish that uncertainty, and the upbraidings of a guilty conscience could inflict upon him. Again, they despatched letters to Milan; and again were they fated to be disappointed; no answer was returned, and despair now actually took possession of their bosoms. It seemed as if it were to be their destiny to be constantly miserable, and when even the smallest gleam of comfort burst in upon them, it was quickly obscured by some cloud heavier than the one which darkened their peace before.

No one felt the uncertainty of the fate of Ela and Fanny more keenly than Maria, and hours and hours did she pass in reflecting upon it, and in trying to attribute their silence to their letters to some feasible cause; but in this she was unsuccessful; she knew too well the anxiety which Ela would feel, to make them acquainted with what had taken place, and whether there was any prospect of their succeeding in discovering the place where Fanny was confined, to suffer her to have remained so long silent, had not something particular occurred to prevent her having a chance of writing. Lord Helvendon, too must have met with some accident, and his, amiable mother also, or certainly one of them would not have neglected to write ere now, and to give them all the particulars that they were so anxious to know. It was a dreadful mystery, and the more Maria sought to unravel it, the further did she became entangled in the mazes of perplexity.

" Alas!" she exclaimed, " dear Fanny, and unfortunate Ela, are we never fated to behold each other again? Indeed, it seems as if fate had denied that we should remain in ignorance of what has become of you, and the end that you have met with. Fain would I make a sacrifice of almost every happiness I possess, could I be certain that you still live, and that you are in safety. But it is madness to think of such a thing: the villain who has been the cause of this misery, has been too successful in his iniquity, to give us any reasons to hope. Oh, may every curse attend him for the suffering his crimes have brought upon so many; and may the Almighty bring him to a sense of his guilt before he dies, so that he may suffer all the anguish that a heavily loaded conscience can inflict. But retribution must, it will overtake him for his enormities, and the voices of the victims of his cruelty will not call to heaven in vain.

Thus ruminated Maria, in whose bosom was created a tumult of anguish, which she felt convinced nothing could ever entirely destroy. It was a source of redoubled anguish to Walter, also, to behold the grief under which she suffered, and he was fearful that it would take such an affect upon her spirits as would, ultimately, impair her constitution. He therefore tried every argument he could think of to endeavour to allay the vehemence of her sorrow, and to lead her to hope that something would ere long take place to bring about the restoration of Ela and her daughter to them, and to consign the Marchese Vivaldi to that punishment which his offences merited. But how little did he actually believe what he gave utterance to;—what little reliance did he place in that hope which he tried to impart to the bosom of his cousin. It was very evident something very serious had happened, or they would have been certain to have heard from one of them; and yet it was very singular that the Marchese Vivaldi should be able so effectually to conceal himself, and that a nobleman so well known and in such a place as Milan should succeed in keeping his residence a secret. There evidently must be some deeper scheme of treachery than they had the means of ascertaining, and that he had many accomplices who were faithful to him, and who probably got up fictitious tales for the purpose of misleading those who were in search of him. Perhaps he was not in Milan, or any part of Italy at all, and that while Ela and Lord Helvendon were endeavouring to trace him there, he was exulting in the success of his nefarious schemes, with the unhappy victim of his oppression, in another part of the country. But then, again, Ela and Lord Helvendon could not be in Milan, otherwise they would have been

sure to have answered the repeated letters that were sent to them; and where could they be? For surely they would not go to any other place, without letting them know, and yet months had passed away without their receiving a single line from them. He would willingly have gone over to Italy himself, and endeavour to find out a confirmation, or contradiction of their worst surmises, but that he considered would be almost fruitless; and, besides, could he leave Maria and his father at home, threatened as they had been by the gipsy gang? No there was no other alternative than to leave it to chance, and there was a latent hope still sprang up in his bosom, that those friends for whose fate they were so anxious, were not lost to them for ever, and that the time [was not very far distant when they would meet again. Something seemed to whisper to him, also, that in spite of the hatred with which Ela seemed to view his father previous to her leaving England, should she escape from the fate which had so often threatened her, she would relent in the fierceness of her behaviour towards him, and that ultimately a reconciliation might be effected between them. Oh, how delightful it would be to see that much wished for circumstance take place. What many years of misery would it repay them for. What transport would it be to see the father clasp his daughter to his heart, and utter his benedictions upon her head, and how great would be his (Walter's) rapture, to be able, unrestrained, to press the beauteous Fanny in his arms, and to call her by the endearing name of sister. These ideas were productive of the most indescribable sensations in the breast of Walter, and could he have been assured that they would be realized, he would have been perfectly happy, and could have submitted to the present state of uncertainty and suspense they were enduring without a murmur. But a short time served to dissipate them, and to replace them with the most dismal feelings of despair. There was not a single circumstance, he reflected, to give him reason to hope for such a result; the fate of Ela and her daughter were yet unknown, and even now they might both have fallen victims to the villany of the Marchese Vivaldi, and were perhaps mouldering in the silent grave: or else why this mysterious silence? He could see no reason for it; wilfully he felt certain it was not done, for Ela could never rest so long without easing the mind of Maria, of whom she was as fond as if she had been her own daughter; and Lord Helvendon appeared to entertain too great a respect for the family to be so uncourteous as not to write, whether Ela had it in her power to do so or no. Thus was Walter at one moment raised to the very pinnacle of hope, and, then, the next he was plunged into the lowest abyss of despair.

The summer had now advanced, and the weather was remarkably fine, but still no tidings were heard of the others. In the midst of the trouble this mystery occasioned, it was a source of infinite satisfaction to them all, that they had received no further interruption from the gipsy, Rupert Darwin, or his associates, and the threats that the villain had made use of in the epistle that he had sent to Mr. Wallingford, and the prognostications of the wild gipsy prophetess, appeared to be unworthy of notice, and only made use of in order to intimidate them, and to hold them in continual dread of their vengeance. The inmates of the hall no longer confined themselves within doors, but wandered forth into Rosemary Dell, and among the adjacent scenery, the same as if nothing had ever occurred. The health of Mr. Wallingford had not suffered much improvement; for the uncertain fate of Ela and Fanny preyed so heavily upon his spirits, accusing himself as he did of being the cause of all their sufferings, and whatever might have befallen them, that he was very weak and careworn.

Although the vehemence of Maria's anxiety about those friends so dear to her was unabated, yet she struggled with her feelings sufficiently to enable her to bear the semblance of apparent composure, while in the presence of her uncle and Walter, notwithstanding she could not deceive the latter, who penetrated immediately to her thoughts, and most poignantly did he regret that he had not the means of offering her the least consolation. He tried to withdraw her thoughts from the melancholy subject by repeating the ardent and tender asseverations of his passion, and talking of the future bliss which would attend them in their union. But even this topic failed to have the desired effect; Maria could not but look forward to that event with the most gloomy presages, and which she found it impossible to banish from her mind. Where would be those who would have so largely participated in their happiness on that auspicious event, and who would have endeavoured to increase their felicity? Gloomy imagination answered, "Under the sod, most probably." Besides, there seemed to be a spell upon them, some dreadful fatality to attend them constantly, and ere that period arrived, something might occur to crush all these hopes, and to prevent their nuptials taking place. For permanent happiness they never seemed destined by Fate, and the prognostications that had at various times been uttered by the gipsies, were not only in part verified, but there seemed to be every likely probability of the other portion of them being fulfilled, and she firmly believed that their troubles would end only with their lives.

Thus, daily giving way to despair, Maria became careworn and ill, and Walter was very much alarmed that unless something should transpire to bring them some information of Ela and Fanny, that she would ultimately be confined to her bed, and probably sink a victim to the ravages of sorrow and despair. A circumstance was, however, about to take place, which would greatly change the aspect of affairs, and which came so unexpectedly upon them, that it was some time before they could recover from it. We will proceed at once to relate it.

Walter and Maria had been taking a walk to Rosemary Dell, and were returning home to the hall, when they saw a peasant coming towards them, and who, by the haste he made, seemed to have something of importance to communicate. He held a letter in his hand, and when he observed Walter and his cousin he bowed, and made a sign, intimating that he had something to say to them.

"What can be the matter, now?" said Walter, as he quickened his pace to come up to the man; "no new calamity, I hope."

Maria trembled with apprehension; but before she had time to make any reply, the man had come up to them.

"Sarvant, Measter Walter," said he, bowing very low; "I thought, mayhap, I should be meeting you as I came back; I have been to the hall, and have got a letter for you, from ——, but dang it, I wur going to let the cat out of the bag. I mustn't say from whom it is."

"Must not say from whom you have brought it?" exclaimed Walter, with a look of astonishment; "what do you mean?"

"What I have said, sir," answered the man; "there is the note, and I wish you good day, Mr. Wallingford."

"Stop! stop!" cried Walter; but the man, who had taken to his heels, after slipping the letter into Walter's hand, was soon out of sight and hearing.

Walter turned the letter over in his hand, and looked at the superscription; he had some recollection of the hand-writing, although it was evidently disguised, but he was unable to bring to his memory when and where he had seen similar characters before. Maria was all impatience and anxiety to know the nature of the contents, for the singular behaviour of the man who had brought it, and the mystery he maintained as to whom he had brought it from, excited her curiosity. Walter was not long, however, in gratifying it. He hastily broke the seal, and read the contents aloud, in the following words :—

"Mr. Walter Wallingford, and Maria Herbert, are earnestly requested to hasten, with the least possible delay, to the Olive Lodge, where they will meet with a most agreeable surprise. They need not fear that any treachery is comtemplated; they will find nothing but friends there. Secrecy and precaution are necessary."

"Well, this certainly is most mysterious," ejaculated Walter, when he had perused the note. "I scarcely know what to think of it. How would you advise, Maria?"

"I am quite at a loss to advise you at all," said his cousin in reply; "the writer of the epistle has certainly chosen a most ambiguous and suspicious plan to forward his invitation. Should it be a scheme of our old enemies, the gipsies, in order to entrap us——"

"Oh, no," returned Walter, "I do not think that, for the Olive Lodge belongs to Sir William Manton, and it is not at all likely that the gipsies would choose a place like that to make their assignation, when it is inhabited by part of Sir William's establishment. But I cannot conceive what necessity there could be for so much secrecy, and why the writer should hesitate to affix his name, or rather her name, for it is evidently a female hand-writing."

"It is curious," observed Maria, "but I should like to know what this unexpected surprise alluded to in the note is."

"Something whispers to me," said Walter, "that this adventure will be productive of pleasure to us both, and I am, therefore, resolved, at all hazards, to risk going."

"If that is your determination, dear Walter," returned Maria, "I will be your companion, and leave the result to Fate. After all, I do not think we shall have much cause to regret having ventured to comply with the request made by the unknown writer of the note."

"I am glad you are of my opinion, my love," said Walter, "so do not let us delay."

With these words, Walter took the arm of his fair cousin, and returned back across the Dell, in the direction of the Olive Lodge.

To the Olive Lodge it was no great distance, and the curiosity of Walter and his cousin being very much excited by the singularity of the adventure, they were not long in making their way to it. As they proceeded, all idea of any treachery being meant them, was entirely dissipated from the mind of Maria, and an indefinite feeling occupied her mind in its place; a presentiment of some approaching joy occupied its place, which she was at a loss to account for. When they arrived within sight of the Olive Lodge, Maria became so agitated that she was compelled to pause for a few seconds.

"What can be the meaning of this, dear Walter," she observed, "I cannot imagine; but I feel confident that some particular and unexpected circumstance is about to happen to us, which will not only create our most infinite surprise, but also pleasure."

"And so I think likewise, my love," said Walter, joy and hope animating his features. "I am positive, from the tenor of the note, and also the characters in which it is written, that the writer of it is not unknown to us."

"And yet, it is strange," observed Maria, "that, whoever they may be, they should make such a mystery of their business with us, and that they did not come to the hall, instead of making an appointment to meet us at the Olive Lodge. I am quite at a loss to imagine who they can be, and what can be their motives for such mysterious conduct."

"Oh, it is only some whim or the other, done with no other object than to cause us an agreeable surprise, as the note states," replied Walter. "Depend upon it, we shall find, when we get there, some of our old friends."

By this time they had arrived at the Lodge, and, having pulled the bell, the gate was soon opened by old Martin, the grey-headed porter, who had at one time lived in the family of Mr. Wallingford, and took much interest in the affairs of that family. When he beheld Walter and Miss Herbert, his features were irradiated with an expression of pleasure.

"Ah! Mr. Walter Wallingford," said he, "I am very glad to see you, and also you, Miss; —there is such a surprise for you;—oh, dear, how rejoiced you will both be, and glad enough I am of it, for, God knows you have suffered enough from one annoyance and the other, first by those confounded gipsies, and——"

Walter interrupted the old man's prolix harangue, by gently desiring him, with a smile, to acquaint the persons who had sent for them, that they had arrived and awaited their pleasure.

Old Martin hurried away with much readiness, and presently returned to the parlour into which he had ushered Walter and his cousin, and desired them to follow him. They did as he had requested, and, after ascending one flight of stairs, Martin tapped at a door, which was thrown open in an instant, and the feelings of the lovers may be conceived, but cannot be described, when Ela and Fanny rushed forward eagerly to meet them. Maria was so overcome with the tumult of delirious joy which rushed to her heart as she embraced that loved girl, whom she had never expected to see again in this world, that for a short time she was deprived of the use of speech, and nearly fainted; while poor Fanny, who was in the same situation, was relieved by a passionate flood of tears, which flowed fast, and joined those of Maria, who pressed her more vehemently than before to her bosom, and could scarcely believe that it was reality, but that she was deluded by some blissful dream.

In the meantime, Ela and Walter were scarcely in any better condition than the other two, and stood gazing at each other 'or a second or two in a state of stupified amazement, unable to articulate a syllable. At length, however, Ela embraced the young man with the same affectionate ardour as if he had been her own son, and then her feelings of joy found vent in a copious torrent of tears.

"Merciful God!" at length ejaculated Maria, after a pause, gently withdrawing herself from the arms of Fanny, and gazing intently upon her lovely features, "is it possible that we meet again, or is it only some wild chimera? Do I, can I once more behold her who my fears had consigned to the cold and silent grave?—Speak to me, dearest Fanny, and convince me that my happiness is not illusive!"

"It is not, it is not, my own dear Maria, my sister, for such must I for ever call you, as such love you," replied Fanny. "It is, indeed, Fanny, who, after so many months of suffering, has providentially been rescued from the power of that villain who would have destroyed her virtue and happiness for ever. Fanny is restored to her friends, and from them she trusts to the Almighty that she may never again be separated!"

"Heaven be praised!" ejaculated Maria, raising her eyes fervently, as she again clasped the form of Fanny to her heart; "this is, indeed, a surprise, a pleasure that we never expected;—it seems scarcely possible!"

Maria now turned away from Fanny, and then flew to the arms of Ela, who embraced her with the most indescribable transport, and her tears flowed so fast, that for a few seconds her utterance was choked, and she could only continue to hug Maria more closely to her bosom.

"The joy of this moment," said Ela, at last, "more than compensates for all the sufferings we have endured for so many years; let us hope that our happiness may never again be interrupted; at any rate, I firmly believe that we have nothing to apprehend from our old enemies, the gipsies, or the Marchese Vivaldi."

Walter and Maria exchanged looks of pain, as the idea of how futile were these hopes passed rapidly through their minds, but they said nothing at the time, and only reiterated the wishes of Ela, and again gave free vent to the feelings of delight and ecstasy that filled their bosoms.

"But, my dearest friends," observed Ela, as a ray of pleasure illumined her features, "I have not introduced Fanny to you in her real character;—in her you now behold Lady Helvendon."

Deep blushes overspread the cheeks of Fanny at this announcement, and the surprise of Walter and Maria was so great, that it deprived them of the power of giving expression to their congratulations upon so cheerful a subject.

"And now,' added Ela, stepping towards the foldings doors, "I must introduce you to two others, for whom I bespeak your friendship, and whom, I know, will soon be found worthy of your esteem and regard."

As she spoke, she threw open the doors, and a tall, elegantly dressed, handsome young man, and a middle-aged lady, of noble and affable appearance, advanced towards them, whom we need not say was Lord Helvendon and his mother. The greeting was one of the most fervent description, and the manners and appearance of Lord Helvendon and his mother were so prepossessing and amiable, that they immediately took possession of their esteem. We should fail, were we to attempt to describe the emotions of delight evinced by all parties on this blissful and unexpected meeting, and Walter and Maria gazed with feelings of pleasure and admiration upon the appearance of Fanny, upon whose countenance no traces were left of the sufferings she had undergone since they had before met; but her beauty seemed to be improved, and the bloom of health glowed upon her cheeks, and sparkled in her eyes, that shone forth with more than redoubled lustre. Never could beings have been better formed to come together than Lord Frederick and Fanny; worthy alike of one another, both from their personal and intrinsic merits, and it required no penetration to observe that they loved each other with all that passionate fondness, which two young and virtuous hearts are capable of experiencing.

And with what delight did Lady Helvendon, (for so we must in future call Fanny) behold Walter, that brother for whom she felt all the affection that the most fervent heart can feel; and when she saw the ardour and sincerity with which he returned her sentiments, she felt the most indescribable delight, and could have remained enfolded in his arms for ever. Never had she imagined she should behold Walter or any of her friends again, and she could not but feel the most unbounded gratitude to Omnipotence for the miraculous manner in which she had been preserved from the many dangers in which she had been involved, and restored, uninjured, to liberty and her friends. There was another being on whom the thoughts of the poor girl were fixed, but she trembled to repeat his name, and hesitated to mention it in the presence of her mother. Need we say that being was Mr. Wallingford, to whom her heart clung with the most unbounded affection, notwithstanding the manner in which he had behaved to her. Could she have been permitted to embrace him—to call him father, and to hear the blest title of daughter bestowed upon her by him, how happy would she have been! what care would then have tormented her mind?—She would then have but one wish left ungratified, and that was a reconciliation between her mother and Mr. Wallingford: that effected, her happiness would be complete. But such a hope she feared, was not fated to be realized, although there were times when she could not help encouraging an idea that such a presentiment —that such a joyful consummation would, some-time or the other, take place. Walter could read the thoughts that were passing in her mind, and earnestly did he sympathise in her feelings, and mentally did he pray that her wishes might some-time, and that ere long, be gratified.

"But why have you remained so long quiet, and returned no answers to the numerous letters we have sent to you?" asked Walter of Ela —"why did you not appease that dreadful state of suspense and anxiety in which we were all placed, by the uncertainty of your fate?"

"I will explain the circumstances that rendered it necessary for us to act in the manner we have done, in the narrative which it is my intention anon to give you," replied Ela; "let it suffice for the present, that the Marchese Vivaldi, who has been so determined a persecutor to Fanny, is no more; and that we have every prospect of our peace not again being interrupted, for from what we have heard, we have every reason to suppose that Rupert Darwin and his associates are exterminated."

"I am sorry to disappoint your hopes," said Walter; "but we have too good reason to believe that the villain and several of his companions are still living; and it is not long since that he was in custody in the gaol here, after having attempted to murder Maria, and her attendant, Clara. My father has also, but a few months since, received a threatening letter from Rupert, and been visited by one of the gipsy tribe—a female—who gave utterance to the most awful predictions, and which, for some time, made a deep impression upon him. However, it is a long time now since we have heard anything of them, and something may have happened to render their guilty schemes, for the future, unsuccessful."

The countenance of Ela and the others underwent a great change when Walter gave them this information, and it appeared to shock Fanny materially; Ela, however, soon recovered her usual self-possession, and then ob-served—

"I am sorry to hear this; for while there is a probability of the wretch being still alive, there is everything to dread. I am confident that nothing will ever be able to quench the fierce spirit of revenge that inhabits his bosom for me and mine; and however groundless may appear my apprehensions, and in spite of the improbability, seemingly, of his being enabled to elude the vigilance set on foot to detect him, the many artifices the gipsy tribe can make use of to accomplish their ends, and

the skill and ingenuity with which they are invariably managed, render them generally successful. I was not altogether satisfied that our enemies were no more, and it was that which partly induced me to preserve so much secrecy on our return to England, and to send for you and Miss Herbert in the manner I did, so that not the least suspicion might be con-veyed to those we have so much reason to dread. Sir William, who is a friend of Lord Helvendon's, was the first person we could think of resorting to on our arrival, and I do not think we could have chosen a better place for the meeting than this lodge. We have not yet made up our minds whether we will continue in this neighbourhood, where we could purchase estates, or go to London: but in either place it makes very little difference; for should our enemies be still alive, they are equally to be dreaded in the crowded and busy neighbourhood of the me-tropolis, as in this quiet and secluded part."

"But where will you remain for the present, my dear madam?" inquired Walter; "there is not room enough to accommodate you in this lodge."

"True," answered Ela, reflectingly; "and, indeed, we have not yet made up our minds, although, by-the-by, we have no time to lose."

"Oh, for my part," said Fanny, "I cannot like any place which will again separate me from my dear Maria, and the rest of my friends. I shall not be happy without we fix our residence somewhere in this quarter, unless Walter, and Maria, and——" my father she would have said, but she suddenly checked herself, "unless they remove from home, then wherever they go, there also should I like to follow."

Maria reflected for a few moments, when she suddenly remembered the house which Doctor Hartley had bequeathed to her, and imme-diately made an offer of it, and proposed their going their, until Lord Frederick had completed his arrangements, and settled his affairs, which the long residence of himself and his amiable mother from England, had put somewhat out of order. This proposition was, of course, gladly acceded to, and the mind of Fanny was set at rest. The house was a very commodious one, built in the Elizabethan style, and was ca-pable of affording every accommodation to a large family. It had been in the possession of the ancestors of the worthy doctor for several generations, and although it had so long stood the effects of time, it was quite unimpaired, and seemed likely to remain so for many years to come.

The mutual congratulations that now passed between them were unbounded, and it would be impossible for us to describe as we would wish, the scene which took place. So sudden

—so completely unexpected was the whole affair, that it seemed quite impossible to be true, and they were unable to give due expression to the sentiments that filled their bosoms. One circumstance particularly pleased Walter and Maria, which was, that although

Ela made no inquiries after Mr. Wallingford, she seemed to listen with interest whenever his name was mentioned, and to have banished from her mind all those violent feelings of hatred and malevolence that had formerly inhabited it towards him. When the change

ELA, DISGUISED, TELLING THE SERVANTS THEIR FORTUNES.

in his behaviour was mentioned, and the kindness and affection with which he now treated Maria, and the assent he had given to the nuptials of her and his son, an expression of pleasure passed over her features, and her heart was evidently softened towards him.

We need not say with what delight Walter and Maria observed this, and they did not despair but that in time all the happy results that they wished would take place.

After some time passed in the most cheerful conversation, the carriages were ordered, and they immediately took their departure to the Old House (for such was the name that the late Doctor Hartley's residence went by), and thither Walter and Maria accompanied them.

Walter and his cousin, as may be imagined, were extremely loth to part from Ela, Fanny, and the others, that night; but at last, fearful that Mr. Wallingford would feel very much alarmed at their prolonged absence from the hall, and anxious to make him acquainted with what had happened, they bade them an affectionate good night, promising to call again at an early hour the following morning, to learn the particulars of what had occurred to Ela and her daughter, since they had last heard from them.

As Walter and Maria proceeded towards Wallingford Hall, they gave free indulgence to the expression of their joy and astonishment at the safe return of Ela and Fanny; and endeavoured, but in vain, to conjecture by what singular and providential means these events had been brought about, and they thought that they could never feel sufficiently grateful to Providence for having interposed to rescue Fanny from the danger by which she had been threatened, and for having united her to a man who would have it in his power to protect her, and who, by his innumerable excellent qualities, was so well worthy of her. Her deliverance, after so many months being torn from her friends, and when there seemed not to be the slightest hope of her ever being again restored to them, seemed to be miraculous, and they could not form any idea by what means it had been effected. What a terrible weight had been taken off their hearts by this circumstance, and their bosoms, which but a few hours before had been the abodes of despair, were now filled with the greatest happiness.

"I told you, dearest Maria," observed Walter, as they proceeded towards home, "I told you that I had a presentiment there was some sudden and joyful surprise in store for us, and you see how happily my predictions have been verified; but never did I imagine that it would be the restoration of that dear girl, over whose uncertain fate we have been so long mourning. We can never sufficiently return our thanks for an event which we did not believe would ever have happened."

"I cannot give utterance to the joy which inhabits my bosom when I think of it," returned Maria, "and then how well and beautiful the poor dear girl looks, and what amiable beings are Lord Frederick and his mother; they must inspire every one with esteem the moment they behold them."

"You say right, dear Maria," replied Walter, "and I am delighted to think that Fanny has at length obtained the hand of a nobleman who seems in every way qualified to

contribute to her happiness. My sister is worthy of possessing the most virtuous and affectionate heart, and I am convinced, that in becoming Lady Helvendon, she has in her husband found a treasure beyond all price."

Maria could not but partake of the wishes and the ideas of Walter in this respect, and she expressed herself accordingly.

"How surprised and delighted my uncle will be," she remarked, "when we inform him of what has occurred. The uncertainty of the fate of Fanny and Ela, I know most severely preyed upon his spirits, and he seemed to reproach himself with being, in a great measure, the cause of the many troubles by which they have been beset. Their return to England will be a great relief to his mind."

"It will, indeed," said Walter, "and there is only one thing wanting to render us all quite happy."

"What is that?" asked Maria.

"A reconciliation between my father and Ela; that brought about, we may enjoy the happiness which has thus so suddenly and unexpectedly befallen us, without any alloy."

"Ah! Walter," observed Maria, "that would, indeed, be a gratification to us all; such a consummation is what I have long thought upon, and wished might take place. Neither do I see that we have any right to consider it entirely hopeless; time has evidently softened, if it has not entirely destroyed the violent passions of Ela, and especially now she finds that Mr. Wallingford repents of his former errors, and has altered so materially in his disposition and manners, she will most likely be easily prevailed upon no longer to cherish those sentiments of revenge that formerly occupied her breast, and which have been productive of so many evil consequences, both to my uncle and those connected with him. I sincerely hope that such an event may take place, and it shall not be for want of exertion on my part, if it does not occur."

"I thank you fervently for this, my dear Maria," said Walter, "and will assist you all that is in my power in so good a cause."

"In which something tells me that we shall succeed," rejoined Maria. "But there is still another thing that we have cause to regret, and which must give all those who are interested in it, considerable uneasiness, and that is the uncertainty of the fate of Rupert Darwin and his associates, and whether they are yet living to put the threats they have made use of into execution."

"To be sure," replied Walter, "that is a subject of some uncertainty, and there cannot be any doubt, if Rupert Darwin be still alive, he will follow up his implacable spirit of vengeance with unabated determination, more especially against Ela and her daughter; but I trust that something will occur to frustrate any designs they may have in contemplation, and to get rid of the parties who have been the cause of so much trouble."

They had now arrived at Wallingford Hall, and found Mr. Wallingford in a state of considerable alarm at the length of their absence from home.

" I was informed," said he, " that there had been a man here inquiring for you, and saying that he had a letter which he could not deliver to any other person than yourself; and fearful that he might have overtaken you (as he was informed the way you had taken), and that some treachery was intended you and Maria, I have not long since despatched several persons in different directions in quest of you. But what's the matter, Walter, you look confused—something must have happened ?"

" Something, my dear father, has, indeed, taken place, which will, doubtless, create no little astonishment in your mind," answered his son; " you must prepare yourself for a surprise, but, I trust, it will be an agreeable one."

" What do you mean, Walter?" inquired Mr. Wallingford, eagerly.

Walter, in as brief a manner as possible, told him what had taken place; and when he had finished, he clasped his hands vehemently together, and raising his eyes towards heaven, exclaimed, in tones that sufficiently bespoke his sincerity—

" God be thanked; it has taken a weight off my heart, which was almost too much to bear, and which must have shortly brought me to the tomb! But where are they? Let me hasten to them, that I may—— Fool!" he added, suddenly recollecting himself, " how madly I talk;—I must not go to welcome them ; they would receive me only with reproaches, and Ela would, probably, repeat the maledictions she has so often showered down upon my head!"

" Oh, no, my dear sir," interposed Walter, when he heard him hit upon the very subject that was then occupying his thoughts; " indeed I think you judge too severely of Ela and Fanny ; the latter, I am certain, loves you with an affection as sincere as it is ardent ; and the former, violent and guilty as her former conduct may, and, doubtless, has been, is a far different woman now, and there would not, in my opinion, be any great difficulty in bringing about a reconciliation between you."

Mr. Wallingford started, and gazed at his son for a short time, with a stupified look of incredulity.

" Reconciliation !" he repeated, and he shook his head despairingly, " reconciliation between me and Ela ?—Oh, no, no, that can never be ;—I know that she could never forgive me, and that my treatment of her, but of which I now sincerely repent, has engendered in her bosom that feeling of hatred towards

me which nothing can ever destroy, and that——"

" Nay, my dear father," interrupted his son, " you must not give way to this idea ; Ela is strangely altered since last you saw her, and I firmly believe that such a happy result is more than probable."

" Heaven send that your surmises may be verified, Walter," said Mr. Wallingford, energetically, as a gleam of hope passed over his countenance ; " there is scarcely any sacrifice that I would consider too great to receive the pardon of Ela, and to be able to press poor Fanny to my heart and call her daughter. All my former feelings of accursed pride are now stifled in my bosom, and could you but read my heart, Walter, you would see how anxious I am to make all the reparation in my power for the evils of which my folly and indiscretion have been the cause."

" I can—I do read your heart, my dearest father," ejaculated Walter, joyfully, " and no one can rejoice more than I do at the wishes you express, and of the sincerity of which I have such unquestionable reasons to believe. Ela will yield, I know she will, and we shall yet be all united together in one family."

" But how has this event been brought about ?" demanded Mr. Wallingford ; " in what manner did Ela discover and rescue her daughter from the power of the Marchese Vivaldi, and——"

" I know not," replied Walter, " at present ; but, to-morrow, Ela has promised to furnish me with every particular, and I will afterwards endeavour to prevail upon Ela, accompanied by her daughter, to pay a visit to you here, where everything may be arranged as we can most heartily desire."

Mr. Wallingford expressed by his looks his gratitude for this, and Walter soon afterwards took his leave of him for the night. But there was no sleep that night for Mr. Wallingford ; no, his mind was to busily occupied with the thoughts that crowded it, to suffer him to yield to the influence of the drowsy god, and the more he ruminated upon the joyful and unexpected circumstances, the more bewildered was he to understand what had occurred to save poor Fanny from that fate to which they all imagined she had fallen a victim. But that she was saved, and restored to the arms of her mother, no one could more sincerely rejoice than he did; and his mind, which had before been continually harassed with afflicting thought, now felt as if it were lightened of nearly all its woe ; and the words which Walter had given utterance to, respecting a reconciliation with Ela, had created in his bosom a hope that, ere long, even that happy result would be accomplished. Towards Fanny, who had been so long deserted, and left to suffer every privation, at the same time that she ought to have experienced every happiness and luxury, his heart warmed with the most fervent passion, and he felt that his happiness would be complete, if he could be permitted, without restraint, to show her all those marks of affection which he had neglected for so many years. Besides, Fanny was no longer the little despised, wandering, mendicant gipsy, but Lady Helvendon, the wife of one of the richest noblemen in the country; and although Wallingford endeavoured to persuade himself that that circumstance had no influence over his mind, it cannot be denied that he reflected upon it with a strong feeling of that pride which was so firmly engrafted in his nature that nothing could eradicate it. The influence of Lord Helvendon might promote the interest of Walter, and this thought again aroused his ambitious views as regarded the senatorial prospects of his son, but he quickly endeavoured to crush them, fearful of the danger they might again lead him into. For some time he was so surprised at the return of Ela and Fanny, or rather Lady Helvendon, that he could scarcely bring his mind to believe it was true; and such was his anxiety to behold them, that he was almost tempted to brave the displeasure of Ela, and insist upon accompanying Walter and Maria to the Old House in the morning, and to force himself into the presence of Ela; but at length he became somewhat composed, and determined to await the issue of Walter's interview with her, well knowing the influence which he and Maria possessed over her.

"Oh," he soliloquised, "could I but be assured of her forgiveness, and be permitted to acknowledge her child as mine, and to receive her fond endearments, methinks I could pass the residue of my days in calm tranquillity, and should be able to forget the many troubles I have suffered for years back. Could I but see Ela once more, the gentle, kind, contented being which she was when I first became acquainted with her, I should be amply repaid for any future sacrifice I might have to make."

The night passed away, as we have before observed, without Mr. Wallingford being enabled to gain any sleep, and as soon as they had partaken of their morning's repast, during which time Mr. Wallingford had talked in the most earnest manner upon Ela and Fanny, and urging his son to be certain not to neglect to endeavour to further the object he had in contemplation, with all the energy he was capable of, which, of course, Walter promised to do, the latter and Maria arose to take their departure for the Old House, Maria, with one of her sweetest smiles, observing—

"Do not despond, my dear sir, I beg of you; something tells me that there is yet much happiness in store for you, and that all you now wish will be quickly accomplished; at any rate if my humble exertions, added to those of my cousin, can bring about so desirable a result, depend upon it we will readily make use of them."

The tears came to the eyes of Mr. Wallingford as Maria spoke. He took her hand, and pressed it fervently between his. His looks expressed more than language could possibly have done, he turned away to conceal his emotion; and Maria left the hall.

"Alas!" exclaimed Mr. Wallingford, "fool, blind, that I was, not to be able to appreciate the many virtues of that amiable girl before; what many pangs could I have saved both her and myself. But it has been my accursed fate to treat with scorn and disrespect those who were my most ardent, my most sincere friends."

Again he ran over in his mind the remarkable events of the last few months, and when he ruminated upon the marvellous restoration to liberty of Fanny, after she had been so long incarcerated, and when her fate seemed almost certain, he could scarcely believe it true; in fact, it all partook more of the character of those improbable events that are often introduced into the pages of a romance, than what had actually taken place, and although it was not at all likely that Walter or Maria would attempt to deceive him, particularly on that point, he would not be perfectly satisfied until he had himself once more beheld them. There was a mystery, notwithstanding, about the whole affair, which he could not solve. Why had Ela and Lord Helvendon maintained such a long silence, when they must have been aware of the intense anxiety and suspense they must have felt to learn the fate of Fanny and in fact, even the most trifling circumstances connected with the affair; and in spite of the numerous letters that they had dispatched to them, soliciting all the information they had it in their power to give? It seemed as if they had, at last, totally become indifferent to the feelings of Walter and Maria, (himself, he did not feel any surprise about,) and were so completely absorbed in their own pursuits, as to forget there were such beings in existence. They might say it was done with an intention of surprising them; but surely there could be no excuse for conduct which they must be aware would be productive of much pain. But then he again thought that, in all probability, they had acted only from motives of prudence, and were fearful that by some accident or the other, their letters might fall into the hands of their enemies, if they should any of them be living, and be the means of running them into danger. Altogether, he was at a loss to comprehend rightly what had given rise to the conduct which Ela and the others had pursued, and anxiously awaited the explanation which Ela had promised his son and Maria to give of the whole affair.

To say that he felt the most unspeakable delight at the return of Ela and Fanny to England, and the union of the latter, would be describing his sentiments in language by far too feeble; of the family, and the character of Lord Frederick Helvendon, Mr. Wallingford had ever heard much in praise, before the events had transpired that brought him acquainted with Ela and her daughter, and he was prepared to meet him with all that warmth of friendship which his numerous intrinsic merits deserved. He pictured to himself the happiness, the domestic bliss, which, in all probability, was in store for Fanny: beheld her with a family of smiling children around her, and Ela watching, with all that intense feeling of delight, which may be imagined, but only those who have experienced it can form an adequate idea of;—the innocent gambolings of the offspring of that daughter, who had shared with her so many vicissitudes, privations, degradations, and narrow escapes from destruction, and who, at length, having triumphed over them all, presented a bright example of what determined integrity, and persevering virtue can ultimately overcome. Then, suddenly, while these reflections passed in his mind, they would all at once become overclouded, as an idea occurred to him that probably those bitter and malevolent enemies still lived, from whom they had already suffered so much, and that they only awaited an opportunity to blight that happiness which they fondly hoped was permanent. The same dismal and torturing misgivings darted upon his mind that had formerly harassed him, and in spite of his efforts to the contrary, he could not help feeling a melancholy foreboding that Ela or himself, or, at any rate, one of them, if not more, was fated to fall by the hand of the wretch, Rupert Darwin;—who, probably, was only now watching an opportunity of making his diabolical schemes certain, and would make his appearance when he was least expected, and at a time when they were unable to resist him.

These gloomy thoughts dashed the cup of happiness away from the lips of Mr. Wallingford soon after it was raised to them, and unable to remain alone in the hall, he quitted it, and almost unconscious of whither he was going, bent his footsteps in the direction of the Old House, where Walter and Maria had long since before arrived.

Ela and Fanny greeted the cousins with the most rapturous affection, and they could not but dwell with the greatest delight upon the countenance of Fanny, which, after a night's rest, appeared more beautiful than it had the day before. Indeed, the great change which had taken place in the looks of Fanny, was most extraordinary, and could only be equalled by the alteration in her situation and prospects in the world. She was no longer the timid, blushing, uninformed girl she had formerly been, but instead of that she must have immediately excited admiration in every breast, for a more beautiful, graceful, self-possessed, and intelligent woman, could not well be imagined; but the heart of Fanny had undergone no change with her appearance; no, it throbbed with the same ardent affection towards those beings from whom she had ever experienced such unbounded kindness, and must continue to do so until its pulsations should have ceased for ever.

Lord Helvendon, her husband, seemed to adore her, and his happiness only dwelt on her smiles. He was a man that needed but to be known, to command the utmost esteem and friendship, for his urbanity and general affability of disposition could only be equalled by that of his amiable mother; between him and Walter, a friendship sprang up in the course of a few hours which nothing but death could destroy, and they were as intimate as though they had been all their lives accustomed to each others company.

Ela greeted Walter and his cousin with much warmth of feeling.'

"This is a happiness that I never expected would occur to me again, but a few weeks since," she ejaculated, "here we are all assembled, uninjured, after being exposed to so many dangers; and there is not one, who——"

"Oh, yes," exclaimed Fanny, hastily, and forgetting in the power of her emotions, the precaution she had ever used upon that painful subject, "there is one whose presence is wanted to render our happiness complete, that is one——"

"Hold, hold! child," interrupted Ela, with much emotion, "I know what you would say; but not now, do not mention it now. Think you that *he* cares or thinks of us, unless it be with contempt and hatred?"

"Oh, yes, yes, he does think of you, dear Ela," ejaculated Walter, eagerly, and glad of the opportunity which was thus afforded him of broaching the subject; "you wrong him greatly, for well do I know my poor father's feelings, and that his thoughts are constantly fixed upon you and Fanny. You cannot have the least idea of the remarkable change which has come over him, and——"

"Heaven send that what you say may be true," interrupted Ela, fervently, and her countenance undergoing a singular alteration as she spoke; "but no matter, let us waive this subject for the present, pray."

"And why now, dear Ela?" urged Maria, in accents of sweetness and persuasion. "Alas, why cannot the past be buried in oblivion, and a reconciliation effected between you? It is the only cloud which now darkens the horizon of our happiness; and what is to prevent that being dispersed?"

"Forget the past?" repeated Ela, while a frown passed over her countenance, and she seemed for a moment to feel all that bitter resentment against Wallingford, which had formerly occupied her breast, and led her on to such acts of violence; but it quickly vanished, and she added, in milder accents—"Ah! Maria, little can you conceive, and may you never experience how hard it is to forget the past, and when that past presents so many reminiscences of heartless duplicity and treachery. But it is not a time nor a place to talk of this; let us change the subject—some other time, perhaps—nay, Walter, I must beg of you not to insist upon pursuing it."

Walter, of course, obeyed, but he felt considerably sanguine upon the ultimate success which would attend his exertions in so desirable and praiseworthy a cause; he could see from the manner of Ela altogether, that it caused a violent struggle with her passions to conquer it altogether, that her resentment towards his father was much softened, and that there was every hope of that reconciliation he was so anxious to bring about, being finally settled to the satisfaction of all parties.

"It is the intention of my mother," said Lady Helvendon, "with the permission of Maria, to make the Old House her residence, until Frederic shall see after his estate, which has been long left to neglect, and is situated not more than twenty miles from this; she will not, therefore, be prevented from indulging in one of her principal gratifications, and which she has so often pined after since we have been away, namely, that of once more rambling among those scenes which for so many years formed our haunts."

"But in doing so, will she not be running into the most imminent peril?" reflected Walter, who could not help thinking at that moment upon the very positive manner in which Ela had formerly asserted it to be her belief, that, sometime or the other, she should most certainly become a victim to the dire and dreadful vengeance of the gipsies. However, the determined and natural air of obstinacy which characterized Ela, rendered him tenacious of mentioning his thoughts and fears to her; and she seemed to have a total indifference to all advice, and to be utterly reckless of what might take place, as though she had made up her mind to the worst, and, to a certainty, that nothing could save her from the fate which her own imagination had predicted to her. After all, could he have truly read the thoughts of Ela, Walter would have found that she would have been much happier rambling about in the verdant fields and green lanes, where the gipsies' tents used to be pitched, than in the midst of every luxury and enjoy-

ment that wealth could purchase. This was a circumstance which Fanny well knew, and it caused her many moments of bitter anguish, for she had every reason to dread the worst from such a predilection; but although she had at various times sought to dissipate such thoughts from her mother's mind, she had every reason to believe that her efforts were attended with very little success; however, she trusted to that powerful magician, Time, to effect what she so ardently wished, who has the mighty influence of turning the most dismal prospects into those of joy and peace; and she could not help thinking that the interest she would naturally feel in her domestic felicity, would gradually estrange her thoughts from the subject, and make her forget all that had happened to her in the bliss of the present.

After some other unimportant conversation, besides that which we have mentioned, Ela, at the earnest request of Walter and Maria, prepared at once to gratify their curiosity, as to the circumstances that had attended Fanny, (with the greatest portion of which we have already made the reader acquainted,) the manner in which they had at last succeeded in discovering her retreat, effected her restoration to liberty, and brought about that happy union between her and Lord Helvendon, which had been so often prevented, by the most unfortunate events. We will make her narrative the subject of our next chapter.

CHAPTER LXVIII.

"Thou art a villain, Hermann,
Ay, a most shameless villain, one who's pride
It is to revel in debauchery, and
To mock to scorn the hapless being
Thy power hath destroyed!"

THE STUDENTS.

"The last letters you received through the medium of Lord Helvendon," continued Ela, after having related a few particulars with which the reader is already acquainted, "informed you, I believe, of the unsuccess which had hitherto attended my inquiries after my unfortunate daughter, and the villain who we were now satisfied held her in his power against her will; and many were the weary days and nights that I passed in the research, and the privations and insults I received, for I was compelled to disguise myself in mean apparel, to conceal my real character from the inquisitive eyes of the inhabitants, for it was by acting in this secret manner that I felt convinced that I alone could hope to elicit the information I required, and elude the danger which might have threatened me, not only from the Marchese Vivaldi, but from any of my other enemies whom I might chance to meet with in the course of my travels. Every day, however, only brought a renewal of my despair; and at length, almost without the slightest ray of hope, and filled with the most dreadful apprehensions, which I need not attempt to describe to you, I returned to the Castello di Alancantaros, where I received the letters that had come from you, and which at first were by no means calculated to decrease my anguish. Well did I know what must be the sufferings of yourself, Walter, and Maria, at the melancholy and mysterious disappearance of Fanny, more especially as you and Maria were separated from each other, and had yourselves no other means of imparting consolation to one another than by letter. I pictured to myself the distraction of Maria at the uncertainty of the fate of that poor girl to whom she had been attached, with all the affectionate regard of a sister, and my own sorrows were rendered doubly poignant. Then again, the probable awful situation of my child, (who had been so many times preserved in such a wonderful manner from danger,) fallen as she had into the hands of the wretch Vivaldi; what could she do to resist his diabolical desires? how could she save herself from the violation with which the villain threatened her? And, oh, should he have triumphed in his nefarious wishes, her fate would be even more terrible than that of death! Bur yet I could not think it possible that such was the case!—in fact, I did not dare to do so, for had I, I should have gone mad! Many were the curses and maledictions which I heaped upon the miscreants head, and my most fervent wish was that I might have an opportunity of wreaking upon him my vengeance. What rendered the circumstance still more mysterious, was the secrecy which Vivaldi had been able to maintain as regarded the place where he had concealed himself and the hapless object of his persecution; but these I was determined to use the most indefatigable means to discover; and such is the cunning and skill with which the gipsy tribe ever go about the accomplishment of their wishes, that, notwithstanding the present unfavourable aspect of affairs, I had not the slightest doubt that I should ultimately succeed, at any rate, in finding out the place of their retreat, and if the wretch had succeeded in effecting the gratification of his nefarious desires, that I should have it in my power to amply revenge the crime upon the villain's head. Should Vivaldi thus far have triumphed, nothing short of his life's blood would have satisfied my vengeance; but I need not describe to you, my dear friends, what the gipsy's passions will prompt them to; no danger is too great, no crime sufficiently revolting to gratify their hatred, when they have received a deep and irreparable injury, and I must admit that, notwithstanding the extraordinary change in my circumstances, my sentiments in that respect are unaltered; but

surely such an insatiable thirst for retribution under such circumstances, must admit of every excuse. What parent could calmly submit to the destruction of her child's virtue and not seek for vengeance upon the head of the seducer?—But I become tedious.

"I once more set out on my melancholy search after my unfortunate child, sometimes clothed in male apparel, and at others, resuming the garb of my own sex, but so altering the appearance of my features, and cladding myself in such mean attire, that it would have been impossible for any person to detect me, unless it had been some one connected with the wandering tribe to which I formerly belonged. Sometimes I was a feeble old woman, at others a burly old farmer;—at one time I assumed the character of a gay young gallant, and went into the *elite* of society; at others, I was a wretched looking mendicant, who seemed to be tottering on the verge of the grave and dying of want. To-day, I was a Spanish officer; to-morrow, a simple rustic. But I should tire your patience were I to endeavour to mention all the various disguises I assumed, and the troubles, insults, and annoyances I endured, the various societies I mingled with, in the hope of being able to elicit something which might guide me to the retreat of the Marchese Vivaldi, and give me reason to hope that I might ascertain the fate of my daughter, or, probably, be able to rescue her from the villain's power, spotless and unscathed, as when he had first borne her away. The vicissitudes I had to encounter would have broken many stronger spirits than mine even, but Providence supported me through the trial, and thanks be to it, has enabled me to triumph. Throughout the whole of my progress, and in spite of the many circumstances that had occurred to perplex me, I never absolutely gave way to despair; in fact, in my most melancholy moments, a latent hope would spring up in my breast, that something ere long would transpire to restore my poor Fanny again to my arms. And so great was the confidence that I could place in the strength of her virtue, that I knew she would rather suffer death than fall a victim to the licentious passions of the Marchese Vivaldi; and I could hear of her death with less anguish, under such circumstances, than that she lived, but that the villain had triumphed in his iniquitous designs. But yet it was strange that a nobleman so well known as he was, who had gained such an unenviable notoriety in the field of gallantry, and what is termed fashionable life, should be able to conceal himself with such success;—it was very evident, I thought, after several days having wandered about from place to place, without meeting with any success, that he could not be in Spain, and I, therefore, despatched a letter to the Castello Alancantaros, informing my friends of the bad success which had hitherto attended me, and the determination I had formed of going to Italy, requesting Lord Helvendon, if he could make it convenient, to join me at Milan, as I might be enabled to advance my plans much better if I had his assistance, and, in fact, as I considered it was absolutely necessary that I should have the aid of some other individual in an affair of such moment, and in which no one could be more deeply interested than his lordship.

"It was at this time Lord Helvendon forwarded to me, my dearest Maria, to the place at which I was then staying, the affectionate letters that had come from you and Walter; and I need not inform you, how heartily I was grieved at their contents, and how deeply I felt the commiseration you expressed, and which I knew to be so sincere, in my complicated misfortunes, and the uncertainty of the fate which had befallen poor Fanny. What would I have given could I have been enabled to impart to you any consolation; but alas! how greatly did I need it myself, and what could I say which could alleviate your distress, or decrease the poignancy of my own?—It is really astonishing how I mustered up fortitude sufficient to support myself during this heavy trial, and I cannot help often wondering at the calmness I ever evinced, the coolness and deliberation with which I always went about the most difficult stratagems I had laid for the furtherance of my plans, and the self-possession I maintained, under the most peculiar circumstances in every society into which I had occasion to mingle. I had to endure many insults and rude remarks, but contumely and vulgarity were nothing new to me, for I had met with enough of it during my association with the gipsies, and had consequently become quite inured to it. As I have before stated, I mixed in all classes of society, thinking in one or the other to meet with some intelligence that might throw some light upon the mysterious subject which so engrossed my thoughts, and singular enough, I never by any chance encountered any person that I knew, or who might have any idea of the business I was upon or the deceptive part I was playing.

"Having received an answer from Lord Helvendon, expressive of the state of distraction into which his mind was thrown by my letter, and promising to join me with the least possible delay at Milan, where we might concert plans for the furtherance of our wishes, I quitted Spain, and made my way towards my native country. My proceeding was slow, in consequence of the time it occupied me in arranging my plans, so as to gain all the information I could on that subject of such vital and agonising importance to my heart, but for a long while nothing whatever transpired to give me any hopes of ultimate success, although, as I before stated, I could not divest my mind of all

hope, nor help indulging in the idea that I and my unfortunate daughter were fated to meet again, and under circumstances less lamentable than might be expected from her present supposed perilous situation.

"I know that the Marchese Vivaldi—for what reason he had never said to any of his friends—had, some months before, disposed of his estates in Italy, and it was believed at that time that he had made up his mind to reside entirely in Spain; recent circumstances, however, had altered that arrangement, and it was a matter of uncertainty, apparently, to every one whom I encountered, at least, whither he had now gone.

"The marchese was well known at most of the places where I stopped in the course of my travels, and I had frequently to listen to anecdotes of his amours, which would have exhausted my patience, had it not been that I listened anxiously with the hope of hearing something concerning Fanny, but it was a considerable time before my wishes were gratified. Weeks, months, rolled away, alas! how heavily with me, and still I suffered but very little change in my fortune, and what I must have endured, both mentally and bodily, may be much better conceived than I can describe it to you. Rest to me was a stranger sleep never closed my eye-lids only for a very brief space of time, and then I could not help my mind being continually haunted by the form of Fanny, and the most dreadful ideas relating to her, and what had become of her flitted perpetually before my imagination. At length, after meeting with several adventures, which would be foreign to the present subject I am detailing, I arrived at Milan, and there found Lord Helvendon, who had arrived there some days, and was waiting anxiously to receive me. Although I had suffered much with fatigue, he seemed astonished at the fortitude and composure I exhibited, and had expected to find me, no doubt, the very image of despair. He looked dreadfully pale and agitated, and it did not require long to discover how much he had suffered. He expressed his fears that our efforts to discover and liberate the poor girl, would be unsuccessful, and he declared that it was only the hope he entertained of meeting, some time or the other, with the miscreant Vivaldi, that made him anxious to cling to life; that he only longed for vengeance on his head; and then, so disgusted had he become with the world, now she whom he prized beyond everything else it contained, was lost to him, apparently for ever, that he cared not how soon he left it altogether. Harassed and bewildered as my bosom was, I could not help endeavouring to console him all that was in my power, and having partially succeeded, we set more coolly about seeking to devise some plan or other to further our designs, and affect the realisation of the object which we had so deeply at heart. Lord Helvendon lost no time in seeking a private interview with the proper authorities of the place ; and acquainting them with the circumstance, solicited their assistance and advice. They informed him they were quite ignorant of the place where the Marchese Vivaldi was at that time residing, but gave it as their opinion that he could not be in the country, as it would be almost impossible for a nobleman like him to remain incog. They,

however, promised to use their best exertions to discover him, and to make the strictest investigation into the case, and if Fanny was found to be really held in his power by forcible means, to demand her immediate restoration to her parent, and to bring the marchese to justice for his forcible detention of her.

"These promises sounded all very fair at the time, but we have good reason to believe since, that the authorities were only deceiving us, and that they knew perfectly well at the very time where the Marchese was living; in fact, it is not probable that they could, by any possibility have been ignorant of it, as it was almost in the immediate vicinity. But Vivaldi was wealthy, and those persons were his friends, and as depraved and unprincipled as himself, and they not only connived at his villany, but were, no doubt, resolved to baffle us all they could. In spite of all their efforts, however, we were fortunately, at last, enabled to succeed, and Fanny is restored to that liberty and happiness from which she thought she was ever estranged. By degrees, we began to suspect those persons of duplicity, and accordingly determined to be upon our guard, and to keep a strict watch over their actions. It was at this time that we considered it prudent to forbear answering any letters that might come from you, for fear it might lead to a discovery, and prevent the accomplishment of that upon which rested our sole hopes of future peace. You may easily guess, my dearest friends, the many pangs this cost us, knowing full well the misery and suffering we should inflict upon you, and the many doubts and terrible fears that would haunt your imagination; but, under all existing circumstances, that course seemed to us to be the most prudent that we could adopt, and we endeavoured to reconcile our minds to it, although it cost us many bitter moments.

"Lord Helvendon, the better to drown suspicion, pretended to leave the country, and took obscure lodgings in a mean street in the town, where we conferred together occasionally without any dread of listeners. I assumed the disguise of a lame mendicant, and went upon two crutches, going from house to house, and racking my brain for stratagems to bring about the accomplishment of our designs. But day after day elapsed, week followed week in rapid succession, and still we were no more forward than we had been. One day, however, when I was standing at the door of an hotel, asking alms of the persons who came out, by way of a preliminary to my getting hold of some of the servants, and eliciting from them the names of the persons stopping there, a circumstance occurred which was the cause of bringing about the discovery we had so long been endeavouring to make. Several persons, menials of some description, had gathered about the entrance to the hotel, and were engaged in conversation. I stopped, and pretending to be still begging, I listened attentively to what they were saying.

"'Don't tell me, Pietro,' said one of them; 'I know he is there; I saw him enter the Pallado Montalversino weeks ago; besides, don't my Constance live there? I repeat, that the Marchese Vivaldi has not only taken up his residence there, but that he has brought

with him one of the prettiest girls that eyes ever dwelt upon. Constance has seen her, although she keeps her very sly and snug to himself, and she (who is a very good judge of beauty) says she is as handsome a girl as ever the sun shone upon; but very sorrowful, and I don't wonder at it, for I dare say the marchese has forced her away from her friends against her will; he is a terrible fellow for that.'

"You may judge my emotions upon hearing this! I almost sank into the earth, and it was a wonder my feelings did not so overcome me as to cause me to betray myself. I held my breath, fearful of losing a syllable. Here, then, the so long sought after mystery was unravelled, the villain Vivaldi was discovered at last; and my Fanny, my own darling, much injured Fanny was living!—Living? Yes, but what must be her sufferings! My God! at that moment I felt a sensation creep through my veins which I had never experienced before; I could have shed tears of joy, of ecstasy, and sorrow, but I restrained them."

Here the feelings of Ela so overcame her, that she could not speak for a few seconds tears rushed to Fanny's eyes, and throwing herself into her mother's arms, they gave free vent to the powerful emotions that struggled at their hearts, while Walter and Maria were as deeply affected as they were themselves, but did not offer to interrupt them.—After a pause, during which interval they had succeeded in partially recovering themselves, Ela proceeded in the following words:—

"'Well,' observed the man to whom the speaker had been addressing himself, 'to be sure, the Marchese Vivaldi is a rare fellow for petticoats, but I do hold with his wild and dissipated ways; no doubt the friends of this poor young lady, whoever they may be, are sadly grieved at her being torn away from them, for I know how I should feel myself if it were my case.'

"'Nonsense, Paolo,' said the other, 'you are as particular as an old woman; what won't a pretty girl tempt a man to do, I should like to know? I don't see much harm in what the marchese has done. If I were situated like he is, and in such good circumstances, I am very much mistaken if I should not do the same as he has myself upon every opportunity.'

"After this brief colloquy, which you may guess, my dear friends, that I listened to with the most intense emotion, the men walked on, and as soon as I had sufficiently recovered from the state of agitation into which I had been thrown by so sudden and unexpected a circumstance, I made my way to Lord Helvendon with more expedition than accorded with my apparent crippled state, and made him acquainted with what had taken place. His surprise and delight may be better conceived than language could describe it, but his indignation was so greatly aroused against the villain Vivaldi, that he would that instant have made his way to the Pallado, and not only have demanded the instant liberation of Fanny, but have satisfaction upon the Marchese for the outrage of which he had been guilty, had I not reasoned with him, and shown him the imprudence there would be in such a step. I felt convinced that the most likely way for us to succeed in our object, would be by stratagem, for, unless we used caution, the Marchese would contrive to escape, and carry with him the victim of his persecution, and the authorities being evidently his friends, we must not look for any aid from them. It was a great trial of the patience of Lord Helvendon to submit to this plan, but reason showed him the necessity of it. I must also admit that I was very little more patient than he was, every delay of a moment seemed like a day to me ; and now that I knew Fanny was alive, my mind was tortured to a state of distraction until I had her once more restored to my arms. I reflected upon what she must have suffered, and what she most probably still suffered, and my resentment against the Marchese Vivaldi increased, and I felt as if I could, at that moment, have plunged a knife in his heart, and have exulted in the deed. I thought upon Fanny's situation ; had she been able to resist the guilty importunities of Vivaldi? It was so long since she had been in his power, that it appeared almost impossible that he would not have forced her to a compliance with his diabolical desires ere now, and should such be the case, alas! her situation would be even more horrible than as if she had suffered even death. But I could not bear to reflect upon this long together, or madness would have seized upon my brain, and I should have been rendered quite incapable of acting with that prudence and caution which the circumstances required ; I, therefore, endeavoured to think the best, and my confidence increased by degrees, for certain was I that Fanny would never have survived disgrace.

" I and Lord Helvendon now consulted coolly together in what manner it would be most prudent for us to act, and what was the most likely way of gaining Fanny's restoration to liberty, and bringing Vivaldi to punishment. We suggested many schemes which we rejected as soon as formed, and it was some time ere we could come to any satisfactory decision. At length, however, it was agreed that I should assume my old character of a fortune-teller, and endeavour to gain access to the Pallado, under the pretext of telling the fortunes of the domestics ; when I might elicit such information as might enable us to accomplish our object

without much difficulty, and without running any of those dangers that might be apprehended if we went a more hasty and incautious way to work.

" The next day was the time we fixed upon for me to put my scheme into execution, and I longed most impatiently for its approach. As night came on, my anxiety was most unendurable, and finding it impossible to remain at home, I walked forth, and with hurried steps, made my way towards the Pallado Montalversino. It was a magnificent edifice, but there was but one casement in which I could observe any light, all the others were involved in complete darkness, and there was a stillness about the place, which would make a person almost imagine that it was uninhabited, save by some one who was left in charge of the building.

" How my heart throbbed as I walked round the edifice ; this, then, was the prison of my poor child, who was probably at that moment enduring all the sorrow that it is possible for a person to imagine, and mourning her separation from that parent who she little thought was at that time so near to her. What agony filled my bosom at this thought. I felt as if I could almost bound through the strong walls of the building, and snatch my persecuted daughter to my heart. I walked round and round the Pallado several times, and minutely examined every part of it, but I could see no chance of gaining access to it only by stratagem. In what part of the building, I thought, was Fanny confined ?—Probably in that apartment in which I saw the light glimmering, she was incarcerated, the victim to the relentless persecution of the Marchese Vivaldi. This idea increased my agitation, and I remained with my eyes fixed upon the casement for several minutes. Oh, could I but see her !—could I contrive, by any means, to let her know that I was near at hand, what a relief would it be to me, and what hope and fortitude would it inspire in the poor girl's bosom. She would then rest assured that I, having discovered where she was confined, and in whose power, would not lose any time or means of effecting her immediate liberation. But I had no means of doing this. I was in my private clothes, or, had I been in disguise, I might have contrived, perhaps, to have got an interview with one of the servants, and thus have managed, by the dint of artifice, to have done as I wished ; but now I could not think of anything that afforded the least chance of success, and my emotion increased to such a pitch that I could scarcely contain myself. I paced backwards and forwards with the air of a maniac, and gave vent to my feelings in tears and exclamations. I had lost all that self-possession and caution upon which I usually prided myself, and was completely bewildered, and uncertain and undecided in which way to act.

"While I was thus occupied, I heard footsteps approaching, and I hastily hid myself in a porch, in order that I might observe who the individual was. I felt a strong foreboding dart across my mind at the time that it was the Marchese Vivaldi, and I was soon convinced that I was not mistaken. A short time afterwards the villain advanced towards the Pallado. Yes, the wretch—the destroyer of my peace, the miscreant who had torn my child from my arms, and had probably become her seducer, stood before me!—My blood rushed scalding hot through my veins;—my heart seemed to rise into my throat;—and, unable to resist or restrain the violence of my feelings, I darted from my place of concealment, and rushing upon him, just as he reached the gates of the Pallado, I seized him, with more than feminine strength, by the arm, and vehemently exclaimed:—

" 'Wretch!—villain!—seducer!—where is my child?—Restore that girl to her mother's arms, from which your cruelty has so long torn her!'

"The Marchese started back aghast upon beholding me, and he was so confused and bewildered, that he was deprived of the power of speech for a few moments, but, at length, releasing himself from my hold, he ejaculated:—

" 'Mad woman, why do you obstruct me?—Release your hold;—away with you!'

" 'Nay,' I exclaimed, vehemently, as the villain tore himself away from my grasp, and pulled the bell violently, 'you shall not escape me thus. Give me my child, I repeat, for I know that you hold her in your power; miscreant!'

"He struggled hard to escape from my grasp, but at that moment I seemed to be endowed with almost superhuman strength, and retained my hold, almost shrieking—

" 'My child, my Fanny—restore her to me! —I would sooner perish than——'

"Just at this moment, and when I had succeeded in snatching a poniard from the bosom of the Marchese, which I verily believe, at that time, I should have plunged into his heart, the gates were thrown open by the domestic, the Marchese tore himself, by a violent effort, from my hold, and, before I could follow him, which I attempted to do, the gates were again closed, and the villain, with an exulting and ironical laugh, vanished from my sight into the Pallado.

"I stood for a few minutes after he had gone, and in the phrenzy of the moment, for the manner in which I had been disappointed half drove me frantic, I breathed a thousand curses and maledictions upon his head, and was determined, by some means or the other, not only to rescue my daughter from his power, but have ample vengeance upon the wretch Vivaldi. But of what avail was my standing there? I could effect no good, and probably might run in danger from the vengeance of the marchese. This idea called me to reason, and I repented having been so rash in attacking him. Perhaps, now, when he was aware that I was acquainted with the place of his retreat, and that my daughter was in his power, he would adopt immediate plans to bear her far away, and to prevent all possibility of my being able to track them, before I had an opportunity of adopting any steps to frustrate his designs. My mind was racked to torture by these ideas, and with one last sad look at that casement, in which I imagined, (and the impression was very strongly imprinted upon my mind,) that Fanny was confined, I left the spot, and bent my way with trembling footsteps towards home, eager to impart to Lord Helvendon what had occurred, so that we might take immediate measures to prevent the consequences I had so much reason to apprehend, and to adopt such effectual means as would cause the liberation of Fanny, without any more delay. I had not proceeded far on my way, when I found myself suddenly seized, my arms were pinioned behind, and a mantle was thrown over my head. I was hurried along at a rapid pace for some distance, and such was the confusion into which such an unexpected event threw me, that I was unable to speak for a short time, or to offer the least resistance to the ruffians who held me. At length, however, I succeeded in partly forcing the mantle away from my head, and then I found that I was in the power of two bravoes, who, I had not the least doubt, were hired by the wretch, Vivaldi, to follow me, and take away my life. Frantic at my perilous situation, I screamed aloud for help, and struggled desperately to release myself from their hold, but in vain, they hurried me along, and with dreadful threats and imprecations, enjoined me to silence. However, I totally disregarded what they said, and I have often since wondered that they did not instantaneously bury their poniards in my heart; but Providence protected me, or else I must have fallen beneath the hands of such reckless villains. I called for help with all my might, and still struggled hard to tear myself from their hands. They hurried me towards a river, and a dreadful idea immediately rushed upon my mind: they intended to drown me. Such desperate situations, as the one I was then in, will arouse even the most nerveless into action, and I renewed my cries and struggles, with yet more strength and determination than ever. The bravoes, however, had forced me on the bridge which crossed this river, and were endeavouring to lift me over the balustrades; my strength was almost exhausted; another minute, and I must have fallen a victim to their murderous designs, when I heard a loud voice calling on them to hold, and strengthened by the hope of help, I clung to the balustrades, and resisted all the efforts of the wretches to tear me from them. It was unaccountable to me, and has often been the subject of my thoughts since that time, that they then did not make use of their poniards, and the only conclusion I can come to is, that they were unarmed, and yet it is singular that ruffians of their description should run any such risk. However, while they were still exerting all their strength to force my hands away from the balustrades, and to throw me into the river, the person who called on them to hold, came up, and attacking them fiercely, they took to flight, and my astonishment was not a little excited, when I beheld Lord Helvendon. He had been alarmed at the length of my absence from the place where we were staying, and having come forth to seek me, had heard my screams, and fortunately came up at the critical time which I have been describing, and rescued me from the power of the wretches, who would otherwise have taken my life.

The pleasure of his lordship, when he discovered who it was he had preserved, may be easily conceived, and we made our way towards the place at which we were staying, with all the precipitation we could. On the way thither, he eagerly inquired of me where I had been, and what had caused me to fall into the power of the bravoes. It was some time before I could find strength sufficient, or conquer my emotion enough to satisfy his curiosity; but when I did—when I informed him that not only had I discovered that it was true that the Marchese Vivaldi was actually at Pallado Montalversino, but that I had seen him, and that he was the cause, in my opinion, of what had happened to me, his astonishment and exasperation were almost indescribable.

" ' The villain !' he exclaimed, ' I will seek him immediately, and severely shall he suffer for his guilt, and for the misery he has doubtless caused my adored Fanny. He shall not, by heaven he shall not, triumph in his iniquities, and carry on his nefarious practices with impunity.'

" ' Be not rash, my lord,' I interposed, ' for it is not by the means you propose, that we shall be able to effect our object. I regret that my feelings prompted me to reveal myself to the marchese, for before we can decide upon any plan to prevent him, he may have departed from the Pallado with his victim, and borne her whither we may seek in vain to find her. Recollect the months that have already elapsed in endeavouring to find them out. I agree with you, that some plan must be adopted without further delay, and what I would suggest to you, is, that you would immediately set spies to watch the Pallado, and to see that nothing takes place to realise that which we apprehend.'

" ' You are right,' observed Lord Helvendon, recollecting himself, and becoming more calm and composed ;—' I perfectly agree with your suggestion, and when I have seen you home, will lost no time in putting it into effect. But what plan do you afterwards propose to adopt, in order to rescue Fanny from the danger by which she is, at present, surrounded ?'

" ' I have a design in my mind, which we will confer upon anon,' I replied, 'but let us now make the best of our way home, and lose no time over a business of such momentous importance.'

"Lord Helvendon did as I requested, and quickening our pace, we arrived at the retired place in which we lodged, for the purpose of concealment and to prevent suspicion being excited. Lord Helvendon did not delay an instant, when he had seen me to the door, but hurried away to put the scheme into execution, and in a very short time he returned, and informd me that he had succeeded in getting the assistance of persons on whom he could depend, and had placed spies, in various directions, round the Pallado, so that nothing could occur outside but which he must be immediately made acquainted with.

"We sat up for some time, consulting upon the plan we should adopt, and at last we agreed to hold ourselves in readiness, in case of instant steps being required to be taken, and then to delay any further proceedings for a day or two, so that the suspicions and fears of the marchese might be in some measure allayed, and being taken by surprise, our object might be attained with one half the trouble and danger we had, at present, to apprehend.

"I agreed perfectly with the propositions of Lord Helvendon, although, notwithstanding the propriety of them, my patience was quite exhausted with the various delays that we found it necessary to take place. Besides, if Fanny, I ruminated, should have been able hitherto to resist the power of Vivaldi, might he not, now that he knew I had found him out, and that he very probably might soon lose her, become desperate, and force her to yield to his desires, in spite of all the resistance she might offer? As this idea flitted across my imagination, my mind became distracted, and I could scarcely support myself. At last, however, after many powerful efforts, I succeeded in somewhat composing my feelings, and having uttered a fervent prayer to the Almighty for His aid and protection in our undertakings, I and Lord Helvendon separated for the night, promising to meet at an early hour in the morning, to confer further together.

"Sleep, however, was denied me, and I did not offer even to retire to my couch, but sat up during the whole of the night, reflecting upon what had taken place, and dwelling upon the painful situation of my unfortunate daughter, and reflecting upon what means it would be possible to concert to save her. My misery, my anguish, I need not, I am certain, attempt to describe, for fully aware am I that you, my friends, can form a sufficient idea of it; I traversed my chamber with agitated steps the whole of the night, and when the morning dawned, I felt so uneasy, that it was with difficulty that I could be persuaded by Lord Helvendon to postpone my visit to the Pallado, and to insist upon seeing the Marchese Vivaldi, and demanding the restoration of my child. Lord Helvendon, however, somewhat appeased my anxiety, by visiting the authorities, and after pretty plainly expressing his sontiments upon their conduct, demanded their assistance whenever he might require it, to enforce a compliance with our wishes. They appeared confused at his manner, and it was very evident to be seen that we had not judged of them incorrectly. They, at first, pretended to be indignant at the accusations of his lordship, but they afterwards changed their tone, and promised him all the aid in their power.

"But I found it impossible to rest at home, and the next day determining to disguise myself as well as I could, and to go to the Pallado, for the purpose of reconnoitering, and to see if I could ascertain anything more to forward the plans which I and Lord Helvendon had formed to gain the restoration of Fanny to liberty.

"I assumed the character of a gipsy sybil, and my feeble step and tottering gait were sufficient to deceive those who knew me well. I came by a different way to the Pallado, and walking down an extensive avenue which led up to it, I examined with the deepest interest, and the utmost emotion, the windows of the building, hoping to behold Fanny at one of them."

"And I was at one of them, all the time," interrupted Fanny, "but it was in a room at the top of the Pallado, and most likely it was not possible for a person to distinguish any object there. Ah! well do I remember that day, and the emotions which filled my breast when I once more beheld that beloved parent whom I had began to despair of ever seeing again! You can easily imagine what I must have suffered at that time, especially when I was uncertain whether my mother was aware of my being confined in the Pallado, and I had no means of making it known to her. I could not make her hear me or observe me, and before I had scarcely time to satisfy myself that it was her, she was gone, and I was left in a state of doubt and agony, which is utterly indescribable. No sleep could I

gain that night, and my emotion was such that it is a wonder my strength did not sink under it. The marchese visited me the next day, and I could not help noticing the change in his manners. He seemed to be violently agitated; and spoke to me in a more bold and determined manner than he had previously done. He informed me that it was not his intention to suffer me to tamper with his wishes any longer, and that in fact, if I did not consent to become his mistress the following day, he would force a compliance with them. Good God! what sufferings were then mine, for I was certain that if Providence did not interpose to save me the villain would most assuredly keep his word; and then of what use would be liberty to me, when I was debased, degraded, my happiness for ever destroyed? Never could I live to know my own shame, and I earnestly prayed to Heaven, either to prosper the efforts I knew my poor mother would make for my deliverance, in time, or suffer me to die, rather than fall a victim to the guilty passions of the marchese. But I must apologise for thus interrupting my mother's narrative."

Fanny ceased, and her mother resumed her detail in the following words—

"Although some secret impulse caused me to fix my eyes with more earnestness upon that particular casement, at which Fanny has since informed me she stood, I did not observe her, but so great was the impression upon my mind, that it was in that part of the building she was confined, that I could not remove from the spot for several minutes. A tumult of the most distracting feelings agitated my bosom at this moment; oh, that I possessed the power of magic, I reflected, that I might bid the doors of the Pallado fly open, and rush to the arms of that dear girl from whom I had been so long and so unjustly separated. What was the wealth, the riches, I now possessed, and to know that Fanny was in the power of a villain; suffering every poignant anguish, and probably degradation? Willingly would I have resigned everything I possessed, and have become again the same poor wandering outcast which I was formerly, could I by so doing have obtained the restoration of my daughter in safety, and uncontaminated or disgraced! But while I thus reflected, my indignation against the wretch Vivaldi became absolutely insupportable, and I uttered curses, deep and frequent upon his head. By what cursed illchance was it, that I had not had the means of wreaking my vengeance upon him when I met him the night before? Why had I not a knife that I could have buried in his base and polluted heart? Methought it would have been rich food for me to banquet on his dying agonies, and——"

Here the passions of Ela became so vehement that they choked her utterance; and her listeners, just as they knew she had cause for resentment against the Marchese Vivaldi, could not help feeling shocked at the fierce sentiments of revenge which still at times held ungovernable sway over her mind. Ela observed their looks, and read their thoughts in a moment, for she instantly became more calm, and in milder tones proceeded—

"Pardon me, my dear friends, if my words are violent; but you must make some allowance for me, when you reflect upon the many sufferings that I had been subjected to, the injuries that had been inflicted upon me, the torturing suspense I had for so many months endured, and the manner in which my mind had been racked and goaded. Yes, yes; I know, I am certain you will pardon me for any violence of language I may make use of. Remember it is an injured parent that speaks, strong with all the passion that nature has ingrafted in her heart, whose child is a portion of her very existence, and that every pang inflicted upon her child is worse than racking her frame with the most terrible tortures. But I become tedious, and must proceed with my narrative.

"Having, by a powerful effort, conquered the emotions that had taken possession of my mind, and so discomposed me, I went round to the front of the Pallado, and resuming the same tottering gait which I was in the habit of doing when I was thus disguised, I did not find much difficulty in gaining admittance to that part of the building which was appropriated to the use of the servants. Here I contrived to arrest the attention of the silly girls to the marvellous things that I prognosticated would befall them, and in the course of the same, in the most ingenious manner, endeavoured to elicit all that might prove useful to me in the designs I and Lord Helvenden had in contemplation. I learned that the marchese had evinced much uneasiness of manner since the night before, and it was supposed that something had happended to disturb his mind. He had also given orders to his domestics to prepare to leave the Pallado at a minute's notice, and intimated that it was his intention to depart from thence on the day after the morrow. This was important news to me, for I saw that there was no time to be lost in putting the project I and Lord Helvendon had in contemplation into execution, and had I not gained this information we might have remained in fancied security for a day or two longer, and until it had become too late to save Fanny from the fate which threatened her.

"Upon the subject of Fanny, however, the servants maintained the utmost caution, and affected the greatest ignorance about her alto-

gether. Of course, I could not venture to put direct questions to them, for fear of exciting suspicion, and could only elicit the information I obtained by stratagem. Oh, how my brain burnt to encounter the marchese, and to demand of him that child he had so brutally and unjustly robbed me of; to express to him the nature of my feelings, and to seek for retribution. But what could I do, here, alone as I was, and without any assistance immediately at hand?—Had I persisted in having an interview with the Marchese Vivaldi, I must have betrayed myself; and there could not be any doubt but that he would take effectual means of preventing me from interrupting him in future, and of silencing me for ever.

"But you may judge of a mother's feelings, when she knew herself to be in the same house with that daughter from whom she had been so long separated, and whose fate, if not already decided, hung upon a complete thread, and yet could not come near her, or enfold her to my bosom. I lingered in the place as long as I possibly could, until I could not advance any pretext for remaining, and I then took my departure. During the time I had been there, although I heard that the marchese was in the house, I had not seen him, and it was fortunate that I did not, for I am convinced my feelings would have overpowered my prudence, and that I should have disclosed myself to him.

"On quitting the Pallado, I made the best of my way home, revolving in my mind, as I proceeded, all that I had heard, and ruminating upon the course, under all the circumstances, which it would be advisable for us to pursue. There was only one that I could see, and that was, to seek the promised assistance of the authorities without further delay, and then to enforce the restoration of Fanny from the villanous marchese, and bring him to that punishment his offences had incurred, and which they so justly deserved. This I suggested to Lord Helvendon, and he totally approved of my plan, and set about it immediately, resolving, that the following morning, at the latest, should be the time set apart to put it into execution. I have no occasion to endeavour to describe to you his lordship's emotions upon that occasion, as you may readily conceive what they were; that is, if you do my son the justice which I have every and the strongest reasons to believe. How impatient he was once more to embrace the darling object of his affections, to be assured that, although she had been subjected to every misery which her abduction must occasion her, she was still pure and uncontaminated as when he beheld her last;—it would be presumptuous in me to seek to do so, especially when Lord Frederick is present, and is so well capable of answering for himself.

"It was arranged that I should gain access to the Pallado on the following morning, in the same manner as I had done that day, and contrive, by some means or the other, to await in the hall until the marchese should come that way, when I should fly to the door, give immediate admittance to Lord Helvendon, and those whom he would have with him, and being taken by surprise, he would, no doubt, be made an easy prisoner of, and without any resistance being offered by his servants. Safe in the custody of the authorities, the release of Fanny might be obtained without any obstruction, and thus our object gained in the most easy manner.

"There could be no objection offered to this plan, which was perfectly reasonable, and offered every prospect of success. I waited for the arrival of the morning with the greatest possible impatience, and having arisen at an early hour, and arranged my disguise, I set forth for the Pallado Montalversino, while Lord Helvendon went to apprise the authorities of our designs, and to make his way to the place by a different route.

"I shall not trouble you by recounting any particulars that may appear at all irrelevant to the matter; let it suffice that, as on the preceding day, I found no difficulty in gaining access to the Pallado, where I contrived to detain the female servants for some time in conversation, until my patience, as well as theirs, was pretty well exhausted, for I saw no signs of the marchese, although I was satisfied, from what they said, that he was in the Pallado. But, from this state of suspense, I was soon released; the marchese appeared on the grand staircase, and as I saw him descend, my blood rushed so tumultuously to my heart, that it was with the utmost difficulty I could support myself; but the idea of how soon he would be in the power of those he little expected, recalled me to my reason and self-possession, and I stood in the hall until he reached it. He scowled upon the domestics when he beheld me; and then, in harsh and disagreeable tones, demanded—

"'What frightful hag have ye here?—By whom was she admitted?—Am I to have my palace made the refuge for these vagrant wandering imposters?'

"'Imposter in thy teeth, Marchese Vivaldi,' I returned, in a disguised voice, and with a laugh of scorn, 'your destiny is not unknown to me; shall I read it to you?'

"'Out with you, you hideous old wretch!' returned the libertine, pushing me away from him, and hastening towards the hall door, were the servant was waiting to let him out; 'if you are not gone instantly, I will order one of my fellows to horsewhip you from the Pallado!'

"I returned nothing but a scornful laugh to this threat, and the marchese frowning upon me,

and looking haughtily upon those around, made a motion to the porter to open the door. Scarcely, however, had this been done, and the marchese was preparing to issue forth, when Lord Helvendon and the officers rushed forward and surrounded him, and a scene of surprise, consternation, and confusion prevailed in a moment in the hall, which baffles all my powers of description. The servants were completely paralyzed for an instant, and the marchese was so thunderstruck, that he had not the least power to make any resistance.

"'Miscreat!' I cried, rushing towards him, 'you are caught at last;—I told you, just now, that I could read your destiny!'

"'Ah!—by hell, it is Ela,' exclaimed Vivaldi, recognising me in a moment,—'I have been betrayed!—But release me, dastard knaves!'

"'Wretch!' cried Lord Helvendon, almost choked with rage, 'where is Fanny?—What have you done with that poor girl whom you so heartlessly tore from her mother and friends?—Answer me, or I will plunge my sword in your heart!'

"'Mighty brave,' replied Vivaldi, sarcastically, 'and so you would murder a man, who is deprived of the means of defending himself?—I know nothing of the girl you speak of,—if it is the gipsy girl you mean!'

"'Liar!' cried I, 'I know you speak falsely, and would mislead us: but you will benefit nothing by this!—Away with him;—drag the villain to prison, and there let him learn, that a wretch like him, however exalted may be his station, cannot escape that punishment, that just retribution which he has incurred by his crimes.'

"During this time the servants had all stood by in stupified amazement, and did not offer to interfere, but at that moment, I happened to fix my eye upon one of the fellows, who had procured a pistol, and was, apparently, just on the point of discharging it, when I sprang forward with more than the quickness of thought, and just as he was about to pull the fatal trigger, I seized his arm with all my strength, and attempted to wrench the pistol from his hand. In the struggle, the direction of the pistol got altered, the contents were discharged, and the marchese, who had received them in his heart, gave but one bound, and the next instant was stretched lifeless before our horror-tricken eyes.

"The event was so sudden, so unexpected, and so appalling, that we were all rivetted to the spot with wonder, and stood gazing upon the ghastly features of he, who, but a second before, was in the possession of life and health, unable to speak a word; but, at length, the servants, looking aghast at one another, did not offer any resistance, but raising the body of their master in their arms, they bore it to another apartment, while Lord Helvendon directed one of the women to show us the way to the room in which the female prisoner was confined. What trembling anxiety filled my bosom at this moment; in fact, my feelings were too powerful for utterance, and I could scarcely support myself. So quick, and so successful had been all that had taken place, that it appeared more like a dream than reality. Such a tumult of joy rushed to my heart, that I

THE MARRIAGE OF FANNY.

could have laughed and wept at the same moment. The woman conducted us up several long flights of stairs, until we reached the door which opened upon the suit of apartments in which my long-lost Fanny was confined, and here, again, the intensity of my emotions almost overpowered me;—a faintness came over me, my heart throbbed at double its usual pace, and had it not been for Lord Helvendon giving me the support of his arm, I must have fallen. The woman who conducted us, as my daughter has since informed me, was Clotilde, who had been deputed to wait upon her, and she, therefore, had the key of the room. She applied it to the lock, and while she was doing so, I listened with breathless attention, and could plainly hear some one moving about in the apartment beyond;—another instant, and the door was thrown open;—there was a simultaneous scream of joy and surprise;—I recollect seeing the well-know face of my child, pale with care, but suddenly lighted up when she beheld me;—a mist seemed to rise before my eyes;—I remember clasping her in my arms—my lips being fixed upon her cheek with passionate, with indescribable love and emotion, and I recollect no more.

"1 will pass over this scene, which needs no description of mine to bring it vividly to your imagination;—my child, my beloved Fanny, was restored to the arms of that parent she had despaired of ever meeting again upon this earth;—she was restored to him upon whom she had bestowed her warmest love, and that in so sudden a manner, that it appeared to be almost impossible. But what delight was ours;—what expressions of gratitude did we breathe to the Almighty, when we heard, that, notwithstanding the desperate character of the villain Vivaldi, and the determined manner in which he had followed up his importunities, she was given back to us as pure as when she was taken away from us.

"We lost no time in leaving the hated Pallado Montalversino, and, for the present, took apartments at an hotel in the city; being determined to make our departure from Italy at the earliest opportunity. The terrible retribution which had so strangely, and so justly fallen upon the head of the marchese, having been witnessed by the officers who had attended us, they could fully testify that it had not taken place in any guilty manner, and after the many sufferings he had occasioned Fanny and myself, I could not feel the least pity for his fate. The following day we quitted Italy to return to Spain, and in a short time arrived at the Castello di Alancantaros, and you may readily imagine the feelings of astonishment and transport with which Don Ferdinand, and his two lovely daughters, Elvira and Inez, received us. Our transport was so unbounded, that it was several days before we became in any way composed.

"When we had somewhat recovered, we determined that the nuptials of Fanny and Lord Helvendon should take place in the chapel of the Castello, without any more delay; and, accordingly, they were solemnized with all that magnificence befitting their rank. Soon after this joyful event had taken place, I mentioned to my daughter and her husband my wish to return to England; and after having,

in some degree, conquered the regret they felt at quitting our kind friends at the Castello Alancantaros, and whom, in all probability, we shall never behold again, we left Spain, and embarked once more for England—trusting that we should have nothing more to apprehend from those enemies who had before annoyed us; namely, Rupert Darwin, and his infamous associates. Before we left Spain, however, we exacted a promise from Don Ferdinand di Alancantaros and his two daughters, the lovely Elvira and Inez, that they should pay us a visit to England in the course of a few months, and I trust nothing will transpire to prevent them from fulfilling this promise, for we, certainly, are much indebted to them for the many kindnesses we have received at their hands, and I would not that our correspondence should be terminated so abruptly.

"Nothing particular occurred to us on our way to England, and you, my dear friends, may readily imagine with what feelings of delight we once more beheld those shores, where, although we had met with so many troubles, dwelt all that we sincerely or most ardently loved in the world! We pictured to ourselves the surprise, the transport you and Walter would experience, Maria, when you became acquainted that Fanny was still living, and waiting with open arms once more to embrace those dear friends from whom she had been so long separated, and who she never expected to behold again; and as these thoughts filled our bosoms, we could scarcely contain our joy.

"I believe I have now detailed every circumstance that has occurred to us since we left England, at any rate, every circumstance which is of interest and importance, and I will therefore conclude with a fervent prayer to the Almighty, that we may be suffered, in future, to live in peace, and no more be persecuted by those remorseless enemies, who have so severely wrung our hearts."

"Amen!" simultaneously ejaculated both Walter and Maria, and they then once more congratulated Fanny and her mother upon their fortunate escape from the many dangers by which they had been threatened, and joined in expressing their admiration of the justice of Providence, who, at the very moment when the villain, the Marchese Vivaldi, thought himself most secure, and on the eve of the accomplishment of his diabolical desires, had brought down a just, but awful retribution upon his head, and terminated his career of iniquity.

The Marchese Vivaldi was immensely rich, and Don Ferdinand di Alancantaros being the only relation he had living, (although he was a very distant one) had the whole of his property devolved upon him, which he fixed upon his two daughters, and, consequently, they became two of the wealthiest heiresses in Spain.

When Ela had concluded her narrative, and the friends had passed some time in conversation upon various topics, Walter once more seized an opportunity of introducing the name of his father, and urging Ela to endeavour to stifle entirely those fierce and almost ungovernable feelings of revenge that had hitherto inhabited her breast towards him—to seek to forget the past—to be assured of the sincerity of his present compunction, and not to mar that happiness which might otherwise be universally theirs, by turning a deaf ear to the importunities of Mr. Wallingford, and refusing to pay any regard to his intreaties, mar that feeling which would otherwise be so universal. To these arguments, Lord and Lady Helvendon and the others joined theirs, and it cannot be expected that they could fail to make a most powerful and affecting impression upon Ela.

She listened to them for some time in silence, but it was very evident that her feelings were undergoing a very powerful struggle—her bosom heaved with emotion, her countenance became pale and red alternately, and there was an expression in her eyes which gave the beholders every reason to hope that ultimately she would suffer her better feelings to predominate over the powerful passions of her nature. Walter, who noticed the advantage they were gaining, determined not to lose so excellent an opportunity of furthering their designs, and, therefore, in accents of the most impressive and persuasive description, he observed—

"You will consent, dearest madam—I am certain you will not, you cannot remain inexorable or deaf to the solicitations of those dear friends, who, you must be certain, in urging their suit, have only your happiness and best interests at heart. Heaven knows, my poor father has suffered enough for the youthful indiscretions of which he was guilty; but do not embitter his last days, or refuse to him that forgiveness, without which he will never again be restored to peace. Oh, Ela, had you but seen him in his hours of bitterest sadness, when the past would rush upon his brain, how severely he has reproached himself for his guilt, and breathed his wishes for the happiness of yourself and Fanny, you would not hesitate for a moment, I am convinced, in pronouncing his penitence sincere, and would no longer hesitate to pardon him. Heavy has been the punishment my father has already undergone, and——"

"And what has been his suffering after all, to that of his victim and his child?" interrupted Ela, hastily, and her countenance becoming flushed, as a momentary feeling of her former hatred and implacable revenge darted through her bosom; "were they not driven to herd with wretches more savage than the beast of the forest—exposed to want,

disgrace, contumely, and all the horrors attendant upon that life of shame and misery? Were they not in rags, in penury, and abject destitution, at the very time when he, who had been the cause of all they endured, was master of every enjoyment, and possessed of every luxury that pampered pride and indolence can covet? Yes, yes, it was so! and who was there to pity the poor outcast Ela, or her child, then? Did he come forward to——"

"Oh, yes, yes," interposed Walter, with much emotion; "indeed you wrong him; from the first moment my father saw you again at Rosemary Dell, his heart was stung with pity and remorse, and you know full well that he tried all that was in his power to persuade you to place Fanny under his protection."

"Ah!" exclaimed Ela, "I well remember; he would have torn my poor girl from me;—he would have deprived me of the only happiness that was left me in life;—the only being that made me cling to it. He would have brought her up to hate me, and Ela would probably have remained the wretched, despised, and bereaved outcast, until death had terminated her sufferings. But he did not succeed,—he did not triumph in his designs, and Ela Beranzio and her daughter yet live to love and adore each other, and to look upon the past with a smile of contempt."

"True, dear mother," said Fanny, throwing her arms round her mother's neck, and looking imploringly in her face;—"we can, indeed, look back with contempt upon the sorrows of the past; and there is but one thing wanting to render our future happiness complete;—need I say that that is a reconciliation with my——, Mr. Wallingford, I mean. Nay, my dear mother, do not turn a deaf ear to my solicitations;—I know you have not the heart to do so;—you will forgive him, and we shall all again be reconciled!"

"Oh, yes," urged Maria, joining her entreaties to those of the beauteous pleader who just ceased speaking:—"I am certain your mother will not refuse to render us all so happy!—I can add my testimony to that of my cousin, that my poor uncle is sincerely penitent, and that all the reparation in his power he would willingly make you."

Ela shook her head in a melancholy manner, and remained silent for a few seconds;—it was a violent struggle with her feelings, but it was very clear to be seen that she was gradually yielding to the persuasions and arguments of her friends,—her eyes filled with tears, and Walter, Fanny, and Maria, seizing upon this opportunity to urge more vehemently their persuasions, followed up their arguments with everything which they could possibly adduce.

"Heaven knows," observed Ela, in tones of gentle melancholy, "Heaven knows, that if his sufferings have been half as great as mine, he has been sufficiently punished;—and how can I doubt the sincerity of his compunction, after the assurances I have received from you all to that effect?—I have been violent;—but the intensity of my miseries have driven me to it;—and you all know that I have had ample cause for feeling that powerful sentiment of hatred and revenge that have urged me on to many acts which I have afterwards deeply regretted. But, indeed, it is not in my nature to—I—a strange faintness comes over me, and in spite of all my struggles to master it, my—— Oh, Wallingford, your children have triumphed; I do, indeed, forgive you, and may Heaven do so likewise!"

During the time this conversation was going on between the friends, they had quitted the house, had wandered into the gardens attached, and had taken a seat in an alcove at the further end. At the moment that Ela had given utterance to the words before described, they heard a rustling near them;—the foliage was torn asunder, and the wonder of every person present may be easily conjectured, when Wallingford rushed hastily forward, and threw himself at Ela's feet. We have before stated that he left Wallingford Hall, almost immediately after his son, and had wandered unconsciously in the direction of the Old House. He continued to walk on, deeply wrapt in thought, until suddenly looking up he found himself beneath the garden wall, which separated it from the road, and the gate being open, he could not resist the temptation which seized upon him to enter. He had not proceeded far, when he heard voices, they proceeded from the alcove, and with the deepest interest and curiosity he listened, when he heard his name several times repeated. We need not attempt to describe the emotion at the conversation which he overheard, and the final decision of the much-injured Ela. He could scarcely believe the evidence of his senses, and such was the tide of joy that rushed to his heart, that he could scarcely support himself.

"Ela!—too kind!—too forgiving woman!" he ejaculated;—"can I hear aright?—And will you, indeed, pardon the man who has been the cause of so much bitter anguish to you and to Fanny—my own Fanny?—Oh! this is a happiness too great, too unexpected!"

Ela made several powerful efforts to speak, but it was some minutes before she could sufficiently vanquish her agitation to do so;—at length, extending to Wallingford her hand, which he pressed fervently to his lips, and with a look which expressed more than words could have done, she said—

"Rise, Wallingford;—we have both erred, and severely have we been punished for our errors. I pardon you all the injuries you have

done me, and may we both live to make that atonement to Heaven, which a sincere repentance can alone do."

What a moment of indescribable transport was this to every one present!—Wallingford started to his feet;—he looked at Ela for an instant in silence;—her countenance softened into all that expression of gentleness and beauty which had marked her character when they first became acquainted with each other, and rushing to Ela's arms, they embraced as vehemently as if nothing had ever occurred to interrupt their affection. Fanny and the others stood trembling by; and the former's countenance expressed a variety of feelings of the most powerful and blissful character. Her eyes were fixed upon the face of Mr. Wallingford, and tears filled them;—Mr. Wallingford saw her;—he read her thoughts;—he understood the nature of her feelings;—he gently released himself from the arms of her mother;—he looked a moment at the latter, as if he would seek her sanction;—a tear answered him.

"My child! my daughter!" he exclaimed, with a burst of passionate fondness, and in an instant Fanny, for the first time, felt herself pressed to the heart of her father, and was permitted to call him by that endearing title.

We must pass rapidly over the scene which followed this joyful event, and which we will rather leave to the imagination of our readers. It was one of the most blissful days that any of them had for some time experienced, and nothing could exceed the joyful change it wrought in the spirits of Mr. Wallingford and Ela, who now calmly sat and engaged in conversation upon the passing events, and seemed fully to have made up their minds to forget the past, and to bury all their sorrows in oblivion. But none felt greater transport than did Lady Helvendon and her brother, Walter Wallingford; that brother who she was now permitted to acknowledge, and whose love for her she was certain could only be equalled by that which she felt for him. And Maria, too, how abundantly did she participate in their raptures, and she could not resist the tears that overflowed her eyes, from her joy-surcharged heart. There was no impediment to Lady Helvendon and her visiting Wallingford Hall, and in Walter, Maria, and the others, being together as often as their convenience would permit; and in the society of those whom they loved, they anticipated the most uninterrupted happiness!

'Ah! no," reflected Walter, "until we are perfectly assured that Rupert Darwin, and our other enemies, are exterminated, we cannot calculate upon a continuance of peace."

These ideas, however, Walter kept confined

to his own breast, for he did not wish to make his father and the others uncomfortable so soon after the reconciliation so long prayed for had been accomplished and the day passed away in the most delightful manner ; and to have seen the wonderful alteration that was effected, in Mr. Wallingford and Ela especially, no one would ever have imagined that they had recently been so heavily afflicted.

It was late before the carriage, which Mr. Wallingford had sent for, arrived at the Old House to convey himself, his son, and Maria, to Wallingford Hall; and then how loth were they all to separate! Mr. Wallingford especially, who in the society of Ela and Fanny, particularly the latter, had become so entranced, as to be totally regardless of the lapse of time.

"Alas!" he soliloquised, mentally, "what a blessing has my false pride so long deprived me of; how many hours of rapture might I have secured to myself, instead of misery, had I acted as virtue and integrity ought to have dictated! What a weak fool I have been; and at the very time when I was flattering my vanity and pride, I was making a sacrifice of those pure and uncontaminated joys, that could alone bring me ultimate happiness! Oh! Ela, I feel that I have deserved all you have caused me to suffer, and that I can never sufficiently repay you for the bliss you have this day conferred upon me. If the spirit of my sainted Amelia is allowed to look down upon the earth, I am certain that——"

"What lights are those moving yonder?" suddenly interrupted Walter, pointing in the direction of Rosemary Dell, towards which they were fast approaching.

Mr. Wallingford and Maria looked towards the spot whither Walter pointed, and was astonished to behold two or three lights, (which seemed to proceed from torches carried by some persons moving direct for the high road,) glaring at no great distance from them.

"It is stange," remarked Wallingford, as an inward dread came over him; "what can be the meaning of this?"

"Listen," said Maria, as the carriage approached nearer the spot from whence the lights that had attracted their attention had first seemed to issue; "it is the sound of several voices singing!"

The trio listened in the greatest amazement.

"By Heaven! it is the gipsy chorus!" exclaimed Mr. Wallingford, turning very pale, and laying hold of his son's arm;—"I remember it well!—Good God what fresh trouble is in store for us?—Are we never to be able to get rid of these wretches?—I thought our happiness was too great to last long!"

"There must be some mistake, my dear sir," said Walter, evincing nearly as much alarm as his father; "it is very improbable that the gipsies should again make their appearance in the Dell, in this bold and open manner."

"I tell you, Walter," said Mr. Wallingford, "that I am not mistaken; well I recollect the occasion on which I heard that chorus before, and—but hark!—you may distinguish the very words!"

Walter and Maria did listen with the most breathless attention, and the following well-known words of the gipsy chorus were then distinguished :—

"We gipsies lead a life of glee,
    Fal de ral lal lal lal la ;
There's none more blithe or gay can be,
    Fal de ral lal lal lal la !
In our coarse built tent, when the fire burns bright,
We gather around its cheerful light;
And our cup we quaff, devoid of strife,
Then, oh! how merry is the gipsies life.

" We sigh not for the halls of state,
    Fal de ral lal lal lal la ;
In our own free tent there are none so great,
    Fal de ral lal lal lal la !
No care on the gipsy's brow is seen,
And he sleeps on his grassy couch so green,
With a heart more light than ever was know
To beat in the breast of the heir to a throne !"

As the last words of the chorus were given utterance to, the singers approached so near the vehicle, that the inmates could plainly distinguish them, and it was then proved, beyond a doubt, if even the words of the song had left a doubt behind, that they were of the gipsy tribe, and with packages at their backs, and some of the women with children behind them, seemed as if they were travelling to some place where they designed to pitch their tents. But surely they could not in the neighbourhood of Rosemary Dell, unless they were a different tribe to those that had been in the habit of coming thither, and even in that case, it did not seem at all likely to them that they would be ignorant of what had taken place there before, and the danger they would run in by so doing, and they were, therefore, fain to persuade themselves that they were making their way to some country fair, and that they had nothing to apprehend from them. Both Walter and his father too, as they passed the carriage, had an opportunity of more closely observing them, and of watching them all narrowly; they were certain that there were none of the same gipsies among them that had belonged to the gang of which Rupert Darwin was the chief; but still the appearance of any of the tribe in the neighbourhood was enough to excite the apprehensions of Mr. Wallingford, his son, and Maria, particularly under the present circumstances—so soon after the return of Ela and her daughter, and when they took into consideration the events that had no great while since taken place, and the threats of Rupert Darwin, and the prognostications of the wild Gipsy Sybil. Maria trembled violently, but Walter endeavoured to reassure her, and he partially succeeded. Upon observing the carriage, the gipsies made a sudden stop, and looked eagerly after it, but, at a signal from a stout man, who appeared to be the leader of the party, they once more moved on, and Mr. Wallingford having desired his coachman to drive on as quickly as possible to Wallingford Hall, they were soon out of sight, and the last faint tones of the gipsy chorus died gradually away upon the air.

When Mr. Wallingford and the others arrived at the Hall, they called together the domestics, and asked them if they had seen anything particular to excite their suspicion in the neighbourhood, since they had been absent that day, or whether they had seen anything of the gipsies? To this the servants answered in the negative, and appeared to be not a little surprised at the inquiry. They were, however, ordered to be upon their guard, and to keep a strict watch, in case the Hall should be attacked; and Wallingford resolved to make the magistrates acquainted with the circumstance in the morning, although he could not help thinking that the persons who had been kept for weeks back on the look out, could not have been very vigilant, or they would have been sure to have learned the circumstance as soon as they.

Walter Wallingford having become more composed, endeavoured to tranquillise the fears of his father, and sought to persuade him that the gipsies they had seen were in no way connected with those they had such good reason to dread, and that they should hear no more of them. The apprehensions of Mr. Wallingford, however, were powerfully aroused, and Walter discovered that it was not such an easy task to quell them, as he at first calculated upon, and his father again became almost as distressed and fearful as he had been previously to his meeting and reconciliation with Ela.

Maria's fears too were naturally very much aroused, for the bare name of a gipsy was sufficient, after all they had encountered from them, to create terror in their bosoms, and they had seldom or ever been seen but their appearance was almost always sure to be the harbinger of some approaching calamity. But her fears were excited more upon Ela and Fanny's account, than her own, and this circumstance taking place so soon after the return of the latter and her mother to England, made a double impression upon her mind. It seemed as though some fatal spell pursued their footsteps whichever way they went, and that no sooner did the prospect of happiness begin to dawn upon them, than some fresh misery was at hand to overwhelm it with the heavy clouds of sorrow.

Mr. Wallingford, his son, and Maria, sat for some time after their return to the hall, conversing upon the event which had so seriously alarmed them, and it was not until he had made several very powerful efforts that Walter could in any way succeed in appeasing the fears of his father, and in convincing him of the utter improbability that the gang which they had reason to dread, if any portion of it really existed, being so bold as to venture into a quarter in which they must be aware there were snares laid in every spot to entrap them, and where they would be sure to be defeated by numbers; but he did, at length, partially succeed, and after seeing that all the doors were properly secured, they separated for the night.

Maria, in spite of all her efforts to the contrary, could not help feeling the greatest uneasiness at the circumstance we have been relating, and she longed for morning, that she might again hear of Ela and Fanny, to know that they were safe and to apprise them of what they had seen, so that they might be upon their guard, and be prepared to resist any danger which might threaten them.

The window of Maria's chamber overlooked the gardens of the hall, and upon which the moon was now shining brightly. She, not feeling inclined to retire to rest immediately, took a seat by it, and in a pensive mood, gazed upon the scenery beyond, which was rendered clearly distinguishable by the brilliancy of the moon's lumens. She partly opened the window to admit of the zephyrs which came fresh from the bosom of the lake, (it being very close and sultry), and she had scarcely done so, when she thought she heard something rustling in the grass immediately underneath it. She involuntarily drew herself back behind the curtains of the window to prevent being seen, although she could observe all that passed in the garden herself, and she had scarcely done so a second, when her eye fell upon the shadow of a human form upon the grass, and presently afterwards she saw the tall figure of a woman moving about near the window of the back parlour. Maria trembled with terror as she gazed upon this form, more especially when she distinguished in its gaunt and bony figure that of one of the gipsy women, whom she knew to belong to the tribe of which Rupert Darwin was, or had been, the chief.

The woman moved stealthily along for a short distance from the place where she had first appeared, and, folding her arms across her chest, remained fixed, and appeared to be examining the house and the windows minutely. Maria was so completely overcome by this circumstance, occurring as it did only two or three hours after they had seen the gipsies, that she could scarcely prevent herself from screaming aloud with fear. She continued to watch the woman closely, and was at a loss in what manner to proceed, or how to act.

Should she alarm the inmates of the house before they could be made to understand the nature of her fears and the cause of apprehension, the woman would in all probability be gone, and she would, most likely, be accused of giving way to the effects of some frightful dream. Then again, if she suffered it to pass off in this manner, might not the woman have accomplices at hand, who might gain access to the hall, and murder them all before they had the means of making any resistance? Certain it was that the intentions of the gipsy were no good; but how she had contrived to gain access to the gardens of the hall, surprised and puzzled Maria, and that, too, without being observed by the persons who for some months past had been placed there to keep watch; and it appeared very clear that (notwithstanding the apparent plausible protestations of the men on a former occasion, when they were examined by Walter and Mr. Wallingford) there must be some treachery among them, and, consequently, while their bitter enemies remained in existence, they were not safe one minute from another.

The state of Maria's mind during the time these thoughts were rapidly passing in it, it will be no very difficult thing to conjecture—she started at the least breath of wind, and thought it was some one moving in the hall; but still she kept her eyes fixed upon the woman, who did not offer to alter her position for a few minutes, and seemed to be intently gazing upon the different windows. At length, however, she started as if she had been suddenly alarmed at something, and darting behind a cluster of trees, became lost to the view, and the following moment Maria heard the barking of a dog, which she had no doubt was one that Mr. Wallingford had lately ordered to be kept chained up in the grounds. In a short time all was again quiet.

Maria, however, still continued at the window for a few minutes, and gazed as far as her eyes could stretch into the gardens; but not beholding anything more to excite her attention, she withdrew from it, and closed the shutters. Notwithstanding she felt tired and sleepy, she could not make up her mind just yet to retire to rest; but, stepping lightly from her chamber on to the lobby, she listened as attentively as she possibly could to hear whether there was anything moving about; but all was quite silent, and she, therefore, returned to the room, and securely fastening the door, committed herself to the care of Providence; after which she arose and went to bed—but not to sleep. No; busy thought, and the strange and alarming events of the evening, kept her waking, and she sought, but in vain, to form some conjecture as to what had been the woman's intentions in coming to the gardens of Wallingford Hall, and in what manner she had obtained the said entrance. Perhaps she was some wandering vagrant, whose object was robbery, and no personal violence to the inmates; but that she had been frustrated in her designs by the barking of the dog, and had thus, being alarmed, decamped as quickly as possible. Still there was something in the demeanour of the woman which made her reject this idea almost as soon as she had formed it, and her fears increased to an almost insupportable degree, when she reflected that, in all probability, her being foiled this time in her evil intentions would not prevent her from making another attempt at some future opportunity. She was glad, however, that she had seen her, as it would enable her to put her uncle and Walter upon their guard against any surprise, and would cause them to use greater precaution than they had done lately.

Her mind was too much disturbed to suffer her to obtain much sleep on that night, and she was extremely glad when the radiant sun ushered in the morn. She immediately arose, and as she did not hear any of the family stirring, she descended into the garden, and walked on in the direction which she had seen the woman take on the previous night. When she reached the spot where Carlo, the dog, was chained, and who, knowing her, did not offer to make any noise, she paused, and looked round her. The dog came forth from his kennel as far as his chain would permit him, and frisking about her, wagged his tail, licked her hands, and gave every other demonstration in his power of the pleasure he felt at seeing her.

"Poor, faithful Carlo," said Maria, patting his head, "I suppose you want your liberty; and, therefore, I will not keep you long in suspense."

With that Maria removed the chain from Carlo's collar, and suffered him to go at large, and apparently grateful for the same, he jumped gaily about her, but speedily altered his action, and commenced pawing and raking among the grass.

"What's the matter now, Carlo?" cried Maria, stooping down and looking more narrowly at the spot to which the dog seemed to direct her attention, and, much to her astonishment, she picked up a pistol, which was loaded, and which had, no doubt, been dropped by the gipsy woman in the hurry of making her escape on the night before.

If this surmise were just, here, then, was a clear proof of the guiltiness of her designs; and Maria shuddered with horror as she gazed upon the deadly weapon, and reflected upon the determined manner in which the gipsies pursued their diabolical schemes of vengeance, although they might be quiet, and appear to abandon them for awhile ; and all those fears which before had occupied her breast, returned with full force upon her mind.

An hour had now pretty well elapsed since she had arisen, and she therefore returned to the hall, and sought the presence of her uncle and Walter, as may be expected, with much trepidation depicted in her manner. When she had detailed the events we have been describing, their astonishment and consternation was very little short of that which she evinced; and the loaded pistol which Maria had found in the garden, was not only proof sufficient that she had not been mistaken, but that the gipsy woman had really been in the grounds as she had described, but also that her intentions were of the most desperate kind.

"The wretches will not rest," said Wallingford in tones of despair, "until they have satiated their deadly vengeance in the blood of all or some of us. It is remarkable that so soon after the return of Ela and Fanny, they should again make their appearance."

"It is indeed, my dear sir," replied his son, "but some immediate steps must be taken in this business. Let us directly summon the men hither, to whom we have committed the charge of the grounds. It must be as Mary suggests, in spite of all their specious assertions on a former occasion of a similar description, that some treachery must exist amongst them ; and until that evil is remedied, we shall not be safe an hour together."

"But, for goodness sake," observed Maria, "before you do anything else, let us drive over to the Old House, and she that our friend there are all safe. I am under terrible apprehensions for them."

"And so am I, my love," said her uncle ; "so if Walter will take upon himself the examination, and the dismissal, I think, of these fellows, you and I will drive over there at once."

"I perfectly approve of that plan," said Walter, "and I shall not be long before I follow you. I think, myself, it would be advisable to discharge the whole of the men we have at present engaged, since it is very evident that there is no reliance to be placed in them, and to get a fresh set in their place."

"Exactly so, Walter," said his father ; "however, I will leave everything to you, and I know you will act with your usual prudence and discretion."

The carriage being, by this time, ready, Mr. Wallinford and Maria stepped into it, and it was driven off with great haste towards the Old House. On the way thither they conversed, of course, upon the events which had so recently taken place, and which so suddenly put an end to the sanguine expectations of uninterrupted happiness which they had formed the day before ; and Mr. Wallingford again protested it to be his firm belief that it was the fate of at least one of them to fall by the hands of the gipsies ; and he was also convinced, in his own mind, that Rupert Darwin was concealed somewhere in the neighbourhood, and was only waiting an opportunity of putting his diabolical designs into execution.—Maria, although she could not but think exactly as her uncle did upon this subject, endeavoured all in her power to persuade him to the contrary, but her efforts were entirely ineffectual.

"And yet it is strange," observed Mr. Wallingford, after a pause, " it is very strange, if, as I suspect, Rupert Darwin is somewhere about the spot, that, instead of entrusting the woman with the perpetration of the deed, he did not attempt to commit it himself, especially, when it is not likely that he would have found any greater difficulty in gaining access to the gardens than she did. It is very strange; in fact, it is a mystery which I am perfectly at a loss to fathom."

"I, too, sir, have ruminated upon that," said Maria, " and am of your opinion, that it is very ambiguous altogether. However, let us hope that time will unravel it, and that it will not be attended with such dreadful results as those which you apprehend."

By this time they had arrived at the Old House, and the fears of Mr. Wallingford and his niece were soon dispersed when they beheld Ela and her daughter up at the drawing-room window, who waved their hands to them.

"Thank God! they are at present safe !" ejaculated Maria, fervently.

"At present," reiterated Mr. Wallingford, with emphasis, and sighing.

Having alighted, they were speedily ushered into the presence of Ela, Fanny, and Lord Helvendon and his mother, who expressed their surprise that Mr. Wallingford and Maria should pay them so early a visit, and eagerly inquired the reason that Walter did not accompany them.

The looks of both prepared them for the news they were about to impart to them.

"Something has happened to disturb you, I am certain of it," said Ela ; " alas ! how soon are all our air-built hopes of happiness fated to be destroyed."

"Oh, surely nothing has happened to my brother," said the beauteous Lady Helvendon; her countenance betraying the extreme agitation and suspense of her mind.

Mr. Wallingford, as well as he was able, requested them to compose themselves, and then deputed Maria to impart to them that intelligence which was so well calculated to revive their terrors.

Fanny, Lord Helvendon, and his mother,

listened to the communication with the most painful interest; but Ela heard it all with a calm demeanour, and an expression of countenance which expressed a very different sentiment, but not less intensity of anguish; and when Maria had concluded, she remarked—

" I knew it would be so; I always said it; and yet, fool that I was, to suppose that permanent happiness upon this earth could ever be mine, or peace, long together. The blood-hounds have scented out their prey again, and they will not rest this time until they have glutted on

THE MYSTERIOUS HAG AT THE MANOR HOUSE.

their blood.—In vain you may endeavour to thwart them, in vain you may seek to elude them; one or more of us is doomed to fall by their hands !"

Mr. Wallingford strove, but in vain, to repress a groan as Ela gave utterance to these awful

predictions, and a dead pause ensued, each one being at a loss what to say in refutation of the observations of Ela. It was a pause of much anguish to all of them, but at length Lord Helvendon broke the painful silence, by remarking—

" Really, after all I cannot help thinking that these fears are entirely groundless and fallacious ; there must be some means of setting them at defiance, unless they are supernatural beings altogether. At any rate, it shall be no fault of mine if they escape."

" You may imagine so, my lord," said Ela, " but have we not learnt, from woeful experience, how little reliance we ought to place upon such an opinion ?"

" At any rate, we will use every precaution that the circumstances may suggest, to endeavour to discover the wretches, and bring them to punishment," said Lord Helvendon ; " and it strikes me, very forcibly, in spite of all you have said, and notwithstanding what has formerly occurred, that we shall not be unsuccessful in our endeavours."

" Walter is at present instituting every inquiry into the matter," observed Mr. Wallingford, who, by a powerful effort, had sufficiently combatted his own fears to appear more composed than could have been anticipated ; " the magistrates are, by this time, I dare say, acquainted with what has taken place, and officers will be dispatched in all directions in pursuit of the gipsies. The boldness of the wretches in entering the neighbourhood so openly, is what principally astonishes me."

" They are insensible to shame or danger," observed Ela ; " you ought, however, to have learnt that fact by this time."

" Why, it certainly would appear so," returned Mr. Wallingford ; " but all their power and reckless daring, could not rescue the father and brother of Rupert Darwin from the fate which had been awarded to them for their bloody and inhuman crime ; and, therefore, why should we despair of being also able to triumph over these miscreants ?"

Wallingford spoke this in a tone of hope and confidence, but he was far from feeling those sentiments. However, he noticed the pale looks of Fanny and Maria, and the intense agony which reigned in the bosom of Ela, and he was anxious to do all in his power to appease their anguish.

" Mr. Wallingford speaks very reasonably," remarked Lord Helvendon, catching eagerly at the observations of the former, " and I think we ought to place much confidence in his remarks ; to believe otherwise, is to invest these wandering wretches with a power more than mortal. Come, come, Fanny, my love, do not give way to despair. Trust me, the time is not far distant when all our enemies will be destroyed, and then our peace of mind will not again be interrupted."

Lady Helvendon turned her sparkling eyes upon the countenance of her husband with an expression of the deepest affection, but although she sought to conquer the feelings that had so depressed her heart, she found it a task more arduous to accomplish, than she had strength to do at that time.

" I will endeavour, dear Frederick," she said, " to profit by your advice, and to conquer what may seem to be an unwarrantable weakness ; but you must admit that my mother and myself, who are so thoroughly acquainted with the character of these people, must be better qualified to judge of the consequences likely to result from their vengeance than you, who have never mingled with them ; and, therefore, the fears we entertain are the more excusable. Heaven grant that your ideas may be verified.'

Every one present responded to this prayer, and none more heartily than Maria, who had been a silent listener to all the arguments and opinions that had been advanced, and could not help—in spite of her apprehensions—considering that the opinions of Lord Helvendon and her uncle were very reasonable, and, therefore, sought all that it was in her power to conquer the apprehensions she had indulged in since the previous night.

" At any rate," observed Ela, " admitting the force of your arguments, while we entertain fear, we are sure to use caution ; and were we entirely to set our minds at rest, we might become so careless as to fall into the very snares we might otherwise avoid."

" I perfectly agree with what Ela has just now remarked," said Mr. Wallingford ; " but I think it is most probable that the gipsies are ignorant of your having returned to England, much more the place of your present retreat. Therefore, if you remain close to the house, you may, most likely, be able effectually to elude them."

" Perhaps so," returned Ela, carelessly ; " although, I must confess I am not so sanguine upon that subject as you appear to be, Mr. Wallingford. They have spies in every direction, and it would not take them long to discover the place where we are at present concealed. However, you say that Mr. Walter is at present using all the precautions that can be made, and I know of nothing further that can be done just now."

The subject was changed at this period ; but although they conversed upon different topics, it was very evident that the one alarming subject of the gipsies engrossed their minds, and nothing could divert their thoughts from it. Mr. Wallingford, however, by dint of extraordinary perseverance, contrived to appear the most tranquil of them all, with the exception of Lord Helvendon, and it was a truly gratifying sight to those who had witnessed his sufferings for so many years, and who had feared that they should never more behold a smile upon his brow again. Often were his looks fixed upon the countenance of Ela, and in those glances were expressed more than all the vows of compunction he had made. When their eyes met, a feeling of gentleness beamed in the face of Ela, which reminded him of their early and unfortunate love; and he could almost imagine that what had subsequently taken place, was only a frightful vision, and that Ela was the same virtuous, gentle, and affectionate being she was when first they met. These were moments of transport that he had not experienced for years before, and could the illusion but have lasted, he could have forgotten that sorrow had ever been his.

Ever and anon his gaze would be directed towards Fanny, and whenever it was, it would encounter the eyes of the beauteous woman fixed upon the features of her father, with all that passionate fondness her heart was capable of feeling. Then would a pang of reproach shoot through Wallingford's heart, when he recollected the miseries to which she had been exposed through his perfidy; and in such moments he would doubt whether his offences had not been too heinous for forgiveness; but hope, and the smiles of Fanny, who seemed as if she could penetrate to his thoughts, quickly restored him, and his mind might be said to be almost at rest.

CHAPTER LXIX.

"By all th' infernal hosts!
I will pursue the darling object of my soul,
Even unto the death!"

AFTER two or three hours passed in the manner we have been describing, Walter arrived at the Old House, and was received with much eagerness and pleasure. In answer to his father's questions, he informed them that he had given information of the circumstance to the magistrate, who had given instruction for every necessary inquiry to be set on foot. He had also strictly examined all the persons who had been employed to keep watch at Wallingford Hall, but had not been able to elicit anything of the least importance. Suspicious, however, of their fidelity, he had, according as Mr. Wallingford had suggested, dismissed them all, and had employed others. From all that he had been able to ascertain in the neighbourhood, no one had seen or heard anything of the gipsies, and they seemed to listen to what he stated respecting them, with incredulity and astonishment. He, therefore, ventured to state an idea which had often occurred to him, and which the recent event tended in a great measure to confirm, namely, that many of the inhabitants of the places adjacent to Rosemary Dell and Wallinford Hall, were in colleague with the gipsies, and were paid to keep their movements secret, to give them all the information they could gather

together, and to mislead and deceive those whom they wished to destroy.

"No doubt of it," remarked Ela, "it is not at all likely that every one with the exception of yourselves, should be ignorant of the gipsies being somewhere in the neighbourhood, when they entered the place in the bold and open manner you have described to us. This shows at once, how dangerously we are all situated, and how difficult is the task to be upon our guard, when we actually know not who are our friends and who are not. Depend upon it, long ere this our retreat is as well known, as if we had employed the beadle to announce the same in the public market-place."

A pause ensued after this, no one being at that time possessed of any argument to combat this opinion; and after various suggestions for their mutual safety, and the detection of their enemies, they once more endeavoured to divert their thoughts from the painful subject which had hitherto so entirely occupied their minds, and to discourse upon other topics. Thus the day passed away, and as soon as evening had thrown its shades upon the earth, Mr. Wallingford, his son, and niece prepared to return to Wallingford Hall; but it was with heavy hearts that they did so, more especially Fanny and Maria, who having been so long parted from each other, were loth now to separate. At length this matter was arranged to the satisfaction of all parties, and it was agreed that Maria should remain at the Old House for a few days, over which they had placed a guard similar to that which was engaged to watch the hall. Mr. Wallingford and Walter then, after an affectionate parting with them all, quitted the mansion, and drove on their way towards home.

"It pleased me much, my dear father," observed Walter, when they had got a short distance on their way home, "to see you overcome your fears sufficiently to act with such composure and presence of mind as you have done to day, and I trust that in future you will be able to conquer that weakness which you have hitherto evinced, a weakness occasioned by the many troubles you have encountered, and their rapid succession upon each other."

Mr. Wallingford sighed, as his son made these remarks, and after a pause said—

"Oh, Walter, would that my firmness were sincere; but in spite of all my efforts to the contrary, a weakness as you may designate it, I find it utterly impossible to banish from my mind the melancholy forebodings that have so long haunted my mind, but which, on my reconciliation with Ela Beranzio, became greatly allayed. The recent circumstances that have taken place, you cannot be surprised should have renewed these melancholy ideas, doubts, and apprehensions ; and notwithstanding I struggle all that is in my power against it, I cannot help thinking that the crisis of my fate is near at hand."

Walter shuddered, as Mr. Wallingford uttered these words in a tone of unusual solemnity, and although he despised all superstitious notions, there was a strange indefinite feeling came over him, which resisted all his efforts to shake off.

" My dear sir," he remarked, at last, " I am astonished to hear you speak thus, and pardon me, if I presume to opine that common reason is opposed to such wild and tormenting ideas. I can make every allowance for the uneasiness which it was only natural to suppose the re-appearance of the gipsies would occasion you ; but I cannot be so blind to probability, as to imagine that the wretches, powerful as they may be in their lawlessness, will be able long to elude the hands of justice, or that they can actually set at defiance every force and law. I pray you, sir, to endeavour to become a convert to my opinion, for it is only by prudence and caution that we can hope to frustrate those designs that are invariably so artfully devised."

" In the latter observations," replied Mr. Wallingford, " I entirely agree with you, and you will find that whatever may be my opinions, I shall never forget the caution and prudence of which you speak ; but—hark ! I thought I heard a cry of distress."

" So did I," said Walter, looking from the carriage window eagerly, " it seemed to me to proceed from some person not far from this spot ! Hark ! there it is again. I am confident that I am not this time mistaken ; but yet it is so dark that it is impossible to distinguish anything."

" What can be the meaning of this ?" said Mr. Wallingford ; " some unfortunate has evidently been, or is being ill-treated. William," he added, calling to the coachman, " stop a minute."

William obeyed, and alighting, came to the door of the carriage, and observed—

" If you please, sir, some one is kicking up a hubbub, that's very certain, and it seems to come from the Dell ; I shouldn't at all wonder but them confounded gipsies have been up to their tricks again. It's a man's voice that's quite clear."

" Suppose you and the footman proceed to the spot from whence the cries appear to come," said Mr. Wallingford, " and endeavour to ascertain what is the cause."

" What me—me—me—me, sir ?" stammered out the coachman, evincing the utmost consternation.

" Yes, to be sure, William," returned his master, " come, don't delay, man, or there is no knowing what may be the consequences."

" Lor bless you, sir," returned the alarmed coachman, " to attempt such a thing would be perfect madness ; suppose it should be the gipsies, and we quite unarmed, what would become of us ? Why we should all be barbar-ous ly murdered, and no mistake."

" Psha ! booby !" exclaimed Walter, impatiently, and alighting from the vehicle. " Will you attend me, sir ?" he added, speaking to his father ; " Thomas will accompany us, and we can leave this clown in charge of the carriage until our return. We must not suffer any fears of the consequences, to intimidate our minds, when the life of a fellow creature is probably at stake ; fortunately here are a brace of pistols in the carriage, which I took good care to place there this morning before you left the hall, for fear anything should happen to render their services necessary."

Walter took one of the pistols and his father the other, and attended by Thomas, the footman, who was armed with the coachman's whip, they directed their steps towards the place from whence they imagined the sounds to issue.

It was a very dark night, and they could not perceive anything many paces before them. They, therefore, advanced with caution, and looked carefully around them, so that they might be upon their guard against any surprise which might suddenly befal them. After forcing their way through a thicket, they seemed to be evidently near the place where the distressed party, whoever it might be, was, and presently they were startled by an exclamation of terror from Thomas, who had accidently got a little in advance of them, and staggering up to them with a pale visage, was terribly alarmed.

" Why, what in the name of patience is the matter with you, Thomas ?" interrogated his master, Mr. Wallingford, " what has frightened you, man ?"

" Oh—oh—oh—oh, sir," faltered out Thomas, his teeth still chattering, " there is somebody hanging—some person is hanging to the tree."

" Mur—der ! mur—der ! fi—re !" exclaimed at that moment a voice of stentorian qualifications, " oh, lord save me ! will nobody come and release me ? Must I hang here like a dried haddock ? Help, help !"

" Help, help !" reiterated a second voice ; " good lord deliver us, poor unhappy sinners, or we are dead men to a certainty."

" I certainly know those voices," said Walter, as he and his father walked up to the spot to which the terrified footman pointed ; " why, as I live, it is Farmer Fallowfield and Knobbs hanging suspended from the tree."

And those unfortunate individuals it was sure enough ; their hands and arms pinioned, fastened back to back, and suspended by the arm-pits to the stout branch of one of the trees. They were almost dead with exhaustion and terror, but when they recognised Walter and his father their joy at the prospect of release became unbounded.

"Why, what in the name of wonder brought you in this singular and dangerous plight?" demanded Mr. Wallingford.

"Oh, these infernal gipsies!" cried Fallowfield; "but for the love of Heaven, release us from our present predicament, or we shall be dead men in a few minutes. We will tell you all about it."

At the mention of the gipsies, Mr. Wallingford and his son exchanged glances, and the former especially, evinced much emotion. They, however, with the assistance of Thomas, the footman, complied with their wishes, and having released them, assisted them to the carriage, in which having placed them, they told William to drive with all the speed he could make to Wallingford Hall.

By the time they had arrived there, and two or three glasses of wine had been administered to them, they were sufficiently recovered to gratify the eager curiosity of Walter and his father, as to the manner in which they had found them, and Farmer Fallowfield having taken upon himself to be spokesman, as Knobbs did not pride himself particularly upon his eloquence; after some little difficulty they were enabled to gather the particulars, which were briefly that Mr. Fallowfield and Knobbs, (who, it must be understood, were particular old cronies,) were on their way to the village ale-house, where they were accustomed to meet in the evening to discuss the politics of the day, and other equally important matters, they were suddenly met by several of the gipsy tribe, who immediately knew them, and, having owed them an old grudge, after having so belaboured them that they thought they had not got a whole bone in their skin, they served them in the manner we have described Mr. Wallingford and his son to have discovered them, and there left them.

Mr. Wallingford and Walter listened to this account with much regret; for here was another most convincing proof that the gipsies were in the neighbourhood, and were, doubtless, only awaiting a fitting opportunity to put their villanous designs into execution. But still they were by no means taken by surprise, as the recent circumstances that had taken place did not give them any reasonable room to doubt, but that their old enemies had contrived to secret themselves in the neighbourhood. They enjoined Fallowfield and Knobbs to keep a good look out, and to make them immediately acquainted with any suspicious circumstance which might come to their knowledge.

"It is very evident," said Mr. Wallingford, "that these wretches have some means of secreting themselves, which appears to set at defiance all our efforts to fathom; for my own part, I have racked my brain in reflecting upon it, and seeking to arrive at a just conclusion, until I am completely tired, and I am now as much in ignorance as I was at first. What plans to adopt for our security I know not, for it seems as if there were no way whatever to frustrate their designs, which, it strikes me, are not far off being accomplished."

Walter remained silent for a minute or two, for he was, in fact, at a loss what reply to make; he had exhausted all his arguments, in seeking to calm the apprehensions of his father, and now he really saw so much reason for the said fears, that notwithstanding all his efforts to the contrary, he found it impossible to erase the impression from his own mind; at any rate, they could not take any more precautions than they had hitherto done, and they must, therefore, leave their fates in the care of Providence.

"To give way entirely to despair, my dear sir," at length Walter said, "is to become weak, and is giving our enemies a signal advantage over us. Besides, it is arraigning the justice of the Almighty to believe that He will allow the guilty machinations of such miscreants to succeed, and permit them to triumph over the innocent. This last circumstance which has happened to Knobbs and Farmer Fallowfield, will doubtless render them and others more vigilant, and cause them to use every effort to discover the secret haunt of the gipsies, and to apprehend them."

"Ah! no," returned Mr. Wallingford, shaking his head, "the fellows are by far too cunning and designing for them; and I do not think, if even we should discover their retreat, that we should find it a very easy task to take them. You well know their desperate character, and that they would to a man, and woman too, fight to the last, and rather die than be taken."

"Yes, yes, I know well indeed the truth of what you say," returned Walter, "but we must hope for the best."

At this juncture a servant entered, and informed them that Fallowfield and Knobbs had returned again, and requested to speak to Mr. Wallingford and his son.

"What can they want now?" said the former, when he had told the servant to usher them in; "some fresh occurrence, I suppose, to add to our alarm."

Before Walter could make any reply to these observations, the farmer and the constable entered, their countenances evincing that they had in some measure recovered from their terrors, although their bodies were still smarting from the treatment they had received at the hands of the gipsies.

"Well, my good men," said Mr. Wallingford,

impatiently; "what brings you back to me so soon again? Have you any fresh information to impart?"

"Oh, yes, sir," replied Knobbs, who took upon himself to be spokesman on this occasion, "we forgot to mention one very pertikler circumstarnce, and which is of the greatest consekens I des say to you, sir."

"Well, well, what is it, Knobbs?"

"You had better let me tell it, Knobbs," remarked the farmer, preparing to put his powers of oratory into motion; "you go such a roundabout way, that we shall never get to the facts, and his honour cannot have his time occupied in this manner, you know."

"No, no, I'll tell it," said Knobbs, peremptorily, and exhibiting some indignation at the observation of his companion, which he considered was an imputation upon his eloquence it behoved him to rebut with all possible despatch; "do you think I'm not capable of telling a story as well as you, Mr. Fallowfield?"

"Ay, that you are, Mr. Knobbs," replied the farmer, with a grin, and a sagacious wink of the eye; "why, I'd back you against any man in the county for telling a story; you be quite famous for it."

Knobbs did not appear to relish the wit of Farmer Fallowfield, if anything could be understood from the very grim looks with which he eyed him; however, the farmer wanted no one to participate with him in what he, doubtless, considered to be a very rich joke, for he could more than enough laugh at it himself, and for at least a dozen persons besides; and this hilarious ebullition he gave evident symptoms of being about to indulge in, to no very limited extent, when Mr. Wallingford, who saw that unless he at once entered his protest against it, there was no knowing when the matter would be explained, demanded whether they had really anything to impart or not, if not they had better retire as soon as possible, as he had other business to attend to. The two worthy pot-companions perceiving that he was displeased, winked at each other, and Fallowfield having yielded the point to Knobbs, that individual went on to give the following explanation—

"I beg pardon, sir, I'm sure, for having kept you so long; but you see, sir, Mr. Fallowfield seems to think himself such a very cleaver man—"

"Whoy, dang it," interrupted Farmer Fallowfield, with some asperity of manner; "if you—"

"Come, come, no recrimination," said Walter, "but let us hear at once what you have got to relate."

"Very well, sir," said Knobbs, "if you will only let me tell it my own way, and do not allow me to be interrupted by Fallowfield, I'll

tell you the whole truth in a few words; it's summat o' vary great importance too—vary great importance, indeed, to your father."

"Well, well, come to the point at once," said Mr. Wallingford, his patience completely exhausted by the prolix manner in which the parish constable took to impart the information he had for them.

"That's the very thing I've been coming at all this time, sir," replied Knobbs; "you must know, sir, that after we had been *attacted* by the gipsies in the manner we have before told you, and *sarved* as you found us; when they had left us and had got a little way, one of them turned back suddenly, and coming up to me, he looked as black as a thundercloud, and ten times more dangerous, and shoving a letter into my bosom, he said:—

'"There is a letter, varlet; if you should see Squire Wallingford, deliver it to him, and tell him to maik well the contents, for the writer is no vain boaster, and as sure as he now lives, the threats contained in that letter will be fulfilled.' With that the fellow gave me a cuff on the cheek, by way of a parting remembrance. I presume, and then left us. Here is the letter, sir."

Mr. Wallingford took the epistle hastily from Knobbs, and drawing his son aside, broke the seal, and read the following words to him:—

"SQUIRE WALLINGFORD,—Thou mayest repose thyself in fancied security—thou mayest think that the gipsies have forgot their oath of vengeance against thee and thine;—but thou shalt shortly find that thou art mistaken. Ere many weeks, many days perhaps, are fled, the threats which have been so long held out, shall be accomplished, or Rupert Darwin will die in the attempt. Ela and her daughter, too, may tremble; the place of their abode is known, and their enemies are on the alert, to put those designs against their life, they have so long had in contemplation, into execution, and no power on earth shall save them, while the world contains such a being as—

"RUPERT DARWIN."

"P. S.—Your spies and all are perfectly useless. We are near them at the same time that they are using the most vigilant and deep laid schemes to trepan us; and we laugh at them for their pains. Tremble,—

"No power on earth can e'er abate
The gipsy's unrelenting hate!
To thwart him, he'll all schemes defy,
Those he hath doom'd shall surely die"

"The villain! the daring villain," exclaimed Walter, when his father had finished reading the letter.

"Ah! sir! you may say that," observed Knobbs, "they are *willians*, sure enough;

and not only *willians*, but complete devils, saving your honour's presence, all the whole lot of them. I really do not think they are human beings, at least, that Rupert Darwin, as he is called, for he do not seem to care a pin for anything, and there is nothing at all that hurts him. See how easily he broke out of prison, when he was chained and fettered all over; and yet he got them off, and wrenched out the iron bars of his cell, as if they had been ginger-bread; take my word for it, sir, if ever there was a devil, that Rupert Darwin is one."

"He is a most reckless scoundrel," said Mr. Wallingford; "but was he among those who so maltreated you, Knobbs?"

"Oh, no, your honour," answered the constable, "and a very good job that he was not, for although I am not daunted or frightened at trifles, I would as soon have seen old Beelzebub himself as that fellow; I fancy we might both have reckoned our business settled had that been the case,"

"Yes, I reckon we mought," returned Farmer Fallowfield, "for the very sight of Rupert Darwin is enough to frighten a person to death, let them be ever so courageously inclined; and I do firmly believe it would have been the death of me."

"No doubt of it," said Knobbs.

"But did you recognize in those who ill-used you, any of our old enemies, the gipsies?" demanded Mr. Wallingford.

"Can't say that I did, sir," replied Fallowfield, "but it seems they knew us well enough, as the soreness of our bones can full testify, and they seemed to have resolved to have their bellyful of vengeance against us. Why, one of the wretches actually proposed sticking us on the top of a haystack, and having a game at cock-shy at us."

"Ah! the *willians*, that they did," said Knobbs.

"Well, is that all you have to tell us?" asked Mr. Wallingford.

"Yes, your honour," answered Knobbs, "and enough too, I think."

"Well, well, I thank you for your information," observed Mr. Wallingford, "and here is a guinea for you. Keep a sharp look out after these daring rascals, and the least thing which may come to your knowledge, calculated to excite suspicion, do not fail to make me immediately acquainted with it."

"Oh, you may depend upon that, sir," said Farmer Fallowfield, "we will keep a sharp look out, as you say, after the desperate ruffians, and it shall not be our fault if they are not apprehended."

Mr. Fallowfield might have reversed his promise, and said, that—"it should not be their fault *if they were taken*," and then he would, most unquestionably, have been considerably nearer the mark, for he, at any rate, had firmly made up his mind never, by any chance or persuasion, to wander near the spot where any of the gipsy tribe might be lurking, and if, by accident, he should encounter them, to make the best possible use he could of the active legs which nature had provided him with. Upon this point, the farmer and his companion, constable Knobbs, agreed remarkably well, and having both promised Mr. Wallingford and his son things quite contrary to their determinations, they made their *congees*, and took their departure from the hall.

The circumstance of the letter created but very little more uneasiness in the mind of Mr. Wallingford or Walter, who, had there been nothing more to excite their apprehensions, would have been inclined to treat it as a mere idle piece of vain boasting, or an attempt at intimidation; but this was an event of minor importance, and it was only from other circumstances that their principal fears arose. After Fallowfield and Knobbs had taken their departure, Mr. Wallingford and Walter sat up for some time, conversing upon this occurrence, and the different ideas it gave rise to, and when they had arose to separate for the night, they had arrived at no more satisfactory conclusion than when they first sat down to discuss the matter.

The principal thing in the letter, which caused them pain and alarm, was the statement as regarded the gipsies being acquainted with the residence of Ela and Fanny; and they determined to ride over to the Old House at an early hour on the following morning, and make them acquainted with the particulars, and thus put them on their guard, and warn them of the danger which threatened them.

The night passed away without anything taking place to alarm them, although, after all that had recently taken place, neither Mr. Wallingford nor his son could sleep long together; for they knew not how close their enemies might be to them, or what hour might be the time selected by them for the perpetration of their cruel, their bloody intentions. It was dreadful to be always kept in this state of dread and suspense; and thus to have the mind continually placed upon the rack; but Walter endeavoured to conquer the fears he saw too much reason for, for the sake of his father, and taking all the many trying and bewildering circumstances into consideration, he certainly succeeded much better than could have been anticipated.

The following morning, after partaking of a hasty breakfast, Mr. Wallingford and his son, in accordance with the resolution they had formed on the previous night, rode over to the Old House, and they found them there, exhibiting a great deal of alarm, with the cause of which they were speedily made acquainted. It seemed that soon after Walter and his father had quitted the Old House, the night before, and while Ela, her daughter, Maria, Lord Helvendon, and his mother were still seated in the parlour of the house, they were suddenly aroused by a peal of rude laughter outside, and directing their attention to the window, they were completely thunderstruck on beholding the tall figure of a gipsy woman, standing before it, and gazing upon them with looks of ferocity, but more especially at Ela and Fanny, at whom her eyes seemed to dart glances of hatred and vengeance. Having waved one of her hands with a menacing gesture, they perceived, for the first time, that she held a pistol in the other, and they were all so petrified to the spot with astonishment, that they did not offer to avoid the danger, although it was so near them. Another moment, and the woman seeming to take a deliberate aim at Ela, fired.—But the quick eye of the latter had watched the action, and with the rapidity of lightning, she shrunk down, and escaped, the ball penetrating the wainscot. Aroused to a full sense of the danger, Lord Helvendon sufficiently recovered from the confusion and surprise into which the circumstance, and the unparalleled effrontery of the gipsy had thrown him, snatched a gun from behind the door, and hastily quitted the house. When he left the parlour, the woman was still standing at the window, and gazing with looks of fiendish and malicious disappointment upon Ela and the others;—but although to quit the room was scarcely the work of an instant, when his lordship got into the garden, she was gone, and he could not perceive any traces of her. He rushed hastily through the grounds, totally regardless of what might be the danger by which he might be encompassed, or reflecting she might have accomplices at hand; but he saw nothing whatever to excite his suspicions, and after examining minutely every nook and corner of the gardens, he returned to the house, where he found Ela and the others, as may be expected, in a state of great alarm, more especially Fanny, whose fears were created more for her mother than herself, and who paid but little attention to the gentle soothings and expostulations of Maria, who, although she offered them, gave utterance to them with a very bad grace, inasmuch, as she was in a very little better condition than she was herself. All doubts of the truth of the gipsies being near the spot, and that they must have spies about to make them acquainted with every circumstance, as soon as it took place, were now at an end; and what security had they from the vengeance of the miscreants?— None at all!—What would become of them that night? They trembled to think of it;—

for they had not the least doubt but that the woman, finding herself foiled in the attempt she made upon the life of Ela, would return, accompanied by numbers, and make an attack upon the house, and they could not offer a sufficient formidable force to repel the said attack, for there were only two or three male domestics in the house, and they could not boast, they had every reason to believe, of the most redoubtable courage. If, then, their fears were realised, nothing could save them from destruction. Could they manage by any means to leave the house secretly, they might contrive to escape to Wallingford Hall, which would afford them a more secure shelter for the present; but it was madness even to think of such a thing; for independent of the doubt their was as to whether or not Wallingford Hall had not been already attacked by the sanguinary wretches, might they not encounter them on the way, and then their lives would be sure to fall a sacrifice? They had no other alternative than to secure all the doors, and barricade the windows, as well as they could, and then the servants arming themselves with such implements as they could lay their hands on, at the moment, awaited the issue of the alarming adventure, in a state of uneasiness, which the reader will find it no difficult matter to imagine to himself.

However, hour after hour glided on, and nothing further took place to excite their fears, and it seemed at last pretty evident that the gipsies had abandoned their design, at any rate, for that night, if, indeed, it had been as Ela was inclined to imagine, namely, that they would make an attack on the house, and, satiate their vengeance at last with their blood. Still, however, they kept an unwearied watch, and did not offer to retire to their chambers; and the men servants were regaled with an extra allowance of ale to sharpen their courage, if their services should happen to be required, and to enable them to act with more determination. But all passed off without any further interruption, and the morning dawned at length upon them, much to the relief of all.

Just as Mr. Wallingford and his son entered the room, Ela had been proposing to Lord Helvendon that they should drive over to Wallingford Hall, to make them acquainted with what had taken place to put them on their guard, and to consult with them what was best to be done, and what plans it would be advisable for them to adopt, under the pressing and critical circumstances. Mr. Wallingford and Walter were very much shocked, when they heard of this diabolical attempt at murder, and they were completely at a loss what to do; although it was with feelings of dread they were compelled to own that the gipsies were too cunning and subtle for them, and that they firmly believed they would never abandon their projects, until they had accomplished their wishes, even if it cost them their lives the next minute.

"It is very evident to me," said Ela, "from what I have seen and heard, that Rupert Dar-win has joined a new tribe; for every one who has seen them state positively that they are not the same gipsies from whom we have experienced so much misery and annoyance."

"I am of the same opinion," observed Mr. Wallingford, "and Farmer Fallowfield, and

WALLINGFORD HALL IN AFTER-DAYS.

Knobbs, the constable, confirm the idea. But if that be the case, I should imagine we have not so much reason to fear, because it is not very likely those who are strangers to us can imbibe the same feelings of hatred and vengeance that actuated the others."

"Ah, Wallingford," answered Ela, "much as you have seen of these lawless people, from sad experience, you are yet almost ignorant of their real character, or otherwise you affect to treat the matter more lightly for fear of increasing my alarm. The death of Mark Darwin and his son, was considered not merely as an injury to the particular gang to which they belonged, but to the whole fraternity of the wandering race; they are all equally sworn to one another, and must take up the cause of one of their people if their assistance should be required. The gang of which the Darwins and their accursed race were for so many years the principals, was estimated above any other, and the Darwins were held in great repute, so that the simple word of Rupert will be sufficient to command them all to his assistance; he is the spark that can fire the train, and bring down the vengeance of the miscreants with overwhelming fury. Thus you see by what imminent danger we are surrounded, and what little chance there is of our being ultimatey able to escape."

"It is a most lamentable thing," said Mr. Wallingford, sighing, when he reflected that he was the origin of all the misery,—"surely no persons were ever so situated as we are before."

"It is useless to give way entirely to despair," said Lord Helvendon,—"we must be prompt in our decisions, and come at once to some determination. I suggest that we leave this part of the country with all possible expedition."

"But whither would you advise us to go?" asked Ela and Mr. Wallingford.

"I do not think that we can find a place of greater security than London," returned Lord Helvendon; "there, if even the wretches were to pursue us, where there are always so many persons about, they would never venture to molest us."

"I approve of his lordship's proposal," remarked Walter, "and would advise our making immediate arrangements for our journey to the metropolis. We can settle there until we have reason to believe we have no farther cause to apprehend danger, and in the meantime, the vigilance of our friends here must not be abated, and we may then hope that our fears will not be long before they are set at rest."

"Under existing circumstances," remarked Ela, "I do not think we can do better, than adopt Lord Helvendon's and Walter's suggestions; we have but few preparations to make, and shall be ready to depart from hence this very day."

"And must we again travel, my dear mother?" said Fanny, in a melancholy tone. "Alas! when shall we be permitted to rest?"

"You see the urgency of it, my love," said her husband;—"but I am sure we must all alike feel the inconvenience and annoyance to which we are put. But it cannot be helped, and, therefore, it is useless for us to murmur at it. What say you, sir?" he continued, speaking to Mr. Wallingford,—"do you approve of the plan I have proposed; and will

you accompany us; or do you prefer remaining behind, and running the risk of the consequences?"

"Why," replied Mr. Wallingford, "I certainly much regret the necessity which compels us to such a course, for I am neither disposed nor in health fit to travel; but so firmly am I of your lordship's opinion, that in London we should be secure from the wretches, that I not only agree to become your companion, but advise that our journey be not only commenced this day, but immediately; for should any of the gipsies be lurking about, and see us depart, they would not venture to make any attack upon us in open daylight. Your arrangements, you say, Ela, can shortly be made, so also can be mine; I, therefore, think it advisable that you lose no time, but when you have everything complete, we will all of us return to the hall, where post-horses can be procured, and we can depart on our journey without any more delay."

To this proposition every one assented, and deeply regretting the painful circumstance which compelled them to the step, Ela gave immediate instructions to her domestics, and the few preparations necessary were soon completed, and they announced themselves ready to depart to Wallingford Hall. Previous to their doing so, however Mr. Wallingford sent a man to reconnoitre round the neighbourhood, to see if any suspicious looking persons were lurking about, and he having, after awhile, returned, and informed them that the coast was clear, they walked forth, stepped into their carriages, and leaving the Old House in the charge of persons competent to look after it, were driven off to Wallingford Hall.

Post-horses were soon obtained, and old Anthony and his wife being once more left in charge of the hall, and instructed to communicate to them all the information they could obtain, addressed to them at Mr. Goodwin's, London, whither they at present proposed going, in less than an hour the whole party were on their way to London.

Every mile our travellers proceeded their spirits revived, as it took them farther and farther from the place were their implacable and desperate enemies lurked to satiate their vengeance; and by the time they had arrived at the end of the first stage, they had become perfectly tranquil, and could converse freely upon the course they purposed pursuing.

CHAPTER LXX.

"There's a cloud o'er thy head, which shall
    burst ere long,
Retribution shall come for each earthly wrong;
Thou mayst hie thee to some distant land,
But tremble, for know that thy fate is at hand.
No power shall save thee the deadly blow
Which shall lay the proud lord of Wallingford
    low."

THE journey to London was performed without anything occurring worthy of being mentioned in these pages, and they were soon settled in a spacious mansion in St. James's Square. Anthony wrote to them several times, and informed them that, although a strict search had been kept up, nothing whatever had been seen of the gipsies since they quitted the neighbourhood. As months passed away in this manner, without anything occurring to disturb their peace, and the young women mingled freely in the gaieties of the metropolis, their spirits revived, and they began to hope that they should yet be able to look forward to a certainty of happiness, and trusted that, in a short time, they might, with safety, return to the neighbourhood of Rosemary Dell: which notwithstanding the many troubles they had there experienced, was still endeared to them all, by many blissful associations. Ela, too, became, as it were, quite another being, and whatever might be her thoughts upon the subject, she endeavoured always in the presence of Fanny and her friends, to appear to have entirely banished all fears of the gipsies from her mind. Towards Wallingford, too, she also behaved with the most marked kindness, which plainly evinced that her forgiveness of him was perfectly sincere, although to forget the many sorrows he had occasioned her, she felt to be utterly impossible.

Three months only after they had quitted Rosemary Dell, Walter Wallingford led his beloved Maria to the altar of St. George's Church, and every one who was present at the union were enthusiastic in their admiration of the beauty of the bride and bridegroom, and heartily wished them every happiness in the wedded state that heaven could bestow.

All the many sorrows they had formerly experienced were now forgotten by all parties, in the bliss of the present moment, and several days were given up to the most unbounded festivity and rejoicing, Mr. Wallingford also sent orders to Anthony to give all his tenants and dependants a feast upon the joyful occasion, and ordered that there should be such rejoicing as the event called for. All were alike invited to share in the hospitality of the absent gentleman, and all were treated alike with the same liberality and benevolence, who held a place in the memory of Mr. Wallingford and the newly married couple.

But within a few days of the nuptials, Mr. Wallingford was again observed to become very gloomy and thoughtful, and it was quite evident that he was again brooding over the past, and giving way to the same melancholy forebodings that had so often racked his mind. In vain Walter and the others tried to arouse him from this state of feeling, by every means in their power; he did indeed affect to yield to their remonstrances and soothings, but it was clear to be seen that he only assumed what he did not really feel, for the purpose of appeasing their anxiety and apprehensions towards him.

Twelve months glided swiftly away, and Lord Helvendon, having by that time had all his arrangements at Walthorp Abbey (his estate) completed, intimated his intention of retiring there from London, and invited Mr. Wallingford and his son and daughter to accompany them thither. However, they declined, for the present, accepting the invitation, Mr. Wallingford's health being in too delicate a state to permit him to travel, and he not being inclined to leave London for the present. Lord and Lady Helvendon, with Ela, and the mother of his lordship, therefore, took their departure for Walthorp Abbey, while Mr. Wallingford and Walter and his wife remained behind, until such times as the strength of the former had been recruited, when, as all apprehensions of any harm from Rupert Darwin and the other gipsies were at an end, they determined once more to return to Rosemary Dell.

Three months more were passed by Mr. Wallingford, his son, and daughter, in London, and then the former feeling so much better, both in constitution and spirits, they prepared for their departure to Wallingford Hall. A week, however, previous to this, they received a communication from Ela, announcing the confinement of Lady Helvendon, her daughter, and the birth of a son and heir to the title, wealth, and honours of that ancient family. She further stated, that there was so much riot at Walthorp Abbey, since the above-mentioned joyful event, owing to the influx of visitors and friends of the father, to congratulate the happy parents on such an auspicious event, that she was completely tired, and longed for a few weeks' quiet; she, therefore, intended (if they purposed returning to Rosemary Dell,) to become their visitor for a short time, and requested them to write and let her know all the particulars, so that she might be aware in what way to act.

They were very well pleased at the intentions of Ela, (or Mrs. Beranzio, as she was now called,) and immediately wrote off to her, informing her of their designs, and expressing a wish that she would join them soon after their return to Wallingford Hall. The day after they had despatched this epistle, they left

London, and in due course once more arrived at Wallingford Hall.

It was very remarkable that never since the appearance of the gipsy woman to Ela and the others, and her daring attempt upon the life of the former, had anything either been seen or heard of the wandering tribe, and it was, therefore, concluded that they had abandoned their villanous designs, and had gone to another part of the country, where they were not so well known, and might carry on their predatory deeds with less fear of being detected and punished. There were moments, however, when Mr. Wallingford's mind would become distracted by all those doubts and fears which had tormented it so long, to an almost insupportable degree, and at such times all the arguments of his son and daughter, or of Ela, were of little avail.

In order to afford him all the recreation in their power, and to endeavour to divert his thoughts from the melancholy subject which almost continually engrossed them, they frequently rambled forth amongst the beautiful scenery in the neighbourhood of Rosemary Dell, and there, in the comtemplation of the charms of nature, sought to dissipate all recollection of the sorrows that had before so heavily afflicted them. Upon all of these excursions, Ela was their companion, and she took especial pains to amuse and occupy the mind of Wallingford.

It was on a lovely summer's day, that they had taken their seat upon a green knoll, and Maria, who had brought one of her favourite authors with her, was amusing them by reading choice passages from it, when they were suddenly startled by a rustling among the bushes immediately behind them, and they had scarcely time to turn round and look from whom the noise proceeded, when the report of a pistol was heard; Mr. Wallingford uttered a loud groan, and was immediately stetched a bleeding corpse at their feet.

"Damnation!" cried Rupert Darwin, for it was the monster, "I have again missed my mark.—It was not meant for him, but for thee, base, accursed, and hated wretch!—Ela Beranzio, behold the last, the only living foe of the gipsy race that thou hast; and who has come here fully determined to accomplish that vengeance for the wrongs thou has done him, in thy blood! This to thy heart!—Die! die!"

Walter and Maria, maddened with horror, were leaning over the body of the unfortunate Wallingford, and as the miscreant, Rupert Darwin, gave utterance to the above words, he drew a knife from his bosom, and rushed ferociously upon Ela, endeavouring to plunge it to her heart. She was, however, prepared to meet him, and seizing his arm with masculine strength, as it was raised in the air to inflict the deadly blow, and with a wild, and almost super-human laugh of exultation, buried it in the murderer's heart. He fixed upon her one ghastly look of agony, his eyes immediately became glazed in death, and he fell by the side of his unfortunate victim!

CONCLUSION.

It was some time ere Water and his wife, Ela, and their other friends, could erase from their recollection this horrible catastrophe, but at length, years mellowed the violence of their grief, and they became more calm and composed.

Ela lived many years afterwards, and to become the grandmother of a numerous family emulating the virtues of their parents, who, were revered by all who knew them.

Mr. and Mrs. Wallingford lived in the enjoyment of every domestic happiness, and to behold their childrens' children around them, possessed of all those intrinsic qualities that ennoble mankind, and is the only true source of earthly joy.

LONDON: PRINTED AND PUBLISHED BY E. LLOYD, SALISBURY-SQUARE, FLEET-STREET.

www.ingramcontent.com/pod-product-compliance
Lightning Source LLC
Chambersburg PA
CBHW080942020726
47505CB00009B/2118